More praise for LONDON

"Rutherfurd is a skilled storyteller with respect for his readers. He doesn't cast them adrift in a maze of characters and thousands of years. . . . He juggles his immense cast with great poise and momentum. . . . Climb aboard the Rutherfurd time shuttle in 54 B.C.; 827 pages later meet Sarah Bull, a young archeologist excavating a Roman site near the Thames in 1997. . . . No tourist will look at the ancient but chaotic city [of London] through quite the same eyes after following its history through two millennia."

—*The Washington Post Book World*

"Engrossing . . . Entertaining . . . Real people dance across the pages, as multidimensional as Rutherfurd's invented characters."

—*Miami Herald*

"What a history! . . . Rutherfurd spent long hours researching this work in the Museum of London. The results show in his keen sense of place. . . . LONDON is a long summer soak of a book, one to sink into. . . . You can be entertained by its drama *and* instructed by its history."

—*St. Louis Post-Dispatch*

"Few literary novels tell us as much about the history of modern humans, or have such charity."

—*Daily Telegraph* (London)

Please turn the page for more reviews. . . .

"REMARKABLE."

—*Virginian-Pilot*

"You'll love this writer's way of coaxing you into the hearts and minds of jealous Plantagenets, Elizabethan hangers-on, newlyweds visiting the Crystal Palace, and young hopefuls in the working class at the start of World War II."

—*The Dallas Morning News*

"As Chaucer knew, a good tale well told is the best way of passing a tedious trip, be it by the bridle path to Canterbury or jumbo jet across the seas. So wherever you journey this summer, LONDON: THE NOVEL will be the best of companions."

—*Raleigh News & Observer*

"There are elements of Dickens in Rutherfurd's writing as he describes the struggles of the poor in a society that had few safety nets. . . . LONDON is the kind of novel that even those who say they never read fiction will enjoy."

—*The Register-Herald*

“A VIGOROUS, COLORFUL NARRATIVE.”
—*Kirkus Reviews*

“Rutherfurd is an acknowledged master of the epic historical novel. . . . [who] has proven yet again that his technique of telling a huge story through many, many small ones produces rich, stirring, and unforgettable novels.”

—*The Readers Showcase*

“[An] all-encompassing fictional history of London . . . Rutherfurd does not flinch at a challenge. . . . [His] whirlwind historical tour is an appropriate purchase for all collections.”

—*Library Journal*

“Readers with imagination may even come away with the sense that great cities aren’t just places but living beings with hearts and souls.”

—*Publishers Weekly*

By Edward Rutherfurd:
Published by The Ballantine Publishing Group

SARUM
RUSSKA
LONDON

LONDON

Edward Rutherfurd

FAWCETT CREST • NEW YORK

This book is dedicated to the curators and staff of the Museum of London, where history comes alive.

A Fawcett Crest Book
Published by The Ballantine Publishing Group

http://www.randomhouse.com

Library of Congress Catalog Card Number: 97-97186

ISBN 0-449-00263-2

This edition published by arrangement with Crown Publishers, Inc.
CROWN is a trademark of Crown Publishers, Inc.

Manufactured in the United States of America

First Ballantine Books Edition: April 1998

10 9 8 7 6 5 4 3 2

Contents

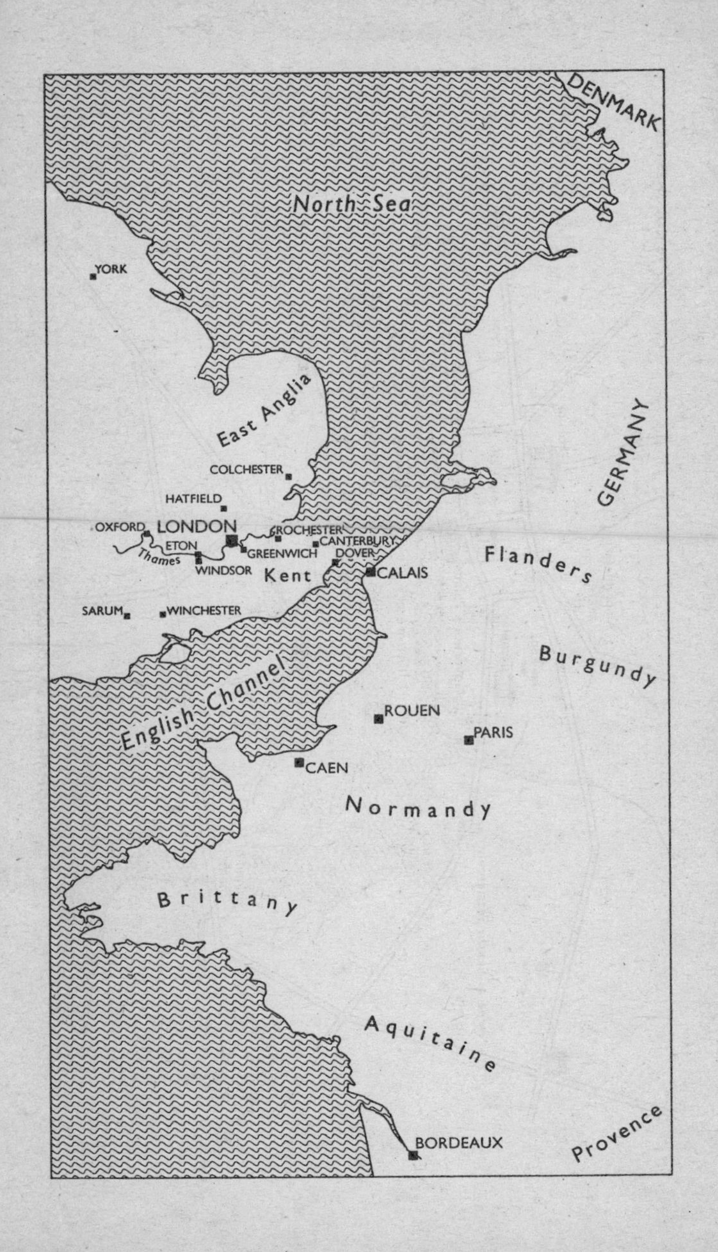
DENMARK
North Sea
YORK
East Anglia
GERMANY
COLCHESTER
HATFIELD
OXFORD
LONDON
ROCHESTER
CANTERBURY
ETON
GREENWICH
DOVER
Thames
WINDSOR
Kent
CALAIS
Flanders
SARUM
WINCHESTER
Burgundy
English Channel
ROUEN
PARIS
CAEN
Normandy
Brittany
Aquitaine
BORDEAUX
Provence

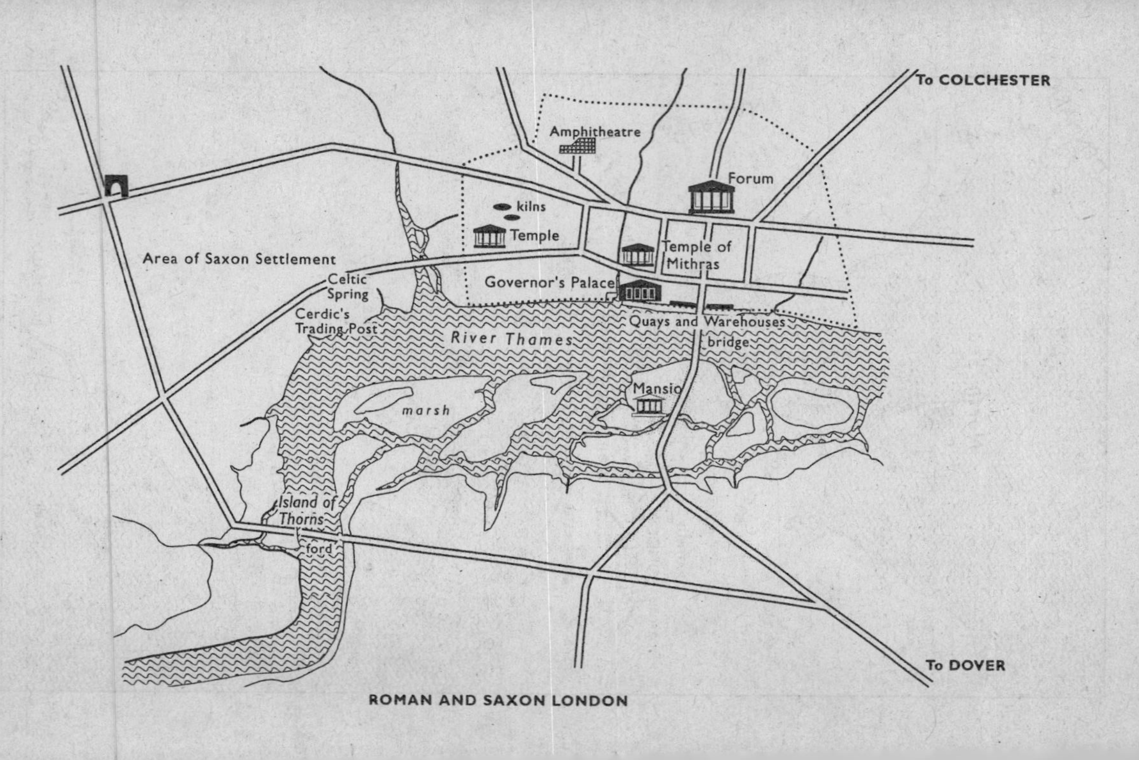

ROMAN AND SAXON LONDON

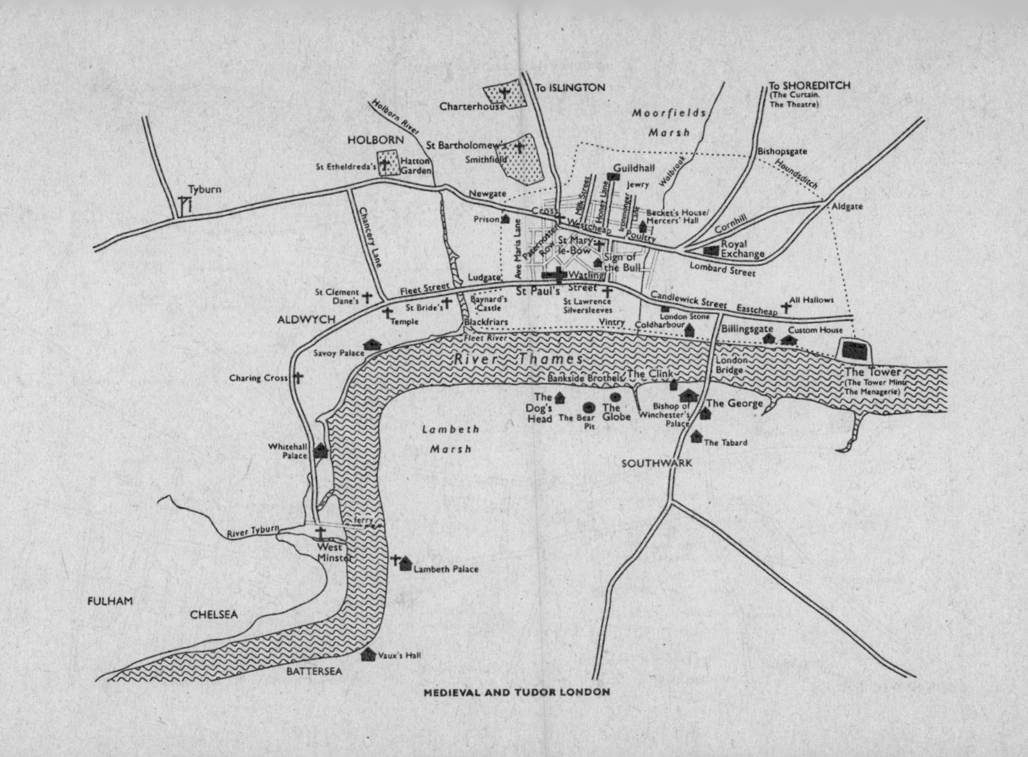

MEDIEVAL AND TUDOR LONDON

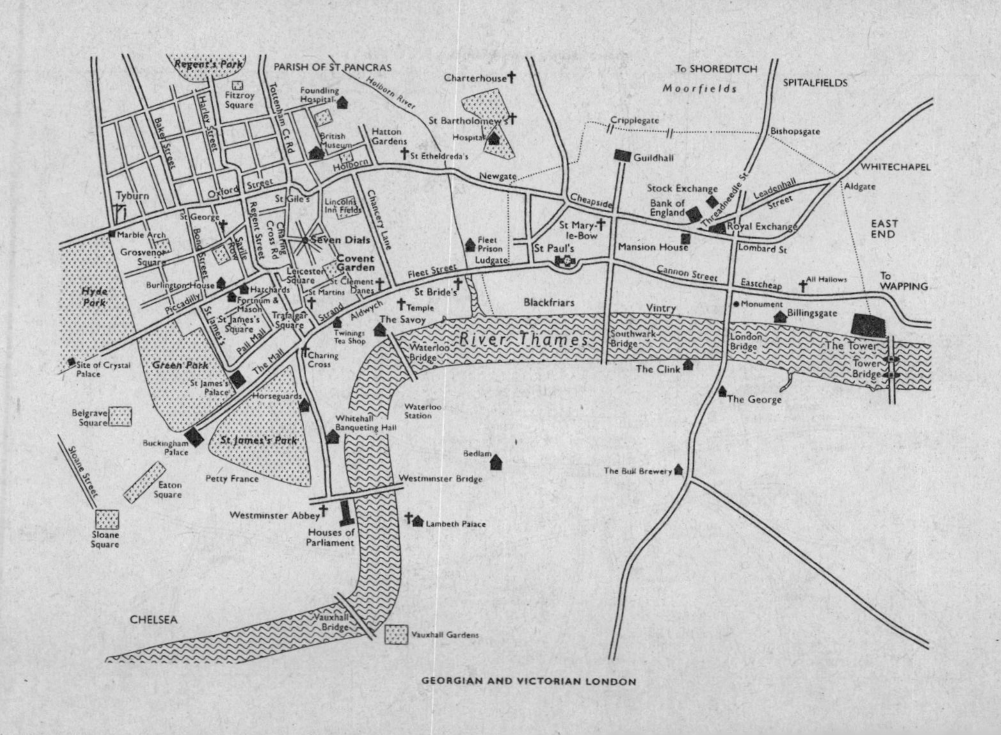

GEORGIAN AND VICTORIAN LONDON

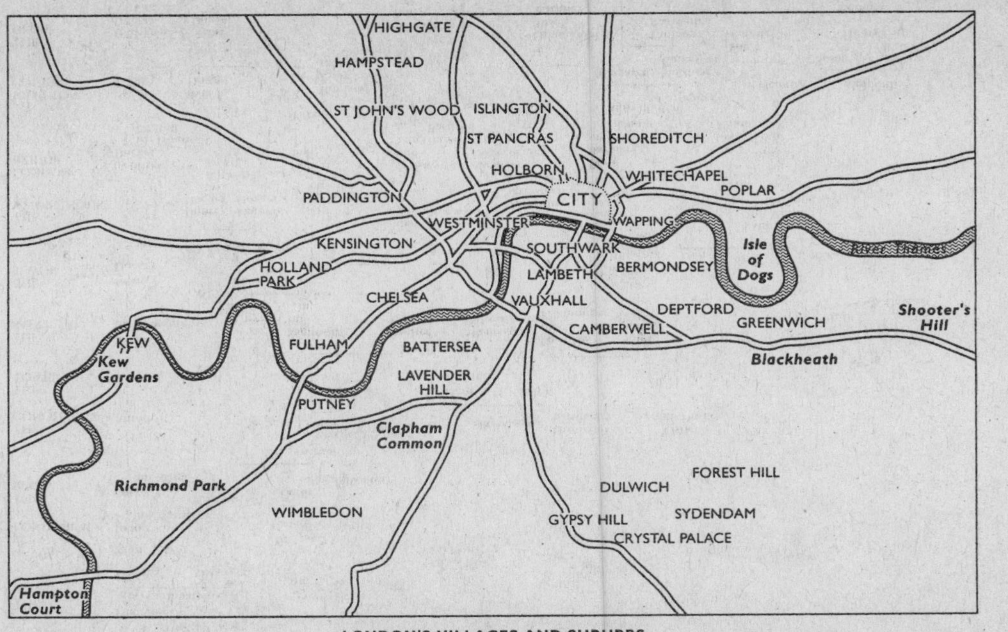

LONDON'S VILLAGES AND SUBURBS

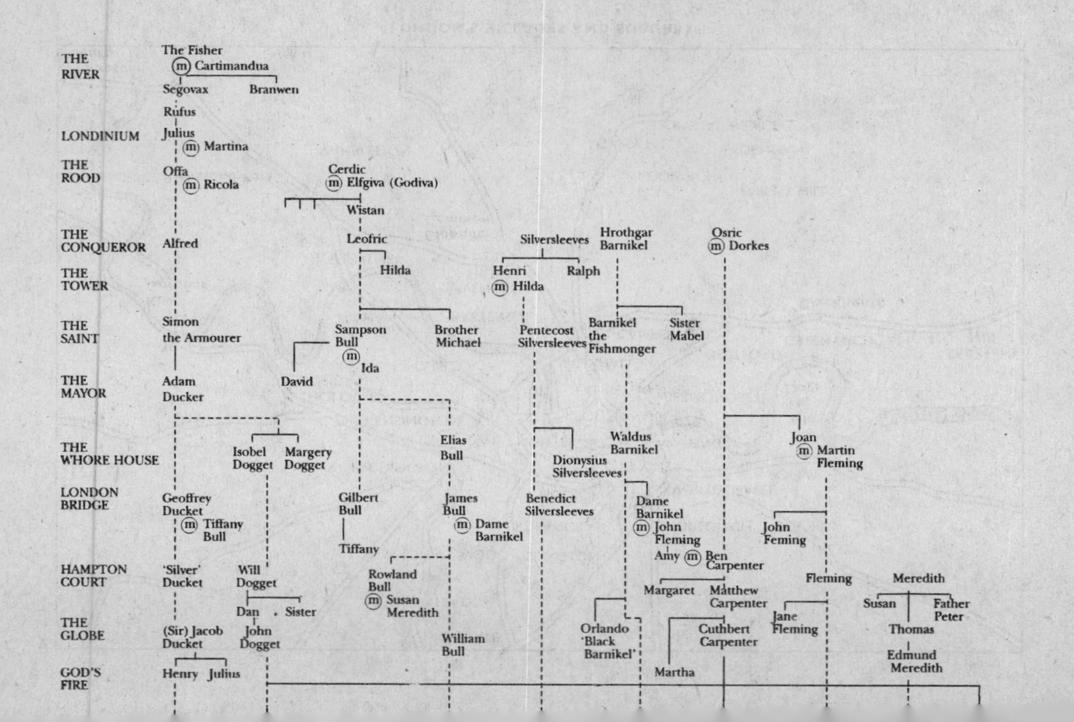

THE RIVER
The Fisher
(m) Cartimandua
Segovax
Branwen
Rufus
LONDINIUM
Julius
(m) Martina
THE ROOD
Offa
(m) Ricola
Cerdic
(m) Elfgiva (Godiva)
Wistan
THE CONQUEROR
Alfred
Leofric
Silversleeves
Hrothgar Barnikel
Osric
(m) Dorkes
THE TOWER
Hilda
Henri
(m) Hilda
Ralph
THE SAINT
Simon the Armourer
Sampson Bull
(m) Ida
David
Brother Michael
Pentecost Silversleeves
Barnikel the Fishmonger
Sister Mabel
THE MAYOR
Adam Ducker
THE WHORE HOUSE
Isobel Dogget
Margery Dogget
Elias Bull
Dionysius Silversleeves
Waldus Barnikel
Joan
(m) Martin Fleming
LONDON BRIDGE
Geoffrey Ducket
(m) Tiffany Bull
Gilbert Bull
Tiffany
James Bull
(m) Dame Barnikel
Benedict Silversleeves
Dame Barnikel
(m) John Fleming
John Feming
Amy (m) Ben Carpenter
HAMPTON COURT
'Silver' Ducket
Will Dogget
Rowland Bull
(m) Susan Meredith
Margaret
Matthew Carpenter
Fleming
Meredith
THE GLOBE
(Sir) Jacob Ducket
Dan
Sister
John Dogget
William Bull
Orlando 'Black Barnikel'
Cuthbert Carpenter
Jane Fleming
Susan
Father Peter
Thomas
GOD'S FIRE
Henry
Julius
Martha
Edmund Meredith

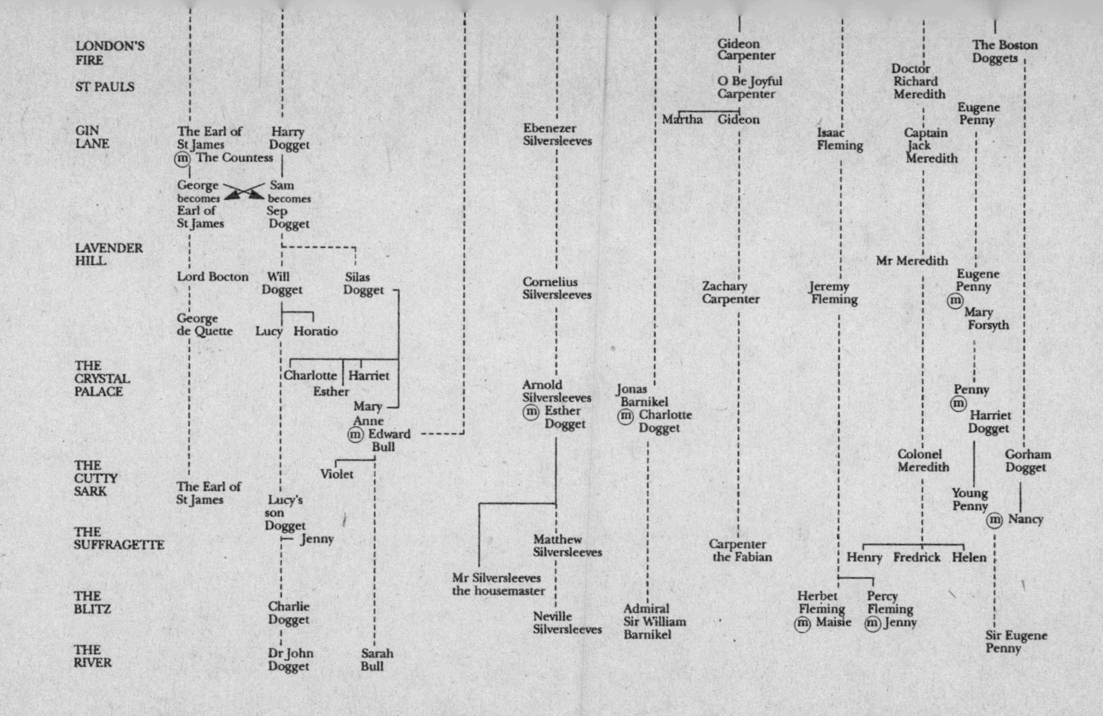
LONDON'S FIRE
ST PAULS
GIN LANE
LAVENDER HILL
THE CRYSTAL PALACE
THE CUTTY SARK
THE SUFFRAGETTE
THE BLITZ
THE RIVER
The Earl of St James (m) The Countess
Harry Dogget
George becomes Earl of St James
Sam becomes Sep Dogget
Lord Bocton
Will Dogget
Silas Dogget
George de Quette
Lucy
Horatio
Charlotte
Harriet
Esther
Mary Anne (m) Edward Bull
Violet
The Earl of St James
Lucy's son Dogget
Jenny
Charlie Dogget
Dr John Dogget
Sarah Bull
Ebenezer Silversleeves
Cornelius Silversleeves
Arnold Silversleeves (m) Esther Dogget
Matthew Silversleeves
Mr Silversleeves the housemaster
Neville Silversleeves
Jonas Barnikel (m) Charlotte Dogget
Admiral Sir William Barnikel
Gideon Carpenter
O Be Joyful Carpenter
Martha
Gideon
Zachary Carpenter
Carpenter the Fabian
Isaac Fleming
Jeremy Fleming
Henry
Fredrick
Helen
Herbet Fleming (m) Maisie
Percy Fleming (m) Jenny
Doctor Richard Meredith
Captain Jack Meredith
Mr Meredith
Colonel Meredith
The Boston Doggets
Eugene Penny
Eugene Penny (m) Mary Forsyth
Penny (m) Harriet Dogget
Gorham Dogget
Young Penny (m) Nancy
Sir Eugene Penny

Preface

London is, first and foremost, a novel. All the families whose fortunes the story follows, from the Duckets to the family of Penny, are fictitious, as are their individual parts in all the historical events described.

In following the story of these imaginary families down the centuries, I have tried to set them amongst people and events that either did exist, or might have done. Occasionally it has been necessary to invent historical detail. We shall probably never know, for instance, the exact place where Julius Caesar crossed the Thames: to this author, at least, the site of present-day Westminster seems the most logical. Similarly, though we know the political circumstances in which St Paul's was founded by Bishop Mellitus in 604, I have felt free to make my own guess as to the exact situation at Saxon Lundenwic then. Much later, in 1830, I have invented a St Pancras constituency for my characters to contest in the election of that year.

But generally speaking, from the Norman conquest onwards, such a rich body of information has been preserved not only concerning London's history but also the life stories of countless individual citizens, that the author has no shortage of detail and only needs, from time to time, to make small adjustments to complex events in order to aid the narrative.

London's chief buildings and churches have nearly always kept their names unchanged. Many streets, too, have retained their names since Saxon times. Where names have changed, this is either explained in the course of the story; or if this would be confusing I have simply used the name by which they are best known today.

Inventions belonging to the novel are as follows: Cerdic the

Saxon's trading post is placed roughly on the site of the modern Savoy Hotel; the house at the sign of the Bull, below St Mary-le-Bow, may be presumed to stand on or near the site of Williamson's Tavern; the church of St Lawrence Silversleeves near Watling Street might have been any of several small churches in this area which disappeared after the Great Fire; the Dog's Head could be one of a score of brothels along Bankside.

I have, however, allowed myself to place an arch at the location of today's Marble Arch, in the days when this was a Roman road junction. It is not impossible that there really was such an arch—but its remains have yet to be found!

Of the fictional families in the story, Dogget and Ducket are both quite common names, often found in London's history. Real individuals bearing these names—in particular the famous Dogget who instituted Dogget's Coat and Badge Race on the Thames—are occasionally mentioned in the text and clearly distinguished from the imaginary families. The derivations of the fictional families' names and their hereditary physical marks are, of course, entirely invented for the purpose of the novel.

Bull is a common English name; Carpenter is a typical occupational name—like Baker, Painter, Tailor and dozens of others. Readers of my novel *Sarum* may recognize that the Carpenters are kinsmen of the Masons in that book. Fleming is another frequently encountered name and presumably indicates Flemish descent. Meredith is a Welsh name and Penny can be, though is not necessarily, Huguenot. The rarer name of Barnikel, which also appears in *Sarum*, is probably Viking and its origin associated with a charming legend. Dickens made use of this name (Barnacle) but in a rather pejorative way. I hope to have done a little better for them.

The name of Silversleeves however, and the long-nosed family of this name, is completely invented. In the middle ages there were many more of these delightful and descriptive names which, sadly, have mostly died out. Silversleeves is intended to represent this old tradition.

A writer preparing a novel on London faces one enormous difficulty: there is so much, and such wonderful material. Every

Londoner has a favourite corner of the city. Time and again one was tempted into one or another fascinating historical by-way. There is hardly a parish in London that could not provide material for a book like this. The fact that *London* is also, to a considerable extent, a history of England, led me to choose some locations over others; but I can only hope that my choice will not prove too disappointing to the many who know and love this most wonderful of cities.

Embankment, a favourite corner of the city. Time and again I was tempted into one or another fascinating historical byway. There is hardly a part of London that could not provide material for a book like this. The fact that London is also, to a considerable extent, a history of England led me to choose some locations over others. So I can only hope that my choices will not prove too disappointing to the many who know and love this most wonderful of cities.

Chapter 1

The River

Many times since the Earth was young, the place had lain under the sea.

Four hundred million years ago, when the continents were arranged in a quite different configuration, the island formed part of a small promontory on the north-western edge of a vast, shapeless landmass. The promontory, which jutted out in a lonely fashion into the great world ocean, was desolate. No eye, save that of God, beheld it. No creature moved upon the land; no birds rose in the sky, nor were there even fish in the sea.

At this remote time, in the south-eastern corner of the promontory, a departing sea left behind a bare terrain of thick, dark slate. Silent and empty it lay, like the surface of some undiscovered planet, the grey rock interrupted here and there only by shallow pools of water. Under this layer of slate, deep in the Earth, pressures still more ancient had raised up a gently shelving ridge some two thousand feet high, which lay across the landscape like a huge breakwater.

And thus the place long remained, grey and silent, as unknown as the endless blankness before birth.

In the eight geological periods that followed, during which the continents moved, most of Earth's mountain ranges were formed, and life gradually evolved, no movements of the Earth disturbed the place where the slate ridge lay. But seas came and departed from it many times. Some of these were cold, some warm. Each remained there for many millions of years. And always they deposited sediments hundreds of feet thick, so that at last the slate ridge, high though it was, became covered, smoothed over and buried deep below, with scarcely a hint that it existed.

As life on Earth began to burgeon, as plants covered its surface and its waters teemed with creatures, the planet began to add further layers formed from this new, organic life it had brought into being. One great sea that departed about the time of the extinction of the dinosaurs, let fall such a prodigious quantity of detritus from its fish and plankton that the resulting chalk would cover much of southern England and northern France to a depth of some three hundred feet.

And so it was that a new landscape came into being, above the place where the ancient ridge lay buried.

It was a different shape entirely. Here as other seas came and went, and huge river systems from the interior drained out through this corner of the promontory, the chalk covering became shaped into a broad and shallow valley some twenty miles across, with ridges to north and south, and opening out in a huge V towards the east. From these various inundations came further deposits of gravels and sands, and one, a tropical sea, left a thick layer of soft deposit down the centre of the valley, which would one day be known as London clay. These floodings and withdrawals also caused these later deposits to be formed into new, somewhat lesser ridges within the great chalk V.

Such was the place that was to be London, about a million years ago.

Of Man, there was still no sign. For a million years ago, although he walked upon two legs, his skull was still like that of an ape. And before he appeared, one great process had to begin.

The ice ages.

It was not the forming of frozen layers upon the Earth that altered the land, but their ending. Each time the ice began to melt, the ice-filled rivers began to churn and the stupendous glaciers, like slow-moving, geological bulldozers, gouged out valleys, stripped hills, and washed down the gravel that filled the riverbeds created by their waters.

In all the advances to date, the little north-western promontory of the great Eurasian landmass had been only partly covered by the ice. At its greatest extent, the ice wall ended just along the northern edge of the long chalk V. But when it did reach this far, about half a million years ago, it had one significant result.

At this time, a great river flowed eastwards from the centre of the promontory and passed some way to the north of the long chalk V. When the advancing ice began to block its way, however, thwarted, the cold, churning river waters sought another outlet, and about forty miles west of the place where the slate ridge lay, they burst through a weak point in the long chalk ridge, making that narrow defile known today as the Goring Gap, and flooded eastwards down the centre of the V that was so perfectly formed to receive them.

In this way the river was born.

Somewhere, during these later comings and goings of the ice, came Man. The dating is uncertain. Even after the river came through the Goring Gap, Neanderthal Man had still to develop. Not until the latest Ice Age, a little over a hundred thousand years ago, did Man as we know him evolve. At some time during the ice wall's withdrawal, he moved into the valley.

Then, at last, somewhat less than ten thousand years ago, the waters from the dissolving Arctic ice-cap swept down, swamping the plain on the promontory's eastern side. Cutting through the chalk ridges in a great J-shape, they washed right round the base of the promontory into a narrow channel running westwards to the Atlantic.

Thus, like some northern Noah's Ark after the Flood, the little promontory became an island, free but forever at anchor, just off the coast of the great continent to which it had belonged. To the west, the Atlantic Ocean; to the east, the cold North Sea; along its southern edge, where the high chalk cliffs gazed across to the nearby continent, the narrow English Channel. And so, surrounded by these northern seas, began the island of Britain.

The great chalk V, therefore, no longer led to an eastern plain but to an open sea. Its long funnel became an estuary. On the estuary's eastern side, the chalk ridges veered away northwards, leaving on their eastern flank a huge tract of low-lying forest and marsh. On the southern side, a long peninsula of high chalk ridges and fertile valleys jutted out some seventy miles to form the island's south-eastern tip.

This estuary had one special feature. As the sea tide came in, it not only checked the outflow from the river, but actually reversed it, so that at high sea tide the waters ploughed up the narrowing funnel of the estuary and a considerable distance upriver too, building up a huge excess volume in the channel; as the sea tide ebbed, these waters flowed swiftly out again. The result was a strong tidal flow in the lower reaches of the river with a difference of well over ten feet between high- and low-water marks. It was a system that continued for many miles upstream.

Man was already there when this separation of the island occurred, and other men crossed the narrow, if dangerous, seas to the island in the millennia that followed. During this time human history effectively began.

54 BC

Fifty-four years before the birth of Christ, at the end of a cold, star-filled spring night, a crowd of two hundred people stood in a semicircle by the bank of the river and waited for the dawn.

Ten days had passed since the ominous news had come.

In front of them, at the water's edge, was a smaller group of five figures. Silent and still, in their long grey robes they might have been taken for so many standing stones. These were the druids, and they were about to perform a ceremony which, it was hoped, would save the island and their world.

Amongst those gathered by the riverbank were three people, each of whom, whatever hopes or fears they may have had concerning the threat ahead, guarded a personal and terrible secret.

One was a boy, the second a woman, the third a very old man.

There were many sacred sites along the lengthy course of the river. But nowhere was the spirit of the great river so clearly present than at this quiet place.

Here, sea and river met. Downstream, in a series of huge loops, the ever widening flow passed through open marshland until, about ten miles away, it finally opened out into the long, eastward funnel of the estuary and out to the cold North Sea. Upstream, the river meandered delightfully between pleasant woods and lush, level meadows. But at this point, between two of the river's great bends, lay a most gracious stretch of water, two and a half miles long, where the river flowed eastwards in a single, majestic sweep.

It was tidal. At high tide, when the incoming sea in the estuary reversed the current, this river road was a thousand yards across; at low tide, only three hundred. In the centre, halfway along the southern bank where the marshes formed little islands, a single gravel spit jutted out into the stream, forming a promontory at low water, and becoming an island when the tide was high. It was on the top of this spit that the little crowd was standing. Opposite them, on the northern bank, lay the place, now deserted, that bore the name of Londinos.

Londinos. Even now, in the dawning light, the shape of the ancient place could be seen clearly across the water: two low gravel hills with levelled tops rising side by side about eighty feet above the waterfront. Between the two hills ran a little brook. To the left, on the western flank, a larger stream descended to a broad inlet that interrupted the northern bank.

On the eastern side of the two hills, there had once been a small hillfort whose low earthwork wall, now empty, could serve as a lookout post for vessels approaching from the estuary. The western hill was sometimes used by the druids when they sacrificed oxen.

And that was all there was. An abandoned settlement. A sacred spot. The tribal centres were to the north and south. The tribes over whom the great chief Cassivelaunus was master lived in the huge eastern tracts above the estuary. The tribe of Cantii, in the long peninsula south of the estuary, had already given that region the name of Kent. The river was a border between them, Londinos a sort of no-man's-land.

The very name was obscure. Some said that a man called Londinos had lived there; others suggested that it might refer to the little earthwork on the eastern hill. But nobody knew. Somehow, in the last thousand years, the place had got the name.

The cold breeze was coming up the river from the estuary. There was a faint, sharp smell of mud and riverweed. Above, the bright morning star was beginning to fade as the clear sky turned to a paler blue.

The boy shivered. He had been standing an hour and he was cold. Like most of the folk there, he wore a simple woollen tunic that reached to the knees and was fastened at the waist with a leather belt. Beside him stood his mother holding a baby, and his sister little Branwen, whom he held by the hand. For it was his task at such times to keep her in order.

He was a bright, brave little fellow, dark-haired and blue-eyed, like most of his Celtic people. His name was Segovax and he was nine. A closer inspection, however, would have revealed two unusual features in his appearance. On the front of his head, on the forelock, grew a patch of white hair, as though someone had dabbed it with a brush of white dye. Such hereditary marks were to be found amongst several families dwelling in the hamlets along that region of the river. "You needn't worry," his mother had told him. "A lot of women think it's a sign that you're lucky."

The second feature was much stranger. When the boy spread his fingers, it could be seen that between them, as far as the first joint, was a thin layer of skin, like the webbing on a duck's foot. This too was an inherited trait, although it did not show itself in every generation. It was as though, in some distant, primordial time some gene in a fish-like prototype of Man had obstinately refused to change its watery character entirely, and so passed on this vestige of its origins. Indeed, with his large-eyed face and his wiry little body, the boy did somehow make one think of a tadpole or some other little creature of the waters, a quick survivor down the endless eons of time.

His grandfather had also exhibited the condition. "But they cut the extra skin away when he was a baby," Segovax's father had told his wife. She could not bear the thought of the knife, though, and so nothing had been done. It did not trouble the boy.

Segovax glanced around at his family: little Branwen, with her affectionate nature and her fits of temper that no one could control; the baby boy in his mother's arms, just starting to walk and babble his first words; his mother, pale and strangely distracted of late. How he loved them. But as he stared past the druids, his face broke into a little smile. By the water's edge was a modest raft with two men standing beside it. And one of them was his father.

They shared so much, father and son. The same little tuft of white hair, the same large eyes. His father's face, scoured by crease lines almost resembling scales, made one think of some solemn, fish-like creature. So dedicated was he to his little family, so knowledgeable about the river, so expert with his nets, that the local people referred to him simply as the Fisher. And though other men, Segovax realized, were physically stronger than this quiet fellow with his curved back and long arms, none was kinder or more quietly determined. "He may not be much to look at," the men in the hamlet would say, "but the Fisher never gives up." His mother, Segovax knew, adored his father. So did he.

Which was why, the day before, he had formed the daring plan that, if he managed to carry it out, would probably cost him his life.

Now the glow along the eastern horizon was starting to tremble. In a few minutes the sun would rise and a great shimmering ray of light would come dancing from the east along the stream. The five druids facing the crowd began a low chant while the people listened.

At a signal, a figure stepped out from the crowd. He was a powerfully built man whose rich green cloak, golden ornaments and proud bearing declared him to be a nobleman of importance. In his hands he carried a flat, rectangular metal object whose burnished surface glowed softly in the gathering light. He handed it to the tall, white-bearded druid standing in the centre.

The druids turned to face the glowing horizon and the elderly figure in the centre stepped forward and on to the raft. At the same moment, the two waiting men – Segovax's father and another – stepped on to the raft behind him and with long poles began to push the raft out into the broad stream.

The other four druids chanted, a droning sound that mysteriously grew, spreading out over the waters as the raft drew further away. A hundred yards. Two hundred.

The sun appeared, a huge red curve upon the water. It grew, its orb flooding the river with golden light. The four remaining druids, silhouetted against it, suddenly seemed to have grown into giants as their long shadows leapt into the waiting crowd.

The senior druid was out in midstream, the two men with

their long poles keeping the raft steady in the current. On the northern bank, the two low hills were bathed in the sun's reddish light. And now, like some ancient grey-bearded sea god rising up out of the waters, the tall druid on the raft raised the metal object over his head so that it caught the sunbeams and flashed.

It was a shield, made of bronze. Although most weapons on the island were made of iron, the more ancient and easily worked bronze was used for ceremonial arms requiring delicate workmanship, such as this. And a masterpiece it was, sent with one of his most trusted nobles by the great chief Cassivelaunus himself. The pattern of swirling lines and the inlaid precious stones represented the finest of the wondrous Celtic metalwork for which the island was famed. It was the most important gift the island people could make to the gods.

With a single, sweeping gesture, the druid hurled the shield high over the water. Flashing, it made an arc through the air before falling into the gleaming path laid down by the sun across the water. The little crowd let out a sigh as the river silently took its offering and moved on.

But as the old druid watched, something strange occurred. Instead of sinking out of sight, the bronze shield remained suspended just below the surface of the clear water, its metal face glinting in the light. At first the old man was astonished, until it occurred to him that the reason was very simple. The metal was beaten very thin. It was backed with a light wood. Until the wood became waterlogged, the ceremonial shield was destined to remain hovering there, covered only by a film of water.

Something else was happening too. While the dawn silently approached, the tide had turned. The current was now flowing not downriver, but upriver, from the estuary to a point several miles further upstream from Londinos. Slowly, therefore, beneath the cold, translucent wave, the shield was moving up the stream, as though being gently pulled by some invisible hand towards the island's interior.

The old man watched and wondered what it meant. Did it portend good or evil, in face of the terrible threat?

The threat came from Rome. Its name was Julius Caesar.

Several folk had made the island of Britain their home in

the thousands of years since the ice's great retreat. Hunters, simple farmers, the makers of stone temples like Stonehenge, and, in more recent centuries, tribes who belonged to the great Celtic culture of north-west Europe. With its bardic poetry and song, its rich and echoing folklore, its astonishing and fantastic metalwork, the life of the islanders was rich. They dwelt in stout round timbered huts with warm thatched roofs. Their larger settlements were surrounded by palisades or rings of high earthwork walls. They farmed barley and oats, kept cattle, drank ale and heady mead distilled from honey. Behind the soft northern mists, their island remained a place apart.

True, for many generations, traders from the sunlit Mediterranean world had ventured to the island, bringing luxuries from the south in exchange for furs, slaves and the island's famous hunting dogs. In recent generations, a lively trade had developed through a harbour on the southern coast where another river descended from the ancient abandoned temple of Stonehenge. But although British chiefs liked, occasionally, to obtain wine, or silks, or Roman gold, the world from which these luxuries came was still far over the horizon and only vaguely apprehended.

But then the classical world produced one of the greatest adventurers that history has ever known.

Julius Caesar desired to rule Rome. To do so, he needed conquests. Just recently he had swept northwards all the way to the English Channel and established the huge new Roman province of Gaul. Now he had turned his eyes to this mist-shrouded island of the north.

Last year, he had come. With a modest force, mainly infantry, Caesar himself had disembarked below the white cliffs of Britain's south-eastern shore. The British chieftains had been warned; but even so, it was an awesome thing to behold the disciplined Roman troops. The Celtic warriors were brave, though. Swooping down with horses and chariots they managed to catch the Romans off guard several times. A storm damaged Caesar's fleet. After a series of skirmishes and manoeuvres in the coastal region, Caesar and his troops left, and the chieftains were triumphant. The gods had given them victory. When exiles warned them "That was only a reconnoitre", most Britons did not believe it.

But then news had begun to filter across. A new fleet was

being built. No fewer than five legions and some two thousand cavalry were rumoured to be under orders. Ten days ago, a messenger to the chiefs had paused at Londinos. His message was brief, and definite.

"Caesar is coming."

The offering had been made. The crowd was dispersing. Four of the druids were returning, two to the south and two to the north of the river. As for the oldest druid who had made the offering, it was the task of Segovax's father to row the priest up the stream to the druid's home two miles away.

Having bade a quiet farewell to all those assembled, the old man was about to step into his boat when he turned and let his eyes rest upon the woman. It was only for a moment. Then, with a sign to the humble fisherman, he was on his way.

Only a moment, but long enough. Cartimandua trembled. They said that the old man knew everything. It might be true. She could not tell. Holding the baby on her hip, she pushed Segovax and Branwen ahead of her as she made her way across to where the horses were tethered. Was she doing right? She told herself she was. Wasn't she protecting them all? Doing what she had to? But the sense of terrible guilt, the anguish, would not leave her. Was it really possible that the old druid her husband was rowing had guessed about the nobleman?

She waited for several minutes by the horses until the men from the great chief came. He was amongst them. Seeing her waiting, he turned aside and paused.

Young Segovax looked at the noble with interest, for this was the man who had stepped forward to hand the druid the shield. He was a stout man with a thick black beard, hard, shrewd blue eyes and an air of blunt authority. Beneath his green cloak he wore a tunic trimmed with fox fur. Around his neck the heavy torc – the Celtic circlet of gold – signified his high rank.

It was not the first time the boy had seen him. The powerful commander had twice visited the area in the last month, each time staying a night at the hamlet opposite Londinos. "You are to be ready," he had ordered the men after inspecting their weapons. "The great chief Cassivelaunus expects our forces to gather near this point. I shall prepare the defences." Now,

Segovax's mother, leaving her son to stand with Branwen and the baby, was moving forward to speak to him.

The noble watched her thoughtfully as she approached. As was his habit, he considered her sexual potential. She was certainly, as he had observed at their first meeting, a striking creature. Her thick, raven-dark hair fell past her shoulders. Her body was slim, on the tall side, but with heavy breasts. Breasts a man might dream about. He was aware of the small, sinuous movement her body made as she approached. He had noticed it the first time they met. Did she always move that way, or was it just for his benefit?

"Well?" he said gruffly.

"Our agreement is still good?"

He glanced across at the children, then his eyes flicked towards the dugout in which the woman's husband was rowing the old druid. They were well out in the stream now. Her husband knew nothing. His eyes continued to take her in steadily.

"I already told you so."

He could see her now, in future years. That pale face with its narrow cheekbones would become haggard, the seductive eyes sunken. Her passion would turn perhaps to obsession, perhaps to bitterness. A troubled spirit. But good, very good, for a few more years.

"When?" She seemed relieved, but still anxious.

He shrugged. "Who knows? Soon."

"He must not know about it."

"When I give orders, they have to be obeyed."

"Yes." She nodded but stood there uncertainly. She's like an animal from the wild, he thought. Only half tame. He indicated that the interview was over. A few moments later he was riding away.

Cartimandua turned back to her innocent children, who knew nothing of her terrible secret. But soon they would know. And an even more terrible thought crossed her mind. Would they still love her then?

The druid's eyes scanned the water as the dugout moved upstream. Had the shield been received by the river yet, or was it still hovering in the stream? He glanced also at the modest man rowing him. He could remember this fellow's father, with webbed hands like the little boy's. And his father before that. The druid sighed. Not for nothing did the people of that region call him the father of the river.

He was very old, almost seventy, yet still powerful, still an imposing figure. He stood nearly six feet tall – a giant compared with most men. His full white beard reached down to his waist, whilst his head of silver hair was bare except for a simple gold band round his forehead. His eyes were grey and watchful. It was he who performed the sacrifice of the oxen once a year on the western of the twin hills of Londinos; he who prayed in sacred groves in the oak forests of the region.

No one knew when the druid priesthood of north-west Europe had first begun, but there were more in Britain than ever, since in recent years a number had come across the sea to take sanctuary in the mist-shrouded island. It was said that the druids of Britain safeguarded the purist tradition of the ancient lore. In the interior of the island there were strange circles of stone, temples so old that no one could say even if human hands had built them, and in these, long ago, the druids were said to have met. But along the river they usually worshipped in small wooden shrines, or in sacred groves of trees.

Yet this ancient druid, it was said, had a special gift denied to other priests. For the gods, years ago, had given him second sight.

He had been in his thirty-third year when this strange gift had come to him. He himself could not say whether its possession was a gift or a curse. It was not complete. Sometimes he had shadowy premonitions, sometimes he saw future events with terrifying clarity. And sometimes, he knew, he was as blind as other men. As the years passed, he had come to accept this condition as neither good nor bad, but merely part of the order of nature.

His home was not far away. At the western, upstream end of the great two-and-a-half-mile stretch of water lay one of the river's many majestic curves, this one making a full right angle to the south before veering eastward again. Just around this corner, a bifurcated stream had created a low rectangular island off the river's northern bank. It was a quiet place where oak, ash and thorn trees grew. Here, in a single, modest hut, the druid had chosen, for the last thirty years, to live alone.

Often he travelled around the hamlets along the river where

he was always reverently welcomed and fed. Sometimes he would abruptly summon a villager, like Segovax's father, to row him many miles upriver to some sacred site. But usually a little column of wood smoke would announce that he was on his island, a silent presence, so that the folk in the area considered him a guardian of the place, like some sacred stone that despite the lichen growing upon it remains unchanged by the seasons.

It was just as they were entering the curve, with the island now in view, that the old man caught sight of the shield. As before, it was still glinting softly just below the surface, inching its way upstream towards the river's distant heart. He gazed at it. The river had not exactly rejected the offering. But it had not accepted it either. The old man shook his head. The sign seemed to match the premonition which had come to him a month ago.

His second sight had told the druid other things that morning. He had not realized what young Segovax was going to do, but he had perceived Cartimandua's terrible dilemma. Now he also foresaw what fate had in store for the quiet fisherman before him. But it was a much greater and more terrible event that his premonition had been concerned with. Something he still did not fully understand. As they neared his home, he remained deep in thought. Could it really be that the gods of the ancient island of Britain were going to be destroyed? Or was something else, something he could not comprehend, to happen? It was very strange.

All that spring Segovax waited. Each day the boy expected messengers on foaming horses to appear, and each night he gazed at the stars and wondered, Are they crossing the sea now? But no one came. From time to time, rumours of preparation had reached the hamlet, yet there was no sign of invasion. It seemed as if the island had relapsed into quietness.

The little hamlet where the family lived was a delightful spot. Half a dozen circular huts with thatched roofs and earthen floors were surrounded by a wattle stockade that also included two pens for livestock and several storage huts raised on stilts. It stood not at the tip of the spit where the druids had waited, but about fifty yards back. At high tide, when the spit became an island, the hamlet was cut off, but no one minded.

Indeed, when the place had first been settled a score of generations ago, this watery protection had been one of its attractions. The ground itself, however, being gravel-based like the twin hills opposite, was firm underfoot and dry. With the warmer spring weather, some of the marshy ground along the southern bank dried; horses and cattle grazed there; and together with the other children, Segovax and his little sister would play in these meadows strewn with buttercups, cowslips and primroses. But the best feature of the little promontory was the fishing.

The river was broad, shallow and clear. Many kinds of fish teemed in its waters. Trout and especially salmon abounded. The spit was a wonderful place from which to run nets out into the sparkling waters. Or the boys would venture along the marshy banks by the base of the spit to certain places where it was always easy to trap eels.

"Those who live here," his father had told him, "will never go hungry. The river always provides." Sometimes, when they had set their nets, he would sit on the shore with his father, gazing across at the twin hills on the far bank. And, seeing the ever-changing ebb and flow of the tide as once every day the current flowed upstream from the estuary, paused at high water, and then ebbed back towards the sea again, his father would contentedly remark: "You see. The river is breathing."

Segovax loved to be with his father. He was so anxious to learn, and his father so happy to teach. By the age of five he had known all about setting snares in the nearby woods. By seven he could thatch a hut with reeds from the marshes nearby. As well as setting nets, he could stand stock-still in the shallows and expertly spear a fish with a sharpened stick. He knew many of the stories of the innumerable Celtic gods and could recite the ancestry not only of his own family but of the island's great chiefs for many generations. Recently he had begun to master the more important of the huge web of marriages, descents and oaths of loyalty that bound tribe and tribe, chief and chief, village and family in friendship or enmity all over the Celtic island. "For these," his father explained, "are things a man must know."

To these, in the last two years, his father had begun to add another skill. He had made the boy a spear. Not just a sharpened stick for fishing, but a proper spear, with a light shaft and a metal tip. "If you want to be a hunter and a warrior one day," he told the boy with a smile, "you must first master this. Though be careful when you use it," he had added cautiously.

Hardly a day passed when the boy did not go out and hurl the little spear at a mark. Soon he could hit any tree within range. Before long he was searching out more difficult targets. He would aim at hares, usually without success. Once he had been caught with little Branwen dutifully holding a target on the end of a stick at which he was throwing the spear. Even his kindly father was furious with him for that.

His father was so wise. And yet, as he had grown a little older, Segovax had begun to sense something else. Though he was wiry, his father, with his thin face, his rather straggly brown beard and his curved back, was not as physically strong as some of the other men. Yet in any communal work, he always insisted on doing as much as any of them. Often, after he had toiled for long hours, he would look pale and strained, and Segovax would be aware that his mother was glancing at him anxiously. At other times, when folk sat round the fire on summer evenings, drowsy with ale and mead, it was his father, in a voice that was quiet but surprisingly deep from so slight a body, who would sing to them all in the poetic voice of their people, strumming sometimes on a simple Celtic harp. At such moments the strain would dissolve and his face would take on a look of magical serenity.

And so it was that at the age of only nine, Segovax, like his mother, not only loved and admired his father, but knew in his heart that he must also protect him.

There was only one thing in which, in the boy's view, his father had failed him.

"When will you take me downriver, to the estuary?" he would ask every few months. Always his father replied: "One day. When I'm not so busy."

For Segovax had never seen the sea.

"You always say you will, but you never do," he complained, and sometimes sulked a little.

The only shadows that fell across these sunlit days were the occasional dark moods of their mother. She had always been mercurial and so neither Segovax nor his sister was much troubled. But it seemed to the boy that recently her moods had been harder to account for than usual. Sometimes she would scold him or Branwen for no reason, then suddenly seize the little girl and clasp her tightly, before just as quickly sending her away. Once, having slapped them both for some offence, she burst into tears. And whenever his father was there, the boy would see his mother's pale face watching him, almost angrily following his every move.

As spring turned into summer, no further news came of Caesar's movements. If the legions were still massing across the sea, no one came to the hamlet by the river to tell them. And yet, when the boy asked his father, "If the Romans come, do you think they will come here?", his father always quietly answered: "Yes." And then, with a sigh: "I think they must." For a very simple reason.

The ford. It lay by the island where the druid dwelt. At low tide, a man could walk from there to the southern bank with the water only reaching up to his chest.

"Of course," his father would add, "there are other fords, further upstream." But, coming up from the estuary, this was the first place where the river could safely be crossed. Descending from the ancient tracks along the great chalk ridges that strode across the island, travellers since time out of mind had made for this pleasant spot. If this Roman Caesar landed in the south and wished to strike up into the wide lands of Cassivelaunus beyond the estuary, then the simplest course would bring him to this ford.

"Soon," the boy told himself, "he must come here." And so he waited as a month passed. And then another.

It was in early summer that the incident occurred after which, it seemed to Segovax, his mother's behaviour became stranger.

It had started quite innocently one afternoon with a childish quarrel. He had gone for a walk with little Branwen. Hand in hand they had crossed the meadows on the southern bank and started up the slopes behind, to the edge of the woods. For a while they had played together; then, as usual, Segovax had practised throwing his spear. And then she had asked.

It was a small enough thing. He had promised her that she could throw his spear. Nothing more than that. But now he refused, though whether because he thought she was too small after all, or because he felt like teasing her, he could not afterwards remember.

"You promised," she protested.

"Perhaps. But I've changed my mind."

"You can't."

"Yes I can."

Little Branwen, with her tiny, athletic body, her bright blue eyes; Branwen who would try to climb trees even he hesitated to tackle; Branwen with her temper that not even his parents could control.

"No!" She stamped her foot. Her face began to go red. "That's not fair. You promised. Give it to me!" And she made a grab at the spear. But he cleverly switched hands.

"No, Branwen. You're my little sister and you have to do what I say."

"No I don't!" She shouted the words with all the force of her lungs, her face now puce, tears welling from her eyes. She made another grab, then swung her little fist, hitting him on the leg with all her might. "I hate you!" She was almost choking with rage.

"No you don't."

"Yes I do!" she screamed. She tried to kick him but he held her off. She bit his hand and then, before he could catch her, she ran up the slope into the trees and vanished.

For some time he had waited. He knew his little sister. She was up there, sitting on a log probably, knowing he would have to come looking for her. And when he finally found her, she would refuse to move so that finally he would be reduced to pleading with her. At last, however, he had made his way up into the woods.

"Branwen," he had called. "I love you." But there had been no reply. For a long time he had wandered about. She could not be lost because wherever she was, she had only to walk downhill until she came to the meadows and marshes above the river. She must, therefore, be hiding deliberately. Again and again he called. No answer. There was only one conclusion. He guessed now what she had done. She had given him the slip, trotted home to their parents and told them he had gone off and left her alone, so that he would get into trouble. She had played that trick on him once before. "Branwen," he called once more. "I love you." And then, under his breath: "I'll get even with you for this, you little snake." Then he had gone home. To find to his surprise that she was not there.

But the strange thing had been the reaction of his mother. His father had simply sighed, remarked, "She's hiding somewhere to annoy him," and started out to find her. But his mother's response had been entirely different.

She had gone completely white. Her jaw had dropped in horror. And then, in a voice hoarse with fear, she had shouted at them both: "Quickly. Find her. Before it's too late." Nor would Segovax ever forget the look his mother gave him. It was almost one of hate.

It was the least favoured of the pack, the last in consideration, the last, always, to eat. Even now, in summer, when its brethren were so well fed that they often did not trouble to attack the game they saw, this one retained a thin and mangy look. When it had set off from the ridge to scavenge below, none of the brethren had bothered to object, but had merely watched it leave with incurious contempt. On this warm afternoon, therefore, the gaunt grey shadow had slipped silently down through the woods towards the habitations of men. It had caught some poultry down there once.

When it saw the little fair-haired girl, however, it hesitated.

It was not the custom of the wolves to attack humans, for they feared them. To hunt a human alone, without the sanction and aid of the pack, would bring a savage reprisal from the leader. On the other hand, this killing need not be found out. A tempting morsel, all to itself. She was sitting on a log with her back to it. She was humming to herself and idly kicking the log with her heels. The wolf edged closer. She did not hear.

As Cartimandua strode up the hill she was still deathly pale. She had been running. She had sent her husband by a different path. Segovax, now frightened, was already out of sight. She was breathing heavily, but this agitation was nothing to the terrible fear in her mind, where one thought had formed to the exclusion of all others.

If the girl was lost, then all was lost.

The passion of Cartimandua was a fearsome thing. Sometimes it seemed beautiful; more often it was like an ache that would not go away, and sometimes it was blank and terrible, gripping and then hurling her forwards so that she was helpless. So it was now. As she raced up the slope with the sun on her cheek, it seemed to her that her passion for her husband was endless. She desired him. She wanted to protect him. She needed him. She found it hard to imagine her existence without him. As for their little family and the baby, how would they manage without a father? Besides, she was ready to have more children. She passionately desired that too.

She had no illusions. There were already more women than men in the hamlets along the river. If there were fighting and he was killed, her chances of finding another man were poor. Her passion had driven her; motherhood and the preservation of her family had made her reason harshly. She had to. And so she had come to her terrible and secret decision, the agony of which had been with her all spring like a haunting and reproachful echo.

Had she done right? She told herself she had. The bargain was a good one. The girl might be happy; probably she would be better off. It was necessary. It was all for the best.

Except that every day she found she wanted to scream.

And now – this was the terrible secret of which her husband and children were unaware – if anything happened to little Branwen, her husband would probably die.

Branwen heard the wolf when it was only twenty feet behind her. Turning and seeing it, she screamed. The wolf watched her, ready to spring forward. But then it paused. For something surprising happened.

Branwen was terrified, but she was also quick-witted. She knew that if she ran the wolf would have her in its savage teeth in an instant. What could she do? There was only one chance. Like all the village children, she had driven cows. Even running cattle could be turned by a man waving his arms. Perhaps, just possibly, she could face the creature down. If she did not show fear.

If only she had a weapon, even a stick. But she had nothing. The only weapon she possessed was the one she often used at home and which nearly always seemed to work. Her temper. If I can pretend to be angry, she thought. Better yet, if I could just get really angry. Then she would not be afraid.

And so it was that the wolf suddenly found itself confronted by a tiny child, her face red and contorted with rage, waving her little arms and hurling obscenities that, although unintelligible to the wolf, conveyed their sense clearly enough. Stranger yet, instead of running away, the girl was advancing. Uncertain for a moment, the wolf backed away two paces.

"Go. Get away!" the little girl shouted furiously. "Stupid animal. Clear off!" And then, doubling herself up just as she did when she threw a real tantrum at home, she positively screamed: "Get out!"

The wolf backed off a little further. Its ears twitched. But then, watching her carefully, it stood its ground.

Branwen clapped her hands, shouted, stamped her foot. She had actually succeeded in working herself up into a real fury now, though at the same time she was carefully calculating the battle of wills. Did she dare make a rush at the wolf to make it turn and run? Or would it snap at her? Once it bit her, she knew she was finished.

Watching, the wolf sensed her hesitation and understood the bluff. It took two steps towards her, growled, and crouched to spring. Desperately the little girl, knowing that the game was up, bellowed at it in rage. But she had stopped coming forward. The wolf crouched lower.

It was just at this moment that the wolf saw another figure appear behind the girl. The animal tensed. Did this mean hunters were coming? It glanced right and left. No. There was only this single figure, another man-child. Unwilling to abandon this easy prey, the wolf crouched once again. The man-child was only carrying a stick. The wolf ran forward.

The searing pain in its shoulder took the wolf completely by surprise. The boy had thrown the pointed stick so fast it had taken the quick-moving animal off guard. The pain was sharp. The wolf stopped. Then, puzzled, suddenly found it could not go on. Then sank to the ground.

Segovax did not want to tell the grown-ups about the wolf.

"If they find out," he explained, "I'll get in even more trouble."

But the little girl was beside herself with excitement. "You killed it!" she cried joyfully. "With your spear!" And he saw that it was useless.

He sighed. "Come on then." And they began to descend the hill.

It was his mother's reaction that was so mystifying. At first, while his father kissed them both and patted his son on the back, she had said nothing, staring across the river as if the little reunion before her was not taking place. But after his father had gone off to skin the wolf, she turned and fixed her eyes upon Segovax with a terrible, haunted look.

"Your sister nearly died. Do you know that?" He gazed miserably at the ground. He knew there would be trouble. "You would have killed her by letting her go up there alone. Do you understand what you did?"

"Yes, Mother." Of course he understood. But instead of scolding him, Cartimandua had let out a low, despairing moan. He had never heard such a sound before and he looked at her awkwardly. She seemed almost to have forgotten him. She was shaking her head and clutching the little girl at the same time.

"You don't know. You don't know at all." Then she had wheeled round, uttered a cry almost like an animal's wail, and walked away from them both towards the hamlet. And neither he nor Branwen knew what to think.

The terrible bargain had been made when the noble from the great chief Cassivelaunus had first come to plan the river defences that spring. Perhaps the idea would not have occurred to her if it had not been for a casual remark he had made to the women of the hamlet while he was inspecting the weapons of the men.

"If the Romans come to the ford here, you'll all be moved upstream." The dark-bearded captain did not like having women near a battle. In his opinion, they got in the way and distracted their men.

But the remark was enough to set her thinking, then to give her inspiration. That evening, seeing him alone by the fire, she had ventured up to him.

"Tell me, sir," she asked, "if we go upstream, will we have a guard?"

He shrugged. "I dare say. Why?"

"All the people round here trust my husband," she stated. "I think he would be the best one to accompany us."

The noble looked up. "You do, do you?"

"Yes," she said quietly. She saw him smile to himself as one who, having authority, has known every kind of proposition.

"And what," he asked gently, as he gazed at the darkened waters, "would make me think that?"

She stared at him. She knew her attractions.

"Whatever you wish," she replied.

He was silent for some time. Like most military commanders, he did not bother to count the women who offered themselves to him. Some he took; others not. But when his choice came, it was a surprise.

"The fair-haired little girl I noticed beside you this afternoon. She is yours?"

Cartimandua nodded.

And in just a few, brief moments, she had given little Branwen away.

It was all for the best. She had told herself so a thousand times. Branwen would belong to the captain of course. Technically, she would be a slave. He could sell her or do what he liked with her. But the fate of such a girl might not be bad. She would be at the court of the great Cassivelaunus; if the captain liked her he might free her; she might even make a good marriage. Such things happened. Better than waiting around this village where everything was so dull, Cartimandua reasoned. If the girl could learn to control her temper, it could be a fine opportunity.

And in return, her husband would not fight the fearsome Romans, but come with her to safety up the river.

"You will all go upriver," the captain had told her bluntly. "You will deliver the girl to me at the summer's end." Meanwhile, all she had to do was to hide the bargain from her husband. For though she knew he would never agree, once it was done, it would be too late. An oath was an oath in the Celtic world.

No wonder, therefore, that from the day when the wolf nearly killed her, Cartimandua kept the girl always at her side.

Still no news was heard of Julius Caesar.

"Perhaps," Segovax's father cheerfully remarked, "he will not come."

For Segovax, these summer days were happy. Though his

mother continued in her strange, dark mood and kept poor Branwen always at her side, his father seemed to delight in spending time with him. He had mounted one of the wolf's pads for the boy, and Segovax wore it round his neck like a charm. Every day, it appeared, his father was anxious to teach him some new skill of hunting, or carving, or guessing the weather. And then, at midsummer, to his surprise and delight his father suddenly announced: "Tomorrow I shall take you to the sea."

There were several kinds of boats in use upon the river. Normally his father used a simple dugout hollowed from an oak trunk for setting his nets along the bank or crossing the river from time to time. There were rafts, too, of course. The boys of the hamlet had made their own the previous summer, mooring it out in the stream and using it as a platform from which to jump and dive into the river's sparkling waters. There were also little coracles, and occasionally Segovax had seen traders from upriver come by rowing long boats with high, flat-boarded sides that the Celtic islanders also knew how to make skilfully. But for a journey like this, the little hamlet owned one vessel that was especially appropriate. It was kept under cover and tended by his father. And if the boy had any lingering doubts about whether the long-awaited journey would actually take place, they were finally dispelled when his father told him: "We'd better test it on the river. We shall take the wicker boat."

The wicker boat! It consisted of a shallow keel, with broad ribs made of light timber. But this delicate framework was the only hard material in the vessel's hull. Over the frame was stretched a coat not of wood, but of osier woven into stout wickerwork. And over this, to provide the necessary waterproofing, was a coating of skins. Traders from over the seas had long admired the wickerwork of the Celtic Britons. It was one of the island's minor glories.

Though only twenty feet long, the wicker boat had one other refinement. In its centre, secured with stays, was a short mast on which a thin leather sail could be raised. The mast was nothing more than a small, freshly cut tree trunk, carefully chosen so as not to be too heavy, and with a natural fork left at its top as a head for the halyards. Charmingly, it was also the custom to leave some sprigs of leaves growing at the top of the mast, so that the little wicker boat seemed almost like some living tree or bush floating upon the waters.

Primitive the vessel certainly was, but also remarkably convenient. Light enough to be carried; flexible but sturdy; stable enough, despite its shallow draught, to be taken out to sea if necessary. The oars and tidal flow would propel it about the river, but its little sail could be a useful additional source of power – enough, given its lightness, to overcome the river current if the wind was anywhere behind it. For an anchor, it had a heavy stone set in a wooden cage like a lobster basket.

They carefully inspected the little vessel, raised and set the mast, and for several hours that afternoon they tried the boat out upon the river. At the end of which time his father remarked with a smile: "She's perfect."

High tide came some while before dawn the next day, and so it was just at first light that father and son pushed the wicker boat out from the spit and caught the ebb tide that would carry them downstream for many hours. There was also, by good luck, a gentle breeze from the west, so that they could hoist the little leather sail and, using a broad oar to steer, sit back and watch the riverbank pass by.

As they slipped away into the stream, Segovax turned round to see his mother by the end of the spit, her pale face watching them depart. He waved, but she did not wave back.

The river beyond Londinos did not widen quickly, and before it did so, the boy knew they must pass through one of the most striking features in its long and winding course.

For though, in its great journey from the island's interior, the river made many a huge meander, it was just past Londinos that it entered a series of big, tightly packed loops that formed a sort of double S. About a mile from Londinos's eastern hill, it began a big curve towards the north before swinging completely round to the right and almost doubling back on itself as it went south. At the bottom of this southern curve, still only three miles as the crow flew from the eastern hill, the river's course passed directly beside the high ground on the southern bank, which rose from the riverside in a large and gracious slope. At this point the river veered clean round north again, and then, after a mile, back once more.

As they passed through the loops, his father watched Segovax with amusement. Every so often he would ask, "Where is Londinos now, then?" Sometimes it lay to the left, sometimes to the right, sometimes behind. Once, when the boy became confused, he laughed aloud. "You see," he explained, "though we are going away from it, Londinos at this moment is actually ahead of us!" It was a feature of the river well known to those who sailed upon it.

The day was clear. As they progressed downstream, Segovax saw how, just as at Londinos, the water of the river was so clean and clear that the bottom was visible, sometimes sandy, sometimes mud or gravel. At mid-morning they ate the oatcakes Cartimandua had sent with them, and for drink scooped up the sweet-tasting river water with their hands.

It was as the river began gradually to open out that the boy obtained for the first time some sense of the great chalk V in which he had been living.

In Londinos itself, the chalk ridges were not immediately obvious. There were the slopes behind the hamlet, of course. These rose in a series of low ridges for about five miles until they reached a long, high line with sweeping views. But this ridge, formed mainly of clay, lay just within the curving lip of the great chalk downs to the south, and masked them from the world of the river. Similarly, on the river's northern side, the boy was familiar with the gentle wooded slopes, intersected by streams, that formed a background to the twin hillocks by the riverbank. He could see the rising terraces behind those, and the series of promontories and ridges, several hundred feet high, that extended several miles into the distance. But of the great chalk escarpment that veered away north-eastwards behind these inner ridges of clay and sand, he was unaware.

Now, however, a dozen miles downstream from Londinos, a very different landscape had begun to reveal itself. On the left side of the river, where the northern edge of the great chalk V was already more than thirty miles away, the banks were low and marshy. Beyond the banks, his father explained, lay the huge flat wastes of forest and fen that swept round for a hundred miles and more in a vast, bulging curve to form the eastern coast of the island with its endless, wild seascapes by the cold North Sea. "That's a vast, raw land," he remarked to the boy. "Endless beaches. Winds that cut you in half when they come from the east across the sea. Chief Cassivelaunus lives up there." He shook his head. "They're wild, independent tribes," he remarked. "Only a powerful man like that can master them."

But if he looked to his right now, to the southern bank, what a contrast. At this point, the great chalk ridge on the south side of the V was approached by the river. Now, instead of gentle slopes, the boy found himself sailing beside a steep, high bank, behind which there rose, hundreds of feet high, a great, striding ridgeway that extended eastwards as far as the eye could see.

"That's Kent, the land of the Cantii," his father cheerfully told him. "You can walk for days along those chalk ridges until you get to the great white cliffs at the island's end." And he explained the details of the island's long, south-eastern peninsula and how, on a clear day, you could look across the sea to the new Roman province of Gaul. "There are rich farms in the valleys between the ridges," he said.

"Are they as wild as the tribes on the north side of the estuary?" Segovax asked.

"No," his father smiled. "But then they're richer."

For a while they continued in silence, the boy filled with wonder, his father meditative.

"Once," his father said at last, "my grandfather told me something strange. There used to be a song when he was a boy; it said that one time, long ago, there was a huge forest out there," and he gestured eastwards, in the direction of the sea. "But then there was a great flood and the forest's been buried ever since." He paused as they both considered this idea.

"What else did he tell you?"

"He said that at that time, when people first came here, all the land up there" – and now he pointed north – "was covered in ice. It was frozen all the time. And the ice was like a wall."

"What happened to the ice?"

"I suppose the sun melted it."

Segovax looked north. It was hard to imagine this green land dark and frozen all the time.

"Could the land freeze again?"

"What do you think?"

"I don't think so," Segovax said confidently. "The sun always comes up." He continued to stare at the scenery as the boat progressed down the river, which slowly grew wider. His father gazed affectionately at his son, and said a silent prayer to the gods that, after he was gone, the boy would live and beget children in his turn.

It was mid-afternoon when they came in sight of the estuary. They had just rounded a large bend. The river was already a mile wide. And there it lay before them.

"You wanted to see the sea," his father said quietly.

"Oh yes." It was all the boy could say.

How long the estuary was. On the left, the low shoreline began its slow curve, opening ever wider; on the right, the high chalk ridges of Kent stretched straight to the horizon. And between them, the open sea.

It was not quite as he had expected. He had supposed the sea would seem, somehow, to sink away towards the horizon, but if anything the open expanse of waters appeared to swell up, as though the whole ocean was not content to stay where it was, but was anxious to move swiftly forward and pay the river a visit. He gazed at the sea, saw its choppy waves and the patches of darker water that lay across it. He smelt the rich, salty air. And he felt a huge thrill of excitement. Ahead of him lay this great adventure. The estuary was a gateway, and Londinos itself, he now realized, was not just a pleasant place by the river, but the starting point for a journey that led to this wonderful, open world. He stared at it, rapt.

"Over there on the right," his father remarked, "there's a big river." And he pointed to a place some miles along the high coastline where, behind a headland, the great Kentish stream of the Medway came down through a break in the chalk ridge to join the river.

For another hour they drifted down the estuary. The current was becoming slower, the water more choppy. The wicker boat began to bounce about, water slopping over its side. The water seemed greener now, darker. The bottom was no longer visible, and when he scooped some water into his mouth, the boy found that it was salty. His father smiled.

"Tide's turning," he remarked.

To his surprise, Segovax suddenly found that the motion of the little boat was making him feel queasy. He frowned, but his father chuckled.

"Feeling sick? It gets worse if you go out there." He waved towards the sea. Segovax looked at the distant, rolling waters doubtfully. "But you'd still like to go?" his father asked, reading his thoughts.

"I think so. One day."

"The river's safer," his father remarked. "Men drown out there in the sea. It's cruel."

Young Segovax nodded. He was suddenly feeling very sick. But one day, he secretly vowed, however sick it made him, he would taste that great adventure.

"Time to go back," his father said. And then: "There's a bit of luck. The wind's changing."

It was indeed. With a hidden kindness, the wind had dropped and then shifted to the south-east quarter. The little sail flapped as the fisherman put the boat about and started inching back.

Young Segovax sighed. It seemed to him that no day in his life could ever be as perfect as this, alone in the wicker boat with his father, in sight of the sea. The water was gradually getting smoother. The afternoon sun was warm. He felt rather sleepy.

Segovax woke with a start as his father nudged him. They had been progressing very slowly. Though an hour had passed since he had closed his eyes, they were still only just entering the bend of the river, the open estuary behind them. As he woke, however, he gave a little cry of surprise, and his father muttered: "Look at this, now." He was pointing to an object not half a mile away.

Upon the river, they saw a large raft slowly making its way from the north shore. Some twenty men with long poles were pushing it across the stream. Behind them, Segovax could see, another raft was setting off. But what was remarkable was not the large rafts, but their cargo. For each carried, strapped to its deck, a single magnificent chariot.

The Celtic chariot was a fearsome weapon. Pulled by swift horses, it was a light, stable, two-wheeled machine, capable of carrying a fully armed warrior and a couple of helpers. Highly manoeuvrable, these chariots could dash in and out of a mêlée while their occupants darted spears or shot arrows right and left. Sometimes warriors fixed scythe blades to their wheels, which cut to pieces anyone who came close. The chariot on the raft was magnificent. Painted red and black, it gleamed in the sun. Fascinated, Segovax gazed at it while his father turned their boat to accompany this wonder to the southern bank.

But if the boy was taken with the raft and its shining cargo, it was nothing compared with his excitement when, as they neared the shore, his father suddenly exclaimed: "By the gods, Segovax. Do you see that big man on the black horse?"

And when the boy nodded, his father explained: "That's Cassivelaunus himself."

The next two hours were thrilling. While he was made to wait by the wicker boat, his father was busy speaking with the men and helping them get the rafts to shore.

For as Segovax sat waiting by the little boat, no less than twenty chariots were brought across the river and some fifty horses as well. These horses were no less magnificent than the chariots. Some, the largest, were to carry individual warriors. Others, small but swift, were for the chariots. All, he could see, were carefully bred. A quantity of men crossed, too, with cartloads of weapons. Some of them were splendidly arrayed in brightly coloured cloaks and jewellery of shining gold. The boy's heart swelled with pride to see this noble show of his brave, Celtic people. But best of all was when the great chief himself – a huge figure in a red cloak and with long, trailing moustaches – summoned his father over and spoke with him. He saw his father kneel to the chief, saw them exchange words, saw the great man smile warmly, place his hand upon his father's shoulder and then give him a small brooch. His father, a humble peasant but a valiant man, recognized by the greatest chief on the island. Segovax blushed for joy.

It was well into the afternoon when his father came over to him. He was smiling, but seemed preoccupied. "Time to go," he said. Segovax nodded, but sighed. He could have stayed there for ever.

Soon, however, with his father working the oars, they were making good progress back up the river. Looking behind, Segovax saw the last of the rafts being pulled ashore.

"Are they going to fight soon?" he asked.

His father glanced at him with surprise.

"Didn't you realize, boy?" he said quietly. "They were on their way to the coast." He pulled steadily on the oars. "The Romans are coming."

Little Branwen watched her mother curiously. She had been asleep when Segovax and her father left, and the day had promised to be quiet and rather boring. Her mother had spent the morning making a basket, sitting with some of the other women in front of the hut, talking quietly while the children played. And there, no doubt, they would have stayed all afternoon, had it not been for the druid's visit.

He had arrived quite unexpectedly, rowing himself in a dugout, but then one could never account for the old man's comings. With the quiet authority of his ancient order, he had commanded the people of the hamlet to give him a cock and three chickens to sacrifice, and then to accompany him to the sacred places across the river. And so, obediently, not knowing what instinct or premonition had caused the old man suddenly to leave his island, the villagers had followed him, on rafts and coracles, across the broad stream that sunny afternoon.

They had not gone directly to the twin hills of Londinos, but had first made their way to the broad inlet where the stream descended the western flank of the hills. Disembarking on the left side of the inlet, they walked up the bank to a spot about fifty yards from the stream. There was nothing much to see except a group of three rough stones, about as high as a man's knee, which were set around a hole in the ground.

It was a sacred well. No one knew when or why it had first been opened up. It was fed not by the river but by a little spring. And in this deserted well, it was said, a certain benign water goddess dwelt.

Taking one of the chickens, the druid murmured a prayer while the people watched, expertly slit the bird's throat, and dropped it into the well, where a moment later they heard it splash into the water deep below.

Next, returning to their boats, they crossed the inlet and walked up the slope of the western hill. Here, just below the summit on the river side, there was a bare expanse of turf with a fine view over the water. In the centre of this grassy spot there was a little circle cut a few inches into the ground. This was the ritual killing place. Here the druid sacrificed the cock and the other two chickens, sprinkling their blood on the grass within the circle and muttering:

"We have shed blood for you, gods of the river, earth and sky. Protect us now in our hour of need." Then he took the cock and the chickens, and, telling the villagers they could now return home, made his way across to the other hill to commune with the gods alone.

And this, for the people of the hamlet, should have been the end of the matter. They had been dismissed. As they trooped down to their boats and rafts, they were content that they had done all they should.

Except for Cartimandua.

Branwen continued to observe her mother. She was strange; the little girl knew that.

Why else, just as everyone was getting into their boats, should Cartimandua suddenly have begged one of the men to leave a coracle there for her, and then abruptly started back up the hill with Branwen and the baby again? Why, while the rest of the hamlet had reached the southern bank, had they spent all this time searching the two hills for the druid, who had mysteriously vanished? And why was her mother so pale and agitated?

Had the little girl only known it, the reason for Cartimandua's behaviour was all too simple. If the druid had so abruptly and unexpectedly called for these sacrifices, it could only mean one thing. With his special powers and his contact with the gods, the priest had divined that danger was very near. Her own dreadful hour, therefore, had arrived. The Romans were coming. And once again, with a terrible force, the agony of her dilemma had thrust itself before her.

Had she done wrong? What could she do? Hardly knowing what to say or what to ask, she had returned in search of the druid. Surely he could guide her, before it was too late.

Yet where had he gone? Carrying the baby, and dragging little Branwen along by the hand, she had traversed the western hill, crossed, by stepping stones, the little brook between the twin hills, and mounted to the summit of the eastern hill, expecting to find the old man there. But there was no sign of him, and she was about to give up when she saw a thin column of smoke coming from the far side of the hill. She hastened towards it.

There was one other curious feature of the place called Londinos. On its downstream side, the eastern hill did not fall away evenly. Instead, a spur continued, before curving round and descending to the river. Thus, on the hill's south-eastern flank, there was a sort of natural, open-air theatre, with a pleasant, grassy platform by the riverbank providing the stage, and the hill and its curving spur the auditorium. The slopes around this spacious stage were grassy and dotted with a few trees; the platform itself covered only with turf and some bushes. It was here, by the riverside, that the druid had built a little fire.

From the slopes above, Cartimandua watched, but hesitated to go down. This was for two reasons.

Firstly, from where she stood, she could see what the druid was doing. He had extracted bones from the birds he had sacrificed and was placing them in the fire. That meant he was telling oracles – one of the most secret rites the Celtic priests performed, and one that should not be audaciously interrupted. The second reason concerned the place itself.

It was the ravens.

On the curving slopes around this riverside site, for as long as anyone could remember, there had dwelt a colony of ravens.

Cartimandua knew, of course, that if you treated them well, ravens were birds not of evil, but of good omen. Their powerful spirits, it was said, could defend the Celtic tribes. Probably that was why the druid had chosen this spot to read the oracles. Yet as she gazed at them, Cartimandua could not suppress a shiver. The large, black birds with their powerful beaks had always frightened her. How grim and ungainly they looked as they flapped and hopped about on the turf, making their horrible, deep, croaking caws. If she ventured down there, at any moment she would expect one of them to walk over to her, grasp her hand or leg in its vicious claws, and hammer a hole in her flesh with its brutal beak.

But the druid had looked up and seen her. For a moment he gazed at her, apparently annoyed. Then he silently beckoned her to come down.

"Wait here," she suddenly said to little Branwen, handing her the baby. "Wait and don't move." And taking a deep breath, she walked down the slope past the ravens.

As long as she lived, Branwen remembered the long minutes that followed. How afraid she had been, standing at the top of the grassy slope, alone with the baby, watching her mother and the old man below. Even though she could see Cartimandua, she did not like being left in this strange, eerie place, and if she, too, had not been afraid of the ravens, she might have run down to her mother.

She saw her talking earnestly to the druid; saw the old man slowly shake his head. It seemed, then, that Cartimandua was pleading. At last, gravely, the old druid took several bones out of the fire and inspected them. Then he said something. And suddenly, a terrible sound came from below, echoing so loudly that it caused the ravens to rise, startled into the air, and descend with cross, croaking sounds. It was an awful, wailing scream that might have come from a desperate animal.

But it came from Cartimandua.

Still, no one had guessed his secret. Segovax felt pleased with himself. Ever since their return, Londinos had been a hive of activity. The dark-bearded noble had already arrived by the time they reached the hamlet, and his father had immediately been sent with the other men to the ford just up the river. Indeed, so busy had the men been that his family had hardly seen the fisherman from that time.

The preparations were extensive. They were driving pointed stakes into the riverbed at the ford. Men from every hamlet within miles had been summoned to cut down trees so that all along the bank of the druid's island they could build a stout wooden palisade.

News came daily now, as fresh men arrived at the ford from all quarters. The news was sometimes confusing.

"All the British tribes have sworn to follow Cassivelaunus," one fellow stated, whilst another declared: "The Celtic tribes across the sea in Gaul are going to rise. We'll soften Caesar up here. Then they'll cut off his retreat." But others were less confident. "The other chiefs are jealous of Cassivelaunus," some wiser heads remarked. "They can't be trusted."

Yet at first the reports were good. Caesar had landed by the white cliffs on the south coast and started to march through Kent, but straight away the island gods had struck. As before, a huge storm had nearly wrecked his fleet, forcing the Roman back to the coast to repair it. When he began to march once more, the swift Celts in their chariots had harried his line, swooping down, wasting his troops. "They'll never reach the river at all," people were saying now. Still, the busy work went on.

For Segovax, it was a time of suspense – a little frightening, but most of all exciting. Soon, he felt sure, they would come. Then it would be time for his secret plan. "The Celts will smash them, of course," he proudly explained to Branwen. He sneaked off along the riverbank until he came to a place where he could watch the preparations. By the second morning, they were floating extra timbers down the stream.

Cartimandua was now in a daze of terror and confusion. If Branwen left her side, she grew anxious. If the baby cried, she rushed to it. If Segovax disappeared, as he so often did, she would search for him frantically and hug the embarrassed boy to her as soon as she found him.

Above all, she would glance continuously in the direction of the ford where her husband was working. For two nights now, the men had camped there, and though she and the other women had brought food, it had been impossible to talk to him.

If only she could make sense of it all. If only she understood what the druid's terrible words had meant.

Perhaps she should not have approached the old man that day. He had certainly not wanted to speak to her. But she had been so anxious, she had been unable to help herself. "Tell me," she had begged, "what is to befall me and my family?" Even then he had seemed to hesitate, until at last, almost with a shrug, he had drawn some bones from his fire, inspected them, and nodded in a way that somehow suggested that he had seen what he had expected. Yet what did it mean?

"There are three men whom you love," he had told her bleakly. "And you are going to lose one of them."

Lose one? Which one? The three men could only be her husband, Segovax, and the baby. There were no other menfolk in her life. He must mean her husband. But hadn't she saved him? Wasn't he coming safely upriver with them if the Romans came?

The day after he had arrived, she had sought out the dark-bearded noble as he was directing the men preparing the defences. Was their bargain still good? she had demanded. "I have already told you," he had answered impatiently, and waved her away.

What could it mean, then? That some new accident was to befall Branwen to destroy the bargain? Or was it not her husband at all? Was something going to happen to Segovax, or the baby? In a new agony of doubt she felt as if she were an animal, trapped with her young, trying desperately to shield first one and then another from the advances of snapping predators.

Finally, after several days of suspense, news came that Cassivelaunus had massed his hordes for a huge pitched battle.

They were streaming in now, warriors of all kinds: foot soldiers, horsemen and charioteers. Contingent after contingent arriving hot and dusty at the ford.

Some spoke of treachery, of chiefs who had deserted. "The Romans bribed them," they said. "May they be cursed by the gods." But if they were angry, they were still not downhearted. "One defeat is nothing. Wait until the Romans taste our vengeance." Although when Segovax ventured to ask one of the men in the chariots what the Romans were like, he answered frankly: "They stay in formation." And then: "They are terrible."

There were no more defences in the south now. The river was the next barrier. "The battle will be here," the boy's father told him on a brief visit to the hamlet. "This is where Caesar will be stopped." The next day the women of the hamlet were told: "Be ready to evacuate. You leave tomorrow."

Segovax watched carefully the next morning as his father put on his sword. Usually it was kept wrapped in skins from which, twice a year, his father removed it for inspection. At such times Segovax was allowed to hold it, but not to touch the blade. "You'll rust it," his father would explain as he carefully oiled it before putting it back in its wood and leather scabbard and wrapping it up again.

It was a typical Celtic weapon. It had a long, broad, iron blade with a ridge down it. At the hilt was a simple crossbar, but the pommel was carved in the shape of a man's head that stared out fiercely at the enemy.

As he watched, the boy was strangely moved. How worn his father looked after the backbreaking work of the last few days. His spine was bent in a way that suggested he had been in some pain. His arms seemed to hang more loosely than usual. His soft, kindly eyes were tired. And yet, vulnerable though he might be, he was brave. He seemed almost eager for battle. About his whole body and face there was a determined masculinity that overcame his physical frailty. As he took his shield down from the wall and collected two spears, Segovax thought his father was transformed into a noble warrior, and this made the boy proud, for he wanted his father to be strong.

Thus prepared, the fisherman took his son to one side and spoke to him gravely. "If anything happens to me, Segovax," he said quietly, "you will be the man of the family. You must look after your mother and your sister and brother. Do you understand?"

A few moments later, he called little Branwen over and started to tell her to be good, but the absurdity of the idea made him laugh, and he contented himself with giving her a hug and a kiss instead.

And now all was ready. By the end of the spit, the party was waiting to leave. Four large dugouts contained the women and children of the hamlet. There were also two rafts carrying provisions and their movable belongings. The men of the hamlet stood by, awaiting final orders from the noble in charge, who was coming down the river now, from the palisade.

Minutes later the dark-bearded captain was there. His hard, shrewd eyes glanced around, taking them all in. Cartimandua, standing in the boat with her three children, caught his eye. He nodded imperceptibly.

"Seems in order," he remarked gruffly. Surveying the men, he quickly picked out three. "You will go with the boats as guards." He paused. "All the hamlets will assemble five days upriver. There's a fort there. You'll be told what to do next."

Then he glanced at her husband. "You go too. You're in charge. Post a watch each night." And he turned to go.

It had worked. She felt a flood of relief. Thank the gods. For the moment, at least, they were all safe. She started to sit down in the boat. And so, for an instant, she hardly realized that her husband had failed to move.

She looked at the other women in the boat with their children. She smiled, then noticed that her husband was speaking and began to listen.

"I cannot."

The captain was frowning. He was used to being obeyed. But Segovax's father was shaking his head.

What was he saying? Suddenly she became aware. How could he be refusing to go?

"It's an order," the noble said sharply.

"But I swore an oath. Only days ago," the fisherman was explaining. "To Cassivelaunus himself. I swore to fight with him at Londinos."

They all heard him. Cartimandua heard herself gasp, felt herself go very cold. He had not mentioned an oath. But then, she realized, she had scarcely seen him since his return.

"An oath?" The captain looked perplexed.

"Look, he gave me a brooch," the fisherman went on. "He told me to wear it in battle so that he would know me." And he produced the brooch from the pouch on his belt.

There was silence. The captain gazed at the brooch. The fellow might be only a simple villager, but an oath was a sacred thing. As for an oath to a chief . . . The brooch, he could see, was Cassivelaunus'. He looked at Cartimandua. She had gone an ashen colour. He looked at the girl. A pretty little thing. But there was nothing to be done about that now. The bargain was off.

He grunted irritably, then pointed to another man. "You. You're in charge instead. Get going." Then he was gone.

As the fisherman watched the boat with his wife and children go off, he felt a sense of melancholy, and yet also of satisfaction. He knew his little son could see that he was not as strong as other men. He was glad that he should have heard, in front of everyone, about his oath to the great British chief.

* * *

The boats went slowly. As they rounded the bend, Segovax gazed at the forces gathering there. They had been coming fast. Already there was line upon line of chariots; behind the palisades were scores of little fires around which groups of men gathered. "They're saying that when Cassivelaunus arrives tomorrow," his father had told him, "there may be as many as four thousand chariots." How proud he was to think of his father as part of that great array.

They left the ford and the druid's island behind, went southwards for another half-mile and then the river curved again, to the right, so that the boy could no longer see the battle lines. On each side were mud flats and islands, green and heavy with willow trees.

Branwen, leaning her head against him, had fallen asleep in the sun. His mother, staring out at the water, was silent.

As the river meandered through a broad, level valley of meadows and greensward dotted with trees, Segovax realized now that the river was flowing against them, downstream. There was no longer any tidal flow in from the estuary. They had passed out of reach of the sea.

They camped under willow trees that night, then proceeded on their way joined by the folk from another hamlet. Once more they passed a quiet sunny day working their way slowly up the pleasant stream. Nobody noticed that, as evening fell, a new air of excitement came over Segovax. How could they guess that now, at last, it was time for his secret plan.

Segovax crept through the darkness. There was no moon, but the stars were bright. Nobody stirred. The night was warm. They had made camp that night on a long, thin island in the stream. As the sun set, the sky had had that hard, red colour that promises a fine day to come. Everybody was tired by the journey. They had all made a big fire, eaten and then lain down wherever they were to sleep under the stars.

He heard an owl. Moving carefully, his spear in one hand, he made his way down to the water's edge.

The people from the other hamlet had brought with them two small coracles, one of which had a pointed prow like a canoe. The moment he had seen it, he had known that this was his chance. It was lying on the muddy bank now. It was so light, he found that he could easily drag it with one hand. He had just begun to slide it into the water when he heard a familiar patter of little feet on the mud behind him. It was Branwen. He sighed. She never slept.

"What are you doing?"

"Sssh."

"Where are you going?"

"To Father."

"To fight?"

"Yes."

She greeted this tremendous news with silence, but only for a moment.

"Take me with you."

"I can't. Stay here."

"No!"

"Branwen, you know you can't come."

"No I don't."

"You don't know how to fight. You're too little."

Even in the dark, he could see her face begin to pucker and swell and her hands bunch with rage.

"I'm coming."

"It's dangerous."

"I don't care."

"You'll wake everyone."

"I don't care. I'll cry." This was a very real threat.

"Please, Branwen. Give me a kiss."

"No!"

He hugged her. She hit him. Then, before she could wake anyone, he pushed the coracle into the water and stepped inside it. Moments later he was paddling swiftly out of sight, down the stream into the darkness.

He had done it. Ever since the news of the invasion had come, just before the druid had offered the shield to the river, he had secretly planned this expedition. Day after day he had practised with his spear until he achieved an accuracy that few adults could equal. And now his chance had come at last. He was going to fight beside his father. He can't very well send me away if I suddenly arrive just as battle is beginning, he thought.

The night was long. With the current flowing behind him, and with the little paddle to help, he was able to slip down the river at two or three times the speed the boats had made coming up. In the darkness the banks seemed to race by.

But he was only nine. After an hour his arms felt tired; after two they were aching. He pressed on, though. Two hours later, in the deepest night, he began to long for sleep. He had never been up so late. Once or twice his head fell forward and he came awake again with a start.

Perhaps, he told himself, if I was just to lie down for a little while, but an instinct also warned him: do that and you will sleep until midmorning. He found that if he kept the vision of his father before him, it gave him strength. In this way, resting his arms now and then, and thinking always, hour after long hour, of his father waiting for him upon the battlefield, he was given the power to press on. They would fight together, side by side. Perhaps they would die together. It seemed to him that this was all in the world he desired.

As the dawn began to lighten the sky, he entered the start of the river's tidal flow. Luckily, it was on the ebb, and so it carried him swiftly down, towards Londinos and the sea.

By the time the sun was up, the river was getting much wider. An hour later and he was approaching a familiar bend. Even his lack of sleep was forgotten in the excitement as he began to turn it and came in sight of the druid's island, less than a mile ahead. Then he gasped in amazement.

In front of him, the Romans were crossing the river.

The force that Caesar had assembled for the conquest of Britain was formidable indeed. Five disciplined legions – some twenty-five thousand men, with two thousand cavalry. He had lost only a few men in the south-eastern peninsula of Kent.

The alliance of British chiefs was already beginning to crumble. Caesar's intelligence was excellent. He knew that if he could break Cassivelaunus now, a number of important chiefs would probably start to come over to him.

But this river crossing was a serious matter. The day before a captured Celt had told them about the stakes in the riverbed. The palisade opposite was stout. The Romans had one great advantage, however.

"The trouble with the Celts," Caesar had remarked to one of his staff, "is that their strategy doesn't match their tactics." So long as the Celts harried his line with their chariots in a game of hit and run, it was almost impossible for the Romans to defeat them. Given time, they could wear him down. Their strategy, therefore, should have been to play a waiting game. "But the fools want a pitched battle," he observed. And here the Romans would usually win.

It was a simple question of discipline and armaments. When the Roman legions locked their shields together in a great square, or, in a smaller detachment, locked their shields over their heads to form the ancient equivalent of a tank, they were quite impregnable to the Celtic infantry, and even the wheeling chariots found it very hard to break them. Looking across the river, therefore, to where the Celtic horde was drawn up on open ground, Caesar knew that his only serious obstacle was the river. Without more ado, therefore, he gave the order: "Advance."

> There is only one place to ford the River and even that is difficult.

So Caesar wrote in his history. There was, of course, nothing intrinsically difficult about the ford, but Caesar, as a good politician and general, was not likely to admit that.

> I at once ordered the cavalry to advance and the legions to follow. Only their heads were above water, but they pushed on with such speed and vigour that infantry and cavalry were able to make the assault together.

It was hardly surprising that neither Julius Caesar nor anyone else noticed a little coracle, several hundred yards upstream, beaching on the river's muddy northern bank.

By the time he found himself on solid turf, Segovax was a small brown figure caked in mud. He did not care. He had made it.

The Celtic line was less than a mile away. How splendid it looked. He scanned the thousands of figures for a sight of his father, but could not see him. Dragging his spear and making a squelching sound as he walked, he slowly advanced. The river was full of Romans now. The first formations were grouping on the northern bank. Huge concerted shouts arose from the massed Celtic forces. From the Romans, silence. Still the boy moved on.

And then it began.

Segovax had never seen a battle before. He had no conception, therefore, of the incredible confusion. Suddenly everywhere men were running, whilst chariots wheeled about at such speed that it seemed as though in a matter of seconds they might bear down across the meadows upon him. The Romans' armour seemed to glint and flash like some terrible, fiery creature. The noise, even from where he stood, was tremendous. Amidst the din, he heard men, grown men, screaming with cries of agony dreadful to hear.

Above all, he had had no idea how big everyone would seem. When a Roman cavalryman suddenly appeared and cantered across the meadow a hundred yards from him, he was like a giant. The boy, clutching his spear, felt completely puny.

He stopped. The battle, now half a mile away, was edging towards him. Three chariots rushed out, straight at him, then careered away. He had not the faintest idea where, in this terrifying mêlée, his father might be. He found that he was trembling.

Now half a dozen horsemen, all together, were chasing a Celtic chariot that was wheeling about only two hundred yards away.

A galloping cavalry charge is a fearsome thing to behold. Even trained infantry, formed in squares, usually shiver. An unruly crowd, faced with charging horsemen, will always flee. Small wonder, then, that the boy, suddenly aware that an entire army was moving towards him, should have found himself so frightened that he could not go on. He started to back away. Then he fled.

For weeks he had prepared. All night he had paddled downriver to be with his father. And now here he was, only hundreds of yards away from him, unable to run to his side.

He stood, shaking, by the riverbank for another two hours. Below him, beached on the mud flat, was the little coracle into which, if the battle came closer, he was ready to jump. White with fear, he felt terribly cold. The day seemed to echo like a nightmare. As he gazed at the huge battle going on across the meadows, he realized with horror: I must be a coward.

"If only," he prayed to the gods, "my father does not see me, a coward, now."

But there was no danger of that. Upon the Romans' third rush his father had fallen, sword in hand, as the gods had revealed that he would.

Segovax remained there all day. By mid-afternoon the battle was over. The Celts, brutally broken, had fled northwards, pursued some distance by Roman cavalry, who mercilessly hacked down all they could. By early evening, the victors had set up camp just to the east, near the twin hillocks of Londinos. The battlefield – a huge area strewn with broken chariots, abandoned weapons and bodies – was empty and eerily quiet. It was upon this desolate field that, at last, Segovax ventured forth.

Only once or twice before had he seen human death. He was not prepared, therefore, for the strange greyness, and stiffening heaviness of the corpses. Some were horribly mutilated; many had missing limbs. The smell of death was beginning to permeate the place. The bodies were everywhere: in the meadow, around the stakes and palisades: in the water around the druid's island. How should he find his father amongst all these, if he was there? Could it be he would not recognize him?

The sun was already reddening when he came upon him near the water. He saw him at once, because he was lying on his back, his sweet, thin face gazing up at the sky, his mouth, wide open, giving him a vacant, pathetic air. His flesh was blue-grey. A short, broad Roman sword had opened a frightful gash in his side.

The boy knelt beside him. A red heat seemed to rise in his throat, choking him and filling his eyes with hot tears. He put his hands out and touched his father's beard.

And was so racked with sobs that he was not aware he was no longer alone.

It was just a small party of Roman soldiers, accompanied by a centurion. They had come to search for any fallen Roman weapons. Seeing the lone figure, they walked towards him.

"A scavenger," one of the legionaries remarked in disgust. They were only twenty feet away when the boy, hearing the clinking of their armour, turned and looked at them with terror.

Roman soldiers. The evening sun was glowing on their breastplates. They were going to kill him. Or at least take him prisoner. He glanced round frantically. There was nowhere to run to. He had only the river behind him. Should he make a dash for that? Try to swim away? They would catch him before he could get into the current. Segovax glanced down. His father's sword was lying beside him where he had fallen. He stooped, picked it up, and faced the approaching centurion.

If he's going to kill me, he decided, I may as well fight.

The sword was heavy, but he held it firmly, his young face set. The centurion, frowning slightly as he continued to advance, indicated that he should put the weapon down. Segovax shook his head. The centurion was very close now. Calmly he drew his own short sword. Segovax's eyes grew large. He prepared to fight, hardly knowing what to do. And then the centurion struck.

It was so fast, the boy hardly saw it. There was a metallic bang, and to his astonishment his father's sword had gone from his hand and was already lying on the ground again, while his wrist and hand felt as if they had been wrenched apart. The face of the centurion was calm. He took another step forward.

He's going to kill me, the boy thought. I'm going to die by my father after all. Though now, seeing the grey corpse beside him, there no longer seemed anything attractive in such a death. Anyway, he thought, I'll die fighting. And once more he scrambled to grab the sword.

To his horror, he could hardly lift it. His wrist hurt so much that he needed both hands. Swinging the sword wildly, he was vaguely aware of the centurion's calm face watching him. He swung again, hitting nothing. And then he heard a laugh.

He had been so intent on the centurion that he had not noticed the approach of the riders. There were half a dozen of them, and they were now staring down at the little scene curiously. In the middle of them was a tall figure with a bald head and a hard, intelligent face. It was he who had laughed. He said something to the centurion, and everyone laughed with him.

Segovax went red. The man had spoken in Latin, so he had no idea what he had said. Some cruel joke perhaps. No doubt, he supposed, they proposed to watch him die. With a huge effort he swung his father's sword again.

But to his surprise, the centurion had sheathed his own sword. The Romans were moving away. They were leaving him alone, with his father's body.

Segovax would have been surprised indeed if he had known the words that Julius Caesar had just spoken.

"Here's a brave young Celt. He still won't give up. Better leave him alone, centurion, or he might kill us all!"

On his father's tunic, Segovax saw, was pinned the brooch that Cassivelaunus had given him. Reverently he took it, with the sword, and started to leave, pausing only once, for a last look at his father's face.

In the months that followed the engagement at the river, Caesar did not take over the island of Britain. Whether he intended to occupy it there and then has never been clear, and he was far too wily to make it plain in his own account.

The British chieftains had to supply extensive tributes and hostages. Caesar claimed a triumphant success. By autumn, however, he and his legions had returned to Gaul, where trouble was brewing. In all likelihood, realizing that his conquests had run too far, too fast, Caesar had decided to consolidate his rule in Gaul before taking over the island at a later date. Meanwhile, life on the island returned, for the time being at least, to something like its normal state.

The next spring, though it was half expected, neither Caesar nor any Romans came. Nor in the summer.

Except once. For on a summer's day that year, the inhabitants of the hamlet looked out early one morning to see a strange sight. A ship was advancing up the river on the incoming tide, and it was unlike any they had ever seen.

It was, in truth, not very large, although to the people of the hamlet it seemed so. It was a squat sailing vessel, about eighty feet long, with a high stern, a low bow, and a mast amidships that carried a big, square sail made of canvas sewn with rings through which the brails for gathering the sails were neatly passed. A smaller mast, sloping over the bow, carried a little triangular sail for extra power. Its sides were smooth, made of planks fastened to the ribs with iron nails. It was steered not with one but two rudders, placed on each side of the stern.

It was, in short, a typical merchant vessel of the classical world. Its swarthy sailors, and the rich Roman who owned it, had ventured into the river out of curiosity.

They rowed ashore to the hamlet and approached the villagers politely. They made it clear that they were anxious to see the place where the battle had been fought, if it was thereabouts. After some hesitation, two of the men agreed to show them the ford and the druid's island, which they inspected. Then, finding nothing else at Londinos to interest them, they left on the ebb tide, having paid the people of the hamlet for their trouble with a silver coin.

It was a visit of no historical significance whatever. A fleeting visit from a ship riding on a tide of much greater history, making a detour to an almost nonexistent place to satisfy a rich man's curiosity.

But for young Segovax, it meant everything. With fascination he studied the outlandish boat moored so tantalizingly in the stream before him. Avidly he inspected the silver coin, gazed at the god's head upon it, understanding that its purpose was more than ornamental, though he could not exactly guess its use and value. Above all, as he watched the ship depart downstream again, he remembered that precious day when he had seen the open sea with his father.

"That's where the ship is going," he murmured aloud. "Out on that sea. One day, maybe it'll come here again." And secretly he dreamed of going on it, Roman though it was, whatever its destination might be.

Strangely, it seemed that it was Segovax, more than the rest of his family, who suffered. It had come as a great surprise to the boy when, after three months of uncontrollable grief, Cartimandua had suddenly taken up with another man. The man was from another hamlet, and was kind to the children. But still his own grief would not depart. Who knew how long it might have persisted had it not been brought to a close at the end of autumn by a small event?

There was, in the Celtic world, a great feast that took place at the start of winter. This was Samhain, a time when the spirits were active upon the earth, arising from graves, visiting the living, reminding men that the community of the dead who kept the ancient habitations demanded recognition from later trespassers too. It was an exciting but rather frightening time, at which feasts were prepared and important oaths made.

A few days after Samhain, on a mellow, misty afternoon, the boy and his sister had decided to play at the end of the gravel spit by the hamlet. Now, however, having tired of their games, Branwen had gone away, and the boy, feeling suddenly melancholy, was sitting on a stone, gazing across the river at the hills of Londinos opposite.

He had taken to sitting like this recently, especially since the visit of the strange ship. He found comfort watching the river's slow, tidal breathing. Here, at dawn, he could watch the golden light of the rising sun strike the little eastern hill, and at sunset watch the reddening glow of its departure upon its western counterpart. Here, it seemed to him, the rhythm of life and death made a perpetual and satisfying echo. He had been there some time when he heard a footfall and saw, approaching him, the old druid from his island.

The old man had been looking frail of late. The battle of the previous year had been, some said, a great shock to him. Yet still, in the year since Caesar's departure, he made his quiet, unannounced rounds of the hamlets. Now, recognizing the boy sitting sadly alone, he paused.

Segovax was surprised that the druid should wish to speak to him. He rose politely, but the old man waved him to sit down again, and then, to the boy's still greater astonishment, calmly sat down beside him.

But if Segovax had supposed that the presence of the druid might be a little frightening, he was surprised once more, and very pleasantly. Far from being alarming, there was an inner calm about him that was comforting. They talked for a long time, the priest gently questioning, Segovax replying with greater confidence, until, at last, and with a strange sense of relief, the boy told him all about the terrible day of the battle, and what he had seen, and even of his cowardice.

"But battles are not for children." The druid smiled gently. "I do not think you are a coward, Segovax." He paused. "You think you let your father down? That you failed him?"

The boy nodded.

"But he did not expect to see you there," the old man

reminded him. "Didn't he tell you to look after your mother and sister?"

"Yes." And then, despite himself, and thinking of the new man his mother had taken, he burst out tearfully, "But I've lost him. I've lost my father. He'll never come back to me again."

The old man gazed across the river, and for a time said nothing. Although he knew the boy's grief was as useless as it was understandable, Segovax's sense of loss touched him in ways the boy could not have dreamed of. Indeed, it reminded him only too well of anxieties and mysteries that had troubled him for a long time now.

It was a strange thing, this possession of second sight. Though it was true that sometimes he was granted a direct vision of future events – just as he had known the fate of this peasant's family before the Romans had come – his gift was not so much a sudden illumination as part of a more general process, a special sense of life that had become more pervasive as he grew older. If, for most men, life was like a long day between the sunrise of birth and the sunset of death, to him it appeared differently.

Instead, to the old druid, this life seemed more and more dreamlike. Outside it lay not darkness, but something light, very actual; something he felt he had always known, even if he could not describe it, and to which he would return. Sometimes, with awful clarity, the gods would indeed show him a piece of the future, and at such times he knew he must keep their secret from other men. But usually he stumbled forward through life with only a vague sense that he was part of something predetermined, that had always been so. The gods, he felt, were guiding him towards his destiny, and death was only a fleeting thing, part of a larger day.

But here was the strange and disquieting thing. In the last two years, the gods themselves seemed to have been signalling to him that even this larger destiny, this encompassing shadow world, was coming to an end. It was almost, he sensed, as if the ancient island gods were preparing to withdraw. Was the world coming to an end? Or, he wondered, did the gods, like men, pass on, falling as leaves to the ground?

Or perhaps, he thought, as he sat beside this simple boy with his tuft of white hair and his webbed hands, perhaps the gods were just like streams, flowing invisibly into the larger river.

Quietly, then, putting his hand on the boy's shoulder, he ordered him: "Bring me your father's sword." A few minutes later, when Segovax had brought the weapon, the old man, with a huge blow, broke the iron sword upon the stone.

For this breaking of swords was a ritual custom among the Celts.

Then, taking the two pieces of the sword, the druid put one arm around the boy and with the other hurled the broken sword high out into the stream. Segovax watched as they splashed far out in the waters.

"End your grief," the druid said quietly. "The river is your father now."

And though he could not speak, the boy understood, and knew that it was true.

Chapter 2

Londinium

AD 251

The two men sat facing each other across a table. Neither spoke as they went about their dangerous work.

It was a summer afternoon – the ides of June by the Roman calendar. Few people were about in the street outside. There was no breeze. Inside, the heat was oppressive.

Like most ordinary folk, the two men did not wear the cumbersome Roman toga, but a simple knee-length dress of white wool, fastened with clasps at both shoulders and held in at the waist with a belt. The larger man wore a short cape of the same material; the younger preferred to leave his shoulders bare. Both wore leather sandals.

The room was modest, typical of that quarter, where thatched frame houses and workshops huddled round courtyards off the small streets. The clay and wattle walls were plastered white; in one corner was a workbench, a rack of chisels and a hand axe, proclaiming the occupant to be a carpenter.

It was quiet. The only sound was the gentle rasping of the metal file in the larger man's hand. Outside, however, at the end of the narrow street, someone was keeping watch. A necessary precaution. For the penalty for their activity was death.

At the place where the two gravel hills stood by the riverbank, there was now a great, walled city.

Londinium lay peacefully under a clear blue sky. It was a gracious place. The twin hills by the river had been transformed into gently swelling slopes with graceful terraces. At the summit of thc eastern hill rested a stately forum, its sedate stone buildings reflecting the sunlight with a pale stare. From the forum, a broad street led down to a stout wooden bridge across the river. On the western hill, just behind the crown, a huge, oval-shaped amphitheatre dominated the skyline, and behind that, in the north-west corner, lay the headquarters of the military garrison. Down on the riverfront were wooden wharves and warehouses, whilst on the eastern bank of the brook that ran down between the hills were the pleasant gardens of the Governor's Palace. And the whole ensemble – temples and theatres, stucco-covered mansion houses and tenements, red-tiled roofs and gardens – was enclosed on its landward sides by a fine, high wall with gates for entrances.

Two great thoroughfares crossed the city from west to east. One, entering by the upper of the two gates in the western wall, strode across the summits of the two hills before exiting through an eastern gate. The other, entering through the lower western gate, ran across the upper half of the western hill and then sloped down to cross the brook and continue past the Governor's Palace.

This was Londinium: two hills joined by two great streets and enclosed by a wall. Its waterfront was more than a mile long; its population perhaps as much as twenty-five thousand. It had already been standing there for about two hundred years.

The Romans had waited to come to Britain. After the battle by the river, Caesar had not come a third time. Ten years later, the great conqueror had been stabbed to death in the Senate in Rome. Another century had passed before, in AD 43, the Emperor Claudius had crossed the narrow sea to claim the island for civilization.

Once begun, however, the occupation had been swift and thorough. Military bases were immediately set up in the main tribal centres. The land was surveyed. It did not take long for the canny Roman colonizers to interest themselves in the place that went by the Celtic name of Londinos. It was not a tribal capital. Just as in Caesar's time, the main tribal centres lay to the east, on either side of the long river estuary. But it was still the first place where one could ford the river, and therefore the natural focus for a system of roads.

However, the Romans were interested not so much in the ford as in another feature entirely, one that lay close by; for when the Roman engineers saw the two gravel hillocks on the north bank, and the gravel promontory that jutted out into the stream opposite, they came to an immediate and obvious conclusion.

"This is the perfect place for a bridge," they reported. Downstream, the river grew wider, opening out into a pool. Upstream, the banks were marshy. "But the crossing here is quite narrow," they pointed out, "and the gravel bed gives us a firm foundation to build on." Better yet, the tidal flow continued past this point, allowing ships to pass easily up- and downstream on its ebb and flow, and the inlet between the hillocks where the little stream came down was a convenient harbour for smaller vessels. "It's a natural port," they concluded.

Tamesis, they called the river, and, Latinizing the existing name, they called the port Londinium.

It was inevitable that, as time went on, this port should increasingly have become the focus of activity on the island. Not only was it the centre of trade, but all the roads radiated from the bridge.

And the Roman roads were the key to everything. Ignoring entirely the ancient system of prehistoric tracks along the ridges, the straight, metalled roads of the Roman engineers struck across the island, joining tribal capitals and administrative centres in an iron framework they were never entirely to lose. From the white cliffs of Dover in the south-eastern peninsula of Kent, up through Canterbury and Rochester, ran the road known as Watling Street. To the east, above the broad opening of the estuary, lay the road to Colchester. Due north, a great road led to Lincoln and on to York; and in the west, past Winchester, a network of roads joined Gloucester, the Roman spa of Bath with its medicinal springs, and the pleasant market towns of the warm south-west.

In the summer of the year 251, the province of Britain was calm, as, for two centuries, it had usually been. True, in the early days a huge revolt led by the British Queen Boudicca had briefly shaken the province; for a long time, too, the proud people of Wales had troubled the west of the island, whilst in the north the wild Picts and Scots had never been subdued. The Emperor Hadrian had even built a great wall from coast to coast to lock them up in their moors and highland fastnesses. More recently, it had also been necessary to build two strong naval forts on the east coast to deal with troublesome Germanic pirates on the seas.

But in the increasingly troubled world of the sprawling empire, where barbarians kept breaking through the frontiers in eastern Europe, where political strife seemed endemic and where that very year no fewer than five emperors had been proclaimed in one place or another, Britain was a haven of peace and modest prosperity. And Londinium was its great emporium.

At this moment, however, young Julius had almost forgotten the awful threat from the law as he considered what the man with the file had just said to him. For although Sextus was his partner and his friend, he could also be dangerous.

Sextus. He was a swarthy, heavy-jowled man in his late twenties. The dark hair on his head was already thin. His face was clean-shaven, or rather plucked, in the Roman manner, except for a pair of thick, curly, muttonchop sideburns, of which he was very proud and which some women, at least, found attractive. These good looks were a little modified by the fact that the middle of his face seemed to have been squeezed together, so that his dark brown eyes looked out as if from under a ledge. His manner was slightly ponderous, and his shoulders appeared to be rather heavier than the gods had originally intended, causing him to stoop over his work and to make a bobbing motion when he walked.

"The girl's mine. Keep your hands off her." The warning had come quite suddenly, out of nowhere, whilst they worked in silence. Sextus had not even looked up as he spoke, but there was a flat finality to his voice that told Julius to be cautious. He was surprised, too. How had Sextus guessed?

The older man had often taken young Julius out drinking and introduced him to women, but he had always been a mentor, never a rival. This was something new. It was also full of risk. His partnership with Sextus in their illicit business was the only way Julius could get his hands on the extra money he wanted. It would be foolish to jeopardize that. Sextus knows how to use a knife too, he thought. But even so, he was not sure he was going to obey the order.

Besides, he had already sent the letter.

* * *

When women saw Julius, they smiled. People sometimes took him for a sailor; there was a freshness and innocence about him that suggested a young mariner just on shore. "He's a manly fellow," the women would laugh.

He was twenty, just under medium height – his legs were a little short for his body – but very strong. His sleeveless tunic revealed a wiry torso hardened by training. Julius was very proud of his body. He was a good gymnast, and down in the port where he worked unloading the boats he had already made a name for himself as a promising boxer. "I've never been beaten yet by anyone my size," he would claim.

"You can knock him down," the bigger men would say admiringly, "but he just keeps getting up."

His eyes were blue. His nose, though it started on its downward journey as though it intended to be aquiline, suddenly became flattened just below the bridge. This was not, as might be supposed, the result of boxing. "It just grew that way," he would cheerfully explain.

Julius was marked, however, by two more striking peculiarities. The first, shared with his father, was that while his head bore a mass of black curls, at the front he had a patch of white hair. The second was that his hands had webbing between the fingers. It did not greatly worry him. Down at the port they affectionately called him "Duck" because of it. Often when he boxed they would cry: "Come on, Duck. Knock him in the water, Duck." A few wits would even quack when he won.

Above all, it was his personality that the women liked. There was something so merry, so full of life in those blue eyes that looked out so eagerly upon the world. As one young matron was heard to remark: "There's a nice young apple, just ripe to be plucked."

Julius's infatuation had not begun at once. Two months had passed since he and Sextus had first seen the girl. But once seen, she was not easy to forget.

There were all kinds of people in the port of Londinium. Vessels came in bearing olive oil from Spain, wine from Gaul, glassware from the Rhine, and amber from Germanic lands by the eastern, Baltic Sea. There were Celts of all kinds, blond Germans, Latins, Greeks, Jews, and olive-skinned men from the Mediterranean's southern shores. Slaves in particular might come from anywhere. The Roman toga might be seen beside a costume full of African colour and another bearing Egyptian ornaments. The empire of Rome was cosmopolitan.

Even so, the girl was unusual. She was two years older than Julius, and almost as tall. Her skin was pale, her hair yellow, but instead of being long and piled with pins like the other girls, it grew in tight curls close to her head. This and her slightly broadened nose indicated her dark-skinned ancestry. Her grandmother had been brought as a slave to Gaul from the African province of Numidia. She had small, very white teeth, rather uneven. Her eyes were blue, shaped like large, rounded almonds, and they had a strange, smoky quality. When she walked, her slim body had a wonderful, rhythmic grace denied to the other women of the port. They maliciously said her husband had bought her in Gaul, but nobody really knew. Her name was Martina.

She had been sixteen when the master mariner had decided to marry her. He had been fifty, a widower with grown children of his own. He had moved from Gaul to Londinium the previous year.

Julius had seen the mariner. He was a large, powerful man, strange to look at. His head was completely devoid of hair, and a profuse network of tiny broken veins all over his body and face made his skin look blue, as if tattooed. He and the girl lived on the south bank of the river, in one of the little houses strung out along the roads that led from the bridge towards the southern coast.

The trade of the port was busy. Despite his age, the mariner was active and often away in Gaul or visiting the ports by the great River Rhine. He was away now.

Julius had reason to be hopeful. Sextus was quite successful with women. He had been married, but the girl had died and he seemed in no great hurry to marry again. In his slightly patronizing way he had told Julius that he meant to have the mariner's young wife, and Julius had thought no more about it. Sextus had found out about the mariner's sailings and discovered how to get into his house at night unobserved. He liked to plan his seductions like a military operation. The girl, however, was hesitating. "The fun of the chase," Sextus had remarked, and continued his campaign.

So it had surprised Julius when, parting from himself and Sextus by the bridge one day, the girl had squeezed his hand. The very next day, down at the quay, she had gently but deliberately brushed him as she walked past. Soon after, she had remarked casually: "Every girl likes to get a present." Though she had said it to Sextus, she had glanced at him, Julius was sure of it.

But he had had no money that day, and Sextus had given her some sweetmeats. A few days later, when Julius had tried to speak to her alone, she had smiled but walked away, and after that ignored him.

It was then that his infatuation began. He started to think about Martina. As he unloaded the boats, her smoky eyes seemed to hover in the rigging. In his mind's eye, he saw her rhythmic walk and it appeared infinitely seductive to him. He knew that Sextus was closing in on her, but the mariner had been at home until recently and he was almost sure his friend had not succeeded with her yet. He imagined himself instead of Sextus slipping into her house under cover of darkness. And the more he brooded, the more this infatuation developed a life of its own. That wonderful musky scent – was it something she put on, or did it emanate naturally from her body? Her feet had seemed a little large to him at first, but now he found them sensual. He longed to feel her short hair, to take her head in his hands. And more than anything, he thought of that long, lean, flowing body. Yes, he would like to discover that.

"But would you want her if she didn't run away? That's the question to ask yourself about a woman." Julius had never mentioned the girl to his parents, but this was the remark his father had suddenly made the other day. "I can see some woman's leading you a dance," he had continued. "I hope she's worth it." Julius had laughed. He didn't know. But he meant to find out.

And Sextus's warning? It was not in his nature to make cold calculations. Julius was too full of life to weigh the risks of all his actions. Besides, he was an incurable optimist. It'll all work out, he decided.

The fat girl sat by the street corner. She did not want to sit there, but they had told her she must. She had brought two folding stools with her, upon which she had slowly let herself down. They had given her a loaf of bread, some cheese and a bag of figs. Now she sat, placidly enough, in the warm sun. A little dust had collected on her. By her feet, a litter of crumbs and fig skins suggested that she had consumed the bread and cheese and five of the figs.

She was eighteen, but had already grown to a size that would have been impressive in an older woman. Her first two chins were well developed and a third was taking its place beneath them. Her mouth was wide and turned down at the sides, where a little juice from the figs had gathered. She sat with her legs apart, her dress falling loosely over her bosom.

It always seemed to Julius that there was something mysterious about people who were very fat. How did they come to be that way? Why were they usually so content to remain so? To such a fit young fellow it seemed very strange. Indeed, when he looked at the fat girl he occasionally used to wonder whether behind her massive passivity, there might lurk a secret rage. Or could the mystery be deeper yet? At times it was almost as though, knowing something about the universe that was hidden from the rest of mankind, the fat girl was content. To sit, eat, and wait. In expectation of what? Who knew? Yet perhaps the greatest mystery of all was this: how did the fat girl come to be his sister?

For sister she was. From the age of about nine, though, she had gradually grown bigger and bigger, retreating from the busy world of sports and games that Julius and his friends enjoyed in a way that baffled her family. "I don't know how she got like that," his father would say in puzzlement. Though round and rubicund now, he had never been fat; nor had Julius's mother. "My father always said he had an aunt that was very big," he would remark. "Maybe the girl gets it from there." Wherever it came from, it was clear that her condition was there to stay. She and Julius had had little to say to each other as the years progressed; indeed, she seldom spoke to anyone, though she was amenable enough to do things like keep watch without asking questions, as long as she was given something to eat.

Now, therefore, as the afternoon wore slowly on, she sat eyeing the empty street and dipping into the bag from time to time to draw out another fig.

All was quiet. Five hundred yards away, beside the amphitheatre, a sleepy grunt came from one of the lions brought there from overseas. Tomorrow the games would be held – a big affair. There would be gladiators, a giraffe from Africa, and fights with bears from the mountains of Wales, as well as local boars. Most of the population of Londinium would crowd into the great arena to see this splendid spectacle. Even the fat girl would waddle in there.

At the street corner it was very warm. The fat girl felt the hot sun and lazily pulled her dress to cover her breasts. There was only one fig left now. She took it out, placed it in her mouth, bit it so that the juice appeared on her chin, wiped the chin with the back of her fleshy hand, dropped the fig skin on to the ground where it joined the others, and then put the empty cloth bag over her head to shield it from the sun.

Then she sat and stared at the whitewashed wall opposite. She had nothing more to eat; it was getting very boring. The glare of the wall made her want to shut her eyes. No one at all came by. Most people were having their siesta.

Just for a moment she closed her eyes. The bag rested, limply, on her large head. By and by, the bag began to rise and fall rhythmically.

The soldiers came swiftly through the streets. There were five of them, accompanied by a centurion. The centurion was a big, corpulent man with grizzled hair; in the peaceful province he had seen little real action in his career, but a knife wound from a brawl years ago had left a scar from the top to the bottom of his right cheek that gave him the look of a veteran, and commanded a certain respect and fear in his men.

Their rapid march made little sound on the dusty street, but the gentle clinking of their short swords against the metal studs on their tunics gave warning of their presence.

It was Julius's fault. If someone knocked him down in a boxing match, he got up cheerfully enough to fight again. It did not occur to him to hold a grudge. It was his weakness that because meanness was not in his own nature, he failed to see its presence in others. And so he had never noticed the look in the eyes of the fellow he had defeated ten days before. Nor would it have occurred to him that his opponent might open the purse he had carelessly put down that day and take note of a particular silver coin it contained.

> Julius, the son of Rufus, who works in the port, has a silver denarius. How did he get it? His friend is Sextus the carpenter.

That was the anonymous note the authorities had received. It might, of course, mean nothing. But they were coming to find out.

Julius grinned to himself. If there was one thing he needed in his young life, it was money. His pay at the docks was meagre; by getting friends to place bets on him when he boxed, he could often make some extra. But at this moment, he and Sextus were making money in the simplest way possible.

They were forging it.

The gentle art of forging coins was simple, but required great care. Official coins were struck. A blank metal disc was placed between two dies – one for the top face, the other for the underside. The dies were engraved and their impression stamped – that is, struck – on the disc. Julius had heard of forgers who could actually copy this process to produce counterfeits of the highest quality, but for that you had to be able to engrave the dies yourself, which was far beyond the skill of Sextus and himself.

Consequently, most forgers did something a little less convincing but very much easier. They would take existing coins – which might be new or old – and by pressing each side of the coin into damp clay they would make two half-moulds. These were then fitted together with a little hole in the side so that when the clay was dry and hard, molten metal could be poured through it into the mould. Break open the mould after cooling, and there was quite a passable counterfeit coin.

"Except, of course, you don't just make one at a time," Sextus had explained. "You do it like this." Taking three moulds, he had placed them together in a triangle, the holes in the three moulds all facing the gap in the middle. "Then you add another layer of three on top, like this," he demonstrated. "Then another." And he showed Julius how to stack the moulds up to form a tall, triangular column. "All you need to do then," he said, "is to pack clay round the whole thing, and pour the molten metal down the middle so that it flows into all the moulds."

When Sextus first proposed this illicit business to his young friend, Julius had been doubtful. "Isn't it a bit risky?" he had demanded. But Sextus had only stared at him from under the ledge of his brow. "Lots of people do it. You know why?" He had grinned. "Not enough coins."

This was only too true. For more than a century, the entire Roman Empire had experienced an ever-increasing rate of inflation. As a result, there were not enough coins to go round. Since people needed coins, there were many forgers. The private minting of cheap, bronze coinage was not technically an offence; however, forging high-value gold and silver was a serious crime. Yet even that did not deter the illicit trade and as a result nearly half the silver coins in circulation at this date were probably counterfeit.

Sextus obtained and melted the metal; Julius made the moulds and poured the molten ore into them. Although Sextus had showed him how to do this, the older man was not in fact very good at these operations. He was always making mistakes: either the ore failed to flow into the moulds properly, or he could not break his moulds off cleanly afterwards. Several times he had mixed up the two halves of the moulds when he put them together so that coins would come out with an obverse that did not match the face. Despite his webbed hands, Julius did the work neatly and precisely and thanks to him the quality of the coins had improved dramatically.

"But how do we make them really look and feel like silver?" That had been Julius's second question when they began. At this, the rocky terrain of his friend's face had seemed almost to crumble as he chuckled: "They don't need to. There's little enough silver in the real ones."

For in trying to supply even part of the coinage needed, the imperial mints had run so short of precious metal that they had debased their own currency. The valuable silver denarius nowadays contained as little as 4 per cent of actual silver. "I use a mixture of copper, tin and zinc," Sextus had told him. "It looks fine." But the exact proportions he would never divulge.

On the table before them now lay a pile of coins, each silver denarius representing a small fortune to the young man who unloaded boats for a living. Up to now, being cautious, they had made mostly bronze coins and a few silver, since any show of sudden wealth might look suspicious. But there would be a huge amount of betting and gambling at the games tomorrow, and the possession of a few silver coins could be more easily explained. Today, therefore, they were acting boldly. His one-third share would be enough, Julius reckoned, to set him up in a small business of some kind.

There was only one problem. How would he explain the money to his parents? Already they were both suspicious of Sextus. "You stay away from that one. He's up to something," his mother had said, having taken a special dislike to his friend.

Well, that was a problem to be solved later. Julius at this moment knew only one thing. The very next morning, before the games began, he was going to buy the girl a gold bracelet with his new-found wealth.

And then? It was up to the girl. She had had his letter.

There was, besides, one further consideration of a more serious kind. It had come from his father, Rufus.

For some months, that cheerful man had secretly been concerned about Julius. At first, he had hoped the boy would be a legionary, as he had been. It was still the best and most secure employment in the Roman Empire. You retired young with a good position and some stake money to start a business. But when Julius had failed to show any interest, he had not pushed him. "He'll pick up bad company, like that Sextus," his wife had warned, but she was a congenital pessimist. "He's not ready to settle down and he can't come to much harm here," he had replied. All the same, he had started to have pangs of conscience. It was time he did something for the boy. He wondered what.

Rufus was a gregarious fellow, a member of several associations. Just the day before he had heard of an interesting opportunity for a young man. "There are two men I know," he had eagerly told his son, "who might be able to put you in the way of a useful little business. They'd stake you too." He had arranged for Julius to meet them that very night.

So by morning, Julius considered, he'd have his share of the money they were forging now, and maybe a business opportunity as well. I might not even need Sextus so much, he thought. It was another argument for going after the girl.

All in all, it seemed to him, things were going rather well.

The soldiers arrived suddenly and without any warning. There was a crash, a sudden cry from outside, and then pounding on the door.

They seemed to be everywhere. He saw the flash of a helmet through the window. Not waiting for a response, they were already battering on the door with their swords. The wood was beginning to split. Julius jumped up; then, for the first time in his life, he panicked.

It was not what he had expected. He had always thought that when people panicked they ran about in a sort of frenzy, but on the contrary, he simply found that he was unable to move. He could not speak properly; his voice was hoarse. He stood helplessly, staring. This lasted for perhaps five seconds; to Julius it seemed like half a day.

Sextus, however, was moving with a speed that was astonishing. Leaping to his feet, he snatched a bag from the workbench and, with a single movement, swept the entire contents of the table into it – coins, moulds, everything. Racing to the cupboard in the corner, he threw it open and cleared the shelves of more moulds, nuggets of metal, and a collection of coins Julius did not even know he had.

And then suddenly Sextus had him by the arm. Propelling his stunned friend into the kitchen behind, he glanced out into the little yard. They were in luck. The legionaries sent to cover the rear of the house had made a mistake and blundered into the yard of the workshop next door. They could be heard knocking over a pile of tiles and cursing. Sextus shoved the bag into Julius's hands and pushed him outside. "Go! Run!" he hissed. "And hide the stuff." Julius, snapping out of his panic as abruptly as he had fallen into it, found himself leaping up over a wall, dropping into the yard on the far side, and slipping into the little maze of alleyways that ran behind the houses. The bag, stuffed in his tunic, made him look pregnant.

Before he had even started along the alley, the soldiers had broken down the door and burst into the house, where they found Sextus the carpenter, apparently just awoken from an afternoon nap, blinking at them in amazement. There was no sign of any forging. But the centurion was not deceived. He made for the back of the house.

It was then that Julius made his dangerous mistake. He was about a hundred yards down the alley when he heard a deep-throated bellow. Glancing back, he could see the big centurion, who, despite his weight, had clambered with agility on to the top of the wall and was scanning the alleys. Catching sight of Julius scurrying along, he had shouted. Now, as Julius turned, he saw the centurion calling to the legionaries below him: "That's him. That way. At the double." The centurion's scarred face, which Julius could see clearly, made it even more terrifying. He fled.

It was not difficult to lose the legionaries in the alleys. Even with his burden, he was faster than they were. Only some time later, as he walked down an empty street, did it occur to him to ask why he had looked back. "If I saw him," he muttered, "then he could have seen me." The patch of white hair on his head was a certain giveaway. The centurion had been shouting to the legionaries when Julius had looked at him, but had then turned.

"So the question is," he murmured sadly, "how much did he see?"

Martina stood by the southern end of the bridge. The summer day was drawing towards its end. The glare on the white-washed houses of the city opposite had faded, leaving only a pleasant glow. In the west, purple clouds gathered along an amber horizon. The breeze touched her cheek softly.

She held the letter in her hand. A boy had brought it to her. It was written on paper, which was expensive. The hand-writing was as neat as Julius could make it. It was written in Latin. She had to admit, she was excited.

Not that such communications, even between humble folk, were unusual. In the Roman city of Londinium, literacy was the norm. Though they usually spoke in Celtic, most towns-people knew Latin and could write it. Merchants wrote contracts, shopkeepers labelled goods, servants received written instructions and walls carried Latin graffiti. All the same, this was a love letter of sorts, and as Martina read it again she felt a little tremble go down her body.

If you come to the bridge at noon tomorrow, during the games, I have a present for you.
I think of you night and day. J.

Though he had not signed his full name – a sensible precaution should the letter go astray – she knew who the author must be. The young boxer. She nodded thoughtfully, and wondered: What was she going to do?

Time passed. Bathed in the evening glow, the city's red-tiled roofs, pale walls and stone columns presented a cheerful aspect. Why should Martina feel a touch of melancholy? Perhaps it was the bridge. Stoutly built of wood on high, heavy piles, this fine piece of Roman engineering stretched two-thirds of a mile over the water. Now, as the river turned wine-red in the sunset, the bridge's long, dark form reminded Martina of her own lonely journey through life. For she had been alone in the world when she met the mariner in Gaul. Her parents were dead; he had offered her a new life, a home and security. She had been grateful; in a way she still was.

How proudly the mariner had shown her the city. She had especially admired the long line of wooden quays built out into the river. "They're all made of oak," he had informed her. "There are so many oak trees in Britain that they just cut a huge beam from each tree and throw the rest away." They had walked up the broad street from the bridge to the forum. She had found the square impressive, but what really astounded her was the single, huge building that ran across the entire north side. This was the basilica – the vast hall and office complex where the city council and judges met. As she gazed, awestruck, at the five-hundred-foot nave, her husband had told her: "It's the biggest in northern Europe." There was so much to see: the courtyards and fountains of the governor's mansion; the several public baths; the many temples; and the great amphitheatre. It was thrilling to feel herself part of such a metropolis. "Rome is called the eternal city," the mariner remarked, "but Londinium, too, is part of Rome."

And though she could not express it, the girl had gained a sense of what it meant to be part of a great culture. For the classical culture of Greece and Rome *was* the world, from Africa to Britain. In Rome's public places, the arches and pediments, columns and domes, colonnades and squares had a proportion, a sense of mass and volume, space and order, that was profoundly satisfying. Roman private houses, paintings, mosaics and sophisticated central heating provided comfort and repose. In the peaceful shadows of her temples, the perfect geometry of stone met the inner mystery of the sanctum. The known and the unknown had been married for centuries in Rome. The forms Rome produced were destined to echo throughout the world for two thousand years and would continue to resonate, perhaps, as long as humans survived. It was the gift of a historic culture that, though the girl could not have said such things, she instinctively knew them. She loved the city.

Often the mariner sailed to Gaul with British household pottery, returning with rich, red Samian bowls decorated with lions' heads, cedar barrels of wine, and great amphorae filled with olive oil or dates. These last were mostly for the houses of the rich, but the mariner kept some for himself and they lived well. Sometimes he would also export barrels of oysters from the huge oyster beds in the estuary. "They used to be taken all the way to the Emperor's table in Rome," he remarked.

When he was away, she loved to go for solitary walks. She would go to the island by the ford. There, where a druid had once dwelt, there was now a pretty villa. Or she would leave by the upper western gate and walk two miles to a great crossroads at which there stood a fine marble arch. Or sometimes she would stroll up to the ridges to the south and admire the view.

She had only gradually wondered if she was unhappy. Perhaps she was just lonely.

She often prayed for a child. There was a complex of temples near the summit of the western hill, including one to Diana, but she did not think the chaste goddess would help her. Most women went to the numerous shrines to the Celtic mother goddesses; she had tried them to no avail. One shrine she found comforting. Leaving the lower western gate, the road crossed the stream and then passed by a sacred well where a Celtic water goddess lived. It seemed to Martina that the water goddess heard her, and was kindly. But no child came.

She had not positively known she was unhappy until one day that spring.

The house in which they lived lay in the city's southern annexe. It was a pleasant spot. As the wooden bridge reached the gravel spit that protruded from the southern bank, it continued on raised supports for some way, so that when the tide came in and turned the spit into an island, the bridge remained comfortably clear of the water. On reaching the marshy southern bankside beyond, the road was built up on a base of huge logs laid crosswise, with an earth and metalled surface above. It was just as she was walking along this that she had stopped to watch some workmen by the marshy edge of the river.

They were building a revetment along the riverbank. It was a large structure: great hollows made of oak timbers jointed to form a square, and then filled in. It rose well above the high-water mark, almost like a dike or a wharf. As she watched, she realized something else. The revetment had eaten several feet into the river, narrowing it slightly. When she had remarked upon this to one of the workmen, he had smiled.

"That's right. We've taken a little back from it. Maybe another year we'll take more." He laughed. "It's like a woman, you see. We use the river and we tame her. That's the way of it."

She had wandered across the bridge, thinking about it. Was that the story of her own life? The mariner was never cruel. But why should he be? He had an obedient young wife to look after him whenever he came to port. Was he kind to her? Fairly. She knew she should not complain. On reaching the other side of the bridge she had turned right and walked eastwards along the waterfront, past wharves and warehouses, until at last, just past the wharves' end, she had come to the eastern corner where the river was met by the city wall.

It was a quiet spot. By the angle of the wall there was a large bastion, but it was deserted now. Above, the spur of the eastern hill curved round until it reached the wall, making this riverside corner into an empty quarter-bowl, a sort of natural open-air theatre. On the slopes, the ravens walked about as though waiting in the silence for some play to begin.

Alone in that space, she had gazed at the high city wall in front of her. It was certainly admirable. Pale ragstone, brought up the river from Kent, had been neatly squared to make the outer face. The centre, nearly nine feet thick at the base, was packed with stone and mortar infill, and every three feet or so, two or three courses of red tile were laid through the entire thickness of the wall to strengthen it further. The final result was a splendid structure some twenty feet high with thin red stripes running horizontally along its length.

And suddenly, unbidden, it came to her with terrible, absolute clarity that she was not happy and that, after all, her life had become a prison.

Even so, she might have continued indefinitely if it had not been for Sextus.

At first she had been repelled by his advances, but they had made her think. She knew other girls with older husbands who secretly took lovers. As Sextus persisted, something in her began to stir. Perhaps it was excitement, perhaps she just wanted to end her sadness, but gradually she had allowed the thought to form. Might she, too, take a lover?

It was then that Julius had come into her mind.

It was not just his boyish looks, his bright blue eyes and obvious physical prowess. It was the faint briny smell of him, the way his powerful young shoulders bent to his work and the sweat glistened on his arms. Once she allowed the idea to take hold, she found an almost aching desire to have him possess her. I'll take the bloom off his youth, she smiled to herself. Cunningly she had teased him, first advancing then pretending to withdraw while she flirted mildly with Sextus. She found she was taking a huge pleasure even in the game.

When his letter came, "I have him," she murmured. Yet now that the moment had arrived, she was also afraid. What if she were caught? The mariner would doubtless be vengeful. Did she really want to risk everything for this boy? For a long time, therefore, she had gazed across the river as the sun went down, wondering what to do, before at last deciding.

The mariner was away. The faint, sensuous melancholy of the evening had worked upon her. I can't be sad any more, she thought. Tomorrow she would go to the bridge.

"Your turn."

Julius came back from his reverie with a start. Was his father looking at him strangely? He tried to concentrate on the board in front of him and slowly made his move.

He was safely home. It was a cheerful domestic scene. He could see his mother and sister in the adjoining kitchen, preparing a feast for their neighbours after the games tomorrow. As usual, he and his father were sitting on folding stools in the main room of the family's modest house, playing their evening game of draughts. Yet all the time he kept wondering whether the soldiers would come.

He glanced towards the kitchen. He had not been able to speak to his sister since he had run for his life. What had the fat girl seen?

On the kitchen wall hung a brace of duck. On the scrubbed table, a side of beef, the favourite British staple, a huge bowl of oysters from the river, and a bucket of snails that had been fed on milk and wheat and would be fried tomorrow in oil and wine. In a broad, shallow bowl a soft cheese was curdling. Beside it were spices for a sauce. The diet the Romans had introduced into Britain was appetizing indeed: pheasant and fallow deer; figs and mulberries; walnuts and chestnuts; parsley, mint and thyme; onions, radishes, turnips, lentils and cabbage. The island Celts had also learned to cook snails, guinea fowl, pigeons, frogs and even, occasionally, spiced dormice.

Mother and daughter worked in silence. The older woman, quiet and humourless, prepared. The fat girl tried to eat, whilst her mother, without changing her expression or pausing in what she was doing, protected the family's food by slapping her. Julius saw his mother go to the bowl of eels. Slap. Having inspected them, she said a few words to the girl, who moved to the cupboard, and went back to the sauce she was preparing. Slap. Then his mother moved to the window for a moment. The fat girl succeeded in getting a piece of fresh bread into her mouth. Slap. The fat girl munched contentedly.

Had his sister seen the soldiers? Did she know what had happened to Sextus? Had she told his parents? It was impossible to guess. He supposed she must know something. When could he ask her?

The last few hours had been torture. As soon as he had got well away from his pursuers, Julius had tried to take stock of the situation. That it was he, rather than Sextus, who had caused them to be under suspicion never occurred to him. Had his friend been arrested? He did not dare return yet to find out. Had Sextus incriminated him? Carefully he worked his way towards his home. If Sextus had given him away, the soldiers would surely come there.

It seemed to him that the safest plan was to wait until the morning and then encounter Sextus in the street on the way to the games. Until then, he must somehow try to act as though nothing had happened.

But where to hide the bag? That was a problem. Somewhere safe, not connected with himself. Some place where he could easily retrieve it later. He cast about, but found nothing.

Until, skirting the summit of the western of the two hills where the little temple of Diana stood, he glanced at one of the pottery kilns that shared the site. Beside it was a heap of waste, rejected pots and other rubble that had obviously been undisturbed for some time. Waiting until there was no one about, he had sauntered over to the pile, pushed the bag quickly under the rubbish, and moved swiftly away. No one had seen him. He was sure of it. He had gone home.

But he felt little confidence. And as he looked once more from his father's cheerful face to his mother's, he knew why.

For if Rufus was merry and red-faced and loved to sing, his wife was none of these things. Her hair, now neither blond nor grey, was pulled in a tight bun. Her eyes were grey and never shone. Her face, unchanged since his childhood, was phlegmatically pale, like pastry before it is cooked. She was kind enough, and he believed that she loved them all, but she spoke little, and when her husband told a joke she never laughed but only stared. It often seemed as though, like a boring but habitual duty, she carried about with her the burden of some glum memory.

Celtic memories were long. Only two centuries had passed since Boudicca, the tribal queen, had revolted against the conquering Romans, and her family had been of Queen Boudicca's tribe. "My grandfather was born in the reign of Emperor Hadrian, who built the wall," she would state, "and his grandfather was born in the year of the great revolt. He lost both his parents." She still had distant cousins in the remote countryside who farmed just as their Celtic ancestors had and spoke no word of Latin. Hardly a day went by without her uttering some dismal warning.

"Those Romans are all the same. They get you in the end." It had been like a litany all his childhood.

Click. A sharp sound from the draughts board interrupted these observations. A series of clicks and a triumphant bang.

"Wiped him off the board." His father's red face was grinning at him. "Dreaming about women?" He began to gather up the draughts. "Time to go in a little while," he added more seriously, before disappearing into his bedroom to get ready.

Julius waited. The meeting with his father's friends at the temple that evening was important. Very important. He must try to forget about the day's events and prepare himself. "Just show that you're businesslike and ready to learn. That's all you have to do," his father had counselled him.

He tried to concentrate, but it was difficult. Surely he had taken every precaution he could. And yet there was still one thing that was bothering him.

The bag. All evening, he now realized, the bag had lain there, in the back of his mind, silently haunting him. At first he had been so afraid the soldiers might come that he was glad the bag was hidden where no one could connect him with it. But now he guessed that in the barracks, as everywhere in the city, the soldiers would be preparing for the games, and he became more and more confident that they were not coming. For that night, at least, he was probably safe.

Which left the bag. Of course, it was well hidden. But what if by some fluke they decided to clear up the rubbish? Or some scavenger should discover the coins and steal them? A picture of the precious bag, out there in the night, hovered before his eyes.

And so it was that he suddenly made a decision. Slipping quietly out of the house, he made his way swiftly through the streets to the kilns. It was not far. There were people about, but the pile of rubble was in the shadows. For a moment he could not find the bag, but then he did. Holding it under his cloak, he hurried back home. Carefully he entered and went to his room. The two women in the kitchen did not notice him. He pushed the bag under his bed, where there were already two boxes of his possessions. It would be safe there until morning. Moments later, he was awaiting his father by the door, ready to go out.

The night was clear and full of stars as Julius and his father crossed the city to the meeting. The family's house was situated near the lower of the two gates in the western wall, and so they took the great thoroughfare which led from that gate, across the side of the western hill and down the incline to the brook that ran between the hills.

It was not often that Julius saw his father nervous, but just for once he sensed that he was. "You'll be fine," the older man muttered, more to himself than to his son. "You won't let me down." Then, a little later: "Of course, it's not a closed meeting tonight, or you couldn't be there." And finally, squeezing his son's arm tightly: "Just sit quietly, now. Don't say anything. Watch." They had reached the brook. They crossed the bridge. Before them lay the Governor's Palace. Their destination lay up a street on the left.

At last, ahead of them in the darkness, there it was: a dark building standing alone, its doorway lit on each side by burning torches. Julius heard his father give a little hiss of satisfaction.

Though he was an easy-going man, there were two things of which Julius's father Rufus was fiercely proud. The first was the fact that he was a Roman citizen.

Civus Romanus sum: I am a Roman citizen. In the early decades of Roman rule, few natives of the island province gained the honour of full citizenship. Gradually, however, the restrictions were eased, and Rufus's grandfather, though only a provincial Celt, had managed by service in an auxiliary regiment to earn the coveted status. He had married an Italian woman, so Rufus could also claim that there was Roman blood in the family. True, when Rufus was a child the Emperor Caracalla had opened the gates and made citizenship available to nearly all freemen in the empire, so that in truth there was nothing to distinguish Rufus from the modest merchants and shopkeepers amongst whom he lived. But he still took pride in telling his son: "We were citizens before that, you know."

But the second, and far greater, source of pride lay in the doorway with the flickering lights.

For Rufus was a member of the temple lodge.

Of all the temples in Londinium, though many were larger, none was more powerful than the Temple of Mithras. It was situated between the two hillocks, on the eastern bank of the little brook, about a hundred yards up from the precincts of the Governor's Palace. Built recently, it was a stout little building, rectangular in shape and only sixty feet long. One entered from the eastern end; at the western end was a small apse containing the sanctuary. In this respect it resembled Christian churches, which at this time also had their altars at the western end.

There had always been many religions in the empire, but in the last two centuries the mystery cults and religions from the East had become increasingly popular, two especially: the religion of Christianity and the cult of Mithras.

Mithras the bull-slayer. The Persian god of heavenly light; the cosmic warrior for purity and honesty. Julius knew all about the cult. Mithras fought for truth and justice in a universe where, in common with many Eastern religions, good and evil were equally matched and locked in an eternal war. The blood of the legendary bull he killed had brought life and abundance to the earth. The birthday of this Eastern god was celebrated on 25 December.

It was mysterious, for the initiation rites were shrouded in secrecy, but it was also staunchly traditional. Its followers made small blood sacrifices in the temple, in the time-honoured Roman manner. They were also bound by the old, Stoic code of honour to keep themselves pure, honest and brave. Nor was membership of the lodge open to everyone. The army officers and merchants with whom the cult was popular kept it exclusive. Only sixty or seventy people could even get into the Londinium temple. Rufus had good reason to be proud of his membership.

By comparison, the Christians, though expanding rapidly, were a very different crowd. Julius knew some down at the docks, but like many Romans, he still thought they were some sort of Jewish sect. And anyway, whatever its precise nature, Christianity, with its emphasis on humility and the hope of a happier afterlife, was clearly a religion for slaves and poor people.

Julius had never been in the temple before; even his presence in the lodge that night, he realized, was some sort of preliminary test. As they reached the door, went down three steps and entered, he hoped he would pass.

The temple consisted of a central nave flanked by pillars, behind which were side-aisles. The nave itself, nearly fifty feet long, was only twelve feet wide, with a wooden floor; wooden benches were fitted in the aisles. They were motioned to one at the back, Julius looking about him curiously.

The burning torches cast an uncertain light; the aisles were in deep shadow. As other men came in and moved forward to their benches, Julius realized that he was being inspected, but he could not always see the faces of those who passed. At the far end, at the front of the little apse between two columns, stood a fine statue of Mithras, his staring face like that of a rather strong-featured Apollo, his eyes upturned towards the heavens, a pointed Phrygian cap upon his head. Before the statue was a modest stone altar upon which the offerings were made. It had a dip in the top, to receive the blood.

Slowly the temple filled. When the last member of the lodge had arrived, the doors were closed and bolted. Then everyone sat quietly. A minute passed; then another. Julius wondered what came next. At last, a lamp flickered at the far end; he became aware that something was moving, and with a faint rustle, two figures emerged from the shadows of the aisles. They were strange indeed.

Both wore headdresses that entirely hid their faces. The first wore a lion's head with a mane that hung around his shoulders. The second was altogether more eerie, and as he gazed, Julius felt a tiny shiver go down his spine.

This man was taller. What he wore was more than a headdress, for it reached almost to his knees. Made of hundreds of large feathers that faintly rustled and creaked, it was in the shape of a huge black bird with folded wings and a huge beak. This was the Raven. "Is he a priest?" Julius whispered to his father.

"No. He is one of our number. But he's leading the ceremony tonight."

From the far end, the Raven now began to move down the nave between the seats. He walked slowly, his great tail brushing the knees of the men he passed. Every few feet he would pause and address a question to one of the members in what was obviously a ritual of some kind.

"Who is the master of the light?"

"Mithras."

"Whose blood enriches the earth?"

"That of the bull, slain by Mithras."

"What is your name?"

"Servant."

"Are you of our number?"

"Beyond death."

As the Raven moved slowly down the nave and back again, it seemed to Julius that the eyes looking out of the sockets above the beak were paying particular attention to him. He suddenly became afraid that the Raven might ask him a question, to which, of course, he would have no reply. He was glad when, having given him, it seemed, a parting glance, the Raven returned to the sanctuary again.

So it did nothing to make him feel more comfortable when, leaning over so that he could speak directly into his ear, his father whispered: "That's one of the men you're going to meet tonight."

The rest of the ceremony was not long. The Raven said a few invocations, the Lion made some brief announcements concerning the membership, and then the meeting broke up into an informal gathering, with small groups collecting in the nave.

Julius and his father remained near the back. Around them, Julius observed, were other relatively humble members, obviously like his father rather pleased to be there, but he could also see several prominent and influential citizens. "The lodge can fix almost anything in this city," Rufus whispered proudly.

They continued to wait quietly, chatting to those close by. Several minutes passed. Then Julius felt his father nudge him. "Here he comes," he muttered. "You'll do fine," he added nervously. Julius gazed towards the west end.

The man who had been the Raven was a large, imposing figure. He had taken off his costume and was making his way down the nave, nodding to members here and there with an air of friendly authority. In the soft light, Julius could see that his head was grizzled, but it was only as he came closer that Julius saw, with a sudden, cold panic, the scar running from the top to the bottom of his cheek.

The eyes of the centurion were fixed on him. Their stare was harsh. Julius felt himself go white. No wonder the Raven had seemed to be observing him so closely. He's recognized me, Julius thought, and I'm done for. He could scarcely look up as his father, with a nervous little laugh, introduced him.

At first Julius did not hear anything. He was conscious of nothing except the centurion's eyes upon him. Only after several moments did he realize that the soldier was quietly speaking to him. He was talking about the river trade, of the need for a bright young fellow to bring pottery from the interior of the island to the port. The pay for such a fellow would be good. A chance to trade on his own account. Was it possible that the centurion had not recognized him after all? He looked up.

There was something strange about the centurion. Julius noticed it now, though he could not say exactly what it was. As the large man stared down at him, Julius was aware only that behind those hard eyes lay something else, something hidden. Not that it was unusual for such a man to have business interests. The legionaries were well paid and no doubt the centurion intended to become a substantial merchant, even a landowner, after he retired. In the meantime, his duties in the capital were mainly ceremonial, together with some light police work. He had time to make investments. As he talked, however, Julius found that his first impression grew even stronger: there was more to the centurion than first appeared. The bluff soldier was a man of secrets. Perhaps they concerned the Mithraic lodge; maybe something else. Julius could only wonder what.

A little nervously he answered the questions the centurion put to him. He tried to give a good account of himself, even if he felt awkward. It was impossible to tell what impression he was making. Finally, however, the centurion nodded to his father. "He seems all right," he remarked, and gave the older man a smile. "You'll bring him to the lodge again, I hope." Rufus blushed with pleasure. "As far as this river business is concerned, I'm satisfied. But he'll have to work with my agent." He glanced about with a hint of impatience. "Where is he? Ah yes." He gave a smile. "Stay there. I'll bring him over." And he moved away to where some figures were standing in the shadows.

Rufus was beaming at his son. "Well done, boy. You're in," he whispered. It seemed to the older man that this evening was bringing everything he could wish.

He was surprised and a little confused, therefore, to observe that the expression on Julius's face, far from showing joy, had just changed to one of amazement and horror. Whatever could be the matter?

For as the centurion returned, Julius had got his first sight of the agent. And though, for a moment, he had told himself it was impossible, as they drew closer there was no doubt. There before him, in the soft light of the temple, his blue face forming into a smile, stood the mariner.

A quarter-moon had risen as father and son returned home through the streets that night. Rufus was in a merry mood. Nothing was better, he thought, than a father's pride. He had long ago given up with his daughter, but now, with his son, he could truly feel that he had done a good job.

The centurion had taken the boy on. The mariner had said that he liked him. "You could be set up for life," he told Julius contentedly. If his son seemed a little thoughtful, he supposed there was no harm in that.

In fact, Julius's mind was in a whirl. The centurion had not recognized him; he must thank the gods for that. But what about the mariner? He had the impression he had only just got back, but he had not dared to ask. Had he been home yet? Could he have seen the letter? Should he warn Martina, to make sure she destroyed it? It was too late for that, he thought. The mariner was probably halfway home by now.

As for their affair, even if the mariner remained in the dark, could he really think of a relationship with the wife of the man on whom his business career now depended? The idea was absurd.

And yet. He thought of that body; he thought of that rhythmic walk. He went on thinking as he went along.

The house was dark when they arrived back. His mother and sister had gone to bed. His father bade him an affectionate goodnight and retired. For a time Julius sat and thought about the day's events, but came to no conclusion. Realizing that he was tired, he too decided to go to bed.

Carrying a small oil lamp he went into his room and sat on the bed. He took off his clothes. Before lying down, he reached under the bed to feel the precious bag, yawning as he did so. Then he frowned.

Vaguely irritated, he hauled himself off the bed and knelt on the floor. He put his arm under the bed and pushed the boxes aside. Then he put the lamp on the floor, and stared in disbelief.

The bag had gone.

The figure moved quietly in the darkness. There were few lights here, on the south bank of the river. Crossing by the wooden bridge, he had continued southwards a little way past the big tavern for arriving travellers, and past the baths, before striking off into a lane on the right. Unlike the streets of Londinium across the river, only the main street here was metalled. Walking on the dirt, therefore, his sandalled feet made no sound. His cape was pulled over his head.

When he came to the familiar little house, he paused. The whitewashed walls glimmered in the pale moonlight. The front door, he knew, would be bolted. The windows were shuttered. There was a courtyard at the back, though, into which he slipped.

From its kennel, the dog came swiftly out and barked, but then, recognizing its master, quietened. Standing in the shadows, man and dog waited for a while to make sure that no one was stirring. Then the hooded figure climbed on to a water butt and, with surprising agility, got on to the tiled wall running along the side of the courtyard to the corner of the house. The slanting moonlight cast shadow lines beside the ridges of the terracotta tiles that covered the roof, making a strangely geometric pattern as the hooded figure walked skilfully along the top of the wall to the square, dark space of a window whose wooden shutters were open.

The mariner entered his house quietly and made his way to the door of the room where Martina was sleeping.

He had been suspicious for about a month. It was hard to say why: something in his young wife's manner; a preoccupied look; a tiny hesitation in their lovemaking. Certainly nothing much. Another man might have ignored it. But the mariner's mother had been Greek and from her he had imbibed, in childhood, a sense of fierce, proud possession that lay under the surface of all his dealings with men and women alike. "He's patient as can be when he sails," those who voyaged with him would say, "but if someone cheats him, he must have blood."

The mariner did not think the girl had been unfaithful. Not

yet. But he had decided to make sure, and so he had played the oldest trick known to married men and pretended to be away when he was not.

Carefully, now, he opened the bedroom door.

She was alone. The faint moonlight fell across the bed. One of her breasts was uncovered. He looked at her and smiled. Very well. She was not deceiving him. He watched her breathing softly. The room gave no hint of the presence of any other in the house. All was well. As quietly as a cat, the thick-set mariner moved round the room, glancing at her as he went. Perhaps he would give her a pleasant surprise and climb into the bed with her. Or perhaps he would steal away and observe another night. He was just debating these two courses in his mind when he noticed a piece of parchment on a table near the bed. Picking it up, he moved to the open window.

There was light enough from the quarter-moon to read the letter Julius had sent. The signature gave him no clue as to the identity of the sender, but that did not matter, since the note gave a place and a time. Gently he replaced the letter and made his way out of his house.

For once Julius's mother had acted with remarkable swiftness.

The fat girl had not seen the soldiers. She had slept through their visit and finally, finding no one about in the workshop any more, she had waddled home, arriving late. It was this late arrival, together with something in Julius's manner, that had made her suspicious. A few extra slaps had got from the fat girl that the two men had set her to watch the street for soldiers. Then the older woman was sure. "That Sextus has got him into trouble," she muttered.

As soon as Julius and his father had left, therefore, she had searched his room. She had found the bag at once, seen its terrifying contents, sat for over a minute in a state of shock, and then announced: "We've got to get rid of these." But where?

For once, she was grateful that her daughter was fat. "Stick this under your clothes," she ordered. Then, putting on her cloak, she and the girl had set out.

At first she thought of throwing the bag in the river, but that was not so easy. There were people about on the waterfront. Instead, therefore, she led the girl along the main thoroughfare to the nearby gate in the western wall. All the city gates were supposed to close at dusk, but on warm summer nights this rule was often relaxed. Young people liked to wander out, and so no one paid the slightest attention as the fat girl and her mother passed through. They had only gone a little way, however, before they stopped. The road ahead led over a bridge to the shrine where the water goddess dwelt, but there were several couples in sight that way. On each side of the road, as at all the city gates, was a cemetery.

"Give me the bag and go back now," her mother ordered. "And tell nobody about this, especially not Julius. You understand?" When the girl had waddled away, she turned into the cemetery. She looked about for an open grave, but found nothing. Continuing through the cemetery, she came out at the other end, passed by the outside of the upper western gate, and continued to wander along a path that ran parallel with the city wall.

It was a quiet place. The wall, with its horizontal tile stripes, looked ghostly. Below, about four yards out from the wall, a deep defensive ditch made a broad shadow like a black ribbon along the ground. There were no guards on top of the wall: she was not being watched. She took her time, passing the corner of the city and skirting the long northern section of the wall. She passed a gateway that was closed, and continued on her way. About six hundred yards further on, she saw what she wanted.

The little brook that descended between the city's two hillocks was divided into several tributaries in its upper reaches, and in three or four places these tiny rivulets passed under the city's northern wall through neatly engineered tunnels with grilles across their entrances. For a moment she had considered dropping the bag into one of these watercourses, until she remembered that the grilles were regularly cleaned and the channels dredged. Just past one of these tunnels, however, she noticed that someone had recently emptied a large quantity of rubbish into the ditch that ran outside the wall. Unlike the watercourses, the ditch was not well kept up. She had never seen anyone clear it out.

She paused only a few moments to look about. Satisfied she was not observed, she flung the bag into the ditch and heard it fall amongst the rubbish at the bottom.

Continuing on her way as if nothing had happened, a little

further on she found the main northern gate wide open, and passed unnoticed into the city.

Julius gazed at the long line of city wall. His hands fell helplessly to his sides and he shook his head. The quest was futile. Over the wall, on the far side of the western hillock, he could see the curving top storey of the amphitheatre. The morning was clear: no breeze, not a cloud in the pale blue sky. It would be hot in the amphitheatre's huge bowl that day.

Where was the money? He had been out at dawn and he still hadn't the faintest idea what his mother had done with it.

Had the fat girl lied? He did not think so. When he had crept to her bedside in the middle of the night, put his hand over her mouth and held a knife against her throat, she had been frightened enough. She had said that his mother had dumped the bag somewhere outside the western wall, but three hours of searching had not yielded a clue. He had gone out through the western gate. He had visited every place he could think of before finally returning. And now the city was stirring. Soon people would be flocking towards the amphitheatre. And he was penniless.

What was he going to tell Sextus? Though he had planned to encounter him on the way to the games, he was not so sure that he wanted to see him just yet. Would Sextus believe him? Or would he suppose Julius had stolen the money and cheated him? Hard to say. Nor did he relish going home to encounter his mother. "I'd better lie low until this evening after the games," he muttered. Perhaps everyone would be in a better temper by then.

Which left the girl. He sighed. He had promised her a present, and now he had no money. What could he do about that? Nothing. Anyway, he reminded himself, the whole business was too risky. "And she probably won't come to the bridge now in any case," he muttered. The whole thing made him sad, and having nothing else to do just then, he sat down on a stone near the road to ruminate.

Several minutes passed. Once or twice more he muttered, "I'm broke," and "Forget the whole thing." But somehow even these statements did not satisfy him. Gradually, another thought began to take shape and to grow.

What if she did come to the bridge after all? It was quite

likely that she had hidden the letter. The mariner probably suspected nothing. What if she took the risk herself and came to the bridge, and he was not there to meet her? What if he let her down?

He shook his head. He knew very well. "If I don't have her, someone else will," he murmured. Sextus probably.

He thought of her body. He wanted her, certainly. He thought of her all alone by the bridge and suddenly the whole business seemed bathed in a warmer light. He felt his heart begin to beat more rapidly.

Just as every pugilist in the port knew, Julius would never stay down if you knocked him out. It might not be wise, it might not even make any sense at all, but his deep inner optimism soon rose to the surface again as naturally as the buds appear in spring.

After a short time, therefore, he seemed to pull himself together. A few minutes more and he nodded to himself with a faint smile. A little later he grinned and got up.

Then he made his way towards the gate.

Martina was up early that morning. She prepared the room, brushed her short hair, washed and scented herself carefully. Then, before dressing, she inspected her body. She felt her breasts, which were small and soft; she ran her hands down the firm lines of her legs. Satisfied, she began to dress. She slipped on a pair of new sandals, experience having taught her that the leather would give off a faint smell that, combined with the natural scents of her body, was attractive to men. She pinned a small bronze brooch at each shoulder, and as she did so noticed a little fluttering of the heart which told her, if she had had any doubt about the matter, that she was going to make love to young Julius that day.

Then, wrapping in a handkerchief a few sweet cakes to eat during the morning, she set out from the house and joined her neighbours as they made their way over the bridge to the games.

She was conscious of a lightness in her step that she had not felt for a long time.

It had been strange to have the city all to himself. By mid-morning it seemed that the entire population had gone to the games. Now and then Julius would hear a great roar from the amphitheatre, but for the rest of the time the cobbled streets were so quiet he could listen to the birds. In a cheerful mood, he had wandered down alleys, enjoying the pleasant aroma of freshly baked bread from a bakery, or the rich, thick smells emanating from some nearby kitchen. He had sauntered down handsomely paved streets past the fine houses of the rich. Some of these had their own private bathhouses; many had walled compounds around them, enclosing little orchards where cherry trees, apples and mulberries grew.

And everywhere he had been looking. He was going to meet the girl at noon and he had promised a present. He did not want to go empty-handed.

So he was going to steal it.

Surely there would be an opportunity somewhere. Almost the entire population was in the amphitheatre. It should only be the work of a moment to slip into some unguarded house and take something to satisfy her. He did not like to steal, but at the moment it seemed the only way.

However, it had been harder than he had expected. He had entered a few modest houses only to find nothing he liked. The rich houses had all seemed to contain elderly servants or fierce guard dogs and twice already he had been forced to flee.

A little discouraged, he had wandered down to the quay. At first he tried along the western side, but without any luck. He passed the bridge and tried the eastern side. Here, too, the lines of low warehouses were all closed up. He went by a small fish market whose stalls had been empty since dawn. It was just after this that he came to a much larger building, the sight of which made him pause.

This was the imperial warehouse. Unlike most of the others, it was stoutly built of stone. It was guarded by soldiers night and day. Into this official depot came all the supplies for the governor, garrison and administration. Sometimes these cargoes were valuable. Three days ago, Julius had helped unload a vessel containing several great chests of gold and silver coins – pay for the troops – all officially stamped and sealed. The weight of each chest had been amazing and the men had had a terrible time transferring them to the quay. For Julius, who understood all too well the astounding value of this cargo, it had been a vivid reminder of the power and wealth of the state. The empire might sometimes seem to be veering towards chaos, but the deep, underlying might of the eternal city and its dominions was still awesome to behold. He grinned to himself. If I could spend a few moments in there, he thought, my money problems would really be over. But after his narrow escape from the legionaries the day before, Julius was nervous of authority and now did not care to walk past the warehouse.

As he turned back up the broad street towards the forum, Julius was beginning to think that he would have to do without a present after all. Reaching the lower thoroughfare, for no particular reason he turned left towards the Governor's Palace, where a sentry guarded the entrance. The street was otherwise empty.

It was there that Julius had his idea. It was so simple, so daring, that it was insane. And yet, as he considered, it seemed to him not only that it might work, but that it was positively logical. "It's just a matter of timing," he muttered, to reassure himself.

Unlike the private houses he had investigated, the Governor's Palace was a public building. Apart from the guard on the gate, the entire staff had probably sneaked off to the games. And even if I were found in there, he thought, I could probably make some excuse, say I was waiting to petition the governor or something. The neatness of it made him smile. After all, who would ever think of robbing the governor himself? Ducking into the corner of an alley, he settled down to reconnoitre for a while.

The street side of the palace consisted of a ragstone wall, in the centre of which was a handsome gateway leading to a large courtyard. In front of the gateway, on a marble plinth, stood a tall, narrow stone, almost the height of a man. This was the central marker from which all the milestones in southern Britain took their distances.

The sentry seemed to like standing in front of the stone, surreptitiously resting his back against it, but every little while he would slowly march along the empty street, turn, and march back to his resting place.

Julius watched carefully. The man took twenty-five paces in one direction, then, after a pause, twenty-five in the other. To make sure, Julius watched again, then a third time. It was always the same. He calculated his moves carefully. There would just be time.

When the sentry began his next turn along the street with his back to him, Julius moved quickly out, and, keeping the stone between him and the sentry for cover, ran swiftly and silently forward, ducking into the shadow of the gateway just before the fellow turned.

It took him only a moment to slip into the courtyard. On the far side, under a portico, was the main door of the residence. It had been left open. He walked boldly in. And found himself in another world.

Perhaps no civilization has ever invented better homes for its richer classes than the Roman villa or town house. The governor's mansion was a splendid example of the latter. The high cool atrium with its pool of water set the tone of stately repose. The sophisticated system of underfloor central heating – the hypocaust – kept the house warm in winter. In summer, the stone and marble interior was cool and airy.

As was common in the better houses in Londinium, many of the floors had beautiful mosaics. Bacchus, god of wine, was depicted here, a lion there; dolphins graced one hall, whilst elsewhere there were intricately woven geometric patterns.

After an admiring glance at the splendour of the main rooms, Julius moved quickly to the smaller chambers. These, too, though more intimate, were fine. The walls were mostly painted in panels of ochres, reds and greens, with the lower panels in some cleverly painted to look like marble.

Julius knew what he was looking for. It had to be something small. If the mariner's wife were seen with a valuable piece of jewellery it would excite comment and lead to trouble. He wanted a single, modest object; something so small they would probably think it had just been lost.

It did not take him long. In one of the bedrooms he found on a table a mirror of polished bronze, some silver brushes and three jewelled brooches. There was also a beautiful necklace made of huge uncut emeralds set in a gold chain. The emeralds, he knew, would have come from Egypt. He picked it up and admired it. Just for a moment he was tempted to steal it. He could never dispose of the emeralds, of course – they would be far too conspicuous – but he could melt down the gold. Then he put it down again. It seemed a pity to destroy such beautiful workmanship.

Beside it, however, was exactly what he needed: a simple gold bracelet without any markings. There must be a thousand like it in Londinium. That was what he would give Martina. Picking it up, he slipped quickly out.

The house was still silent, the courtyards deserted. Hugging the wall, he made his way towards the gate. All he had to do now was to get past the sentry who had resumed his watch in the street. As long as he doesn't come into the courtyard now, he prayed. He edged to the inside of the gateway.

He could see the sentry's back as he lounged against the stone. As far as he could judge, the street was empty. He waited until the sentry set off again, to the left this time, towards the brook. Then, quick as a flash, he darted out, making for the right.

But as an extra precaution, Julius did a cunning thing. After a few yards, instead of running forwards he turned and, as fast as he could, walked backwards, his face towards the retreating sentry. Five, ten, fifteen rapid steps. And it was just as well. This time, for some reason, the sentry finished his patrol and turned early. At which point Julius, instead of retreating, started to walk forwards, casually coming to meet the sentry, so that it appeared he was approaching the gate for the first time. The soldier looked surprised, wondering where he had come from, but as the young man was walking towards him, he thought nothing more about it and the two men passed each other with a nod. A few minutes later, Julius was on his way back to wait at the bridge with his present.

He wondered if the girl would come.

Sextus descended the broad street that led from the forum down to the bridge. He was frowning, and the fact that he had been unable to find Julius at the amphitheatre had not improved his temper.

Was his young friend avoiding him? The thought would not have occurred to him except for a chance remark he had overheard the afternoon before.

When, after bursting into the house, the soldiers had raced to the back looking for accomplices, he had heard them spot Julius, but was relieved to see that his friend had got away. It was soon clear that they had not got a decent look at him. Then, however, a few minutes later, he had heard two soldiers chatting as they searched his bedding in the next room. "There's nothing here," one had grunted. "I think this was a hoax. Someone just took a dislike to this fellow and wrote the letter."

"But what about the young one? Was that him running away?"

"Maybe. Maybe not. He's young anyway. Respectable family. If anyone forges, it's this carpenter."

The young one. Respectable family. It had to be Julius they were talking about. The young fool must have given them away somehow. Sextus cursed. "If they get to him, he'll probably crack," he groaned. "Then I'm done for."

Though he wanted to, he had not dared go to Julius's house that night in case he was followed, but he had expected to find him at the amphitheatre this morning. So when he failed to appear, Sextus had begun to be seriously worried. Had the authorities got to him? Had he given the game away? Finally, when he had stealthily approached Julius's house, he had found it deserted. What did that mean? He had finally returned to his own house, in case Julius had gone there, then he had looked around the forum. Now, as a last resort, he was going to try the quay.

Suddenly, only a hundred yards ahead, there the young fellow was, walking towards the bridge. Sextus hurried forward. Julius was so engrossed in where he was going that he did not even notice Sextus until he was close behind. He turned. Seeing Sextus, his face fell.

Immediately Sextus was on his guard. "Is everything all right?" he asked. He saw Julius hesitate before reluctantly but truthfully telling him exactly what had happened.

Sextus did not believe a word of it. He prided himself on the fact that he was no fool. This story was utterly improbable, whereas certain other things were very clear. The young man was avoiding him. Thc moncy was gone. Only two explanations were likely, therefore. Either Julius had stolen it, or he had betrayed his friend, in which case the authorities probably had the bag of moulds to use as evidence in court. No doubt Julius would be let off for testifying against him.

Sextus's face was a mask, though, as he listened to Julius's awkward explanation. He said nothing, letting the young man justify himself. When he had finished Sextus concluded that his friend was a poor liar.

He decided to try a direct approach. "Have you been talking?" he asked bluntly. "To the soldiers?"

"No. Of course not."

Sextus considered. He'd know that soon enough anyway. He drew a knife from his belt, and showed it to Julius.

"Find the money by sundown," he said calmly, "or I'll kill you." Then he turned on his heel and walked away.

A little before noon, they brought on a gladiator and a bear. The gladiator was skilled with the net. The betting was two to one that he would kill the bear. He was due to fight another gladiator that afternoon, however, a popular champion, and for this second contest the betting was five to one that he would die. For a bet that he would win both you could, at this moment, get twenty to one. The bear was paraded around the arena first. The crowd was in a good-humoured mood. Tension and excitement would mount only when blood was seen.

Martina rose quickly. Across the arena, in the governor's box and the tiers nearby, she could see the important men of the city in their togas and the women in their long dresses of fine silk, their hair piled high in elaborate coiffures. As she made her way back to the stairway, she felt a little tremor run through her.

They may be in the fine seats, she thought, but none of them will be getting what I am going to get this afternoon.

A few moments later she emerged from the shadowy tunnel of the stairway into the bright glare of the street. She made her way towards the forum. She did not notice that, two hundred yards behind her, the mariner moved quietly out of a doorway and started to follow.

Julius waited. He was standing by one of the pair of big wooden pillars that marked the northern end of the bridge. It was almost noon.

The interview with Sextus had left him worried. He thought the older man probably meant what he said, but how could he recover the bag? Perhaps if he told his mother about the threat she would relent, though he was not sure about that. In any case, he decided, it was useless to worry about it now. He had other business on hand.

There was a roar from the amphitheatre on the hill away to the left; a faintly contemptuous note in the sound told him that an animal must be getting the better of a human.

Julius gazed up the broad street towards the forum. If the girl was coming, she would turn into it before long. At present the street was empty; so was the quay. He could feel his heart beating. "If she comes now," he murmured, but did not complete the sentence. If she appeared now, he was certain she would be his that afternoon. He trembled with excitement. And yet – this was a strange thing – for all his anticipation, part of him was still nervous, almost hoping that she would stay away.

Several minutes passed; still there was no sign of Martina, and Julius was beginning to think that perhaps, after all, she might not come, and maybe it was just as well, when his attention was distracted by a small movement from along the quay to his right.

It was nothing much, just some soldiers with a donkey pulling a small cart. He watched them idly as they came slowly along the waterfront towards him. It occurred to him that the little cart must be heavy, because he saw the donkey slip once and stop. But perhaps the animal was just being obstinate. He glanced up the street again: still no sign of Martina.

The soldiers and the donkey were two hundred yards away now. There were only three men: one leading the donkey, two behind the cart. Because he was standing behind the wooden pillar, they did not see him, but as they drew closer, he could make out their faces under their helmets. One of them, it seemed to him, looked familiar.

And then, with a start, he realized why. The man bringing up the rear was none other than his acquaintance from the day before. The centurion. He looked at the big man curiously. Why, he wondered, should the centurion be escorting a donkey cart through the streets in the middle of the games?

The cart was covered with a canvas sheet. One corner had worked loose, however, and Julius could see the top of an amphora of wine sticking out. Obviously, for some reason, the soldiers were taking provisions from the official warehouse to the fort that day. No doubt they were having a feast in the barracks that night. The cart started to turn into an alley that led up the hill.

His thoughts returned to Martina. A little wave of lust passed through him. Where was the girl?

And then something happened. At first glance it was nothing of importance. As the cart entered the alley, one wheel hit a bump and a small item from the load fell off. For a moment it lay in the dust before one of the soldiers hurriedly scooped it up and pushed it back under the cover. As he did so, however, Julius noticed two things. The object glinted dully in the sun. And the centurion looked quickly to the right and left to make sure no one had seen. On his face was an expression Julius was sure he recognized. It was one of fear – and guilt. For the object that had fallen off the cart was a gold coin.

Gold. There could be whole sacks of coins on that cart. No wonder the donkey had stumbled trying to pull it. And why should the soldiers be surreptitiously moving gold along a deserted street and up an alley? The thought was so astounding that for a moment Julius couldn't believe it. Yet no other explanation made sense. They must be stealing it.

He remained quite still until the cart had passed into the alley and out of sight. The street ahead was still empty: no sign of the girl. Suddenly he felt very cold; his mind was in a whirl. Then, very quietly, he moved out from the bridge and towards the alley.

Cautiously, he kept his distance. For several minutes, moving from corner to corner, he pursued their zigzag course. There was no question; they were taking care not to be seen.

Several times he hesitated. If the soldiers were stealing bullion and they saw him following them, he knew what would happen. But already the outline of a plan had started to take shape in his mind. They've got to be planning to hide the gold somewhere, he reasoned. If he could just find out where, he could pay the hiding place a visit himself. Just one of those sacks would make Sextus forget he ever lost the bag. He could just see his friend's happy face. A thought struck him and made him grin. "We'd have no need to forge coins if we had real ones," he chuckled to himself. With wealth such as this he could buy Martina anything she wanted.

Keeping roughly parallel with the main street, the soldiers' route through the side alleys took them up the slope of the eastern hill towards the forum. Here they came to the upper of the two great thoroughfares that crossed the city. Taking an alley that ran parallel with it, they turned left.

"They're going west," Julius muttered, "but where to?" He could not guess. Judging it safer, he went into the main thoroughfare and began to walk down it, intending to track the cart's progress at the next side street.

After tracking the cart down the incline between the two hills, Julius saw it come out into the main street ahead of him. He paused, not wanting to be seen, while the soldiers continued across and started up the slope opposite. They were over a quarter of a mile ahead with the amphitheatre looming over the summit behind them, when they turned abruptly into an alleyway on the left and vanished. Julius hurried forward, not wanting to lose track of them. A minute passed; two. He was almost there.

It was then, glancing up the slope, that he saw her.

Martina was coming down the street towards him, walking with a swinging step. She was smiling to herself. She was two hundred yards away and had not seen him.

Julius stopped and gazed. So she was coming to the rendezvous after all. His heart leapt. As he watched her approach, all his doubts dissolved. She's beautiful, he thought. She wants me. Perhaps she even loves me. A wave of joy and excitement swept over him. It was as though he could feel her body, smell her even. He wanted to run forwards to meet her.

But if he went to Martina now he would lose valuable time. At any second that cart could disappear in the maze of alleyways and courtyards. And then he'd have lost the gold.

"The girl will wait," he murmured to himself. "The gold won't." And he ducked into a gateway.

For several minutes he made his way cautiously along one lane after another, working his way westwards. Just before the slope levelled off at the top, there was a handsome street, colonnaded on one side, that ran from the upper thoroughfare southwards to the lower. It, too, was empty. He crossed it. It was in a narrow alley beyond that, nearing the temple of Diana, that he saw the little cart and the donkey.

They were unattended. There was no sign of the soldiers. He stayed by the corner and waited. No one came. Could the soldiers have abandoned the cart? Surely not. He looked about, trying to guess where they had gone. All along the alley were small yards, workshops and little storehouses. They might have gone into any one of a dozen. The cover was still over the cart. Had they already unloaded the gold, or was this only a temporary halt? Still no one came.

If they've unloaded, then I should scout around to see if I can find where they went, Julius considered. It seemed pointless to wait there all day. Cautiously he moved forward and approached the cart.

He reached it and glanced around. There was no sign of anyone. He lifted the cover and looked in.

The cart was almost empty. Only three amphorae of wine remained, and some sacking. He reached in and felt around under the sacking, until his hand encountered something hard. He pulled. It was heavy. Grinning to himself, he reached in with his other hand. And lifted out a single sack of coins.

It was not large. He could hold it in his two cupped hands. But even this was a fortune. No need to bother about the rest. One sack like this was enough. It was time to run.

A shout behind him. He half turned. The soldier was almost upon him. Instinctively, he dropped the sack, ducked his head, dodged round the cart, and ran. As he did so he heard another voice. And, he thought, a third. The centurion.

"Get him."

Straight up the alley. Left. Then right. A moment later he was in the great thoroughfare. He ran across it, looked for another alleyway, found one and fled up it.

They knew he had seen the gold. He was a witness. They had to kill him. As he ran, he thought fast. Where could he go? Where could he hide from them? Their voices were still there; they seemed to be to his right and left at the same time. Then he had an idea. It was his only hope. He pushed himself forwards, gasping for breath, as their footfalls echoed close behind him.

* * *

Martina waited by the bridge. There was not a soul to be seen. Just below, the wide, clear waters of the river flowed silently by, glinting in the sunlight. From the bridge, she could see the fish, silver and brown, moving about beneath the surface.

The fish had company. She was alone.

Martina was furious, as only a young woman can be who, having prepared herself to be kissed, finds herself ignored instead. She had been waiting for an hour. Now and then she had heard huge roars from the distant crowd as the gladiators fought. She disliked the killing, but that was not the point. He had sent her a letter and promised a present. She had taken a great risk and now, humiliated and frustrated, was going to be left standing there like an idiot until she decided to crawl away. She waited a little longer, then shrugged. Perhaps something bad had happened to young Julius. Perhaps.

"I'll forgive him if he's broken his leg," she murmured to herself, "but not if it's anything less." If he thought he could ignore her, just let him see how she would repay him.

She was in a receptive frame of mind, therefore, when to her surprise she saw a familiar figure come out from the shadows of a side street and approach her.

Seeing her alone, it was second nature to Sextus to approach Martina. As for her, seeing the man she had avoided for the faithless Julius, it was only natural that she should welcome him now with a kiss. If Julius were anywhere near, she hoped he would see it. To make certain, she kissed Sextus again.

Sextus was a little surprised that this girl he had been pursuing should suddenly seem so warm towards him. His conceit told him it was to be expected; his experience told him not to ask for reasons. He smiled pleasantly.

He discovered she had come from the bridge. Had she seen his friend Julius down there? he enquired. No, she told him with a wry smile, Julius was certainly not in that area. "Perhaps he's at the games," she suggested. "Shall we go and see?" And she linked her arm in his.

It was a pleasant walk for Sextus. He had business to attend to with Julius, but he did not want to waste this unforeseen opportunity. By the time they came in sight of the amphitheatre, he had arranged that he would come to her that night.

If I'm not in jail, he thought, I'll be in heaven.

"Better not be seen going into the amphitheatre with you," he lied cleverly, as they drew close. "Until tonight then." Then he slipped away to wait for his former friend. In his hand, he felt the knife.

The evening was warm and a pleasant pall of sweat and dust hung in the air as the great amphitheatre was emptied. The crowd was well satisfied. They had eaten and drunk on the long, curved terraces; they had seen lions, bulls, a giraffe, all manner of beasts; they had seen a bear maul a man and two gladiators had died before them. Londinium might seem far from Rome, but at these moments, beneath the serried arches in the theatre of stone, when men saw the beasts of Europe and Africa and watched men fight, the imperial capital of the ancient, sunlit world seemed no further away than a cry over the southern horizon.

Julius moved with the crowd. They had probably saved his life. Having managed to get about a hundred yards ahead of his pursuers, he had raced out of a lane, across a short cobbled space and dived through a doorway into the amphitheatre. Round the huge circular passage in the walls he had run, up two flights of steps, and then through a narrow doorway into the upper terraces. Two gladiators were fighting. People had stood up to see the kill. He had been able to slip in and find a place without anyone taking any notice.

All afternoon he remained there. Many times he scanned the audience, half expecting to see the legionaries looking for him. He had not dared to venture out in case they were waiting, but now, as he emerged with the crowd, he saw no sign of them. With luck, they had not got a proper look at him.

Maybe I've made it, he grinned to himself.

But what to do next? His parents would be starting their feast with the neighbours very soon. All day they must have been wondering where he was and they would be expecting him now. Indeed, after all the danger of the last few hours, the safety of his cheerful home seemed inviting.

But there was still the matter of the bag of forged coins. His mother knew about it. Sooner or later he was going to have to discuss the business with her – and with his father too, no doubt. He dreaded it, but braced himself. "Anyway," he muttered, "she's got to tell me what she's done with them so that I can get Sextus off my back."

Julius sighed. Sextus had given him until sundown. The sun was sinking now. I'll just have to stall him until the morning, he decided. In the meantime, I'm quick on my feet, he said to himself. And besides, he grinned, he's got to find me first.

He allowed himself to go with the crowd that had flowed into the upper thoroughfare and was mostly drifting towards the eastern hill. As he went, his mind returned to Martina. Was she there somewhere? Would he be able to make it up to her? Perhaps. Certainly there was no need to give up hope.

And then, once again, as he had so many times during the long afternoon, he thought of the gold.

To have held that sack in his very hands! To know that even now it was close by, resting in some cellar probably, not yards from where he had seen the cart. Would the legionaries still be there, guarding it? Surely not. If they had stolen the gold they would keep well clear of the place for the time being.

But then another thought occurred to him. Perhaps they would not leave it there. In a day or two, they might return and start to disperse the gold. Why leave it all in one place where it might be discovered and lost? At the very least, there was a chance the gold might not remain there for long. If I want to get my hands on it, I'd better start looking soon, he concluded. And then laughed softly. I wasn't going home anyway.

He stepped into a side street and discreetly returned to where he had seen the cart standing. There were a few people about, but no sign of the soldiers. He scouted the area carefully. There seemed to be half a dozen places where the cache could be hidden. He would have to break into them. Dusk would be coming soon. He would need an oil lamp. Cautiously, he went upon his way.

He did not know that he was being followed.

It was only after nightfall that Julius's mother began to be concerned. The neighbours were enjoying their meal. The fat girl had just consumed her third chicken. Her husband, Rufus, his round, cheerful face now red as a berry, was telling his friends a funny story. But where was the boy?

"He's after some woman," Rufus had told her with a grin

when his son had failed to show up when the feast began. "Don't you worry."

But then she had not told Rufus about the coins yet. And what had that Sextus got to do with it? She did not like the heavy-browed fellow.

The stars were out as Martina waited. She hardly knew what she felt now. Her fury with Julius had subsided since the afternoon. Perhaps something had happened to him. Had she been too quick to blame him?

And now Sextus was about to arrive.

Part of her was excited. After all, he was a man. It was the thought of a man, that warm summer night, that made her tremble with anticipation. And yet, did she really want Sextus, with his deep-set eyes and muttonchop whiskers? Perhaps not very much. "It was the young boxer I wanted," she confessed aloud.

But Sextus was coming, and she felt sure that if he arrived, she would not be able to get rid of him so easily. She sighed. At that moment she hardly knew what she wanted.

Under the bright stars, the little boat slipped silently downstream on the ebbing tide. The air was warm, even on the river. Round the great loop beneath the city of Londinium it went, gliding unnoticed through the waters as they drained silently towards the eastern sea.

The body in the bottom of the boat lay still, its face towards the night sky. The knife wound that had killed him had been made so cleverly that he had scarcely bled at all. Now the body was weighted so that it would sink to the bottom of the river and stay down.

It took skill, all the same, to dispose of a body in the water. The river had secret eddies and currents, a hidden will of its own, and a body sunk in one place, even weighted down, might mysteriously be conveyed to some other spot entirely where it might be found. On such occasions, it was necessary to know the river's secrets.

But then the mariner knew the river very well.

He had been surprised, at first, to see his wife and Sextus greet each other with kisses. He knew Sextus by sight, knew his name. And the letter, he recalled, had been signed with a J.

But then he had realized his mistake. It must have been not a J but a poorly made S.

He had killed Sextus while the carpenter was trailing his friend Julius through the alleys in the gathering dusk.

He had only to decide what to do about Martina now. His first instinct was to punish her in a way she would not forget. In his mother's country she would have been stoned to death. But he was wiser than that. After all, he might not find it so easy to replace her. He had had his revenge on her lover. He would treat her with kindness, and see what happened.

In the autumn of the year 251, the theft of a considerable amount of gold and silver coinage was discovered.

The centurion who was ordered to lead the investigation under one of the governor's most senior officials, was unable to discover anything.

Shortly after this, the centurion and a number of troops from the garrison at Londinium were abruptly transferred by the governor to aid in the rebuilding of the great fortress of Caerleon in Wales. No date was set for their return.

For Julius, however, events went well. The question of the bag was not raised by his mother, and the mysterious disappearance of his friend Sextus seemed to end the matter.

His business with the mariner prospered. Better yet, satisfied that he had dealt with his wife's lover, the mariner never had the least suspicion of the affair that began between Julius and Martina the following spring. And when the mariner was lost at sea a year later, Julius not only took over his business but married his widow too.

On the birth of their second son, to the great delight of his father Julius became a full member of the Temple of Mithras.

It was also at about this time that strong rulers emerged once more in Rome, and both in the empire and in Londinium it seemed, for the time being, that things were returning to normal.

Yet one thing continued to trouble Julius. Again and again, since the day of the games, he had returned to the place, searching high and low, by day and night. When the centurion was suddenly sent away, he was sure he could not have taken the heavy treasure with him. Somewhere, therefore, within a short distance of the spot where he had last seen the donkey cart, there might still be hidden a cache of coins whose value it was hard even to calculate. Months went by, years, and still he searched. On long summer evenings, he would stand by the quay or on the ramparts of the great wall of Londinium, watching the departing sun, and wonder.

Where, by all the gods, was that gold?

Chapter 3

The Rood

604

The woman stared at the sea. Her long hair fell loosely over her hunting dress, which flapped in the wind. The bright autumn sun was still in the east.

Her last moment of freedom. For three days she had delayed in this wild place that was her refuge, but now she must return. And decide. What answer would she give her husband?

It was *Haligmonath* – holy month – as they called the old Roman month of September in the pagan countries of the north.

The place where she was standing lay on the huge, curving coastline beyond the Thames Estuary where England bulges out some seventy miles eastwards into the waters of the cold North Sea. Before her, the great, grey sea. Behind her, huge, flat tracts of fen and heath, wood and field stretching to the horizon. And to her right, the long, desolate beaches that continued southwards for fifty miles before they curved into the wide entrance to the Thames.

Her name was Elfgiva – "The faeries' gift" in the Anglo-Saxon tongue. Her richly embroidered dress proclaimed her a noblewoman. She was thirty-seven, with four grown sons. Her complexion was fair, her face handsome, her eyes bright blue. Although strands of silver had stolen into her golden hair, she knew she was still a fine-looking woman. I could still have another child, she thought. Even the daughter she had longed for. But what was the use of that if this terrible business remained unresolved?

Though the two servants waiting with the horses could not see the anguish on her face, they could guess her feelings. They felt sorry for her. The whole household knew how, after a quarter-century of happy marriage, the master and mistress had suddenly fallen out.

"She's brave," one groom whispered to the other. "But can she hold out?"

"Not against the master," the other replied. "He always gets his way."

"True," the groom agreed. And then, with admiration: "But she's proud."

It was not easy for a woman to be too proud amongst the Anglo-Saxons of England.

Profound changes had taken place in the northern island of Britain during the last two centuries. The first was that, since the empire of Rome had effectively collapsed, Britain had ceased to be a Roman province. The second was that, like most of the empire, it had been invaded.

There had always been barbarians at the empire's gates, but Rome had either repelled them or absorbed them as mercenaries and immigrant settlers. From about 260, however, as the sprawling empire fragmented into regions, the incursions grew harder to control. And around the year 400, the many tribes of eastern Europe, stirred up by the appearance of the terrible Huns from Asia, began a long series of huge migrations west. The process was a gradual one. But slowly the Goths, Lombards, Burgundians, Franks, Saxons, Bavarians, Slavs and many others, settling beside the existing populations, established their tribal territories and the old order and civilization of western Europe had been completely disrupted.

It was soon after 400 AD that the hard-pressed Roman emperor withdrew the garrison from Britain, sending the island provincials only the bleak message: "Defend yourselves."

At first, the islanders coped. True, there were raids from Germanic pirates, but the island's ports and towns had defences. After a few decades, they started employing German mercenaries to protect them. Gradually, however, with the old trade from the Continent disrupted, things began to slide. Regional leaders sprang up. The mercenaries settled and sent messages to their kinsmen overseas that the island province was weak and fragmented.

They were north Germans – tribes from the coastal regions of today's Germany and Denmark – Angles, Saxons and others, including, probably, a related tribe known as the Jutes. Most of these people were fair-haired and blue-eyed.

They came in a steady stream, extending their hold on England from east to west. Sometimes they were successfully resisted. Around the year 500, a Romano-British leader held the West Country against them, and his name, discovered by chroniclers long after, gave rise to the legend of King Arthur.

But despite these valiant attempts to preserve the old Romano-British world, within a century and a half of their first coming, the immigrants were masters of the English land. Wales in the far west and Scotland in the north they failed to colonize. Elsewhere, except in some place names and river names – Thames from Tamesis, for instance – even the old Celtic and Latin languages largely died out. The settlement evolved into several famous kingdoms: the Angles set up Northumbria and midland Mercia; in the south lay the Saxon kingdoms of Wessex in the west, Sussex in the centre, and Kent in the old peninsula of the Cantii. The huge, low-lying eastern tract of land across the estuary from Kent was divided in two: in the northern half were the Angles of East Anglia; in the south, the East Saxon King of Essex.

It was from East Anglia that Elfgiva was returning to her husband.

It was her childhood home. Every year she went there to visit her father's grave. This time, in particular, she had hoped the visit would give her strength, and in a way it had. How happily she had wandered along the open coast where the broad flats and beaches were broken only by the long, low lines of sand dunes before they merged with the shallow waves. How she had enjoyed the salt breeze that came in, harsh and bracing, off the sea. They said the East Anglians lived longer than others because of it.

A little way inland lay the burial ground, a series of mounds, a few feet high, by a clump of furze and small trees whose tops had long since been brushed to flatness by the winds. She had spent several hours there during her visit. The largest of the mounds was her father's grave.

How she had loved and admired him. He had travelled all over the northern seas and taken a Swedish bride. Such a bold seafarer had he been that when he died they had buried him in his boat in full regalia. She could hear his deep voice still. As he lay there now, with his long beard spread, was he dreaming of the heaving seas? Perhaps. And did the gods of the north watch over him? She had no doubt of it. Were they not in his very blood? Had not their people given their names to the days of the week? Tiw, the war god, had Tuesday, in place of Mars in the Roman calendar; Woden, or Wotan as the Germans called him, greatest of all gods, had the middle day, Wednesday; Thunor the Thunderer, Thursday; Frigg, goddess of love, Friday, in place of the Roman Venus.

"My great-grandfather was the youngest brother of a royal line," he would remind her, "so we are descended from Woden himself." Nearly all the royal families of England claimed descent from Woden. No wonder her father's endless strength had seemed to come from the sea and sky itself.

Wasn't this the heritage she had passed on to her own four sons when they were in the cradle? Hadn't she taught them that they were children of the sea and the wind and of the gods themselves? What, then, would her father have said to her husband's new and shameful demand? As she stood by his grave she had known very well. Which was why, if the visit had given her strength, it had brought her no comfort.

Her husband had demanded that she become a Christian.

The man and his pretty young wife were standing together in the middle of a circle of villagers by the river. Both were terrified.

Like the rest of them, the couple were dressed in simple smocks and leggings bound with thongs of twine. Except that two women were pulling the leggings off the girl. In a moment they would pull off the smock as well.

The crime and the trial – such as it was – had taken place the previous day; the sentence would have been carried out then, too, if the village elder had not decided to wait until they had a snake. They had one now.

The woodsman carefully held the adder just beneath its head. In a moment he would hold it close to a small charcoal fire, just to tease it.

On the ground in front of the girl was a large sack already weighted with stones. As soon as her clothes were off, the fair-haired girl would be forced to get into it. They would then toss the adder in, tie up the top, and watch the sack's convulsions as the adder struck her. When the elder said so, they would throw the sack in the stream and let it sink.

This was how they punished a woman for witchcraft.

There was no question about their guilt: they had been caught in the act. No man would speak on their behalf. Admittedly, the young fellow had protested that his wife was not involved, but there was no need to take any notice of that. He had come from their cottage before he did it, and she had been in there. In the eyes of the village, that made her guilty.

"She must have told him to do it," some said. "She didn't try to stop him," others qualified. Either way it made no difference. The ancient laws – the *dooms* – of the Anglo-Saxons were harsh and unyielding. "Put her in the sack," they cried.

For the young man, Offa, there was more sympathy, even though his own sentence was assured. No one could deny he had shown spirit. The facts were simple. The village elder, a tall and cunning man, had taken a fancy to young Offa's wife. He had tried to seduce her and come close to rape before her screams had stopped him. That was all. No harm had been done. But Offa was in love with his wife, and she with him. He could not bear the thought of the assault. Some in the village considered that he had slightly lost his reason.

If he had just attacked the elder it would not have been so bad. Disputes between parties were usually settled by payments. If you cut off a person's hands, it would cost so much; their arm, so much more. Though it could mean a blood feud, even a death was often settled with a man's family forcash. But that was not what the young fellow had done. Egged on, no doubt, by his wife, he had come out of his cottage the previous day and stuck a pin into the elder. This was another matter altogether. It was witchcraft.

Though the sticking of pins into the effigies of victims was a common form of witchcraft, another method was to stick the pin directly into the victim himself, as is still told in the tale of Sleeping Beauty, and then pray not that the victim would sleep but that the wound should fester until death was brought on. This was the terrible crime of which Offa was accused. Being of little account, he had not stood a chance.

He was an eager fellow, twenty years old, wiry, smaller than most of the sturdy Saxon villagers, brown-haired where they were fair, although, like them, his eyes were blue. A certain quickness in his thoughts and temper were further signs that his blood was Celtic rather than Saxon. He had two distinguishing marks: just above his forehead was a patch of white hair, and between the fingers of both hands was a curious webbing. Though his name was Offa, the other villagers usually referred to him as Duck.

It was a century and a half since his family had departed the once Roman city of Londinium. Small-time merchants, they had served in the militia when the legions left and watched with concern the city's decline. They had still been there in 457 when thousands of people from Kent had streamed in to escape a huge force of Saxon marauders. Although, on that occasion, the formidable walls, strengthened with extra bastions and a great stout wall along the waterfront, had protected them, it had proved to be the city's last hour of glory, the beginning of an end that came quite swiftly. The Saxon farmers who took over the land had no use for cities. The old metropolis, its purpose lost, sank into decay and emptied. A generation later, Offa's family were impoverished; another and they drifted away. Offa's grandfather had eked out a living as a charcoal-burner in the forests of Essex; his father, a jolly fellow and a wonderful singer, had been adopted by this small Saxon village and allowed to marry a Saxon girl. These villagers, then, were Offa's people: he had no others.

It was a small place, just a forest clearing really, but set beside one of the many streams that followed modest, meandering courses through woods and marsh down to the lower reaches of the Thames. There were a few brown thatched huts, a long wooden barn, two fields, one ready to harvest, the other fallow, a meadow, and an area of open grass where four cows and a shaggy horse were idly grazing. There was a black painted boat by the riverbank. Oak, ash and beech trees stood sombrely around. Pigs snouted for nuts and acorns on the soft forest floor.

Once a Roman road from Londinium to the east coast had passed only a mile away, but its line was grown over now. The village was not entirely cut off, however, for a winding track through the forest brought occasional travellers, and over the stream there was a small wooden bridge.

Young Offa was one of the poorest of the villagers. He did

not possess the peasant's full quota of land, the yardland. "I've only a farthing," he had warned his bride when he courted her – a quarter of a yardland. To support himself, he worked for others. Still, he was free. A Saxon peasant in a village. Yet now, as soon as they had drowned his wife, they were going to inflict a punishment perhaps worse than death upon him.

"Let him bear the wolf's head," the elder had pronounced. Let him live like the wolves in the forest – friendless, alone. An outlaw. That was the terrible punishment they reserved for a freeman. An outlaw had no rights. If the village elder came after him to kill him, he was free to do so. No one in the area would take him in. He must wander where he could, to survive or die alone as he pleased. That was the *doom* of the Anglo-Saxons.

Ricola, his wife, was naked now. She looked at him. Her cheerful, round face was very white. He knew she loved him, but her expression said only one thing: You did this to me. I'm going to die. You aren't.

Some of the men were leering at her. They could not help it. After all, she had a delicious young body. Pink and white flesh, a trace of puppy fat, soft young breasts. Two men held open the sack. The man with the adder was grinning. Saxon justice was harsh.

"Woden," the young man murmured, "save us." And he looked around in desperation.

Surely their lives could not end like this.

Elfgiva and her party rode slowly. It was only a day's journey, and she still felt confused. It was not just the question of denying her faith, though nothing was dearer to her. There was something else: she had an instinctive sense of foreboding. And the closer she was to home, the worse it became. What did it mean? Was it a message from the gods?

How dreary the clouds seemed. They had come from behind her and now they masked the sun. The travellers were passing through a stretch of wilderness: small trees, burnt grass, brown bracken. Elfgiva remained deep in thought. As she pondered, she remembered her father's words, many years ago. "When a voyager begins a journey, he prepares his ship, decides upon his course and sets sail. What else can he do? But he cannot know the outcome – what storms may arise, what new lands he may find, or whether or not he will return. That is destiny, and you must accept it. Never think you can escape destiny."

Wyrd they called it in Anglo-Saxon. Destiny. *Wyrd* was invisible, yet governed all. Even the gods were subject to it. They were the actors; *Wyrd* was the story. And when Thunor's thunder rumbled across the sky and echoed in the mountains, behind that sky, containing that echo, lay *Wyrd*. It was neither good nor bad; it was unknowable. You felt it all the time, in the earth, the rolling sea, the cavernous grey sky. Every Anglo-Saxon and Norseman knew *Wyrd*, which decided life and death and gave to their songs and poetry a resonant fatalism.

Destiny alone would decree what was to happen when she met her husband.

"I shall decide what to say when I see him," she murmured aloud. She would pray to Woden and Frigg that night.

They were passing through a wood when they came to the stream. It was deep. Irritated, she realized that if they tried to ford it she was going to get very wet. For several minutes, therefore, she cast about to see if she could find a better crossing. It was just then, seeing the small bridge, that she also caught sight of the strange little gathering and urged her horse into a canter.

Moments later, Offa was surprised to find himself staring at a handsome lady whom the gods had just caused to appear out of the forest upon a fine horse.

"What did she do?" The lady was gazing down at the naked girl with curiosity. The village elder quickly explained. Elfgiva gazed around the crowd. The sight of the snake and the sack made her tremble. She looked carefully at the young couple again. It was chance that she should have come across this hamlet hidden in the woods. Why should fate have brought her there just then? To save a life perhaps. As she looked at the couple, her own troubles did not seem so terrible. She even felt envious in a way. They were young. The young man loved the girl almost, it seemed, to insanity.

"What will you take for them?"

"Lady?"

"I'll buy them. As slaves. I'll take them away."

The village elder hesitated. It was true that for certain crimes a man might be turned into a slave, but he was not sure in this case what the proper *doom* should be.

Elfgiva took a coin from the pouch that hung at her waist. The Saxons had no coins of their own, but used those of the traders from across the English Channel. The coin she took out was gold. The entire village stared at it. Few had ever seen such a thing before, but the elder and several of the men had a shrewd idea of its value.

"You need them both?" he asked. He had rather wanted to see the naked girl in the bag with the snake.

"Yes."

The elder could see at once what the village wished him to do. He signalled to the women to release the girl, who hurriedly began to dress herself.

"Cut their hair," Elfgiva ordered one of her servants. This was the mark of all her slaves, but Offa and his wife were so shaken by what had been about to happen that they submitted meekly. As soon as it was done, Elfgiva handed the elder the coin, then turned to the young couple. "You belong to me now. Walk behind," she ordered. And she began to ride away, across the little bridge.

They travelled for some time in silence. Offa noted that they were heading almost due west.

"Lady," he called out respectfully, at last. "Where are we going?" At which Elfgiva briefly turned her head.

"You've probably never heard of it," she said. "It's just a little trading post, far away." She smiled. "It's called Lundenwic." Then she turned back again.

Whatever destiny might finally decide, there was little doubt that Elfgiva's fate that morning lay in the firm hand of the powerful figure who, unknown to her, was at that moment riding exactly parallel to her course only twenty miles to the south.

All those who knew her husband would have agreed, "She may be brave, but no one gets the better of Cerdic." Two events – one that had taken place the day before, the other which Cerdic planned for the following morning – would have convinced them: "She doesn't stand a chance."

Cerdic rode steadily. Though it was only twenty miles as the crow flies, he might have been a world away, for he was on the other side of the Thames Estuary, riding along the great chalk ridges of the kingdom of Kent.

The contrast between the two sides of the estuary could not have been greater. Whereas the huge tracts of East Anglia were low and flat, the narrower peninsula of Kent was divided by the huge ridges that ran eastwards until they ended abruptly in the tall white cliffs that stared over the sea. Between those ridges lay great valleys and sweeps of country – rolling, open fields in the eastern parts, and in the western, bosky woods, smaller fields and orchards.

If Elfgiva was from the wild, free coast, Cerdic was from ordered Kent. And there was the difference.

His family had been there since the first Saxon and Jutish settlement. Their estate, in the west, was still their true home, but as a young man Cerdic had also set up a second residence at the little trading post of Lundenwic on the River Thames. From there he received and shipped goods and set out with a string of packhorses to visit all parts of the island. It was a trade that had made him rich indeed.

He was a large, bluff man, a Saxon to the core, fair-haired, blue-eyed, with a hint of temper about him. Whilst his beard was full, the hair on his head was thinning, and his complexion suggested that, when angry, he could become flushed even to apoplexy. At the same time, his broad, Germanic face had high cheekbones that suggested a measured, even cold strength and authority. "Strong as a bull, but hard as an oak tree," his men used to say of him. It was also generally agreed that, like his father before him, he would live to be old: "They're too shrewd to die in a hurry, that family."

Two other character traits, always strong in his ancestors, were especially noticeable in Cerdic. One was that, once given, he had never been known to break his word. As a trader, this had become a great asset to him. The other, though it was sometimes the subject of wry amusement to his friends, was more often viewed with awe and even fear.

To Cerdic there were only two sides to any issue. Whatever he had to decide – a course of action, a man's character, a question of guilt or innocence – as far as Cerdic was concerned, there was a right answer and a wrong answer, and nothing in between. Once his mind, which was an intelligent one, was made up, it snapped shut like an iron trap. "Things are only black and white to Cerdic, never grey," his associates would say.

None of this boded well for his wife. At this moment, Cerdic was on his way back from the court of his traditional lord, good King Ethelbert of Kent, in the city of Canterbury.

Where they were Christians.

In the days when young Offa's ancestor Julius had forged his coins in Roman Londinium, Christianity had been an unofficial cult, subject to occasional persecution. Then, in the following century, thanks to the conversion of the Emperor Constantine, Christianity had become the empire's official religion, and Rome the Catholic capital. In the province of Britain, as elsewhere, churches were built, often on the site of pagan temples. The British Church was of some consequence. Even decades after the Romans had left the island, British bishops were still attending faraway Church councils. "Though we had to pay their travelling expenses," the Italian bishops recorded, "because they're miserably poor."

But then the Anglo-Saxons came, staunch pagans all. The British Christians struggled, became cut off, and then silent. A century passed, and more.

Not that all was lost. Missionaries arrived. From Ireland, recently converted by St Patrick, came Celtic monks, intense in spirit, rich in Celtic art. Monasteries were established in the north of the island, near the border with the Scots. Nevertheless, most of England still belonged to the Nordic gods. Until now.

For in the year of Our Lord 597, the monk Augustine had been sent by the Pope to convert the Anglo-Saxons to the true faith. His mission had taken him straight to Canterbury, in the south-eastern peninsula of Kent.

It was certainly a convenient place. Situated at the centre of the peninsula's tip on a small hill, Canterbury had since Roman times acted as a hub to which the Kentish ports like Dover – which lay only twenty miles across the Channel from the European Continent – were all connected. Coming from Europe, Canterbury was the first place of significance a traveller reached. Far more important than its geography, however, was that good King Ethelbert of Kent, whose principal residence this was, had married a Frankish princess, and her people had already been converted. It was the presence of this Christian queen that really drew the Church to Canterbury and gave it its opportunity. In those times the rule of conversion was simple: "Convert the king. The rest will follow."

"And you, my good Cerdic, I know I can trust absolutely." Only yesterday, the grey-bearded King Ethelbert had put his hand on his shoulder whilst Queen Bertha had smiled approvingly. Of course they could trust him. Hadn't his ancestors been loyal companions of the first Kentish kings? Hadn't King Ethelbert given rings – the most intimate token between a lord and his men – to his own father? "We are always so glad to see you," the queen had said, "at our court at Canterbury."

The court of the Kentish king was, by the standards of ancient times, a rustic little place. Where once, in the days of Rome, the provincial town had had a small forum, temple, baths and other buildings in stone, there now stood a large stockaded enclosure, in the centre of which was a long, barn-like building with timber walls and a high thatched roof. This was King Ethelbert's hall. A short distance away, however, was another, simple enclosure, and in the centre of this stood an altogether more remarkable building. For although it, too, seemed little more than a barn and was smaller than the king's hall, it was built in stone.

Canterbury's cathedral was built by the monk Augustine himself. It was possibly the only stone building in Anglo-Saxon England at the time. Primitive though it surely was, in these first few years of its existence this little building marked a turning point in the island's history.

"And now we have Canterbury as a base," the queen had said eagerly, "the missionary work can really begin." And she smiled at her husband.

"You see," the king explained, "your position makes you particularly useful." The plan for the rest of the island, Cerdic had now discovered, was ambitious. The missionaries planned to strike right up the east coast to the north. Their first goal, however, was to secure both banks of the Thames Estuary, which meant, after Kent, converting the Saxon King of Essex. "He's my nephew," King Ethelbert explained, "and he's agreed to convert out of respect for me. But," he made a wry face, "some of his followers may be more difficult." He fixed his eyes firmly on Cerdic. "You're a loyal man of Kent," he went on, "but you trade from Lundenwic, which is on the north shore, part of my nephew's kingdom, technically. I want you to give the missionaries every help you can."

Cerdic nodded. "Of course."

"There's to be a bishop there, you see. And a new cathedral," Queen Bertha added enthusiastically. "We shall tell the new bishop to rely on you."

Cerdic bowed. Then, thinking of the various residences of the Essex king, enquired: "But where does this bishop plan to build his church?" Only to find the king laughing.

"My dear friend, I see you haven't understood." He smiled, but with a serious look in his eyes. "The cathedral is going to be at Lundenwic."

It was late afternoon when Cerdic arrived at his destination for that day. Since leaving Canterbury he had followed the line of the old Roman road – now an overgrown, grassy track – that led along the northern edge of the peninsula until it reached the mouth of the River Medway, where there lay a modest Saxon settlement known as Rochester. Here, instead of continuing on the old Roman road along the estuary towards the former city of Londinium, he had turned inland, mounted the steep ridge that strode across the northern part of the peninsula, and made his way across it for some time until he emerged on the high ground's southern edge. Then he smiled. He had come home.

The estate that had been the home of Cerdic's family for the last century and a half lay just below the crest of the great ridge. It consisted of a hamlet and, some way distant, a single thatched hall or farmhouse beside which were wooden outbuildings surrounding a courtyard. From these buildings the ground descended in a long, graciously wooded slope to the valley floor. This was the place known as Bocton.

The Bocton estate was extensive. There were fields, apple orchards, and productive oak woodlands. It also contained a quarry – unused since Roman times – of Kentish ragstone.

But the feature that made the place so outstanding, and which, whenever he saw it, caused Cerdic's hard face to break into a mellow smile of deep satisfaction, was the view. For, gazing southwards from Bocton, one looked right across the huge, sweeping valley – that glorious, wooded landscape, some twenty miles across – known as the Weald of Kent. Bocton and the several estates along this long ridge shared this magnificent view, one of the finest in southern England. It was not just the house, but this huge, rich outlook over the Weald that was in his heart when Cerdic the Saxon said: "I'm home."

But this time he had not come only to see the view. He had come to pay a visit to another estate, not far away, the following morning. The purpose of this visit he had told no one at all.

It was astonishing how quickly Offa and Ricola recovered from their ordeal. Like two puppies who had fallen into water and shaken themselves dry, the young couple had accepted their new situation and regained their spirits before they had even reached their new home.

"We won't be slaves for long," Offa assured his wife. "I'll think of something." And though Ricola was the more practical of the two, she quite believed him.

The day after their arrival Offa was sent to help the men, who were harvesting in the meadow. "You'll work under my husband's foreman and do whatever he tells you," Elfgiva explained, although as her personal slave he would be at her disposal whenever she wanted him. As for Ricola, she was sent to help the women.

At the beginning the pair were too occupied to think of anything very much. All the same, Offa had time to observe, and what he saw pleased him. Unquestionably, the little trading post of Lundenwic was a delightful spot.

It was certainly not a place of great importance. The ford nearby was a useful place to cross the river, but it lay in a tribal no-man's-land between the Saxon kingdoms of Kent and Essex, and had no other significance.

When the Saxons had finally made a small settlement there in the time of Cerdic's father, they had ignored the great empty ruins of Londinium on the twin hills nearby; they had also, because it was rather marshy, avoided the ground by the island and ford upstream. Instead, they had chosen a pleasant spot, just halfway between the two, where the river curved and the northern bank sloped down some twenty feet to the water. Here they had built a single wharf. This landing place they now called Lundenwic: *Lunden* from the old Celtic and Roman name of the place, Londinos, and *-wic*, meaning in Anglo-Saxon "port" or, in this case, "trading post".

Above the wooden jetty, a small group of buildings included a barn, a cattle pen, two storehouses and the homestead of Cerdic and his household, surrounded by a stout wattle fence. All these buildings, large or small, were single-storey and mostly rectangular. Their walls, made of post and plank, were low, only four or five feet high, and strengthened on the outside by a sloping earth bank, turfed over. Their steep thatched roofs, however, rose to a height of nearly twenty feet. Each building had a stout wooden door. The floor of Cerdic's hall was slightly sunken, so that one stepped down on to the wooden floorboards covered with rushes. The space inside was warm and commodious but rather dark, since when the door was shut the only light came from the vents in the thatch, made to let out the smoke from the fire in the stone hearth near the centre of the floor. Here, the entire household gathered to eat. Beside the hall were several small huts, including one, the smallest of all, where Offa and Ricola were quartered.

And how delightful the place was. The grassy north bank was high enough to afford a good view of the great sweep of the river, including the marshes on the opposite bank. Less than a mile away to the right lay the ford, whilst to the left, no further away, one could just see through the trees a hint of the huge Roman ruins upon the twin hills. Across the river from them a gravel promontory jutted out from the south bank. "That's the best place to fish," one of the men told him. Of the sturdy Roman bridge that had once crossed between these points, the only sign was some rotting timbers on the southern side.

Lundenwic might be small, but as Offa soon discovered, it was surprisingly busy. "The master spends more time here than at Bocton," the men told him. Boats would come down the river from deep in the island's interior, and as Cerdic's activities increased, ships would even make their way up the estuary from the lands of the Norsemen, the Frisians and the Germans. In the stores, Offa found pottery, bales of wool, beautifully worked swords, and Saxon metalwork. There were also kennels: "They always ask us for hunting dogs," the foreman explained. More intriguing, however, was another building set a little apart. Like the other stores it was a stout hut with a thatched roof, but it was long and narrow, and for some reason its roof was low, leaving only just enough headroom for standing up. Down each side were small pens that might have been for pigs or small livestock. Attached to the posts were chains.

"What are the chains for?" Offa asked. The foreman gave him a sidelong glance. "They're for our best cargo. The one that makes the master rich," he quietly replied.

Offa understood. Once again, as it had been before the Romans came, the island had become well known for its slaves. They were sold all over Europe. Indeed, just before he sent the monk Augustine to the island, it was the Pope himself who, seeing the fair-haired English slaves in the marketplace in Rome, had famously pronounced: "They are not Angles, but angels."

The supply was always plentiful. Some were the losers of occasional conflicts between the various Anglo-Saxon kingdoms; a few might be criminals. But the majority of slaves came to that condition not through war, or even the raids of cruel slave-traders, but because, whether they were unwanted or there were too many to be fed, they had been sold by their own people.

"The Frisians come for a load every year," the foreman remarked, and then added with a grin: "You're lucky it was the mistress who bought you and not the master, or you'd be on the next ship!"

It was on the second day of his return that Cerdic gave Elfgiva his ultimatum. He did so in private. Not even his sons were aware of what passed between them. His message was as blunt as it was simple.

"If you will not obey me, then I am going to take another wife."

"As well as me?"

"No. Instead of you."

And Elfgiva stared at him with a terrible, dull pain, knowing that he meant it.

He was within his rights. The laws of the Anglo-Saxons concerning women were simple. Elfgiva belonged to her husband. She had been paid for. He could add other wives if he wished, and if she committed adultery not only could he throw her out, but the other man would have to compensate him and provide another wife. If, however, he just chose to replace her, this too was allowed.

This was not to say that all Saxon women were downtrodden. Elfgiva knew some wives who ruled their husbands entirely. All the same, if he chose to use it, the law was on Cerdic's side.

"The choice is yours," he explained. "When this bishop comes here, you must be baptized with our sons. If you refuse, I shall feel free to act as I wish. It's up to you."

Indeed, as far as Cerdic was concerned, he was acting properly and morally. To Cerdic, the issue was very simple. As a loyal man of King Ethelbert, he had become a Christian, having been baptized earlier that year. However much he might feel sorry for her, as his wife Elfgiva's duty was to do the same if he asked. The fact that they had loved each other as man and wife for so many years only made her refusal all the more disloyal. The more he considered it, the clearer it became to him: there was a right course and a wrong course; black and white. Elfgiva's duty was clear. Whether anybody liked it or not, there was nothing further to be said.

That the Christian Church frowned upon both polygamy and divorce was something Cerdic did not know. But this was not his fault. The Catholic missionaries, although usually men of fearless courage and deep dedication, were also wise, and in the matter of ancient customs they usually followed a simple rule: "First convert them to the faith, then start to change their customs." It would be many generations before the Church would be able to wean the Anglo-Saxons from polygamy.

The girl in question was young, the daughter of a fellow like himself with a fine estate not far from Bocton. "I'd thought of her for one of your sons rather than you," her father had remarked mildly when Cerdic had called upon him the day before. This, indeed, was the arrangement the two men had privately come to. If Cerdic put away his wife, the girl should marry him; if not, his eldest son. She was a nice, sensible and pretty young Saxon who liked the ordered life of Kent, to which she so entirely belonged. She also agreed to be baptized.

I should have married a girl like that in the first place,

Cerdic had thought to himself as he rode from Bocton towards Lundenwic. She'd never have given me trouble like Elfgiva, from her wild East Anglian shores.

She was young, too. Was that part of it? Hadn't he suddenly felt youthful again, rejuvenated by the presence of this fresh fifteen-year-old maiden who might be his? Perhaps. Did he secretly fear the loss of his strength? No, he told himself, not for a long time yet. In any case, he reminded himself, if Elfgiva behaved like a proper wife, she had nothing to fear.

So it was, faced with this humiliating ultimatum, that Elfgiva listened and bowed her head. She did not even ask who the other woman was. She said nothing at all.

The day after his conversation with Elfgiva, Cerdic decided to deal with his sons.

In a way, he was rather looking forward to it. Although he was quite determined that they must submit, he would be disappointed if they did not show some resistance.

They're young bulls, he told himself. But I dare say I can still master them. Now, standing before them, in front of his hall, he spoke sharply. He did not choose, at this stage, to tell them about his threat to their mother, but he explained about the arrival of the bishop and King Ethelbert's request. "We are all his men," he reminded them. "You will therefore take this new religion as I have."

The four young men stood there awkwardly. He could see they had been discussing the matter amongst themselves, for now they all turned to the oldest, a stalwart fellow of twenty-four, who spoke for them.

"Is it really our duty to forswear our own gods for the king, Father?"

"The king's gods are ours. I'm his man. The King of Essex has already promised to follow King Ethelbert," he said, to encourage them.

"We know. But did you know that the King of Essex's sons are refusing to follow their own father? They say they won't worship this new god."

Cerdic reddened. He had not heard this, but he saw the implication well enough.

"The Essex princes will do as their father tells them," he said firmly.

"How can you ask us to worship this god?" the eldest suddenly burst out. "They say he let himself be nailed on a tree and killed. What sort of a god is that? Are we supposed to desert Thunor and Woden for a man who couldn't fight?"

Cerdic himself was a little vague about the details of Christianity and this point had worried him too. "Christ's father could send floods and part seas," he assured them. "And the King of the Franks has had notable victories since he became a Christian." But he could see they were not impressed. "This is your mother's doing," he muttered, and waved them away.

It was a week later that Elfgiva received a sign.

She had gone riding with her youngest son, Wistan. As she often did, she had followed the curve of the Thames a short distance upstream to the island beside the ford. It was a spot she liked. The small Roman villa on the old Druid's island had vanished and the ground was all overgrown now, except for the track across it to the ford. Thorney, the Saxons called it, because it was so full of bramble bushes. Perhaps it was the somewhat desolate air that attracted Elfgiva to the place.

The day was fine, the sky clear blue, a few white clouds scudding by, throwing their moving shadows on the river. Since the breeze was rather cold, Elfgiva was wrapped in a heavy brown woollen cloak. On her raised left hand she wore a thick leather glove, upon which, with curling claws and curving beak, was perched a hooded bird of prey.

Like many Anglo-Saxon women of her class, Elfgiva enjoyed hawking. On Thorney, she often had good hunting. She also liked to have Wistan near her. He was only sixteen, but of all her sons, it was he who most resembled her. When his brothers went hunting he would often good-naturedly join them, but he was just as likely to go for a walk by himself or sit down to carve a piece of wood, which he did well. She suspected he was the one who loved her best; she also knew that if the other three were defiant over the question of religion, he was deeply troubled. She had therefore used this opportunity to urge him: "Obey your father, Wistan. It's your duty." When he had replied, "I will if you will," she had shaken her head sadly. "It's not the same. I'm older."

"Do you mean to refuse him then?" he had asked, but she

had not yet replied. Instead, since they had now arrived at Thorney, she began to hawk.

As she reached over and flicked off the falcon's hood, Elfgiva almost caught her breath at the magnificent, hard beauty of the bird's tawny eyes. In a flash, it unfurled its wings and rose as she gazed after it, envying its ease.

High the hawk flew, into the heavens. How free it was: free as wind over water. It soared into the open sky, braced against the breeze like a sail on the sea; then dipped, slipping silently, plummeting on to its prey.

Elfgiva watched as the hawk caught the bird. As she saw the luckless victim fluttering helplessly in the falcon's claws, she felt a sudden sense of sorrow and foreboding. How cruel life was, and how transient. It was then, in a momentary flash of absolute clarity, that she understood.

The hawk in the air was free. So was Cerdic. Even if the question of the new god was not just an excuse for him to turn from her – and she was sure that this was all it was – it made no difference. Something had passed within him. He had taken the step away from her into freedom, and once that was done, nature, cruel but inevitable, would take over. Even if I give in now, she thought, in another year or two he'll find some other excuse. Or he'll keep me, but take younger wives as well. I shall be crushed, just like that bird in the falcon's claws. Not because Cerdic is cruel, but because, like the falcon, he cannot help it.

That was *Wyrd*. She knew it with all the ancient, pagan wisdom of the Nordic gods.

What should she do then? Refuse to give in. After all, if she were cast off for her loyalty to the gods, at least there was dignity in it. As she looked up to the hawk descending from the clear blue sky, she inwardly uttered the cry of married women down the ages: If I cannot have love, at least leave me my dignity.

As they rode home that day, she contented herself with urging Wistan once more: "Whatever happens, promise me you will obey your father." More she would not say.

Offa was still full of plans, but he too had met an obstacle – in his wife.

When he had been at Lundenwic ten days, Wistan and one

of his brothers had taken a boat upstream to collect supplies from a farmstead a few miles away, and Offa had gone with them. He had been delighted with what he saw. Soon after leaving the bend by the ford, the left and right banks broke up into a system of marshy islands.

"That's Chalk Island on the right," Wistan had told him. Except that in Anglo-Saxon, in which "island" was rendered "eye", the words "Chelch Eye" made a sound roughly like "Chelsea". "Opposite is Badric's Island." This time "Badric's Eye" came out roughly as "Battersea". Everywhere along the marshy banks of the Thames, Offa discovered, there were more of these *eyes* and the even smaller islands, mud flats really, known as *eyots*.

There were already numerous tiny settlements, a farm here, a hamlet there. These, too, bore characteristic Saxon names with endings like *-ham* for a hamlet, *-ton* for a farm, and *-hythe*, meaning a harbour. Soon after passing Chalk Island, Wistan had again pointed to the north bank, where smoke was rising above the trees. "That's Fulla's-ham," he explained. "And up there," he pointed to a higher spot a couple of miles north, "there's Kensing's-ton."

But what had impressed Offa most, as they progressed upstream, was the lush richness of the land. Behind marsh and mud flat he saw meadowland, pasture and, further off, gentle slopes. "Does the land continue far like this?" he cautiously asked Wistan.

"Yes," came the reply. "Pretty much all the way to the river's source, I believe."

When they had returned that night, therefore, he had said to Ricola: "When you feel ready, I think we could run away. Upriver. The living is good there. If we go far enough I'm sure someone will take us in."

But here, to his surprise, Ricola had flatly opposed him.

Though she was still very young, Offa had already noticed in his wife a cheery independence of spirit that he found attractive. She had established a light-hearted banter with the men. Once, to his horror, she had even made a disrespectful remark to the foreman, but with such good humour that he had just shaken his head and smiled. "She doesn't put up with any nonsense, that one," the men laughed.

He had assumed, therefore, that she would be as anxious as he was for freedom. But he was wrong.

"You must be mad," she told him. "What do you want to go wandering through the forest for? So we can be eaten by the wolves?"

"It isn't forest," he countered. "Not like Essex."

She shook her head. "It doesn't make sense," she said.

"But we're just slaves here," he protested.

"So what? We eat well."

"But don't you want to be free?" he demanded.

And now she truly surprised him. "Not much," she said. Then, seeing his astonishment: "What does it mean? We were free in the village and they would have drowned me with that snake." She shuddered at the memory. "Run away from here and we aren't free anyway. We're outlaws. Frankly," she smiled, "being a slave here isn't so bad. Is it?"

Of course, he could not deny that her earthy practicality was right. In a way. But though the young fellow could not have expressed himself in abstract terms, the notion of independence acted powerfully upon him. It was something as primordial as the need for a fish to swim about in the sea.

"I don't want to be a slave," he said simply, but for the time being they discussed the matter no more.

In the meantime, he soon found something else to occupy his mind. A few days after the trip upriver, some of the men went across to the little promontory on the southern bank to do some fishing. As he had worked hard, Offa was allowed to go too.

It proved to be an excellent place for fishing. Jutting well out into the flow of the Thames, the spit had enough bushes and small trees to give the fishermen cover so that they could set nets in the water and throw out baited lines. Under the clear surface, Offa could see the silvery fish gliding about. However, the sight that really attracted his attention lay over the water. There before him, no longer masked by trees, lay the huge, ruined citadel that had been Londinium.

It was a remarkable sight. Although the riverside wall built by the city's last inhabitants had badly crumbled, the original, landside wall was still standing, and within this great enclosure, across the twin hills, lay the ghostly ruins.

"A strange place," one of the men remarked, following his gaze. "They say it was built by giants."

Offa said nothing. He knew better.

That Offa should know more than these Saxons about the Roman city was not surprising. Only four generations had passed since his family had left the deserted city. And though neither he nor his father had had more than the vaguest conception of what such a city might look like, he had always known that it was huge and contained splendid buildings of stone. He also knew something else. True, it was only a family legend, and like most oral folklore it was a tantalizing mixture of the vague and the precise. But for three centuries, this simple and fascinating piece of information had been passed down from father to son.

"My grandfather always said," Offa's father had told him, "that there are two hills in the great city. And on the western hill, there's buried gold. A huge treasure."

"Where on the hill?" Offa had asked.

"Near the top," he said. "But no one could ever find it."

Now, directly before him, lay the city, with its two hills.

While the men were fishing, he took the boat and slipped across.

Londinium had been empty for more than a century, but its crumbling walls, with their red, horizontal stripes, were still huge and impressive. The two western gateways remained intact. Between them, at various points along the wall, mighty bastions jutted out. Behind, looming over the summit of the nearer hill, the great stone circle of the amphitheatre, which now had a jagged breach in its side, stood against the sky like a surly sentinel, as though to say: Rome has departed only for a day. She will return. The stream on the western side now bore a Saxon name – the Fleet – though further up they called it the Holebourne. Walking up the slope, he passed through the gateway.

Into a ghost city. Before him stretched the broad Roman thoroughfare, now covered with grass and moss, so that his footfalls fell silently. The Saxons, having no understanding of Londinium, had left the place alone. But they passed across it from time to time, and even drove cattle through, and as a result, upon the ancient pattern of the two great east–west thoroughfares and the grid of streets and alleys between, a new and more rustic pattern had been imposed. As far as possible, this series of cattle tracks and pathways led directly across the ruined city from one gateway to another, but because they frequently encountered obstacles, such as the huge circle of the amphitheatre, they had come to form a winding pattern, full of bends and curious turns that would seem strange and illogical once their Roman causes had vanished.

He had the whole place to himself. He briefly visited the high ground by the city's south-eastern corner, but, encountering the ravens, quickly withdrew. For no special reason, he followed the rivulet that ran between the twin hills to where it passed under the city's northern wall, and, climbing the parapet, observed that due to the Roman ducts under the wall having silted up, a great marsh had formed on the wasteland along the city's northern side.

Climbing down to the quay again, one thing puzzled him. The silent waters of the river came over the edge of the ruined quays which seemed meant to have been set higher. Could the city, over time, have sunk or the river grown higher?

His observation in fact was perfectly correct. Two dynamics had been at work to produce this phenomenon. The first was that even now the Arctic ice-cap, extended by the last Ice Age, was continuing to melt, causing the sea, and hence all water levels, to rise gently. The second was that in the huge march of the Earth's geological plates, the south-eastern side of the island of Britain was being tilted very gradually downward into the sea. The combined effect of these factors meant that the level of the Thames near its estuary was rising approximately nine inches each century. Since his ancestor Julius had forged his coins in the year 250, the river had risen some two and a half feet.

"But where's that gold?" he demanded aloud, as though the empty city might tell him.

He had investigated the puzzling remains of the Temple of Mithras, returned to the forum, and then taken the upper of the two great thoroughfares across the city towards the western hill. He had walked along ruined colonnades, gazed at tumble-down houses with trees growing through where windows had once been, poked his head into alleys filled with bushes as though the disposition of these relics might give him a clue as to where the treasure lay. Several times he had closed his eyes, muttered a prayer to Woden, and turned in a circle, hoping the god might point him in the right direction.

Men use divining rods to find water, he said to himself now. Perhaps you can divine gold underground the same way. But what kind of rods would do it? For an hour and more he tramped around before the light began to fade. "But I'll come back another day," he muttered. And another. After all, it was something to do. Besides, he never gave up. He decided, however, to say nothing about his quest, even to Ricola.

And so, at Lundenwic, they came towards the end of *Haligmonath*, the holy month.

Another reason why Ricola was unwilling to leave was that she was becoming attached to her mistress.

Perhaps it was because the girl was a new face, or because she had suffered misfortune, or because Elfgiva had always wanted a daughter, but whatever the reason, the older woman took a liking to Ricola. She would often summon her on some pretext, sometimes only to sit with her, but often to braid her hair or brush it, for which the girl had a talent. And Ricola was glad to do so.

Since Elfgiva was the first woman of the noble class the girl had met, she observed her closely. Not only was her dress different – a long girdled gown instead of the ordinary woman's modest tunic – but her whole manner subtly marked her out. What was it? "She gets cross just like I do. She laughs. She may be a bit quieter than me, but so are lots of women I know," the girl explained to Offa. "Yet she is different. She's a lady." Gradually Ricola began to reach a conclusion. "You know what it is. It's as if she is being watched all the time."

"I suppose she is. By all the people who work for the master."

"I know. And I dare say she knows it. But," Ricola's brow furrowed, "there's something else. Even when I'm alone with her. She doesn't care a rap what I think of her. I'm just a slave. She's too proud for that. But even then she thinks she's being watched. I can feel it."

"By the gods, I dare say."

"Maybe. Actually, I think it's her own family. Her dead father, his father, the whole lot of them, generations back. She has to behave because she thinks they're watching her. That's what I reckon it is." She nodded with satisfaction. "And all the time, just walking around like you and me, that's not just the Lady Elfgiva you're looking at. You're looking at the whole bunch of them, all the way back to the god Woden himself, I dare say. They're all there in her mind, you see, whatever she's doing. That's what it's like being a lady."

Offa looked at his wife wonderingly. He could see what she meant. "So would you like to be her?" he asked.

Ricola gave an earthy laugh. "What, and have that lot to carry around on my back all the time? I'd sooner get in that sack with the snake! It's too much trouble."

But while Offa chuckled at her common sense, she remarked more seriously: "It's terrible for her really, you know. You see, I've watched her. I told you the master's done something bad to her. I still don't know what it is, but she's really suffering. Only being a lady, she's too proud to let it out."

"Well, there's nothing we can do," Offa said.

"No," his wife agreed. "But I wish there was."

A further bond developed between Ricola and her mistress when Elfgiva permitted her to join in an activity the girl had never seen before.

Even at this early date, the Anglo-Saxon ladies of England were famous for their needlework, but embroidery was practised only by women of the upper class, for the simple reason that the materials used were rare and expensive. With fascination, therefore, when the afternoon drew in Ricola would sit at Elfgiva's feet as, holding her work close to a lamp, the noblewoman went about her task.

"First you must take a length of fine linen," she explained. "Some people in the king's court even use silk. On this you trace the whole design." To Ricola's surprise, Elfgiva did not take the marker herself, but instead sent for Wistan. "He draws a better line than I," she said.

And what designs, indeed, the young man drew. First, down the centre of the cloth, he made a single, long, curving line. "This is the stalk," he announced. Then, branching off from this stalk, he made smaller stalks, always with the simplest curves, and upon these he made the outline, still with the purest simplicity, of several kinds of leaves and flowers, so that when he had finished, in the centre of the bare linen was a design that was so organic you could almost feel the nature of the plants, and yet so entirely abstract it might have been Oriental.

Next he indicated some stars and crosshatching as modest decoration within these forms. Finally, leaving a bare, echoing space around this plant form, he began to design a border. This, too, was masterly. Tightly controlled, geometric flowers, birds, animals, all manner of pagan and magic symbols appeared, as precise and neat as if they were links in a bracelet. From the inside of the border, like crocuses pushing rudely through the unbroken ground in spring, strange plants with elegantly curling, scroll-like leaves, and blunt little trees, insistent and sexual, broke into the edge of the central space as though to say: Art is order, but nature is always greater. Which was, perhaps still is, the essence of the Anglo-Saxon spirit.

Only then did Elfgiva put the linen on to a frame to begin the slow work of embroidery. She began with the centre.

Working with bronze needles, she would cross-stitch the details of the leaves. For these she used a variety of coloured silk threads. "When the Frisians come for slaves," she explained, "they always bring me silk from the south." Not content with this, however, she also used threads of gold and, to make the embroidery even richer, in one or two places she added seed pearls as well. At last, when this process was completed, she took a heavy cord of green silk and laid it down along the curving line of the stalk. Then she couched it in place, passing a silk thread over it from the back of the linen. To finish, she stitched extra lines of coloured silk along all the main outlines.

"Next we start to tackle the border." She smiled. "That will take many months."

Finding the girl's fingers were nimble, Elfgiva would often let her put in a stitch or two, amused to see the slave girl's delight in the process. She even let the girl bring Offa in, to show him what they were doing.

And all the while Ricola studied the older woman, admired her stately ways, and, each day, asked some questions about her dress, or the life of the court, or the estate at Bocton, adding a little to her stock of knowledge. At the same time, she studied ways to make herself useful. "You want us to be free," she reminded her husband, "and if she likes us enough, one day she could give us our freedom, you know." She smiled. "We just have to be patient. It's a waiting game."

As for Elfgiva, she, too, was playing a waiting game of a kind. She had quickly realized that even though Cerdic had so deeply hurt her, she must deny her pain. "If your husband strays," the older women had told her long ago, "there is only one thing to do." It was a fact of married life, for better or worse, that the only way to keep a straying husband was to entice him to bed as quickly and as often as possible. All other approaches that reason or morality might suggest were, unfortunately, futile. She had acted accordingly. She had not sulked, or argued, or been cold towards him, but each night after the evening meal set out to seduce and satisfy him. More than once they had awoken at sunrise in each other's arms and she had lain quietly listening to the birds at dawn, thinking that perhaps, after all, he was contented, that the simple operation of inertia, that greatest of all friends to the married state, might keep him at her side. Even now, at this late hour, she still found herself secretly praying to the gods of her ancestors: "Let me have another child." Or if not that: "Give me time. Do not let this bishop come just yet." And so the next month passed.

Blodmonath, the month of blood, the Saxons called November. *Blodmonath,* when the oxen were slain before the winter snows and the last of the leaves, crisp with hoarfrost, fell to the ground hardening after the autumn rains.

Early in *Blodmonath*, a ship had come to the trading post. It had crossed the sea from the Frankish lands beside the River Rhine, and Offa had been told to help unload it.

It was the first time he had seen a proper seagoing vessel, and the boat fascinated him. Although the Saxons had well-constructed rafts and even broad rowing boats upon the Thames, this ship was in another class entirely.

The most immediately striking feature was the keel. Starting as a great wooden ridge high above the stern, it descended in a graceful, curving line to the water, made its long way down the centre of the vessel and then rose once more in a magnificent prow that arched proudly above the water. Wistan, as it happened, was standing just by Offa as he gazed with admiration at this lovely sight. "It's just like the line you drew for the Lady Elfgiva's embroidery," the young slave cried out in a flash of inspiration, and Wistan agreed.

Across the spine of the keel the vessel's wooden ribs were fitted, and on to them were laid overlapping planks fastened with nails. Long though the vessel's lines were, Offa realized that with the broadening allowed for at the centre, the ship had a considerable capacity. It had only two small decks, fore and aft; otherwise it was open. It had a single mast on which a sail could be raised on a crossbar. But its real power lay in the half-dozen long oars projecting from each side.

This was the longship of the northern world. Similar vessels had brought the Saxons to the island. Elfgiva's father lay buried on the East Anglian coast under such a one.

The cargo also intrigued Offa: fine, wheel-turned grey pottery; fifty huge jars of wine; and, for the king's household, six crates of a strange, clear material he had never seen before. "It's glass," a sailor told him. In the northern lands by the Rhine they had been making wine and glass since Roman times.

In this way, for the first time, Offa received a hint of that great heritage from across the seas – the heritage his own ancestors had known, and which had once filled the empty, walled city where he liked to roam.

A few days later, however, he received a far more significant visit from the Roman world.

He had sneaked off again into the empty city and spent an hour or two on the western hill. Since he had time – perhaps a lifetime, he ruefully realized – to investigate the place, he had decided to proceed methodically, concentrating on one small site at a time, searching it thoroughly until he was sure it had yielded all its secrets, before proceeding to the next.

That afternoon, halfway up the hill on the river side he had found a promising little house with a cellar. Using an improvised shovel, he was on his hands and knees picking away at the debris when it seemed to him that, some way distant, he might have heard voices calling. Emerging, therefore, he looked up the hill.

The brow of the western hill on the river side was much barer than the rest. The tile kilns had long ago crumbled away, though there were still plenty of tile fragments sticking through the soil to attest their former presence. The little temples were only a few stumps of stone now, marking the bases of their columns. The area around formed a sort of grassy platform with a view over the river.

On this plot of ground he now saw two men, one of whom, presumably a groom, was holding their horses. The other, a shortish figure in an ankle-length black robe, was pacing about, apparently looking for something. At once, his heart filled with misgiving, Offa thought: They must have come to look for the treasure. He wondered how they had found out. He was just about to duck out of sight when the black-robed figure looked up, saw him, and pointed.

Offa cursed inwardly. What should he do now? The man was still pointing at him, and since they had horses he did not think he would be able to escape them. "Better act stupid," he muttered, and slowly advanced.

The figure in black was the most curious man Offa had ever seen. He was not tall, and had a large, clean-shaven oval face and grey hair that, being tonsured, left the top of his head bald. He looks like an egg, thought Offa.

Indeed, as he came close, the man's small features and tiny ears reinforced that impression. Offa could not help staring, but the man seemed unconcerned and smiled slightly.

"What is your name?" he enquired. He spoke English, as the Anglo-Saxons called their language, but with a strange accent Offa could not place.

"Offa, sir. What's yours?" the slave boldly asked.

"Mellitus."

Offa frowned at the curious name, then looked about.

"You are wondering what I am doing here?" the strange man enquired.

"Yes, sir."

In answer Mellitus showed him the beginnings of an outline he was making with stones on the ground a few yards away. It looked like the foundation line for a small rectangular building of some kind. "This is where I am going to build," he declared.

It was certainly a pleasant site, with a good view down the hill in three directions.

"Build?"

The strange man smiled again.

"Cathedralis," he replied, using the Latin word. Seeing Offa's look of bafflement, he explained: "A temple to the true God."

"To Woden?" Offa asked, but the man shook his head.

"To Christ," he answered simply.

And then Offa understood who the stranger was.

He had known, of course, everyone had been told, that a man from Canterbury was going to come there. A bishop, whatever that was. At any rate a man of great importance. Offa stared at the monk in his black habit with surprise and doubt. He's nothing much to look at, he considered. All the same, he'd better be careful.

"What'll you build with, sir?" he asked. He supposed he might be forced to cart a lot of timber up the hill.

"These stones," Mellitus said, and indicated the Roman masonry and broken tiles that lay all around.

Why here? Offa wondered, but remembering that the stockmen had told him they used to sacrifice bulls in the big round space nearby, he assumed it was a religious precinct, so merely nodded politely.

"And what are you doing here?" the stranger suddenly asked.

Immediately Offa was on his guard.

"Nothing much, sir. Just looking."

"Looking for something?" The man smiled. Offa noticed that his brown eyes, though rather soft, had a curious, perceptive light in them. "Perhaps I can help you find it," Mellitus said gently.

What did this stranger know? Was he just, as he said, designing a building as he paced, eyes on the ground? Or did he have some other intention? Was it possible that somehow he knew about the buried gold? Was he really offering to help Offa find it, or was he trying to find out what Offa knew? Evidently, this bishop was a cunning fellow, to be treated cautiously.

"I must go to my master, sir," Offa muttered, and started to move away, conscious that Mellitus was still watching him.

Why should the bishop have chosen this deserted citadel near an isolated trading post to build his cathedral?

The reason was simple and it lay in Rome.

When the Pope had sent the missionary Augustine to the island of Britain, he had never meant him to tarry more than briefly in Canterbury. After all, why, except for the opportunity offered by the Frankish princess, should the pontiff have more than a passing interest in the peninsula of Kent? He desired to convert the whole island. And what did he know of Britain? That it had been, until unfortunately cut off, a Roman province.

"The records are clear," the archivists told him. "It is divided into provinces, each with a capital: York in the north, Londinium in the south. Londinium is the senior." Consequently, when Augustine and his colleagues, reporting upon the kindness of the Kentish king and on Londinium, protested that the place was empty, the response from Rome was unequivocal: "Let the king have a bishop in Canterbury. But set up York and Londinium at once." Roman tradition must be maintained.

This was why Bishop Mellitus now stood in the deserted ruins of Londinium. In a way, it occurred to the monk, there were advantages in the situation. It was by a growing trading post, yet set apart in this ancient and majestic place that surrounded it like a vast cloister. The site, by the old temples, was impressive. The little church to be built there would be his cathedral; its patron saint had already been chosen.

It would be called St Paul's.

The bishop stayed at Cerdic's hall that evening. His party was small: apart from himself there were just three servants, two young priests and an elderly noble from King Ethelbert's court. Though Cerdic was anxious to prepare a feast for him, the missionary begged him not to.

"I am a little tired," he confessed, "and I am anxious to continue on to the King of Essex. Next month I shall return here to preach and to baptize. After that, you may prepare a feast." He did, however, announce that the following morning, before continuing on his way, he would say a Mass at the place where the new church was to be built. Until then, Cerdic begged the bishop and his party to take over his own hall for the night, while he and his family retired to the barn.

Early in the bright, sunny morning, Bishop Mellitus led his little party to the empty city. One of the young priests took with him a flask containing wine, the other a bag containing barley bread. The nobleman from King Ethelbert's court carried a simple wooden cross about seven feet high. At the site on the hill, they stuck the cross into the ground. There, Mellitus and his two priests prepared to say a simple Mass.

Cerdic looked around him with satisfaction. It was an intimate occasion. He and King Ethelbert's noble would receive the bread of the communion while his family watched. He felt proud to be part of such an occasion. "I'm sure I'm the only man north of the Thames to have been baptized," he remarked to the nobleman. In due course, when the cathedral was built and ready to be dedicated, he thought it likely that the kings of Kent and of Essex would attend with their courts. Then he, too, having helped the bishop as he built it, would have a place of honour amongst them.

Only one thing had irritated him. The night before, his two eldest sons had asked him if they could be excused from the event. "Why?" he had demanded. "We wanted to go hunting," they casually replied. He had been furious. "You will all accompany me and behave yourselves," he thundered. And when the boys had asked him to explain what the ceremony meant, he had been so angry that he had only shouted: "Never mind what it means. You'll show respect to your father and the king and I'll hear no more about it." But glancing at them now, wearing their finest cloaks, their fair hair and young beards neatly combed, he decided that, all in all, they were a credit to him, and he approached the Mass in better humour.

The service was not unduly long. Mellitus preached a brief sermon in which he dwelt on the qualities of the Saxon King of Kent and the joy that they should all feel in this place of worship. He spoke Anglo-Saxon rather well, with feeling and eloquence. Cerdic nodded approval. Then came the communion itself. The bread and wine were consecrated. The miracle of the Eucharist took place. Proudly Cerdic stepped forward with the other noble who had been baptized.

It was then that Elfgiva, understanding little of these foreign rites but thinking to please her husband who, perhaps, still loved her, urged her four sons: "Go and do as your father does." Which, after hesitating, they reluctantly did.

So Cerdic's four sons, blushing a little, tramped forward to where the Roman priest was serving communion and, glancing at each other uncertainly, knelt before him to receive their due. Cerdic, who was already kneeling, did not see them approach, and, not expecting them to be there, was unaware of their presence until, just after he had risen and turned to go, he heard the bishop's voice.

"Have you been baptized?"

The four sturdy fellows looked at him mistrustfully. Mellitus repeated the question. He guessed they had not.

"What does this beardless wonder want?" muttered the youngest.

"Just give us the magic bread," the eldest said, "like you did our father," and he indicated Cerdic.

Mellitus stared at him. "Magic bread?"

"Yes. That's what we want." And one of the four, meaning no harm, reached out to grab one of the pieces the priest held in a bowl.

Mellitus drew back. Now he was angry. "You treat the Host in this way? Have you no reverence for the body and blood of Our Lord?" he cried. Then, seeing the four strong Saxon youths look utterly mystified, he turned furiously towards Cerdic and demanded in a voice that seemed to echo off the city walls: "Is this how you instruct your sons, wretched fellow? Is this how you respect your sovereign Lord?" Cerdic, thinking the bishop was referring to the king, went scarlet with shame and humiliation.

A terrible silence fell. Cerdic looked at his sons. "What are you doing here?" he enquired, through gritted teeth, of the eldest. To which the boy shrugged and, indicating his mother, "She told us to come up for the bread," he said.

For a moment Cerdic did not move at all. He was too shocked. The truth of the matter was that not only had he failed to instruct his sons and to control his family, but that he was in fact a little uncertain about the niceties of the communion anyway. He had followed his king. He had supposed it was enough. Yet now he had been shamed before the king's man, humiliated by this bishop, shown up as a weakling and a fool. He had never thought of himself as either. The pain was terrible. His throat felt very dry, his face red. Almost choking, he motioned to his sons to rise, which they did awkwardly. Then he walked back to where Elfgiva was standing. And as he did so, and glanced at her, it suddenly seemed to him that this was all her fault. None of this would have happened but for her obstinacy and disloyalty. Now she had sent his sons to disgrace him. If, at the back of his mind, he realized she had not done it deliberately, it no longer seemed to make any difference. It was her fault; that was the point.

Coldly, deliberately, he struck her across the face with the flat of his hand.

"I see you no longer wish to be my wife," he said quietly. Then he strode over to his horse and rode down the hill.

A few hours later, a group of five riders came along the track from Lundenwic and, emerging from the trees, rode towards the little river now called the Fleet that lay below the Roman city's western walls. Instead of crossing the wooden bridge, however, they went a short way upstream, dismounted, and walked down to the Fleet's grassy riverbank, where Mellitus and his priests awaited them. There, watched by Cerdic, the four young men undressed and, at the priests' command, jumped one by one into the freezing water.

Bishop Mellitus was merciful. He did not force any of them to stay in for more than a moment, but made the sign of the cross over each and let them hastily clamber out, shivering, to dry themselves. They had been baptized.

Cerdic watched calmly. After the disaster of the Mass it had taken all his powers to persuade the furious bishop not to leave at once. Finally, however, deeming it best for his cause, Mellitus had agreed to delay his onward journey a few hours and to perform this important ceremony for these pagan youths.

"I dare say," he remarked with a smile to his priests, "that we shall be called upon to baptize worse fellows than these before long."

As Cerdic saw them emerge dripping from the water, he

had another reason for quiet satisfaction. The rage he had thrown at his sons when they returned to the trading post had proved effective. He had reasserted his authority. Without another word about hunting, they had gone meekly to their baptism.

Only one person was absent from the scene.

Elfgiva had remained alone in the hall, silently weeping.

By the next day, everybody knew. A groom had been sent down into Kent with a message: the master wished to claim his new bride. The Lady Elfgiva was to be cast aside. Despite the long weeks of tension between master and mistress, the entire household reeled from the shock. Yet nobody dared say a word. Cerdic went about looking silent but grim. Elfgiva, tall and very pale, moved through the days with a stately dignity that no one liked to invade. Some wondered if she would stay there in defiance of Cerdic. Others thought she would return to East Anglia.

Yet for Elfgiva the most painful aspect of the business was not the rejection, or even the humiliation of her position. It was not what had happened, but what did not happen.

For as she waited for her sons to protect her, or at least to protest, there was only silence.

True, the three eldest came to her, each in turn. They commiserated: they suggested that perhaps, if she converted, there might be a reconciliation. But even this they said without conviction. "The fact is," she murmured to herself, as she stood staring at the river one day, "they fear their father more than they love me. And I do believe they probably love hunting slightly more than they love their own mother."

Except for Wistan. When he had come to talk to her, the sixteen-year-old had broken down with grief. He had been so upset with his father that she had had to urge him for her sake not to enrage Cerdic further by attacking him.

"But you can't just accept this," he protested.

"You don't understand."

"Well, I can't," he vowed, and would say no more.

Three days after this conversation, Cerdic, walking along the lane from Thorney, was not entirely surprised to see young Wistan standing in his path awaiting him.

Assuming a grim expression, the merchant walked towards him with scarcely a nod, expecting to freeze the boy into silence. But Wistan stood his ground and spoke firmly.

"Father, I must talk to you."

"Well I don't need to talk to you, so get out of the way." It was said with the cold authority that made most men tremble, but bravely the boy moved to bar his path.

"It's Mother," he said. "You can't treat her like this."

Cerdic was a burly man. Not only that, he had force of character and all the tricks of authority. When he chose, he could be very frightening indeed. Now, he glowered at his son and fairly bellowed.

"That is a matter for us, not for you. Be quiet!"

"No, Father, I can't."

"You can and you will. Out of the way!" And using his far greater weight he knocked the boy aside and strode furiously down the lane, his eyes blazing with fury.

But that boy's the best of the lot, he thought to himself secretly as he marched along.

It did not change his view about Elfgiva, however.

Four days after he had left, the groom Cerdic had sent to Kent returned with the reply from the girl's father. Cerdic's new bride would be delivered to him at Bocton, two weeks after the midwinter feast of Yule.

It had always been the habit of Cerdic and Elfgiva to return to the Bocton estate well before the great Saxon Yuletide celebrations, but on receiving this news, the merchant announced briefly: "I shall celebrate Yule here at Lundenwic. Then I shall go to Bocton for the rest of the winter." The signal was clear. The old regime was to end. A new one was to begin.

As the household adjusted to this information, a change of mood began to take place at the trading post. At first it was almost imperceptible, but as the days went by there was no mistaking it.

Elfgiva was still there. Technically, since Cerdic had not yet sent her away, she was still his wife. However, in some indefinable way, people started to behave as though she had already left. If she gave an order, for instance, it would be politely obeyed, but something in the other person's eyes would tell her that the servant was already thinking about how to please the new mistress. "It's as though I've become a guest in my own home," she murmured to herself. And then, with bitter irony: "One who's starting to stay too long."

Yet if everybody else was wondering when she would leave, she herself had still to make up her mind about what to do. She had a brother in East Anglia. But I haven't seen him for years, she reminded herself. There were some distant kinsfolk living in a village a few miles from her childhood home. Could she go there? "Surely Cerdic can't just send me out into the forest?" she cried. For the moment, though she hardly realized it, a strange lassitude crept over her. I'll decide before Yuletide, she told herself. And did nothing.

Cerdic, too, said nothing. She did not know what he wanted nor how he meant to provide for her. He merely left her, still his wife in name, in a kind of limbo.

Ricola found that she was often with her mistress now. Although Elfgiva was usually reticent and dignified, occasionally, in her loneliness, she stooped to sharing a confidence with the slave girl. Ricola was certain the rift between Cerdic and his wife was complete. "The master's not sleeping with her any more," she told Offa. "I'm sure of that." She braided and brushed Elfgiva's hair with a secret tenderness. And once, after Elfgiva confided that she hadn't decided where to go yet, she cautiously asked: "If the master means you to leave, Lady Elfgiva, then why hasn't he made arrangements about it?"

"It's quite simple," the older woman explained with a sad smile. "I know my husband. He's a cautious merchant. He'll divorce me as soon as he has the new girl in his hands. Not before. He'll wait until then."

"I'd just leave," Ricola blurted out. To which the older woman said nothing.

But this uncertainty left one problem which Offa brought up with Ricola one night. "If she's sent away," he demanded, "what do you think will happen to us? You and me?" He looked perplexed. "She bought us. Does that mean we go with her?"

"I should hope so," the girl cried indignantly, surprising herself by the strength of her feeling. "She saved my life," she added, to explain her vehemence. And then, staring at Offa she asked: "Don't you want to stay with her?"

At first Offa could only reply by looking puzzled. Where

would Elfgiva take them? He thought of the dark Essex forest; he had no wish to go back there. He thought of what little he knew about the huge cold openness of East Anglia. And he thought of the rich, lush valley of the Thames, and of the empty city with its hoard of gold.

"I don't know," he said at last. "I don't know at all."

As the days passed, there were two events in Ricola's life that she did not discuss with anyone. The first concerned the merchant.

It was just a week after the baptism of his sons that he first looked at Ricola. It was nothing much. She had been emerging from the main house, stooping under the heavy thatch of the little doorway just as he strode up from the jetty. She had passed close to him, and he had looked at her.

She was neither surprised nor shocked. She was sensual; she accepted sensuality. He hasn't had a woman in a week, she thought, and passed on. Nor did it worry her too much when it happened the next day. Better keep clear of him, she decided, and better not tell Offa, she added to herself with a grin.

The second event was more pleasant. At the end of *Blodmonath*, she realized she might be pregnant. But I'll wait another month, just to be sure, she thought contentedly. Though she did wonder now, a little anxiously, where and how they would be living when the child was born.

Offa continued to do all he could to please the master. He also managed to sneak off once or twice to the empty city, where, having fashioned himself a little pick and shovel, he burrowed into places that seemed promising. It was after returning from one of these secret expeditions one evening that he witnessed the arrival of a new cargo at the trading post.

There were half a dozen slaves. A tough, ugly-looking merchant was leading them along, but Cerdic greeted him civilly enough. "You come late in the year," he remarked.

The men were fine, dark-haired fellows tied to a rope. Their cropped hair and depressed looks proclaimed their new condition. "The King of Northumbria raided the Scots last year," the merchant explained. He grinned. "Captives. I had a hundred when I left the north. This is what's left."

"The dregs?"

"Take a look. They're not bad."

Cerdic inspected them. He did not trouble to cavil about the merchandise. "They seem sound," he agreed. "But I'll probably have to feed and house them all winter. Slave traffic usually starts in the spring."

"You can work them yourself."

"Nothing much for them to do once the snows come, is there?"

"True. What's your price, then?" People liked doing business with Cerdic because he was straightforward and never wasted time. Offa saw the two men go into Cerdic's hall together. Before long, the merchant had left.

For the moment, the six fellows were housed in the slave quarters and chained up each night. During the day they were exercised, and one or two were set to work hauling wood or repairing one of the storehouses. Offa watched them, wondering what their final fate would be, and felt sorry for them.

A whole day passed before anyone realized that young Wistan had disappeared. Nor did anyone know where he had gone, except that he had told one of his brothers he wanted to go hunting. It was strange in itself for him to go hunting alone, and when he did not return, Elfgiva was worried. Cerdic was more sanguine.

"It must be a girl," he said curtly. "He'll be back." When another night passed, he remarked grimly: "He'll have some answering to do to me, for going off without permission." But another day and night passed without any sign of him.

Wistan had risen early. By the first grey light of dawn he was by the waste ground at Thorney, crossing the ford. It was low tide. His horse only had to swim a short part of the crossing, and when Wistan emerged on the southern side he was hardly wet. His route took him a mile or so to the south, first on to the slopes above the marshy ground. Then he turned eastwards, keeping roughly parallel with the river.

It was a clear, cold day. As he rode over marsh and through oak woods, he could see the dim ruins of the empty city two miles away on the other side of the river. The ground began to rise after that into ridges that grew progressively higher. Two or three miles more and, as the sun broke over the horizon, he had a splendid view of the sweep of the glinting river as it made its great series of bends towards the estuary. At the bottom of the long slope down the ridge, beside the riverbank, was a tiny hamlet known as Greenwich. Ahead, the ridge broadened out, the light oak woods giving way to a great expanse of open heath. Across this he followed the hard, turf lane that covered the metalled Roman road and which would lead him, by the afternoon of the following day, to the settlement of Rochester.

He was going to see the girl.

He slept the next night at Bocton. Then, early in the morning, with a fond look at the magnificent view over the Weald, Wistan rode on to her home.

He knew her family, of course, but as it happened he had not seen the girl for some years. Indeed, he thought wryly, last time I saw her she was just a skinny child like me. It was hard to believe his father was about to marry her.

It was mid-morning when he reached the place, but he did not go up to it. Instead he remained some distance away in the trees, watching. At last he saw her come out of the homestead and, by good fortune, take a path that led into the trees not far from where he was.

At least he supposed it must be her. As she drew nearer, he hardly recognized her, for in place of the skinny girl was a young woman. And a lovely one at that. Nearly as tall as he, still with a little down on her lip, her golden hair done up in a plait, her blue eyes bright and intelligent, this beautiful creature of almost fifteen was only ten yards from him when he softly called her name.

"Edith."

She did not start when the gentle-eyed young fellow with his first beard stepped on to the path before her, though she looked surprised. She gazed at him evenly, then smiled.

"Don't I know you?" To his surprise he blushed. "You're Wistan," she said and smiled. He nodded. "What are you doing here?" She looked curious. "And why are you in the woods?"

"Will you promise not to tell anyone I came?" he asked.

"I don't know. I suppose so."

"I'm here . . ." He took a deep breath, suddenly aware of the enormity of what he was doing. "I've come to tell you we don't want you."

They talked for almost an hour. It was not difficult for her to make him tell her everything. To his relief she was not angry. "So you've come to try to save your mother?" she summarized. And then, with a smile: "You've told me so much about your father, also, I suppose you've come to save me too."

He looked confused and she laughed. Then she heard voices calling for her.

"You must go," she said suddenly. "Go now."

He nodded as she turned.

"And what will you do?" he called softly after her.

But she was already walking swiftly through the trees.

Thunor's day, the day of the Thunderer.

A week had passed since young Wistan had reappeared. Cerdic had made a show of fury and threatened to whip him, but the boy's excuses that he had gone hunting, met friends and got lost were so entirely unlikely that the merchant had grinned to himself and chuckled to the stockmen: "I told you it was some girl." Once or twice he had even given the boy a friendly, if somewhat knowing, look.

But now, at noon, like a thunderclap from the grey skies, had come the news. His young bride had changed her mind. The messenger from her father, clearly embarrassed, regretted that there had been a mistake. She was not coming.

He knew how upset his youngest son had been. Now, seeing the boy pale, he guessed at once. It only took a few moments' savage confrontation for the truth to come out. In an apoplexy of fury he seized a stock whip, and if Wistan had not fled after a few blows, Cerdic might almost have killed him.

The next question was, what to do? He toyed with the idea of sending for the girl again, demanding that her father keep his word, but decided it would be undignified. Besides, he admitted to himself, if he was trying to avoid the kind of trouble his otherwise loyal Elfgiva had been giving him, why insist upon marriage with a young girl who, it seemed, was already capable of giving trouble?

For several days he stomped about the trading post in silent fury. Wistan wisely remained out of sight. Gradually, however, as his anger lessened, he began to feel a sense of weariness. Despite himself, he secretly missed the comfort of his old marriage. At least, he thought wryly, it was better than chasing after young girls who changed their minds.

But if, once or twice, he allowed himself to gaze thoughtfully at Elfgiva, she made no answering sign, instead remaining stiff, cold and numb in his presence.

A whole week passed before, striding into the hall where his wife was sitting with the pretty slave girl, he informed her calmly that if she would follow the example of her sons and be baptized, he would end his search for a new wife and take her back. "Perhaps," he said kindly, "you would like to think it over for a day."

A moment later, he was storming out in a greater rage than ever.

She had refused.

Ricola gazed at her mistress for a long moment before she spoke.

"You're mad. You know that?"

Even a week before such words from slave to mistress would have been unimaginable, but much had passed between the two women in those last days.

Alone in the whole household, it was Ricola who had sat with Elfgiva on those nights when, unable to hide her grief entirely, the older woman had allowed silent tears to run down her face. It was to the slave that Elfgiva had turned when young Wistan had fled from his furious father into the woods. Ricola had sent her husband to find the boy and they had hidden him in their tiny hut for the night. "It's the one place the master won't think of looking for him," she had remarked with a grin. And when Cerdic was down at the jetty that morning, it was Ricola who had smuggled Wistan in to see his mother and had heard him plead with her: "I stopped the girl coming. Won't you be baptized now, and go back to him?"

So Elfgiva did not rebuke the girl for her impertinence; she just stared into the fire, and said nothing.

The truth was, she did not know what to do. The sight of her youngest son pleading, the thought of all he had done for her, moved her profoundly. How could she refuse him after such a show of love? Yet it was not so easy. Had anything really changed? They beg me to give in today, she considered. They tell me it will be all right. But what about tomorrow? Won't my husband get restless? Won't it be the same all over again, and even more painful?

She listened to Ricola urging her, "If you don't convert, then he's sure to look for another wife. Otherwise he'll look a fool again. I mean, maybe he'll throw you over one day, but that's a risk you have to take, isn't it? Better than losing him now." And shaking her head the girl said firmly: "You're just looking a gift horse in the mouth. You've nothing to lose."

"Except my dignity." The girl looked doubtful. But then dignity meant less, Elfgiva supposed, if one were only fifteen and a slave.

And so, for some time, the two quietly sat together without coming to any conclusion, until at last Elfgiva, growing weary, sent the girl away. Ricola went, but not before turning by the door and saying fearlessly: "He's not so bad, you know, your husband. If you won't have him, just remember all the other women that will." That, the earthy girl considered, would give her mistress something to think about.

As Yuletide approached, a new animation came over the people at Lundenwic. Offa helped the men drag a huge log into Cerdic's hall, where it would slowly burn for many days, a token that, though the sun might depart, here on earth the Anglo-Saxon fire in the hearth would smoulder on until spring returned. Ricola helped the women. At the Yuletide feast there would be venison. Brought in from the store would be great jars of fruit preserved from the summer – apples, pears and mulberries. There would be drink, including that speciality of the Saxons known as *morat*, made of honey and mulberry juice.

And each day, as they worked and the time of the festival drew near, the women gossiped together and wondered: Will the Lady Elfgiva still be there?

As for Elfgiva, she found herself perhaps more torn than ever. As Yuletide drew close, happy memories of that season came flooding back. She had nowhere to go to. Her husband had bluntly offered, once more, to have her back. Even on his terms she might have done it. She understood well enough how absolute his duty or his pride, whichever it was, must always be to him. But was she allowed no pride, no self-respect, in return?

If he would only beg me, she mourned to herself. If he would only show tenderness, even a little regret. But he left her there, like some poor animal tethered and forgotten in a storm.

It was one evening during this critical time that Ricola the slave formed a plan to save her mistress. It was typical of her entire outlook on life: down-to-earth, sensuous, cheeky and, it had to be admitted, extremely brave. When he heard it, Offa was horrified.

"Now it's you who's gone mad," he cried.

"But it would work," the girl insisted. "I'm sure of it. Just so long as we get it right." She smiled. "Think of all she's done for us. Anyway, what've we got to lose?"

"Everything," he replied.

The rider from King Ethelbert of Kent took them by surprise; his message even irritated Cerdic somewhat.

"Bishop Mellitus is returning, as he promised, to preach," the messenger declared. "You are to gather all the folk from round about to hear him."

"At Yuletide?" the merchant cried. "Why come at Yule of all seasons?"

But he did as he was asked, and when, two days later, the bishop and a party of ten priests and two dozen noblemen of Kent appeared, Cerdic had assembled a goodly company of some hundred people from the hamlets along the river to meet them.

"Today is Saturday," Mellitus announced. "Tomorrow I shall preach and then baptize."

The rest of that day was spent in feverish activity. Accommodation had to be readied for all the company. There was hardly a yard of floorspace in any of the outbuildings that would not be covered with a straw bed or a blanket. Everyone was hard at work, including Elfgiva, who was directing the household exactly as she had always done, so that more than once Cerdic glanced at her with quiet admiration. Great sides of beef were brought in from the stores. And when, during these proceedings young Wistan somehow miraculously appeared, hard at work, Cerdic decided to ignore it.

Only one ripple might have disturbed this pleasant scene. This was when, not unnaturally, some of the monks began to look askance at what was clearly going to be considerable feasting, both in the austere, pre-Christmas season of Advent, and on the Sabbath eve. But Mellitus, smiling, told them: "This is not the time to worry about that." Then, scandalizing one or two still more, he remarked: "I for one shall eat a hearty meal tonight with our Saxon friends."

And so he did.

Towards noon on that Saturday, accompanied by some hundred and fifty people, Bishop Mellitus entered the empty city and walked up the hill to the site of his future cathedral of St Paul's. He brought with him no communion bread, but to aid him in his work he did bring one remarkable object, which was carried before him.

It was a large wooden cross. It was certainly striking just in its size, for planted in the ground it stood some twelve feet high, lending a dignity to the hillside scene as great as in any church. What was truly remarkable about the cross, however, was the magnificent carving upon it.

In the centre of the cross, his arms stretched out flatly, the figure of the crucified Christ gazed out with hollowed eyes that somehow conveyed to the onlooker both the Roman hierarchy of heaven and hell and the grim Norse sense of fate. But what really caught the attention of the Saxons gathered there was the rest of the workmanship. For on every spare inch around the figure of the Saviour were, wonderfully carved, all the geometric plants, birds, animals and beautiful interlaced designs that had long been the glory of their Anglo-Saxon art, and which from now on, joined to the Continental, Christian figures and symbols, would be the glory of the Anglo-Saxon Church.

This was another great rule of the missionaries: "Do not destroy what is already entrenched. Absorb it."

Which was precisely why the good Bishop Mellitus had come to Lundenwic on the Saxon feast of Yuletide. Centuries ago, had not the Christian Church done its best to convert Rome's pagan, sometimes obscene, midwinter festival of Saturnalia into a more spiritual Christian festival? Had not, somehow, the birthday of the Persian god Mithras – 25 December – been converted to the birthday of the Christian Lord?

"If the Anglo-Saxons like Yuletide," Mellitus had explained to his monks, "then Yuletide must become Christian."

Now, standing before his Saxon wooden cross, Bishop Mellitus surveyed the congregation gathered before him.

Everyone was there. Farmers, stockmen, even Offa and Ricola, and the Lady Elfgiva had all come. Uncertain at the last minute who to leave behind to guard them, Cerdic had also ordered the captive slaves from the north to be brought and tethered at the back of the crowd.

These simple folk then, nearly all pagans, were to be his flock. They would come, perhaps, from time to time to the little stone cathedral he would build in the middle of this deserted citadel. He must love them and cherish them and, if God gave him grace, even inspire them.

The missionary bishop was a realist but also a man of faith. As he always told his priests: "Our Lord saved the world. You must learn to accept a humbler role. If, when you preach, you save a single soul, you will have done well." As he gazed out at the rustic crowd, the bishop smiled to himself. "Which of these souls shall we save?" he murmured. "Only you, Lord, could even guess."

Offa watched with fascination. The service was not long. The ten priests sang psalms and other responses in Latin, so that Offa had no idea what they were about. The singing was strangely nasal, though it had a melancholy, haunting quality amongst the cold grey ruins. Growing a little bored, the young fellow might have stolen away before the end had it not been for his sudden curiosity when the bishop with the head like an egg began to address the little crowd not in Latin, but in Anglo-Saxon English.

And what English. As Mellitus got under way, young Offa was amazed. He remembered from their meeting that the strange priest spoke the island tongue, but this was astonishing. He must have been studying with the poets who sing to the king, he thought.

Anglo-Saxon English was a language of tremendous richness. Its vowels, which could be mixed together in many ways, gave it subtle moods and echoing tones. Its Germanic consonants could declaim or whisper, crack and crunch. Even in formal verse, the lines varied their stresses and length, falling into the natural rhythm of the scene the poet wished to evoke. It was the tongue of Nordic sagas and of men who lived by the sea, river, and forest. When poets recited, their listeners could almost feel the swinging axe, see heroes fall, sense the deer in the thicket, or hear the singing saw of the swans' wings over the water. Above all, the art of the poet lay not in rhyme but in the clever use of alliteration, to which this strong tongue so obviously lent itself, searching its riches for an endless supply of evocative repetitions.

And this the preacher had already begun to master. How simply and sweetly he spoke. He talked of the coming of the Lord upon the Earth: this man god who, it seemed, had opened the way for mankind to enter the wonderful place he called heaven. Not only heroes who had died in battle, not only kings and nobles, but poor men, women and children, even slaves like himself, young Offa discovered. It was astounding.

And who was this Lord? He was a hero, yet more than a hero, Mellitus explained. He was like Frey, the priest said, only greater. And he was born in winter, in this very season. Born in midwinter, but bringing promise of a new spring, an everlasting life to come.

Offa knew about Frey. This was a handsome young god of the Anglo-Saxons, kindly and loved by all. Fervently, using these Anglo-Saxon terms, the bishop declared: "The Frey of mankind, this young hero was God Almighty. It is He who washes our sins away with water, the laver of life." This Frey, then, the one they called Christ, had been sacrificed upon a cross – a rood as the Anglo-Saxons called it.

"Reared up on the Rood, He rose again," the preacher cried out. "He sacrificed Himself for our sins, and gave to us life everlasting." How wonderful it sounded. Mellitus was doing his work well.

Why had this Frey been raised upon a cross? Offa was not sure. But the spirit of the preacher's words was clear. Somehow this young god had given himself for them all. It was strange but wonderful. For the first time in his life Offa had a sense that fate itself, the grim, unknowable *Wyrd*, might instead be something reassuring, happy. It produced in him a feeling of ineffable joy that made him tremble.

And – this was the message of the bishop that day – if Christ could lay down His life for men, how much more should they be ready to sacrifice themselves, to be reconciled one with another, in order to be worthy of Him? "There is no place for unkindness, for obstinacy, for ill will amongst us," he said. "If you have quarrelled with your neighbour, your servant or your wife, go now and make amends. Forgive them and beg their pardon in turn. Do not think of yourself. Be ready to sacrifice your own desires. For the Lord has promised us, He will protect us, He will lead us through even the darkness of death so long, only, as we believe in His name." And in the manner of the Anglo-Saxon poetry that was its inspiration, he ended his sermon resoundingly:

> High on the hill in sight of heaven,
> Our Lord was led and lifted up.
> That willing warrior came while the world wept;
> And a terrible shadow shaded the sun.
> For us He was broken and gave us His blood
> King of all creation Christ on the Rood.

For a moment the little crowd, spellbound, was silent. Then there was a gentle murmur almost like a sigh. The Roman priest had touched them.

Offa stared in wonder. Those words about reconciliation and forgiveness – didn't they refer to Cerdic and his wife? As for the rest, the promise of heaven, the demand for sacrifice, to his astonishment it seemed to the young fellow that in some way he did not yet understand, they were meant for him. Flushed with emotion, still half trembling, he stayed there until the service was over.

Now the bishop led his flock to be baptized, not, this time, to the Fleet outside the wall, but to the little brook that ran down between the city's two hills. They were all invited to come forward, and under Cerdic's stern eye his entire household did so. Offa and Ricola and even the rather puzzled northern slaves stepped into the little stream, watched with satisfaction by those already dripping from this brief ordeal. Cerdic, his sons and the noblemen from Kent, already Christian, looked on with a sense of duty performed.

It was at the very end of this process that Cerdic's stern look fell upon Elfgiva.

In truth, she was not at this moment sure what she wished to do, for like Offa, and despite all her resistance, she had found herself strangely touched. The bishop, though he did not know it, had spoken directly to her heart. Was there really a hope greater than that offered by the bleak, harsh gods of her Nordic heritage? Was it possible that the great destiny behind the skies might be suffused with a love that could comfort sufferers such as she? Had she been alone, had Cerdic not been watching her, she might have stepped forward with the rest. But his eyes were upon her, hard and unyielding as ever. She hesitated. All he wants, she thought, is surrender.

Bishop Mellitus was coming up from the stream now, straight towards her. He glanced up, saw her hesitation, saw her husband's grim face and, remembering the unhappy scene he had witnessed between them some weeks before, went quietly to her side and beckoned Cerdic to him.

"You wish to be baptized?" he gently enquired of Elfgiva.

"My husband wishes it."

Mellitus smiled, then turning to Cerdic he announced: "I shall baptize your wife, my friend, when she comes to me with a good heart. When she desires it – as I hope she will – and not before." With more firmness, he added: "You must show Christian charity, Cerdic. Then she will obey you willingly."

And hoping that by this show of understanding he might have improved things between them, he turned back to his duties.

Cerdic begged Mellitus to rest at Lundenwic until the next day, but although it was the Sabbath, the bishop was anxious to continue on his way. "Some of the brethren await us in Essex tonight," he explained. "A good ride from here." Soon afterwards, he and his party were riding across the city, taking the track that led to the eastern gate. Meanwhile, Cerdic and the others slowly made their way back along the pathway to Lundenwic, with Offa bringing up the rear.

Towards evening it grew a little warmer. After the preacher's moving words, a certain quietness descended on the settlement. It seemed to young Offa that men and women alike were walking about with a softness in their expressions. That night he fully expected his master, his heart opened, to comfort and be reconciled with his wife. But though he was sure that the merchant had been no less affected than the others, Offa saw that Cerdic still went off to sleep in another of the huts, leaving Elfgiva alone.

So it was that, late at night as he lay in Ricola's arms, Offa, still profoundly moved by the day's events, murmured to his wife: "I was thinking about the master and mistress."

"Yes."

"We owe her so much. I mean, she saved our lives."

"That's right."

"It's such a shame. If only we could do something."

"Like what I said the other day? Is that what you mean?"

"I don't know. Something."

While her husband slept, Ricola lay awake, thinking, for a long time.

The main feast of Yuletide fell on the eve of the year's shortest day, two days after Mellitus had left.

The eve of the shortest day, the year's midnight. How brief the hours of daylight seemed. Grey clouds came in from the west, closing over the river like a blanket. As the men set up the trestle tables in the hall and banked up the fire, they all agreed that there would be a blizzard before the feast was done. Indeed, by midday the western sky had taken on that orange tinge that signals the coming of snow.

Ricola was busy. She baked bread, made the oatcakes, and helped the two women turn the great haunches of venison over the fire. How good the meat smelled as it slowly hissed and the smoke rose into the thatch. But all the time she was doing these things, the girl was thinking about her plan. And the more she did so, the more she told herself it would work, whether Offa believed her or not.

The plan that Ricola had formed, and which had so horrified her husband, rested on two very simple assumptions. The first, that she knew men. The second, that she understood her mistress.

"It's this way," she had explained to Offa. "I've watched her. She can't make up her mind. She thought she'd lost him; now she knows she could have him back. She wants to give in, but she's so afraid of losing him again that she can't bring herself to make the move. And he won't either because . . ." She searched her mind for the reason, was not sure if she saw all the possibilities, and settled on: "Because he's a man." Then she grinned. "You know what she's like?" She stood up and gave a wonderful imitation of a woman teetering on a river-bank, unable to make up her mind whether to jump into the stream. "That's how she is," the girl concluded. "She's so close. All she needs is a little push." She smiled at him again. "Just one little push, Offa. That's all."

"And who's going to do that?" he had asked.

"We are," she had replied, almost severely.

Now, it seemed, was time to do it.

"I understand her," Ricola had claimed again. "And as for him, that'll be easy enough."

"But if it goes too far. If it doesn't work . . ." The possibilities were horrifying.

"It will," she promised. "Just do as I say."

There were about a dozen guests at the feast. They had gladly come to Lundenwic, to Cerdic's generous table.

In the hall, many lamps were lit. The long table was crowded. Even the household slaves – Offa, Ricola and four others – had been allowed in to join the festivities. All around were merry faces flushed with ale. One of the stockmen had just given the company a song. As the light faded, a few tiny flakes of snow had fallen, lying like a powdery frosting upon the thatched roof before slowly dissolving. The sky was still orange.

Offa was still nervous. All the time, Ricola's words kept echoing in his ears.

"It's nothing, silly. He's just been giving me the eye recently. It's only natural. But we can use that. Don't you see?"

Was his wife right? The dangers seemed so terrible to him, but Ricola had been reassuring: "She's my friend. She won't be angry with me. If we do nothing and the mistress gets sent away, where does that leave us? Out with her, or worse."

Until the sermon, he had refused to think about it. Even now, he could not quite say why he had changed his mind. Had it been a sense that they should take a risk for this woman to whom they owed their lives? Or had it been something more general, a feeling he had taken from the preacher that somehow, thanks to this wonderful new god, everything would be all right? Only believe in His name, the preacher had said. He believed. He was sure he did. The Frey would protect them.

But now he was beginning to wonder again. He tried to put such thoughts away. Gradually, as the warmth from the venison and the thick, spicy ale spread pleasantly inside him, he began to feel that, after all, Ricola was right. There would be a fleeting incident. If it worked, well and good; if not, no harm would be done. He reached for the wooden beaker before him and drank some more ale.

The master, too, was eating and drinking well. He seemed content, if watchful. Elfgiva, wearing a fine gold band around her neck and looking, it seemed to Offa, as beautiful as any of the younger women, was graciously serving her guests with mead and ale. Everyone thanked her and raised their beakers to their host, swearing oaths of friendship and loyalty. Everything appeared as it should.

More than once, Offa noticed, Cerdic, flushed with warm mead, looked across at Elfgiva. Just let her look back at him, Offa silently prayed. One little look of surrender was all that was needed. If she would just give in that night, Ricola's charade would be unnecessary and they could all go to their beds happy.

But though Elfgiva played her part she gave Cerdic no sign, and his face darkened. Other men would be with their wives that night, but not, it seemed, the merchant. Offa sighed. The plan would go ahead. As the feast wore on, he thought about it numbly.

It was almost the end of the feast when Ricola made her move.

People were drifting in and out. Men who had drunk a quantity of ale would step briefly outside. Already one or two couples, red-faced and well fed, had staggered off, not to return. When Cerdic went outside, and Ricola and Offa slipped out after him, nobody even noticed.

A short time later, Cerdic, returning, noticed the slave girl standing alone by the door of her hut. A faint light from the lamp inside showed her outline in the darkness; it also caught her short, fair hair, giving it a strange glow. She's a pretty little thing, the merchant thought. The woollen shawl she was wearing round her shoulders had slipped, revealing the top of her breasts, which were small but well formed. If she was cold, she did not seem to notice it. Cerdic paused.

"Where's your husband?"

She gave him a smile and nodded towards the hut.

"Sleeping. He'll sober up tomorrow."

He grinned. "All alone tonight then?"

She glanced up at him, pausing for just a fraction of a second before answering, "Looks like it."

He began to turn away, but then did not. He looked at her thoughtfully. He felt a warmth stirring inside him. Other men were sleeping with their women that night, yet the master of the house would sleep alone.

Why should he?

The plan was simple enough. Crude, even. But not entirely stupid.

"All we need to do is let her see him coming after me. Nothing more."

"Then she'll blame you," Offa had protested.

"No." Ricola had shaken her head. "Not if we do it right. He'll be wanting a woman. She'll know that. I'll be looking frightened because he's the master and I don't know what to do. You go and get her. Say I sent you, like I'm asking for help."

"She'll be angry with him."

"Maybe. But he's still her man. She isn't going to have him sleeping with her own slave right in front of her. She'll put a stop to that quickly, and there's only one way a woman can do that."

"So she'll just take him off to bed herself?"

"She knows she can have him. This time she has to decide: take him or he grabs another woman. Move or not. On the spot. She's his wife. If she's half a woman, she's got to make a move. After all," Ricola wisely added, "if she was really ready to let him go, she wouldn't still be here now." This was the plan. The little push Elfgiva needed.

Through the darkness, Offa looked across the yard from the barn where he had been hiding. They were only twenty paces away and he could see them clearly enough by the dim light of the doorway. Ricola was playing her part well, laughing at something the master had just said, head a little thrown back. She was friendly, naturally warm, enticing without actually provoking him. She saw Offa as he slipped inside.

It was quite simple, but he had to be quick.

It was hot in Cerdic's hall. For a second the air, thick with smoke, stung his eyes. The fire and lamps lit the scene with a warm glow. It was not as easy as he had expected to get to where Elfgiva was sitting. The table ran down the centre of the little hall. Halfway along, his path was blocked by two of the stockmen who had decided to pass out together in a heap, quietly snoring. Unable to skirt them, he climbed over instead. They did not notice.

At last he came to his mistress's side, ready to say the words Ricola had made him rehearse carefully. He leaned forward.

But Elfgiva was talking to an elderly farmer from upriver. When the slave tried to speak to her, she waved him away. Since, however, the young fellow seemed insistent, she told him to wait. Politely she continued the conversation with the old farmer, who was telling her an interminable story. It was boring, but one must show respect. The farmer's ancestor had killed no less than three men in battle, including a considerable chief from the north, before Elfgiva looked at the slave again and noticed that he was getting very agitated.

The message Offa had rehearsed was very simple. "My wife sent me, lady. She begs you to help her. She does not want to offend the master." A loyal slave in an awkward position. He could leave the rest to her, Ricola had told him.

But time was passing. The farmer seemed well set to tell Elfgiva about his ancestor's brothers too. Offa became anxious. When, at last, with a faint show of impatience, Elfgiva turned to him, he became confused.

"My wife –" he began.

"I shall not need her tonight." Elfgiva smiled and started to turn away.

"No, lady. My wife –"

"Not now." Again she was turning from him.

"My wife, lady," he tried, a little desperately, then, forgetting his lines: "Your husband and my wife . . ." He gestured towards the door.

She frowned at him. "What are you talking about?" She smiled at the farmer quickly.

"They sent for you," he blurted out, now hopelessly confused. And at last she shrugged, excused herself, and a moment later was moving towards the door.

What was keeping Offa? Ricola had calculated everything so carefully. She needed the merchant to go just so far and no further, but time had passed and Cerdic was getting excited. She wondered what to do. More time passed. The merchant had put his hand on her shoulder. Either she must fight him off now and provoke his anger, or . . .

Still they did not come. Cerdic's smile was growing. She almost winced, tried gently to remove his hand, which had found her breast. Not yet, she wanted to scream. Not yet.

But he was stooping to kiss her.

When Elfgiva emerged from the low doorway into the darkness of the yard, she saw clearly enough the figures of her husband and the slave by the entrance of the little hut. Her husband was kissing the girl, who showed no sign of struggling. Her shawl lay on the ground beside her. As they disengaged and glanced towards her, Cerdic smiled with a mixture of guilt and triumph. But the girl, in a ridiculous pantomime of pushing him away, looked at her with fear.

At that moment, Elfgiva remembered only one thing. What had the little slave so impertinently said to her the other day? "If you won't have him, others will"? Something like that. And now the girl thought she could take him herself.

Elfgiva shrugged. She was hurt, of course. She was furious. But if her husband chose to amuse himself with a slave, she thought with bitter contempt, it was a matter beneath her notice. Paying no more attention to Offa or the lovers, she turned back to the feast, followed by the young fellow, who was trying to say something. She did not even listen.

For this was the one thing that poor Ricola had not fully understood. Her mistress might confide in her when she was in distress, but to the high-born Saxon lady, the girl was still only a slave. She was not a rival. Hardly even an embarrassment. She was a chattel to be used for the night if her husband had nothing better to do, to be discarded at will. Elfgiva could, even in these circumstances, dismiss her from her mind just as she wished.

Which was exactly what she did now. As she made her way back up the table to the garrulous farmer, Elfgiva merely waved young Offa away.

By the time the young fellow went outside again, Cerdic and Ricola had vanished.

That night seemed long to Offa. The wind had dropped. In the earlier part, as he sat by the door of his hut, he could see figures passing out of the hall opposite or stumbling about in the yard. Occasionally he heard the faint murmuring of a drunken laugh from somewhere. Was he hearing the merchant and Ricola?

There was nothing Ricola could do. He realized that. Even if she resisted, the merchant was bigger and far stronger, and as slaves he and Ricola had few rights. The irony of the situation struck him. As a freeman back in the village he could have stood up to the elder. He could at least have demanded compensation. But by losing his head and then his freedom, he had ensured that the same thing could happen again, and that this time he would be helpless.

He moaned at his own stupidity.

For a little while he had vainly hoped that perhaps Ricola might manage to escape from the merchant. Perhaps Cerdic would be too drunk, or she would somehow be able to give him the slip. It was a faint hope at best. As the night deepened and Ricola did not appear, it passed.

He wanted, against all good sense, to go and look for them. Where were they? In the barn perhaps? Or one of the huts?

"What would I do anyway?" he muttered to himself. "Stick a pin in him too?" As he considered the hopelessness of the situation, and his folly in letting Ricola start this whole business, he shook his head. "I'd never have done it if it hadn't been for that preacher," he murmured. "Much use his new god's been to me." It seemed to him that the Frey on the Cross was a powerless god after all.

As she lay in Cerdic's powerful arms, Ricola was thoughtful. Her mind had drifted to her husband, then to Elfgiva. What would tonight mean to them all? To her marriage, her position with her mistress, her future relationship with the merchant? She ran her hand softly over the merchant's chest, feeling the blond hair. She wanted to go, but he was still only half asleep and his strong arm gently restrained her. In the early hours, he became wakeful once more.

One thing at least Ricola knew. Within her she already carried a tiny life – the life that belonged to her and Offa alone and which, come what may, she must protect.

Ricola might have been very surprised, however, if, in the vague greyness of the midwinter dawn, she could have seen her mistress.

Elfgiva did not sleep. She had lain awake, tossing restlessly. Again and again, the events of the evening had passed before her eyes and it was not long before her anger gave way to another, simpler emotion. Regret. Why didn't I just stop him? she asked herself. And then, as if addressing another: He was yours, and you turned him away.

She was hurt, yet she felt sorry for her husband too. She knew his needs, but she had refused them. And why? Loyalty to her gods. Fear of humiliation. Pride. But was her pride bringing her any happiness? Was humiliation worse than this mess? As for those ancestral gods and her loyalty to them, had Woden, Thunor and Tiw brought her any comfort during this winter night? It seemed to her that they had not.

A little before the first hint of light, she wrapped a heavy fur around her and walked down the slope to the water's edge. The river made little sound. In the darkness it looked black. Hunching her shoulders, she sat on the jetty and stared at the water.

What would her father have done? He would have set sail for some distant shore, trusted in his gods and braved the sea. But her father was a man. As the night wore on, the old seafarer seemed less and less relevant. And yet perhaps that vigorous old soul might have approved when, as the water began to turn from black to grey, she stood up, straightened her shoulders and proceeded briskly up the slope.

Young Ricola had been right after all. Her ruse had worked, even if later than she had planned. Elfgiva had decided to take control of her marriage again.

* * *

That morning, therefore, it was with a sense of relief and warm pleasure that Cerdic listened to his wife, who announced firmly: "I will follow your new god. Tell your priest he can baptize me." To which, however, she added: "The slave girl goes."

He grinned and embraced her.

"The girl goes," she repeated.

He shrugged as if it were of no account. "Whatever you want," he said. "After all, she belongs to you."

Unknown to any of them, one other event had taken place during the long watches of that winter night.

This was the arrival of a visitor.

As the dawn arose over the long Thames Estuary, a single longship had come stealing up the river on the incoming tide. Now, on this dull, damp day, it had just entered the great bend downstream from the settlement.

As his squat, seaworthy vessel came in sight of the jetty at Lundenwic, the small, hard man standing near the bow looked ahead of him with anticipation. He was in his forties, with a rather brutal face, and a patchy grey beard that was clipped very short. Of all the Frisian traders, he was the only one who would make the journey to the island at this bleak and dangerous time of the year. He did so because he was fearless, clever and greedy. He bought his merchandise cheap because he saved their owners the cost of housing and feeding them in the winter months, and he was usually the only man who could supply any goods that might be urgently needed before the spring. His traffic was in human beings. All along the north European coastline it was known: "That cunning Frisian's the only one who can supply winter slaves." He reached Lundenwic at midday.

When he saw the Frisian ship, Cerdic smiled. "I thought he'd come," he remarked to the foreman.

"You were counting on it," the foreman responded with a grin.

"True." When Cerdic had bargained for the slaves from the north he had let the merchant think he would have the expense of keeping them all winter, and so had got a much better price. "I never said I couldn't sell them until the spring," Cerdic reminded the fellow. "I only said the slave trade usually begins in spring."

"Of course." Cerdic never lied.

By mid-afternoon the Frisian had inspected the northern slaves and agreed a good price. He was surprised and delighted when, as a goodwill gesture, Cerdic offered him two more slaves – a man and a woman – at a discounted price. "I just want to get rid of them," Cerdic explained. "But they won't give you any trouble."

"I'll take them," the Frisian said, and put them in chains with the rest.

There was a little trouble, though. At sundown, the girl started screaming that she wanted to talk to her mistress. But it seemed that the mistress had no wish to speak to her, so the slave-trader gave her a quick whipping to quieten her down before going to the hall to eat with Cerdic. After a night's sleep, he would depart on the ebb tide.

In the Anglo-Saxon calendar, the longest night of the year was known as *Modranecht* – mothers' night.

It had been a long time since Cerdic and his wife had slept together, but now, when they did so, the merchant experienced a sense of homecoming, and as for Elfgiva, it seemed to her in the depths of that long night that something had opened again within her. Something wonderful and mysterious.

The next morning, she awoke with a quiet and special smile.

The boat was ready to leave.

It was a Norse longship with a rising keel, very like the one Offa had unloaded that autumn. Its wide draught would allow the slaves to sit in the central section and stretch out their legs. To ensure they gave no trouble, their ankles would be manacled.

Still Ricola was thinking desperately. All night she had lain in the slave quarters hoping for some reprieve. She had tried to speak to Elfgiva. A few moments with her – that was all she needed – and she could have explained everything. She was sure of it. But ever since Cerdic's men had come to seize her and Offa the previous morning, it was as though her mistress had disappeared entirely. For Elfgiva and her husband the two slaves had, quite suddenly, ceased to exist. When she had protested, tried to scream her message to the people outside the slave quarters, the Frisian had cruelly whipped her. After that, no one had come to the slave quarters. No one.

Surely somebody would take pity on her. Wistan at least, if not his mother. She guessed that this isolation must be deliberate. Either Elfgiva or her husband had given orders. She and Offa were not to be approached. No contact at all. They wanted the two slaves out of their lives.

And yet if Elfgiva only knew her secret. If she could just let her mistress know that she was pregnant. How could she as a woman fail to sympathize? As dawn at last arrived and she thought she heard people moving about, her hopes grew a little and focused upon a single, vital point. Somehow, between the slave quarters and the Frisian's boat, she had to get this one message to Elfgiva. No matter how many blows the Frisian rained upon her with his cruel whip, she had to tell her.

An hour passed. The light was stealing under the door. After a while it opened and the Frisian entered. In silence, he fed them barley cakes and water before disappearing. Some time passed, then he reappeared with four of his eight sailors and led them all out into the cold, grey morning.

There were, as she had guessed there would be, a number of people on the bank waiting to see them leave. She saw the stockmen, the foreman, the women with whom she had worked every day. But not one of Cerdic's family. Not even one of the four sons. If they were watching, they were out of sight.

At the top of the bank she passed close to one of the women. The cook.

"I'm pregnant," she whispered. "Tell the Lady Elfgiva. Quickly!"

"Stop talking," the Frisian called out curtly.

Ricola looked at the woman beseechingly.

"Don't you understand?" she cried out softly. "I'm pregnant."

A second later she felt a searing pain across her shoulders, and then the Frisian's hand on the back of her neck, pushing her forward. Twisting her head painfully, she managed to look back at the woman. The cook's broad Saxon face was pale, a little frightened perhaps, but she did not move.

Something distracted the Frisian now. He removed his hand and started to the front of the line. Ricola was passing the foreman now.

"I'm pregnant," she called to him. "Won't you just tell the mistress that? I'm pregnant."

He stared at her as calmly as if she were a piece of livestock. Crack! The whip came hissing down again. Once, twice, catching her on the neck, making her scream with agony.

Now she was beside herself. She had nothing to lose. No dignity left. Never mind the pain.

"I'm pregnant!" she screamed at the top of her lungs. "Lady Elfgiva! I'm pregnant! Can't you understand? Pregnant! I've got a child!"

The fourth blow cut into the first. Deep. For a second she almost passed out. She felt strong arms dragging her down the bank while she babbled uselessly: "A baby . . . I'm having a baby." Her whole body was shuddering with the shock and the pain. But still nobody moved.

Some five minutes passed while she sat in the boat, coming back to her senses. The Frisian's sailors were calmly loading stores. The Frisian himself, directing his men, seemed to have forgotten her. It was as though her outburst had never taken place.

Surely when she had shouted her message it must have echoed all round the trading post. Surely Elfgiva, or at least one of the family, must have heard. She looked at the northern slaves in front of her. Their faces were resigned, almost deadened. They, at least, had no hope. Some distant Frankish farm or Mediterranean port awaited them. They would be worked hard until they grew weak, then, quite possibly, be worked harder still until, having given every ounce of value they had, they dropped. Unless they were very lucky.

And what did they do with a pregnant woman? Did they let her stay with her husband? She thought probably not. And with the child? Whoever bought her might let it live. More likely – she could hardly bear to think of it. More likely, she had heard, they drowned the child as soon as it was born. What use was a baby to a master?

Her eyes caught sight of the boat's high, curving prow. How cruel it seemed, like some great, cold blade about to strike through the waters. Or the beak, she thought, of some ominous bird of prey. She turned her gaze back to the bank.

Lundenwic. The last place where any of their feet would touch Britain's soil. Lundenwic, the wharf from which the Anglo-Saxons sold their sons and daughters. Grey, grim Lundenwic. She hated it, and all those faces so calm upon the green bank.

"Doesn't seem to worry them that we're going like this, does it?"

She suddenly realized that in her desperation she had not spoken to Offa since the night before. Poor Offa who had stuck a pin in the village elder, who had gone along with her misguided plan. Offa, the father of her baby that was probably to die. She looked at him, but he said nothing.

Now the Frisian was returning. The sailors fore and aft were ready to cast off. It was all over. Shaking her head in defeat, she gazed at the bottom of the boat, and so did not see Elfgiva coming down the grassy bank.

She had heard.

But it was not only Ricola's cry that had brought her down. It was the cry together with something else – the something that had passed between husband and wife in Cerdic's hall that mothers' night, the tiny seed of joy in that long midwinter night. When Elfgiva awoke that morning and stretched, and felt her husband kiss her, and then heard the girl's cry, it was this new and secret warmth that caused her to take pity on poor Ricola and her husband.

Soon afterwards, therefore, to their great surprise the couple found themselves back in the homestead, standing before their mistress outside the long, thatched hall.

There was little conversation, however. Elfgiva was brief. She silenced them at once when they started trying to explain themselves. She had no wish to hear. "You're lucky not to be on the slave ship," she informed them. "And now you may count yourselves luckier still. I am giving you back your freedom. Go where you want, but never show your faces at Lundenwic again." Imperiously she waved them away.

Soon afterwards, Cerdic, watching them down by the jetty, was tempted to give the girl a present, but thought better of it.

* * *

The snow came that afternoon, a steady, soft snowfall that blanketed the riverbank.

Offa and Ricola had not gone far. Down by the ford on the island called Thorney, in the shelter of some bushes, Offa had constructed a crude hut. The snow was a help. Working quickly, he was able to build up snow walls around it, so that by the time darkness set in, he and Ricola were warm enough in a little hovel that was half brushwood and half igloo. In the entrance, he made a fire. They had a little food; the cook had given them barley bread and a packet of meat left over from the feast that would last them for a few days. But soon after nightfall, a hooded figure on horseback approached their little camp and dismounted, and by the firelight they saw the friendly face of young Wistan.

"Here," he said with a grin, and swung down a heavy object he had been carrying behind his saddle. It was a haunch of venison. "I'll come tomorrow to make sure you're all right," he promised before riding away.

And so the young couple began their new life out in the wild. "Now we can let our hair grow," Offa reminded Ricola with a smile. "At least we aren't slaves any more."

Using fat from the venison, Offa did what he could to make some oil to rub into the welts around her neck and shoulders. She winced as he touched them, but said nothing as he went to work.

They made no mention, then or later, of the night she had spent with the merchant. But when he asked her, "Is it true you're pregnant?" and she nodded, he felt a sense of both joy and relief. Somehow the merchant's intrusion into his life seemed marginal now.

"We'll manage here for a few days," he said. "Then I'll think of something." The river was long. Its valley was lush. The river would look after them.

Another new life also began by the river that midwinter. By the second month of the year, Elfgiva became certain that she had conceived.

"I'm sure it was on *Modranecht*," she told her husband, to his surprise and delight. She also had a feeling, which she did not share with him, that this child was a girl.

There was only one duty that Elfgiva knew she still had to perform. It was not until the fourth month of the year, when the Anglo-Saxons celebrated the ancient festival of *Eostre*, to welcome the spring, that Bishop Mellitus returned to supervise the construction of the little cathedral church of St Paul's. Work now proceeded rapidly. Cerdic and the local farmers provided extra labourers and under the supervision of the monks, and using the Roman stones and tiles that lay all around, they built the walls in a modest rectangle with a tiny circular apse at one end. Lacking the skills to attempt anything more sophisticated, they made the roof of wood. Standing near the summit of the western hill, it looked very well.

And it was just before the *Eostre* feast that Elfgiva, watched by her sons, was led by her husband to the little River Fleet, where she knelt by the bank while Bishop Mellitus anointed her head with water in the simple rite of baptism.

"And since your name, Elfgiva, means 'Gift of the Faeries'," the bishop remarked with a smile, "I shall baptize you with a new name. Henceforth you shall be called Godiva, which means 'Gift of God'."

The same day he preached another sermon to the people of Lundenwic in which he explained to them in more detail the message of the Passion of Christ, and how, after the Crucifixion, this wondrous Frey had risen from the dead. This great feast of the Church calendar was of supreme importance, he told them, and always fell about this time of the year.

Which is why, in the years to follow, the English came to refer to this all-important Christian festival by the pagan name of Easter.

The conversion of the Anglo-Saxons to Christianity, and the re-establishment of the old Roman city of Londinium – or Lunden as the Saxons called it – did not continue without interruption.

A little over a decade later, when both the kings of Kent and Essex were dead, their people revolted against the new religion, and the new bishops were forced to flee.

But once the Roman Church had established a hold, it did not give up lightly. Soon afterwards, the bishops were back. Over the next century or so, great missionary bishops like Erkonwald went into the remotest forests, and the Anglo-

Saxon Church, with its several notable saints, became one of the brightest lights of the Christian world.

In the centuries that followed, Lundenwic continued to grow into a substantial Saxon port. Only long afterwards, in the time of King Alfred, did the Roman city take over from it again; after which the old trading post a mile to the west was remembered as the old port – the *auld wic* – or Aldwych. But this was far in the future. For several generations after Cerdic, the walled enclosure of Londinium remained a place apart, with only a few religious structures and, perhaps, a modest royal hall. Certainly there were few houses on the western hill when Godiva's daughter used to wander there as a girl. But she could always remember how she used to see, every month or two, a cheerful fisherman with a white patch of hair on the front of his head cross from the spit of land on the southern bank in a little dugout boat, accompanied by his several children, who would all go wandering about in the ruins, studying the ground.

They were a secretive folk, though. She never found out what it was they could possibly be looking for.

Chapter 4

The Conqueror

1066

On January 6, the feast of Epiphany, in the year of Our Lord 1066, the greatest men in the Anglo-Saxon kingdom of England gathered on the little island of Thorney just outside the port of London to take part in extraordinary events. Everyone was there: Stigand, the Saxon Archbishop of Canterbury; the king's council, the Witan; the powerful burghers of London. They had been keeping vigil for two weeks.

But nothing, that cold winter morning, was more remarkable than the place where they met.

For generations, a modest community of monks had dwelt on the little island by the old ford. Their church, dedicated to St Peter, was just big enough for themselves and a small congregation. Now, however, a new building had taken its place by the river. There had been nothing like it in England since Roman times. Set in a wide, walled precinct, its ground plan in the shape of a cross, this new church of chalk-white stone dwarfed even the old cathedral of St Paul's on its hill in the city nearby. Because the monastery on Thorney lay just west of London, it had come to be known as the West Minster, and so this new landmark would thereafter be called Westminster Abbey.

Only twelve days before, on Christmas morning, the frail, white-bearded King Edward, whose life's work the Abbey was, had proudly watched as the archbishop hallowed the new building. For this pious work, he would become known as Edward the Confessor. But now the vigil was over. His work done, he was free to seek eternal rest. They had buried King Edward in his Abbey that morning, and as they emerged from the church, the great men knew that the eyes of all Christendom were upon them.

From the papal court in Rome to the fjords of Scandinavia, it had been an open secret that the English king was dying. He had no son. At that very moment, adventurers in Normandy, Denmark and Norway were making their preparations, and every court in the northern world was buzzing with the single question: "Who will take up the crown?"

The hooded figure watched them silently, unnoticed.

Wrapped in heavy cloaks, the two men were standing outside, somewhat sheltered by the great Abbey just behind. It was said that nothing could shake their friendship, but he did not believe that. Enmity lasts. Friendship is less certain. Especially at such times as these.

A light snow had begun to fall as, a hundred yards away, the members of the Witan made their way across the enclosure to the long low hall by the riverbank that had been the dead king's residence, and where they would now choose the new king. Beyond, the river wore a choppy yet sluggish look that suggested the tide was about to turn. Less than two miles away, across the mud flats of the river's huge bend, the walls of London and the long wooden roof of the Saxon cathedral of St Paul's could just be seen through the falling snow.

The figure on the left was well set, about forty, his thinning hair compensated for by a rich golden beard. Like his ancestor Cerdic, who had shipped slaves from the ancient trading post now called the Aldwych, he had a broad chest, a broad, Germanic face, an air of cheerful, sturdy self-control, and hard blue eyes that could spot a short measure of goods at a hundred paces. He had a reputation for being very cautious, which some found a virtue, others a fault. But no man had ever known him break his word. His only weakness was a painful back thanks to a fall from his horse, but he was proud that only those closest to him knew he often suffered. He was Leofric, merchant of London.

If Leofric was burly, his companion was a giant. Hrothgar the Dane towered over his Saxon friend. A great mane of red hair grew upon his head; his huge red beard was two feet wide and three feet long. This massive descendant of the Vikings could lift a grown man with each hand. His periodic rages, when his face became as red as his hair, were legendary. When he pounded his fist upon the table, strong men blanched; at his bellowing roar, lines of doors along the street would hastily close. That this rich and powerful noble was nonetheless held in affection by his neighbours might, however, be expected from his ancestry. Two centuries before, his great-great-grandfather had earned a reputation as a fearsome Viking warrior who disliked killing children. His order before each raid of *"Bairn ni Kel"* – "Don't kill the children" – was so well known that it became a nickname. Five generations later his descendants were still generally referred to as the family of Bar-ni-kel. Since he lived on the eastern of London's two hills, and traded from the wharf below called Billingsgate, he was usually referred to as Barnikel of Billingsgate.

The Saxon's green cloak was trimmed with red squirrel fur, but Barnikel's blue cloak was trimmed with costly ermine from the Viking state of Russia, a sign that he was rich indeed. And if the Saxon owed the wealthy Dane a debt of money, what was that between friends? Leofric's eldest child, his daughter, was due to marry the Norseman's son next year.

Few things gave Barnikel greater pleasure. Whenever he saw the girl his huge face softened and broke into a smile. "You're lucky I chose her for you," he would tell his son with satisfaction. Demure, with a pleasant smile and soft, thoughtful eyes, she was only fourteen, but she had learned thoroughly the business of running a household, she could read, and her father confessed that she understood his business almost as well as he did. Already the huge red-bearded Dane felt like a father to her. He looked forward eagerly to the time when she would sit at his family table – "Where I can keep an eye on you, and make sure my son is looking after you properly," he would tell her jovially. "As for Leofric's debt to me," he confided to his wife, "don't tell him, but when the marriage takes place I'm going to cancel it."

As the Witan went into session the two men waited, stamping their feet in the cold.

The hooded figure watched them thoughtfully. Both men, he knew, had much to fear that day, but it seemed to him that the Saxon was in the greater danger. This suited him very well. He had no interest in the Dane, but the Saxon was another matter. He had sent Leofric a message the day before. As yet, the Saxon had not replied. Soon, however, he would have to. "And then," the figure murmured, "he'll be mine."

* * *

A Saxon and a Dane. Yet if anyone had asked either Leofric or Barnikel to name his homeland, both would have replied, without hesitation, that they were English. To understand how this was, and the nature of the choice before the Witan that fateful January morning in 1066, it is necessary to consider certain important developments that had taken place in the northern world.

In the four centuries since St Augustine's mission to Britain, though Celtic Scotland and Wales remained apart, the numerous Anglo-Saxon kingdoms had slowly begun to coalesce into the entity called England. But then, two centuries ago, in the reign of good King Alfred, England had nearly been destroyed.

The onslaught of the fearsome Vikings upon the northern world lasted several centuries. These Norsemen – Swedes, Norwegians and Danes – have been called merchants, explorers and pirates. They were all those things. Emerging from their fjords and harbours, they wandered the oceans in longships to form colonies in Russia, Ireland, Normandy, the Mediterranean, and even America. From the Arctic to Italy, they traded furs, gold and whatever else they could lay their hands on. With fierce blue eyes, flaming beards, heavy swords and mighty axes, these adventurers drank hugely, swore oaths of loyalty to one another, and bore tremendous names like Ragnar Longhair, Slayer of Tostig the Proud, as though they were still heroes from the Nordic legends of old.

The Vikings who swept across England in the ninth century were mostly Danish. They entered the walled trading centre London and burnt it. But for the heroic battles of King Alfred, they would have taken over the whole island; even after Alfred's victories, they still controlled most of the English territory north of the Thames.

The area where they settled came to be known as the Danelaw. Here, the English population had to live by Danish custom. Yet this was not so bad. The Danes were Nordic folk, their language like Anglo-Saxon. They even became Christians. And while in the Saxon south the poorer peasants gradually became serfs, the freebooting Danes led a more open life where peasants were independent, belonging to no man. After Alfred's descendants had gradually regained control of the

Danelaw and reunited England, the men of the south would still say, with a shrug: "You can't argue with a northerner. They're independent up there."

However, things were seldom peaceful in the tumultuous northern world, and just before the year 1000, the Danes again descended upon the rich island.

This time they were in better luck. The English leader was not Alfred, but his inept descendant Ethelred, who, because he usually failed to take good advice – *raed* in Anglo-Saxon – was known as Ethelred *Un-raed*, the Unready. Year after year, this foolish king paid them protection – Danegeld – until at last the English, sick of him, accepted the Danish king as their monarch instead. As Leofric's grandfather had remarked, "If I'm going to pay Danegeld I'd like to have some order."

Nor was he disappointed. The reign of King Canute, who shortly succeeded to the thrones of both Denmark and England, was long and exemplary. His strength was feared; his simple common sense was legendary. The Danish Barnikel family found a ready welcome at his court, but so had Leofric's grandfather and many Saxons like him. Impartially ruling England as an English king, he brought unity, peace and prosperity to the land, and if his son had not suddenly died soon after succeeding him, forcing the English Witan to choose pious Edward from the old Saxon line, England might have remained an Anglo-Danish kingdom.

Nowhere was this marriage of Saxon and Danish cultures more successful than in the growing port now known as London. Lying on the old borderland between Saxon and Danish England, it was natural that the two cultures should merge there. Though the assembly of all the citizens, summoned three times a year by the great bell to the old cross that stood beside St Paul's, was still the Saxon Folkmoot, the court where the city fathers regulated the city's trade and commerce had a Danish name: the Hustings. Whilst some of the little wooden churches were dedicated to Saxon saints like Ethelburga, others bore Scandinavian names like Magnus or Olaf. And along the lane that led to Westminster lay a rural parish of former Viking settlers called St Clement Danes.

On this cold winter morning, therefore, both Barnikel the Dane and Leofric the Saxon were united by a common desire: they wanted an English king.

* * *

One might suppose from his pious name that Edward the Confessor had been revered. He had not. Not only was his character petty, but he was foreign. Although Saxon born, he had been brought up in a French monastery and had taken a French wife, and whilst used to the long-established communities of French and German merchants in London, the burghers and nobles had not taken to the Frenchmen who infested his court. His Abbey said it all. Saxon buildings were usually modest timber structures full of intricate carving. Even the few stone churches sometimes looked as if they were meant to be made of wood. But the Abbey's massive pillars and rounded arches were in the stern Romanesque style of the Continent. Not English at all.

The final insult, however, had been William of Normandy.

The Witan had three choices. Only one, a nephew of King Edward's, was legitimate, but he was a youth, brought up abroad by a foreign mother and without a following in England. "He won't do," Leofric declared. Then there was Harold. Not royal, but a great English noble, a fine commander, and popular.

And then there was the Norman.

It was generations since Viking adventurers had colonized this northern coastal region of France. Merging with the local population, they were French-speaking now, but their Viking wanderlust remained. The last Duke of Normandy, having no legitimate heir, had left a bastard son to succeed him.

Ruthless, ambitious, probably driven by the sense of his illegitimacy, William of Normandy was a formidable adversary. Marrying into the family of Edward the Confessor's wife, he saw the chance to succeed the childless monarch and make himself king. From across the English Channel, he was claiming that Edward had promised him the throne. "And knowing the king, he probably did," Barnikel remarked gloomily.

But now the two men fell silent. The Witan was emerging.

"Look down upon our humble prayers and bless this Thy servant whom we, with humble devotion, have chosen to be King of the Angles and Saxons." So ran the prayers they used as they held the crown over the new king's head. Then came the coronation oath, in which the king promised peace, order and mercy. After this, the bishop, invoking Abraham, Moses, Joshua, King David and Solomon the Wise, once more asked God's blessing and anointed the king with oil. Only then was he invested with the crown of good King Alfred and given the sceptre for power and the rod for justice.

In this way, just hours after the funeral of King Edward, the traditional English coronation for the first time took place in Westminster Abbey. As Leofric and Barnikel looked at the well-built, brown-bearded figure whose clear blue eyes stared out boldly from the throne, they felt a new hope. Saxon King Harold would do very well.

It was as they came out of the Abbey at the end of the service that Barnikel of Billingsgate made his great mistake.

The hooded man who had been watching them was positioned near the door. His head was bare now, the hood pushed back on to his shoulders.

He was a strange figure. Standing close to one of the church's massive pillars, he might have been taken for a statue, a dark excrescence of the stone. His cloak was black and furled around him like the wings of a bird. His uncovered head revealed that his face was clean-shaven and his hair cut in a close-cropped circle well above his ears, in the current Norman fashion. But it was another feature that was truly remarkable. Emerging from his pale, oval face was a nose of notable dimensions. It was not so much broad as long; not pointed but rounded at the tip;.not red but somewhat shiny. A nose so distinctive, so serious, that with his head tucked down it seemed to descend into the folds of his cloak like the beak of some ominous raven.

As the congregation started to move out, he remained where he was, and this time the two friends saw him. He bowed.

Leofric returned the bow briefly.

The Saxon is careful, he thought. So much the better. But the Dane, flushed with relief, turned to him with a contemptuous growl.

"We have an English king, thank God. So keep your great French nose out of our business." He stomped out, while Leofric looked embarrassed.

The strange figure said nothing. He did not like people referring to his nose.

Leofric stared at the girl. Then he grimaced. After standing about in the cold all day, his back was hurting abominably. But it was not the pain that made him frown.

How innocent she looked. He had always thought of himself as a decent man. A man of his word. A good father. How, then, could he betray her like this?

He was sitting on a stout oak bench. Before him, on a trestle table, a fat-burning lamp smoked continuously. The hall was spacious. The timber walls were roughly plastered; on one hung an embroidery depicting a deer hunt. There were three small windows covered with oilcloth. The wooden floor was carpeted with rushes. In the middle stood a large brazier full of smouldering charcoal, its smoke drifting into the thatched roof above. Below was a large basement for storing goods; outside, a yard surrounded by outbuildings, and a little orchard. An improved version, in fact, of the old homestead of his ancestor Cerdic over at the Aldwych.

Again he considered the message he had received the day before. He was not sure what it meant, but he thought he guessed. And if he was right? Perhaps there was a way out. But he could not see it. He must do this terrible thing.

"Hilda." He beckoned. How obediently she came.

Outside the snow had stopped. Only a pall of cloud remained, beneath which the city of London lay quiet.

Though Winchester, in the west, was still the senior Saxon royal seat, the London of Leofric the merchant was a busy place. Over ten thousand people – traders, craftsmen, and churchmen – dwelt there now. Like some huge, long-neglected walled garden, the ancient city had gradually been reclaimed. King Alfred had restored the Roman walls. A pair of Saxon villages, each with its own market, which the Saxons called *cheaps*, and a crude grid of streets had spread over the twin hills. Wharves appeared, and a new wooden bridge. Coins were minted there. But with its thatched and timbered houses, its barns, halls, wooden churches and muddy streets, Saxon London still had the air of a large market town.

Reminders of the Roman past remained, though. The line of the lower of the two great thoroughfares across the city was still discernible. Entering through the western gate, now called Ludgate, it crossed the western hill below St Paul's and ended on the riverside slope of the eastern hill in the Saxon market of East Cheap. The outline of the upper Roman street was vaguer. Passing through the western wall at Newgate and crossing above St Paul's, it lay under the long, open space of the West Cheap, but then, as it struck across to the eastern hill, it vanished ignominiously into some cowsheds where a Saxon track now led up to the eastern summit, known, because of the grain grown on its slopes, as Cornhill.

Of the great forum, not a trace remained. Of the amphitheatre, there was only a low outline in which some Saxon buildings had arisen and ash trees grew. Here and there, however, a broken arch or a marble stump might yet be found sheltering by a wattled fence, or brushing the thatched roof of some busy workshop.

The city's only impressive building was the long, barn-like, Saxon structure of St Paul's, with its high wooden roof. The most colourful place, the long stretch of the West Cheap, ran across from the cathedral, and was always full of stalls.

Halfway along the West Cheap on its southern side, beside a tiny Saxon church dedicated to St Mary, a lane led down to an old well beside which stood a handsome homestead which, for some reason already forgotten, was graced with a heavy hanging sign depicting a bull. And since it was his hall, people would often refer to the rich Saxon merchant who lived there as Leofric, who dwells at the Bull.

She stood meekly before him, dressed in a simple woollen smock. What a good girl Hilda was. He smiled. What was she? Thirteen? Her breasts had just formed. Her leggings, bound with leather thongs, showed well-shaped calves. She was a little thick in the ankle, he considered, but that was a minor fault. She had a broad, unworried forehead, and though her fair hair might be a little thin, her pale blue eyes had a calm innocence that was charming. Was there fire within? He was not sure. Perhaps it did not matter.

The problem for both of them lay on the table in front of Leofric. It was a short stick, nine inches long, scored with notches of various widths and depths. This was a tally. The notches marked his debts and showed that Leofric was facing ruin.

How had he got into this mess? Like other large London traders, he had two main lines of business. He imported French wine and other goods through a merchant in the Norman city of Caen, and he sold English wool for export to the great clothmakers of Flanders in the Low Countries. The trouble was that recently his operations had grown too large. Small fluctuations in the price of wine or wool could be critical to his fortunes. Then a cargo of wool had been lost at sea. The loan from Barnikel had helped him over that problem. "But even so," he confessed to his wife, "I owe Becket in Caen for the last shipment of wine, and he's going to have to wait for his money."

The family had always kept the old Bocton estate in Kent. Many successful merchants in London had such estates; Barnikel himself had a big landholding in Essex. At present, it was only the revenues from his land that allowed Leofric to keep his business going.

And here was the danger.

"For if England is attacked," he reasoned, "and Harold loses, then many estates, including my own, will probably be confiscated by the winner." Either way, the harvest might be lost. With his finances on a knife edge, it could mean ruin.

Leofric pondered. He glanced to the corner where his wife and son sat in the shadows. If only little Edward were twenty, old enough to marry well and fend for himself, instead of ten. If only it were not necessary to provide a dowry for his daughter. If only his own debts were less. How like him the boy already looked. What must he do to protect those estates for him?

And now this message, strange and disturbing. How much did the long-nosed Norman know about his business affairs? And why should the fellow want to help him? As for his offer . . .

Leofric was not used to moral dilemmas. For the Saxon, as for his ancestors, a thing was either right or wrong, and that was the end of it. But this was not so easy. He gazed at Hilda and sighed. Her life should be simple, even placid. Could he really consider sacrificing her to keep his son's estates? Many men would, of course. In the Anglo-Saxon world, as all over Europe, daughters were bargaining chips in all classes of society.

"I may need your help," he began.

He spoke for some time in a low tone, and she listened quietly. What did he want her to say? Did he want her to protest? All he knew was that when he had finished, he heard her gentle reply with a sinking heart.

"I will do whatever you wish, Father, if you are in need of help."

Gloomily he thanked her and then motioned her away.

No, he decided, he could not do it. There must be some other way. But why, he wondered, did some accursed little voice inside him caution: You never know what may happen?

It was just then that his thoughts were interrupted by a neighbour's voice calling from outside.

"Leofric. Come here and look!"

He watched the chessmen thoughtfully, as though they might move of their own accord. In the candlelight, his long nose cast a shadow on the chequered board before him.

For a moment his mind returned to the events of that afternoon. He had planned his moves, considered every eventuality. He only had to wait a little longer. Since he had been waiting for twenty-five years, he could afford to be patient.

"Your move," he remarked, and the young man sitting opposite reached forward.

Both sons resembled their father. Both were sombre; both bore the burden of the family nose. But Henri had his father's brains, which the slightly larger and more thickset Ralph had not. Ralph was out in the town somewhere. Drinking, probably. Henri made his move.

No one knew exactly when the game of chess had first reached England. Certainly King Canute had played. Originally from the Orient, in the West it had undergone certain alterations. The Oriental king's minister had become a queen, whilst the pair of magnificent elephants bearing howdahs – strange figures to the Europeans – had been transformed, because the shape of the howdah vaguely resembled a mitre, into a pair of bishops.

The hall in which this game of chess was being played was rare indeed in Saxon London, for it was built of stone. It was situated just below St Paul's, at the top of the steep hill down towards the Thames. This was London's finest quarter, where several great churchmen and nobles had their houses – a sure sign that its owner was a man of some importance.

A quarter of a century had passed since he had come to London from the Norman city of Caen, where his family were prominent merchants. Such a move was not unusual. At the mouth of the brook that descended between the city's twin hills, there lay two enclosed wharves. On the eastern side was the wharf of the German merchants; on the western side, that of the French-speaking merchants from Norman towns such as Rouen and Caen. Chiefly engaged in the lucrative wine trade, these foreigners had been granted many commercial privileges and some settled permanently and became burghers of London.

Would he have stayed here if he had not lost the girl in Caen? Probably not. He had been so sure she was his; he had loved her since she was a child. What had he loved? Was it her little snub nose, so different from his own heavy protuberance? As the years passed, that was the only thing he could precisely recall about her, yet deep within him, the sharp remembrance of that pain remained like a lodestar to guide him on his way.

And to have lost her to a Becket. Whenever his family's hatred of these rival merchants had begun, it had certainly existed by his grandfather's day. It was not just a question of business. There was something in their character. And it was not just that they were quick, lively, clever and charming, though that was bad enough. They all had a truculence, a deep-seated egotism that irritated many, and which his family had learned to loathe.

She had been his. Until one day, round a corner, he had heard young Becket talking to her. They were laughing.

"How will you kiss him, my dear? The nose is an impenetrable barrier – don't you see? A fortress that no one has ever got past. It's magnificent, of course. One admires it like a mountain. But don't you know that since Noah's Flood, no member of that family has ever been kissed?"

He had turned away. He was fifteen. The very next day, she had been cool towards him. A year later she had married young Becket. After that, his home town had become hateful to him.

The years of Edward the Confessor had been good for him.

In London he had married and prospered, made useful friends in Edward's cosmopolitan court, and become a valued benefactor of St Paul's cathedral, a man of importance.

He had also gained a new name.

It had happened one morning soon after his marriage. Walking along the stalls in the West Cheap he had paused at a long table where some silversmiths were working. Fascinated, he had leaned over the table to watch them, and remained there some time. It was when he was finally moving away that the voice had called out: "Look, that one must be rich. He's got silver sleeves."

Silver sleeves. He thought about it. Silversleeves. And since it made no reference to his nose, and suggested he was rich, he decided to adopt it. Silversleeves: a rich man's name. "And soon I'll deserve it," he had promised his wife.

Now, as Silversleeves gazed at the chessboard, he allowed himself a faint smile. He loved chess, with its play of power and its secret harmonies. In his years of trading he had learned to look for similar patterns in his business. And had found them. Sometimes subtle, often cruel, the affairs of men were like an elaborate game to Silversleeves.

He enjoyed playing chess with Henri. Though Henri lacked his father's deep strategy, he was a masterful tactician, brilliant in improvising sudden solutions. Silversleeves had tried to teach his younger son too, but Ralph could not follow the game, getting into embarrassed rages while Henri looked on with mild contempt.

If he was secretly disappointed in Ralph, however, Silversleeves never showed it. Indeed, like many a clever father he felt a protective affection for his stupid son, doing his best to make the brothers friends and assuring their mother: "They will share my fortune equally."

Nevertheless, it was Henri who would one day run the business. Already the young man thoroughly understood the details of making, shipping and storing wine. He also knew his customers. And at quiet times like this, Silversleeves could share other, deeper thoughts with him to improve his understanding. This evening, his mind full of the calculations of the last few days, he decided to broach a most important subject.

"I have an interesting case to consider," he began. "A man with debts." He gazed at his son thoughtfully. "Who, generally, is stronger, Henri – a man with cash or a man with debts?"

"A man with cash."

"Suppose, though, that a man owes you a debt and can't pay?"

"He'll be ruined," Henri replied coolly.

"But then you lose what you lent him."

"Unless I seize all he has in payment. But if that's worth nothing, then I lose."

"So as long as he owes you money, you fear him?" Seeing Henri nod, he went on. "But now consider this. What if this man *can* in fact pay you what he owes, but chooses not to? Now you fear him because he has your money, but since he *can* pay, he does not fear you."

"I agree."

"Very well then. Suppose now, Henri, that you need that money badly. He offers to settle for less than he owes. Do you take it?"

"I might have to."

"Indeed you might. And now, do you not agree, he has made money out of you? Therefore, because of the debt he owed, he was stronger."

"It will depend on whether he wants to do business with me again," Henri said.

Silversleeves shook his head. "No. It will depend on many things," he replied. "On timing, on whether you need each other, on other opportunities, on who has more powerful friends. It is a question of hidden balances. Just like this game of chess." He paused deliberately. "Always remember this, Henri. Men trade for profit. They are driven by greed. But debt is about fear, and fear is stronger than greed. The true power, the weapon that defeats all others, is debt. Fools search for gold. The wise man studies debt. That is the key to all business." He smiled, then reached out his hand again. "Checkmate."

But Silversleeves's mind was on a greater game, the game in which debt would be a weapon and which he had been secretly playing for the last twenty-five years against Becket, the merchant of Caen. In this game, he was about to make a devastating move. Leofric the Saxon was going to serve his purpose very well. He had only a little longer to wait. Then there was the Dane. The great, red-bearded lout who had insulted him that day. Barnikel had been peripheral to the game, a mere pawn, but he could be fitted in. The plan would take care of Barnikel quite beautifully, so perfect was its hidden symmetry.

He was still smiling when Henri stood up, went to the window and called to him excitedly: "Father, look! There's something in the sky."

In the last hour the clouds had cleared to reveal a cold, hard winter night of stars, in the midst of which was now a most extraordinary sight.

Silently it hung in the sky, its tail stretching behind it in a long fan. All over Europe, from Ireland to Russia, from the islands of Scotland to the rocky shores of Greece, men looked up at the great, bearded star in horror and wondered what it meant.

The appearance of Halley's Comet in January 1066 is well recorded in the chronicles of the time. It was universally agreed that it must be a portent of ill omen, of some disaster that was about to befall mankind. In the island of England especially, threatened from so many sides, they had good reason to be afraid.

The boy with the white patch in his light brown hair gazed up at the great comet with fascination. His name was Alfred, after the great king. He was fourteen, and he had just taken a decision that infuriated his father and filled his mother with grief. He felt her nudge him now.

"You oughtn't to go. That star's a sign, Alfred. You stay put."

He chuckled and his blue eyes twinkled. "You really think that God Almighty sent that star to warn me, Mother? You think He wants the whole world to look up and say, 'Ah, that's God warning young Alfred not to go to London'?"

"You never know."

He kissed her. She was a warm, simple woman and he loved her. But he had made up his mind. "You and Father will be fine. He's already got one son to help in the smithy. There's nothing for me around here."

The harsh light from Halley's Comet illuminated a pleasant

scene. Here, in the flat, low-lying landscape twenty miles west of London, the Thames meandered through lush meadows and fields that now gleamed frostily in the starlight. A mile or two upstream lay the village of Windsor, a royal estate; nearby, a hill jutted over the stream like a watchtower, the only prominent feature in that placid landscape. These delightful surroundings had been the family's home ever since good King Alfred's reign, when they had fled there from the woods north of London to escape the marauding Vikings. It was a decision they had never regretted, for the land was rich, the living good.

One other factor made their lives pleasant. As the boy's father always reminded him: "We can go to the king himself if we want justice. Never forget, Alfred, that we are free."

This was crucial. By now, the organization of the Anglo-Saxon countryside was broadly similar to the rest of north-western Europe. The land was divided into county shires, each with a shire reeve – the sheriff – who collected the king's taxes and oversaw justice. Each shire was divided into hundreds, each hundred containing numerous estates. These were in the hands of thanes or lesser landowners, who, like the lords of Continental manors, held their own courts over their peasants.

But when it came to the peasantry, Anglo-Saxon England was a special case. While, in general, European peasants were either serfs or free, in England it was far more complex. There was a bewildering variety of legal statuses. Some peasants were slaves, mere chattels. Others were serfs, tied to the land and subject to a lord. Still others were free, paying rent only. Some were half free but paid rent, or free but owed particular services, and there were many other categories in between. Nor, of course, were men fixed in their positions. A serf could become free, or a freeman, too poor to pay his rent and taxes, descend into servitude. The resulting kaleidoscope pattern, as court records show, was often bewildering.

About their own status, however, the family of young Alfred was very clear. Apart from that brief and long-forgotten interlude when their ancestor Offa had been a slave of Cerdic the merchant, they had been free. True, they were only modest cottagers; their land was just the tiny smallholding known as a farthing. "But we pay a money rent, in silver pennies," Alfred's father could truly claim. "We don't labour for the lord like serfs."

Like every free man in the land, therefore, young Alfred proudly wore in his belt the symbol of his treasured status: a fine new dagger.

Since his grandfather's day, the family had been the village smiths. By the age of seven, Alfred could shoe a horse. By twelve he could swing the hammers nearly as well as his older brother. "You don't have to be big and strong," his father told his sons. "Skill is what matters. Let your tools do the work for you." And Alfred learned well. The fact that, like his grandfather, he had the family's webbed fingers did not seem to trouble him. At the age of fourteen, he was as good as his brother who was two years older.

"But there isn't work for two smiths in this village," he pointed out. "I've tried all the villages around – Windsor, Eton, even as far as Hampton. There's nothing. So," he declared proudly, "I'm going to London."

What did he know about London? Truth to tell, not much. Certainly he had never been there. But ever since he was little and had learned the family saying, "There's buried gold in London," the city had possessed a magic significance for him. "Is there really gold there?" he used to ask his parents.

It was no surprise, therefore, when his father scornfully remarked: "You think you'll find buried gold, I suppose."

Perhaps he would, he thought irritably. And when his mother timidly asked him when he meant to go, he suddenly felt inspired to answer: "Tomorrow morning."

Perhaps the strange star was speaking to him after all.

By the approach of Easter 1066, the kingdom of England had become agitated. The Saxon fleet was being hastily prepared for sea patrol. The king had taken direct charge of it.

The reports were coming in daily. William, the bastard Duke of Normandy, was preparing to invade. Knights from all over Normandy and its neighbouring territories were flocking to him. "And worst of all," Leofric informed Barnikel, "they say he has the Pope's blessing." Other adventurers – the Norsemen – were also threatening. The only question was when would the first blow be struck, and how?

Early one morning at this perilous time, when a cold night had left a frost upon the rutted streets, Barnikel the Dane was making his way from Leofric's house to his own on the eastern hill.

He had just passed over the little stream that ran down between the twin hills, and which, since it came through the city's northern wall, was now called the Walbrook, when he was arrested by a pitiful sight.

The lane lay along the line of the lower Roman thoroughfare. On his right, on the Walbrook's eastern bank, the Roman Governor's Palace had once stood, though the memory of its elegant courtyards was long gone now, covered by the German merchants' wharf. Along the street where sentries once patrolled, there was now a line of stalls and workshops belonging to the candlemakers. Candlewick Street, they called it. Of imperial grandeur there was not a trace – except for one curious object.

Somehow, the old milestone marker that had stood by the palace gate had remained, like the obstinate stump of some ancient oak, rooted for nine hundred years or more in its place by the side of the street. And because they were vaguely aware that this familiar though mysterious object came from the city's antiquity, the citizens referred to it, with some respect, as the London Stone.

It was beside the London Stone that Barnikel saw the pathetic little figure.

It was three days since Alfred had eaten. His filthy woollen cloak was wrapped tightly around him as he huddled by the Stone. His face was very pale. At the moment his feet were numb with cold. Later, if he could warm them somewhere, perhaps by a brazier, they would hurt.

The first month he had been in London, Alfred had been a young fellow seeking work, only he had found none and had no friends to sponsor him. By the second month he was cadging food. By the third, he was a vagrant. The people of London were not especially cruel, but vagrants threatened the community. Soon, he realized, someone would report him. For all he knew he would be dragged before the Hustings court, and then what? He did not know. So, as he heard the heavy footfall approaching him, he huddled even closer to the cold stone. Only when he was addressed did he look up, and saw, towering over him, the largest man he had ever beheld in his life.

"What is your name?"

Alfred told him.

"Where are you from?"

"Windsor."

"What is your trade?"

Again, Alfred told him. Was he free? Yes. When had he last eaten? Had he yet stolen? No. Only one barleycake, which had fallen on the ground. The questions continued like a catechism until finally the huge red-bearded man gave a snort, though what it signified Alfred did not know.

"Get up."

He did so. Then, unaccountably, he fell down. He shook his head and tried again, but once more his legs buckled. At that moment, more astonished than frightened, he felt the Dane's massive arms lift him up and toss him over one shoulder as though he was a small sack of flour, while the big man began striding along the street towards the East Cheap, humming to himself.

Not long afterwards Alfred found himself in a large homestead with a steep wooden roof on the far side of the eastern hill. Better yet, he was in the hall, before a huge brazier, where a quiet, grey-haired, broad-faced woman was heating a big bowl of broth that smelt, to him, like all the good meals he had ever eaten.

While she was getting this broth, Alfred looked around the hall. Everything in it seemed huge, from the great oak chair to the stout oak doors, and on the wall hung a mighty two-handed battle-axe. The Dane was standing on the other side of the brazier, so that Alfred could not see him very well. By and by, he remarked: "We'll feed you, my young friend, but then you must go home to where you came from. Do you understand?"

He had not liked to say anything, but since the Dane repeated his question, and since it seemed wrong to lie, he found the strength to shake his head.

"What! Are you defying me?"

It was a roar. Suddenly Alfred was afraid the huge Dane would change his mind and not feed him after all. Nevertheless, he found the courage to reply: "Not defying you, sir. But I'll not go back."

"You'll starve. You'll die. You know that?"

"I'll get by." He knew it was absurd, but there it was. "I'm not giving up, sir."

This was met by such a loud shout that he feared the massive Viking was about to strike him, but nothing happened.

Now the woman was ladling the broth into a smaller bowl, and motioning him to draw up to the table. As he did so, he was aware of the huge fellow moving towards him.

"Well," the deep voice demanded of his wife, "what do you think of him?"

"He's a poor-looking thing," she replied mildly.

"Yes. And yet," Alfred heard him chuckle, "in this boy dwells the heart of a hero. You hear that? A mighty warrior." With a great guffaw, he gave Alfred a clap on the back that almost sent him into the bowl of broth. "And do you know why? Because he won't give up. He just told me. He means it. The little fellow won't give up!"

His wife sighed. "Does this mean I have to keep him?"

"Why of course," he cried. "Because, young Alfred," he declared to the boy, "I have work for you to do."

All that summer, the Saxon fleet cruised up and down the English Channel. There was only one raid, on the port of Sandwich in Kent, which was quickly beaten off. After that, nothing. Over the horizon, William the Norman was biding his time.

For young Alfred, however, despite this danger, these months became the happiest of his life.

He soon came to know the Dane's family. Barnikel's wife, though strict, was kindly; they had several married children, and the eighteen-year-old son who was to marry Leofric's daughter still lived in the house. He was a stalwart, quiet version of his father and taught young Alfred how to tie sailors' knots.

It seemed to amuse the Dane to take the country boy about with him. His house on the eastern hill overlooked the bare, grassy slopes where the ravens dwelt and was close to a Saxon church called All Hallows. Each morning he would stride down the lane to Billingsgate to inspect the little ships and their cargoes of wool, grain or fish. Alfred liked the wharf, with its bracing smell of fish, tar and riverweed. Even better, though, were the visits to the western hill where Leofric lived. Now he was no longer a vagrant, what a joy it was to wander from St Paul's along the West Cheap, where each of the little lanes that came to meet it seemed to have its special trade – Fish Street and Bread Street, Wood Street and Milk Street, all the way to the Poultry at the far end – and hear the cries not only of the sellers of these products, but also of spicers, shoemakers, goldsmiths, furriers, quiltmakers, comb-makers and dozens of others. Only one thing had surprised him, and this was the number of pigsties along the stalls. It was a feature of city life that he had not expected, but Barnikel explained: "The pigs eat up the rubbish and keep the place clean."

Thanks to Barnikel, Alfred now began to understand more of London's character. In some ways the city was rural still. The Saxon settlement did not fill the huge walled enclosure; there were orchards and fields as well. Around the city lay great estates owned by the king, his chief men or the Church, and these landowners' estates existed inside the city walls too. "The city's divided into wards," the Dane told him. "About ten on each hill. But some of the wards are privately owned. We call them sokes." He reeled off the names of several nobles and churchmen who held these estates within London.

Yet London was still a world of its own. As he watched and listened to Barnikel each day, Alfred found himself constantly amazed. "The city is so rich," Barnikel explained, "that it's taxed like a whole shire." Proudly he listed all the liberties that the city had won: trading concessions, fishing rights over miles of the Thames, hunting rights over the whole county of Middlesex that lay on its northern side and many others.

But it was not these things, but rather something else – something in the air, yet something very tangible – that truly impressed the sharp-eyed boy. For a time he could not find words to summarize this perception, but then one day, in a chance remark, the Dane provided them.

"The walls of London touch the sea," he said.

Yes, the boy thought. That is it.

Resting as it did at the head of the long Thames Estuary, looking daily to the sea, the great walled settlement had for generations been a home to seafarers and traders from all over the northern world. And though they obeyed the authority of the island's Saxon or Danish kings, these men of the seas did not expect to be interfered with too much. They organized their own guilds to regulate trade and defence. They knew their value to the king, and this was recognized. A great merchant like Barnikel's grandfather, who had made three voyages to the Mediterranean, had been created a nobleman. Three generations of Barnikels had served as captains of the city's Defence Guild, which could produce a formidable force. The city's walls were so mighty that even King Canute had respected them. "No invader can take London," these Anglo-Danish merchant barons liked to boast. "And no king is king unless we say so."

It was London's pride that Alfred sensed. "For the citizens of London," the Dane explained, "are free."

It was an old English custom that if a serf ran away to a town and lived there unclaimed for a year and a day, he was free. True, there were serfs and even slaves in the households of some of the landowners and rich merchants, though most of the apprentices were, like himself, free. But in London, he discovered, the word "free" meant something more. A merchant who paid his entrance fee, or an artisan who had completed his apprenticeship, became a freeman of the city. They had the right to trade, set up a stall, sell goods and vote at the Folkmoot. They paid the king's taxes; and all others, whether they came from the next county or beyond the sea were "foreigners" and could not trade there until they had been awarded citizenship. No wonder, then, that the Londoners cherished their freedom. As the boy felt his dagger at his side, he flushed with pleasure to think he was to be part of it.

After a week, when Alfred's strength had fully recovered, Barnikel turned to the boy one morning and remarked: "Your apprenticeship begins today."

The quarter to which the Dane now led him lay just outside the city's eastern wall. Here, a little stream ran down to the Thames, and along its banks were numerous workshops. It was a busy area, controlled by the city's Defence Guild. As they approached a long wooden building and Alfred heard the familiar sound of hammer on anvil, he supposed that he was to be apprenticed to a blacksmith. It was only after they entered and he looked around him that his heart almost missed a beat.

They were in an armoury.

Of all the tradesmen, to a boy brought up as a blacksmith, the armourer was the prince of craftsmen. Gazing round at the coats of chain mail, the helmets, shields and swords, Alfred was speechless.

The master armourer who now approached was a tall, bony-faced man with a stoop. His mild blue eyes were kindly, but as he noticed the curious webbing on the boy's hands he turned to Barnikel doubtfully. "Can he do the work?"

"He can," the Dane answered firmly. And so Alfred's apprenticeship began.

Perhaps no days in his life were ever happier. As the newest apprentice, Alfred was set to work on menial tasks – fetching water from the stream, stoking the fire and working the bellows. This he did without question and nobody took much notice of him.

At the end of the first day he went back with the other apprentices to their lodgings. Usually apprentices were not paid, but lived free in their master's house, but the armourer was a widower who disliked this arrangement. Instead, on the slope of Cornhill his sister had a house, divided into tenements, and just behind it lay outbuildings where the noisy apprentices lodged together.

The armoury being large, there were eight other apprentices of varying ages, and as he performed his duties, Alfred had a chance to observe them. One struck unevenly with the hammer; another gripped the tongs too tightly, introducing stress into his work. Another used a chisel badly. He noticed all this but kept his thoughts to himself.

On the third day, however, he was given a small piece of work to do: some metal filing and a dented helmet that needed hammering out. He did both jobs carefully and handed them to the master, who took them without comment.

The next day, the master called him to help another apprentice, a year older than himself, who was putting rivets in a helmet. Alfred held the helmet while the other put the rivet in. Then the master said: "Let the new boy try." With ill grace the older apprentice changed places. But when Alfred began to rivet, he made a complete mess of it. With a grunt of irritation the master turned to the older boy. "Show him how to do it," he remarked, and walked away.

But if Alfred thought that was the end of the matter, he was wrong. That evening, as the apprentices were leaving, the master called him over and, hovering by the forge, asked him in a soft voice: "Why did you do that?"

"Do what, sir?"

"I've watched you. You hold a hammer as if it's part of your arm. You deliberately made a mistake today. Why?"

Alfred looked at him carefully, then confessed. "I've worked at my father's forge since before I can remember, sir. But I'm new here, and I nearly starved before Barnikel brought me to you. If the other apprentices get jealous, they could make my life hell. Even drive me out." He grinned wryly. "So I want them to think they're teaching me until we're friends."

He blushed, afraid this might sound conceited. "I'm only a smith, though," he added quickly. "I want to learn to be an armourer."

The master nodded thoughtfully. "Work hard, Alfred," he said quietly. "And we'll see."

As the weeks went by, besides learning his craft, his work in the armoury taught young Alfred something of great significance for the Anglo-Saxon kingdom. If the fleet was readying itself to defend the island at sea, preparations on land were a very different matter. "We've been expecting an attack ever since winter," he remarked in astonishment, "yet nobody's ready."

The English kingdom had no standing army, nor forces of hired mercenaries. Her army was the *fyrd* – a levy of landowners and peasants. Not a day passed without some flustered Saxon landowner appearing with equipment in need of urgent attention: a blunt sword or battle-axe; a heavy, round Saxon shield with straps on the back that always needed replacing. Alfred could hardly believe they were so disorganized.

Above all, they would bring in their armour.

The armour of the warriors of Anglo-Saxon England was the same as that used all over Europe: the coat of chain mail. Known probably since the Bronze Age, the principle of chain mail was simple and convenient. Small, riveted rings of metal, usually about four-tenths of an inch in diameter, were linked together to form a long shirt that reached past the knees. Being loose and flexible – unlike the later suits of plate armour – a coat of chain mail could be altered to fit different wearers. Many of the coats Alfred saw had belonged to the wearers' fathers. They were valuable – ordinary foot soldiers could seldom afford them – and treasured accordingly.

But they had two disadvantages. They became worn and torn, and above all, the large surface area of so many links made them very prone to rust. As the most junior apprentice, Alfred was given the tedious job of cleaning them, so that soon, whenever the owners of these garments appeared, a cheerful cry would go up from the other apprentices: "Alfred! Rust!"

Still, he was happy. The other apprentices had quickly accepted him. Nor did Barnikel forget him. Every week he was summoned to the Dane's hall for a hearty meal, and though he was only a poor apprentice in a rich man's house, he felt almost part of the family. He also came to know Leofric's daughter, who was often there, and so admired her gentle simplicity that by midsummer he was half in love with her himself.

It was towards the end of June that his life at the armoury began to change.

They had been told to produce a dozen new coats of mail. Alfred found this prospect exciting, though the master cursed the short notice and the other apprentices groaned. Before each coat of mail could be begun, however, there was one miserable task to perform, and this was to make the wire for the links.

How he hated it. A long, thin iron bar was heated in the forge to soften it, and then its end was worked through a steel draw plate with a hole in the middle. The heaviest apprentice would begin, dragging the rod through the plate; then repeating the process again with another plate which had a smaller hole. And again; and again, so that the rod was stripped and stretched as it came through. But once it was reduced, the later drawing out was done by Alfred. Holding the thick wire in gripping tongs attached to a broad leather belt around his waist, he would haul himself backwards across the workshop floor like a man in a tug of war, until his whole body was aching.

At the end of one day of this activity, the apprentices were leaving to go drinking together when the master called out: "I need help. Alfred will stay behind."

There was a sympathetic laugh from the others as he brusquely ordered the boy to tend the bellows, and for another two hours he kept Alfred busy with menial tasks before sending him home.

A few days later the same thing occurred, except that this time the master made another junior apprentice stay too and kept them both occupied for three hours before letting them go.

The making of a coat of mail fascinated Alfred. It was so simple, yet so exacting. First the wire was formed into rings with open ends. This was done by winding it round a metal spindle and then making a cut down the length of the coil. The newly formed rings were then pushed through a tapering hole in a steel block to force one of the ends neatly to overlap the other. The rings were softened in the brazier and then, while hot, each was put in a mould and given two taps with a hammer to flatten the overlapping ends. Now, using piercing tongs, one apprentice punched a tiny hole through the flattened ends. "That's where the rivet will go," he explained. After that, another prised the ends gently apart again so that the rings could be linked together, and tossed them into a bucket of oil. "Always use oil," the master admonished them. "If you put hot iron in water it cools too fast and becomes brittle."

But what astonished Alfred was how at the end of this process, the work had been so precisely done that he could never see any difference between the rings. In fact the links rarely varied by more than twelve-thousandths of one inch.

The third time the master ordered Alfred to stay late, the other apprentices groaned, and two of them even offered to take his place. But the master only grunted, "The newest apprentice does the dirty work," and waved them away.

This time, however, after an hour, the master called Alfred to him. Speaking little, he made the boy perform each of the tasks – winding and cutting, overlapping, piercing and opening – correcting him when necessary, nodding quietly once he had got it right. Then, leading the boy to a large trestle table in the middle of the workshop, he instructed: "Now watch."

The art of the master armourer was like that of the master tailor. First he would lay out the open rings in rows so that each could be linked to four others – two diagonally above and two below. The shape of the coat was like a long shirt, with elbow-length sleeves. The lower part was slit back and front for ease when riding. The top was formed into a hood that could be pushed back off the head on to the shoulders. The neck was slit like the top of a shirt and tightened with laces, whilst a flap, held in place with a strap, usually came across the front of the hood to protect the mouth.

Whereas a tailor could cut and fold his cloth, the armourer had to rearrange the rings geometrically, and this arrangement resembled nothing so much as a knitting pattern. Here, a link would be joined to five others instead of four; there, one would be left dangling loose. When finished, however, so close and intricate was the workmanship that it was almost impossible to find the different joins.

For several hours now, Alfred had watched enthralled as the master showed him how this was done, demonstrating the geometry, the lines of stress, the need for ease of movement in the metal shirt that had already protected fighting men for over a thousand years. As he worked by lamplight, the master explained: "Always rivet the same way, from the outside. You can feel why." When Alfred ran his hands over the coat, he realized that the outside was rough, while the inside, where the rivets were flattened and which would rest against a leather undercoat, was smooth as cloth.

On some of the rivet heads the master would stamp his personal mark. And then the coat of mail was complete.

Or almost. One thing still remained. The iron used by the medieval armourers was relatively soft. To toughen it for battle, it had to be case-hardened. Now, therefore, the master rolled up the finished garment in crushed charcoal, packed it in an iron box, and put it into the forge. Soon it glowed red-hot.

"The iron and charcoal interact," he explained, "and the iron turns to steel. But you must not heat it too long," he warned, "or it gets brittle. You want the outside to be hard as diamonds and the inside to remain flexible."

Then, having shown him these mysteries of his art, he let the boy go home.

From this time on, at least once a week Alfred was summoned to stay behind. And while the other apprentices supposed he was operating the bellows or pulling wire, the master quietly taught him the techniques that were normally reserved for the senior apprentices only. Often, they worked together late into the night, Alfred's hammer and tongs and pincers flying to their task. They spoke to no one of these sessions, but the boy had an instinct that Barnikel was kept informed by the master, although he could not be sure that this was so.

The crisis broke in September.

The events that were to change the face of England for ever were made possible by a simple and regrettable fact. In September, it being the month of harvest, the men manning the English fleet announced that they had to go home. Nothing King Harold could say would stop them. Accordingly, Alfred, Barnikel and Leofric stood on the quay at Billingsgate one morning and watched the last of the little sailing vessels tie up. From which moment, as they all knew, the Anglo-Saxon kingdom lay open to invaders.

They struck almost at once.

The invasion planned by William of Normandy could hardly have gone better. His timing was perfect. Two weeks after the English fleet put in, the King of Norway led an attack on the shores of northern England and took York. King Harold raced northwards and, in a well-fought battle, smashed the invaders. However, he and his army were now two hundred and fifty miles away from the south coast – where William promptly landed.

His army was not large, but it was formidably trained. Some, the élite, were retinues headed by great magnates with famous names like de Montfort, but most were men for hire, landless knights from Normandy, Brittany, France, Flanders and even southern Italy. Thanks to William's staunch support of the Church, they rode under the papal banner. On arrival at the bay of Pevensey, near the little settlement of Hastings, they built an earth and wooden fort and set out to reconnoitre.

In Alfred's memory, the events of the next few days were forever blurred. The king returned to London. The city was arming. The Staller – the head of the city's Defence Guild – and his captains were commandeering every able-bodied man they could find. Each day Barnikel stormed into the armoury with fresh demands, and they worked all night.

But one small scene always remained in the boy's mind with clarity. It took place one evening in Barnikel's hall, after the Dane and Leofric had returned from a big council meeting with the king. The Dane was agitated, the Saxon thoughtful.

"How can he hold back?" Barnikel cried. "Strike now!"

Leofric was less sanguine. "The army's exhausted after the march south. Our London contingent is brave, but it's no good pretending they're a match for trained mercenaries. However, if we burn all the crops between here and the coast and destroy his transport, we can starve them. Then," he added grimly, "we should kill them all."

Barnikel grunted in disgust. "This family will fight."

Yet, as Alfred subsequently learned, the more cautious advice was exactly the course that King Harold's wisest counsellors urged upon him.

Soon afterwards, on 11 October, for reasons that are not entirely clear, before half the reinforcements he needed from the shires had arrived, King Harold of England marched out of London towards the southern coast at the head of about seven thousand men. In place of honour, by the king's standard, marched the Staller, Barnikel and the London contingent. Barnikel's son went with him. Leofric, because of his injured back, could not go. The Dane was carrying his two-handed battle-axe.

Despite all their efforts, young Alfred noticed that not all the London contingent were well armed. One man, wearing a foolish grin, was carrying a window shutter instead of a proper shield.

Leofric hesitated. Could he bring himself to go in?

It was evening, the hour after vespers, and he had come to that important quarter on the western hill just below the quiet precincts of St Paul's. Several days had passed since the king and the army had left. No word had come. The city was quiet, waiting anxiously for news.

Behind him, the long wooden roof of the Saxon cathedral loomed over the thatched houses. On his left stood the guarded courtyard of the London Mint. Ahead, the narrow lane, carpeted with yellowed leaves, sloped down steeply towards the river. A faint smell from the cathedral brewhouse nearby mingled agreeably with the scent of wood smoke in the still, damp air. A church bell was tolling. And in the west, the sky was reddening, deep crimson like a rich man's cloak.

The house of Silversleeves was quietly impressive. The stone hall facing him was not large, but well built, with an outside staircase leading to the main floor. Slowly and with misgiving, he went up.

Silversleeves and his two sons greeted him politely. It was strange how, inside their own hall, their clean-shaven faces and long noses seemed less out of place. Indeed, though his own knee-length green gown was of the best cloth, Leofric could not help noticing that their longer Norman gowns were decidedly elegant.

A great fire burned at one end of the room. At the other, a tall window was filled not with oiled parchment like the windows in his own house, but with green German glass. The hangings on the walls were rich. On the table, instead of smoking lamps stood large and expensive candles of sweet-smelling beeswax.

Several other people were there – a Flemish merchant, a goldsmith he knew slightly, and two priests from St Paul's. He noticed that the last two especially were treating Silversleeves with deep respect. There was also one other group, the reason for whose presence the Saxon could not immediately guess. Sitting on a small oak bench in the corner furthest from the fire, three poor and undernourished lay monks were watching the proceedings with mournful interest.

Excusing himself while he completed his business with the others, Silversleeves left Leofric near the fire with his two sons, which gave the Saxon some opportunity to study them. Henri, who at once began a polite conversation, seemed agreeable enough. His brother, Ralph, however, was not. Silent, awkward and sullen, nature seemed in him to have debased the family's features. His nose was long, but also brutal; his eyes were strangely puffy; where his brother's hands were long, his were gnarled and clumsy. He stared at Leofric suspiciously.

All Leofric knew, as he gazed at them, was that one of these two young men apparently wanted to marry his daughter.

So troubled was he by this thought that for a few moments

he entered a kind of daze, and at first did not quite take in what Henri was earnestly telling him. "A great day for my family . . ." he was saying. "My father is building a church."

A church! Now Leofric was all attention. He gazed at Henri in wonder. "Your father is endowing a church?" The young man nodded.

The Norman must be rich indeed, far richer than Leofric had realized. No wonder the priests were treating him with such respect.

There were already more than thirty churches in the Anglo-Danish city. Most were small Saxon buildings with wooden walls and earthen floors; some were little more than private chapels. But to found a church was a sure sign that a family had ascended to fortune.

Silversleeves, he learned, had just acquired a plot of land below his own holding. A good spot on Watling Street, above the area of wine warehouses known as the Vintry. "It will be dedicated to St Lawrence," Henri explained. He smiled. "I dare say," he coolly added, "that since there's another St Lawrence nearby, they'll call it St Lawrence Silversleeves." This custom of double names commemorating both a saint and a founder was already becoming one of the features of London churches.

Nor was this all. That very day, the young man added, another solemn consecration had taken place: that of the merchant himself. "My father has taken holy orders," he said proudly. "So that he can officiate at the church."

It was not uncommon. Whatever the piety of Edward the Confessor himself, the English Church during his reign had sunk into a complete and cheerful cynicism. True, the Church was still a mighty institution. Its lands were everywhere, its monasteries like little kingdoms. A man on the run could still seek sanctuary in a church and not even the king could touch him. But morality was another thing. Priests were frequently and openly living with, in effect, common-law wives, and left their church livings to their children or even gave them as dowries. Rich merchants took orders, as Silversleeves was doing, and might even, if they fancied the dignity, become canons of St Paul's. Indeed, it was in the pious hope that William of Normandy might reform these abuses that the Pope had given the planned invasion his blessing.

Whatever the Pope may have thought, however, it was clear to Leofric that the house of Silversleeves was grown powerful indeed.

Several minutes passed before the priests and merchants left, then Silversleeves himself advanced towards Leofric.

"So that we can take our time," he said pleasantly, "I hope you will sup with us this evening."

From behind a screen came three serving women, who spread a large white cloth upon the table. They brought two earthenware pitchers, knives, spoons, bowls and drinking vessels. Once this was speedily and quietly done, Silversleeves motioned him forward.

It happened that this was a fast day in the calendar of the Church; at this hour, devout men ate only a light collation of vegetables with their bread and water. Since Silversleeves was now a priest, Leofric resigned himself to a harsh diet, but in this, too, he underestimated his host. At last turning his gaze upon the three depressed lay monks, who were still sitting on their bench in the corner, Silversleeves beckoned them to approach. "These good men fast and say penances for us," he blithely explained. And giving to each of these worthies a silver penny, he waved them away and they sadly retired. Then he said grace.

The meal began with a capon brewet – a rich broth with spices on top.

It was the practice of those times for men to sit along one side of the table only, the food being served from the other, as though across a counter. Leofric found himself placed on Silversleeves's right, with Ralph beside him. Henri was furthest away, on his father's left. The brewet was served in a two-handled bowl placed between each pair of diners, courtesy demanding that one should share with one's neighbour. It fell to Leofric, therefore, to dip his spoon into the same bowl as Ralph.

If only the fellow ate more pleasantly. Leofric was accustomed to all kinds of table manners amongst the bearded Norsemen of the port, but for some reason the little dribble of food that came from the corner of Ralph's clean-shaven yet brutal mouth filled him with a particular repugnance. Not to seem wanting in the courtesies, his silent companion also offered him his goblet to share, which Leofric was naturally bound to do.

Still, the meal was impressive. Silversleeves kept his table like a French noble. After the brewet came a porray – a soup of leeks, onions and other vegetables cooked in milk. Then a civet of grilled hare cooked in wine. As was the custom, the tablecloth was long, so that the diners could use it as a napkin, and Leofric was impressed to notice that, whether because of the mess Ralph made, or whether it was simply another example of his host's magnificence, the cloth was changed between every course, just as if he had been dining with the king.

Silversleeves himself was a fastidious eater. He rinsed his hands frequently in a bowl of rose-water. He ate slowly, taking small bites. And yet, Leofric observed, it was extraordinary how much food he put away in this decorous fashion. The wine in the two earthenware pitchers was also excellent – the most prized, from the Paris region. Leofric drank just enough for it to seem to him that as they rose and dipped over their food in the glow of the candlelight, the three noses beside him had become even longer than before.

Finally came a frumenty, a custard dish with figs, nuts and spiced wine. Only then did Silversleeves broach the business in hand.

He began indirectly. They had been speaking generally of the invasion, and what news they might expect to hear. "Of course," he said meditatively, "as a Norman, I know some of William's men." And he named de Montfort, Mandeville and several of the Norman duke's closest confidants. "Whoever wins," he remarked, "it will probably be the same for our business."

But not, Leofric thought bleakly, for mine.

For a few moments Silversleeves was silent, letting the Saxon think his own, sad thoughts. Then, with a smile, he came smoothly to the point.

"One of my sons," he said easily, "wishes to marry your daughter." Before Leofric could frame a suitable response, he gently continued: "We seek no dowry, except the alliance with your good name."

Leofric gasped. This was as astonishing as it was courteous. But it was nothing compared with what followed. "I can also offer an arrangement that might be of interest to you. If this marriage takes place, I should like to take over your two debts, to Barnikel and Becket. You need never concern yourself with them again." At which he dipped his nose into his beaker of wine and then stared politely at the tablecloth.

For several moments Leofric was completely speechless. When, in his message, Silversleeves had stated that he could be of help to him, the Saxon had realized that the Norman was powerful, but this was far beyond anything he had dreamed of.

"But why?" he asked simply.

Silversleeves gave what might have been a sentimental smile.

"All for love," he said softly.

To be free of his debts. Perhaps an alliance with this Norman might even save the estate if William should triumph.

"Which son wants my daughter?" he asked gruffly.

Silversleeves looked surprised. "I thought you knew. It is Henri."

And Leofric was so relieved it was not Ralph, he scarcely troubled to notice that young Henri's eyes were cold.

Yet even with this prospect opened up before him, he knew he could not. Hadn't he given Barnikel his word? It was now, for the first time in his life, that just for a moment the honest Saxon experienced a truly base thought. If by chance the Dane or his son were to be killed in battle, then he would be free of his promise and the family fortune saved.

"I will consider the matter," he said weakly, "but I fear —"

"We shall await your decision," Silversleeves interposed smoothly, and raised his beaker. "There is, by the way, one small condition," he began to add.

But what this was, Leofric did not discover. At this moment, one of the lay monks burst in at the door, and as Silversleeves looked up in annoyance, the fellow cried out wildly:

"Sirs! The king is dead. The Duke of Normandy has beaten him."

"Where?"

"At a place by the coast. Near Hastings."

The Battle of Hastings, which so profoundly changed the course of England's history, took place on Saturday, 14 October.

William of Normandy had several advantages. He attacked

at first light, surprising King Harold. He had formidable contingents of bowmen and trained cavalry, neither of which the English king possessed. Also the English hilltop position was too narrow, allowing the bowmen to concentrate their fire with deadly effect.

Yet even so, the battle went on all day. The bowmen failed to break the English defence. When the cavalry charged, they wilted before the tremendous two-handed axe blows from men like Barnikel, which bit through their chain mail. They fled, and only William himself prevented a general rout.

Hour after hour they continued. Twice the cavalry advanced and pretended to flee, luring many of the English down the hill into a trap. Gradually, as their leaders fell, the English were worn down, but even then, as the long, grey afternoon began to darken, their battle line was still standing, and might have held till nightfall, had not a single arrow, loosed, it is said, at random, chanced to fall into the socket of King Harold's eye, wounding him gravely. Minutes later he had received a deathblow.

Then it was over. The Staller of London, badly wounded, was carried from the field. Amongst the little group of stalwarts with whom he had fought by the king's standard, Barnikel and his son survived to accompany him.

It was two months later, on a bright December morning, that, in the churchyard of St Paul's, where the Folkmoot had just finished meeting, several hundred of London's citizens witnessed a curious scene.

Barnikel of Billingsgate was red in the face. He was glowering at his friend Leofric, and he had just bellowed, in a voice that could be heard halfway down the West Cheap, a single, terrible word:

"Traitor!"

Not that his rage was directed only at the Saxon merchant. The huge Dane was furious with them all.

The weeks after Hastings had been tense. William could not immediately press home his advantage: his troops were weakened after the battle; disease broke out in his camp. He had to wait at the coast for reinforcements. Meanwhile, contingents from the north and other shires had finally begun to arrive in

London. The Witan hastily named the legitimate heir, old Edward's foreign nephew, as king.

"Why don't we strike again?" Barnikel would roar.

Yet even to young Alfred the situation had been plain enough. The city was full of armed men, but there seemed little direction. The Staller, still wounded, was carried about in a litter. The young prince, king in name only, was seldom seen. The northern nobles were talking of returning home. Even the apprentices heard rumours that the Archbishop of Canterbury was secretly negotiating with the Normans.

On 1 December, William of Normandy had finally made his move. Advancing up the old Roman road of Watling Street, through Canterbury and Rochester, his advance guard had reached the southern end of London Bridge itself. The wooden bridge was defended; the city gates closed. The Normans had contented themselves with setting fire to the houses on the southern bank before retiring. "He's too clever to attack the bridge," Leofric remarked. "He'll wear us down instead."

Which was precisely what the Norman did. Slowly flanking the city, he crossed the river upstream, beyond Windsor, and then circled to the north, burning the farms as he went. "A few more days," Leofric had grimly noted, "and he'll come to our land." By mid-December both the archbishop and even the Staller had made visits to his camp, and the Saxon merchant judged: "The city will hold out for terms."

The terms came. All the city's ancient rights and privileges would be respected. William of Normandy would be a father to them. That morning, beside St Paul's, Leofric the merchant, with grim common sense, had not hesitated to state his position: "We should accept."

Even the Staller agreed. London would yield to William and there was nothing Barnikel could do about it.

"Traitor!" he shouted again. And then half London heard him say: "As for your daughter, keep her. My son will marry no traitor's child. Do you hear?"

Leofric heard. In the circumstances, sad though the business was, he supposed he should thank his stars.

"As you wish," he replied, and walked away.

It was three days later when they brought Barnikel the news of Hilda's betrothal to Henri Silversleeves. For a few moments he could not believe it.

"But you told him we didn't want her. You refused the marriage," his son pointed out miserably.

"He might have known I didn't really mean it," the Dane moaned, before it occurred to him that Leofric had.

And then Barnikel of Billingsgate became very angry indeed.

It was generally agreed by the inhabitants of Billingsgate and All Hallows that there had been nothing like it in their lifetime. Even old men who could remember the entire reign of King Canute and would swear they had seen Ethelred the Unready, confessed they had witnessed nothing better. People stood in their doorways or leaned out of their windows; a few desperadoes who had run up from the wharf gathered, ready to scatter in a moment, only thirty paces from Barnikel's door.

The Dane's rage continued for more than an hour. The next day, when his family ventured back into the house, they could not prevent their neighbours from entering with them to survey the damage he had wrought. It was awesome.

Three barrels of ale smashed, seven earthenware pitchers, six wooden platters, two beds, a cauldron, five wooden stools, fifteen pots of preserved fruit, a chest. Twisted beyond all further use: three meat hooks and the spit on which the meat was roasted. Broken: the shaft of a double-handed battle-axe. Further destroyed or greatly reduced: a trestle table, three wooden window shutters, two oak doors, and the larder wall.

Even his Viking ancestors, they said, would not have disdained these efforts.

The coronation of William the Conqueror of England was fixed for Christmas Day 1066. It took place in the sacred church of Westminster Abbey.

Silversleeves and Leofric attended, standing side by side. The marriage had been fixed for the following summer. Leofric was free of his debts. The sole condition on which the Norman had insisted turned out to be that Leofric should henceforth import his wines through Silversleeves and cease to do business with Becket, the merchant of Caen. Leofric did this with some regret, but it seemed a small price to pay.

It was with some surprise that, two days after the coronation, young Alfred, chancing to meet Barnikel in the East

Cheap and remarking that the Norman king was making himself master of London now, received this admonition:

"Wait and see."

Unusually for the Dane, it was said very quietly. Alfred wondered what it meant.

Chapter 5

The Tower

1078

And now by the riverside, below the slopes where the ravens dwelt, a new presence was beginning to rise.

It had always been a quiet place, this south-eastern corner of the city where the ancient Roman wall came down to the Thames and the spur of the eastern hill created its natural open-air theatre by the water. A few fragments of the old Roman buildings had stood there, like guardian sentinels, or actors from some antique drama, turned to stone. But if the croaking ravens on the slopes had been expecting entertainment from the grassy stage below, then they had been waiting for the play to recommence for nearly a thousand years.

Until King William came.

For now, on this sheltered green, a large earthwork had been formed, behind which were the beginnings of a new building. From its foundations alone, it was clear that it would be massive.

It was made of grey stone. And it was called the Tower.

When King William I conquered England, he made a very understandable mistake.

Although there were still rivals for the island kingdom, he had assumed that his nobles, who were not so great in number, would settle and live peaceably with the English, side by side. After all, wasn't that what had happened with the Danish King Canute? And even though he spoke French, wasn't he, William, a Norseman too?

To begin with, all his actions had been conciliatory. England kept her Saxon common law, London her privileges, and though, as was normal throughout the medieval world, some estates had been confiscated to provide for his followers, many

English nobles had in fact kept their lands during those early years.

So why the devil couldn't these cursed English be reasonable? For twelve years now there had been challenges to the Norman king. First there had been English revolts; Scotland had threatened; the Danes had invaded. More than once it had looked as though William might lose his new island kingdom. And each time, those Anglo-Saxon nobles he thought he could trust had proved to be false, and the harassed Norman had been forced to bring more mercenaries from overseas, and to reward more of these foreign knights with estates confiscated from a new set of Saxon traitors. So it was that, over more than a decade, the old English nobility had been replaced. And with truth the Conqueror could claim: "They have only themselves to blame."

These were also the years when another innovation began to change the face of England.

At first the Norman castle at London was quite a modest structure: a simple, stout wooden tower built on a high earth mound and surrounded by a palisade. This was the Norman motte-and-bailey. It was simple but strong, and it overawed any town. Such castles had already been built to garrison Warwick, York, Sarum and numerous other English boroughs. But at the two key eastern defensive sites, here at London and at Colchester on the east coast, something more ambitious had now been planned: a massive castle keep, not of wood, but of stone. Its message to the Londoners was bleak.

"King William is your master."

It was morning. Under a hot August sun, the labourers were swarming like so many ants on the building site by the river.

Ralph Silversleeves stood with a whip in his hand. Before him, the young labourer was gazing up hopefully, holding out the small object like a religious offering.

"You did this?"

The young fellow nodded, and Silversleeves stared at it thoughtfully. The thing was remarkable. No doubt about it. Then he looked at the supplicant again. It gratified him to know that the youth's entire life now lay in his hands.

The Conquest had been good for Ralph. All his life he had known that he was the family fool. Though he would, one day, inherit equally from his father, it was still his clever brother Henri who would run the family business. He admired Henri; he wished he could be like him. But he knew that he could not. He was useless, and people laughed at him.

But with the coming of King William, things had changed. His father had obtained a position for him with no less a figure than the magnate Geoffrey de Mandeville, the king's chief agent in London. Now, for the first time in his life, Ralph could feel himself a fellow of consequence. The fact that Mandeville only used him for jobs that were menial and brutal did not trouble him. "I am a Norman," he could say. One of the new élite. For the last year he had been the overseer at the new Tower of London.

"So, Osric," he said coolly, "what are we going to do with you?"

He was a small fellow, only sixteen years old, but his hard life and the disfigurement he had suffered had already given him an ageless look. His short legs were bandy, his fingers stubby, his solemn eyes set in a head that was too big for his body.

He came from a village in the west of England, near the ancient settlement of Sarum. Not long after the Conquest, the village had passed into the hands of one of William's greatest magnates. Though they were good craftsmen, amongst the hundreds of peasant families on the magnate's vast landholdings, young Osric's had been of no special significance, and the great magnate would never have known of his existence if Osric had not foolishly set a snare to trip the horse of one of his knights, who as a consequence had broken his arm. The boy might have expected death, but King William, still hoping to ingratiate himself with his English subjects, had told his followers to show clemency. So they had only slit young Osric's nose.

In the midst of his solemn face, therefore, there was now a sad little reddish-blue mess. He breathed through his mouth. And he hated all Normans.

Since the magnate had also been granted the manor of Chelsea, upstream from London, he had sent the boy there. A year later, his steward had sold Osric to another magnate, none other than Geoffrey de Mandeville. Now the boy was not sure whether he was a serf or a slave. But one thing he did know: if he gave any trouble, Ralph Silversleeves would cut off his ears.

He waited nervously, therefore, whilst the surly overseer considered his verdict.

As the sun beat down, it seemed to Osric that the site where they were standing was like a huge, mysterious forge. The grassy platform was like a great green anvil; the carpenters, with the tap-tapping of their hammers echoing softly round the slopes, might have been so many elfin blacksmiths.

Within the curve of the high ground, the Tower lay in its own, inner enclosure. Just east of it was the ancient Roman wall; on its western and northern sides, the earthwork rampart and palisade of the wooden fort had been left in place. Within the enclosure stood several workshops, storehouses and some stables.

Beside the riverbank were moored three large wooden barges, one full of rubble, the second piled with ragstone from Kent, and the third containing a hard, pale stone from Caen in Normandy. Gangs of men were dragging handcarts from the river up to the foundations of the Tower.

They were massive. The keep itself was over a hundred feet square, and whenever he stared down into the growing foundations, young Osric's heart sank. The trench that stretched before him each morning seemed endless. Not only was it long and deep, its width too was amazing: at their base, the walls of the new Tower were as much as twenty-six feet wide. As the masons quietly tap-tapped on the anvil of London, whole bargeloads of stone disappeared into this vast cavity like molten ore into an enormous open mould.

How hard the work was. For months he had hauled the carts up the mound until his small back was almost breaking. Often, his face red from the heat and exertion, his mouth and eyes full of dust, he would try to rest his weary body until a flick of Ralph's whip or a kick from one of the foremen sent him miserably back to his task. His stubby hands, once raw, were now covered with calluses. Only one thing made his life bearable, and that was to watch the carpenters.

There was a great deal of work for carpenters on a building site like this. There were wooden ramps, hoists and scaffolding; in due course there would also be beams to make, and floorboards. Whenever he had a spare moment, he would hang around them, watching all they did. It was only natural. Coming from a family that had always supplied the village with craftsmen, he was instinctively drawn to such men. And in their turn, the carpenters, sensing his ability, would let him wander among them and sometimes show him the tricks of their trade.

How he longed to work with the carpenters! It was this desire that had inspired him to make his courageous move. Thanks to a kindly craftsman, he had been practising on ends of wood for three weeks, and now, at last, he had produced something to be proud of. It was quite modest, a simple joint of two pieces of wood, but so perfectly planed, so neatly fitted, that any one of the carpenters would have been happy to call it his own work.

This was the offering he had placed in Ralph Silversleeves's hands with the plea, "Could I not help the carpenters, sir?"

As Ralph turned it over in his large hands, he was thoughtful. If this serf of his master's could be turned into a good craftsman, Mandeville would no doubt be glad of it. Certainly this squat little fellow with his large head and his split nose was of no particular value as a heavy labourer. At that moment, Osric was about to get his heart's desire.

But for one fatal mistake.

"So, you think you could be a carpenter?" Ralph idly enquired.

Supposing it would help his cause, Osric replied eagerly: "Oh yes, sir. My older brother is a fine craftsman. I'm sure I could be one too." And then wondered why a strange flicker almost like a wince of pain passed across the overseer's face.

Poor Osric. He could not have known about the nerve he had struck. If I can never hope to equal my clever older brother, thought Ralph, why should this miserable fellow hope to equal his?

Calmly, therefore, and, it seemed, with a kind of grim pleasure, the big-nosed Norman delivered his verdict.

"Your brother is a carpenter, Osric. But you are only a beast of burden, and so, my little friend, you shall remain."

Then, for no obvious reason, he flicked his whip across the boy's solemn face before sending him back to work.

* * *

The two men sat facing each other across a table. For a while neither of them spoke as they considered their dangerous work, though either could have said, "If we get caught, they'll kill us."

It was Barnikel who had called the meeting in his house by the little church of All Hallows, which now overlooked the rising Tower, and he had done so for a simple reason. For the first time in the ten years of their criminal activities, he had just confessed: "I'm worried." And he had outlined his problem.

To which Alfred had just offered a solution.

When Alfred the armourer looked back, it often amazed him how easily he had been drawn into the business. He had hardly realized it was happening. It had all started ten years ago, the summer that Barnikel's wife had suddenly died. All Barnikel's friends and family had rallied round, taking turns to keep him company. His children had encouraged the young apprentice to go too. Then, one evening, just as he was leaving, the Dane had put his huge arm round Alfred's shoulders and muttered into his ear: "Would you do a little job for me? It could be dangerous." He had hardly thought about it. Didn't he owe the Dane everything? "Of course," he had replied. "Your master the armourer will tell you what to do," Barnikel had said quietly, and left it at that.

The situation at the time had often been tense. King William's hold on his lands was by no means secure yet. In London, Mandeville was edgy and curfews were frequently imposed. Meanwhile the needs of the Norman garrison kept the armourers occupied. Many times after the evening curfew bell had signalled the end of labour, Alfred and his master had toiled on alone.

And then one autumn evening, the master had remarked to Alfred, "I've one more job tonight. But you can go." When Alfred volunteered to help, the older man had continued quietly: "This one is for Barnikel. You don't have to stay."

In the short silence that followed, Alfred had understood. "I'll do it," he had said.

After that fateful night, master and apprentice had often stayed late in the workshop. Since their work was ostensibly for Mandeville, their strange hours gave rise to no suspicion. All the same, they were careful, always barring the door and keeping their official work on hand so that they could hide the illicit arms and display the regular ones while the door was being opened.

For Alfred, it was wonderful training. There was almost nothing now that he could not tackle. Helmets, swords, shields and spearheads he made by the dozen. The fact that he had concealed his skill from his fellow apprentices now came in doubly useful. For while they knew that he had made progress, those who saw him by day would have been astonished to see how at night, side by side with the master, his fingers flew. As they stored the arms they produced secretly under the floor, only one thing had puzzled him. Who exactly were these weapons for?

Then, one night, Barnikel had come with packhorses and removed the arms. Where he was going he would not say. Soon afterwards, however, a huge rebellion had broken out in the north and east of Britain, the Danes had landed in support, and in East Anglia a brave English noble named Hereward the Wake had led a revolt.

On that occasion, King William had ruthlessly crushed the rebels and devastated much of the north. Four years later, the Danes had tried again. This year, with William's son in rebellion in Normandy, more rumours were flying.

Alfred had also noticed something else. Each time, the request for arms had come not at the time of the revolt, but many months before.

Yet this should not have surprised him. After all, the great Nordic network – that huge pattern of Viking settlements linking traders from the Arctic to the Mediterranean – was very much alive. Beyond the Thames Estuary lay the vast highway of the northern waters, where the voices of the sagas echoed still, and scarcely a month passed without some new whispers stealing around the seas. Barnikel the Viking trader still heard many things.

And now, with the king over the sea in Normandy, it seemed that Barnikel knew something else. In the last three months they had made spears, swords and a huge quantity of arrowheads. Who were they for? Was Hereward the Wake still at large in the forests, as some believed? Were Norsemen even now making ready their Viking longships? No one knew, but the king was rebuilding his Tower in stone, and Mandeville, it was said, had spies in every street. No one, so far as he was aware, suspected the armourer, but it was plain that, this time, Barnikel was concerned.

The last decade had changed Alfred too. He was a fully fledged armourer now. Before long, he would take over from the old master. Four years ago he had married; already there were three children. He was more cautious nowadays. Of course, if Barnikel was right, if King William was ousted by a revolt and replaced, perhaps, with a Danish king, then his secret work would, no doubt, be well rewarded. But if he was wrong . . .

"The trouble," Barnikel had explained, "is that I daren't risk the packhorses any more. There are too many spies. We need something else."

It was then that Alfred had made his suggestion.

Now, having considered it, the Dane nodded his huge red beard. "It might work," he agreed. "But we'd need a good carpenter we could trust. Do we know one?"

Two days later, on a quiet summer evening, Hilda made her way down the hill from St Paul's and passed out of the city through Ludgate.

The Tower was not the Conqueror's only new castle in London. Though on a much smaller scale, here on the city's western side a pair of new forts were being erected beside the gate nearest the river. But their looming presence did not affect Hilda's mood. Indeed, she was smiling, for she was going to meet the man she called her lover.

It was fortunate, Hilda realized, that she had never loved her husband. Thanks to this, she had suffered no great disappointment, since she had always seen him for what he was.

And what was he? Henri Silversleeves was clever and hard-working. She had observed him in his business dealings. If he lacked his father's sense of strategy, he was a master of the swift stroke. He despised Ralph, though he had learned to be polite to him. "Why Father insists he inherits half the family fortune, I can't think," he had once remarked to her. "At least, thank God, he hasn't any children of his own." Henri's passion, she knew, was for the Silversleeves fortune. It was like a fortress of which he was the constable, and which she knew he would never surrender. And so competent was he that nowadays his father frequently spent time at an estate he had obtained near Hatfield, a day's journey north of London.

For Hilda's family, the marriage had achieved its objective. When the Conqueror confiscated most of the estates in Kent, her father, Leofric, had lost Bocton, just as he had feared. But Silversleeves had come to the rescue, and it was a joy now to see her father, free of his debts, building a solid fortune to hand on to her brother Edward. Yes, she thought, she had done the right thing.

As for herself? She lived in the fine stone house near St Paul's. Henri had already given her two children, a boy and a girl. He was thoughtful. He paid her every attention. Indeed, she supposed that Henri might have been a good husband if it had not been for the fact that his heart was entirely cold.

"You certainly have a fine position," Leofric had remarked to her. It was true. She had even met the king, for the Silversleeves family had attended him several times at the king's hall at Westminster when he held court there at Whitsun. King William, bulky, florid, with a large moustache and piercing eyes, had addressed her in French, which, thanks to her husband, she now spoke prettily, and had been so pleased with her replies that he had turned to his entire court. "You see," he had declared, "here is a young Norman with an English wife proving that the two can live contentedly together." And he had beamed at her. "Well done," Henri had whispered, and she had felt proud of herself.

The following year, however, a less happy incident had occurred in the same place.

Her father's attitude to the Norman king was pragmatic: "I don't like it, but he's probably here to stay, so we must make the best of it." Consequently, on hearing that the king wanted falcons for his hunting, Leofric had gone to great trouble and expense to find a magnificent pair of hawks, and when Hilda and her husband were next summoned to court, he brought them and gave them to her with the instruction: "Present them to William from me."

With delight, therefore, she had watched as her husband's servants carried in the two heavy cages and the king exclaimed with pleasure: "I've never seen finer ones. Where did you get them?" And she had been completely unprepared when Henri, in front of her and without a blush, had quickly interposed:

"I searched far and wide, sire."

Then he had smiled at her.

She could not contradict her husband in front of the king. She could only stare at him. But after a moment, as a cold pain shot through her, she felt something die. Perhaps, she considered afterwards, she might have forgiven him if he had not smiled at her.

So now, as she walked out to meet her lover, she felt only a sense of duty for Henri. Nothing more.

Just across the wooden bridge over the Fleet, where once there had been a sacred well, there now stood a little stone church dedicated to a Celtic saint often associated with such watery places: St Bridget, or, as she was called in this case, St Bride. And by the little church of St Bride's, which stared across to Ludgate, he was waiting for her patiently.

Barnikel of Billingsgate was in love.

The Conquest of England had hit the Dane hard. The lands he owned in Essex had been taken by the Normans. For a while he had wondered if he would be ruined, but he had managed to hold his business together in London, and to his great surprise Silversleeves had remained scrupulous about paying him the interest on Leofric's old debt. Even his youngest son, whom he had so passionately intended for the Saxon's girl, had made an excellent marriage. The boy lived with his father-in-law now, whose business he would in due course take over. "Things could be far worse," his wife had liked to remind him. But then she herself had suddenly died and for some months afterwards the Dane had felt the heart go out of him.

Since then two things had kept him going. The first was his secret battle against the Norman conquerors. That he had vowed to continue until his dying day.

The second was Hilda.

They had been shy of each other at first, both regretting the family rift, but once Barnikel's son was married, they felt less awkward when they met in the West Cheap and often paused to exchange a few friendly words. Learning where she took her evening walks, he had fallen into the habit of strolling out across the Fleet at times when she might be there. For a long time, even a year after his wife had died, the Dane had supposed he felt only a fatherly affection for her, while she, perceiving the truth far sooner, said nothing.

Only once, five years ago, had he dared to go further. She had been looking tired and sad one day, and suddenly he had demanded: "Does he mistreat you, your husband?"

She had paused before giving a sad, wry laugh. "No. But what," she asked, smiling, "would you do about it?"

Forgetting himself for a moment, the Dane had moved close and said fiercely: "I would take you away from him."

To this declaration she had merely shaken her head, murmured, "I may not see you if you say such things," and he had never made any advance again.

And so, year after year, this relationship of chaste lovers had continued. It was agreeable, she thought, knowing herself to be imperfectly loved at home, to be appreciated by an older, wiser man. And for his part, Barnikel found that this role of an ardent suitor who, perhaps, was not quite without hope brought its own particular kind of joy.

He came forward eagerly, therefore, wearing a new blue cloak, with a lightness in his step, and together they walked westwards towards the Aldwych and the old churchyard of his Viking ancestors at St Clement Danes.

How cavernous the cellars would be. As the foundations grew, the outline of the huge Tower's interior was already clear.

Approaching the site from the riverbank, the whole of the left half of the interior was taken up by a great hall. The right side was divided in two: a long, north–south, rectangular chamber occupied the rear two-thirds of the space, leaving the front, south-eastern corner for a smaller chamber. This corner would contain the chapel.

The builder of this mighty project was Gundulf, a distinguished Norman monk and architect who had recently been brought to England and made Bishop of Rochester in nearby Kent. With him Gundulf had brought all his knowledge of the fortress-building of Continental Europe and King William had already set him to work on several projects. Indeed, the great Tower of London was itself one of a pair, its nearly identical sister being in the Essex town of Colchester.

Much as he hated the drudgery of his work, Osric could not

help being fascinated by the details of the building growing around him. The base level would form the cellars, which were roughly at ground level on the river side of the building, but because of the slight slope in the ground, were almost completely underground along the back wall.

The stone was laid in layers: first Kentish ragstone, which was only rough-hewn or rubble, then a layer of flint to strengthen it, then more ragstone. Everything was bound with mortar made from various materials to hand. On a number of occasions, cart-loads of ancient Roman tiles from the surrounding area had been brought to the site and he had been put to work with the men who were hammering and grinding them into powder to make the binding cement. When the tiles were used, the mortar in the wall had a reddish tinge, and one of the labourers had grimly remarked:

"See. The Tower is built with English blood."

The pale Norman stone from Caen was for corners and dressings only. "It's especially hard," the foreman had told him, "and being a different colour, it makes the building look neater."

As the cellar walls began to rise, Osric observed other things. Although one could walk from one huge room into another, there was no door in the outer wall. The cellar would only be reached, he discovered, by a single spiral staircase set in a turret in the north-eastern corner. As for windows, when he asked the foreman, the fellow had smiled and pointed to one of two narrow insets high in the western wall. "Watch those," he said. Once the masons started work on these places, Osric had realized that each was to be an opening in the shape of a slim wedge that grew narrower towards the outside.

"There won't be room for much of a window," he had remarked to one of the masons, and the fellow had laughed.

"It'll be just a slit," he answered the boy, "no wider than a man's hand. No one will get in or out through there."

Two other features of the cellar also concerned Osric. The first was a large hole in the floor of the main, western chamber. At first he had been puzzled by this, but he soon learned its purpose, for since he was one of the smallest labourers, Ralph had promptly chosen him to go down into it. "Dig," he had curtly ordered. And when the boy had foolishly asked "How far?", Ralph had cursed him and explained:

"Until you find water, you fool." Although the Thames flowed nearby, and there was also a well not far from the bank, it was essential that the king's castle should have its own secure water supply within its mighty walls. Day after day, therefore, Osric had gone down with pick and shovel, lowered by ropes, sending the earth and gravel he dug up to the surface in a bucket. Deeper and deeper into the bowels of the Tower's mound he had gone until at last he had come to water. When they measured the well he had dug, they found it was forty feet deep.

But it was the other feature that filled his heart with dread.

The very day after refusing to let him be a carpenter, Ralph had suddenly called out, "Osric, since you are good at working down holes, I have a new job for you." And before the little fellow's face even had time to fall: "The tunnel, Osric. That's the place for you."

A necessary feature of any large fortified building was its drain, and the Tower of London's was intelligently conceived. Beginning in the corner, below a hole in the floor not far from the well, it was to run underground, sloping gently down for some fifty yards until it reached the river. At low tide the drain would be tolerably dry, but at high tide, the Thames water would flood the drain and flush it out.

It was a low and narrow space, with just enough room for a few small fellows like Osric to use their picks in a crouching position. Each day he went down and dug away for hours while the loosened earth was dragged back up the tunnel in open sacks, and carpenters put up supports to keep the roof from collapsing. How many days or weeks it would take to bore this hole before the masons could move in to wall and roof it, Osric did not know. All he knew was that he felt like a mole in the ground and that his back was continually aching.

It was after a week of this that he made a second, hopeful attempt at freedom.

Bishop Gundulf of Rochester was a large man. His head was bald. His face was fleshy. Both his body and his manner of speech could best be described as rotund. But there was also a certain briskness in his movements, giving an indication of the very quick mind that made him an excellent administrator. If he experienced any distaste or amusement that late August afternoon as he stood facing the slow-witted overseer, nothing of it showed on his face. It was time to be tactful.

He had just changed the design of the Tower of London, and Ralph Silversleeves was going to have to rebuild it.

At first Ralph could not believe it. He gazed at the huge foundations already rising. Could it really be that the fat bishop wanted him to remove the tremendous mass of stone and begin all over again?

"It is only the south-east corner, my friend," the bishop said in a soothing tone.

"It's twenty-five bargeloads of stone," Ralph retorted furiously. "And for God's sake why?"

The reason for the alteration was simple enough. The sister castle at Colchester had a semicircular projection towards the east at this same corner. The designer of the London Tower, seeing how well it looked, had decided to do the same thing here as well.

"It will form the apse of the royal chapel, you see," Gundulf continued blandly. "It will be a noble construction. And the king is delighted," he added.

If the slow brain of the overseer had registered this last hint, it did not show.

"It will add weeks to the work. Months more likely," he said sullenly.

"The king is anxious that the work should proceed swiftly," the bishop replied with firm politeness. It was an understatement: after a decade of trouble in England, William wanted the new stone castle of London completed without delay.

"Not a chance," Ralph grunted. He hated being bullied by clever men.

Gundulf sighed, then struck.

"I said to the king only the other day how willing you were, how well suited to your great task," he remarked. "I shall be seeing him again shortly."

Since even he could not fail to see the implied threat, Ralph shrugged sulkily. "As you wish," he muttered, and began to move away.

"I shall tell the king," the bishop smoothly concluded, to punish the surly fellow for boring him, "that you will be able to complete the new task on exactly the same schedule as before. Not a day will be lost," he called gaily. "He will be very pleased."

Only moments after this, young Osric made his move.

Osric had often seen the portly bishop before, when Gundulf came to inspect the work.

Like many people in high position, Bishop Gundulf had easily assumed that mantle of cheerful politeness which protects and eases the path of those in public life. As he went round the building site, his courteous nods, even to the serfs, cost him nothing.

It was natural enough, therefore, that the little serf working miserably in the dark tunnel should have formed the plan he had.

Every instinct, even a physical craving in his fingertips, told him he should be a craftsman. Could this be wrong? Or had God decided he must suffer like this for his sins? The one thing he was sure of was that Ralph Silversleeves was no agent of God: he was the devil. But Bishop Gundulf, who was in charge of everything, was a man of God, and he looked kindly. Surely even a humble serf like him might approach a man of God?

Anyway, he thought, I've nothing else to lose.

He had waited for an opportunity. Now, as he came out from his shift in the tunnel and saw the bishop standing in front of the building site, he decided to take his chance. Running over to the carpenters' workshop, he seized the piece of work he had done and shyly approached the great man.

Bishop Gundulf was surprised when he saw the earnest little figure caked in earth standing before him with his lump of wood. Nevertheless, he asked kindly, "What is it, my son?"

In a few words Osric explained. "This is my work. I want to be a carpenter."

As he gazed at the serf, it was not difficult for Gundulf to guess the rest. The work, he saw, was good. His eyes strayed towards the carpenters' workshop. Perhaps he should place the boy there to see what they could make of him. And he was about to stride over there when he heard a cry of rage behind him.

It was Ralph.

The moment he caught sight of them, he had realized what

Osric was up to. Already in a furious temper about the change of plan, the sight of the wretched little serf going to Gundulf behind his back was more than he could bear. As he raced to the bishop's side, his cry of rage was practically a howl.

"He says he wants to be a carpenter," Gundulf observed mildly.

"Never."

"The craftsman's talents are a gift from God, you know," the bishop remarked. "We are supposed to use them."

And then Ralph had his inspiration.

"You don't understand," he replied. "We can't trust him with a knife or sharp tools of any kind. He's only labouring here because he tried to kill one of the king's knights. That's why they slit his nose."

"He doesn't look very dangerous."

"But he is."

Gundulf sighed. He was not sure he believed the overseer. On the other hand he'd given him enough trouble for one day. And the work on the Tower must go smoothly on.

"As you wish," he said with a shrug.

And so it was that Osric, though he did not understand what they were saying, since they spoke to each other in Norman French, perceived that the last hope in his young life had been extinguished.

A few moments later, held by the ear, he found himself back at the entrance to the tunnel. Ralph was shouting at him.

"You think you'll be a carpenter behind my back, do you? Well, look around you. This earth and this stone are what you are going to dig and carry for the rest of your life, little carpenter. You'll do that and nothing else until your back breaks." He gave a grim smile. "This Tower will be your life, Osric, and it will be your death, because I shall make you work building it until you die." Then he threw him bodily into the tunnel with the curt order: "Work another shift."

So intent was he upon this important task that Ralph Silversleeves did not take any notice of the other people standing around. Even if he had, there was nothing remarkable about the presence of Alfred the armourer.

In fact, Alfred was inside the Tower for a good reason. He had been told that he would be making the great metal grilles that would fit over the drain and the well, and he had come by to get an idea of the size of these cavities.

With mild interest he had watched and listened as Ralph raved at the solemn little fellow. After Ralph had gone, he walked over to the tunnel entrance. On the ground he noticed the little example of Osric's woodwork, which had fallen when Ralph had thrown him down. Alfred picked it up thoughtfully.

And that night, following a long conversation with young Osric, he told his friend the Dane: "I think I've found the little fellow we need."

"Can you trust him? With your life?"

"I think so."

"Why? What does he want?"

Alfred grinned.

"He wants revenge."

Revenge was sweet. The plan was not without risk, but Osric felt confident. Above all, he felt proud.

Secretly, at night, he would sneak out of the labourers' quarters by the Tower and make his way to the Dane's house nearby. There, in a storeroom at the back, he and Alfred would work, his stubby fingers instinctively feeling their way forward so that soon, by careful trial and error, he had evolved a piece of carpentry so neat, so ingenious and so deceptive that the master armourer cried out: "You are a craftsman indeed!"

The task the Dane had set him was to convert a huge wagon he possessed so that he could conceal arms in it. But where he had expected the little carpenter to design a secret compartment under the cart, Osric had hit on a more ingenious solution. "If they search you, that's the first thing they'll look for," he had pointed out. Rather than touch the floor of the wagon, he had instead concentrated on the solid beams that made its frame. Working with care and sheer inspiration, he had hollowed these out, preserving their outside appearance with stops and sliding panels, and doing so with such thoroughness that a quite remarkable quantity of dismantled swords, spearheads and arrowheads could be snugly lodged within. By the time he had finished, his work was invisible.

"The cart itself is built of arms!" Barnikel exclaimed with

delight, hugging the little carpenter so warmly that for a moment Osric feared he might not breathe again.

He would be taking out a consignment, the Dane told Alfred, the following week.

It was quite by chance that, two days later, Hilda had an encounter with Ralph. It took place on the hill from Ludgate to St Paul's, and Hilda was in a very bad temper. This, however, had nothing to do with Ralph.

Her anger was caused by an embroidery.

It was in those years, in King William's England, that the largest and most famous piece of needlework that has probably ever been undertaken was made. The Bayeux Tapestry, as this extraordinary work was called, was not, in fact, a woven tapestry at all, but a huge embroidery of coloured wools stitched, in the time-honoured Anglo-Saxon manner, on linen. Though only about twenty inches high, it was an astounding seventy-seven yards long. It pictured some six hundred humans, thirty-seven ships, as many trees, and seven hundred animals. And it celebrated the Norman Conquest.

More than this, it was the first known example of English state propaganda. Arranged in the form of a huge, Anglo-Saxon strip cartoon, its stylized figures depicted, in dozens of scenes, the Norman king's version of the events leading to the Conquest and a detailed account of the Battle of Hastings. It was commissioned by the king's half-brother, Odo, who, though bishop of the Norman city of Bayeux, which yielded him a fine income, was also a soldier and administrator just as ruthless and ambitious as the king himself. And it was embroidered by English women, mostly in Kent, before it was finally stitched together.

There were good reasons why this magnificent work of art should so infuriate Hilda. She had not wanted to take part, but Henri had forced her to join the ladies who had been meeting in the king's hall at Westminster to work on the project. "You will please Bishop Odo," he had said, even though it was Odo who had been granted half of Kent and one of Odo's knights who now occupied her own family's ancestral estate at Bocton. Henri knew this, but did not care. The tapestry, with its vivid portrayal of events, always reminded her painfully of the loss of her old home, of her country, and of the long years of service to her husband's cold and cynical nature.

As she returned from the ladies at Westminster that morning, therefore, Hilda's anger was still raging.

And then she saw Ralph.

It was clear that he was excited. His heavy face was animated, his normally dull eyes were shining as, unasked, he fell into step beside her.

"Would you like to know a secret?" he began.

Sometimes Hilda felt sorry for Ralph. Partly it was because Henri despised him, but perhaps more it was because he was still unmarried.

Indeed, he had no woman. Sometimes he would cross the bridge to the south side where a small community of whores dwelt along the bankside, but even these ladies, it was said, were not enthusiastic for his blunt attentions. Occasionally she had suggested finding him a wife, but Henri had discouraged her. "Then he'll have heirs to inherit," he would remind her. And once he had remarked drily: "I look after the family money. And I intend to outlive him." So as the curious fellow strode by her side, she forced herself to give him a smile.

If he had not seen his sister-in-law quite so soon after his meeting with the great Mandeville, Ralph might not have been so indiscreet. He liked Hilda. "I'm not such a fool as Henri thinks," he had once plaintively told her. Now, flushed with excitement, he could not resist the chance to impress her.

"I have been given an important mission," he said.

The conversation between Ralph and Mandeville had been brief but important. It was the business of the great magnate to be well informed, and little that passed in south-east England escaped his notice. From the interview, Ralph learned that there were indeed fears of further trouble in the countryside. "In the rebellion of three years ago," Mandeville had told him, "we think they got arms from London. We want to put a stop to that."

Having considered the matter, Mandeville had decided that to oversee the little operation he had in mind he needed a man who was suspicious, small-minded and ruthless.

"It's a good opportunity for you to show what you can do,"

he informed Ralph as he explained the plan. "You will need to be patient, and you will need spies."

"I'll tear apart every cart that leaves London," the overseer cried.

"You will do no such thing," Mandeville replied. "In fact, I want you to relax the inspection of goods leaving the city." He smiled. "The trick is to lull their suspicions. Have men posted in the woods instead, and when they see any suspicious shipments, follow them. We don't just want to stop the arms. I want them to lead us to any rebels. Above all, tell nobody. Do you understand?"

Indeed he did. A position of trust. A secret commission. Bursting with pride, Ralph had walked through the city. It was hardly surprising that, seeing Hilda and anxious to impress her, he had instantly decided:

"I can tell you, of course, because you're my own family."

If it had not been for her irritation over the morning's needlework, Ralph's confidence might not even have interested her. But now, as she looked at his heavy face, a brutish version of her own husband's, and thought of the wretched English – her own people – whom he would trap and no doubt kill, she experienced a feeling of revulsion.

The truth was, she realized, that she had become sick of them all, of Henri, of Ralph, of the Normans and their rule. There was, of course, nothing she could do about any of it. Except, perhaps, for one thing.

"You must be very proud," she said to Ralph as she left him.

She was due to go up to her father-in-law's estate at Hatfield the next week, where she would stay for a month. It was not a prospect she relished much, and so she had arranged to enjoy a quiet walk with Barnikel that evening, knowing it was the last they would have for some time.

When they met at St Bride's, therefore, and began their usual stroll towards the Aldwych, she quietly confided to him everything that Ralph had told her, adding: "I know, after all, that you are no friend of the Normans. So if you know who should be warned, will you do it?"

It was then, on seeing Barnikel's evident dismay at the news, and shrewdly guessing he must be more closely involved than she had realized, that Hilda, with a sudden and generous impulse, caught the older man's arm and softly asked: "Is there some way, dear friend, that I can help you?"

The road north from London first passed across marshy meadows and fields and then, as the ground began to rise, entered the forest of Middlesex near the old Saxon village of Islington.

Ten days after his meeting with Mandeville, a hot Ralph Silversleeves, accompanied by a dozen armed riders, rode southwards out of the forest in a lather of frustration.

He had just come from a meeting with his men, and it had not been a happy experience. His spies had found nothing. "Not so much as a pitchfork," one of them told him grumpily. "Maybe they were tipped off," he had added. "Impossible!" Ralph had cried. When another had asked him, "Are you sure you know what you are doing?" he had struck the fellow in a fury.

Now, as he rode back, he could sense that the men behind had little confidence in him. Somehow, he had no idea how, he had the feeling that he had been duped. He was even becoming suspicious of his own spies.

And then he saw the wagon.

There was clearly something suspicious about it. It was large and covered, and was obviously carrying a heavy load as it creaked along, pulled by four big horses. Beside the driver sat a figure in a hood.

It was now that Ralph lost his presence of mind. It seemed to the overwrought Norman that at last he might have found his quarry. Forgetting entirely his instructions from Mandeville, he rode straight at the wagon, as though it might take wings and fly, bellowing at the driver to stop. "Halt and uncover, you traitors," he screamed. "You dogs!"

Only as he drew up, panting, beside them, did the mysterious figure throw back her hood and cast at him a look of utter scorn. It was Hilda.

"Idiot!" she cried so that all his men could hear. "Henri always told me you were a fool." Then, whipping back the cover from the wagon, she revealed its harmless cargo. "Flagons of wine," she shouted. "A present from your own brother to your father. I'm taking them up to Hatfield." And she made as if to strike him with the driver's whip so convincingly that he backed away hastily, puce in the face.

There was laughter from the men. Humiliated and enraged, Ralph shouted for them to follow, and without even glancing behind, rode quickly down the lane towards London.

Five weeks later, by the church of St Bride, where no one seemed to be about, Barnikel of Billingsgate allowed himself to place a chaste kiss upon the forehead of his new conspirator.

Then they walked contentedly along the riverbank.

It did not occur to either of them that this time they were being discreetly followed.

1081

It was in his twentieth year that Osric became aware of the girl. She was sixteen.

He did not tell anyone about her. Not even his friend Alfred the armourer.

It was curious to see the two men together. Alfred was master of the armoury now. The shock of white hair over his forehead had become almost invisible since the rest of his hair had gone grey. He had become rather stout. He gave orders to his apprentices in a voice of authority, and his wife and four children obeyed him in all things.

But he had not forgotten the day when Barnikel had found him starving by the London Stone, and so, trying to pass on that kindness to another, he did all he could to help his poor little friend. Not only did his family see to it that Osric had a square meal at least once a week, but he had even offered to buy the serf his freedom several times. Here, however, he had been unsuccessful. By one means or another, Ralph had always contrived to stop him. "I'm sorry," Alfred had told the young fellow. "There's nothing I can do."

Though based on little enough, Ralph's hatred for the serf had by now hardened into a habit. "In a way, Osric," he had once sneered, "I think I almost love you." It was perfectly true. The little labourer was a living object he could hurt whenever he wished; if Osric loathed him in return, it only gave him more satisfaction. And nothing gave him greater pleasure than thwarting Osric's attempts to break free. "Don't worry," he promised, "I'll never let you go."

She was small. Her long dark hair was parted in the middle; her skin was white. The only colour in her face came from her lips, which were small but red. All of which suggested, though Osric did not know it, that her ancestry was Celtic, perhaps Roman too.

The labourers were quartered in a series of wooden buildings set along the inside of the old Roman wall by the riverbank. Here they had been left to make their own arrangements. Some, like Osric, claimed nothing more than a particular patch of straw. Others, having found women, had with bits of wood or bales of straw constructed for themselves what privacy they could, so that by now whole families had colonized this or that corner of the place. They were a motley collection. Some were serfs sent by landholders who owed service to the king; some were slaves; a number, like Osric, bore mutilations that showed them to have been guilty of some crime. Discipline was lax. Ralph cared little for what passed amongst the labourers so long as they worked.

Her father had been the cook and while he was alive they had eaten well. But two years ago he had died, and since then their life had been hard. Her mother, used for sundry odd jobs, was sickly, her hands increasingly swollen and aching from arthritis, and with no one else in the world to help them, the girl had to do what she could to protect her. A sickly serf woman without a family did not live long in these times. The girl's name was Dorkes.

He had first noticed her in December. The labourers were kept working at the Tower in all weathers, but that winter had been particularly harsh, and one day, two weeks before Christmas, the order was given: "Stop work."

"When it freezes like this," the foreman explained to him, "the wet mortar turns to ice and then it cracks." The next day, many of the serfs were sent back to their villages while the men remaining were led out and told, "Now we have to cover the walls."

It was a big but necessary task to insulate the huge open tops of the walls. It was also a smelly one, for the material used was a mixture of warmed dung and straw. "But it works," the foreman assured him, and soon the huge, grey walls were crowned with layers of manure and thatch.

Despite the cold, at the end of each day Osric was anxious to wash himself and so he would quite often go down to the Thames bank and jump into the water fully clothed before hurrying back to the barn where he could strip and dry his clothes by the brazier. It was at this time that he became aware there was another person in the camp who also went down to the water, at dawn and at dusk, to wash herself. This was Dorkes.

She was very clean, and very quiet. Those were the first things the little fellow noticed about her. Also that she seemed physically rather underdeveloped. A little mouse, he thought, and smiled at her. But he did not, just then, pay her any other attention. He had other things to think about.

Since his job for Alfred and Barnikel three years before, there had been no more adventures. Apart from the outbreak in the north, England had remained quiet. Whatever Barnikel had hoped for when he shipped the arms, it appeared to have come to nothing. Osric suspected that the old Dane had continued to stockpile arms, but he was not sure.

His life was bearable, though. Most of the time, of course, there was the sheer daily drudgery – pulling carts of rubble, hauling buckets of stone up to the masons, or carrying wood from the carpenters. Gradually, however, he had added another activity.

Ever since he had discovered his skill with Barnikel's wagon, the little fellow, almost unable to help himself, had taken to picking up bits of wood or begging timber ends from the carpenters. Sitting by the light of the brazier in the evenings, he would then carve them. Every week or so he turned out something – a little figure, a child's toy – and soon even the carpenters and masons were referring to him as "the little craftsman". It was said affectionately, though with some amusement, as if he were a sort of mascot. After all, he was not a member of their craft; he was only a beast of burden. Still, he did not mind, and as he went about his daily business, they would often show him what they were doing and explain it to him.

And here was the strangest thing. Despite the fact that he

was being sacrificed to the building of the Tower, whenever he entered its grim walls, Osric found that he was fascinated.

The great cellars were finished now, covered over with huge rafters and floorboards, except for the south-eastern corner, which had a vaulting of stone. The spiral stairs down to the cellars were already sealed off with a massive, iron-studded oak door locked with a large key made by Alfred the armourer. "The arms for the whole garrison will be stored down there," the foreman told Osric.

The walls of the main floor were growing rapidly. As was usual with such Norman strongholds, the main entrance was on this level, a handsome doorway in the south wall, reached by a high wooden staircase on the outside. Though almost as thick as the cellar's, the walls of the main floor were punctuated with numerous recesses leading to narrow windows and other apertures. Two of these especially intrigued the young labourer.

The first was about ten feet across, in the western wall of the main hall. One could walk right into it, as though it was a small room, and looking up inside, Osric could see that it went up about twelve feet, and that just below the top there was a small hole in the wall leading to the outside.

"Whatever is it for?" he asked the masons.

They laughed. "It's for the fire," they explained. And when he looked mystified: "The king's hall will be above this room, so instead of a brazier in the middle which will send smoke up through the floorboards, he wants these fireplaces. They have them in France, you know. There's to be another in the eastern chamber."

And so it was that in the Tower of London the kingdom of England received its first fireplaces. They did not have chimneys, however. The smoke just went out through a hole in the wall.

Two other cavities, these ones in the northern wall, also seemed curious. Each narrow little passage led to the outer edge of the wall, where, in a nook, there was a stone bench with a hole in it. "Look through the hole," one of the masons suggested, and when he did, Osric found himself gazing down a short, steep chute into open space with a twenty-foot drop down the outside of the north wall. "The French call it a *garderobe*," the mason explained. "You've guessed what it's for?" And when Osric nodded: "We fit a wooden gutter down the chute that overhangs the wall. That way you get a clean drop to the cesspit below. You'll be digging that later."

Osric considered the thing. "Draughty on your backside."

The mason laughed. "Encourages people not to hang about."

It was in June that the incident occurred. It was nothing really. One warm evening, a group of men who had been drinking were sitting by the riverside when little Dorkes came down to the water. She did not stay there long, only scooping up the clear water to wash her arms and face before returning. But as she passed the men, her eyes carefully looking at the ground, one of them, a little drunk, tried to grab her round the waist, calling out: "I've caught a mouse. Give us a kiss."

Another girl might have laughed it off, but Dorkes did not know how to handle a drunken man. Burying her chin in her chest, she shook her head and tried to break free. The man's hands felt for her small breasts as he grinned at the others.

And then something hit him.

Osric, coming on the scene, did not wait to argue, but threw himself so violently at the fellow that although the little labourer was only half his size, the man was knocked to the ground. For a moment after, Osric thought the bigger man or his friends might go for him or throw him in the river. Instead, a cry of laughter went up.

"The little craftsman's a fighter!" Then: "Osric, we didn't know she was your girl!" From that day it was a regular joke on the building site. "How's your girl, Osric?"

It caused him, for the first time, to look at her.

There were plenty of opportunities. Sometimes he would watch her when she went down to the river in the early morning. As it was summer, she wore only a simple shift, so that when, like most of the women, she stepped into the stream fully dressed to wash, he got a good idea of her body as she came out. He discovered that she was not, as he had imagined, flat-chested, but had small, nicely formed breasts.

At nights, as she sat with her mother by the fire, he would

sit a little way off and study her face. Before long, what had seemed a pale, unremarkable profile became beautiful.

But more even than these features, he now saw something else. Timid she might be, but with what quiet determination she defended her mother as, with every passing month, the poor woman became more useless thanks to her crippled hands. Always keeping her dignity, never begging, Dorkes would do little jobs for people for which she would be paid with food or even an item of clothing, thereby keeping herself and her mother from destitution.

Ever since he had defended her, the girl had been friendly towards Osric. Quite often they would chat together, or walk about. Sometimes he would see her gaunt mother with her helpless, gnarled hands watching them, but it was hard to tell what she was thinking, and since she never granted him more than a sad nod, he seemed unlikely to find out. Dorkes knew, of course, that the men teased him about her, but she did not seem to mind. But Osric noticed that despite her quiet smile, she was still guarded with him, whether from timidity or for some other reason he was not sure.

He fell in love in July. He could not say exactly why. One evening he was watching her and he felt a sudden wave of protective tenderness. The next day he kept looking about to catch sight of her. That night he saw her in his dreams, and by the following day it seemed to him that his entire life would somehow have meaning if he could live with her.

"And then," he murmured to himself, "I could look after her." The thought was so exciting that even the miserable sheds where they lodged seemed to the little fellow to be bathed in a warm new light.

A few days later he and Dorkes met Ralph Silversleeves together.

It was Ralph's habit to walk around the site early in the morning, before work began. Sometimes he stopped to investigate the lodgings; usually not. Always, though, as if it were his personal castle, he walked proudly round the outside of the growing Tower. He had just done this when he encountered the two young people walking up from the river.

Ralph had heard the men's jokes about Osric and the girl, but as he considered the little labourer such a miserable object, he thought it hardly likely that any girl would look at him. Now, seeing them together, he suddenly wondered: could it possibly be true? Could the miserable Osric have a woman when he, Ralph, had none? Seized with a sudden fit of secret jealousy, he gazed at the girl and then remarked: "Whatever are you doing, walking round with this poor little runt?" And to Osric: "Why don't you leave this pretty girl alone, Osric? You'll embarrass her with your face, you're so hideous." Then, giving the boy a quick cut across the back with his whip, he moved on.

Neither of them spoke. "I always ignore him," the girl whispered after a moment.

But though he knew Ralph was his enemy, the Norman's words had given Osric a shock, and he kept silent.

At low tide, there were several places along the banks of the Thames where the clear water collected in pools. That same afternoon, when the sun was shining so brightly that you could see the sky in the water, Osric slipped down to the river alone.

As the years had passed, once he had forgotten the pain of having his nose slit and grown used to his awkward breathing, Osric had not thought much about his appearance. Nor, in a world almost without glass, was there much likelihood of him catching sight of himself. But now, in one of these pools, he gazed in surprise at his own reflection.

Then he burst into tears.

He had not known that his hair was already thin. He had forgotten how the little mess that had been his nose was a smudge of purple which made him look ridiculous. As he stared at his overlarge head, his bent little body and the disfiguring blotch in the middle of his face, he wanted to wail out loud, but for fear of attracting attention he choked it back and instead, in a stifled little whisper, told himself, "It's no good. I'm a freak."

Duly humbled, he went sadly to his work.

Yet in the days that followed, though at first he wanted to put his hand in front of his unsightly face whenever he saw her, he was never able to detect the revulsion he supposed the girl must feel. If she was hiding it, she did it very well. She smiled at him quietly, just as she always had.

He began to look at other men, assessing their disadvantages. One had a limp, another a crushed hand, a third a running sore. Perhaps, he consoled himself, I am not the most ill-favoured of all.

If only she could love me, he thought. He would protect her. He would die for her. In this state of mind, three more weeks of his life passed.

The masons were working on what would become the chapel crypt now. It was a large space, about forty-five feet long into the eastern apse. Already they had started to build the vault.

Osric enjoyed watching this. First the carpenters made big, semicircular arches of wood that were raised on scaffolding like a series of humpback bridges. Then the masons would clamber on top and lay the stones, each carefully cut into a wedge shape with the broad end upwards, so that when the stones were all slotted into place, the arch held itself up with tremendous strength.

But before long, he was witnessing another new feature of the Tower.

One morning he arrived to find the masons grumbling about "another cursed change". Moments later Ralph appeared and angrily told him to go and fetch his pick. Soon he was hard at work.

The wall between the crypt and the chamber on the eastern side of the Tower was over twenty feet thick. After the masons had cut a narrow entrance into this wall from the crypt, Osric and three other men were told to dig into the rubble filling within the wall and hollow out a chamber. And so, with the carpenters providing props to hold up the masonry over their heads, they dug away for days, like miners going into a rock face, until they had created a hidden chamber about fifteen feet square. "It's like a cave," Osric said, and grinned. And the analogy was apt, for the walls of a medieval castle were not there simply to divide spaces. They were complete entities, into which men could cut and burrow as into a mountain.

"This will be the strongroom," Ralph told them, "where valuables will be kept." It was to be fitted with a massive oak door.

* * *

On an overcast Sunday morning at the start of autumn Osric declared his love.

Along the old Roman wall beside the Tower there were stairs leading up to the battlements, and since there was no work being done that day, Osric and the girl had gone up there to enjoy the view of the river. It was pleasantly quiet, and finding himself alone with her, the little fellow was suddenly so overcome with tenderness for her small pale form that he gently put his arm round her waist.

And immediately felt her freeze. He turned to look at her, but she drew away. Then, as she glanced up nervously at his face and saw his sad, solemn eyes, she shook her head and gently but firmly removed his arm.

"Please don't do that."

"I thought, perhaps . . ." he began.

Again she shook her head, then took a deep breath.

"Osric, you've been very kind to me, but . . ." Her brown eyes gazed at him calmly. "I do not love you."

He nodded, feeling the hot misery rise in his throat. "Is it because . . . ?" He wanted to say, "Because of my face?" but found he could not.

"Please go," she said. And when he hesitated: "Go now."

Of course. He understood. Osric went back down the stairs and into the lodgings, where, for a long time, he sat quietly on his straw bed and wept silently because he was ill-favoured.

He would have been surprised to know that, if anything, the grief of the pale little girl still staring out from the wall was greater than his, for her dilemma was not at all what he supposed.

Indeed, though Dorkes had noticed his disfigured face at first, she had scarcely thought about it after that. She admired his courage and she liked his kindness. But what, she calmly and sadly asked herself, was the use of that? Osric had nothing. Even the meanest serf in a village had a hut to live in and a plot of land to work for himself. Osric had only a bed of straw. What would his life be? Hauling stones for Ralph Silversleeves who hated him, until he dropped. And what had she? A crippled mother to look after. With a man in her life, how could she care for her? Osric certainly couldn't. Anyway, she had seen the crude couplings that took place in the lodgings, the ragged, half-starved children who scrabbled about in the hay and mud. "They live like vermin," her mother had once remarked. "Don't you do that."

Her only hope was that a craftsman or one of the serfs sent temporarily from an estate might like the look of her. If not, she would provide for her mother as best she could. And after that? Perhaps I shan't live long, she thought.

Consequently, she had been cautious with Osric, anxious to give the poor little fellow kindness but not too much hope. That morning, she had done, quickly and firmly, what she must, and had sent him away. Now, gazing out over the long city walls and back at the massive, rising Tower, she cursed the fate that had locked her in this grim prison.

Above all, Osric must not guess the secret she had been living with now for all these weeks, which was that she loved him.

In the days that followed, when Osric and Dorkes saw each other they smiled as usual but rarely spoke. Both kept their feelings to themselves. Here, it seemed, the matter rested. But not quite.

It was Alfred's wife who first noticed the change in Osric. Normally his weekly meals with the armourer and his family were happy occasions. Alfred had built a new house for himself adjoining the armoury, a stout, timber-framed structure consisting of a large main room with a loft divided into two parts, one for himself and his wife, the other for their six children. The apprentices slept in an outbuilding at the back.

Alfred's wife was a jolly, comfortable woman, the daughter of a butcher, and she presided over her noisy household with all the ease and confidence of a woman who has a loving husband and exactly one over the number of children she had always hoped for. However miserable his daily existence, Osric had usually cheered up by the time he reached the house, and often brought some little present he had carved to please the children.

"You're a mother to the fellow," Alfred would tell his wife.

"So much the better," she would reply. "God knows he needs one."

So, when, towards the end of summer, she noticed that Osric was not himself, she was concerned. He seemed abstracted and ate little. Could it be, she asked Alfred, that the poor boy was in love? Alfred did not think so. But when, in the autumn, Osric came in looking pale as death, saying not a word and unable to eat at all, she became worried. She tried gently questioning him, but got nowhere. "Whatever it is," she told Alfred, "it's bad. Ask at the Tower. Try to find out."

A few days later Alfred reported back. "They say there's a girl he seemed quite friendly with. I saw her actually. Quite a pretty little thing, in a timid sort of way! I even spoke to her."

"And?"

"Oh. They were just friends, nothing more. She told me so herself."

At which his wife shook her head and smiled. "I'll talk to her," she said.

She was surprised, therefore, by Osric's behaviour when he came to eat with them the very next evening.

He still seemed pale, yet there was something, some secret, that appeared to be giving him an inner excitement. Unless he had made it up with the girl, she could not think what it might be.

Above all, no one had ever seen him eat so much. When she produced a dish of stew, he had four helpings. Offered ale, he drank three tankards. He consumed twice as much as one of the normally ravenous apprentices. "Look at Osric," the children cried. "He's going to burst!"

"Are you building up your strength for something?" Alfred asked him.

"Yes. I need all the food I can get tonight," he replied, refusing to say why, and when he finally left no one was any the wiser. But he departed contentedly, and that night, as he lay on his bed of straw, he smiled as he contemplated his plan.

There was a mist hanging over the riverbank the next morning as Ralph made his usual rounds. People were stirring in the lodgings but they appeared only as vague figures, their coughs and voices sounding faint and disembodied in the clinging dampness. Even the great square of the Tower loomed indistinctly, as though in the mist some huge, phantom ship had strayed on to land.

Ralph grunted. He had been to visit the ladies of the south

bank the night before, but though they provided physical release, nowadays they gave him less and less satisfaction, and he had wandered back across the bridge at dawn in a bad temper.

Besides, something else was annoying him.

Where the devil was his whip? It had mysteriously vanished two days before. He had only put it down for a few minutes, and though he had issued horrible threats, none of the workers at the Tower seemed to have any knowledge of it. Over the years he had grown so used to the feel of it in his hand that now he felt curiously awkward, almost off balance, as he strode about. "If I don't find it soon," he muttered irritably, "I'll have to get another one."

He did not bother to visit the sleeping quarters, but, as was his habit, stalked around the looming mass of the Tower, occasionally glancing towards the slopes as if to check that the ravens out there in the mist were still standing sentinel to protect those dark, damp walls.

He had just turned the corner when he saw his whip.

It was lying on the ground near the wall, undamaged by the look of it. Presumably the thief, having grown frightened, had found this way to return it to him.

With a faint smile, he moved across and bent down to pick it up.

Osric had been waiting for nearly an hour.

He knew his plan was dangerous, but all that week as he had thought about it, he had asked himself what he had to lose. Dorkes did not want him. The rest of his life contained nothing to look forward to. What could they do to him that they had not already done? Wasn't there some satisfaction, however small, in striking a blow at the overseer who had so humiliated him?

So now, watching from his vantage point, he carefully calculated the moment for the blow to fall, took a deep breath, tensed himself and, through gritted teeth, muttered:

"Now."

Osric's efforts the evening before had not been in vain. Indeed his stomach had been so full he had wondered if he would burst. The soft, warm evacuation that sprang from him now and sailed down the north face of the Tower from the *garderobe* on which he sat was certainly greater by far than anything he had ever produced before. Having held himself in readiness for so long, the discharge burst out with wonderful concentration. Soft, full, yet compact, it fell in blissful silence towards its mark.

A second later, Osric, peeping down the chute, saw to his delight that his delivery had landed precisely on the overseer's head.

From below there was as cry of terror, then, as Ralph put his hand up, of stupefaction, and then, as he saw and smelt what was on his hand, of utter horror. But by the time he looked up to the orifice above, its occupant had vanished.

With a scream of rage, the Norman raced round the building and up the staircase. He rushed to the *garderobe*, then ran from the hall to the chamber, the crypt, and even into the darkness of the strongroom. He found nothing. Bellowing in fury, he returned to the main hall, and was about to cast about further when a sudden and even more awful thought occurred to him.

In a few moments, the first of the masons would be entering the Tower to begin their work. They would see him covered with this smelly and unsightly mess. He would be the laughing stock of the Tower, of all London. With a cry of despair, therefore, he raced out of the building and, moments later, was glimpsed running into the morning mist towards the city.

Osric waited. His legs, pressed hard against the wall, held him securely in a sitting position some ten feet up in the shadows of the great fireplace. He heard Ralph's cries and smiled. He heard the Norman's disappearing feet.

Then, after a time, he came down.

A few days later, Dorkes, to her great surprise, found herself accosted by the cheerful armourer's wife. At first, as they walked together towards Billingsgate, the girl was reserved and noncommittal, but gradually, as the older woman's warmth and understanding conquered her, she admitted a little; and finally, without wanting to, she broke down.

Yet none of this was as surprising as what happened next.

Calmly and kindly the woman explained to her that she and her husband were Osric's friends; she told her how Alfred had tried to buy Osric out of serfdom. "He may even succeed one day," she added. Then she made her offer.

"We'll look after your mother. Even Ralph doesn't want a pair of useless hands. We'll see she doesn't starve, and if Ralph allows, we'll take her in to live in our house."

"But . . ." The girl hesitated. "If I have children and Osric . . ."

The woman completed the sentence for her. "If Osric dies?" She shrugged. "In so far as possible, we'll look after them. I don't think they'll starve." She paused. "You may get a better offer, of course. If so, you should take it. But it's something at least." She smiled. "My husband is a master armourer. He has some standing here."

As they walked back, Dorkes was silent. She hardly knew what to think or what to say. But at last, being young, and weary, she replied: "Thank you. Yes."

And so it was that a few nights later, Osric looked up in astonishment to see, by the soft glow of the brazier, a small, pale figure approaching him.

A year passed before Dorkes's mother was taken into the armourer's house. During this time the main floor of the Tower was completed and the huge oak rafters for its ceiling prepared.

Osric and Dorkes, having made what private space they could for themselves in the lodgings, lived together undisturbed. There was no marriage ceremony, no official sanctification of any kind, but in those conditions none was expected. The other inhabitants of the place referred to Dorkes simply as young Osric's woman, and to him as her man. There was nothing more to say.

Except when, a short while after her mother had left, Dorkes quietly told Osric that she was going to have a child.

As the months continued to pass, it seemed to Alfred the armourer that he and his wife had done a fine thing and that, all in all, life in Norman London was tolerable enough.

Or would have been, but for a nagging problem that now began to grow: one which, if he could not solve it, threatened to engulf them all.

On a late autumn morning in the year of Our Lord 1083, Leofric the merchant, who dwelt by the sign of the Bull in the West Cheap, stood near his house in momentary indecision.

The two sights that claimed his attention were so interesting to him that he kept turning his head from side to side as he tried to watch both.

The first was a half-built church.

For if the Conqueror had brought castles to England, he had also brought something else of great importance: the Continental Church. After all, he had promised the Pope that in return for his blessing, he would reform the English Church, and he was a man of his word. At the earliest opportunity, therefore, he had removed the Saxon Archbishop of Canterbury and replaced him with Lanfranc, a Norman priest of the greatest distinction. Following his first inspection of his new flock, Lanfranc's verdict was simple: "Disgraceful." And he set about cleaning things up.

Some years before, there had been a fire along the West Cheap. Leofric's house had been spared, but the little Saxon church of St Mary at the top of the lane had been burnt to cinders. Now, Archbishop Lanfranc himself had ordered it rebuilt, to serve as his own church in London.

Halfway along the Cheap, therefore, just behind the stalls of mercers, drapers and ribbon-sellers, a small but handsome church was now rising. Like the Tower in the east, it was square, sturdy and built of stone. The crypt, which was mostly above ground, was already completed. It had a nave, four bays long and two aisles. Even the vaulting was stone, though here the builders had also used some Roman bricks they had found nearby. But the most striking feature, which had already impressed the inhabitants of the city, was that like those of Westminster Abbey, the stout arches of this little church were in the impressive, Romanesque style – rounded like a bow. As a consequence, even before the building was done, the church had acquired the special name it was to keep: St Mary-le-Bow.

Hardly a day went by without Leofric watching the progress on this fine new building for at least an hour. It might be Norman, and on his doorstep, but it pleased him.

The other sight, however, was becoming stranger every moment.

On the northern side of the Cheap, not a hundred yards from where he was standing, lay the narrow street of Ironmonger

Lane. And by this corner, for five minutes at least, a most curious figure had been lurking. His hood was pulled over his head. He was stooping in a futile attempt to conceal his height and, presumably, his identity; and from his hood peeped out the edge of a large, red beard.

But why should he be lurking there? For up Ironmonger Lane there lay only one quarter – a new one – known by the name of its most recent inhabitants: the Jewry.

As well as his military followers, William the Conqueror had brought one other group with him to England: the Norman Jews. They were a privileged class. Under the king's special protection, but discouraged from entering most occupations, this community had come to specialize in the making of loans. Not that the merchants of London were any strangers to simple finance. The loan and its necessary accompaniment, interest, had long existed there, as they had always done in any place where there are merchants and some kind of currency. Leofric, Barnikel and Silversleeves had all undertaken loans bearing interest or its equivalent. But this community of specialists was a novelty in the Anglo-Danish city.

So why should Barnikel be lurking there? It was not simply his dress but also his actions that were so strange.

First he would advance a little way up the lane, then stop, turn, shuffle back to the bottom, then turn again, press forward, receive some inward check and come back down again. Leofric watched his old friend do this three times before, fearing that he might have gone mad, he started towards him. But evidently Barnikel had caught sight of him, for with a strange agility he scuttled off down the Poultry and vanished behind some stalls, leaving Leofric to ponder the question: What could the Dane be up to?

It was Hilda who discovered the answer the very next evening as she walked with Barnikel past St Bride's, towards St Clement Danes.

Little had changed for Hilda. Her life had been quiet. There had been one more child. If it was possible for a disappointed woman to mellow, she had done so. Her chaste rendezvous with the Dane by the banks of the Thames were perhaps her greatest pleasure.

Recently, though, she had noticed a change in her friend. It was not just that he was preoccupied; suddenly he appeared older. The grey hairs in his red beard seemed more noticeable; a slight tremor in his hand told her that some nights he drank too much.

Her father had let her know about the curious scene he had witnessed by the Jewry, so now, when she judged the moment was right, she gently asked her old friend if anything was the matter. At first he would not tell her. But when they reached the little ruined jetty at Aldwych, she made him sit on a stone, and there, gazing sadly over the Thames, he at last confessed.

His debts had slowly grown, it seemed. She suspected his secret activities had been part of the cause, but did not ask. Since the Conquest, many Danish merchants had suffered from competition with the Normans. Recently there had also been heavy taxes on Londoners to pay for King William's castle-building. Barnikel was not ruined, but he needed money. "So soon I must go to the Jewry," he said bleakly, and shaking his head explained: "I have lent, but I have never had to borrow before." It obviously distressed him.

"But doesn't Silversleeves owe you money?" she asked, remembering her father's old debt.

He nodded. "He pays the interest."

"So why not claim it back?" she demanded.

He rose. "And let the Norman know I need it? Let him see me crawl?" Suddenly he was almost his usual self again. "Never!" he thundered. "I'd sooner go to the Jews."

And Hilda could only marvel, as most women do, at the vanity of men. But she thought she saw what to do.

And so, later that day, she visited her father and suggested to him: "Go to Silversleeves. Don't tell him Barnikel's in trouble, or that I told you. Just say that the debt's been on your conscience and ask him to repay it. He'll do it for you, and if it happens naturally, Barnikel needn't guess."

Leofric nodded his agreement. But before she left, he looked at his daughter thoughtfully.

"You're fond of him, aren't you?"

"Yes," she answered simply.

Leofric continued to gaze at her. For years he had wondered what her relationship with the Dane might be, but had never dared to ask. "I'm sorry I made you marry Henri," he said softly.

She returned his gaze. "No you're not," she said, and smiled. "But just do as I ask." Then she left.

Not long after this, a rift between Alfred and his friend and patron Barnikel began to open. It happened very privately.

They were standing in Barnikel's hall on a quiet evening. Little had changed. The great two-handed battle-axe still hung on the wall. Everything was as usual – or would have been if Alfred had not just repeated, still more firmly, the words he had spoken a moment before to the huge, red-bearded figure who was glaring at him furiously.

"No. I dare not." It was the first time Alfred had ever tried to refuse him.

Barnikel had once more been hearing voices from over the sea. Nor had he imagined them. The voices were very real. Indeed, in the closing months of 1083, King William of England was more worried about his new island kingdom than he had ever been.

The cause was a vast, northern conspiracy. Its origin was Denmark, where a new king, another Canute, was anxious for a Viking adventure. Even now his envoys had begun to negotiate with the Norman Conqueror's rivals, the envious King of France and the swashbuckling King of Norway.

Even the Conqueror's own family were not always reliable. His son Robert, aided by the French king, had already tried to rebel once, and recently William had been forced to put his half-brother, Odo, the fighting Bishop of Bayeux, in jail for suspected treason.

"And if all these come together, then even William may find it's more than he can handle," the Danish envoys were quick to point out.

Hardly surprisingly, such rumours were a source of delight for Barnikel. He might be sinking into debt. He might be growing old. "But in a year or two, we could have a Canute on the throne of England again," he cried to Alfred enthusiastically. "Think of that!"

How, then, could Alfred hesitate?

For a long time now, Alfred had been concerned about his relationship with the Dane. Five years had passed since they had last shipped arms. Five years in which England had been quiet. Five years in which Alfred had become the trusted master armourer at the Tower. He had even made a coat of mail for Ralph and a sword for Mandeville himself. He had raised his family, and lived in security.

True, every month or two Barnikel had come to him and asked him to make arms. Never very much at a time. Easy enough to accomplish without arousing suspicion and to hide in the several spaces he had devised under the floor of the armoury. Without telling even his wife, Alfred had continued to oblige the Dane out of loyalty. "I still owe it to him," he told himself. But as time passed and his family grew, he did these commissions with ever increasing reluctance. And a month ago, when he had surveyed the full size of the hoard hidden under the floor, he had been horrified.

"You could equip a hundred men," he whispered to himself. For the first time, he experienced a real sense of panic. If ever the Normans raided the armoury and found these arms? I could never explain that away, he thought.

"I'm frightened," he confessed to Barnikel.

"Then you're a coward."

At this Alfred only shrugged. He was much too fond of the Dane to take offence. Besides, there was a further consideration.

"I also think," he admitted, "that it's all becoming a waste of time. The truth is," he said quietly, "that most Englishmen have accepted William now. They might not even fight for the Danes."

Barnikel let out a roar of rage. And yet he could not altogether deny it. London, of course, would make its own terms with any king, but in several of the minor rebellions over the last ten years, the English in the countryside had actually fought side by side with the hated Normans, putting down the rebels – for the simple reason that such insurrections threatened to damage the harvest.

"You're a traitor," Barnikel angrily declared. And at this Alfred did bridle.

"If so," he retorted, "then what are your children?"

It was a sharp blow and it hurt the Dane. Alfred knew very well that the Dane's grown sons had shown little interest in joining their father in his secret activities. "If the King of Denmark arrives, we'll be Danish," the youngest son had once told him. "But not before." It was a sensible position to take, but Alfred knew that Barnikel had been deeply disappointed.

Perhaps it was because he saw how hurt the old man was that, a few minutes later, Alfred gave in and agreed to do as Barnikel asked. But he did so with misgivings.

In December of that year, Barnikel of Billingsgate was greatly surprised to find himself politely summoned to a meeting with Silversleeves.

There was no denying it. If Alfred had become independent, the long-nosed Norman had nowadays become nothing less than splendid. A man-at-arms stood by the gateway to his house. Two clerks busied themselves at a table in his fine stone hall. He was a canon of St Paul's. Archbishop Lanfranc himself had called upon him, and though that stern reformer had seen the clerical merchant for exactly the disgrace he was, he was too wise to do more than drily admonish the generous canon and patron of St Lawrence Silversleeves. Barnikel tried not to be impressed, but it was difficult.

The Norman greeted him with the utmost courtesy, begged him to sit down, and, looking down his nose at the table between them, gravely addressed him.

"It has long been on my mind, Hrothgar Barnikel, that I owe you the debt I took over from Leofric. I hope you will acknowledge that I have always discharged my obligations in this regard."

Barnikel nodded. Much as he disliked the Norman, he could not deny that for ten years he had paid the agreed interest on the nail.

"For a long time I have wished to discharge this debt," Silversleeves went on, "but the sum is large." Barnikel glanced at him suspiciously. He had heard of the Norman's tactic of forcing creditors to accept less than they were owed. To his surprise, Silversleeves continued blandly: "I believe, however, that if you could accept my offer, I am now in a position to repay the debt in full." Raising his head, he smiled.

For a moment Barnikel was too stunned to react. The debt repaid in full? He thought of his embarrassing visit to the Jewry that autumn. So far even he, who would not have shrunk from any battle, had not summoned up the courage to go back there. "What did you have in mind?" he asked gruffly.

Silversleeves picked up a parchment from the floor and unrolled it on the table. "Something that might interest you," he said. "An estate that has just come into my hands. You may know of it. It's called Deeping." Which surprised the Dane even more, as he did indeed know of the place.

It lay on the east coast about fifteen miles from the estates he himself had lost at the Conquest. Though he had not been there, he knew well that the land along that coastal strip was rich, and the Saxon charter before them indicated that, if anything, the estate might even be worth more than the debt he was owed.

"Please consider the matter at leisure if you wish," Silversleeves said. "Though I have an agreement drawn up if you are interested."

Barnikel, looking at him and then at the charter, heaved a sigh.

"I'll take it," he said.

It seemed that after all things were looking up.

Indeed, for Barnikel, in the year that followed the whole world became bathed in a new light. A dangerous light to be sure, but to the Dane each distant rumble, each faint flash upon the horizon, brought promise of the great conflagration for which his Viking soul was longing.

In the winter a great tax was raised. It fell heavily on London, but even in the countryside not a village was spared. Throughout 1084 the tension rose. Extra defences were prepared along the eastern coast. News came that the huge Danish fleet would be ready to sail by the next summer.

As the spring of 1085 began, word spread in London: "King William is bringing over an extra army of mercenaries from Normandy." In the city, a curfew was strictly enforced. And on their walk one day, Hilda warned Barnikel: "Ralph is posting spies in every street."

Which only made Barnikel relish the challenge all the more.

For when Alfred had declared that resistance to Norman rule was over, he had, in fact, been wrong. The Dane knew of fifty or sixty men who, if they thought there was a chance, would probably be ready to act. Some of these were men from Kent, where the greed of Odo had made the Norman rule unpopular; others were Danish merchants like himself who, since the Conquest, had been hit by the increasing influence of Continental merchants; others were dispossessed Saxons hoping to regain their lands.

It's just a question of waiting until the time is ripe, Barnikel told himself with satisfaction. Then I'll be ready.

The blow to these plans came in the month of May, from an unexpected quarter.

For Osric these were happy times. His first child was a healthy girl, who brought him great joy. Thanks to Alfred and his family, she never wanted for food or clothing. It seemed to him that only one thing was needed to complete his family happiness. "One day," he said to Dorkes, "perhaps there will be a boy as well."

In another way, the deepening political crisis in England also improved his life. With the work on the Tower progressing rapidly in its established routine, Ralph had become occupied with other duties for Mandeville, and his supervision of the work usually consisted of only a brief daily inspection. Labourers and masons went about their tasks with a sense of relief, and, as the high walls of the Tower rose, Osric's work settled into quite a pleasant daily rhythm.

And how fine it was. The upper and final storey of the Tower would be the most magnificent by far. "The royal floor, I call it," Osric liked to say.

It was, in fact, a double floor. Although many centuries later, an extra floor would be inserted halfway up, the original apartments soared to a height of nearly forty feet. The western half would be taken up by a huge hall, most of the eastern by the royal chamber. Twenty feet up, round the outside wall of both rooms, there would run an internal gallery like a cloister, where courtiers could stroll, gaze out through small windows at the River Thames, or look down through the Norman arches into the great rooms below. There were more *garderobes*, and in the eastern chamber another fireplace, though the huge main hall would be warmed in the traditional manner by the great braziers in its centre.

But noblest of all, in the south-eastern corner, was the chapel.

It was very simple, with a rounded apse in the eastern wall. Its space was divided by a double row of thick, round pillars, making a short nave and two side aisles, with a gallery on the upper level. Its arches were rounded, its windows just wide enough to bathe its pale grey stone in a pleasant light. It was dedicated to St John. It was perhaps here, in this simple, sturdy chapel in the great castle keep by the river, that the spirit of William the Norman conqueror of England could most perfectly be felt.

And the main arches were just nearing completion when, one evening in spring, Osric received an unexpected message that Barnikel wanted to see him.

Two people had thrown the Dane's plans into confusion. The first was Ralph Silversleeves.

As preparations for the expected invasion went forward, not only had King William sent for mercenaries from the Continent, he had also told Mandeville to prepare the Londoners. Which meant a new task for Ralph.

For once, the surly Norman had set about his work with intelligence. His men went from house to house collecting arms. All weapons of any description were taken and their owners warned that if they were found concealing anything afterwards, the punishment would be terrible. The Normans moved swiftly. Perhaps the only weapon they missed was Barnikel's great two-handed battle-axe which, to his family's horror, he obstinately insisted on hiding.

Since many of the weapons were in poor repair, they were taken to the armourers, where guards were posted to make sure nothing was removed. After this, they would be taken to a secure store. "And then I shall search the armourers as well, just to make sure they aren't hiding anything either," Ralph boasted to his family one evening.

"And where will you store all the arms, finally?" Hilda asked.

Ralph grinned. "In the Tower," he replied.

It would be the first time the Tower had been used. While building was in progress, the garrison of London remained dispersed at the Ludgate forts and other places, but the great cellar, sealed off from the rest of the Tower, could serve as a store. Ralph had already had another mighty door placed at the bottom of the spiral stairs for extra security, and this, too, Alfred had fitted with a heavy lock. "A guard at the top door to the staircase, that's all I need," Ralph remarked. King William would be pleased to know that his great castle was already in use.

By the following day, Hilda had told Barnikel everything.

If the threat of having the armoury searched made Barnikel and Alfred nervous, in the end it was the armourer's wife who brought the crisis to a head.

Wandering into the armoury late one night, she had surprised her husband just as he was concealing a sword in the hiding place under the floor. When, after her initial horror, she had forced him to tell her everything, she had given the armourer an ultimatum: "How could you put us all at risk? You must stop helping Barnikel. For good. And the arms must go."

Alfred soon discovered that on this matter, his usually comfortable wife was implacable. "If not," she told him, "I go."

Here lay the problem. Although Alfred was secretly rather relieved at this excuse to end the dangerous business, there remained an obvious difficulty. "Ralph's men guard the outside of the armoury. His spies are everywhere. Where can we hide the arms now? And even if I wanted to dump the arms in the river, how would we smuggle them out?"

Neither he nor Barnikel could think of what to do until the Dane, remembering Osric's ingenuity when they had smuggled the arms before, at last suggested: "Let's ask our little carpenter. Perhaps he'll have a bright idea."

And it was after listening to them carefully and thinking for some time, that Osric came up with a suggestion which caused the huge old Dane to gasp and then roar with laughter before crying:

"It's so outrageous, I do believe it might work."

Tap. Tap. As softly as he could. The little hammer and chisel echoing around the huge, cavernous cellar in the darkness. Tap, tap. Sometimes he held his breath, hardly able to believe that the short, sharp sounds could be muffled even by the thick walls of the Tower.

Tink, chink, he softly dislodged the mortar. Tap, scrape, he gently removed a stone. All by the light of a little oil lamp in the pitch-black cellar below the crypt. Tink, tink, like a busy gnome Osric burrowed in the bowels of the mighty Norman keep.

It was the strongroom he had made three years earlier that had given him the idea. "The wall beside the crypt was about twenty feet thick," he pointed out to Barnikel. "So if there was enough space in there to make a strongroom, then there must be the same amount of space in the wall of the cellar directly below." After careful calculation, Barnikel and Alfred had told him that they needed a space about five feet by eight feet to store all the illicit arms they had. Could he create such a thing?

"I'll need a week," he replied.

Tink, chink. All through the night, Osric eagerly went about his work.

It was not difficult for him to sneak into the empty Tower at night. Alfred had provided him with keys to the cellar doors. But there was very little time. As soon as he started to take arms into the cellar, Ralph would post guards on the door. Each night, therefore, until an hour before dawn, the little labourer worked, carefully loosening the stones to create a small space he could crawl into before cutting into the softer rubble behind.

This rubble he carefully placed into a sack, which he dragged from the crypt cellar, down the eastern chamber, round into the bigger western chamber and then over to the well, dropping it in there before returning. At the end of each night, he replaced the stones in the wall and fixed them with a shallow layer of new mortar that he hoped would not be noticeable in the cellar's darkness. Tidying the floor carefully, he then departed.

And so he continued, night after night. Apart from the fact that he sometimes seemed sleepy at his daily work, no one was any the wiser.

Only one thing worried him. "I'm going to put so much rubble down the well," he told the Dane, "I'm afraid I might block it." But each night when he let down the bucket, it continued to enter the water easily and come up clean. And by the end of the week, as he had estimated, there was a small secret chamber just high enough for him to stand up in hidden within the cellar wall.

Which left him one, final task.

On the last night, instead of going to the wall, he went to the big western cellar. In the corner, over the great drain, was the stout iron grille Alfred had made. So that the drain below could be cleaned and repaired, this grille opened on a hinge and was locked in place. Using the key Alfred had provided him with, Osric unlocked the grille and let himself down with a rope. Entering the long passage, he bent almost double and worked his way down it for fifty yards until he came to the outlet in the riverbank. This, too, was guarded by a thick metal grille.

His timing was good. It was low tide and the passage was nearly dry. He encountered nothing except for a few rats. The great bars of this grille could not be opened with a key, however, and so for the rest of the night Osric worked around the masonry until he had prised it loose. Then he carefully fixed it once more, but this time with thin mortar so that with accurate hammer blows in the right places he would be able to push it open from either side. Finally, he returned to the cellar, locked the grille, and left.

From now on, he would be able to get into the Tower cellar from the river, through the damp and narrow tunnel.

"Ralph won't think of that," he had pointed out to his friends. "After all, who wants to get into the Tower cellars except me and the rats?"

Three days later they stored the arms in the Tower. Everything went smoothly as, under close armed guard, three carts went from each of the several armouries to the Tower.

When they came to Alfred, however, he was not ready, and with some irritation they went away, to return later. In fact, it was not until the very end of the day that Alfred was ready to load all the arms, carefully wrapped in oiled cloths, on to the carts.

Noticing that there was an even larger quantity than they had been told to expect, the guards, accompanied by Alfred himself, went as quickly as possible to the great keep.

A number of men were needed to carry the heavy loads up into the Tower and down the spiral staircase into the cellar, where they were stacked against the walls. When Alfred peremptorily called to Osric, who was standing nearby, to help, nobody took any notice. Even Ralph, as he watched the arms go into the great fortress, was not suspicious. After all why should he be, when the weapons were going into the Tower?

Nor, at the end of the day, when they locked the two doors to the cellar and set the guard on the main floor, did anyone notice that Osric had vanished.

All night he laboured. It had to be done carefully. As quietly as he could, using the tools Alfred had smuggled in for him, he worked the stones loose to gain entry to the secret chamber. Then he began to move the arms.

Alfred had arranged everything cleverly. Each rolled cloth contained a second in which an illicit weapon was wrapped. Even after all the illegal weapons had been removed, therefore, there appeared to be just as many arms as before. One by one, Osric extracted the swords, spearheads and other arms and took them round to the hiding place. Two hours before dawn, he had stacked everything in there. Then he put the stones back in the wall and, as before, fixed them with a little mortar.

After this, the plan was simple. All he had to do was unlock the grille over the drain and clamber in. Putting his hand up through the bars, it would be easy enough to lock it after him and make his way out to the riverbank, opening the grille there and then fixing it behind him.

He tarried, though. First he threw dust at the freshly rebuilt wall to conceal the wet mortar. Then, lamp in hand, he checked round again and again to make sure that there was no other sign of his having been there. Dawn was approaching when at last he satisfied himself he could go. He was just halfway down the great western cellar when, suddenly, he heard the heavy oak door at the bottom of the stairs creak open behind him.

Ralph had been unable to sleep. He was too excited. The king himself had already expressed his pleasure about the arms operation and now, in the early dawn, Ralph had decided to survey his work.

Holding a torch high over his head, he walked down the huge western cellar where the arms had been stacked. With a smile he looked at them. A fine collection, all secure.

Then he saw Osric. The little fellow was asleep, sitting on the floor with his back to the wall. What the devil was he doing there? Ralph lowered the flaming torch near Osric's face until his eyes blinked open. And then Osric smiled.

"Thank God you've come, sir," he said.

He had been left down there, it seemed, the evening before. "I hammered on the door and shouted," he explained. "But nobody came. I've been here all night."

Suspiciously Ralph looked around, then searched him.

All the time, Osric was inwardly thanking the Lord that, as well as all his tools, he had thought to throw the key of the grille into the well behind him.

Finding nothing suspicious, Ralph considered the situation. The fellow must be telling the truth. How else could he have got there? Besides, what could he do down there anyway? And then, because the long-nosed Norman was in such a good humour anyway that morning, he did something most unusual. He made a joke.

"Well, Osric," he said. "This makes you the very first prisoner of the Tower." Then he let him out.

Later that day, Barnikel murmured with even greater satisfaction: "The arms are in the one place in London where no one would ever think of looking for them. And thanks to that drain, we can get them whenever we want."

But the Dane's satisfaction at this triumph was short-lived.

By the month of June, London was full of mercenaries. Every day the invasion was expected. The city was more nervous than it had been since 1066. July came. August. Soldiers came and went. Every sail upon the estuary seemed a threat. Rumours flew. "Yet still they don't come. I can't understand it," Barnikel grumbled. And then, gradually, word began to filter through. "Something's happening. There's been a delay. He isn't coming."

England waited, but still no Viking ships hove into sight.

The collapse of the great Danish expedition of 1085, which might, indeed, have meant the end of Norman rule in England, remains a historical puzzle. The vast fleet was assembled. The new King Canute was ready and eager to sail. And then some kind of disagreement took place. Exactly how or why has never been entirely explained. Certainly the next year Canute was murdered. Whether the disputes were genuinely internal or cleverly fostered by the agents of William of England will never be known. But whatever the true reason, the fleet did not sail.

Autumn departed and the Tower grew. Cold Christmas came, and as the Dane trudged down to the riverside, he saw only the bleak outline of the great stone square, dark in the snow. A sense of uselessness and lassitude descended upon him.

But it was for spring that fate had reserved her grim surprise.

Even in the autumn, Barnikel had suspected he was being cheated. Just after Michaelmas, when he had asked for the rents from his new estate at Deeping, the steward there had sent a derisory amount. When he demanded an explanation, the man had returned a message that made no sense at all. "Either this fellow is a fool or he takes me for one," swore the Dane, and if it had not been for a heavy fall of snow he would have gone to sort him out there and then. As soon as the snow cleared in early spring, therefore, he set off.

It took him several days. First he had to pass through the thick forests beyond London, then travel across the huge, flat wilds of East Anglia. The east wind was damp but bracing.

On the day he arrived, however, it had dropped to a light breeze and the sky had partly cleared. It was a pleasant March morning by the time he came to the coastal hamlet of Deeping.

Where he was unable to believe his eyes.

"What the devil happened?" he asked the sullen steward. The fellow only answered: "You can see."

For the hamlet and its green were standing alone, not amid broad fields, but marooned, surrounded on three sides and gently lapped by the salty waters of the grey North Sea.

"It came in another fifty yards this year," the steward told him. "Another two years and we reckon the whole village will be gone. It's like this for five miles along the coast," he explained. And then, with a kind of dour satisfaction on his long, pale face, he added: "There's your estate, sir." He pointed eastward. "All in the sea."

Seeing that it was so, poor Barnikel bellowed: "I've been cheated by that damned Silversleeves!" And then: "I've been cursed."

But why, he wondered in bafflement, why was the sea rising?

In fact, it was not. Or hardly. Although, even now, the final thawing of the last Ice Age was still fractionally raising the sea levels of the northern world, the true cause of this flooding lay in that other long-standing phenomenon; the tilting of England. This was what Barnikel really saw, the slow geological tilt that drives the coast of East Anglia down and raises the water level in the Thames Estuary. It was because of this that, here and there along the low-lying east coast, the land was being waterlogged and taken back by the northern seas of his Viking forefathers.

He stared east and shouted curses at the sea, still more at cunning Silversleeves, but knew there was nothing he could do. "I made my mark and seal on it," he cried. The document was legal. He had been duped.

He would have been even more bemused had he understood the true origin of his misery.

When, long ago, Silversleeves had taken over Leofric's debt to Becket, the merchant of Caen, he had simply been continuing the long process by which he secretly came to control all his old rival's trade with London. Only last Christmas, when Becket was owed for six separate shipments, the subtle Canon of St Paul's had suddenly stopped all payments and refused all supplies. "And that," as he explained to Henri, "should ruin them by Easter." Thanks to his foolish insult of twenty years ago, Barnikel had been added to this process, rather as an architect might add a side chapel to complete the symmetry of an otherwise perfect building.

Wiser, poorer and suddenly older, Barnikel returned sadly to London with an unremitting sense that the Normans had won. Upon reaching his house at Billingsgate he did not break a single door, but instead took to his bed for three weeks, during which time he drank far more ale than he should have. He did not come to himself again until Hilda, having tried unsuccessfully three times, at last gained admittance and, with her own hands, made him a bowl of sustaining broth.

In the year 1086, prompted partly by his need for extra revenue during the panic of the previous year, one of the most remarkable administrative feats in history was begun by William, the Conqueror of England. It was an amazing testimony not only to his thoroughness, but still more to his domination of his own feudal magnates. Certainly no other king in medieval Europe ever dared attempt such a thing.

This was the Domesday survey. William ordered it on Christmas Day, 1085. Village by village, the entire countryside was to be investigated by his clerks; every field and coppice measured and valued, every free man, serf and even the livestock counted. "He didn't miss a pig," men said, with a mixture of awe and disgust. At the end of it, King William would have the basis for the most efficient tax assessment seen until modern times.

In this respect, William was uniquely fortunate. Most feudal lords in Europe gave only grudging obedience to their monarch, and would never have tolerated such an inquisition. Even William never attempted such a thing in his own duchy of Normandy. But the island of England was different. Not only did he claim it belonged to him by conquest, but most of the landholders were now his own men, bound to him personally, and obedient. He could, therefore, be thorough.

On a bright morning in April, Alfred the armourer arrived at the hamlet near Windsor that he had left as a boy. He had meant to visit his family for some years, and now, as he approached the familiar bend in the river, he felt quite excited.

It was thanks to his father that he still had an interest in the place. In the years following the Conquest, the smith had acquired the tenancy of a number of strips of land on the manor, for which he paid a money rent. On his death he had left some of these to Alfred, who paid the rent while his brother arranged for the land to be worked. It brought the Londoner a modest extra income, for which he was glad, and also preserved a link with his childhood. Now, knowing that the Domesday surveyors would shortly be in the Windsor area, he had decided to go there to make sure his land claims were properly recorded.

It was a pleasant, lively scene that he found. The great field had already been ploughed. The seed had just been scattered and now, before the birds could eat it, the field was being harrowed. Four great carthorses were dragging the big wooden frame with its toothed underside across the heavy soil, covering the seed, while a gaggle of children followed, shouting and flinging stones to drive away the greedy crowds of birds.

There was the old forge with its wooden roof, his father's anvil and the sharp, familiar smell of charcoal. Nothing had changed.

And yet it had. Though his brother and his family greeted him warmly enough, there was something, something he could not quite put his finger on, that disturbed Alfred. Was it a tension between his brother and his wife? Was there a hangdog look about the fellow? He wondered what it was about, but had no time to ask, for the surveyors had already arrived.

There were three of them: two French clerks and a fellow from London who helped to translate. The reeve, the landlord's steward, was taking them round. Their practised eyes noted everything.

They had nearly finished when they got to the smithy. One of the clerks had gone with the London man to inspect the meadow, and as the other went round the cottages with the reeve, it was clear that he was anxious to leave. They paused politely, however, to inspect the forge. The clerk glanced enquiringly at the reeve, who, indicating Alfred's brother, remarked: "A good cottager. He does labour service for his land."

Alfred stared. How could this fellow be so careless?

"You pay rent," he prompted his brother. But his brother only looked sheepish and said nothing as the clerk made a note on his slate.

"And this one?" They were looking at him.

"I am Alfred the armourer, of London," he announced firmly. "A free citizen. I pay rent."

The steward nodded, confirmed the rent, and the clerk was about to write it down when his colleague called him away to show him something by the meadow. While he was gone, Alfred turned upon his brother.

"What does this mean?" he demanded. "Are you a serf?"

And then it came out. Times were hard; there was not enough work for the smithy and too many mouths to feed. His brother spoke sullenly, without conviction, before ending with a shrug.

Alfred understood. Free men paid rent; they also paid the king's taxes. It was not uncommon for a free peasant, unable to cope with these burdens, to pay his lord with labour instead and become a serf. "What difference does it make?" his brother weakly demanded.

In practice, in his day-to-day life, not much. But to Alfred that was not the point. It meant that his brother had given up. Then he glanced at his brother's wife and saw the thought in her eyes: if this rich brother from London gave us the land he had here, which he doesn't need, we'd be better off.

At that moment Alfred experienced the curious sensation that is often felt by successful men with poor relations. Perhaps it was meanness, or a deep instinct for survival, or a fear of contamination, or just impatience, but he felt a sudden rage. And if an inner voice reminded him that he, too, might have starved if it had not been for Barnikel, he countered this at once. When my chance came, I took it, he reminded himself. So it was that, gazing at them with disgust, he merely remarked: "I hope our father cannot see you now."

When the French clerk returned he did not ask any more questions. After a rapid glance at the other cottages, he prepared to leave. Only then did he recall that he had been about to write down something about the fellow with the white patch in his hair. What the devil had the man said he was? "Damn these English," he muttered. "They make such a confounded muddle of everything."

For despite the thoroughness of the Domesday survey, the French clerks who compiled it were frequently baffled by what they found.

"Is this man a slave, a serf, or free?" the orderly, Latin-trained clerks would ask. In return, they would very often receive an account of curious, indefinite arrangements that time and custom had wrought and which even local people could scarcely disentangle. How could they put these Anglo-Saxon uncertainties into the clear categories that their document demanded? Often they were unsure, so they would resort to some general category whose legal status was deliberately vague. One of these was the category of *villanus* – a villein – a term that carried no specific legal sense at this date, and meant neither serf nor free man but merely "peasant".

The clerk frowned. He could not remember what the fellow with the white flash in his hair had said, but he recalled that the man beside him, who looked like his brother, was a serf. He sighed, therefore, and noted: *villanus*. And so it was that Alfred appeared in the great Domesday Book of England as a small, nameless mistake. It did not seem important, at the time.

1087

In August 1086, a great and symbolic meeting took place eighty miles west of London at the castle of Sarum. There King William was presented with the huge volumes of his Domesday Book and all his chief men did homage to him. It was supposed to be an occasion to celebrate, but even at this time there was a sense of melancholy in the air. The king was growing old. He was very corpulent; when he hoisted himself into the saddle, it was with a groan. His enemies were as many as ever, the most notable being the jealous King of France. Seeing him now, ageing and unwell, the great men of the kingdom were filled with a new foreboding.

For if few loved William, all feared him. If he was brutal, he kept order. What, then, would become of his Norman lands and his English kingdom when the great Conqueror was gone?

They would fall to his sons. To Robert, dark and moody. William, called Rufus for his red hair, a clever, cruel fellow. Unmarried still, it was said that he preferred the company of young men in his bed to that of women. And Henri, the youngest, devious and unknowable. There was also their ambitious half-uncle, Bishop Odo of Bayeux, still waiting in the jail in which King William had put him. What, indeed, would happen with such fellows as these free to roam after the Conqueror had gone?

In the spring of the new year, things grew worse. Cattle disease broke out in the west and spread rapidly. In late spring there were terrible storms and it was feared the harvest might be ruined. Once more, King William was fighting on the Continent, and his agents were already trying to raise new taxes.

It was not surprising, therefore, that in London, amongst the merchants who contemplated the future, there should be careful calculation. As the months went by, there were many secret conversations. Nor was it surprising that some of them involved Barnikel.

Even in dark days, however, a small ray of light may warm some corner of the world. And so it was that in the spring of 1087 Osric learned that Dorkes was pregnant again.

It was her third pregnancy. After their daughter there had been another girl, this time stillborn. But this healthy bundle kicking inside her so vigorously seemed different somehow. Osric noticed that she was carrying this baby differently too. And in his heart he was certain: it would be a son.

A son. Osric was only in his twenties, but in those harsh times a labourer could not expect to live for very long. In the comfort of his house, a rich merchant might live to be old indeed. But Osric would probably be dead at forty. He had already lost three teeth.

A son who would be grown, with luck, before his father died. A son who might have a better life. "Maybe," he said to Dorkes, "if he has better luck than me, he'll be a carpenter."

"And what will you call him, if he's a boy?" she asked.

To which, after a little thought, he replied: "I'll give him the name of our greatest English king. I'll call him Alfred."

But perhaps the most astonishing event that took place that year concerned Ralph Silversleeves.

In the month of August, just when another storm made it quite certain that the harvest would be ruined, he announced that he was going to be married.

He had met the girl in May. She was a large blonde creature, the daughter of a German merchant then residing at the German wharf by the mouth of the Walbrook. Her father was even quite rich. She had a large, flat face, large blue eyes, large hands, large feet and, as she cheerfully told anyone who cared to listen, a large appetite. Finding herself sturdy and unwed at the age of twenty-three, she had spotted Ralph and decided that she liked his clumsy ways; and nothing had given Ralph greater pleasure than the look of delight on his father's face, and the astonished disbelief on Henri's, when he had told them.

On a chain around his neck he proudly wore a talisman she had given him depicting a rampant lion. She said it was how she thought of him. They were to be married before Christmas.

Her name was Gertha.

That summer, there was one other important change in the Silversleeves family, but it happened so quietly that not even a ripple appeared on the surface of their lives.

During the month of June, Hilda realized that her husband was unfaithful. She could not say for sure when it had begun. The gap between them had slowly grown wider, until one day she discovered that, if the truth be told, neither of them wished any longer to cross it. She guessed there might be other women. Then, one evening in June, he went out and indicated he might not return that night.

Since her father Leofric had been unwell recently, she went to stay with him in her old home by the sign of the Bull. A few nights later, Henri went out again. By then she was sure.

When, at last, the impending crisis came, it did so rather unexpectedly.

Following the storms that ruined the harvest, the weather grew hot and dry. The heat of that wasted summer continued late into a tinder-dry September, and it seemed to most men that some conflagration was likely.

At the end of summer, in the year of Our Lord 1087, while besieging a French castle of no great importance, William, Duke of Normandy and King of England, was wounded. The wound festered. Very soon it was clear that William was dying.

Around his deathbed his family gathered. To Robert was given Normandy; to William Rufus, England; to young Henri, money. Odo, the dying king's half-brother, was released from prison. Thus the stage was set for a generation of jealousy, intrigue and murder. Some days later, after a long, hot journey across country to the Norman ancestral church at Caen, the putrid corpse of King William the Conqueror, so swollen that it could not be forced into its coffin, burst over the bystanders, scattering entrails and much else besides.

Meanwhile, as quickly as he could, Rufus crossed the Channel to be crowned in England.

Two weeks later, on a warm, dry, October day, a small group of men paid a call on Barnikel the Dane at his house by All Hallows. When Barnikel heard what they wanted, he smiled. "I can provide what you need," he said. "I have it all under lock and key." Then, secretly, he sent for Osric.

Barnikel the Dane had no idea that his luck had just run out.

Ralph Silversleeves could hardly believe his good fortune. What a chance, if things worked out, to impress the new Norman king.

He understood the political situation, because Mandeville had patiently explained it to him.

"Robert will try to seize England from Rufus, because he wants to rule over as much as his father did. Odo will probably support him. If so, he'll be able to bring in a huge party of knights from Kent. To my knowledge, because they don't like Rufus, a number of the other barons are ready to join them. And you can be sure there's a party in London ready to go with them if they think there's profit in it. But," the magnate continued, "most of the sheriffs and the countryside want the King of England, not the Duke of Normandy, to rule over them. So we are backing Rufus." He had looked at Ralph bleakly. "Our job is to keep London quiet. Find the conspirators. Find their arms. Rufus will be grateful if we can turn something up."

The next day, out of the blue, had come this unexpected piece of information, which, when he had thought it over carefully, caused Ralph to summon a dozen spies to him and declare: "We're going to set a trap that will catch them all."

Osric stood by the riverside and smiled. Everything was going to be all right.

Behind him, the grey mass of the Tower loomed. The great royal floor was almost completed now. Already, the first of the huge oak timbers that would stretch right across the building to take the roof had arrived at the site. The only trees big enough had been found nearly fifty miles away, and had to be shipped there by river. It would take another two years to complete the roofing, but even so, in the afternoon sun the great, grim keep seemed to suggest that already, Norman though it was, it had as much right to be there as the Celtic ravens on the slopes.

Osric looked around him. The place where the Tower drain came down to the riverbank was well hidden, some carpenters' huts screening it from view. Barnikel's boat could pull right up to the grille and be loaded unseen. It would take only a few moments to open the grille. Then it was up the passage to the inner grille, for which Alfred had once again supplied the key.

While Barnikel kept watch by the boat, he would empty the secret chamber and bring out the arms. Before the autumn dawn, they would be on their way down the river with nobody the wiser.

Exactly who the arms were for, he did not know and did not ask. As far as he was concerned, if the Dane said they were needed, that was good enough. The risk, he judged, was slight. It was one more blow against the Norman king. Besides, as he declared to the Dane: "What a present, anyway, to welcome the birth of my son."

The birth was very near. Two days ago he had thought Dorkes was going into labour. Certainly, before the week was out, the child would be born. He and Dorkes were both sure it was going to be a boy.

The operation at the Tower was set to take place the following night. Satisfied that everything was in order, Osric was looking forward to it.

That same evening Henri had gone out, intimating that he might not return. So, leaving the children with the servants at home, Hilda had decided to spend the night at her father's house. She had already passed a pleasant hour there when, while the evening sun was still glowing, she slipped out for a stroll along the West Cheap.

It was just as she was returning by St Mary-le-Bow that she saw the German girl, who immediately hailed her. Hilda sighed. As a Saxon, she usually felt at home with the city's German merchants, who were good-hearted and hardworking. She liked her future sister-in-law, too, but found her exhausting. Today Gertha was radiating enthusiasm.

Hilda asked after Ralph.

"He is very well. He is wonderful. I have just seen him." Beaming at Hilda, she seemed positively excited by the memory. "He is so clever." And then, apparently unaware of the look of bafflement that crossed Hilda's face at this news, she took Hilda by the arm, pressed her into the wall of St Mary-le-Bow and, suddenly becoming very confidential, imparted a still more surprising, and much more interesting, item of information.

"He told me not to tell anyone," she whispered, "but we are family." She glanced round to make sure they were not overheard. "Can you keep a secret?"

Faint stars were just appearing over the little church of All Hallows, and in the great hollow below deep shadows were gathering round the Tower like a moat when Hilda came quietly to the stout thatched homestead of Barnikel the Dane.

As he moved about, lighting the lamps, she watched him thoughtfully. There was more grey than red in his beard now. When she had first given him the bad news, she had been distressed at how old and tired he had looked. But now he seemed stronger again. Taking a jug from a table, he poured them each a goblet of wine.

She gazed, half sorry for him, yet half admiring.

"What will you do?" she asked.

It was a poor peasant in the forests of Essex who had given Ralph his clue. He had been found with a sword, and they had taken him to the castle at Colchester. They were curious as to how he obtained the weapon and questioned him closely. He had borne it bravely, but after the joints of his fingers had been crushed he had been persuaded to talk.

He had owned the sword for a long time, since he had lived in the forest with Hereward the Wake's men. But that had been more than fifteen years ago. "And those people are all dead now," he said.

The guard at Colchester had sent the fellow to London, giving Ralph the chance to question him. The fellow did not tell him much. Except for one thing. The arms, he admitted, had come from London, where there was a man whom the rebels trusted. About this man he swore he knew nothing, until, just before he died, he remembered one detail: "He had a red beard."

It was not much. God knew, there were plenty of men with red beards in the old Anglo-Danish city. Plenty of Normans had red beards, come to that. But gradually, as Ralph considered all the facts he knew, a pattern began to form in his mind.

A hater of Normans; a member of the old Defence Guild; a friend of Alfred the armourer. Then there were other things he knew. The pieces fell into place until he cried with rage, "I've been duped," and then, with a smile of cruel satisfaction: "But now I can catch them all."

And so he had set his trap.

"Tomorrow morning he's going to come at dawn. He's going to raid this house, your store at Billingsgate, and Alfred's armoury. If he finds arms, he's got you. If not, his spies are going to watch you to see if you lead them to anything," Hilda said anxiously.

As he listened, the old Dane had only nodded. "They'll find nothing," he assured her. "As for our being watched . . ." He shrugged. "There will just have to be a slight change of plan."

And then he told her about Osric and the secret of the Tower.

As she listened, and realized the danger that the old man and his friends were in, she felt nervous, and then moved. "Why are you doing it?" she asked.

It was simple, he explained. If Robert became king, he would have huge territories to control. "And he's not the man his father was." Norman rule would weaken. "And then . . ." The heirs of the old English line were still alive. So were King Harold's family. For some time he showed her all the things that might happen until at last, with a smile, she shook her head.

"You just don't give up, do you?"

He grinned, almost boyishly. "I'm too old to give up. If an old man gives up, he dies."

"Do you feel so old?" she asked, genuinely curious.

"Sometimes." He smiled. "Not with you." And she blushed, knowing this was true.

There was a low fire in the brazier in the centre of the room. He stoked it a little and then sat down beside it in a big oak chair, motioning her to a bench, and for several minutes they sat there, quite contentedly, in silence. She noticed that in repose his face, though it did not look younger, had a vigour about it, like that of a splendid old lion that has not lost his force. Meditatively, he drank his wine.

What a strange evening it was, she thought. She had done all she could. She should probably go. Yet she felt no inclination to depart. Her father always fell asleep by sunset. God knew where her husband was. After a short while, without a word, she pulled the bench close, leaned across, and laid her head on his chest.

He did not move. Then, after a few moments, she felt his great, gnarled hand begin to stroke her hair. It was surprising how gentle and how comforting it felt. She started to play with his beard, and felt him chuckle.

"I expect many women have done that in your life," she said softly.

"A few," he replied.

"What a pity – " she began, and then stopped.

"What?"

She had been about to say, "What a pity I never married your son." Instead she replied, "Nothing," and he did not press her.

As the minutes passed, she found herself considering her life. Henri's cold image arose. Putting it out of her mind, she thought: I'd rather have married this older man, even as he is now, with his magnificent courage, and his big, warm heart. And suddenly, wanting to express her affection and to do something for him, she moved round and, smiling softly into his eyes, kissed him on the lips.

She felt him quiver. She kissed him again.

"If you go on doing that . . ." he whispered.

"Do," she said happily, rather to her own astonishment.

* * *

It had been a long time since Barnikel had made love and he had supposed that such a thing might no longer easily come to pass. Yet as he rose and took in his arms the young woman whom he had loved first as a daughter and then as a woman, all doubts seemed to vanish.

As for Hilda, experiencing for the first time the slow and delicate caresses of an older man and brought gently and lovingly to ardour, she found a warmth that was infinitely touching.

They stayed together until the early hours, when she stole back through the streets to her father's house and slipped up to the chamber where he was asleep.

And so, after a dozen years, Barnikel's last love was consummated.

Soon after dawn, as Barnikel had requested, she slipped out of her father's house and delivered two messages. One to Alfred. One to Osric.

And it did not occur to Hilda that on both her journey to Barnikel and her journey back, she had, as usual, been followed.

It was not until mid-morning that Ralph Silversleeves, accompanied by half a dozen men-at-arms, visited Barnikel at his warehouse at Billingsgate. Politely the Norman informed the Dane that they must make a search, and Barnikel, though he shrugged irritably, let them go about their business. Three of the men then went up to his house by All Hallows.

They were thorough. They took two hours, but at the end of the morning they gave up. At the same time, a man arrived from Alfred's armoury. They had found nothing there either.

"I hope you have now set your mind at rest," the Dane remarked to Ralph drily, taking the grimace he received in reply as a sign of assent.

As Ralph left, however, he had such an overwhelming sense of having been duped that once on the quay he told his men: "There are arms here somewhere. We're not giving up." And he was as good as his word. To the fury of the boatmen, he started inspecting their cargoes. Four more of the little warehouses were investigated. They went up the street and moved along the East Cheap, poking at carts and stalls, first to the terror of the traders, soon to their jeers. But if Ralph had ever been afraid of making a fool of himself, he did not seem to care now. Red-faced and determined, he ploughed on, moving eastwards towards the Tower.

It was in the early afternoon, within the lodgings by the Tower, that a new life entered the family of Osric the labourer. It brought him such joy that as he stood outside, gazing over the Tower into the sky, the squat little fellow was unable to speak for several minutes.

For he had been right. He had a son.

Barnikel was restless. He had been in his house all afternoon. The events of the last twenty-four hours had been taxing, and during the afternoon he had felt tired. Now, however, unable to bear his confinement any longer, he finally ventured out into the East Cheap to take the air.

It was still warm, although in the west the sky had turned a deep magenta. The stallholders in the market were packing up as he strolled along the East Cheap in the direction of Candlewick Street. It was just before he reached the end of the market that he saw Alfred walking calmly towards him.

Both men thought quickly. If they were being followed, it would be wisest to do nothing suspicious. They prepared to pass each other, therefore, with nothing more than a polite nod, and would have done so if, at that precise moment, a small figure had not suddenly rushed to join them, tugging at their sleeves with urgency.

It was Osric. He had been walking about the place for almost an hour in a daze of happiness. He had been told by Hilda at dawn that he must avoid Barnikel, but on seeing his two friends together, the little fellow had been so excited that for a moment he had forgotten everything and run up to them, his round face glowing.

"Oh sir," he cried, "oh Alfred. I have such news." And as Alfred paused and Barnikel looked down, he burst out: "I have a son!" Then he beamed at them as if they were all at the gates of Paradise.

So the two men, who in their own crisis had quite forgotten

Osric's family concerns, gathered round laughing and hugged the little fellow.

There was no moon that night, and a thin pall of cloud blown by a rising wind from the west was now hiding even the stars. As the boat slipped up the dark river, the only light came from a small fire that had started somewhere on the city's western hill.

Softly the boat bumped into the mud by the entrance to the Tower drain.

Osric was alone. His response to the Dane's message that morning had been simple. Since Barnikel was being watched, he had better stay in his house. "I can manage alone," he said.

Carefully, therefore, he tied the boat up to a stake and then worked away to loosen the grille. Before very long, he had wriggled into the drain. Cautiously, disturbing only the rats, he crept up the dark tunnel towards the black and cavernous womb of the London Tower. Hoisting himself up with a rope, he reached the grille above, unlocked it, and made his way through the cellar.

Hilda sat in her chair. In her hands was a piece of embroidery, but she was finding it hard to concentrate. Henri had come home early that morning, but apart from a polite enquiry after her father, they had spoken little. All day she had waited in suspense. Now she tried to embroider while Henri played chess with his youngest son and occasionally glanced at her in his cool, detached way.

The evening was quiet. Some way off, by the West Cheap, a fire had started at dusk and had spread to several houses. Such things were common in London, however, and she had thought no more about it.

But her heart did jump when, two hours after dusk, Ralph arrived to pay them a visit.

By now, all London had heard of his exploits in the East Cheap that morning, but although Henri looked amused and Hilda anxious, nobody said anything. Indeed, by now the surly fellow seemed not so much angry as thoughtful. Nodding to them all and taking a pitcher of wine, he sat on a bench opposite Henri and gazed morosely into the fire for some time before speaking. When, at last, he did, Hilda felt herself go cold. "I have a problem, Henri," he said.

"What is that?"

Ralph took a draught of wine, then looked up slowly. "A spy," he said quietly. "Close to me." Hilda felt her hand tremble. "You see," he went on, "I nearly made a big catch today. Arms. I'm sure they were there."

"Perhaps you just made a mistake."

"It's possible," Ralph admitted. "But I have an instinct, you see. I think the conspirators were tipped off."

"By whom?"

Ralph was quiet for a moment. "By someone who knew my plans." He looked straight at Hilda. "Who do you think could have done it?"

Hilda knew that she had gone very pale. She rested her hands in her lap and stared back at him. Did he know, or was this an innocent question? Was it a bluff to catch her out? But why should he suspect her? Her mind raced over the possibilities. "I've no idea, Ralph," she said. But despite herself, it seemed to Hilda that her voice had shaken.

They were both looking at her now, Ralph and Henri. She longed to get up and leave them, but dared not do so. Who knew how long the agony might have continued, had it not been for an unexpected interruption.

It was Gertha. Her face was flushed from her evening walk and she was beaming with pleasure to see them all. Oblivious to the tension in the room, she went straight to Ralph, kissed him, laughed loudly as he blushed awkwardly, then took the talisman he wore into her large hands and cradled it for a moment.

"The fire out there is growing big," she remarked, and Hilda prayed that this would change the conversation. But her prayer was not answered.

Turning to Ralph, Gertha remarked: "So you did not arrest the red-beard?"

Ralph grunted. "Something happened."

"You will catch him. Won't he, Hilda? He is so clever."

Once again, Hilda realized that they were all looking at her. She stared at the German girl numbly. Was this some horrible trap? Had Gertha already told Ralph that she had known about his raid the night before? Was she about to do so now? Instead, however, to her equal horror, Gertha went on: "I saw him this evening in East Cheap with his two friends, hugging each other and laughing."

Ralph's jaw dropped. "Which friends?"

"The man who makes armour. Alfred, yes? And also a little man with a round head. No nose." She laughed. "Maybe they think you won't catch them, but you will." Then, giving his head a kiss, she happily announced, "I go to my father now," and was gone.

In the silence that followed, nobody spoke. Hilda, staring down at her embroidery, felt her mind in a whirl. How the girl had seen the two men with Osric she had no idea. What it might mean, she dared not think. At last, she glanced towards Ralph.

He was sitting very still, staring at the fire. He seemed to have forgotten her, but his face was working, as though in pain. How could he have overlooked that link? Yet it was so obvious. Barnikel the friend of Alfred. Alfred the friend of Osric. Osric, the wretched little serf he had found in the Tower cellars. The Tower cellars, where the arms were stored. The Tower cellars, for which Alfred had made the locks.

And suddenly he saw it. How they had done it, he could not imagine. Nor why. But now, jumping up from his seat, he cried out aloud:

"The devils. I know what they've done. I know where the arms are hidden!"

"Where?" asked Henri quietly.

"The Tower itself!" Ralph shouted. Then, to Hilda's terror, he added: "I'll go there now."

And he rushed out of the house, followed by Henri.

Hilda ran swiftly. In the darkness, it seemed to her that she flew. Past the long shadow of St Paul's she ran, then down the western hill towards the Walbrook.

She knew she must hurry. It might even be too late. But whatever the risks, even if there were spies watching his house, she knew where she must go.

She must tell Barnikel. He would know what to do.

So great was her urgency, she scarcely noticed that the fire which had started earlier had now been spread by the wind all the way along the line of the West Cheap and was attacking some of the houses on the eastern hill.

Nor did she notice something else much stranger. As she ran down the hill, other feet were running softly not far behind her.

She crossed the little bridge over the Walbrook and started along Candlewick Street. It was empty now. She was panting so hard that she could hear nothing else. Her chest was hurting. Reaching the London Stone, she paused for a moment to catch her breath and heal the stitch in her side. She leaned forward, her hands on her knees.

The strong hands took her completely by surprise as they suddenly grabbed her, pinned her arms, and threw a cloak over her head. Before she had time to scream, they were dragging her swiftly into an alley.

The job was easier than Osric had thought. He had soon established a rhythm. First he took all the arms out of the chamber and across to the grille. Letting them down into the drain was not as hard as he had imagined; it took only half an hour. After this, he dragged them in bundles down the black passage until he reached the faint outline of the grille in the riverbank.

Two hours after he had entered the cellar, he was ready to load the arms on to the boat.

Only one thing had surprised him. Each time he had come down the passage towards the grille, it had seemed to him that the sky outside was lighter. Though he had somewhat lost track of time as he worked, he knew it was still only the first half of the night. It could not possibly be the light of dawn he was seeing. So when, finally, he stepped out on to the mud, he received a shock.

Blown by the wind, the fire that had begun on the western hill had developed a huge and terrible life of its own. Not only were the wooden buildings of London tinder-dry; not only was there a wind behind the leaping flames; but once it reaches a certain critical point, a great fire creates a wind of its own. So it was that on this night in the autumn of 1087, the huge fire had taken hold. Crackling and roaring, it had advanced across the eastern hill, along the spur behind the Tower and round to All Hallows.

As he emerged from the tunnel, it was the noise that Osric noticed first. A dull, continuous roar coming from the city. Only as he reached the boat and turned round did he see it.

It was an astounding sight. Hissing, crackling, sending up explosions of sparks, the fire was leaping up like a single flame round the rim of the curving slopes above. Here and there a flare suddenly rose as though some huge, unseen dragon was lurking behind the hill, breathing flames as it devoured the city. And looming up before this encircling ring of fire was the great, black shadow of the Tower.

It was a striking picture, but he had no time to look.

Ignoring the flashing and spluttering flames on the hill above, he dived back into the blackness of the tunnel.

Ralph hurried down the hill. Below him, lit by the flames, stood the huge mass of the Tower.

His progress had been delayed. Twice as he hastened across the western hill he had been forced to pause to direct people who were trying to contain the fire. Whatever his faults, he was a man of action. Using a chain of men from the garrison at Ludgate, he had attempted to save a house by passing buckets of water from a well. "Douse your roofs," he had cried to the people in Poultry. At the Walbrook stream, he had made another concerted attempt to hold the fire. But even as they watched, the great red monster had flown hissing and spitting across a hundred-foot gap from one thatched roof to another. Finally realizing that it was useless, he had hurried on through streets of panic-stricken people, feeling the flames behind him as he ran ahead of their roar towards the great, grim silence of the waiting Tower.

In a few bounds, he was up the wooden staircase. With hardly a glance back at the encircling flames, he strode through the doorway into the main hall, calling for the guard.

There was no sound. He went through the chamber, heading towards the stairs to the cellar. There was a torch burning in an iron bracket, but no guard. Ralph cursed. No doubt the fellow had gone to look at the fire. Seizing the torch to light him on his way, he unlocked the door and went down the spiral stairs.

At first, as he gazed around the chamber and the main western cellar, he saw nothing.

Then he noticed the open drain. So that was it. Taking up a position with his sword, he waited for someone to come up. Nobody did. He waited a little more, straining to hear. After a while, fearing that perhaps the conspirators might already be making their escape, he cautiously lowered himself down. Holding the torch in one hand and his sword in the other, he advanced along the passage.

More than half the weapons were stowed away. It would not be long now before the loading was done. After that Osric had one trip back up the passage to make sure he had not dropped anything. The tide was starting to come in. So much the better. It would be easier to get the heavy boat off the mud.

He was just bending over the boat, stowing some spears, when he heard a sound behind him, turned, and saw the familiar, long-nosed face of Ralph Silversleeves emerging from the passage.

The Norman straightened up and smiled. "Alone, Osric?" he asked. Then, glancing around: "I think so." Seeing Osric's astonished face, he calmly went on: "You are arrested, Osric, in the name of the king," and, advancing across the mud, he pointed his sword at the little fellow's midriff. "You thought you could deceive me with your friends, didn't you?" he hissed. "But soon, perhaps in there," he jerked his head towards the Tower, "you are going to tell me all about it."

The flames were leaping higher than ever above the slopes. From somewhere behind All Hallows there was a great crack and a billow of flame. The red flashes lit the Norman's face, half pale, half in brutal shadow.

It was now that poor Osric made his foolish move. Scrambling into the boat, he snatched for a weapon. A moment later, his face ghostly white, his eyes larger and more solemn than ever, he faced the Norman again. In his hand was a spear.

Ralph watched him. He was not afraid. The serf lunged at him furiously, but he stepped back. He let Osric clamber out and advance towards him while he gently retreated up the bank, each step taking the little fellow further away from the arms still in the boat.

How pathetic Osric looked. Ralph saw the hatred in his eyes: it radiated from his whole body, the pent-up loathing of a man who has suffered two decades of oppression. Ralph did not even blame him. He just kept his eye on the tip of the spear. Another backward pace. He was halfway up the path now, at a clear advantage. Thanks to the flickering red light rising so fiercely above the Tower, the spear gleamed, easily visible, while the serf blinked at the glare in front of him.

Osric lunged.

It was so easy. With a single, swift blow from his sword, Ralph cut off the spearhead, leaving Osric with nothing but the shaft in his hands.

"Well, little man," he said softly, "are you going to kill me with that stick?"

Osric's large, round face was so woebegone, his eyes so desperate and serious; an open, pathetic smudge where his nose should have been; a broken shaft where the spearhead had gone. Uselessly, yet unable to give up, he took another pace forward, jabbing at the Norman with his broken weapon.

Ralph grinned. "Do you want me to kill you, so you can escape torture?" he asked. "Would you like that?" He chuckled. He needed the serf alive, but it amused him to frighten him.

He raised his sword.

How startled Osric looked. How amazed. Was it the sword flashing before him? The prospect of death? The huge red wave of fire that had just risen behind the Tower? Who knew? Ralph started to bring his sword down.

But it was not the fire, nor the sword, but another astonishing vision that had caused Osric to gasp in amazement. It was a great, red beard and a pair of blazing eyes, a huge figure from out of the shadows that now arose, blocking out even the Tower, and, surrounded by a great halo of fire, his arms upraised like some avenging Viking god, swung the mighty double-handed battle-axe through the flame-filled sky, and smote down upon the Norman's head, smashing the skull and cleaving even his torso in two down to the bottom of his ribcage.

Barnikel had come.

Half an hour later, they buried Ralph's body.

It had been Osric's idea, and it had seemed appropriate. Dragging it up the passageway wrapped in oiled cloths, they had carried the body to the secret chamber where the weapons had been stored, and placed it in there. Then, carefully, Osric had sealed up the wall again and they had left, leaving no trace, locking and refixing the grilles behind them. It pleased him to think of the Norman locked in there for eternity.

Soon afterwards, he guided the boat into the stream, towards the place where other hands would disperse the weapons.

Barnikel, meanwhile, walked back through the city. His own house at All Hallows was already in flames. He did not care. There was nothing he could do to save it. The fire had spread everywhere now, from the stalls in Candlewick Street all the way up to Cornhill. But the most significant event of that night was announced when, crossing the Walbrook, Barnikel heard the cry: "The fire's got St Paul's. It's coming down." Which caused him, at that moment to smile. For in his hand he held the talisman and chain they had ripped from Ralph's broken body. And now he knew where to put it.

One thing about that evening remained a mystery.

Just as the Dane and Osric were taking the body away, the labourer had turned to the old man. "By the way," he demanded, "how did you come to turn up here so conveniently?"

Barnikel smiled. "I got a message. I came as fast as I could. As I didn't see Ralph on the way to the Tower, I came here." He grinned. "At just the right time."

"But who sent the message?" the little fellow persisted.

"Oh, I see. Yes, that was certainly lucky." He nodded. "A fellow came. From Hilda."

Which was a mystery.

1097

It was one summer evening ten years later, as Hilda sat in the hall of the house by St Paul's, that the mystery was solved.

Looking back on her life, she usually supposed that she was contented. Certainly, it had to be admitted that over the last decade things had generally worked out for the best. Osric had gone, though she sometimes saw his little son, who lived with Alfred and his family now. Barnikel too. But she was glad of that. A month after the great fire of eighty-seven he had suffered a huge stroke down at Billingsgate Wharf and had crashed out of this life into the hereafter. A year later the expected rebellion in Kent and London had taken place and been utterly crushed. "Thank God he wasn't there to make a fool of himself," she often murmured.

And now old Silversleeves had gone too. Two months before, on a wet April night, a merchant had arrived at the stout stone hall of Silversleeves with a written message for the old man. An hour later a servant had approached the master to find him sitting stiffly in his chair, apparently still reading the message on the table before him. Except that he was dead.

The Canon of St Paul's had been buried in St Lawrence Silversleeves with every obsequy and honour. Three days later she and Henri had moved into the house, and in the coming weeks even she had been astonished to discover the full extent of the fortune he had bequeathed them.

There had been peace too, for Rufus reigned securely now. Recently he had built a huge hall of his own at Westminster, a fitting companion for the Confessor's Abbey. He was strengthening the fortress beside Ludgate. And when she glanced up from the courtyard of her house, she could see, on the site where the Saxon St Paul's had burnt down that fateful night, the outline of a great Norman cathedral, massively built in stone, that would soon dominate the entire skyline, just as the Tower dominated the river.

Yet whenever she stared at St Paul's and remembered that great fire, she always found herself pondering certain mysteries.

The talisman belonging to Ralph had been found in the cathedral's charred ruins. But what had he been doing there? And whose were the mysterious hands that had held her for two whole hours that night before she had been just as suddenly released near the Walbrook only to see half London burning? She had never been able to solve either puzzle, and she had not supposed that she ever would.

Now that their children were grown, it often happened that Hilda and her husband were alone in the evenings, and they had long since evolved a habit of politely ignoring each other by which they could tolerate the other's presence quite comfortably.

Hilda, therefore, was quietly doing her embroidery; Henri was sitting by his father's chessboard, playing against himself.

This evening, however, Hilda was irritable. The reason, she thought, was the house. She had always felt uncomfortable in the stern, stone hall. She wanted to go outside, or else to find some more intimate, congenial place. Blaming her husband for all this, she occasionally glanced at him with an expression of dislike.

It was after he had made some twenty moves on the chessboard that Henri, aware of her angry looks, calmly turned his eyes towards her and remarked: "You should try to conceal your thoughts."

"You have no idea what is in my mind," she snapped, resuming her needlework, then, after a few cross passes of the needle, added: "You know nothing about me at all."

Henri resumed his chess, his face lit by a faint half-smile. "You might be very surprised by how much I know about you," he replied.

"Such as what?" she shot back.

For a few moments he said nothing. Then, very quietly, he said: "Such as that you were Barnikel's lover. And that you helped him commit treason."

For half a minute there was silence in the stone hall, broken only by the faint tap of a chess piece moving.

"What do you mean?"

Henri did not look up from the board. "Do you remember the night of the great fire? I'm sure you do. You spent the night before it with Barnikel."

She gasped. "How do you know?"

"I had you followed," he remarked mildly. "I had you followed for years."

"Why?" Suddenly she felt very cold.

Henri shrugged. "Because you are my wife," he replied, as though that answered everything.

Her mind went back to the evening of the fire. She frowned. "The night of the fire. Somebody grabbed me . . ."

"Of course." He smiled. "I guessed you were running to Barnikel. It was too risky. You could have been arrested." He paused. "Besides, it worked out perfectly. You couldn't have set things up better."

"I don't understand."

"It wasn't a good idea for Ralph to get married."

"Ralph? He died at St Paul's."

"I don't think so. I think he encountered your friend Barnikel at the Tower." Henri smiled. "My father often said that when I played chess, my strategy was indifferent but my tactics were good. He was right." He paused. "You see, my dear wife, it was you who gave me the chance. When you were obviously about to warn Barnikel, it occurred to me, after my men stopped you, to send your message to warn Barnikel after all. So one of my men went. He said he came from you and told him to kill Ralph when he reached the Tower. Since Ralph disappeared, I feel sure he did." The master tactician gently sighed. "Either Ralph would arrest your lover or your lover would kill Ralph. Either way, a neat move."

"*You* killed Ralph."

"No. I assume Barnikel did that."

"You are the devil."

"Perhaps. But please consider that if Ralph had married and had heirs, your own children's inheritance would have been cut in half."

"You should be arrested."

"I committed no crime. Which is more, my dear, than I can say for you."

She got up. She felt ill. She had to get out of that accursed hall.

Minutes later, she was walking down the hill to Ludgate, then out, across the Fleet, and past St Bride's. She let the soft breeze from the river below brush her hair. She did not stop until she reached the old jetty at the Aldwych.

And as she sat on the ground and stared along the river, first round the curve to Westminster, and then along the stately stretch to the placid Tower, she thought of her rich children, and the passing of the years, and realized to her astonishment that she was not even angry any more.

That, she now saw, was for her personally the meaning of the Norman Conquest.

It would have surprised her, some minutes after she had gone, to see her husband.

He was still sitting at his chessboard, but having concluded his game, he had taken out a piece of parchment, which he was now studying carefully. It was the message his father had received just before he died. As he read it once again, Henri's face was calm, but his lips had twisted into a faint half-smile.

The message announced that the Becket family of the Norman city of Caen were planning to move to London.

Chapter 6

The Saint

1170

A June morning in the Palace of Westminster. In the long chamber beside the king's great hall, all was quiet and orderly.

By the door a few courtiers murmured in hushed tones; in the centre, quill pens scratching softly upon parchment, ink supplied by the monks of Westminster Abbey, seven scribes were busy at their writing desks. From the far end, at the table where some of the most powerful men in England were sitting, came a curious clicking sound. They were moving the chequers.

How grave they looked. How awesome. The treasurer, the justiciar, the Bishop of Winchester, Master Thomas Brown and their clerks. Noblemen and sheriffs trembled before them.

Halfway down the chamber, with his back to the wall, stood a quiet young man with a very long nose. The men at the table knew him well. A promising clerk. But, why, on this warm June day, should his face be as white as a ghost's?

His name was Pentecost Silversleeves.

They knew. They were looking at him. They all knew about the night before.

The Palace of Westminster. In the century since the Conquest, the small island of Thorney, now a kind of royal platform beside the Thames, had become magnificent. It was entirely surrounded by a wall. Several bridges crossed the Tyburn stream that flowed around it. The great Abbey of Edward the Confessor still dominated the place, but nowadays was accompanied, as though it had acquired a little sister, by the modest Norman church of St Margaret, which stood beside it to serve the local parish.

Westminster had also increased its dignity when, a few years previously, the Pope had canonized its founder, Edward the Confessor. Like France and several other countries, England now had a royal saint. His tomb, moved to the centre of the Abbey, had become a shrine, and Westminster was confirmed as the spiritual centre of the kingdom.

But perhaps the most obvious change had taken place by the riverbank, for here stood the great hall.

Westminster Hall, rebuilt by William Rufus, was one of the largest royal halls in Europe. Over eighty yards long, it needed two lines of central pillars to hold up its massive wooden roof. So large was it that under its high, Norman windows the king's judges could hold three sessions simultaneously in different corners. Beside the great hall stood the courtyards, chambers and living quarters of the royal palace. Although the king himself was usually travelling around his huge domains, increasingly his administration was to be found in this one location. And of all its different offices, none was better known or more dreaded than the court now in progress.

"A hundred then."

Master Thomas Brown spoke quietly. A clerk moved one of the chequers. The court proceeded imperviously while a sheriff sitting at one end of the table nodded nervously. After the throne, this table, known as the great Exchequer, was the most important piece of furniture in the kingdom.

It was a curious thing to look at. Ten feet long and five wide, it had a ledge four fingers high running round its edge, giving it the appearance of a gaming table. Covering its surface was the black cloth marked into squares by white lines that gave the court its name.

Depending on the square it occupied, a chequer might represent a thousand pounds, or ten, or even the humble silver penny that was a common labourer's daily wage. The chequered cloth was, therefore, nothing more than a kind of abacus, a primitive manual computer on which the revenues and expenses of the kingdom could be reckoned and reviewed.

Every year, at the spring and autumn feasts of Easter and Michaelmas, the sheriffs of the counties of England came to the Exchequer to render their accounts.

First, in an outer chamber, the sacks of silver pennies they brought were tested for quality and counted. If good, twenty dozen pennies weighed a pound. Since the Normans called the English penny an *esterlin*, which transcribed into Latin became *sterlingus*, the unit of account had become known as the pound sterling.

Next, the sheriff was given a tally – a hazel stick cut with notches to mark the amounts he had paid in. To provide each party with a record, the stick was then split lengthwise from just below the handle; the two tallies being known as the foil and counterfoil. Since the sheriff's counterfoil, which established the amount to his credit, was always the longer piece, including the handle, it was also known as the stock.

In this manner, in the twelfth century, the terms Exchequer, sterling, counterfoil and stock entered the language of English finance.

Finally, after satisfying the Chancellor of the Exchequer at the great table, the sheriff's transactions would be recorded by the scribes.

This was a slower, but all-important process. The scribes would begin by making a draft on tablets of waxed wood, which they scraped with a stylus. The drafts would then be fair-copied on to parchment.

Parchment was not merely plentiful at this time, it was cheap. True, the finest, unblemished vellum made from the scraped and stretched skins of calves was rare and highly prized, but vellum was only needed for such works of art as illustrated books. For ordinary documents, the supply of skins from cattle, sheep or even squirrel was almost unlimited. In England's Exchequer, the cost of parchment was less than the ink. "And sheepskin parchment is best," Master Thomas Brown would wisely declare, "because if anyone tries to tamper with the record, it almost always shows."

There was, however, one feature of the English system of record-keeping that was peculiar to the island. Usually, parchment records were folded and made into books. When William the Conqueror had surveyed his new kingdom, it was into mighty volumes that his Domesday Book had been made up. In the generations following, however, for some reason English record-keepers had decided to preserve the Crown's accounts rolled into cylinders instead, for which reason they became known not as books but as the Rolls, or, often, the Pipe Rolls.

The coins themselves were, at this date, still kept in the treasury – the *thesaurus* as the Latin clerks termed it – in King Alfred's old capital of Winchester. But until conveyed there, they were stored in the chapel known as the Pyx in Westminster Abbey next door.

Such was the Exchequer.

Was he screaming? Was he shouting out the awful truth? He put his hand up to his mouth to make sure, then held his tongue between his teeth.

The nightmare of the night before.

Pentecost Silversleeves was a very strange young man.

His biblical name, as it happened, was the least unusual thing about him, for in the religious revival that had swept London in recent generations it had become rather popular. His father, Henri's grandson, now head of the Silversleeves family, would have preferred something Norman, but then a certain widowed aunt who had become a nun made it clear that she would provide a legacy for a son of that name. So Pentecost it was.

His looks were typical of his family: dark hair, a large, long nose, and mournful eyes. But nature had decided to deal Pentecost Silversleeves several particular blows. His shoulders sloped forwards; his hips were broader than his chest; his limbs were weak. As a boy, he had seldom been able to catch a ball thrown to him, and never in his life had he been able to hang by his arms. However, these physical shortcomings were compensated for by phenomenal mental gifts.

When Master Thomas Brown tested the young clerks – "Thirty-five knights must be paid five pence a day for sixty days. What is the total cost?" or "The county of Essex owes three hundred pounds. There are forty-seven knight's fees. How much per knight?" – Silversleeves was forbidden to reply. He needed neither abacus nor writing tablets. He knew the answers instantly. He knew the entire contents of the Pipe Rolls, not because he had tried to memorize them, but because he had that kind of memory.

Such gifts should have made him a fine scholar, yet he had failed to excel. His parents had sent him first to the school at St

Paul's, then to another, then to the smaller school that had started at St Mary-le-Bow. At each he learned just enough to get by. Always his teachers complained: "It comes too easily to him, so he won't really work."

He had been sent to Paris. Here were the greatest scholars in Europe. Only recently, the famous Abélard had lectured, until his illicit affair with Héloïse had led to his castration and disgrace. Fellow Englishmen, like John of Salisbury, who had studied there had risen to high office and were today men of letters. It was a golden opportunity. A man who completed his studies in Paris was called, by courtesy, *Magister* – Master. Yet somehow young Silversleeves never completed his studies. He drifted briefly to Italy, then returned home. No one called him Master.

What did he know? He had mastered the basic trivium: grammar, meaning Latin, rhetoric and dialectic. Since the days of the Roman Empire, these had formed the foundation of the European educated class, the common language of which was still Latin. He had also studied the quadrivium of music, arithmetic, geometry and astronomy, which meant he knew a little Euclid and Pythagoras, could name the constellations, and believed that the sun and the planets revolved in a complex pattern around the Earth. His study of divinity allowed him to quote biblical texts, in Latin, to buttress any argument. He could expose a dozen half-forgotten heresies. He knew enough law to prove to an abbot what money he owed the king. In Italy, he had been to a lecture on anatomy. Plato and Aristotle were no strangers to him. In short, he knew only what was necessary, and no more.

But if not a *magister*, what was he? The answer to this was simple. He was a clerk, a man in holy orders.

This was not surprising. In a world where few could read, all education was in the Church's hands. It was normal, therefore, for a young man who had finished his schooling to have his head shaved in a monk's tonsure and be admitted to the minor orders.

Technically, young Silversleeves was a deacon. As such, he was free to marry, enter business, do as he pleased. Later, should it suit him, he could enter the higher orders. In the meantime, he could claim all the privileges of the Church.

As the Christian inheritor of the ancient Roman Empire, the Church's influence and network throughout Europe was vast. And whether they were saintly or corrupt, scholars or scarcely able to get through the Lord's Prayer in Latin, all society's educated men had the Church to thank for their learning. Even if there were occasional schisms, even if at this moment the German emperor was trying to promote a rival claimant of his own for the Holy See, the fact remained that the Pope was the direct inheritor of St Peter. With an authority far older than theirs, he could admonish feudal kings. Bishops walked with the greatest nobles in the land. In a feudal society where it was hard to change classes, a clever man, even the son of a lowly serf, might still rise through the Church to the pinnacles of society – and at the same time, it was presumed, serve God as well.

There was one more element in this special relationship between the State and the educated class of churchmen. Centuries of donation meant that throughout Europe the Church was the greatest landowner. And though, a generation after the Conquest, most of the spare land in England had already been granted to feudal families, Church land was always available to provide huge incomes for the senior clergy of the day. If the king needed to reward his friends or servants, the solution was obvious:

"Let's make him a bishop."

In this way a curious but necessary system had developed. While certain bishoprics usually passed to men of impeccable piety and distinction, others often passed to great royal servants and statesmen. The present Bishop of Winchester was both a kinsman of the king and a statesman. Royal officials often held the sees of Salisbury, Ely and several others. Numerous officials had incomes from lesser offices – archdeaconries, canonries and rich livings. And at this moment, the Chancellor of England and the Archbishop of Canterbury were actually the same man, the king's great servant, Thomas Becket.

Its own reformers might not approve of such practices, but on the whole the Church went along with it.

One day, perhaps, young Silversleeves too might become a bishop.

* * *

Why had he gone with them? Did he even like them?

No, but they were the young bloods of London – men from leading merchant families like his own. Once a month they went out. Black hoods. Daggers and swords. One time, over to the stews across the river. A whore at sword point. They made her give it to all of them for nothing. How she cursed! And the peasant they had found in the woods. They had taken him for such a ride in his cart. A moonlit night. The fellow was so frightened he thought he was bewitched. They drove him into a stream and left him there. How they'd enjoyed reliving that one.

There was no harm in it. All the young bloods were playing these pranks. It was just the fashion. Nobody took it too seriously. The more daring the better.

But why did he go along?

"You look like a woman," they used to chant at school. They used to laugh at him. "And you act like one too." That stupid song. He'd shown them. He went with the wildest gang now. No one got caught.

Until last night.

"We have to do something special." That's what Le Blond had said. "After all, it's coronation day."

Coronation day. A strange business that had been. Perhaps if it had not been so strange, he might not have gone out drinking with his friends afterwards. He might never have gone along.

They were all so drunk. How else could they have gone to the wrong house? Dear God. It wasn't the baker at all. It was an armourer. A fellow with a coat of mail, strong as a blacksmith. What a fight he had put up. They were only going to steal the fellow's shirt. Just a trophy.

Then the apprentice. That wide-eyed boy with a knife. And then . . . He could not bear to think of it. His hands were clenched. Try to relax.

Nobody had seen him. They had all run. The hue and cry had been raised. They'd scattered. Nobody could have seen him.

•

The coronation that had taken place in Westminster Abbey the previous day, 14 June 1170, had been remarkable for two reasons. The first was that the young man being crowned was not, in fact, the king.

After the Conqueror's sons Rufus and Henry I, and a period of feudal anarchy while the heirs in the female line fought for supremacy, the English Crown had settled upon an extraordinary man. Henry II had inherited England and Normandy through his mother, the Conqueror's granddaughter. By a spectacular marriage he controlled the vast lands of Aquitaine in south-west France, including the rich wine region of Bordeaux. From his French father, he had also inherited the fertile region of Anjou, which lay between his Norman and his wife's domains. The King of England was thus master of a feudal empire that stretched up Europe's Atlantic coast from Spain to Scotland and threatened even the jealous king of France.

From his father he had inherited two other things. The first was a curious family name. A certain ancestor, it was said, had worn in his cap not a feather but a flower, a sprig of broom. *Plante à genêt,* they called it in French. In English, Plantagenet.

He had also inherited the Plantagenet family temperament. Brilliant and restless, the sharp-eyed Henry was seldom in one place for more than a few days as he laboured to secure and expand his empire. He was a wonderful administrator. Already he was transforming English justice, his trained judges offering his subjects royal courts instead of the unreliable ones of the feudal barons. His administration was strict. That very year half the sheriffs of England were trembling as the clerks of the Exchequer suddenly arrived to inspect their affairs. No wonder young Silversleeves's father had admonished him: "If you would only work and serve the king well, the whole world would be at your feet."

But there was another side to the Plantagenets. Even by the standards of those dangerous times they were ruthless and devious. Some said they were descended from the Devil. "From the Devil they came," the great Bernard of Clairvaux had grimly remarked, "and to the Devil they will return." Their fits of temper were legendary.

King Henry II also had four turbulent sons. It was to secure the succession to the English throne, therefore, and to prevent anarchy, that he had summoned his family and magnates to Westminster Abbey to witness the coronation of his eldest son whilst he himself was still alive. "Perhaps," the onlookers hoped piously, "this will bring some order to this devil's brood."

The other strange feature of the ceremony was that Thomas Becket, Archbishop of Canterbury, the priest who should have officiated, was not even present. He had fled the country.

Becket. Cursed name. Cursed family. Strike them down and they rise up again like serpents.

A dark night. That was what reminded him of Becket. Another dark night long ago. And another crime. A terrible one.

Had his own family done it? Were they born criminals?

No. He could not accept that. If the Beckets drove men to dark deeds, it was they, the cursed Beckets, who were to blame. It must be so.

The enmity between the Beckets and the Silversleeves had not simply continued from the preceding century, it had grown worse.

When Gilbert Becket, a prosperous mercer, and his family had arrived in London, the Silversleeves, still living in their stout stone hall in the shadow of St Paul's, were rich, proud and respected. But when they had haughtily declared of the newcomers, "They're interlopers," no one seemed to take much notice. This was not really surprising. Already at that time London's leading citizens included many new arrivals from France, Flanders and Italy. Names like Le Blond and Bucherelli soon became English as Blunt and Buckerell. The Beckets moved into a substantial house on the West Cheap, just below the Jewry. They bought a dozen other houses. They prospered. But when young Silversleeves's grandfather, confidently expecting to be chosen for an important city position, had seen Gilbert Becket chosen instead, the old bitterness had turned to flaming hatred.

Who had started the fires? The first had begun at the Beckets' house on the very night their son Thomas was born. The second, many years later, began elsewhere but destroyed most of their property. And then the rumours had begun. "It was the Silversleeves," people began to whisper. "They started those fires. They ruined the Beckets." It was outrageous. It cast a pall of suspicion over the entire Silversleeves family. However hotly Pentecost's father had denied it, the hissing rumour spread and could not be quenched. Gradually a new and even more insidious thought crept into the mind of this gloomy family. "The Beckets started the rumour," they decided. "They'll torment us to the grave." It did not make him any less resentful when young Pentecost secretly asked himself: could it be true?

And still those Beckets would not lie down. Londoners remembered young Thomas Becket very well. Thomas of London, he often used to call himself. A lazy fellow who, like young Silversleeves, had never become a *magister*. He became a clerk, though, and despite his father's ruin got himself noticed. He was good at that, always making friends and dropping them, as the Silversleeves family liked to point out. Then the old Archbishop of Canterbury had taken him into his household. He charmed the king. He had a talent for that too, with his tall good looks, his elegance and his brilliant eyes. He must have served his masters well, even brilliantly, for suddenly, to all London's astonishment, at the age of only thirty-seven he was made Chancellor of England.

Pentecost had once seen him riding down the West Cheap with his retinue. He had been magnificently dressed in a cloak lined with ermine. Jewels had flashed on his tunic. Even the men who rode with him looked like dukes. "He's got style," his father had conceded gloomily. And then, with irritation: "Look at him. He takes on more airs than the king."

But the surprise of Becket's rise to the chancellorship was nothing compared with the general stupefaction when, seven years later, he was made Archbishop of Canterbury. Thomas, the worldly servant of the king, Primate of all England? And to remain the king's chancellor as well?

"The king wants the Church under his thumb," young Silversleeves's father had remarked. "With Becket there, that's what he'll get." It was sensible enough, if a little shocking.

And then the strangest thing had happened. Pentecost remembered it well, that day he had returned home from school to find his father's courtyard full of people talking excitedly.

"Becket has turned against the king."

Of course, for a king and an archbishop to quarrel was not

unusual. For the past one hundred years, a great debate had been taking place across Europe as to how Church and State should exercise their authority. Were the great feudal bishops subject to kings or not? Could a pope depose a king? There had been angry words, even excommunications. In England only a generation earlier, Rufus's callous treatment of the Church had forced the saintly Archbishop Anselm to leave the kingdom for several years. Certainly, Henry II was just the kind of monarch to provoke one of these quarrels. But Becket? The king's own man?

"He's given up all ostentation," the reports came. "He lives like the simplest monk." Had the ambitious and worldly Londoner really turned pious? Why should he suddenly have had a blazing row with Henry over the Church's rights and then left the country?

"I can explain it," Pentecost's father had said. "It's typical of a Becket. He's found a new role to play. He's just showing off as usual."

Whatever the cause, the dispute had been dragging on for several years. The two men, once such friends, were now the bitterest enemies. Which was why King Henry had had his son crowned not, as was his right, by Canterbury, but by the Archbishop of York. Like everything Henry did, it was carefully – in this case viciously – calculated. It was the final insult.

"Poor Becket," Silversleeves had remarked the day before with satisfaction. "That must really have hurt. I wonder what he'll do now."

Pentecost Silversleeves might have continued pondering this interesting question had there not, at this moment, been a sudden commotion at the entrance.

The short, sturdy master craftsman with the close-cropped brown beard and white patch in his hair burst through the courtiers in the doorway and fairly bounced into the chamber. He was wearing a bright green tunic and green leggings. His face, as red as his soft leather boots, was so puffed up with fury that he looked like an indignant cockerel. Behind him loomed two large bailiffs.

Seven startled scribes, quill pens still in hand, turned to stare. The courtiers, uncertain what to do, hesitated. The grave figures at thc Exchequer table, surprised at this unseemly interruption, gazed down the chamber silently. But the craftsman was not concerned with them. He was shouting.

"There he is. That's the one. Seize him!" The furious fellow pointed at Pentecost.

An astonished silence.

"Of what is he accused?" The awesome voice of the justiciar, personal representative of the king himself.

And then, ringing round every corner of that hallowed chamber, came the terrible reply:

"Of murder."

The large, broad-faced man gazed around him with satisfaction. The other men in his little hall bowed respectfully, and Alderman Sampson Bull smiled back. This was going to be the best day of his life.

Everything about Alderman Sampson Bull was red. He was wearing a long red gown, a red hose, a red tunic with gold cuffs and a painted leather belt. On his head was a large red beret. His face, whose strong jowl carried two days' growth of fair beard, was ruddy. Only his eyes were blue. With his head thrust forward from his bulky frame, his appearance matched his family name.

The name itself had come about gradually. After the Conquest, the family had been content to adopt the Norman way, adding their father's name, with the prefix Fitz, to their own. But this system had one disadvantage. Whilst Leofric's son was Edward FitzLeofric, his grandson was Richard FitzEdward, and Richard's son was in his turn Simon FitzRichard. If three or four generations were living at any one time it could become very confusing. Since the family always lived by the sign of the Bull, however, they were often known more simply as the family of Bull.

Sampson Bull was a man of importance. Since his father's death two years earlier, he had been head of the family. A rich mercer – a wholesale merchant dealing in wool and cloth – at the age of thirty he had already been chosen as alderman of his ward in the city. And it was no small thing to be an alderman. The government of London that was now taking on a settled form consisted of three levels. The lowest was the parish, often very small, but which might contain a few citizens of importance. Of greater significance were the twenty or so wards. Each ward had its own little council, the wardmote, consisting of its leading citizens, who also came together to form the city's greater council. But at the pinnacle were the aldermen, one for each ward. Sometimes they still owned whole areas of their ward; often they kept their post for life. They organized the militia. And it was these men, like so many feudal barons, who made up the city's all-powerful inner council. Sampson Bull was of this inner group.

The London over which they ruled was larger than before. Many more houses had appeared along the roads leading out of the city; whilst on the western side, outside Newgate, where the River Fleet became the Holborn, the city's new outer limit was marked by stones known as the city's bar. But if nowadays the streets of London and its trading were regulated by proud merchants like Sampson Bull, those grim sentinels of the Norman Conquest still remained. Standing guard over the city in the west were the fortifications by Ludgate; in the east, the mighty Tower. The castles of London belonged to the king and his magnates, and both still spoke that single, surly word: "Obey".

But as Alderman Bull completed the business of the wardmote and dismissed its members with a wave of his hand, he was not thinking about the king. He had a far more cheerful subject on his mind. Minutes later, as he walked up the gentle slope of Cornhill, he allowed his mind to dwell upon it pleasantly.

Bocton. He was going to get it back.

•

It was a century since Leofric the Saxon had lost the ancestral Kentish estate to a certain St Malo, follower of the Conqueror, and the Bulls had assumed it was gone for good. But twenty years ago young Jean de St Malo had gone on the Second Crusade, mortgaging his estate to do so. The crusade was a disaster; the knight had returned broken, and after years of struggle had finally given up. Bocton had just passed to his creditor. Yesterday, that gentleman had called upon the alderman to acquaint him with the situation.

He was a short, neat, elegant man. He wore a black silk cloak and a skullcap. His name was Abraham.

"As soon as I realized it had been in your family, I came to you," Abraham explained. "As you know, I can't keep the place anyway."

And Bull, with a grin, replied: "Thank God for that."

There were many moneylenders in London nowadays. Expanding trade, the huge scale of operations in the Plantagenets' sprawling European empire, and the overseas expenses of the crusades all needed financing. Norman, Italian and French moneylenders provided huge sums of money; so did that most Christian, crusading order, the Knights Templar; and so did the Jewish community of England. Their methods were not markedly different, with one exception. While most moneylenders held estates, and the Templars even became specialists in land management, the Jews were still prohibited from owning land. So when a Jewish financier repossessed an estate, he always sold it.

Abraham named a price. Bull explained that once his ship returned he could pay it. "And Bocton will be ours again," he had told his wife and children. A crowning achievement.

Had he any doubts that the voyage would be a success? None. Did he trust Abraham to wait a little? Certainly. His word was good. Was there anything that worried the merchant about the transaction? Well, perhaps. There was one discordant note sounding at the back of his mind.

He had not told his mother. But that was a problem for another day.

His journey up Cornhill had been for a particular purpose and now, having reached the summit, he looked down upon the second reason for his cheerfulness that morning.

It was a small sailing ship. At a time when most cargo was carried overseas by foreign merchants, Bull had, the previous month, become one of the few Londoners to own his own vessel. Though the sleek, many-oared longships of the Norsemen were still to be seen, his own stout little ship was of the south European type more often used in London now. Broad-beamed, deep of draught and usually propelled by a single mainsail, it was clumsy and slow, its rudder set at an angle at the stern's side, so that the vessel was steered rather as a riverman steers his boat with a single oar. However, the cog, as it was called, could also sail with a small crew in all weathers, and carried a prodigious load.

In the bowels of this particular ship rested a third of Bull's fortune in the form of wool bound for Flanders. When it returned laden with silks, spices and luxury goods, the profits from the voyage would give him enough spare money to make the most important alteration to the family's status and fortunes since the Norman Conquest.

How gaily the little cog passed before the Tower. Bull had come to the top of Cornhill so that he could see the whole panorama of the Thames's great, shining path towards the estuary. The cog entered the long stretch of the Pool of London and approached the river's huge curve.

And then something strange happened. Suddenly the cog seemed to lurch. A second later, its prow veered towards the southern bank, it drifted sideways, began to turn about crazily, and then, as though some unseen hand had caught it, held fast.

Alderman Bull, understanding at once what had occurred, let out a bellow of rage that must have carried all the way down to All Hallows and even to the river below.

"Kiddles!" he shouted. "God damn the king!"

Then he rushed down the hill.

Treasonable though this sentiment was, there was hardly an alderman in London who would not have echoed it. The city's ancient fishing rights had long been vested in certain great offices, and the fishing for many miles downstream now belonged to none other than the king's servant, the Constable of the Tower. Since the Thames teemed with fish, the rights were valuable and were therefore cynically let for the constable's maximum profit. As a result, the river's broad waters were cluttered with nets, weirs, booms and traps of every kind. Scarcely a month went by without some ship being fouled. These obstacles were known as kiddles. And though the larger merchants never ceased complaining, even to the king himself, about the damage to shipping, only vague promises were ever made and the infuriating kiddles remained.

By late that afternoon, the cog was back at the wharf, its rudder broken, and at least a day's sailing lost while it was repaired. The nets, Bull discovered, belonged to a red-haired fishmonger named Barnikel, whom he knew slightly, and who very reasonably remarked, "I'm sorry about your cog, but I paid the constable a fortune to fish there." Furious though he was, Bull could hardly argue.

But one thing Bull did know. And he knew it with precisely the same sense of black and white, right and wrong, of his ancestors. He had been cheated. The king and his constable, contemptuous of the city's leaders, were operating a system that was unfair, a racket. It was all he knew and all he cared about. Standing alone on the wharf and staring along the waterfront towards the Tower, he made a quiet but solemn vow.

"I'll stop them one day."

It might reasonably be supposed that fate had completed her work in ruining the best day in the life of Alderman Bull. Certainly he supposed so, as he trudged bitterly home that evening. But that would have been to underestimate the powers of providence.

On his arrival home, the alderman found his family waiting anxiously for him at the door. Imagining it was on account of the ship, he told them tersely that the rudder would be mended. It was then that his mother, gently shaking her head, revealed, "I'm afraid there is something else." And at his impatient look: "You must be calm, Sampson, not angry."

"What about?"

"Well." She paused nervously. "It's about your brother."

He had been seventeen when he began. Ten years had passed. Now, as he faced the furious abbot, he trembled.

"You are breaking your vows," the abbot thundered.

He trembled, but he did not give way.

Brother Michael was a pure and simple soul. Three years younger than Sampson, he could not have been less like him. Where his older brother was thickset, Michael was tall and spare; prayer and meditation had softened his broad Saxon face; his head was tonsured; and in all his actions he was quiet and mild. Yet now, with the whole monastery against him, he was firm.

Why had he become a monk? Had it just been a youth's revolt against his father, his coarseness and endless talk of money? Not really. He knew he was no worse than others. Was it because of Sampson, the older brother he had revered as a boy but whose small, blunt cruelties had come to shock him? Was it a yearning for the protection of his pious mother's simple faith as she prayed to the Blessed Virgin every day?

No. It was an inner voice that had prompted him, a growing sense of the emptiness of the world around him, a need to shake off its grossness and find purity and simplicity. Just as a pilgrim desires to touch a fragment of the Holy Cross at a shrine, so Michael needed to feel the living presence of his God each day. And he knew he could not do so in the world.

This was not particularly surprising. Whatever the Church's quarrels and compromises with kings, a great new tide of religious emotion had been sweeping across all Europe in recent generations, and had reached the shores of England. The great Cistercian monasteries, led by that stern monk known as Bernard of Clairvaux, had spread their simple religious communities and sheep farms from the Mediterranean to the bleak moors of northern England. A sudden enthusiasm for the Blessed Virgin Mary had sprung up. The roads to Europe's holy shrines were thronged with pilgrims. Above all, in the last seventy years Christendom had thrilled to a new call to rescue the Holy Land from the Saracens in that great series of adventures, the crusades.

In London, too, this fervour was evident. The bells rang out, and time was reckoned not by the hours but according to the seven monastic services of the day. New churches and other foundations were clustering about the city. On the Thames riverside near the Aldwych the crusading Knights Templar were building the great headquarters already called the Temple. Near Westminster Abbey there was now a hospital dedicated to St James. So many and so flourishing were all these, that more than a fifth of London's population was in religious orders of some kind.

When young Michael said he wanted to be a monk, therefore, his father had been disappointed but not shocked. After a few months, seeing that his son was steadfast in his purpose, he had obtained a place for him in the aristocratic community of Benedictine monks at the great house of Westminster Abbey, to which he had accordingly made a handsome donation, remarking hopefully, "The king's palace is right beside him. Monks have been known to make fine careers." And there, in the ancient and royal Abbey of Westminster, in the company of the black-robed monks, Michael had passed ten happy years.

He loved Westminster, the grey abbey, the great hall, the atmosphere that came from having religious cloisters, royal chapel and the courtyards of the royal administration side by side. He loved to walk out into the surrounding fields or gaze over the River Thames as it flowed by. How pleasant it was to be in a place so silent and peaceful and yet at the centre of things.

He had been happy when he had taken his vows. "These three vows," the old monk who prepared him had explained, "will for the rest of your life be like friends to accompany you along the path to God. Poverty first," he went on. "Why do we take the vow of poverty?"

"Because Our Lord said, 'Where your treasure is, your heart will be also.' And also, 'Sell all thou hast and follow me.'"

"Exactly. You cannot love worldly goods and God at once. We choose God. And the vow of chastity?"

"He who follows the flesh neglects the soul."

"And obedience?"

"To set aside my own pride and desires."

"And to be guided by those wiser than you. For you need a guide upon your journey." These three vows, the old man reminded him, were taken by every monk in Christendom. "Like dear friends, you must be constant to them, and they will protect you."

Brother Michael had taken his vows and kept them. Indeed, they were now dearer to him than anything else. And if, from time to time, he saw that not all the monks at Westminster were chaste, or obedient, or even poor, he knew it was only a human frailty and prayed for them, and himself, the more.

He had been happy, too, when, just a year after his arrival, the Pope, having read the great *Life* of the monarch that the Abbey had prepared, together with many supporting documents, had at last acceded to the petitioning of the monks and canonized their former patron, Edward the Confessor. He had been happy when they set him to work making copies of manuscripts with the scribes, for he came to love books and the Abbey had a fine library. And, like any loyal monk, he had been happy at the growing prestige of his house. "We are even older than St Paul's," the brethren assured him. "St Peter himself came to Britain and founded this monastery here." It gave him a thrill of religious excitement to think that he stood upon ground hallowed even in the days of the apostles.

But as time went by, there were things that troubled him.

Wasn't the Abbey, with its ever-increasing lands, just a little too rich? Didn't the monks live a little too well? What had happened to the vow of poverty? When the scribes proudly showed him the great charters that granted the Abbey's possessions, were they not a little too obsessed with them?

For years he had put such doubts from him. Life at Westminster was delightful. Why question it? And then, two months ago, something had happened.

He had worked happily in the scriptorium for years now, copying manuscripts. He had even developed a fine hand. But the keeping and care of the monastic records was a task reserved for the more senior scribes. So he was honoured one morning when one of them, motioning Michael to join him, asked for his help. In his hand he held a charter that, Michael saw at once, came from an ancient Saxon king. "What are we going to do?" he asked. And was greatly astonished by the answer.

"Age it," the monk had replied blandly. "You know, dust, oil, brine." He smiled. "It'll be old in no time."

Only then had Brother Michael begun to understand.

In the month that followed, he had looked over most of the charters held by Westminster Abbey. As he sought information, he had asked naïve questions and spent hours in minute study. By the end of that time he had gone to thc abbot and announced with a terrible gravity:

"I have discovered that at least half the charters in the Abbey are forgeries."

Never in his life would he forget what happened next.

The abbot had laughed.

In fact, the situation at Westminster Abbey was substantially worse than Brother Michael had realized. The great *Life* of Edward the Confessor was largely a work of fiction. As for the Abbey's claims to be older than St Paul's, there was no proof at all. This being the case, it was clearly God's will that the missing documents bc provided.

So they had forged them. And still a constant stream of documents came forth. In an age when such forgeries, especially in the Benedictine order, were common all over Europe, the English Abbey of Westminster was the undisputed master of the craft. Charters of land grants, royal writs giving tax exemptions, even papal bulls – some were so well done that they would not be detected for centuries. All attested the Abbey's rights and its almost incredible antiquity.

A few days later, after the abbot had told him not to concern himself, the same monk had again asked for his help. This time Michael had refused.

Within a very few weeks the situation had become intolerable. They reminded him of his vow of obedience and of his loyalty. He prayed for guidance. But he could not escape the dilemma.

All these charters are really about increasing the Abbey's privilege and wealth, he reasoned to himself. How does that square with my vow of poverty? As for obedience, if I cannot obey with good conscience, what sort of obedience is that? He was out of sympathy with the great house and they all knew it. There was only one proper course of action. And so he had stood once more before the abbot and calmly told him: "I'm leaving."

"You are proud," the abbot thundered. "Who are you to question us?" Then, as almost any well-meaning monk would have done, the abbot pointed out with sweet reasonableness, "Do you not see? What we do is for the glory of God. When we write history or tell the lives of the saints, it is not just to inform men of what occurred, but to illustrate and expound the divine plan that men may better understand. Similarly, if it is God's will that this Abbey's rights and antiquity be known, we are right to furnish the proof so that sinful men may be convinced of the truth."

Yet still Michael could not agree. The pragmatic common sense of his Saxon ancestors stood in the way. Either it was or it was not an ancient charter. Either he was telling the truth or it was a lie. "I'm sorry, but I wish to leave," he repeated.

"And where will you go?"

Brother Michael bowed his head. That was something he had already arranged. As he told the abbot, however, that worldly-wise monk stared in astonishment and declared: "You must be mad."

The crowd fell silent. It was still early. At a nearby monastery the bell for the morning service of terce had just finished ringing. At a sign from the bailiff, young Henry Le Blond reluctantly removed the cloak from his shoulders and stepped forward. Despite the fact that it was a warm summer morning, he shivered.

Hidden in the crowd, Pentecost Silversleeves watched with horror.

The place where they stood was a large, open space, about four hundred yards across, that lay just outside the north-west corner of the city wall. Today, its muddy surface caked dry by the sun, it looked like a huge, dusty parade ground. On its western edge the ground sloped down to the gully along which the Holborn stream flowed before it became the Fleet. Near the centre stood a group of elm trees and before them a horse pond.

This was Smithfield. On Saturdays there was usually a horse market there, and sometimes executions took place at the elms. At the horse pond, beside which the crowd of four hundred was now standing, certain important judicial proceedings were held.

By the water's edge, as well as the man, naked but for a loincloth stood two other youths, two bailiffs, a dozen aldermen, a sheriff, and the Justiciar of England himself.

A master craftsman had been attacked and one of his apprentices killed. The culprits were all known because, in the hope of getting off lightly, they had turned king's evidence and all accused each other. The crime had taken place the very night of the prince's coronation. King Henry had been so angry that he had ordered his representative to deal with the matter personally. "I want them all tried," he had stipulated, "within three days."

Now, at a nod from the justiciar, the bailiffs tied the young man's hands behind his back and bound his feet. Then, taking hold of his ankles and shoulders, they lifted him up and began to swing him.

"One!" the crowd roared. "Two! Three!" Le Blond's body

arched through the air and splashed into the water. Suddenly silent, the crowd watched expectantly.

Henry Le Blond was on trial for his life.

There were many kinds of trial in England. In civil disputes, freemen could choose trial by jury before King Henry's impartial justices, but for serious felonies like murder or rape, which carried a penalty of death, the matter was felt to be too grave to leave to the imperfect judgement of men. So, despite the fact that many churchmen no longer approved, these cases were submitted directly to the judgement of God through the ancient trials by ordeal. For women this usually meant holding a red-hot iron and then seeing if the burns healed innocently or festered with guilt. For men it meant the speedier ordeal of trial by water. It was very simple. If young Le Blond floated, he was guilty.

Surviving this ordeal was difficult. To prove innocence, he must sink, and the best chance of doing that was to reduce buoyancy by expelling all the air from the lungs. But then, of course, if he wasn't quickly fished out he would drown. Frightened men instinctively took a deep breath and floated. The crowd watched in silence. Then roared.

Henry Le Blond was floating.

It should have been him. He should be there with Le Blond and the other two. Oh God!

But Pentecost Silversleeves was free, for a very simple reason: he had taken holy orders.

Of all the Church's privileges, none was more useful than the right of any clerk in orders, no matter how humble his status or how great his crime, to be tried by the ecclesiastical courts. Such men were known as criminous clerks. It was a system open to abuse, and in his dispute with his former friend Becket, nothing had infuriated King Henry II more than the archbishop's refusal to reform it.

"Your Church courts either find their own people innocent, or they give them a few penances and nothing more. You are defending the most utter rogues," he had charged.

"The privilege of the Church must be sacrosanct," Becket would respond. "It's a matter of principle."

True, those guilty of serious crimes were supposed to be stripped of their orders and handed over to the king's courts for punishment. "But even that you oppose," King Henry had protested. "It's outrageous." And many sensible men in the Church thought he was right. Nevertheless, Becket had refused to give in, remaining in exile instead, and the matter had still to be resolved.

The trial of Pentecost Silversleeves had taken place the day before, at a hearing hastily called and held in the hall of the Bishop of London's house at St Paul's. It had been a dour proceeding.

Gilbert Foliot, Bishop of London, was an aristocrat. His black robe was silken. His gaunt and yellowed face was like antique vellum drawn across a skull. His hands were thin as claws. He had no time for criminal clerics, nor for Becket, whom he regarded as a vulgar fool. As his hawkish eyes rested upon the trembling, long-nosed clerk, he had felt only contempt. "You should be handed over to the king for execution," he had remarked drily. But there was nothing he could do about it.

For the ecclesiastical court still followed the ancient rules of oath-swearing. If an accused cleric said he was innocent and could provide enough reputable witnesses to swear to it, then he had to be found not guilty. Despite the fact that Pentecost's accomplices, now suffering the king's rougher justice, had all named him, the Silversleeves family had produced two priests, an archdeacon and three aldermen, all of whom either owed them favours or were subject to blackmail, to swear upon oath to the bishop that young Pentecost had never been near the scene of the crime.

"I am therefore obliged," Foliot had said with a look of contempt for Silversleeves and his witnesses, "to find you innocent. And since technically you are innocent, you cannot be handed over to the king's justice." Then, with a cold menace, he had added: "However, I reserve the right to take my own view of this matter, and I tell you this: neither you, nor your mendacious witnesses, will ever, if I can prevent it, receive any preferment in this diocese again." With which he had waved them away.

* * *

The other two had floated. They were all guilty. Now, upon the king's particular orders, the sentence was to be carried out at once. Silversleeves trembled.

It was just then that he caught sight of the stout figure with the white patch in his hair. He was only thirty feet away and he had just turned round. Silversleeves tried to duck, but the master craftsman had seen him and a second later was jostling through the crowd. It was useless to try to get away. Silversleeves froze.

Simon the armourer was a conservative fellow. He lived in the house and followed the craft of his great-grandfather, Alfred. He still held several strips of land in the hamlet near Windsor, for which he paid rent. And he was proud of his skill as a master craftsman.

But he was far from the rich wholesale merchants, the aldermen, who ran the ever-growing city. "They never dirty their hands with work like we do," he would say. "They hardly ever touch their goods. Their children are too proud to work at all, half of them. Think they're nobles." Here he would spit. "But they aren't. They're just merchants, no better than me."

The intrusion of the young bloods into his house and the murder of his favourite apprentice had not only shocked and saddened him, it had positively infuriated him precisely because of the contempt for his class that it showed. "They're no better than us. They're worse," he had raged. "They're just criminals." And that was just what he would show them to be. Justice would be done. He had come to Smithfield that day to witness his revenge.

But watching the young men as they were found guilty, and knowing what was to follow, he could not help feeling a pang of remorse. "They did a terrible thing," he muttered. "But even so. Poor devils."

Then he had seen Silversleeves.

He did not hurry, or make a scene. Carefully making his way through the throng, he came up to the long-nosed young man trying so uselessly to ignore him, sidled close until his beard was brushing Pentecost's ear, and gently whispered: "You're slime. You know that, don't you?" He saw the scarlet blush start across the youth's pale cheek. "You're a murderer too, as much as them. But you're worse. Because they're going to die and you aren't, Judas. You're too much of a coward." He saw Silversleeves stiffen. "Slime," he whispered again, softly, then moved away.

Pentecost stayed to see the hanging. In a near daze, he forced himself, with fascinated horror, to watch as the three young men, all stripped, were led to the elms over whose high branches ropes were now tossed. He saw the nooses fitted, saw the three hauled up as the crowd cried out "Heave", saw his friends' beseeching faces contort and turn red, then purple, saw their bodies frantically kicking in the air, and saw one of their loincloths fall down pathetically. Then the three pale bodies hung limply, gyrating slowly in the faint breeze.

An hour later, when Silversleeves entered, the Exchequer court was hard at work. Normally by now the Easter session would be over, but with the extra business of the prince's coronation there was still much to do. Grateful for something to take his mind off the executions, Pentecost made himself busy.

How quiet and normal it seemed, the scribes bent to their tablets, the faint click and murmur from the great table at the far end. Only gradually did he realize that the silence was unnatural. The scribes were studiously ignoring him. If he glanced towards them, the courtiers by the door looked awkward. He knew what it meant: it was embarrassment for a person who has just become an official outcast. He tried to take no notice, but after a while he went out. He walked about the Palace of Westminster for some time, his head bowed, trying to sort out the pictures that crowded into his mind.

His parents when he had told them. His mother, tall, pale, shocked, unable to comprehend that her son could do such a thing. His father, terrible in his silent anger, but effective in getting his son cleared. The trial. The bishop's eyes. The bodies turning in the breeze. The silence in the Exchequer chamber.

He was finished as a cleric as long as Foliot lived, but what about the Exchequer? Was he really finished there too, all for one youthful indiscretion? It was too early to know. "Perhaps it will pass," he murmured.

He had just come to this conclusion when, turning into a broad passage, he looked up to see two painters at work on a wall.

Many of the walls in the chambers around Westminster Hall

were painted; this one consisted of a series of moral scenes from the lives of Old Testament kings and prophets. In the centre, half finished, was a single wheel.

The two painters were obviously father and son. Both were short with bandy legs, stubby hands, large round heads and solemn eyes. They gazed at him placidly as he paused to admire their work. "What is this wheel to be?" he asked.

"This is the wheel of fortune, sir," the father replied.

"And what does that signify, fellow?"

"Why, sir, that a man may rise to fame and fortune, then just as quickly fall again. Or the other way round. It signifies that life is like a wheel, sir, always turning. And it teaches us to be humble, sir. For even when we are high, we may be brought low."

Silversleeves nodded. Every literate man knew about the wheel of fortune. It was the Roman philosopher Boethius, much admired in contemporary schools, who, himself cast into prison after a political reverse, had urged a stoic acceptance of fate and likened men's fortunes to a constantly turning wheel. So popular had the idea become that even humble painters like these, who knew nothing of the philosopher, knew all about his wheel. He smiled to himself. How apt. He would be philosophical about his own reverse. No doubt if he was down now, the wheel would turn again. He passed on.

It was a few minutes later, standing in the huge, cavernous space of Westminster Hall, that he saw a group of men coming towards him. There were half a dozen of them, in rich cloaks; they were walking quickly to keep up with the figure in the middle. And as soon as he saw who it was, Silversleeves caught his breath and ducked behind a pillar.

Unlike his courtiers, King Henry II of England was as usual simply dressed in plain green hose and jerkin, like a huntsman. Of medium height and strongly built, he might have inclined to fat if his ceaseless, driven activity had not always burned it up. This morning, as at all times, he was brisk, trim and all-seeing.

Perhaps, if Pentecost had not tried to hide behind his pillar, he might have been ignored. Instead, as he instinctively pressed himself against the grey, Norman stone, he heard a harsh voice call out in French: "Bring me that man." King Henry did not like people hiding from him.

A moment later, they were face to face.

Though he worked in Westminster Palace, Silversleeves had never seen King Henry close before. This was not surprising. His northern kingdom occupied only part of Henry Plantagenet's time, and even when he was on the island he was constantly travelling from place to place, hunting as he went.

A freckled face. Norman, ginger hair, close-cropped and flecked with grey. Dear God, the Conqueror's great-grandson. Hands nervously twisting a length of twine. A restless Plantagenet, too. A terrifying combination. Eyes grey and piercing.

"Who are you?"

"A clerk, sire."

"Why were you hiding?"

"I wasn't, sire." A stupid lie.

"You still haven't told me your name."

"Pentecost, sire."

"Any more? Pentecost what? Of where?"

It was no use. "Silversleeves, sire."

"Silversleeves." Henry Plantagenet frowned, searched his mind, and remembered. "Silversleeves. Aren't you one of those louts who attacked my armourer?" Silversleeves was very pale, Henry's eyes suddenly harder than stone. "Why weren't you hanged this morning?" He turned to the courtiers. "Weren't they hanged?" The courtiers nodded. "Why hasn't this one been hanged? Why weren't you hanged?"

"I am innocent, sire."

"Who says so?"

"The Bishop of London, sire."

For a moment King Henry was silent. Then a flush began to appear just below his left ear, quickly spreading over his face. There was a sound like a snort from his nose. Silversleeves noticed that the courtiers were starting to back away.

"A criminous clerk," he hissed. A rogue hiding from the king's justice behind the skirts of the Church. It was the very matter that had poisoned his relationship with his old friend Becket. A criminous clerk skulking in his own hall at Westminster. He snorted again.

And then Silversleeves had the privilege of witnessing the

other characteristic for which the king's family was famous: a Plantagenet rage.

"Viper!" King Henry's face had suddenly become so suffused with blood that it darkened to ochre, as though some wooden effigy from an antique royal tomb had come to life. His eyes were so bloodshot they seemed to glow. He brought his face close to Pentecost's until they almost touched, and in his nasal French, beginning in a harsh whisper and rising to a furious shout, he spoke his kingly mind.

"You long-nosed son of a whore! You hypocritical, half-baked priest. You think you've dodged the gallows?" Here his voice began to rise. "You think you can cheat the king, you crapulous toad? Do you?" He glared straight into his eyes. "Well? Do you?"

"No, sire," Pentecost stammered.

"Good!" His voice rose further. "Because you shall not. By the bowels of Christ, I promise you, you shall not! I, personally, will have your case reopened. I'll pluck you from the bishop's skirts. I'll slit you open. You'll hang until you rot. You understand?" And now, summoning all his Plantagenet fury: "You shall taste my justice, you stitched-up sack of slime. You shall smell death!" The last was not so much a shout as a guttural scream that echoed all round the cavernous spaces of Westminster Hall.

Pentecost Silversleeves turned and fled. He could not help himself. He fled down Westminster Hall from the Court of Common Pleas, past rows of pillars to the Court of the King's Bench and out through the great, ribbed doorway into the yard. He fled out past the Abbey, through the water gate and over the Tyburn stream; he fled along the banks of the Thames to the Aldwych and beyond; he fled past the Temple and over the River Fleet; he fled into the city up Ludgate Hill; he fled into the sanctuary of St Mary-le-Bow. And there he sat quaking for upwards of an hour.

On a warm afternoon near the end of September, a man and a woman sat quietly on a bench in front of a large range of buildings along the eastern edge of Smithfield, and waited. The man, who wore a grey habit and sandals, was Brother Michael.

The woman was an ageless twenty-two. She was short and

stout; her face wore a perpetual frown of friendly determination; her left eye stared out at a rakish angle; and only her red hair, pulled severely back, gave a clue that she was one of the Danish family of Barnikel. Perhaps the faint air of confusion behind her determination hinted at something else. "I have to think very hard," she would often say, "because otherwise I get things all muddled up." But this did not take away from the central feature of her personality: she knew her own opinion. She, too, wore a grey habit. She was called Sister Mabel.

The buildings behind them were comparatively new. Less than five decades had passed since a worldly courtier, loved by the king for his wit and his jests, had suddenly experienced a vision, turned from the world and founded the priory and hospital dedicated to St Bartholomew. The priory was rich and grand. The hospital was humble.

It was to the Hospital of St Bartholomew that Brother Michael and Sister Mabel belonged. Now she turned to him.

"Perhaps he will not come." She was not afraid, not for herself, but she was afraid for gentle Brother Michael. "You take care," she had earnestly warned him. "He has a black heart." The jaws of hell were already open; the fiends would drag him down. For the man they were awaiting was, she was sure, the wickedest in London. And their task that day was to save his soul.

"He'll come," Brother Michael said serenely. Then, with a smile: "Mother will make him." And then, seeing her still looking doubtful: "I'm not afraid, Sister Mabel, with you to protect me."

Mabel Barnikel was the sister of the fishmonger who had inadvertently caused such damage to the ship of Alderman Bull. Many people thought her a joke. Yet if they laughed at her behind her back, they were wrong to do so, for she was a humble soul.

She had always, ever since childhood, listened very carefully to anyone she thought was wise, trying as hard as she could to make sense of the puzzling world she saw around her. As a result, when she did finally satisfy herself that she had got an idea straight, she clung to it with all the doggedness of a shipwrecked man who has found a raft in perilous seas.

She was thirteen and just going through puberty when she had discovered that she was in danger of suffering hellfire. The reason for this sad state of affairs was very simple. She was born that way.

"The trouble is," she would state matter-of-factly, "I'm a woman."

It was the parish priest who had explained it to her. He had preached a sermon on the subject of Adam and Eve and used the occasion to deliver a stern warning to his female parishioners. "Women, if you would save your souls, remember Eve. For it is the nature of woman to incline to frivolity and the sins of the flesh, and mortal sin as well. Women are in special danger of hell."

He was a white-haired old man whom Mabel revered. The sermon alarmed her, and the next time she saw him she had begged him to explain: "Why are women more likely to sin, Father?"

The old man had smiled kindly. "It is in their nature, child. God has made woman the weaker vessel." It was an old belief, dating back to St Paul himself. "It is man who is made in God's image, my child. Man's seed produces his perfect likeness. Woman, being only the container in which the seed matures, is therefore inferior. She may still reach heaven, but, being inferior, it is harder."

Several days passed while Mabel digested this authoritative information. Certain things still puzzled her and so, afraid he might be angry and apologizing to him for her confusion, she once more approached the kindly old man and asked: "If man's seed produces his perfect likeness, how is it that women are born as well as men?"

Far from being angry, the priest had placed his hand on her shoulder. "A very good question," he told her. "You see, some of the seed is defective. But – and this is one of the wonders of God's creation – it is necessarily so, to provide vessels by which mankind may continue. Is that all?"

"I also wondered, Father," she continued humbly, "if a child is born of man's seed only, why is it that children often resemble their mother and not just their father?"

To her relief he positively beamed. "God's providence is wondrous indeed. Why, child, you think like a physician. The answer to your question is not certain but the great philosopher Aristotle" – he smiled at this evidence of his own learning – "was of the opinion that while it grows in the womb, the unborn child drinks fluid from the mother which may have some effect. So you may take it that this is the reason."

"Tell me one last thing, Father," she asked meekly. "If it is so hard for a woman to be saved, what must I do?"

Now the priest frowned, not because he was irritated, but because he did not know. "It is hard to say," he replied at last. "Pray earnestly. Obey your husband in all things." He paused. "There are those, my child, who say that it is only virgins who can easily pass into heaven. But that is not a path for all."

From this kindly conversation, Mabel came to understand three things: that women were inferior; that she herself might have some talent for the arts of the physician; and that virginity was the likeliest path to heaven. Few of her contemporaries would have doubted the first or last of these statements.

It was not surprising, therefore, when, a few years later, realizing she had little chance of ever finding a husband, her earnest nature should have made her desire to enter the religious life. Here, however, she met a difficulty that might have been insuperable: "Our family are only fishmongers," she acknowledged.

The decline of the Barnikel family from their glory in Viking days had been steady and probably inevitable. Since the Conquest, the old Danish families of London had lost their hold, pushed steadily aside by incoming merchants from Normandy and the growing network of German Hanseatic ports. The present Barnikel of Billingsgate was a fishmonger, meaning not that he sold fish in the street, though he did have a stall, but that he dealt in fish and other cargo for shipping. And though he was a prosperous and respectable fellow, albeit one given to occasional rages, he and his fellow fishmongers enjoyed a status about the same as the richer craftsmen and far below that of wholesale merchants like Bull and Silversleeves.

Yet why should this be such a problem? It was a commonplace of the time that by adulthood nature provided a greater supply of women than of men – about 10 per cent more in England at this date. By Mabel's generation, this difference had been increased by the growing number of men entering holy orders and, at least in theory, a life of celibacy. It might have been expected, then, that many women would also choose the religious life.

But it was not so. True, there were the great nunneries, but they were few, select, and expensive to enter, the preserve of noble families and the richest merchants. And though the Catholic Church might be content to idealize a few pious noblewomen, given its view of women in general as weaker vessels there was little interest in expanding the female orders. As for the humble merchant and craftsman, the spare women of the household were absolutely necessary to his economy, working in the house and helping him at his trade.

Mabel, therefore, was too lowly born to serve God in any formal capacity.

But she was persistent. She heard of a nunnery that took lay sisters to perform menial tasks. Some of the crusading orders were even using women nurses. Finally, a place was found for her in the hospital attached to the rich priory of St Bartholomew. No donation was required.

And she was happy. She liked tending the sick. She knew every herbal cure, real or otherwise, that the hospital used, and was always on the lookout for more. In the larder she kept a veritable treasure-trove of jars, pots and boxes. "Dandelions to clean the blood," she would explain, "cress for baldness, wort for fever, water lilies for dysentery." For the truly sick, she would bring holy water from the rich canons regular in the priory, or she would help a struggling invalid across London to touch some holy relic that was, she knew, his only hope of a cure or, better yet, of eventual salvation.

And then there was Brother Michael. From the moment she had set eyes on him early that June, she had felt sure he was a saint of some kind. Why else should a rich merchant's son desert Westminster Abbey not for the rich priory, but for her poor sister, the hospital? How she admired his quiet, stately ways, the fact that he read books and was wise.

Yet as one month passed, and then a second, she realized that not everyone shared her opinion of him. Some, like his wicked brother, even thought him a fool. This made her angry. "He's just too good for them," she would mutter. So that while she continued to revere him, she also began to feel protective.

But now Brother Michael was looking towards the city gate and waving.

"Here he is," he remarked pleasantly, as Alderman Bull strode towards them.

The wickedest man in London was in a very bad temper indeed.

He would not have come there at all if it had not been for his mother. For weeks now she had been begging him, "Be reconciled with Michael before I die." When he replied irritably that she was not dying, she would only answer: "You never know." Finally, he had been able to stand it no longer.

Why did his mother always take Michael's side? She had done so ever since his brother was born. Personally he had never thought so much of his younger brother. When he had gone into the monastery at Westminster, he had been contemptuous. But when he had left that June, his fury had known no bounds. "The donations we made," he shouted, "completely wasted!" He had not spoken to Michael since.

But that was not the real reason why his mother had plagued him to see Michael. He knew the true cause very well.

It was Bocton. Despite the delay caused by the kiddles, his ship had completed her voyage successfully. Negotiations with Abraham had taken time, but tomorrow the agreement would be concluded. Which was exactly what so shocked his pious mother.

"Can't you see it's a crime?" she had protested. "You'll be damned for all eternity." And many in London would have agreed with her.

A crusader was a holy pilgrim, ready to suffer martyrdom in God's righteous war. In the eyes of the Church, his crusade absolved him from his sins and gave him a place in paradise. Though the repossession of the estates of bankrupt crusading knights was one of the commonplaces of that century, many considered it a serious moral crime and sought laws to protect crusaders from their creditors.

"To take advantage of a crusader like that. And to do it with a heathen Jew!" She had thrown up her hands in despair.

And then, having had no success, she had secretly gone to see Michael.

At first it seemed to Brother Michael that things were going well.

Sampson Bull, whatever his faults, was a man of his word. He had promised to come and be reconciled. He would do his best. He had prepared himself for the ordeal and even forced a smile on to his face.

It was a long time since he had bothered to visit St Bartholomew's, and as Michael escorted him round, he could not help admiring the place. The priory consisted of a large Norman church, cloisters, a refectory and richly furnished monastic buildings. Not only was the priory well endowed, but every August, at the feast of St Bartholomew, it held an important cloth fair at Smithfield, from which it enjoyed a handsome profit. The members of the community, known as canons regular, were a small but distinguished company who lived in pleasant comfort.

The church itself was a noble structure with a broad, high nave, massive pillars, Roman arches and barrel vaults. The more intimate choir was especially fine, with a two-tiered screen of rounded pillars and arches forming a semicircle at the eastern end behind the altar. As the early autumn light filtered softly into this mellow interior, even the red-faced alderman was affected by its atmosphere, a mixture of Norman strength and Oriental warmth that conjured up images and echoes of the Host, the chalice, and of knights on crusade to the Holy Land.

Yet even though he tried to be agreeable, Bull could not help it if certain things began to irritate him. Somehow the sight of his brother's bare toes and the faint slapping sound of his sandals upon the flagstones annoyed him. And why did this Barnikel woman with her strangely squinting eye keep staring at him so malevolently? As they toured the cloister, he was already breathing heavily.

Then came the moment Bull dreaded: they entered the hospital.

St Bartholomew's Hospital was quite separate from the priory. Its brothers and sisters were not canons regular but a much humbler order of folk. The main building, to which Brother Michael now cheerfully led them, was a long, undecorated, rather narrow dormitory like a cloister walk, with a simple little chapel at one end.

Like most hospitals at that time, Bartholomew's had begun as a hospice, a place of rest for weary travellers and pilgrims.

But that had soon changed and Brother Michael and Sister Mabel were proud of their collection – now numbering over fifty – of the sick and helpless. There were three blind men, half a dozen crippled to some degree, several senile old women. There were men with ague, women with boils, the ill and suffering of every kind. As was the custom of the age, they were placed two, three or even more to a bed. The alderman looked at them with horror.

"Are any of them lepers?" he asked. Only a month before, a leprous baker had been discovered selling bread in the city.

"Not yet."

Bull shuddered. What was he doing here? And what was his own brother, who might at least have upheld the family honour in a prestigious monastery, doing in such a disgusting place?

It was as they came out into the sunshine that Brother Michael made his move. The alderman had to admit that he did it with grace. Taking him gently by the arm and leading him a few paces away from Mabel, he began quietly: "My dear brother," he said with obvious sincerity, "I'm sure our mother plagued you, but it has still touched my heart to see you here. You must forgive me, therefore," he smiled, "if now, for a moment, I try to save your immortal soul."

Bull grinned ruefully. "You think I'll go to hell?"

His brother paused. "Since you ask, yes."

"You wouldn't want Bocton back in the family?"

"It is family pride, my dear brother, that is blinding you to your sin."

"Someone else will buy Bocton if I don't."

"That doesn't make it right."

They had turned round and were pacing back towards Mabel, whom they had both forgotten for a moment. It was then that Bull, with a sigh and a shake of his head, uttered the terrible words: "It's all very well to lecture me, Brother Michael, but you're wasting your time. I'm not afraid of damnation. The fact is, I don't believe in God."

Mabel gasped.

Yet it was not such a shocking statement. Even in that religious age there were plenty of men who had doubts. Two generations before, King William Rufus had made no secret of his hearty scepticism about the Church and all its religious claims.

Thinkers and preachers still found it necessary to argue the case for God's existence. In a way, Bull's view that with their endowments, their special courts, and all the accretions of the centuries churches were nothing more than the creation of men was testament to a certain fearless, if brutal, honesty not so very different from his brother's.

But not to Mabel. She knew Bull was avaricious; she knew he scorned his saintly brother; she knew he planned to rob a crusader with the help of a Jew. Here, now, was the final proof of his absolute wickedness.

It was, for Brother Michael, one of the charms of Mabel's character that it had never in her life occurred to her not to say what was on her mind. But even he was a little startled when, fixing the burly alderman with her straight eye, she burst out: "You're a very wicked man. You'll go to hell with the Jews. You know that?" She wagged her finger, not afraid to admonish the Devil himself. "You ought to be ashamed of yourself. Why don't you give money to the hospital instead of robbing pilgrims who are a lot better than you could ever hope to be?" And she stared at him so hard it seemed she expected him to give in.

It was a mistake.

For months Bull had listened to his mother's complaints. Now he was not only being lectured at by Michael, but he was being attacked by this madwoman whose brother had almost destroyed his ship. It was too much. The blood rose to his face; his head hunched down like a bull about to charge; his shoulders bunched with rage. Then he exploded.

"Damn your hospital and your lepers, and your old hags covered in their own filth. Damn your monks and your stupid crusaders and your hypocritical priests. Damn you all. I tell you this, Brother," he roared at Brother Michael, "if ever I need a religion, then by God I'll be a Jew."

It was not original. It was exactly what King William Rufus had once threatened to do when some complaining bishops were boring him. But it served to shock Mabel well enough. She had already crossed herself seven times before he reached the word "Jew".

He had not finished, though. His parting shot, after only a second's pause, was reserved for his brother.

"You were born a fool. You're a fool now. What do you do

with your life? You make no money because you took a vow of poverty. You never have a woman because you took a vow of chastity. You never even think for yourself because you took a vow of obedience. What for? Who knows?" And then, as if suddenly inspired: "What's more, I don't even believe you can keep your stupid vows." He grinned furiously. "So I'll tell you what I'll do. I'll even put it in my will. Send for me, or my successors, on your deathbed. Swear before God and a priest that you have never broken your vows from this day to your ending, and by God I'll give Bocton to Bartholomew's. There now."

And with this astonishing challenge, he wheeled round and stamped away towards the city gate.

"Oh dear," said Brother Michael.

During the autumn of 1170, news of an unexpected event began to filter back to England.

Days after his encounter with poor Silversleeves, King Henry II of England had hurried over to Normandy, where he had met with the exiled Archbishop of Canterbury. There, Becket, probably spurred by the humiliation of knowing the heir to England had been crowned without him, had at last become reconciled with his king. Soon, there were rumours that Becket was coming back. But he did not appear.

For the Silversleeves family it was an anxious time. Pentecost did not dare show his face at the Michaelmas Exchequer. What did the new turn of events mean? Had the king agreed not to prosecute criminous clerks, or would Becket hand them over? They tried to get information from Normandy, but no one knew. October passed. Then November. Finally, at the start of December, the news came flying up from Kent: "He's here."

He did not come like a lamb. Becket might have made peace with the king, but not with the bishops who had insulted him by crowning the prince in his absence. Within days he had excommunicated the Bishop of Sarum and Gilbert Foliot, the contemptuous Bishop of London. The English Church was in an uproar. "It's worse than when he was away," his opponents protested. Foliot and his supporters sent messengers across the sea to Normandy, to let King Henry know what was passing in his kingdom.

One of them was also paid, by the Silversleeves family, to keep them informed.

In the mid-afternoon of 30 December 1170, Pentecost Silversleeves, dressed in several layers of clothes to keep himself warm, was engaged in a curious activity. With a pair of waxed and polished beef shin bones attached to his feet by leather thongs, he was pushing himself along with the aid of a stick. He was skating.

London's skating rink lay just outside the centre of the city's northern wall. Even now, eight hundred years after the Romans had left, the old watercourses, through which the Walbrook stream passed under the wall were still choked with rubbish, so that the undrained area outside remained a marsh. Moorfields, they called it. A morass in summer, in the harsh midwinter it froze into a vast, wild skating rink where Londoners came to enjoy themselves. It was a cheerful scene. There was even a man selling roasted chestnuts on the ice. But Pentecost was not cheerful.

For the news the messenger had just brought from Normandy was very bad.

"The king's going to arrest Becket. Foliot has won," his father had told him that morning. "That's bad for you: Foliot hates criminous clerks as much as Henry does."

"Perhaps the king's forgotten me by now."

"No. He still speaks of you. So," his father concluded grimly, "there's nothing for it. You'll have to abjure the realm." And his mother had begun to cry.

Abjure the realm. Leave the kingdom. It was the only way a criminal could escape justice. But where could he go? Nowhere in Henry's vast domains. "You could go to the Holy Land on pilgrimage," his mother had piously suggested. But this did not appeal to Pentecost in the least.

Mournfully therefore he pushed himself about, and the sun was dipping when a fellow came running out from the city, shouting the message that, within a month, would echo all round an astounded Europe.

"Becket's dead. The king's men have murdered him."

And Pentecost ran home, to find out what it meant.

* * *

The murder of Archbishop Thomas Becket took place before the altar of Canterbury Cathedral, at vespers on 29 December in the year of Our Lord 1170. Monastic historians, who at that date reckoned the new year from Christmas Day, often give the year as 1171. The details remain ambiguous.

Four junior barons who were of the party sent to arrest Becket, went on ahead, confronted the archbishop themselves, and in a scene of the utmost confusion, killed him. Having heard Henry cursing Becket in one of his rages, they thought he would be pleased.

But it was the aftermath that really shocked the world. For when the frightened monks began to strip the archbishop's body, they found to their astonishment that, concealed under his clothing, the proud prelate had been wearing the rough hair shirt of the penitent. Not only that, it was crawling with lice. Now, suddenly, they saw him in a new light. The chancellor turned churchman, the unexpected martyr, was not what he had been content to appear. This was no obstinate actor. His rejection of his former worldly life had been far more complete than anyone had guessed. "He was a true penitent after all," they cried. A son of the Church.

The word began to spread, and with gathering force. London proclaimed the merchant's son a martyr. Soon all England was saying it, and clamouring for him to be made a saint, no less. The chorus grew throughout Europe. The Pope, having already excommunicated the murderers and their accomplices, gave ear.

For King Henry II of England it was a catastrophe. "If not culpable, at least responsible," the greatest churchmen declared. To escape the growing storm, Henry quickly went on campaign to Ireland. As for the issue of the Church's privileges, over which he had fought Becket so long, King Henry was quiet as a mouse.

In the autumn of the year of Our Lord 1171, there was a great rejoicing in the house of Silversleeves.

"I've talked to the justiciar and to the Bishop of London in person," Pentecost's father was able to announce. "The king's fight with the Church is dead. As for criminous clerks, he's terrified of even mentioning them. You're safe. You can even go back to the Exchequer."

For the first time in many generations, they blessed the name of Becket.

That the world was full of wonders, Sister Mabel never doubted. God's providence was everywhere. The astonishing revelation of Becket's sanctity was, for her, just another example of a process that was all the more splendid because she could not explain it.

Even Alderman Bull's angry promise to his brother, which the monk had not taken literally, was to her an article of faith. She knew Brother Michael was good. She knew Bull should not have acquired Bocton. "You'll see," she assured Brother Michael, "the hospital will get that legacy."

"On my deathbed," Brother Michael gently reminded her.

"That's right," she replied, cheerfully.

Yet even Sister Mabel was puzzled by the extraordinary event that took place on a bright, damp April morning in the year of Our Lord 1172.

She had been over to the Aldwych. She had heard there was a leper there, but she could not find him, and was just returning across the empty space of Smithfield when she saw an unusual spectacle.

It was a procession – a considerable one, coming down the western edge of Smithfield. The cortège was beautiful. A great company of knights and ladies on richly caparisoned horses led the way. Minstrels with pipes and tambourines ran beside them. Everyone seemed to be smiling and happy. Further behind, she could see, was a long procession of ordinary folk. But who could they be? What was the reason for this glittering throng? She stepped boldly forward and tried to ask one of the passing riders, but he rode by as though he had not seen her.

It was only then that she noticed the strange thing. Just before reaching the city gate, the sparkling company was vanishing.

She stared. There was no mistake. Horses and riders were dissolving as though they had passed into some unseen mist, or into the ground under London itself. Turning back to the horses passing by, she now realized something else. Their hooves were making no sound.

And then she understood. It was a vision.

She knew about visions, of course. Everyone did. But she

had never expected to see one. To her surprise, she was not frightened. The riders, though she could almost touch them, seemed to be in a separate world of their own. Now she noticed that some of them were not knights and ladies, but humble folk. She saw a stonemason she knew, and a woman who sold ribbons. To her astonishment, she suddenly caught sight of one of the patients from the hospital dressed in a shining white robe, his thin face strangely serene.

After a little time, the riders had all passed by, but now came the mass of folk behind them. They were a very different crowd – all conditions of men and women, from furious fish-wife to shattered lord. Most were on foot, their dress ragged, their faces wan. Beside them walked not minstrels but the strangest creatures Mabel had ever seen. They resembled men, except that they had long legs like a bird's with claws for feet, and curved tails. They stalked beside the crowd, occasionally prodding them with the tridents they were carrying in their sinewy hands. Though their sharp, hard faces were human, Mabel noticed that they had different coloured skin – some red, some green, others mottled. "They must be demons," she murmured, and stepping forward to a green-and-white one passing by she demanded: "What's this procession?" And this time she had better luck.

"Human souls," the creature replied in a nasal voice.

"Are they dead?"

"No. Living." He paused for a moment. "The ones in front are going towards heaven. These," he prodded a bloated monk, "are on their way to hell."

"Have they committed such terrible sins?" she asked.

"Not all. Some have yet to commit them." He made a high-pitched, bird-like squawk. "But we have them in our hands already. We're leading them towards temptation, and then to their doom." He began to move on.

"Will any of them be saved?" she called after him.

He did not turn around, but gave a raucous chuckle.

"A few," his voice came back. "Only a few."

For some time she watched these desolate pilgrims crowding by. She saw numerous people she knew and murmured a prayer for each. Once or twice she called out to try to warn them, but it seemed they did not hear. Then she saw Alderman Bull. He was sitting on a horse, but the wrong way round. He was dressed, as usual, in red, and his huge frame looked as powerful as ever. But she noticed that his face and his hands were covered in boils, and shook her head sadly. She knew he would get to hell, and she did not even try to call out to him.

But nothing had prepared her for what followed.

Only a few paces behind the heavy alderman, his pale face looking tragically sad, walked a still more familiar figure, the sight of which caused her to gasp. It was Brother Michael.

How could it be? He walked slowly and deliberately, as was his habit. His head was bent down, not in reflection, but in sorrow and shame. His eyes seemed to be fixed upon something just in front of him, as though he were hypnotized. What, she wondered, could he possibly have done? She cried out to him. She ran along beside the procession, calling to him again and again. Once, it seemed to her, his head raised as if he might have heard, but then, as though pulled by some unseen force, it bowed down again as he continued his dismal march.

She stood by the side of the lane and wondered. She could not believe Brother Michael had committed any grave crime. Was there some sin he was going to commit?

And then it also occurred to her: If he's bound for hell, I'm sure I must be too. And she searched amongst the passing souls, but could not see herself, try as she might.

And then the vision vanished.

Chapter 7

The Mayor

1189

In the summer of 1189, King Henry II of England died, and the heir he had crowned having predeceased him, he was succeeded by his second son, Richard.

Thus began a period of several years that has entered the realm of legend. For what chronicle in England's history is better known than that of Robin Hood and the greedy Sheriff of Nottingham, of good King Richard, away on crusade, and his evil brother, John? It is a fine tale and it grew out of real events.

But the true account of those years, though a little more complex, is even more interesting. And it took place, mostly, in London.

News travelled quickly wherever he went. Already that August morning a little crowd had gathered in a semicircle before the fine new gateway to await his coming. No one was more excited than the boy standing at the front.

David Bull looked much as his father Sampson had at thirteen: fair, broad-faced, with a ruddy complexion and bright blue eyes that were now shining with excitement.

Before him stood the gateway to the Temple. Of all the religious houses whose great walled compounds were arising throughout the city, none were more splendid than those of the two crusading orders. These military religious organizations serviced the logistical needs of the Holy War. To the north of Smithfield were the Knights of St John, who were responsible for the hospitals; here, on the slopes above the Thames, about halfway along the lane that ran westwards from St Bride's to the Aldwych, lay the precincts of the powerful order that arranged the great convoys of money and supplies, the Knights Templar.

Through the gateway could be seen their stout stone church, recently built and instantly recognizable because, like all Templar churches, it was not rectangular but round. And from this church, at any moment, the greatest hero in Christendom was going to emerge: King Richard the Lionheart.

In every age the warrior has been a hero. In recent decades, however, a subtle change had begun to permeate the world of the knight. The crusades had given him a religious calling; the new Continental pastime of jousting had added pageantry; now, from the warm, southern, French-speaking courts of Provence and Aquitaine had come a fashion for ballads and tales of courtly love, together with sophisticated manners new to the northern world. The perfect knight of this new dispensation was warrior, pilgrim and lover. He prayed to the Blessed Virgin, yet the lady in her bower was his Holy Grail. He jousted, and sang too. It was a heady mixture: religious, gallant, erotic. It was the dawn of the age of chivalry, whose fullest expression would be the tales of the legendary King Arthur and his Knights of the Round Table, now being translated for the first time from Latin and French into English.

And Richard the Lionheart was the new age's champion.

Brought up in his mother's cultivated court in Aquitaine, he could compose a lyric as well as any minstrel. He loved to joust and was a formidable warrior, siege expert and castle-builder. Even those closest to him, who knew he could be vain and cruel, acknowledged that he had unrivalled style and charm, as well as the gift of command. Soon, in response to the pleas of the Templars and others valiantly holding out against the Saracens in the Holy Land, he would depart upon that most sacred of all knightly adventures, the new crusade.

The crusade. Even the old jealousy between the King of France and the Plantagenets was to be shelved. The King of France and Richard were to crusade together as brothers. There was an added, mystic quality about the English king's expedition, for it was said he was to carry the ancient sword of King Arthur, the magical Excalibur itself, upon his journey.

It was a time to rejoice. The old king's last years had been sad. The outcry over Becket had increased until finally poor Henry had gone in penance to be publicly whipped at Canterbury. Becket had even been made a saint. Then Henry's beloved mistress, the Fair Rosamund, had died. His wife and children had turned against him; two of his sons, including the heir, had died. But these sad times were over, and now heroic Richard had come to England to be crowned.

All London shared in the excitement. Looking past the Temple precincts to the River Thames beyond, David could see a flotilla of seagoing vessels that were to take an adventurous party of Londoners – not noblemen, but the sons of merchant families like his own – on the king's crusade. No wonder, then, that everyone was anxious to catch sight of the hero.

Now the church door was opening. A cheer went up as, accompanied by only six knights, a tall, well-built figure in a cloak of blue and gold stepped quickly into the sunlight, which gleamed upon his golden hair. With a firm, athletic step he strode to his horse and, scarcely troubling to rest his foot on the squire who bent to help him mount, swung himself easily into the saddle and rode towards the gate.

David Bull was aware only of a hard, Plantagenet face. Until a tiny piece of magic occurred. Passing through the gateway, Richard the Lionheart briefly rested his gaze upon the little crowd. Seeing the boy, almost without thinking he looked straight into his eyes and smiled. Then, knowing full well that by this simple ruse the youth was now his for life, he clapped his heels to his horse, and rode away towards Westminster.

It was a full minute later that David Bull, gazing after him, murmured to himself: "I'm going with him. I must go on crusade." Then, thinking of his father's awful fury: "Uncle Michael will help me. He'll speak to Father."

Half an hour later an observer standing on London Bridge might have noticed a curiously dismal sight. A long-nosed man on a piebald palfrey was leading an elegantly mounted lady and two packhorses over the quiet waters of the Thames and into the city of London. The man was Pentecost Silversleeves. The lady was Ida, the widow of a knight, and despite herself she had just started to weep, which was not surprising, since she was about to be sold.

As she looked at the city before her, it seemed to Ida that the world had turned to stone. The great walled enclosure of London seemed like a vast prison. On the left, she could see the thickset stone fort by Ludgate. On the right, down by the waterside, the grey, square mass of the Tower, surly even in repose. All stone. Over the two low hills of London covered with houses loomed the dark, high, narrow line of Norman St Paul's, dreary and forbidding. Even in the water beside her she noticed, as she glanced sideways over the wooden parapet, that they had started to build massive piers for a new bridge which, she rightly guessed, would also be made of stone. And now, as the horses' hooves clip-clopped softly on the wooden bridge in the morning quiet, the sound of a striking bell came over the water with a solemn, sullen sound as though it, too, were made of stone, to summon stony hearts to stony prayer.

Ida was thirty-three. She was the daughter of a knight, the widow of a knight, and everything about her proclaimed her to be so. Below her stiff headdress her dark brown hair was fastened in a bun and covered by a wimple. Behind her veil was a long, handsome face. Beneath her broad-sleeved, trailing gown was a slim, pale body with small breasts and long legs. She had always known, modestly but definitively, that she was a lady. So why was it that no one, not even King Richard, seemed to care? For, on the king's orders, this long-nosed clerk was taking her to be married to a vulgar merchant about whom she knew nothing except that his name was Sampson Bull.

"Can't you tell me anything about him?" she had impatiently demanded of Silversleeves the day before.

After a little thought, he had only replied: "They say he has a very bad temper."

How could they treat her this way? The reason was very simple. Thanks to the good management of his father, King Richard the Lionheart was one of the richest monarchs in Christendom – certainly far richer than his rival, the King of France. But a crusade was a costly business. When, two years before, the Pope had proclaimed the Third Crusade to liberate Jerusalem from the Muslim ruler Saladin, King Henry II had levied a special tax, the Saladin tithe. But even that was not enough, and before his arrival King Richard had informed his Exchequer that it must raise all the cash it could.

Richard, as it happened, had hardly set foot in England before. "Frankly," he told his inner circle, "England seems wet and dull. But," he cheerfully added, "we love it for the huge income it yields us."

In the summer of 1189, therefore, everything was for sale: sheriffdoms, trading privileges, tax exemptions. "If you can find me a buyer," he remarked, "I'll sell London itself." Amongst the king's assets were numerous heiresses and widows, who, through the accidents of feudal vassalage, were his to protect and to bestow as he saw fit. This meant that when cash was urgently needed, he could sell these aristocratic ladies to the highest bidders.

Silversleeves understood his new king's needs perfectly. Ida was the seventh widow he had ferreted out and sold within the space of less than six weeks. He was proud of this transaction. Ida was poor. She brought no estate with her. If Pentecost had not known that the rich widower Bull was looking for a noble wife, Ida would probably have been unsaleable. Now, however, because her impending marriage would help pay for the Third Crusade, Pentecost could turn and, seeing her tears, coolly remark: "Never mind, madam. At least you're being sold in a good cause."

It was a short while later, as they passed into the West Cheap and rode down the line of gaily coloured stalls, that Ida received the final shock. Just before they drew level with the little Norman church of St Mary-le-Bow, Silversleeves turned to her and, indicating a group of merchants by the church door, remarked: "That's him. The one in red." And then Ida, seeing the coarse, red face and heavy-set frame of her future husband, fainted.

As the bystanders revived her, Pentecost watched idly, but his mind had already strayed from the luckless young widow. There were much more important things – urgent things – to occupy his thoughts, the chief of which was his own career.

On the surface, his prospects looked bright for the first time in twenty years. Not only was his old enemy King Henry at last removed from the scene, but something else quite wonderful and unexpected had occurred. He had found a patron.

William Longchamp was a self-made man. Tough, efficient, deeply ambitious, he had already risen high in the service of the Plantagenets and acquired great wealth. At the time he had met Silversleeves he was contemplating his next big move, and he needed a creature to serve him who would be entirely dependent on his good will.

It had always puzzled Pentecost that, however hard he tried, his superiors at the Exchequer had never seemed to trust him. When Longchamp had suddenly taken him up, therefore, he had been as much amazed as delighted. "If I serve him well," he eagerly told his wife, "he could make us rich." Not that he was poor. His father having died some years ago, Pentecost was in possession of a large fortune. But he also had a large and increasingly determined wife as well as three children who, though the eldest was only sixteen, were already anxiously enquiring about the size of their inheritance. The news he had heard the day before from his patron was thus exciting indeed. "Longchamp is going to be Chancellor of England," he had told his family. "He's having to pay the king a huge price for the office, but the deal's as good as done." His wife had kissed him. "And just think what he can do for us then," the children had cried as they clapped their hands.

There was only one problem. Richard the Lionheart would be crowned in less than ten days. Soon afterwards, he would leave his kingdom to depart upon his heroic crusade to the Holy Land. But would he ever return? Many thought not. The mortality rate for crusaders was high. Whilst many died fighting, still more died of disease or accidents on the long and perilous journey to the East. And even if he lived, what would he be returning to? As Silversleeves considered this, he did not like it.

The situation in the Plantagenet empire was complex. There had been three candidates for King Henry's vast inheritance: Richard, his brother John, and their nephew, Arthur. Richard had inherited the entire bulk of the empire, Arthur had been given the ancient land of Brittany, but John, dark and hard to know, had only received some rich estates, including parts of the west of England, in return for a promise to stay out of the island kingdom while his brother was away. Worse yet, from John's point of view, was that if Richard died without a son, the whole empire was to pass not to him but to the boy Arthur.

It was dangerous. No question. An empty kingdom. A discontented brother. There were other factors, too, that needed taking into account. As Silversleeves ran these over in his mind, he decided he liked the situation even less.

But of one thing he was certain. Whatever treachery lay ahead, he was not going to be on the wrong side. The vision of the preferment he had once dreamed of was rising before his eyes. He was going to be careful. Very careful. "And," he reassured his wife later that morning, "I shall do whatever I have to."

It was early afternoon when Sister Mabel entered St Paul's cathedral for her usual visit to her confessor. Today, for once, she had something to confess.

Ever since her vision years ago, Mabel had known that the Devil had plans for poor Brother Michael, and perhaps for her too. As for her, she had of course been aware of her friend as a man, but the monk's austere ways had always set him apart. Now, however, when the serpent had come, he had been so cunning, and so quick, that he had caught her unawares.

It had been a Saturday morning, the day of the horse fair, and Smithfield was crowded. She and Brother Michael had walked round, admiring the horses in the pens, and were just making their way back to the hospital when suddenly there was a cry of alarm, followed by a woman's scream. Turning to look, they saw a large, bay stallion careering through the scattering people. A second later he had broken into a gallop and was coming straight towards them. It did not take Brother Michael long to think. Throwing himself into the horse's path, he caught the bridle. At first, the stallion ploughed on. Two other men joined him. There were more cries, confusion, a ripping sound. A few moments later, his cassock almost entirely ripped off, Brother Michael led the stallion back across Smithfield, grinning like a boy.

And then she realized she had never seen his body before. She had thought of him as tall and thin, but here, laughing merrily and casting the tattered cassock from him, was an athletic, well-built man as perfectly proportioned as any she had seen. With a recognition that hit her suddenly and almost physically, she murmured: "Lord God but he's beautiful."

For the first time in her life, Sister Mabel experienced physical desire. She knew it was the Devil who sent it. She prayed night and day. She tried to close her mind to the man under the cassock, but what could she do? She was with him every day. For three weeks, to the exclusion of almost everything else, she was aware of his physical presence: the sound of his footfall, the smell of the sweat on the cuffs of his habit; the often matted fringe of hair on his tonsured head. Then even this seemed to merge into a more general love for him that was so intense she caught her breath if he even came into the room. Now, finding herself completely powerless before this engulfing emotion, she had gone to confess.

Beneath one of the dark, soaring arches of St Paul's, therefore, a rather surprised young priest asked her: "Has anything taken place?"

"No, Father," she answered sadly.

"Pray to our Blessed Mother the Virgin Mary," he told her, "and know in your heart that you will not sin."

But here she surprised him. For, devout though she was, Mabel had the practical sense of those who treat the sick. "That's no good," she answered, "because I probably shall." Which left the young priest, despite himself, somewhat curious as to what would happen next.

For three desperate days Ida tried to avoid her marriage. In her eyes, her fate was truly appalling. It was not just that Bull was heavy, coarse and a complete stranger. It would have been just as bad if she had liked him. The chief cause of her agony was purer than mere personality: Sampson Bull was of the wrong class.

It was termed disparagement, this forced marriage of heiresses and widows to men of lower rank: a magnate's daughter to a middling baron, a baron's to a humble knight, or even, as with Ida, a modest knight's daughter to a rich merchant. Nothing, in her world, could be worse. It was humiliating.

She went to the Exchequer and saw the justiciar himself, but no one was interested. Had she no powerful friends?

There was one, slim chance. The squat little western fort by Ludgate known as Baynard's Castle had long been held by the powerful feudal family of Fitzwalter, and to the Fitzwalters she could claim – just – a family connection. It was very distant, but it was all she had. So she went there.

The young knight who spoke with her was polite. The lord was busy. She explained that she was his kinswoman and that the matter was urgent. He advised her to come back in an hour.

After going to St Bride's to pray, she duly returned, to be told, apologetically: "The Lord Fitzwalter has gone out." The next day she saw only the doorkeeper, who also advised her to return. This time she waited near the entrance, but an hour later was again told that she had just missed him. Clearly her kinsman had no need of poor relations. She had lost.

The ceremony took place in St Mary-le-Bow. It was mercifully brief. Only the family attended and Ida was glad enough to return quietly to the Bull house afterwards.

Once there she took stock of her situation. As she looked at the merchant, she felt discouraged. On his face she could see only one emotion: satisfaction. And she was right, for if in retrieving Bocton Bull had fulfilled a lifetime's dream, in marrying Ida he had set a crown upon it. Not only had he reclaimed his Saxon estate, but he was edging into the Norman upper class that had supplanted him there. Nor was he alone. Several London merchants had already made such alliances. "And one day," he explained to young David, "she can help us find a noble wife for you too." In a generation, the Bulls of Bocton might become greater in the land than they had ever been. No wonder Bull looked pleased with himself.

As for Bull's family, his mother appeared to be a kindly, pious old woman, but was obviously not in the habit of talking much. The boy, David, who stared at her so shyly, seemed a much better prospect. She could see at once that he was a brave, frank fellow who must be lonely. When she gently said she was sorry he had lost his mother and hoped he would let her try to take her place, she saw his eyes moisten, and she was touched.

The surprise was Brother Michael. How amazing that the blunt merchant should have such a relation. She looked into Michael's kindly, intelligent eyes and liked him at once. Time had wrought a fineness in his face. She discerned his purity. Having always admired religious men and found herself attracted to them, she went up to him and begged him to come and visit her very soon, causing the monk to blush.

But she still had to sleep with the merchant, and here Sampson Bull was clever. He knew very well Ida's feelings for him and her repugnance for the marriage, but was not discouraged. He saw it as a challenge. When, therefore, they were alone in the bedchamber and it was the hour when she must submit to him, he took his time. This first night, Ida, conscious of her new station and that the boy was in a chamber nearby, let the merchant do what he must in silence. The second night, bathed in a sweat, she bit her lip. The third, despite herself, she cried out with pleasure. Later, asleep, she was not aware that the merchant, looking down at her pale body with a certain grim amusement, murmured gently: "Now, my lady, you've really been disparaged."

On the morning of 3 September 1189, King Richard I of England was crowned in Westminster Abbey. The coronation had one unusual feature. The gallant crusading king, having suddenly developed a fear that the sacred rites might somehow be polluted or endangered by witchcraft, had the day before ordered that the coronation was to take place in an atmosphere of particular purity.

"No Jews or women are to be admitted to the service."

Brother Michael hesitated. He told himself it was because of the boy. Why had he promised to raise the matter of the crusade? He knew it was futile, and it would only make his brother furious.

Relations between the brothers had improved in recent years. If Sampson was still irreverent, he seemed to have reconciled himself to his brother's life. A little before she died, his mother had summoned Michael and placed a considerable sum in his hands. "I want you to use it, on behalf of the family, but for religious purposes," she had told him. "It grieves me that your brother Sampson is still a lost soul, but you of course I can trust. Keep it until you know what to do, and I'm sure God will guide you." For some years he had remained the guardian of this money, and it gave him pleasure to think that when he was sure what to do, he would be able to make use of it. Michael had half expected his brother to protest, but when the alderman had heard, he had only laughed. When Bull's wife had died a year ago, and Brother Michael had visited almost every day to keep his and David's spirits up, Bull had one day given him an apologetic look and remarked: "I must say, Brother, you've behaved uncommonly well." No, he really did not want to have an argument now.

But there was something else.

It was nearly twenty years since his brother's crude challenge, yet the words still came back to him: "I don't even believe you can keep your stupid vows." But he had. Was it so difficult? His vow of poverty had been easy, of course; there was no wealth at St Bartholomew's Hospital. Obedience, too, had been easy enough. And chastity? That had been harder. He had been tempted by women, especially in the beginning. But with time the practice of celibacy had become not only a habit but a comfortable one. His work had brought him joy. I believe, he had thought to himself when he passed the age of forty, that I am safe. So why, now, did he hesitate at the door of his brother's house? Was it some instinct warning him of danger?

The coronation had taken place without interruption. Sampson Bull had attended the service in Westminster Abbey; then, while King Richard feasted with his court in Westminster Hall, the rich merchant had returned home for a more modest meal, to which he had invited his brother.

The conversation was cheerful. Though several times Brother Michael saw his nephew staring at him anxiously, he was in no hurry; and he found his gaze returning to Ida. What did she make of this marriage to his coarse brother? Could she be happy? It was hard to know what she was thinking, he decided. Only when the meal was nearly over, and he could not put it off any longer, did he finally broach the subject of the crusade. And held his breath.

To his surprise, however, Bull showed no sign of anger. Instead, he leaned back, closed his eyes for a few moments and smiled.

In truth, Bull had half expected it. The crusading fever was at its height. He knew that boys of David's age often conceived a passion for religion that usually passed, and if the boy had a desire for adventure, so much the better. Opening his eyes again, therefore, he remarked: "So you want to go to the Holy Land." Then, turning back to the monk, he mildly enquired: "Are you so anxious, Brother, that this boy should die?"

Brother Michael flushed. "Of course not."

"Yet many who go to the Holy Land," the merchant truly observed, "do not return." The monk was silent. "But you want the boy to save his soul? Which is hard to do in London, I suppose."

The merchant sighed. How was it, he often wondered, that men ran after ideals and ignored reality? Some who went on crusade were honest pilgrims, some were seeking adventure, some profit. Many would never even reach the Holy Land, dying first of disease or even, as with the last crusade, fighting other Christians. Nearly all would be ruined. Where, in all this, was the ideal? Lost in the journey.

It was at just this moment that young David gained an unexpected ally. The more Ida saw him, the more she liked the boy. The thought of losing him on a dangerous crusade horrified her, but as the daughter of a knight she understood him. Only the day before he had confided his secret to her, and when she had replied, "You're rather young," and seen him flush with shame, she had cursed herself. Now, therefore, she calmly intervened:

"I think you should let him go." It was the first time she had crossed her husband. She wondered what would happen.

Bull did not respond at once, frowning while he considered how to deal with this new development. Finally he observed with a trace of cruelty, "You were sold against your will, madam, because of a crusade, yet you still support them?"

"It's the principle that matters," she proudly replied. Then, very calmly, she smiled at Brother Michael.

How beautiful she was, he thought, how noble. With her pale white face, her large brown eyes, how sublimely above this merchant's house she was. He noticed with approval that young David was also gazing at her admiringly.

It was seeing their admiration that tempted Ida to make a foolish mistake, for now, turning to her husband with a trace of contempt, she remarked: "But since it concerns principles, you would not understand."

Deserved or not, it was an insult, and at once she realized she had gone too far. For a moment Bull was silent. Then he began to redden.

"No," he replied dangerously, "I wouldn't." She saw the veins beginning to stand out on his forehead. She noticed Brother Michael and David looking anxiously at each other. With a little tremor of fear, she realized that she was about to experience for the first time the merchant's famous temper.

Who knew what might have happened next if, at this moment, a servant had not burst into the hall, knocking over a pitcher of wine in his haste, and cried out: "Master! There's a riot!"

Men were running through the streets. Brother Michael made his way swiftly along the West Cheap and up Ironmonger Lane, from where he could hear shouts. One of the timber and thatch houses had been set alight. He found the dead body of a man lying in the street. Then he came to them.

There were about a hundred – men, women and children. Some were ruffians, but he saw two respectable merchants he knew, also some apprentices, a tailor's wife and a pair of young clerks. They were breaking down the door of a house. Someone had just thrown a lighted torch on to the roof, and a rough voice was crying out, "Round the back. Don't let him get away." When he asked one of the merchants what was happening, the man replied: "They attacked the king at Westminster. But don't worry, Brother. We'll get them."

It was the Jews.

The London riot of 1189 began as a simple, stupid mistake. While Richard and his knights were feasting, the leaders of the Jewish community had, with the best intentions, arrived at Westminster Palace to make a presentation to the new king. Since women and Jews had been forbidden to attend the coronation, the men at the door mistook this for some kind of attack and started shouting. Some hot-blooded courtiers rushed out, swords drawn. They struck. Several Jews fell. The commotion spread, and within the hour men were gathering in the city.

It did not take much to start a riot. In this case, as the whole city was in a fever for the Lionheart's crusade, the excuse was obvious.

"What's the use of a crusade if we let these foreign infidels live off the fat of the land right here in London?" the merchant now demanded angrily. Turning around, he shouted: "It's a crusade, lads. Kill the infidels!"

It was at exactly this moment that the Jew came out of his house. He was an elderly man with pale blue eyes, a narrow face, and a long grey beard. He wore a black cloak. As he looked at the mob before his door, he shook his head in disgust and mumbled a prayer. It would not save him.

A roar went up. The crowd surged forward.

Only then did Brother Michael realize who the old man was. It was Abraham, the Jew who had sold his brother the Bocton estate.

It did not take Brother Michael long to decide. It seemed to him there was nothing else to do. He rushed forward. The crowd, seeing he was a monk, let him through and a moment later he was standing beside the old man, his hand raised as though to restrain them.

"Well, Brother," a voice cried, "will you kill him, or shall we?"

"No one shall kill him," he shouted. "Go home."

"Why not?" they cried. "Isn't it right to kill an infidel?"

"Yes, Brother," he heard the merchant's voice. "Tell us why?"

And for a moment, to his own surprise, he could not remember.

Of course his humanity told him it was wrong, but that would not protect the old man now. Wasn't all Christendom supposed to fight the unbelievers, Muslim, Jew and heretic alike? What was the proper reply? Stumped for a moment, he looked helplessly at the old man, who softly murmured: "We're waiting, Brother."

Then, thanks be to God, it came to him. The great monk Bernard of Clairvaux, that indefatigable founder of monasteries, the man who had inspired the previous crusade and who all Christendom declared a saint, Bernard himself had formulated the doctrine concerning Jews:

> It is written that at the last the Jews also shall be converted to the true faith. If, however, we kill them, then they cannot be converted.

"The blessed Bernard himself said the Jews must not be harmed," he shouted. "For they are to be converted." Triumphantly he smiled at the old man.

The crowd hesitated. The two men could feel its mood in the balance. Then, glancing up for a second to heaven, Brother Michael did something he had never done before. "In any case," he shouted, "it makes no difference. I know this man. He has converted already." And before anyone could think of anything to say, he seized the old man by the arm, pushed him through the hesitating crowd, and marched him down the street, not even looking back until they had crossed into the West Cheap.

"You lied," Abraham remarked.

"I'm sorry."

The old man shrugged. "I'm Jewish," he said wryly. "I shall never forgive you." Which, though Brother Michael did not understand it, was a bitter Jewish joke.

They were not safe yet, however. The mob behind, now doubtless looting Abraham's house, might change its mind, and there would be other mobs about too. Thinking quickly, the monk told Abraham: "I'll take you to my brother's house."

But here again he was due for a shock. Encountering Bull, who was standing by St Mary-le-Bow in the company of Pentecost Silversleeves he explained what he wanted, only to be told by the merchant, "Sorry. I don't want my house burned down. He must go elsewhere."

"But you know him. You got Bocton from him. He could be killed otherwise," Brother Michael protested.

Bull was adamant. "Too risky. Sorry." And he turned his back.

To the monk's surprise, it was Pentecost Silversleeves who solved the problem. "We shall take him to the Tower," he announced. "The Jews are being protected there by the constable. Come on," and he started to lead them in that direction. When, however, Brother Michael remarked that the Exchequer clerk at least showed some humanity, Silversleeves gave him a bland look. "You don't understand," he remarked coolly. "I'm protecting him because the Jews are chattels of the king."

Not all the king's Jewish chattels were so lucky. There were numerous assaults, and the mobs also, naturally, looted the houses of these rich foreigners. Before long, as news of the London riot spread, other towns started similar atrocities, the worst of which took place in York, where a substantial congregation was burned alive. King Richard was furious and had the perpetrators severely punished, but the London riot of

September 1189, the first of its kind in England, was to mark the start of a gradual erosion of the Jewish community's position that would have tragic consequences for a hundred years.

For Brother Michael, however, the image that remained, hauntingly, in his mind from that day was not of the angry mob, nor even of Abraham.

It was of a pale, proud face, a pair of large, dark brown eyes, and a long white neck.

If Sister Mabel kept cheerful, it was partly because early that year an important new interest had been added to her own life. She had a child.

Not of her own, but as near as she could get.

Sister Mabel never did things by half. When Simon the armourer suddenly died, leaving a widow and an infant son, she not only comforted the mother, she virtually adopted the little boy. As it happened that her brother the fishmonger had young children, she arrived at his house one day with the little fellow in her arms and announced, "Here's a playmate for our babies." The boy's name was Adam. With his webbed hands and his white tuft, the Barnikel family soon dubbed him 'little duck', or 'ducket', and before long Adam Ducket he became.

Mabel was delighted with the arrangement. Hardly a day went by without her finding some cause to visit Adam and his mother, and indeed, the widow was glad enough of her assistance. "For his two daughters from his first wife," she explained to Mabel, "are both married and they aren't interested in us. That's for sure."

In other ways, though, the widow was lucky. Many of London's humbler craftsmen owned little more than the tools of their trade, but whilst the armoury itself had been taken by a new master, Simon had left his widow a tiny, four-room house by Cornhill, and through letting out two of the rooms and working hard as a sempstress, she could get by.

There was also the other inheritance. It was on this account that, thanks to Mabel, a small event now took place which was to have quite unforeseen consequences for the Ducket family. It concerned the little parcel of land at Windsor.

His widow had never understood why Simon had continued to hold these few acres, which yielded little return, but no subject had been closer to his heart. "My father had them, and his before," he used to declare. "They say we were there in the days of good King Alfred." To him the importance of this ancestral link was self-evident. Each year he had ridden the twenty miles to pay his rent and arrange with his now distant cousins, still serfs, alas, to work the land for him. Just before he died he had made her promise: "Never give up our land. Keep it for Adam."

"But what am I to do about it?" she asked Mabel. "How would I even get there to make the arrangements?" Her answer came when Mabel appeared at Cornhill one morning with a small horse and cart belonging to her brother. "It smells of fish a bit," Mabel remarked, "but it'll do. You go to Windsor. We'll look after the baby while you're gone." And so Adam's mother set out to secure his inheritance.

She reached the hamlet on the second day. The place had changed little since the Domesday survey. She had no difficulty in recognizing her husband's kin, for as soon as she arrived, she saw a fellow in the lane with a white patch in his hair just like her husband's. And if, at first glance, she thought the fellow looked a little shifty, her fears were soon set to rest when he not only turned out to be the head of the family, but that very evening offered her a solution to her problem. "You don't want to come out here every year," he explained. "And there's no need. We'll work the land as usual. But from what it yields we'll settle your rent with the lord's steward and afterwards one of us will come to London with the balance for you." He grinned. "I've two sons and a daughter who all want to visit London. You'd be doing me a favour if you would let them lodge with you a few days."

By the next morning, the whole matter was settled with the steward and the widow was able to return, delighted with the easy way this tiresome business had been taken off her mind.

For Ida, the month of September passed pleasantly enough. The house of which she was now mistress had been enlarged in recent decades and was now a substantial building. Like most merchant houses, it was constructed of wood and plaster. Bull conducted his business on the ground floor; there was a fine upper floor where the hall and bedchamber were situated;

and an attic floor where young David and the servants slept. However, two other features of the building, common to most of the houses in London then, gave the place its character.

The first concerned the construction of the different floors. Having completed the ground floor, the builders had not continued upwards in a straight line. Instead, the upper storey was actually larger in area than the one below, jutting out several feet into the lane, above the heads of the passers-by. Few houses, as yet, had more than two storeys, but in those that did the third storey came out even further, making the narrow lanes almost like tunnels.

The other feature was that the overhanging front and sides of Bull's house were supported by horizontal timbers that were no more or less than the great branches of pollarded oaks. These were used exactly as they were, uncut, sometimes even with the bark left on, and as a consequence, though hugely strong, they were by no means straight. The result was that all these timbered houses had a lopsided look, as if they were about to collapse, although in reality they could stand for centuries so long as they did not burn down.

The last risk was their weakness. Fire was endemic. That very year an ordinance had been made requiring the citizens to rebuild their ground floors in brick or stone and to replace their thatched roofs with tiles or other less flammable material. But as Sampson Bull had declared: "I'll be damned if I'll do it in a hurry. The expense is huge."

Though used to running an estate, Ida found that she had plenty to do. If there were no serfs to supervise, she was nevertheless expected to take some part in her husband's business, and within days she found herself glancing with a sharp eye at sacks of wool, bales of cloth and rolls of imported silk, just as before she would have inspected the grain or the feed for the cattle. The servants, thank God, were friendly. The two girls who worked in the kitchen seemed genuinely delighted to have a mistress again, and on the first Saturday Bull took her to Smithfield to purchase a fine new mare.

But her greatest pleasure came from young David. It had not taken them long to become friends. During the day he went to school at nearby St Paul's, but in the evenings she would sit with him. It was obvious that for over a year the boy had had no one to talk to at home. All she had to do was listen kindly and in no time he was sharing every confidence. She understood his grief that he could not go on the crusade. She promised him things would get better. She had never been a mother before and found she enjoyed it.

And then, of course, there was Brother Michael. Once a week, at her insistence, he came for a meal. Secretly she wished it could be more often.

Only two weeks after the coronation, however, this new rhythm of life was interrupted when Bull suddenly announced, "We're going to Bocton for a few days."

It was nightfall when they arrived, but she liked the place at once. The knight who had lived there had left a modest stone hall with a fine yard and large wooden outbuildings. It was not unlike the manor she had lived in before. But her astonishment came the next morning when, soon after sunrise, she stood and gazed out at the magnificent, sweeping view across the Weald of Kent. It was so lovely it made her gasp. "We always had this place," Bull remarked softly, "until King William came." Just for a moment, Ida felt a sense of kinship with him.

Her stay there was pleasant, if brief, but her feelings were mixed. She was glad Bull had such an estate, yet it reminded her poignantly of the life she had lost. And perhaps it was this sense of loss that caused her, soon after her return to London, to make the first major mistake of her marriage.

It happened on Michaelmas Day. She was returning home in the afternoon when she heard from the outside voices raised in anger. Moments later she walked in and found, to her surprise, three figures: Sampson Bull, red in the face, sitting at an oak table; Brother Michael; and, pale and faintly contemptuous, Pentecost Silversleeves. However, this was nothing to the shock she felt on hearing what her husband was saying.

"If this is how King Richard rules, then let him go to hell," the merchant thundered. And then, to her horror: "London will get another king." At which poor Ida blanched, for this was treason.

The reason for it was simple enough, though. It was about taxes. If the tension between the monarch and the city was ancient, it also had well-defined limits. The city's annual tax was termed the farm. When the king was weak the city could negotiate a reduction in the farm, and choose its own sheriffs to collect it. When the king was strong, the farm went up and the king named the sheriffs, though not without reference to the citizens. As for its collection, this was done in whatever way the great men of London deemed best. The arrangements were announced at Michaelmas.

"And do you know what this cursed Richard has just done?" Bull thundered. "No sheriffs. He's just sent in his stewards, like this creature here," he gestured to the long-nosed Exchequer clerk, "without so much as a by-your-leave. They're to bleed us for everything they can get. It's iniquitous."

The description was wholly fair. Silversleeves, using a sound and ancient principle, had just demanded an outrageous sum from the merchant. "Start high," the Exchequer men had agreed, "and let them beat us down." After all, the king's crusade must be paid for.

But a member of the knightly class did not speak treason lightly, and Ida quietly reproved her husband: "You should be careful what you say about the king."

In the months following, Brother Michael often blamed himself. If I had just led her out, he would think, she would not have heard. I should have guessed the way things would go. However, partly because he was curious to listen himself, he had not. And certainly, nothing in her life had prepared Ida for what came next.

For, quite coolly, her husband now addressed himself to the clerk.

"The king's a fool. The barons of London are not to be trifled with like this."

Ida knew that the rich London burghers liked to call themselves barons, but had always supposed it a piece of foolish pretension. However, if she expected a sharp reaction from the king's man, none came. Silversleeves knew better. A strong king like William the Conqueror or Henry II could dominate the city, but during the anarchic period before King Henry, which older folk could still remember, the Londoners in their huge walled city had been capable of holding the balance of power in the kingdom. Besides, the cautious Exchequer man, though determined to do his master's work, was equally anxious in these uncertain times to make as few enemies as possible. To Ida's surprise, therefore, he now sat down opposite Bull at the oak table and remarked in a voice that was almost apologetic, "Richard, you must understand, knows nothing of England, and cares less."

"Then the city will oppose him."

"The king is powerful at present," Silversleeves observed. "I think you'll have to pay."

"This year, yes. Next year, perhaps not. After that," Bull looked at him steadily, "we shall see." He shrugged. "With a bit of luck he'll be killed on crusade and we'll be rid of him."

Ida gasped. But far from protesting at this, as she thought he must, Silversleeves instead leaned forward and confidentially asked, "We all know this is a mistake, but tell me honestly, how bad is London's reaction going to be?"

Bull considered for a few moments before delivering his verdict. When he spoke, his voice was grave. "If the king won't play by the rules, if he turns his back on custom," he looked Silversleeves carefully in the eye, "we won't stand for it."

To Ida the words seemed rather foolish. To Pentecost they were frightening. Custom was everything in England. The old common law that governed every manor and village in the kingdom might not be written down, but the Norman conquerors had wisely never attempted to touch it. Similarly, the customs of London might not be formally set out, but every king since William had respected them. This was the code the Norse and Saxon burghers of the city lived by. Within its limits, they were flexible. Break the code, and cooperation would end. Ida only dimly guessed this. Pentecost had known it from his cradle.

It was then that Bull added something that to Ida sounded even stranger, though in time the curious word he used would become as familiar to her as it would be loathsome.

"Frankly," he remarked, "it wouldn't surprise me if this didn't lead to a commune."

Silversleeves went pale.

A commune. Ida had only a vague idea of what such a thing might be, although in fact, as an institution, it was not new. In Normandy, the ancient city of Rouen had possessed a commune for half a century, and other European cities had versions of it. In the past, the barons of London had been known to raise the idea from time to time, though never with much success.

For the commune was every burgher's dream. It meant, in effect, that the city became a self-governing unit with almost no interference from the monarch. A kingdom within the kingdom, electing its own governor, who was usually called by the French term of mayor. But there was another feature of the Continental commune of which Silversleeves was well aware.

There were three main ways in which the king obtained his income. The first was the yearly farm from the counties; the other two were occasional taxes, levied for special purposes as the king and his council thought best, one of which was the aid, in theory a gift given to the king by all his feudal barons, the other the tallage, a flat, per capita tax paid by all the king's freemen, especially those in towns.

In feudal Europe a commune was treated as though it were a single, feudal baron. The farm was paid to the king by the mayor, who raised it as he thought fit; the aid was paid similarly. But since the commune was a single, feudal baron, when it came to the tallage, it was as though all the thousands of freemen within the city's walls had vanished. They were no longer the king's men; they belonged to a baron called London. No tallage was payable. The commune was, in reality, a form of tax haven not for the rich but for ordinary citizens. No wonder, then, that the Exchequer clerk regarded it with horror.

"Would you support a commune?" he asked.

"I would," Bull gruffly replied.

Ida had listened to this disloyal conversation with mounting horror. Who did these arrogant merchants think they were? Perhaps if her visit to Bocton had not sharply reminded her of her former state, she might have kept silent. If she had been the widow of a magnate, familiar with the power of the great European cities, she would have known better. But she was only the widow of a provincial knight; nor was she clever. So, with nothing but the prejudices of her class to sustain her, she now addressed her husband with disdain.

"You are speaking of the king!" she protested. "We owe him obedience." Seeing their astonished looks, she burst out: "You call yourselves barons? You're nothing but merchants. You talk of a commune. It's an impertinence. The king will crush you, and quite rightly. You should pay your taxes and do as you're told." Then, finally, "You forget your place."

Within this speech lay all the pain of her own humiliation, and a reminder to them that, whatever they might do to her, she was still a lady. Flushed and angry, Ida felt rather proud. It did not occur to her that every word of it was absurd.

For a moment Bull was completely silent, staring down impassively at the heavy oak table. Then he spoke.

"I see I made a mistake when I married you, my lady. I had not realized you were so stupid. But as my wife I believe your place is to obey me, so get out."

As she turned, white and shaking, she saw young David at the door, watching her.

In the weeks that followed, the relationship between Ida and Bull remained cold. Both were secretly hurt by the exchange, and like other couples who discover they despise one another, they retreated into a state of armed neutrality.

Brother Michael continued to come to the house. He did what he could to make them cheerful, and prayed for them, but he was not sure if he had much success. As for David, if Ida wondered what he made of the dispute, it soon became clear, for only days afterwards, sitting quietly with her one afternoon, he asked: "Is my father wicked?" When she replied that of course he wasn't, he persisted, "But surely he shouldn't speak against the king?"

"No," she admitted frankly, "he shouldn't." But she refused to discuss it any further.

Only one thing during this period gave her a small satisfaction. Despite her failure to interest him before her marriage, she did not give up in her attempt to claim kinship with the Lord Fitzwalter. Once, cleverly trapping him as he came from a Mass in St Paul's, she forced him to acknowledge her existence. Meanwhile, by referring to him frequently as her kinsman, she could see that she had impressed several of her husband's friends, who displayed in her presence a faint social discomfort which, at this time, was her greatest pleasure.

And so autumn proceeded into winter. In early December, King Richard crossed the sea to Normandy, and England was quiet.

* * *

It was one winter's night that Sister Mabel nearly sent Brother Michael to perdition. Or so, in after years, she liked to think.

Midwinter had come to London, and all the world was seeking warmth. At St Bartholomew's it was the feast of Christmas. Darkness had fallen and there was a quarter-moon. The priory roof was covered with a mantle of snow; the interior of the cloister was a pale, staring square. After the service of compline, the canons held a feast. There was swan, spiced wine, three kinds of fish, and sweetmeats. Even the inmates of the hospital were fed by the light of smoking lamps what morsels they could manage, and throughout the establishment there was a sense of good cheer.

So perhaps it was not surprising that, having drunk more than she realized, Sister Mabel felt a little flushed; nor even that, as they passed through the cloister where a brazier was burning, she should have suggested to Brother Michael that they sit by its warmth and talk a while.

They sat quietly in the glow from the charcoal. Brother Michael, too, was feeling relaxed. They spoke of their families, and by and by it came about that she asked him if he had ever loved a woman. "Yes," he answered, he supposed he had. "But I took my vows to this," he said, indicating the long cloister of their religious home.

"No one would have married me," she confessed.

And it was then, with a giggle, that Sister Mabel made her move. Pulling up her habit to a little above the knee, she gave him a curious smile and stuck out one leg. "I used to think my legs were all right," she said. "What do you think?"

It was a strong, plump little leg with freckled skin and surprisingly few hairs, and those so fair that they scarcely showed. A pretty enough leg, many would have said. Brother Michael gazed at it.

There was no mistaking her intention, but he was not shocked. Indeed, he was touched. Realizing that this was the first and only sexual advance Mabel would make in her life, kindly Brother Michael kissed her gently on the forehead and remarked: "A fine leg indeed, Sister Mabel, with which to serve God."

Then he quietly rose and walked away through the cloisters and out of St Bartholomew's into the great, blank emptiness of Smithfield.

Two days later, having consoled herself with the thought that if the Devil was after Brother Michael, he had failed this time, she told her confessor cheerfully, "It's over for me. I shall go to hell and there's nothing you can do about it. But Brother Michael's still all right."

On the last night of December, a secret meeting took place.

The seven men who arrived separately and unnoticed at the house near the London Stone were all of the rank of alderman. At their discussion, which lasted an hour, they not only agreed upon what they wanted, but devised the strategies and tactics they would use. "The first thing to be addressed," their leader announced to general agreement, "is the question of the farm." But there were other, deeper matters also to be considered.

It was towards the end of the meeting when someone remarked that what they needed was a stooge, that Alderman Sampson Bull, after a moment's thought, declared: "I know exactly the man. Leave it to me." When they asked him who, he smiled and answered:

"Silversleeves."

Nor was it simply chance that only days later messengers came to London with important and frightening news.

John, the king's brother, had arrived on England's shores.

APRIL 1190

Pentecost Silversleeves gazed at the Barnikel family. They did not like him, but that did not matter. They were not important. There was the stout, red-haired fishmonger and his children, another woman he did not know holding the hand of a little boy, and that curious creature Sister Mabel.

"It's not fair," Sister Mabel protested.

He knew that.

"I paid for those nets," the fishmonger reminded him.

"I fear," Pentecost said smoothly, "there will be no compensation."

"Then there's one law for the rich and one for the poor," Mabel stated in disgust. At which Silversleeves smiled.

"Of course," he said.

Kiddles. The perennial problem of the Thames. Not that on

this occasion Barnikel's nets had actually damaged Bull's ship, but the sight of them in the river one morning had infuriated the rich merchant. He had spoken to Silversleeves, who had spoken to the chancellor, and within a day their removal was ordered, despite the fact that the fishmonger, who, though not poor, was only a modest trader, had paid handsomely for the right to have them there. As soon as he left, Silversleeves would hasten to inform Bull of what had been done. Which was only natural, since for the last three months Alderman Sampson Bull had become his greatest friend.

How slowly, almost imperceptibly, it had all begun. At first there had been only whispers, vague rumours, but he knew how to read the signs, and by March he had been sure. It was John.

Why had King Richard relented and allowed his younger brother to enter England? Because he despised him. Indeed, in comparison with the rest of his family, John cut a poor figure. Where his father flew into rages, John had epileptic fits. Where Richard was tall, fair and heroic, John was dark, stout, stood only five feet five, and was an unlucky soldier. Occasionally brilliant, he did everything by fits and starts, and Richard was not afraid of him. But, like any Plantagenet, he coveted his brother's throne.

To all outward appearances, he did nothing. Richard was still only two weeks' journey away, collecting his forces on the Continent and consulting with his fellow crusader the King of France. John remained on his vast estates in the west of England. Hunting and hawking mostly, the reports said. But Silversleeves was not deceived. He's biding his time, he concluded, before he strikes. And he knew who the target would be.

His patron, Longchamp.

To begin with it had seemed that all was going so well. The chancellor had succeeded brilliantly, becoming in his master's absence the most powerful man in England. For his assiduous devotion, Pentecost had already been rewarded with a handsome benefice or two. The future might have been bright indeed, had it not been for one problem.

"Longchamp's arrogant. That's the trouble," Pentecost told

his wife. "He's made enemies." The chancellor had, unfortunately, made no secret of his scorn for some of the great feudal families. "And they mean to bring him down," the Exchequer clerk lamented.

"They must not succeed," his large wife cried. "He's worth a fortune to us."

The signs were small, but ominous. If any knight or baron ran foul of the chancellor, it was not long before a report came that they had gone to visit John. There were other rumours too. As early as January a merchant had remarked to him, "They say John's agents are already in London," though when he had asked who, the man had refused to say. Pentecost had been watchful, but was unable to discover anything.

How lucky, then, that he had become so friendly with Bull.

He could hardly say how it had happened. A casual invitation to the merchant's house. A few chance encounters. If he had analysed it, Pentecost might have concluded that Bull had begun the friendship. Anyway, he was glad of it. "No one knows what's going on in the city better than he does," he told his wife. "I mean to stay close to him."

He had even tried to make friends with Bull's family. To Ida he was studiously polite. She would never be his friend, but she was somewhat mollified by the fact that nowadays he always bowed to her and addressed her as a lady. The boy David was easier. To him, Pentecost always said stoutly, "I'm the king's man." He took the boy round the Exchequer once, telling him, "Here we do the king's business." But for Bull himself, nothing was good enough. Today's incident of the kiddles was just one more way to persuade the powerful alderman that he and his master, Longchamp, were his friends. "And you'll tell me about anything you hear," he always requested.

It was as he was leaving, that Pentecost suddenly noticed that the little boy holding the woman's hand looked vaguely familiar. For a moment he frowned in puzzlement, but then he realized what it was: the child had a white patch in his hair.

"Who's he?" he asked. Mabel told him.

Pentecost walked back towards Bull's house thoughtfully. He had not known that Simon the armourer had left a son. It seemed to him the news was good. There was a score to settle there. Father or son, it was all the same to him; and since the son was so young, that gave him plenty of time to think of something appropriate. Before long he was smiling, then grinning from ear to ear.

So when he entered Bull's house, it was a shock to find the merchant looking grave. And when, after thanking him for his help over the kiddles, Bull took him by the arm and told him, "I think there's something you ought to know," poor Silversleeves went quite pale.

Brother Michael realized he was losing the battle during the month of May. That was the month the stranger came.

His name was Gilbert de Godefroi and he was a knight. His manor was called Avonsford, near the western castle of Sarum. And he was staying in Bull's house.

His presence there was not so surprising. Whilst humble pilgrims lodged in hospices, a travelling knight would normally stay with a merchant. When, therefore, Godefroi arrived with a letter from a West Country merchant Bull knew, it was only natural for the alderman to offer him hospitality. The knight slept in the merchant's hall, his groom in the stables.

Gilbert de Godefroi was in London to set his affairs in order before departing on crusade. He was tall and middle-aged. His face was sad and stern, his manner somewhat dry. They did not see him much, for he rose at dawn each day, and having been to prime, the first service at St Paul's, he would ride to Westminster or exercise his horses in the woods at Islington; and after eating little in the evening, would retire. Upon his surcoat was a cross in red to mark the fact that he was on crusade. He was a perfect knight. Also a widower.

Godefroi had been there for four days when Brother Michael met him at the weekly family meal. He was impressed at once by the knight's dignified manner. Young David was obviously in awe of him, and even Bull was quieter than usual, but what the monk could not have anticipated was the change in Ida.

That she paid the knight attention was proper: he was their guest. That she served him first was only courtesy. That she had dressed herself in the flowing robe of a lady, this, too, was understandable. But it was more than that. Ida was transformed. It was as though she had been a traveller in some strange country and had at last encountered someone who spoke her own tongue. Indeed, in the remarks she addressed to the knight she seemed almost to say aloud: "But these others would not understand." Her husband she appeared to have forgotten entirely, and she hardly, Brother Michael thought, even notices me.

The knight said little and the monk left, deeply troubled. It grieved him to see Ida make a fool of his brother. And she's making a fool of herself too, he thought.

In fact, it was worse than even Brother Michael had guessed. From the moment the knight had come, Ida had claimed his attention. She had let him know at once what quality of person she was and how she had been disparaged. She told him her ancestry, hoping to find a common connection. When she retired with Bull at night, her large brown eyes gave the knight a look that said: "Rescue me." She even tried to join him at his prayers. All of which things Bull watched in silence.

By the next week, it seemed to the monk that the situation was even more serious. I must do something, he thought. So, upon some pretext, he returned again the next day, and the next, and it was on these visits that a further, and even graver, aspect of the business appeared.

For if Ida made approaches to the knight, young David was in love. Brother Michael watched as, day by day, the fair, fresh-faced boy followed the stern knight around. David would watch Godefroi practise with his sword and mace, or help his groom, a young fellow only a few years older than himself, to clean the knight's mail to keep it from rusting. He was fascinated, too, by the knight's shield, which had a white swan depicted on a red background. This choosing of a personal coat of arms as an adornment in jousting was a knightly custom that had sprung up in the last few decades, and it seemed to the boy further proof that Godefroi was a hero, an impression that was confirmed when, now and then, the knight himself paused to talk to him in his quiet, serious way. When he swung into the saddle of his magnificent charger, however, it seemed to David Bull that the knight was almost a god.

It was as Godefroi clattered out of the yard one morning, watched by David, Brother Michael and Ida, that the boy turned to his stepmother and remarked, "I wish my father was like that."

Ida only laughed. And then she said the hurtful thing.

"Don't be silly," she told him. "Just look at your father. You can see at once that he's only a merchant." Then, with a sigh, "Nobles are born, not made." Though, to cheer him up she added: "I'll find you a noble wife. Perhaps your son could be a knight."

And so the London merchant's son came to understand that not only was his powerful father wrong in his attitudes, not only was he of lower rank than the feudal knight, but God had actually created him inferior. He had not known this before.

But it was true. Except in London itself, Norman and Plantagenet rule had produced one huge change in English society. The Anglo-Saxon noble had boasted of his warrior ancestry, but his nobility had actually derived from his wealth. A man with enough land was noble; rich London merchants became thanes. In time of war, they had led the old English levy drawn from their fields.

Their Norman supplanters were quite separate from the English people. Godefroi might run his estate at Avonsford like his Saxon predecessor, but he had another in Normandy. He could speak English, but his first language was still French. He did not lead his peasants to war, because the old, untrained English levy was hardly used any more. Lionheart's troops were hired – tough archers from Wales and the terrifying *routiers*, the mercenaries from the Continent. The knight might be rich, or very poor. Bull could have bought even Godefroi twice over. But he belonged to a separate, European, military aristocracy, a caste united in a vast cousinship that looked upon all others with disdain. It was a perception of nobility that, once rooted in the island of Britain, would haunt its society.

Alderman Sampson Bull saw, cannily, that his family could, over time, buy and marry its way into this nobility. Ida knew it too, but regretted the fact. As for young David, when he looked at the knight he saw only magic. And from now on, when he looked at his father, he would see him as base and, despite the fact they were father and son, secretly despise him. This was Ida's latest gift to her husband.

All this the monk observed, and he grieved. It was at the next family visit, however, that the real shock came.

After the meal, he had gone outside with his brother and the boy. The hall was quiet; Ida had gone to supervise the larder; his old mother was asleep in a corner; and the knight was sitting alone in silence. Only by chance had Brother Michael gone back and seen them.

Godefroi was standing, as quiet and motionless as ever. Ida had re-entered and was standing in front of him, saying something softly. Then she reached out her hand and touched the knight on the arm. With that tiny gesture, it seemed to Brother Michael that he knew. Turning pale, he backed out.

The awful dream came that night. He saw her pale body intertwined with the knight's, saw her long neck stretch in ecstasy, saw him possess her. He saw her dark eyes, her long hair falling over her breasts; he heard her utter a small cry. And awoke with a huge, cold anguish that caused him first to sit bolt upright, then to pace his little cell. Nor did he find it possible to sleep again, but paced up and down the five night hours before dawn with that same terrible image of Ida's love-making continuing all the time, now this way, now that, before him.

It was soon after dawn and the birds were in their full May chorus when he made his way across Smithfield and down towards St Paul's. There, by the door, as a single bell summoned a few chaste souls to prime, he saw the silent figure of Godefroi approaching.

When the pious knight heard what he had to say, he did not even deign to show surprise. "You accuse me of adultery, monk?" he coldly enquired. "You suggest I should leave? I have no need to leave." And he strode into St Paul's without another word.

Had he been wrong? Brother Michael put his hand on his forehead. Did he really suspect this pious knight? Confused, he returned, hardly knowing what to think.

Three days later, Gilbert de Godefroi was ready to depart. Ida offered him her glove to wear as a gage upon his journey – a courtly gesture from the knightly world. But this he refused with a solemn look, reminding her: "I am a pilgrim to the Holy Land." And Brother Michael sighed with relief.

With the departure of the knight both Ida and young David seemed to grow listless. David even became quite unwell and his studies began to suffer. In midsummer, therefore, the Alderman asked Brother Michael to give his son some help.

No one could call young David a scholar, but he was curious enough, and pleasant; and for his uncle he had a huge respect. "You are so learned," he would say in genuine amazement, which encouraged the monk to tell him all he knew.

Brother Michael's knowledge of the world was typical of a moderately learned man of his time: a pleasant mixture of fact and folklore culled from the library he used to enjoy at Westminster Abbey. He could give his nephew a good account of the great patchwork of states that made Europe, with its ports and rivers, its cities and shrines. He could speak knowingly of Rome and of the Holy Land. But at the edge of this huge medieval world, his knowledge began to blur into fabulous terrains beyond.

"South of the Holy Land lies Egypt," he could correctly inform David, "from which Moses led the Jews across the desert. And by the mouth of the great River Nile lies the city of Babylon." This was the name the medieval world gave to Cairo.

"And if you travel up the Nile?" the boy eagerly asked.

"Then," the monk confidently told him, for he had read it in a book, "you come to the land of China."

About London's history, he could also instruct his nephew. "London was founded long, long ago," he explained, "long before even Rome. A great hero called Brutus first built it. Then he journeyed on and founded ancient Troy." He told him how the Romans had come and gone and how King Alfred had rebuilt the walls.

"And who were the kings before Alfred?" the boy asked.

"There were many ancient English kings," the monk replied. "But the most famous, long ago, were two. One was good King Arthur with his Knights of the Round Table."

"And the other?"

"The other," he could affirm, "was old King Cole." For so, in the history books, it was written.

Often, as he instructed the boy, Ida would come and sit beside them.

On a fine early autumn day Sister Mabel might have been expected to be in a good humour. Yet this morning she was not.

The cause of her fury was to be found in a small church she had just been visiting.

The church of St Lawrence Silversleeves was a handsome little building, which stood on a narrow plot between a rope-maker's house and a bakery. Down the hill in the Vintry were the Thameside warehouses of the Norman wine merchants, over which one could see the river. It was built in stone, except for its roof, which was wooden; it was four bays long and could, had its congregation ever been so many, have conveniently contained a hundred souls. Sister Mabel had just been to visit the curate of this modest church.

The curate of St Lawrence Silversleeves was a poor sickly fellow with a wife and two children. Technically, of course, since he was in holy orders, the long-suffering woman with whom he lived was not called his wife but his concubine. But few, even amongst the strictest churchgoers, would have considered his moral crime a grave one. Most of the curates in London were married – because if they did not have a wife, they would starve.

The situation at St Lawrence Silversleeves was typical. The Silversleeves family appointed the vicar, who enjoyed the income from its endowment. If there was no one in the family who wanted the position, it would probably go to some friend or connection. He, like as not, would be vicar of several other churches as well, all of whose incomes he accumulated. And to carry out the duties of each, he would appoint a curate, to whom he paid a pittance – so small that if the wretched fellow did not have a wife to earn their keep, he could scarcely put wood on the fire.

The curate of St Lawrence Silversleeves was thirty-five. His hair was grey and sparse, and he suffered from dizzy spells. His wife, who worked in the bakery next door, was stouter but suffered from varicose veins. And his two sallow daughters reminded Mabel of nothing so much as a pair of broken candles. They all lived together in a huddled little tenement behind the church; and so miserable were they that, one Christmas two years ago, even the Silversleeves family had given them a shilling.

Sister Mabel went to them as often as she could. Today, after a busy session with pestle and mortar in her larder, she had brought a philtre of wood lettuce to cure the man's failing vision and betony for his giddy spells. She brought savine for his wife's swollen feet and whey bread because both their children had worms. She had spent an hour with them dispensing these medicines and her own, blunt comfort, and now she had emerged with a single thought in her mind. "Damn that Silversleeves. He must do something for them. I shall make him."

She went to his house but he was not there. "I'll find him," she muttered, as she tramped back towards Smithfield. And just as she entered that broad, open space she did indeed catch sight of him. He was standing not far from the gateway to St Bartholomew's church, talking to Brother Michael. "Got you," she whispered with satisfaction; and she hurried across, her basket bumping against her leg. But she was only twenty paces from them when she stopped dead in her tracks, blinking in astonishment at what she saw.

For there, standing just behind the two men, as clear and as solid as the priory behind, was a strange, green and white figure, with a bird-like face, a curving tail, and a trident in his hand. There was no mistaking him: it was that very demon she had spoken to, years ago, when she had had her vision. And now – there was no mistaking this either – his beaked face was gloating. He's come for Silversleeves, she thought, without remorse. Well, serve him right.

But then, as she watched, she saw to her horror that the green and white demon was not looking at Silversleeves at all, but putting his long arms around saintly Brother Michael. And Brother Michael was entirely unaware.

When the seven men met in secret soon after Michaelmas that year, it was agreed that Alderman Sampson Bull deserved congratulation.

"You handled Silversleeves perfectly," their leader declared. And indeed, Bull did feel that his performance had been masterly.

Not that he had lied. No Bull ever did that. "But I may," he confessed, "have exaggerated a little." And Pentecost had been so willing to believe.

When he had told the Exchequer clerk that spring that John's envoys had opened negotiations with some of the leading aldermen of London, Silversleeves's fright had been wonderful to behold. It was in fact true that some discreet conversations had taken place, but John was not yet confident enough and nor were the aldermen ready to do more than hint at mutual interest. But by allowing Pentecost to suppose that a fully fledged conspiracy was already afoot, Bull had galvanized him into action.

"For with these monstrous tax arrangements in force," he warned Pentecost, "I can't imagine the city will fail to support John in any attack upon your master."

From that day, Bull had been able to play the Exchequer clerk like a fish that had been hooked. No one was more active in counselling the chancellor as to the dangers of offending London. Hardly a week went by without Pentecost meeting Bull and anxiously asking for news, to which the thickset merchant would always reply with some vague but frightening statement such as, "John is everywhere," or "Things look bad for Longchamp."

Silversleeves was assiduous. By midsummer, the aldermen had been receiving hints that their campaign was working. And now, just days before, at the Michaelmas Exchequer, had come the wondrous news.

"Everything!" Bull had cried in triumph to his friends. "Everything we wanted. The king's new taxation completely abolished. The farm back at the low rate. Two sheriffs of our own choice." To Silversleeves he solemnly announced, "London is in your debt, Master Silversleeves." And then, to the clerk's further, anxious enquiry, "Why should London support John when we have such a friend as Longchamp?"

So it was fortunate, now, for Silversleeves's peace of mind that he was not at the meeting in the house near the London Stone, and therefore did not hear the leader of the group, after congratulating Bull, announce with a bland smile to his colleagues:

"And now my friends, as to the next step, all we need to do is wait."

For news had reached him that very day that King Richard the Lionheart had finally left the Continent and had set sail on the distant Mediterranean Sea, beyond any chance of recall.

Adam's mother never heard from her relations at Windsor again. Despite all they had said, none of the family ever came to London, which meant that she never received any money. After more than a year had passed and no word had come, she had promised herself that she would go down there the following year to look into the matter. Or perhaps, she thought, the year after that. It was a long way.

When Adam was five she told him: "Your father had some strips of land in a village. We're supposed to get something from them." It meant nothing to the little boy then, and in time, as his mother let the business lapse, he would forget it entirely.

David Bull's sickness returned that autumn. He suddenly became so pale and thin that his father was seriously worried. "We Bulls are never ill," he said firmly; but the boy only seemed to get worse. Everything was tried, including Mabel's herbal cures; and for a time, whether thanks to the herbs or Brother Michael's prayers, he appeared to rally. The month of December passed. But then in January, the illness came back.

First it had snowed, then become bitter cold; the streets of London turned to ice; they sprinkled cinders in the lanes. And each day, wearing thick boots, the monk crunched sadly down to the house by St Mary-le-Bow. Not all Sister Mabel's herbs could save the fifteen-year-old David Bull, it seemed, and even the tough merchant shook his head with tears in his eyes and said to his brother: "It seems that our family is finished." By the end of the month, as the boy lay like a pale ghost in the chamber, Ida told him: "Fight, David. Remember, I'm going to find you a noble wife." But to Brother Michael she whispered: "I love him as my own; but there are only your prayers now between him and death."

Day by day Brother Michael prayed. More than once, he found his brother, head bowed in misery, kneeling by his side. Sometimes David watched dully, sometimes he slept. Each day, the monk thought, close as he was to giving up, there remained in the boy a tiny strand, like the thinnest ray of sunlight, that persisted, and it was upon this, always, that he tried to concentrate his attention. If only poor David's pale, thin frame could somehow be brought to stand in the shaft of light; if he could feel its warmth bathing his whole body: if I could just accomplish that, the monk thought, then I believe he would either fly like an angel up to heaven, or be cured.

If young David were to die, therefore, the least he could do was try to prepare him. This turned out to be easier than he had thought. For whether it was because he feared death or was prompted by the monk's spiritual presence, several times, as he sat with him, the boy had seemed eager to talk. He asked about heaven and hell and the Devil. One day he wanted to know: "If my soul seeks God, then why does it love the world, which is so far from heaven? Does that mean the Devil has taken me over?"

"Not exactly," the monk told him. "Worldly desires, the desires of kings, and courts, the lust for riches, even the love of woman –" and for a moment he thought of Ida – "these are in truth only a perversion of your desire for eternal things. They are the worldly illusion of that far greater court, the court of God."

"If so, then why should I fear to leave this Earth?" David asked.

"You should not, if you are ready and have served God," the monk replied.

"I should have liked to have gone on crusade," the boy said with a sigh. "But as it is, I have done nothing."

A day later, he asked the monk about his own life. What had led him to a religious house? "A sense of vocation, I suppose," Brother Michael answered. "Which just meant," he explained truthfully, "that I no longer wanted anything but to be closer to God." But the boy did not reply to this, seeming very weak. Yet he held on to life, day by day. A week later, it began to grow a little warmer. Still David clung to life, and still his uncle prayed.

Then, one day, for no reason he could explain, Brother Michael knew that the boy would live. He confided it to Ida, who was so moved that she kissed him. That morning, as he returned from the house, on a little patch of grass he saw a snowdrop growing by St Paul's.

It was in the middle of February that Sister Mabel finally understood the meaning of her vision. She had once again revisited the curate at St Lawrence Silversleeves; despite getting nowhere in several attempts to persuade the Exchequer clerk to help the poor family, she was doing the best she could for them herself. She had decided to pay young David Bull a visit after this, and, in her usual cheerful way, had stomped up to the Bulls' hall and walked in through the door when she saw them sitting together near the window. In that instant she perceived the truth.

There was no demon this time: just three very human figures. The boy was at the table with a handsome book before him. Brother Michael, sitting quietly beside him and guiding the boy's hand over the complex calligraphy, was explaining a difficult passage of Latin. Ida, opposite, was not touching the saintly monk, but was looking at him with adoration. And now, gazing with horror at the three of them Mabel realized the unnatural love which was growing and which would catch them unawares.

She gave young David some medicine, then departed, and wondered what to do. She prayed, yet got no guidance. And then, meeting the monk in the cloister that evening, she told him bluntly: "You must beware, Brother Michael, of an unnatural love."

It was rare indeed for Brother Michael to be angry, but just for a moment he was tempted. Yet then, remembering Mabel's own attempt one Christmas night to lead him astray in this very cloister, the kindly monk had compassion. She was jealous, he realized, but what good would it do to throw that in her face? As for his feelings for Ida, he was confident enough.

"We all have to be careful," he rebuked her gently. "I assure you that I am. But I think, Sister Mabel, that you should not say this to me again."

Then he left her; and poor Mabel could only return to her cell and pray again.

JUNE 1191

The nightmare had begun. It was even worse than Pentecost had imagined.

Prince John had done his work well. At the start of the year, Silversleeves reckoned, there had not been a baron in England with any kind of grudge against the chancellor, who had not become John's friend. Then, in the spring, John had begun to move.

First it was one of the southern castles that he claimed was his; then an important northern sheriff refused to obey the chancellor; then, in March, a messenger had arrived in London with still more ominous news: "John's seized the castle of Nottingham." It was one of the most powerful strongholds in the Midlands. "He's gone hunting in Sherwood Forest as if he were king already," it was said. Since then there had been constant rumours. John himself was moving about the kingdom, collecting supporters from half the shires. One of the barons was amassing a dangerous force on the borders of Wales. Indeed, in the city they were asking only two questions: "Will the chancellor face down the brother of the king?" and "Will John attack London?"

Silversleeves gazed at the scene before him. In front of the Tower a small army of men had been set to work. Already they had hastily erected a new and quite impressive-looking wall around the Tower precincts. They had also dug a huge ditch outside that. But as he studied these constructions, Pentecost could only feel discouraged. Longchamp might be a talented administrator, but as one of the workmen had remarked to the clerk, "He's not a castle-builder." Even Pentecost could see that the foundations of the wall were too shallow, its masonry too thin to withstand a proper attack. As for the ditch, it was meant to be a moat, but when Longchamp had tried to flood it a few days before it had been a disaster. At present it contained nothing more daunting than an inch or two of mud. Only the week before, as if in preparation for a more serious disturbance, there had been a small riot in the East Cheap. It had been put down easily enough, but Pentecost suspected John's agents might have been behind it.

Would London stay loyal to the chancellor? God knew he had given the Londoners all they wanted. Yet he was so tactless. The previous month his hasty works at the Tower had destroyed a fruit garden belonging to one of the aldermen. "But he left me to go and apologize," Silversleeves had complained.

"London is still loyal to the king, whether they like Longchamp or not," Bull had promised him.

But then where was King Richard now? Was he somewhere on the dangerous seas or in the Holy Land? Was he even alive? Nobody knew. If only there were some word from the Lionheart.

* * *

That spring had been a strange time for Brother Michael. All around him, the world seemed threatening. The crusader king was far away. Who knew what his brother John was up to? And yet, by some wonderful alchemy, Brother Michael was happy. For David Bull was getting well again.

Often now, he and Ida would take the boy for a walk. At first David could only manage a few steps. But by late March he and the wiry monk were walking so vigorously that Ida would declare with a laugh: "You two boys go off together. I can't keep up with you."

Once, on a warm late April day, as they were passing the Aldwych, where some bold youths were diving into the Thames from the bank, David suddenly surprised his uncle by running down, stripping, and diving in too. Though he shouted to him to stop, Brother Michael could not help feeling joy at seeing his body, slim and elegant, but strong and healthy once again. Afraid that he might still catch chill though, the monk had dried him vigorously and, after a scolding, put his arm round him to keep him warm as they walked briskly home.

But despite these flashes of high spirits, David was often pensive. He liked to pray with the monk nowadays, and continued to question him about religion. Once or twice, with a sad look, he admitted: "My life has been spared by God: but I'm not sure for what." And when in May, Ida and Bull went down to Bocton for the month, David, on the excuse that, with the spring revels, this was a pleasant season to be in London, lingered there in the company of his uncle.

Exactly when it was that Brother Michael knew what he must do, he was not afterwards sure. Perhaps he had somehow known it the night after David dived into the Thames; perhaps it was a few nights after Bull and Ida had left, when he had arrived at the house to find the boy at prayer. But one thing he knew: he would not allow the boy to lose his soul. If God had brought David back from death, it must be for a special purpose. No matter what rift it might cause with his brother, he would do his duty. "I shall save him," he decided.

And then he realized something else. If this was what God had intended, providence had put into his hands exactly the means to make it possible: his mother's legacy. The circumstances exactly fitted her instructions. The money would be used for the benefit of the family's religion. "You will know what to do," she had told him. And now he was sure he did.

In the middle of June he went quietly to Westminster Abbey, requested an interview with the abbot, and made the arrangements.

These suited him very well. Whatever objections he may have had to the life of the Abbey in his youth, they seemed less important now. Ida, he was sure, would feel its noble setting to be appropriate. As for himself, having spent a lifetime in the service of Bartholomew's, it seemed to him that he had earned a rest. The least he could do was keep an eye on David. Their entrance to the Abbey would be secured, and their comfortable maintenance assured, by the generous donation which Sampson Bull would never have provided. It was, he concluded, providence indeed.

So it was, on a warm May night, when the spring moon was almost full, that with a clear conscience and singing heart Brother Michael went to his nephew and said: "I think you may have a vocation for the religious life. What do you think?" At this remark from the saintly man he so admired, when his own young mind was so uncertain, David could only blush with pleasure and gratefully cry: "Oh yes. I do."

With a heart flowing with love greater than he had ever known before, good Brother Michael suggested: "If you join the great Abbey of Westminster, I will be there also with you, as your guide."

In the happy consciousness of these events, saying nothing of his plans to anyone as yet, Brother Michael awaited the return of his brother and Ida. That Bull would be angry he had no doubt. Yet remembering how broken he had been when he had thought his son was lost, it seemed to the monk that perhaps, even at this late stage of his life, the unbelieving merchant's heart might be softened. After all, he planned to say, Bull could at least be glad he was safe and sound in the monastery nearby – where, God knows, he can always visit him, he thought.

As for Ida, he had no doubt that seeing her stepson safe in the bosom of the Church, she would feel the same joy and gratitude as he. When a message came that they would return in June he waited, half nervous and half expectant, to give them the wonderful news.

* * *

"What have you done?"

He had never seen her like this before. Her pale, noble face had become as hard as a knight's. Her large, brown eyes looked at him with scorn, as if he were an impertinent peasant to be cut down.

"The work of God . . ." he began.

"David a monk? How would he have children?"

"We are all the children of God," he said, abashed.

"God has no need of my step-son," she retorted with furious contempt. "He will marry into a noble family."

He stared at her first in horror, then some anger. "Would you put family pride before God and your son's happiness?"

But she cut him off abruptly. "Let others be the judge of that, you meddling old virgin," she suddenly shouted. "Get out of this house and go back to your wretched cripples and your cell." And, half dazed, poor Brother Michael found himself stumbling out. An hour later, after a rapid conversation with her husband in which they found themselves in the most perfect agreement, Ida left again for Bocton, taking David with her.

Yet the true humiliation of Brother Michael came that afternoon when, sitting in a bemused state in the cloister of St Bartholomew's, he confessed his troubles to Mabel. "I can't understand it," he muttered, shaking his head. Mabel, sorry though she was for him, was also firm. "I tried to warn you," she said, "about unnatural love."

Thinking of Ida's scornful eyes he replied sadly: "I don't think I'm in love with her any more."

Mabel frowned. "Her? You mean Ida?"

"Who else?" He looked up in surprise.

"Why, David! The boy. You fell in love with a boy, didn't you, you naughty old man?" And she gave a chuckle, as though it was amusing.

So stunned was he by this outrageous and revolting proposition that Brother Michael was entirely speechless for a moment or two. Then a great rage welled up in him, but before this could take form in words, like some vast, cold chasm opening before him, into which not only the wave of his anger but the whole of his life seemed suddenly to fall, Brother

Michael saw before him the horrible realization that it was true. In his innocence, he had not known.

Bent double with the shame and pain, he got up and left her, and shuffled like an old man to his cell.

Young David Bull completed his recovery at Bocton. He loved the old manor with its sweeping views and went for long walks round the woods and fields with his father. He read knightly tales with Ida who was at her best as mistress of the manor. Perhaps the spirits of his Bull ancestors passed on to him some of their own, solid strength. He had never known such contentment.

Nor it seemed had Ida and his father. The crisis of David's illness, and Ida's fury with poor Brother Michael had evidently drawn them together. As they discussed improvements to the old place, inspected the orchard or just sat on a bench in the sun, gazing over the Weald together, they seemed for the first time to have become man and wife. The subject of his father's merchant outlook was no longer mentioned – unless it was implied when Ida promised to find David a noble wife – and this seemed to amuse the alderman rather than irritate him. And there was so much going on in the wider world that summer that the subject of the monastery was practically forgotten.

The trouble caused by treacherous Prince John seemed to have subsided. In July, the Archbishop of Rouen had concluded a peace between John and Longchamp. England was quiet again. And not only was the crusading King Richard alive and well, but reports in August announced he had married a beautiful princess who, surely, would give him the heir his loyal kingdom needed?

One day Silversleeves came from London to have a talk with the merchant, to which David listened with great interest.

"Was Richard wise to marry this princess?" Bull asked.

"On the whole," Silversleeves replied, "I think so. She comes from Navarre, you see, which lies just south of his own Aquitaine, so by this alliance, Richard lessens the chance of the French king attacking him from that direction. I'd say it was a sound move."

David was slightly puzzled by this. He was not a fool, but like his Saxon ancestors he liked things to be clear. Either a man was your friend or your enemy. He could not be both. "But surely," he asked the Exchequer clerk, "King Richard and the King of France are sworn friends? They are brothers on crusade."

Silversleeves smiled sadly. Given the vast Plantagenet empire running down France's western flank, the kings of France and Plantagenet England could never be more than temporary friends. "He's only Richard's friend for the moment," he replied.

David looked sad. "I'd die for King Richard," he said bluntly. "Wouldn't you?"

Silversleeves only hesitated a second before smiling and answering, "Of course. I am the king's man."

But, a few days later, as he was preparing to return to London, even this conversation was swept from the boy's mind as another, truly miraculous piece of news arrived – proof, surely, that in this year of the Third Crusade God was sending a message of bright hope to the English and their valiant crusader king.

News had just come from the western abbey of Glastonbury that the monks had discovered the tomb and the remains of King Arthur and his Queen Guinevere in the ancient abbey grounds. Could any sign be clearer, or more wonderful, than that?

There was no more time. It was many years since Pentecost Silversleeves had experienced a state of panic, but now, on the afternoon of 5 October, he was near it. In his left hand was the urgent summons from his master and patron; in his right, another piece of parchment. Both were equally frightening. And both posed the awful question: which way should he jump? Still he hesitated.

The crisis had broken quite unexpectedly in mid-September, and because of it the Michaelmas session of the Exchequer had been moved fifty miles up the Thames to Oxford. But that quiet castle town, with its little community of scholars, brought no peace to Silversleeves now.

The cause of the wretched business was a bastard; the problem, that he had been made Archbishop of York.

It was common enough, of course, for the king's bastards to be made bishops; it gave them an income and something to do. The appointment of one of King Henry II's many extra sons as archbishop would not have mattered, except that he was a known collaborator of John's and had been expressly forbidden to enter England by King Richard.

So when, last month, he had landed at Kent, the chancellor had been right to insist he swear allegiance. When the cunning fellow refused, Longchamp's mistake had been to throw him in jail.

"The whole thing was a deliberate trap," Pentecost judged. If so, his master had fallen into it. To John's delight, there was an outcry. The archbishop, though quickly released, was hailed a martyr, like Becket himself. John and his party had protested, and even now a great council, meeting between Oxford and London, had summoned Longchamp to explain himself. "They mean to get him this time," Silversleeves moaned.

Yet nothing was certain. Many in the council were suspicious of John. The chancellor still held several castles, including Windsor. The key, as usual, would be London. Which way would the city go? Silversleeves was not surprised, therefore, at the urgent message from his master summoning him to London at once.

But what of the parchment in his other hand?

At first sight it looked like any of a hundred Exchequer records. Until you looked in one corner. For there, nestling inside a large capital letter, was a neatly drawn caricature of the chancellor. It was a work of art, and it was vicious. Longchamp's heavy features had been accentuated until he looked like a coarse and fleshy gargoyle. His mouth was dripping as if he had eaten more than he could contain. The thing was not just a caricature, it was contemptuous, insulting. And this was the chancellor himself. No Exchequer scribe would dare leave such a thing in the records unless he were sure, very sure, that the chancellor was doomed. "So what does this scribe know that I don't?" Pentecost wondered aloud.

But the parchment contained something even worse. In the margin beside the capital was a second caricature, this one of a dog that the chancellor was holding on a leash. The face of the dog, with its greedy, slobbering mouth and long nose, was also, alas, unmistakable. It was himself.

So – they thought he was doomed too. If they were right, he

should desert his patron now. Quickly and firmly. As an exercise, he quickly went over all the chancellor's actions. Were there any secret crimes he could denounce if he fled to Longchamp's enemies? Were there any in which he himself was not implicated? Only two or three, but in an emergency they would have to do. On the other hand, if Longchamp survived this crisis and he had deserted him, Pentecost would have lost all hope of reward, probably for ever. For several agonizing minutes, he considered his future.

Then, carefully taking his knife, he cut away the offensive corner of the parchment and walked out. By evening, he was on his way to London.

On 7 October, at the house by the sign of the Bull, Ida spent the hour around noon quietly. She was glad to do so after the disturbances of the last two days.

First, Longchamp the chancellor had arrived from Windsor with a troop of men the day before. He was in the Tower now, securing the fortifications. Parties of his men were patrolling the streets. Then, this morning, news had come that the council, Prince John, knights and men-at-arms were advancing towards the city and should arrive by evening. "They intend to depose the chancellor," the messenger reported.

But that might not be so easy. If the city stayed loyal to Richard's man and closed the gates, there would not be much the council could do. Not that she cared for Longchamp much, but he was loyal to Richard. "And anything," she remarked to her husband, "is better than that traitor John." Bull himself had gone out two hours earlier. A meeting of all the aldermen and the greatest men of the city had been called to decide what attitude they should take towards the council. Ida waited anxiously.

And then there was the other matter, which she had not yet told him about.

So when Ida heard someone in the courtyard, it was her husband she was expecting. It was with surprise, therefore, that, a moment later, she saw a different figure entirely.

It was Silversleeves. She had never seen him like this before.

* * *

Bull strode rapidly past St Paul's. He was wearing a cloak of the deepest blue, lined around the collar with ermine. His broad face was set in a bluff expression that gave little away, but his heart was singing. Everything had gone to plan.

The meeting of the aldermen had taken place in a chamber behind closed doors. There had been careful discussion, of course; several strategies had been suggested. But the group of seven had been well prepared. Months of working discreetly on the minds of their colleagues had now come to fruition. Their arguments had been cogent. They knew what to do, and how. The meeting had finally agreed to place everything in their hands, and at this moment a messenger was quietly slipping out through Ludgate.

Only one other thing had been agreed. If the strategy of the seven was to work, then discretion was advisable. The bargaining position must not be revealed. Absolute silence about the meeting would need to be maintained. "And then," Bull muttered with deep satisfaction, "the day will be ours."

He was surprised, when he reached home, to find Pentecost Silversleeves awaiting him. A glance told him that the Exchequer clerk was in a sorry state. He had been pacing up and down the courtyard for almost an hour. Rushing up to the merchant now, he begged him for news.

Though his face showed nothing, the merchant thought quickly.

"You are on your way to Longchamp?" he asked. Silversleeves nodded. "Then you may tell him," he said carefully, "that London is loyal."

Minutes later, the relieved Exchequer clerk was on his way to the Tower, leaving Bull alone with his thoughts.

Did I lie? Bull wondered. No. No Bull ever lied. "I just said London was loyal," he said out loud.

He had not said loyal to what.

It was shortly after dark when young David Bull saw the strange little procession. All afternoon he had been watching from Ludgate for signs of the approaching forces, but though there was a rumour that they were close to Westminster, he had not seen them. At dusk the gates had been shut.

So who were the party of twenty hooded horsemen being led quickly through the quiet streets by men with torches and lanterns? He saw them near St Paul's and followed them curiously down the incline towards the Walbrook. At the London Stone, the procession paused. Three of the riders went up a lane opposite; some of the others dismounted. Still curious, David drew closer. There was no one else in the street. The horsemen were clustered together and he did not quite dare approach them, but after a moment he noticed a large figure holding a lantern detach himself from the group and go towards the shadowy lane. Running up behind him, David touched his arm and softly enquired, "Can you tell me, sir, who are these men?" And was amazed, as the figure turned round, to see in the glow of the lantern the large, heavy-set face of his father.

"Go home!" Bull hissed to his startled son, and then, in a low voice, "I'll tell you about it later."

Obediently David turned to go. Unable to resist, however, he hesitated for a moment. "But who are they, Father?" he whispered.

He was truly astonished when his father muttered, "It's Prince John, you fool. Now go."

It had been a relief to Ida to hear that her husband and his fellow merchants were loyal. Alone that afternoon, she had even quietly congratulated herself. Clearly, her influence had begun to do some good. Crude merchant though he was, there was decency in Bull. She would express her approval that evening.

There was also the other matter to discuss, she thought. It would be well to talk about that too.

At first, then, when David came in that evening and told her what had happened, she could not quite believe it. "You must have misunderstood," she told him. But as an hour passed, and then another, she began to wonder. What could it mean? What was her husband up to? As she thought of the aldermen dealing with the treacherous prince, her face became pale and taut. When Bull finally arrived her large brown eyes fixed upon him and she asked her simple question in a voice that was low and icy.

"What have you done?"

He was not abashed, glancing first at her, then at David.

"A deal," he answered coolly.

"What kind of deal?"

"The best in the history of London," he cheerfully replied.

"You dealt with the traitor John?"

"With John. Yes." Was his calm contemptuous?

"The enemy of the king. What deal?"

Bull ignored his wife's tone, as though he was so satisfied he did not much care what she thought of him, and answered her easily enough.

"Tomorrow, madam, Prince John will officially enter the city with the king's council. We shall open the gates and welcome him. Then the city will give Prince John and the council its full support in deposing Longchamp. If necessary, we shall storm the Tower."

"And then?"

"We shall join the council and swear to recognize John as King Richard's heir instead of Arthur."

"But that is monstrous," Ida cried. "You effectively give England to John at once."

"Not in law. The council rules. But in practice you may be right."

"Why have you done this?" Her voice was hoarse with dismay.

"The deal, you mean? Oh, it is excellent." He smiled. "You see, in return for London's cooperation at this critical time, Prince John has granted us something we greatly deserve."

"Which is?"

"Why my dear, the commune, of course! London is now a commune. We shall choose our mayor tomorrow." He beamed at them both. "London is free."

For just a moment Ida was too stunned to speak. It was worse, more cynical, more wicked, than anything she had imagined. The happy weeks of the summer at Bocton were forgotten. She erupted.

"London a commune," she shouted. "So that you merchants can strut and call yourselves barons and pretend your mayor's a king? For that you have sold England to that devil John?" She stared at him with rage. "You traitor!" she screamed.

Bull shrugged, then turned around. And because he did so, he did not see young David Bull, staring through tears at his father not only with shock but, for the first time in his life, with hatred, before he rushed out of the house.

* * *

Pentecost and the four horsemen rode through the dark streets. He had decided to join the patrol in case he could learn any further news, but everything was quiet.

His meeting with Longchamp had heartened him. The chancellor might be a dark, coarse-featured fellow, but one had to admire his cool resolve. All his castles, Pentecost learned, were well defended. The dispositions at the Tower were excellent. "And tomorrow at dawn, you are to ensure that all the gates of London stay closed, upon my order," he told Silversleeves. The clerk had also helped him begin a letter to King Richard, setting out John's treacherous game in detail. "If, as you tell me, the city will stand firm, we can probably frighten John off," Longchamp remarked. "And then," he added with a grin, "we must find you another estate, my friend Silversleeves," the prospect of which had greatly increased the clerk's valour.

The patrol had reached the foot of Cornhill and was about to return to the Tower when it met three knights riding up from the river. Wondering who they were, Pentecost listened idly as the patrol leader, glad of something to do at last, told them to identify themselves. He was surprised when, after a slight hesitation, one of the knights responded with: "Who may you be?"

"The chancellor's men. Identify yourselves." Again there was a slight pause. He heard one of the three knights mutter something, and another laugh. Then came the reply.

"I am Sir William de Montvent, fellow. And your master is a dog!"

John's men. What could it mean? He had no time to think. The sound of swords drawn, a pale flash of steel in the dark, and the knights were running their horses at them.

What happened next took place so quickly that afterwards Pentecost could never quite remember the sequence of events. As the three knights rushed, he instinctively tried to wheel his horse to run away. But there were cobbles underfoot. His panic made him act so suddenly that his horse slipped and fell, and he was lucky, as he crashed on to the hard ground, to fall clear.

By the time he struggled up, two of the three knights were already a hundred yards away. He heard the clash of steel.

Then he looked up. The third knight was gazing coolly down at him, his sword drawn. He laughed. "Fancy a little swordplay?" he asked. "I'll come down then." And in a leisurely manner, he began to get down from his steed.

Terrified, Pentecost did not even have time to think. As he clambered to his feet and drew his sword he saw, for just a second, that as the knight dismounted he had his back to him. He lunged, and by good fortune struck deep into the fellow's side. A mortal blow.

With a cry the knight fell. Pentecost looked at him, aghast. The knight was on the ground staring up at him, groaning softly and very pale. He looked about, wondering what to do. The others were already round a corner, out of sight.

It was just at this moment that, from the direction of the West Cheap, a single figure came wandering dejectedly through the shadows towards him. Pentecost peered nervously, then murmured in surprise. It was David Bull. Pentecost hesitated. Should he hide? It was too late. The boy had recognized him and was hurrying up. Catching sight of the fallen knight as he drew close, David gasped. "He attacked me," Silversleeves said quickly.

And then the boy said the words that caused Pentecost to grow paler than the dying knight. "Oh sir," he cried, "do you know what has happened? My father and the aldermen have sold London to Prince John."

Silversleeves stared. "Are you sure?"

"Yes. He told me so himself. There's to be a commune." He was so distressed he was near to tears again. Gazing miserably at Silversleeves he asked; "Is it all over, then?"

Now Pentecost had to think very fast. Glancing down, he saw with relief that the knight was dead. He looked up and down the street. Those knights would be back soon to find their companion. Had anyone else seen the killing? He did not think so.

"All is not lost," he told the boy. "The chancellor's here. We have men."

"You mean you'll still oppose Prince John?" The boy brightened. "You'll fight for Lionheart?"

"Of course," said Pentecost. "Won't you?"

"Oh yes," cried David Bull. "I will."

"Good. Take my sword," Silversleeves said, handing it to

him. "I'll have his." Reaching down, he picked up the fallen knight's weapon. Once more, he glanced around. All was silent.

Then, with a single, easy thrust, he plunged the knight's sword into David Bull's heart.

A few moments later, having put the sword back in the dead knight's hand and closed his fingers around it, he went to get his horse. Fortunately the animal was still sound. Then, making a small detour, he waited in a nearby alley to watch.

It turned out as he had thought. After only a few minutes the other knights, having chased the patrol to the Tower, returned to find their companion. From his hiding place, he could hear their voices.

"By God," one cried, "he's been killed by a boy."

"The boy attacked him from behind. Look."

"He managed to kill the little brute before he died, though." And they picked up the body of their comrade and rode away.

Not long afterwards, Pentecost arrived at the house of Alderman Sampson Bull.

"I've come to ask a favour," he told Bull. "I've left Longchamp. He's finished. Would you put in a good word for me with John and the council? After all I did for you?" And, feeling a little guilty at having misled him earlier, Bull grudgingly agreed. "All right. I'll do my best."

"You are a true friend," said Silversleeves.

"By the way," Bull remarked, "my boy went running out into the street a little while ago. You haven't seen him, have you?"

"No," Pentecost replied, "I haven't."

On 7 October in the year of Our Lord 1191, a momentous event took place in the history of London. After being summoned to the churchyard by the great bell of St Paul's, the ancient Folkmoot, of the citizens of London, met to hear the council, in the presence of a large body of magnates and, of course, Prince John, depose Chancellor Longchamp. At this meeting John was proclaimed heir to the throne. But most wonderful of all, it was declared that, subject to the confirmation of King Richard – should he ever return – London was to be a commune. With a mayor.

During this happy ceremony, a red-faced Alderman Sampson Bull stood somewhat apart from his fellows, who tried not to look at his large body shaking almost continuously with silent tears.

When the tragedy of his son had become known to him the previous night and he had returned home with David's body, it was perhaps not surprising that, in his grief, he had blamed Ida. "It was you who turned him against me and filled his head with nonsense," he cried in anguish. "Now see what you have done. Get out of my house," he bellowed, "for ever." When she refused, he struck her.

So guilty did she feel, so shocked and sorry for the merchant as she witnessed the full extent of his agony, that she let him strike her. Nor did she say anything when, as she stumbled up, he struck her again, breaking two of her teeth.

But the third time, before the blow fell, she begged him: "Do not strike me again." And as he paused, she told him the thing she had been about to tell him for a little while: "I'm pregnant."

Strangely, in his pain that day it was his brother Michael to whom Bull went for comfort.

1215

The castle of Windsor was a pleasant sight. Constructed over the last century, it occupied a single hill, covered with oak woods, and rose like a guardian over the placid meadows by the River Thames. It commanded a magnificent view of the hamlets and countryside around. Around the broad summit, above the trees, there was a high curtain wall with battlements. But where the Tower of London was square and grim, this other great royal castle further up the Thames had a sedate, almost kindly presence.

Silversleeves had only gone three miles from the castle gates when he wished he hadn't. The sun had been out when he left that June morning, but now it was raining hard. As the lush meadows all around roared with the din of falling water, and the raindrops gathered on the end of his nose, he cut a sorry figure.

The truth was, as every new Exchequer clerk was told

nowadays: "Old Silversleeves is a bit of a joke." It was not simply his age. After all, the mighty Earl Marshal, one of the greatest officers of the kingdom, was still fighting in the saddle at over seventy. But poor Silversleeves, with his stooping shoulders and his nose that seemed to grow even longer with advancing years – Silversleeves whose half-century at the Exchequer had never led to advancement – Silversleeves was certainly an object of fun. The legend of Henry II chasing him out of Westminster Hall was now told in several amusing versions. His last-minute changes of allegiance were cautionary tales. And if it were not for the fact that he carried the entire Exchequer Rolls in his head and could compute sets of figures quicker than most men could blink, he would probably have been retired years before.

But at least he could console himself he had been important enough to be present at the great meeting three days before in the meadow near the castle called Runnymede.

King Richard the Lionheart had not been a good king. He was never in England. When he had died in battle and his brother John succeeded, some people had hoped things would get better. Certainly no one could have predicted the disasters of John's reign. He had murdered his nephew, poor young Arthur of Brittany. Then, in a series of ill-judged campaigns, he had lost almost all his father's empire across the Channel. Henry had quarrelled with Becket, but John managed to quarrel with the Pope so thoroughly that England was placed under an Interdict. For years, there had been no Masses; you could hardly even get a decent burial. Finally he had managed to offend so many of England's powerful feudal families that a determined group had decided to rebel and bring him to order.

The result had been Magna Carta, the great charter to which John had been forced to swear three days before at Runnymede.

In some ways it was a conservative document. Most of the conditions it placed on the king and the basic liberties it asserted for the people were no more than the long-established conventions of feudal society and old English common law. John was being put on notice that he must abide by the rules. Some improvements were made, though: widows could no longer be forced, as Ida had been, to marry. There were clauses, too, protecting men against imprisonment without trial. But one set of provisions was truly radical. Instead of the ancient council – the group of great nobles who had always expected to advise the king – the rebels now insisted there should be a named council of twenty-five men, including the Archbishop of Canterbury and the Mayor of London, to make sure the monarch abided by the charter. If he did not, they would depose him.

"It's unheard of!" Silversleeves had remarked to one of the rebel barons. "No monarch has ever submitted to such a thing. "Why," he added, "England would then be just like a commune. Your twenty-five barons would be like so many aldermen, and the king no more than a mayor!"

"I quite agree," the nobleman replied. "It was London, my dear fellow, that gave us the idea."

Nor was London itself left out of the charter. Strangely enough, though they were determined to preserve their privileges, the aldermen had not held out for their right to have a commune. The reason for this had been explained to Silversleeves by Bull. "It's the taxes." He grinned. "You see, we soon found that since a commune is treated like a single baron when it comes to taxes – which meant that the other citizens wanted the richest of us to pay a bigger share. But if the king taxes each citizen individually, we aldermen don't get hit so hard. So we don't want the commune so much as we thought we did, after all!" But the mayor was another matter. The king's charter confirmed him in perpetuity. "He'll never be taken from us now," Bull assured him. One other small clause was added. It was number thirty-three.

> Henceforth all kiddles shall be completely removed from the Thames and the Medway and throughout all England, except on the sea coast.

After over forty years of waiting, Alderman Sampson Bull had triumphed over the king.

Looking for a place to shelter, Silversleeves now took a lane that led to a hamlet he had not visited before. Riding up to a cottage, he demanded entrance. Only after he had begun to dry out did he notice something rather curious abut the peasant family who were his reluctant hosts: the father had a white patch in his hair. He remained with them an hour, until the shower passed; after which he paid a call upon the steward of the estate in which the hamlet lay.

When he returned to London later that day, Pentecost Silversleeves was smiling.

Life had treated Adam Ducket well. He was a member of the fishmongers company now, a modest craft guild, but nonetheless a respectable position. There had been sadness, true: his first wife had died in childbirth several years before, but his old patron Barnikel had a daughter, Lucy, of marriageable age. They were due to marry in the spring.

On a dull November afternoon a messenger with strange news arrived at the house of Adam Ducket on Cornhill. It was not merely strange, it made no sense at all.

He was summoned to appear before the Hustings court in two weeks' time. "I've done nothing wrong," he said to the messenger. "What's it all about?" When he discovered, at the house of the mayor the next day, he could not believe his ears.

The ancient court of the Husting generally met on a Monday. The place of its meetings was a simple stone hall, of quite modest dimensions, with a steep wooden roof, that stood in the ward known as Aldermanbury, just above the Jewry. The ground beside it was rather more open than elsewhere, with several courtyards, and it was also noticeable that the streets around this area had a curious curve. Until a few generations before, the outlines of a Roman amphitheatre had still been visible upon the site, but this was now entirely forgotten. The little stone courthouse, where the mayor and aldermen met, was known as the Guildhall.

Inside the Guildhall on a cold November morning, with Barnikel and Mabel beside him as supporters, Adam Ducket faced the mayor and aldermen of London. And also his accuser: Silversleeves.

The last ten days had been like a bewildering dream. The accusation had come from nowhere, from a man he scarcely knew, even by sight. He was not even accused of a crime. It was more incomprehensible than that. "They say I'm not who I think I am," he told Mabel, "and I can't prove it."

He had tried. He had ridden down to the hamlet near Windsor the very day after hearing the accusation. But to his astonishment, the distant cousins he had never visited before, and the landlord's steward, confirmed his guilt. "If only my mother were still alive. Maybe she could have told me something," he cried. But no one could help him.

Silversleeves had begun. Thin, stooped, and an object of ridicule he might be; but now, entirely in his element, he became strangely impressive. "The accusation, Mayor and Aldermen, is very simple," he declared. "Before you stands one Adam Ducket, fishmonger and supposed citizen of London. My duty today is to tell you that I have discovered he is an impostor. Adam Ducket he is. But a citizen of this noble commune," he used the word with a deep bow of respect, "he may not be. For Adam Ducket is not a freeman. He is a serf."

The great men of London sighed wearily. "Give us your proof," they said.

They were by no means uncommon, these accusations of serfdom, and they were heard by the London courts for many generations. True, in theory, a serf might run away and live in a town, unclaimed, for a year and a day: at which point he became free. But such runaways were not common, and were likely to be treated as vagabonds unless they had money. Besides, the freemen of London had their own families to employ, their own guilds to protect. They were a proud community. And one thing – custom was very clear on this – which the freemen of London would not tolerate was the presence of servile men amongst the citizenry. "We are barons," they said, "not runaway serfs." As for an actual serf trying to masquerade as a citizen – it was unthinkable.

Nonetheless, the men sitting in judgment sensed that there was probably some game of personal vengeance here, and they were cautious. "Your proof," the mayor warned, "had better be good."

It was. In quick order Silversleeves produced Adam's cousins whom he had brought up from Windsor. Then the estate steward. Both swore that Adam held the strips of land, which his father before and his forebears had held, not by rent, but by servile labour service. "Just," his father's cousin declared, "like us."

In a way, they were telling the truth. For as the years of Adam's childhood had passed, neither he nor his mother had bothered about the place, and his cousins had fallen into the habit of paying the rent for Adam's land in labour instead of cash and then keeping all the modest profits for themselves. Ever since the steward had been there, which was now twelve years, he had known that Adam's strips owed labour service, which his cousins provided for him. Therefore, even though he was living in London, he was still in this matter a serf. It was obscure, it was highly technical, but in the feudal world it was such technicalities that mattered.

"I was told I had cousins who were serfs, but that we were always free," the young man protested. And indeed, on his visit to the hamlet he might have found one old man who could have testified to that effect – except that he had died the week before.

Now Silversleeves produced his masterstroke. It had suddenly occurred to him a few days before. "I have even consulted the great Domesday Book of King William," he blandly informed the court. "And there is no word of any such free holding. The members of this family were always serfs." The fact that a century and a half before a hurried Norman clerk had made one of the few errors in that great compilation and forgotten to record Ducket's ancestor as free was something Silversleeves neither knew nor cared.

The mayor was silent. The aldermen looked grave. And then Sampson Bull spoke up. "There's something wrong here," he said gruffly. "This man's father was Simon the armourer, a respected citizen" – he gave the Exchequer clerk a stern look – "with whom, as I recall, Silversleeves had a quarrel. If Ducket is Simon's son, then he's a citizen by right, and that's that."

There were looks of relief. Nobody liked this case.

But Silversleeves was not a royal clerk for nothing. "If Simon was a citizen," he said, "he probably shouldn't have been. But either way it's irrelevant. Because, Mayor and Alderman of the city, Adam Ducket holds his land by labour service *at this very moment*. He is a serf, *now*." He paused to survey them carefully. "Or are we to change the ancient custom of London, and make this serf a citizen?"

Here even Bull could not argue. Ducket was a serf, no question. As for Silversleeves's canny suggestion that they were changing London's sacred customs – that had gone home.

The mayor spoke. "I'm sorry, Adam Ducket," he said. "This is a bad business and you may not even be to blame. But we can't have serfs as citizens. You must leave us."

"What about my craft? I'm a fishmonger."

"Oh, I'm afraid you'll have to leave off that," the mayor replied. "You're not a citizen."

As Barnikel and Mabel went out with him, Adam turned to them helplessly. "What am I to do?" he cried.

"We'll help you," Barnikel promised.

"But what about Lucy?" he asked.

And now Mabel, second mother though she might have been, spoke in the true voice of London.

"This is terrible, Adam," she said sadly, "but we can't have Lucy marrying you any more. You're not a citizen."

And so, after a very long wait indeed, Pentecost Silversleeves finally had his revenge.

1224

There was no doubt about it: things were getting better. As she surveyed the world around her in the seventy-fifth year of her robust life, Sister Mabel could not avoid feeling cheerful.

England was at peace. After continued strife between the barons and the king, John had suddenly died, leaving his son, only a boy, to rule with the help of a council. The council governed well. The great charter and its liberties had twice been confirmed. London had a mayor. If they had failed to avoid the tallage tax, the new administration, keeping out of foreign wars, had not needed to levy much money anyway. "We're not even in trouble with the Pope at the moment," she would cheerily add.

In London, too, there had been several recent improvements. The most striking, perhaps, was the great lantern tower that had just been completed above the nave of St Paul's. Breaking the long, narrow line of the building, it added a new grace and dignity to a dark mass that had loomed over the western hill rather like a barn. But what had given Mabel even more pleasure in the last three years had been the arrival in the city of two new kinds of religious folk, unlike any that had been seen there before: the friars were busy building their modest lodgings at that very time; the followers of St Francis, the Franciscans or Greyfriars, and the Dominican Blackfriars.

"I like these friars," Mabel would say. "They work." The Franciscans, dedicated to personal poverty, cared for the poor. The Blackfriars were committed to teaching. The Greyfriars she especially liked. "Everything can be improved," she would say. "So long as we all keep busy." And it was no doubt with this in mind that she had undertaken her mission that day.

They were a strange couple, as they inched their way along. Mabel, solid and bustling, even if a little slower, and the stick-like figure who moved stiffly beside her, holding her arm. Thin and pale as a dusty old stick of chalk, bent at the shoulders as if he had been snapped, it still appeared that Silversleeves would live for ever.

He was completely blind, and every week, Mabel would take him for a walk. "You can't sit in here all day," she would tell him in the stout stone hall below St Paul's. "You get out and take some exercise or you won't be able to move." Their expeditions fell into two parts. First she would lead him on his little palfrey to some convenient spot. Then she would make him walk. Then lead him home again.

Today, however, she had a special object in view as she led him towards the river. She was going to take him on London Bridge.

Perhaps of all the changes in London in her lifetime, this was truly the finest. For where once, crossing by the old wooden bridge over half a century before, Ida had observed the great stone piers of a new bridge appearing in the water, now that work was nearing completion. It had taken a long time. Thirty years had passed before a roadway had joined the mighty piers, and then that had been damaged by fire and work had had to start again. But now it was a splendid sight. Nineteen great stone arches crossed the Thames. The bridge they supported had recently been so widened that houses were starting to appear upon it, with the road, broad enough for two carts to pass, running between them. And in the centre of the bridge there was a little stone chapel, dedicated to St Thomas Becket, the city's martyred saint.

They had left the palfrey by the church of St Magnus, at the northern end of the bridge, and Mabel was walking the old man across.

"Where are we?"

"Never you mind."

"What street is this?"

"The road to heaven. Or hell."

He frowned. "I want to go back."

"You always say that." She edged him towards her object.

"You're up to something," he complained. And he was right. For Mabel had a mission; and she was determined to succeed. It concerned her poor old acquaintance, the curate of St Lawrence Silversleeves.

The man himself was long since dead, of course. So was his wife. One of the daughters was an invalid in the hospital now, but the other was eking out a miserable living in a hovel not far from the church. The Silversleeves family refused to do anything for her. Mabel had protested to Pentecost and to his children, but nothing had been done. She was so incensed that she nearly stopped seeing the old man, but she secretly enjoyed the challenge. "I'll get something for that curate's daughter," she swore. And since she had taken a great liking to the little chapel on the bridge, she had decided to bring the old man there.

Reaching it now, she made him enter, then took him to a bench, and made him sit.

"What is this place?"

"A church. Now listen to me." And for several minutes she gave him a piece of her mind about the curate, concluding: "I can't make you see with your eyes any more, old man. I've no herbs for that. But I can make you see your sins. Now you just kneel there and have a good pray until you decide to do something for that curate's daughter."

"And if I don't?"

"I'll leave you here," she said.

So grudgingly he got down on his knees, while Mabel went to another bench and prayed in silence to the martyred saint.

The miracle – for such Sister Mabel could only take it to be – occurred a little while after. She had been deep in thought when a thin voice came from where Silversleeves was kneeling.

"I can see!"

"What's that, old man?"

He was gazing at the palms of his hands. "I can see!"

She went over to him. It was true. He could. She crossed herself. "The saint has obtained us a miracle."

He smiled, despite himself, in an almost child-like manner. Then gave a little laugh. "It seems he has. A miracle. I can see!"

"Will you give something to that poor woman now?"

"Yes," he said, bemused. "Yes, I suppose I will." He looked around the chapel. "Extraordinary. I can really see!" Then he frowned. "What chapel is this? Do I know it?"

The chapel of St Thomas."

"Thomas?"

"Becket, of course," she said. "Who else?"

A month later, just before dawn, Brother Michael, tended lovingly by Mabel, departed very peacefully from this life. If he had been unable to claim his wager from his brother, there was no need. Bull had long since given generously to St Bartholomew's.

After she had said some prayers by his body, Mabel went out to walk a little while in the cloisters. The light at that early hour was uncertain, but as she turned the south-eastern corner, she had no doubt about the figure she saw for a moment at the other end of the walk. The long-tailed demon even turned its head to look at her. She was pleased to see that, having come for its prey, it was slinking away now, empty-handed.

Chapter 8

The Whorehouse

1295

They had promised her she would still be a virgin tomorrow. It was around noon, however, that she began to grow suspicious.

All that dull November morning the girl had sat wrapped in a shawl, on a bench in front of the brothel. Opposite, across the water, were the wharfs below St Paul's. To the left, between the river and Ludgate, where the little fort of Baynard's Castle used to stand, lay the huge precinct taken over by the black-robed Dominicans and now called Blackfriars. It was a pleasant view, but, to the girl that day, it seemed full of a vague menace. Her name was Joan, and she was fifteen.

She was a neat little person: her brown hair was pulled back carefully to reveal an oval face; her skin was pale and very smooth; her hands and feet were small and a little fleshy, hinting at the modest plumpness of her body which, she realized, men often found attractive. But it was her quiet, rather solemn eyes which told you that she was one of that busy family of craftsmen, descended from Osric, who had laboured at the building of the Tower.

Not that this mattered any more: not since early that morning when she had taken her terrible decision and crossed the river. Her father, as soon as he discovered, would never speak to her again. She had no doubt about that. As for her mother, she was sure it would be the same. Yet even this, she thought, she could bear, for if she had given up her home, her family, and every shred of reputation she possessed, she had done it to save the life of the young man she loved. She was going to save him tomorrow. If she could just last out till then.

There were eighteen stew-houses, as the brothels were known, standing in a long line by the south side of the Thames opposite St Paul's, along a strip of reclaimed marsh known as Bankside. Some were extensive structures, arranged round courtyards, with pleasant gardens stretching back to Maiden Lane. Others were of a drearier kind – tall and narrow, with overhanging plaster and timber storeys that appeared to be sagging under long years of dingy waterside debauchery. And in these various accommodations, each leased and run by a brothelkeeper, some three or four hundred prostitutes plied their trade.

Halfway along the line, the Dog's Head, where Joan had just come to reside, was of middling size, its plaster painted red, with a high thatched roof and a large sign hanging over the door depicting a dog's head with a huge tongue. At the far end, upstream, the brothels ended with a large house, partly of stone. This was the Castle upon the Hoop. Downstream, just past the brothels, lay a large stone building with its own waterside dock and steps: the London manor of the Bishop of Winchester. Within its precincts it included a small but busy prison, known as the Clink.

The whole area, manor house, Clink, all eighteen brothels and the handsome profits therefrom, belonged to and was ruled by the bishop.

The area south of London Bridge had always been a place apart. Since the long-forgotten days of Rome, the road from Dover and Canterbury had met the other roads from the south to cross the river there. Since Saxon times, it had borne the name of Southwark and formed a borough of its own, independent of the city. As such, it had also been a refuge where vagrants and those in trouble with the law were usually left to their own devices. The borough of Southwark stretched for some way along the river. By London Bridge, there was a market. Further west, an old church, St Mary Overy, from which a ferry crossed the river. Then the bishop's manor and Bankside. And how long had the brothels been there? As long as the borough, it was said. Indeed, they were still often known by their Saxon name – the *hor-hus* – the whorehouse.

The bishop's estate in Southwark was extensive. Like the old private wards that had once featured in the city opposite, it was actually a feudal manor, within whose bounds the bishop dispensed justice and ruled as absolute lord. And since such jurisdictions were also called "liberties" and this one contained the prison called the Clink, the whole estate was known, even in official documents, by a curious name: the Liberty of the Clink.

The Liberty of the Clink was well run, as were the eighteen brothels. Nearly a century and a half before, in the reign of Henry II, the Bishop of Winchester, who as it happened was also Archbishop of Canterbury just then, had decided: "My brothels are a mess." And so, aided by his able assistant, he drew up a thorough list of regulations for running them which, in Latin and in English, was preserved for future centuries in the diocesan library. "To the honour of God and according to the laudable customs and regulations of the land," the document concluded; and so excellent were these rules that afterwards, when the city of London had been granted permission to have its own official brothels in Cock's Lane near St Bartholomew's, it was the bishop's regulations which applied there too, while the prostitutes themselves were still cheerfully referred to as "Winchester Geese". And whether or not he personally should be thanked for these rules, the Archbishop's assistant when they were made was none other than that great Londoner, Thomas Becket.

But now the brothelkeeper and his wife were approaching her. He was a large, balding man with a black beard that always seemed to be greasy; she was a square woman, whose broad, yellowish face made Joan think of a sweating cheese. And the moment she saw them, she guessed. "You promised . . ." she blurted out. But they were both grinning. She was completely in their power.

Desperately the girl looked around. It had been the Dogget sisters who had thought of the whole idea; the Dogget sisters who had promised to protect her. Surely they had not abandoned her now? Yet where were they?

"There's a customer for you, dear," the square woman said.

Everyone in Southwark knew the Dogget sisters. One was called Isobel and the other Margery, but nobody – not even the brothelkeeper of the Dog's Head where they worked – could tell you which was which. For Margery and Isobel were identical twins.

They were tall and stringy, with thick tresses of black hair, big black eyes, big buck teeth, and voices that, whenever they laughed, made a surprisingly deep sound, like a donkey's braying. Yet, with their slim bodies and rather heavy breasts, they possessed a remarkable sexuality. And if all this was not enough to mark them out, over the centre of their foreheads, in their black tresses, each had a streak of white.

They dressed identically, always; their conversation was identical, they rented rooms side by side in the Dog's Head where they sold their bodies; and, if a client wanted, they would, for a modest discount, make up a party of three that could, if the client had the stamina, last all night.

The Dogget sisters belonged to a small tribe that infested Southwark, and whose presence there derived from a simple, human, mistake. For eighty years ago, when poor Adam Ducket had lost the freedom of London, he had made a foolish choice. In his hurt and bitterness, when the Barnikel family had offered to help him, he had utterly refused. "If they don't want me for their daughter, I'll take nothing from them," he had angrily declared. Within a month of his trial, he had drifted across to Southwark where he set up a market stall that failed. Then he had worked in a tavern, married a serving girl, and in time had a brood of children who ran barefoot in the streets. Thus, within a generation, the proud family of modest London citizens had sunk into that underclass which had been found in the larger cities of the world since history began. The two sisters belonged to a family of five and they had a dozen cousins. They all lived in Southwark; and they were all, without exception, cheerful, irrepressible, and disreputable.

They were also called Ducket – except for the two sisters, whom fame had brought a new, professional name. So well known were they, and so associated with their particular whorehouse, that they were nowadays universally known as "the Dog's Head girls". Which had already started to lapse into another old English name not unlike the one they were born with: Dogget, they became. Some Duckets, a little embarrassed by their reputation did not mind this distancing of the name. The girls accepted it cheerfully. The Dogget sisters, therefore, they unashamedly were.

The Dogget sisters were a kind-hearted pair; but if there was one thing they loved best, it was an adventure. So when, two days before, they had come upon Joan in floods of tears outside St Paul's, and made her tell them her story, they had been intrigued. "We must help her," they said together. And whether it was Isobel who had suggested it to Margery, or the other way round, they had come up with the extraordinary plan that Joan was now following, and which, risky though it was, had been working so beautifully until this moment.

The only trouble was that for the last hour they had completely forgotten her. The problem lay with Margery.

"Does it hurt?" The two sisters had gone to a quiet place on the slopes a mile away from Bankside. Now they were gazing sadly at the little sore.

"It burns," said Margery.

"That's it, then," said Isobel. "They'll find it." The bishop's bailiff and his assistants inspected all the girls once a month. If they had any kind of disease, they were thrown out of the Liberty. Even a bribe was probably useless. For, most Londoners agreed, it was one of the advantages of the Church running the brothels that the bishop's inspections were thorough. And Margery very clearly had the burning sickness.

It was a form of syphilis, though less severe than the strain which would appear in later centuries. When it had first come to Britain is uncertain; but, though the infection may have been brought by returning crusaders, there are clear indications of its presence on the island from as early as Saxon times.

But what could they do? If Margery were thrown out of the brothel, her livelihood would be gone.

"I wish," she said, "that the king hadn't thrown out all the Jews."

If there was one thing that everyone on Bankside agreed upon, it was that the old Jewish doctor had been the best; and many Londoners had similar memories. For whether it was because they had better access to the ancient knowledge of the classical world and the Middle East, or whether they were simply better educated and less prone to superstition, it was true that the Jewish community had often provided the best physicians. The old Jewish doctor on Bankside had known how to treat the burning sickness with mercury; and now nobody did.

The Jewish community had completely disappeared. Ever since the anti-Jewish riots at King Richard's coronation a century before, the bad feeling towards the Jews in England had been growing. This gradual process of persecution was not primarily caused by the community's financial activities. For though it was true that some Church philosophers declared that the charging of interest was usury, and therefore a sin, this ignorance of elementary economics was not general, even in the Church. Bishop administrators and the abbots of great monasteries made extensive use of Jewish loans. Indeed, a huge rebuilding recently completed at Westminster Abbey had been financed in this way. To their amused astonishment, a group of Jewish financiers had once been offered the relics of a saint – which assured a profitable flow of pilgrims – as security for a loan.

But three things had been against them. The first was that the Church on religious grounds had waged a long campaign across Europe against them; the second, that like all creditors, they had become unpopular with the large number of barons and others who were deeply in debt. And the third had been the king. The reign of King John's son Henry III had lasted over half a century, that of his son Edward nearly another quarter already: and both had frequently needed funds. Nothing had been simpler, therefore, than to fine the Jews. But so often and so severely had this occurred that by the last decade nearly every Jewish financier had been ruined. Their place, meanwhile, had been taken by Christian moneylenders, especially the great Italian finance houses promoted by the Vatican. In short, the king had not needed the Jews any more. And so, in the year of Our Lord 1290, in an act of convenient piety, King Edward I of England had cancelled the remaining debts, and greatly pleased the Pope by expelling the entire Jewish community from his island kingdom.

Unfortunately, the doctors had gone too. And so that November morning the Dogget sisters considered their plight which, in the absence of the Jewish doctor's mercury, looked grim indeed. As for little Joan, whose life they had turned upside down, they had, just then, completely forgotten about her.

Martin Fleming sat very still in the cell. "Better say your prayers," the gaoler had said that morning. But try as he might, no prayer would form in his mind. All he knew was that they were going to hang him tomorrow, and it did not help that he was innocent.

Martin Fleming was only one inch taller than the girl he loved, but it was his curious shape which people really noticed. For in every place where most people bulged outwards, Martin Fleming caved in. His little chest was sunken; his face reminded you of the inside of a spoon. His whole appearance was so puny and concave that everyone assumed he must be weak of mind as well. Few knew that within the soul of Martin Fleming was a secret obstinacy that, once set, was as immovable as a mountain.

As his name suggested, his family were Flemings – men from Flanders. This was common in London. That great, cloth-making territory just across the sea between the French and German lands was not only England's trading partner, but also the greatest source of immigrants to the island. Flemish mercenary soldiers, merchants, weavers and artisans – sometimes called Fleming, more often acquiring Anglicized names – merged easily into the English mainstream and usually prospered. But Martin's family had not. His father was a poor horner whose trade, thinning horn until it was translucent when it was used as casing for lanterns, brought him only a pittance. So when the wonderful opportunity had arisen, his father had urged him: "Take it. I can't do much for you." And though the position itself was humble: "You never know what a man like that might do for you, if he likes you."

If only he had.

At first young Martin had been so pleased to be working for the Italian that he had hardly noticed that all was not well. The Italian was rich, one of the moneylenders who had supplanted the Jews and whose base was the lane in the city centre just below Cornhill which – since many of them came from the north Italian territory of Lombardy – was already known as Lombard Street. A widower, whose son ran the business in Italy, the Italian lived alone and used Martin on all manner of errands. He paid him well, if grudgingly.

"But he always thinks I'm cheating him," Martin complained. Whether it was because the Italian understood English badly, or just his mistrustful nature, Martin could never discover, but there was always trouble. If he delivered a message, he was accused of loitering; if he went to the market for food, his master said he had kept some of the money for himself. "I should have left him," he said mournfully, afterwards. But he had not. For he had something else on his mind.

Joan: she was not like the other girls.

When he was eighteen, Martin had discovered that most of the girls laughed at him because he was puny. On May days, when many a young apprentice received a kiss, and sometimes more, he got none. Once, a cruel group of girls even taunted him as he passed. "Never been kissed. Doesn't know how," they chanted.

Another boy might have been crushed. But Martin with his secret pride told himself he despised them. What were they anyway? Only women. Fickle, weaker vessels – wasn't that what the preachers in church called them? As for their smiles, their kisses, and their bodies – he shrugged. It was all the work of the Devil. As the poor young fellow brooded, his sad defences grew stronger. By the time he was a young man, still unkissed, he had come to believe, with a secret righteousness: "Women are unclean. I want none of them."

Joan's father was a decent, solemn craftsman. He painted the huge, elaborate wooden saddles of the rich and the nobility. His two sons worked with him; he had reasonably assumed his daughter would marry a craftsman of the same kind. So what the devil had she seen in the young Fleming, who had so few prospects? As would any reasonable father in his position, he had discouraged her. But the girl was quietly insistent, for a very simple reason: she was loved. In fact, she was worshipped.

Martin had been working for the Italian for six months when he noticed her. He had been on an errand to the Vintry wharves and was walking up towards West Cheap when he saw her sitting outside her father's workshop at the bottom of Bread Street. Yet what had made him stop and talk to the girl? He could hardly say. Some silent voice within must have prompted him. Whatever it was, he had walked that way again the next day. And the next.

Little Joan was different. She was so quiet, so modest. She did not seem to find him ridiculous. When her calm, serious eyes looked up to his, it made him feel manly. And above all, he soon discovered there was nobody else. If he wanted her, she was his, and his alone. "She is pure," he said to himself. Which, indeed, she was. She had never even been kissed.

And so he courted her. The absence of rivals gave him the confidence he needed and as that confidence increased, he became protective of her. He had never felt strong before, and it was thrilling. The first flush of courtship makes some young men conceited. It even makes them cast about, to see if they can be as successful elsewhere. But Martin knew that women were unchaste and not to be trusted, except for Joan. And the more of her goodness he saw, the more determined he was never to let her go. Not a week passed without some little present; if she was happy, he would match her mood; if sad, he would comfort her. No one had ever paid her so much attention before. So it was not surprising that six months later they both wanted to marry.

But how? The saddle-painter had only a little to give his daughter, young Martin's father less. The two men met and sadly shook their heads. "He says there's no one else for him," the horner explained apologetically. "Joan's just as bad," the other replied. "What are we to do?" At last an agreement was reached, by which the young people were to wait two years in the hope that Martin might improve his position. After that: "Who knows," Joan's father said hopefully, "maybe they'll change their minds."

And then the disaster had occurred.

In a way, it had been Martin's fault. The rules were simple enough. All common folk should be indoors after dark. If a servant went out, he must have his master's permission. Even the taverns were supposed to be closed. This was the curfew, typical of medieval cities. Not that anyone took much notice; and apart from two sergeants at the city gates, and the beadle of each ward, there was no one to enforce it anyway.

One October evening, when his master was away, Martin had slipped out to a tavern. Two hours passed before he returned to the darkened house in Lombard Street and surprised the thieves. There had been two of them. He heard them as soon as he entered. Thinking of nothing, except that he must protect the Italian's property, he rushed to the back of the house where they were, making such a noise that they fled. He chased them up an alley, where one dropped a small bag.

Then they vanished. Martin picked up the bag and began to walk home.

It was a few minutes later that the beadle had emerged from the shadows to ask him if he had permission to be in the streets after curfew. And inspected the bag.

When the Italian returned the next day, nothing would persuade him that Martin had not tried to rob him. For the bag was found to contain several gold ornaments he had kept hidden. Poor Martin never had a chance. "I've caught this young man trying to rob me before," he told the justices at the trial. It was enough for them to find him guilty of theft. The penalty for theft was death.

There were three main prisons that belonged to the city, all by the western wall: the Fleet, Ludgate, used mainly for debtors, and Newgate. None of them consisted of more than a few stone rooms, usually crowded. The regime was simple. Prisoners could pay the gaoler for food, or their family and friends, if any, might visit and pass food and clothing to them through a grille. Otherwise, unless passers-by took pity on them, or the gaoler gave them a little bread and water out of kindness, they would starve.

Martin Fleming had been in Newgate for a week now. His family had fed him, Joan had come to visit him each day, but he had no hope. Sometimes rich people could buy pardons from the king, but for a fellow like him, that was not even a possibility. Tomorrow he was going to die; and that was that.

So he hardly knew what to make of the strange message he had just received. It was Joan's brother who had brought it, delivering it verbally, through the iron grille.

"She says to tell you that tomorrow everything will be all right."

"I don't understand."

"Nor do I. But she said something else. However it looks, nothing will be what it seems. Just do as she says. She was very insistent about that. Told me to repeat it. It won't be what it seems and you have to trust her."

"Where is she now?"

"That's just it. She's gone. Told me to tell the family not to expect her until tomorrow. She's vanished into thin air."

"So you've no idea what this is all about?"

"Beats me," her brother shrugged. Then he left.

And what, Martin wondered, would be all right? Death?

Some time earlier – about an hour before noon – a tall, fair-haired man in his late twenties had stood before a door on the first floor of the house of William Bull. A servant had sent him up there, but now, faced with the awful prospect, his courage failed him. He hesitated. From the other side of the door, he heard a grunt. Then, nervously, he tapped.

William Bull sat on his privy and ignored the tap at the door. He was thinking.

The privy, which had been built on to the upper floor of the house by the sign of the Bull, was a splendid affair. It was a small square room with a shuttered window; the walls and the door were covered with green baize; the floor with fresh, scented rushes. The orifice itself, which opened on to a chute with a ten foot drop, was fashioned out of polished marble, upon which, in the shape of a ring, was a thick, red cushion which had been embroidered with a design of fruit and flowers in red, green and gold. The last king, Henry III, had conceived a passion for sanitation which led him to build as well as his many churches, the most extraordinary number of *garderobes*, or privies. Nobles wishing to be fashionable had followed suit, and Bull's father, a baron and alderman of London, had installed his own, upon which he sat as though upon a throne, a merchant monarch proud of all he did.

It was also a good place to think. And that morning, William Bull had much on his mind. In particular, there were two decisions to make – one small, the other large. So large, in fact, that it would entirely change his life. Yet strangely enough, after the unspeakable events of the day before, it was the big decision that was easier.

When he grunted, he had just made it.

Another tap at the door. He frowned. "Come in then, damn you, whoever you are," he growled.

It was, as his household knew, his habit to give interviews in this sanctum. But now, seeing who it was, his face darkened into a glower. "You," he snarled. "The traitor." And his cousin winced.

Elias Bull was ten years younger than William. Spare where the merchant was thickset, fresh-faced where William had a blotchy cheek and heavy jowl, he was a weaver, but he made a poor living. "I wouldn't trouble you," he had confessed at their last encounter, "but it's for my wife and children. As you know, our grandfather cut my father off with a pittance." All he needed was a little help. "Is it right," he had asked William, "that the sins of the father should be visited upon the son?" William, in genuine surprise, had answered: "Yes."

The long reign of King Henry III had not gone well for the Bull family. It had started happily enough while the council had run England wisely and efficiently for the boy king. There had been no wars of consequence. England's mighty wool trade was booming. The city, under its mayor and oligarchic council of aldermen, had prospered. "If only," William's father used to say, "that boy had never come of age. Or if only," he would add, "he hadn't been a Plantagenet." For was there ever a Plantagenet born without dreams of empire? Young Henry had England and still possessed the lands of Aquitaine, around Bordeaux; but he dreamed of more.

And finally he had come to grief, just like his father John: a series of foreign entanglements that were vastly expensive had aborted; a large section of the barons, led by the great Simon de Montfort, had rebelled, and had set up a new council to govern the king, as though he were a child again. Montfort had called a huge assembly of barons, knights and even burgesses, which he called a Parliament. For a few short years it had even looked as if some new kind of kingship, subject to a great council, might develop in England. And in the midst of this turmoil, the awful thing had happened.

There had been dozens of riots in London before. But this one was different. It was not just the poor folk or hot-blooded apprentices. Solid citizens – fishmongers, skinners, traders and craftsmen – had led the ancient Folkmoot in an organized rebellion against rich dynasts like the Bulls. There were riots; a party, led by a furious young fishmonger called Barnikel, had even smashed the door of Bull's house and tried to set light to it. Worse still, Montfort had let these radicals depose the aldermen and elect new, vulgar fellows of their own. And this disgraceful state of affairs had continued for some time until at last Montfort had been killed, the king returned to power, and the old patriciate managed to get control of London again.

Worst of all – the thought of it still made Bull clench his

fists in fury – his father's own brother had joined these rebels. A number of young idealists, or opportunists, from other patrician families had done the same. "But that doesn't make it any better," William's father had told him. "A traitor is a traitor, and that's that." The young radical had been cut off from the family for ever. And now, for the third time this year, here was the traitor's wretched son, pestering him for help. It was an outrage. But then his brow cleared, and he even grunted with a hint of pleasure. For after the great decision he had just taken, this visit was rather appropriate. I am growing cruel, he thought. But he saw no reason why he should deny himself a modest revenge.

As the merchant stared fixedly at his unwitting victim – to whom at that moment and in his present posture he appeared like a large and rather frightening toad – he said abruptly: "I'll give you three marks if you go away." This was enough to improve the family's meals for some time, but not enough to make the slightest change in their circumstances. Elias looked anguished. "But if you come and find me here in a year from today," William shrugged, "perhaps I'll even give you the inheritance that might have been yours. Now get out," he suddenly cried, "and shut the door after you." At which poor Elias Bull, much mystified, departed.

The cruelty of William's little joke lay in the one fact he had withheld: the big decision he had just taken.

In a year's time, he would not be there. The Bulls were leaving London. For good.

In a way it was not surprising. Even his father had said: "The city is becoming intolerable." The problem for his father, apart from the rebellion, was contained in a single word. Immigrants. It was natural, in the booming prosperity of that century, that London should have swollen. But the stream of immigrants had turned into a flood: Italians, Spaniards, French and Flemings, Germans from the growing network of northern ports known as the Hansa, not to mention the merchants and artisans flocking in from the regions of England. Worse yet, with the exception of the Hansa men, who kept themselves apart, they were mixing and marrying with exactly the craftsmen who had been such a confounded nuisance under Montfort. "These vulgar upstarts and foreigners are crowding us out," the old patrician claimed.

For William, the process was summed up by an event that took place a year before old King Henry died. The little steeple over St Mary-le-Bow had come down in a storm and smashed a nearby house the Bulls owned. Normally this would have been quickly repaired; but his father had hesitated, then decided to sell. A year later, together with three smaller houses of the Bulls, it was being shared by a dye-master from Picardy and a Cordova leather-seller from Spain. Then, in nearby Garlick Hill, some vulgar tanners had moved in. These were small things, yet a sign of the times. But the final blow had been when his own house, previously in the aristocratic parish of St Mary-le-Bow, had been made part of the tiny parish of St Lawrence Silversleeves. A mean little church, not worthy of the patrician Bulls. Nothing could disguise the fact that the family was in retreat.

If the long reign of Henry III had been bad for the family, the last twenty years under his son Edward had been a nightmare. No English king was ever more impressive than Edward I. Tall and powerful, with a noble face and a flowing beard, his only peculiarities were a drooping left eyelid and a lisp when he spoke. A vigorous law-giver and commander, he was both intelligent and cunning. The leopard, they called him. And having seen his father's often pathetic rule, he was determined to impose his own, iron will. He was usually successful. Already he had subdued the Welsh, secured their land with huge castles, and given them their first, English Prince of Wales. Soon he would march north, to hammer the Scots as well. And if there was one body of men in his kingdom he disliked, it was the proud patrician aldermen of London who elected their own mayor and thought they could make kings.

His attack had been cunning. For what merchant could deny that Edward was his friend? His laws were just and good for trade. Debts were regulated, taxes simplified, with a new but reasonable duty on wool exports that could mostly be passed on to the foreign customers. "Yet look at what he's quietly done to us patricians," William would point out. "He's pushed the best wine trade to fellows from Bordeaux; the biggest wool dealers are either Italians or men from the West Country." And while his father had always made huge and profitable sales of luxury goods to the Wardrobe, as the royal purchasing office was called, William could not sell them a thing. "We've been sidestepped," he bitterly concluded. "That leopard's run round us."

Yet even this was only the softening up. The real assault, which had begun ten years ago, was devastating. For suddenly, on the pretext of improving law and order, King Edward had dismissed the mayor and put in his own warden. The aldermen had been aghast. But they got no support from the Londoners. And then King Edward had set to work. A barrage of ordinances followed: records, courts, weights and measures – all reformed with Edward's usual thoroughness. "I suppose," Bull conceded, "our sort of rule may have been a bit slack." But the sting was in the tail. "His laws give any foreigner the same trading rights as ours," Bull stormed. The king's Exchequer court abruptly moved into the Guildhall, where the aldermen's Husting court had always held sway. Two years ago, when the aldermen had finally protested – "What about London's ancient privileges?" – the warden had coolly thrown them out of office and replaced them with new men, chosen by the Exchequer. "And do you know who these new fellows are?" Bull stormed. "Fishmongers, skinners, smelly little craftsmen." The Montfort rebels were back.

Yet even then, the old guard had not quite given up. They had ruled London for centuries, after all. Many, indeed, had looked to Bull – a respectable figure not yet tainted by office – as a possible champion. Recently he had thought he saw his chance.

A year ago, to help pay for the coming Scottish campaign. King Edward had overstepped the mark by abruptly raising the customs on wool. This new tax, known as the *maltote*, was so severe that all London had protested. And while the city was still simmering, the post of alderman for Bull's own ward suddenly fell vacant.

He had been assiduous. "In my father's day," he remarked to his family, "we owned so much of this ward that the aldermanry was ours for the asking." But he made no such assumptions now. Swallowing his pride, he had courted the lesser merchants and craftsmen; he had made himself agreeable to the king's warden. Even one of the vulgar new aldermen quietly confessed to him: "We need a sound man of standing, like you." As the day drew close, no one from the ward had troubled to challenge him.

And yesterday the day had come. Discreetly, happily, his sense of family history lending him a dignity of which he was rather proud, William Bull in a fine new cloak had presented himself at the Guildhall to be chosen.

The Exchequer man who waved him away had scarcely troubled even to be polite. "We don't want you," he said curtly. "We've chosen someone else." When Bull, mystified, had protested – "But I'm unopposed" – the fellow had only snapped back, "Not from your ward. From Billingsgate." An outside man. It was unusual, though sometimes done.

"Who?" he had asked, mortified.

And then the reply, quite casual. "Barnikel," the fellow said.

Barnikel. That cursed, low-born fishmonger. Barnikel of Billingsgate, alderman of the Bulls' own ward! For several minutes he stood outside the Guildhall, almost unable to take it in. And now, as he brooded about it once more, he knew: it was too much to bear.

The great decision was made: it was time to go.

Which left the smaller decision.

It should have been easy – and pleasant too. The message from Bankside had certainly been intriguing. A virgin at the Dog's Head. A rarity indeed. Only the most favoured customers were being told: you could be sure of that. Though his own excursions to the whorehouse were only occasional, he was still a patrician, and the brothelkeeper was always as respectful as he was discreet.

So why did he hesitate? A pang of guilt. Was it really necessary to feel guilty? As if in answer to his thoughts at that moment, there was a thump at the door, followed by a querulous voice. Inwardly he groaned.

"What are you doing?" His wife.

"What the devil do you suppose?" he thundered.

"No you aren't. You've been in there an hour." Was this, he asked himself, any way to address a middle-aged merchant of distinction? "I know what you're doing," her voice went on. "You're thinking." He sighed. The rows between his great-grandmother Ida and her husband were part of family legend:

but surely, he thought, no Bull had ever had to put up with a wife like his. "I heard you," she called. "You sighed."

He had tried, over twenty miserable years, to love her. After all, he daily reminded himself, she had given him three strong children. But it was not easy and, in the last few years, he had quietly given up. Grey, gaunt, insistent, she complained if he was out and harassed him if he was home. No wonder, he thought to himself, if he sometimes sought a little quiet solace on Bankside. Now therefore, if only to relieve the tedium, he told her his big decision.

"We're leaving London. We're going to live at Bocton." He paused, heard her gasp, and added for good measure: "All year round."

In fact, Bull's plan was not unusual. While London merchants had often retired to their estates in the past, a number of his own patrician contemporaries, finding the competition in the city too hot, had stopped trading and turned into country gentlemen. Thank God there was still a substantial fortune. He would simply buy more land. But now he heard a cry of disbelief.

"I hate the country." He smiled. He knew. "I shall stay here in London," she protested.

"Not in this house," he said cheerfully. "I'm selling it."

"To whom?"

That, as it happened, was the easy bit. For if there was one feature of the booming city that all men remarked upon, it was the astonishing increase, since his childhood, in the number of drinking establishments. In a city with a resident population of around seventy thousand, there were already some three hundred taverns serving food and drink, not to mention another thousand little brew-houses offering a beaker of ale. Some of the taverns were quite large affairs, offering sleeping quarters for the city's many visitors too; and some of their owners had made fortunes. Only a month ago an enterprising fellow who owned two of these had told him: "If you ever want to sell your own house, I'll give you a good price." So now Bull informed his wife: "I'm selling to a taverner."

"You beast." She began to cry. He cast his eyes to heaven. "You brute!"

"I'm going out," he said, and prayed for silence. But there

was only a brief and hostile pause, and then that dreadful, plaintive murmur.

"I know where you're going. After some woman."

It was too much. "I wish to God I were," he bellowed back, thumping both hands on the embroidered cushion. "Shall I tell you where I'm going? I'm going to get the city sergeants. And when I come back with them, we're going to put you in a scold's bridle. And then I'll have them lead you through the streets. That's where I'm going."

It was not a pretty thing, the scold's bridle. Foul-mouthed women were sometimes sentenced to wear the little iron cage that fitted over the head, with a cruel iron bit that went in the mouth to immobilize the tongue. Encased in this, unpopular women would be paraded about, in the same way as other malefactors were put in the stocks. He heard her weeping, and felt ashamed.

He made up his mind. It was too much. He would stand no more. A moment later he was striding past her and out of his house. And so it was, just after noon, that William Bull arrived at the whorehouse on Bankside, and, accompanied by the grinning brothelkeeper, strode towards Joan.

He was, the man assured him, the very first to get there.

Joan looked at William Bull.

He was, she supposed, about forty. She saw a large, burly man in a cloak, with thick calves, hide boots folded over below the knee, and a florid face, who was obviously used to being obeyed. Already he had rewarded the brothelkeeper for the pleasure of taking her virginity.

It was quiet. At that hour of the day there were few customers about, and most of the prostitutes were either out or sleeping. Of the Dogget sisters there was no sign.

Suddenly, she became angry. Striding over to the brothelkeeper, she cried, "You promised me no customers until tomorrow, you filthy liar."

Bull looked questioningly at the man's wife.

"It's nothing, sir," that worthy woman called. "She's just a little nervous." To Joan she hissed: "You'll do as you're told."

"And if I refuse?"

"Refuse?" the brothelkeeper spat.

"You don't understand, dear," his wife cut in. She tried a motherly smile. "This is an important man. A good customer."

"I don't care."

The smile vanished. The two little eyes in the cheese-like face were cold. "You need a whipping."

"You've no right to do such a thing."

The arrangement of the brothel was that each girl rented her room. Apart from this obligation, in theory she was free to come and go as she pleased. In practice, of course, the brothelkeeper had a hold of some kind over almost every one of them.

"Maybe." The brothelkeeper was cool now, and deadly. He stepped closer, and she could smell the stale food on his beard. "But I can call the bishop's bailiff and throw you out of the Liberty within the hour. You'll get no work after that."

And that was just what must not happen.

"I'll do it then," she finally said. And she turned, and forced herself to smile at William Bull.

The wooden staircase went up the outside of the brothel for two storeys, on each of which there were three chambers, which had been subdivided into pairs of cubicles by wooden partitions. Stepping in at the second storey, Joan and the merchant entered a narrow passage between wooden walls. It was dark. A few paces down the passage there was a little internal flight of stairs, hardly more than a ladder really. Feeling her way, she began to mount them.

Joan's room was an attic set in the gable of the house. Though very small, at least there was no cubicle beside it, so no banging and grunting would be heard. There was a little window, the upper part covered with parchment to let in light, the lower with a stout wooden shutter. When she had opened the shutter that morning, and felt the cold, damp air on her face, Joan realized that she could see straight across the river and even, over the rooftops of Blackfriars, catch a glimpse of the top of Newgate. It had comforted her to think that she could see the place where Martin Fleming was.

The rushes on the floor had not been changed in months and they stank. She had managed, however, to persuade the brothelkeeper to give her fresh ones to put down, though he had grumbled at the expense. It was, therefore, as such places went, a reasonably pleasant little attic into which the merchant, breathing a trifle heavily after his climb, was led.

The bed was a mattress stuffed with straw. It lay in the middle of the floor. Joan dropped her shawl. She had not yet acquired the striped garb of her trade, but was simply dressed in a plain, long-sleeved undergown of linen, over which was a sleeveless smock with a pattern of flowers. She took the circlet off her head and her hair fell loose. She looked towards the window, stepped across and pushed the shutter open. A hundred yards away, the river was moving sluggishly. Her back to the merchant, she realized that she was trembling slightly. Had he noticed?

In her mind was only one thought. How can I delay him? Wasn't there, even now, some way out?

"You are really a virgin?" His voice behind her.

She did not turn round, but nodded.

"Are you frightened?" The merchant's voice was gruff. But did she detect a hint of awkwardness in it? A trace of guilt? She turned.

He had taken off his cloak and was already undoing the buttons on the chest of his tunic. Evidently he meant to get on with the business in hand. She looked at his broad, hard face. Was there any sign of kindness there?

"It won't be so bad," he said.

And then it occurred to her. There was, after all, just one way in which her awful situation could be turned to advantage. It was a very small chance, but if she was bold – perhaps, just possibly, he might cooperate.

She mustered all her calm.

"I want you to do something," she said. He looked down at her. Then she told him.

"You want what?" He was staring at her with stupefaction, but she did not flinch.

"Let me explain," she said.

It was an hour after noon that a single, robust figure, grinning from ear to ear, bounced out of the old royal palace, bounced to his horse, bounced into the saddle and rode off towards the city, with the ancient Abbey of Westminster looming behind him.

In the year 1295, the Abbey of Westminster presented a most curious appearance, for when pious King Henry III had decided to rebuild it, he had made one unfortunate miscalculation. Notwithstanding the huge sum raised by the Jews, or the pawning of the jewels that Henry had intended for St Edward the Confessor's sumptuous new shrine, he had run out of money. The magnificent eastern half of the church, the choir and transepts and a little bit of the nave rose splendidly, its soaring arches in the pointed Gothic style. But then, suddenly, the nave dropped sharply to the far more modest height of the Confessor's old Norman church. And so it had remained for a quarter-century: two churches, in different styles, joined in a way that made no sense at all. Another century would pass before work restarted, more than another again before it was completed. For the reign of no fewer than twelve of England's monarchs, the sacred coronation church was to be a mess.

But if Waldus Barnikel had glanced back at the old Abbey, which he did not, he would have seen nothing wrong with it. Because that day, it seemed to him, everything was perfect. "I am," he had just remarked to the king himself, "the happiest man in London."

Waldus Barnikel of Billingsgate was as round as a ball. It was as though nature, having decided to confine the towering strength and temper of his ancestors into a smaller space, had realized that so much fermenting energy could only be contained, with any hope of avoiding an explosion, in a perfect and solidly constructed sphere. He was clean-shaven, though his red hair hung halfway down his neck, and he wore a fur hat. He radiated confidence.

As well he should. For hadn't the common fishmongers raised their craft fraternity to the city's heights? Already he was wearing the red robes of an alderman. Henceforth, all men would call him "Sire". As for the humiliation of the proud, patrician Bulls whom he had hated all his life: "My soul is soaked in honey," he confessed. Indeed, he need not even be in awe of the Bulls' wealth nowadays. For Barnikel was rich.

His route to riches was typical of the fishmongers. Soon after the reign of King John, the family had acquired a small fishing vessel, then another. By the time Waldus was born, they not only had a warehouse at Billingsgate wharf and a huge stall in the market with six men behind the counter, but most significant of all, like several of the more successful

London fishmongers, they had also set up a second base of operations. This was at a small but busy port called Yarmouth, nearly a hundred miles away on the eastern coast, where they had two more fishing vessels and a half share in a highly profitable cargo ship. And it was in Yarmouth that Barnikel had met his wife, his great fortune, and also become part of a curious historic movement.

The great territory of East Anglia had kept its ancient character in the centuries since the Conquest. True, outsiders had arrived – chiefly Flemish weavers, whose skills had been turned to good use. But in essence, the vast tracts of pasture, wood and fen were still the Danelaw: land of Angles and Danes, homesteaders and merchants; isolated, independent, open only to the great east wind that came in from the echoing sea. Like the rest of England that century, East Anglia had grown rich; and most notably had begun to export its own cloth, of two types, each taking the name of the village which was its centre of manufacture: Kersey in the southern part, and in the northern, the little town of Worsted.

It was natural therefore that when Barnikel had met a rich young heiress from Worsted, a descendant, like him, of seafaring Vikings, he should have married her. This doubled his fortune. When he took her back to London, her whole family had come too.

Of all the many groups who flocked into London in that generation, many were merchants from East Anglia. As Barnikel had recently remarked: "People are even starting to talk differently. They all sound like my in-laws!" But he did not perceive that this slight shift in London's local accent was the signal of a deeper quirk of history. For whether by chance or by destiny, in the late thirteenth century, the Norsemen were coming to London again, not as Viking seafarers, but as their solid, middle-class descendants.

He was a rich merchant. He still sold fish, to be sure; but his ships also carried furs and timber from the Baltic, and grain, and even wine. Then, yesterday, an alderman. And today? Nothing had prepared him for the summons that morning. It had come from King Edward himself.

Only a short while before, he had stood before the tall, grey-bearded monarch, and the royal eyes had gazed steadily straight into his.

"I need you," the king had said. "I need you for my parliament." And the fishmonger had blushed, hardly able to believe the honour. A Barnikel in Parliament.

When King Edward I of England had decided to hold parliaments, as he called them, twice a year, and usually in Westminster, he displayed his usual cunning and sagacity. Remembering the humiliations of his father and grandfather, whose obstinacy brought them under the thumb of baronial councils, he had been much cleverer. No one would ever be able to say that Edward ruled without advice. Whenever there was a matter of special importance to decide, he summoned not only the council of barons but the other parties to be affected. If it concerned the Church, he summoned representatives of the clergy; if trade, then burghers from the towns; if general military service, then local knights. And sometimes all these together. Such parliaments also witnessed the dispensing of royal justice, of which the king in council was also the court of last resort. True, the king often made laws by himself too, with only his inner advisers. But he never went too far. He always had his parliaments as a sounding board.

Just as he used the lesser merchants to break the power of the mayor of London and his oligarchs, so, with his parliaments, the monarch could limit his feudal magnates – which he did time and again, by statutes – and to a lesser extent he could break the Church as well. And so in the reign of King Edward I of England, the great institution of Parliament first began to take shape: not – God forbid – to place power in the hands of the people, but to strengthen the long political arm of the king.

By chance, the day before, one of the London burgesses due to attend had fallen sick. "So I asked for you," King Edward told Waldus with a smile.

Of course, there was a reason. Barnikel was no fool. If the king wanted merchants at this Parliament, it meant he wanted taxes from the towns. If he was ready to flatter a newly made alderman, he must want a lot. Well, so be it.

But he had asked for him, Barnikel, by name.

No wonder then if Waldus Barnikel was ready to celebrate that afternoon. And this was exactly what he next proposed to do. For just before he left to see the king, he too had received a message from Bankside. About a virgin. And it was with cheerful eagerness, therefore, that he hurried now upon his way.

Waldus Barnikel normally went to the Dog's Head once a week. He had done so for nearly five years. As constant as he was regular, he always slept with one of the Dogget sisters.

Their name amused him because, quite unrelated to them, there was now a highly respectable but humourless goldsmith of the same name in the city. "Saw your cousins across the river," Barnikel would tease him, from time to time.

He had been planning to go to Bankside today anyway. For, with typical clear-sightedness, King Edward had already understood the great truth which the history of nearly all future legislative assemblies would prove – that prostitutes and politicians are inevitably drawn together. "If I leave a lot of knights and burgesses hanging around in the city," he observed, "they're sure to go off whoring and get into trouble." And so, when Parliament sat at Westminster, the Bankside brothels, at least officially, were closed. It might be some time, therefore, before he could go again.

As for the news of a virgin at the Dog's Head, it was indeed amazing. "And I'll have her," he murmured with mounting excitement. He'd give the Dogget girl a present too, though, to keep her happy.

Only once, for a moment, did he pause. The broad, muddy lane from Westminster ran parallel with the river and less than half a mile from the Abbey it turned right, as the Thames made its final curve by the Aldwych to enter the great, straight sweep that led past London. At this turning there stood a tall, handsomely carved stone monument surmounted by a cross, before which Barnikel now paused to say a brief prayer.

The cross had been there only some five years, since King Edward's wife, to whom, most unusually for a monarch, he was both devoted and faithful, had died in the north. A great cortège had set out to bring her body to Westminster, and twelve nights it had rested on the way: the last stage, before its formal entrance to the Abbey, had been here, at the road's turning. So great was Edward's devotion, that he had ordered a stone cross erected at each stopping place. There was another, in the West Cheap, by Wood Street. And since this spot was known by its old English name of, roughly, Charing, meaning the turning, this touching little monument was known as Charing Cross.

Barnikel had respected the queen; but he paused at the cross because, on the day it was erected, his own dear wife, having given him seven children, had died in childbirth with the eighth. It was because he had never found a replacement for her that Barnikel had not remarried, but preferred instead to go to Bankside once a week. As he always did, therefore, he said a prayer for her at Charing Cross and then rode on for his rendezvous. He had no qualms of conscience as he did so. His wife had been a cheerful soul. She would have approved. He pushed his horse into a canter.

As they approached the Dog's Head, Isobel and Margery were still not certain what to do. They had visited a doctor in Maiden Lane who was said, for a bribe, to keep his mouth shut, and he had confirmed their fears at once. "It's a leprosy," he said. So all such contagious sores were called. After bathing it in white wine, he had given Margery an ointment which, he swore, would cure her. "The chief ingredient," he remarked cheerfully, "is the urine of a goat. Works every time." She thanked him, doubtfully.

"I could go away for a bit I suppose," Margery said. She had never been away from her sister before. "I can pay the rent, and we're supposed to be closed tomorrow anyway, because of Parliament." In fact, the brothelkeeper usually arranged some discreet services for which he required the sisters.

"I shall pray," said Isobel.

Isobel was religious. The dispensation allowed to its prostitutes by the Church was uneven. They could receive communion, for instance; but they must be buried in unconsecrated ground. Though whether this meant that the dead were more liable to moral contamination than the living Isobel did not know. Even so, she believed that God might forgive her sins in this harsh world and that, in the end, she would be saved. But she knew that Margery's condition must not be discovered. "You'd better not work tonight," she said. "We can decide what to do in the morning."

With such urgent affairs on their mind, they still had not

remembered about little Joan. As they drew near the stew-house, they did so, with some shock. For the girl was standing outside, between two men and the brothelkeeper. Something, clearly, was badly wrong.

Waldus Barnikel was very angry indeed; Bull was smiling blandly and the brothelkeeper was looking embarrassed.

"You offered me a virgin," the new-made alderman thundered.

"She was, this morning," the brothelkeeper apologized. "I thought you'd come sooner, sire," he added.

"And so I would have done," the alderman declared, looking contemptuously at Bull, "but I have been with King Edward. He was speaking to me about the Parliament," he explained as a final reminder of his superiority to the patrician.

"She's only been had once," the brothelkeeper said, with a nervous glance at Bull.

"By me," Bull remarked with quiet satisfaction.

The new-made alderman and Parliamentarian glared.

"You think I would want her after that old fart?" he cried, glowering at the hated patrician; and the brothelkeeper wondered if this would lead to blows. But Bull seemed content to witness the fishmonger's fury.

"Seems I got in first," he said bluntly.

"You cur!" Barnikel cursed the brothelkeeper. "This is how you treat a good customer. I'll go elsewhere in future, by God I will."

"So you don't want her?" Bull asked.

"No more than I want a dog!" Barnikel roared. And then paused, uncertain what to do next. He had come there to celebrate, and quite emphatically wanted a woman. But seeing the girl standing side by side with his old enemy who, he now knew had got there first, his pride would not allow him to touch her. What should he do?

Just at this moment he noticed the Dogget sisters, who had now arrived.

"I'll have the Dogget girl," he said gruffly. "The one I always have."

"Which is?" The brothelkeeper was so alarmed by the turn of events that, for a moment, he had forgotten. Barnikel glared at him.

"Margery, of course."

The sisters looked at each other in consternation. They had but one thought in their mind. If the alderman caught anything from Margery there would be all hell to pay. He'd tear the brothel down. They would probably both be thrown out. There was no time to talk. One of them stepped forward.

"It's always me he wants, never my sister," she said with a smile. "Come on up, big boy," she cried.

There would be no problem. Margery had told her, long ago, exactly what it was he liked.

But for the real Margery, remaining below, there remained one puzzle. She had been preparing herself hastily to apologize to poor Joan. They had promised to protect her. And look at what had happened.

Yet now, amazingly, there was no reproach in her eyes. In fact, she was laughing. And as Margery Dogget stared at her, Joan smiled up at Bull and kissed him on the mouth.

"Shall I walk you to the bridge?" she said.

Joan parted from Bull just before the bridge, knowing that she had been lucky. More than lucky. Many men, having heard her story, would have laughed, or frankly disbelieved her. But Bull had done neither. At first he had stood there, stunned. Then he had shaken his head and told her: "That's the bravest thing I ever heard of in my life." Then he had chuckled. "All right," he said. "I'll help you. Do you really think you can get away with it?"

"I must," she said quite simply.

The law was clear enough. There was only one way, short of a pardon, that a condemned man in London could escape the hangman's noose. And that was if he was claimed by a whore.

There was a precise ceremony to be followed. The woman must appear publicly before the justices, dressed in the striped white dress and hood which were the official garb of the profession, and carrying a penitential candle in each hand, and offer herself as the prisoner's bride. If the condemned man in London agreed to marry her, he was set free and the marriage took place forthwith. The Church, though it ran the brothels, applauded the saving of a life from sin; the authorities doubtless took the same view. Few cases are recorded of this happening, though whether the prostitutes were unwilling to leave off a profitable occupation to be the wives of paupers, or whether the men preferred to swing rather than marry such women is unknown.

The Dogget girls' scheme was to do precisely this. Joan must become a prostitute for a day. She must be taken in properly at the Dog's Head, her name registered with the bailiff. Then she could claim her man. They had thought it the greatest adventure they had ever come up with in their life.

"But I can't actually go with the men," the girl had objected. "I just couldn't." She had shaken her head. "As for Martin . . ." This was why she had not dared tell him the details of her plan. He would certainly have refused, and given the game away. She thought of her betrothed's sad yet fiercely proud little face. "If he even thought . . ." her voice trailed off.

"We'll protect you," the sisters had promised. "We can get you through a night untouched." They had gone into fits of giggles at the thought. "What a joke," they had cried. "What a trick."

But Joan's objections were also the potential weakness of the plan. She did not think the authorities would enquire too closely about the short time she had spent in the brothel. After all, the dishonour of appearing in the despised dress, even once, as a registered whore was enough to brand her for life. But she supposed that if they discovered she had never acted the part at all, they might take a different view. She had worried about this also, all morning, but could not see what to do.

As she faced the florid-faced merchant in her little attic room, the idea came to her. First, if she told him everything, would he take pity on her instead of forcing himself upon her? And secondly, ingeniously, would he let the brothelkeeper and if necessary the authorities believe that she really had played the part?

For William Bull, gazing at this strange, solemn little person, the affair had been astonishing. That she would even dare to do such a thing! "My God," he said, after agreeing to help, "your young man's a lucky fellow. Mind you," he added, thinking with sudden embarrassment of his wife, "if it ever came to the question, I'd prefer to tell the justices in private that I'd had you. But I dare say that could be arranged. If the brothelkeeper thinks I did, that should be enough."

"But there's one other thing," she said. "After they've released Martin, you must tell him what really happened. I wouldn't want him to wonder . . ."

Bull grinned. "Of course," he said. But even he had not dreamed of the wonderful coincidence when, at last, he and the girl had come down. There was that cursed fishmonger Barnikel, puce with rage at finding that Bull had been there before him.

So extraordinary was the whole business, so sweet the revenge on Barnikel, that Bull found as he returned across the bridge that he felt quite as contented as if he had had a dozen virgins.

I might even go to bed with my wife, he thought, so happy was his mood.

Joan, meanwhile, equally contented, had been in no hurry to go back. First she had walked a little further along the river; then wandered about by the market; she had gone for a while into the church of St Mary Overy, and said a little prayer for Martin Fleming, before a statue of the Virgin. Then, taking her time, she had returned towards the Dog's Head.

No one, she felt sure, would bully her any more that day. Besides, the Dogget girls were there to protect her now. An early November dusk was falling as she approached the brothel door.

Dionysius Silversleeves stared at the lion and snarled. The lion shook its shaggy mane and snarled back. Silversleeves went a little closer and snarled again. Then, taking a deep breath and drawing back his thin head like a snake about to strike, he darted his long-nosed face forward, yellow teeth bared, and let out a sound which was somewhere between a roar and a screech.

The lion became furious. He batted the bars of his cage with his forepaws, gave another, huge snarl of rage and finally, in vexation, emitted a roar that echoed all around the precincts of the Tower.

Silversleeves squealed with delight. "You're not playing, are you?" he said. "You'd really like to eat me, wouldn't you?" It was a ritual he went through every evening when he had finished work; and few things in life gave him greater pleasure.

Dionysius Silversleeves was twenty-nine. His hair was dark, his nose long, his body thin; his cheek was red, his eyes were oddly bright, and he had acne.

The fiery pimples were everywhere: on his neck, on his forehead, on his shoulders, around his chin, and all over his long nose which, after he had been drinking, glistened with them. When he was young, his parents had told him that these would pass; but now not even the passing of the centuries could calm these eruptions. "It's the humours in my body," he would cheerfully grin. "Hot and dry. Like fire." Perhaps, who knew, it was this same unbalanced combination of the elements that compelled him, every evening, to tease the lions.

The first London zoo was situated at the outer gateway, just above the river on the western side of the huge complex of the Tower. Begun in the last reign, it consisted of a number of those wild animals which it then amused the monarchs of Europe to give each other as presents. Years before, there had been a polar bear on a chain, a gift of the King of Norway. The Londoners used to watch it catching fish in the river. There had been an elephant, too; until it suddenly died. But there were always lions and leopards in cages beside the bastion near the entrance, known as the Lion Tower.

The menagerie was not the only innovation. In the last two reigns, a huge transformation had taken place at the old fortress by the river. The Conqueror's square keep now stood in the middle of a great open space. Around this was a massively constructed curtain wall with battlements and a series of bastion towers, several like miniature castles themselves. This was the inner ward. Outside it, on the three landward sides, was a broad corridor – the outer ward – enclosed by a second splendid curtain wall. And around that was a huge moat, broad and deep, which turned the Tower complex into an impregnable island that could be reached on foot only by drawbridge and a series of enclosed yards and towers, including the Lion Tower at the south-western corner. It closely resembled the great castles with their rings of walls that Edward had recently built to hold down Wales. So powerful and impressive was it that the overall layout would never be changed again.

Pious King Henry III had decided that the great Norman keep at its heart should have its appearance altered, and had accordingly insisted that its entire outer surface be given a limestone whitewash. Now, instead of grey stone, the Londoners saw a great, white castle, staring pale and luminous out over the river. Long after the whitewash had worn away, it was known as the White Tower.

Only a decade before, the royal Mint had been moved from its ancient quarters below St Paul's to the Tower, and it was now housed in a series of brick workshops in the outer ward between the walls. Here Silversleeves passed his days. He was happy. The Mint at the Tower was one of only six mints in the kingdom, and it was by far the most important. Apart from ordinary wear and tear, and the needs of ever-expanding trade, the old coinage of the previous reign had been debased and King Edward was determined to establish a coinage that would enhance his kingdom's trade and repute throughout Europe.

As clerk to the Mint, Silversleeves came to know every one of its activities. There was the assay, where the coins were tested for the Exchequer men. This was done by careful weighing, melting, and then mixing with molten lead, which carried any impurities to the bottom and allowed the true silver content of coins and bullion to be checked. There were the huge vats of molten metal that made his red face glow brighter than ever; the moulds for making the blank coins, and the dyes which the moneyers would strike with a single, clean blow of a hammer. "One blow, one new coin," Silversleeves would contentedly muse as he walked through halls that rang with the sound of tapping.

Then there was the room where the coins were counted – the farthings, four to a penny, the silver pennies, and the newest addition to England's coinage, the special and rare heavy fourpenny piece called the groat. Whether it was because of the heat, the noise, the constant business, or the fact that it was money, which he so loved, that was being made, Dionysius Silversleeves counted himself lucky in his work and a happy man.

Best of all, when he came away from his work, he had not a care in the world. He had two elder brothers to carry on the family line. They were far less rich than a few generations ago, and had abandoned the former family wine business. But they had more than enough money to care for their widowed mother.

So when Dionysius left work in the evenings, he was free to do the one thing he enjoyed best of all: he pursued women.

Of course, they were always whores. Most other women, though he sometimes tried, would not look at him. But in his pursuit of the former he was relentless. There was not a stew-house on Bankside, nor in Cock's Lane, that did not know him. Even in a little alley off the West Cheap, known as Gro-peleg Lane, where some unlicensed prostitutes resided, he would turn up every month or so, "like a bad penny," the women would remark.

And now Dionysius was going off to Bankside as usual. But tonight he was looking forward to something special.

A virgin at the Dog's Head.

It had been an afterthought on the part of the brothelkeeper to send him a message and Silversleeves had guessed as much. But it did not worry him. With a laugh, he moved close to the cage of the irritated lion.

"I'm going to have a virgin tonight," he told the beast. "Which is more than you are. So there!"

She won't be a virgin by now, he thought to himself – but never mind. After all, what was the point of a new-minted coin if it was never used at all? Moments later, crossing the draw-bridge out of the Tower, he was on his way.

Darkness had fallen. The curfew bell had sounded. The ferry-boats had all withdrawn across the river and tied up on the London side – this was the rule, so that no Southwark thieves could slip across the water into the city. The watch was posted on London Bridge and the city prepared to pass another quiet night under the protection of the king's ordinances.

They were lighting the lamps at the Dog's Head. The red-painted plaster walls appeared ochre by the lantern's light, and the wooden sign was creaking in a breeze that had just got up as Silversleeves arrived.

The brothelkeeper had forgotten about Dionysius until that moment. He was standing, warming himself by the charcoal brazier in the middle of the long, low-ceilinged room where the girls met the customers. Nearly all the girls had already gone up, for in the late afternoon a number of men had arrived, including two burgesses up to London for the Parliament, in order to enjoy a last fling before the place officially closed.

Only two girls remained in the room, including Isobel Dogget, who was sitting alone on a bench, as Silversleeves strode in, looked right and left, grinned and demanded:

"Where's your virgin, then?"

The brothelkeeper seemed doubtful and glanced at Isobel, who shook her head.

"I'm sorry, sir, but she's not available," he said. "And curfew's sounded. You're too late." This was a significant point. Once the bell had gone and the ferries withdrawn, customers with the girls were supposed to remain with them until dawn, to prevent their roaming about the streets. If Joan had a customer, then she was taken for the night now. "How about one of the other girls, sir?" he suggested.

Silversleeves glanced around. "These old hags? I can have them any time. I came here for fresh meat." He grinned. "Tell you what. Soon as she's done, tell her customer he can have one of the others for free to follow. I'll pay. Then you give her to me. How's that?"

But again, after a moment's pause, the brothelkeeper shook his head.

If the brothelkeeper had not hesitated for that instant, if his eyes had not momentarily flicked towards Isobel again, Silversleeves would probably have admitted defeat. But he noticed, and at once a look of cunning came across his face.

"What's the game?" he cried. "What are you hiding, brothelkeeper? Are you trying to cheat me?" Whatever Silversleeves might be, he was also sharp. He moved over to the brazier where the brothelkeeper was standing. The pimples made tiny shadows on his face in the charcoal's glowing light. "I could make things awkward for you," he said quietly to him. Gently he took the fellow's beard and gave it a little tug. "I could mention your small party next week."

The party was being held for a group of burgesses up for the Parliament. Girls would be supplied, of course. It was illegal, but the brothelkeeper had forgotten Silversleeves knew about it. "I don't want trouble," he muttered.

"Of course you don't, and nor do I," the other replied. "So are you going to let me have this girl or not?"

The brothelkeeper shrugged. He couldn't see why this girl, now that she'd started well enough, shouldn't work like any other. "She isn't a virgin any more," he remarked, in case this was going to cause any further problem. "She had a customer this afternoon."

"Doesn't matter. Who, by the way?"

The brothelkeeper hesitated, but decided not to risk any more trouble from this devious fellow. "Bull the Merchant," he unwillingly replied.

"Really?" Silversleeves chuckled. "The old dog. Now go and get her, will you? There's a good fellow."

The brothelkeeper turned.

"She's sick." Isobel Dogget was standing. Her harsh voice rang out angrily. "Leave her alone, pimple face."

Silversleeves stared. "What's the matter with her? And don't call me names," he added, "or the bishop will fine you."

"Go to hell. I'm telling you she's sick."

"Bull too rough with her?" he mocked.

"Never you mind. You're not getting your hands on her. Leave her alone," she shouted, to the brothelkeeper this time.

But now that worthy man had had enough.

"No. You fetch her down," he told the girl, while Dionysius laughed.

Joan and Margery Dogget were alone in the little attic room when Isobel came up. By the lamplight, Joan was trying on a striped shift of Margery's that she would have to wear for the ordeal tomorrow. It was far too long, and the Dogget girl had just cut it and roughly hemmed it to her satisfaction.

"You'll do us all proud," she said with a laugh. And then to Isobel, as she appeared: "Maybe we'll all find husbands at the gallows."

When Isobel told her the problem below, however, she cursed and poor Joan went very pale. "I can't do it," Joan said, "not after all this."

"And wait till you see him," Isobel added ruefully.

"We've got to think of something," Margery said.

The two sisters sat down together on her mattress on the floor, with their chins resting on their hands. For what seemed like an age to Joan, they sat there in silence. But then they began to mutter. A little later, there was a pair of hoarse laughs. Then more muttering. Then they looked up cheerfully.

"We've got a plan," said either Isobel or Margery. And they told her what it was.

* * *

"We promise she'll come," the sisters said, as they sat one each side of Dionysius upon a bench. And when he looked suspicious: "I swear to God," said one. "She's coming," said the other.

"What we need", said Margery, "is food." "And wine," said Isobel. "Let's sup," they cried.

At this the brothelkeeper frowned. The stew-houses were not supposed to sell food and drink since this encroached on the tavern-keepers. But Silversleeves was smiling now. He jingled some new-minted coins in his pouch.

"I haven't eaten since morning," he said. "I need a full belly for wenching."

Reluctantly the brothelkeeper went off and reappeared with a flagon of wine, bread, and the information that his wife would shortly bring them a bowl of beef.

"Drink up, girls," Dionysius said cheerfully.

"We'll make a night of it," they agreed. They filled his beaker.

The brothelkeeper's wife soon appeared with a large bowl which she set on the table in front of them. It smelt good. Silversleeves dipped his nose over it and inhaled with pleasure. He began to eat.

There was still no sign of the girl, but he was not concerned. Perhaps she was, in fact, with a client and finishing off. Perhaps she had been sleeping. He did not care. He was not a man of too many niceties. If the sisters swore she would arrive, he did not think they would dare cheat him now.

Unless. As they filled his beaker of wine it did occur to him that, since they had been so determined to protect this new virgin from him, they might be trying to drink him under the table. He smiled to himself. Whatever his faults might be, a weak head for drink was not one of them. He could drink this flagon and another. But he'd still have the girl. He finished the bowl of beef. They brought him a huge apple tart. That, too, he could manage. But before he did, he sent Margery off to find the girl.

"I've waited enough," he told her, as Isobel poured more wine.

When Margery returned a little while later she was smiling. "She's coming," she promised, and poured them all some wine.

After further time had passed, however, and another beaker had been poured, a little too quickly, Silversleeves was beginning to become suspicious and angry. "Damn you," he muttered. "I'll fetch her myself."

And then she came. And he gasped.

Her hair was hanging loose. Her small feet were encased in sandals. She wore a nightgown of bright red silk that almost exposed her small breasts and which had a long slit up one side, through which her pale, slightly plump leg appeared. It was Isobel's best gown. The girl was not wearing anything else. Even the brothelkeeper could not suppress a little intake of breath, and his wife gave the girl a thoughtful look. She smiled at Silversleeves, walked boldly over to him, sat calmly on his knee, looked at the food on the table, and announced: "I'm hungry."

And now Silversleeves relaxed. The girl was his. A tasty dish indeed. He beamed at the brothelkeeper's wife. "More food," he cried, "and wine."

As the evening wore on, Dionysius realized that he had never been happier in his life. This girl was the first fresh, clean woman he had ever had. She was certainly going to be his. She was sitting in his lap and her arm was round his neck. She even appeared to like him. His habitual, aggressive good humour began to give way to a kind of bonhomie. "I'm sorry to make you wait," the girl had said, "but we have all night." Indeed they had. He was so happy now that he was even content to wait. The room seemed bathed in a warm and pleasant glow. And when, a little later, she whispered – "If you want to know, I'm still a little nervous" – he had actually been touched, and patted her knee. "No hurry," he said, and even sang a song.

Then they had all sung songs, and drunk some more, and her head nestled comfortably on his shoulder and even his own, hard head had been spinning a little when, some time in the night – he had not kept track of the time – he noticed a rattling of the shutters. He looked up, past the contented faces around him.

"What was that?"

"Wind," the landlord said, then made a face. "East wind." As though to confirm the fact the shutter rattled again.

Dionysius got up; the girl seemed half asleep. He swayed

a little, but grinned. "Time to go upstairs," he said. The girl stumbled beside him as he made for the door. For some reason, the Dogget girls were coming too.

The cold hit him like a hard blow as he stepped outside. During the hours he had been inside, a great, stark, November night had moved from the cold North Sea, across the flatlands of East Anglia and up the Thames Estuary to London. Coming from the close, smoky room by the roasting brazier, having drunk more than even he realized, it hit him so hard that he reeled. He blinked. The lantern by the entrance had gone out. His head swam. He shook it in an effort to clear his brain and felt for the wall that would lead him to the stairs.

But even then, though he could scarcely see her red nightgown, he held Joan by the wrist. "Come on, my pretty one," he heard his own voice, strangely, cry. "This way to paradise." He began to ascend the staircase.

Why did everything seem so crazy? Pitch darkness. The moaning wind. The staircase that creaked and swayed. The entire Dog's Head, it seemed to Dionysius, was moving about in an unaccountable way. Perhaps the brothel, sign, staircase and all, was about to take wing and spiral over Bankside into the black sky. He fought down the swaying sensation.

And then the two women. The Dogget girls.

Two, pale, flapping shapes, like ghosts, calling to him, pulling him with their hands. One, seizing him by the arm, on the first landing, crying: "Come with me. Sleep with me, lover." Twice, three times she had tugged at him, and he felt the coarse cloth of her pale dress pressing against him until he managed to throw her aside. Then it had been the other as soon as he had entered the passageway on the second storey, her arms suddenly found his neck, dragging him past the little stair to the attic and somehow, he scarcely knew how, managing to pull him into a room, even while he still held little Joan, and murmuring incoherent words of love and lust to him. "Take me. Oh take me any way you want me." He had to wrestle with her, and knock her down before he could break free. There had been voices, bangs, footsteps and then, silence.

Then at last, still holding on to Joan in the darkness, he stumbled back to the narrow stairs to the attic, pushed her up ahead of him, and, shaking his head to remain conscious, he followed her up.

It was pitch dark in the little room up in the gable. For a moment he thought he was going to faint. But he heard her, on the mattress in the middle of the floor and moved towards the sound until he tripped on the mattress and fell.

For a moment he had lain there, wondering if he could move. God knows, he wondered, if I can do anything now. He groped and felt her leg, under the soft silk of the nightrobe.

"Let's wait until morning," he heard Joan say; and, for fully a minute, his head was swimming so much that he thought that might be best. But then, with a grunt, he half-smiled.

"Oh no. You're not getting out of it now," he muttered. He put his hand down. Yes, he smiled, he could. And with a sleepy grunt, and a groping hand for preamble, he levered himself up and in drunken triumph, pressed home his advantage quickly in mounting excitement and then, with another grunt of satisfaction, that turned into a long sigh, rolled over and fell asleep. It was done.

A few moments later, the door softly opened and closed.

When he awoke the next morning, it was just in time to see her flitting out of the room. She turned and smiled briefly at him as she went.

The little crowd that had gathered outside Newgate was in a cheerful mood. The hanging of five thieves, even if they lacked notoriety, was still an event. It was a fact hard to deny that the majority of mankind like to watch a hanging. With the concourse of great folk gathering in Westminster for the Parliament, it promised to be a pleasant day of amusement.

The studded door of the prison house beside the gateway was still closed, but already the tumbrel was there. It was a funny little cart, quite low, with two spoked wheels and only a single horse to pull it. Around it ran boarded sides which the condemned men standing in the cart could hold on to. This way, as it made its slow progress the short distance to Smithfield and the hanging trees, the crowd could get a good look at them. The tumbrel from Newgate often made a little detour through the streets to give amusement.

William Bull gazed round the crowd. Immediately opposite the door he saw a group of people with sad, strangely concave faces. These, he guessed, must be the family of Martin Fleming. Near them he saw some short, solemn-looking craftsmen with large round heads that seemed too big for their stocky bodies. These must be members of Joan's family. The day was fine; the wind had ceased, but it was chilly.

Over on the right, standing alone but with a good view of the proceedings, was a tall figure in black. This must be the Lombard, come to see justice done. Or vengeance. Bull stamped his feet and pulled his cloak tighter about him.

The studded door of the prison was opening. The crowd muttered expectantly. Some figures began to emerge. First came one of the king's justices, a knight, who would supervise the proceedings; next one of the city sheriffs. Both strode to their horses, which grooms were holding for them. Out came a bailiff; then another. And at last, the prisoners.

Of the five men, four were poor craftsmen and one, by the look of him, a vagrant. The craftsmen all wore shirts, jerkins and woollen hose or leggings. The vagrant had bare legs and what seemed like a patchwork of rags covered his body. The five all had their hands free, but they were manacled around one ankle and attached to a chain. Silently they climbed up into the tumbrel, followed by the bailiffs. One or two voices in the crowd called out words of recognition and encouragement. "Be brave, John." "You'll be all right, lad." "Well done." Martin Fleming was the third man.

He saw his family, stared at them sadly, rather blankly, but gave no other sign. Nor, in their grief, did they cry out to him. But his eyes wandered over the rest of the crowd as though looking for something.

An ostler stepped forward, ready to lead the horse. But now, just as he did so, there was a new and excited murmur from the back of the crowd, which began to part. The sheriff glanced irritably towards the commotion, then his face took on a look of surprise. He said something to the king's justice, who also turned in his saddle to stare. But their surprise was nothing to the look of horror and stupefaction which now appeared on the pale face of Martin Fleming as he gazed at the apparition coming towards him.

Joan walked slowly but steadily. On her head was a white striped hood, to go with the white striped dress she wore, the humiliating garb of the common prostitute. In each hand, a long, lighted candle, sign of the penitent. Her feet were bare, despite the cold, as she moved towards the tumbrel. Before it, as the king's justice and the sheriff gazed down at her, she stopped.

"I am Joan, a whore," she said in a clear voice that every ear in the crowd could hear. "Will Martin Fleming marry me?" And she looked at the young man, straight in the eye, with a look that said: "Remember. Remember the message. You have nothing to fear."

The crowd, stunned, had momentarily fallen silent. Now an excited buzz began. The prisoners gazed at her. The bailiffs and ostler stared at her. And the sheriff and the justice looked at each other.

"What do we do about this?" the sheriff asked.

"Damned if I know," the knight replied. "I've always heard of this sort of thing but I never thought I'd see it."

"Is she within the law?"

The knight frowned. "I rather think she is." He glanced down into the tumbrel at Martin, for whom he had felt rather sorry, then suddenly he grinned. "I'll be telling this story for years."

Now there were voices in the crowd. The knight turned. A stocky little man with a large head had stepped forward. His face was white with agitation, and he was gesticulating wildly.

"This is my daughter," he cried. "We're a respectable family." There were laughs and catcalls. "She only left home a day ago." More cries. "It only takes a night," someone yelled. "She's a virgin, I swear," the painter shouted. The crowd erupted with laughter. Joan looked neither to right nor left but only stared at Martin Fleming.

Her father was right. Bull had not harmed her, and nor had Silversleeves. The plan of the night before had worked perfectly. While Dionysius was wrestling with one of the Dogget sisters in the darkness, the other had run up to the little attic room, slipped on a silk nightdress like the one Joan was wearing, and lain down on the bed, while Joan herself, entering ahead of Silversleeves, had hid under a blanket in the corner where she had stayed, holding her breath, until it was over and he had fallen asleep. It was the Dogget girl the drunken fellow had mounted in the darkness, and in the early hours of that morning, the two sisters had sat downstairs together, rocking with laughter at the joke. "It worked," they cried. "It worked. What a jape."

"We'll be there to watch you save your boy from hanging," they had promised Joan at dawn that morning. As yet, however, there had been no sign of them, for the simple reason that, at this moment, the two Dogget sisters were still happily asleep.

Looking down at Joan and her agitated father, the justice spoke firmly to the craftsman.

"Either she is, or she isn't a prostitute," he said. "I don't see it makes much difference for how long." He turned to Joan. "Can you prove you're a whore?" he mildly enquired.

She nodded. "At the Dog's Head on Bankside. Ask the bishop's bailiff."

The justice glanced at the sheriff. "We can put this boy back in the gaol until we've checked," he remarked. "We can always hang him another day, I suppose, if she's lying."

The sheriff nodded. He was rather enjoying the scene.

Further deliberations were now interrupted by a savage cry. It came from the Lombard, who had just understood what was going on. "No," he shouted, striding forward. "This girl," he searched for a word. "No whore. She to marry him anyway. This is play acting. *Commedia*." He looked furiously at young Fleming. "He is a thief. He got to hang."

The justice gazed down at the Lombard, decided he did not like him, and turned reluctantly to Joan. "Well?" he asked.

And it was just then, unlooked-for, that help came from an unexpected quarter: a red, pimply face, grinning cheerfully, burst out of the crowd. It was Silversleeves.

No one had noticed Dionysius arrive. Indeed, he had not planned to be at Newgate at all, or even remembered that there was to be a hanging that morning. He had been walking out to Westminster, to watch the gathering for the Parliament, when just past St Paul's he had noticed a small stream of people on their way to Newgate. He had arrived just in time to see Joan approach the tumbrel, had witnessed the argument, and now, vastly intrigued, and relishing his own part in the business, he saw his chance to make a dramatic intervention. They'll be talking about me all over London, he thought as he stepped forward.

"It's true, sirs," he cried out to the justice and the sheriff. "I'm Dionysius Silversleeves, of the Mint." Now they would all know his name. "She is a whore. I had her last night."

Catching sight of William Bull, and pointing to him, he cheerfully called out: "And so did he!" He beamed at them all, delightedly.

Joan's face turned to horror. This was not what she had intended. She thought furiously. She knew she must make them believe she was a whore, but kindly Bull had been going to do that. Thrown off balance by the interruption she looked guilty and distressed. And then what about poor Martin, watching all this from the tumbrel. What must he think? In an agony of fear, she stared at him, willing him to trust her, to understand.

At that moment, she heard the justice speak.

"By God, we've forgotten something." He turned his gaze upon Martin Fleming now. "It seems, young man, that this girl is a whore. Now then. If she is, are you ready to marry her?" He paused. "It means you go free, you know," he added kindly. "You won't hang."

And Martin Fleming only stared ahead.

He could not speak. He could hardly even think. On his way to death, to which he had resigned himself, his Joan, his pure and beloved, had appeared in the loathsome dress of a whore. It was so unimaginable that for moments he had been unable to comprehend what was going on. "Nothing will be what it seems." He remembered the message. But how was that possible? "You must trust her." He wanted to. Perhaps, against all appearances he might have, had it not been for the look he had just seen on her face. There was no mistaking it. The look was one of guilt and confusion. And even though she was now staring at him desperately, mouthing something, he was sure he understood the awful truth.

She was a whore. She might have done it for his sake. She must have. But she was a whore. At the moment of death, for a crime he had not even committed, this ultimate horror of horrors had been sent him by a God whose great, blank cruelty he could not begin to understand. The one girl he had dared to trust was like them all. Indeed worse. It was all filth, he thought; all bitterness, all useless. As he looked up, now, into the clear, cold, blue sky, he decided: No more. I want none of it, any more.

"No, sir," he said. "I don't want her."

* * *

"No!" Joan was screaming. "You don't understand." But the tumbrel was already moving.

"That's it then," remarked the justice, as he rode away.

What could she do? How could she speak to him? She tried to run after the tumbrel, but strong arms were holding her back. She tried to fight them off. "Let me go," she screamed. Why were they holding her? Who were they? She twisted her head, to see the grave, stern face of her father and her two brothers.

"It's over," they said.

And she fainted.

William Bull rode swiftly.

He was not very pleased at being publicly exposed by young Silversleeves, though he did not blame the girl for that. Nor did he quite understand what had happened. Had the fellow from the Mint taken her virginity? If he had, it must have been by force. Whatever was going on, he sensed there was foul play.

But one thing he did know: he had given his word. "I said I'd help her," he muttered. And that was enough. He would try. And the only course left now, that he could see, offered only a slim chance. "He can hang last," the justice had told him. "I will give you one hour."

He was going to try for a royal pardon. The Warden of London might give it him. And he was at the Parliament.

The great Palace of Westminster was thronged with people when he arrived. Magnates and lesser barons in sumptuous robes, knights and stout burgesses like himself in heavy cloaks and furs. No one stopped the doughty merchant as he strode in.

He had no plan. There was no time. "I must find the Warden of London," he cried. "Does anyone know where he is?"

Several minutes passed as he made his way through knots of men before someone helpfully pointed to a place at one end of the palace, where a small dais had been erected, covered with a purple cloth. And there Bull saw the warden, talking to the king. "Oh well," Bull grimaced to himself. "In for a penny . . ."

King Edward I of England gazed impassively as the large and flustered merchant stated his case to the warden, whose conversation with the monarch he had dared to interrupt. A possible miscarriage of justice. A pardon begged. Such things did happen. The fellow at the gallows now. No wonder the man was sweating. The condemned a poor man, no relation of this solid London patrician, who was prepared to pay. Most unusual.

"Well?" King Edward intervened. "Do we grant it or not?"

"We could, sire," said the warden, doubtfully. He knew he had the king's confidence, and did not much care for the patrician Londoner. "But the man robbed was a Lombard. He's very angry, too."

"A Lombard?" King Edward turned his eyes full upon Bull. They glowered so that even that powerful man blanched slightly. Then he delivered his crushing judgement. "I will not have my foreign merchants bothered. No pardon." And he waved Bull away.

"He's one of the patricians you wanted to break," the warden told him as Bull withdrew. "A wise decision."

It was no good then. With a sense of failure, and of sorrow for the girl and her luckless lover, Bull rode slowly back towards the city. He passed Charing Cross, and turned west along the lane. He hated to give up, but he could not see what else he could do. Had he been a praying man, he would have prayed for inspiration.

It was just as he reached the Aldwych that he saw the company of riders. Upon the site where his ancestors' homestead had once stood, there was now a fine new complex of buildings. In the previous reign it had been given to the king's uncle, the Italian Count of Savoy, and so this sprawling aristocratic residence was generally referred to as the palace of Savoy. In front of the Savoy the riders had momentarily paused to greet some others. They were, Bull saw at once, a group of London aldermen, going to the Parliament. Just those very fellows who had supplanted him and his friends. Another cruel reminder, he realized, of his impotence.

"If one of these damned people had pleaded for that boy to the warden," he muttered, "I dare say they'd have succeeded." He was just about to wheel his horse to avoid them, when in their midst he observed the hated Barnikel himself. "He even saw the king," he cursed, thinking of the day before. "He could probably get anything he wanted."

Then it struck him. There was, after all, one remote chance for Martin Fleming. One man who just might change the monarch's mind.

"Oh damn," he said. "Oh damn and a thousand curses." This was going to hurt. "But a life's a life," he comforted himself, and humbly rode towards the fishmonger.

"Another fellow begging for this boy?" the king stared at the fishmonger in astonishment. "Who is he to have such friends?"

But Barnikel did not flinch. Though he had no particular interest in Fleming, he knew what it had cost the patrician to come begging to him like that. And if he succeeded and demonstrated his own triumph over the fallen Bulls, well then, so much the better.

"You are asking a favour from me already, are you, Alderman Barnikel?" the monarch coolly demanded, as he surveyed him from under his drooping eyelid. "You know that the favours even of kings usually come at a price?"

Barnikel nodded. "Yes, sire."

King Edward smiled. "We have a busy Parliament ahead," he remarked. "Remember, Alderman Barnikel," he added meaningfully, "that I shall be relying on you."

The fishmonger smiled, "Yes, sire."

The king summoned a clerk.

"Go with him," he said. "I should think you'd better hurry."

And so it was, a quarter of an hour later, that a greatly astonished Martin Fleming, as he stood under the elm tree upon Smithfield with the noose already round his neck, saw William Bull, Alderman Barnikel, and a royal clerk, riding swiftly towards them with a cry.

"Royal pardon."

The marriage of Martin and Joan Fleming took place a few days later, in the porch of the riverside church of St Mary Overy in Southwark.

Though Martin was fully satisfied by now of his wife's purity, it had required a long conversation with Bull to overcome his horror at Joan's action in becoming a prostitute, even in name. As for his family, and hers, neither had got over it and neither had come to the wedding.

So it was that Alderman Barnikel stood by Martin, and William Bull gave the bride away, and the two Dogget sisters acted as bridesmaids, and the priest thought he had never seen anything like it in his life.

Perhaps the most remarkable thing of all, was that young Martin Fleming was the only man in the church that day who had never slept with either of the Dogget sisters.

Margery Dogget and her sister Isobel left London the next day. They had a reason for absence which not even the bishop could quarrel with. They went to Canterbury on pilgrimage.

While they were away, Margery continued to use the ointment the doctor had given her. To her great surprise, by the time they got back, it seemed to be working.

The Parliament of 1295, often referred to because of its broad composition as the Model Parliament, successfully concluded its business by Christmas. The barons and knights granted the king a tax of an eleventh of their movable goods, the clergy a tenth, and the burgesses, stirred no doubt by a passionate and loyal speech from Alderman Barnikel, a generous seventh.

The alderman might also have been amused to discover, the same day, that Isobel Dogget had come to the reluctant conclusion that he was going to be a father.

"I'm definitely pregnant and I'm sure it's him," she told her sister.

It was just after Christmas that Dionysius Silversleeves began to experience a burning sensation in his private parts.

It was Margery, not Isobel, that he had slept with.

Chapter 9

London Bridge

1357

As the medieval world approached its final flowering two things could be said with certainty. The first was that earthly life, so rich and exciting, was also fleeting. War, disease or sudden death came behind every footfall. The second, which provided some comfort, was that the order of the universe was known. More than twelve centuries had passed since the great astronomer of classical times, Ptolemy, had described it, and with such ancient authority, how could there be any doubt?

At the centre of the universe was the Earth. And though simple men – and even some mariners who feared to sail over the edge – supposed the Earth to be flat, men of learning understood that it was a globe. Around this central Earth, the universe was arranged in a series of concentric spheres – translucent and therefore invisible to men – upon each of which moved one of the seven planets: the haunting Moon, swift Mercury, lovely Venus, the Sun, warlike Mars, fearsome Jupiter, sullen Saturn. Their motions around the Earth followed an elaborate dance whose pattern the astronomers could predict. Outside these lay yet another sphere in which the stars were set which also rotated, but incredibly slowly. "And outside all these," the scholars declared, "resides a still greater sphere, whose motion causes all the rest to turn. This sphere, the *Primum Mobile*, is moved by the hand of God Himself."

Nor were the heavens indifferent to men below. Comets and shooting stars were messages from God. Though the Church was uncomfortable with the pagan superstition of astrology, most Christians paid heed to the signs of the Zodiac. Each planet had a character and its influence upon men was undoubted. Similarly, all matter was composed of the four elements – air, fire, earth and water – and to match them, the year had four seasons and men four humours. All things in God's universe were connected in this mystical way.

And if, in this ordered universe, the Earth was at the centre, then was there a place upon Earth's surface which could be called the focal point of the whole system? Here opinions differed widely. Some said Rome, others Jerusalem. The Christians of the East might claim Constantinople, the Saracens Mecca. But ask a true Londoner, and he could tell you at once. The centre of the universe was none of these. It was London Bridge.

By now, London Bridge was far more than just a crossing. In the century and a half since it was rebuilt in stone, the long platform on its nineteen arches had grown a massive superstructure. Down the centre ran a carriageway wide enough for two laden carts to pass; on each side were lines of tall, gabled houses jutting out over the river, and some of these buildings were joined across the thoroughfare by footbridges. Only one of the nineteen spans was not built upon and this was a drawbridge, so that even the tallest masted vessels could pass upstream. There were two big gateways. At one, all "foreigners" entering the city paid tolls. In the middle, enlarged into a two-storey building, was the old chapel of St Thomas Becket.

The bridge had, besides, one other particular feature: so massive were the piers supporting the arches that it acted as a kind of dam. When the tide was flowing slowly upriver, this was hardly noticeable, but when the tide was flowing downstream and the full weight of high tide water and the river current met this partial dam, it was held in check. At such times, the level on the downstream side of the bridge fell several feet below that of the pent-up waters on the upstream side, and each archway turned into a seething mill-race as the water rushed furiously down. Sometimes the more daring watermen would put their boats in to shoot these rapids, but it was a dangerous pastime. One mistake, a capsize, and even a strong man might be drowned.

Upon London Bridge, the heads of traitors were stuck on spikes for all to see. National triumphs were marked by gorgeous processions over the water. The bridge was the focal point of the city and of all England.

* * *

On a sunlit day in May, Gilbert Bull's burly form had been crammed into a short, waist-length tunic and blue and green hose.

The bridge was festooned with garlands. On the city side, the mayor and aldermen were waiting in their red robes and furs, the city's two gold and silver maces carried before them. Attending them were the leaders of the guilds, some in their liveries, others carrying banners depicting their crafts. There were the canons of St Paul's; the Black Friars; the Grey Friars and monks, nuns and priests from a hundred parishes, dressed as sumptuously as their orders allowed. All around, standing upon every vantage point, thousands of spectators strained to catch the extraordinary sight.

A King of France was being led captive to the city.

In recent decades, the ancient conflict between France and the Plantagenets had entered a new and different phase known, by later historians, as the Hundred Years War. By accidents of marriage and genealogy, the Plantagenets could now assert a claim to inherit the French throne; and though the French denied the claim, English monarchs would henceforth, for generations, add the French *fleur-de-lys* to their royal coat of arms.

The English had also become astoundingly successful. King Edward III, worthy grandson of mighty Edward I, whom he rather resembled, had hammered the French repeatedly. His eldest son, the gallant Black Prince, leading the English knights and archers at the famous battles of Crécy and Poitiers, was the greatest hero since Lionheart. Not only were the southern lands of Aquitaine and the Bordeaux vineyards secure under the English Crown, but in northern France, the Channel port of Calais, whose burghers had begged for their lives in chains before King Edward and his queen, was English now, a depot and customs point for England's mighty wool trade on the European mainland.

Most remarkable of all, the wars had even been profitable. England's merchants had been able to continue their huge trade – with Flanders, the Hansa ports of the Baltic, with Italy and Bordeaux – almost uninterrupted. There were profits from supplying the armies too. And the successes against the

French had brought in so much plunder and ransom money from captured knights that for years King Edward had not needed to tax his people at all.

Now, on a bright May morning, the King of France himself, a gallant and charming fellow, captured in battle the previous year, was coming as a captive guest to London. And here came the heroic Black Prince, worthy leader of his father's new order of chivalry, the Knights of the Garter, riding with exquisite courtesy beside the captive monarch on a little palfrey, as though he were his squire. No wonder, seeing these matchless flowers of chivalry, that the Londoners flocked to greet them. "His ransom," they declared, "will be stupendous."

It was just as the procession reached the mayor that Gilbert Bull, standing on the slope behind, took a decision and, turning to the girl at his side remarked:

"I've decided to marry you."

The girl looked up at him.

"Do I get a say?" she enquired.

"No," he answered pleasantly. "I don't think so." At which she smiled. She wanted a husband who would take the decisions. And he smiled too, because she was exactly what he needed.

When, sixty years before, William Bull had retired in disgust to his estate at Bocton, he had stopped trading and devoted himself to country matters. So had his son and grandson. But in the next generation, when there were two healthy sons and only one estate, something had to be done. In Continental Europe, the estate might have been split. But English kings, finding this made it harder to collect their feudal dues, had increasingly insisted upon primogeniture, inheritance by the eldest son. And if Bocton went to the eldest son, then what about his younger brother, Gilbert?

There was the Church, of course. But the priesthood was now almost entirely celibate, and young Bull had no desire for that. Then there was a military career. At the age of fourteen he had gone with the Black Prince and fought at Crécy. The experience had been as thrilling as it was frightening; but it had also given him a chance to see the harsh reality of medieval warfare. "The truth is," he told his father upon his return, "when they're not on campaign, our soldiers and their captains roam around the French countryside. If I find a patron I might rise; otherwise I'd be little better than a brigand."

"You'd better go to London, then," his father said.

Trade. Here again, England was a special case. When a French noble married a merchant heiress, as many did, he took her merchant money, but never touched trade himself. But though Norman and Plantagenet kings had imported knights into England who shared these attitudes and who still formed the bulk of the upper aristocracy, these Continental impositions had never quite struck root. It was only a little more than a century after the Conquest that Bull the merchant had bought back the Bocton estate. A century later and William Bull had retired to it. Before Gilbert was born, the Bulls of Bocton were wholly indistinguishable from the other gentry, some of whom were Norman knights, and others former aldermen, who lived on the Kentish estates around them. They spoke French as well as English, could write some Latin, rendered knight-service for their land, usually in cash, and might even affect aristocratic prejudices. But they knew where their wealth came from and their younger sons were still thought of as gentlemen when they returned to London to make a fresh fortune. Sometimes they were given positions at court, or sent on missions where gentlemen were needed. Even while England was still feudal, therefore, the socially mixed society of the Anglo-Saxons and Danes was quietly reasserting itself on the northern island.

Young Gilbert Bull had gone to London. He had become a trader in linen and imported cloth, a mercer. With money and family connections he soon prospered. And now he had chosen a wife.

His choice could not have been more sensible. The daughter of a prominent goldsmith with gentry connections, she would bring a handsome dowry. She was short, pleasant-looking and if the large dark rings around her eyes made her look a little worn, her temper was cheerful. She shared all his opinions about life and, as far as he could see, would give him no trouble at all. They were destined to be very happy.

Gilbert Bull was a very agreeable fellow. Everyone said that he was sound; like a true Bull, he never broke his word; and if, in private, he sometimes liked to read books or indulge a taste for mathematics, these were small weaknesses which he had under complete control. Was there no flaw, then, in his ordered universe? Perhaps only one: a dark memory, shared with many others, that made him too cautious, too anxious to control the world around him. But as he would say himself, with typical soundness, no one is perfect.

1361

It was spring, and the sign of the Zodiac was Taurus, the Bull. For the previous two evenings, the planet Venus had risen over the horizon, glowing with love.

There had been a shower earlier that morning, but now a moist breeze from the south was driving the puffy clouds across a pale blue sky; over the river, London was glistening in the warm sun, and steam was coming up from the ground as two men stood at the southern end of London Bridge and looked at the baby.

It was propped up in a sitting position against an empty barrel beside the busy road. It appeared to have been fed, and wrapped in a white shawl which was still fairly clean. The baby seemed to be contented, but there was no sign of any parents.

"Abandoned, do you think?" the younger man asked. He was not yet twenty, but already his dark brown beard was dividing into a fork. He had a broad, intelligent face and eyes which seemed to take in everything. His companion nodded. Whoever had placed the infant there was probably hoping some passer-by would take pity. "How old would you say?"

"About three months," Bull replied.

"He's looking at you, Gilbert." There was something about the little baby, even now, that suggested he was a boy; and certainly, he was gazing at Bull's burly figure with interest. "It's a pity to leave him," the younger man continued. Unwanted babies sometimes ended in the river.

Bull sighed. He had a large house. He could certainly afford to take the child in. "I'd save him," he said, "but the risk . . ." There was no need to finish the sentence. They both understood.

The baby might mean death.

* * *

The dark memory. Thirteen years had passed since it first arrived. The astronomers had warned of a terrible calamity, but had not been heeded.

The year before, the harvests had been bad and many poor folk in London had gone hungry. Winter had been harsh. And then the rain had come. Rain for days on end. Rain enough to make the Thames overflow and climb halfway to Ludgate; rain in rivers down the slope of Cornhill, and in streams along the gutters in the West Cheap; rain washing over the runnels as it poured down the lanes and turned the alleys into pools of black mud; rain filling cellars with slime whose smell came up, pungent through floorboards; rain in undercrofts drowning rats. The rain seeped down into the very roots of the city. But no city, not even London, could contain so much moisture, and when at last it ended, the old place could only sweat with the evil accumulation, and exude, under a yellowish sun, a ghastly, damp, unhealthy breath.

And then, at the start of that summer of 1348, came the plague.

It had already devastated much of Europe, and it travelled with astonishing speed. The Black Death had swept up the island of Britain and killed, perhaps, a third of the population. When it struck, it was sudden. Terrible sores and swellings appeared; fever followed, choked lungs and usually, within a few days, an agonizing death. The Great Mortality, it was called.

For Gilbert it was the dark memory. The day it reached London, he had left for Bocton and there he remained for a month with his family. Upon his father's orders, the estate on its ridge had been virtually sealed off. The occupants of the manor and its hamlet did not leave, nor did any visitors come. Together, gazing over the great panorama of the Weald of Kent, they had waited. And by the Grace of God, the plague had passed them by.

When he did return, he found the world had changed. In the countryside, the Black Death had made labour so scarce that, with landlords competing for men to work the land, the old system of tied serfs had already broken down, never to recover. In the cities, whole streets of houses and tenements were empty. And something else had happened. A girl he had loved had gone with all her family. No one could even tell him where they were buried.

Despite the trauma, the city recovered with astonishing speed. Nothing could stop the trade of London. Fresh immigrants came in. The children of the survivors began to fill the yawning gap. Life seemed to have returned to normal. But the plague had not passed. It had only gone into hiding. For more than three centuries, like some terrible blight, it would suddenly appear and shatter the bright life of the city for a season before abruptly vanishing once more. Though where and how it dwelt meanwhile – whether in some dark, infected part of the city's bowels, or brought back by the damp wind in a cloud – no man knew. In that spring of 1361, it had appeared again. Several London parishes had suffered. There had been many deaths in Southwark. And if this baby had been abandoned, the chances were that its family had died of plague. Bull was reluctant to touch it.

"There haven't been any new cases for a week," his friend remarked. "If this baby were infected, he would have died by now. I'd take him myself, except that I'm a bachelor." But still Bull did not step forward.

They had not noticed the cart approaching, nor the puddle of water close by. As the cart passed by, it splashed them. The younger man leaped to one side with agility, but Bull was less fortunate, and a moment later was gazing down at his mud-splattered red cloak, his face a picture of woe.

And then the baby laughed.

The two men stared in surprise; but there was no mistaking it. The little round face was looking up at Bull with obvious amusement. "What a cheerful little fellow," the younger man said. "Do let's save him, Gilbert." And so Bull picked the baby up.

A few minutes later, as the two men parted in the middle of London Bridge, Gilbert Bull gazed at the little bundle he was holding in his arms. "Now see what that damned fellow had made me do," he murmured with a smile. He had known his young friend for some years now: he had a junior position in the king's service, though his father and grandfather had dealt in wine. Before that, however, Bull assumed that the family must have been shoemakers, since their name came from the

French word for shoes, *chaussures*. He was very fond of young Geoffrey Chaucer.

"Your name is Ducket. Ours is Bull." It was the first sentence he remembered being addressed to him. How large and impressive the merchant had seemed as he spoke the words, not unkindly, but firmly. Until that moment, the little boy had vaguely supposed that he was part of the family. Now he understood that he was not. It had been the day their daughter was born, when he was five.

Yet who exactly was he? It was kindly young Chaucer who had discovered the baby's identity a few days after he was found. "I asked around," he told Bull, "and it seems the neighbours found him in a tenement where a poor family called Ducket had all died of plague. A miracle he lived, really. They left him by the bridge to be picked up, just as we thought." More puzzling had been the baby's first name. Since no child could enter heaven unbaptized, and since infant mortality was high, babies were usually christened quickly after birth. "I asked at all the local churches," Chaucer reported. "But not a thing." And when they wondered what to do, he grinned. "Call him Geoffrey," he said. "I'll be his godfather."

When he was three – this was the custom – the boy had been confirmed into the Church. After that, he had not seen much of his godfather for some years, since Chaucer was often away. Yet even if he was only a foundling, without a real family, his childhood was happy. Bull was always scrupulously fair and his wife, in her quiet way, was prepared to act as a somewhat distant mother. Indeed, only one thing worried him.

He was odd. There was a funny white patch in his hair which people stared at. Worse, the curious webbing of skin between his fingers appeared to be strange as well. Often, he would look surreptitiously at people's hands to see if they had this webbing too. But they never had. Once he had discovered that the cook's assistant, a fat girl who seldom spoke, was also called Ducket, and he had asked her eagerly, "Are you of my family?" But she had only munched a ginger cake and finally told him: "I dunno."

Gilbert Bull's house stood near the middle of London Bridge on the upstream side. It was four storeys high with a tall, steep tiled roof. It was constructed of timber and plaster and, like many of the better houses now, its dark oak beams were elaborately carved. A dozen curious little gargoyles of human or animal faces peeped down cheerfully from overhanging corners into the busy street. The ground floor contained a counting house. On the main upper floor, a splendid solar, a living room with a large fireplace and chimney looked out over the river. The top half of its big window was filled with tiny panes of greenish glass. Coal burned in the fireplace. Known as sea coal since it was brought from the north by ship, it gave more heat and smoked less than timber. Above this floor were bedroom chambers, and above those, the attics. The cook slept in the kitchen on the ground floor; little Geoffrey Ducket, the servants and the apprentices, in the attic.

But the busy kitchen was his favourite place; the great spit by the fire which was always lit; the blackened old iron kettle; the huge wooden vat of water, filled from a bucket lowered into the sparkling Thames each morning; the leather tank of live fish from which the cook would make her selection; the heavy pot of honey she used for sweetening; the pickling tub and the spice cupboard where he would go to open the jars and sniff the aromas.

Still more amusing, once a month, was to watch the women do the laundry. A big wooden trough was placed in the middle of the kitchen floor, filled with hot water, caustic soda and wood ashes, and linen shirts and sheets were soaked, pounded, rinsed and then run again and again through a mangle until they were stiff as a board. The cook showed him how to clean fur as well. "This is the fluid I use," she explained. "I take wine, and fuller's earth." She used to let him sniff this and he would start and jerk back his head at the pungent smell of ammonia. "Then I mix in some juice from green grapes. And, you see, every stain comes out."

He would hang about by the kitchen doorway to watch the pedlars coming by with their wares just after the service of terce in the morning. And for special amusement, from the little courtyard where they lowered the bucket into the river, he would throw sticks down into the Thames and then rush dangerously across the crowded thoroughfare and into another yard where he would try to see them as they came shooting out under the arch on the other side.

But the best times of all were spent with his hero.

There were usually apprentices in the house, friendly, but too busy to take much notice of the little foundling in the kitchen. Except for one. A decade older than Ducket, with curly brown hair, brown eyes, a devil-may-care attitude coupled with a kindly charm, to the boy he seemed a god. The younger son of a rich old gentry family from the West Country, his father had sent him to join the merchant élite of London. As the cook would say with approval: "That's a real young gentleman." But Richard Whittington was still an apprentice. In the old days, rich men or the sons of citizens bought or inherited their citizenship. Now they almost always obtained it through the guilds. They had always set the standards, quality, working conditions and prices, trade by trade. No craftsman or merchant could operate without guild membership. But nowadays the guilds dominated the wards, the common council and the inner council of aldermen. From the humblest craft guilds to the great merchant guilds like the Mercers who vied with each other for control of the city's politics, the guilds were London.

Whittington liked little Ducket. The foundling had such a cheerful spirit that the apprentice often played with him. He taught him to wrestle and box and soon discovered something else: "no matter how often he goes down, he gets back up again," he said approvingly. "He never gives up."

Sometimes he would show him the city. The plague might have made gashes in the population, but London still seemed to be bursting with life. And everything was such a wonderful jumble. They would dive into an alley and find some great nobleman's house, with his coat-of-arms fluttering on a silken banner from the windows, while to left and right clustered the hanging wooden signs of bakers, glovemakers and taverns. Even the house of the Black Prince himself was in a street full of fishmongers, and great wicker baskets of herbs hung by his gate, to lessen the smell. Rich, middling and poor jostled side by side; so did the sacred and the profane. The great walled enclosure of St Paul's might set the cathedral apart; but by the little church of St Lawrence Silversleeves, the surrounding tenements, which had been emptied by the Black Death, had collapsed and their yard had been turned into a midden where poor folk went to relieve themselves – and whose resulting stench obliged the curate to keep a handkerchief before his face as he hurried through the services.

Once they made a longer expedition. This was to find the origin of the city's fresh water supply.

Since the tidal Thames was often salty, it was not always good for drinking. Once, the Londoners had used the little Walbrook or the nearby Fleet; but neither of these was wholesome. Apart from the discarded pelts from the skinners' workshops, there were too many houses with *garderobes* hanging over its narrow stream to make the Walbrook pleasant; as for the Fleet, it was a dirty river now. Upstream lay the tanneries where leather was cured and whose effluent made the Fleet stink of urine and ammonia. Then, by Seacoal Lane, the coal barges unloaded, and their dust darkened the water. At Newgate, butchers from the shambles would come out and empty offal and entrails into the stream. By the time the Fleet passed the watermill which stood at its junction with the Thames, it was not a pretty sight.

So in the middle of the West Cheap stood a curious building, shaped like a miniature castle tower; from its sides, through narrow pipes of lead, came constant streams of clear fresh water, brought there by a little aqueduct. It was known as the Great Conduit. Whittington and the boy followed the line of the pipes one Sunday afternoon all the way across to the sparkling spring which fed it, on a slope just north of Westminster, two miles away.

But if, to the boy, these were marvels, they did not seem to satisfy his hero at all.

"Disgusting," he would say of a place like St Lawrence Silversleeves. "This has got to be cleaned up." As for the Great Conduit: "One conduit for a city this size? Totally inadequate. The city must put this right. Or one day I will." When he asked how Whittington would accomplish such things, the young man calmly replied: "I shall become mayor."

"How does one become mayor?" he asked one day.

For answer, Whittington pointed to a stout building in the Cheap, just below where the Jewry had once begun. "Do you know what that is?" he asked.

On the site where the family of Thomas Becket used to live stood a handsome chapel, with a hall above, dedicated to the memory of the London saint. "That's where the Mercers Guild meets," Whittington explained. "First you become a member; then perhaps the warden; and then they make you mayor. The guild, that's the thing." And Ducket looked at the building and thought that to be a mercer like Bull and Whittington must be the finest thing in the world.

When he was seven, young Geoffrey Ducket was sent to school at St Mary-le-Bow. He had been a little fearful of this, but when he got there he received one pleasant surprise. Though the children were taught to read and write Latin, of course, the classes were now being conducted in English.

Bull was astonished. In a conversation which the little boy did not overhear, he complained to Whittington: "It was Latin and the birch in my day. What's the matter with them?"

"All the schools are starting to teach in English now, sir," the young gentleman laughed. "After all, even at court they speak English."

The merchant was not convinced though. "I suppose it's good enough for a foundling," he grumbled.

And then there was the girl. A wavy mass of dark hair, a pale little face with a rather pointed nose, small red lips, grey-blue eyes. Theophania, the priest had solemnly baptized her, using the Latin form of her name. But never, after that day, was she known as anything but simple, English, Tiffany. Bull adored her.

Ducket had paid little attention to her until she was five, when Whittington's stay in the house came to an end; but in the years that followed he was often her companion and, remembering Whittington's kindness to him, tried to be kind to her in turn. Besides, it was pleasant to have someone who looked up to him and followed him around so faithfully. He would even break off from some game of ball or wrestling to play hide-and-seek with her or, as she loved best of all, to carry her on his shoulders across the bridge and back. Sometimes he would take her fishing and they would catch a trout or one of the salmon with which the river was so plentifully stocked.

Of all the things a young man could do, the most daring and dangerous feat was at London Bridge. One day, when Ducket was eleven, Whittington casually remarked to him: "If you watch the river tomorrow morning, you might see something of interest." It could only mean one thing. No one had done it in months.

The next morning, hand in hand, he and Tiffany stood at the big upstairs window. It was a fine day and the Thames was sparkling, but thirty feet below them the water eddied impatiently by the great stone pier and poured down with a terrifying roar through the channel. "Will he be safe?" Tiffany whispered. "Of course he will," Ducket said. But secretly he was not so sure. Maybe I shouldn't have let her see this, he thought.

There was Whittington, with two friends in a long boat, standing in the stern and sculling with a single oar as if he had not a care in the world. Dear God, how brave he looked! As he approached, he glanced up, smiled and gave a cheerful wave. He was wearing a blue neckerchief. Then he coolly set the prow of the boat at the centre of the arch, and sailed into the race.

It was just now that Ducket realized that Bull was standing behind them. His big face looked stern. "Damned young fool," he said, but Ducket thought he detected approval in his voice. "Better see if he's alive," Bull said as the boat disappeared below them, and he led the two children out and across the bridge to the downstream side. Whittington had already been carried well away and was nearly level with Billingsgate. He had taken off his kerchief and was waving it over his head in triumph. Tiffany watched, her eyes very wide. She turned to Ducket. "Would you do that?"

He laughed. "I don't think so."

"Would you do it for me?" she persisted.

He gave her a kiss. "I would for you," he said.

When Ducket was twelve, Bull summoned him into the big upper room.

"It will soon be time you were apprenticed," he said with a smile. "I want you to think about what you'd like to do. You can choose what you want."

The great moment. He had been waiting for it for years.

"But I already know," he blurted out. "I want to be a mercer." Like Whittington. Like Bull himself. He looked at the merchant happily, and only after several moments wondered why the smile had died on his face.

Gilbert Bull was an intelligent man. For a second, he had thought the boy was being impertinent, then realized: he did not understand. How shall I tell him? he thought, and knew it was kinder to be firm at once.

"That is impossible," he said. "The Mercers Guild is for merchants, people with money. If you were a Whittington, or . . ." he almost said "a Bull," but thought better of it. The truth was that there were poor apprentices, even in the élite Mercers Guild, but he had no intention of placing this foundling there. "You've no money, you see," he said bluntly. "You must learn a craft." And he sent the boy away to think about it.

Ducket did not stay downhearted for long. A few days later, he was walking round the city, poking his head into this workshop or that, always cheerful and always curious. "God knows," he muttered to himself, "there's choice enough."

Glovers making gloves. Saddlers making saddles. Lorimers making bridles. Coopers making barrels. Turners making wooden cups. Bowyers making bows. Fletchers making arrows. Skinners dealing in furs. Tanners curing leathers – the stench of the tanneries decided him against this. Then there were the shopkeepers – bakers and butchers, fishsellers and fruiterers. He could see himself as any one of these.

The issue was resolved, however, from another quarter entirely.

Though he was vaguely aware that Bull's friend Chaucer had been his godfather, young Ducket seldom thought of the courtier. After all, he was usually away. But he heard the merchant speak of his progress from time to time. This had been considerable. From a humble page, the wine merchant's son had progressed through the various stages of a young gentleman at court, making himself both useful and popular. This last came to him easily, for he had a naturally sunny temperament. "Amazing fellow. Never loses his temper," Bull remarked.

"He knocked down a friar once," his wife gently observed.

"All students do that," Bull replied.

Chaucer had gone on campaign several times, been ransomed once, and studied enough law for any official appointment he might get. He also possessed one other talent: he could turn a pretty verse in French to please a lady or celebrate a great event. Lately, he had even experimented by rendering some verses into the Frenchified version of English spoken at the court – a daring novelty that the royal circle found charming. He had been included in a diplomatic mission, to broaden his experience. And a little while ago he had also received another significant reward.

In the large and sophisticated court of King Edward III, it had become usual to find aristocratic wives for rising young courtiers from the middle classes, and Chaucer, the popular wine merchant's son, had been favoured with the daughter of a Flemish knight. "Yet doesn't the fellow have the devil's own luck?" Bull had cried happily. For Chaucer's amazing good fortune was that his wife's sister, Katherine Swynford, was the acknowledged mistress of no less a person than King Edward's younger son, John of Gaunt.

There were numerous royal sons, all handsome fellows who sported the long, drooping moustaches that were fashionable. If John of Gaunt was shorter and broader than his heroic brother the Black Prince, he was still an impressive figure, and almost certainly more intelligent. By his first marriage he had secured the vast estates of the dukedom of Lancaster; by his second, to a Spanish princess, a claim to the throne of Castile. But his real love, to whom he was as quietly devoted as any husband, was Katherine. Geoffrey Chaucer therefore had married into the outskirts of the Plantagenet royal house.

John of Gaunt lived in the huge palace of the Savoy, by the Aldwych. And it was from there one summer's day, as Ducket and little Tiffany were walking out to Charing Cross, discussing the merits of being a butcher over those of a bowyer, that a man with a forked beard strolled, who, as soon as he spotted the boy's white patch, came over to them with a smile and asked: "How does my godson?"

Nor, when Ducket told him about his problem, did he hesitate for more than a moment before declaring: "But I think I've got the very thing for you."

A week later, it was all arranged. Ducket prepared to leave the house on London Bridge and move into his new master's. On a summer morning, with a spare hose and two new linen shirts provided by Bull's wife, he set off cheerfully to his new home. Though this was less than a mile away, it was a parting nonetheless. As she stood by the door, little Tiffany asked him: "Will you come back to see me every week?" He promised he would. "Will you miss me? Every day?" "Of course I shall."

Even so she stayed by the door for a long time as he went upon his way.

As for Geoffrey Chaucer, he smiled to himself. "Your master is a kind fellow," he assured the boy; "but the household is, you might say, unusual." More than this, however, he would not divulge, preferring to leave his godson curious.

1376

On a wet spring morning, Dame Barnikel faced her eleven-year-old daughter Amy across the matrimonial bed and prepared for battle.

Dame Barnikel's bed was a splendid affair. It was by far the most valuable piece of furniture in the house – a huge four-poster. It was made of oak. Upon it she had already had two husbands. In the taverns of Southwark, the betting was five-to-two for a third within seven years. The first man, they said, had died of exhaustion. The bed had a thick mattress stuffed with down. At its foot rested a huge wooden trunk, banded with iron, in which all the bedclothes were kept and which, when Dame Barnikel had sat on it to close it, packed the contents so tight that any unfortunate fleas who had failed to jump out were instantly suffocated.

For several seconds she eyed the girl, who wilted stubbornly under her gaze. Then she began.

"You're very pale," she announced gruffly. She paused now, searched for words and found them. "You look," she suddenly roared, "as if you'd been kept under a pot."

But this was not the real issue on her mind; that followed soon enough.

"This young man of yours. This carpenter. He won't do at all." She gave the girl a firm look. "Just you forget about him," she growled affectionately, "and you'll feel better."

As Dame Barnikel looked at the girl, she inwardly sighed.

How like her father Amy was. Though more strongly built, she had the same thin, concave face and, as far as one could tell, the same tendency to silence.

When people saw John Fleming and Dame Barnikel together, they could never believe they were man and wife. It was no wonder: with his spoon-like face and spindly body they never thought he could stay the course. As for why, only a year after first being widowed, she had married this quiet grocer, it remained one of the mysteries in an otherwise ordered universe.

But Dame Barnikel, at thirty, was magnificent. Half a head taller than Fleming, with her dark red hair pulled back like an Amazon, even Bull, who was a harsh critic, admitted she was a fine-looking woman. Silent she was not. Her voice would boom an indiscretion across the street or share a secret in a husky growl; once a month she would get drunk, and then, if crossed, she could roar like a Viking in battle. Above all, she loved to dress in bright colours.

Sometimes this led to trouble. Since the reign of Edward I, there had been a number of laws regulating dress. Not that this gave offence in an ordered society. A merchant, for instance would think it impertinent to wear the red robes of an alderman; nor was his wife likely to put on the elaborate head-dress and flowing silks of a lady of the court. Indeed, the main offenders against the laws were the more fashionable nuns who, in winter, were apt to forget their vows of poverty and trim their habits with costly furs. But Dame Barnikel took no notice of these laws at all. If a headdress, a bright silk or a rich fur took her fancy, she wore it. And when the beadle, more than once, came to complain to Fleming, the grocer only shrugged and suggested: "You talk to her." At which the beadle would hurriedly leave.

Her daughter's interest in Ben Carpenter had only begun in the last year. The girl was young and Carpenter still an apprentice, but Dame Barnikel was taking no chances. Many girls married at thirteen and betrothals, even for humble folk, could come years before that. She was going to put a stop to it at once.

"He's not good enough," she stated firmly.

"But he's my cousin," the girl objected. For what it was worth, this was true. One of the grandsons of the saddle painter whose daughter had rescued the Fleming boy eight decades before had become a carpenter and taken the name of his new occupation. Thus, as could easily happen amongst such craft families, two branches were called respectively Painter and Carpenter – and both were distantly related to Amy. Dame Barnikel, however, treated this information with a snort.

"Father likes him."

This was the problem. For some reason Fleming had taken a liking to the solemn craftsman; otherwise, Dame Barnikel could easily have sent the fellow packing. It was a point of honour with her, however, to respect her husband's opinion in matters concerning their daughter.

"The reason you like him," she told the girl, "is that he's the first boy who's taken an interest in you. That's all."

Dame Barnikel was often puzzled by Amy. She herself had been born a Barnikel of Billingsgate. At thirteen she had married a tavern-keeper. Widowed, at sixteen, she had married Fleming. Yet so great was her force of character that she had never been known by any name but Barnikel, to which, as though she were the wife of an alderman, even the aldermen themselves would usually add the prefix Dame. "I'd be afraid she'd cut my head off if I didn't," Bull once laughed.

From her first husband she had inherited the George tavern in Southwark which for fifteen years now she had run herself. She was a member of the Brewers Guild.

Such arrangements were not uncommon in London. Widows often had to continue the family business; many a little backstreet brewhouse was run by a woman. There were women members of several guilds and many female apprentices in the crafts where weaving or sewing was involved. Normally, if a widow married a man with a different trade, she was supposed to give up her own. But Dame Barnikel had announced she would continue – and none of the brewers had dared to argue.

Amy took no interest in the business; she preferred to help in the house; and if her mother suggested she try a craft of her own, she would quietly shake her head and say: "I just want to get married." As for Carpenter – every time Dame Barnikel saw the little craftsman with his bandy legs, his head too big for his body, his large round face and solemn eyes, she would mutter: "Dear God he's dull." Which was exactly, she guessed, why Amy liked him.

"You'd do much better with young Ducket," she said. She had taken a liking to her husband's apprentice. He might be a funny-looking fellow and a foundling, but she admired his cheerful spirit. The girl seemed to like him too, but so far had not turned her gaze from the gloomy craftsman. "Anyway," she concluded, "the real problem is much worse than that."

"What do you mean?"

"Can't you see, girl? The poor fellow's moonstruck. He's not right in the head. You'd be a laughing stock."

At which poor Amy burst into tears and fled from the room, while Dame Barnikel tried to decide whether she had actually meant what she had said or not.

James Bull, at the age of eighteen, was a credit to his race. Tall, sturdy, fair-haired, broad-faced, his Saxon ancestors would have recognized him as one of their own immediately. In all his dealings, his staring blue eyes told you at once that he was absolutely honest. Not only did he never break his word, he never even thought of doing so. Indeed, if any adjective in the English language summed him up it was: forthright.

In the modest ironmonger's business which the family still ran, everybody swore by him. His parents relied upon him, his young brothers and sisters all looked up to him; and if, for three generations, the business had never produced more than enough to feed the family, they all felt confident that James would lead them to greater things. "Everybody trusts him," his mother would explain with legitimate pride.

Even so, his parents had some misgivings about his plan to visit his cousin Gilbert Bull. It was over eighty years since the family of ironmongers had encountered the rich Bulls of Bocton, and humiliation seemed likely. James's plan to transform the family fortunes might excite his brothers and sisters, but his mild-mannered father was not so sure.

James, however, was confident. "He can't possibly mind," he told his father, "when he sees that I'm honest."

And so it was, on a bright spring morning, that he set out for the big house on London Bridge.

* * *

As Gilbert Bull made his way back from Westminster he felt a sense of heaviness.

The long reign of Edward III was drawing to its close, and, sadly, it was not a dignified ending. Where were the triumphs of yesteryear? All whittled away. The French had once again managed to claw back nearly all the territory the Black Prince had won. The most recent English campaign had been an expensive waste of time and the Black Prince himself, having fallen sick on campaign, had died a broken man in England that very summer. As for the old king, in his dotage now, he had taken up with a young mistress, Alice Perrers, who in the manner of such women had infuriated the judges by interfering with their work and the merchants by spending their tax money on herself.

But worst of all, for Bull at least, was the Parliament which had just ended.

The practice of calling parliaments, used so cunningly by Edward I, had become more or less an institution during the long reign of his grandson Edward III. It had also become customary for these great assemblies to split into three parts. The clergy would hold their own convocation in one place; the king and his extended council of barons, the Parliament proper, would usually meet in the Painted Chamber of Westminster Palace; and the knights of the shires and burghers, rather patronizingly called the Commons, would gather until sent for in the octagonal Chapter House of Westminster Abbey.

The Commons had also subtly changed. The previous century, the burghers from the towns had only been summoned there occasionally, when needed; but now they were a regular fixture. At least seventy-five boroughs usually sent men, who sometimes outnumbered the knights. London generally sent four, Southwark another two. And in recent years, a further sophistication had evolved: it was expensive to send a man to Westminster, where he might have to stay for weeks. So some boroughs began deputing London merchants to represent them. "After all," they could truthfully say, "these fellows are merchants. They know what we want." Many a borough, therefore, instead of its own timid provincials, was represented by a London man. Rich men; men with connections amongst the nobility; men with centuries of London independence behind them. Men like Gilbert Bull. That year he had represented a borough in the West Country.

Yet he was not glad he had done so. For if historians have called the Parliament of 1376 the Good Parliament, they have done so with hindsight. To those who took part, it was a melancholy affair.

Everybody was angry. The government had lost a war and was looking for money; the Church, which owned a third of England, was already being pressed for contributions by a needy Pope.

Even before the chancellor's speech, Bull had realized the session would be difficult. It was usual for some members to bring petitions with them, for redress of grievances, but this year everybody seemed to be carrying a scroll of parchment. As they crowded into the Chapter House and sat, tightly packed round the walls, there was an air of expectancy. They took an oath: "Our discussions shall be private, so that every man feels free to speak his mind." But Bull was still astonished when, as soon as this was done, an ordinary country knight strode to the lectern in the middle and calmly declared: "Gentlemen, the money we voted last time has been squandered. Until we are given a proper accounting, I think it's time we refused to pay."

The ailing king, half paralysed by a stroke, had not come to the council chamber, and so it was John of Gaunt who received the Commons men in the council the next day. Normally only two or three of the Commons men stood humbly before the king and barons. Yet this time, not only had they chosen a speaker to represent them, but the entire Commons insisted on standing with him in a solid and threatening phalanx in the Painted Chamber. Worse yet: addressing Gaunt in the formal Norman French that such occasions still required, the Speaker coolly informed him that the Commons was not satisfied with the handling of funds. "In short, some of the king's friends and ministers have misused them, sire, and we demand that they be brought to account." Until they were, the Speaker said, the Commons refused even to discuss whether they would grant the king any money at all. It was not a petition. It was a demand. It was an impertinence. It was unthinkable.

But the king was weak and the humble Commons were going to have their day.

They went on for weeks. The Commons accused ministers, who were found guilty and dismissed. They even – ultimate impertinence – had the poor old king's mistress, who had certainly lined her pockets, sent away. This process of accusation by the Commons at once acquired a name. In Norman French it was *ampeschement*: it meant embarrassment. Spoken in English it became: impeachment.

The Commons got everything they wished. And though John of Gaunt secretly vowed to get even with them, and in particular cursed the London contingent, whom he rightly held responsible, the Parliament finally closed without granting more than half the taxes needed.

So another landmark in English constitutional history was made. Just as London had won her mayor and the barons their charter, now the humble Commons had imposed their Speaker and the practice of impeachment. In this way the first miles down the long road towards a later democracy were paved, not with ideals, but with opportunism and a series of medieval tax revolts.

Yet as he went home on the last day of the Good Parliament, Bull felt nothing but depression. The sight of the old king being savaged by the Commons men had only reminded him of his own mortality. It was also the spirit of the thing he did not like. It was against the proper order of the universe. So he was not in a good temper when he reached his home to find James Bull awaiting him.

Young James was forthright.

"So are you suggesting," the rich merchant replied, "that if you marry my only daughter and I die, this would ensure my fortune staying in the family? Your name being Bull, that is."

The honest young man nodded.

"I thought it was a good idea, sir," he said.

"But what," Bull enquired, "if I were to have a son? Or do you not think that likely?"

James looked at him with a faintly puzzled expression.

"Well I shouldn't think it's likely now, sir, is it?" he said.

There had been three occasions, since Tiffany was born, when Bull had thought he might have an heir. His wife, who was often poorly, had always miscarried. But he still secretly hoped for a son, and it was still, in theory, not too late. He looked at the frank young man with no pleasure, therefore, and paused, gazing out over the Thames for nearly a minute before replying.

"I'm grateful to you for bearing me in mind," he said quietly. "And should I need you, I will send for you. Good day."

Some time later, as his family crowded round him to ask how the interview had gone, young James Bull, his honest blue eyes only slightly puzzled, replied:

"I'm not sure. But I think it went rather well."

Geoffrey Ducket liked his master Fleming and the grocery business. Chaucer had persuaded Bull to settle a small amount of money on the boy, which he promised to give him when he had completed his apprenticeship. "Then," Chaucer explained, "Fleming will either let you take over, or you can start up on your own."

It was only recently that the ancient Company of Pepperers, who dealt in spices, had merged with a group of general wholesalers who, since they sold in gross quantities, were known as the "grossers". The new Grocers Guild was large and powerful. They and the Fishmongers vied with the Wool and Cloth Guilds for the city's greatest offices. But of all its many members, few were more modest than John Fleming.

He had a little stall in the West Cheap, by Honey Lane, though he kept his goods in a storehouse behind the George. Every morning he and Ducket would leave Southwark and push their brightly painted handcart across London Bridge. And when the bell of Mary-le-Bow signalled the end of trading, they would return and Ducket would lock their modest takings in a little strongbox he kept under the floor of the store.

Ducket loved the store. Before long he could go round it with his eyes shut and, opening any sack or box, tell by the smell what it contained. There was the sweet smell of nutmeg, the rich aroma of cinnamon. There were saffron and cloves, sage, rosemary, garlic and thyme. There were hazelnuts and walnuts, chestnuts in season, there was salt from the salt beds on the east coast, dried fruit from Kent. And of course, there were the little sacks of black peppercorns, the most valuable commodity in the grocer's trade. "All the way from the Orient, by way of Venice," Fleming would say. "This is the grocer's gold dust, young Geoffrey Ducket. Purest gold." And his eyes would take on a faraway look.

Fleming was scrupulous. He would weigh every item with the utmost care on the little scales he kept on the stall. "I've never been taken to the Pie-Powder court in my life," he would say of the little court where the city authorities dealt with complaints in the market each day. He had never sold short measure by so much as a clove.

Once, soon after Ducket's apprenticeship began, a fellow was found guilty of selling stale fish. He and his master watched as he was led along the Cheap on a horse with two bailiffs carrying a basket of fish behind him. At the end of the Poultry, opposite Cornhill, stood the wooden stocks. A heavy wooden yoke was put across the man's neck and then, as he stood immobilized, they burned the fish under his nose and left him there for an hour before releasing him. "It doesn't seem so terrible, does it?" Ducket remarked. But Fleming gazed at him with his thin, sad face and shook his head.

"Think of the shame," he said. And then, very quietly: "If they'd done that to me, I would have died."

Ducket soon discovered another peculiarity of his master. Though Fleming did not possess any books of his own, and would anyway have struggled with the Latin or French in which they were all written, he had a fascination with all forms of learning and would seek out those who had it and do his best to engage them in conversation. "Time spent with a man of learning is never wasted," he would say earnestly. And if Ducket's godfather Chaucer were mentioned, he would declare: "There's a distinguished man. Go to see him whenever you can."

The George was one of over a dozen inns on the main street of Southwark known as the Borough. It lay on the east side near the Tabard. And though the bishop's brothels were not far away on Bankside, the George, like the other inns, was a respectable house patronized by people coming up to London on business and by pilgrims about to take the ancient Kent road to Rochester and Canterbury. Behind the tavern was a small brewery. Over the main door, as was the custom at most inns, there was a stout pole, seven feet long, on which hung a small bush. Inside was a large hall where, at night, poorer travellers would sleep; around a little courtyard on three floors were chambers for the better off. In the evenings the place was always busy, with trestle tables set up in the hall.

Over the George, Dame Barnikel splendidly presided. In the mornings, she might be seen emerging cheerfully from the little brewery where, like most tavern-keepers, she brewed her own ale. In the evenings she sat by the bar where ale and wine were served. Behind the bar but always within reach was a heavy oak club in case of trouble-makers. On the bar before her, a huge and ancient Toby jug in the shape of an alderman. While she acted as master of ceremonies, Amy helped serve the guests; but Dame Barnikel never allowed Fleming to do anything. "He has his business and I have mine," she would explain.

But Dame Barnikel was happiest of all when she was brewing ale, and sometimes she would let young Ducket watch her. Having bought the malt – "it's dried barley," she explained – from the quays, she would mill it up in the little brewhouse loft. The crushed malt would fall into a great vat which she topped up with water from a huge copper kettle. After germinating, this brew was cooled in troughs, before being poured into another vat.

And now the real miracle began, as Dame Barnikel approached with a wooden bucket of yeast. "God-is-Good, we call it," she explained. For the yeast caused fermentation, producing froth and – this was the miracle – more yeast. "We sell it to the bakers," she said, "whenever we brew." And often the apprentice would see her, growling contentedly to herself as she breathed the thick, rich aroma from the frothing vat and spooned the yeast in, murmuring: "Manna from heaven. God-is-Good." Dame Barnikel's rich barley ale was renowned.

As for his master's daughter, he liked the quiet girl, but for the first two years he was in the household they had not spent much time together. He, after all, was a humble apprentice and she a shy, eleven-year-old girl. In the last year however, since Carpenter had come into her life and she had gained self-confidence, their relationship had grown into an easy friendship; and the three of them would often walk out to Clapham or Battersea together, or go swimming in the river on a warm summer afternoon. And if recently he had noticed that she was really not bad-looking, he had not troubled to think much about it.

It was on a pleasant day, shortly after the Parliament had ended, that he accompanied Amy and Carpenter on an excursion, to Finsbury Fields, a pleasant stretch of drained ground just outside the city's northern wall, where the Londoners practised archery.

Although the first, rudimentary firearms had just begun to be seen, English weaponry still meant the massed longbows, made of best English yew wood, which had wrought such devastation at Crécy and Poitiers. The Londoners had a formidable contingent of bowmen, of whom Carpenter hoped to be one. Ducket watched with interest therefore, as Carpenter took up his position, bow in hand, arm extended, back straight and waited eagerly for him to loose the first arrow.

But nothing happened. The stocky fellow just stood there, perfectly still. When Ducket asked, "Aren't you going to shoot?", he only answered: "Later." And after a further pause, seeing Ducket puzzled, he said quietly: "Pull my arm."

With a shrug, Ducket did so. But to his surprise, the arm remained rigid. He pulled again: still nothing. And, strong though he was, the boy found that short of knocking him down, he was utterly unable to break the bowman's position.

"How do you do that?" he asked.

"Practice," Carpenter replied. "And patience." And when Ducket asked how long he could stand like that, he said: "An hour."

"You try," Amy suggested. But after a couple of minutes Ducket began to fidget, and soon he could stand it no more. "I'm off," he said. When he looked back, Carpenter was still there, perfectly still, with Amy sitting on the ground, watching him admiringly.

He was rather surprised, returning to the George, to find Dame Barnikel, arms impressively folded, waiting for him. "I want to talk to you," she began. She fixed him with a baleful look. "How do you think young fellows like you get a start in life?"

"Hard work," he suggested, but this elicited only a snort.

"Time you grew up. They marry the master's daughter, of course. Bed," she suddenly roared. "That's where it all gets done. Get in the right bed and you're set up for life." Even now, Ducket was not sure what she meant, but her next words left him in no doubt. "Do you really think I'm going to pass all this," she waved at the George, "to that moon-faced little Carpenter? Do you think I want him to marry my daughter?"

"I think she likes him," he offered.

"Never you mind. You just get in there," she ordered. "You take that girl from him. Don't you take no for an answer, if you know what's good for you." And she stomped off, leaving Ducket uncertain what he should do next.

If there was one matter about which Bull felt he could congratulate himself, it was the upbringing of his daughter. With her fluffy hair and her soft but bright eyes, Tiffany was such a pretty little thing that she almost compensated for his lack of a son.

Tiffany was eleven when she was told it was time to think of a husband. It happened on her father's birthday, one sunny afternoon in June. It was the first time she had been dressed as a grown-up.

Her mother, who had looked rather tired of late, had brightened as she took this business in hand. First she slipped a silk undergown over the girl's head; this had close-fitting sleeves with silk-covered buttons all the way from elbow to wrist. On top went an embroidered gown of blue and gold that brushed the floor. Then, despite her protests, she parted Tiffany's dark hair in the middle, pulled it very tight, made two plaits which she then wound and pinned into circles over her ears. "And now you look like a young woman," she said with pride. The effect was simple and charming. And though Tiffany had no breasts to speak of yet, and was quite small, as she saw the effect in her mother's little silver hand-mirror, she smiled with pleasure. The outer gowns had slits like pockets at the hips, and as she slipped her small hands into these, between the soft silks, it made her feel deliciously feminine.

A large company had gathered at the house. There were several prominent mercers. Young Whittington had come. At Tiffany's request, Ducket too, neatly dressed in a clean, simple linen shirt, had also been invited. Chaucer could not be there since he had an appointment at court, but he had come by in the morning with a present that had given Bull huge delight.

There was also one other couple, whom she had never seen

before: a young man and a nun. The nun, she learned, was named Sister Olive and came from the convent of St Helen's, a small but fashionable religious house just inside the city's northern wall, where rich families often placed their unmarried daughters. Sister Olive had a pale face and a long nose; when she smiled, it was with becoming piety; her large, soft eyes were modestly downcast. Her companion was her cousin, a pale, long-nosed and serious young man called Benedict Silversleeves. Both, it seemed, were distant kinsfolk of Tiffany's mother. The girl found them rather intriguing.

If at first she felt a little shy in her adult dress, she was soon put at ease. Whittington came over and made much of her; Ducket gazed with a frank admiration that greatly pleased her. Several of the merchants and their wives came to talk to her. She was rather flattered too when Sister Olive came across the room, raised her brown eyes, composed her mouth into a demure smile and told her that the dress was very becoming. "But you must talk to my cousin Benedict," the nun then said. And before the girl knew what was happening, she found herself being gently led across the room. It made her blush for a moment, for she had never spoken to a strange young man before, in these new, adult circumstances. More unnerving still, it seemed he was important. An old London family, a student of law, destined to go far: the nun had imparted all this information before they even reached him. "And of course," she added quietly, "he is pious."

She was relieved, therefore, when the young man made himself pleasant. His expression towards her was grave, but very courteous. He spoke of the latest city affairs, of the rapidly deteriorating health of the old king, of things she would know about, asked her opinion and seemed to value it. She felt flattered and grown-up. She decided, looking at him, that, if his nose was long, it gave him a certain solemn distinction; his dark eyes were intelligent, if a little mysterious. His tunic and hose were black and of the very best Flemish cloth. She did not quite know if she liked him, but she had to admit that his manner, if a little formal, was faultless. After a while, he politely excused himself and went over to talk to her mother about the merits of certain shrines.

But the highlight of the party, which Bull soon called them to inspect, stood on the table in the centre of the room. This was the present he had been given that morning. "And trust clever Chaucer," Bull cried in delight, "to think of such a thing." Indeed Tiffany had never even seen such an article before.

It was a curious object. The main component was a circular brass plate, about fifteen inches in diameter, with a hole in the middle through which there was a pin. On the edge of the plate, at the top, was a ring so that the plate could be held up or hung, and on the back was a sighting device by which the user could measure the angle of objects in the heavens. There were also a number of discs that could be fitted into place over the pin on the front side. Both sides were covered with lines, calibration marks, numbers and letters which, to Tiffany, looked like so many signs of magic.

"It's an astrolabe, and its object," Bull proudly explained, "is to read the sky at night." He began to show them how it worked. But after a minute or two, while his listeners tried to follow, he too began to become confused by the intricate lines and after a while, shaking his head with a laugh, he confessed: "I'll have to take lessons, I'm afraid. Can any of you do better?"

Benedict Silversleeves stepped forward. He spoke in a quiet, rather dry voice, but so simply and clearly that even Tiffany found that she could follow every word. He explained how, depending upon where you stood on the surface of the Earth, and upon the time of year, you would see a different segment of the heavenly spheres above.

"And the astrolabe, which was known to Ptolemy in ancient times," he said, "is like a moving map."

He showed easily how, by taking sightings and reading the marks on the astrolabe, you could select which of the discs should be fitted over the pin on to the front plate, and how each disc carried a diagram of the constellations as seen at a different latitude and season. He even showed how, using the astrolabe, you could not only identify the stars above but follow the sun and the planets through their courses. Dry though his delivery was, it seemed to the girl that she could almost hear the geometric music of the spheres.

"And so," he concluded, with quiet propriety, "by this little brass disc, and some mathematics, we may discern the still greater motion of the *Primum Mobile*, and the hand of God Himself."

The whole company applauded. Even Bull, though he had not at first much liked the look of the young lawyer, could not fail to be impressed by such luminous intelligence, and later, when the party broke up, he invited him to call again.

That evening, after the company had gone, he was still in an expansive mood when he turned to Tiffany and remarked: "I've been wondering, Tiffany, to whom we should marry you."

In fact, he had already thought about it many times. "In an ideal world," he had told his wife, "I'd have been happy to see her marry one of Chaucer's children. But as he's only just started a family, that's no good." He had dropped broad hints to young Whittington, but the rumour was, alas, that the young man had another prospect in mind. Socially, he would have been glad of a knight. "But not a fool."

Now, gazing affectionately at his docile wife and obedient daughter and, without thinking about what he was saying, Gilbert Bull expansively remarked:

"I want you to think about it Tiffany, but I shall never force you. The choice will be yours. You may marry whomever you wish."

It was not a concession many fathers in his position would have given. Though, so impressed had he been by the performance with the astrolabe that he could not resist adding casually: "You might do worse, I dare say, than consider young Silversleeves."

Not everyone was so impressed. As the guests made their way out on to London Bridge, that evening, Whittington turned to Ducket, and pointed at the lawyer who was walking a little way in front of them.

"I hate that fellow," he remarked.

"Why?" asked Ducket, who had felt, rather humbly, that the clever young man belonged in a different world from his own.

"I've no idea," Whittington snorted. "But he's no good." At the end of the bridge, as Silversleeves turned left towards St Paul's, he hissed in a whisper the lawyer could not fail to hear. "Why doesn't someone clear up St Lawrence Silversleeves? It stinks." Benedict Silversleeves, however, did not turn to look at them. "Humbug," Whittington muttered.

If the thought of her future husband occupied Tiffany's thoughts, she was not sure quite what to do about it. In the coming months she and her girl friends would sit in the big window overlooking the waters of the Thames that rushed under the bridge, and discuss the merits of all the men they knew. One boy they all wanted to marry.

Shortly after Bull's birthday, Edward III had finally died, and the Black Prince's ten-year-old son Richard was proclaimed king; with his uncle John of Gaunt as his loyal guardian.

"He's the same age as us," the girls all said. Young Richard was undeniably handsome. His features were clear-cut; his bearing, even at such a young age, was gracious. If he was opinionated, only those closest to him knew it. "And his eyes," one girl said with a rapturous sigh, "look sad." They had all seen him. But how to meet him?

Kings did not marry merchants' daughters however, even if they had a fine house on London Bridge. "Perhaps your father will find you someone you like," Tiffany's mother said soothingly. But though Tiffany did not object, she remembered his promise. "He said I could choose," she said meekly.

Ever since he had joined Fleming, Ducket had kept his word to Tiffany and called to see her every week. Sometimes they would sit in the kitchen with the cook, but if the weather was fine they would go out. One bright October day that year, they went to see Chaucer.

Ducket had seen more of his godfather recently for Chaucer had a new position nowadays, that kept him in London. He was Comptroller of Wool Customs.

The London Customs House was a huge, barn-like building that stood on the wharf between Billingsgate and the Tower. The royal regulations that covered all wool exports insisted that they only pass through certain ports – this was the great Staple organization of England. And the Staple port of London was one of the greatest. On any day, hundreds of sacks of wool would arrive there to be checked, weighed and paid for. And only when duty had been paid would they be tagged and stamped with the royal seal, supervised by

Chaucer himself before being loaded and allowed to proceed downstream. Ducket enjoyed visiting Chaucer here, watching the men hauling the sacks to the weigh-beam, as the wool-fluff, which always covered the great wooden floor, constantly stirred. Chaucer would show him the endless sheets of parchment on which he and his clerks kept the records – "just like the Exchequer," he explained – and the strongboxes where the money was kept. Once, soon after he had seen the astrolabe at Bull's, and asked his godfather – "What exactly is this *Primum Mobile* that makes the universe turn?" – Chaucer had laughed and answered: "Wool." For despite the increase in clothmaking, the mainstay of England's economy, on which, ultimately, all the trades of London depended, was still the vast export of raw wool to the Continent of Europe.

On this occasion however, they found the customs man just as he was leaving for his home, and so they went back there with him. Chaucer's lodgings, which came with the customs position, were delightful. They stood beside the Aldgate entrance to the city in the eastern wall, a few hundred yards from the Tower, and they included a large and handsome room over the gate itself, with a splendid view towards open fields down the straight old Roman road towards East Anglia. There they found his pleasant, dark-haired wife busy with a baby, and Chaucer led them to the big rooms upstairs.

The room was certainly pleasant, and yet, as Tiffany whispered to the boy with a nudge: "What a mess." There were several dozen books – a large collection by any standards – piled here and there on tables. Some were bound in leather, others not, some written in handsome calligraphy, others in hands so crabbed it made one's eyes swim to read them. But it was not the books that were so untidy, but the pieces of parchment. There were sheets everywhere, in stacks or singly, some neatly copied but most half-written and covered with corrections.

"This is my retreat," Chaucer smiled apologetically. "Here I read and write every evening."

Tiffany knew about his literary activities from her father, and thinking of her own schooling she asked: "How many lines can you write in an evening?"

"I throw so much away," he confessed. "Sometimes I can hardly get a line out."

"So I don't think," Tiffany said to Ducket afterwards, "he can be very good at it."

It was after they left Chaucer and walked along the old road outside Aldgate for a little way that Tiffany, who had allowed herself to start musing about her husband, suddenly turned to Ducket.

"Do you know," she remarked, "I've never been kissed. I suppose you know how." He did. "Do it, then," she said.

Ducket found Benedict Silversleeves waiting for him on his way home at the southern end of London Bridge. Whatever Whittington might think, to him the young lawyer was impressive.

Silversleeves could not have been more polite. He spoke quietly and with dignity. He happened to be walking out of the Aldgate that afternoon, he explained. "So I think you know what I saw."

Ducket blushed. He hoped, the lawyer went on, that the apprentice would forgive him, but he hoped, equally, that Ducket was not trying to take advantage of a young girl from a very different station in life – "and who is, you see, my kinswoman." What could he say? That she asked him to? Any apprentice would have thought that was low. "You may feel it's none of my business," Silversleeves continued, "but I think it is."

No, Ducket could not fault the man. Silversleeves was acting properly and he felt ashamed.

"Well, there we are," the lawyer said. "Goodnight." And perhaps, Ducket thought, he'd better not see little Tiffany for a while.

More than a year had passed since his interview with his rich cousin, but James Bull was not discouraged. "The girl's still young," he told his family; and he still hoped to receive, at least, an invitation to the merchant's house some day. His mind had been on just this subject – and on the beef pie his family was to eat that day – when, entering the city through Ludgate on a wet November afternoon, his attention was caught by a pretty young girl, carrying a basket and hurrying home. It was Tiffany.

Having seen her, he hesitated for only a moment. For after all, he told himself, she cannot mind as long as I am honest. With a clear brow, therefore, he strode forward and placed himself in her path. It was just starting to rain.

"I'm your cousin James," he informed her. "I expect your father has told you about me."

Tiffany frowned. She knew she had many relations and did not want to seem rude. On the other hand, she had never heard of him.

"What would he have told me?" she asked cautiously.

James looked down at her, uncertain how to proceed; but since his rule was to be truthful, he blurted out:

"I think the idea was that I should marry you." And wanting to seem encouraging: "I told him I'd be interested."

"But I don't know you," she protested; and, realizing that this, in her world, was not a sufficient objection she explained: "You see, my father has said I can marry whom I like."

"You mean," he asked in amazement, "he said you could choose your own husband?" Could the rich merchant really have said such an eccentric thing? "Are you sure?"

"Yes."

"I suppose," he said with a frown, "that puts me at a bit of a disadvantage."

"I might get to like you," she suggested.

"Perhaps." But he looked doubtful.

"You should never give up," she smiled.

"Really?" He continued to gaze at her as the rain started to fall rather insistently. "Better go," he said, and moved off.

James Bull went out and got drunk that night. It was not a thing he had done before. He wandered down to Southwark, entered the George, for no particular reason, and sat alone drinking ale. He did not attract the interest of Fleming, since he did not look like a learned man, but halfway through the evening Dame Barnikel came and sat with him for a while. "You look down in the mouth," she said, and asked him what was the trouble.

"Never you mind," she told him. "A handsome fellow like you will find a girl."

"Sometimes," he confessed, "I think I'm a bit simple. Being honest, I mean." She told him not to worry and gave him another jug of ale. But later in the evening she came and sat down again beside him.

"Do you see that man over there?" she muttered, and indicated a tallish, swarthy man in the far corner, who had a woman each side of him, and who smacked his lips when he drank. "He always gets the women. But do you know what he does? He's a highwayman. Robs pilgrims, they say, on their way through Kent. And do you know where he'll be in five years' time? Swinging on a gallows, I can promise you. So you just stay honest the way you are. You'll be all right." And she gave his shoulder a friendly pat.

As he went to sleep, very drunk, that night, James Bull saw, with a measure of contentment, the swarthy highwayman swinging, while he watched with a girl on his arm: Tiffany, he supposed. The thought gave him courage enough to mutter in his sleep: "I'll show them."

If James Bull had been discouraged, for Tiffany, soaked though she was by the time she got home, the interview had been an agreeable revelation. This business of being sought in marriage, she realized, might be rather enjoyable. And when at Christmas her father asked her if she had any thoughts about the matter, she begged him, with every show of meekness, if she might have a few years more to consider: to which he agreed easily enough. "After all," he remarked to his wife that night, "with my fortune, I dare say we could find her a husband even if she were fifteen." And there, for the time being, the matter rested.

1378

While the threat of further war with France, now aided by Scotland, continued to perturb the young king's council, the latest development was even more infuriating: French pirates were freely attacking English merchant vessels and the council seemed impotent. The king's uncle, John of Gaunt, proud if well-meaning, had led an expedition to the French coastal region, but got nowhere and came home looking a fool. Yet no sooner was he back than a mere London merchant, an enterprising fellow called Philpot, of the Grocers company, had equipped a small flotilla at his own expense, routed the pirates, and sailed back in triumph to the city.

"Our own guild," Fleming cried to Ducket in triumph. "He should be made mayor." And from that day Fleming would say proudly to his apprentice: "Gaunt is royal; but Philpot is the better man."

But after this triumph, there was a setback. One night, another royal uncle, Gaunt's youngest brother, had been attacked with his companions by a gang of ruffians near the city. The prince decided it was a plot by the Londoners, and nothing the mayor and aldermen could say would convince him otherwise. Their failure to admit guilt or bring anyone to trial infuriated him.

"The royal princes have been insulted," he claimed. And John of Gaunt agreed. "It's time," the princes decided, "to teach those impertinent Londoners a lesson."

Kings had threatened the Londoners with troops before, and levied fines, and even redirected trade to weaken powerful merchants; but the tactic used by the royal uncles to teach the city respect was new.

It began on a bright morning, shortly before winter set in. Ducket and Fleming had just set up the stall when a group of horsemen came jingling along the Cheap. One of them drew his sword and knocked a great earthenware bowl of stewed fruit to the ground, where it broke. Instead of apologizing, his companions merely laughed and rode on. A moment after this strange display, a large cart laden with equipment lumbered after them. Only a few minutes later, as Whittington hurried by, did they learn what this meant.

"Didn't you know? The princes decided last night. They're going to withdraw from the city."

Within an hour a stream of people started to emerge from the city: knights and men-at-arms, grooms leading strings of horses, servants driving wagons piled with household effects. A cortège of elegant ladies, accompanied by squires, drifted past, and headed towards Ludgate.

"They mean to ruin us," Fleming cried in despair. It was true. With their vast landholdings and their huge retinues, half the wealth of England flowed through the hands of the princes. And into the hands of every tradesman in London.

In the days and weeks that followed, the full extent of the crisis became plain. The West Cheap was half empty. "All the grocers are hit," Fleming reported, "and the fishmongers and butchers even more." But it was not until shortly before Christmas that the Londoners decided what to do. "They're going to bribe the royals to come back," Whittington told Ducket, and when the boy looked baffled, he explained: "A huge present from the city. All the big men are contributing. Bull's giving four pounds." Even a rising young mercer like Whittington himself was going to contribute five marks. "It's called buying your customers," he said wryly.

Ducket pleased his master Fleming well enough, but he knew that as far as Dame Barnikel was concerned, his performance was less satisfactory. He had not succeeded in winning Amy's heart, nor did he think he would. Not that he had tried very hard. Either she likes me, or she doesn't, he thought. If he made advances and they were unwelcome, it would make relationships in the household impossible.

Soon after Christmas, Carpenter and Amy went to see her parents. The proposal they made was simple enough. They wished to be betrothed; but since, at thirteen, Amy was not yet a woman and the solemn young craftsman was anxious to establish himself as a master of his trade before entering what he called "the dangerous state of matrimony", he had asked Amy to wait for three years before the marriage should take place. "But perhaps you think that's too much to ask," he had suggested to her parents. "No, no. Not at all," Dame Barnikel had hastily assured him. "You can't be too careful." And if she had not seen Amy glaring at her, she might have advised him to make it five. While to Fleming, later, she growled: "Please God she'll grow out of him by then."

Fleming himself was quite content with the arrangement, and Amy clung to it with silent determination, as if the carpenter were a raft in a stormy sea. To her the issue was settled.

But not, it seemed to Dame Barnikel. A little later, coming home early one day, Ducket had just wheeled the cart into the yard at the George when he saw Dame Barnikel hovering by the door. As soon as he did so, he cursed his stupidity. He had forgotten. It was the time of the month when she got drunk.

Dame Barnikel's red hair was loose; with bloodshot eyes she was staring at her daughter like a beast about to eat its prey. The girl quailed before her.

What Dame Barnikel had been saying, Ducket never discovered, but as soon as she caught sight of him, she turned with a strange half-smile. "You're just the man we need," she cried. And before he knew what was happening, Ducket found his arm in a powerful grip. "You too," she muttered and, seizing her daughter as well, began to haul them towards the storehouse. Taking no notice of their protests, she opened the door and shoved her daughter inside. Then she began to push Ducket as well, and though he was certainly stronger than most young fellows his size, he found that against Dame Barnikel he was completely helpless. She picked him up and tossed him into the store as easily as if he were a child. "Time you two got to know one another," she growled. A moment later the door was banged shut, and bolted, and they heard Dame Barnikel departing.

It was cold in the store. They both sat in silence for a time. Finally, it was Amy who spoke.

"She wants me to marry you."

"I know," he said. For some minutes more, neither said anything.

"Do you think Ben Carpenter's mad?" she asked at last.

"No." He waited a while. "Are you cold?" She did not reply, but he moved closer and, putting his arm round her, discovered she was shivering. And there, for another hour, they sat together in silence until Fleming discovered them and let them out.

The mystery began a few days afterwards.

Fleming had seemed rather low of late. With business in the market so meagre, Ducket had several times noticed him drifting into fits of abstraction at the stall; and if he could not find anyone to talk to in the evenings, he would sit by the fire with his head bowed, looking so sad that Ducket informed him: "You look as if you're waiting for bad news on the Day of Judgment."

Ducket was glad, therefore, one evening when Fleming

seemed about to slip into one of these moods, to see an unexpected figure appear in the tavern. It was Benedict Silversleeves, well wrapped in a large black cloak, who had just returned up the cold road from Rochester.

Though he was rather in awe of the young lawyer, and though the last time they had spoken had been when Silversleeves rebuked him for kissing Tiffany, Ducket did not hesitate now. Fleming was depressed; Silversleeves was exactly the sort of educated man his master liked to talk to. He went across the room, introduced himself, and invited Silversleeves to join his master by the fire.

The lawyer could not have been more obliging. If he remembered Ducket's crime, he gave no sign of it. With a goblet of mulled wine in his hand, he went over to the little grocer, and in no time at all the two men were so deep in conversation about abstruse matters that Ducket was able to slip away without even being noticed. Several times, however, when he glanced over at Fleming, he saw upon his master's thin face a look of delight which told him that, tonight at least, the grocer had truly found a man of education.

He did not know what hour it was when he was awoken by the noise. It was nothing much: just the sound of a door being scraped open. A door that should not be opened. He sat up with a start.

Moments later Ducket was out in the yard, moving silently towards the store. The door was ajar and there was light coming from inside. He crept closer, wishing that he had a weapon. Cautiously he looked in.

It was Fleming.

He had not spoken to his master after Silversleeves had left. He had seen him talking to one or two other people, and he had appeared perfectly normal; indeed, he had seemed rather cheerful. Once he had seen him go out with a tall fellow who, Ducket assumed, wanted directions to Bankside. He thought that the grocer had turned in later with the rest of the household. Yet something must have happened. How else could he explain what he saw now?

Fleming was in a trance. He was standing quite alone, facing the door. But although he was staring straight at Ducket, he did not seem to see him. There was a lamp on one of the sacks. Fleming's hands were cupped in front of him, and filled with precious peppercorns. At last he became aware of Ducket and gazed at him with a look of rapt ecstasy, as though he were a visiting angel. Then he spoke.

"Do you know what these are?" he asked.

"Peppercorns," the astonished apprentice replied.

"Yes. They are peppercorns. And are they precious?"

"Of course. Most expensive item we carry."

"Ah." He nodded. Then, slowly but deliberately he opened his hands and let them spill on to the floor. Ducket was horrified. But Fleming only smiled. "Worthless," he said. "Worthless." And as Ducket came forward to start picking them up, he took him by the arm with a confidential urgency.

"But," the grocer now whispered to his apprentice, "what if a man were to discover the secret of the universe? What would peppercorns be then?" Ducket had to confess he did not know. "But I do," said Fleming softly. And then gazing at him in the faint light: "Is my wife a fine woman?" Ducket agreed that she was. "And isn't this a fine place?" With a sweep of his thin hand he indicated the whole of his wife's domain in the surrounding shadows. "It is indeed. And all hers." He shook his head and gave a strange little laugh. "Nothing," he said, apparently addressing the sacks around him. Then, suddenly staring at the boy with a wild look: "Soon, Ducket, you shall see such wonders."

After this, he stood gazing into space with such a vacant expression in his eyes that Ducket hardly liked to interrupt him, and stole back to bed.

The next morning the grocer seemed perfectly normal, and Ducket did not think it was his place to mention the incident to anyone. But he wondered, all the same, what it might mean.

It sometimes puzzled Tiffany, and secretly hurt her, that Ducket so seldom came to see her, despite the promises he had once made. One kiss, she thought, and he almost vanishes. Was it so terrible? Though she was always modest, she had resolved to kiss other men, if only, she thought, to get better at it.

As she neared thirteen, her father had ensured that a succession of men came to the house on London Bridge. Though Whittington, alas, had found a wife, he brought several other young mercers of good family; three aldermen had sons of the right age; there was an Italian vintner, a rich German widower, a Hanseatic merchant, who rolled his eyes and was soon dispatched, and at least a dozen other suitable fellows. There was even a young noble, heir to a huge North Country estate; but though he was handsome, both father and daughter agreed he was too stupid.

Indeed, as the months went by, a new relationship had evolved between Bull and his daughter. Naturally, there were many things she preferred to discuss with her mother; but while she always treated her father with a meek respect, Bull was surprised to find himself sharing confidences with the girl. He had never set much store by the opinion of women before, and certainly not that of a mere girl; yet now, having no other child to dispose of, and having given her so much choice in the matter, he became fascinated by what was passing in her mind. "Do you know what she really thinks of young so-and-so?" he would say to his wife proudly. Each time he brought in a new prospect, he awaited her verdict with curiosity. "When the time finally comes, I'm sure she'll make a good choice, guided by me," he said. Meanwhile, he found himself in no particular hurry to give the girl away. "They're none of them good enough for her," he sometimes declared.

One suitor, however, he continued to look upon with more favour. This was Silversleeves.

The strategy of the young lawyer had been extremely proper. "I must tell you," he had said to Bull, "that though my family is ancient, my fortune is only modest." It was generations since the family had moved from the old Silversleeves house below St Paul's. His widowed mother, who had died recently, had only inhabited a tenement in Paternoster Row, just west of the cathedral. "But," the young man confessed, "I am ambitious." As they both knew, in the last decades, the study and profession of law in London had started to rival the Church as a path of power. Many young men nowadays, preferring to marry honestly rather than take vows of celibacy, were following this route, and there were lawyers now side by side with bishops in the highest offices. "Your daughter is adorable," he would say to Tiffany's mother. "Should I ever find favour in her eyes, I should strive night and day to make her happy."

But wisely he also confided to Bull: "I admire your generosity, sir, in allowing your daughter to choose. But between ourselves, if I could not earn your blessing, I should not feel comfortable in trying to recommend myself to Tiffany." To Bull's wife, every few weeks, he brought a thoughtful gift.

To Tiffany herself, he was an agreeable friend, but it was natural that the girl should admire him. His fortune might not, as he said, be large, but he was always dressed in the finest cloth, and he had a fine horse. He could talk about any subject. He could be amusing. And when he spoke about the affairs of the day with her father, she could see that Bull respected his opinion.

"He's certainly the most intelligent of all the men I've met," she told her mother one day.

"And?"

"I don't know. I think I'm too young," she replied.

Tiffany hardly knew how to put it herself. Something, perhaps, was missing. When she read the romances of knights dying for the love of their ladies, she experienced a strange sense of excitement: yet she hardly knew whether this sensation belonged to adulthood or was merely childish. Once, speaking of a romance she had read, she asked her mother: "Do such men really exist?"

"Well," her mother paused before replying. "Have you ever met such a man?"

"No."

"You mustn't be too disappointed, then," the older woman said, "if you never do."

"Then," Tiffany decided, "I don't want to marry until I'm at least fifteen."

As Ducket considered his life, in the early spring of 1379, one thing concerned him: he was seventeen, but he had never had a woman.

He had kissed, to be sure. When it came to wrestling or boxing, he had proved his manhood to his fellow apprentices many times. But when, as they sometimes did, his friends went off to the stews on Bankside, he always made some excuse and left them to it. This was not because he was timid; but the seediness of the place and the risk of disease offended him. Sometimes, as he was healthy and well made, he thought he had noticed women glance at him appraisingly; but he was not quite sure how to approach them.

He could not confide this problem in Fleming, Bull, or even his worldly godfather Chaucer. But one day at the start of April, after they had chanced to meet in the Cheap, he asked the advice of Whittington, who remarked: "I might be able to help you there. Give me a week or two."

With some excitement, therefore, ten days later, the boy met his friend at a tavern, down behind St Mary-le-Bow. But when he entered the crowded tavern, Whittington met him with a long face. "A delay," he murmured apologetically. "I've been trapped. You'll have to help me make polite conversation for a while until this person leaves. Then we'll see what we can do." And to his chagrin, as Whittington led him to a table, Ducket saw that the cause of the delay was none other than Silversleeves' cousin, the long-nosed nun from St Helen's, whom he had once seen at the house on London Bridge. "For God's sake not a word about what I'm up to," Whittington whispered.

Ducket found it hard to concentrate. More than once he surreptitiously glanced around to see if he could spot the woman who, he hoped, he was there to meet, but without success. Meanwhile, for the nun's benefit, Whittington was putting on a display of serious good manners that almost suggested he was on the way to Mass. For her part, Sister Olive asked the boy about himself and something in her smile seemed to indicate approval.

Shortly afterwards she indicated that she wished to leave. Whittington politely escorted her to the door and accompanied her outside. He was gone for a few minutes, presumably taking her up to the West Cheap, and then he returned and sat down. "Sorry about the interruption," he apologized. Then, with a grin, he turned to Ducket.

"And now, my friend, to other matters. Are you ready for your woman?"

At the doorway, Ducket took his arm: "You're sure . . ." he began.

"She's clean. I promise."

"Have I seen her?"

"I saw you looking around for her," Whittington laughed. "But she had a good look at you. She likes you." And he led him into the courtyard outside. There was a small wooden staircase there which led up to a chamber overlooking the little walled orchard. A faint light came from under the door. "Up there, young Ducket," said Whittington. "The gates to Paradise!" And without another word he strode up the alley.

So this was it. Would he know what to do? Would his manhood fail him? His heart was thumping as he made his way slowly up the stairs, and opened the door to the chamber.

The room was pleasant. There was a thick rush mat on the floor. On the right stood an oak chest, glowing in the soft light from the lamp that rested upon it. On the left, the window shutters were closed. In the middle of the chamber was a four-poster bed piled high with mattress and covers.

And upon the bed, quite naked, with her dark hair now down to her shoulders, lay the slim, pale form of Sister Olive.

It was Whittington who told Bull. In fact he told several people. He could not resist it, not because he meant any harm to Sister Olive but just to annoy her cousin Silversleeves.

Bull was furious. "That nun should be thrown out of her convent," he cried. "As for Ducket, I'll have him put in the stocks." And it was only Chaucer, visiting later that day, who calmed him down.

"My dear friend," he reminded him, "there are nuns in this city of the deepest devoutness. There are also, at St Helen's, several women who have no vocation for the religious life but who find themselves in a cloister because their families put them there. If Sister Olive is not perfect, she's very discreet; and I shall box Whittington's ears when I see him for giving her away. Be merciful."

"And Ducket?"

Chaucer smiled.

"From what I hear," he said, "I should imagine he had a very nice time."

A few days after this, Silversleeves, passing Ducket in the street, gave him a look that could have killed. Nor did it make it any better when, the next time he called upon Bull, the merchant, biting his lip, remarked: "Always a lot of scurrilous rumours about London, my dear fellow. Never listen to them myself."

The only person in the household with whom the matter

was not discussed was little Tiffany. For a day she could not discover what the shouts and whispers had been about. Her mother looked vague when she asked; no one else would tell. But at last the cook told her; after which, Tiffany considered the matter alone by herself for some time.

So, she thought: he knows. The thought was strangely exciting.

But that summer Tiffany learned that her childhood friend might have moral flaws of an altogether more serious nature. These might never have been suspected, but for a new development that now took place in England.

When the young king's council, still desperate for money that spring, had gone as usual to the city for help, they had received a rebuff. "We've just paid a fortune to get our royal customers back," the London men pointed out; and the sum they offered the council was quite inadequate. "Other means must be found," the council decided. And so it was that, when the summer Parliament met, a different expedient was hit upon. "It's a poll tax," Silversleeves explained to Tiffany. "The principle's quite simple. Every adult in England – man or woman, noble, free or serf – will have to pay a tax per head."

Simple, certainly; but also revolutionary. For the paying of tax in medieval England had always been the privilege of the free minority in society. The citizen of London paid; his poor apprentice did not. A rich miller in the country, if a free man, would pay tax. But the humble serf, once he had rented the lord of the manor his feudal service and paid a few pence to the Church, was quit.

It was true, at the same time, that traditional life in the countryside was changing. In the last generation, since the Black Death, the old feudal system had been splitting at the seams. There was such disruption, and such a labour shortage, that serfs were hiring themselves out as free labourers and acquiring the tenancies of their own farms without much hindrance. And though the authorities had tried, through the hated Statute of Labourers, to stop this movement and to hold down wages, they had only succeeded in angering the peasantry without stopping the process. The old shackles of serfdom were dissolving; the world of free yeoman farmers and wage labour was beginning. But even if, in a way, the general poll tax was just a recognition of this new reality, such logic has never been a good enough reason for a tax. "It's against custom," was the cry.

There had been a modest attempt at a poll tax two years before, but this was far more ambitious. The richest men in the kingdom would pay large sums. "But even poor peasants will pay several days' wages," Silversleeves explained.

"Do you think there will be trouble?" Tiffany asked him.

"Yes. There could be," he admitted.

The collectors arrived unexpectedly at the George early one summer morning, just as Ducket was loading the handcart. And since the grocer was nominally the head of the household, Ducket was sent to fetch him.

Since their strange night-time encounter, it seemed to Ducket that his master had been less abstracted and rather more cheerful than before. True, he would sometimes look worried at the stall, but that was natural when the trade in the market was still so poor. Only one aspect of his behaviour had changed. In the last few months he had taken to disappearing. It did not happen very often: perhaps once in ten days, and always in the evening. Ducket however, assuming his master was enjoying a solitary walk now the weather was warmer, had not thought much about it. Indeed, as he went to fetch Fleming, the only question on his mind was one of idle curiosity: I wonder if he'll try something on?

The truly remarkable feature of the poll tax was the amount of evasion. It was astonishing. Spinsters, grown-up children, apprentices, servants, mysteriously vanished from households all over the land. Cottages suddenly fell empty. In some areas, with the collusion of local collectors, entire villages simply disappeared. If one believed the returns, it would seem that the Black Death had just struck again. About a third of the population of England was missing.

Would Fleming try to conceal Amy, the boy wondered? It was too late for the grocer to try to hide his apprentice. And how much would they demand? Though the poorest peasants were only assessed a groat – a day or two's pay for most of them – many merchants in London were being charged a whole pound or more. Would Dame Barnikel be assessed as a wife or as an independent trader?

But the one thing he had not expected was that Fleming, looking very pale, should, after much hesitation confess: "I can't pay. I've no money." And when the collectors had laughed and told him to try another story, the shaken grocer had gone to his strongbox in the store and returned with only half a mark. At which point Ducket at least, staring at his master's face, realized that he was speaking the truth. The grocer was destitute.

"But how?" Dame Barnikel was too concerned to be angry. She had paid the poll tax, which had amounted to two marks, and now, in the privacy of their bedchamber, she was gazing at him in puzzlement.

"Trade's been so bad," he mumbled.

"But even so. You had savings, didn't you?"

"Yes," he said absently. "Yes. I thought there was more." He shook his head. "I just need a little time," he muttered.

"Never mind that," she frowned. "Do you mean there should have been more in the strongbox?"

"Yes, of course." He hesitated, shook his head again. "I can't understand it," he said awkwardly.

"Could someone have stolen the money?"

"Oh no. I don't think so." He seemed confused.

"Who knows where you keep the box?"

"No one except you and me. And Ducket." He frowned. "No one stole it."

"Then why isn't there any money?" she demanded. But still the grocer had no answer.

Two days later, Bull took his daughter Tiffany into his confidence.

"I've had Dame Barnikel here," he explained. "She came to ask me if I had ever had any indication that young Ducket might be a thief." He looked at Tiffany seriously. "I know you used to be fond of him, but I want you to search your mind very carefully. Can you think of anything he has ever said or done that might suggest he has these tendencies?"

"No, Father." She thought for a moment. "I really can't."

"Dame Barnikel thinks," Bull went on, "that there's been a theft and that Fleming may be protecting the boy." He pursed his lips. "On no account must you mention this to anyone, especially Ducket. Dame Barnikel's going to keep an eye on him. If he's innocent, there's no need to say anything more. Let's hope he is." He shook his head. "But you never know with a foundling. Bad blood. . . ."

The only other person to whom, after some thought, Bull mentioned this painful subject was Silversleeves. He trusted the young man's discretion; but he also reasoned that, since Ducket had embarrassed the lawyer, Silversleeves might well choose to remember if there were any rumours about the apprentice. But the lawyer, after a few moments' pause, gave an answer that, it seemed to Bull, was greatly to his credit.

"I've no reason to like the fellow, sir," he said. "But I've never heard that said of him. He may be foolhardy, but I think he's honest." He looked at Bull. "Don't you?"

But Bull could only shrug.

"I shall pray for him," said Silversleeves.

It was the spring of 1380 when Amy noticed that Ben Carpenter had something on his mind. At first he seemed unwilling to confide in her, but when he did, she was taken aback. For it seemed that Carpenter was worried about God.

In fact, the solemn craftsman's concern was not so strange; in the last few years, the question of religion had often been on men's lips, not only in the religious houses but in the streets and taverns of London. The cause of this unusual interest, however, was a rather unlikely figure: a quiet, middle-aged scholar of modest attainments at the still infant university of Oxford. His name was John Wyclif.

At first Wyclif's views had not been outrageous. If he complained about corrupt priests, so had all Church reformers for centuries. But gradually he had evolved more dangerous doctrines. "All authority," he pointed out, "comes from God's Grace, not from Man. If evil kings may be deposed by the Church, then why not corrupt bishops and even popes too?" And if this displeased the Church authorities, it only provoked the Oxford scholar to be more extreme. "I cannot even accept," he declared, "that the miracle of the Mass takes place when the hands of the priest are impure."

This was shocking. Yet it was another of his conclusions that really infuriated the Church. "It cannot be right," he decided, "that the scriptures may only be interpreted to the faithful by often sinful priests. Hasn't God the power to speak directly to every man? Why shouldn't the people read the scriptures for themselves?"

This would never do. The Catholic Church had always reserved for its preachers the right to declare the Word of God to their flock. "Besides," it was asserted, "the Bible is in Latin, and therefore beyond the comprehension of ordinary folk." It was to this that Wyclif made his most outrageous response.

"Then I will translate it into English."

It was not surprising that Wyclif was popular with the Londoners. Though Holy Church had dominated the medieval world for centuries, never before had her presence in the city been so pervasive. Dark old St Paul's loomed over everything; there was a church in almost every street, whole areas of the city were given over to the huge walled monasteries, convents and hospitals of the various orders and the fine houses and gardens of abbots and bishops graced the suburbs. Men, most men anyway, believed in God, in heaven and in hellfire. Guilds and individual merchants, more than ever, were endowing chantry chapels in churches, where Masses would be said for their souls. Every spring, the taverns of Southwark saw bands of pilgrims on their way to Becket's shrine at Canterbury.

But the Church was also worldly. It owned a third of England. On any day in the streets, one could see portly Blackfriars, and even Franciscan Greyfriars, who lived too well and preached too little. There were priests who sold pardons; there were scandalous convents. And in recent years, the Church had been split once again, with two rival popes each claiming the other was an impostor, or even an Antichrist. Like any huge and powerful institution, the Church was a natural target for satire. This cheeky fellow Wyclif from Oxford appealed to the Londoners' robust common sense. It was all summed up by Dame Barnikel one evening when she eyed a portly Blackfriar who was drinking in the George and remarked:

"If this fellow Wyclif translates the Bible, Fatty, I'm going to find out what you've been hiding from me."

The Church declared Wyclif a heretic; Oxford censured him. But that was all. John of Gaunt himself, who enjoyed irritating bishops, gave the reformer his protection. And so

Wyclif quietly continued his work, with other scholar friends, preparing an English Bible.

Most Londoners cheerfully agreed with Wyclif, but Carpenter thought about these matters more seriously. In the long hours, when he stood at his archery practice or laboured at his woodwork, the quiet craftsman had been turning everything over in his mind.

"Something bad is going to happen," he warned Amy. "I don't know what it is, but God will probably send a sign."

But he continued to go about his work; he courted her as usual. Whatever storms might be brewing, it seemed to the girl that their own little ship sailed on, sound and steady as usual. At times, she wondered if Carpenter brooded too much, but she knew that she could rely on him.

Young Ducket had continued to lead a carefree life. For some time, unknown to the talkative Whittington, he had enjoyed the favours of Sister Olive. Gaining confidence, he also slept nowadays with several other women in the town. But certain things puzzled him. Though business in the market was better and Fleming seemed more cheerful, he would still disappear from time to time, and on one of these occasions Ducket found him the next morning, his eyes bloodshot and his hand bandaged from a severe burn. "An accident," he had muttered, but declined to say more. Stranger yet was the behaviour of Dame Barnikel. While Amy was friendly enough, her mother seemed to have changed towards him. Her eyes were watchful. She was cold. He had no idea why.

But he did not allow these matters to worry him. If people around him behaved oddly, he accepted it cheerfully. In less than two years, his apprenticeship would end, and then he would have to make serious decisions. Until then, he thought, I might as well enjoy myself.

During the year there had been another disastrous expedition to France. The council chose the Archbishop of Canterbury to be chancellor that year, and that well-meaning but not very wise man, faced with a huge bill, decided with Parliament to levy another poll tax. But this one was to be different. Instead of making a small levy on the poorer folk and a high one on the rich, the archbishop for some reason designed a flat rate tax. The rich would pay proportionately less; the poor, three times as much as they had before – an entire shilling a head.

"We shall actually pay less," Dame Barnikel pointed out to her family, "because we were well enough off to be assessed high last time. But do you realize what this means for the peasant? A shilling for himself. Another for his wife. Say they have a fifteen-year-old daughter still at home. She counts as an adult. Another shilling. Altogether, several weeks' wages. How the devil are they going to find that?" She shook her head. "Bad business."

On a December day, in 1380, when the city was covered with snow and the river rushed silently under London Bridge, Ducket, dressed in thick woollens, was just approaching the small church of St Magnus by the bridge's northern entrance when he saw them coming towards him. They were both wearing rich, fur-trimmed cloaks and fur hats; they were walking side by side, and laughing. Silversleeves and Tiffany were so taken with each other that they did not notice him.

It was some time since he had seen Tiffany. Ever since his conversation with Silversleeves he had kept to his policy and paid her only occasional visits as a reminder of their childhood friendship. "You'll be married long before I am," he had once cheerfully remarked to her.

The long-nosed young man, his face flushed in the cold, looked almost handsome. Tiffany's face was turned up to his, and her eyes were shining with amusement. A moment later, they saw him. There was not a trace of awkwardness in Tiffany's smile, but only kindness; and in Silversleeves's greeting, the comfortable jocularity of a man who, lucky in love, meets another man who cannot possibly be a rival. And wasn't it natural? Wasn't the lawyer a clever young fellow of good family, with a fine future before him – a worthy husband who had every right to this charming girl upon whom Ducket had no claim at all?

Why then, as they passed on, should the apprentice suddenly have felt such violent, astonishing emotion? A flash of warmth, an instant of the most complete and certain knowledge: she was the one.

But it was impossible. He had no right. It was pointless. He could not, he would not, fall in love with Tiffany Bull.

* * *

It was the eve of St Lucy's, the winter solstice, the midnight of the year. A long, deep night, dark as nothingness, in which all manner of things might be concealed: which was as well, for behind these tightly closed shutters was concealed no ordinary mystery, nothing less than the secret of the universe itself.

That the secret of the universe was, at present, within the city's bounds, was due to a minor alteration of geography. For with the passing of time, the city limits had progressed well beyond its ancient walls. At various points along the approach roads, these new boundaries were marked by chains across the road to force the traffic to halt and pay tolls. These gateways were known as the city bars. On the western side there were two: about half a mile out from Ludgate, on the lane now called Fleet Street by the old precincts of the Knights Templar, lay Temple Bar. A similar distance out from Newgate, was Holborn Bar.

It was here, between the Holborn and Temple Bars, that the most learned men in London were gathered together, in the lawyers' quarter. There had been hostels, known as Inns, for lawyers in the vicinity for a long time. But in recent decades, the ever-increasing number of legal men had been flocking to the area like gathering starlings. Already some of their communal lodgings and schools were acquiring permanent names: Gray's Inn, Lincoln's Inn; even the Temple precincts too, their crusading order having been disbanded, were now leased to these sharp-eyed and chattering fellows. Down the centre of this quarter, running from Holborn southwards to Fleet Street, was the narrow thoroughfare known as Chancery Lane. And it was by Chancery Lane, in a small lodging on the upper floor whose windows, had they not been shuttered, would have given out on a tiny, enclosed courtyard, that the secret of the universe, like some subtle legal contract, was being minutely investigated to see what it could yield.

Fleming watched spellbound, his concave face turned towards the glowing coals in the fire, as the dark figure before him went about his work. The Sorcerer wore a black robe on which were sewn, in golden thread, images of the sun, moon and planets. On a table in the centre of the room was a score or so of bowls, jars, phials, beakers and retorts. As the Sorcerer moved about, at one moment he seemed like some strange and dangerous bird, at another like a priest at his devotions; but always his ministrations were awesome and hypnotic.

"You have the mercury?"

Trembling, the grocer handed over a little phial which contained two ounces of the liquid metal.

"That is good." The Sorcerer nodded his approval. Then, very carefully, he measured out one ounce, which he transferred to a small earthenware crucible. "See to the fire," he ordered.

Obediently taking the bellows, Fleming stoked the fire while the other hovered over the table.

With what care the Sorcerer went about his work. From one bowl he took iron filings, from another, quicklime; to these he added saltpetre, tartar, alum; brimstone, burnt bones, and moonwort from a jar. Then a miraculous powder, hugely costly, whose ingredients he would never divulge; and lastly, as though in kindly recognition of his visitor's calling, he ground up one of the precious peppercorns the grocer had brought him the week before, and added that too. For another five minutes, his face half in shadow, he mixed and warmed this magical brew until, finally satisfied, he reverently poured a little of it into a phial and, turning, allowed his eyes solemnly to rest on the concave face of his pupil.

"It is ready," he softly intoned. Little Fleming felt his breath grow short.

"You are sure?" he ventured.

The alchemist nodded.

"It is the Elixir," he whispered.

No wonder Fleming trembled. In the Elixir was the secret of the universe. And now, oh dear heavens, they were going to make gold.

The art or science of alchemy in the medieval world was based upon a very simple principle. Just as the celestial spheres rose in order towards the vault of heaven, just as there were orders of angels from the mere winged messengers to the radiant seraphim who dwelt beside the Godhead, so every element in the natural world was arranged in a divine order, ascending from the grossest to the most pure.

Thus with metals too. The philosophers recognized seven metals, each corresponding with a planet: lead for Saturn, tin for Jupiter; for copper, Venus, for iron, Mars, Mercury and its planet shared a name, silver for the Moon and gold, purest of all, for the effulgent Sun.

But here was the wonderful mystery: with the passing of time, no man knew how long, the warmth of the Earth would gradually refine each of these metals, stage by stage, into a purer form: iron into mercury, mercury into silver until at last, at the very end of time, all should finally have passed into purest gold, their ultimate and perfect state.

"But what," the philosophers asked, "if a way could be found to hasten the process, to sublimate a base metal from its gross condition into its purest golden form?" And so it was not surprising that, just as men sought cures by making pilgrimages to shrines, or knights in stories sought the Holy Grail, so the men of science known as alchemists sought some substance that would cause metals to transform themselves from their base to their purest state. This magical stuff, whatever it might be, must surely contain the secret of the universe. It was known as the Elixir or the Philosophers' Stone.

And Silversleeves had found it.

It was five years since Benedict Silversleeves had become a practitioner of the magic art of alchemy, and Fleming was only one of a number of clients – each of whom believed that he alone shared the secret – who were greatly in awe of him. For he was very good at it. Not only could he astonish even learned men with his knowledge, but he really could transform base metals into precious. At least, all his clients thought he did, for they had seen him do it.

The actual performance of the miracle was very simple; and though he had devised many cunning variants of the trick, Silversleeves always favoured the easiest of all. This was what he did now.

Pouring a few drops of the Elixir into the crucible, he placed the latter on the fire. Watching it earnestly he began to stir it with a long, thin stick. As a special concession, for a moment or two he even allowed the grocer to stir as well. What Fleming did not know was that inside the stick, before he arrived, Silversleeves had inserted granules of purest silver, held in with a little wax filling at the tip of the stick. As the crucible was stirred, the wax melted and the granules of silver ran out. It was a trick that could be performed with any metal.

And so it was, time after time, that his clients had seen iron appear in molten lead, or silver apparently made from iron, tin or mercury. Only one thing they had never seen. The production of gold.

For this was the Sorcerer's cleverness. If he could transform base metal into silver, then surely, one day, he would succeed in achieving that last step, and make gold. Their faith was strong, and their greed was even stronger. Like men drunk with gambling, they came back to him again and again. With money.

"It's not the iron or the mercury," he would explain. "Besides, you can bring that. But it's the powder for making the Elixir. It costs a fortune. For that I need your help." Indeed, he could not make so much as a grain of it for less than five marks.

The Elixir was composed mostly of chalk and dried dung, and so Benedict Silversleeves, until he found preferment in his profession, made a very good living indeed.

Why did he do it? When he informed Bull that his fortune was modest, he had made a huge understatement of his real position: in fact, a downright lie. For by the time his widowed mother died, so shrunken were the family's resources that he was practically penniless.

It did not do for a young man to be penniless. A rich merchant might welcome a younger son of a gentry family into his house: the family's wealth gave the boy some standing, and there was usually some financial help to get him started. He might accept an ambitious fellow from an old London family like Silversleeves, and with good prospects, on the assumption that he had some means behind him. But take that same young man and make him penniless, and he became an adventurer, an object of suspicion and of scorn. And so it was that Silversleeves had invented his modest fortune; his fine horse and rich clothes all paid for by his secret gulling of poor fools like Fleming. He must keep this up, moreover, all through the long and delicate courtship of a wealthy bride. If nothing else, his patience and his nerve were exemplary.

Fleming had been easily caught from the first moment he had begun to converse with this scholarly young man in the

George. Month after month he had bought more of the powder, watched metals sublimate themselves to silver, secretly eroded his savings until he could not even pay the poll tax. And still he had dreamed. For when at last the gold came through, they would live a life of such ease. Why, he could buy the George, the Tabard, every inn from Southwark to Rochester and on to Canterbury too. Dame Barnikel could do as she pleased. He would give her all the furs and gorgeous clothes that she wanted. How she would bless him, love him, even respect him as other wives did their husbands. And Amy should marry a gentleman. Or, if she preferred, Carpenter. What happiness would be theirs. His heart in his thin frame swelled; his concave face glowed. And perhaps, this very night, it would all come to pass.

Most of the charlatans who practised this criminal activity would explain their failure by some defect in the equipment, or in the ingredients supplied. Silversleeves, however, had a more elegant solution.

"The Elixir is perfect," he would say. "You've taken the silver we made and had it tested. You know it's pure. But the final transition to purest gold – that's hard. Even the Elixir must operate with the benefit of the planets and the stars. When all are in the right conjunction, we shall succeed, I promise you." It was for this reason – and the fact that he had decided to buy Tiffany a new hood that afternoon – that as dusk had fallen on that dark day at the midnight of the year, he had sent a fellow to the grocer with an urgent message.

"Mercury is in the ascendant. Come tonight."

The great cataclysm of 1381 took Geoffrey Ducket by surprise. But then very few people in England saw it coming either. The spring of that year had passed rather quietly. If Fleming had seemed subdued, the youth, knowing nothing of his master's addiction to alchemy, thought little of it. He visited Tiffany once or twice, and heard in the Bull household that Silversleeves was seen by the whole family with ever-increasing favour.

True, he heard the stories of discontent in the countryside. The new and outrageous poll tax was causing problems. The peasants were furious; there was widespread evasion, especially in the eastern counties. But this did not affect him much.

In March the poll tax returns were inadequate. And this time, the boy king's council was determined to act. Ducket heard the news one morning. "They're sending the tax collectors back into Kent and East Anglia." Rich and sturdy Kent, close to the capital, shared much of the robust London spirit. But East Anglia, besides its ancient independence, had a particular problem with the poll tax. For whereas in the more feudal counties, most villages had a lord of the manor who might, out of kindness or self-interest, help the poorer peasants with the tax, in East Anglia, with its pattern of small independent homesteads, there were fewer manorial lords and the peasants were hit hard.

During April and May, reports of the collectors' activities came frequently. The city of Norwich had been hit: six hundred furious tax evaders had been found within the walls of this one town. Out in the East Anglian countryside, over twenty thousand had been caught and forced to pay – more than one adult in ten!

At the start of June, the reports became more ominous. "They've killed three tax collectors in Essex." A day later: "There are five thousand peasants on the move. They're sending messengers across to Kent." And sure enough, before sundown the rumour ran along the stalls in the Cheap: "Kent is rising." On the morning of 7 June, Ducket heard a report that the rebels had attacked Rochester Castle. He did not believe it; but seeing Bull in the street later on, he asked him. "True, I'm afraid," the merchant grimly confirmed. "I've just heard that half the peasants from around Bocton have gone down there. They've elected a leader too," he grunted. "Some fellow called Wat Tyler."

England's great Peasant Revolt had begun.

While the men of Essex were massing, and the rest of East Anglia preparing to rise, Wat Tyler led his men swiftly down the old road to Canterbury. The archbishop, whom they blamed for the poll tax, was not there, so they sacked his palace and broke open his prison. Then Tyler turned them round. It was time to go to the boy king.

Besides giving Tyler a chance to organize his men, the march to Canterbury had had one other important effect. At the archbishop's prison they had liberated a preacher named John Ball, who had long been in trouble with the Church for his inflammatory and unorthodox preaching in the country-side. No scholar like Wyclif, who would have abhorred him, he agitated for radical reform of the whole kingdom and to many of Tyler's followers he was a folk hero. With Tyler as general and Ball as prophet, the enterprise was becoming a peasant crusade.

And now London began to tremble, for the twin forces approaching from the east were formidable: from the north side of the Thames Estuary came the men of Essex; up the south side, Tyler's men. Each horde numbered tens of thousands. The boy king and his council joined the frightened archbishop in the safety of the Tower; but they had no troops that could handle such huge numbers of rebels. The arch-bishop, hopelessly out of his depth, begged to resign the chancellorship, and no one else knew what to do.

Ducket and Fleming were just closing the stall on Wednes-day afternoon when the word came. "They've arrived. The Essex men are going to camp at Mile End." This was only two miles outside the Aldgate entrance to the city. "Tyler's at Blackheath." About the same distance on the Thames's southern side. All down the Cheap, the traders were hurrying home, and the grocer did likewise. As they crossed London Bridge they were told: "The mayor's giving orders to raise the drawbridge here tonight." All down Southwark High Street, people were boarding up their houses, and at the George, Dame Barnikel met them with a grim expression. In her hand she was carrying a huge club. They stored the goods, locked up, and barred the gate to the courtyard. It was all they could do. Dame Barnikel, having inspected the premises, nodded her approval.

"Where's that girl?" she asked impatiently. Amy, it seemed, had slipped out somewhere. A few minutes later, however, she reappeared and went quietly indoors, and her mother, after a satisfied grunt, took no more notice of her. But when Ducket entered the kitchen he suddenly felt his arm caught, and pulled, and found himself in a corner, face to face with Amy. He realized that she was unusually pale.

"Help me," she whispered. When he asked what the matter was: "It's Ben," she cried softly. "I can't find him. I'm so afraid he'll get himself hurt."

"I shouldn't worry," he reassured her. "He can't be far. And none of the rebels have entered the city yet," he added. But at this she only shook her head.

"You don't understand," she hissed. "It's the other way round." And seeing him baffled: "I think he's gone to join them. I think he's at Blackheath."

Ducket enjoyed the walk. As it went towards the south-east, the Kent road rose gently from the valley floor up the series of terraces that led to the higher ground, until, at the point where the river completed its big southern loop at the hamlet of Greenwich, it emerged on the sweeping ridge above. Here, on a broad plateau running eastward under open skies, lay the great expanse of heathland known as Blackheath.

He joined a stream of people along the way. Whether they wished to join the rebels all were there out of curiosity, they were coming out from the villages all around: from Clapham and from Battersea behind him, from Bermondsey and Deptford down by the river. Considerable numbers of the Essex men from Mile End had also taken ferries across the river to fraternize with the men from Kent. Yet even so, Blackheath took his breath away.

He had never seen a crowd like this before and could hardly guess their number: fifty thousand, perhaps? The huge, informal camp, bathed in the warm light of the early summer evening, spread across the heath for over a mile. There were a few fires alight, a scattering of tents and some horses and wagons; but most of the folk there were just resting on the ground, having walked sixty miles from Canterbury. They were country folk. Ducket saw broad, sunburned faces, peasant smocks, stout boots. In the June warmth, many wore no leggings. Everywhere there was the rich, pleasant smell of folk who had been working on farms. But most noticeable of all was their temper. He had expected to find a sullen and angry army; yet few of the peasants carried arms, and they seemed cheerful. It's more like a holiday than a battle, he thought.

He was afraid he would never find Carpenter, but after a quarter of an hour he spotted him, talking to some Kentish craftsmen. Hoping the solemn fellow would not mind that he had followed him up there, Ducket went over to him.

Carpenter seemed delighted to see him. He looked more animated than usual. After introducing the apprentice to his friends, he took him by the arm and led him across to a spot from where they could see a figure on horseback, giving directions to some men. "That's Tyler," the craftsman said, and Ducket gazed at the sturdy figure. He was wearing a leather jerkin, with bare arms, and his swarthy face had already assumed a look of command.

When Ducket suggested gently that Amy was concerned about him, and that Dame Barnikel was getting ready to defend the George Inn against the rebel horde when it attacked, Carpenter only laughed. "You don't understand," he said. "These good people," he gestured around him, "are all loyal. They've come to save the kingdom. The king himself," he explained, "is coming to a parley here tomorrow, and once he's heard us, everything will be all right." He smiled. "Isn't it wonderful?"

To Ducket this sounded unlikely, and he might have been tempted to argue, if there had not, just then, been a movement on the southern edge of the gathering. Some men were drawing up an open cart. A whisper seemed to be running through the whole camp; and already people were starting to get up and walk, as if drawn by some unseen hand, towards the cart. "Come on," said Carpenter.

They got a good position, well forward, and did not have to wait long. Only minutes later, Tyler appeared; riding beside him on a grey mare came a tall, large-boned man in a brown cassock who, having dismounted, leaped up on to the cart. Straight away, he raised his hands and, in a deep voice that carried right across the heath, called out:

"John Ball greeteth you well, all." And fifty thousand souls fell silent as a mouse.

The sermon of John Ball was unlike anything that Ducket had ever heard before. The theme was very simple: all men were born equal. If God had meant there to be masters and servants, He would have made it so at the Creation. Unlike Wyclif, who said that all authority must derive from God's Grace, the popular preacher went much further. All lordship was evil; all wealth must be held in common. Until it was so, things would never go well in England.

But what language! Truly this preacher knew how to speak

to the English heart. With rhyme and heavy alliteration he called out the phrases that could be remembered by every hearer. "Pride reigneth in palaces," he cried. "Government is gluttony. Lawyers are lechers." And at each phrase, Ducket could see Carpenter beside him nodding and muttering: "This is true. This is just."

"Why is the lord warm in his manor and poor Peter Ploughman frozen in the field?" Ball demanded. "Now is the time," he cried menacingly, "for John Trueman to chastise Hobbe the Robber. Take courage today. You shall smash them. With right and might. Will and skill." It was the thick, strong, echoing language of their Anglo-Saxon ancestors. Then, returning to that simple biblical theme, he chanted loudly, so that not a man there could fail to hear, that couplet for which his sermons were famous, and which has remained like a haunting cry in the folk sayings of England ever since:

When Adam delved and Eve span
Who was then the gentleman?

As he came to his conclusion with a loud Amen, the crowd let out a mighty roar. And Carpenter, his eyes solemnly shining, turned to Ducket and said: "Didn't I tell you everything would be all right?"

Ducket had hoped to persuade Carpenter to return home after this, but the craftsman would not hear of it. "We must wait for the king," he declared. So, cursing under his breath, Ducket remained to spend the night in the huge camp under the stars. As he moved about the camp, talking with these men from the countryside, he learned much. Many, like Carpenter, meant no harm at all. They had come to help the king set the world to rights. All that was needed, they assured him, was to rid the land of all authority. "Then," they assured him, "men will be free."

To Ducket the idea seemed strange. In London, he knew what freedom meant. It meant the city's ancient privileges, the city walls which protected Londoners from the king's soldiers or foreign traders and craftsmen. It meant that an apprentice could become a journeyman, and perhaps a master. It meant the guilds, the wards, the aldermen and mayor, as fixed in their places as the celestial spheres in the heavens. True, the poor folk might protest about the rich aldermen from time to time, especially if they evaded taxes. But even they knew the need for authority and order: without these, where was London's freedom?

Yet in these countrymen he divined a quite different sense of things: an order not made by Man, but vaguer: the order of the seasons. The order of Man, to them, was not a necessity, as it was to the Londoner, but an imposition. "Who needs a master on the land?" asked one fellow. They dreamed of being free peasant farmers, like the Anglo-Saxons of old.

Ducket noticed something else, too. Asked where they came from, nearly all these peasants spoke of themselves proudly as men of Kent, or Kentish men, as if they were a tribe. Had he been across the Thames with the Essex men, it would have been the same. Angles, Jutes, the various groups of Saxons, Viking Danes and Celts – England like every country in Europe was still a patchwork of old tribal lands. And that evening Ducket began to understand what every wise ruler of England knew, that London was a community, but that the counties, in time of trouble, would always revert to a more ancient order.

If the men from Kent meant no harm to the king, as Carpenter assured him, Ducket was not so sure about their other intentions. When he asked one fellow what he thought of the sermon, the man replied: "He ought to be Archbishop of Canterbury."

"He will be," said his companion grimly, "when we've killed this one."

Ducket mulled over these words as he went to sleep.

The dawn promised another fine day, but Ducket felt hungry and there did not seem to be any food in the camp. He wondered what would happen next. The sun had not been up long, however, when the whole company, on an order from Tyler, began to move over the edge of the heath and down the broad, handsome slope to the Thames at Greenwich. As they did so, Ducket realized that the huge horde of Essex men was gathering across the river opposite them.

They waited an hour. Another passed, and Ducket was [illegible]dy to leave when he saw a large and handsome barge, [illegible]mpanied by four others, being rowed down the stream towards them. It was the boy king. Ducket watched, fascinated, as the barge drew near. It was full of richly dressed men, the great ones of the kingdom, he supposed. But there was no mistaking the tall, slim, flaxen-haired youth who stood at the front for all to see. Richard II of England was fourteen. A few months before, having reached his majority, he had taken the reins of government into his own hands. His council, led by the terrified and hopeless archbishop, had begged him not to go. But the son of the Black Prince had courage. He was a fine figure, Ducket thought, standing there in the morning sunlight.

The roar that greeted him was huge and echoed across the river. The figures in the barge, except for the boy king, looked frightened. The barge was stopped about twenty yards from the bank. Then the young king raised his arm, the crowd hushed, and in a clear voice he called out to them.

"Sirs, I have come. What have you to say to me?" Ducket noticed that he had a slight stammer.

In answer came another roar in which Ducket could make out many cries. "Long live King Richard." "Bless the king." And more ominously: "Give us the archbishop's head." "Where are the traitors?" After a few moments, Ducket saw Tyler order some men to row out to the royal barge with a petition. He saw the king read it. "Tyler's asking for the heads of all the traitors," someone said close by. Then Ducket saw the king shrug, shake his head, and the royal barge turned round.

"Treason," the crowd now roared. "Treason!" as the barge departed. Then came the cry: "Let's march."

English history would have been changed if the men on the bridge had only listened to Bull. Purple in the face, he stood in the middle of London Bridge, watched anxiously from the house by Tiffany, his wife and the servants, and bellowed at the alderman on the horse: "In the name of God, man, do as you were told. Raise the drawbridge."

He was absolutely correct: the mayor's instructions had been explicit. Yet as the huge horde from Kent swept through Southwark, this alderman in charge of the bridge refused his orders. "Leave it down," he said.

Why? Was it treachery, as many later said? The charge made no sense. Fear of the mob if he crossed them? Possibly.

But the day before, three of his fellow aldermen had gone out to Blackheath and reported back that Tyler and his men were loyal and harmless. It seems they had persuaded him and that now he had completely misread the situation.

"Don't provoke them," he said. "Let them through."

"Idiot!" Bull shouted, rushed back to his house and started to bar the door and close every shutter. Minutes later, the house, with the Bull family inside, was engulfed in the moving mass.

Twice Ducket had hoped to stop his friend. As they swept towards the George, he caught sight of Dame Barnikel, standing grimly before the door with a club. He had tried to steer Carpenter towards her, for she could certainly have stopped him; but a sudden surge from behind carried them past. At London Bridge there was a crowd waiting to cross, while others were streaming along the south bank instead, towards Lambeth. "Turn back," he begged. "There's sure to be trouble." But Carpenter refused. "No trouble," he said. "You'll see."

And amazingly, as they crossed into the city, he seemed to be right. Tyler's orders had been strict: no looting. The Londoners were cautious, but friendly. The men from Kent began to wander through the streets and Ducket saw them stop and pay for food and drink as they went by. The main body drifted along the Cheap, past St Paul's and out through Newgate to Smithfield, in whose large space they set up camp. The good temper of the previous day seemed to have returned. By late morning, Ducket left his friend and, curious to see what else was happening, wandered right across the city. At Aldgate, he found the gate open and a steady trickle of Essex men from Mile End coming through. Chaucer was there too, watching them with a wry expression. "I don't know why the gate opened," he said. "They don't seem to be after my books, anyway." And he glanced up at the big room over the gate.

Ducket told him all he had seen and heard. "Could the peasants really take over?" he asked.

"It has been tried in other lands," Chaucer said, "but never successfully." He smiled. "Doesn't it occur to you that Tyler ould make himself king and soon his chief followers would he new lords? As for today," he went on, "there will be le."

"How do you know?" Ducket asked.

"Because these fellows have nothing to do," the poet replied.

He was proved right that afternoon. Ducket had not been back at Smithfield with Carpenter for an hour when he realized the crowd was getting restless. A few started singing. Something else was happening too. Mobs of Londoners had come to join them. Some were just apprentices, there for the fun; but others were of an uglier sort. Soon there were shouts, of anger. And then, whether on Tyler's orders or of its own volition, the whole crowd suddenly gathered itself up and began to stream towards Westminster. Just before Charing Cross, they came to the huge, sprawling palace of the Savoy, the residence of no less a person than John of Gaunt. And now they had a target.

The whole Savoy was blazing. Soon, the huge symbol of feudal privilege by the Thames would be smouldering ashes. The looters – mostly London ruffians – had also been busy, despite Tyler's orders. Ducket had watched in fascination, but also sadness, for it was a fine building; at his side, Carpenter had also watched, with a dazed look on his face, murmuring from time to time: "Yes, it must go. This is what must happen." And, supposing his friend could come to no harm there, standing in the crowd, Ducket had walked a short way towards the Temple, where some of the lawyers' lodgings were being fired, before coming back again to find that Carpenter had vanished. He looked about, could see no sign of him, and then glanced at the Savoy.

What could have possessed him? Who knew? The carpenter's solemn figure was walking into the courtyard as though in a dream. Others, too, were in there, tearing any loot they could carry from the flames; but the craftsman made no such move. As though hypnotized, he was entering one of the buildings, drawn by the flames. Ducket's act of heroism was purely instinctive. He did not stop to think. He ran.

It was bad luck that the building should have collapsed just as he got there. He saw Carpenter fall, leaped in, managed to drag him out and was considerably burned himself in the process. Carpenter had been knocked unconscious. With the help of another fellow Ducket managed to lift him and carry him away.

Half an hour later, Carpenter having come round though still burned and shaken, Ducket left him with the good brothers at St Bartholomew's Hospital, and started off towards the George, to let Amy know what had happened.

James Bull was not a man to give up. True, his rich cousin had never sent for him in the last five years. True also, a year ago, judging her to be old enough to receive such things, he had sent flowers to Tiffany, together with a lumbering poem that had never been acknowledged. But how could he bring himself to the attention of his cousin and earn his approval?

When James Bull saw Tyler's men enter London, he knew exactly what he thought. Most Londoners hated the poll tax. Many sympathized with the men from Kent. Some had gone to join them. But James had no such ideas. They were troublemakers. He did not have to think about troublemakers, he knew, deep in his bones what needed to be done. They must be put down. And in this, indeed, he proved himself to be a true Bull. Keeping his distance, but eyeing them with deep suspicion, he had followed their progress to the Savoy. Now, as he watched, he saw what he could do.

Later, he felt sure he had done his best. He had dragged three would-be looters out of the burning Savoy, and only stopped when the crowd made it plain that if he did it again they would lynch him. Then he had gone off to look for support. Finding none of the city sergeants or anyone else in authority, he hurried back towards Ludgate in the hope of finding some men-at-arms. After all, if he wanted to make a name for himself and impress his cousin on London Bridge, he needed to do something remarkable, and in front of witnesses. As he passed the burning Temple and reached Chancery Lane, he had seen Silversleeves on a fine horse. "Carry me to the Tower. We must get help," he cried, but the lawyer only gave him a silent look and then rode swiftly off, to the west, down a lane that avoided the Savoy by a good half-mile.

So it was an unexpected piece of good luck, just as he [folded corner]hed London Bridge, to see one of the rebels walking [folded corner] There could be no mistaking it: the white patch in his hair; the burned hands. He ran forward, threw himself on the man, and as they went down held him fast, with a cry: "Got you." Yet surely it must have been providence that, as the winded rebel tried to struggle free, James saw, approaching from the bridge, the burly form of his rich cousin, to whom he cried out: "Sir, help me. This fellow was looting the Savoy."

He was rather surprised when the merchant, after asking if he was sure, turned to the rebel as if he knew him and, with a look of thunder declared: "So, Ducket. You shall pay for this."

The hours passed slowly in the kitchen of the house on London Bridge. Bull had ignored Ducket's protests. Though if young James Bull, who had hurried on to the Tower, could have heard the merchant's comments he would have been pleased indeed. "Capital fellow. Grown up sound, I must say. I may have misjudged him when he was younger." Bull's words to the apprentice, however, were bleak: "You'll stay under lock and key until I can hand you over to the proper authorities," he told him. The doors were locked, the windows barred and shuttered. Only one person remained with him, and this was the fat girl. "You watch him," Bull said. "If he tries anything, raise the alarm."

From time to time, Ducket would look at the fat girl. At one point, having nothing better to do, he tried to explain to her how Amy had sent him after Carpenter, the things he had heard and seen, and lastly how, far from looting, he had rescued Carpenter from the flames. "So you see," he concluded, "I'm not guilty of anything at all." But the fat girl continued placidly eating and said nothing.

This regime lasted all the next day. The cook was briefly in the kitchen in the morning. She spoke little but told him the king was going to Mile End. Then the house was quiet for some hours. But later Ducket heard the sound of a great crowd approaching. From the clamour, it seemed something was happening close by. Next came a huge roar. Then the sound of a crowd departing. An hour later the cook appeared again. "They got into the Tower and killed the archbishop," she said. "They've stuck his head on a spike in the middle of the bridge."

That evening, Bull himself appeared. He looked at Ducket with disgust. "Your friends have been successful," he said drily. "The king has granted charters abolishing serfdom. In return, they have not only murdered the archbishop, but they are roaming the streets setting fire to houses and killing anyone they don't like the look of. About two hundred innocent people so far. I thought you'd be pleased." Then he banged the door furiously and locked it.

The following morning was Saturday. The early hours passed quietly. Then, in mid-morning, he heard people running in the street. There were cries, but not like yesterday's. People being called by name. He heard someone at Bull's door. Hurried conversations. After a while, the voices died away. Two hours passed. More cries. Cheers. People in the street laughing. A horse clattering up to the door. Someone entering the house with, it seemed to him, a heavy tread. And then, half an hour later, the kitchen door opened and Bull appeared.

"It seems," he said calmly, "that the king has pardoned you."

James Bull saw it all.

At the Tower, after capturing Ducket, James had not found anyone ready to go to the Savoy; but his eagerness to serve the authorities was so obvious that no less a man than Alderman Philpot procured him a horse and arms. "You can make yourself useful," he said. From that time, he hardly left Philpot's side. And so on that fateful Saturday, he witnessed the astonishing climax to the Peasants' Revolt.

Early that morning, after going to Mass at Westminster, King Richard II of England, together with a small retinue of nobles, the mayor of London, Philpot and some other aldermen, rode to Smithfield, to parley with Wat Tyler.

It was a calculated risk. So far, the rebels had shown no desire to harm the boy king himself. But they could destroy London. Reports were also arriving of risings all over East Anglia. "The whole country could go," Philpot told James. If young King Richard could persuade Tyler's men to disperse, huge bloodshed might be avoided. "Or they may change their [illegible]nds and kill him," Philpot remarked grimly.

[illegible]hen they arrived, they found Tyler and his men drawn up [illegible] western side of the broad space of Smithfield. The little [illegible]hind the king stopped in front of the tall, grey buildings of St Bartholomew's. The horde, pressing round the side of Smithfield, was a fearsome sight, and even James found he was trembling. But the son of the Black Prince, with the Plantagenet blood of Edward I and the Lionheart, rode out into the centre, alone. And Tyler came to meet him.

Seeing a space just in front of him, James managed to edge forward until he was only just behind the mayor's shoulder. Despite his efforts at the Savoy, he had not actually seen Tyler before, but now he was only sixty yards away and James could see the man's features clearly. He gazed, fascinated, at the swarthy face. It seemed to him Tyler might have been drinking. And then he frowned.

Tyler wasted no time. Greeting the king in a friendly but abrupt manner, he now issued his demands. All lordship must be abolished. There were to be no more bishops, except one – John Ball. The vast estates of the Church must be confiscated and given to the peasants. And all men should be equal, under the king. Richard rode back to his cortège. James heard him in muttered conversation with the mayor and others. He heard the king say: "I'll tell him we'll consider them all." Then Richard returned to Tyler.

But it was not the king upon whom James Bull's eyes remained fixed. It was Tyler. He was racking his brain. Where had he seen that face?

On receiving Richard's response, Tyler grinned. He called for a jug of ale. One of his men brought it. He raised the jug to his lips, gulped it down crudely. Smacked his lips in triumph.

Of course! It was when the fellow smacked his lips that the memory came back. A night, long ago in the George. A swarthy man like this one, who smacked his lips. Could it be the same? Yes, he was almost sure of it. And then James Bull entered English history.

"I know that fellow," he blurted out, his voice ringing across Smithfield. "He's a highwayman from Kent."

Whatever he might have expected, nothing could have prepared James for the effect this produced. Tyler stared. Next, whether it was true, or he merely felt insulted, he went red. And then suddenly he lost his head. With a roar of rage he seemed to forget the king, spurred his horse, and pulling out a dagger as he came, dashed straight at James. "I'll have you dead," he yelled. James blanched, but hardly had time to think.

There was a scuffle in front of him. Swords flashed: he saw the mayor's, then a squire's. There was a scream. Tyler's horse wheeled round, raced back and, just before it reached the king, Tyler crashed to the ground and lay there, streaming blood.

There was a terrible silence. The rebels gasped. James heard Philpot mutter: "They'll kill us all, damn it."

But he had reckoned without the boy king. For now the fourteen-year-old King Richard II performed an extraordinary feat of coolness and courage. Raising his hand, and walking his horse forward straight into the midst of the huge rebel crowd, he called out to them.

"Sirs, I will be your captain. Follow me." He headed towards some fields that lay to the north. The crowd paused. James held his breath. Then the rebels followed him.

The next hour had been frantic. The mayor, Philpot and the other loyal men had dashed round London. At last, taking heart, the men-at-arms and the Londoners from every ward formed up in ranks. While the king kept the rebels occupied at a parley, the London force surrounded them.

And suddenly it was all over. The rebels surrendered. The king was safe. The mayor and Philpot were knighted on the spot. The head of Tyler replaced that of the poor archbishop on London Bridge. Wisely, however, King Richard had ordered that all his humble followers, whatever they had done, should be unconditionally pardoned.

But, flushed and excited as he was, James Bull's real triumph came when he rode over to the house on London Bridge to give them the news and, for the first time, was ushered upstairs to find the merchant, his wife and Tiffany all in the big room.

"Now tell us, my boy," his kinsman said with a smile, "tell us everything just as it happened."

The great Peasants' Revolt of 1381 was over. For some time outbreaks continued in East Anglia and elsewhere, but with the failure at London, the head of the revolution was severed. As for the promises of the boy king to the peasants, they were immediately and entirely forgotten. As he himself curtly informed a deputation of peasants a little later: "Villeins you are: villeins you shall remain." The stars had returned to their courses, the orders of society were back in their proper spheres. But one important political lesson had been learned, which would not be forgotten for many centuries. Bull put it succinctly: "Poll taxes mean trouble."

It was two days after Tyler's death, when order had safely been restored, that a foaming horse and rider clattered up to the house on London Bridge. It was Silversleeves. His joy at seeing Bull seemed to be huge.

"Thank God, sir, you're safe," he cried. "And dearest Tiffany?" He sighed with relief. "I've been so worried." He had been in the West Country on business, he explained. "But as soon as I heard about Tyler, I came as fast as I could." He rushed upstairs, even allowing himself to hug his beloved. "How I wanted to be with you!" he cried. Bull was touched.

But one person towards whom Bull's heart remained hard was Ducket. "He was with the rebels; that is enough," he said. "He is a traitor." And to the apprentice himself, when he released him from his confinement he said coldly: "I do not care what your part was in this. I will keep the commitments I made to you when you were apprenticed to Fleming, because I gave my word. But you are not to come to his house again."

One month later, Benedict Silversleeves and Tiffany Bull were betrothed. At Tiffany's request, the marriage was not to take place until the following summer.

When James Bull heard that Tiffany was betrothed, he looked very thoughtful. "That's it then," he said at last. If, in his inner heart, he had known that the last five years of hoping had been a waste of time, his sense of family duty and of his own worth had never allowed him to acknowledge it. And now, just when, for the first time, he had at last got into his kinsman's good graces, it was all over. Suddenly, he realized, his life had no particular object. He began to frequent the George. Not that he drank heavily, or failed to attend to his business, but there were still many hours when a man might sit morosely by himself; and this is what he did.

Dame Barnikel noticed him, and remembered vaguely seeing him like this once before. Now, rather curious, she kept an eye on him and pointed him out to Amy.

"A man," she told her daughter, "is what you make of him." Not, she reflected to herself, with a sigh, that she had been able to make much of poor Fleming. "But now that young man," she said, "needs looking after." After a while she decided to take him, as she put it, under her wing. Whenever James came in, he found the formidable landlady wreathed in smiles. "Here's this handsome man again," she would say in her deep voice, as she sat him down. She positively purred at him. She even made the big, spare fellow feel attractive. "There," she would say to Amy afterwards, as the girl stood awkwardly by. "You must learn to bring a man out; you never know what may be in there."

Sometimes, she had to admit to herself, Amy wondered how she would accomplish this with Carpenter. Of course, she still admired his quiet strength; but the experience with Tyler's revolt had disconcerted her. When he had returned from St Bartholomew's, he had had nothing worse than some burns and a massive bump on his head. But who knows what might have happened to him if it had not been for Ducket? Nor had he changed his views. "It was London ruffians who did the looting," he told her. "We still live under a godless authority. One day it will have to change." She was not sure what she felt. But he was still her man. And so she knew she must be glad when, shortly before Christmas he announced: "I think we might marry in the summer."

To many in England, after the calamities of the previous twelvemonth, the start of the year 1382 seemed to promise a new and brighter hope. In January a happy event took place. Richard II, the brave boy king, was married to Anne, a plain but kindly princess. She was almost as young as he, and had come, enduring a dangerous sea crossing, from the distant land of Bohemia, in eastern Europe. To the delight of all it was obvious that, as in a fairy tale, the young king and Anne of Bohemia had fallen instantly in love.

In the Bull household there was a hope that they might be similarly blessed.

In the last week of February the fat girl decided to speak. If there was a reason why she chose to do so then, it was buried deep in the folds of her person. "Ducket wasn't in the riots," she remarked, quite suddenly, to Tiffany in the kitchen one day. "He was saving a man's life."

When Tiffany told her father about this, he was not very encouraging. "I'm sorry," he said, "but I'm not convinced.

The fat girl only had the tale from Ducket himself. And whatever he says he was doing, there's no doubt he was at the Savoy. Besides," he went on, "you may recall Dame Barnikel's suspicions about the theft of money. I'm not prepared to revise my opinion, and," he gave her a hard look "you're to stay away from him, if you please." To which Tiffany bowed her head meekly and said nothing.

Then she sent a message.

Ducket came as appointed to the church of St Mary-le-Bow.

It was over six months since he had been barred from the house; and now, as she gazed at his familiar face, his cheerful eyes and jaunty shock of white hair, she felt a sudden pang of guilt. Even if her father was right, how could she have let so much time pass without even attempting to see him? How must he have felt, an outcast, without even a show of friendship from her? And now, knowing what she did, she felt even greater embarrassment. But when she told him what she had heard, he showed no sign of resentment. "I'm glad you feel it's safe to talk to me now," he laughed. "It's funny though," he confessed, "how everyone's been so cool towards me in the last couple of years. I don't know why."

But Tiffany did. And suddenly, thinking of her father's and Dame Barnikel's suspicions, and looking at his smiling face, she knew as certainly as she knew anything in the world that he could not have done what they thought.

"I think," she said, "there's something you should know."

During the Easter season, in the year 1382, several copies of a very dangerous book were infiltrated into London. Since books had to be written out by scribes, the number of copies was limited; but the authorities were alarmed nonetheless.

The book was the Bible. It was a literal and not very pleasing translation, made partly by Wyclif himself, mostly by other hands; even its authors viewed it only as a first attempt. But it was in English; and men like Carpenter could read. This was the frightening thought. "An English Bible," Bull told his wife, "means sedition." With John Ball's sermons still ringing in the people's ears, and the terrifying rebel horde such a recent memory, the idea of simple folk reading the Bible and making their own sermons struck terror in responsible men.

The followers of Wyclif now came to be known by a pejorative nickname, which meant either mumblers or layabouts: the Lollards. Wyclif's Bible was called the Lollard Bible. And both were dangerous.

Ben Carpenter wanted a Lollard Bible. He had been able, so far, to obtain the Book of Genesis. Like many Lollard bibles, it was prefixed by a series of Lollard tracts; and he had read both tract and scriptural text, slowly but successfully, twice so far. He did not bring it to the George since Amy said it would annoy her mother, who had ceased to like Wyclif since the revolt. But several times he had conducted Amy to a quiet spot and read her chapters on each occasion. "When the weather's warmer," he promised her, "we can walk out in the evenings and I can read it to you for longer."

A wet spring night, rather cold for May. Gusts of wind rattled the shutters as Ducket made his way out past Ludgate. He had waited patiently for this chance, two months from the day when Tiffany had warned him of Dame Barnikel's suspicions, and now he was careful to keep his quarry in sight.

Of course, it might be nothing. There might be no link at all, but he could not help thinking that Fleming's lack of money must be connected with his strange disappearances. And whatever Fleming was up to, if he wanted to clear his own name he had better find out. Ahead of him, the grocer crossed the Fleet bridge and continued westward towards Temple Bar.

The rain was blowing in his face, making it difficult to see. Just before Temple Bar, Fleming suddenly turned right and started up Chancery Lane. This was not a quarter that Ducket often visited and he wondered where the grocer could be going. He tried to draw a little closer. A gust of wind smacked a sheet of rain into his face. He wiped his eyes.

Fleming had vanished.

Taking a chance that he might be detected, he ran up Chancery Lane. A hundred yards; two hundred. There was no sign of him.

"He can't have gone any further," he muttered, and began to retrace his steps. "He's got to be in here somewhere." There were houses on both sides of the street. With their high gables and curved timbers they seemed to be looming towards him in the darkness. He realized that already he had passed a score of alleys and yards into which Fleming could have stepped. Here and there, a little light seeped out of a doorway or window, but that was all. I must keep looking, he thought. Even if I only see him coming out of somewhere, it will probably tell me where he's going next time. Ignoring the driving rain, he wandered up and down.

Half an hour passed. An hour. And then, just as he had entered a small yard, he heard a shutter bang open, looked up, and saw a face framed for a moment in a lighted window.

Fleming watched the glowing fire with mounting excitement. This time, he thought, it is going to happen.

It had to happen. In another month it would be his daughter's wedding. And what had he to give her? Nothing. He thought of his wife. How long was it since she had had a good opinion of him? Only money would solve it. So, once again, he had taken all the spare money he had in the box and brought it to Silversleeves. The alchemist had seemed confident too.

"This will be the last time I do this," he had informed the grocer. "I shall not need to any more." And seeing the grocer wondering if this meant they would make gold, he smiled. "Yes, my friend," he said, sending up a secret prayer of thanks for Tiffany and her wealth, "soon I shall be very rich indeed."

It was hot in the room. Silversleeves, dressed in his magic cloak, bent over his work. Slowly he mixed the ingredients of the Elixir, adding for good measure a little salt and garlic. Time passed. The atmosphere in the room grew closer, the fire hissed, while outside the rain lashed the shutters. At last he was ready. "Stoke the fire," he ordered the grocer.

It was while Fleming was doing so that the wind burst open the shutter. With an impatient gesture, Silversleeves had motioned him to fasten it, which had caused Fleming to lean out of the window. Then his eyes had been drawn back to the fire.

Already the crucible was bubbling. "Do you think . . ." Fleming began; but Silversleeves raised his finger to his lips. Longing to say something, the grocer stood on tiptoe with anticipation as he watched the crucible trembling on the coals.

The rain roared on the shutters. He was vaguely aware of a creaking sound near the door. The crucible hissed.

But then something strange began to happen. He felt the movement clearly, and so did Silversleeves, who looked up in surprise: not only was the crucible bubbling furiously and shaking, but now the beakers and bowls on the table were starting to tremble too. The door and window began to rattle; the crucible jumped. The floor itself was moving in a giddy fashion. The walls, the whole house, amazingly, started to sway.

"Dear God," he cried in ecstasy, "this is it!" This must be what happened when the miracle of alchemy was accomplished. Why, for all he knew, the planets might be whirling wildly too, the celestial spheres themselves be shaking as madly as the house. Perhaps – a thought terrible, yet sublime – Silversleeves had just caused the world to end. Certainly the alchemist was looking alarmed.

And then the door opened.

Ducket stared open-mouthed. The last few moments had been strange indeed. First he had dived across the courtyard, up a rickety outside staircase and on to a landing, groping his way in the blackness. Then the whole house, and all the houses round, had started shaking.

Ducket had never been in an earthquake before, nor had he ever heard of such a thing – which was hardly surprising. The great earth tremor of May 1382 was one of the very few recorded in London's history, and, though it did no serious damage, it frightened the Londoners very much indeed. But he had no time even to consider the earthquake as he gazed in. This was not a prostitutes' quarter, but he had supposed his master might be with a woman of some kind. Or perhaps a circle of men playing dice, or some game that might have caused the grocer to lose money. He had meant to open the door very cautiously, hoping to get a glimpse of what was going on and then, if necessary, beat a hasty retreat. But the sudden movement of the earthquake had caused him almost to fall against the door just as he lifted the latch. It swung open, and now, as he blinked in the strange light, he saw Fleming, staring as if he were a ghost, and by the fire a magician. Yet not a magician. He frowned. He was looking into the face of the pious and respectable Silversleeves – and his face, at this moment, was neither respectable nor even fearsome, but was a picture of embarrassment and guilt. "What are you doing?" he cried.

"Why Ducket," the grocer said, relieved now that he realized who it was, "didn't I say that one day you should see wonders?" His face took on a look of angelic happiness. "Oh Ducket, come and see. We have just made gold."

Then Ducket, who had heard of alchemy, turned upon Silversleeves. "You devil," he shouted. And the lawyer cowered.

Ducket was quite surprised, afterwards, at how easily he had taken charge. At first, it had been difficult to make the grocer realize he had been duped.

"Don't you know," Ducket cried, "that all these fellows are frauds. They can't make gold. They just make you think they can so that you pay them. The whole thing's a trick." He strode over to the crucible. "Where's this gold?" he demanded. "There's none here." Even so, it was only after Ducket, with the threat of a bloody nose, had forced Silversleeves to tell his victim the truth, that the poor fellow began to comprehend. "He has stolen all my money then," he murmured.

"And he must give it back," Ducket said stoutly. But by now the lawyer was beginning to recover his composure. "All gone." He smiled sweetly.

Yet if Ducket might have expected Fleming to be angry, or threaten Silversleeves with exposure, he had overlooked one thing: the victim was guilty too. Now, with tears in his eyes, Fleming appealed to him.

"I've always been good to you, Ducket," he begged. "So promise me, you'll never tell a soul what I have done." He hung his head. "If my wife and Amy ever knew . . . I couldn't bear that, Ducket. Will you promise me?"

Ducket hesitated. He saw Silversleeves smirk. Of course, the cunning lawyer thought he'd got away with it. He turned on him.

"I'll tell all London," he said evenly, "unless this devil makes me a promise first. You give up Tiffany," he told Silversleeves. "Give her up or I'll expose you for exactly what you are."

"I don't think that's necessary." Silversleeves had gone pale.

"I do. So choose," Ducket replied, and watched the struggle taking place in him.

"All right," the lawyer said at last.

The next morning, while all London was discussing the earth tremor and assessing the damage, Ben Carpenter enjoyed an astonishing stroke of good fortune. A man he had been discreetly meeting near St Paul's, instead of the Book of Exodus which he had been hoping for, produced nothing less than an entire bible, all translated. Not only that, the man quoted Ben a price which, though high, was within his means.

He had a bible. He could hardly believe it. True, it had consumed a part of his savings; but it was the only book he would ever need to purchase in his life. He wrapped it in a cloth, put it in a bag, and carried it home.

Some discretion on his part was necessary. With the suspicion of Lollards still as high as ever, a Church synod meeting at Blackfriars only days ago had again vigorously condemned all Wyclif's beliefs as heresy: even the possession of a Lollard bible was deemed suspicious. He put it away carefully, therefore, in a cupboard.

And just as he did so, a thought occurred to him. Ever since the previous summer, it had been on his conscience that he had never properly expressed his gratitude to Ducket for saving his life at the Savoy. He had wanted to make him a present of money: but Ducket refused it. Often the craftsman had wondered what favour he could do for his friend. Now, lying in the cupboard in front of him, was the answer. Reverently, but with a happy smile, he took out the Book of Genesis.

Silversleeves went out to kill Ducket late that afternoon.

It was a calculated risk. Though he did not think Fleming would talk, he had no doubt that, as soon as Ducket discovered he still intended to marry Tiffany, he would. He had, of course, no intention of giving the girl up; and with Ducket out of the way, he would probably be safe. The logic, he found, was unanswerable. Ducket must die.

He felt a little nervous, nonetheless, as he took a spare dagger and concealed it under his tunic.

To make sure that nothing was suspected, he next went to

the house on London Bridge, where he received a friendly welcome. Nothing in Tiffany's eyes suggested that she had heard anything about him. On his way out, he met Bull, who was as affable as usual. "I wonder, sir, if we might fix a day for the wedding," he ventured. "Certainly, before June is out," the merchant agreed.

When Silversleeves reached the Cheap, Ducket and the grocer were just taking down the stall. He hovered at a distance, considering his next move.

How did one kill a man? He had never done such a thing before. Clearly he must not be seen: he would need a private place, perhaps after dusk. It would probably be best to come at him from behind. But then, what to do with the body? Leave it? Hide it? Drop it in the river? Without a body, no one would even be sure there had been a crime. It would all depend on what chances he could get, he supposed; with some apprehension he began to follow him.

The two men started off as usual, pulling the handcart along the Cheap. They passed along the Poultry and headed across to Lombard Street, which would take them towards the bridge. But just as they reached Lombard Street, a squat figure, obviously a craftsman, hailed them and came over to speak to Ducket. After a few moments, the man and Ducket started to walk back towards the Cheap, while Fleming continued home with the handcart. Following carefully once again, Silversleeves found himself retracing his steps until the couple dived down the lane behind St Mary-le-Bow and went into the tavern there.

Luckily the place was crowded. Though he saw them at once, sitting together at a table, they did not notice him. He bought a jug of wine and watched them thoughtfully. The craftsman seemed unusually happy, even excited; he was calling for more ale. Just after it arrived, glancing around him with a trace of furtiveness, he handed a package to Ducket. A present of some kind, judging by the expectant look on his face. Ducket began to open it.

Very carefully Silversleeves edged closer.

It was a book. He could not quite read it from where he stood. Ducket had turned the first few pages. Both men's heads were bowed over it now. For a moment, Ducket tilted the book. And, though he was nearly ten feet away, Silversleeves could see the single, large word that ran across the top of the page: GENESIS. It must be a Lollard bible.

He drew back quickly. A Lollard tract. What use could that information be to him? His clever brain considered it rapidly, from every angle. Then he smiled: a delicious smile. It might not be necessary to kill Ducket after all.

The evening was well advanced when Ducket strolled down towards the bridge. The Book of Genesis, safely in a bag, bumped on his shoulder. He did not want it, really, but had not had the heart to tell Carpenter. The solemn fellow had given it to him with such pride.

When he saw the two men advancing towards him, he took no particular notice. The first he recognized as one of the city sergeants who maintained law and order; the other was Silversleeves, whom he decided to ignore. Only as they drew close did he realize that they meant to speak to him.

"I'll see what's in the bag, please," the sergeant said. Ducket hesitated, then shrugged. Apprentices did not disobey a city sergeant. Reluctantly he handed over the bag and the sergeant pulled out the book, handing it on to the lawyer. "What does it say?" he enquired.

It only took Silversleeves a moment to examine it.

"This is the Book of Genesis," he declared. "And it is accompanied by a Lollard tract. It is all heresy," he added gravely. "I think you ought to hold on to it."

"You can't do that," Ducket burst out. "I've broken no law." He saw the sergeant look at Silversleeves.

In fact none of them knew whether the possession of this material was technically legal or not. But there was no doubt about the danger of Lollard apprentices. "You should keep it," the lawyer stated firmly, "until we know whether he's to be charged or not. It's evidence." And the sergeant nodded.

"Where did you get this book, lad?" he asked.

Ducket considered. If the wretched thing was really illegal, he did not want to get poor Carpenter into trouble.

"I just found it."

"Evasive reply," said the lawyer. "Guilt."

"You rogue," cried Ducket in exasperation. "What are you up to?"

"Upholding the law and Holy Church," Silversleeves replied blandly. It was too much.

"You devil," Ducket cried. "You necromancer!"

"Ah," Silversleeves smiled. "Necromancer. You Lollards say that the Mass is nothing but magic. Note that, sergeant."

"I shall know where to find you, lad," the sergeant said.

When Bull heard what Silversleeves had to say, he was very angry indeed. "Of course you did right to tell me," he declared.

"I was not sure," Silversleeves explained. "I wouldn't have mentioned it at all, but I know Ducket is connected to you, and I feel he may be being led into evil ways. Could you not help him? Personally," he added, "I think the young fellow is entirely harmless."

"No," Bull cried, "you are wrong. There's been too much. Theft. Insurrection. Now Lollardy. If you've a fault, Silversleeves, you're too kind. And you say he slandered you too?"

"Necromancer." Silversleeves laughed. "A meaningless word. The heat of the moment. I thought," he added, "that if it should come to arrest, you might speak up for him."

"No sir." Bull shook his head. "Not after this. In fact, I may have to take sterner measures."

"Oh dear." Silversleeves looked concerned.

"He is due to receive a sum of money when he completes his apprenticeship," Bull explained. "I no longer think I should give it to him." He sighed. "Bad blood, my dear boy. Bad blood." Then he clapped the lawyer on the back. "To happier subjects. Marriage in three weeks. Get ready."

That night, very carefully, Benedict Silversleeves destroyed all evidence that he had ever attempted to turn base metals into gold.

Fleming had gone out. There was no one to talk to. As Ducket sat in the George the following morning, it seemed to him that there was an inevitable order in the universe. You could not make gold from a base metal; and a low-born foundling could never rise above his sphere.

He was penniless: cut off completely. Bull had not even troubled to tell him in person but sent a message to Dame Barnikel who had broken the news to him. A young grocer with no money. What could he do? The Grocers Guild sometimes gave reputable young members some capital to help them get started; but what sort of reputation had he now?

"All is not lost," Dame Barnikel had said. But she had said it with neither great friendliness nor conviction.

He was greatly surprised therefore, a little before noon, to see Tiffany. She was wearing a pale violet gown and a little ruffled cap. Her breasts were just covered and he noticed how charmingly she had filled out. She sat down beside him.

Dear God, how downhearted he looked. She had never seen him like this before. And it's we, she thought, my own family who have done this to him.

"You probably shouldn't be seeing me," he said.

"Probably," she replied. "But I'm always going to. Always. No matter what." And she took his hand.

To his embarrassment, he cried. They sat together for an hour. She persuaded him easily enough to explain how he was given the Lollard bible – though he still refused to say by whom. But how Silversleeves had come to know, Ducket had no idea.

"I'm sorry," she frowned, "that it should have been Silversleeves. I am sure," she explained, "that he only meant to help you. I will have him speak to Father again and make it all right. We are to be married, you know," she added, "in three more weeks."

"You are? When was that arranged?"

"Last evening. Just after he encountered you."

And now Ducket understood. Of course. The cunning lawyer had broken their bargain; but first, how neatly he had discredited him. Nothing he said now would be believed, because it would be set down to malice. He could be sure the lawyer had covered his tracks, too. Yet he must save Tiffany.

"Would you believe me," he said at last, "if I told you that Silversleeves was not what he seemed?" And he began to talk.

He told her, without mentioning Fleming by name, how he had discovered Silversleeves. He told her that the lawyer had defrauded people, and that he was a most accomplished liar. He told her all he could. He watched her bow her head and look deeply thoughtful. At last she spoke.

"You say terrible things about the man I am to marry. Yet

you don't say who his victims are. You give no proof." She looked up at him with distress in her eyes. "How can I believe you?"

How indeed? Why should she? What had he ever done to make her trust him more than Silversleeves? And if she doubted him, what possible chance had he of convincing Bull or anyone else? As he gazed at her now and remembered that day when he saw her with Silversleeves on the bridge, he realized with a force which smote him so hard it hurt, that he loved this girl, completely unattainable though she was to a poor boy like him, more than anyone else in his life.

"If you come here tomorrow," he said, "I will give you proof."

Yet could he? This question occupied his thoughts as soon as she had gone. Silversleeves clearly had gambled that the grocer would not talk. He had to persuade him. If he swore Tiffany to secrecy, would Fleming talk? Surely he'd see he must save the girl from Silversleeves. But even that might not be enough. Bull would demand explanations. Would Fleming be prepared to tell him too? And would Bull believe him? There was no doubting Silversleeves's bland ability to lie. He sighed. Just now, he could not think of anything better.

He waited for Fleming to return.

It was exactly noon when Fleming finished the letter he had been writing. It was not long, but he was satisfied with it. He placed it on the box of peppercorns, then went to the door of the storeroom and fastened it. The other piece of private business he had to conduct required some care and he did not wish to be disturbed.

He smiled. With luck, it seemed to him, he might have found a solution to everybody's problems.

They found Fleming that evening, when Dame Barnikel and Ducket had tried to get into the storehouse. He was hanging by a rope he had tied to a rafter. His letter was very simple.

> I am sorry about the Poll Tax money, and all the other money too. It was me that stole it. I was trying to make more for you and Amy. Please don't ask any more.
>
> I want young Ducket to take over the business. He has

been a good friend to me, and very loyal. He tried to save me but it's too late. You can trust him.

When Dame Barnikel read the letter she only glanced briefly at Fleming. Then she turned to Ducket.

"You understand all this?"

"Yes."

"He says he stole the money."

"He didn't really mean to. I promised him I'd never tell."

"I thought you stole it," she said honestly.

"I know. I didn't, though."

"He didn't have to do this," she remarked. But Ducket understood that he did. For though the rope around poor Fleming's neck was the visible cause, the apprentice knew that in truth his sad little master had died of shame.

"You'd better take over, then," Dame Barnikel said gruffly.

None of this was any help to Ducket, the next morning, when Tiffany arrived. "I've lost the person who might have convinced you," he told her simply. "I've no proof."

"So I have to take your word for it?"

He nodded. "I've nothing else," he said.

After Tiffany departed, he did not move for some time. He did not know what she would decide. But one thing he did know. He would never let her fall into the clutches of Silversleeves. If necessary, he thought, I shall have to kill him.

Dame Barnikel was not often contrite; but the next morning, as she sat on her great bed and talked to Amy, she was.

"I can't get over how wrong I was about that boy," she growled. "He's a little hero. Look at what he's done. Saved Carpenter's life. Suspected of theft. Took the blame for your father. Tried to save him too, apparently. Then Bull cuts him off. I bet there's a good explanation for that too. And never a whimper. He's a plucky, loyal fellow," she concluded warmly. "Loyal." And she noticed that Amy did not disagree.

She rose. "I've got to see about your poor father's funeral, now," she said. But at the door, she paused. "I know you want to get away from me," she said quietly. "But don't marry Carpenter. You know you don't love him."

* * *

The preparation for a wedding is a joyous thing. There were the dresses to be made, and nightdresses too. There were trunks of linen to be aired. Though it was still two weeks away, the cook and the fat girl had already started their preparations in the kitchen. Bull and Silversleeves had just taken a pleasant house on Oyster Hill, near the bridge, where the young couple would commence their married life. Even Chaucer had been pressed to use his influence at court to secure the promising lawyer a lucrative position.

Yet for Tiffany, though she smiled, the days went painfully. What conflicting emotions she felt. Could it really be that her childhood friend, the brave young fellow she loved like a brother, was lying? When she looked at the calm face of her future bridegroom, Ducket's charge seemed impossible. Yet would Ducket invent such a slander? Was it in his nature? Or was that nature, as her father believed, fatally flawed after all? Which of them did she really know – the foundling or the clever lawyer who had courted her?

She had thought of telling her father about Ducket's accusation, but she knew what his response would be. And wasn't his judgment sound? Few men in London had a better reputation.

Yet, every day, as she watched the preparations for the marriage, something else still troubled her. Even if everything they said about young Ducket was true – that he was a liar, and Silversleeves a paragon of virtue – the question still came to her: what did she feel for Silversleeves? She admired him of course. He was pious, kindly, everything he should be. He seemed devoted to her. Yet despite this, her mind kept returning to that other conversation she had had with her mother long ago, when she had asked her: were there no perfect knights to marry? You'll never meet one, her mother had said. So that was it: she was marrying Silversleeves and her parents were pleased.

If only a voice within her, first in a whisper, then every day a little louder, were not urging her: stop. Stop before it's too late. But as she watched the preparations so rapidly advancing she thought: it already is too late.

Amy Fleming had made her own decision more easily. With the death of her father, it was natural that her marriage to Ben Carpenter should be temporarily postponed. Carpenter himself had suggested they consider the autumn, but now Amy secretly decided otherwise.

It was not her mother's words but her father's sad little note that had finally swayed her. His ringing endorsement of Ducket, his desire for the brave fellow to take his place, his message that they should trust him. Was he trying, in his own way, to tell her something before he departed?

She knew she did not love Carpenter, but he had always seemed secure, while Ducket, so carefree, was a risk. The events of the last twelvemonth, however, had given her pause for thought. Carpenter at the Savoy; Carpenter with his Lollard texts. Were the solemn craftsman's obsessions going to lead them into trouble? And now, she discovered, even her quiet father had been in trouble too. Yet who had saved both men, or tried to? Ducket, whom her father urged her to trust. It was Ducket, after all, who was the strong one. Ducket the brave.

She supposed he would marry her. After all, he had lost everything else. If Fleming wished him to run the business, he could hardly do it with no money. Her father's message had been for Ducket too. Marry my daughter, it said. But she decided to proceed carefully – to ascertain Ducket's position first.

She had just come to this conclusion one morning when she saw Tiffany Bull approaching the George. Supposing she might want Ducket, she met her at the entrance to the yard and told her that he was minding the stall at the Cheap. But to her surprise, the merchant's daughter shook her head.

"Actually," she said, "it is you I came to see." And with a glance around she enquired: "Could we speak privately?"

Though she had seen Tiffany, Amy had never spoken to her before, and she observed the rich girl curiously. She admired the fine, silk clothes, so different from her own, noticed the dainty way that she sat down. It was strange to think that once her simple young Ducket had lived in the same house as this creature from another world. It was even more surprising when, with pain in her eyes, the girl said simply: "I need your help. You see," she added frankly, "I've no one to turn to."

Tiffany told her story as shortly as she could, while Amy listened. "So you see," she concluded, "Ducket has made these charges against the man I am to marry. I find it hard to believe them. No one else does. Yet if any part of them is true . . ." She spread her hands. "In two weeks Silversleeves will be my husband." She looked at Amy earnestly. "You have seen Ducket every day for years. You must know so much more about his life than I do. Have you any idea if all this could be true?"

Amy gazed back at her. How strange. If she had thought she had problems herself, it seemed to her now that the dilemma before this rich girl, who apparently had everything, was worse. "I'll gladly tell you all I know," she said.

Tiffany listened intently as Amy outlined the apprentice's story. She explained how she had begged him to find Carpenter during the revolt and how he had saved the craftsman at the Savoy. "That was all true, then," Tiffany interjected. "I was sure it was." Then, sadly, Amy explained the strange circumstances of her father's death and his message about Ducket. "So you see," she continued, "he didn't steal anything." But it was another aspect that especially caught Tiffany's attention.

"You say your father took money and lost it, but didn't explain how. And Ducket knows, but won't tell."

"He promised Father he wouldn't."

"But he warned me Silversleeves was a necromancer who defrauded people. Then when your father died, he said he couldn't prove it any more."

The two girls looked at each other.

"Silversleeves," they both said at once.

"That's it then," Tiffany said, "I'm not marrying him."

"We've no proof," Amy pointed out. "He'll deny it."

"Too bad," Tiffany said. And then she smiled.

"You shouldn't be smiling," Amy said. "You've just lost your husband." But with a strange sense of relief, Tiffany suddenly laughed. "Never mind," she grinned. "I never really liked him."

It was curious, Amy considered, how she should already feel a bond of friendship. She leaned forward conspiratorially. "I'll tell you something," she confided. "I'm planning to ditch my man Carpenter too, only nobody knows."

"Really?" Tiffany liked the girl more and more. "Have you someone else in mind?" And now Amy smiled broadly.

"Why, Ducket, of course," she said.

* * *

The sun was setting and the reddish glow along the river was touching the green grass in the window as Tiffany stood before her father that evening and told him what she wanted. At first he did not believe her.

"But the marriage is all arranged," he said in bafflement. "You can't back out now."

"I must, Father," she said.

"Why?" He suddenly turned on her suspiciously. "Have you been talking to Ducket? He's been spreading rumours."

"I know," she answered calmly. "But that's not the reason." Strictly speaking it was true. Amazed by such words from the daughter on whose obliging nature he had always been able to count, Bull made an effort to be conciliatory. "Can you tell me what is the matter, then?" he gently asked. And she, thinking that he might understand, cried out, "I do not love him, Father."

For a moment or two, Bull said nothing. He pursed his lips thoughtfully. Was this just a sudden panic before a wedding? He knew that girls were sometimes prone to these unreasonable fits. When he spoke, he was firm.

"I'm afraid you must marry him," he said, "and that's the end of it. Let's not discuss it any more." And from the look in his eye, Tiffany realized that this was going to be even more difficult than she thought.

"You gave your word," she cried. "Now you're breaking it. You promised I could choose."

This was too much. First an absurd demand, then an insult. No Bull ever broke his word.

"You chose," he roared at her. "You chose, young Miss, and you chose Silversleeves. Now it's you who want to break your word to him. I won't allow it."

"I hate him," she cried back. "He's a villain." She had never fought with her father before in her life.

"Too good for you, I see," he shouted. "But you'll marry him anyway." And then, with a bellow that almost knocked her off her feet: "Enough! Get out of my sight or by God I'll thrash you before you reach the altar."

Yet still, to his amazement, she held her ground.

"I will not speak the vows. I'll appeal to the priest. You cannot force me, no matter what you do."

"Then I'll send you to a nunnery," he yelled.

"Send me to St Helen's then," she cried in exasperation. "At least I'll have some fun." And she rushed from the room, leaving her father puce in the face, and stupefied.

An hour later, Tiffany was in her room at the top of the house, with the door bolted from the outside. "She will stay there until she sees sense," Bull declared. Only the fat girl was allowed to go up with a jug of water and a bowl of gruel.

So three days passed. Her mother, supposing that it must be a case of nerves, went to talk to her and returned looking helpless. The preparations for the wedding, at Bull's insistence, continued. Nor was Silversleeves even told about the trouble when he called. "She'll come round, or I really will send her to a convent," Bull told his worried wife. But as the days passed, even he began to grow discouraged until, at the end of the fourth day, he was so uncertain that he did something he had never done in all their married life. "What do you think I should do?" he asked her.

"I think," she said quietly, "you will have to send her to a convent or let her have her way."

Tiffany's room was a good place to think. It was directly above the big upstairs room and had a pleasant view up the Thames so that she could sit and watch the traffic on the river by the hour. There, as the days passed quietly, she had plenty of time to consider.

What did she want? At first, she hardly seemed to know herself, except that she had no desire to marry Silversleeves, or be a nun. By the second day, she began to realize. By the third, she knew, and it all seemed so simple, so natural, that she wondered if she had not known it all along. But how could she bring it about? She did not know.

She would have to play for time.

She spoke quietly. Her voice was meek and small.

"I have always obeyed you, Father. If you loved me, you would not condemn me to a life of unhappiness." She waited. When at last he replied, his voice was gruff.

"What do you want, then?"

Now she looked up at him. Her eyes were soft.

"I wish you would help me," she said. "I am so confused. I beg you, give me a little time."

"For what? To choose another husband?"

"To be sure of my heart."

Bull paused. He had no wish to see her in a convent. God knows, he wanted grandchildren. He also had some knowledge of the human heart. Doing his best to set aside the embarrassment he felt towards Silversleeves, he tried to guess at his daughter's real state of mind. Was she sure about Silversleeves? Even if she chose someone else, mightn't she change her mind again? Few fathers in his position would have allowed their daughters so much freedom; it had probably been a mistake. He announced his decision.

"I will make a bargain with you," he said, "but it will be the last." Then he told her what it was, and left, bolting the door behind him.

After he had gone, Tiffany looked pale, and thoughtful. It was not at all what she had wanted. Yet what could she do? It seemed that she would have to gamble everything on a single throw of the dice.

When Ducket received the message the following morning, he questioned the fat girl closely. But the message she delivered had been typically brief.

"That's all she said? Come to the house this evening?"

"I've to let you in."

"What's going on?"

"I dunno."

"You must know something."

"Cook says Tiffany's got to marry or go to a convent."

"Who?"

"The long-nosed one, I s'pose." She watched him impassively. "You coming?"

"Of course I will," he cried, as she waddled away.

If anyone had been observing as the guests arrived at the house of Bull the merchant that evening, they might have noticed a curiously high proportion of eligible young men. There were several middle-aged aldermen with their wives, two of whom had brought daughters, also a widow and even a priest. But there were seven or eight bachelors.

No one knew of any particular reason why they were there. Before noon that day, the merchant had invited as many as he judged necessary. Besides Silversleeves, who looked very comfortable and at ease, standing in the middle of the upstairs room near Bull's precious astrolabe, there were four sons of merchants, a young mercer and a draper, both from solid gentry families, and even the young fellow with a great estate. The only exception in terms of eligibility was the figure who, tall, red-faced and a little flustered, had clumped up the stairs behind the others. Chancing to see James Bull in the street, that afternoon, the merchant, with a shrug, had invited him too. He was, at least, a kinsman.

As it was almost midsummer, there were still hours of daylight left. It was warm; the lower half of the big window had been thrown open, allowing in a pleasant waft of air, cooled somewhat by the river which, the tide having just turned, was rushing with a roar through the channel far below. The company was relaxed; even James Bull, who to give himself confidence in such society had been thinking how honest he was all afternoon, soon began to feel at ease. The master of the house chatted to everyone affably.

Tiffany entered. How charming she looked. Perhaps she was a little pale, but she went over to Silversleeves, greeted him affectionately, and began to mix with the other guests. She even came and talked to James. From time to time her gaze strayed towards the door, but nobody noticed. Her father smiled at her and she at him.

For this meeting was their bargain. "I'm not telling anyone," he had told her the day before, "because I'm not going to embarrass either Silversleeves or myself. But this much I'll promise you. If you like any of the other young men in the room, you can marry them. They've all expressed an interest before. I'll break it to Silversleeves. But if you don't choose anyone else, then it's Silversleeves, or a convent. I shan't go back on this," he had said with a stare. "You have my word." And she had known he meant it.

It had been a bitter blow. She had intended to bring him round to the idea gradually; but there was no chance of that now. So she had planned her great gamble. She hoped it would work.

She was going to point to Ducket.

Yet even then, there was still one terrible danger – a flaw which, if she were wrong, would bring the whole plan down in ruin. What if Ducket did not want her? What if, that very day, he had promised himself to Amy? She had not dared tell the fat girl too much when she sent her to Ducket. She had not even dared to send a letter. And now, as there was no sign of him, she even began to wonder: did the fat girl deceive her? Had her father, who smiled at her now, already forestalled him? Where was he?

Ducket took his time. He had watched the guests arriving, and had waited. He did not want to meet anyone when he approached the house; if Silversleeves or Bull caught sight of him, he would certainly be thrown out. He would let them get started first.

There was another reason why he allowed himself to pause. These might be his last moments of freedom. He did not know exactly why Tiffany had summoned him, but he feared the worst. Silversleeves or a convent: that was what the fat girl had said. Why all these people were arriving he did not know but no doubt he would soon find out.

He had wondered if Silversleeves would be there, and had come prepared. The knife was concealed, stuck in his belt under his shirt. As soon as he was sure how things stood, he would use it.

Silversleeves must die. If possible he would follow him out and do it somewhere discreetly, but if, for some reason, he had to, he would do it here. As for his own fate, he shrugged. I'll swing, he thought grimly.

He was just contemplating this when he saw a latecomer hurrying to the door. It was the priest Bull had invited. And now, with a shock, it seemed to him that he understood. "My God, he's going to marry them right away," he muttered. The company were gathered to witness it. His heart beating hard, he hastened to the kitchen door.

He could hear the sound of voices as he followed the fat girl up the familiar stairs. She had given him an old gown of the cook's and a little linen cap to hide his give-away hair. He carried a platter of food as well. Fortunately he was clean shaven, so if he kept his head down and stayed at the back of the room, people would probably assume he was a serving girl.

At the top of the stairs they paused. The fat girl stood in the doorway, as a signal to Tiffany. Looking past her, Ducket could see that there were at least twenty people in the room.

Then Tiffany came over. She slipped round the fat girl, and

a second later, Ducket found himself gazing into her face. She looked pale, her eyes a little frightened.

"Thank God you've come." She was trembling. "I told father I didn't want to marry Silversleeves. But he said . . ."

"I know. A convent. Don't worry. It'll be all right."

"You don't quite understand."

"Tiffany." Her father's voice was calling.

"Tell me," her eyes gazed into his searchingly, earnestly, "tell me Geoffrey Ducket – I have to ask, you see – do you love me? I mean, could you? You see . . ." He cut her short.

"Enough to die for you," he promised. It was the truth.

She was about to say more, but her father's voice was heard again. Closer. She gave a desperate little shrug, turned, moved quickly round the fat girl and stepped forward to meet him. A second later they had moved away.

Ducket entered the room. No one seemed to be looking at him. He edged forward. He saw Silversleeves, standing a few paces in front of the table on which the astrolabe lay. Just in front of him, he also saw James Bull, and silently cursed. Another figure who could recognize him. Fortunately however, an alderman and his wife stood between himself and these two. Keeping his head down, he was able to get closer. Holding the platter in his left hand, he reached under the folds of his dress for the dagger. He had it. He wasn't taking any chances. He prepared to make his rush.

Tiffany and her father had drawn a little apart from their guests for a moment and were standing close by the window. Though her father had looked at her enquiringly, it was Tiffany who had begun the conversation.

"Father, you said that if I could not bring myself to marry Silversleeves, I might choose another in the room?"

"I did."

"There is a man in the room of whom you have a low opinion. Nor have we ever spoken about him as a husband. And yet, Father, I truly love him. Will you allow me to marry even him? For if not, I shall have to go to the convent."

Bull glanced around. The only man who seemed to fit the description was James Bull. Could his daughter really have fallen in love with the clumsy fellow? It was certainly a disappointment.

"You are sure? Rather than the convent?"

"Yes."

He shrugged. At least, he thought, he's honest. "Very well," he sighed.

"It is Ducket," she said. And pointed.

"What?" Bull's face was red. His bellow shook the room. The whole company had turned, to follow his gaze.

Ducket went pale. They were looking at him. He had been recognized. He clenched the hidden knife. There was nothing for it. Before they threw him out he must strike. He started towards Silversleeves, pushing past the alderman in his way.

And then something happened.

With a roar of rage, Bull turned upon Tiffany and, swinging his large arm, struck her face with the open flat of his hand so hard that she seemed to fly from him like a wounded bird. There was a general gasp.

Then a cry, as Tiffany, spinning away, crashed against the open window, lost her balance, and fell out.

"My God!" Bull, suddenly ashen, leaped to the window. The whole room seemed to surge forward, as Tiffany, with a faint cry, dropped like a bundle of clothes the thirty feet into the waters of the Thames below.

The sequence of events that followed lasted only a matter of seconds from beginning to end, yet, to most of those present, they seemed to happen rather slowly.

Tiffany's dress had lessened the impact of her fall and she was only briefly submerged. Though stunned as she came up, she could see that one of the bridge's great piers was only yards away and she struggled desperately to reach it before the current took her to the point where the waters began their irresistible rush into the channel. She was vaguely aware of a voice far above crying – "Hold on" – as she managed to seize the long riverweeds that grew upon its sides. But already the current was pulling, tugging at her dress. The weeds were slippery. Frantically she held on, but knew she could not do so for long. Yards away, the churning waters roared and foamed; the current seemed to be urging her, ever more insistently, to join it in the headlong ride to death.

Above, in the big room, all was confusion. What should they do? Bull was struggling to get out of his heavy robe; his wife, about to lose a husband as well as a daughter, was gasping for breath. Silversleeves, with a look of deep piety, sank to his knees and began to pray, while James Bull, waving his arms wildly, cried out: "A rope! Fetch a rope!" Clambering across the room, he knocked over the table, stamping, in his haste, upon the astrolabe and crushing its delicate mechanism entirely.

But it was Ducket who, dropping the knife and ignoring Silversleeves, ran to the window and launched himself out into the air just as, below, Tiffany's fingers lost their grip.

A second later he followed her, into the raging torrent.

Bull the merchant had many faults, but ingratitude was not one of them. Nor, indeed, was moral cowardice.

Some hours later, when Tiffany was sufficiently recovered to talk, he spent some time at her bedside, listening while she spoke to him earnestly. Then he went down to the kitchen where, in dry clothes, Ducket was sitting by the fire, and asked the apprentice to accompany him to the big room.

"I have thanked you for saving Tiffany's life, which you certainly did, and I do so again," he began. "But I now believe, after talking to Tiffany, that I owe you an unqualified apology for doubting your character. I ask your forgiveness." He paused. "It seems also that my daughter is very anxious to marry you instead of that rogue Silversleeves. Her judgement is obviously better than mine." And now he smiled. "The question is, Ducket, would you consider it?"

Ducket and Tiffany were married a week later. It was a happy occasion. Whittington stood beside the bridegroom. Chaucer made a speech.

The rich merchant, before giving his daughter to the foundling, had made one stipulation. "Since I have no son, and you will enjoy a large fortune from me, I ask one thing: that you, Ducket, should take the name of Bull." To which the couple had readily agreed. It was therefore Geoffrey and Tiffany Bull who now started their new life together, in the pleasant house already picked for them, on Oyster Hill by London Bridge.

One other happy event also took place a month later. On the eve of her daughter's wedding to Carpenter, Dame Barnikel made an announcement.

"I'm going to marry James."

She had decided she could make something of him; and James Bull for his part, it seemed, had concluded that, if not the fortune he had dreamed of, the George Tavern was a good and solid business. "He's going to become a brewer," she told the guild, and they did not dare to argue. And so the Bull Brewery was born.

As for the prospect of being a bride again, she became quite girlish about it.

1386

The idea was Chaucer's.

He had been worried about his friend Bull of late. Tiffany was married; two years ago, Bull's wife had died. The merchant was feeling rather lonely. Once or twice Chaucer had got the impression that his old friend might have been drinking. And so, in the spring of 1385, he had been delighted when fate provided him with a new official position, and the perfect excuse to take Bull out of himself. "You're coming with me," he said. "To Kent." For Chaucer had just become a Justice of the Peace.

The role of Justice of the Peace had been evolving for some time. It was a good, commonsense system, in which local gentlemen of the shire, aided by professional sergeants-at-law to advise on the legal niceties, presided over the county courts; and Geoffrey Chaucer was eligible because as a royal servant he had been granted a small estate in Kent.

Bull had finally agreed, but before he left, there had been one important decision to make. Who should manage his affairs while he was gone? Since marrying Tiffany, the foundling had exhibited a surprising aptitude for business and before long Bull had found real pleasure in teaching him all he knew, but one thing had displeased the merchant. Though the young man had agreed to dispense with his own name of Duckct, and take that of Bull, he had refused to join the Mercers Guild, despite the fact that Bull could have got him in. "The Grocers Guild is where I served my apprenticeship," he declared, "and it's the trade I know." Nothing would change his loyalty. The fact that the Grocers were currently running the city and the Mercers were not did not make Bull any happier, and Bull was not sure he wanted to put his affairs entirely in the younger man's hands just yet. The solution he hit upon, however, suited everybody. He called in Whittington.

Whittington was in his thirties now, a man of substance already and a member of the Mercers Guild. He and young Ducket had always been friends. "I want you to watch over my affairs jointly while I'm away," he instructed them. "You can always send for me if you're in any doubt." Feeling confident in the arrangement, he had departed cheerfully enough.

How delightful it was to be in Kent. Just for a moment, when he had met the justices at Rochester Castle, Bull had been afraid he might not enjoy himself. They were a large party, who, apart from the five sergeants-at-law, were mostly courtiers or members of the greatest landowning families in the shire. Rich as he was, Bull had never moved in these circles; but Chaucer came immediately to his rescue. "Gentlemen," he smiled, "I am such a newcomer to this county myself that I asked my dear friend here to ride with me and guide me. He was born a Bull of Bocton, an ancient Kent family, I believe." The effect was instantaneous. "Been here longer than we have," one landowner declared. "It must be your brother I know," smiled another. By the end of that day, they let him feel as if they had known him all his life.

As Chaucer had foreseen Bull had no time to brood, for they were constantly on the move. There were investigations, into the administration of an heiress's estate, or the land grants of a monastery; they carefully checked the coastal defences in case of French attack. But above all, it was the simple business of administering justice, in towns, in villages and on manors all over the county, that delighted Bull and his friend the poet.

A tax-collector had been beaten up, a yeoman's barn set on fire, a miller robbed of his flour, a peasant had refused labour to his lord. They came before the court, stated their case and were questioned in simple English. Local juries provided information, local customs were observed, and justices like Chaucer handed down verdicts. Yet the greatest joy for Bull was to discuss the day's events with the poet in a tavern or manor house in the evening.

Chaucer was a little portlier of late; his goatee beard contained a few grey hairs; his face and hooded eyes were sometimes red. He looked, and was, a comfortable fellow. And he missed nothing. "Did you notice the wart on that friar's nose?" he would suddenly ask. "That reeve had been making love to the miller's wife – did you see how she looked at him?" He would chuckle. "The more despicable they are, the more you seem to like them," Bull once chided him. But Chaucer only shook his head. "I love them all," he said simply. "Can't help it."

Yet, as time went by, there was one thing that troubled Bull. Strangely enough, it did not concern his own affairs, but those of Chaucer. He was so respectful of his friend's accomplishments, however, that for a long time he did not dare to bring it up. His chance came, at last, in April.

The two men had paid a visit to Bocton, where Bull's brother had welcomed them with his family, and it was as they rode in the warm spring sun down the Canterbury road the following morning that Chaucer broached his idea.

"It's an idea for a huge new work," he explained. "I've written so much conventional courtly verse. But for a long time now I've wanted to try something completely different. Look at all these folk we've been seeing day by day in court. The yeomen, the millers, the friars, the fishwives. What if I could let them speak, as well as the courtly folk." He grinned. "A great big work, a huge stew, a feast."

"But how do you make the speech of the common folk into a poem?" Bull objected.

"Ah," Chaucer cried, "I thought of that. What if each one of them told a tale, a little story like the Italian author Boccaccio uses. As they tell the stories, they also reveal themselves. Don't you see the neatness of it?"

"Except that common folk don't sit around telling stories like lazy courtiers," Bull remarked.

"Oh, but they do," his friend responded. "They do it when they travel together. And when do men and women of all conditions travel together, my dear Bull? On this very road." He laughed aloud. "Pilgrims, Bull. Pilgrims setting out from taverns like the George or the Tabard on their way to Becket's shrine at Canterbury. I could tell dozens of stories and fit them all together. I shall call it the Canterbury Tales."

"Wouldn't it be very long?"

"Yes. It will be my life's work."

And it was now, at last, that Bull saw the opportunity to say the thing that had been troubling him.

"If this is going to be the crowning work of your life, my dear friend," he said, "then will you allow me to beg of you one thing?"

"Of course," Chaucer smiled. "But what?"

"For the love of God," the merchant implored him, "don't let your talent be wasted and all your work be lost."

"Meaning?"

"Write it in Latin," Bull cried.

In fact, Bull's request was perfectly sensible and many would have agreed with him. When Geoffrey Chaucer wrote his verses in English, he was taking a huge risk. For in a sense, the English language did not really exist. True, there were related dialects all over England, but a man from Kent and a man from Northumbria would hardly have understood each other. When a northern monk wrote the tale of Sir Gawain and the Green Knight, or the poet Langland wrote of Piers Ploughman in the countryside, their work, though English, was thick with the Norse alliteration and the desolate echoes of ancient Anglo-Saxon, which sounded rustic and even comical to the courtly Chaucer. Yet what was the language he used? Part Saxon English, part Norman French, full of Latinate words, falling as lightly as a ballad by a French troubadour, Chaucer's English was the idiom of the court and the better classes in London. Not only that: aristocrats were just as likely to switch to French or learned men to Latin when they conversed. And even London English was constantly changing. "It's changed since I was a boy," Bull reminded his friend. "I dare say my own grandchildren will hardly understand your verses. Latin is best," Bull urged, "because it is eternal." Men all over Europe read and spoke it and, it could safely be assumed, would always do so. "You are like a man," Bull said, "throwing himself into a river and swimming when he should be building a noble bridge of stone. Don't let your life's work be swept away. Leave a monument, for future generations." It was sound advice; nor was Chaucer in the least annoyed.

"I'll think about it," he said, as they rode upon their way.

* * *

Few trading activities are more profitable, and few more hated, than the stratagem of cornering a market. Buy up the entire quantity of any commodity that is in great demand, create an artificial shortage, and sell at a high price. Such operations usually have to be large and involve a ring of merchants. In medieval London, the practice was called "forestalling". Technically, it was illegal.

Young Geoffrey Bull, formerly Ducket, and Richard Whittington, gentleman mercer, were more subtle.

The situation in which Bull had left them was remarkable. First, they had the use of Bull's huge business – the rents coming in from properties near the bridge; the exports of wool to Flanders, the imports of cloth; and there were profits from long-standing dealings with the Hansa merchants too. But it was not just the cash at their disposal that was so exciting. It was Bull's credit. "With this sort of credit," Whittington remarked, "a man could make huge speculations."

They did. But the system they operated was entirely of Ducket's devising. For the unusual feature of Bull's arrangement was that the two guardians of his fortune came from different guilds – not only that, but from guilds which were, just then, on extremely bad terms. When, therefore, Ducket's group of grocers purchased a huge quantity of a commodity, and Whittington's group of mercers bought up most of the rest, those in the marketplace assumed they must be rivals. Cleverer still, the two men were always careful to leave a little so that some of the middling traders could benefit from the rise in prices they were engineering. The two men went for luxury goods whose prices were not regulated and which could not be quickly replaced.

Peppercorns. Furs from the Baltic. An entire cargo of silk from the Orient. In the space of months they had swooped upon each of these – buying up, holding back in warehouses, letting out a little at a time at inflated prices. Between the autumn of 1385 and May 1386, the two men struck five times. By the end of this period, Whittington was a major figure in the Mercers; and Geoffrey Bull, formerly Ducket, was already a rich man in his own right.

* * *

It was Tiffany's idea. "I wouldn't have had the nerve," her husband confessed. "We're doing this behind your father's back." But Tiffany was determined.

"Leave Father to me," she said.

So on a bright afternoon in June 1386 Geoffrey Bull, formerly Ducket, nervously left his house on Oyster Hill and walked westward two hundred yards to the great house known as Coldharbour, whose gardens ran down to the river, and which was the place of business of one of the most awesome officials in the kingdom. "I bet they throw me out," he muttered, as he entered the forbidding gateway.

If the ten months since Bull's departure had allowed Geoffrey Bull, formerly Ducket, to make his fortune, his good luck in the last few weeks had almost taken his breath away.

The mighty Grocers Guild controlled the city. The mayor was a grocer, as were key aldermen. Like all successful organizations, its leaders looked to the future. And when they looked at Bull's son-in-law, they liked what they saw. His recent activities had impressed them. A number of middling members of the guild, who had been part of the ring, had profited nicely. "He is also going to inherit a huge fortune from Bull," an alderman pointed out. "Who would prefer him to transfer to the Mercers," someone else reminded them. "Can't have that," the alderman said. Like every man concerned with politics or charity, he knew that rich men must be cherished. "Better do something for him, then," he said.

So it was that Geoffrey Bull, formerly Ducket, found that he had been made an officer of the Grocers Guild – a remarkable feat for a fellow just short of twenty-six years old. Two weeks later, a vacancy having occurred, he found he was also a counsellor for his city ward. "You realize," Tiffany delightedly told him, "that this is the first step to being an alderman?"

Yet, despite all this good fortune, there was one thing that made him discontented. He felt guilty that it should do so since, he was the first to admit, none of his success could have happened but for his marriage. But all the same, it had rankled. Whatever I do in my life, he thought, I shall always have to call myself Bull. Always Bull. Never Ducket.

Yet it was not he, but Tiffany who had brought it up one day.

"You hate it, don't you?" she said. He denied it, but she shook her head. "Yes you do." And then she surprised him. "I hate it, too," she declared.

It was perfectly true. She was proud of being a Bull, and proud of her fortune. But even so, it had often secretly irritated her that to her friends she was the girl who had married beneath her. Once she had overheard a young woman saying: "Tiffany's husband? He's the one with the patch in his hair and the funny hands. The Bulls couldn't find her a proper husband, so they fished him out of the river." The words had shocked her. "No," she had wanted to tell her. "It was he who saved me from the river." She had wanted to smack the girl's face, but instead she inwardly resolved: I'll show you. I'll show you I have a husband to be proud of, and a better man than yours.

The College of Arms in Coldharbour was an awesome place. The cobblestone courtyard behind the gateway was brushed twice a day. The main building, facing the gate, was of stone below and timber above. Its great oak door was waxed and polished to a discreet glow. And having been admitted by a servant in gorgeous armorial livery, young Geoffrey Bull, formerly Ducket, found himself in a fine hall below whose timbered roof hung the colourful standards of many a knight and lord. After a short wait, a clerk, also in livery, conducted him through two more rooms to a grand, square chamber, in the middle of which, behind a dark table, sat no less a personage than the master of the royal heralds. Richard Spenser, Clarenceaux King of Arms and Earl Marshal of England. He gestured to the young man to state his business, which, after a moment's nervous hesitation, Geoffrey did.

"I wondered, sir," he concluded, "if I might have a coat of arms." And blushed.

A mere merchant, a humble little fellow without even a yard of land to his name, asking for a coat of arms just as if he were a knight, nobly born, of ancient lineage? A tradesman, venturing into the heraldic holy of holies, amongst the banners of barons, earls and Plantagenet princes? Absurd. Intolerable. An outrage.

Except, of course, that in England, it was not so at all.

For just as London merchants could turn into country gentlemen, and the gentry's younger sons could turn to trade, so in the dignities it awarded, feudal society's appearances often masked a more practical reality. Even the coveted order of knighthood was not sacrosanct. A century before, Edward I had insisted that rich merchants become knights, so that they would then owe the feudal tax which paid for his army of mercenaries. And in the matter of heraldry, the system was more flexible still.

It was, after all, an artificial invention. Until the joust had become popular in the time of Lionheart, many nobles had never heard of a coat of arms. But it had soon become the fashion. It was colourful, dignified, heroic, even romantic. And as in every sphere of medieval life, steps had been taken to give the new fashion a proper order. Under the heralds, the College of Arms became like a huge, royal guild, with conditions of membership, regulations, and its own mystery – the rules and art of heraldic design. No wonder then that the dignity of arms was eagerly sought. A man with a coat of arms, no matter who he was, secretly felt himself to be one of King Arthur's knights. His ancestors, however prosaic, became unsung heroes. He and his family, inscribed in the heraldic rolls, joined the immortals.

It was natural that the heralds should recognize the proud men who, even now, still referred to themselves as the barons of London. A mayor or alderman of London was entitled to a coat of arms. Bull had one from his father. An officer of one of the great guilds would merit consideration. When, therefore, the Earl Marshal stared at Geoffrey, he was not outraged, but only surprised.

"You are rather young for such a dignity," he reasonably pointed out. "But then," he added, "you are young to have become an officer of the Grocers Guild and a ward counsellor. How did you do it?"

Though he did not mention all his activities with Whittington, Ducket did explain that he had married Bull's daughter, and advanced because of it. He also admitted his own humble birth. "I suppose I shouldn't have come," he said.

"Though your humble birth is against you," the herald told

him, "it is not a bar to your achieving arms. We are more interested in the dignity you have attained. One thing, however," he continued, "is not clear to me. Are you seeking permission to use the arms of your wife's family or to establish a new coat of arms of your own?"

"I want to return to using my own name, sir," he said. "I want a coat of arms for the family of Ducket." For here was the heart of the matter. Once he had that, not even Bull could take his name away.

The herald looked at him and pondered. The august surroundings of Coldharbour generally produced, even in the proudest merchants, a certain discomfort. He could guess the courage it must have taken Ducket to walk through the door. The young fellow was not, so far as he could see, some cocky little upstart. He seemed to possess humility. Yet one puzzle remained. "Forgive my asking you," he gently enquired, "but how on earth did you manage to marry the daughter of a rich merchant like Bull?"

So Ducket told him, while the herald stared.

"You dived into the Thames under London Bridge, when it was in full spate?" he queried. "These things can be checked, you know," he softly warned.

"Yes sir," the young man replied.

And now the Earl Marshal of England burst into laughter.

"That's the most splendid thing I've heard in years." And with a smile of approval: "Well, Counsellor Ducket, you certainly seem determined to behave like one of the Knights of the Round Table. We shall have to see what we can do. Go with my clerk now," he ordered, "and he will explain."

A few minutes later he found himself in a long, busy room with a work table down the middle, half like a monastic library, half like a sign-painter's workshop. "Now good Master Ducket," the clerk began, "you shall see the wonderful mystery of heraldry."

"First," the clerk explained, "your arms will have a background colour. Except," he smiled, "that in heraldry we do not say colour, we say 'Tincture'." He pronounced the word in a French manner. "The chief Tinctures are blue, which we call Azure; green, which is Vert; red, Gules; black, Sable; purple, Purpure. There are two metallic tinctures: gold, which is Or, and silver, Argent. We also depict certain furs, the most liked being Ermine.

"This background we call the Field. You can partition the Field with lines – divide it into two halves of four quarters. You can make a chequerboard of it or have bands running across it, which we call bars. Whatever else you add upon it is called a charge. You can have a cross, for instance, or swords, axes, arrows, horseshoes, knots, harps. Here's a knight who's chosen a battering ram. Or you can have trees, flowers, stars."

"What about animals?" Ducket asked.

"Ah," the clerk beamed. "Yes indeed." And turning over some great sheets of parchment: "These," he said contentedly, "are only a few." Ducket gasped. It was astonishing. There were depictions of lions, leopards, bears, wolves, stags, hares, bulls, swans, eagles, dolphins, serpents. But not only that, each was shown in a variety of different attitudes: rising up on hindlegs (this he learned was Rampant); sitting, crouching, turning; upper half only; head only. The combinations seemed endless. Nearby he noticed another clerk working up a design of two lions rearing up as though about to fight. "Lions Rampant Combatant," his guide advised. "But you haven't seen the best of all," he said, and taking Ducket to another pile of drawings he began to spread them out. "These," he said fondly, "are the heraldic monsters."

How exotic they were. Some were familiar: a magnificent dragon, a handsome unicorn. But others were more curious: a griffin, half lion half eagle; a cockatrice, cock in front, tailed dragon behind; the heraldic panther, which breathes fire; a sea-lion, which was shown as a lion with a fish's tail; and of course a mermaid.

"So," the clerk concluded, "have you any thoughts as to what you might like? A mermaid perhaps? A griffin?"

"I wondered," Ducket answered, "if I could have a duck."

"A duck?" The clerk looked disappointed.

"In a river," Ducket said.

It turned out to be not as simple as Ducket had supposed. His first suggestion, a green duck on a blue background was instantly vetoed. "You can't put one colour on top of another," the clerk explained. "You put gold or silver on a colour, or a colour on gold or silver. It shows up better. We often suggest a river by some wavy bands across the field," his guide suggested. "Let me show you."

And so it was, some time later, that Ducket found himself gazing at a sketch of a shield. The background was silver – which could also be shown as white. Across the middle ran two thick wavy bands of blue, for the river. And there were three red ducks, two above and one below the blue wavy bands. All of which, naturally, had to be given the correct heraldic description, known as the Blazon.

"Argent, two Bars Wavy Azure, between three Ducks Gules," the clerk announced firmly. "The arms of Ducket."

The figure who stood before the court in Rochester Castle had clearly seen better days. His black coat was badly stained. The tunic, though of expensive material, was worn. He was, perhaps, not aware that in the back of his hose there was a small, round hole through which the flesh could be seen. Chaucer and the sergeant-at-law accompanying him looked at the fellow curiously. It seemed to the poet that he had seen him before. The fellow's name was Simon le Clerk. He said he came from Oxford.

His defence, it had to be said, was good, and he made it soundly, in the tones of an educated man.

"The truth is, your worshipful and learned sirs, that I did indeed take money from this miller here." With a trace of distaste he indicated a stout and vulgar looking fellow. "He made a wager with me which I won. I considered him sober at the time, but if he wishes to plead that he was not, and it pleases your worships, I will return the wager, which was exactly half of what he says I took. The rest of his charge," he shrugged disdainfully, "that I am a magician, a necromancer, and that I promised to turn base metal into gold, is absurd. Does he offer any evidence? Where are the tools of my nefarious trade? What beakers and crucibles? What concoctions and elixirs? Have any such things been found upon me or at my lodgings? Of course not, for they do not, and never have existed. There is not a shadow of proof for his assertions which are, I suggest, as base as the metals he claims I turn to gold. In short, your worships, it is he who seeks, in this preposterous matter, to manufacture gold – not I."

The judges smiled. It was neatly put. The miller was

shaking his head and looking furious, but it was obvious he had no evidence to offer.

"Pay back what you won," Chaucer ordered, "and let the matter be closed." And the sergeant-at-law was just nodding in agreement when Bull arrived.

"Good God," he cried, "it's Silversleeves."

It was the last day of his sojourn with Chaucer. A year had passed since he had left London and, ever since the start of July, he had been feeling it was time to return. He had just been visiting the noble cathedral of Rochester that morning before making his way up to the castle where he was to bid goodbye to his friend.

It did not take him long to tell what he knew, after which Chaucer summed up once more, but rather differently.

"From the words of a witness of unimpeachable character," he told Silversleeves, "we now learn that you have given us a false name, that you come from London, not Oxford, and that you were suspected of exactly this crime before. We have, therefore, your word against the word of this miller. And I must tell you that this court believes the miller." He turned to the sergeant-at-law. "Is that good law?"

"Good enough."

"Then," pronounced Geoffrey Chaucer, Justice of the Peace, "I sentence you to repay this miller the entire sum he says you owe, and to spend tomorrow morning in the stocks." He thought for a moment. "With a crucible hung round your neck." English justice was commonsense, if nothing else.

It was in a cheerful mood that Gilbert Bull the merchant rode back towards London and his house on the bridge. He had not told them he was coming.

She had forgotten how angry he could be. As Tiffany stood before her father, three days after his sudden arrival, in the big upstairs room of the house on London Bridge, she felt almost like a child again. Red-faced, his blue eyes glowering, he seemed even larger than she remembered him. And he was in a towering rage.

"Treachery!" he roared. "Your husband's a Judas. I was right all along. Never trust a foundling. Bad blood." He pointed at her. "You're no better though, you little Jezebel!"

"It's not treachery," she protested. "Our children are still your grandchildren."

"Oh but it is treachery," he cried. "It's the fortune of Bull you expect to inherit, not of Ducket."

"I did not realize you felt so strongly, Father."

"Then why did you do it behind my back?" he roared.

It had been when the cook had referred to Geoffrey as "Master Ducket" that he had discovered. "You mean Master Bull," he had corrected. "Oh no sir," she had said, "he's Master Ducket now." And it had all come out.

It was hard for Bull to say what had hurt him most: the deception they had used, the loss of his name – his immortality – in future generations, or the fact that thanks to Ducket's brilliant business success, they no longer needed him. He would have scorned, in any case, to say such things. But there was one thing he could say, the most terrible indictment that any Bull could make of another man.

"He broke his word," he cried. And then, as Tiffany went very pale, he told her exactly what he intended to do.

"At his age?" At first Ducket did not believe it.

"Why not? He's still vigorous."

"But to start all over again?"

"It's my fault," Tiffany said. Her father's sudden arrival had caught her off-guard. She had meant to break the idea of Ducket's name change to him gently, at the proper time. But there was no excuse. She had been so busy thinking of pleasing the one man that she had grown careless of the other.

"Does this mean I have to go back to being Bull?"

"No good," she said. "He doesn't trust us any more. He thinks we'd change it back again, after he's gone."

"Perhaps he'll alter his mind?" But Tiffany shook her head.

For Bull intended to marry again. "And if I have a son," he had told her coldly, "it is he, and not you and Ducket, who will inherit."

But it was now, to his surprise, that Ducket saw a side of his wife that he had never seen before. For she shook her head, and her soft brown eyes suddenly went very hard.

"I don't think you quite understand," she said quietly, "how much money we're talking about."

"What can we do then?" he asked.

"We've got to head him off," she said.

Dame Barnikel was rather surprised towards the end of the first week in August, to receive a visit from Tiffany. Since she only knew her slightly, Dame Barnikel was equally surprised when the girl indicated that she wanted to speak to her confidentially. But they sat down at a table, and after a little small talk, Tiffany broached the subject.

"I'm worried about my father," she began.

Her description of the rich merchant was touching: a lonely widower, in need of the companionship of a woman of mature years. "Or," Tiffany said quietly, "perhaps there are married women who might like a discreet friendship. He is in very good shape for his age. I wondered," she said, "if you might know of anyone."

Dame Barnikel frowned.

"Let me get this straight," she said. "You're trying to find your father a nice mistress."

"Yes."

"You're asking if I might know of anyone?"

"I know your judgement is good, Dame Barnikel." Tiffany paused. "Actually," she said, "I think he's always had rather an admiration for you."

It was not her first port of call. Dame Barnikel was in fact the third woman with whom Tiffany had had a similar conversation. She probably would not have ventured into so vulgar a place as Southwark if she had met with better luck so far. But she had heard her father in the past refer to her, albeit with a laugh, as a fine woman. By now she was ready to try anything. As to her strategy, it was very simple. "He must either marry a woman past childbearing, or find a mistress he can't marry. Which means she must be married already," she had told Ducket. And when he wondered aloud if she could bring it off. "I've got to," she said.

"You're thinking of me?" Dame Barnikel asked.

"It just crossed my mind."

"You couldn't let him find his own woman?"

"I'm so fond of him. I don't want him to get hurt."

Dame Barnikel looked her straight in the eye.

"Lot of money at stake?" she said.

"Yes."

And now Dame Barnikel laughed.

"I don't think so," she said. "I've got a perfectly good Bull of my own."

And so the two women parted, the one to tend to her husband, the other to her inheritance.

Tiffany's problem was solved not by her own efforts, but by help from another quarter.

Of all the members of the Commons who had gathered by the start of October for the opening of the new session, few were more quietly distinguished than one of the knights of the shire chosen for the county of Kent. For it was in this capacity that Chaucer, wool comptroller, soldier, diplomat, poet, Justice of the Peace and now representative of his county made his one appearance in that hallowed institution. Though he had not actually received the accolade of knighthood, he was, by convention as a county representative, referred to as a knight of his shire.

Upon this notable occasion, it was entirely natural that Richard Whittington, mercer and gentleman, should have given a small feast in his honour at his house. It was also natural that he should invite their mutual friend Bull to be one of the party. And it was typical of his character that, as he considered what other guests to invite, he should have borne in mind the grave problem currently faced by his friend and erstwhile colleague Geoffrey Ducket.

So it was a rather pleasant surprise for Bull to find himself sitting next to a woman whose quiet and subtle sensuality, as the evening progressed, he could not fail to appreciate. He was flattered also that she seemed to take an interest in him.

"I believe," Whittington murmured to him at the end of the evening, "she's quite unattached at present." While to Ducket the next morning he remarked with a laugh: "The beauty of it is, they certainly can't marry."

There was no small excitement when it was rumoured that Bull had been seen purchasing a posy of flowers which, they had reason to think, he intended to present to Sister Olive.

1422

As the new century had begun, it was generally agreed in London that few families were more fortunate than that of Ducket. There were seven healthy children; Ducket himself continued to increase his own considerable fortune; and Tiffany became a far greater heiress than even she had hoped to be.

For in the year 1395, first the heir to Bocton and then his grief-stricken father had died. The lovely old Kent estate had passed to Gilbert Bull, the surviving brother, who became the richest member of his family who had ever lived. Since, as he pointed out, he could not have very many years to enjoy the place, he quit the house on London Bridge, which Tiffany and Ducket took over, and went to live at his childhood home, where he remained. His affair with Sister Olive had lasted eight years and had been an unqualified success. Given her convenient and sensual availability, his desire for the rigours of matrimony soon left him. As he saw his merry grand-children, he could not fail to be taken with them; and his family pride was somewhat mollified when it was pointed out to him, by one of the heralds at the College of Arms, that since Ducket had his own arms, and Tiffany was, as he put it, an armorial heiress, the arms of Bull and Ducket could be joined, leaving Bull at least a heraldic immortality for future generations. As he looked out from Bocton across the glorious sweep of the Weald of Kent, it seemed to Bull that the years of his retirement were bathed in a soft and gentle light.

Yet, before he found final rest, some shadows were to cross even this pleasant landscape.

Despite its early promise, the reign of young Richard II had ended badly. Many at court felt that the young man's brave success at the time of the Peasants' Revolt had gone to his head. Whatever his courage, he had shown none of the Black Prince's ability as a commander. Wildly extravagant, some of his ideas, like the handsome new roof for Westminster Hall, were admired; others, like his reckless spending on his favourites, were not. And suddenly, shortly before the century's end, his behaviour had become so erratic that, after a huge row over his feudal inheritance, John of Gaunt's son Henry had taken up arms and deposed him.

Henry IV, of the House of Lancaster, as his branch of the royal family was called, had governed well. But the business had offended Bull's sense of propriety all the same. The new king had usurped another's rightful place. The order of the universe had been disrupted. "In the long run," he warned his family, "it will lead to trouble."

A deeper shadow had come a year later, in 1400.

Plague. It had returned to London in the summer. Despite their protests, Bull carried his family to Bocton. There on the high ridge, just as when he was a youth, he had waited until it was past. Only when he was sure it was safe, in late October, did he venture back with them to London. To find that the darkness, once again, had taken from him one he loved.

Chaucer had found a pleasant little house for his retirement, at Westminster, just between the palace and the Abbey with a charming walled garden all around. He had only been there a year, working on his Canterbury Tales when, quite suddenly, in that summer of the plague, his life was snuffed out.

"Why didn't I think of him? Why didn't I bring him to Bocton?" Bull cried in misery. Though when he went to the house, it was not clear to him whether his friend had died of the plague or of something else. The gardener said plague; the monks said not.

"But I can promise you this," one monk assured him, "he made a good death. He repented of all his works at the end, you know. Impious and ungodly, those tales were. He said we should burn them all," he added with satisfaction.

"Did you?" Bull asked.

"Those we could find," the monk replied.

Could his friend, Bull wondered, in the last extremities of pain, have cried out such a thing? Who knew? But as he considered Chaucer's huge and panoramic work, unfinished at his death and so hopelessly, so mistakenly, in English, it hardly seemed to him to matter.

"It will all be lost or forgotten anyway," he said sadly as he left the house.

The bells were tolling for vespers as he was led back through the Abbey. "Would you like to see his grave?" the monk kindly enquired, and led him to the place.

"I'm glad, at least, he is buried in the Abbey," Bull said.

"He was an ornament to England. I'm pleased to see you recognized it."

But the monk shook his head.

"You misunderstand, sir," he explained. "He is here because of his house." He smiled. "He was an Abbey tenant, you see."

Bull died five years after that and Bocton came to Tiffany. She went there more often than Ducket, though he too came to love the Bulls' ancient place.

"But my home is in London," he would truthfully say. And he lived there contentedly. He saw his friend Whittington become mayor not once, or even twice, but a legendary three times. He saw him build many of the things he had always said he would, including a new water fountain. In his will, the mayor even provided for sanitary public lavatories not far from dirty old St Lawrence Silversleeves.

He watched James Bull's brewery prosper from its modest beginnings at the George to a great affair which supplied beer to the troops of the next king, Henry V, when they went to fight at Agincourt. He saw England, in its old conflict with France, once again triumph as it had in the days of the Black Prince. He saw his own children grow up and grow rich until it was nearing the time when he, too, should depart.

Yet even now, as he grew old, and remained in the house on London Bridge, his greatest pleasure of all was to watch the river, not only in the evening out of the big window that faced upstream, but better yet, in the early morning, standing by the road on the Southwark side not far from the spot where he had first been found, from which vantage point he could gaze for an hour or more at the great stream of the Thames flowing eternally towards the rising sun.

Chapter 10

Hampton Court

1533

She should not have entered the garden. She should have walked past when she heard the whispers. Hadn't her brother warned her about such things?

A sultry August afternoon; a clear blue sky. In its great deer-park beside the Thames, a dozen miles upriver from London, the huge, red-brick Tudor palace of Hampton Court lay in the warm sun. Across the green spaces before the palace, she could hear the distant sounds of the courtiers' laughter. Further away, amongst the parkland trees, the deer moved delicately, like dappled shadows. There was a faint scent of mown grass and, it seemed, of honeysuckle in the gentle breeze.

She had walked away to the riverbank, wanting to be alone, and it was only now, as she came past the hedge, that she heard the whispers.

Susan Bull was twenty-eight. In an age which admired pale, oval faces, her features were pleasantly regular. People said that her hair was her best feature. When not pinned up, it hung very simply close to her face, only curling a little at her shoulders. But it was the colour that everyone remembered – a dark, rich brown with a hint of warm auburn that gave it a lustrous sheen, like polished cherry wood. Her eyes were of the same colour. But secretly she was more proud of the fact that, after four children, her body had not lost its slim shape. Her dress was simple but elegant: a starched white coif on her head, under which her hair was neatly tied, and a pale brown silk gown. The modest gold cross that hung round her neck suggested, correctly, that she loved her religion, though many a lady would have made a similar show of piety at the court, where it was quite the fashion.

She had not wanted to come here. The courtiers always seemed so devious, and she hated any kind of falseness. Nor would she have done so if she had not felt she must. She sighed. It was all Thomas's idea.

Thomas and Peter, her two brothers: it really was astonishing how different they were. Thomas, the baby of the family: quick, brilliant, charming, wilful. She loved him of course, but with reservations. Large reservations.

And Peter, comfortable, solid Peter. Though actually her half-brother from an earlier marriage, he was the one to whom she felt closer. It was Peter, the eldest of the Meredith family, who had taken the place of their father when he died young. Peter who was still, and always would be, the family conscience. She had not really been surprised when he had entered the priesthood, leaving young Thomas to pursue the things of the world.

There had been no better parish priest in London than Father Peter Meredith. A good height, balding and pleasantly stout by his forties, his comforting presence was as familiar as it was welcome to his flock. He was a clever man and, but for a streak of laziness in his youth, he might have been a fine scholar. His parish of St Lawrence Silversleeves was not a place for an ambitious man. Yet he was content. He had restored the little church with its dark rood screen, and under his wardenship, it had gained two fine new stained glass windows. He knew the name of every child in his parish; the women liked his bonhomie because they knew he observed his vows of celibacy; he could drink with the men but keep a genial dignity. After giving the last rites, he would always hold the dying person's hand until they were safely gone. His sermons were simple, his conversation matter-of-fact. He was a solid Catholic priest.

Only the previous year he had fallen sick, quite seriously so, and after a time announced: "I can't keep up the pastoral work any more." He had chosen to retire to the great Charterhouse monastery in London; but before doing so had decided to make a pilgrimage to Rome. "See Rome and die," he had cheerfully remarked, "though I shan't die yet, I dare say." He was still there now. And she had had to write to him for guidance about this business today. For the twentieth time, that morning, she had read his reply.

I can only tell you to follow your conscience. Your religion is strong. Pray therefore, and you will know what to do.

She had prayed. Then she had come here.

Somewhere in the great labyrinth of Hampton Court was her dear husband Rowland. It was an hour since Thomas had led him in there – to what they both knew would be the most important meeting of his life. She had never seen him so on edge. For three days he had repeatedly been sick and looked so deathly pale that, if she had not been used to his intense and nervous constitution, Susan might have thought that he was really ill. He was doing it for her and the children, but for himself too. Perhaps that was why she wanted him to succeed so much.

Peter's greatest gift of all to her had been her husband. It was Peter who had found Rowland, Peter who had quietly sent him to her with a message: *This is the one*. "Damn it, they even look the same," Thomas had complained. For it was true that Peter and her husband with their stout build and prematurely balding heads did look rather similar. But despite this superficial resemblance there was an important difference. Even if the monk was the older and wiser of the two, gentle Rowland had a quiet ambition which, she knew, Peter lacked. "I couldn't have married a man without ambition," she confessed.

As for the physical side of their marriage, that too, she felt confident, could hardly be bettered. Yet she smiled when she thought of the early days. How devout, how hesitant they had been! How seriously they had both tried to follow the rules and make their intimacy a sacrament. It was she, after a short while, who had decided to take charge.

"But you are wanton," he had said, looking rather surprised.

"I need something to confess," she had replied. And many times since then their own priest, with a smile they did not see, had given them each a little penance and a kindly absolution.

Now Rowland had his chance. If the interview which Thomas had arranged was successful, there was no denying what it might mean. An outlet for his talents; a respite from their endless worries over money; perhaps even modest riches one day. When she thought of the children she told herself: it must be right.

There was one other consolation. Whatever she might think of courts, she knew they were a necessary evil, the courtiers only servants. Behind them lay the all-important figure whose cause they would really be serving. Her father's friend; her brother's benefactor; the man she had been brought up to love and trust all her life.

Good King Henry, England's pious king, head of the house of Tudor.

The Plantagenet dynasty had collapsed in that terrible series of family feuds between John of Gaunt's House of Lancaster and its rival the House of York, known as the Wars of the Roses. So many royal princes had been killed, that an obscure Welsh family, married by chance into the old royal house, had emerged. When he killed the last Plantagenet, Richard III, at the Battle of Bosworth, fifty years before, Henry's father had established the Tudor dynasty on England's throne.

Susan could still remember the day – she had been five, a year before her father died – when he had taken her to court; and how, advancing across the great hall had come the most splendid figure she had ever seen. Big and broad-chested in his jewel-encrusted tunic with its huge, rolled shoulder-pads, Henry was a magnificent giant. His tightly fitting hose revealed the powerful legs of an athlete; and between them, padded to emphasize the bulk of his sexual parts, a bulging cod-piece. Her heart missed a beat when suddenly a pair of tremendous arms scooped her up, raised her high, and she found herself looking straight into a large, handsome face with a pair of wide-set, merry eyes and a square-cut, reddish-brown beard.

"So this is your little girl," the mighty monarch had smiled, as he brought her to his face and gave her a kiss. And, even at her age, Susan knew that surely this was everything a man could be.

No prince in Europe was finer than Harry of England. England might be small – at under three million, her population was only a fifth of that of the now united kingdom of France – but Henry made up for the deficiency with lavish style. Mighty sportsman, accomplished musician, occasional scholar, tireless builder of palaces – he was everything a Renaissance man should be. At Flodden, his armies had crushed the Scots; at the gorgeous pageant of the Field of the Cloth of Gold, he had made a peace with the equally splendid King of France. And most important of all, at a time when Christendom was facing its greatest crisis in a thousand years, Harry of England was devout.

It was early in Henry's reign that Martin Luther had begun his religious protest in Germany. Like the English Lollards before, the Lutherans' original demands for Church reform had soon grown into a huge challenge to Catholic doctrine. Soon these Protestants were denying the miracle of the Mass and the need for bishops, and were saying priests could marry. Shockingly, some ruling princes were even sympathetic. But not good King Henry. When German merchants had infiltrated Lutheran tracts into London, he had stamped them out. A translation of the New Testament by Tyndale had been publicly burned seven years before at St Paul's. And the scholar king had personally penned such a splendid rebuttal of the heretic Luther that the grateful Pope had given him a new title: Defender of the Faith.

As for Henry's recent problems with the Pope over the question of his wife, like many devout people in England Susan had great sympathy for Henry. "I believe he is doing his best in a very difficult position," she would declare. Besides, the business might still be resolved. "I'm not prepared," she said, "to judge him yet."

The grounds that lay before Hampton Court, known as the Great Orchard, were typical of those around such houses – an elaborate network of formal gardens, gazebos, arbours and private places which King Henry, who loved such displays, had been decorating with all manner of heraldic beasts, sundials and other ornaments in painted wood or stone.

It was chance that, as she walked by a high, green hedge enclosing one of the gardens, she should have heard the whispers. Then she thought she heard a laugh.

Daniel Dogget stood by the landing stage at Hampton Court, looked down at his squat wife and her sturdy little brother, and wondered.

It was quiet. Out in the stream, white swans glided and black moorhens bobbed, as though that summer would never cease.

Dan Dogget was a giant. Over two centuries had passed since Barnikel of Billingsgate had visited the Dogget sisters on the Bankside and left one of them with a baby. The child took on the Barnikel stature, but the sisters' colouring and name. His children, apart from their size, were hardly distinguishable from their cousins of the old Ducket family, except by their slightly different name; but by the time of the Black Death, when little Geoffrey Ducket was taken in by Bull, it was this other, Dogget branch of the family that had mainly survived. Dan Dogget was six foot three; big-boned and spare in build, with a huge mane of black hair with a flash of white over his forehead. He was the strongest waterman on the Thames. He could break a chain across his chest. Ever since the age of twelve, he had been allowed to row with the men; by the age of eighteen he could out-curse any of them – a notable achievement, for the watermen of London were legendary for their loud mouths. At twenty, not a man would fight him, even in the roughest of the waterside taverns.

"So what will you do?" the little man asked again. Receiving no reply, he delivered his considered opinion. "You know your problem, Daniel? You've got too many obligations." To which Dogget only sighed, but said nothing. Not that he had ever complained. He was devoted to his tubby wife Margaret and their brood of happy children; he was kind to his sister's family; and now, when poor Carpenter's wife had died giving birth to her fourth, he had brought his own wife and children upriver from Southwark to the lodgings at Hampton Court where Carpenter was working. "They can live with you until things get sorted out," he had offered, and Carpenter's gratitude had been obvious. But if only this were all. There was still the matter of his father.

It was a year since he had let the old man live with them in Southwark – and a year that he had regretted it. Old Will Dogget might be a standing joke to his friends, but after his last drunken escapade, Dan confessed: "I can't handle him any more." What was to be done with him, though? He couldn't just throw the old man out. He had tried his sister, but she wouldn't take him. He sighed again. Whatever the answer was, he thought, you could be sure of one thing. "It'll cost money." And short of stealing, there was only one way he could get that: which was why, now, his eyes were scanning the barges moored by the jetty. Could one of them provide his answer?

Though they came in many sizes, all the Thames passenger barges conformed to the same basic pattern. In construction, they were essentially Viking longboats with a shallow keel, and planks laid, in the overlapping clinker fashion, in long, sweeping lines. Inside, they were divided into two parts: the fore section, with benches for oarsmen; and the aft section where the passengers reclined. The variations upon this theme, however, were many. There were the simplest row-boats, the broad and shallow wherries, which one or two oarsmen could send skimming across the river between Southwark and the city. There were longer barges, with several pairs of oars and, usually, a canopy over the passengers. These frequently had rudders and a man to steer as well. And there were the huge barges of the great city companies, with entire superstructures for the passengers, magnificently carved prows, and a dozen or more pairs of oars to pull them, like the gilded barge of the Lord Mayor, as he was now called, which led the yearly water procession.

Daniel loved the waterman's life. The work might be physically hard, but he was built for it. The feel of the blades dipping neatly into the water, the surge of the boat, the smell of the riverweed – these brought him a contentment that could not be bettered. Above all, as he fell into the slow, powerful rhythm, he would experience a huge warmth swelling up in his broad chest as though, like the river's flow, his strength were endless. How well he knew the river – every bank, every bend, from Greenwich to Hampton Court. Once, rowing a young courtier, the fellow had sung a pretty ballad with a chorus:

Sweet Thames, run softly
'Til I end my song.

This had so pleased him that often, on a still summer morning, he would find himself murmuring the words as he slipped down the stream.

There was plenty of work. Since London Bridge was still the only road across the Thames, and it was frequently congested, there were always wherries hurrying across the river at the city and at Westminster. For longer journeys, too, the river route, if not quicker, was certainly more comfortable. Many a courtier due at Hampton Court in the morning would spread out on cushions in one of the noble barges and let the watermen, dressed in gorgeous livery, row him upriver through a warm summer night. It was much better than setting out at dawn down the rutted lane known as the King's Road, that led past Chelsea towards the royal palace. Sweet Thames run softly. On such journeys as these, with gratuities in addition, the watermen were well paid.

If only he could get work on one of the fine barges, he could make a very different living. But, "You're so big," he was told, "it's hard to pair you." And for the good jobs, even in the humble Watermens Guild, you needed connections. "Which is what I haven't got," he would sigh. Somehow, though, he had to find a way, if only to save his old father. Then his troubles would be over.

The two men were laughing as they walked through the great courtyard, their footsteps echoing softly against the brick walls. It was time to rejoice.

Rowland Bull was laughing with relief. The interview had gone better than he could have imagined. Even now, he could hardly believe that they had said: "We want you." It was no small thing for a conscientious lawyer to hear from the Chancellor of England himself. Rowland Bull, son of modest Bull the brewer of Southwark was needed at the heart of the kingdom. He was flattered. As for the income – it was more than he had dreamed. If he had had doubts about the worldliness of the court, when he thought of his little family and how this would transform their lives, it seemed to him that it must be God's will. He turned.

"I owe all this to you."

It was hard not to like Thomas Meredith. Slim and handsome, with his sister's colouring, he was the family's worldly hope. The Merediths were Welsh. Like other Welsh families, they had come to England with the Tudors. Thomas's grandfather had fought at Bosworth; his father might have risen at court if he had not died when Thomas and Susan were children. But King Henry had not forgotten the Merediths and had given young Thomas a position with the powerful royal secretary, Thomas Cromwell, where he seemed born to succeed. He had studied at Cambridge and the Inns of Court; he sang and danced well; he fenced and drew a bow; he even played the royal game of tennis with the king. "Though I make sure I lose," he smiled. At the age of twenty-six he was altogether charming.

If Rowland Bull wanted to sum up the influences that had brought him so far, he could do so precisely. Books, and the Merediths.

The books were easy to explain. It had been a member of the Mercers Guild, a fellow called Caxton, who had brought the first printing presses to England from Flanders and set up shop at Westminster, just before the Wars of the Roses came to an end. The effect had been astonishing. A flood of printed books had soon appeared. Caxton's books were easy to read. In place of illuminations they often had lively black and white woodcuts; and above all, compared to the old hand-produced manuscripts, they were cheap. Bull the brewer, though he liked to read, would never have owned several dozen books otherwise. And so it was that Rowland, the youngest son, had been allowed to bury his nose in Chaucer, the stories of King Arthur, and a score of sermons and religious tracts; and it was this love of books that had finally led him away from the brewery to become a poor Oxford scholar and then to study the law. It was the books, too, that had caused him as a young man to contemplate the religious life.

But all the rest was the Merediths. Wasn't it Peter, the man he respected above all others who had told him: "There are other ways to serve God, you know, than in holy orders." Wasn't it Peter who, when he had feared he could not keep a religious vow of chastity, had smilingly remarked: "Better, according to St Paul, to marry than burn." Through Peter he had discovered Susan, and a happiness he had never dared to hope could be his. And if, from time to time, he still yearned for the religious life, it was the only secret he ever kept from the wife with whom, now, his duty lay. As for today, his thanks were due to Thomas Meredith, and he gave them gladly. He trusted him.

But that August afternoon there was more important news which, after the summer of uncertainty, was today being whispered throughout the palace. As they came out of the courtyard through a heavy archway, Thomas nudged his brother-in-law and remarked, with a grin: "Look up."

The arch was certainly fine. If the previous century had been darkened by the Wars of the Roses, its compensating glory had been its architecture – in particular that very English culmination of the Gothic style known as Perpendicular. Here, the tiers of pointed arches gave way to a purer structure of simple, elegant shafts between which hung not walls but great curtains of glass; and above this the ceiling, nearly flat now, spread out in the lovely fan vaulting, a lacework in stone, the finest examples of which were in the chapels at Windsor and at King's College, Cambridge.

The ceiling of the archway also had a fan vault; and it was there, amidst the delicate tracery, that Thomas and Rowland could see, lovingly entwined, the two initials which, this summer, were bringing a new hope to England: H, for Henry and A, for Anne.

Anne Boleyn.

When, after two decades of affectionate marriage to his Spanish wife, Katherine, Henry still had no legitimate heir except his sickly daughter Mary, he was understandably alarmed. What would become of the Tudor dynasty? No woman had ever ruled England: wouldn't it dissolve into chaos, like the Wars of the Roses? Nor was it surprising if, as a loyal son of the Church, he finally began to ask himself: why? Why was he being denied the male heir his country needed? What had he done wrong?

One possibility existed. Had not Katherine, however briefly, been his elder brother's wife? For before the poor boy's untimely death, Arthur, the then heir had first been married to the Spanish princess. So wasn't Henry's union forbidden? At this juncture he had met Anne Boleyn.

She was an English rose. The Boleyns were a London family; Anne's grandfather had been Lord Mayor. But two brilliant marriages had allied the former merchant family with the upper aristocracy, and a stay at the French court had given her an elegance and wit that were captivating. Soon Henry was in love; before long he was wondering whether this bewitching young woman could provide a healthy heir.

And so it was that, impelled by desire as well as the needs of state, he decided: "My marriage to Katherine has been cursed. I shall ask the Pope for an annulment."

It was not as shocking as it seemed; indeed, Henry had every reason to assume it would be granted. The Church was not without mercy. Grounds were sometimes found to release couples trapped in impossible marriages. The laity manipulated the rules too: an aristocrat might marry a cousin within the forbidden degree of relationship, knowing the marriage could be annulled; some even made deliberate mistakes in their wedding vows, leaving a loophole to have them declared invalid. But all this aside, the Pope had a clear desire and responsibility to help England's loyal king create an orderly succession if he could.

It was therefore amazingly bad luck that, just as Henry appealed for help, the Pope himself should have been virtually taken prisoner by another, even more powerful Catholic monarch: Charles V, Holy Roman Emperor, King of Spain, and head of the mighty Habsburg dynasty, whose aunt was none other than Katherine. "The Habsburgs would be insulted by an annulment," he declared; and as Henry's messengers arrived, the Pope was told: "Say no."

The ensuing negotiations were part tragedy, part farce. Henry's minister, the great Cardinal Wolsey, was broken by them. As Henry pressed, the poor Pope prevaricated. Everything was tried. Even Europe's universities were canvassed for their opinions. Earthy Luther laughed: "Let him commit bigamy." The Pope himself discreetly suggested that Henry should divorce and remarry without his sanction – presumably hoping to regularize it later. "But that would be no use," Henry pointed out. "The marriage, and the heirs, must be clearly legitimate." To frighten the Pope, Henry even commanded the English Church to subject their courts to him and stopped their taxes going to Rome. But still the pontiff was helpless, clamped in the iron Habsburg jaws.

Then, in January 1533, time ran out: Anne was pregnant.

With a new archbishop, Thomas Cranmer, who believed his case was good, Henry acted. On the authority of the English Church alone, Cranmer annulled the marriage to Katherine and married the king and Boleyn.

Many protested. Old Bishop Fisher of Rochester refused to

sanction it. Thomas More, the former chancellor, was disapprovingly silent. A religious fanatic, the Holy Maid of Kent, prophesied that the wicked king would die, and was arrested for treason. But the embarrassed Pope himself, who had confirmed Cranmer in office, still hesitated to say whether he agreed with the new marriage or not.

What were a pious and educated couple like Rowland and Susan Bull to think? Their devout Catholic king had fallen out with the Pope. Such things had happened before. They understood the politics of the situation. The faith, as such, was not really affected. "He may have acted wrongly, but he is doing his best for England," Susan said. "It will all be resolved in the end," Rowland hopefully declared. And especially, he thought, as he walked through the arch with Thomas Meredith, after the wonderful news that day.

The astrologers had predicted it; Anne herself, sitting inside the palace with her ladies making smocks for the poor, admitted that she felt sure; and that very morning the doctors had unequivocally declared that the unborn child was a boy. England at last was going to have an heir. And who, devout or not, Pope or not, was sensibly going to quarrel with that?

So it was with his heart full of happiness that Rowland Bull hurried out to find his wife that August afternoon.

There were red and white roses in the garden. It seemed very quiet as Susan Bull stepped in.

She had gone several paces when she saw the man and the woman. They were to her right, in an arbour, and they were looking at her.

She did not know the woman – a lady of the court, clearly. Her blue silk dress was raised above her waist. Her white stockings were down to just below her knees. Her slippers were still on, but her pale, slim legs were clasping the haunches of a large man who held her. The man remained fully dressed except in one particular: the brightly coloured flap of his cod-piece had been undone. It was a convenient aspect of that part of masculine attire.

King Henry VIII of England had found it so this afternoon. It was a pity that, surprised in the act, he had automatically disengaged, with the result that now, to her astonishment, and hardly aware of what she was doing, Susan Bull found herself staring at the king in his nakedness. And he at her.

For several seconds she was so shocked that she did not move, but stood there staring idiotically. The woman who, expecting her to retire discreetly, had not altered her position, with a look of annoyance now lowered her feet to the ground while King Henry, to her amazement, calmly turned to face her.

What should she do? It seemed too late to run. Unaware that she was even doing so, she put her hand up to the cross she was wearing. How was one supposed to behave? Should she curtsy? Her body seemed paralysed. And then King Henry spoke.

"So, Mistress: you have seen the king today."

She realized: it was her cue. This was the moment to say something amusing, to make the business pass off lightly. She racked her brains. Nothing came. Worse: without thinking, she had allowed her eyes to wander.

She couldn't help it. She might have been taken aback by the sight of Henry, but now, as her gaze travelled down and she remembered the king's reputation as a lover, she found herself thinking: he is no different from my husband. Rather less in fact. She also noticed something else. The shirt that Henry was wearing had come partly undone. The splendid figure she remembered lifting her up as a child was still recognizable, but time had taken its toll upon Henry; the thirty-four-inch waist of his prime had swelled to almost fifty-four, and the great, hairy, overhanging gut of which she caught a glimpse did not seem very appealing. She looked up to his face.

And Henry smirked.

That was what did it. She had seen that look before. Most princes had mistresses: it was to be expected. But this was different. After all the difficulties – the putting aside of a loyal wife, the problem with the Pope, the marriage to Anne – now with the all-important heir almost born and his new queen probably not a hundred yards away, this overweight king was casually indulging himself in a garden where anyone might see. That look said it all: guilty but triumphant, it was the greedy grin of the lecher. The heroic and pious king she had revered was suddenly a shadow; in the flesh, under the harsh light of the sun, she saw he was merely vulgar. She felt disgust.

Henry saw it. Very coolly, he fastened the cod-piece back in place while the lady, with practised swiftness, rearranged her dress. By the time he looked up again, the grin had vanished. "Methinks this lady has a sullen look." The voice was quiet, and dangerous. He addressed the words to his companion, who gave a little shrug. He stared at Susan. "We do not know this lady," he said with deliberate evenness; and then, loudly: "But we like her not!" And suddenly, remembering his power, Susan felt herself go cold.

"What is your name?"

Dear God. Had she just ruined her husband's career before it had even begun? Her heart sank.

"Susan Bull, sire." She saw him frown. His memory, as every courtier knew, was formidable, but it seemed the name of Bull meant nothing. "Your name before marriage?" he abruptly demanded.

"Meredith, sire." Had she destroyed her brother too?

But there was a just perceptible change. His brow seemed to clear a little.

"Your brother is Thomas Meredith?"

She nodded. He looked thoughtful.

"Your father was our friend." He gazed at her carefully now. "Are you our friend?"

He was offering her a chance, for her father's sake. She knew she must take it. "Kings," Thomas had once said, "have only friends or enemies." Whatever her private feelings at his behaviour, she could not let her family down. She made her deepest curtsy.

"I have been Your Majesty's friend all my life," she said. And then, with a smile: "When I was a little girl, Your Majesty held me in his arms." It was, she hoped, everything it should be: friendly yet submissive.

Henry watched carefully. He was an expert in submission. "See to it that you remain so," he said quietly, and motioned that she should withdraw. But then, with one of those astonishing transformations that are the prerogative of kings, he suddenly decided to continue.

"You did wrong to come upon us in such a way," he remarked gravely. It was a gentle, but firm rebuke. She bowed her head. From this moment, she instantly realized, in the royal mind, the incident would be marked down as her fault, and in no way his. It was always so with Henry. Any courtier could have told her. She began to withdraw.

Just as she reached the entrance to the garden, she turned and, thinking to reassure him of her loyalty blurted out: "I saw nothing, sire, when I was here."

And the instant she said it, she realized her terrible mistake. By her thoughtless words she had just implied that he had something to hide, that, even for a moment, she had enjoyed a moral superiority over him. It was an impertinence. It was dangerous. He scowled and waved her to be gone; and so, miserably confused, she backed away, wishing that the ground of Hampton Court would open up and swallow her.

As she came away, she was trembling, not so much at the threat to herself and her family but because she had discovered in that horrible moment that in the innermost heart of the kingdom, stripped of the pomp and pious façade, lay a hideous corruption.

Dan Dogget waited and tried to look calm; but it was not easy, under the circumstances.

It was a cloudy September day; a sharp wind was passing across the waterfront at Greenwich and the grey-green Thames waters were choppy.

Nothing had altered in the last few weeks. Margaret and the children had settled in well enough at Hampton Court, but he still hadn't found a berth for his truculent old father.

It was six weeks since he had first rowed Meredith, with two of his family, from Hampton Court one August evening; but straight away he had judged he was a coming man. At journey's end, he had offered his services again, and before long had become Meredith's regular boatman, picking him up whenever required. He had even put a fresh coat of paint on the boat and made sure he was cleanly turned out on each occasion; and the young man seemed to like the arrangement. In doing this, the waterman had no definite plan, but as his father would say: "Get on the right side of a gentleman and he may do you some good." A week ago, an opening had come. Meredith had casually remarked that he was surprised such a fine-looking fellow was not working on one of the smarter barges. During the trip, from Chelsea to the city, Dan had explained his predicament. Meredith had said nothing, but two days later, on his way to Westminster from Greenwich he had remarked: "And if I could help you, good fellow, how would you serve me?"

"Why sir," Dan had eagerly replied, "I'd do whatever you ask. But I think," he added regretfully, "that you cannot help me get a barge."

The young courtier had smiled. "My master," he said quietly, "is Secretary Cromwell." Square-jawed, surly-eyed, a man so compact he was like a boulder: everyone knew that, since the fall of Wolsey, it was Thomas Cromwell who ruled England for the king. Dan had not realized how well connected the young man was.

So when, just as he left him that morning, Meredith had casually remarked "I may have news for you today", he had left the waterman in an agitated state.

When Dan Dogget considered the two great Tudor palaces on the Thames between which he plied his trade, they always seemed like two different worlds. Hampton, nearly twenty miles away upstream, amidst its lush meadows and woods, felt as though it was deep inland. But as soon as he passed the Tower, and entered the river's great eastern loop, his heart began to beat with a different pulse. He would take a deep breath, and think he smelt a salty breeze; the sky seemed somehow wider; he was on his way to the open sea where everything was possible.

The palace of Greenwich shared this bracing air. Beside the old hamlet, its brown brick walls and turrets stretched right along the waterfront. It had a great tiltyard – for though, since the Wars of the Roses, improved firearms had made heavy armour out of date, Henry loved the dangerous sport and pageantry of the joust, in which he took an active part himself. There was a huge armoury on the eastern side of the palace, and a short distance upstream lay the Tudors' new dockyard of Deptford, where seagoing vessels were fitted out and the air was redolent of tar.

Dan Dogget had always loved the place. He wondered if it would be lucky for him today.

* * *

Thomas Meredith's career was progressing well. Thanks to a friendship recently formed with the new and still youthful Archbishop Cranmer, he had been allowed a privileged place at the christening of the new royal baby in the chapel in Greenwich Palace today. The baby had been wrapped in a purple mantle with an ermine train. With several other courtiers, Thomas had stood with a towel to receive the baby naked from the font. Cranmer had been godfather. They had given the baby a resounding and royal name: Elizabeth.

The birth of the eagerly awaited heir had turned out to be an unpleasant surprise: it was a girl. Queen Anne Boleyn was embarrassed; the court, considering all the king had been through, was shocked; Henry himself put the best face on it he could. The baby was healthy. There would be others. For the time being therefore, in the eyes of the English Church, the baby was heiress to the throne since, by annulling the king's first marriage, Cranmer had made Princess Mary, technically, illegitimate. As for the view from the Vatican, it was impossible to say, since the Pope had still not given his decision between the king's two marriages.

As he approached the wherry, Meredith smiled to himself. Here was his waterman, looking expectant. He took his seat without a word. Dogget cast off. Deciding to keep the fellow in suspense a few more minutes, Meredith waited until they were opposite the Deptford docks before he spoke. "Well, fellow, do you still seek a barge?"

"Aye, sir. But what barge?"

He saw the courtier smile. "Why, the king's barge, fellow," he quietly replied.

For a moment, Dogget was so astonished that he forgot to make his stroke. He stared open mouthed at Meredith. He was not sure exactly how much these lucky aristocrats of his trade were paid, but probably double what anyone else got. The king was also constantly moving up and down river, with Greenwich as his favourite residence, and with less frequent trips to Richmond and Hampton Court. He began to stammer his thanks, but Meredith raised his hands.

"It may be that I can find a lodging for your father too," he continued, and seeing Dan gasp, he smiled again.

If asked why he, a young man already making friends with the greatest men in the kingdom, should concern himself with a humble waterman, Thomas Meredith would have had no trouble explaining himself. It was the courtier's instinct – the same instinct that made him find Rowland his place with the chancellor – that you cannot have too many friends. Who could guess what service, at some future date, this fellow could do him in return? The art was to have dozens of such people, in every place imaginable, upon whom you could call.

"I am much in your debt, sir," the awestruck Dogget said.

A week later, Meredith was as good as his word.

Perhaps in all London at this time, no place was more respected than the large grey-walled monastery that lay a short distance east of old St Bartholomew's Hospital just outside the city wall. As well as the communal buildings, its chief feature was a large courtyard surrounded by little houses, each with its own tiny garden; and each of these was the cell of an individual monk. Its inhabitants, the Carthusians, were not the most ancient of orders; but unlike most others, no word of scandal had ever been whispered about them. Their rule was strict. Silence was maintained except on Sundays. The monks did not go out without the prior's permission. They were above reproach. This was the Charterhouse.

A curious little procession formed outside its gateway that sunny day. At its head was Thomas Meredith. Behind him came a couple who had, until shortly before, been tending their stall in the street nearby – a profitable little venture selling crucifixes, rosaries and a splendid collection of brightly painted plaster figures. The man, whose name was Fleming, was of medium height, with a rather concave face; his wife as tall as he and stout, had for some minutes already been heaping praises upon the courtier, and the monks, for their wonderful kindness to her father: which was no doubt in order since she herself, for more than five years, had refused to take any interest in the old man. And bringing up the rear, his arm firmly held by Daniel who was now splendidly dressed in the livery of the king's watermen, came Will Dogget.

He was somewhat stooped now, or he would have been as tall as his son. Though dressed in a clean shirt and tunic, and with his long grey beard freshly brushed, there was something vaguely disreputable about the old man's walk which suggested that, after a lifetime of cheerfully doing as he liked, he was liable at any second to veer off in pursuit of pleasure. But now he had come to live in the Charterhouse.

There was not a religious house in London without its quota of dependants. Ruined gentlemen living quietly in furnished monastic cells; widows who did laundry or just swept the cloisters; to say nothing of the gang of hungry folk who were fed at the gates each day. Even the sternest critics of the more lax monastic orders would readily admit that they all fed and cared for the poor.

Though his brother Peter had not returned to the London Charterhouse yet, Thomas Meredith knew enough of the monks to beg a place for the old man. He would sleep in a cell with two other old fellows and work in the garden.

"You're to behave yourself, now," his son admonished him a few minutes later. "If you get thrown out of here, that's it. I'm not taking you back." To all of this, in his habitually cheerful manner, Will Dogget listened with a smile. "Though God knows how long he'll last," Dan remarked to his sister when they got outside.

Before leaving he went over to Meredith and bowed to him. "How can I repay you, sir?" he said.

Meredith smiled.

"I'll think of something," he said.

For Susan too, this was a happy time. In late summer, she and Rowland took a little house in Chelsea. It was charming, made of brick and oak beams with a tiled roof. There were two chambers on the upper floor, attics, outbuildings and a pleasant garden that led down to the river.

During the first weeks that Rowland had worked for the chancellor, she had often thought about her meeting with the king. Had it been a mistake to hide it from Rowland? Was it right that they should be at court at all? Yet as time went by, these fears began to recede. No hint of trouble ever came: Rowland would return from Westminster, where he spent most of his time, with stories only of the kind treatment he received there. The house was delightful; their new income gave her a sense of ease she had never known before; the children were happy. Gradually, reassured, she began to put the whole business out of her mind.

The family had slipped easily into a natural rhythm of life.

Her eldest daughter, Jane, now ten, was her chief helper in the house; but every day, without fail, while the two little girls played, she would make her sit down for three hours to work on her books, just as she had been made to do. Jane already had a good command of Latin, and if, sometimes, she complained to her mother that many of her friends could only just read and write English, Susan would tell her firmly: "I don't want you to marry an ignorant man; and believe me, a happy marriage is a sharing of minds as well as of other things."

But sweetest of all was to watch young Jonathan. The girls were all fair, but with his fine, dark hair and his pale, intense little face, he was clearly an eight-year-old version of his father. He had now started to go to school at Westminster. Often his father would take him in the mornings, and she would watch as the two of them set off to walk down the lane together, hand in hand; or sometimes, if he rode, Rowland would put the boy in the saddle in front of him. Once or twice, having seen them go off like this, she had felt such a wave of happiness and affection that it had brought a lump to her throat.

Peter was still away, and she missed his company and his wise counsel very much. Yet her brother Thomas stepped in to take his place. He and Rowland often met now, and Rowland would bring him home. These were happy evenings, when he would play with the children, who loved him, and tease everybody gently; and though she had always thought he was too worldly, she could not help laughing at some of the witty things he said and admiring his intelligence when he discussed his life at court.

Sometimes, as the three of them sat before the fire, the talk would turn to matters of religion; and here things would get especially lively, with both men on their mettle.

Susan sensed that behind Thomas's bantering tone and worldliness, there was a concern for a simple faith that she had not realized before, and she liked him for it. Some of his views on the laxity and superstition that had crept in to the Church, she could almost share. Though sometimes he went too far.

"I cannot see by what right we deny the faithful an English Bible," he would say. "I know," he cut Rowland off, "you will cite the Lollards and say that left to their own the people will lead themselves astray. But I can't agree."

"Luther began as a reformer and ended a heretic. That's what happens when people set themselves up against the wisdom and authority of the ages," Rowland replied.

Susan could not help feeling that in the reformers, and especially those who went over to Protestantism, there was a certain arrogance. "They want everybody to be perfect," she complained. "But God rewards us all for doing our best. The reformers want to force everyone to be like them and they think no one can be saved otherwise."

But Thomas was still not to be swayed. "Reform will come in one way or another, sister," he would reply. "It must."

"At least one thing is sure," Rowland would say with a smile. "There will be no Protestants in England if King Henry has his way. He hates them."

Of that, Susan thought, there could be no possible doubt.

But if Thomas Meredith was glad to bring happiness to those around him, he was preoccupied by a rather different meeting. It had taken place two days before the royal christening. A very private meeting. With his master, Cromwell.

The royal secretary never ceased to fascinate Meredith. An expert courtier, closest adviser to the king, you would scarcely have guessed he was the son of a humble brewer. He had not risen, like Bull, through scholarship but by his ruthless grasp of affairs. And yet there was always something else about him – some secret reticence, perhaps a secret set of convictions. Only a very few men, Meredith guessed, even got a glimpse of these.

They had been alone in an upstairs chamber when the royal secretary had murmured to him that he had news from Rome. "The Pope," he had informed the young man, "is about to excommunicate the king." Thomas had expressed concern, but Cromwell had merely shrugged. "He has to really, to save face, after all Henry's done." Then he gave a wry smile. "Yet His Holiness still does not say who, in his opinion, is Henry's true wife."

It was clear, however, that the secretary had some purpose in telling him this. Cromwell's eyes, though set very wide apart, were small and Meredith felt them upon him now like a pair of dividers. "Tell me," he said quietly, "what you think of this news."

How carefully he had answered. "I regret it when any man, even a pope, cannot agree with my master the king."

"Good." Cromwell looked thoughtful. "You were at Cambridge?" Thomas nodded. "Friends with Cranmer?" Nothing escaped the secretary. Thomas agreed that he was. Cromwell seemed satisfied; but he had not finished. "And tell me, my young friend," he continued softly, "this news of excommunication: is it good or bad?"

Meredith looked him straight in the eye. "Perhaps it is good news," he answered quietly.

Cromwell grunted, but both men knew that this had been an invitation. The secretary had given him his confidence, had referred to the secret which, though neither of them had ever spoken the thought aloud, they had long since guessed they shared. The secret which Meredith could not tell his family and Cromwell could not tell the king. The next few months, Thomas Meredith thought, would be interesting.

1534

Only once, during the first year at Chelsea, was Susan's peace of mind threatened; and that problem, she thought proudly, she had handled rather well.

It had been an April day which had started poorly, with a messenger coming from the Charterhouse bearing a letter that had just arrived from Peter in Rome, and which announced that, having been ill there, he would not be returning to London for some months. It was sad news. But even this had been driven from her mind by the sight, in the middle of the afternoon, of her husband riding dejectedly towards her, ashen pale and accompanied by Thomas, who was looking unusually solemn. She ran out to meet them.

"What's the matter? Are you in trouble?" she asked Rowland. "No," Thomas replied. "But he may be tomorrow." And he led the way inside.

In her determination to raise her family in an atmosphere of peace, Susan had deliberately kept her mind off the affairs of the world. The political events of recent months, though she regretted them, had not seemed alarming, partly because they were expected. Forced, at last, to choose between the mighty Habsburg monarch and the island King Henry, the Pope had reluctantly issued his excommunication. Then in March, still more regretfully, he had declared that Spanish Katherine, and not Anne Boleyn, was the English king's true wife. Henry had been ready: an Act of Succession, already prepared, was presented to Parliament by Secretary Cromwell and was quickly passed. With it came an oath, recognizing Anne's children as the rightful heirs, with a preamble which denied that the Pope had authority to change these arrangements.

"We cannot allow doubt about the succession now," Henry declared. "My subjects must all take the oath." In London, the aldermen were to administer the oath to each citizen and then report to Greenwich; elsewhere, Cromwell's officials would see to it.

Susan thought the business distasteful but necessary. Better, she supposed, an agreed succession – even if it did prolong the embarrassment with the Pope – than a dispute over the Crown; and from what she heard, most people felt the same. The Londoners might grumble but none, so far as she knew, had refused to obey the king's law. It was a shock to her therefore when, as soon as the two men got inside, Rowland blurted out: "It's the oath. Three men have refused it. They've been sent to the Tower." And seeing her still puzzled: "I'm to take it tomorrow."

"And he thinks," Thomas added, "that he should refuse it too."

Susan suddenly felt weak, but she kept calm. "Which three men?" she asked. A certain Doctor Wilson, they told her: she had never heard of him. And old Bishop Fisher, too.

"That might have been expected," she countered. Having been the one bishop who had originally refused to sanction Henry's new marriage, the saintly old man could hardly change his mind now. It was the third name, however, which caused her heart to sink: "Sir Thomas More."

For Rowland, she knew, the former chancellor – scholar, writer, lawyer and sternest of Catholics – was a man to be admired and followed.

"What will happen to them?" she asked.

"Fortunately, according to the Act, refusing the oath is not treason," Thomas said. "But no doubt they'll cool their heels in the Tower for a while. Anyone who follows their example . . ." he looked at Rowland and then grimaced. "The end of his position. The end of all this," he indicated her beloved house. "Awkward for me too, as a brother-in-law."

Rowland looked uncertain. "Yet More is a lawyer. He must have his reasons."

At which Susan let out a snort of disgust. For, devout though she was, if there was one man in London whom Susan Bull had come thoroughly to dislike, it was Sir Thomas More.

History, not without cause, has often dealt kindly with Sir Thomas More. Yet, in his own day, the antipathy Susan felt was probably more common. In her own case, there were several reasons. Since his retirement two years before, he had spent almost all his time at his house by the river at Chelsea, not half a mile from their own. While she saw his bustling wife and members of his extensive family, the great man, busily writing, was rarely visible; and though people who knew him said he was kind and witty, on the few occasions when she had encountered him, she had found the pale figure with his greying hair to be remote, and also sensed that he had a rather poor opinion of women. Her real objections to him, however, dated back to the period when he was chancellor. For it was then that a more disturbing side of his character had become evident.

He had a passionate dislike of heretics. Though not in holy orders, he had more or less appointed himself as the king's religious watchdog. A lawyer to his fingertips, he had seemed to like the role of prosecutor as well as judge. Time and again, suspected heretics had been taken by river to Chelsea for interrogations, which he often conducted in person. His integrity and intellect were never in doubt, but even Susan, devout though she was, thought him obsessive. "He's not a bishop," she had complained. "And besides, it isn't English." Unlike some countries, England had always been mercifully free of heresy-hunts. So now she protested: "More is a bigot."

"Consider," Thomas cut in. "This oath is not a matter of faith: it concerns only the succession. Now, does the Pope name the heir to the English Crown?"

"Of course not."

"Very well then. Consider further: where does this oath come from – the king alone? No. It was enacted by Parliament." He smiled. "Do you set yourself up against Parliament?" This, Thomas knew very well, was the key to the business – the key that his master Cromwell had so carefully used.

The Parliament of England was still essentially medieval. But for a strong king like Henry, it had one particular use. It could confirm the royal will, in a manner that could not be gainsaid. For who could deny that when the House of Lords, which included the bishops and abbots too, and the Commons spoke together, it was with the united voice, temporal and spiritual, of the whole realm?

"Let me put you a case," Thomas drove his advantage home. "If the king and Parliament enacted that I, Thomas Meredith, should be the next king, could you or the Pope deny it?" Rowland shook his head. "Well then."

"But it's the preamble," Rowland still objected. "Doesn't it deny the Pope's authority over the sacrament of marriage?"

"It's arguable," Thomas at once conceded. Indeed, the wording had been an elaborate compromise between Cromwell and the bishops, and the exact sense was deliberately unclear. "But the bishops accept it. And even," he urged, "if the bishops are wrong, we all know the thing is necessary because of the impossible position the king and the Pope find themselves in."

It was a strong argument, and seeing her husband hesitate, Susan now struck. "You must take the oath," she said firmly. "You cannot destroy your career and family. Not for this. It isn't enough."

"I suppose you're right." He nodded, then smiled. "I know I can trust your judgement," he said.

Did she, Susan wondered, truly believe she was right? Or did instinct tell her that Fisher and More had correctly seen to the heart of the matter? She remembered the Henry she had seen in the garden, then swiftly put the vision out of her mind, and thought of her children instead. She could not see them hurt.

All that evening, after Thomas had gone, though Rowland seemed outwardly calm enough, she knew from his pallor that his conscience was troubling him. Once or twice he remarked to her with a sad smile: "I wish Peter were here." And she wished she could think of something she could say to put his mind at rest.

She was glad, early the following morning, when looking out from their chamber she saw a barge emerge out of the mist on the river, and a few moments later welcomed her brother at the door. He was grinning.

"I just thought I'd tell you," he announced. "I went to the Charterhouse last night. They are all taking the oath." In fact the strict Carthusians had only agreed with the gravest reservations, but he saw no need to go into that. "So," he said cheerfully, "if the Charterhouse, where Peter is going, can do it, so can you."

And now she saw Rowland's face relax at last. Thank God, she thought, for Thomas.

When Dan Dogget reported for duty one bright morning in May, he was in a cheerful mood. He was certainly a handsome sight. A scarlet jacket laced with gold, white hose, gleaming black shoes with silver buckles and, on his head a smart peaked cap of black velvet: the summer livery of the king's watermen suited his splendid figure very well.

The months since he had joined the royal barge had been happy indeed. The pay was everything he had hoped for; and on ceremonial occasions the bonuses could be huge. Only one matter had given him any difficulty. He had never had to submit to discipline before. When the barge-master curtly told him what to do, he sometimes experienced a kind of bafflement, and more than once he had caught himself longing for the cheerful anarchy of his father. I suppose, he acknowledged to himself, I'm more like him than I thought. But he managed to keep his feelings under control.

He was taken aback when, as soon as he arrived at the Greenwich waterfront, the barge-master told him: "You're off duty today, Dogget. I've a message here that says you're to go to the Charterhouse. Your father's there?" Dan nodded and the master grinned. "Seems your old man's giving a bit of trouble. You'd better be off there."

It was worse than he had feared. When he arrived at the monastery, Dan found the sub-prior awaiting him, and also his sister. "The prior is most displeased," the man informed him. "Lord have mercy on his soul, poor old man," his sister offered, with aggressive piety. "It's up to you, Dan," she added firmly.

It had been an event for the Charterhouse monks: the younger ones had never seen anything like it. For Will Dogget in his cups was still a memorable figure. He had gone into a local tavern and made some acquaintances there who had bought him drinks. He had drunk there and at other taverns for some hours. He had given them a song and then at last, having consumed far more than he had done for many months, he started back towards the Charterhouse.

It was dark and the big outer gateway was closed when Will Dogget staggered up. When his good-natured banging failed to elicit any response, he had decided to see if he could break the gate of the monastery down. When a greatly perturbed young monk had finally opened the gate, the old man had walked sorrowfully over to a little nut tree in the yard, sat down with his back to it and had given them a few verses of a waterman's ditty the language of which had certainly never been heard in the Charterhouse before.

"We cannot have this," the sub-prior explained. The old man would have been ejected that morning if his daughter had not sworn by all the saints whose images she sold that she could do nothing for him.

When he reached his father, Will raised himself to a sitting position, and gave Dan a half-reproachful, half-guilty look.

"Well," he sighed, "your sister won't have me. The monks are telling me I'll have to go and live with you again."

"You can't," Dan said firmly. "I've no room."

Help eventually came from the prior himself. "Your father is not a bad soul," he told Dan with commendable frankness. "But," he continued gravely, "the work of this monastery is serious. Your father may remain on one condition: that he stays within our gates."

Dan looked at his father's face. He didn't rate the chances highly.

Susan Bull's nightmare began on a perfect summer day.

It was one of the things Susan liked about Rowland that, while his career and marriage had led him towards the gentle class in society, he was not in the least ashamed of his family of brewers; and every few months they would pay a visit to the old brewery at Southwark. Thomas had accompanied them on this occasion, and after showing him round the extensive premises which the brewery occupied now, the family had all repaired to the old George Inn where the business had first begun.

Susan had been feeling rather mellow. The danger she had feared in April had receded. Whether they liked it or not, hardly anyone else had refused the Supremacy oath; and though Fisher, More and Doctor Wilson were still confined to the Tower, no further action had been taken against them. The mood of the court was also lighter. "The king and Queen Anne are happy together," Thomas reported. "Everyone is sure there'll be a male heir sooner or later." Above all, Rowland seemed to be contented. The crisis with his conscience now past, he was enjoying his work and their life together had been especially happy.

It was a jolly party, consisting of the three visitors, Rowland's old father and his two brothers. Susan always felt comfortable with the Bulls. Unlike Rowland, who with his dark hair and balding head looked more like a Celtic Welshman, they had remained true to the family type, with fair hair, blue eyes and broad Saxon faces. They were solidly conservative in all their opinions; but if they lacked Rowland's intellectual gifts, it was obvious that they were as proud of him as he was of them, and soon Thomas was cheerfully assuring them: "Such a fine scholar as Rowland can't fail to be chancellor one day."

Thomas was at his best. He gave them vivid depictions of the gay life of the court, the jousts, the sports, the music. He told them funny stories about all the great folk there. Rowland's father was curious about the painter Holbein, who had already made portraits of many of the greatest figures in England. "Do you know," Thomas told them, "his painting of King Henry is so lifelike that the first day it was hung one of the courtiers, who didn't know it was there, gave a huge start and bowed to it!"

He even made his dour master Cromwell sound delightful. "Cromwell is tough," he conceded, "but he has a fine mind. He loves the company of scholars and Holbein often dines with him. But do you know who his closest friend is? Archbishop Cranmer himself." He grinned at Susan. "We courtiers are not all so bad," he said.

For a long time, in the old tavern where Dame Barnikel had once presided, they enjoyed each other's company so much that by mid-afternoon when they decided to return by river to Chelsea, they were all a little drunk.

How well everything looked, Susan thought, as their barge skimmed up the stream. The surface of the water was like liquid glass; the sky was blue, the air was still. There was no doubt that the Tudors had improved London. As they passed the mouth of the Fleet, narrower now thanks to repeated encroachments, she looked with approval at the king's new waterside hall by Blackfriars and, across the Fleet, reached by a bridge, the little palace of Bridewell for important foreign visitors. She smiled at the Temple enclosure and at the green lawns of the great houses, each with its own river steps. True, the old palace of the Savoy had lost its ancient glory – it had never recovered from Wat Tyler's destruction more than a century before and the site contained only a modest hospital now. But just as they approached Westminster there was another huge building site, the splendid new palace which King Henry was going to call Whitehall.

By Westminster, she realized that Rowland was really rather flushed. She did not mind. He was humming softly to himself, but quite tunefully. His eyes were glazed. As for Thomas, he seemed to find everything amusing.

It was a few minutes later, after they had passed Westminster and were drawing level with the archbishop's Lambeth Palace on the opposite bank that Rowland nudged her and pointed. By Lambeth steps, she now observed, a handsome barge had tethered and its occupants were about to walk through the big brick gatehouse to the palace.

"There goes Cranmer," he said, and Susan watched curiously as a tall, handsome figure emerged from the barge. But her attention was soon caught by something else. For as the men were unloading a quantity of baggage, she noticed that four of them were carrying a large box, almost like a coffin.

"Do you suppose someone has died?" she said.

And then, for no good reason that she could see, Thomas started to giggle.

"I can't see what's so funny," she remarked. "People do die, you know." But now he burst out laughing. "I think," she said crossly, "you might explain."

"Cranmer's little secret," he muttered, then grinned. "Hush."

"You're drunk," she sighed. His eyes were bloodshot.

"Maybe, sister." He was quiet for a few moments. The coffin went through the gatehouse. Then he chuckled again. "Do you promise not to tell," he said confidentially, "if I tell you what's in that box?"

"I suppose so," she said reluctantly.

"Mistress Cranmer," he grinned. "That box contains his wife."

For a moment Susan could not speak. Priests sinned, of course, although the English clergy had in fact been rather free of this kind of laxity recently. But for the archbishop to keep a woman . . . "Cranmer has a doxy?" she queried.

But Thomas was shaking his head. "Not a doxy. She's his lawfully wedded wife. His second, actually. They were married before he became archbishop."

"But does King Henry know?"

"Yes. Doesn't approve. But he likes Cranmer. Needs him too, to legitimize the Boleyn marriage. So he's made Cranmer promise to keep it a secret. That's why Mistress Cranmer is never seen. When he travels, she goes in a box." He laughed again. His words were a little slurred. "Don't you think it's funny?"

Susan looked at Rowland, but he was still humming, apparently not quite aware of what was being said. Just as well, she thought. "She must be a loose sort of woman," she said with disgust.

"Not at all," Thomas replied. "Very respectable. Cranmer married her when he was studying in Germany. I believe her father's a pastor."

"Germany?" She frowned. A pastor? It took her a moment to realize the implication. "A Lutheran pastor?" she asked. "Do you mean," she continued, amazed, "that this woman, who is married to our own archbishop, is a Lutheran?" And then an even worse thought occurred to her. "But what does this mean about Cramner? Is *he* a covert heretic?"

"A modest reformer," he assured her. "No more."

"And the king? Surely he doesn't secretly sympathize with the Protestants?"

"Good heavens, no," he cried.

She supposed it was so. She noticed, though, that the conversation had sobered him. He even looked a little anxious. But she would probably have left the matter there if she had not suddenly had a terrible flash of perception.

"And you, Thomas," she turned on him. "What are you?"

Yes, he was sober now. She looked into his eyes, but he dropped them and did not answer.

For Thomas, as for many others, the conversion had taken place when he was a student – though to call the radical change in his beliefs a conversion was not quite proper, since he had not actually joined another faith.

Indeed, the process had been subtle. Part of it he had felt free to admit to Susan and Rowland in their conversations at Chelsea: the scholar's desire to purify the scriptural texts, the intellectual's scorn for idolatry and superstition. But beyond this lay something far more radical and dangerous, and for Thomas at least, the inspiration for these other ideas could be summed up in a single word: Cambridge.

Of the two great universities, Cambridge had always been a more radical place than traditionalist Oxford. And when Cambridge men, inspired by the Renaissance scholar Erasmus, turned their gaze upon the creaking old colossus of the medieval Church, they soon stripped it down to its mechanical essentials; even the most hallowed doctrines were examined.

Thomas never forgot the first time he had heard the central doctrine of Transubstantiation – the miracle of the Mass – attacked. He had known, of course, that Wyclif and the Lollards had questioned it. He was aware that heretical Protestants in Europe were now denying it. But when he heard a respected Cambridge scholar in action, he had been shaken.

"Discussion of this question," the scholar had pointed out, "has usually been about details. Does God really grant a miracle to every priest every time? Or, more philosophically, how can the Host be both bread and the body of Christ at the same time? But all this," he stated confidently, "is unnecessary speculation. My case is far simpler. It rests on what the Bible actually says. In only one of the four Gospels does Our Lord tell his disciples to re-enact this part of the Last Passover Supper, and all He says is: 'Do this in remembrance of me.' Nothing more. It is a commemoration. That is all. Why, then, have we invented a miracle?"

By the time he left the bracing East Anglian air of Cambridge, Thomas Meredith was no longer a believing Catholic.

If pressed to define his allegiance, he would have had to say he belonged to the party of reform. It was a broad group. Though Cambridge was its intellectual base, there was a little circle around the rising scholar Latimer at Oxford, too. There were progressive churchmen like Cranmer, some prominent Londoners, aristocratic sympathizers at court, including some of Queen Anne Boleyn's relations; and even, as Thomas had discovered, Secretary Cromwell. It was also an élite. The majority of English folk were attached to the old, familiar ways. As usually happens, the reformers were not answering a cry from the people: they had merely decided to improve them.

"I'm not sure if I'm a Lutheran or not," Meredith had recently confessed to Cromwell, "but I do know I want to see religion radically purified." There was only one man in England, however, who could change the religion of the people: the king. How could the reformers hope to move the self-proclaimed Defender of the Faith towards their camp?

"Opportunity," Cromwell said. "It's that simple. After all," he reminded him, "who could possibly have foreseen, when it began, the amazing outcome of the Boleyn affair? Yet for us reformers it was an astounding gift, because it is causing the king to break with Rome. We can build on that."

"The king may be excommunicated," Thomas objected, "and he may tolerate Cranmer's tendencies because he likes him, but he still seems to hate heretics as much as ever. He hasn't moved an inch towards reform."

"Patience," Cromwell grunted. "He can be influenced."

"But how?" Thomas cried. "By what arguments?" At this, Cromwell had only smiled.

"I see," he remarked with a shake of his head, "that you still know nothing of princes." He looked him calmly in the eye. "If you want to influence a prince, young man, forget arguments. Study the man." He sighed. "Henry loves power. That is his strength. He is hugely vain. He wants to look like a hero.

That is his weakness. And he needs money. That is his necessity." His small eyes bored into Thomas. "With these three levers we can move mountains." And now he smiled. "We may even, young Thomas Meredith, bc able to bring a religious reformation to England." He patted the young man's hand. "Give me time."

Now therefore, as Thomas gazed into his sister's worried face, he wondered what to say. He was already sober enough to realize, with a shock, that he had allowed himself to say too much. He must somehow backtrack.

"I'm not Protestant," he assured her. "Nor is anyone at court." He smiled. "You worry too much."

But she had seen his eyes. And for the first time in her life, she knew he was deliberately lying to her. And though she said nothing, it gave her great pain to know, whatever cynical schemes might or might not be going on at court, that from that day she could no longer trust her brother.

Shocked and disappointed as she was, Susan did not let this matter dominate her thoughts. Rowland, fortunately, had not really taken in their conversation. Nor did she enlighten him. If Thomas was, in some sense, secretly lost to her, she did not want to place the burden of her feelings on her hard-working husband. I must be a good wife and a support to him, she reminded herself.

Only sometimes, when she found herself in the house alone did a sense of desolation visit her. It was, she recognized, a moral loneliness. She would dearly have liked to correspond, at least, with Peter; but his last letter had told her that he was now well enough to undertake a pilgrimage to some of the greatest shrines so she did not even know where to write to him. Meanwhile, she continued, from time to time, to welcome Thomas to the house, and watch him play with the children, and pretend that all was well.

It had been her idea to visit Greenwich. She had always wanted to see round the greatest palace, and learning that King Henry was away one autumn day when both Thomas and Rowland had business there, she had suggested that she accompany them.

She enjoyed the day. Thomas had conducted them all round

the great waterside palace. He had even procured a chamber inside the palace where they could spend the night before returning to Chelsea in the morning.

A little before sunset the three of them walked up the broad, green slope behind Greenwich Palace. For a short while they had strolled across to the edge of Blackheath and then returned to the top of the slope to watch the sun go down. It was certainly a fine sight. Above, the sky was clear; from the east, a faint cool breeze was coming up from the estuary, while in the west, grey clouds with burnished edges lay in long streaks above the horizon. Below her, the turrets of the palace caught the sun's rays; to the left, in the middle distance, Susan could see all London laid out and beyond that, the golden ribbon of the Thames wandering westward. After they had gazed several minutes, when the sun went behind a cloud, turning the scene to greyness, Thomas suddenly pointed at the Deptford dockyard just upstream, and cried: "Look."

No monarch had done more to build a navy than Henry VIII of England. There were several ships, including the great six-hundred-ton *Mary Rose*; but the pride of his fleet was the *Henry, Grâce à Dieu*, the mightiest English warship yet to float. This vessel, detaching itself from the cluster of masts by the Deptford wharfs, had just glided into the river.

As the four-masted ship moved out towards midstream, Susan found herself watching spellbound. It was certainly huge. The *Great Harry*, the sailors affectionately called the mighty vessel. "Weighs over a thousand tons," Thomas murmured in a voice of awe. The ship seemed to dominate the whole river.

Then, suddenly and unexpectedly, the *Great Harry* unfurled not its everyday, but its ceremonial sails, which were painted gold. And at the same moment, as if in response, a cluster of the sun's rays burst out through a gap in the western cloud, catching the ship and its sails magically in a pool of red gold light on the darkening river, so that it floated there like a fairy ship, gleaming, unreal, and so lovely that Susan caught her breath. For over a minute this vision lasted, until the sun was covered again.

This was the magical vision Susan would have carried away with her if the master had not decided on one more manoeuvre. Just as the sun withdrew, along the whole length of the ship's side two lines of traps abruptly burst open and from these dark cavities ran out the muzzles of a score of cannon, so that in an instant the great ship was transformed from a golden phantom to a grim, brutal engine of war.

"Those cannon could reduce the palace to rubble," Thomas remarked admiringly.

"Magnificent," Rowland agreed.

But the warship filled Susan with dread. It reminded her of the other transformation that she had witnessed in a garden the summer before. It was as if the golden ship and the dour vessel with its dull, threatening cannon were two faces of the king himself. And while the men remained contentedly watching as the *Great Harry* moved slowly downstream, she felt a strange uneasiness, and a little shudder passed through her that, she told herself, was only caused by the breeze which now felt cold, coming from the east.

They were standing in a hallway, whose dark wooden panelling was glowing softly in the candlelight when the young man came up to Thomas.

"Secretary Cromwell will need you first thing in the morning," he murmured. And then with a smile: "It's been decided. We're to draft the new Act of Parliament at once."

Wondering what this might be, she had glanced at Rowland; but he evidently did not know. Then she noticed, even in the shadow, that Thomas was blushing. "What Act of Parliament?" she quickly enquired.

The young man looked uncertain for a moment, but then grinned. "It won't be a secret after tonight anyway," he said, "so I can tell you. It's to be called the Act of Supremacy."

"What's to be in it?" she asked.

"Well," he replied cheerfully, "Thomas knows better than I, but the main provisions are these." He began to explain.

At first, as she listened, Susan was not sure what the purpose of this new Act was. It seemed to recapitulate all the things, in his dispute with the Pope, that Henry had already done – the appropriation of Rome's revenues, the succession provisions, and much else besides. But gradually, as he continued, her eyes grew wide with astonishment.

Rowland finally spoke. "No king in history has ever made such claims!"

By his new title of Supreme Head of the Church, Henry now intended not just to take all revenues, appoint bishops and even abbots – these things had been tried before by powerful and greedy medieval kings. He also meant, personally, to decide all doctrine, all theology, all spiritual matters as well. It had never even crossed the mind of any medieval king to do that. He intended, effectively, to be king, Pope and church council all rolled into one. It was outrageous. And almost like a final insult, giving him the title of Vicegerent, he had put Cromwell in charge of the entire body of the Church – priests, abbots, and bishops, they were all to answer for everything they did to the king's hard-faced secretary.

"Henry's making himself the equal of God!" Rowland protested. "This," he said quietly, "would be the end of the Church as we know it."

"Henry is a good Catholic," Thomas replied defensively. "He will protect the Church against heresy." Susan said nothing.

"But what," Rowland pointed out, "if the king changes his mind? What if Henry decides to abolish relics? What if he decides to alter the form of the Mass? What if he suddenly becomes a Lutheran?"

Nobody said anything.

"There's to be another Act, you know," the young man went on. "A Treason Act. Anyone who even argues against anything in the Supremacy Act will be guilty of treason. That'll mean death," he added unnecessarily.

Susan began trembling, and she looked at Rowland. "We are not traitors," she said, her voice as steady as she could make it. "We shall obey the Act if it is passed."

But Rowland was staring at the floor.

As the weeks went by and the Supremacy Bill began to make its way through Parliament, she knew how Rowland was feeling. She felt the same way too, but she knew she must not show it. Indeed, she even found herself in the strange position of defending the king, of siding with her brother, who she suspected was a heretic, to deflect her husband's criticisms.

"In practical terms it changes nothing," Thomas repeatedly assured him. "Not only is Henry a staunch Catholic, but even the most modest reforms would have to get past the bishops and Parliament. The faith is safe."

There was less opposition in Parliament than Susan might have expected. Partly, she realized, this was because of an attitude expressed to her by the wife of a neighbour one day. "Better to have our own Harry of England in charge of the Church than some Italian in Rome who knows nothing about us," she had remarked. Others, Susan suspected, even amongst the bishops like Cranmer, might be covert reformers who thought their cause might stand a better chance in a separate English Church than under the Pope. But above all, as she watched ruthless Secretary Cromwell in action, she understood all too well the fundamental reason why Parliament was submitting to the will of the king. It was fear. And remembering that vision of the *Great Harry*, that golden ship with its concealed banks of murderous cannon, she knew in her heart that the grim ship of state meant to sail on.

"We must obey the law," she would say quietly.

There was only one small consolation. Unlike the succession legislation of the spring, there was no talk of forcing everyone to take any new oath. If any of Henry's subjects wished to defy the new Act publicly, it would be treason; but if they disagreed, they could at least suffer in silence.

And that, Susan realized, was exactly what her dear husband was doing. He went about his work mechanically; though, after a period of looking deathly ill, he regained some of his usual colour, the spring went out of his step. As autumn turned to winter, he seemed to sink into a sad and silent gloom, and even alone in their bedroom, while the affection remained, the joy was all gone. As for her, trying to conceal the fact that she knew he was right, and knowing that she must do whatever was necessary to preserve her family, she would gaze at her children, and endure.

If only, she thought as the year drew towards its close, if only Peter were here.

It was a cold December afternoon and Susan had gone to the city. She had walked down Paternoster Row, a little street by St Paul's where several booksellers had stalls, to buy a volume for Rowland as a present for Christmas. Pleased with her purchase, she strolled along Cheapside and on an impulse had turned down the little lane by St Mary-le-Bow.

A few moments later she entered the church of St Lawrence Silversleeves.

How warm the little parish church seemed with its dark rood screen, its stained glass windows, and its figure of the Virgin before which half a dozen candles were flickering. The whole place was redolent of incense. How well the church expressed her brother's kindly parish ministry. If she closed her eyes she could almost imagine that he was there.

So it was with a little cry that she turned to see him standing behind her.

1535

In the month of January 1535, a disturbing report reached Secretary Cromwell from Rome. Poor, hesitant Pope Clement had died some months before and there was a new pontiff. No word had been heard from him, until the secret report had come, but when it arrived it was shocking.

"He means to depose you," Cromwell told the king.

Letters, it seemed, had already been sent to the King of France and the Habsburg emperor. For all his shows of strength, if either, let alone both of these mighty powers were to invade the island to take his kingdom away from him, Henry would be in dire peril. Would they do such a thing?

"They might be tempted," Henry judged, "if they think the country is split and that people would rise up to greet them."

"What do you wish me to do?"

"Simple," the king smiled. "We must show them, once and for all, who is master in England."

It was a February day, cold but bright, when Peter finally came from the Charterhouse to visit the family at Chelsea. It was remarkable, Susan had noticed, how even the fact that Peter was in London again had changed the atmosphere in the house. She felt a sense of security and well-being; Rowland also seemed more cheerful; and whatever her doubts might be about Thomas nowadays, she determined to put them aside on this occasion at least. "We'll have a family reunion," she declared. "Thomas must be there too." For days before, she had bustled about the house preparing, making sure that everything, wood, pewter and metal, was cleaned and polished until it gleamed. She sewed fresh lace on the children's clothes and by the time the day arrived she felt proud of herself.

The main celebration of the day would be the family dinner, served soon after noon; and in place of honour, as for any English family that could afford it, would be the great roast. "A swan," Rowland had decreed. Londoners of sufficient means were permitted to keep their own swans on the Thames and since last year he had been the proud possessor of several.

"We shall be eating it for a week," Susan had laughed. And early that morning she was up preparing the huge bird.

He came by barge and had hardly stepped out on to the little landing stage before he was raising the children, each in turn, into his arms. He smiled warmly at them all, and taking his sister by the arm, advanced up the path very cheerfully towards the house.

Like the experienced parish priest he was, his eyes missed nothing. He praised the little garden, admired the house, expressed delight at the modestly growing library. He had made friends with the children in minutes.

Thomas arrived at the end of the morning and soon after midday they all assembled at the big oak table. It gave Susan great happiness to hear Peter say a simple grace for them and to watch Rowland carve the great swan. Thomas, too, was smiling.

"You still look alike," he remarked to the two men.

"I still have the advantage in weight," Peter replied.

"Not by much," Rowland laughed.

All through the meal Peter kept them entertained with his accounts of Rome and of the other religious sites and shrines he had visited, which included Assisi in Italy and Chartres in France. "I should have liked to journey to the great shrine at Compostela," he remarked. "But Spain was just too far."

"And did you see any miraculous cures performed by these relics?" Thomas asked with a trace of mischief in his voice.

"Yes. A woman was cured at Assisi," he answered quietly.

They sat a long time at table, talking easily on such cheerful topics. Despite what the cynics at court or the secret heretics might do, Peter would have words of calm and wisdom; and suddenly, even the king and his misfortunes and her anguish about the Supremacy seemed less important. These things would pass. The faith would remain. This was the comforting message Peter would bring. She was sure of it.

But as the February afternoon grew dark and the children left to play upstairs, Peter turned quietly to Thomas and, with a faint glint of reproach in his eyes, enquired: "So Thomas, is the rumour we hear at the Charterhouse true?" And seeing that Susan and Rowland did not understand, he gently explained: "The king and Secretary Cromwell are planning to take a special interest in us."

It was, it had to be confessed, a logical step. Peter himself explained it very simply. "Henry wants to ensure that he is absolute master in his own house. His Supremacy Act has been passed by Parliament and accepted by his bishops – many of whom, of course, are his own men. But there are still a few thorns in his side which irritate him. There are More, Fisher and Wilson. But there are also the sterner religious houses, such as the Charterhouse and some of the friars, who took the oath only with reluctance in the spring. Since any dissent is now treason, Henry has just had the bright idea of frightening all these tiresome people into taking an oath of some kind – we haven't seen it yet – which presumably will admit all his claims to Supremacy. Then he'll have proved his point." He paused and looked sternly at his brother. "Have I got that right, Thomas?"

"It's a new idea," Thomas said. "It's only the people you mention who'll be asked for an oath. The rest of us," he glanced at Rowland, "will be left alone."

"We are honoured to be singled out," Peter said drily.

Susan saw Rowland frown. "What will you do, Peter?" he asked.

"I shall do what the prior tells me to. That is my duty since I have joined the order."

"And what will that be?"

"I don't know. He's going to meet the heads of the other Carthusian houses. I imagine he'll consult the brethren too. That would be proper."

For a moment nobody spoke. Then Rowland quietly asked: "If you were prior, Peter, what would you decide?"

"Me?" He did not even hesitate. "I should refuse."

Susan went cold. "You can't mean that!" she cried. "It would be treason!"

"No," he said quite coolly, "not really. Parliament can decide many things. It can decide the succession, certainly. But Parliament is not competent to alter Man's relationship to God. If they insist on calling it treason, I can't help it. As for me, don't forget that I took vows to a higher authority long ago." He looked at her kindly and his tone was matter-of-fact. "There's no getting round it, you know. Henry's trying to become the spiritual authority and he can't. I'm sorry. And as for this Cromwell business, this Vicegerent," he pronounced the word with mild contempt as he gazed steadily at Thomas. "The Church spiritual to be run by the king's lackey? Obscene. Of course I can't accept it."

"You would court death?" Thomas asked in surprise.

But his brother only shrugged with a trace of impatience. "Court it? No. Why should I court it? But what would you have me do? Swear to this nonsense?" He turned to Susan and Rowland. "This is the trouble with being in power, like Thomas here. It's very difficult, you see. They want to get things done and sooner or later they always forget their principles." He turned back to Thomas. "Either something is right, or it's wrong, my friend."

"So what," Rowland said very quietly, "should a man like me do?"

Susan looked at Peter in anguish. He saw and understood, but his expression did not change as he surveyed the two of them calmly. "I think," he said, with consideration, "that there's no necessity for the laity to intervene. It's the monks who are being challenged, and it's up to us to respond."

"But if it's wrong," Rowland began, "surely any Christian . . ." His voice trailed off.

"We are warned not to seek martyrdom," Peter replied gently. "It's a spiritual error." He smiled. "A family man like you, with those God-given responsibilities –" He reached across and placed his hand over Rowland's. "I should leave it to the monks. That's what we're there for."

Susan sighed with relief.

"What if I were asked to take an oath?" Rowland asked. "You won't be," she cut in. But Rowland was not satisfied. He looked uncertainly at Peter. Please God, Susan thought, let him give the right answer.

Peter gazed at him thoughtfully. "You have a wife and children," he said gently. "I cannot tell you what to do."

It was not enough. She waited, in vain, for more. And now, looking with terror at the two men, so alike, she almost cried aloud: oh, why, Peter, why did you have to come back?

The two men were standing in the Great Hall at Hampton Court and Carpenter was proudly showing Dan Dogget his handiwork. It was an extraordinary structure. The palace at Hampton had originally been built by Wolsey and it was large then, but Henry seemed to make it huger every year; and of all his additions, none was more splendid than the hall. It took up the entire side of one courtyard and was three storeys high. At one end, a vast window, like one of the great curtains of glass in a Perpendicular church, let in a pleasant light through its stained glass. The outside brickwork was painted and even the mortar between the bricks was picked out in grey. The floor was of red tile, the walls hung with great heraldic tapestries. But most spectacular of all was the mighty hammerbeam roof. And it was to this now that Carpenter was proudly pointing.

The English hammerbeam was not just a roof, it was an institution. Invented in the Middle Ages, this useful piece of engineering had proved so pleasing to everyone that it was to last, even when not really needed structurally, for centuries. Soaring, yet sturdy, elaborately carved and painted, yet massively solid, it was everything the English liked. There was the great early hammerbeam in Westminster Hall. Every London guild or livery company that could afford a hall would want one; Oxford and Cambridge colleges boasted sumptuous examples.

The wooden hammerbeam roof was simply a series of partial arches – exactly like wall brackets – arranged one on top of, and jutting out from, another. By building a line of these brackets out from each side of a wide hall, and joining them above with a great beam, a big space could easily be crossed and a heavy roof supported.

It was, indeed, magnificent. There were eight of these mighty oak hammerbeam arrangements down the length of the hall, dividing the roof space into seven compartments. At the foot of each was a huge wooden corbel; from the end of each bracket a heavy wooden pendant hung in the space overhead. And all these, together with many of the other details, were elaborately carved in gleaming, oaken magnificence.

"I did some of those," Carpenter said.

So perfectly were the accounts of the works at Hampton Court kept that every scrap of painting, carpentry and masonry carried out during those years was detailed with the name of the craftsman and what he was paid. Carpenter was thus already, as perhaps all men are, immortal without knowing it.

"So what news of your father?" the craftsman asked his brother-in-law, as they left the Hall together. "Has he kept to quarters?"

And now Dan was able to surprise him. "It seems," he said, "he's reformed."

It was Father Peter Meredith's arrival in the Charterhouse that seemed to be the cause of this miracle. No one could say quite how he had done it: perhaps it was his spiritual influence, or perhaps he just kept the old man company; but within a week Will Dogget had attached himself to the priest. As long as Father Peter's around the old man seems perfectly happy. It's the most remarkable thing I've ever seen.

"Better hope the priest stays there," said Carpenter.

Outside Newgate and a little way westward across the Holborn there was a modest stone church dedicated to St Etheldreda, a saintly Anglo-Saxon princess in the island's early Christian days nearly a thousand years before. During the Middle Ages, the bishops of Ely had built their London mansion beside it, surrounding the whole with a big walled enclosure and using the church as their chapel; but it was still open to any of the faithful who chose to venture for spiritual refreshment within its old grey walls.

On a bright day early in March Rowland Bull, coming from the Charterhouse and intending to walk down Chancery Lane on his way to Westminster, caught sight of the roof of St Etheldreda's over the bishop's wall and, on a sudden impulse, decided to go in.

Spring was in the air as he passed through the gateway. The first green buds were on the trees; beside the path to the chapel were little clumps of white and violet crocuses; and on a grassy bank, some yellow daffodils. There was a faint, sharp smell of freshly turned earth in the damp air. St Etheldreda's consisted of two parts: the upper, raised well above ground level was a handsome chapel with a fine window taking up much of its western wall; the lower, called the crypt, was only a few steps down and, though smaller than the chapel above, was often used for services. Finding this lower space empty, Rowland went in.

The crypt was a quiet place. On his left was a small altar beside which, in the shadow, he could see the tiny red glow of the Host. At the far end, on his right, set in the upper part of the wall, was a window of green glass which provided the crypt's soft illumination. Just below it was an old stone font with Saxon carving. In the middle of the floor were some benches and kneeling pads, where Rowland knelt down to pray.

There were so many things troubling his mind. His meeting with Peter had brought him no comfort. The Charterhouse monks were praying for guidance. The prior was going to ask Cromwell to let them take a less objectionable oath. "But he'll refuse," Peter had predicted. "He's got to break us." Either the Carthusians would yield to Henry's will, or be found guilty of treason. Even now he found it hard to believe: the saintly Charterhouse monks, going like criminals to execution? The idea was so outlandish it seemed unreal. Could King Henry really do such a thing? "Certainly," Peter had said. "Who will stop him?" But a traitor's death? That was a fearful thing: the lucky few went to the block, but most died by the harsh old medieval way – hanged first, taken down still conscious, their bowels cut out and their limbs hacked off before their eyes. He pictured the nerve-searing horror of it and shuddered.

Trying to escape the vision, he allowed his eyes to wander round the crypt, and caught sight of the Host, glowing in the shadows. Christian faith can lead to martyrdom, the little red light seemed to be silently reminding him. Wasn't the religion he held so dear founded upon exactly such sacrifice?

And after the horror, after death – what then? Eternal peace, said the red flame. Salvation. He hoped so. He believed with all his heart it must be so. Yet even for the most devout, there is nearly always the awful doubt. What if it were not so after all? What if a man lost the only life he had, and went into eternal night for nothing? Looking away from that pinpoint of light, his eyes came to rest upon the old font at the other end of the crypt. How peaceful it looked, bathed in the greenish beams from the window; how quietly it seemed to speak of the spring day outside. He thought of his little house at Chelsea, his library, his wife and children. How precious they were. With a sudden vividness, he knew how much he desired life.

For long minutes he remained there on his knees, and once or twice looked upwards and murmured: "Lord: show me the way."

At last, when he received his answer, it was no flash of illumination that came, nor even a silent whisper from the altar. It was the memory of Peter's words that day they had first discussed the question in the little house at Chelsea: "Either something is right, or it's wrong, my friend."

It was not even his lawyer's mind but something much more instinctive in him that finally understood what he must do. A thing was either true or false, right or wrong, black or white. It was not the religious scholar, it was the generations of Anglo-Saxon Bulls in him that knew it. The king's claim was a lie. There was nothing more to say. He was either a Christian believer or he wasn't. That was it. He felt relieved.

But there remained Susan and the children and his moral obligation there. Now his lawyer's mind interposed. That too was a claim that must be satisfied.

As he quietly left St Etheldreda's and walked out through the walled garden Rowland knew what he must do.

Susan stared at Rowland; at first she could hardly speak. It was dark outside, the children were in bed and they were alone. As much to give herself time to think as anything, she went over it carefully: "You think that the Charterhouse monks will refuse the oath?" He nodded. "But you believe that the king, even now, means to require the oath only from those, like the monks, who opposed him?"

"I think so."

"You do not suppose he would require it of you."

"I took it before. Why should he trouble me?"

"But if, by chance, the king altered his mind, and asked for the oath again . . ."

"We must decide what I should do."

"So you have come to me, because you owe a duty to me as your wife, and to your children." She nodded thoughtfully, and then, looking up, quietly spoke the terrible proposition he had made. "You are asking my permission to refuse the oath? You are asking if you may go to execution?"

And returning her gaze with affection he calmly answered: "Yes."

From almost any other man, she supposed, it would have been a lie, an excuse. Tell me I must not go, he would have been saying. Let me be a coward with dignity. And, at that moment, she almost wished she had married a lesser man. But she knew that Rowland really meant it.

This was her dilemma. In her innermost heart, she knew that Rowland and Peter were right. Yet here, also, was her pain: to know that, for the sake of the God they shared, he would rather leave her all alone. And worse yet, her knowledge as a wife, that if, to save her family, she refused her consent, he would accept it but, very likely never in his life forgive her.

"You must do what your conscience tells you," she therefore said. "I forbid you nothing." She turned her face away, not only to hide her tears, but because she could not bear to see that she had made him happy.

"It will not happen." Thomas Meredith was adamant. "Unless he means to provoke the king deliberately, there is no danger," he assured Susan. "I see Cromwell every day. I know exactly what is intended. The king will bring those who opposed him to heel. If those few, like the Charterhouse monks, still remain obstinate . . ." He grimaced. "I fear it may go hard with them."

"Poor Peter."

"I cannot help him," he admitted sadly. "But Rowland," he continued reassuringly, "is another case entirely. He took the original oath like everyone else. He is not under suspicion of any kind. Does he mean to speak out?"

"No."

"Well then." He smiled. "If his name were ever mentioned, which it will not be, I'll assure Cromwell he is loyal." He grinned. "Trust your brother. I'll protect him."

"You are sure?"

"I'm sure." He kissed her. "You have nothing to fear."

It would be May tomorrow. The afternoon sun was pleasantly warm; there were yellow buttercups and cowslips in the meadows as the gilded royal barge slipped up the stream.

Dan Dogget was smiling. There was no doubt about it, he had been lucky of late. And all thanks to Thomas Meredith. Was he free of worry, then? Almost, but not quite. He glanced back towards the covered cabin in the stern.

The curtains of the cabin were drawn back, since the weather was warm, and the doorway was open so that, from where he sat amongst the oarsmen, Dan could see inside to where, on a broad, silk-covered seat, the two men were sitting: on the left, the big, bearded head of the king; on the right, the broad, pale and rather sulky face of Secretary Cromwell, murmuring something to him. Dan wondered what they were planning to do next.

At last, after the long months during which he had quietly threatened all those who dared to oppose him, King Henry of England had struck with pinpoint accuracy. Only three men – the prior of the London Charterhouse and the priors of the two other houses – had been arrested for refusing to take the oath admitting his supremacy. The oath had not even been administered to the rest of the Charterhouse monks yet. Yesterday, in a private hearing in Westminster Hall, the three priors had been tried, with Cromwell presiding. Cranmer had pleaded for them, the jury had been unwilling to convict, but Cromwell had brushed their objections roughly aside and by noon all London knew: "They've been taken to the Tower. They'll be executed in five days."

But what, Dan wondered, would this mean for him? Would Henry pursue the rest of the Charterhouse monks too? He guessed he would. And would they buckle when they saw the horror that was to come? He thought of Peter Meredith and suspected they would not. And if that happened, what would become of old Will?

With a vague sense of misgiving, therefore, Daniel Dogget rowed the king to Hampton Court.

* * *

He should not have entered the garden. He should have walked past when he heard the laughter. He had not realized that King Henry had arrived.

He had kept his head down recently. He had attended to his duties assiduously; Cromwell had praised him. He had seen little of King Henry but was glad that few if anybody at court had been aware that his brother Peter had joined the offensive Charterhouse. As for the trial that day, word of the result had yet to reach Hampton Court. So it was with shock that he now beheld the king.

There were only a few courtiers with King Henry. Wanting to stretch his legs after the long river journey, he had summoned them to attend upon him and Cromwell as they walked through the orchard. For no particular reason, he had turned into the quiet garden behind its high hedges only moments before Thomas entered.

The king was in a jovial mood. He had been bringing order to his life recently. First there had been the queen. If Anne Boleyn was sometimes moody and jealous of his other loves, time spent with her recently, in the royal business of making an heir, had cured these domestic troubles. Indeed, he suspected she had already conceived. And now this business of the monks. He had just told the courtiers about the forthcoming executions and he could see that behind their polite faces there was a hint of fear. Good. Courtiers should be afraid of the king. Indeed, on the journey from London, he had been discussing whether he should apply the oath again more widely, to seek out any other opponents of his supremacy and strike them down too; but Cromwell had urged caution. "The fewer we have to destroy, the less opposition you will appear to have," he had pointed out. He supposed it was true.

But partly to irritate Cromwell, and partly to watch the courtiers tremble, he had just that moment returned to the theme. "Are you sure, Master Cromwell, that we should not demand the oath again? Why," he allowed his eyes to wander round the little group, "there may be traitors even here, lurking in our midst." He gave a great guffaw of laughter as his hard eye watched the courtiers blanch. And then he saw young Meredith.

Henry liked Meredith. He remembered his father; Cromwell

spoke well of his work. He remembered beating the young fellow at tennis, too. Seeing him now, therefore, hesitating bashfully at the garden entrance, he beckoned to him.

"Come closer, Thomas Meredith," he called with a smile. "We are discussing traitors."

The young man went deathly pale. Now why should he do that?

From the labyrinth of Henry's suspicious mind came a memory, of another encounter in this very garden; which, since it had not been flattering to himself, he had chosen to forget until this moment. A memory of a young woman's reproachful look, a hint of disloyalty and impertinence. Hadn't the girl been Meredith's sister? He thought so. "Remind me, Thomas," he suddenly said, "about the rest of your family."

Thomas stared. How much did he know? Was he thinking of Peter? Probably. He must have discovered that he was at the Charterhouse. That King Henry had Susan in mind, and that he had once encountered her before, in this very garden, he had no idea.

"I have a brother, sire," he began cautiously. "A priest until he became ill, and retired."

"Indeed?" Henry had not known. "And where is he now?"

He must know. It was a trap. Or even if it wasn't, he would probably soon discover. Useless to deceive him, either way.

"In the Charterhouse," he replied miserably.

Everything went very quiet.

"The Charterhouse?" There was no mistaking his surprise. He had not known. His voice was now a rasp. "I hope you do not share their opinions. Their prior is about to die." He glanced at Cromwell.

"Meredith is loyal, sire." Cromwell's reply was instant. Thank God. Henry nodded. "Good." But Thomas knew he did not like these surprises; and Henry clearly had not done with him yet. "What other family have you, Master Meredith?" he quietly continued.

"Only a sister, sire." Surely that could not interest him.

"Married? To whom?"

"Rowland Bull, sire." He tried to keep calm, hoped the sudden trembling that afflicted him had not been noticed.

"Bull?" Henry seemed to be searching his mind. "In the

chancellor's office?" Thomas nodded, as King Henry stared, apparently at the hedge.

Yes. That was the woman. Henry hid a grimace. The one with the look: the living reproach. One did not look at kings like that.

"And are Mistress Bull and her husband loyal?" He turned to Cromwell who in turned gazed at Thomas. They waited for him.

"They are loyal, Your Majesty."

For a few seconds Henry was silent, nodding quietly to himself before he spoke.

"We do not doubt it, Master Meredith." His voice was quietly dry. Then he turned to his minister. "So we think, Cromwell, that Mistress Bull and her husband should take the oath. Let it be done tomorrow morning, before the sun is up. That is our will." It was a command. Cromwell bowed his head. And now, suddenly, King Henry beamed at them all. "We have a better idea yet. Our loyal servant, young Master Meredith here, shall go to administer the oath to them himself. See it is done. How's that?"

And he let out a great laugh that echoed round the garden.

The barge had left Hampton Court before dawn. For hours only the muffled sound of the oars had broken the silence as it passed through the greyness; and the mist was still swirling around Thomas's feet as he reached the threshold of the little house at Chelsea. Once again Susan was dully repeating: "He will not take the oath."

They had been arguing for over half an hour, in urgent whispers. Rowland, still unaware of his presence, had not yet come down; the children were sleeping. Again and again she had reproached him: "You promised this would not happen. You promised."

There was only one thing he did not understand. So desperate, so guilty had her reproaches made him feel that, to defend himself, he had tried to explain to her exactly how he had come upon the king in the garden, and how Henry had so unexpectedly started to ask about his family. She became suddenly thoughtful then, and quiet, before at last she softly said: "Then it was my fault, too."

What had she meant by that? Above all, what were they to

do? "I shall take the oath," Susan said simply. He knew she believed in it no more than Rowland. Yet wasn't there a chance, when Rowland saw her submit, came face to face with the awful consequences of his decision for his family, that he might take the oath after all? But Susan only shook her head and in a voice made small by her rising tears, answered: "No. He won't."

Which left him one alternative. He had considered it last night, and all the way down the river from Hampton Court. He had prayed it would not be necessary: the risks were terrifying and it might not even work. But as he looked at his sister and saw her pain, it seemed to him that he must try.

The sun had already dissolved the mist as far as the river's edge when Rowland took the oath. He did so calmly and without fuss, then smiled at his wife who looked back at him with relief.

"I had not thought I could," he remarked. And best of all, his conscience was clear.

Thomas Meredith smiled. "I'm glad," he said.

It had not been so difficult. He had taken the greatest care, made Rowland repeat the words after him so that his lawyer's mind could precisely understand their significance; and then, satisfied that his religion was not compromised, Rowland had sworn the oath.

Thomas had simply administered the wrong oath.

Or, to be precise, he had doctored it. The oath he had administered to his brother-in-law was hardly different from the one he had been prepared to swear about the succession the previous year. Above all, after a brief mention of Henry's supremacy, he had added a crucial saving clause: "As far as the Word of God allows." It was an old stand-by of the Church, this little clause, and they both knew it. With this qualifier, good Catholics could, if necessary, disclaim any improper interpretation the king might place upon the oath in the future. With it, Henry's claim to supremacy became virtually meaningless. Had even the Charterhouse monks been allowed this saver, they too could have sworn in good conscience.

"I am surprised the king allowed the disclaimer," Rowland remarked.

"It's a special dispensation," Thomas lied. "Those who opposed him publicly are being given a tougher oath. But nobody wants to embarrass loyal men like yourself. You mustn't discuss it though. If anyone asks, just say you've taken the oath. You know what you've sworn to: that's enough." And though Rowland frowned a little, he agreed to abide by this.

Let's just pray, Thomas thought, that it works.

"I must go now," he said aloud. "I have to report to the king." And then turned in surprise, as he saw Susan, with a look of horror on her face, staring out of the window.

Cromwell did not trouble to knock on the door. He stepped straight in. Two assistants hovered just outside while two men-at-arms waited by his barge.

"I have administered the oath," Thomas began, but Cromwell cut him short.

"Rowland Bull," the secretary's face was turned to the lawyer. The small, deadly eyes seemed to see no one else. "Do you accept the king's supremacy in all matters temporal and spiritual?"

Rowland was very pale now. He glanced at Thomas for guidance, then at Susan. "Yes," he replied hesitantly. "As far as the Word of God allows."

"Word of God?" Cromwell shot a glance at Thomas then stared at Rowland. "Never mind the Word of God, Master Bull. Do you or do you not, without any disclaimer, acknowledge King Henry as Supreme Head in matters spiritual? Yes or no?"

There was an agonizing pause.

"I cannot."

"As I thought. Treason. Open and shut case. Say goodbye to your wife." He called outside to his assistants. "Bring the guards."

And only then did he turn to Thomas. "You fool," he muttered. "Thought you'd save him with a let-out clause, then tell the king he'd taken the oath?" Thomas was too shocked even to answer. "Don't you realize," Cromwell growled, "the king wasn't interested in this fellow. He was testing you. Wanted to see what you'd do. He was going to send someone else to give him the oath afterwards, to check up on you." He grunted. "I've just saved your life." Then, turning back to Rowland:

"Your life, I'm afraid, you have just lost." He nodded curtly to Susan. "You can give him some clothes. He's going with us now, to the Tower."

Father Peter Meredith received two visitors at the Charterhouse that day. He was a little unwell, so he remained seated in his cell while old Will Dogget brought them to him. The first was Susan. She was very quiet as she stood before him, yet he thought he detected a faint note of reproach as well as desperation in her voice. Her request was simple.

"You want me to persuade him to take the oath?" he asked.

"Yes."

"Isn't it too late anyway?"

"There still has to be an official trial with a jury. If he submits now, the king might accept it." She made a sad little shrug. "It's our only chance."

"And you think my voice might make a difference?"

"You're the one man he respects. And," there was no mistaking the reproach in her voice now, "it was your opinion he was following when he refused the oath."

He looked down at the floor for a moment.

"I think," he replied softly, "he was also following his conscience. For the sake of what we all believe in."

He could not blame her if she ignored this mild rebuke. However devout, she was after all a mother fighting for her family. But now she had a surprise for him.

"You don't really understand," she said. And she explained how she had met the king in the garden, and how Thomas had encountered him in the same place. "You see," she went on, "those chance encounters, the fact that you are a Charterhouse monk: in a way, it is you and I who have brought this on Rowland. He was never meant to be given the oath at all."

Peter sighed. Why did providence work in such strange and cruel ways? It was God's plan, of course. But why, he wondered sadly, must the design be so obscure, even to the most faithful? "I will go to see him," he said at last. "But I cannot tell him to disobey his conscience. I cannot imperil the man's soul, which, I promise you, is immortal."

She was not comforted, and he had not thought she would be. Yet, he had to admit, her final words had caused him pain.

"Do you know what they will do to him? Do you understand?" She gave him such a bitter look. "It is easier," she had said coldly, "for you." Then she had gone.

Easier? He doubted it. The word was that the three priors would be executed in days – not with a merciful beheading but in the most savage way. When the monks had had a chance to witness that, the king's commissioners would come to the Charterhouse to offer the oath to the community. "These things are like phantoms, sent to frighten us and test our souls," an old monk had said. But did Susan really suppose that, sitting hour by hour in his cell, he did not think of it?

It was evening when Thomas came.

At first, when he saw the worldly young courtier in the doorway, Peter could not help a feeling of irritation. True, Thomas looked distraught; but then, Peter thought, whatever his grief about Rowland, he was still Cromwell's man.

"No doubt," he said to Thomas quietly, "you have come on the same errand as our sister." He sighed, and then added a little drily: "This combination of a brother in the Charterhouse and your sister's husband refusing the oath cannot be very good for your career."

Thomas only shook his head. "I've just come from court," he said. "Even if Rowland takes the oath now, the king will not accept it. Treason has been spoken. He is going to destroy him." He sat down, and buried his face in his hands. "And it's all my fault."

"Yours?"

"I brought him to court. I put him in this position."

"He took a stand for his faith."

"Yes," Thomas agreed. "But only because, on a whim, the king decided to test my loyalty, not his. Henry wasn't interested in him."

"If he dies," Peter said quietly, "he will still be a martyr, you know."

But to his surprise, Thomas could not agree even to this.

"To you and to Rowland it is an act of faith. Of course. But I'm afraid it will not be seen to be. Don't you realize, Peter? When the Charterhouse monks are executed, they will be martyrs. All England will know it. But Rowland is not important. No one has heard of him. They will quietly execute him one day with some common criminals – an obscure royal servant who committed treason. That is how it will be. A private piece of royal vengeance. That is all that anyone will know or care."

"God will know and care."

"Yes. But His cause is being served by the monks, I dare say. Poor Rowland is just an innocent, a loyal family man, who happened to be in the wrong place. It's all a mistake." For several moments he was silent. Then he sighed. "I have a confession, brother."

"Which is?"

"I am a secret Protestant."

"I see." He tried to hide his disgust.

"That, and serving Cromwell make me feel doubly guilty, therefore. I abandon my family's faith, then cause Rowland's death."

"Perhaps you should feel guilty, then."

"Yes." Thomas looked down at his hands sadly, but then suddenly gazed up, straight into Peter's eyes. "And what am I, brother? A man who lives the evil life of the court and enjoys it? I hold my faith in secret because I am afraid. Henry burns Protestants. I cause Rowland's death, I leave my sister alone, ruined, and with four children. And I ask myself, brother, is my own life worth a tenth of any of yours? I think not. I tell you frankly, if I could die in Rowland's place, I'd do so. I wish to God I could."

Peter saw that he meant it; and found that, for all his faults, he could love him again. "If only," he said without any malice, "you could." But there was nothing anyone could do for Rowland now.

Peter slept little that night. Time and time again he tossed and turned on his bed so that old Dogget, who had taken to sleeping by the door of his cell since he had been ill, more than once came in to see if he was all right.

He thought of Susan and her children. He thought of the terrible death that awaited poor Rowland and, no doubt, himself; and, despite all his attempts at prayer, Father Peter trembled, like any other man.

He was not sure what hour it was when he awoke from a fitful sleep with a new idea in his mind. As he lay there, staring up into the darkness, he wondered what to make of it. He went over it again, carefully, and it seemed to him that it might work, though with heavy risks for those involved. There was, however, another difficulty: was it a crime to deny God's Church even one of her martyrs? For as a priest, Father Peter Meredith faced a terrible dilemma: he did not know if he was doing right or wrong. One thing was clear. He himself, now, was in danger of losing his immortal soul.

Nonetheless, shortly after dawn, he woke faithful Will Dogget, and sent him with a message to summon Thomas.

Thomas listened very quietly until Peter had finished.

"There are great risks for you," the priest said.

"I accept them."

"It would take a strong man," Peter remarked. "Stronger than you or I."

"That can be arranged."

"Then the choice is yours."

"But," Thomas hesitated before continuing softly: "It is the final thing of all that I cannot do."

"I'm sorry," the priest said simply. "You must."

That afternoon, Thomas Meredith met Dan Dogget. He had a debt to call in.

"I told you," he said with a smile, "that I'd think of something."

Susan watched Rowland as he stared out of the stone window and wondered how he could be so calm. Especially considering the scene taking place below.

He had not been calm at first. How terrible it had been, that Mayday morning, only three days ago, as they had approached the Tower. How his heart sank as the barge headed in, not to the ordinary dock by the old Lion Gate, but towards another entrance entirely – a small, dark tunnel in the very centre of the Tower's long waterfront. The Traitors' Gate.

A heavy portcullis creaked up to receive him as they passed under the wharf. They crossed a pool, then a pair of huge iron-barred watergates swung slowly open as they entered a dimly lit dock under a great bastion. The Traitors' Gate. Abandon hope, they said, if you come to the Tower that way.

A few minutes later they had led him up through the great

inner wall, to a chamber in the enlarged turret on its inner side that was known as the Bloody Tower.

And so he had made the acquaintance of the Tower of London. It was a strange place, a world of its own. Outwardly it had not grown much in recent centuries, except for the wharf which had steadily encroached on the river; but within its walls, over the centuries, there had been innumerable additions – a hall here, a new set of chambers there, additional wall-towers and turrets of brick or stone to house the ever-growing community who dwelt therein.

And a remarkable community it was. Apart from the small army of workmen and retainers, cooks, scullions and washerwomen required to service the place, and the lieutenant, constable and other ancient officers, there was the Mint and its keepers, and the Master of Ordnance, whose gun foundries were on the wharf but whose stores lay safely within the walls. To add yet more colour, the new Tudor order of gentlemen-bodyguards to the king, the yeoman warders, were headquartered at the Tower and were often to be seen in their magnificent crimson uniforms. There was still the royal menagerie of exotic beasts and lions whose occasional roars, breaking the silence, could sometimes be heard from the south-west corner. And lastly, of course, the ravens on the green whose dark croaks announced what none could gainsay, that it was they alone who were the true, ancestral guardians of the place.

The prisoners were few in number and almost exclusively of the upper class – courtiers or gentlemen who had offended the monarch in some way. Sometimes, it was true, they might be made to suffer, though use of the rack or other tortures remained extremely rare in England, but more often than not they were housed in modest comfort as befitted their estate.

His own reception had been polite enough. The Lieutenant of the Tower, a courtly man, had paid him a brief visit. Although loyal to his monarch, Rowland suspected, he was secretly appalled by Henry's actions. Sir Thomas More and Bishop Fisher were confined in the Bell Tower, near the entrance, he learned. Doctor Wilson was elsewhere, and the three priors in yet another lodging. After this, though brought his meals by whatever guard was on duty, he was largely ignored. He was, after all, of no importance. He was left alone with his thoughts.

He had tried to be calm. But how could he be, given the terror of what was surely to come for himself and the fear for his family?

By the end of the first day he had twice been sick and was so pale that the constable was told he might be dying. The next two days, despite visits from his wife and children, he was hardly better. Yet now, as he looked out at what was passing below, pale though he was, he almost smiled, and turning to Susan remarked:

"Come and see this wonder."

The three priors were being led out to execution.

They were allowed to walk from their lodging to the outer gate. From there they would be taken across London to the awaiting gallows. They were accompanied by the lieutenant and a respectful group of yeoman warders, who were evidently determined to give them a few last moments of dignity before the ordeal that lay ahead; and they had just passed the green where the ravens strutted when Susan, unwillingly, joined her husband to watch them.

"See how meekly and cheerfully they go," he murmured. "The lambs of God." He smiled at her. "I think," he went on gently, "that is what faith really means. They know, you see. They know they are doing right." He paused as the little party went quite close beneath the window. "That's what martyrs leave behind, isn't it? For all of us to witness. A message stronger than words." He smiled. "I suppose they are the stones, in a way, of which the Church is truly built."

Susan said nothing.

Rowland continued to watch. He now felt the calm which, after a long agony of anticipation, men often feel when they are at last brought face to face with a great terror. A sense, curiously, of relief.

Last night Thomas had given him some other news when he had visited. "When the executions are done," he had said, "they are going straight to the Charterhouse to give the oath to the rest of the monks."

Peter. He too, then, would soon be in his company. Perhaps, Rowland thought, they would be tried together, even die together. The thought comforted him and gave him strength.

* * *

On 4 May in the year of Our Lord 1535, upon the order of King Henry VIII of England, that zealous Defender of the Faith, the execution of the three priors was carried out in the following manner.

From the outer gateway of the Tower, they were placed on hurdles and dragged through the streets. Their journey was a long one, for while the old Smithfield site was still used for executions, another place had gradually become even more popular: the old Roman crossroads a mile to the west of Holborn, where once a marble arch had stood and which now took its name from a little stream that ran nearby, known as Tyburn; the gallows was Tyburn Tree.

The crowds along the way noticed something unusual. Since olden times, since the good old days when Saint Thomas Becket had defied the Plantagenet king, it had been the custom before any churchman was handed over to the civil authority for execution to remove the Church's protection by stripping him of his religious orders. But today, Henry being God's temporal and spiritual representative on Earth, this was no longer necessary. With a gasp the onlookers noticed: "They are dressed as priests."

At Tyburn, where a great crowd awaited by the gallows, King Henry had decided to make this a court entertainment. Not only was he present, but so were the ambassadors of France and Spain. More than forty mounted courtiers accompanied the king, all wearing masks, as though they were going to a carnival.

Before this noble company the three priors meekly came. Offered the chance to recant at the gallows foot, they all refused. Nooses round their necks, they were hauled up and hanged and then, while fully conscious, taken down and cut open. Their bowels were dragged out, then their hearts, and their arms, legs and heads hacked off and raised, and waved about for all that splendid crowd to see. It was savagely done, in the best and oldest way. Then their blood-soaked limbs were taken to be nailed or hung in sundry places.

And so, with the butchering of these, the first of the Christian martyrs who denied the king's supremacy, Henry's Church of England proclaimed its new authority.

Peter attended the executions, then made his way back to the monastery. When he reached it he felt very tired.

Shortly afterwards some of the king's servants arrived with a small package rolled up in a cloth. When it was unwrapped, the monks saw that it was their prior's severed arm. The king's men nailed it to the monastery gate.

It was a little after noon that the commissioners came to the Charterhouse to demand the oath from the community. The monks were all gathered together. The commissioners, who included a number of churchmen, explained to them the propriety and the manifold wisdom of loyal obedience to their king. But all the monks refused. Except for one.

To their great astonishment, looking tired and ill and having, after the horrors of the morning, it seemed, lost heart, the most recent arrival, Father Peter Meredith, stepped forward and, alone of all their number took the oath.

Secretary Cromwell himself informed young Thomas Meredith what had happened; and Thomas should have been glad. "Not only does he live," Cromwell remarked, "but it does you some good: I've already told the king that the only loyal fellow there was your brother." He grimaced. "He himself may not be long for this world though. They tell me he seems very sick."

And so, indeed, Thomas found him when he visited the Charterhouse a few hours later. For while the rest of the community was being subjected to a barrage of threats and persuasion in the chapel and in the refectory, Peter had withdrawn to his cell where he was being tended by old Will Dogget. He seemed now to have difficulty even rising from his bed, and after a few words, Thomas left him.

But it was the other visit he had to make that he dreaded. For a long time he hesitated outside the house at Chelsea, and it was only when one of the children happened to run out and spot him that he was obliged to enter. Even then, he made every excuse to play with the children and avoid the subject before, at last finding himself alone with Susan, he had to break the news.

"Peter has taken the oath."

At first, she did not believe it. "I have been to the Charterhouse and seen him," he told her. "It is true." For long moments she was silent.

"You mean," she finally said, in a low voice, "that after leading Rowland to certain death, he himself has now deserted. He is leaving Rowland to die alone? He led him there," she spread her hands, "for nothing?"

"He is very sick. I think he is very tired."

"And Rowland? He is well, but about to die."

"I think Peter is not just sick. Ashamed. I try to understand."

"No." She shook her head slowly. "That is not enough." After another long pause, with a grief in her voice that almost made him double up with pain, she quietly said: "I do not wish to see Peter again."

And he knew that Peter had taken away everything in which she trusted, that she would never change her mind, and that there was nothing he could do about it.

Dan Dogget glanced up at the sky. He did not often say a prayer but now, surreptitiously, he did so. There was one good thing: his debt to Meredith would be discharged when this strange business was over. "Just let it be soon," he prayed.

It was nearly sunset when they set out. Father Peter had not felt well enough to attempt the journey in the afternoon; but an hour ago he had seemed to gather strength and, on young Thomas's orders, Dan had brought the little cart round to the monastery gate.

The atmosphere in the Charterhouse had been tense. Since the executions the previous morning, Henry's churchmen had subjected the monks to a continuous series of tirades. Earlier, three of the most senior monks had been taken, not to the Tower but to the common jail. "The king is determined to break at least some of them down," he was told. As for Father Peter, his position was strange. Since he was ill, he kept apart in his cell anyway; but it was clear to Dan that the other monks had effectively disowned him. Even the king's men had rather lost interest in him. "He only just arrived," one of the other old lodgers remarked to him. "He was never really one of them, you know." Yet whatever his disgrace within the community, and even though, as they passed through the courtyard, the monks looked the other way, Dan noticed how his father still treated the former priest with reverence and, when Peter prepared to climb into the cart, knelt down and kissed his hand.

Slowly he conveyed the two Meredith brothers across the

city on their melancholy mission. They were going to the Tower to see poor Rowland.

They gained admittance easily at the Tower's outer gate: Thomas was immediately recognized as Secretary Cromwell's man. But the cart had to be left outside and it was now that Dan realized how much they needed him. For during the journey, Father Peter's strength appeared to have ebbed away again. Getting down from the cart with difficulty, he seemed hardly able to walk and though in recent months the monk had lost considerable weight, it took both Dan and Thomas, one on each side, to help him along the cobbled lane between the high stone walls; and Peter was clearly short of breath by the time they reached the Bloody Tower. After Thomas identified himself to the respectful guard, they made their way slowly up the spiral stairway to Rowland's cell.

Rowland Bull was sitting quietly on a bench when they entered. The last red glow of sunset was coming through the narrow window. Some of yesterday's calm had worn off. He had been sick again that morning, but only once. Now he just looked pale as Peter slowly sank down beside him. He was clearly glad to see them nonetheless.

As the two of them talked in low tones, Dan found himself watching them with interest. Brother Peter he had come to know a little, Rowland he hardly knew at all. Seeing them side by side now, he observed with surprise how like each other the two men were; Peter's illness had not only caused him to lose weight but made his face thinner too, so that he and Rowland might have been brothers. It was funny, he thought, but if he hadn't known otherwise, he would have guessed that the former parish priest was the family man, and the lawyer, with his ascetic, almost ethereal expression, was the monk. Perhaps they lived their lives the wrong way round, he mused.

They had been there several minutes before Peter broke the news. "I have taken the oath."

Rowland had not known. He had seen no one except a guard with some food in the last two days. Yet, shocked though he was, after seeming to droop for a moment or two, his reaction was rather unexpected. Gazing earnestly at Peter he said gently: "Was it so terrible for you, too?"

"Do you wish to do the same?" Thomas asked him. "I do not think it can save you, but," glancing at Peter, "with Peter here having done so too, it might soften the king's mood. I could try."

Though he paused for thought, Rowland did not do so for long. "No," he said at last. "I could not take it then; I cannot now."

Peter drew out from under his cassock a little flask of wine and then, with a smile, three little beakers. A little shakily he poured out wine, fumbling slightly with one of the beakers. Managing to control his shaking hand well enough he passed them to Rowland and Thomas.

"In my state of health," he said gently, "I am not sure that we shall meet again on earth, Rowland. So let us drink together one last time." He looked carefully at Rowland, then. "Remember in your hour of agony," he said softly, "you who are more to me than even a brother, it was you, not I, who truly earned a martyr's crown."

They drank, and waited a while, saying nothing more. Then Peter and Thomas Meredith rose up, and did what they had come to do.

Darkness had fallen by the time Dan and Thomas departed with the monk. It was not only sickness but the emotion of this final parting that had suddenly overcome him, for now, unable even to walk properly, he was practically a dead weight between them as they made their way back, very slowly, towards the gate. Seeing Thomas, the guards not only opened the gate but helped them get the monk up into the cart. Once this was done, assuring Thomas that he could manage, Dan drove slowly away to return to the Charterhouse, while the courtier turned round.

"A sad night," he remarked to the yeoman warder in charge of the gate, who nodded his head in quiet agreement. "I shall return and sit with poor Bull a little longer," Thomas told him. "He looks almost as ill as the monk." And he walked slowly and thoughtfully back.

All was still in the Tower that night. Prisoners, custodians, even the ravens were asleep. The grey stone walls and turrets loomed blankly out of the shadows, apparently sightless in the starlight – except for a single faint glow, from the window of one cell, dimly lit by a candle, where two men still remained, keeping watch together. When once the guard looked in, he saw that Thomas was sitting gloomily on the bench while the lawyer, kneeling by the window, was softly murmuring his prayers.

Thomas did not interrupt, though the prayers were long. As he waited, he went over his conversation with his brother three days before. How brave and yet how uncertain the priest had been, in what agony of spirit. "I am denying the Church two martyrs," he had confessed, "if we do this thing. Perhaps," he had sadly remarked, "I shall lose my soul."

Yet surely, Thomas thought, Rowland had offered himself for martyrdom: wasn't that the same? As for Peter, what name did one give the sacrifice, he wondered, of a man prepared to lay down not only his life, but even his immortal soul for his friend?

But now the figure by the window rose from his knees and, with a nod to Thomas, lay on the bed. It was the moment Thomas had dreaded, the thing he had said he could not do.

"You must," the figure on the bed said softly. "We have to be sure."

Taking a blanket, therefore, Thomas went across to the bed, put the blanket over the other's face, and began to press down.

All his life he accounted it a proof of God's mercy that another hand, at that moment, intervened.

There was no doubt what was happening when the courtier summoned the guard. A few minutes later, two sleepy yeomen warders joined them to witness the scene.

The lawyer on the bed was having a massive apoplexy. He was gasping for breath; his face was discoloured; even while they watched he started to sit up, then fell back, mouth open, face strangely sagging. One of the yeomen went over, then turned to Thomas. "He's gone." Then, more softly: "Better this than what he had coming."

Thomas nodded.

The yeoman turned. "Nothing you can do, sir," he said kindly to Thomas. "We'll inform the lieutenant." He ushered the others out, tactfully leaving Thomas alone for a moment.

So that nobody heard Thomas, as he touched the corpse, whisper: "God bless you, Peter."

* * *

It was dawn when Rowland Bull awoke. He found consciousness slowly; his head felt strangely heavy. Thomas was still there. The last thing he remembered was the two of them talking with Peter. And then he frowned. Why was he wearing a monk's habit? He glanced round. Where was he?

"You're in the Charterhouse," Thomas said quietly. "I think I'd better explain."

It had not been difficult really. The sleeping draught Peter had given him had worked even faster than they had expected. Changing his clothes with Peter's had been the work of a couple of minutes. Nor had there been any difficulty taking him out of the Tower. "I'm Cromwell's trusted man, you see," Thomas said. The only problem, which they had anticipated, was getting an unconscious man into the Charterhouse; and for that short journey, Daniel Dogget had simply carried him, bodily, in his mighty arms.

"You'd be amazed how like you Peter looked once he was in your clothes," Thomas continued. "And when a man dies, you see, his looks change anyway."

"Peter is dead? How?"

"I was to kill him. We were going to make it seem he had died in his sleep. It was helpful that they already believed you were ill. But then, just as I began . . ." Thomas looked down for a moment. "I thank God the Lord took him instead. An apoplexy. He had been ill for so long, as you know."

"But what about me? What am I to do?"

"Ah." Thomas paused. "That is the message I have for you from Peter. He dared not write it of course: so I am to tell you. He wants you to live. Your family needs you. He reminds you of what he said: you have already earned the martyr's crown because you were ready to die. By doing this, however, he has prevented you."

"His taking the oath, then . . . ?"

"Was part of the plan. Father Peter Meredith is spared and you must now become him. It will not be too difficult. No one will trouble you here. To the monks you are an outcast. They will avoid you. The king's commissioners are not interested in you; and besides, you are believed to be very sick. Remain in this cell, therefore, Old Will Dogget will look after you. In a little while, I can probably arrange for you to go to another place."

"And if I refuse?"

"Then," Thomas made a face, "both I and the two Doggets, father and son, will accompany you to a terrible death and your wife will not have even me to protect her. Peter hoped you would not do that."

"And Susan? The children?"

"You must be patient," Thomas answered. "For your safety, and for her own, she must believe, truly, that you are dead. Later," he continued, "we will see what can be done. But not yet."

"You have thought of everything."

"Peter did."

"It seems," he said sadly, "that I should thank you all. You risked your lives."

"I felt guilty." Thomas shrugged. "Will Dogget did it because Peter asked, and the old man loved him." He smiled wryly. "Simple souls are nobler, aren't they? As for Daniel," he grinned. "Let's say he owed me a favour."

Rowland sighed. "I suppose I have no choice."

"There was one other message from Peter," Thomas added. "It's a little strange. He said: 'Tell him he may only be a monk for a time. Then he must return to his wife.' I'd have thought that was obvious. Does it make sense to you?"

"Yes," Rowland said slowly. "Oh, yes. It does."

Of all the horrors which marked the birth of Henry's new English Church, one single execution in June that year truly shocked his people.

It was occasioned by the Pope. In May, still urging Europe's monarchs to depose the schismatic English king, the vigorous pontiff made Bishop Fisher, still in the Tower with More, a cardinal. King Henry's fury knew no bounds. "If the Pope sends a cardinal's hat," he vowed, "there will be no head to put it on."

On 23 June, tired and broken, the saintly and grey-haired old Bishop of Rochester was led out on to the green in the Tower of London, and his head was struck off. It marked, most men felt, the passing of an age.

Two weeks later he was followed to the block by the former chancellor, Thomas More. But though it was known that the royal servant died for the faith, his fate was seen more as a political fall than a religious martyrdom and did not make nearly such a powerful impression at the time.

Doctor Wilson, who had originally accompanied the two men, being of no importance, remained almost forgotten in the Tower.

The monks of the London Charterhouse continued their sufferings. Three more were executed and the rest were subjected to constant indignities. Their trials were made all the more painful by the fact that other houses of the order submitted to the oath, and the head of the order in France even sent a message that they should do likewise.

It was hardly even noticed when, one evening in June, upon orders from the office of Vicegerent Cromwell, the cowardly Father Peter Meredith, still very frail, was conveyed out of the monastery to go to another religious house in the north. Old Will Dogget went with him.

In the spring of 1536 a double irony took place. Perhaps, had she remained his wife, or even been more kindly treated, the Queen Katherine, Henry's Spanish wife, might have lived longer. But whether this is so or not, at the start of that year, in a cold house in East Anglia, she died. Had King Henry waited, therefore, he would have been free to marry and need never have broken with Rome at all.

Within months, moreover, Anne Boleyn, the other great cause of the business, having failed to produce the needed male heir, fell into disfavour and was executed. Then King Henry married again. But he did not return the Church to Rome. He liked being Supreme Head, and besides, the money he was now deriving from the Church was considerable.

1538

It was a May morning, but there was thunder in the air.

The two Flemings looked at each other glumly across their little stall.

Neither of them could find words to speak, but more than once they glanced sadly at the Charterhouse as if to say: you have deserted us. Though what the poor old monastery, now empty of inhabitants, could have done it would have been hard to say. Fleming and his wife had no thoughts, however, of such niceties that day. They were too busy pitying themselves. They were taking down the stall for the last time. The business was closed.

The fault was King Henry's. Or, to be yet more precise, that of his Vicegerent Cromwell. For Cromwell was closing all the monasteries.

The Dissolution of the Monasteries was already the most extraordinary affair. For the last two years, up and down the country, the smaller, then the greater houses had been visited by Cromwell or his men. Some had been found guilty of laxity, others merely closed on little or no pretext. The vast holdings of lands, accumulated over the centuries, had thus fallen into the hands of the Church's new spiritual head, who had for the most part sold them off, sometimes allowing his friends to purchase at discounted prices. About a quarter of the property in England was changing hands, the greatest change since the Norman Conquest.

"It has also," Cromwell remarked with satisfaction, "transformed the king's finances." On the strength of it, the Supreme Head was starting to build Nonsuch, another huge palace outside London.

But this was not all. The reforming party in the English Church had received such strength and encouragement from this great cleansing of the past that they had also won Henry's permission to accompany it, this spring, with another purge.

"Superstition," Cromwell and his friends declared: "we must rid England of popish superstition." It was not a wholesale purge, but for weeks now, all over the country, a careful selection of images, statues and relics had been destroyed. Pieces of the Holy Rood had been burned, sanctuaries closed. Even the great jewel-encrusted shrine of London's saint, Thomas Becket had been broken up and its gold and gems taken to the king's treasury. The point was made.

There had been, even Cromwell had to admit, one unfortunate by-product of all this zeal. The monasteries had been host and comforter to an army of the poor. Old men like Will Dogget had been housed; hungry folk had been fed at their doors. Suddenly in London now there were tribes of beggars with whom the parishes could scarely cope. The aldermen had appealed to Cromwell, who had to agree that something must be done.

And then there were the stall holders. What was to become of those who, like the Flemings, trafficked before the gates of every London monastery in all the religious trinkets and images that were now condemned? Nothing, it seemed. "Our occupation's gone," Mistress Fleming declared. Bitterly they packed up their stall.

A few minutes later, as they wheeled their handcart down into Smithfield, another melancholy sight awaited them. In the middle of the open area, a crowd had gathered. Before it a curious little square scaffold had been set up underneath which piles of wood had been stacked. As they drew closer, they could see that an elderly figure was hanging by his arms in chains from the scaffold and that the wood beneath him was about to be lit.

The reformers were doing good work that day. Along with the statues and the images and the superstitious relics, they had found an old man to burn.

Old Doctor Forest had been told he should die years ago. His crime had been that he was confessor to poor Queen Katherine. In his eighties now, he had been left, half forgotten in jail for some years until, as an afterthought, it had been realized that someone had better burn him or he might die of natural causes. Presiding over this little ceremony the Flemings saw a tall, grim, greybearded figure, who, as they drew near, was calling out to the old man: "In what state, Doctor, will you die?"

Hugh Latimer, the Oxford scholar and reforming preacher was a bishop now. If he had any objection to this affair, he certainly gave no sign of it. Gallantly the old man replied that, even if the angels were to start teaching any but the true doctrines of Holy Church, he would not believe them. At which answer Latimer indicated that it was time that he should burn.

But something special had been ordained that morning. Instead of the usual fire, where the victim either suffocated or died of the flames quite quickly, they had decided to dangle the old man over the fire in chains so that he could suffer a slow death that might torture him for hours. Under Hugh Latimer's supervision, this was now done. But the crowd, for once, had had enough. As the flames and smoke rose, a rush of able-bodied men knocked the scaffolding down and within a minute or two, the old man was dead.

Slowly the two Flemings continued on their way.

"It's lucky," Mistress Fleming declared to her husband, "that my brother Daniel makes good money on the royal barge. He'll have to look after us now."

"You think he will?"

"Of course," she said. "He's family, isn't he?"

Just then, she heard a rumble of thunder.

But there was no thunder that morning twenty miles away to the east, in the old Kent city of Rochester: only a pale blue sky and a bright sheen on the water of the River Medway as it went silently to meet the Thames around the point.

Everything was quiet as Susan waited.

It had been Thomas's idea, the previous year, that she should move to Rochester; and though at first she had been hesitant, she was glad in the end to find a pleasant sanctuary in the old place, far from the unhappy scenes she associated with the capital. The children were happy there too. In the modest lodgings near the cathedral, she had discovered a new peace.

But she was not sure about the meeting this morning. Thomas had insisted upon it, and after all his kindness over the last few years, she had not felt she could refuse him. He had even come down, hours before, and tactfully taken the children out for a long walk, so that she could see her visitor alone. But did she want to see him?

Peter. In the first weeks after Rowland's death, she could not even bear to hear his name. When she heard he had left London for the north, she was glad. Once or twice, in the last two years, she had considered writing to him, but had not done so since she did not know what she should say. And now he was coming to see her. All the monks in England, of course, were now without a home. As each monastery was dissolved, they had to leave. Most were being given pensions, not ungenerous. Some had become parish priests; some left holy orders and even married.

"I will see him," she had told Thomas finally, "but you must make one thing clear. I cannot take him in to live with me. I hope he does not think I can."

At mid-morning there was a knock at the door and the

sound of footsteps entering the little house. And then she saw her husband.

Few people in Rochester, in the years that followed, paid any special attention to the Brown family. Her neighbours remembered that Susan Brown had been a pious widow and that she had married again. It was said that her new husband, Robert Brown, had been a monk, but no one seemed certain. He was a quiet man, devoted to his wife and stepchildren, who referred to him affectionately as "father". He became a schoolmaster at Rochester's ancient school; and he seemed happy in his work and in his loving family, though sometimes, it seemed to those who came to know him a little, he wore a rather wistful expression which suggested that he might still secretly hanker after the life of the cloister he had left.

When he died, ten years after coming to Rochester, his wife was so upset that the priest heard her call softly to him, "Rowland," which, he believed, had been the name of her first husband. But the priest knew that, in their grief, people sometimes became confused, and he thought no more about it.

In the decades that followed, no family could have been less conspicuous. Susan was determined to keep it so. The girls married; young Jonathan became a schoolmaster. Their inner faith, of course, was Catholic. But after all that had passed, she advised them: "Whatever happens, keep your own counsel. Be silent."

The final years of King Harry were grim. He became bloated and sick. The fortune he had stolen from the Church was wasted in extravagant palaces and useless foreign ventures to satisfy his craving for glory. Wives came and went. Even clever Cromwell fell from favour and lost his head.

The king had managed to produce an heir in the end, by the third of his six wives. The boy Edward, everyone said, was brilliant but sickly, and it soon became clear that his tutors, Cranmer and his friends meant to take their new boy king even further from the true Catholic faith after King Harry died. But even Susan was astounded when she discovered how far they meant to go.

"Cranmer's Prayer Book," she said to her family, "need not have been so bad. After all, it is mostly a translation of the

Latin rite and I'll agree that his language is beautiful." But the doctrines the English Church were now espousing were no longer just those of reformers. They were entirely Protestant. "The miracle of the Mass is utterly denied," she cried. Priests could marry. "I'm sure that suits Cranmer," she remarked acidly. But, in a way, even more shocking to the senses was the physical destruction which the Protestants demanded. She saw it most painfully one day when, visiting London, she slipped into Peter's little church of St Lawrence Silversleeves.

The change was truly astounding. The little church had been stripped. The dark old rood screen which her brother had loved was gone. They had burned it. The walls were whitewashed. The altar had been taken away and a bare table placed in the middle of the church. Even the new stained glass windows had been smashed. She knew this vandalism had been taking place everywhere, but here in her brother's church it hurt her more. Do they really imagine, she wondered, that by breaking up everything beautiful they can purify their own sinful souls? But despite all these horrors, she stuck to her rule: be silent.

Nor when the Protestant boy king died and his sister Mary came to the throne, did Susan allow herself to rejoice too soon. True, Mary as the daughter of poor, Spanish Queen Katherine, was a devout Catholic. True, she swore to return England to the true Church of Rome. "But her nature is obstinate," Susan judged, "and I fear she will handle the business badly." And alas, that was how it turned out. Despite the protests of her people, she insisted upon marrying King Philip of Spain. The Catholic cause from now on, in the minds of many Englishmen, came to mean that they would be subject not only to a Pope, but to a foreign king as well. Then came the burnings of Protestants. All the leaders of the reform were sentenced. When Cranmer burned, she felt sorry for him. When cruel old Latimer went to the stake she only shrugged. "He did worse to others." But soon the English were calling their queen "Bloody Mary"; and when, after five unhappy years, she died childless, it did not at all surprise Susan that England's religion was still an open question.

There remained only one of King Harry's children, Elizabeth, the daughter of Anne Boleyn, and Susan was sure that she could not return England to Rome. For if the Pope in

Rome were the true authority, then her mother's marriage to the old king must have been invalid. She herself, therefore, would be a bastard and could not legitimately sit on England's throne. The religious settlement that Elizabeth constructed was perfectly logical, therefore. The question of the Mass was described by a formula so mysterious that with enough good will you could read it either way. A degree of religious ceremony was maintained. The Pope's authority was denied, but Elizabeth tactfully called herself Supreme Governor, instead of Supreme Head of the English Church. To Catholics therefore she could say: "I have given you a reformed Catholicism." To Protestants: "The Pope is denied." Or as Susan put it drily: "Bastard child; bastard Church."

Yet even Susan had to admit, Elizabeth was showing wisdom. For as the whole of Europe drew into two huge, and increasingly hostile religious camps, the position of England's queen was not an easy one. While she temporized with the great Catholic powers and even hinted that she might marry one of their princes and return England to Rome, she was faced in London and the other cities with an increasingly Protestant people. This was not surprising. Intelligent merchants and artisans, having once got their English Bible and Book of Common Prayer, liked thinking for themselves. Their trading partners, in the Low Countries, in Germany, even in France, were often Protestant too. Gradually the more extreme forms of Protestantism made headway. Puritans, these people began to call themselves. Even if she had hated the Protestants – and secretly she was in sympathy with them – Elizabeth could not have stopped this development without resorting to tyranny and bloodshed.

So instead, she and her wise minister, the great Cecil, had adopted an English compromise. "We do not seek to look into men's hearts," they said. "But outward conformity we must require." It was a humane and necessary policy; and even Susan, on the whole, was grateful for it. So that, to her own surprise, when the Pope in Rome grew impatient with the English queen and threatened excommunication if she did not return her kingdom to the fold, Susan found herself saying irritably: "I wish he would not."

Only one thing, in those years, drew from her a cry of fury. This was the publication, in 1563, of a single, stout book. It was known as Foxe's *Book of Martyrs*; and it was an astonishing feat of propaganda. For this book, carefully written to evoke every man's pity and rage, described in detail the martyrs of England – by which it meant those Protestants who had perished under Bloody Mary. Of the Catholics who had suffered martyrdom before then, it said not a word. That some of these Protestants, like vicious old Latimer, had been burners and torturers themselves, it conveniently forgot. The sale of the book was prodigious. Soon, it seemed, only Catholic persecution of Protestants had ever existed.

"'Tis a lie," Susan would protest. "And I fear it will persist." It would indeed. Foxe's *Book of Martyrs* was destined to be read in families, to give warning to children, and to shape English people's perception of the Catholic Church for generations.

Yet, apart from this one outburst, the silence of Susan continued. She had had her fill of trouble; she was determined to live at peace. And peace she was granted, at least in this life, except for one minor disturbance.

After a long career at court, where he never really advanced, her brother Thomas took a wife late in life. She was a girl of good family and some fortune, but some small blemish on her character, Susan suspected, had prevented her getting married. She gave him a son, then died. And not long after that, Susan received a letter from her brother informing her that he, too, was not long for this world and intended sending his infant son and heir to Rochester, "where I know you and Jonathan will look after him."

And so it was, in the last years of her life, that Susan found herself with a new charge, a handsome little fellow with auburn hair and, she had to confess, great charm. His name was Edmund.

Sometimes, though, she wondered if he was not just a little too wild.

Chapter 11

The Globe

The long years of Queen Elizabeth I were remembered as a golden age, but to Londoners living at the time they were more varied. Firstly, for the most part, there was peace. Elizabeth was naturally cautious, and thanks to her father's extravagance, she could not really afford to go to war. There was also modest prosperity. All men's lives, even those of the tiny minority in the towns, still depended on the harvest; and Elizabeth was usually lucky with her harvests. There was adventure, too. Though seventy years had passed since Columbus found America, it was not until Elizabeth's reign that English adventurers like Francis Drake and Walter Raleigh set out on the voyages of exploration – in truth, a mixture of piracy, trade and settlement – that began England's huge encounter with the New World.

But the defining event of the reign took place when Elizabeth, having avoided large-scale war for thirty years, was at last, unavoidably, forced into it. The cause was religion. If the Reformation had dealt the Catholic Church a mighty blow, Rome had risen to the challenge: with dedicated orders like the Jesuits, even with the dreaded Inquisition, the Church set out to win back what was lost; and high on the list was the schismatic kingdom of England. Nothing could disguise where Elizabeth's true sympathies lay; and many of her subjects, led by the stern Puritans, were urging her even further into the Protestant camp. Exasperated at last, the Pope told England's Catholics that they no longer owed loyalty to the heretic queen. Indeed he wished there were someone to depose her. One candidate was her Catholic cousin, Mary Queen of Scots. Cast out by the Protestant Scots and held in a northern English castle, this romantic, wayward lady was an obvious focus for any Catholic plots. Unwisely however, she was caught in one of these and Elizabeth had been forced to order her execution. But there was another candidate, mightier by far than foolish Mary.

King Philip of Spain had hoped to obtain the Crown of England for his Habsburg family when he married Mary Tudor. Now he might win it by conquest – a chance to perform a great service for the true faith. "This is nothing less," he announced, "than a holy crusade."

At the end of July 1588, there set out from Spain the greatest fleet that the world had ever seen. The Armada's mission was to land on the shores of England a huge army against which Elizabeth's modest militia would be helpless. Philip was sure that every true Catholic in England would rise to support him.

On the little island, Englishmen trembled. But they prepared to fight. Every suitable vessel made ready at the southern ports. Great beacons were set up on hills all the way along the coast to signal the Armada's approach. As for the Catholics, Philip was wrong. "We are Catholics, but not traitors," they declared. But most memorable of all was the speech Elizabeth made, dressed in full armour, as she came to join her troops.

> Let tyrants fear. I have always so behaved myself that, under God, I have placed my chiefest strength in the goodwill of my subjects; and therefore I am come . . . being resolved in the midst and heat of the battle to live or die amongst you all; to lay down for God, my kingdom and for my people, my honour and my blood, even in the dust.
>
> I know I have but the body of a weak and feeble woman: but I have the heart and stomach of a king – and a king of England too.

As the massive galleons advanced up the English Channel, a huge storm arose, and harried by the little English vessels, the Spanish were confounded; the storm continued day after day until at last they were blown all the way round the rocky coast of Scotland and Ireland where many were wrecked. Only a fraction ever returned home and King Philip of Spain, honestly mystified, wondered if this were a sign. The English had no doubt. "We were saved by the hand of God," men said. The Roman Catholics, henceforth, were seen as dangerous invaders. God, clearly, had chosen England as a special haven: a Protestant island kingdom. And so it would remain.

At the hub of the fortunate kingdom, London bustled as never before. Seen from a distance, the old place looked much the same. The medieval city still rose on its two hills within the ancient Roman walls, and in several places the surrounding fields and marshland still came to the city gates. On the skyline, however, the spire of St Paul's had gone, struck by lightning, leaving only a stubby square tower, somehow less medieval than before; and in the east, the Tower had now acquired four gleaming onion domes at its corners, giving the place a more festive air, like a Tudor country palace.

Within its confines, London had swelled. The houses had grown taller: three or four timbered and gabled storeys now jutted out over the narrow streets and alleys. Unused spaces were being filled up: the old Walbrook stream between the two hills had almost disappeared under houses now. Above all, the great enclosed precincts of the old monasteries, dissolved by King Harry, were being colonized. Parts of the old religious houses were workshops; the huge Blackfriars precinct was rebuilt as fashionable houses. And the population was swelling, not because families were growing – for age and disease, in crowded Tudor London, still took away more than were born – but because of a stream of immigrants from all over England, and from overseas, especially from the Low Countries, where Protestants fled the persecuting Catholic Spanish. At the end of the Wars of the Roses, London had perhaps fifty thousand souls; by Elizabeth's last years, four times that number.

And in busy London there now grew up one of the greatest gifts that the English genius was to leave the world. For in the reign of Elizabeth I began the first and greatest flowering of the glorious English theatre. Yet it is less generally known that in Elizabeth's final years, when William Shakespeare had written only half his plays, the English theatre almost came to an end.

1597

Earlier that spring afternoon, there had been a cockfight and now they were baiting a bear. The circular pit of the Curtain, from which the actors' stage had been temporarily removed, was about fifty feet across, with two tall tiers of wooden galleries enclosing it. The bear was tethered to a post in the centre by a chain which was long enough to allow it to bump into the barriers at the spectators' feet. The bear was a splendid beast: already it had killed two of the three mastiffs which had been set on it and their bodies, pulped and bleeding, lay in the dust. But the remaining dog had put up a tremendous fight. Though a blow from the bear's mighty paw had flung him right across the pit, he would not give up. Weaving and springing he had attacked again and again, savaging the bear's hindquarters, driving it to a frenzy of indignation and even twice sinking his teeth into its throat when it grew tired. The crowd roared: "Well done, Scamp. Go for him, boy!" Bears were seldom killed, but the pluckiest dogs were often saved to fight another day. As the mastiff was called off, the onlookers shouted their approval.

None cried more heartily – "Bravely fought! Noble hound!" – than the handsome, auburn-haired young man in the gallery, surrounded by a group of friends who hung upon his words. He was obviously one of the young gallants of the town. His doublet was richly embroidered, dagged and – this was the fashion – formed into a stiffened curve over his midriff. Though some young men still favoured the medieval hose, which certainly showed off a fine leg and, indeed, the buttocks too, he had gone over to the newest style: a pair of woollen stockings and above these, made of the same material as the doublet, the billowing breeches known as galligaskins, secured at the knee with ribbons. On his feet were embroidered shoes, tucked into outer slippers lest the mud should soil them. Around his neck, a starched ruff, white as snow. Over his shoulders, also matching his tunic, a short cape. It was a fashion, echoing the shape of Spanish armour, that made him look both elegant and manly.

From his waist hung a rapier, its pommel embossed with gold, and at the back, a matching dagger. He wore gloves of soft and scented leather and in his right ear a golden ring.

Upon his head was a high brimmed hat from which there sprouted, like fountains, three gorgeous plumes which added a foot to his height. This was the dress with which, in Elizabeth's last years, a man decked himself out for immortality upon the stage of life. But there was one more prop to make the costume complete. With studied nonchalance, Edmund Meredith held it in his right hand. It was long, curved and made of clay.

It was a pipe. Some years before the queen's favourite, Walter Raleigh, had learned the use of the tobacco plant from the American Indians and brought it back to England. Soon the expensive Virginian weed was all the rage amongst the fashionable. Edmund Meredith, as it happened, did not much like the taste of the pipe, but he always had one with him in a public place, to take away from his nostrils the smells, real or assumed, of the common people: "the garlic-breaths and onion-breaths," as he liked to call them.

And it was during the lull before a pair of fighting cocks was brought into the pit, Edmund Meredith smiled at his friends.

"Shakespeare's giving up. I'm going to take his place," and made his remarkable boast.

Young Rose and Sterne, gallants like himself, applauded. William Bull wondered if he would get his money back. Cuthbert Carpenter trembled, because he was going to hell. Jane Fleming wondered if Edmund would marry her. And John Dogget grinned, because he had no worries anyway.

Nobody took any notice of the dark-skinned man behind them.

Edmund Meredith wanted to cut a figure in the world. He had no other motive, and there was nothing else that he wanted to achieve. But in pursuing his ambition he was single-minded. If the world was a stage, he meant to play a handsome part. He had always known that quiet old Rochester would never do for him, but fortunately his father had left him a modest income on which he could live as a single gentleman. And so he had come to London.

But what to do? How did a young man cut a figure in the world? There was the royal court of course, the great high road to rank and fortune. But the chances of failure and humiliation were high, as his father and grandfather had discovered. The law then. There were more lawsuits in busy London nowadays than ever before, and the best lawyers were making huge fortunes. He had attended the Inns of Court, therefore, and nearly completed his studies. "But law's too dry, too tedious for me," he judged. His cousins the Bulls were brewers. "But I'll not dirty my hands with trade," he vowed.

He liked to write verses. "I'll be a poet, then," he declared. But to be a poet you needed a patron. Without a patron the court and the fashionable world never noticed you; printers, even if they printed hundreds of copies, only paid a pittance. A rich patron, however, pleased by elegant verses dedicated to him and immortalizing his noble house, could be generous indeed. The Earl of Southampton, people said, had paid Shakespeare so well for one fine poem, *Venus and Adonis*, that the fellow had been set up for life. The only trouble was that patrons were also fickle. Poor Spenser, no less a poet than Will Shakespeare, had hung about the court for years and had scarcely made a penny.

There was, however, the theatre. It was amazing really: even in his childhood, the theatre had hardly existed. There were the mummers who enacted Bible stories at religious festivals, or the fellows who would put on a song and dance in the courtyard of an inn like the George; and of course every educated man knew about the drama of classical times. Classical scenes were sometimes enacted at court. But it had only been recently that the great nobles had set the fashion by encouraging troupes of actors to give more elaborate shows to please the queen. Encouraged by their lordly patrons, the actors had begun to discover what they could do. Soon they wanted proper plays. They began to hire writers, and in a few years, as if by magic, the wonder of the English theatre had begun.

"It's a fashion that will pass," some said, but Meredith did not think so. People were flocking to the plays, not just at court, but in London too. The best actors, little more than servants or vagrants before, were becoming popular heroes. Writers were well paid. If a play was successful, the playwright was granted most of the house receipts for one performance. And some – men of learning like Ben Jonson – had won the court's admiration for their brilliant wit. Marlowe too, killed young, alas, had written tragedies in language so re-sounding that men compared him to the ancient Greeks.

And then there was Shakespeare. Meredith liked both the Shakespeare brothers. He saw more of Ned, who acted the minor parts well enough: Will was always so busy that you only saw him fleetingly. But when he did join the crowd at the tavern he was certainly very cheerful company. He had written several comedies which had found favour, and some history plays about the Plantagenet kings as well. "Fustian stuff, but popular," Edmund judged. Will Shakespeare had not yet attempted tragedy and Edmund imagined it was probably beyond him. Except for one play. His *Romeo and Juliet* had been astonishing, and had played again and again. All London knew it. "But I'm sure he must have had help from other hands," Edmund would say. He had done nothing quite like it since. "He's wise enough to know his limitations," Edmund told his friends. For though, with his balding, dome-like head, you might have thought the fellow was a man of learning, this was not the case. "I've a little Latin and no Greek," he had freely admitted. Shakespeare was just an actor with a remark-able wit, and in his secret heart, Meredith could not help feeling that he was cut from a finer cloth and could probably do better.

He had started over a year ago when he contributed some extra lines to a comedy, which had been praised. Even suc-cessful writers like Shakespeare often did light work of this kind and he was delighted with himself. A few months later he was allowed to do a whole scene, and then another. He ex-celled, they agreed, at producing witty repartee in the mouths of young gallants like himself. But six months ago, the Lord Chamberlain's company, the very same troupe that Shake-speare wrote for, had agreed in principle to take an entire new play from him for which, when it was accepted, he would be paid the full fee of six pounds.

"Is it finished?"

He smiled down at the red-haired girl at his side. "Almost."

The play, though he said it himself, was a masterpiece: none of your crude humour for the crowd, but brilliant wit to delight the court and the discerning. It was about a young man like himself. *Every Man Hath His Wit,* it was called. She had already followed each step of its progress over the last few months and now he told her the latest developments of its plot.

There were several things Edmund Meredith liked about Jane Fleming. She was fifteen – young enough to look up to and be moulded by a man like himself. She was pretty, but not such a beauty that she attracted a host of rival suitors. Her family were involved with the playhouse: she shared his love for the theatre. And though her family was modest, she was to receive a small legacy from an uncle. "Enough," he had confided to the Bulls, "to keep a family."

"I'm surprised," said one of those cousins, knowing his ambition, "that you don't look for a real heiress, or a rich widow." Some of the greatest men at court had done that. But Edmund knew his limits. "I'd always be looked down upon. A mere kept man," he reasoned. He was not strong enough to strut through that.

In time, perhaps, he would marry young Jane Fleming.

And then the dark-skinned man behind them spoke.

"I think, young master, I'll come to see your play." They turned, and found themselves looking at the strangest fellow they had ever seen in their lives.

It was hard to describe him. Though his features were negroid, you could only say that his skin was a rich brown. His hair was long and black and hung in heavy ringlets and he was wearing a long, sleeveless leather jerkin that reached down to his knees, with leather boots, red breeches and a white linen shirt. On his wrists were golden bangles. He carried no sword but a long, curved dagger. He was perhaps thirty-five, but his teeth were all there, as sparkling white as his shirt, and it was obvious from the almost indolent way he carried himself, that under the shirt there was a splendid athlete's body. A dark-skinned man was rare in London. His eyes were a perfect blue. His name was Orlando Barnikel.

One of the Barnikels of Billingsgate, a seafarer, had brought him to London as a cabin boy after a voyage to the south, and cheerfully announced to his astonished family: "He's mine." He never offered any further explanation, but the boy's blue eyes seemed to confirm the statement, and when, ten years and several profitable voyages later the seafarer died, he left Orlando quite a tidy little fortune: enough for him to acquire a part-share in a ship which he captained himself. With a crew drawn from every port in Europe, a dead-eye with a pistol, a body as strong and supple as a serpent and a hand fast as a panther, he roamed the seven seas.

He was, of course, a pirate. In another age, he might have been hanged; but then so, very likely, would Sir Francis Drake, and a good many other English heroes. But now the island kingdom had other things to worry about. There was the Spanish enemy to plunder, and since men like Drake offered the hard-pressed queen a share of their profits, if a French or other prize were found on the distant, broad high seas, only a fool would ask too many questions. Anyway, as Elizabeth knew: "You cannot control these salty sea-dogs: they go with the wind." It was Orlando, and many like him, who harried the great Armada to destruction.

Although his colour was dark, he had the spirit of the Viking. His appearances in London were irregular, but whenever he came to the port, he would stride down Billingsgate market to the huge stall where the Barnikels carried on their fishmongering business, and where his cousins, rather proud that this exotic adventurer belonged to them, always gave him a welcome. The Moor, some of the Billingsgate folk called him, by which they meant only that his skin was dark. But those who sailed with him, and the men all over Europe who feared him referred to him as Black Barnikel.

Edmund Meredith knew nothing of this. He stared at him in surprise, but then, seeing the other two gallants watching, he quietly smiled. It was only natural, after all, that a man of wit like himself should have a little sport with the curious stranger. With a sideways glance at his companions, therefore, he began.

"You wish to see my play, sir?"

Black Barnikel nodded slowly.

"I thank you for your kindness then. And yet I cannot help you."

"The reason?"

"Why, that my play, sir, is not made to be seen." And as Barnikel gazed at him, the other two gallants laughed. For they knew what he meant.

There were two kinds of play in Elizabethan London. The common herd liked a spectacle: a battle, a sword fight – the actors were expert at these. Even a cannon was fired sometimes. They liked broad jokes from popular clowns who ad-libbed to the audience, and every play, no matter what the subject, ended with a gig – a song and dance routine. These were the spectacles written, as Meredith and his friends would say, to be *seen*. But for the discriminating, for the more private, courtly audience, there was another kind of play, full of wit and decorous language. The kind that Edmund meant to write. Plays written not to be *seen*, but to be *heard*.

"It will not be played?" the seafarer softly asked.

"Marry, sir, yes."

"I come here to the Curtain," Black Barnikel said.

"Then you shall neither see nor hear it."

"Where should I go then?"

"Why, you may go to the devil," Edmund laughed. "But to hear aught for your good, sir," he continued lightly, "I commend you to a monastery." And the little company applauded.

This little sally was not without wit. For if there were two kinds of play in London, there were also two kinds of theatre. Most playhouses were essentially open-air stages surrounded by a circular gallery. Of the two in Shoreditch, the Theatre and the Curtain, the nearby Theatre which was used by Shakespeare and the Chamberlain's men, was moderately respectable and confined itself to plays; but the Curtain was known for its vulgar entertainments and so like a bear-pit that, as today, it was even used as one. The only advantage of these roofless and noisy buildings was that the acting companies could pack in a large paying audience; but the dream of every serious actor was to perform indoors, before a quiet and attentive audience. In 1597, the lease on the Theatre having run out and renewal refused, it was precisely this that the Chamberlain's men proposed to do.

It was a radical move. Though boy companies from the London schools had put on courtly indoor productions from time to time, this would be the first time in history that anyone had put on serious, professional indoor drama. "We'll have nothing but the finest plays," they decided, and a splendid hall had been found and fitted up in the precincts of the Blackfriars, the former monastery. Edmund planned to have his play performed in this elegant new setting when the indoor productions began later that year.

Black Barnikel's eyes took on an almost sleepy look as he

watched the little group. The brewer, the carpenter and young Dogget did not interest him. He noted the girl's pale freckled skin and her abundant red hair with interest. But though he had seen, and sailed with, and even killed all kinds of men, this clever young popinjay was a type that was new to him. He did not especially mind being teased with riddles. London was full of witty fellows and even the crudest theatre audience expected the clowns to amuse them with quips and conundrums. But behind Meredith's words, he detected a trace of contempt.

"I think you mock me," he gently suggested. And stretching easily, he took out his dagger and gazed at it thoughtfully. "They say that my point is sharp."

The other two gallants put their hands towards their swords, but if Edmund felt any alarm, he had too much spirit to show it. "I intend no mockery, sir," he said. "But I warn you even so that my pen is mightier than your dagger."

"How so?"

"Why, with your dagger, sir, you may end my life," Edmund laughed. "Yet with my pen, I can make you immortal."

"Mere words," the sailor shrugged. "On a stage."

But Meredith was not so easily gainsaid. "Yet what is the world, sir –" he demanded, "if not a stage? And when our life is done, sir, what remains? How shall we be remembered? For our fortune? Our deeds? Our tomb? But give me a theatre – even a pit like this," he gestured round. "I can contain a life within this circle, sir," he cried. "I can show you a man, his deeds, his qualities, his very essence."

Black Barnikel's eyes continued to rest upon the little group. "Do you mean," he asked curiously, "that you could write a play about me?"

"Aye, sir," the other rejoined, "which makes my pen still greater. For not only can I make you immortal," he smiled, "but I can change your very form, sir, turn you into something else, like a magician."

"I do not follow you." The seafarer's eyelid drooped.

"Nay but you shall, like a hound on a leash," he blithely continued. "For this reason. My pen can make you into what it will. Perhaps a hero; or just as well, a fool; one who loved wisely, or a helpless cuckold. Captain or coward, handsome or loathsome. Upon the stage, sir, in the hands of a poet, a character is tethered like that bear upon a chain." And he smiled in triumph.

How fine, how clever he was, thought Jane, as she gazed at Edmund. The dark-skinned stranger rather frightened her, though she could not help stealing glances at him too.

Black Barnikel said nothing. If he felt threatened or insulted, he gave no sign; but had either Jane or Edmund looked more closely, they might have noticed that his eyes were somewhat smoky. Only after a pause, did he softly murmur:

"I shall come to your play then, young master."

The leafy little suburb of Shoreditch lay half a mile to the north of the city, above Moorfields. It was here that the two playhouses lay. For Jane Fleming, it was also the place she had called home all her life.

As she walked into her parents' lodgings an hour later she could not help smiling. She knew her parents were a little strange. "Don't be like them," her uncle used to urge her. But she loved them as they were. And she smiled because the house was like her father: small and thin. Just eight feet wide and two storeys high it stood, jammed between two larger houses, just behind the Theatre. And it was completely full of clothes.

Gabriel Fleming was the trusted keeper of the tiring house – the room in the theatre where the actors changed their costumes – for the Chamberlain's men. The whole family was in the theatre too: his wife Nan, and Jane, who both assisted him, and even Jane's little brother Henry, who had just started as a boy-actor, taking, as the custom was, the female roles. As for the clothes, for reasons of safety Gabriel liked to keep most of the theatre wardrobe in his house.

Nothing was ever tidy. With her parents shuttling between house and theatre, and actors dropping in at all hours, Jane was used to a genial mess. But life was never dull. In autumn and winter the theatre was in full swing, culminating, if the company were chosen, with performances before the queen at the Christmas court. During Lent, when plays were forbidden, she and her mother went over the entire wardrobe, washing, repairing, renewing, and thanks to this she was a first-rate sempstress. Then, after Easter, the performances began again. But it was the summer that she enjoyed best of all; for then the whole company set out on the road. There would be a line of wagons – one loaded with the travelling stage and props, her parents in another filled with costumes, which would also serve as a tiring house at each stop. They would trundle out of London and be gone for weeks, into the surrounding counties. Each time they came to a town, members of the troupe would go ahead to announce their arrival with kettledrum and trumpet. The stage was set up, usually in the yard of an inn so that people would have to pay to enter; and for several days they would go through their repertoire until it was time to move on. Sometimes they turned aside to play in a noble house. And how Jane loved it all – the freedom of the road, the new sights and sounds, the sense of adventure.

"You must get away from the theatre." No wonder her kindly uncle shook his head. The Fleming family were cautious, and proud of it. When the Dissolution of the Monasteries had ruined their old business, they had moved into haberdashery. "Haberdashery is more reliable than religion," Jane's grandfather had solemnly declared, and he bequeathed a sound little business to his three concave-faced sons. Why Gabriel had deserted this for the unstable world of the theatre, his two brothers could never understand. The eldest, with a family of his own, had never spoken to him since; but Uncle, as Jane called him, having remained unmarried, had appointed himself her guardian, constantly gave her advice and, since he was convinced Gabriel would die a pauper, had promised her and little Henry a legacy.

The haberdashery business was good. Buttons and bows, ribbons, sequins, all manner of knick-knacks. The two Fleming brothers also had a workshop making brass pins, as had several others. "That's where we'll find you a husband," Uncle told her. "You want a good pin man. Just leave it to me," he would add with a sigh. "Your parents will never do anything."

But even Uncle was a little impressed by Edmund, who had become a familiar figure at the playhouse. As for his play, she had seen parts of it and thought it wonderful. He was going to be a playwright she was sure – perhaps even, as he said, take the place of Shakespeare.

For nobody really knew what Shakespeare planned. There were rumours that he wanted to set himself up as a gentleman. She knew this was a fine thing to be; but what did it really mean? So many people in Elizabethan London swore they were. In olden times, everyone knew, such men were of the knightly caste; and merchants, as they always had, bought estates to enter the gentle class. This was not all, however. Those styled Master, from Oxford and Cambridge, were gentlemen now; and lawyers from the Inns of Court. For learning must be respected. But best of all, for any man – courtier, lawyer or the apprentice son of a squire – was the claim to be gentle born, not gentle made.

Edmund, his father and grandfather being courtiers, was gentle born. Will Shakespeare was not.

"And yet," Edmund had told her with a smile, "he means to be not only a gentleman made, but gentle born as well!" For though some believed that Will Shakespeare wanted to make his fortune and retire to the life of a country gentleman, and though there was a rumour that he was buying a large house and some land in his native village of Stratford, Edmund through his lawyer friends had discovered something else.

"It's such a good story," he explained. "His father's a merchant whose business got into trouble. He'd applied for a coat of arms two years ago, to make himself a gentleman, but been refused. So what does Will Shakespeare do? He goes to the College of Heralds last year, and re-applies. I'm surprised they considered an actor – I bet it cost Will a pretty penny – but anyway they did. Only Will gets the arms granted not to him but to his father! So now he can go back to Stratford and claim to be gentle born. Isn't that a splendid joke?"

One thing seemed certain anyway. If Will Shakespeare had enough money to do all this, he could probably afford to retire to Stratford any day. "In a year, he'll be gone," Edmund predicted. Jane knew that her father and some of the Chamberlain's men thought so too. Would Meredith's name then replace Will's as the best-known playwright?

And if he were successful, would he still take an interest in her?

Cuthbert Carpenter sneaked home, hoping he had not been seen. Even so, he had made a detour to the church of St

Lawrence Silversleeves, where he had tried to pray. But he had not even stepped inside the door when a sharp voice accosted him.

"Where have you been?"

"To church." It was true.

"And before that?"

"Walking."

"And before that? The playhouse?"

His grandmother. Cuthbert was squat, and she only came up to his chest, but ever since his parents had died, the tiny woman in the black dress had ruled the whole family with an iron rod. Both his brother and he had been apprenticed to strict masters; two of his sisters firmly married off at fifteen and the third, equally firmly, told she must stay and keep house instead. Though he was twenty, and a journeyman carpenter now, Cuthbert still lived in the house and contributed rent to help her. Yet she watched over his morals as though he were a boy, even reporting serious failings to the master for whom he worked. And in truth, Cuthbert was still afraid of her.

For wasn't she in the right? Cuthbert Carpenter knew that those who had impure thoughts risked hellfire. "Those who touch the whore or attend the playhouse will suffer on Judgment Day," she had promised, and he believed her. He had never touched a whore. But the playhouse . . .

He was a good carpenter. Even his stern master agreed. A good worker. But whenever he could, he would sneak off to a playhouse. He had seen *Romeo and Juliet* ten times, and afterwards he felt fear and shame. Yet he kept sinning, and he had even taken to lying about it.

"I have not been to a play," he now replied. Strictly true, but of course misleading. She muttered something, but seemed satisfied – which only made him feel worse.

As night fell, Cuthbert Carpenter vowed: "I will never, ever, go to the playhouse again."

It was already dark when John Dogget led Edmund into the boathouse. They had crossed the river to Southwark some hours before, then stayed drinking at the George; and it was a testimony to their new friendship that the cheerful fellow should have taken the fine young gentleman into his confidence enough to show him the treasure. Not many people knew about it.

The boathouse lay downstream from London Bridge in a group of similar wooden buildings round a little inlet; and by the light of Dogget's lamp, Edmund could see that this was a workshop for the making and chiefly the repairing of boats.

"My grandfather started the business," Dogget explained. Back in King Henry's days, Dan Dogget's youngest son, less of a giant than his waterman brothers and having worked with his uncle Carpenter, had gone into boat repair, where his own son, the present head of the thriving establishment, had followed him, and would one day turn it all over to young John. And John Dogget was contented with his lot. With his flash of white hair and his merry face, he could be seen any day working beside his rubicund father in an atmosphere smelling most agreeably of woodshavings and riverweed. Both men's hands were slightly webbed, but they never found this a problem with their work; and often they would look up and wave as they saw one of their burly waterman cousins go by.

John was popular with both men and women. "If you can make a woman laugh, you'll be all right," his father had told him; and already there were a number of women in Southwark who had been made to laugh by young Dogget. As for settling down: "I'll bide my time," he would grin. Recently, however, one possibility had occurred to him: the Fleming girl at the playhouse. He liked her looks and she seemed to have spirit. "She's got a bit of money coming to her too," he told his father. Although she seemed to have eyes only for Meredith, the young boat-builder was not downhearted. There were plenty of other girls. It was also possible, in any case, that Meredith himself was not really interested in Jane. So he decided to find out more about the handsome gallant and struck up a friendship with him.

"I shall need your help," he said. Leading the way to the back of the workshop, he indicated several piles of planks.

For several minutes, Meredith helped him remove the planks. As he did so, he became aware that, running right across the rear of the building, and carefully hidden under covers, were some large, strange shapes. At last, motioning him to step back, Dogget put the lamp behind a barrel and stepped alone into the shadows. Meredith could not see, but could hear him moving as he pulled the covers off. When he was done, Dogget returned, picked up the lamp, and held it high: so that, by the flickering light, Meredith could see a most remarkable sight.

It was a good thirty feet long. To the fore were benches for four pairs of oars; its long, clinker-built lines swept up into a graceful prow like a Viking longboat of ancient times, every plank polished until it gleamed; but its greatest glory lay aft: there, magnificently carved and gilded, was a large cabin, its velvet curtains and trim all in perfect repair. It glowed quietly in the lamplight.

"My God," Edmund breathed. "What is it?"

"King Harry's barge." Then Dogget grinned. "It's mine."

Shortly before the end of his long life Dan Dogget had come upon the old vessel, in a sorry condition by then. It was not, of course, one of the great state barges, just one of several for daily use that the prodigal monarch had maintained at his riverside palaces. Under Elizabeth's regime, however, when money was tight, it had lain unused for a dozen years until the bargemaster was told to sell it off. Saddened to see its ruin, Dogget had bought it himself and brought it to his son's boatyard and, since his little grandson John had just been born, had cheerfully declared: "It's for him."

Year after year, after the day's work was done, father and then son had lovingly tended it, restoring a plank here, a piece of gilding there, going over it inch by inch as they had brought it back to its former life. Not only timber and gilt but even the rich materials inside the cabin had been restored until, for the last five years, there had been nothing further to do except gaze at it, in all its antique beauty, and guard it like a treasure in a temple.

"Seems a pity she's never used," Dogget remarked in the silence. Too large and grand for ordinary use, yet not quite big enough to serve as one of the city guild barges, John Dogget's royal treasure had long lain there like an unclaimed bride – mature, beautiful, a Cleopatra waiting for her Mark Antony. "I suppose," the boatbuilder said, "you can't think of anything?"

Meredith gazed at it in wonder. "No," he said, "but I'll try."

The next morning, William Bull had been waiting for some time before Edmund sauntered up. But if he was worried, he did not want to show it. For although he was ten years older, he was still rather in awe of his cousin. Edmund had such style.

Without a word they fell into step as they passed through the ancient gateway into the riverside area of pleasant greens and courtyards still known as the Blackfriars, and made their way towards the hall, to which Edmund was carrying the key.

The Blackfriars Theatre was impressive. Down the centre of the spacious, rectangular hall ran rows of wooden benches with backs; around the sides were galleries. The stage, only a little raised, formed a wide platform right across one end so that the gallants like Edmund could seat themselves on stools round its sides in front of the galleries, thus imitating the elegant informality of the court where the players performed amidst the circle of courtiers. The hall had a decidedly Renaissance air, with classical pillars supporting the galleries and a wooden screen behind the stage ornamented with pediments and arches. Bull was impressed.

"We shall all make a fortune," said Edmund proudly.

Whatever else the Elizabethan Theatre might be – a symbol of prestige for noble patrons, a showcase for actors and writers – its entire existence depended on the indisputable fact that it was a business. And of all the entrepreneurs behind the various acting companies, none were more daring than the Burbage family which had conceived the Blackfriars venture. Old Burbage had been a remarkable figure. A master craftsman turned businessman, he had quickly perceived the opportunities of the theatre and had organized the Chamberlain's men into a professional company of actors. He leased a playhouse and financed performances and writers. It was thanks to him that Will Shakespeare had already made a small fortune. And last year, deciding that something more sophisticated was needed, he had leased the Blackfriars.

The concept was simple. The new indoor theatre would seat less than half what the outdoor amphitheatres could hold, but the audience would be select. Instead of a penny, the lowest cost of entry would be a stiff sixpence. No rowdy apprentices or garlic-breaths could afford that. "Even the whores will have to be of the best sort," Edmund remarked with a grin. But the risk had been large. The lease and refurbishments had come to a staggering six hundred pounds. Additional help with the financing had been sought.

William Bull had been flattered when his fashionable young cousin had approached him. "It's an opportunity," Edmund had explained. "I know the Burbages and they've let me in on it. I can put something in for you too, if you like." The brewery was prosperous but dull. Anyway, his brothers never seemed to let him do much. This venture sounded exciting. So William had lent his cousin fifty pounds which, together with five of his own, had enabled Edmund Meredith to cut a very fine figure indeed when he lent it all, in his own name, to the Burbages. And as proof of how well things were going, soon after this, Edmund had proudly told him that he himself had just been commissioned to write a play for the new theatre when it opened, which had made William doubly proud.

Now, however, Bull had started to become a little nervous. Old Burbage had died that winter, but since his two sons, already seasoned in the business, were carrying on as normal, he was not too worried about that. But then there had come another rumour, of objections to the new theatre from some of the residents of Blackfriars, led by alderman Ducket. They were even petitioning to stop it opening. He had heard that the alderman condemned all the theatres as encouraging disorder and Godlessness and that he was threatening to shut them down. The playhouses had a reputation for rowdiness, and Bull supposed the inhabitants of this quiet and select enclave might object to such an intrusion into their midst. Was it true, he now hesitantly enquired?

"Good heavens, yes." Meredith could hardly have looked more cheerful.

"You are not concerned?"

"Not at all," Meredith even laughed. "It doesn't mean a thing. Some of the people here didn't realize what sort of plays, and audience, we shall have here. And how could they? This," he indicated the handsome hall, "has never been done before. Once they realize there'll be no common or poor folk coming here, the whole thing will blow over."

"It will go ahead then?"

"We shall be open before this year is out."

"So," Bull gave a sigh of relief. "I'll get my money back."

Edmund smiled superbly. "Of course."

* * *

No one in the Chamberlain's company, by that summer, was happier than young Jane Fleming. For it had seemed to her, in recent weeks, that Meredith loved her.

His play was done. She thought by now she must know every line. As Edmund approached the end, his excitement had mounted. How proudly he had read her his favourite lines, or asked her: "Is it all right?" And she had always said: "It's wonderful." Certainly, his wit was sparkling.

Once, as she had tried to think of the play as a whole, she had timidly asked: "What exactly is it all about?" But he had started to grow angry, and she had never asked again.

Why should she do anything to spoil the sense of triumph which kept him so attentive to her? Even when he was with his fashionable friends, he hardly ever ignored her.

There was another reason why she felt happy. High summer was approaching. Already, Jane and her parents had been carefully preparing the costumes to be loaded into the wagon. Though she knew it meant she would not see Edmund for a while, she was still excited.

It was on a pleasant July afternoon, as she and Edmund strolled down the lane from Shoreditch that they encountered Alderman Jacob Ducket.

Even on this summer day, he was dressed in black, his white ruff, his silver and diamond-pommelled sword and the silver flash in his hair providing the restrained decoration appropriate to his wealth and stern authority. He was standing in front of Bishopsgate and, perhaps she should have noticed, he was smiling. As they came near, Edmund airily doffed his hat and made an elaborate bow, so nicely calculated between respect and mockery that it made her giggle. But if normally Ducket would have had no time for young Meredith, today he looked at him almost affably and, beckoning him to come closer, gently asked: "You have not heard the news?"

The alderman did not often smile. Indeed, the only visible trace of the cheerful genes of his ancestor who had dived into the river was the silver flash in his hair. Like many of his fellow aldermen, he was a Puritan – in his case of a sternly Calvinistic kind.

It had been a very good day for Alderman Ducket. He had already been to the Bankside theatres. He had enjoyed that.

Now he was going to Shoreditch. Seeing young Meredith, known to be a play-lover, gave him another chance to savour the reaction to his statement. Calmly, then, he informed him: "The theatres are all to be closed."

It was as he expected. The girl looked stunned and Meredith went pale; but Meredith recovered first. "Who says so?"

"The city council."

"Impossible. All the theatres are outside your jurisdiction."

Shoreditch, of course, lay past the city limits. But it was a curious feature of city government that, even after the Dissolution of the Monasteries, their old feudal liberties had never been repealed but passed into the hands of the monarch. The Bankside theatres, therefore, lay in the old Liberty of the Clink. Even Blackfriars was still a liberty. It had long infuriated the city fathers that the theatres continued under their noses yet outside their jurisdiction.

"We have asked the Privy Council to close them all."

"They won't. The queen herself loves the players."

But now Ducket smiled. "Not since *The Isle of Dogs*," he said.

This play, performed by Lord Pembroke's men, had featured pointed, but amusing criticisms not only of the city aldermen, but even of the government. It had been an amazing stroke of luck. For months Ducket and his fellow aldermen had laboured, ensuring the Chamberlain's men's lease on the Theatre in Shoreditch would end. They had even approached Giles Allen, who owned the site and ordered him: "Don't lease it to actors again or we'll ruin you." Since then, Ducket had been stirring up trouble in Blackfriars, but he had achieved nothing definite. And then those fools the Lord Pembroke's men had given him his chance, and he had taken it with both hands. A deputation to the Privy Council had produced a careful report showing how the government had been insulted.

"You are wrong," he said sweetly. "The council is with us."

"But," Edmund protested, "that would mean . . ."

"That the theatre is over," Ducket nodded. "Indeed," he went on, "some of your actor friends had better be careful. They may be considered vagrants."

The threat was not entirely empty. Anyone wandering about the country, with no fixed employment, as actors did, was liable to be whipped and returned to his place of origin; and while Ducket could not touch respectable men like the Shakespeares, some of the poorer actors with only casual employment might run this risk if they attempted to tour. The real point of his remark, however, was the implied insult: the theatre was outside society, its actors mere vagabonds.

"I still don't believe you," Meredith said, and walked on.

But it was true; and by that evening all London knew it. The theatres were ordered to close. Worse yet, poor Ben Jonson, one of the writers of *The Isle of Dogs*, had been put in gaol for contempt, while his fellow author Nashe had fled. In the theatre community people were deeply despondent. "I shall have to go back to haberdashery," Jane's father miserably remarked. The actors were distraught. Even the Burbages, who had repeatedly tried to see the Privy Council, could say nothing encouraging.

Only after a week was there any piece of news.

"We are permitted to leave the city to go on our tour," the company was told. But when someone asked "After that, will we be allowed back?" he was given a shrug and a curt: "Who knows?"

Amid all this gloom, the person who kept their spirits up was not a member of the company at all.

Edmund Meredith was a tower of strength. "This is only done to frighten us," he told them. "The Privy Council has been mocked and it is teaching us a lesson." And when Fleming remarked dolefully that some of the council were as puritan as Ducket, he only laughed. "The court must still be amused," he cried. "Do you suppose the queen means to spoil her Christmas entertainment for the Puritans?" And because he was a gentleman, whose father had been at court, they mostly supposed he must know something that they did not.

Jane loved him all the more when she watched him gaily put heart into the little group of spare actors and small fry who gathered at the Fleming house. She thought what it meant to him, when his hopes were pinned entirely on his own play. There was a nobility in his bravado. Some days later, when the troupe set off in their wagons, and he kissed her goodbye with the promise "We shall come through this together", she had never felt so close to him.

* * *

The summer months were very difficult for Edmund Meredith. He had been proud of his performance in front of the Flemings. He knew he had cut a good figure. But did he really feel confident about the future? Three days after the announcement, things were even more difficult when his anxious cousin Bull came to his lodgings at the Staple Inn to ask about his fifty pounds.

"Keep calm," he had counselled. "This will pass." But after Bull had departed, shaking his head, Edmund experienced a profound gloom. What was to become of his play? And what indeed am I, he thought, without it? What was to be his fortune in men's eyes?

At the end of summer, while the players were still on tour, he encountered Lady Redlynch.

He was introduced to her by his friends Rose and Sterne. Her husband, Sir John, had died the previous year and at the age of thirty, alone and without children, she had nothing much to do. Despite his own depressed state, he felt a little sorry for her.

He need not have worried. Lady Redlynch, having been born a West Country merchant's daughter, knew perfectly well how to take care of herself. Thanks to Sir John, she already had a handsome house in Blackfriars, and she promised to take a personal interest in the business of the new theatre. She had fair hair, wide blue eyes, inviting breasts and, rather charmingly, a voice like a little girl, which vanished entirely when she was in a hurry. Meredith amused her. She liked witty men. She decided to take him as a temporary lover at once.

By late October the situation was still unchanged. The theatres stood empty and silent; the costumes lay unused in the wardrobe. The Burbages had been to the Privy Council again. It was said that Will Shakespeare had been hatching something with his patrons at court, but nothing definite was heard. Each day, actors came to Fleming's house for news and asked: "Is it all over then? Shall we go?" Not yet, they were told. Not yet.

Edmund came by each day. He was admirable. Always light-hearted, yet always calm. He had frequently gone to inspect the Blackfriars theatre, he told her. Everything was ready for performances to begin.

"Just be patient," he urged. "The audience is waiting for the theatre to be restored. They will not be denied for ever."

There was no doubt, Jane thought, that he cut a fine figure. How proud of him she was. There was something else about him too: a new confidence, a sense of potency. She found it strangely fascinating and it sometimes exercised her imagination during those dull days.

It was one of the actors who finally told her that Edmund was sleeping with Lady Redlynch.

In early November Edmund Meredith sent the letter. It was a daring move, but he could not stand the tension any longer.

The affair with Lady Redlynch had been a success. Though they were discreet, the fact that a few men gossiped was enough to make him look a fine fellow in the eyes of the fashionable world. But at times, recently, he had wondered if the affair had run its course. Perhaps he had had enough of her somewhat padded charms. He was also a little afraid. Once or twice he had sensed that she might be considering marriage. He dreaded a pregnancy too. Precautions were few and crude in Tudor England. As a barrier to conception, a lady and her lover might use a handkerchief; but it did not always work.

He thought of Jane Fleming, though this worried him less. She would probably never know; and anyway, if she did, a man with a reputation was all the more attractive to a young girl.

But what about his play? To be a gallant lover was a fine thing, but it still begged the essential question: "What can I say that I am?"

Though he had kept up his cheerful face, over three months after the ban was announced Ducket and the aldermen were still looking complacent and the Privy Council maintained its ominous silence. His friends at court had heard nothing; nor had Lady Redlynch. The usual theatre scene would normally have begun, but the days passed uselessly. And then one day: "I must know," he told Lady Redlynch. He decided to send the message. When Lady Redlynch asked him what sort of missive it was, he answered simply:

"A love letter."

It was written to the queen.

Of all England's rulers, none has ever understood as well as Queen Elizabeth I that the key to monarchy is theatre. Indeed, the Elizabethan court, with its constant public displays, its tours of the counties and its calculated, stage-managed receptions for foreigners, was one of the cleverest theatres ever devised. And at the centre of the stage, gorgeously dressed in brocade encrusted with pearls, a huge lace ruff encircling her neck and head, her gold-red hair piled up or freely flowing, stood Elizabeth – daughter of royal Harry yet born of her people too, the Renaissance princess, and virgin queen whose glittering radiance was a star to every Englishman.

For many years this part, of the virgin queen, had been a necessary role. Threatened by Europe's dangerous powers, she had protected her little kingdom by hinting at marriage with one or another of them. But she had long ago grown used to it. Her courtier favourites, men like Leicester and Essex, had always pretended they were in love with her, and she had pretended to believe them. No doubt, sometimes it was true; for Elizabeth was a woman too. But who can ever say, in statecraft, what is theatre and what is real? One mirrors the other. And so if now, threatened by parliaments who wanted to know her successor, old Elizabeth, face painted, hair dyed, still played the virgin queen, who could blame her? She did it to perfection, rising each season like a phoenix from her ashes, surrounded by gallants who made her withered autumn like a spring.

Edmund's letter was perfect. It was, in fact, the best thing he had ever written. The terms in which he addressed the queen were those of an unknown admirer. Inspired by her he had written a play that might amuse her. Yet now, utterly downcast, he learned that all further plays should lie in darkness, never to be lit by the radiance of her eyes. The conclusion of this protestation was just what she liked.

> But if your Majesty thinks that heaven, of having pleased you, too good for me, then I had rather I, and my poor verses, should remain in perpetual darkness than offend your sight.

* * *

He ended it with the suggestion, almost as though she were a girl again and they were secret lovers, that if there were any hope for him, she should at a certain time and place, where he could clearly see her, let fall her handkerchief.

It was the sort of thing she loved.

Dusk had already fallen but Jane was careful as she made her way past Charing Cross. There were plenty of people about and the couple ahead were entirely unaware of her presence.

The great palace of Whitehall was a series of handsome courtyards surrounded by brick and stone buildings. There were walled gardens, a tiltyard for jousting, a chapel, a hall and a council chamber; also, some lodgings reserved for visitors from the Scottish court, known as Scotland Yard. The palace was, to a large extent, open to the public, and since its gates straddled the road from Charing Cross to Westminster, people came through all the time. The queen allowed her subjects to cross the yard to the river stairs if they wanted a barge. They could even come to see the tapestries on the great stairs or watch the state banquets from a gallery. They could also stand about at times like this in the hope of seeing her.

Edmund and Lady Redlynch passed through the gateway and entered the palace courtyard. Jane followed them.

There were several dozen people gathered in the yard, a number bearing torches. November, despite the cold, was usually a cheerful time at court, for in the middle of the month, on the anniversary of the queen's accession, there was a big pageant at Whitehall and a joust. Some of the spirit of these coming festivities seemed to have infected the crowd, which was in a happy mood. Edmund waited eagerly.

Minutes passed. The torches flickered. And then she came. The doors of a council chamber opened. Two, four, six gentlemen in gorgeous tunics, short cloaks, their hands resting on jewelled swords stepped out. Then pages, carrying torches. And then, six more gentlemen, carrying a litter in which, magnificent in a billowing, jewel-encrusted dress, a huge lace ruff, and wearing a tall feathered hat against the cold, sat the queen. A cheer went up. Slowly, stiffly, her painted face like a mask, she turned and seemed to smile. My God, thought Edmund, thinking of his perhaps too gallant letter, has she grown so frail? Yet a moment later she partly dispelled his doubt, for in reply to the usual cry – "God save Your Majesty" – her voice rang out across the yard, as clear as it had to her troops before the Spanish came: "God bless you, my good people. You may have a greater prince, but you shall never have one more loving."

She said it every time, and it never failed to please.

They carried her across to the doorway that led to the great staircase. After that, for a short while, she was lost to view. But then, at the entrance to the gallery leading to the private apartments, suddenly candles appeared. Then more. And a few moments later, at a slow and stately pace, the little cortège made a decorous procession down the gallery, the queen walking now, the candlelight gleaming on her jewelled dress as she appeared behind one glass window, then another, and then another. It was charming; it was magical; it was haunting; it was, Edmund realized, pure theatre.

And at the third window, there was no mistaking it, she paused, half turned, raised up her hand in silent salutation, and let fall a handkerchief.

Jane followed Edmund and Lady Redlynch back all the way to Ludgate and into the city. Once, as they crossed the Fleet, she heard them laughing. She followed them also as they turned into Blackfriars and went into Lady Redlynch's house.

In the shadows of one of the gateways she watched Lady Redlynch's house for three long hours, until its last lights were out. Then she slipped back through the city and walked in the darkness up the empty lane to Shoreditch.

At dawn the next day, Edmund awoke with a new hope and, thinking of Jane, decided it would soon be time to part from Lady Redlynch; but Jane had not slept a wink, and she was still weeping silent tears.

"We are to present four plays at court."

They were all there in the room – the two Burbage brothers with their heavy-set, clever faces; Will Shakespeare; the other leading actors.

"I told you it would be so." He had gone to the Burbages the morning after the incident with the queen, to put heart into the company. At first they had not believed him. Then word had come from the royal household that the Master of the Revels ordered them to prepare a selection of their best-loved plays for the court festivities at Christmas.

"We shall offer them three by Shakespeare, including *Romeo and Juliet* and *Midsummer Night's Dream*," the elder Burbage went on, "and one by Ben Jonson." He smiled: "If they accept that it will mean the poor fellow's to be forgiven." He paused for a moment. "There's something else, too, even better news in fact. It won't be announced until the New Year, but the ban on plays is going to be partly lifted. The Privy Council will license us and the Admiral's men to continue public performances. So," he summed up, "for us at least, a reprieve."

Edmund felt a wave of excitement.

"So my play can be performed."

There was a cough from one of the actors. The two Burbages looked awkward. For a moment no one said anything, and then, with a quick glance of reproof at his companions, it was Will Shakespeare who spoke.

"My friend," he said, "I fear you must prepare yourself. The news is also bad." His eyes were kind.

"How so?" Edmund asked.

"We have no theatre."

"But the Blackfriars . . ."

Shakespeare shook his head. "We dare not use it."

"Two days ago," Burbage took up the story, "the Privy Council received another letter, from Ducket and many others in the Blackfriars. Hearing that we might be reprieved, they've protested yet again. They will not have us there. And with matters so much in the balance . . ." He shrugged. "The risk's too great."

"Yet Lady Redlynch believes . . ." Edmund began, but paused when he saw the others exchanging glances.

"She was one of those who signed the letter," Burbage gruffly said. "I'm sorry."

For a moment, Edmund could not speak. He felt himself go red. She had deceived him.

Shakespeare came to the rescue. "She has a house there. Ducket's powerful." He sighed. "I for one know that a mistress may change her mind."

"All is not lost," Burbage continued. "For the time being at least, we have a theatre where we can put on some plays."

"Then my play . . . ?"

The awkwardness returned. Shakespeare looked at Burbage as if to say: it's your turn now.

"That's the difficulty, you see," the bearded man went on. "Much as I like your play," he looked unhappy, "in the theatre we shall occupy – it would not suit."

"In short," Shakespeare came in. "We'll have to use the Curtain."

"The Curtain?" The bear-pit. The playhouse for the lowest of the low. Few of the fashionable folk he knew would be persuaded to set foot in it. As for the usual audience, even Shakespeare's bawdiest efforts would be above them. His own sparkling display of courtly wit . . . "They'd hiss it off the stage," he groaned.

"You do agree, then?" Burbage seemed relieved. "If another company wishes to use it, of course," he went on, "you are free to approach them."

"There's only the Admiral's men, our rivals, at present," Edmund said.

"In the circumstances, though," the other Burbage quickly replied, "we could not hold you back." To which the others murmured assent.

It was only then that Edmund remembered his investment. "I lent you fifty-five pounds," he quietly stated.

"And it shall be repaid," Burbage said firmly.

"Only," Will Shakespeare came in, with a rueful smile, "not yet. For the truth of it is we have no money."

It was perfectly true and Edmund saw it must be. Not a penny from the huge Blackfriars investment, no theatre, no plays performed, no income. The court performances would bring something in, but only enough to keep them going.

"Be patient," Shakespeare said. "Our fortunes may improve."

But that was small comfort to Edmund, who had just discovered his mistress had cheated him and whose play was as good as lost. And when the next day he encountered his cousin Bull, who asked him once again how matters stood, he could not bear to face him but muttering quickly that all was well, he hurried away in cowardly flight.

He did, however, summon enough spirit to manage his parting from Lady Redlynch with some style. He sent her a letter professing his admiration in terms of such extravagant hyperbole that, by the time she was through, she could not fail to suspect that he had grown tired of her. He then broke the news: the Blackfriars theatre they had both so fervently hoped for had been destroyed by vulgar hands. His anguish, which he knew she would share, was so great he was retiring from the sight of men.

> And not even the brightness of your eyes nor the loyalty of your heart can draw me back again.

She would, he fancied, understand the message.

But what of poor Jane Fleming? It was two days after the letter that, still in a very melancholy mood, he went up to the house at Shoreditch. He realized he had hardly spoken to her since the encounter with the queen. But on his arrival at the Fleming house, while she was entirely friendly, he found her strangely different. As she went about her tasks, she seemed to take no special notice of him. He asked her if she would like to walk with him. Not now, she said. But later, then. Perhaps some other time.

"Is there a reason for this coldness?" he asked, thinking of Lady Redlynch.

"Why no, sir." She smiled and seemed surprised. "I am not cold."

"Yet you will not walk with me?"

"As you see," she gestured to the heaps of costumes that would now be needed, "I have much to do." Again she went about her work, quite cool, but almost ignoring him. Unwilling to risk rejection yet again, he picked up his hat and left.

1598

The early months of the year had been bleak for Edmund. His literary efforts had gone nowhere. He had taken his play to the Admiral's men, but they had regretfully refused it. "This is too good for us, too fine," they had said politely.

And after that nothing. A month had passed. His gloom had deepened. Then another. The solemn season of Lent had come. Then, the transformation.

At first his friends could hardly believe it. True, he could still be carefree and full of wit, but as for the rest . . . Gone were his fine clothes: his tunic was simple and usually brown; his hat was smaller and held only a modest feather; he even grew a rough little beard. He looked positively workmanlike. When Rose and Sterne protested, he called them popinjays. But most astonishing of all was his announcement: "I'm going to write a play. Not for the court at all, but for the common folk. I shall write it for the Curtain."

After all, it was the only playhouse he had left. Nor would he be put off. Where before he was confident, now he was determined. The Burbages were doubtful that he could do such a thing, but he coolly reminded them that they owed him fifty-five pounds. And when, reluctantly, they agreed he was due a favour and asked him what sort of play he had in mind, he told them. "A history play, with plenty of fighting in it." He had seen such dramas, of course; but now he decided it was time to read and analyse the texts.

Here he encountered a problem. There were almost no texts to be had, for when a play had been written it suffered a curious fate. It was cut up and rearranged into parts, each part being the lines of a particular actor so that he could learn them. The stage instructions went to the keeper of the tiring house so that he could provide props and costumes. Only the author or theatre manager, like as not, retained an entire text which was carefully guarded. Sometimes these texts were printed after a while, but much more often they were not. And the more successful the play, the less chance there was that the author would print it.

There were no laws of copyright. If another company obtained a copy of the play and put on a pirated version without paying the author, there was nothing he could do about it. Texts were valuable property therefore: and if Shakespeare did not have his printed – which indeed he never did in his lifetime – he was not careless of their worth. He was merely protecting his income.

Edmund could, of course, have asked the Burbages for copies of a dozen plays; but, afraid it might betray his lack of confidence, he was reluctant to do so. Another thought did occur to him: when done with, the actors' parts were often kept in the tiring house in case of repeat performances. Fleming could surely put some plays together. So at Easter, Edmund returned to Jane and asked her to find him some scripts.

He found her very busy. The first months at the Curtain had not been easy. Though similar in size to the Theatre, it was far less convenient. The tiring-house was smaller; the stage less good; they regularly had to vacate the place for other entertainments such as cock-fighting. Jane found herself constantly transporting and re-checking the wardrobe.

With so much going on, she had not had time, she told herself, to think of Edmund. She had heard that his affair with Lady Redlynch was over but in the months after Christmas, when his own hopes were so low, he had not been seen about the playhouse and so they had not met. Nor had she thought about the subject of men at all. Except, perhaps, for Dogget.

It was hard to say quite how he had come into her life. She had seen the young boatbuilder before in the company of Edmund; but some time in January she gradually became more aware of him. He often seemed to be about, and he made her laugh; she was grateful for that. But it was a small incident early in February that had really impressed her. A group of theatre people and their friends had been going to the tavern together, Dogget among them. She had had to stay behind because there was so much to do in the tiring house. Without a word, but with a cheerful smile, Dogget had remained and helped her, sorting and cleaning costumes for a full five hours, as if it were the most natural thing in the world. At which she could not help thinking: would Edmund Meredith ever have done that?

A pleasant friendship had developed since then. Dogget would quite often come by and they would walk out together. She felt comfortable in his presence. Late in February he had kissed her, but chastely, as though he expected nothing more. A week later she had remarked teasingly: "I expect you've had a lot of girls."

"Never one," he said, with merry eyes; and they both laughed. Two weeks after that, she indicated that he could kiss her properly and found that she liked this too. So that when, near Easter, her mother had mildly observed – "Young Dogget's courting: you think you'd be happy with him?" – she had answered hesitantly: "I think so. Perhaps."

Indeed, if she had any doubt, it was because of something so absurd that she did not feel she could set any store by it. It was similar to the sensation she experienced whenever the company set off on the road for their summer tour: a desire to see new places, a need for adventure, like some traveller upon the seas. No such thoughts had ever afflicted the Fleming family so far as she knew, nor could she see the point in them. She decided therefore that they must be nonsense, a fleeting and childish fancy. If Dogget and his boatyard in Southwark did not satisfy this vague craving in her for the unknown, she did not think it mattered. She thought she could be happy with him. Then Meredith had reappeared.

Edmund felt pleased as the spring progressed. The play he devised had a stirring subject: the Spanish Armada. There were noble speeches from the queen, from Drake and other sea-dogs. There would be a long re-enactment of the action, in which it would be necessary to fire a cannon numerous times. It would, he was confident, be the noisiest play ever produced in London. The closing speech he intended to model upon the most grandiloquent language of Marlowe, pointing out how God's hand had wrecked the Spanish galleons in the storm. "The common herd will love it," he predicted. "It cannot fail."

By late May, when the first act was done, Edmund felt even more confident. Once again he began to have a vision of himself making a figure in the world; and with this vision came the pleasant realization that he would like to have Jane at his side. It was time to reclaim her. In the first week of June he gave her a posy of flowers. The next week, a silver bracelet. And if, having been neglected, she seemed to hesitate, it did not worry him.

Jane had been pleased at her calm when Edmund first came to ask for help. Perhaps, she admitted, she had been a little intrigued by the change that had come over him; but then so were all his acquaintances. As for the flowers and the bracelet, she took them as thanks for the texts she had procured and nothing else. If he had meant something more, she discounted it, knowing he would only change his mind again and find another Lady Redlynch.

Meanwhile, things at the Curtain were not getting any better. Despite all their efforts, the more fashionable part of their old audience was still reluctant to set foot in the place. There were tensions amongst the actors too. Some, led by the clown, thought they should supply the audience with bawdier entertainments; others, including Shakespeare, were growing impatient with the enterprise, because they wanted to improve the quality of work.

"We're not taking enough money," Jane's father told her one day. The Burbages, he hinted, were in some financial difficulty. "The company will never find its feet again in this place," he concluded. If only they could get back to the theatre. "It's doubly galling," she overheard one of the Burbages remark, "because we even built the place." Some twenty years ago, at the start of the original lease, the Burbages had constructed the wooden building on the site, but with the ground lease up, they still could not set foot in the place. And by early June, her father sadly told her, "There's a chance, I'm afraid, that this season could be our last."

This prospect made Jane close her mind to Edmund. Her reasoning was that if the company closed, and no one would take his play, Edmund would never feel self-confident enough to take a wife. And she judged with considerable maturity that his interest in her was because she was part of the theatre. But Dogget just liked her for herself. She was friendly to Edmund, therefore, but no more.

In midsummer she had promised to go out on the river in the evening with John Dogget, and had been rather looking forward to it. Then, that afternoon, Edmund had come by. He and a party of friends were going to walk up to Islington Woods, to a glade where they would set out refreshments and, very likely, improvise some theatricals. Politely she declined, citing her earlier promise, and Edmund departed. Just after he had gone, she wondered if she should have offered to come and taken Dogget too; but she put this out of her mind. Dogget might have felt cheated; and besides, it was too late.

But as the warm sun gleamed on the water on the way up to Chelsea, and young Dogget, with a happy grin, pulled with his webbed hands on the oars, she felt an unaccountable sadness and even irritation. When they reached Shoreditch again, and Dogget pulled her into the shadows near the darkened playhouse, she could only go through the motions of returning his kiss.

Before they parted, however, she arranged to go out with John Dogget two evenings later, and made up her mind that by then her kisses would be ardent.

On the day after they had left London on the summer tour her father told Jane the sombre news, on condition that she did not tell the actors.

"Shakespeare has given notice. He's told the Burbages that if they don't find him a theatre, he is quitting the stage and retiring." Since Shakespeare now had his property in Stratford, Fleming judged that the threat was real. "He can retire there any day now," he remarked.

"And is there any hope?" she asked.

"A chance, but only a slim one," he told her. "The Burbages have made an offer to Giles Allen, for a new lease on the Theatre. It's so high that he's said to be considering it, even though he fears Ducket and the aldermen. I'm not even sure the Burbages can afford it, but there we are." He smiled wanly. "He'll decide by this autumn. If he says no . . ." He spread his hands. "Pins for me, I'm afraid. And for you, I dare say."

Often in the long weeks of summer as they went from town to town, Jane found herself thinking of the empty theatre. And also, she could not quite deny it, of Edmund and his play.

As Edmund Meredith made his way towards the Burbages' house in the city on a cold October afternoon, he was both thoughtful and cheerful.

Thoughtful because of Cuthbert Carpenter. He had spent the last hour in the George Tavern listening to his troubles. His grandmother was becoming increasingly tyrannical. She had also become convinced that he must be bound for hell, such was Carpenter's liking for entertainments, and had expressed this view to his Puritan master, who, being devout himself, had begun to find fault with Carpenter's work.

"I need to find a new master," he said. "But so many of the

best master carpenters are Puritan nowadays, they may not take me on if my name is blackened. Even if I never set foot in a theatre again, things will still go hard with me."

Edmund had comforted him as best he could, but was not sure what he could do.

He was cheerful, however, for a much more important reason. The play was done – complete down to the last alarum and cannon shot. It was a masterpiece, a mountain of melodrama, bombast and noise. He had sent word to the Burbages two days before, and now they had summoned him to see them. The script of the play was under his arm.

He was surprised to see Shakespeare and three of the others there as well. He had not expected that. Their faces were grave as they looked at him quietly across the oak table. Burbage broke the news.

"I'm afraid the Chamberlain's men have come to the end of their run," he said. "We do not want to continue at the Curtain."

He stared at them. "But my play . . ." He proffered it as though it changed something. "It was written for the Curtain."

"I'm sorry." Burbage made a polite nod towards the now useless sheaf of papers. "We called you here because you are a creditor."

"Fifty-five pounds," the other Burbage said with the respect that such a sum was due.

"We cannot say when, or even if", the first went on, "it will be repaid."

Edmund was flabbergasted. "Are there no other possibilities?"

"We tried for a new lease at the Theatre," Shakespeare explained. "Allen turned us down." He shrugged. And for several minutes, the various principals explained to him the difficulties with which their entire business was beset.

It was not often that Edmund forgot to cut a figure in the world; but without even realizing what he was doing, he buried his face in his hands and almost wept. After a time, nodding to them vaguely, he got up and left.

Slowly he wandered back towards his lodgings, digesting the news. The players had no respectable place to act. There was nothing to be done. He was so upset, he even briefly forgot his own play.

It was just as he reached the Staple Inn that the idea came into his head, an idea which sent him running back towards the Burbages' house. He burst in through the door and, finding them all still at the table, cried out: "Let me see the lease!" He was, after all, a lawyer.

A few minutes later, he made a suggestion. The idea he had had was so daring, so utterly outrageous, so cunning, that for a little while nobody spoke.

"We would have to be careful that no one knew what we were going to do," he added at last. And then Shakespeare grinned.

Of all the changes that took place during the long century when the Tudors sat upon the throne of England, one of the most striking was scarcely noted at all.

It began during the reign of Great King Harry, but did not happen suddenly. Halfway through Elizabeth's reign, however, it was becoming noticeable: England was getting colder.

The mini Ice Age of the sixteenth and seventeenth centuries was never alarming. No ice wall began to advance down the island; the seas did not recede. But over ten decades or so the average temperature of England fell by several degrees. During much of the year, this was not greatly noticed. The balmy days of summer did not cease, and although spring and autumn may have seemed a little cooler, it was only in winter that men really saw a difference. The snows arrived sooner and were more deep. Icicles hung, thick and strong, from the eaves. And above all, scarcely known before even at icy midwinter, the rivers froze.

It was a gentle echo of the distant, frozen past; and a hint for Englishmen, if any were needed that, even though the Renaissance from the warm Mediterranean had come to court, university and theatre, their island still belonged, as it always had, to the north. In December, in the year of Our Lord 1598, the River Thames froze solid.

Nobody took any particular notice of the men who trudged up the lane to Shoreditch as dusk was falling on that icy December day. Some were carrying hammers, others had saws and chisels. Had anyone troubled to observe them, however, they would have seen a surprising thing. Arriving one by one, they all disappeared into Fleming's narrow house. Darkness fell. Two more muffled figures arrived and entered. These were the Burbage brothers. Soon afterwards a slimmer figure, walking with a light step, also went in. The darkness grew deeper.

Cuthbert Carpenter's face was shining. They had fed him meat pies and hot toddy. As he sat on the bench, jammed between a fellow carpenter and a pile of sweaty costumes from *Twelfth Night*, he could hardly stop grinning. This was the most exciting thing he had ever done in his life.

It was all thanks to Meredith, of course. It was Edmund, six weeks ago, who had both found him a new master and just three days ago, given him the courage to do something even more daring: to walk out on his grandmother. But even this was only a minor crime compared to the extraordinary enterprise he was now engaged in. After this night's work, he would surely go to hell. And yet – most amazing and wonderful of all – he didn't care.

An hour passed. By the faint glimmer of the moonlight that crept through the clouds, the shuttered houses of Shoreditch stared out with blank faces, like wardrobes closed up for the night. Not a soul stirred.

At ten o'clock the door of Fleming's house at last opened. The men filed out one by one, some carrying hooded lamps. Silently they made their way across to the looming form of the Theatre and began to move round it. The Burbages reached the doorway.

How strange it looked in the darkness, Cuthbert Carpenter thought. The great empty cylinder of the playhouse seemed suddenly mysterious, even threatening. What if, he wondered, it was a huge trap, and the aldermen of London themselves were waiting in there to arrest them? For a moment, his imagination even conjured up a worse idea: that once inside, the floor of the building would suddenly open to reveal a glowing tunnel down to the pit of hell itself. He put the foolish thought from him, and made his way round the high wall.

There was a muffled crack. The Burbages had broken open the door. Moments later all the men had vanished within the Theatre.

Except for one. Back in the little house, Edmund knew he

was not needed yet. He lay on a bench, covered by a red cloak recently worn by an actor playing John of Gaunt. His eyes were half closed, a smile on his face; and at his side was Jane.

She had almost forgotten about Dogget recently, so close had she and Meredith grown. For if she had been uncertain of Edmund in the summer, the events of autumn had changed that. Indeed, it really seemed to her that she had discovered in Edmund a new man entirely. It was not just that he was a cheerful tower of strength, there was a quiet determination, a thoroughness she had not seen before. For three whole weeks, he had retired to the Staple Inn and studied legal precedent and leases until, at last, he had presented the Burbages with a legal case for tonight's action that, according to the experienced lawyer who reviewed it, could not have been bettered. He was acting now as an unpaid lawyer to the company, saving them a fortune in fees. "And he's not doing it just for his own sake, but for other people too," she remarked to her parents.

The cool daring of the whole business appealed to her, which was no doubt why she leaned forward, kissed him fully on the lips and laughingly remarked: "You look like a pirate."

Tap. Tap. At first the sounds had been carefully muffled. For the carpenters had gone cleverly about their work. Joints scraped free of plaster and loosened, boards prised gently apart, all round the inside of the playhouse, they had worked as silently as possible in the lamplight. Already the stage was reduced to a skeleton. Now, an hour before dawn, it was time for the hammering to begin.

Heads began to pop out of windows. There were cries. Doors opened. Pulling coats round them, neighbours began to emerge – to be met, smiling and even courteous, by Edmund Meredith, who assured them, as if it were the most natural thing in the world, that the noise would soon be over. When asked what the workmen were doing he blankly replied: "Why – dismantling the Theatre. We are taking it away."

And that is exactly what they did. In an exploit unique in theatrical history, the Burbages took their playhouse apart, timber by timber, and removed it to build another one.

The sun was already well up before Alderman Ducket

pushed through the crowd of spectators. His face was white with fury. He demanded to know what was going on.

"We are just taking our playhouse away," Edmund told him sweetly.

"You can't touch it! This theatre belongs to Giles Allen and your lease is finished."

But Meredith only smiled more sweetly still. "The ground belongs to Allen certainly," he agreed, "but the playhouse itself was built by the Burbages. It belongs to them, therefore, every timber." This was the flaw he had so cleverly spotted in the lease.

"He'll take you to court," Ducket protested.

"I agree," Edmund said cheerfully. "But we think we shall win."

"Where the devil is Allen now?" Ducket demanded.

"I do not know," Edmund shrugged. In fact, he knew very well that the merchant and his family had left to visit friends in the West Country two days before.

"I'll soon put a stop to this," Ducket fumed.

"Indeed?" Edmund seemed interested. "On what authority, though?"

"As an alderman of London!" Ducket shouted.

"But, sir," Edmund gestured around, "surely you forget. This is Shoreditch. We are not in London." He bowed politely. "You have no authority here." It was, he often thought afterwards, one of the happiest moments of his life.

By midday, half of the upper gallery had been taken down and the stage had been loaded into carts. Ducket had returned with some workmen to stop them and Meredith had forced them to retire by threatening to charge them with causing an affray and disturbing the king's peace. By dusk they were starting on the lower gallery and no one was bothering to molest them. As a precaution, however, the men took turns posting a watch by the entrance all night, while Cuthbert Carpenter gleefully kept a small bonfire going in the pit so that they could warm themselves.

By New Year's Day, the Theatre at Shoreditch had gone.

The operation was not only daring; it was also necessary. Even without the financial problems caused by the Blackfriars failure, the would-be theatre builder faced one huge problem: the price of wood. It was not surprising. In less than a century London's population had quadrupled and the demand for timber was huge. Above all, the mighty timber of the slow-growing oak, which was needed for a structure to support a boisterous crowd, was at a tremendous premium. The handsome oak-timbered buildings of the Elizabethans were a tribute to their wealth. The huge load of oak that the Burbages now carted away from Shoreditch was worth a fortune.

The site selected by the Burbages for the new theatre was excellent. Occupying a piece of open ground on Bankside, it was in the Liberty of the Clink, but was set apart from the nearby brothels. It enjoyed easy access to the river so that respectable citizens could arrive by barge at the river steps without encountering anything that would offend them. But though the negotiations with the owner of the land were almost complete, the contract was still not signed. It would be necessary to store the timber somewhere for a week or two. There was also one other little difficulty to be avoided.

However angry he might be, Alderman Ducket was a cautious man. He had taken careful advice before he set his trap. The document he intended to use as his authority was signed by several aldermen. The twenty men who would take over the carts were discreetly out of sight. Fortune was also clearly on his side, for his spies had discovered that the Burbages had stupidly decided to move all the heaviest and most valuable oak timbers at the same time. Ten large wagons had been hired.

"When they reach the bridge, they will have to stop to pay the toll. That's when we strike," he explained to his fellow aldermen. "No one can question our authority because they'll be in the city. My men will take over the wagons and we'll impound all the timber on the grounds of suspected theft of property." He grinned. "When Giles Allen returns, the matter can go to court."

"What if Meredith is right, and they win?" one of the aldermen asked.

"It doesn't matter. The case could drag on for years," Ducket pointed out. "Meanwhile," he smiled, "no timber, no theatre. I expect they'll be ruined."

Now, on the last day of the year, he waited patiently by the bridge. It was mid-morning and the wagons were coming.

The procession of wagons approached Bishopsgate at a leisurely pace. Edmund sat in the first one. As he scanned the lane in front of him, he saw nothing suspicious. Even the old fortified gateway into the city looked unoccupied, inviting. From there the street would lead them easily towards the bridge. He smiled.

Just before the gate the first wagon unexpectedly turned left. A few moments later, it was following the lane that led round outside the city wall and ditch. The other wagons followed. Five minutes later, with the Tower some hundreds of yards away on their right, they were bumping along a frozen track that, crossing open ground, led towards the river.

From the entrance to London Bridge, the frozen Thames presented a cheerful sight. Just upstream, some enterprising traders had erected stalls on the ice to make a little fair. Already there were braziers roasting nuts and sweetmeats. Beyond that, opposite Bankside, a huge area had been cleared and parties of youths and children were skating or sliding about. Puritan though he was, Alderman Ducket had no objection to these harmless pastimes and he looked at them with approval.

But then he frowned. Where the devil were those carts? They should have been there by now. Had some fool at the gate held them up? He was tempted to walk up towards Bishopsgate to see; but checked himself. A few more minutes passed. And then he happened to glance downstream.

The ten wagons were all on the ice now; they were several hundred yards beyond the Tower, but even on that grey morning, he could make out every detail. He could even see Meredith sitting in the first cart. For a long moment he watched them, speechless. It occurred to him that, perhaps, the ice would give way. Meredith might even be drowned. But the wagons continued.

Shortly afterwards, they pulled up at John Dogget's boat repair yard where Meredith had arranged for the timber to be stored. From the bridge, the alderman helplessly watched them unload.

* * *

1599

On 21 February 1599, in the city of London, a document was signed which, by good fortune, has been preserved. It was quite modest: a simple lease under which a certain Nicholas Brend, owner of a piece of ground on Bankside, granted the right to build and operate a playhouse thereon. It had one unusual feature: the lessee was not a single party but a group of people, and the lease carefully set out the legal share held by each of them. Half the lease was split between the two Burbage brothers; the other half divided equally between five members of the Chamberlain's company. One of these was William Shakespeare. The new theatre was being owned and operated by a company. Since the term "shareholder" had not yet been coined, a more domestic word was employed. Shakespeare and his fellow investors were known as "the householders". The jointly owned theatre was also to be given a new name. They decided to call it the Globe.

Cuthbert Carpenter knew what his grandmother thought, because he felt duty bound to visit her and his sister once a week. Bankside was Sodom and Gomorrah; the playhouse, the Temple of Moloch. But if, as his grandmother believed, God had already predestined him for hellfire, then there was nothing he could do about it anyway. So he worked on the Temple of Moloch with a will, and was happier than he had ever been in his life.

The Globe theatre was a handsome structure. A huge open drum with an external diameter of over eighty feet, it was not strictly speaking round but, like the other playhouses, polygonal, with nearly twenty sides. In the centre was a large pit and around it, three tiers of galleries. The stage was big, and at its rear was a flat wall with two doorways, one on the left, one on the right, through which the actors made their exits and entrances. Behind the doors lay the tiring house. Above the line of the doors and stretching across the back of the stage was a minstrels' gallery. It was also known, however, as the Lords' Room. For when no music was required during the performance, the fashionable folk liked to sit up there, so that they could both watch the play and be admired by the audience as well.

High over the rear part of the stage was a wooden canopy, supported on stage by two stout pillars at its front corners. The ceiling of the canopy, when completed and painted with stars would be known as "Heavens". Most amusing of all, to Cuthbert, was the special pulley and harness that would be used when one of the actors needed to fly over the stage.

Finally, over the roofline behind the stage, there was a turret from which, on play days, a man would sound a trumpet to let all London know that a performance was about to begin.

And so, through March, April, and into May, Cuthbert Carpenter laboured as the new Globe grew, until at last even its great thatched roof was finished, and the painters started to decorate its outside walls with fake windows, classical pediments and niches, so that it looked like a bright little simulacrum of a Roman amphitheatre. And sometimes, when he visited his grandmother and she asked him sharply where he had been, he would confuse her by declaring:

"I was in the Lords' Room today. And I think, grandmother, that I saw the Heavens as well."

As the Globe neared completion, the whole company felt a growing excitement. All London knew about the daring move across the river. As expected, Giles Allen had started legal proceedings over the removal of the structure, but this had only increased popular interest. Every playgoer in London was delighted to see the Chamberlain's men make fools of the killjoy aldermen. The royal court was said to be highly amused. Even the rival Admiral's men agreed: "You struck a blow for all of us."

As for the building itself and its site, the company was satisfied that it had chosen well. The only disadvantage anyone could think of – and it was a small problem – concerned the access.

In order to reach the new Globe on foot, unless one lived in Southwark, it was necessary to walk over London Bridge. For those coming from the eastern part of the city, this was the direct route anyway; but for those coming from the western side, or the Inns of Court area, it meant either a tedious detour to the bridge, or the expense of a ferry – and even a party of eight would still have to pay sixpence for a wherry big enough to carry them all. "We may lose some of the young lawyers," Fleming remarked to Jane; but with so many other arrangements to be made, no one had time to worry much about this minor matter.

For the Fleming family, the new arrangements meant a move, and during April Jane's father began negotiating with several landlords to secure suitable lodgings near to the Globe, but not too close to the whorehouses.

One afternoon early in May, on her way back from inspecting a little house her father was interested in, Jane encountered John Dogget; and since neither of them were busy just then, they went to the George together.

He was his usual cheerful self. Though they had seen less of each other since the previous autumn, he seemed delighted to be with her. When she told him about the family's forthcoming move to Southwark, he gave her a friendly smile and remarked: "You'll be living near us then. I'm so glad." And she realized that she was glad as well. Indeed, the time in his company went so easily that she hardly noticed that an hour and then two had passed. It was, indeed, only a chance remark of hers that brought it to an end, when, discussing the new Globe, she happened to mention the problem of the costly ferry crossing. For after asking her to go over it again, and pausing thoughtfully for nearly a minute, Dogget's face suddenly lit up with a huge grin. "Come with me. I've something to show you," he said.

The sun was already starting to sink, sending red shafts along the river, when they reached the Dogget yard. With surprise, Jane watched while he dragged planks and timbers away from the back of the boathouse. He lit two lamps, hung them from a beam and commanded her: "Turn your back." She heard him pulling covers off something, while she stared out at the red sky above the water, then his voice said: "You can look now." And to her astonishment, she saw the long, gleaming and magnificently gilded form of Dogget's secret treasure. He beamed at her.

"Could we use this? To ferry people to the Globe?"

He had at last found a role worthy of King Harry's barge.

"We could take thirty. She wouldn't sink," he said.

For another half-hour they tested it, sitting this way and that, laughing happily like a pair of childish conspirators.

It was dusk when he offered to escort her home.

* * *

The play was done.

It was Shakespeare's *Merchant of Venice* that had given him the idea originally. A rogue tries to do a great evil, but the forces of good triumph. Simple enough. But what had especially struck Edmund was that the villain in the play was an outcast, and a striking presence. That was what he needed: a villain who was unusual, memorable, threatening not just because of what he does, but what he is. Someone mysterious. But what? A Jesuit priest? A Spaniard? Too obvious. He had racked his brains for something original, and then suddenly he had remembered the strange fellow who had threatened him at the bear-pit two years before: Black Barnikel, the pirate.

A blackamoor. The pirate moor. What could be stranger, more threatening? The audience wouldn't be able to take their eyes off him.

He made the Moor loathsome, hideous. As terrible as Tamburlaine, cunning as Mephistopheles. His speeches and monologues were magnificent as awful images of evil came spilling out. There was not one redeeming feature in him. At last however, caught in his own toils, he was brought to justice and, after showing himself to be a coward as well, was led away, contemptibly, to execution. When he finally put down his pen, Meredith felt certain: now he would make a figure in the world.

He decided that afternoon to go out. And then he decided to do something he had not done for a long time. He put on his galligaskins, and a white lace ruff, and his hat with the billowing feathers.

Dusk had fallen before Edmund and the lady crossed the bridge. She was being carried by two servants in a covered chair: he was walking beside it, gallantly carrying a lamp to light the way. They had met at a play given by the Admiral's men and then retired to sup with a party of other fashionable folk at a nearby tavern. Until that day, Edmund had only known his companion slightly, as a friend of Lady Redlynch; but it seemed that he was known to her since, noticing him in the playhouse gallery, she had turned and archly remarked: "I see, Master Meredith, you have dressed as a gentleman again." And whatever she might have heard of him from

Lady Redlynch, it was enough, evidently, for her to make it clear to him that evening that his place was at her side.

They had just paused for a moment about a hundred yards north of the bridge when John Dogget and Jane, returning from the boathouse, came in sight of them.

Had they not paused, had Edmund not leaned forward into the covered chair, Jane might not have realized who it was. But in doing so, he held the lamp up to his face. There was no mistaking it. Even from the distance, in the little pool of lamplight, she could see them both: Edmund, his handsome, aristocratic face, half shadowed; the lady, a painted beauty, saying something to him which made him laugh. She saw the lady put her hand out and take his. For a moment, she thought Edmund might draw back. But he did not. She stopped.

It was the same thing, all over again. Nothing had changed. She knew it, with a sudden sickness, in her heart.

At her side, Dogget had not realized whom she had seen and was still chatting happily. She forced herself to walk forward. Dogget was rather surprised when, as they walked, she took hold of his hand.

They were still fifty yards away when Edmund glanced back and saw them. With the lamp still close to his eyes, he would not have recognized them in the dusk if it had not been for the white flash in Dogget's hair. Staring for a brief moment, he saw from her walk that the figure beside him must be Jane.

For a moment he hesitated. He knew the two were friends. Could there be something more that he did not know about? Could they even – the thought flashed across his mind – be lovers? No, he decided. That was absurd. Little Jane would never do such a thing. Dogget was just walking her home, quite innocently. Yet what was he himself doing? Would he be parting from this lady at her door?

He almost went over to them. But then he did not. After all, it might seem as if he was anxious about them: that would be beneath his dignity. As for reassuring Jane – the hypocrisy of the gesture secretly embarrassed him, since he might well spend the night in the lady's arms. No. Let her think what she liked. A fine fellow like himself should do as he pleased. Besides, she might not have recognized him.

A moment later, the lady and Edmund had turned westward across the city, and Dogget and Jane continued northwards.

The little procession that crossed London Bridge one bright noon a week later had a festive air. In the first wagon, filled with costumes, rode Fleming and his son. In the second, his wife presided. The third vehicle was an open cart full of props. Cuthbert Carpenter was perched on top of that to make sure that nothing fell out. In the fourth cart, also full of props, rode Jane, and in the fifth, Dogget.

The contents of the carts were like something for a carnival. There was a throne, a bedstead, a golden sceptre, a golden fleece; Cupid's bow and quiver, a dragon, a lion, and a hell-mouth. There was a witch's cauldron, a Pope's mitre, a snake, a wooden log. Armour, spears, swords, tridents – the bric-à-brac of legend, superstition and story. People gazed and laughed as this extraordinary cargo rumbled by, and those riding in the carts waved cheerfully.

The Globe was ready to open; Fleming had his house in Southwark; and it was time to bring the contents of his store to their new home. And none of the party was more radiant than Jane, for she had made her big decision.

She was bored with Meredith. She had chosen Dogget instead. Since she and the boatbuilder had come to an understanding, she had felt an extraordinary sense of peace and happiness. She was looking forward to telling Meredith.

Two days later Edmund Meredith began to have doubts about his play. More than a week had passed since he had given it to the Burbages. The days passed and he waited in an agony of doubt. It did not help his nerves, therefore, when, two days after his encounter with the actors, he received a visit from William Bull.

"I think it is time that I see the Burbages myself," his cousin said stolidly. "I want my fifty pounds."

"But you must not," Edmund cried. He could not tell William that the Burbages thought the money had all come from him. "It's the worst thing you could do," he blurted out. It had just uncomfortably crossed his mind that if they did not think they owed him money, the Burbages might not put on his play.

"Why?"

"Because," Edmund searched his mind feverishly, "they are subtle. Full of strange humours. Saturnine. Splenetic. The Globe will provide the first profits they have enjoyed in three years and you are not the only man to whom money is owed. I have persuaded them to pay you first," he lied. "But if you come to them now, just when they are occupied with the first performances – why, cousin, put yourself in their place. They will be furious. And," he added, with a splendid indignation, "they would have the right to be so." He looked at Bull and lifted his finger warningly. "Then they would really make you wait."

He saw Bull waver. "You think so?"

"I'm sure of it."

"Very well," Bull sighed, as he prepared to depart. "But I count on you."

"To the death," Edmund said, with a relief he could not describe.

The following day, he had word from the Burbages that his play would be performed next week.

The morning sun was still pale as Jane waited for Edmund outside the Globe, the day before his play. She was dressed in green. A faint, cool breeze coming up the Thames ruffled wisps of her reddish hair.

She was ready. She no longer felt a sense of triumph; indeed, if anything, she felt a little nervous. But she knew exactly what she was going to do. She was going to tell him she was getting married.

He would be along shortly, because this morning was the full rehearsal for his play. The Burbages had certainly done their work properly; he could not complain of that. On the door of the Globe behind her was a printed handbill proclaiming:

THE BLACKAMOOR
by
EDMUND MEREDITH

A thousand had been printed and distributed round the taverns, the Inns of Court and other places where playgoers gathered. They had also employed a crier to announce this and other highlights of the new theatre's opening weeks.

She had heard from her father that there had been some hesitation about putting the play on. One of the brothers had wanted to rewrite it. In the end however, because of the debt and the services he had rendered over the lease, they had decided to proceed, but to do so quickly in the summer pre-season while they were still settling in. The real season would open in the autumn with the new Shakespeare play.

Anyway, good or bad, Meredith's writing was no longer any concern of hers. She composed herself as she saw him coming.

He was simply dressed today. The fashionable clothes were gone; he wore no hat. Instead of his usual saunter, there was a quickness, even a nervousness in his walk. As he came up, it seemed to her that he was grown thinner; and he was white as a sheet. He greeted her quietly. "Today's the rehearsal." He might have said funeral, he looked so woebegone. "They'll hear it all."

To keep their customers coming frequently, the playhouses had a constantly changing repertoire. With repeats of old favourites like *Romeo and Juliet*, and new plays which, if not liked, might get only one performance, actors had to perform several plays a week. Rehearsal times were extraordinarily short and, having conned his own part, an actor might not even know the shape of a play until the final rehearsal.

"What are they saying about it?" he asked.

"I don't know, Edmund."

"They told me," he looked at her hopefully, "that it was so promising they wanted to put it on at once."

"You should be pleased then."

"I've got all my friends coming." He brightened a little. "Rose and Sterne have promised to bring twenty." He did not say that he had even written to Lady Redlynch for support. "But it's the people in the pit I'm afraid of," he suddenly confessed.

"Why?"

"Because," he hesitated, and she was rather shocked to realize that his eyes were almost imploring: "What if they hiss?" And then, before she could even answer, "Do you think Dogget or somebody would bring some friends? To support in the pit?"

"You mean, you want me to ask him?" She paused. The conversation was drifting away from what she had intended. She abruptly changed its course. "Edmund, there is something else I have to tell you."

"Yes? About the play?"

And then she stopped. He looked so frightened, so naked, so far from the confident fellow she knew. No, she realized, she could not tell him now. It could wait. "It will all go well," she said instead. "Have courage." For the first time feeling more like a mother than a lover, she reached up and kissed him.

"Go now," she said. "Good luck."

Throughout this conversation they had not noticed that they were observed thoughtfully by a pair of blue eyes. Blue eyes which, as they now turned away, took on a strange and smoky look.

Black Barnikel had arrived in London only two days before, and he did not plan to stay long. His ship was taking on a cargo of cloth before departing once more. After that, a group of merchants in the Low Countries had chartered him to sail to Portugal. During the last two years his roving life had taken him to the Azores and the Americas. His visits to faraway ports had resulted in two children, about whom he knew nothing, and in a chestful of bullion which, on the recommendation of his Billingsgate cousins, he had deposited in the strongroom of Alderman Ducket for safe keeping. But there was another matter as well, which he had hoped to resolve in London. He had consulted his cousins, Alderman Ducket and several others of his acquaintance there, but their uniform lack of encouragement had left Orlando Barnikel in a very uncertain temper.

He had been intrigued therefore, the previous afternoon, when he had seen the handbill for *The Blackamoor* in a tavern. He remembered his conversation with the young popinjay on his last visit and wondered if this Meredith might be one and the same. Out of curiosity he had strolled across that morning to look at the new Globe and to see what he could find out. Seeing Meredith now with Jane, he remembered his face at once. He remembered the young fellow's girl too, from that day at the bear-pit. There could be no doubt that this was Meredith. And if so, the subject of the play, he guessed, must be himself.

What had the popinjay said – that he could make him into a hero or a villain? To have all London talking of a Moor as a hero would suit his present purposes very well, he thought. Young Meredith might be very helpful to him there. A villain, however, would not suit him at all.

The day was overcast as the crowds approached the Globe. A procession of little groups was crossing by the bridge; on the water, Dogget's new ferry had already made three journeys from the northern side.

Even though the Thames was grey, King Harry's converted barge looked splendid. Its gold and crimson trimming glowed even from across the stream. Above the gilded cabin, a large pennant displaying a picture of the Globe spread itself bravely in the wind. Six burly oarsmen, of whom two were cousins of John Dogget, pulled thirty passengers at a time, paying a halfpenny each. The barge had already been used to advertise the theatre and its productions, carrying handbills for distribution all the way up to Chelsea and down to Greenwich.

From the turret above the Globe's roofline, a trumpet had twice sounded to announce that a play would begin at two o'clock. Evening performances were banned, naturally, since no one wanted crowds in the streets after dark; and even late afternoon productions were forbidden lest they distract the common folk from going to the church service of evensong as they should. Soon after the main midday meal known as dinner, therefore, the Elizabethan theatre had to begin.

One of the bearded Burbage brothers was at the door, watching the audience arrive and quietly counting the take. Entrance to the pit was a penny, to the galleries twopence. The Lords' Room above the back of the stage, entered by a staircase behind the tiring house, was set at sixpence that day. So far the theatre was well under half full, a total of seven hundred altogether: not a disaster, but, unless the play was very well received, not enough to secure a repeat performance. Rose and Sterne, having promised twenty friends, had brought seven. The Lords' Room, as yet, was empty. Lady Redlynch had not come.

But in the tiring house a very different kind of problem had developed.

Edmund looked around desperately. Five actors, including Jane's little brother, stood before him. But where were the other three? Will Shakespeare had excused himself at the start of rehearsals, but that was natural, Edmund supposed, when he was working on his own play. But there had been a full complement at the rehearsal yesterday. "Richard Cowley's sick," one of the others reported. "Thomas Pope has lost his voice," Fleming sadly told him. As for William Sly, no one had heard from him since the previous day. He had simply disappeared.

"Can you double up?" Edmund begged them, as he searched his memory frantically to see how this could be done. After several minutes poring over the script he managed, with a couple of small cuts, to cover for Pope and Crowley; but unless Sly turned up: "We can't do it," he concluded. "It's impossible." He gazed around them, at a loss. His play, all that he had worked for, casually destroyed at this last minute. The audience would have to be given their money back. He could not believe it. The actors, embarrassed, looked at each other in silence. Until Jane's little brother spoke up. "Could you not play a part yourself?"

The actors looked at Edmund curiously.

"I?" He stared blankly. "On the stage?" He was a gentleman, not an actor.

"Seems the best idea," Fleming agreed. They were still watching him.

"But I've never acted," he protested in confusion.

"You know the play," the boy said. "Anyway, there's no one else." And after a long, agonized pause, Edmund realized he was right.

"Oh my God," he breathed.

"I'll get you a costume," said Jane.

They hit him like an engulfing wave as soon as he came on stage, taking him entirely by surprise. He could see them all in the daylight from the big circle of the open roof above: eight hundred pairs of eyes staring at him from the pit below his feet and from the galleries on every side. If he moved to the side of the stage, some in the galleries could almost reach out and touch him. They were all looking at him expectantly.

Not that they would do so for long. Elizabethan actors had to earn the attention of the audience every minute. Bore them, and they would not just become restless in their seats – the folk in the pit and many in the galleries were standing anyway. They would begin to talk. Irritate them and they would hiss. Annoy them, and a hail of nuts, apple cores, pears, cheese rinds or anything else to hand, might land on the stage or on your head. No wonder the prologues to plays often appealed to them, hopefully, as "Gentles All".

But he was not afraid. In his left hand, in a little scroll wrapped around a stick, were his lines, which Fleming had discreetly slipped him as he went through the stage door. It was not uncommon for actors in a new play to bring such prompts with them, and it was hardly visible, but the gesture had seemed absurd to him. He was hardly likely to forget the lines he had written himself. As he waited his turn he glanced around. He spotted Rose and Sterne and noticed their surprise at seeing him on stage. He would have to make up some good reason for this afterwards. He watched the actor playing the Moor. He was speaking tolerably well and Edmund saw with satisfaction that, so far at least, the audience's eyes were riveted on the strange, black figure he had created. His idea had been good, then. But the time for his own speech had almost come now. He smiled, took a step forward, took a breath.

And nothing happened. His mind was a complete blank. He glanced at the actor playing the Moor for a cue. None came. He felt himself go pale, heard Fleming's voice call out something from the stage door, and, shaking with embarrassment, glanced hastily down at the scroll.

So, Sirrah, how does my lady now? How could he have forgotten? It was so simple. A hint of restiveness seemed momentarily to afflict the audience after this fumble. No hissing, just something in the air. But fortunately it seemed to disappear.

The rest of the first scene, which was not long, passed without incident. By discreetly unrolling the scroll in his left hand, and glancing down at it for reassurance, he found that he did not fluff his lines again. The play was settling down.

The strange murmur began in the last minute of the scene.

The Moor was making his first major speech, centre-stage. It was blood-curdling and he had been rather proud of it. But just before he reached the climax of his speech, something else seemed to claim the audience's attention. Edmund saw one or two hands pointing, and nudges being exchanged. The speech ended, not to awed silence, but still more whispers and pointing. He turned to exit, puzzled. And then he saw.

No one had been in the Lords' Room when the play began. The whole gallery above the back stage had been empty. But now, a single figure had entered it, seating himself right in the centre like a presiding judge, and then leaning over the balcony to get a better view – so that, seen from the pit, his face seemed to hang, a sort of strange, stage ghost, over the proceedings. And no wonder the audience had whispered and pointed.

For the face was black, like the Moor's.

"It's him. I'm sure of it." Jane was the one who had gone out to inspect the black stranger from the gallery. "His eyes are blue," she added.

There were seldom any intervals between acts. The second had already begun and Edmund was due to go on again very shortly. As he and Jane gazed at each other, they both remembered the conversation with the Moor only too well. Would he guess that he was the inspiration for the play, Edmund wondered? Of course he would.

"How does he look?" he asked nervously.

"I don't know." She considered. "He just stares."

"What shall I do?" he asked.

"Take no notice of him," she advised.

A minute later, Edmund was before the audience again.

Hard though he found it not to glance up at the black face over the back of the stage, he managed to focus on his lines, and played his part without mishap. The Blackamoor's first great crime – a theft and rape – was unfolding. The audience was following the action expectantly and the actors seemed to be gaining confidence.

Why was it then, towards the end of the second act, that he began to feel uncomfortable. There was plenty of action. The Blackamoor's character and deeds were horrifying. But as the minutes passed, the sensation grew: the play was getting flat.

The third act came. As the evil doings of the black pirate rose to new heights, so did his language. Yet now it seemed to Edmund that the ringing declarations he had so lovingly penned sounded bombastic, empty; and he realized that the audience too was beginning to grow restive. Here and there, he heard faint mutters of conversation: looking up at the gallery, he saw Rose whispering in Sterne's ear. As the act neared its end, he started to search in his mind: something new had to happen by the start of the next act, at least. And with a feeling of cold panic he realized that there were two more acts to follow – and they were just the same. The play had no heart, no soul.

Jane was in the audience too, but if her concentration shifted from the stage, it was for a different reason.

How strange he looked. Time and again, as she watched from the gallery, she found her attention moving from the action of the play to the face behind it.

He never moved, even between the acts. He might have been carved upon the woodwork. His face hung there, expressionless as a mask. Like all Elizabethans, Jane was uncertain whether black people were human beings. Yet as she gazed at him, it seemed to her that there was something noble in that dark, unmoving face.

What was he thinking? There before him the actor, a made-up caricature of his condition, was exposing his villainy to the audience. Was he himself so terrible? She remembered everything about him from that day at the bear-pit: his snake-like body, the sense of danger about him, his dagger. As she stared at him now, she had no doubt that he could be dangerous. And yet, it seemed to her that his eyes were sad.

She should have gone back to the tiring house after the third act; but she stayed, watching him, instead. What was he thinking? And what was he going to do?

The fourth act: within minutes, Edmund knew he was in trouble. The black pirate's villainies were mounting, but, now that the audience had got used to him, and seen through the trick of the play, they no longer cared. Were they going to start hissing? But the audience was in a cheerful mood. Knowing this was a first effort, they were inclined to be kind to the playwright. Towards the end of the act, almost as a gesture of support, there were some hisses and groans each time the Blackamoor appeared. And still, as the final act began, Edmund could see that for some at least, the strange black man at the back inspired more curiosity than the play itself.

Alone in the Lords' Room Orlando stared. He saw them all and understood them; but he did not let them shame him.

He had paid sixpence to enter the Lords' Room, more than any of them. He supposed he was a richer man, quite probably, than anyone in that theatre. He had paid, hoping in his heart to see himself as a hero.

There was no doubt that he was the central character of this play. As soon as he arrived, he saw the audience pointing at him, heard the whispers and the buzz with a feeling of satisfaction. The first scene he saw confirmed this view. The Blackamoor of this play was captain of a ship and evidently a man of some importance. Only kings and heroes, he supposed, had plays written about them. But if, he thought, I am to preside here over this play about myself, I will lean forward, and let them know me and see my face.

By the second act he understood better and by the third act he was certain. He had seen very few plays, but this Blackamoor was clearly a villain. As the fourth act unravelled, he started to feel indignation, then fury. Had this fake buccaneer ever heard the cannons' roar, known the force of a gale, faced death or a mutinous crew? Could he have brought a ship through a storm where the waves came over you like solid thunder, or killed a man in cold blood because he had to, or even guessed what it was to come from six weeks at sea into the arms of a warm and sultry beauty in an Afric port? And, just because he was untutored, only he, the Moorish mariner, in all this audience truly saw, in its entirety, the vulgarity of Meredith's poor play.

Then he remembered, once more, what Meredith had said. "I can make you into a hero, or a villain; a wise man or a fool." So this was the power of the young popinjay's pen. He thought he had the power, in this wooden circle, to make him not only a villain, but to make him worthless.

His face still showed nothing. He felt for his knife.

* * *

The audience had at last had enough. With the fifth act, they could take no more. The play might be terrible, but at least they could have a little fun. As the Blackamoor, attempting his greatest and most terrible crime, was foiled and caught, to be followed by his inevitable trial and execution, they gazed at the actors, considering how best to begin.

Seeing the villains on stage, and the strange, mask-like face of the black man staring out so incongruously from the Lords' Room above him, someone in the pit saw the joke.

"Hang the devil," he cried out. "And the other one too!"

It was a good joke. The audience took to it at once. Here was something of interest. A player pretends to be a blackamoor while a real blackamoor, like a presiding spirit, hovers behind him.

The next lines were cheerfully obvious. "Spare the actor. Hang the blackamoor!"

"Someone must hang for this play!"

"They're partners. Hang both!"

If the pit saw a broad joke, the gallery saw subtler implications. "Spare the blackamoor. Hang the playwright. The play's the crime."

"No," a gallant explained to the audience. "The play's not dull. 'Tis a true report. And behold," he pointed to Orlando Barnikel, "the real villain."

The audience could not contain itself. It rocked with laughter. For a moment the actors could not proceed.

Black Barnikel did not move. His face was still a mask.

It was then that they started throwing things. They meant no harm. Nothing dangerous was thrown. Small nuts, cheese rind, a few early apple cores, one or two cherries. It was all good-hearted. Indeed, wishing to spare the actors, and even the young playwright, too much ignominy, they tossed their missiles towards the blackamoor in the Lords' Room, who, it seemed to them, could provide a harmless focus for this horseplay, and who in any case was somehow the inspiration behind it all. Most of the projectiles fell short. Only two or three landed close or hit him. A moment later, one of the Burbages called back the actors and sent on the clown to give the customary jig. So pleased were the audience with their wit, that they received him with roars of warm approval.

So ended Meredith's play.

* * *

Black Barnikel did not flinch: not a muscle of his face moved, nor did his eyes blink as the missiles flew towards him. He had never flinched, even when lead and cannonballs flew, on the high seas. He despised the nuts, fruit and cheese rinds as much as he despised the throwers. He felt, deep in his stomach, a profound contempt for these people, pit and gallery alike.

Yet Meredith had done his work well. He had come to see a play about himself and been shown this travesty. All London now thought of him not as a rich and daring sea captain, as he wished, but as a villain; and worse even yet, a figure of contempt. Men who would have trembled at his name on the seas were throwing food in his face and laughing at him.

Worst of all was the feeling of desolation – the desolation of a man who, though he has accomplished all that is possible, discovers that he will still, always be scorned; and that, as his Billingsgate cousins had gently hinted to him in their conversation two days before, even in what he thought of as his home, he must always be an outcast. His, was the fate of the mariner for whom there could never be any homecoming.

So what remained? The only thing he had ever truly possessed: his honour. Meredith had dared to insult him. He had killed men for far less. While the clown was still playing, Black Barnikel silently slipped out.

Jane walked with Edmund all the way home to the Staple Inn. She could not leave him alone at a time like this. She linked her arm in his and gave him what warmth she could.

"Was it all bad?" He had not spoken until they reached the bridge.

"Some of it was very good."

He did not speak again until they came out of Newgate. "It was laughed off."

"No. It was the blackamoor in the Lords' Room. That's what set them off. Not your play."

"Perhaps." He grunted. "Where did he go?"

"Who knows?"

When they got to the Staple Inn, she hugged him and gave

him a long kiss. Afterwards, she would be glad that she did it. Then she went slowly back home.

Black Barnikel watched her, as he had since she and Meredith left the Globe. Then he gazed thoughtfully at the high, timbered façade of the Staple Inn.

Dusk had just fallen the following night when the dark figure and his two seamen struck. They did so with great efficiency. They had been lying in wait for some time.

They rolled the body into a small sail and carried it swiftly away. A short time later, they were rowing a boat downstream towards Black Barnikel's vessel, which sailed before dawn on the ebb tide.

The group which gathered a day later at the Fleming house was glum. The business was inexplicable. There had been no message. No one had seen anything. There was no sign of a body. The aldermen who had been informed had already instigated a search. Alderman Ducket, though he did not like any of them, had behaved with courtesy and even kindness, riding over himself a few minutes before to tell them that, as yet, the city sergeants had found nothing. Neither Dogget, nor Carpenter, nor the Burbage brothers could suggest any solution either.

The breeze was coming from the south-west, so they had made good progress down the estuary. By mid-morning they had come to the last great bend in the widening river; by early afternoon they were passing the broad opening of the River Medway on their right while to the left the more distant East Anglian coast had already begun its huge curve and, by later afternoon, was sinking over the horizon.

Jane stood on deck and breathed in the sharp, salt air.

It was kidnap, of course. But as she saw it, Black Barnikel ran no great risk. Who would guess? And if they did, what could anyone do about it? They would soon be far out to sea. After all, she smiled ruefully, he was a pirate.

Orlando Barnikel's original plan, when he arrived in London, had been to find a wife. He was tired of the women of the port he encountered. He had money enough, whenever he chose, to settle down; and often, as he sailed in distant waters, he had thought of his red-haired old father and his burly, friendly cousins at Billingsgate, and considered how he would like to find a bride in the only place in the world, he supposed, which he could call home.

The Barnikels of Billingsgate intimated to him that no girl in London, no matter how humble, could be induced to marry a blackamoor. "I have money," he protested. There were women in some Mediterranean ports who would have had him gladly. But the fishmongers had shaken their heads. "You're our cousin and always will be," they had explained magnanimously. "But marriage . . ." Alderman Ducket had uttered similar cautions.

Orlando had briefly hoped that the unexpected play would cast him in a better light – enough to impress some girl, somewhere. But that, too, had been a bitter illusion.

And so, debating whether to kill Meredith or not, he had come to a different conclusion. Why give these Londoners, who despised him, the opportunity to put his head in a noose one day? His fury, his hurt and his honour might call for Meredith's death, but he had not achieved what he had without being cunning. He could punish the young man another way, and solve his own problem at the same time. Twice he had watched the couple together and seen they were close: he would steal Meredith's woman.

As for the problem of her kidnap, if he ever returned to London, he smiled. "She will say she came willingly with me by the time we go back," he predicted to the mate. He had experience to prove that in many a place.

And so Jane, who had no illusions about what was to come, gazed out at the eastern horizon and, having resigned herself to her fate, felt a strange sense of excitement as they entered the open sea. She thought of her parents, of Dogget and of Meredith with affection, and then, deliberately, cast their images into the wind.

Chapter 12

God's Fire

1603

In the wet and windy days of March 1603 two men, several hundred miles apart on the island of Britain, waited anxiously. Each was expecting a personal signal from God.

In the north, James Stuart, King of Scotland, waited for a messenger. For down south, in a Thameside palace, old Queen Elizabeth was dying. It was no secret. The bright wig she wore, the thick paint on her face, the carefully staged appearances – nothing could now conceal the ravage of time. The creaking play was done. And who should be her heir?

The virgin queen could not bring herself to name her successor, but everyone – the court, the Parliament, the Privy Council – knew that it must be James. His grandmother had been a Tudor, great King Harry's sister, making him nearest by blood. And although he was the son of that treacherous Catholic, Mary Queen of Scots, James himself was free of taint. Placed on the throne of the mother he scarcely knew, he had been trained to reign as a cautious Protestant. The dour Scots council had seen to that. He would suit England very well.

And England would suit James. After the long, bleak years in his poor northern land, the rich kingdom of England seemed to him a warm and pleasant place indeed. Was this the wonderful destiny that God had planned for him and all his heirs to come?

Then, one morning, God's hand was seen. Like a cold draught down a long gallery, blowing curtains, taffeta, silks and gee-gaws before it, time's wind came, and swept through the gallery of the Tudors. A messenger was riding northwards. The Stuart age had begun.

* * *

Just down the lane from St Mary-le-Bow, on the site of a tavern and by the place where once, centuries before, the sign of the Bull had hung, there was a very handsome house. A mixture of brick, timber and plaster, five storeys high and surrounded by a walled orchard garden, its three great gables dominated the tiny parish of St Lawrence Silversleeves below. Alderman Ducket, disgusted that plays had been performed in Blackfriars again, had lived here for the last two years, and as the messenger to James was riding north, he too was about to learn his family's destiny. Cautiously he looked into the cradle where the new-born baby lay. Surreptitiously, so that his wife did not see, he put in his hand. Carefully he felt. Then he smiled with relief.

The curse had been lifted.

Thrice he had been married: three children by the first wife; three from the second; and now this made three more, the ninth child. And all were free of the curse of the webbed fingers. He had never forgotten the day when, as a boy, he had inspected his grandfather's hands and the old man had told him: "My grandfather's were the same. And he had it from his grandfather – the Ducket that dived into the river and married the Bull heiress. Helped him swim, I dare say."

The Ducket family were rich, as rich as any of the Bulls had been. When King Henry had dissolved the monasteries and taken over much of the Church's huge hoard of plate, the alderman's grandfather had acquired so much that he was known as Silver Ducket. But there was no denying their lowly origins. Not that they had ever tried to do so. Descendants of Bulls also, they instinctively scorned any lie; and besides, every generation or two, the webbed fingers had appeared to remind them. They had accepted the fact. But the proud boy could not. His grandfather's hands had shocked him. In his mind, it was as if the grand river flow of the patrician Bulls, to which he felt he belonged, had been joined by a polluted stream. Worse yet, in those increasingly Calvinistic times, he began to wonder – could this even be a mark of God's displeasure, a sign that he and all his blood might not, after all, be members of God's elect?

Yet surely the river was cleansed now. His father had not been disfigured; nor was he. Anxiously, but with growing hope, he had inspected each of his new-born children, the third generation; and now thrice three had come, all whole. The curse had passed. It must be so.

Of course, you still had to be careful. Even the elect had to fight the Devil – the hidden enemy within. It would, for instance, have amazed the actors at the Globe to know that when Ducket had attended their plays, he had enjoyed them. He had crushed this sign of weakness in himself, however, just as firmly as he had tried to crush them. Two years ago when, despite his continued protests, the harmless and courtly boy-actors had been allowed to give occasional performances in the new Blackfriars theatre, he had moved away to his present house, to escape the contamination. But of this he could now be confident: God had shown His hand. As long as he brought his family up carefully, with clear moral precepts, the future was bright indeed.

As he gazed down at his ninth child and third son, he smiled happily and, since he had a taste for the classics, announced:

"Let us call him Julius. A hero's name, like Julius Caesar." Then, gently taking the baby's tiny finger he said quietly: "No curse, my little son, shall ever attach itself to thee."

A month later, proof of the divine favour now attaching to the family came when, riding out with the mayor to greet the new king, Ducket along with his fellow aldermen received the accolade of knighthood. He was Sir Jacob Ducket now, bound by sacred fealty to the monarch. And so with confidence he could give his children these two important lessons: "Be loyal to the king." And perhaps profounder still: "It seems that God has chosen us. Be humble."

By which, of course, he really meant: be proud.

1605

On the eve of 5 November, the day when King James – the first of that name in England, the sixth in Scotland – was to open his English Parliament, it was discovered that a great cache of gunpowder had been hidden in the Palace of Westminster and that a certain Guy Fawkes, together with other Catholic conspirators, intended to blow up king, Lords, Commons and all at the ceremony.

It was a sensation. Sir Jacob Ducket grimly took his family

to St Paul's churchyard to witness some of the executions; little Julius was too young to go, but by the age of four, when the local children built a great bonfire opposite Mary-le-Bow and commemorated the day by burning an effigy of Guy Fawkes, he knew the chant:

> Remember, remember, the Fifth of November
> Gunpowder, treason and plot . . .

He knew what it meant, too, since his father had firmly instructed him, with his third, never-to-be-forgotten lesson: "No popery, Julius. The papists are the enemy within."

1611

It was impossible not to love Martha Carpenter. No one who knew her could imagine her ever acting with malice. Nor indeed could she. Always gentle, always meek, she had never in her twenty-seven years asked anything for herself. When told she must remain at home to look after her grandmother, she undertook it as a duty of love. When Cuthbert left and went to build the Globe, though her grandmother cursed him, she had continued to see him and to pray for his soul. Yet now, as she held out the book to her brother and looked up with her round face and her sweet smile, the blood drained from his face.

"Swear," she said.

Martha shared with many Puritans the quality of hope. Hope was an important virtue, which was about to change the world.

For the Reformation had come not only to destroy. The true doctrine of the Protestants, as they saw it, was one of love, and their best preachers conveyed a message of extraordinary joy.

There were many such men in London. Her favourite as a child had been a Scotsman, a quiet old man with crinkled white hair and the clearest blue eyes she had ever seen. "It is simple," he would tell her. "Strip away the pomp, worldliness and superstition of the Romish Church and what remains? The Truth. For we have the Word of God in the scriptures, the very utterances of Our Lord in the Gospels." When she read the Bible, she realized, God was speaking to her directly.

Several of their neighbours in the little parish of St Lawrence Silversleeves were fellow Puritans. When they met to hear a sermon, or to pray together in each others' houses, they did so in a spirit of charity. Admonition was rare. In Presbyterian Scotland and the Calvinist regions of Europe every parish was organized like this. There were no priests, for each congregation elected its own elders to lead it. Nor were there bishops. The elders in turn elected regional committees to co-ordinate their activities. And it was these developments abroad which had sown the seed of the greatest hope of all: that the kingdom of God might come on Earth.

Of course, the true and perfect kingdom was not due until the world's last days. This was known from the biblical Book of Revelation. But one could at least approach that state. Wasn't it the plain duty of every freeborn Puritan to march with his brethren towards the light and build God's kingdom – the shining city on a hill – here and now? It was, after all, no more than the medieval idea of a commune. But this time a commune for God.

So it was that little Martha, growing up amongst such people, came to possess a dream that would be the guiding vision of her life. When she crossed the river and looked across to London's crowded houses and the dark, Gothic mass of old St Paul's, in her mind's eye she saw God's kingdom, waiting to rise. She saw it so clearly: a shining city on a hill.

She also possessed the virtue of patience. And patience was needed. When King James had come to England from Presbyterian Scotland, the Puritans had hoped: "Surely he will bring the true faith with him." But James had not enjoyed being subject to the Scottish elders, and he realized that the authority of the monarchy depended upon its supremacy over the English Church. The Church of England, with its reformed Catholic faith, its bishops, ceremonies and all the rest, must remain. As King James remarked to his English councillors: "No bishop, no king."

So the Bishop of London still presided at old St Paul's, and in the tiny parish of St Lawrence Silversleeves, the clergyman, aided by Ducket and the other vestrymen, insisted that Martha and the other Puritan parishioners should attend communion three times a year and make a respectful show of outward conformity to the Church.

The book she now pushed towards her brother was the Geneva Bible. It contained the complete scriptures, translated back in King Harry's day into simple English by Tyndale and Coverdale, then revised by the scholars in Calvin's Geneva; and for half a century it had been the beloved guide to every Protestant Englishman. It even had illustrations. True, this very year, on the king's orders, a new translation had been produced, less Calvinist in tone, but also less homely. Though following the beloved Geneva Bible, this new King James, or Authorized version contained sonorous, Latinate phrases which could not please simple Puritans. Like most true Protestants, Martha did not intend to use it.

"Swear."

She had needed patience with Cuthbert. Her grandmother had said he was damned; but she had never given up hope. And gradually, it seemed, her prayers were answered. He had married a sensible girl, not ungodly. At first, though they lived in the next street, her grandmother would not see them; but after a daughter had been born, she had persuaded the old woman to visit them. And what joy it had given her when, after his first son was born, Cuthbert and his wife had asked her to choose his name. She had chosen from the Bible. "Call him Gideon. For he was a warrior for the Lord."

But today was even more special: the culmination of years of patient prayer. It was also a trial that, gentle as she was, she knew she must not shirk.

That cursed theatre. Despite her prayers, after all these years Cuthbert was still being led astray. She had used to blame his friend Meredith, that frequenter of women. But partly also, she now realized, she should blame the playwright Shakespeare. For, however he did it, he appeared to have cast a magic spell over the people of London. *Macbeth*, *Othello*, *Hamlet* – the crowds went to the Globe by the thousand, and poor Cuthbert followed, foolish as the rest. "All London goes," he once protested. "Not all," she had corrected. "And the playhouse is still an abomination unto the Lord." Shakespeare, she had no doubt, would have much to answer for on

Judgment Day. But Cuthbert could be saved, and today she had her chance.

Three weeks ago their grandmother had died, leaving her alone in the house where she and Cuthbert had grown up. Cuthbert's lodgings were small, his family getting larger every year; but her grandmother had been adamant: "The house is Martha's." So, when a few days before, Cuthbert and his wife had come to ask if they might not share this larger space, she had known what she must do.

"I cannot have Cuthbert in grandmother's house if he frequents the playhouse too," she told them. "It is time," she told Cuthbert gently. "I am helping you to break an evil spell."

Poor Cuthbert had thought of his family and now, taking the proffered bible, he swore; and went on his way, sorrowing, but saved. And Martha rejoiced greatly in her heart.

How well Julius learned. Sir Jacob was astonished. Though four of his children had died in infancy, three girls and two boys lived. Two of the girls were married and the elder boy had gone to Oxford at sixteen. But although the girls were inclined to be frivolous and the elder boy lazy, Sir Jacob could find no fault with Julius. He was such a willing boy. By the age of four he would cry – "No popery," or "God save the king" – so boisterously that even Sir Jacob was amused.

He delighted to take Julius out with him. The pattern was invariable. Coming up the lane by St Mary-le-Bow, they would turn right into Cheapside, as the West Cheap was now called. Dressed in a cloak and tunic of sombre hue, with stockings to match and silver buckled shoes, his neatly pointed grey beard jutting over a perfectly starched white ruff, his hat sporting only a single feather, walking a little stiffly but very erect and carrying a silver-topped stick, Sir Jacob Ducket always looked exactly what he was, a Protestant gentleman; and how proudly Julius, now eight years old and dressed in breeches and tunic with a big, floppy lace collar, would walk by his side and receive the bows of the men they passed. Their first port of call, a hundred yards down Cheapside, was always the Mercers' Hall.

The world of the London guilds was more splendid than ever. The greatest of them, including the Mercers, had acquired not only corporate coats of arms but their own ceremonial liveries, and were known as the livery companies. Like others during the Tudor period, the Mercers, still using the old site where Thomas Becket's family house had been, had built a sumptuous banqueting hall, with huge oak-beamed ceilings, and much gilt. "We've always been mercers," his father would remind him. "So was Dick Whittington. And Thomas Becket's father, too, they say." So it was clear to the boy that the Mercers, even more than the other livery companies, must be very close to God.

But their real destination, past Cheapside and the Poultry, and a little way up Cornhill, was the place Julius loved. It lay on the gentle slope of the city's eastern hill, just below the huge site where, twelve centuries before, the vanished Roman forum once had stood. Built in Elizabeth's reign by Sir Thomas Gresham – a mercer, of course – it was a great, rectangular paved courtyard surrounded by open vaulted arches with chambers above, all of brick and stone, in a Renaissance style.

It was called the Royal Exchange. And there, at the start of the Stuart age, Sir Jacob Ducket undertook ventures of which his ancestors could never even have dreamed.

All through the Middle Ages, the huge fleets of the German Hanseatic towns had dominated the northern seas, and the mighty market of Antwerp in Flanders had been the hub of all northern Europe's trade. But during the last sixty years great changes had taken place. Newly assertive English merchant shipping had made such inroads on the Hansa monopoly that the old London Steelyard of the Hansa men had finally been closed; and as the Reformation led Protestant Antwerp into a ruinous war with its Catholic Habsburg overlord, London had grabbed a chunk of the Flanders trade for itself. The new Royal Exchange, where the merchants of London met, was, appropriately, a copy of the great meeting place, or *bourse* of Antwerp.

But the real change was more profound. Sir Jacob's ancestors the Bulls, proud members of the Staple, had exported wool; gradually cloth was added. Silver Ducket had exported more cloth than wool. But these ancient trades were mature and gradually declining. "The increase must come from elsewhere," Silver Ducket had predicted. It was a group of bold

Elizabethan entrepreneurs, mostly mercers, who were at the heart of it: the Merchant Adventurers they called themselves. As the buccaneers like Francis Drake opened up new markets, they hastened to convert them into settled lines of trade. Voyages and convoys were financed; trade charters and treaties sought. Logic swiftly led to the forming of particular groups to develop each new market, but since their business involved large investments in shipping, the risks needed to be shared widely. And as the enterprise was not just a single voyage, but the carrying on of a long-term trade, a more permanent form of business agreement had to be found. Just as Shakespeare and his friends had decided to share the costs of building the Globe and divide the profits year by year, so the adventurous merchants of London were making similar arrangements on a grander scale. Thus, in London, the joint stock company was born.

The Levant Company, the Muscovy Company, the Guinea Company, the East India Company – at the Royal Exchange, young Julius became familiar with every one. Sir Jacob was a Merchant Adventurer with deep pockets and had shares in them all. He would tell little Julius about them, or sometimes read to the boy from the thrilling pages of Hakluyt's *Voyages*. But one day at the Royal Exchange, when his father asked him which of these great ventures he liked the best, Julius enthusiastically exclaimed:

"The Virginia Company."

"The Virginia Company?" Sir Jacob was surprised. When Sir Walter Raleigh had named the great American territory, there had been nothing there except some Indians. Attempts at a trading post had foundered. But in the last few years, believing in the potential of the territory, the Virginia Company had sent out settlers to try again in the huge American wastes, and a rather uncertain bridgehead, called Jamestown, had been established by Captain John Smith. "Why Virginia?" Sir Jacob asked.

How could the boy explain? Was it some instinct carried down from his Saxon Bull ancestors who had founded just such a trading post and settlement on the banks of the Thames a thousand years before? Was it the romantic lure of this huge, undiscovered continent that had sparked his enthusiasm? Perhaps both. But, not knowing how to put his feelings into words, and remembering things he had heard his father say, he answered instead: "Because it will be like Ulster."

Sir Jacob gazed down in delight, for this was exactly what it was meant to be. The plantation of Ulster, in the northern part of Ireland, was a source of pride for Sir Jacob. In this land of wild papists – "little better than animals" – King James had decided to make a great colony of English and Scottish settlers. Land had been offered on easy terms and an agreement made with the London guilds, who put up a huge investment to stock the farmsteads and rebuild the whole city of Derry in return for future rents and profits. The Mercers alone were contributing over two thousand pounds. As for Virginia, wasn't the parallel clear? Weren't the wild papists of Ireland and the heathen Indians of America very similar? Of course they were. The king and Sir Jacob were quite explicit: "Virginia shall be the Ulster of America."

Curious, he questioned the boy further. What did the settlement mean? Did it mean order? Julius nodded: "So that things work." And was it done for profit alone? Julius frowned, "I think it's a place for good Protestants," he said. Did he think, then, that he could serve God, here in the Royal Exchange as well as in the church? At which, after a little thought, the boy smiled happily. "Why yes, father. For didn't God choose us?"

And Sir Jacob was well pleased.

It was a month later that Julius found the sea chest.

It was lying in a corner of the big cellar under his father's house, behind some bales of cloth – a dark old chest crossed by a fretwork of brass bands which had long since grown black, and secured by three great padlocks. He assumed it was old.

Not that this was unusual. If the Royal Exchange represented the adventure of the new, the ancient world was still comfortably all around him. In his own home, there were the heavy four-poster beds from King Harry's reign; a Caxton edition of Chaucer, printed soon after the Wars of the Roses; Silver Ducket's monastic plate, older still. Why, even the oak panelling and the oak ceiling with its ribs and bosses, though installed but ten years ago, seemed to wear the patina of a solid, smoky age. And it was the same at Bocton. Though the façade of the old ragstone house had been remodelled in

Tudor times with a more regular double row of mullioned windows, the estate peasantry still came to pay their feudal fines in the courtroom, the black old cauldrons in the kitchen had been in use since Plantagenet times, and the deer in the park's great silence moved with a grace as ancient as the woods.

But the sea chest looked so mysterious, he asked his father what it was; only to be astonished by the reply.

"It's a pirate's treasure."

A real pirate: more exciting still, a blackamoor. He listened enthralled as his father told of the strange seafarer who had left the treasure in his keeping. "He went away. They say he kidnapped a girl from the Globe, but nobody knows. He's never been seen again. Some say he went to America, others that he's in the southern seas." He smiled. "If he ever returns, I dare say it'll be the three tides for him." Everyone knew what the punishment for pirates was. They were chained to a stake at low tide, downstream from the Tower at Wapping, and left there until the high tide had covered them over three times – a fittingly watery fate.

The role of the old buccaneers had gone. The companies wanted settled trade. They were not even needed in England's defence since King James had now made peace with Spain. The Puritans might dislike any hint of friendship with the Catholic enemy, but the fact was that England could not afford costly wars, and most men knew it. Buccaneers were no longer needed, therefore, to prey upon enemy ships. Men like Black Barnikel belonged in chains.

But Julius could not help being fascinated. In his mind's eye, already, Black Barnikel had become an ogre, huge as a giant in a pageant, with furious whiskers, eyes like fireballs . . . And he might have started to day-dream if his father's voice had not called him back.

"And now, Julius, I want you to learn one very important lesson from this chest." Julius listened obediently. "Consider," Sir Jacob continued, "if this treasure belonged to the king, would I guard it with my life?"

"Of course, father."

"But it was entrusted to me by a pirate who deserves, I expect, to be hanged. Should I look after it therefore?" The boy hesitated. "Yes Julius," his father admonished. "And why?" He paused solemnly. "Because I gave my word. And your word must be sacred, Julius. Never forget."

And Julius never did.

Secretly, though, he wondered what had become of the pirate.

1613

At the end of June 1613 two wonders occurred: first, the Globe Theatre burned to the ground. It happened during a performance of Shakespeare's *Henry VIII*: a cannon let off on stage sent sparks into the thatched roof and set the whole theatre on fire. Cuthbert, who had kept his word and not seen a play in two years, looked sad; but, seeing this was clearly a judgment from God, Martha felt a lightening of the heart.

And secondly, Martha married. Poor John Dogget, Cuthbert's friend with the boatyard, had suddenly lost his wife. With five young children, the fellow was distracted. "He needs a wife," Cuthbert told her; "a Christian woman to look after those children." Hardly knowing what to think, she had agreed to meet the family and found Dogget a hard-working, good-hearted fellow, but overwhelmed with cares, and his children living in disorder. "They love one another, but they scarcely know the scriptures," she remarked to Cuthbert. "You could save them. It would be a Christian duty," he urged. And, touched that he should be so thoughtful of others, she agreed, if Dogget wished, to consider it.

For several days she had hesitated. Southwark held no appeal for her; but she could not deny that the Dogget's need was great, and so, putting her own desires quietly aside, she went to see the boatbuilder.

"You must teach me how to be a wife," she said sweetly, and, for the first time she saw him smile.

"I will," he promised gratefully.

"There will have to be some changes," she gently suggested.

"Of course," the harassed father replied. "Anything you want."

* * *

1615

Early one afternoon, in October 1615, two men prepared for an encounter. Neither man wished to meet the other. One was Sir Jacob Ducket. The man who came to meet him, aged about forty and wearing a dark robe and little white ruff, was in holy orders. Yet there was a certain elegance about him. When he reached the gateway to Sir Jacob's house he paused. Then he sighed and went in.

Edmund Meredith was past his best. Fifteen years of his life had elapsed since the disaster of his play; but what had he to show for them? Three more plays that no one would put on. It was all the more galling because the theatre was more fashionable than ever. King James himself had become patron of the players at the Globe, which had been splendidly rebuilt after the fire. Instead of retiring, Shakespeare had gone from strength to strength. And when he had once complained to the Burbages that Shakespeare had stolen his blackamoor idea for his own *Othello*, they had cruelly reminded him: "There have been a dozen *Macbeths* too, but Shakespeare's is the one people want to see." He still frequented the theatre, but had fewer friends there now; even the Flemings had grown distant. And yet, it was thanks to the Flemings that he had acquired what little fame he had. Or rather, thanks to Jane.

What had become of her? Even her parents had decided she must have been murdered, but some instinct told him she was alive; and because her disappearance coincided in his mind with Black Barnikel's visit, Meredith was the source of the rumour of her kidnap which still vaguely lingered on.

Her real importance though, was for his own reputation. Perhaps he had not much else to think about; or perhaps it began when a fashionable lady (as she always did when she had run out of conversation) remarked, "I believe, Master Meredith, you have some secret sorrow, a lady no doubt"; but within two years of Jane's disappearance, he had begun to grow melancholic at the thought of her, kept her memory about him as a lover keeps a painted miniature, and acquired a reputation as a gallant wit who had lost a great love. He composed some clever yet passionate verses that were widely circulated. The best known began:

Since she I loved was taken away.

Its success had led directly to three brief but fashionably flattering affairs.

But it was no good. As the years passed, there was a new, mercenary hardness about the court. His Elizabethan gallantry was not enough. Women were becoming impatient with him.

"If only Jane had been at my side," he would sometimes sigh. "Who knows what I might have achieved." Indeed, he had taken to thinking of marriage lately. "But I haven't the income." He did not know what to do with himself. And so he had taken holy orders.

This was not as strange as it seemed. Though the Church was not a normal career for a gentleman, several fashionable men, disappointed at court or tiring of the world, had entered it recently; and it was one of these in particular, who had impressed him.

No one could deny that John Donne had made a figure in the world. A gentleman by birth, with a family connected to the great Sir Thomas More, his brilliant poetry and love affairs made him a gallant after Meredith's heart, and the two had often met in London. Donne had also become a favourite of the king; but, probably wisely, King James had said he would only help Donne if he took orders. Donne was eager, therefore, to see others follow where he had been forced.

"You could go far," Donne said, "if you can preach a good sermon." Not only go far, but acquire an audience, even a fashionable one: Edmund pondered this advice, and saw an inviting prospect. It was almost like the theatre.

"I think," he concluded after a week or two, "that perhaps I feel the call." And so he was ordained.

Next, he had to find a living. Here again, Donne offered to help.

"There is one parish vacant. I have spoken to the king, who has spoken to the Bishop of London. You have only to recommend yourself to the vestrymen and, so long as they like you, the living will be yours." He had smiled encouragingly. "You'll hardly find a better position. The leading vestryman is a large shareholder in the Virginia Company. So good luck."

There was only one problem. The vestryman in question was Sir Jacob Ducket.

* * *

Julius watched curiously as Meredith nervously entered the big panelled parlour where the vestrymen sat. His father, thinking it would be good training, had allowed him to stay and observe this exercise of the family's responsibilities.

The old medieval order of London, like the city itself, still preserved its ancient shape. Under their chosen mayor, the aldermen still ruled, one for each of the two dozen wards. Each ward had its own council; and below that, each parish its vestry of the principal parishioners – who effectively chose themselves – and who were responsible for the good order and welfare of their community. They also, in this parish, were accustomed to give the Bishop of London their views upon who should be their vicar. Privately, given his Calvinist leanings, Sir Jacob would have dispensed with the bishop entirely. But since the king wanted bishops, and he was loyal to the king, he considered this the end of the matter. The vestry of St Lawrence Silversleeves consisted of just three men: Sir Jacob, alderman; a draper who was on the ward council; and an elderly gentleman who, very obligingly, had not spoken in three years.

The parish might be small but, thanks to a new endowment given by Silver Ducket fifty years before, it was now a rich little living, not to be bestowed lightly. It was only because of the request of the bishop and a word from the court that Sir Jacob was seeing Meredith, of whom he strongly disapproved; and it was his intention to make short work of him. Dispensing with all courtesies therefore, as soon as Edmund was standing before them, he began:

"Are you still writing plays, Master Meredith?"

"No, Sir Jacob. Not for many years."

"Verse?"

"Some religious meditations. For myself only."

"But no doubt," Sir Jacob's smile was so terse that it might have been a bite, "you keep a mistress."

"No, Sir Jacob." Edmund by now was pale.

"Come, sir," Ducket snapped, "we know what kind of man you are."

"You mistake me," Edmund protested, shaking a little.

"Oh. What, then, has led you to take holy orders?"

Now, thoroughly rattled at seeing his only chance of preferment slipping through his fingers like mercury, Edmund, casting about desperately for something to say, accidentally blurted out the truth: "Because I saw no other way to turn."

It was one of those rare occasions when the truth sounded better than it really was.

From the gentleman on Sir Jacob's right there came a faint and unexpected murmur: "Repentance." The draper, also, was nodding approval. Ducket saw that he had gone too far. He collected himself.

"The question we ask," he said more mildly, but with a quick, admonishing look at his colleagues, "is whether this reformation is sincere."

But Meredith had had a chance to collect himself too. Pausing for a moment, therefore, to look down thoughtfully at the floor, he then raised his head and, gazing soberly at the three men, addressed them very quietly.

"My grandfather, Sir Jacob, was a gentleman at the court of King Henry. My father followed him; and I have never heard it said that my condition was other than gentle too. Even if my word will not suffice you, therefore, I ask you plainly, upon what possible grounds would I take holy orders if not from conviction?"

It was perfect. It was unanswerable. Gently chiding the alderman for calling him a knave, Meredith had put down an ace. For why else, indeed, would any fashionable gentleman choose so humble an occupation? It would have made no sense. Realizing he had played his hand badly, Sir Jacob hesitated. And it was just then, in the little pause which followed, that Julius spoke.

Innocently he asked, from his stool by the fireplace: "Is it true, sir, that the king himself has spoken for you?"

There was silence; then Edmund, as surprised as anyone at the intervention, turned to the boy and, with a most charming and entirely natural smile, replied:

"I rather think he has."

It was over. The draper and the old gentleman were beaming. Sir Jacob was beaten and wise enough to know it at once. Could he really now refuse this courteous penitent supported by the king to whom he himself had sworn undying loyalty? "It seems, Master Meredith," he remarked with the best grace he could, "that you have won us over. But do not forget," he added, as the other two nodded firmly, "that we expect a good sermon."

And, having saved his skin, Edmund was left to reflect that, quite possibly for the rest of his life, he must preach, each Sunday, to Sir Jacob, and that his only real friend was a twelve-year-old boy.

If only, he told himself, Jane had not departed . . .

The Mercers Hall was crowded and buzzing with excitement the following spring. Young Julius, brought there by his father, looked about eagerly. It was to be the first public appearance of the new sensation. Outside in Cheapside a great throng had gathered, hoping to catch a glimpse – and no wonder. Few Londoners had ever seen such a thing before.

The buzz rose. A man had entered at the far end of the hall: solid and handsome, he looked like a provincial merchant. "Rolfe," his father whispered. But immediately afterwards the whole hall fell silent as she entered.

Julius felt a flash of disappointment. She was not at all what he expected.

She was dressed almost like a boy, in a velvet tunic with a big lace collar and cuffs, and wore a plain hat with a stiff brim, from which her dark hair hung in ringlets. In her hand she carried a fan made of ostrich feathers. She walked very upright, taking small steps. And except for the tawny brown skin of her face, which had in any case been touched with rouge, you would never have known she was Indian at all. Her name was Pocahontas.

At least, that is the name of her tribe in Virginia, by which history has chosen to call her. Amongst her own people she was known as Mataoka. When she was baptized a Christian, she acquired the name Rebecca; and since she was truly an Indian princess, the Londoners called her the Lady Rebecca. Indeed, King James himself, so mindful was he of royal status, had expressed some doubt that a princess, even of wild savages, should have married a mere commoner from England. The Indian princess who befriended the settlers had married Captain Rolfe just three years before, and strictly speaking, therefore, it was a plain Mrs Rolfe who was now the first American to visit England.

All London had now heard the romantic story of how, when Captain Smith of Jamestown had been captured by her tribe and almost executed by having his brains dashed out, this Indian girl, only a child, had offered her own head to save his life. There had been no romance with Smith; she was too young. But the ensuing friendship with the settlers had led her to Rolfe, and to be welcomed in England as a heroine.

But she hardly looked like one to Julius. As she moved round the room, speaking a few words here and there, it was hard to tell if her quiet grace were shy or haughty. The organizers were determined that everyone important should get a look at her, but suddenly, bored by the merchants, she came straight towards Julius. A moment later he found a tiny hand outstretched and a pair of almond-shaped brown eyes staring at him with a directness he had never encountered before.

She was smaller, younger-looking than he had realized. He knew she was over twenty, yet she could have been fifteen. And, very aware of the soft down just appearing for the first time on his own upper lip, he blushed. At which the Indian princess burst out laughing, and moved on.

Apart from meeting Julius, the rest of her appearance was as carefully stage-managed as a play. Having completed her tour of the room she was led out, followed by all the company. Outside in the street a platoon of servants, wearing the Mercers' livery, raised her on an open chair, carried on their shoulders so that the crowd could see her, and started to progress westwards along Cheapside, while she waved to them, looking very much the princess. By the time she passed St Mary-le-Bow more than five hundred people were following. And then suddenly she was gone: the chair abruptly lowered, she stepped into the waiting closed carriage at the corner of Honey Lane, the carriage rattled away and a second later vanished up Milk Street. It was so neatly done that the attention of the crowd was left, as it were, in midair, looking for something to which to attach itself. Exactly on cue, a carrying but mellifluous voice was heard from a platform in front of St Mary-le-Bow, causing the crowd to turn. "Behold, the handmaid of the Lord! Today, dearly beloved, we have seen a sign."

It was Meredith. And he was going to preach.

In fact, the Virginia Company was in trouble and the settlement was, so far, a disaster. Only a few shiploads of settlers had gone out; there were rumours of harsh conditions, Indian attacks, starvation; and the company was making a loss. To raise fresh funds, it had even run a national lottery. But the company needed a boost. So, whether the story of Pocahontas and Captain Smith were strictly true, or whether Smith and the Virginia Company had shrewdly invented it, the visit of this friendly, Christianized Indian princess and her English husband was a godsend that Sir Jacob and his friends were using for maximum effect.

The practice of paying a preacher to promote a good cause was common enough; the Virginia Company often employed chaplains. But today, with a crowd of five hundred before him Meredith had the big opportunity for which he had earnestly begged Sir Jacob; and he did not waste it.

The message he had prepared was twofold. The first part, the introduction, concerned Pocahontas; this was to intrigue the crowd. The second, the real purpose of the sermon, was an encouragement to settle in Virginia. He did not try to persuade them it was rich; he assumed they knew it was, and he deployed his several biblical texts accordingly. Finally, rising to a passionate climax, he concluded:

"Come then, and take possession of thy bride, Virginia, thy new-found land."

It was exactly the kind of sermon the Virginia Company favoured. The instant the peroration – which had transfixed the listeners – came to an end, company servants were moving swiftly through the crowds with sheafs of handbills informing prospective settlers or investors how to apply at the company headquarters in Philpot Lane.

Julius, standing with his father, heard it all. He could see that Sir Jacob was highly satisfied, and he was glad, because he liked Meredith. After they had congratulated him, and his father had to go elsewhere on business, he felt too excited to return home directly.

Sir Jacob was still in an excellent temper when Julius returned home; and he smiled indulgently as his son approached him with a piece of news.

"Do you know, father, I saw the strangest thing."

Julius had seen little of Martha Carpenter since she left the parish to marry Dogget. Occasionally she would come to visit her brother and his family, but that was all. As for her new family in Southwark, Julius knew nothing about them. So he had been curious when he saw the little group in Watling Street.

They, too, had come to see Pocahontas and, though Martha distrusted Meredith for once writing plays, they had stayed for the sermon. There was Dogget, five children, the eldest a year or two older than Julius, and an infant that was clearly Martha's. Seeing that Martha recognized him, he went over politely to speak to her; and it was then that he made the discovery.

"The boatbuilder and two of his children have a white flash in their hair, father, just like us. But the strangest thing is their hands. Dogget and one of the children have a sort of webbing, between their fingers." And then he stopped abruptly, for the change in his father was terrible to behold.

For a second, Sir Jacob looked as if he had been hit, and seemed to stagger. The boy wondered if his father was having a seizure. Sir Jacob recovered himself but, still more disconcerting, he stared at Julius with apparent loathing.

"What name? Dogget?" Sir Jacob knew nothing of the humble Doggets of Southwark, nor was there any way he could think of that such people could be connected with him.

Except, of course, for the foundling. Sir Jacob felt a cold wave of fear within him. The orphan; the gutter child. As he stared with loathing, it was not his son that he saw, but a horrifying vision – as though the ground under his feet had opened up to reveal a whole world of subterranean cellars, pits and passages, the dark corrupted ventricles of his own ancestry from which who knew what horrors might worm their way up into daylight to confront him. And no wonder then, forgetting the boy, that he muttered aloud: "The curse."

Julius stared. What curse? What did his father mean?

But all Sir Jacob said, with a terrible force, was: "Do not go near those people. They are all accursed."

Julius stared at his father. "Do you mean the Doggets, father, or Martha Carpenter's family as well?"

And because Sir Jacob, himself, was afraid of the reason, he answered: "All of them." He spoke with such finality that Julius did not dare ask any further questions.

The very next day, Sir Jacob began to make secret enquiries about the Southwark family.

Though the incident puzzled Julius, all thought of it was driven out of his head the following week by an event that brought him huge joy. It happened one morning, as he and his father were riding out of the city together to inspect the venture which, of all Sir Jacob's many investments, was his proudest.

If people were determined to find fault with old London, then they would mention the lack of decent drinking water.

There was the Thames of course. But by the time the butchers had thrown their offal in, the tanners washed their hides, brewers, dyers and others tipped in their excess fluids and to this had been added the natural effluvium of a city of two hundred thousand bodies, the tidal river was less than sweet tasting. The Walbrook had practically vanished under houses; the Fleet stank. True, the old conduit from Whittington's day still functioned and had been added to; but the supply was inadequate and even this, carried in pairs of pails hanging from yokes on their shoulders, had to be taken from house to house by water carriers whose cry, "Water, buy fresh water," echoed every day in the streets.

But now all this was to be changed, and thanks to a single, remarkable man: Sir Hugh Myddelton.

An aristocrat, like Whittington and Gresham before him, from a prominent Welsh family, Sir Hugh Myddelton had made a large fortune in the Goldsmiths Company. He was also a man of boldness and vision. When he had offered to build the city a new water supply, the mayor and aldermen had been more than grateful, and Sir Jacob Ducket had been delighted to purchase a share in the enterprise.

The New River Company, as it was called, was a prodigious undertaking. Expertly surveyed by Myddelton himself, a canal was constructed to bring water from fresh springs some twenty miles to the north. Above the city was a reservoir, and inside the city walls the fresh water could be tapped directly into individual houses. Nothing like it had been seen in England before. So great had been the cost and difficulty of the venture that the king himself had stepped in, purchasing half the shares, and granting the company a monopoly when lesser rivals threatened to spring up. "You need a monopoly," Sir Jacob had explained to Julius, "to make these huge investments possible."

Nothing gave Sir Jacob more pleasure than to ride out of London with Julius and follow the course of this pet project up to the reservoir, from which there was a view of the distant city. They had just set out when they were detained by a cheerful cry. "Father! They told me I'd find you this way." And Julius turned round to see, riding towards them, a tall dark figure, who carried himself with a proud, almost contemptuous elegance. It was his elder brother Henry.

It was three years since they had seen him. From Oxford, instead of returning to London, he had gone to Italy with a friend, studied there a year and spent another in Paris. In that time, he had changed from a sallow student to a man. Dressed in black, with the same silver flash in his hair, you could see at once that he was his father's son. But as he joined them now, and the two men rode along the canal, exchanging news of London, Paris and the French and English courts, it was evident from their bearing and conversation that there was a subtle difference between them. If Sir Jacob was a gentleman, young Henry was an aristocrat; if the Puritan alderman was severe, the polished traveller was hard; if the father believed in order, the son believed in dominion.

As they went along, Julius could hardly take his eyes off him, and his heart swelled with pride to think that this family could be so fine. "Are you now returned for good?" he dared to ask, at last. To his delight, Henry gave him his strange sardonic smile. "Yes, little brother," he promised. "I am."

1620

On a star-filled night in July 1620, a crowd of some seventy people stood in a semicircle by the bank of the River Thames and waited for the dawn. Some of them were nervous, some excited; but as Martha gazed across the glinting water, she felt only a great rejoicing in the glory of the Lord.

For years, godly folk in London had spoken of this enterprise. But who could ever have dreamed that she would be part of it? Who could have foreseen the extraordinary change in the Dogget family? Or the unexpected attitude of the boy. Or, most wonderful of all, the recent but mystifying circumstances that had brought the family to the water's edge this morning. She looked up at her husband and smiled. But John Dogget did not smile.

John Dogget loved his wife. When Jane Fleming had disappeared from the Globe twenty years before, Dogget had been deeply upset, but time had passed, and two years later he had married a lively girl, a waterman's daughter, and had known great happiness until her sudden death. The months that followed, however, had been so miserable that when he married Martha he had scarcely known what he was doing.

He would never forget how he had brought her home on their wedding day. He had tried to prepare the house by the boatyard, but the family had always lived in cheerful chaos, and God knew what she had felt. Nor did their wedding night, though the essentials were duly accomplished, bring her, he suspected, much joy. He went to his work the next morning in a thoughtful and uncertain mood. But returned that evening to a transformation. The house was clean. The children's clothes had been washed. On the table stood a large pie and a bowl of apples stewed with cloves; and from the grate there came the aroma of freshly cooked oatcakes. The family had not eaten so well in a year. That night, overcome with gratitude, he made love to her with tenderness and passion.

How quietly she had won the children over too. She never forced them to acknowledge her, just went about her work, but they quickly noticed that their home smelled fresh instead of stale, their clothes were mended, the larder stocked; an air of pleasant calm descended upon the house. Nor did she ever ask for help; but it was not long before the eight-year-old girl wanted to cook with her, and a few days later the oldest boy, seeing Martha sweeping out the yard, took the broom from her and said: "I'll do it." The following week, as they were working on a boat, he remarked to his father: "She's good."

She still puzzled him. The Doggets were a merry family by nature: hardly a day went by without them finding something funny. But when they were laughing, he noticed that Martha would sit, quietly smiling, because she saw they were happy, but not laughing herself. He began to wonder whether she had seen the joke. And did she really like their sexual life? Certainly she became aroused, but if she always gently welcomed his advances, he couldn't help noticing that she never took the initiative herself. Perhaps she felt it was ungodly. But when she asked him, after three months – "Am I a good wife?" – and he had answered, with real feeling – "None better" – she seemed so pleased that to introduce any hint of doubt seemed unkind.

And in due course they had a child.

The change had come so slowly that for a time he hardly noticed, but gradually he came to understand that something had happened to his family. Even in rowdy Southwark, the better sort of stallkeepers now gave him and his children a polite smile – something they had certainly never done before. Still more startling was the day when the parish beadle, speaking of some noisy drunkards, apologized to him for the disturbance to "godly people like yourselves". But the true turning point had come one day when, pointing to a handsome young waterman and remarking to his ten-year-old daughter, "There's a husband for you," the girl had seriously replied: "Oh no, father, I want to marry a respectable man." He supposed she was right. But something died in him that day.

He discovered something else, too. "I didn't marry a woman," he would wryly say. "I married a congregation." It was not just the prayer meetings, though she went to those; but it seemed that there was an entire network of similar-minded people stretching across all the city wards and far beyond. It was almost like a huge guild to which she could turn for help. It came into play most strikingly on the one occasion when they quarrelled.

It was over the eldest boy. Though brought up to help in the boatyards, he showed no desire to follow his father's trade. The slow work with his hands made him restless, and he announced that he wanted to go to sea as a fisherman. Dogget, knowing that the boatyard was a solid little business, expected Martha to support him; but after a day of prayer, she stated: "You should let him go. Our work is worship," she reminded him. "So if a man hates his work, how can he worship God?"

"He should obey his father," Dogget protested.

"God is his father," she gently corrected. "Not you."

He was so furious, he did not speak to her for days.

Yet a week later, he found himself with Martha at Billingsgate, being ushered into the large, red-bearded presence of no less a personage than the head of the Barnikel family, one of the most prominent men in the Fishmongers Company, who told him: "Found a good berth for your boy. Know the ship's master well." And before Dogget could stammer a reply: "Glad to help. Your wife's good name goes before her."

Now, as the sky grew lighter, those same words seemed to echo in his brain. His wife's good name. But for that accursed good name, none of this would have happened. Yet what could he do? The wherry was coming to take them. And across the water, moored in the stream just below Wapping, he could see the trap into which he was being led.

That stout, three-masted ship called the *Mayflower*.

By noon, they had passed the Medway.

The *Mayflower* was a good little ship: a London vessel, a hundred and eighty tons, a quarter owned by Captain Jones who sailed her – another sign that she was sound. Frequently chartered by London merchants, she had spent much of her time shipping wine in the Mediterranean. Seaworthy, well stocked and with ample space, she was fully prepared to carry her passengers to the New World.

Martha had been approached in the past by agents of the Virginia Company, asking if she and her family would like to settle there. But that was nothing: so had half London. And she had gently pointed out to the men who approached her that there was little point in crossing the Atlantic only to find King James's Church when she got to the other side. But this was different. When she had heard about the little Puritan group who planned to found their own community, not in Virginia, but in the wilderness of America's northern seaboard, she had been fascinated. And try as she might to overcome it, she could not help it: she had felt the pain of envy in her heart. She even mentioned her longing to Dogget. But he had only laughed.

Until help had come from an unexpected quarter. The eldest boy, arriving home from a fishing trip, calmly announced: "Father, there's a new venture going far north of Virginia, to the Massachusetts colony. It's organized by the Merchant Adventurers. We could do well there. Barnikel the Fishmonger thinks so too." And when his father asked him why, he replied with a single word: "Cod."

This, of course, made the whole venture possible. King James, enquiring how the settlers meant to live, and being told they meant to fish, had wryly remarked; "Like the Apostles," but he too knew that the settlement lay near some of the richest fishing grounds in the world. "It's a risk of course," the boy conceded. "But you build boats and I fish." But even so, Dogget had not been enthusiastic.

The mysterious offer came the following day. Though Dogget suspected otherwise, Martha had done nothing to invite it. She was as much in the dark as he, though it was clear that the offer must come from a person, or persons in the Puritan community. Martha even wondered if it might come from Barnikel himself. A message arrived stating that if they wished to join the expedition, a well-wisher was prepared to pay Dogget a handsome sum for the boatyard – far more than it was worth – and to purchase shares in the company for them as well. As his son said to Dogget, in front of the other children: "Where else, father, could you get money for the family like that?" And that was the trouble. He couldn't. A week later, he had reluctantly given in.

The voyage of the *Mayflower* is well recorded. Making her way down the wide Thames Estuary, the little ship proceeded eastward, the long coast of Kent on her right. Then she turned south, rounding the tip of Kent and passing through the Straits of Dover into the English Channel. At Southampton, halfway along England's southern coast, the *Mayflower* was to rendezvous with a sister pilgrim ship, the *Speedwell*. The *Mayflower* reached Southampton just before the end of the month.

The *Speedwell* was a very small ship, only sixty tons. As she came up Southampton Water, she seemed to be low in the water and to move in a curious, ungainly manner. Dogget, staring at her, muttered: "She's overmasted." And as she drew close, an embarrassed silence descended upon the watchers, broken at last by the eldest boy. "That vessel's not seaworthy."

She wasn't. Within an hour they heard: "She needs a refit before she can sail on." Nor was this all. Dogget and his son went aboard her at once only to return, shaking their heads. "They've hardly any supplies."

It was well into August before they finally left Southampton. The weather was fine, however, and the mood was lighter. They passed the sandy coast below the New Forest, then the long cliffs and coves of Dorset. By dawn the next day they were off the coast of Devon when Martha heard a shout.

"They're pulling in." The *Speedwell* had sprung a leak.

At last the *Speedwell* was declared seaworthy again and the two ships set sail. For five days, in a moderate swell, they ploughed slowly westwards. On the sixth day, a hundred leagues out, gazing back at the *Speedwell*, Martha noticed that it seemed lower in the water, and that it was falling behind. An hour later, the two ships turned back.

"The *Speedwell* can't go on. She's rotten," Captain Jones told the assembled passengers, when they had returned to the westerly port of Plymouth. "The *Mayflower* can only take about a hundred of you. So twenty must stay behind."

In the silence that followed, having held his peace for over six weeks, John Dogget spoke.

"We'll stay," he said. His children nodded, even the eldest boy. "We've had enough of you," Dogget said. And Martha could not blame them. Others too now admitted that they would sooner not proceed. "They're not going to make it," the eldest boy confided to her.

And so it was, in the month of September, in the year of Our Lord 1620, that the pilgrim fathers finally set sail in the *Mayflower* from the port of Plymouth, but without the family of Dogget, who returned to London.

On a bright morning in early October, Sir Jacob Ducket was just returning to his house when he encountered Julius. Seeing his younger son give him a slightly uncertain look, he enquired what was on his mind. After a moment's hesitation, Julius told him.

"You remember those people, father, with the funny hands." Sir Jacob frowned. "Well," the boy went on, "I've just seen them again, with Carpenter. I think they've come to live with him."

This came as a great blow to Sir Jacob: because earlier that year, anonymously and through a third party, he had paid them a handsome sum of money to leave. That evening, after sitting alone for some hours with a flagon of wine – a thing he never normally did – Sir Jacob Ducket suffered a stroke. Two days later, it became clear that his two sons, Henry and Julius, must take over his affairs.

It was a familiar sight in those years. Every evening, a little before sundown, she stood there on the low ridge called Wheeler's Hill, gazing eastwards.

What was she looking at? The broad fields below; the winding river? On a clear day you could see the Atlantic, but was she looking for the sea? No one asked. The Widow Wheeler kept her thoughts to herself.

The Wheeler spread was typical of Virginia then – a few hundred acres, a yeoman's farm. Wheeler himself had never made much of it, but his widow had. She ran everything herself, with sweated labour. There were two slaves; but the day of the slave was only just beginning in Virginia. Most of the labourers were indentured English men – some poor, some in debt, a few petty criminals who had ten years of labour to earn their freedom. She had a name for being fair but ruthless. But the real reason for the farm's profit was her choice of crop: for, like many others in Virginia, every yard was given to a single crop whose acres of huge green leaves flapped in the breeze like so many floppy pieces of parchment.

Tobacco. Since John Rolfe, the husband of Pocahontas, had introduced it, the burgeoning of the Virginia tobacco crop had been astounding. A few years ago, twenty thousand pounds weight had been shipped; this year – who knew? – maybe half a million.

From its shaky start, the Virginia colony was growing swiftly. There were several thousand settlers now, taking more land every year. Some of the larger farmers were doing so well they had started importing a few luxury goods from England. But the Widow Wheeler bought almost nothing. Perhaps she was puritanical; perhaps just mean. It was hard to guess for, it had to be confessed, few of her neighbours really knew very much about her.

They would certainly have been surprised to learn that for fifteen years, the respectable Widow Wheeler had lived with Black Barnikel the pirate.

Not, in truth, that this really described their strange, wandering, relationship. Jane herself, during those years, would have put it far more simply: "I'm his woman."

She had been his woman on that first voyage. She had had no choice. She had been his woman when, already pregnant, he had left her to have the child in an African port to which, months later, he had returned, delighted to find he had a son, and showered her with gifts. Five voyages, a dozen ports, three more children. Her years had passed in strange, exotic places, from the Caribbean to the Levant.

And how had she felt? It had been strange at first to be in his power, to know he could probably kill her. She had studied him carefully therefore. Yet she had found him surprisingly tender. Whether she wished it or no, he knew how to bring her to physical ecstasy. Did she not think of escape? He was too cunning to give her the chance. He never went near London. What should she do – abandon her children? She found she could not. Take them home with her to London? What would they, with their strange, dark skins, be there? It was when she thought of this that she guessed at Orlando Barnikel's secret rage, and it was at such times, far more even than those of physical passion, that she recognized that, in a way, she loved him.

The end had come suddenly. After the third child, a boy, she had lost two more babies. Orlando had been much away. She had not conceived for some years. But it was just after the younger boy, aged twelve, had made his first voyage with his father, that Orlando had announced: "I'm sailing to America. Come with me." When they reached Virginia, escorting her off the ship at Jamestown he had put a bag of money in her hand and announced: "It is time for you to leave me now."

She had been almost thirty. Young enough to marry and have a family in a colony like that, where settlers were often in need of wives. He had been right.

Six months later she had found Wheeler, and married. The only catch had been that he had fallen sick and there had been no children. As for Orlando, she had never seen, nor heard of him again. Recently, however, as she stood on Wheeler's Hill and gazed over the plantation, she had sometimes found her eyes wandering, on clear days, towards the blue glint of the ocean.

It was some news she gleaned from one of her own indentured labourers that had caused this change. The fellow had come from Southwark where he knew the Globe well. Having no idea who she was, he had told her that her parents had both recently died and her brother gone away to the West Country. The news had left her with a curious sense of freedom. It made no difference to anyone, she realized, what she did now. She would face no awkward questions.

All the Virginia growers knew that the tobacco plant exhausted the soil. Most plantations at this time were exhausted after seven years. It was not a huge problem, for the whole continent of America lay before the settlers. They just set up a new plantation further inland. In three years, Jane knew, Wheeler's farm would be exhausted and she would have to move. But by then, also, she would have saved a comfortable sum of money. Enough, perhaps, to do something else, she thought, as she gazed towards the sea.

Some people might find Henry proud, but Julius could only admire him for the courageous way he had assumed the leadership of the family. Sir Jacob had never recovered from his stroke: his right side was paralysed and he could not speak. He was a sad sight and some children might have wanted to hide him. But not Henry. On his orders, once a week, immaculately dressed and followed by his two sons, Sir Jacob was carried in a litter to the Royal Exchange so that people could pay their respects to him. "And to our family too," Henry told Julius. "No matter what happens, hold your head high." Henry had style.

His father's incapacity caused a change in Julius's life too. He had been expecting to go to Oxford himself that year, but within a month Henry had informed him: "Young brother, I need you. I can't do all this alone."

Henry soon left the everyday accounting and shipping arrangements to Julius. "You've a head for figures," he said. But Henry made one very shrewd move. "I am buying a parcel of land, just along the ridge from Bocton," he announced one day.

"Whatever for?" Julius demanded.

"To grow hops," came the cheerful reply. "For hopped beer. Everybody's doing it." And he turned out to be right. The

English brewers, having developed a strange darker brew of beer using imported hops, were now finding it cheaper to buy locally if only farmers would produce. A good contract was soon signed with the Bull brewery of Southwark; and in the years that followed, even when trade was poor, the Bocton hop-gardens provided a steady flow of income.

But Henry's true genius, Julius soon discovered, was in making powerful friends. It was amazing how he did it. Within weeks of his return he seemed to know everyone, not only in the city but at court as well. While Julius checked the accounts, often as not Henry would be out hunting, or dining with a great lord, or attending a court entertainment at Whitehall. At first, Julius had assumed that this was only to raise the family's social position. But then one afternoon, striding by in his hunting clothes, Henry had nonchalantly dropped a document on the table: it was a contract, for a huge consignment of silk, signed by no less a person than Buckingham, the most powerful favourite at the royal court. "Friends in the right places," Henry had murmured. "That's all you need."

Monopolies were the thing. Strictly, of course, the great trading companies were monopolies: their charters, giving them exclusive trading rights in distant regions, were probably necessary to make such great investments possible. But the ones Henry spoke of were little, pettifogging affairs. "You want to open an ale-house? You need a licence: apply to a favourite. You need gold thread? A friend of mine has the monopoly. A tiny monopoly, Julius, is still worth a fortune. And all courts do it." The court of the Stuarts, he might have added, more than most.

Yet, as he reached adulthood, it was this very quarter – the royal court – that began to give Julius cause for concern.

There was no use denying it: all was not well between the new House of Stuart and the people of England.

The character of King James did not help. Never very dignified, his old age had become embarrassing. Whether he was actually homosexual, or whether it was just a senile affection for young men, nobody quite knew. "But he actually drools over them," Henry admitted. Fortunately, his heir Charles had both dignity and irreproachable morals, so the Puritan English closed their eyes to the father and looked forward to the son.

True, there were the royal favourites. The greatest, who soon ruled all, was Buckingham, a young man of enormous charm, vapid intelligence and such astonishing good looks that King James had made him a duke. Many felt that Buckingham and his friends had too many monopolies. "Like all favourites, he's offended some of the old nobility," Henry explained. "They're out to get him if they can."

But these were the usual problems of courts and could be dealt with. The real difficulty, much more profound, came to a head less than a year after Sir Jacob's stroke.

The Parliament of 1621 had not begun in a very good temper. For a start, James had not called them in some years. True, that meant he had not asked for money; but for centuries now they had been used to regular consultations. They were feeling neglected. If some of the nobles wanted to attack the rapacious court favourites, therefore, the Commons were in the mood to take part; and no sooner were they assembled at Westminster than they found a way to remind the king who they were. Their method took the court by surprise.

"Impeachment." It was Henry who brought the news. "No Parliament has done that since the Plantagenets."

In fact, the Commons had been rather clever. They had not impeached Buckingham himself, but two corrupt lesser favourites; and the beauty of impeachment was that it was the one prosecution that the Commons and Lords could push through without the king's consent. The message was clear: it was time to deal kindly with the Parliament. But here was the trouble: the learned if eccentric King James had somehow persuaded himself that since monarchs were anointed by God, they ruled by Divine Right – which meant that their subjects must obey them because they could do no wrong. This was the law of God, he said, and it had always been so – a claim that would certainly have horrified a medieval churchman and caused any Plantagenet monarch to burst out laughing. Tudor monarchs took care to have their counsellors in Parliament to manage debates, and Elizabeth had been a master of compromise. But King James expected only obedience. The Commons wrote out a protestation.

"And he's torn it up," Henry reported, with grim amusement.

"So what will happen?" Julius anxiously demanded.

"Nothing," Henry judged. "Parliament is angry, but it knows the king is growing old. There is nothing to fear."

When Dogget and Martha had arrived back in London they waited anxiously to see whether their unknown benefactor, if he was aware of their return, would demand his money back. But, mysterious as ever, he gave no sign. The next question was: what to do? The problem was finally solved by Gideon Carpenter. His father Cuthbert had suddenly died just after they had left; he suggested therefore that he and Dogget should go into business together. They found lodgings close by and a small yard and workshop just by the top of Garlic Hill, and here they set out to repair anything that anyone brought in. Dogget missed his boats, but they were kept busy.

And so it was, on the holy days when they were compelled to attend at St Lawrence Silversleeves, that Sir Jacob would gaze across the little church at the cursed family with impotent loathing – imprisoned both by the stroke that paralysed him and the fact that, even if he could speak and demand his money back, sooner or later people would ask the reason why he had lent it to them. Julius meanwhile, seeing his father trembling with rage at the sight of them, could only conclude that Martha and her family must be very wicked indeed.

Even so, he had meant them no harm that day as he passed out of the city over the Holborn and approached the church of St Etheldreda.

In recent decades a change had taken place there. The old bishop's mansion had become the residence of the Spanish Ambassador, the church his private chapel; and the gardens next door, having belonged to a favourite of Queen Elizabeth's called Hatton, had acquired his name. Just as he reached Hatton Garden Julius saw the carriage of the Spanish Ambassador appear, and, since politeness demanded it, took off his hat and made a bow. He did so, however, with great reluctance.

The position of Stuart England in Europe was the same as in Elizabeth's day. The Continent was still split between the Catholic and Protestant camps. Catholic France was mighty, the Habsburgs of Spain and Austria still determined to reimpose the universal Church of Rome; and Protestant England a small island which could not afford a war. James had to tread carefully. Unlike Elizabeth, though, he had children. And when, recently, his German son-in-law had been turfed out of his lands by Catholic Austria, James reasoned further: "If we make friends with the Habsburgs, perhaps we can persuade them to give the boy his dominions back." Cautiously therefore, approaches had been made to the ambassador of the most Catholic kingdom of Spain.

The Londoners did not like it. The balance of power meant little to them. They did not believe in Catholic friends. "Remember Bloody Mary," they protested. "Remember Guy Fawkes."

The small group of apprentices loitering by Hatton Garden were in a jocular mood. They pointed when they saw the Spanish carriage pass. One of them laughed and made a rude sign, and then the cries came: "Spanish dog!" "Papist!" "We want no papists here."

Julius shrugged. The carriage passed by. He had thought no more about it until the next day, when Henry returned from Whitehall and announced: "The Spanish Ambassador has been insulted. The king is furious."

"But I saw it," Julius told him. "It was nothing."

"You saw it?" Henry had seized him by the arm. "Did you know them? You must tell. The king's sent word to the mayor. The culprits are to be found and severely punished."

Yet Julius hesitated. For one of the young men had been Gideon Carpenter.

It had taken Henry nearly an hour. He told Julius it was his duty, and pointed out that if it was discovered that Julius had failed to report them, the family's prospects at court would be finished for ever. And finally: "Remember, if God has chosen us to be leaders in this city, how do we repay Him if we shirk our public duty."

Henry took the news to the mayor and to the king, who thanked him warmly. The apprentices concerned were whipped with the cat o' nine tails. Such a punishment was not trivial. One of them died. Gideon lived.

From that day on, when the family came to church, Julius could feel Gideon's eyes fixed implacably upon him. Martha, for her part, confined herself to a single, sorrowful statement when she met him the day after the whipping: "This was not right." And in his heart Julius could only wish, like his father, that all of these people, Carpenters and Doggets alike, would depart the parish and even the country for ever.

But if Henry could be harsh, he had continued to work wonders for the family; and just two years after the Spanish incident he arranged another huge step in the family's social rise.

English monarchs had always rewarded their friends with titles. But the Stuarts sold them. It could be lucrative. Buckingham, in James's name, even sold one man a barony for twenty thousand pounds. But rather than inflict too many newcomers on the Lords, the Stuarts hit upon a brilliant idea.

The baronetcy. A baronet styled himself Sir, like a knight. He did not sit in the House of Lords; but his eldest son and the senior heir thereafter would inherit this title, Sir, in perpetuity. Only well-established gentlemen of large income were acceptable, but there were plenty of applicants. And Henry Ducket got one for his father. It cost twelve hundred pounds. A year later, old King James departed life and Sir Jacob followed him soon after; but, if such proof were needed of the purity of his family's blood, he died a hereditary noble. Henry was now Sir Henry.

His progress never faltered in the years that followed. The new king, Charles, had married a Catholic princess in the end, but French, which seemed less threatening. Still very young, and hating Buckingham, she was miserably lonely, but Henry had made friends with her. It proved an excellent move. In 1628, an out-of-work soldier killed Buckingham in the street. With the favourite gone, Charles and his queen came together as never before. And how warmly she spoke to him of "that kind Sir Henry Ducket".

If only the king did not quarrel with his parliaments. But Charles, like his father, believed implicitly in his Divine Right. When he demanded money, they gave him almost nothing. The young king appealed to the country gentry for a loan. "Though some of the sheriffs have got carried away," Henry admitted. "They've actually imprisoned some fellows who refused to lend." Soon Parliament presented a Petition of Right, reminding the king that, since Magna Carta, he could not imprison illegally, nor had he the right to levy taxes without their consent. Their next meeting, early in 1629, provoked a crisis. In the Commons, furious at Charles's attitude, some of the younger and more reckless members completely lost their heads, passing motions against the king by acclaim and pinning the Speaker in his chair. What, Julius wondered, would they all do next?

"And that, as it happens, is something I can tell you," Henry informed him. He smiled wryly. "The Parliament will not be called any more. The king is going to govern without it."

In the year of Our Lord 1630, Edmund Meredith had more important things on his mind than the Parliament. His pleasant, steep-gabled house in Watling Street contained himself, a housekeeper, a maid and a boy. His income was comfortable; his preaching outside the parish – he was much in demand – brought handsome extra fees. If Sir Jacob had tolerated him, Sir Henry, pleased to have a gentleman as vicar, had him to dinner once a month, which pleased him greatly. In earlier years, he had even thought of marrying, except that the presence of children, he rightly felt, might have spoilt the dignity of the household. Yet he wanted to leave.

The truth was, Meredith was getting a little bored. Success had come, but now he felt ready for more. He could still, he believed, make a larger figure in the world; and there was one, huge prize he had his eye upon. John Donne was dying. It might be a year, it might be two or three; but when he went, there would be a vacancy. As Dean of the Cathedral of St Paul's.

Eternal St Paul's. True, the fabric was in a poor state. But it was not the old stone hulk itself that mattered: it was the name. And it was the sermons.

Sermons were given inside St Paul's but by a curious tradition, reverting to early Saxon days, the greatest were given outside, at the pulpit known as St Paul's Cross, which stood in the churchyard. Wooden stands were erected for the mayor and aldermen, as if to view a tournament; huge crowds gathered in the yard. It was the most important pulpit in England.

But how could he get it? Sir Henry, who would have been glad to see his own man in such a place, had spoken to the king; but the person Meredith knew he must really impress was the new Bishop of London. And that might not be easy.

William Laud was a small, red-faced man with a moustache, a neat, grey goatee beard, and an iron will. He was also in total agreement with the king about his Church. He made his views known from the start. "Too many Presbyterians and Puritans in London. Even half the clergy are infected." It was soon clear to Edmund, if he wanted Laud's approval, what he must do.

The first step was to convince the vestry committee. Here he did not anticipate too many problems. Sir Henry and Julius were both on the committee now and they had run the parish in perfect harmony, but, to his surprise, quiet Julius seemed troubled.

"Isn't that," he asked, "like popery?"

"Not at all," Meredith assured him. "The king desires it; and I promise you the king's no papist."

As indeed, he was not. Yet here was the difficulty.

England was Protestant: but what did that mean? On the European scene, that the island kingdom was in the Protestant camp, not to be devoured by the Catholic powers. At home, that many Englishmen, especially Londoners, were Puritans. But the fact remained, her national Church, though slightly modified by good Queen Bess, was still, in its doctrines, the one established by that renegade Catholic, Henry VIII. The creed recited by all loyal Englishmen was perfectly clear:

> I believe in the Holy Catholic Church, the communion of saints, the forgiveness of sins . . .

Good Church of England men then and ever since might say they were Protestant and truly believe themselves so: but the Church of King Henry and Queen Bess was, indisputably, a reformed Catholic Church. Breakaway, schismatic, even heretic, according to Rome – but Catholic.

King Charles I of England believed in the compromise worked out under Queen Elizabeth – that the Church of Rome had fallen into evil ways, that the English Church was purified Catholicism, and that it was the Anglican bishops, nowadays, who were the true inheritors of the apostles. And the law said that every parishioner must attend Sunday service or pay a shilling fine. Few vestries in pragmatic England actually enforced this. The vestry of St Lawrence Silversleeves turned a blind eye. King Charles, however, did not think this way. He expected obedience. If his Church was perfectly reformed, then there was no reason why his people should turn their back on it. If dignified ceremony was proper – and he felt it was – then it must be observed. It was, for him, as simple as that.

Bishop Laud liked ceremony too.

One Saturday, three weeks later, Martha and her nephew Gideon were surprised to receive a visit from the beadle of the ward. They were to come to church, they were told, without fail, the following day. "Why?" they asked. By order of Sir Henry and the vestry, they were informed. Every household in the parish was being summoned. "We'll pay the fine," Martha offered.

"No fines will be accepted," the ward beadle said.

The parish of St Lawrence Silversleeves did not contain a hundred households; but even so, the press in the little church was so great the next day that most people were standing. There was an air of tense expectancy. What were they to witness? Most, looking up at the whitewashed walls, thought the place looked normal enough; but Martha, arriving as late as possible, noticed the difference at once.

"The altar," she whispered to Gideon in horror. "Look."

For decades now, the altar table at St Lawrence had been placed at the head of the little nave, in the Protestant manner. But today it was not there. Someone had moved it into the still tinier chancel, the ancient domain of the priest, withdrawn from the people. They gazed at it in astonishment. Yet even this was nothing to what came next, which was the arrival of the Reverend Edmund Meredith.

The vicar of St Lawrence Silversleeves, in deference to old King James, had long worn the traditional cope and surplice of the priest; but always so simple and sober that old Sir Jacob had never complained. Not so today. It was as though, on his way along Watling Street, Edmund had been drenched by a sudden shower of gold. Indeed, Flemings the haberdashers had sold him no less than forty pounds worth of gold thread and sequins for the making of it – the largest single order since they had supplied the costumes for Shakespeare's *Antony and Cleopatra* at the Globe. The congregation gasped. In shock, Martha and the other Puritans watched as Meredith, transformed into this popish apparition, went through the service.

In silence, they heard the lessons read. And then he rose to preach.

"I want to tell you about two sisters," he announced. "Their names are Humility and Obedience."

Then he attacked with venom. Every aspect of the Puritanism that Martha held dear was ruthlessly dealt with. Bishops, he reminded them, were their spiritual overlords: like kings they ruled by Divine Right. And then came the blow. "It is the will of the bishop that in future all congregations should attend their established church each Sunday. In this parish, this rule shall be enforced." And, staring them down, he ordered: "Hear the word of the Lord, therefore. Be humble. And obey."

They stared back at him, stunned.

It was Edmund's usual practice to stand by the church door to greet his parishioners as they left. Today he did so with the vestry committee at his side. Most of the congregation hurried out without meeting his gaze. A few glared at him.

Julius had watched them all come out, and had started to follow his brother home, when he found himself facing Gideon.

There was no question, he felt awkward in the presence of Gideon. The young man was a sober citizen these days and had become sternly religious. He had also married the previous year. But that awful whipping could never be forgotten and with Gideon's steady, brown eyes upon him now, Julius could not help reddening slightly.

"Your vestry committee authorizes such popery," he said quietly. "But tell me this, Julius Ducket: by whose authority does the vestry committee sit?" Julius, staring at him, hardly knew what to say.

"If the congregation elected the vestry," Gideon stated, "we should have godly men there and a godly minister. You sit in the vestry as though by Divine Right. You have no right. You are imposed upon us." And he turned his back and departed.

When Julius told Henry about it later, Henry was scornful. "That fellow's been whipped once. Perhaps he should be whipped again."

But Julius, upon reflection was not so sure.

As for Meredith, he was happy with his day's work. Three days later a request came from the secretary to Bishop Laud:

the bishop would be interested to see his sermon. Had he by any chance a fair copy?

Two weeks later, when he heard a knock at the door one evening, he half expected that it might be an emissary from that august personage; and so he was mildly surprised when his housekeeper entered the parlour and announced instead that there was a lady who wished to see him. He enquired the lady's name, but it meant nothing to him.

"A Mrs Wheeler."

Moments later, he was face to face with Jane.

There was no mistaking her. The well-preserved woman before him still had the youthful air of the girl he had known. Her figure was fuller and it suited her. The silk dress she wore suggested a woman of means. As he gazed at her in astonishment the memories of what had once been, and of the long years when he had dreamed about her, came flooding back, taking him by surprise, and it seemed to him that here before him was the one long-lost love of his life. And Jane, looking curiously at Meredith's still remarkably handsome face, wondered calmly to herself whether she should marry him.

She had not come to London with that intention. In fact, she had not returned with any definite plans. Her savings in Virginia meant she could live comfortably. And if, but only if, she could find a respectable man, she had thought she might marry again. For whatever else, after her roving life, she knew that she wanted one thing now: peace. Solid, respectable peace. God knows, she thought, I've earned it.

She had assumed that Meredith would either have found himself a rich wife, or possibly drifted into some vaguely theatrical occupation, but here he was, a clergyman and one of the best known preachers in London: handsome as ever, respectable, solid and, surprisingly unmarried. Did she feel a rush of the old emotion she had felt as a girl? Yes. But time had built its fortress round her heart. She surveyed him calmly.

"You are alive." He was still staring in wonderment.

"As you see."

"I always believed it to be so. You are married?"

"I am a widow, sir." She saw his anxious look. "Well provided for. My husband Wheeler had a good farm. In Virginia. There were no children."

"I see." He gazed at her, smiling now. She found that, in her middle age, she could see easily into his mind. She saw that he, too, was struck, that the idea that had come into hers had come into his too.

"It was you and I, once, who were to have married," he said quietly.

"I know." She smiled. "You did not marry either."

"I am curious about one thing," he said, after a long silence. "When you first disappeared, when it was supposed you were dead, you could not have gone immediately to Virginia, for the colony had not then begun." He looked a little awkward. "I had wondered . . . it was so sudden." He frowned. "There was a pirate . . . a blackamoor . . . " He trailed off.

And Jane hesitated. She had not intended to mention Orlando to anyone on her return. After all, why should she? No one in London knew. All she had to do now, faced with Meredith's question, was to lie. So why did she hesitate? Perhaps she wanted to test him a little.

"I ask you to keep this a secret between us," she said at last. "But if you wish to know, it is true. He abducted me." She shrugged. "I had no choice. No one knows. It was long ago."

She watched him now, curiously. She saw him look down, saw something in him wince. Then he looked thoughtful.

"No one," he murmured, almost to himself, "need ever know." Was it, Jane wondered, the thought that a blackamoor had physically possessed her, as he certainly had, that made Edmund flinch? Or was it something more?

Yet the process in the Reverend Edmund Meredith's mind was more finely balanced than that. Certainly, the thought of the Blackamoor was distasteful to him, yet also, since it was now safely past, strangely exciting. But could the Dean of St Paul's have a wife whom the world could even dream had been touched by a blackamoor? The idea filled him with horror. Thinking of John Dogget, so awkwardly in his very parish, he concluded sadly, in a low voice: "But they might suspect."

She guessed that it was over then; a few minutes later, with expressions of regard they parted.

In Watling Street, to her surprise, she met John Dogget.

* * *

It was during the long, quiet years of the 1630s that Julius Ducket had his brilliant idea. It could keep the king free of Parliament for ever.

The end of parliaments? If, to every free-born Englishman such an idea was abhorrent, to a number of people at King Charles's court, and in particular to his French wife, Henrietta Maria, such a thing was desirable and natural. Just across the English Channel, Europe's Catholic monarchs were starting to build up centralized, absolute states. They suffered no indignities from upstart parliaments. Small wonder then if Charles, believing in Divine Right, and Henrietta Maria from France, decided:

"We, too, will build a monarchy like theirs."

So far it was working. England was at peace. King Charles was managing, just, to live within his income. The parliament men had nothing to say. In 1633, Bishop Laud became Archbishop of Canterbury and embarked, nationwide upon a stern enforcement of the English, episcopal Church which, he promised, would be "thorough". Soon "Thorough" became the watchword for the king's entire regime. "The Puritans hate him, but they can always depart for America," Henry remarked. "Laud's the best friend the Massachusetts Company ever had." From 1630, when an energetic gentleman named Winthrop had gone out there, the modest puritan colony in America had been expanding rapidly.

For Julius these had been happy years. He had married a cheerful, blue-eyed girl from a similar family, and soon there were children. Henry, who had shown no desire to marry so far, and who was often at Bocton, had suggested that they occupy the big house behind Mary-le-Bow. Life in London was also agreeable. The absence of Parliament at least meant there had been no new tax demands. There was an atmosphere of progress and prosperity in the city; and outside its walls, just north of Charing Cross two aristocrats, Lord Leicester and Lord Bedford, had started to develop some of their land into large, open squares of houses, with classical façades. One development – Covent Garden – proved fashionable at once and it was to a fine house in Covent Garden that Henry shortly moved, explaining to Julius: "The city's well enough; but Covent Garden's the place for a gentleman to live nowadays."

With Henry's departure, Julius became head of the vestry; and here too he had tried to institute a more cheerful regime. Meredith had failed to become Dean of St Paul's, and with this some of his reforming zeal seemed to have waned. Though the services at St Lawrence Silversleeves were still done in Laud's high church manner, Martha and Gideon were told quietly by Julius that a monthly attendance would be sufficient. They still seethed, but at least he had to watch them less often.

There was one surprise: perhaps to console himself for failing to become dean Edmund Meredith, at the age of nearly sixty, married Matilda, a respectable spinster of thirty, a lawyer's daughter who, religious herself, had fallen in love with his sermons. A year later, they had a child.

King Charles's personal rule had brought the Duckets material gain. They had made several personal loans to the king, always at 10 per cent and always repaid in full. Better yet, as monarchs had often done, King Charles farmed out the customs. In return for a lump payment, Henry had acquired the right to collect the customs duty on several luxury goods. "We're making 26 per cent profit," he boasted to Julius. King Charles's system suited them very well. "Instead of paying Parliament's taxes, we make profits raising money," Henry summed up. "Long may it last."

There was, in fact, only one weakness in the system. It would work just so long as there were no national emergencies. Any armed conflict and the king would have to ask for taxes. "Which would mean a Parliament," Henry would sometimes worry. "So what can we do to be sure that we never come to that?"

This was the problem Julius Ducket solved.

He was standing on London Bridge. It was a summer evening, and as he gazed upstream towards the sun sinking over Westminster, he noticed that its rays were causing the whole surface of the water to gleam, like a huge river of gold. And it had just occurred to him that this was entirely appropriate for such a busy commercial city when the idea came to him.

That was it. Of course: the river of gold. For if one considered the king's financial needs over the last dozen years, what was the most striking feature? Why, their size. A hundred, two hundred thousand pounds – such sums could cause a clash with Parliament. But were they really so huge? To mighty, commercial London? Of course not. Julius himself could easily have gathered together dozens of men worth over twenty thousand pounds. The combined, available wealth of London ran into countless millions. Even the king's emergency needs could easily be met by London, without recourse to Parliament at all. London was a river of gold.

Yet why, Julius considered, was London so hesitant to lend? It was not that the king failed to pay interest. No: the real problem lay in the nature of the loans and their repayment.

Loans to the Crown were nearly always for a particular project. The Londoners might not like it. Equally important, the loans were usually short term, to be repaid out of Crown income in as little as six months – so they could never be very large. But why should things be done this way? Money was money: whether it was invested in a loan to the king or a share of one of the great joint stock companies, it was still the same. It was earning a return. And wasn't the stream of the king's income, which provided the interest for the king's loans, also a constant flow? Then the thought struck him: if I can buy shares in a joint stock company, that promises a constant supply of revenue, then why not buy shares, in a similar way, in the king's debt? If you wanted your money back you could sell your share to another, who would receive the interest in your place. There was no reason why the king should repay the principal for twenty years, as long as he could continue the interest. It was perpetual, like Myddelton's water supply, or the Virginia Company, or the East India, or any of the other great joint stock companies. His appreciation of the idea was not so much mathematical as instinctive: a sense of endless flow. The flow of money, like a golden river, through the city.

Julius Ducket had just invented government debt.

It was a sparkling day under a crystal sky when Sir Henry Ducket took his younger brother downriver to see the king.

It had been Henry's idea. "You must do credit to the family," he had insisted, "if you are to be presented to the king." Henry, therefore, had dressed Julius. Instead of his usual, rather modest clothes, Julius was now sporting a high-waisted, bright scarlet tunic and cape. In place of a simple ruff was a huge, floppy lace collar that came down over his shoulders; his soft leather boots were turned over at the knee; and topping this whole assemblage was a huge-brimmed hat with a great, curling ostrich feather drooping elegantly over the brim. In England, the fashion was known as the 'cavalier' style. And it had to be said, with his moustache and beard curled, Julius looked uncommonly well, so much so that his wife, gazing at him with admiration, burst out laughing, tickled his ribs and cried: "Don't forget, Julius, to come back to me tonight."

"The only thing wrong," Henry remarked, "is that your hair should be longer." His own, in the best court style, flowed over his shoulders. "But you'll do."

As two cavaliers, therefore, the Duckets came down the Thames to Greenwich.

"There is nothing to fear," Henry told him, as they made their way round the old riverside palace. Julius knew this was true; yet all the same, he could not help suddenly groaning: "Oh brother. I am such a rude and simple fellow."

For, it was beyond question, no English court, not even that of great King Harry, had ever attracted such a galaxy of talent. The court masques were masterpieces. Great European artists like Rubens and Van Dyck came to visit and decided to stay. King Charles himself, despite his modest means, was quietly assembling a collection of paintings – Titians, Raphaels, the Flemish masters – to rival any in Europe. The court was cosmopolitan. And, as if to underline this fact, as they walked up the grassy slope behind the palace and turned to look back, Julius was unexpectedly presented with a sight so lovely that he could only gasp:

"Dear God, was ever anything more perfect?"

The Queen's House at Greenwich was just being completed. Because the old Tudor buildings were still there to screen it from the river, Julius had hardly been aware of it before. Its designer, the great Inigo Jones, had already completed one other classical masterpiece – the Banqueting Hall at Whitehall, whose ceiling was being painted that very year by Rubens himself. But fine as it was, amidst the clutter of buildings at Whitehall, the Banqueting House did not show to the same advantage as this.

For the Queen's House was perfect. Set by itself in the outer wall of the old palace gardens, and facing up the park, this gleaming white, Italianate villa, just two storeys high, with three sets of windows at the centre and two each side, looked so neat, so classically perfect, that you might have supposed it was a little model for some casket to exhibit a silversmith's art. "Oh dear," Julius murmured again, "I am such a rustic fellow." At which moment he turned to see, not twenty yards away, the king.

King Charles advanced. Dressed neatly in a tunic of yellow silk, he was also wearing a wide-brimmed hat which, as they hastily made their bows, he politely doffed in reply. He was accompanied by a group of gentlemen and of ladies in long, full-bodied silk dresses. He walked easily, carrying a golden-topped stick. But as he reached them Julius realized that he was tiny. He hardly came up to Julius's shoulder. Yet he was the most aristocratic personage Julius had ever encountered in his life. Everything about the king was as neat as the little gem of a building behind them.

"As it is a fine day," he said pleasantly, "let us speak here," and leading the two men to a grassy knoll where an oak tree provided shade, he stood courteously to listen.

At first Julius stumbled a little with his words as he tried to explain his idea for the royal loan. But gradually he began to gain confidence; and this was helped by the king. If, for instance, Julius through nervousness failed to make a point clearly, King Charles would gently say: "Forgive me, Master Ducket, I have not quite understood . . ." Julius also noticed that the king himself had a slight stammer, which was rather reassuring.

What impressed Julius most was something he could not pin down: there was in this small, scrupulously polite, rather shy man, an almost magical quality that set him apart. It was the royal Stuart charm. And by the time he was finished he found himself thinking: this man truly is not like other men; he is touched, with royalty, by God. Even if he be wrong, he is indisputably my royal and anointed king, and I will follow him.

King Charles, having heard him out carefully, seemed interested. He agreed that he should maintain good relations with the city, and was intrigued by this novel way of encouraging Londoners to lend. "This shall be discussed further," he promised Julius. "Such new methods may have much to recommend them. We do not fear innovation. Though of course," he added with a smile to Henry, "we must also consider what already lies within our prerogative."

It had been, both the brothers felt, a very satisfactory day.

So Julius was a little surprised that autumn when, having heard nothing more of his proposals, he learned that the king had sent to London and the major ports for Ship Money. This contribution of the sea towns towards the cost of the fleet was an ancient and perfectly legal tax, but unpopular. Before Christmas however, King Charles had levied it on all the inland towns as well. "Which is unheard of," Henry admitted. "Though the king claims it's within his prerogative." And then at the start of 1635, King Charles through the royal court of Star Chamber, charged the city of London with mismanagement of its Ulster plantation. "He has confiscated everything," Henry announced, "and fined the city seventy thousand pounds. It is," he remarked wryly, "one way to raise money."

Within weeks, the king's commissioners were asking how much the city would pay to secure a pardon. The city erupted. "It's certainly cunning," Henry said. "The king is still within his prerogative."

But poor Julius remained mystified. How was it possible, after listening so carefully to his proposal, and after agreeing upon the importance of London's good will, for this mild, sweet-mannered king to do such a thing? Half the merchants in the city were now swearing they would never lend to him again. And even Julius had to remind himself more than once:

"He is still my anointed king."

How fortunate she was, Martha thought, to have the respectable Mrs Wheeler to keep an eye on her husband while they were apart. It was Dogget who had first introduced them years before, when they had met her in Cheapside. "This lady comes from Virginia, Martha," he had explained. She learned that Mrs Wheeler had taken pleasant lodgings in Blackfriars; and a few days later she noticed Meredith politely bow as she passed which, little as she liked Meredith, indicated that the lady must be respectable.

Mrs Wheeler was a good listener. If she did speak, it was always sensible and to the point. Martha had only once known her sound frivolous: one day, after she had been explaining to Mrs Wheeler the evils of the theatre, Martha had shortly afterwards come upon her and Dogget laughing together; but when Martha had asked why, after a moment's hesitation she had told her a story that seemed hardly funny at all. Martha supposed that Mrs Wheeler had no great sense of humour.

Mrs Wheeler had become a friend of the whole family. When Dogget's younger son became sick, it was she who came to help Martha sit through the night with him. When Martha's own daughter wanted to become a sempstress, it was Mrs Wheeler, showing an unexpected skill, who taught her most of what she needed. Once, when she asked her if she ever thought of marrying again, Mrs Wheeler only laughed: "I can do well enough without a man." And Martha felt she could quite understand. "A husband is a duty," she agreed.

But one thing she loved to talk to Mrs Wheeler about was America. She could listen by the hour. Always the questions took the same form; after listening politely to a few details of Virginia, she would ask: "And Massachusetts. What did you hear of Massachusetts?"

The fabled, promised land. Martha had never given up her quest. She might say of the *Mayflower*: "Perhaps it was as well we did not go" – for over half the pilgrims who made that fateful voyage had perished within a year – but the dream of the godly commune, the shining city, had never faded from her mind. And indeed, in recent years it was not just in the mind of Martha: many Englishmen saw in that dream no mere hope but a very pleasant reality. The reason could be summed up in two words: Laud and Winthrop.

There could not be any doubt, it seemed to Martha, that Archbishop Laud must be a very wicked man. His grip upon London had increased with every year that passed. One by one the parishes were brought into line. Many clergymen resigned.

"What happened," Martha could well ask, "to the Reformation?"

Not only that: he was worldly. When he rode into London,

he came with a train of fine gentlemen, with lackeys riding before who cried: "Clear the path, make way for the lord Bishop", as though he were a medieval cardinal. He was on the king's council; he had virtual control of the treasury. "Laud and the king are one and the same," men said. But even this worldly pomp did not shock Martha as much as his sacrilege.

"Keep ye the Sabbath." Every good Puritan did. But the king and his bishop allowed sports and games, ladies were permitted to wear finery; once she had even seen some young people dancing around a maypole, and complained to the Church authorities. Nobody cared.

No wonder then if, seeing such outrages, she and countless Puritans like her had longed for a blessed means of escape.

This Winthrop had provided. The Massachusetts colony had continued growing even more rapidly than Virginia; Puritans who had hesitated to take to the seas before were gaining confidence. Word came back with every returning ship: "Truly it is a godly commune."

How Martha yearned to go. The first of her friends to leave were people she had prayed with since her childhood. By 1634 many of her friends had gone. "But you will follow us one day, Martha," they assured her. In 1636, she saw not a ship, but a small flotilla at Wapping, all bound for America. The trickle of emigration was turning into a flood. When Sir Henry had ironically remarked to Julius that Laud was a good friend to Massachusetts, he had spoken more truly than even he realized. Laud and the king might think they were only losing some troublemakers, but in fact during these and the next few years puritan ships were to ferry away no less than 2 per cent of England's entire population to America's eastern coast.

Sometimes she would speak to her family about it, and Dogget would mutter that they were too old. But, as she gently reminded him, they were both still only in their fifties, and people far older than that were making the voyage. Dogget's younger son, who did not seem to know what he wanted to do, was agreeable. As for the elder son, the reports coming back of the cod catches were so astonishing that he had declared: "I'll go if you do." But the person who held Martha back, strangely enough was Gideon – or rather, to be precise, his wife.

Martha had always tried to love the girl. She prayed about it often. Yet she could not quite overcome a certain sense of disappointment. Gideon's wife had given him nothing except girls. They came, with monotonous regularity, every two years. They were given, as might be expected, the virtuous names that Puritans so favoured; and each mildly expressed the family's mounting exasperation about their sex. First Charity, then Hope; then Faith, Patience and finally, when still the awaited son had not arrived, Perseverance. But the thing most difficult to bear was her sickness.

The sickness of Gideon's wife was a curious thing. It seemed to strike her whenever Martha and Gideon broached the subject of America. Its nature was never specified but, as Mrs Wheeler remarked to Martha one day: "She is exactly sick enough not to travel."

Then, to everyone's surprise, at the very end of 1636 Gideon's wife gave birth to a boy. So great was the family's joy that they cast about for a name that would express their gratitude to the Lord. And at last Martha came up with a striking solution. One winter's morning a rather astonished Meredith held the infant at the font, and with a wry glance at the family announced: "I baptize thee: O Be Joyful."

Instead of a name, Puritans would sometimes take an entire phrase from their beloved Bible. It was a clear expression of Puritan loyalty, yet one that even Laud could hardly do anything about. And so O Be Joyful Carpenter, Gideon's son, entered the world.

Gideon's wife could now relax. The first four years of any infant's life were by far the most dangerous. Having delivered herself of such a precious burden, she knew very well that, for some years at least, not even Martha would suggest that O Be Joyful should be risked on the long sea voyage. She became quite healthy.

It was a great surprise to her family, and not least to herself when, in the summer of 1637, Martha performed a criminal act. The sight she had witnessed had finally driven her conscience beyond all endurance, as it had enraged all London.

Although a gentleman and a scholar, Master William Prynne, most people agreed, was a contentious fellow. Three years earlier, he had written a pamphlet against the theatre which King Charles considered an insult to his wife, who was then engaged in some court theatricals. Prynne was sentenced to have his nose split and his ears cut off in the public stocks. Martha was outraged, but there was no public disturbance.

In 1637 however, Prynne was in trouble again, this time for writing against the desecration of the Sabbath by sports and, more dangerous still, for urging that bishops should be abolished. "He shall go to the stocks again," the king's court declared. "Even the stumps of his ears shall be ripped out; and then he shall go to perpetual prison."

"Is all free speech forbidden, then?" the Londoners demanded. "If the king and Laud treat him like this, what will they do to us, who agree with every word he says?"

The day of the punishment itself was a sunny summer's day, 30 June. Drawn along Cheapside in a cart, the tall figure of Prynne, horribly disfigured yet obviously once a handsome man, stood proud and unbowed. "The more I am beat down," he had once declared, "the more I am raised up." And so it was now. A huge crowd cheered him all the way. They threw flowers into the cart. And when the loathsome sentence was carried out, a roar of rage arose that echoed round the city walls and could be heard from Shoreditch to Southwark. Martha returned, trembling.

But it was only when Meredith, in his sermon next Sunday, made reference to the wickedness of those like Prynne who denied God's bishops, that something within Martha suddenly gave way. Standing up, she spoke quietly but clearly: "This is not the house of God."

There was an astonished silence. She said it again.

"This is not the house of God." And then, feeling Dogget tugging at her arm, she calmly proceeded: "I must speak out." And did so.

It was remembered for many years, that little speech in St Lawrence Silversleeves; even though, until the beadle dragged her from the place, it could not have lasted more than a minute. It touched on popery, on sacrilege, on God's true kingdom – in simple words with which every Protestant in the congregation could identify. But most of all, it was remembered for one terrible sentence: "There are two great evils walking this land," she said: "and one is called a bishop, and one is called a king."

"She will surely," they said, "have her ears cut off too."

It took all Julius's powers of persuasion to save her. The Bishop of London would have hauled her to gaol, but Julius could never forget the awkward guilt he felt about Gideon; and so, on the Tuesday following her outburst he carefully explained to her: "I think you must leave the country. Have you any thought of where you could go?"

"I will go," she said placidly, "to Massachusetts."

And so it was, in the summer of 1637, that Martha, her young daughter and both Dogget's sons, prepared to set sail from London. Gideon and his family could not travel yet; and since Gideon needed his help in their little business, it was agreed that Dogget himself would remain in London for a year or so while they decided what to do.

The company that gathered to take ship at Wapping was a varied one. There were a number of craftsmen, a lawyer, a preacher, two fishermen. There was also a young graduate of Cambridge, who had recently inherited money, partly from the sale of a tavern in Southwark. His name was John Harvard.

The last words Martha spoke, as the boat was about to leave, were to Mrs Wheeler. "Promise me that you will keep an eye on my husband."

So Mrs Wheeler promised that she would.

There were many ships that arrived on the shores of Massachusetts in the autumn of 1637. One was the vessel that carried Martha and John Harvard. Many others also came from England, and some from different places.

Hardly anyone noticed the slow old ship which had ploughed its way up from the Caribbean with a cargo of molasses. Indeed, within a season or two, even the harbourmaster and the clerk who noted its arrival at Plymouth would probably have forgotten its existence if the captain of the vessel had not chosen the brief lay-over in port as his time to die. It was memorable because although the hair of the old mariner was white, his skin was black. "Black as your hat," the clerk told his wife.

Orlando Barnikel died quietly because he knew in his heart that he had no true reason to live any longer.

The years after his buccaneering had not brought Black

Barnikel great satisfaction. He had gradually settled into a quieter role as a sea-captain for hire. Men now knew him as a shrewd, skilful old operator, whose ships came through all weathers and who had a knack of avoiding trouble.

Where were his sons? Two, he knew, were dead. One was a Barbary Corsair, a Mediterranean pirate, a lower kind of fellow than he had ever been. A fourth – who even knew? They had gone from him, and come to nothing; it was, he now knew, inevitable for a man who was black in a white man's world.

Before he died, however, he had decided that there was one last debt he wished to repay. And asking for a lawyer, he privately dictated a brief document, which he gave to the mate, whom he trusted, with a simple instruction that it was to be given to Jane, whom he carefully described. "God knows if she's alive or what she's called now," he said, "but I left her in Virginia."

Then, for the hour still left him, he had stared silently out of the window, at the harsh, rocky shore and the cold, unforgiving sea.

1642

Who could ever have believed that things had got so far? In 1637, believing that they had cowed the Puritans in England, King Charles I and Archbishop Laud turned their attention northwards and gave orders that the Church of England Prayer Book and services were straight away to be forced upon the dour Presbyterians of Scotland. Within weeks, all Scotland was aflame. And by the following year, a huge organization had arisen of Scots prepared to die to defend their Protestant cause. They had taken an oath; they were armed; they were ready to march upon England. The name of their endeavour was to ring through Scottish history: the Covenant.

To Charles it was time for stern measures. He called to his side his toughest servant, the trusted lieutenant who for some years had been ruling the unlucky Irish with an iron fist. The Earl of Strafford returned and a force of sorts was put together, but half the troops seemed to agree with the Covenanters.

After more than a year of useless negotiation, Charles reluctantly summoned a Parliament. "For I dare say," he reasoned, "with the marauding Scots at the door, the gentlemen of England will raise a decent army." They demanded to discuss Charles's government, so he impatiently dismissed the so-called Short Parliament within days. "We must hire an army, then," Charles decided. And here began his greatest problem.

Money. He asked the city of London for a loan. No one would lend. Strafford told the merchants: "If we need to we'll get cash by cutting the coinage." As for the city's refusal: "Double the demand, sire," he suggested to the king in the Londoners' hearing, "and hang a few aldermen. That'll do it."

"If only the king had listened to me," Julius lamented to his brother, "about how to raise debt, he would not have been in this position now." But he was. Seeing his weakness, the canny Scots occupied the north of England and would not go away until paid a huge indemnity. Charles therefore had to call Parliament again; and in the autumn of 1640, they were ready for him.

"These parliament men," Henry angrily declared, "are dangerous radicals – no better than traitors. They're in league with the Scots." Of course they were. But traitors they were not, and hardly even radicals. They were mostly country gentlemen of substance who were appalled at Charles's government. One, a senior fellow named Hampden, intended to lead a crusade against Ship Money. Another, a squire from East Anglia named Oliver Cromwell – a distant kinsman, as it happened, of Secretary Thomas Cromwell who had dissolved the monasteries a century before – up to Parliament for the first time, was shocked by what he saw as a godless court. But most important of all, the leader of the pack, was a master tactician called Pym.

"Pym's reasoning is very simple," a stout gentleman informed Julius one day in the Royal Exchange. "As long as the Scots sit tight up north – and they've promised us they will – and we refuse him any money down here, King Charles is trapped in a vice. Can't do anything." He chuckled. "So you see, it's time to squeeze him now."

And squeeze they did. The king's right to customs, stripped away; Parliament must be called every three years; the present

Parliament to sit as long as its members saw fit; the Ulster settlement to be returned to the Londoners. One by one these Acts were passed, humiliating Charles. By November, Strafford had been sent to the Tower; within a month, Archbishop Laud as well.

Yet, as the Parliament went about this grim business in the spring of 1641, Julius was not alarmed. Parliaments had crossed kings for centuries, whenever they dared; caused favourites to fall, even deprived monarchs of their mistresses! The situation was bad, but hardly desperate. Indeed, strangely enough, the sense of disquiet that he did feel came not from the doings of the great men in Parliament, but from a far more humble source, in his own little parish of St Lawrence Silversleeves.

It was not long after the Parliament had begun. Julius remembered the day vividly because William Prynne had just been released from jail and a huge crowd had been leading the earless Puritan hero in triumph through the streets. The shouts of the crowd were still ringing in his ears when, to his surprise, he learned that Gideon Carpenter was at the door; and he was even more puzzled when Gideon, looking at him steadily, showed him a large scroll of paper and asked him: "Do you want to sign?"

"Sign what?" Julius had demanded.

"It's a petition. We have nearly fifteen thousand signatures. For the abolition of bishops and all their works, root and branch." And Gideon pointed to the mass of signatures he had collected.

Julius had heard of this petition. Started by Pennington, a vigorous Puritan on the common council, and encouraged by the Presbyterian Scots envoys who had recently arrived in London, it had been signed by many who had hated Laud and his Church. But whatever the king's troubles with Parliament, Julius could not imagine King Charles even deigning to look at such a document. "Why bring it to me?" he had asked, only to receive a reply that surprised him further. "When you had me whipped," Gideon said quietly, "you didn't give me a chance." He stared at him. "But I'm giving you one."

A chance? What was the solemn young man talking about? "Take it elsewhere," he said curtly. But he still wondered afterwards. Giving him a chance: it was a strange expression. Soon he learned another.

Parliament now turned to impeach Strafford, but its legal grounds were unclear. "We'll accuse him of unspecified crimes and the king must sign his death warrant." To which the city of London added a gentle gloss: "We lend no money till his head is off."

King Charles resisted. In the midst of all this, one April day, when a large crowd had gathered to make their feelings known at Westminster, Julius happened to encounter Gideon. Not wanting to seem discourteous, he remarked to him that, whatever one thought of Strafford, it was hard to see the business going as far as execution. The king just wouldn't have it. So he was astonished when Gideon, instead of arguing, merely smiled and asked:

"Which king?"

"Which king? There is only one king, Gideon."

But Gideon shook his head. "There are two kings now," he said. "King Charles in his palace, and King Pym in the Commons." He grinned. "And I think, Master Ducket, that King Pym will have it so."

King Pym? The parliamentary leader. Julius had never heard the expression before and found it distasteful. "You should be careful what you say," he cautioned. Yet the very next day, he came across a printed broadsheet plastered on the cross in Cheapside, whose heading declared in bold letters: "King Pym Says . . ." And within a week he had heard it a dozen times. Gideon was proved right as well. Within a month, bludgeoned by Parliament and without any funds, King Charles was forced to give way. Strafford was executed on Tower Hill.

But there was still one last, and terrible word that Julius had to learn.

During the summer, little changed. King Pym sat tight in his Parliament. King Charles made one, futile journey north to try to strike a bargain with the Scots, but the Presbyterians did not budge: King Charles remained caught in the vice. The Ducket brothers meanwhile had their own affairs to attend to. Julius and his little family joined Henry at Bocton for the summer, bringing with them several families of children from the parish – including, to his surprise,

Gideon's wife and children – to help with hop-picking. In the great peace of the Kent country, even Sir Henry and tiny O Be Joyful seemed to strike up a friendship as the little boy toddled about in the sun.

As soon as they returned to London, however, it was clear that more trouble was brewing. News had just arrived of a disturbance in Ireland. People had been killed, property burned. King Pym and King Charles alike agreed that troops must be sent to quell the unruly province. But there agreement ended. "I shall control the troops," King Charles declared. It was what kings had always done. "In no circumstances," the parliament men replied, "are we going to pay for troops that the king will surely turn against us."

"To limit the king is not enough," Parliament then argued, "for he could always strike back. We must control him." King Pym, in effect, must be greater than King Charles. Every week some new and more radical proposal was raised. "The army must answer to Parliament alone," they declared. "We should be able to veto the king's ministers too." And, hardly surprisingly, the Puritans among them urged: "No more bishops, either."

By November Gideon was collecting signatures for another petition. "We'll get twenty thousand this time." At Westminster a huge mob was in regular attendance, which Pym and his friends did nothing to discourage.

"I was with some of the sounder parliament men today," Henry told Julius one evening. "And they're getting uneasy too. They want to control the king, but they think Pym is leading them towards mob rule. They'd rather reach some accommodation with the king than go down that slippery slope." At the end of the month, when Pym and his followers forced their Grand Remonstrance through Parliament, incorporating all their radical demands, they only just got it passed, a large minority voting against. "Pym's gone too far," Henry judged. "He won't get another majority unless he learns moderation."

Many of the city aldermen and the richer London families were starting to have similar doubts: "The wards have elected a new common council of troublemakers and radicals." As if to confirm all their fears, just days after Christmas a great mob of apprentices rioted at Westminster and had to be dispersed by troops. And then, for the first time Julius heard the word he was soon to learn to dread. "You know what the troops called the apprentices as they chased them past Whitehall?" Henry asked him. "They saw most of the young devils had close-cropped hair, so they called them Roundheads." He laughed. "Roundheads. That's what they are."

Within days, five hundred young gentlemen from the Inns of Court had offered their services to King Charles, to maintain order. Even the new common council agreed to call out the city's armed men to keep the peace.

Yet just when all sorts of influential people were beginning to have doubts about the opposition to the monarch, Julius, sitting over his accounts in the big house behind Mary-le-Bow, was astonished to see the heavy oak door of the parlour burst open and his brother, of all people, announce: "The king has gone mad."

The actions of King Charles I of England in the first week of January 1642 did not show he was mad, but merely that he had not the faintest understanding of English politics.

On 3 January he sent the sergeant-at-arms to arrest five members of the Commons. The Commons refused him entry. The next day, breaching all etiquette, he turned up himself, and found that the five, including King Pym, and Pennington the Puritan of London, had departed. The Speaker would not tell him where they were – "Your Majesty, I have neither eyes to see nor tongue to speak but as this House is pleased to direct me" – and balked of his prey the king remarked: "I see the birds have flown."

Kings did not arrest members of Parliament for speaking their minds in the House. It was against all custom. It was a breach of Parliament's privilege. From that day to this, when the monarch's representative comes to summon the Commons to the yearly opening ceremony, the door is symbolically slammed in his face. When Charles went to the Guildhall the next day, even the mayor and aldermen, who disliked the radicals, could not help him.

"Privilege of Parliament," they reminded him. "Privilege of Parliament," people cried, as he returned through the streets.

Five days later, King Charles and his queen moved to the safety of Hampton Court. King Pym stayed in London.

* * *

All through that spring Julius waited. There were, perhaps, tiny grounds for hope. Parliament was at least maintaining the fiction of loyalty. It called for troops, but in the king's name, saying they were needed for Ireland. But it was clear that Parliament had a much better idea of how to get the city's support than ever King Charles had. A huge city loan, refused before, was now promptly granted – in return for another two and a half million acres of Ireland.

By April a new militia was being raised: six regiments, no less. "For the king's defence," of course. One day, Julius saw Gideon, solemnly carrying a halberd, leading a little troop of apprentices who were marching down Cheapside. Yet still he persisted in believing that common sense must prevail.

When Henry, who had left with the king at last returned, Julius plied him anxiously for news. "Will the king not seek a compromise?" But Henry shook his head.

"He can't. Whatever his own mistakes, Pym has pushed him too far. You know very well, Julius, we have to maintain order. The Parliament must be taught a lesson."

"He'll raise troops?"

"The queen has left for France with the royal jewels. She's going to pawn them to raise the money."

He left after only three days and by the time he returned briefly two months later, he informed Julius:

"The king's up at York. He's calling all loyal members of Parliament to join him. Some of them are coming." But he also confessed: "The eastern and southern sea ports are all closed to us. The navy seems to be disloyal too."

"Parliament's asked for voluntary contributions," Julius had to tell him. "So much silver plate's come in that they hardly know what to do with it."

In the late summer, it seemed to Julius that a small sign of hope appeared. Some of the king's supporters were producing sensible, reasoned pamphlets that seemed to open the door to compromise. "Perhaps," he told his family, "a settlement will still be reached." But in August, the mayor was removed, and Pennington the Puritan was chosen in his place. And meeting Gideon in Watling Street one day, the solid craftsman cheerfully told him: "We're all Roundheads now." A week later news came that the king had raised his standard in Nottingham. This was the traditional, chivalric way for a king to declare war.

It was in September that Henry came again. He came at dusk. Julius noticed that he now wore a breastplate of armour over his tunic. After a brief visit to his own house in Covent Garden, he spent the night in the house behind Mary-le-Bow and talked to Julius for long hours.

"The north and most of the west are loyal," he told his brother. "Several great lords have promised troops. King Charles has summoned his nephew Rupert to come over from Germany." Julius knew that Prince Rupert was a first-rate leader of cavalry. "There will be one short engagement," Henry predicted. "The parliamentary levies are not properly trained. They won't last five minutes against Rupert." He smiled. "Then we'll bring some order back."

Soon after dawn, Henry quietly left. With him he took, sewn into his clothes and his baggage, no less than three thousand pounds worth of gold and silver coin. When Julius had looked doubtful about the amount, he had given him that splendid, proud look of his and remarked: "We are gentlemen, brother, and loyal to the king. Isn't that," he reminded him, "what father would have wanted?"

The next day, as if in anticipation of sombre times ahead, the mayor and council ordered all the London theatres closed. Before long, parties of trained bands started marching out of the city. The defences round the gate were being strengthened. By the early days of October, everyone was waiting anxiously for news of a battle. None came. Julius realized that he had not seen Gideon Carpenter for some time.

It was on the last Sunday in October that the extraordinary thing happened in St Lawrence Silversleeves.

There had been a battle of sorts in the West Country that week, but it had not been decisive. The trained bands had started trickling back into London to regroup, but King Charles and Prince Rupert were moving across the country very cautiously. News was still fragmentary.

Julius and his family had come into church at the last moment that morning because one of the children had been sick. Julius had hardly bothered to glance round as he hustled them all, as quietly as possible, into the family pew. He did notice, however, that the little church seemed unusually full. Only a minute later, as the silence before the service fell, did he realize something odd.

The altar table was in the wrong place. It had been moved back into the nave.

Then Meredith entered. He was not dressed in his usual gleaming cope. Instead, he was wearing a long black coat and a plain white shirt. He strode to the front of the church; but then, instead of sitting in his usual place, in the chancel, he mounted at once into the pulpit, as though he were about to preach. Julius could only stare as Edmund Meredith began the service.

Except, Julius frowned, that it was not the service. The words were wrong. What had come over the man? He knew the entire Prayer Book by heart. Had Meredith suffered some mental aberration? What the devil was he saying? And then he realized. It was the Directory: the order of service of the Presbyterians. Calvinism – here in his very own church! He glanced at his wife, who was looking shocked and mystified. He could not imagine what Meredith was about, but he knew his duty. He rose. "Stop this at once." His voice rang out clearly and, he was glad to hear, with authority. "Mr Meredith, you have the wrong order of service, I think."

But Meredith was only smiling, blandly.

"The Prayer Book, Mr Meredith," he began. "As head of the vestry I must insist . . ." He was interrupted by the church door opening. Gideon Carpenter, in the dress of an officer, a sword at his side, stepped calmly through it, followed by six armed men. Julius gaped, opening his mouth to rebuke them too, but was pre-empted by Gideon. "You are no longer on the vestry committee, Sir Julius."

"No longer . . . ?" What did the man mean? And why on earth had Gideon addressed him in such a way? "Sir Julius?"

"You did not know? I am sorry. Your brother is dead. You are Sir Julius Ducket now."

"Dead?" Julius just looked at him, taking it in, unable for a moment to speak.

"There is something more, Sir Julius." It was said quietly, without malice. "You are under arrest."

1649

January the 29th. Evening. It had been dark since five in the afternoon. Ahead, a long, star-chilled night, whose cold and silent hours would be a solemn vigil for many. In the grey, blank light of morning, in Whitehall, they would do such a thing as was never done in England before.

Edmund Meredith sat alone. His wife and children were upstairs but not yet abed. On the table nearby lay a stiff black hat with a tall crown and a wide, circular brim. He was still wearing his day clothes – a black, sleeveless jerkin, tightly buttoned down the front from his adam's apple to below his waist; a black and white striped shirt with large, white linen collar and cuffs; black breeches, woollen socks, plain shoes. His silvery hair was cut so that it hung along the lines of his jawbone. This deliberately clumsy and unattractive arrangement was now the fashion amongst the Puritans and he had adopted it unhesitatingly three years before.

He sat in a heavy chair with a padded back, his long fingers pressed together in front of his aristocratic face, his eyes half closed, as though at prayer. But Edmund was not praying; he was thinking. About survival.

He was good at surviving. Though in his late seventies now, he looked twenty years younger. Of his five children living, the youngest was only six, and it seemed Edmund meant to live long enough to see even this boy into adulthood. As for the art of political survival . . .

"It's all," he once explained to Jane, "in the timing." And as he looked back over the last seven years of conflict, he could certainly claim that his own had been good.

He liked talking to Jane. They had known each other too long to have any delusions or secrets. He enjoyed her gentle teasing and she was the only person in the world with whom he dared to be entirely frank.

The most important step had been the first, back in 1642, when he had so shocked poor Julius by switching to the Presbyterian camp. King Charles had still been advancing on London then; many had expected a quick royal victory. "So how did you know," Jane had asked, "which way to jump?"

"I'd looked at the city militia," he had said. "I didn't think Charles would get through that year."

"But what about the long run?" she had challenged. "The king might have defeated Parliament. Then you'd have been out on your ear."

"True," he agreed. "But in the long run I was even more certain Parliament would win."

"Why so?"

"Supply," he had said simply. "The Roundheads had the navy and almost all the ports. Hard for Charles to get reinforcements. Moreover, the ports gave Parliament the customs dues. Above all, the Roundheads had London." He spread his hands. "Long wars take money. London's where the money is." He grinned. "I bet two-to-one on the Roundheads and became a Presbyterian."

And how quickly he had been proved right. Only months later Parliament, dropping all pretence of royal authority, had abolished bishops and done a deal with the Scots: by a Solemn League and Covenant it was agreed that, in return for a Scottish army to defeat Charles, the English would become Presbyterian. Huge numbers of Church of England clergy were thrown out. The London parishes were in turmoil. But Meredith had survived. "Just in time," he had remarked. That same year he had helped take down the old cross in Cheapside. "Such things are superstition and idolatry," he told his congregation. As the dour Scots and the English Parliament slowly hammered out the details of an English Calvinist Church, and the first London council of elders was called, even the sternest Scottish visitors were agreed: "The man Meredith preaches a fine sermon. Very sound."

But that had been some time ago, while the war between Charles and Parliament was still in progress. Things had changed since then – very much for the worse, in his view. And after tomorrow there was no knowing what might happen. He felt pretty sure he would find a way to survive. But then, as he sat alone in his parlour and considered the matter again, it was not himself he was worrying about.

It was Jane. Though God knows, he had warned her.

The candle was still burning in her chamber and by its guttering light Jane looked across at the sleeping form beside her. She was glad he was so peaceful.

But was Meredith right? Were they in danger? Dogget didn't believe it; but then, she thought affectionately, he had always had a cheerful attitude to life. Meredith on the other hand might be a cynical fraud, but his judgement was good. So were they star-crossed lovers – Romeo and Juliet, Antony and Cleopatra? A subject for a play? The idea amused her. Dogget and Jane: a strange pair for a tragedy since, when they actually became lovers, she had been sixty. Even then, she thought it probably only happened because of the war.

Strangely enough, during the entire Civil War, the thing that Jane and many Londoners remembered most was the quietness. For that very first spring the whole area had been sealed off behind a rampart. It was a vast affair. Week after week the Londoners had gone out to dig. Every able-bodied man, including older men like Dogget, had been conscripted and issued with a shovel. They had even toiled on Sundays; and one fine afternoon, when Jane was serving refreshments to the workers, she was told: "A hundred thousand are labouring here this day." The result, completed that summer, was a great earth wall and ditch, eleven miles round, that enclosed the city, all the suburbs on both sides of the river, out past Westminster and Lambeth in the west and Wapping in the east. Not only the suburbs, but great tracts of open ground, orchard and field, even the reservoir for Myddelton's New River water supply, were all within the vast enclosure. The ramparts had entrances, forts and batteries of cannon supplied by the East India Company. They were impregnable. And here, clamped like a tourniquet across the main artery of the nation, the parliamentary opposition made its headquarters for the duration of the war.

If Meredith foresaw the outcome of the Civil War, it was still a long time before he was proved correct. The conflict was slow and halting – a skirmish here, a town or fortified house besieged there, a few pitched battles. Yet, when they emerged from the royal base at Oxford, King Charles and Prince Rupert had proved formidable. In the north, the big port of Newcastle, which supplied most of London's coal, was gained for the king. Also much of the west. Even after the Presbyterian Scots had come down and helped inflict a severe defeat on them at Marston Moor, the message came back: "The Royalists are still in the field." Part of the trouble lay in the Roundhead troops. The trained bands from London were usually the best, but they had still struck their colours and marched off home whenever their pay was late.

The war brought occasional hostilities to other parts of the country, but to Jane, living within the huge earthwork enclosure at London it brought, month after month, only a great silence.

True, once a week, before he had left, she would see Gideon and his men marching proudly off to Finsbury Field or the Artillery Ground outside Moorgate where the city's trained bands would gather. Then the rattle of musketry and the bangs of cannon might go on a whole afternoon. Sometimes great columns of Roundhead troops would depart, returning again, dusty and bandaged, a few weeks later. But most of the time the city was subdued. Half the stalls in Cheapside market were gone. The Royal Exchange was often deserted. With West Country cloth supplies cut off by the Royalists, and little market for luxury imports, the merchants were mostly lying low. Some, suspected as Royalists, had gone to ground entirely. Sir Julius Ducket, it was said, had been completely ruined. As for ordinary folk like herself, though there was food enough, there had been some miserably cold months when the Royalists had stopped the Newcastle coal supply; and the demands, every month, for taxes to pay the troops had sharply depleted her income. Yet, strange to say, she rather enjoyed it. The threatened attack never came and after a while she was sure it never would. Life might be hard, but at least it was different. And then, of course, there was Dogget.

Why hadn't he gone to Massachusetts? It was funny how there had always been some excuse. The first year or two it had been the business; then two of Gideon's children had been sick. "Don't you think you should join your wife?" she had sometimes urged. But he never had. And then, when the Civil War began and Gideon was off soldiering, Dogget really was needed to keep the business going and provide for Gideon's family.

It happened on a September afternoon, just months after the ramparts had been completed. Dogget and Jane had walked out of the old city for a stroll on Moorfields. The sun was shining. It was quiet. In the middle distance, nearly a mile away, she could see the sentries up on the rampart at Shoreditch, like so many little dots against the open blue sky; and it had just occurred to her that, within the great enclosure – she could not say why, but it was so – it was as if they were inhabiting some unreal, timeless place that had somehow separated itself from the rest of the world, when, catching her thought, he half turned to her and remarked:

"It makes you feel young, out here."

Yes, she thought, she did feel young. She smiled.

"You haven't changed much, anyway," she remarked. He was grizzled now, his face lined, but otherwise he was the same John Dogget who had once shown her King Harry's barge.

He nodded. He was looking at her.

"What is it?"

He did not reply. He was still looking at her, smiling.

"Oh." She looked down, and thought for a little as they walked towards the ramparts. Then, after a little while, she had taken his hand and gently squeezed. Neither of them spoke. They had just walked back to the house together, in the huge, afternoon light. And so, in that strange, silent space created by the ramparts of war, their affair had begun: two lovers in their sixties, linked by their past and by long affection, finding comfort, companionship and even excitement, both a little surprised that such things were still possible.

They had been discreet. Only Meredith, clever Meredith, had guessed: and him, she knew, she could trust. Not that it really mattered much anyway. If they brought each other happiness, who cared?

But that had been five years ago, before the great change in events that had brought England to the threshold of the present, awesome crisis. And now, as she looked fondly at the sleeping form beside her, she heard the urgent words that Meredith had spoken to her just days before.

"Soon you will be in danger. Perhaps great danger." He had looked at her earnestly. "Who exactly knows?"

"You." She had considered. "I'm not really sure. People may suspect. But why is it so important?"

He had shaken his head impatiently.

"You don't understand." Then he had looked thoughtful. "Tell me one thing – this is important. Does Gideon know?"

* * *

Gideon picked up his quill pen. The letter to Martha lay before him, but for the hundredth time he hesitated. He glanced across the room at his family. There was his dear wife, in sickness if asked to travel, in health otherwise, quietly sewing; beside her, Patience, soon to marry; Perseverance, still without a suitor. And the light of his life, O Be Joyful, a short, stocky youth now, reading a bible. The boy had shown such talent that, instead of taking him into his own business, Gideon had apprenticed him to the finest woodcarver he could find. But even more than this talent, he was grateful that God had granted his son such a sweet and religious nature. How pleased and proud Martha would be if she could see him now. But this thought, instead of gladdening his heart, only brought him back, uncomfortably, to the letter. And to the agonizing question. Should he tell Martha about Dogget and Jane?

Sometimes he had even tried to pretend to himself that he did not know, that he had not seen them kissing when they thought themselves alone, or seen Dogget disappear into her house. As far as he could tell, few others realized. To his children, Jane was Aunt Jane. And when a neighbour had once innocently remarked – "Dogget and Mrs Wheeler are cousins, aren't they?" – he had just smiled and nodded. God forgive him for the lie. When it was he, Gideon Carpenter, who was supposed to be setting the moral example in the parish of St Lawrence Silversleeves.

For that was his role now. Ever since they had kicked out Sir Julius Ducket and his friends. Three times now, the whole congregation had elected him as one of the vestrymen. And their own moral standards, he was glad to say, were commendably high. More than half the men wore Puritan jerkins and hats; their women wore long dresses of grey or brown, with bonnets modestly tied under their chins.

So why had he allowed this sinful betrayal of the pious woman he revered to continue? Partly, he admitted, it was the fear of a family row and of a possible scandal. But even more importantly, to keep Dogget happy. Without the older man working in the business he would not have felt free – and this was something that Martha, surely, would understand – to serve the still greater cause, whose work would be completed this very next morning. The work of Cromwell and his saints.

* * *

Oliver Cromwell had won the Civil War. After those first inconclusive years, it was the vigorous East Anglian member of Parliament who had gone off, raised his own properly trained troop of horse, the Ironsides, and demanded of Parliament: "Now let me reorganize the whole army."

What thrilling times those had been. Leaving Dogget and his family in London, Gideon had gone eagerly to join Cromwell's force. The New Model Army, it was called. This full-time, trained and disciplined army, its core already battle-hardened, and commanded by Cromwell and his colleague General Fairfax, turned the course of the war. Within a year it had inflicted a crushing defeat on Charles and Rupert at Naseby, and taken one royal stronghold after another. Oxford fell. Charles surrendered to the Scots. The Scots sold him to the English, who kept him under house arrest.

But what mattered to Gideon was that these New Model Roundheads were not just soldiers. They were saints.

For "Saints" was what they called themselves. Some, of course, were only mercenaries; but most were men like himself – men who sought justice, soldiers for Christ, men who were fighting so that now at last, even in England, they might build that shining city on a hill. God was with them, they were sure. Hadn't He given them victory? This knowledge gave them authority; and authority was needed. For if not themselves, who could they trust?

Certainly not the Parliament. Half the time the army had not been paid. The "Saints" knew very well that most of the parliament men just wanted to strike a deal with the king on the minimum possible terms. Certainly not the Londoners. "London," Gideon would sadly admit, "is so big it is a hydra-headed monster." Most of the population supported the Roundhead cause, but you never knew how many secret Royalists there might be. Above all, the Londoners' only real interest was in themselves and in their profits. Once the threat of the Royalist army was gone, they could not wait to disband the "Saints" and settle with Charles as well.

And certainly, most certainly, not the king. Endlessly prevaricating, trying to play one of his enemies against the other, promising anything in the hope that, in the end, he could still return to rule exactly as before, when finally King Charles had managed to foment another rising, the "Saints" had had enough. Despite the Londoners' howls of protest, Fairfax had come down and quartered his army on the city. The treasure of several livery companies was seized to pay the troops. And just a few weeks ago, to Gideon's huge satisfaction, Colonel Pride with a body of troops had gone to Westminster and thrown out all the members of Parliament who were too faint-hearted for the great cause, which was, quite simply, to rebuild England.

In the last two years another heady realization had come upon him. "There is no power left that can stand against us." Cromwell's army was the only true power left in the land. Disciplined and united, it could impose its will. A captive king, a flaccid Parliament: to the saints fell the opportunity, and the responsibility, of fashioning the old country again, on a new model.

But what exactly was that new model to be? Even now, Gideon was not quite certain.

When the Civil War began, he had been clear, like most Roundheads: the king must be reined in by Parliament; the bishops and all their works must go. Some sort of Presbyterian Church he had supposed – not quite so dour and rigid as the Scottish version, though – had seemed desirable. But as the war continued, and the fellowship of Cromwell's army uplifted him, he had begun with his fellow saints to envision a still brighter and better hope. A new world, here in the old. How often, then, he had turned to the letters he had received from Martha; and how they had inspired him with their account of Massachusetts where, unfettered by bishops, the chosen men of each congregation elected not only their pastors but the governors and magistrates as well; where taxes were raised only by consent and where all men lived under strict biblical law. Surely, Gideon thought, this state of Massachusetts must be close to that godly kingdom, that shining city on a hill.

Some of his fellow saints, known as "Levellers", wanted to go further than this, giving every man a vote and even abolishing private property. Cromwell was against this, and so, it was clear from her letters, was Martha.

Right or wrong on these or any other matters, she had been for him all these years like a beacon, steadfastly shining across the ocean; and how he wished she were at his side now, as, after the terrible deed of the coming morning was done, he and the saints prepared to enter the promised land.

So what, now, should he say to her? How much should he tell? Still, in a trembling of conscience, he hesitated before, finally, he began to write.

So it had come to this. Julius sat alone in the panelled parlour for the solemn vigil of the night.

They were going to kill King Charles in the morning. After a shameful mockery of a trial, the Roundheads were going to murder their anointed king.

If Sir Julius Ducket could find any consolation at all in that terrible night, it was this: he had been loyal. "I have kept faith," he murmured, "until the end."

And he had suffered for it. After his arrest by Gideon, he had found himself held under guard with three dozen other prominent Royalist citizens. When asked why, they were told, "You are Malignants," as though they were some disease upon the body politic. The first week they had not even been allowed any visitors; but when at last his wife had been permitted to visit him, he had received another shock. When he suggested that she and the children should go to Bocton she replied: "Bocton? Didn't you know? All the estates of the Malignants have been taken over by the Roundheads. We're forbidden to go near the place."

How depressing those times had been. In the first weeks he had continued to hope that the Royalists would win. Stories came back: Prince Rupert had led another successful charge; the London-trained bands had refused to fight and gone home because they weren't paid. But still he had been held like a criminal. Months had gone by and then at last he had been taken to the Guildhall and ushered into a room where half a dozen Roundhead officers were seated at a table.

"Sir Julius," he was told, "you may go free; but there is a price to be paid."

"How much?"

"Twenty thousand pounds," they coolly informed him.

"Twenty? I'd be ruined," he protested, "Leave me in jail."

"We could fine you anyway," one of them remarked.

And so, early in 1644, Sir Julius Ducket had returned sadly

to his house behind St Mary-le-Bow, to try to begin his life again.

But how were they to live? The fine had consumed almost all his assets. His wife had some jewellery. There was the big house itself, but to sell, even if he had wanted to, would have been very difficult while London was still like a city under siege. He looked about for some business to engage in, but trade was almost at a standstill. Three gloomy weeks passed during which he cautioned his family: "We shall have to be careful not to spend too much." As for the future, he could not see what he was going to do.

It was quite by chance, one March day, that he suddenly remembered the pirate's treasure.

The cellar was dark and smelled musty as he went down, carrying a lamp. He realized it was thirty years since he had last seen the old chest. A mass of domestic objects had piled up in front of the place where it used to lie since then and he wondered if it was even there any more. But after a few minutes he gave a grunt of satisfaction. There it was: covered with dust but still the same, dark and mysterious as ever.

For a moment he hesitated. What was it his father had told him all those years ago? That he would guard his chest with his life. And why? Because he had given his word. His sacred word. But then again, that had been thirty years ago. The pirate had never returned. There wasn't a chance, by now, that the fellow was even alive. Nor was there likely to be any family to claim the chest. Hadn't he been a rover of the seas? The sea chest belonged to nobody. What was in there, he wondered. Money? Stolen silver? A map, even – he smiled to himself – of some distant island where treasure was buried? Taking a hammer and chisel, he set to work. The chest was strong; the old padlocks were solid; but at last, with three great cracks, he managed to break them open. Slowly he lifted the creaking old lid.

He gasped. It was bursting with coins. Coins of every kind – gold and silver, English shillings, Spanish doubloons, heavy dollars from the Low Countries. Many were fifty or sixty years old, from the days of the Spanish Armada and good Queen Bess, but good gold and silver nonetheless. God knows what the treasure was worth. Many thousands of pounds. A fortune. He was saved.

From this moment, the slow recovery of Sir Julius Ducket had begun. He was very careful: after splitting the money up into twenty different bags, he secreted each one in a place where it would not be found. He said nothing, even to his children, about the treasure, but remarking that he had found a little cash, he was able to do some modest buying and selling of merchandise, supplementing the small profits with a little extra from the hoard so that, without drawing attention to themselves, the family were able to live quietly. If he produced one of the antique coins, he would remark casually, "I had this from my father," and the word in London was: "Poor Ducket's broken. He's scraping by on any old coins he can find around his house."

He still had to be careful. Though there were a number of known Royalists like himself in the city, he was also well aware that they were also watched. Gideon, he suspected, knew of every move he made. He would often stand in Cheapside by the stalls, to see if anyone was going down the lane to his house. Yet he was still able to outwit the Roundheads. Once, in late spring, he even managed to slip out of the city on a special errand.

If Julius had felt downhearted at the loss of his brother, and perhaps, still, a little awkward about his use of a treasure that was not strictly his, the secret journey he made to the king's court at Oxford did much to raise his spirits. Together with two other trusted men, he had ridden out of London early one morning dressed as a Roundhead – a disguise they had kept on for more than twenty miles. Sewn into the clothes of the three men were quantities of gold coins provided by Julius from the treasure. Between them they were able to carry almost a thousand pounds. By the following evening they were at the defensive ramparts round the old university city; and the next day, in Christ Church college, Julius was able to present his money to the king in person.

"Faithful Sir Julius." It was the proudest moment of his life when King Charles spoke those words. "We count you amongst our most loyal friends."

"I should gladly fight for Your Majesty," he declared. "But I have no skill at arms."

"We should rather," the king replied, "that you remain in London. We need faithful friends we can rely on there." And for fully half an hour the king had walked with him around the old college quadrangle, asking for all kinds of information about the state of the city and its defences. For his part, the king did not hesitate to give him his confidence, explaining: "Many of my well-wishers would have me compromise my conscience. But this I must not do. I have a sacred duty." It was, however, his final words, just as they were parting, that had gone straight to Julius's heart. "I cannot tell," King Charles said quietly, "how this great matter will turn out. That is in God's hands." He looked solemn. "But if anything should befall me, Sir Julius, I have two sons – two of the blood royal to succeed me. May I ask that you will keep faith with them, as you have with me?"

"Your Majesty has no need to ask," he replied, much moved. "You have my word."

"And I have no subject," the king replied, "whose word is worth more. Thank you, Sir Julius."

Julius was not able to slip through to Oxford again; the London approaches were too closely watched. But from that day, he felt he had gained an inner strength. If his life in London was drab, he was there for a purpose, and he would quietly remind his family: "I have given the king my word."

Even so, in the years that followed, it was not always easy to keep up his spirits. Early in 1645, the Roundheads had executed Archbishop Laud. It was a sign of how far they meant to go. When Cromwell and his army won the war and King Charles was held captive, he had still hoped that a settlement might be reached. Once, when secret messengers from the king had called at his house he had advised them: "If the king would give up bishops, Parliament and the Londoners will surely compromise." But when King Charles failed to give way, he was not really surprised, remembering his words: "I have a sacred duty." As the negotiations dragged on interminably, Julius had wondered how they could ever come to a conclusion.

But he could still scarcely believe the events of the last two months. Only after Pride's purge of Parliament had the full naked power of the army been clearly seen. Having asserted their power, the army men moved ruthlessly. By January the scene was set. The king was brought to Westminster Hall for a trial. "Or a mockery of a trial," as Julius described it. Certainly many of those summoned to sit in judgment upon the king, including several London aldermen, refused to take part. King Charles, true to form, refused to recognize the court's authority, but as he also pointed out, this was not even a court of the Parliament, since the army had thrown out most of its members. The answer of the army's court was to remove him, on both the first and the second day. "He was tried, in effect, in his absence," Julius noted. On the third day the army's henchmen, who insisted on referring to him as "Charles Stuart, that man of blood," arbitrarily sentenced their monarch to death. "We killed the archbishop," they could announce. "Now with the king, our work is complete."

And so it had come to this. In the morning, after this night under the cold stars, they were going to kill their king. Such a thing had never been done before. But if they thought they would change the world thereby, Sir Julius Ducket at least, as he kept his vigil, swore to himself: "They shall not."

It was already the fourth night that the fellow had been staying at the George. He was a gnarled old sea-dog, but he gave no trouble, kept himself to himself. Each day he went out in the morning and did not return until dusk. No one knew what his business might be, though he had confessed to the innkeeper that he had never been to London before; but it evidently kept him busy. When the innkeeper had asked him if he was going to watch the king's execution the following morning, he had shaken his head and replied: "No time." He had only three days left before he sailed.

Twenty years had passed since the first mate had received his commission from Black Barnikel; for twenty years he had carried the pirate's will. But the passage of time meant little to him. He had been asked to deliver it and, if he could, he would keep his word. It had been three years before he could make detailed enquiries after Jane in Virginia, and even then his first search had failed to find any record of her. A year later, however, he had had the chance to spend another ten days in Jamestown, and this time he had more luck. Someone remembered the woman he described, told him she had married Wheeler; and before he left he was fairly sure that Jane and the widow Wheeler were one and the same. They told him she had returned to England. "Said she came from London," one farmer remembered. Ten years back he had been to Plymouth and looked there; five years ago to Southampton, now London.

His method of enquiry was simple and logical. He went from parish to parish and enquired of the clergyman if he had ever heard of a Widow Wheeler. So far he had drawn a blank. But tomorrow, perhaps, he would have better luck. He was going along Cheapside: to St Mary-le-Bow, and to little St Lawrence Silversleeves.

The crowd in Whitehall had begun to gather early that icy morning, but several hours had passed and still the business had not begun. In front of Inigo Jones's beautiful Banqueting Hall, gleaming white even in the pale January morning light, they had erected a wooden platform. The Roundhead troops in their heavy leather tunics and sturdy boots had formed a guard round the platform, and twice now fresh contingents armed with pikes had arrived, forcing the crowd to edge back even further.

What was the mood of the crowd, Julius wondered. Were they stern Puritans like Gideon? Some were, but the majority seemed to be a motley crew – all kinds of folk from gentlemen and lawyers to fishwives and apprentices. Were they indifferent? Had they come just to be entertained? As they waited in the bitter cold, they seemed strangely subdued. He thought of the Banqueting Hall with its magnificent Rubens ceiling. It depicted the king's father James being taken up to heaven – not the first time that a great work of art had been created from a faintly absurd subject; and he thought of what it really meant. It meant the court, the civilized, European world of the king and his friends, the splendid houses, the great picture collection – all to be destroyed by these rude, obstinate Puritan fellows with their brutal God. Was the king waiting in there now? Was he being allowed a last look at the beauty he had created before they cut him down? The crowd had swelled still further; the whole of Whitehall was full of folk. Now mounted troopers were coming and forming up round the execution platform. There was a roll of drums. An upper window of the Banqueting Hall was thrown open; and a moment later, simply but elegantly dressed in cloak and doublet, King Charles I of England quietly stepped out.

How strange. Julius had expected a roar, or even hoots from the crowd; but it remained strangely silent. A clergyman in a long robe followed, then several secretaries and other members of the execution party. Finally, bringing up the rear, with a black mask over his face and carrying an axe, came the executioner.

It was the custom that the condemned man might address the crowd. This had been allowed to Charles Stuart also. Holding a few notes on a scrap of paper in his hand, the king began to speak. How gracefully he did so. The day when he had met him at Greenwich came back into Julius's mind. There was the same calm manner, the careful politeness. He even seemed to be addressing this rabble who had come to gawp at his death as though they were so many ambassadors.

But what was he saying? Julius could see that the secretaries on the platform were making notes, but from where he was standing in the crowd it was hard to hear. Certain phrases he caught. Parliament, he declared, had been the first to begin the conflict over privilege, not he. Monarchs, he reminded them, are there to keep the ancient constitutions, which are the people's freedom. Now, instead, they had only the arbitrary power of the sword in his place. Whatever his own sins might be, "I am a martyr of the people," he cried. "And a Christian of the Church of England," he reminded them, "as I found it left by my father."

Then he was done. They removed his cloak and jerkin so that he stood only in a white shirt over his breeches. They tucked his hair under a cap, so it should not impede the axe and they led him to the block. And it was just then, in the awful silence before he knelt down to the block, that, surveying the faces in the crowd, King Charles caught sight of Sir Julius Ducket, and their eyes met.

How sad those eyes looked, in that noble, kingly face, yet as they held Julius's for a moment, they seemed to contain a question. How could he forget his vow at Oxford, and the king's words – "if anything should befall me" – how solemnly, how tragically prophetic? Looking King Charles straight in the eye, he made a quick bow of his head. There could be no mistaking its meaning. It said: "I have promised." In the moment of his death, King Charles should know that Ducket at least, of all the men in that crowd, would keep faith with his sons. It seemed to Julius that he saw a look of gratitude in reply.

Not even his most bitter enemies could deny that King Charles I of England went to his death with the most remarkable grace. As the axeman struck a single, clean blow, the whole crowd let out a great groan, as if suddenly they understood their awful deed. And as the executioner held up the king's severed head, perhaps Sir Julius Ducket was not alone as he murmured to himself: "The king is dead. Long live the king."

Two days afterwards Sir Julius Ducket received a visit from Jane Wheeler. The document she showed him was perfectly clear. It stated plainly that a certain sea captain by the name of Orlando Barnikel had left her his treasure chest which resided in the safe keeping of his father Alderman Ducket. It also exactly described the chest. There could be no mistaking it. And what in heaven's name, Julius wondered, as he gazed at Jane in stupefaction, was he to do?

Was the old chest with its padlocks burst still lying down there in the cellar? He could not remember. What about the treasure itself? About half was left, but who knew what he might need in the uncertain years to come? What if he were to give her some of it and tell her he had removed it from the chest to hide it more easily? Would she believe him? He suspected not. And that, he thought, would invite people to investigate his own affairs. Those old coins – people would start saying they were the sea captain's instead of his father's. They'd call him a thief.

A sea captain! He knew perfectly well what kind of man had left this treasure to this apparently respectable widow. A blackamoor. A pirate. Stolen money anyway. But of course, if he said that, he would be admitting he knew about the matter. And why, why should this woman, friend of Dogget and the cursed Carpenters, take money which such people in no way deserved and which might yet be needed in the Royalist cause? It could not be right. It couldn't be God's purpose. Hadn't he known since his childhood that it was the Duckets who were chosen by God to do His will, and that these other folk were cursed? Surely the heavenly Father had not altered his priorities? It would be too unjust. Gravely therefore he shook his head.

"I fear, Mistress Wheeler, that this document may be a forgery. I will look through my father's records. If I can find this chest, of course it will be yours. But I must tell you, I have never seen it. Unless," he added, with a flash of inspiration, "it is at Bocton. But then you must ask the Roundheads for it."

Jane stared at him; then she remarked very calmly: "You're lying."

Outraged, Sir Julius asked her to leave. "No one," he declared, "has ever said such a thing to me." But late that night, when all the household was asleep, he went down to the cellar, and found the old chest, and broke it up and burned it in the fireplace, and took the metal remains from the cinders, and buried them before dawn. And hoped, thereafter, to put the business from him.

He could not. A week later, Jane returned.

"Gideon has had Bocton searched," she told him. "The chest was never there. What have you done with it?" His assurance that he knew nothing more about it drew only an angry snort. "You will hear more," she promised.

She was as good as her word. She challenged him again and again. She had a lawyer write to him. She demanded to search the house, which he indignantly refused. A year passed. And another. And still she was not satisfied.

1652

Yes, Martha reflected, she had been blessed with a joyous homecoming. How sweet it was to be reunited with Gideon and his family, with dear Mrs Wheeler, and with her husband too, of course. She wished indeed that she had paid heed to Gideon's urgent letters, and come sooner. But most important of all, it was clear to her now, just as Gideon had told her, that in old England after all – perhaps even more than in Massachusetts – there was a chance to realize her lifelong dream.

Truth to tell, Martha had grown a little disappointed in Massachusetts. She had hardly liked to admit it even to herself while she was there; but as she confided to her friend Mrs

Wheeler: "There has been some backsliding in New England." In Boston and Plymouth, even. And when Mrs Wheeler gently enquired what it was that had tempted some of the colony from the path of righteousness, Martha did not hesitate. "Cod. It's fish that have taken men from the Lord."

The catch off the New England coast had been phenomenal, past all the settlers' wildest dreams. "There are so many fish," they declared, "you can almost walk on the waters." Every year the Massachusetts fishermen were sending between a third and half a million barrels of fish across the ocean to England. "God has granted them such abundance they do not think they need Him," Martha complained. "They are laying up treasure on earth instead of in heaven." Indeed, the growing riches of the men by the coast, and the promise of wealth for the farmers and for trappers who were staking out great land claims in the interior, had so insidiously worked upon men's hearts that there was hardly a church in the colony that had not been affected. "They speak of God, but they think of money," Martha admitted sadly. And some of the fishermen did not even trouble to do that; Martha could never forget, or quite forgive, the terrible occasion when the eldest Dogget son, now a sea captain of some wealth, had turned on her and shouted: "Damn it, woman, I came here to fish, not to pray."

It was not Governor Winthrop's fault, it was not the fault of the good men and women of the congregations, but subtly the character of the Massachusetts colony was taking on the duality it was never to lose: Protestantism and money would walk together henceforth, hand in hand, in New England's promised land.

It was therefore in an uncertain frame of mind that Martha had received Gideon's urgent summons three years before. With the death of the king, he promised her, Cromwell's saints would build a new order, worthy of her. "We need you here," his letter declared. "And your husband too," he had continued, "is greatly in need of your moral guidance." For a year and a half, all the same, she had hesitated before finally, and after much prayer, deciding to return. With her she brought Dogget's younger son, who had failed to achieve citizenship in Massachusetts and thought to try his luck in London, and her own daughter, who Martha feared might be in danger of receiving a tempting offer of marriage from a man who, though godly, was not, she assured her daughter, godly enough.

The England that awaited her was an unfamiliar country. With the execution of the king, the constitution had abruptly changed. The House of Lords was abolished. England was no longer called a kingdom, but the Commonwealth of England, governed by the House of Commons. Nor did anything seem likely to shake the new order. Cromwell, the new state's great general, grew mightier every year. When the eldest son of the executed king, who proclaimed himself Charles II, had tried to enter his English kingdom with an army of Scots, he and the Scots had been utterly crushed. He was living uselessly abroad now. Cromwell had crushed the troublesome Irish too and completely subdued them. It was said he had shed much Irish blood. "But they are papists," Martha said, "so perhaps it was necessary." Even the Levellers in his own army had been brought to heel. The Commonwealth of England was in good order, ready to receive God's law.

Of course, there was much to do. The shining city would not be built in a day. Thanks to Cromwell's one weakness, his religious tolerance, Martha was sad to see that the churches of London remained in some confusion. "Many of these would probably be just as content whether they served a bishop, a Presbyterian assembly or any other form of authority," she shrewdly judged. Nor were the people all as well-behaved as she would have wished. It was hard to promote perfect order in so large a city as London. What mattered was whether a society was striving to improve its morals, whether things were getting gradually better, or worse.

And the rule of the saints astonished her. Never before, in its entire history, had the old city seen anything like it. Even if, as usually happens, the changes were pushed through by an active minority, this godly few had broad support. The Londoners in the street were for the most part so soberly dressed that she might have been in Boston. The Sabbath was strictly observed: no sports were allowed; even going for a walk, unless to church, was frowned upon. No maypoles were permitted. The moral code was strictly enforced by the courts, too, with severe penalties for acts of gross immorality and fines for minor infringements. Her own husband had been fined a shilling, just before her arrival, for swearing a blasphemous oath. "You were rightly reproved, husband," she told him with satisfaction. But best of all, for Martha, was the fact that the playhouses, closed at the opening of the Civil War, had now been boarded up and ordered never to open again. "Not a single play in all London," she smiled. "The Lord be praised."

How blessed she was too, she thought humbly, that her own family should be in such a healthy and godly condition. All Gideon's were safely married now – for even Perseverance had been found a worthy, if silent husband. As for young O Be Joyful, his serious but loving nature was an inspiration to her. "You will be a fine carver of wood," she told him, "because you will carve for the Lord."

The one matter that puzzled her a little was the welfare of her husband. Gideon had been so insistent when he wrote that Dogget needed her moral guidance that, the day after her return, she had taken him aside and asked him what he meant. Whatever it was, Gideon had seemed embarrassed, reluctant to be explicit. "Is it drink?" she asked, "or swearing?" She knew that Dogget was not as strong a soul as she, but he was not a bad fellow and she reminded Gideon: "We must show compassion and forgiveness to our weaker brother, nephew Gideon. All will be well."

It was her duty to love Dogget, but also to help him, she told herself. The first night they spent together he had put his arm round her, which she thought proper; but when, the second night, his hands tentatively started to roam, she had gently though kindly reproved him. "Those things are done for the begetting of children," she said. "But God gives us no cause for such things now." And she had been glad to see that he meekly obeyed.

She had to confess though, she was glad of the presence of dear Mrs Wheeler who would take him off her hands for an hour or two. What a sensible and kindly woman the widow was. If she could not quite approve of her long-standing feud with Sir Julius Ducket – "You should not think of money so much," she felt it her duty to tell her – she did not doubt that Sir Julius was at fault and deserved to be called to account. So she did not often reprove the widow and instead would say to Dogget, "Why don't you go to see Mrs Wheeler for a while?"

* * *

If she had taken Meredith's advice, Jane would have given the business up long ago. "Sooner or later it will come out that Barnikel was a blackamoor and a pirate," he warned. Then you lose your own reputation, and even the Roundheads would take Sir Julius's word over a pirate's. But Jane knew Julius was lying; the businesswoman in her resented being made a fool of. "I don't care," she told Meredith. "I want my money."

It was not easy to know what to do. She did not scruple to harass him every time she saw him in the street, and she would loudly call: "What have you done with my money?" Her lawyers continued to write him letters, but nothing much came of it, and he politely ignored her. Then, in December of that year, seeing the baronet's wife buying meat in the market, Jane suddenly had an idea for a new and ingenious offensive. It was a long shot, but worth a try. She would also need help; but she knew where to get it. She went to see Martha.

It still surprised her that the earnest Puritan had never realized she was having an affair with her husband. Though, she thought with a smile, at their age she would hardly describe it in terms of illicit passion. It was, strictly speaking, a betrayal of their friendship of course, yet even on that count, Jane could not feel very guilty. For years they had lived three thousand miles apart. In her view, the affair was, as much as anything, an act of friendship for a lonely man. And since Martha's return? Well, she had supposed it would end; but a few days after Martha and he were living together Dogget sadly informed her: "She says we're too old for it. God wouldn't approve." And Jane, with a laugh, had given him a kiss. "What are we to do then?" she had smiled.

Sometimes she had even wondered if perhaps Martha did know and chose to ignore it. She clearly has no desire for him herself, she thought, and she seems glad enough to get him off her hands. But then, as she considered Martha's earnest nature she decided: no, she does not know, but in truth she is hardly curious enough even to discover. So the affair continued. Dogget, she could see, was getting an old man now. I bring him life, she realized, and warmth. As for herself – why, the same, to be sure.

They used to meet on Sunday afternoon. Martha and the rest of the family would attend the afternoon service at St

Lawrence Silversleeves or sometimes go further afield to hear a sermon. But Martha did not seem to mind if he remained behind; and then he would go round to the house of Jane Wheeler and spend an hour or two there. Even if he casually mentioned that he had called on her, Martha thought nothing of it.

When Jane outlined her plan to her friend Martha, therefore, Martha was receptive. "You are right," she declared. "Something should be done. I shall speak to Gideon."

On the 25 December in the year of Our Lord 1652, Sir Julius Ducket and members of his family sat down at table in the big panelled parlour, and smiled at each other conspiratorially, because they were about to commit a crime.

First however, as was his habit, before the meal began Sir Julius reverently brought out a small book. No important anniversary ever passed without his quietly reading from it and reminding his family of their duty, and he did so now.

It was an inspirational little volume. Its title, *Eikon Basilike* was taken from Greek and meant "The Image of the King". The simple, moving text was said to be the prayers and reflections of the martyred king; and within three months of Charles's death it had gone through thirty printings. The Roundheads had indignantly tried to censor it. Then they had engaged the great Puritan poet, John Milton, to write a pamphlet against it. But it was no good: even men who supported Parliament but had doubts about Cromwell's new military regime might read the king's book and, finding only sweetness and humble devotion there, begin to wonder if his execution had been just.

For the Ducket family, of course, the issue was not even in question. The book was like a little Bible; the king a holy martyr; and having read a few pages, Sir Julius quietly laid it down and reminded them: "Charles II is our true king; should he die, he is succeeded by his brother James. Remember, we have promised." Then, with happy faces, they set out their Christmas dinner.

They did not hear the soldiers approach the house and enter the courtyard; and they were completely taken by surprise when suddenly, with a bang, the door flew open and Gideon, together with four troopers, marched in and surrounded the table.

Gideon, together with four troopers, marched in and surrounded "Sir Julius," he announced. "You will answer to the magistrates for this." For the crime which the baronet had committed was not the reading of the little book, which he had just had time to slip into his pocket, nor even his words about the king; the crime of Sir Julius Ducket and his family was that they were having Christmas dinner.

For this was another of the improvements that the saints had wrought. "The great holy days should be like the Sabbath," they declared: "times for solemn prayer, not heathen festivals." The English people must be brought closer to God. Anyone caught having Christmas dinner, in the year of Our Lord 1652, was liable to appear on a charge in court. "You have profaned the Holy Day," Gideon said in disgust, then ordered the troops: "Search the house."

"Search the house?" Julius demanded. "Whatever for?"

"Superstitious images. Evidence of popery," Gideon calmly announced.

There was nothing Julius could do about it. For half an hour the Roundheads went from room to room, opening cupboards, chests, turning over mattresses; they even searched the cellar, but they found nothing. Julius was not afraid. Even for a known Malignant, the penalty for eating Christmas dinner would only be a modest fine. Furious at the violation of his home, however, he followed them round, remarking contemptuously to Gideon: "I just want to make sure none of you steals anything."

He was in an upper room when, glancing out of the window, he noticed the two women. Martha and Jane were waiting by the outer gate, looking in expectantly. Martha he could understand. But why Jane? Why should she be concerned about his business? Then he suddenly understood; turning upon Gideon he cried: "You aren't looking for papist images, are you? You're looking for the Wheeler widow's money." And Gideon, just for a second, blushed.

Seeing Julius's wife buy such a large joint of beef in the market had given Jane the idea. They must be planning a Christmas dinner, she had thought. What a perfect excuse. Martha had organized the rest.

By the time Gideon finished, a short while later, Jane had slipped away; so as Julius, white with anger, accompanied him and his men to the gate, he found only Martha standing there. And it was then, enraged almost beyond endurance at what they had done, that he allowed himself to burst out with a cruelty he would never normally have used:

"What a good friend you are, Mistress Martha. You help your friend search for her treasure as well as letting her sleep with your husband." After which, turning on his heel, he stalked back into the house.

Martha stared after him in astonishment. Then she frowned. Then she looked at Gideon. And saw that he was ghastly pale.

In the Puritan London of the Commonwealth, there were many sights to encourage and even inspire the faithful. But none, by the year 1653, could equal the famous preaching universally known as Meredith's Last Sermon.

The years had at last caught up with Edmund Meredith. He was in his eighties now, and he had begun to look it. A sharp illness the previous year had left him so thin and gaunt that people meeting him gave an involuntary gasp, as though they were seeing a ghost. Edmund Meredith walked with death, and rose to the occasion.

His method was simple. As the rule of the saints had produced all the moral bigotry he had feared, and about which he had tried to forewarn Jane, it had also produced a religious confusion so great that even he could not be certain upon which bandwagon he should jump: Presbyterian, Quaker or some other free congregation? Who knew? So he had done the simplest thing of all. He had risen above them. His age only lent conviction to the performance. His language took flight; his gaunt face turned heavenward. The more inspired, the more soul-searing his sermons became, the more absolutely impossible it was to say quite where he stood. Nor did anyone care. Even the most severe and homespun Puritan women, dressed in black and with bonnets tightly tied, felt free to faint. Their husbands in their tall black hats would weep as Meredith's spirit took wing.

For his last sermon Meredith would climb up the steps to the pulpit with such difficulty that, even before he started, the congregation was leaning forward anxiously. With his white hair hanging down to his shoulders – he had grown it long again now – and his hollowed eyes, the very sight of him produced an awed hush. His subject, always, was that of death.

There were many occasions for it: if the season was Lent, a meditation upon Christ's death and resurrection; if Advent, upon the death of the heathen world and the birth of the Christian era. There was nothing in which the seed of death could not be discovered. And, since Sunday afternoon sermons were so greatly in vogue, upon any Sunday when he was in the dying mood, Meredith would refer to the traditional text of evensong:

"Lord, now lettest thou thy servant depart in peace." Gazing out over the congregation, he would stare towards the west window as though, at that very instant, he saw the host of angels coming for him, and cry out: "For mine eyes have seen thy salvation."

He was ready. The congregation could see it. Ready and willing. Indeed, it was clear that he might actually go, at any second, before their eyes. That very possibility made his sermons wildly popular. He was constantly in demand. In the autumn of last year he had preached at St Bride's, St Clement Danes, St Margaret's, Westminster, even St Paul's. Nor did he ever fail to add that dose of humiliation without which no Puritan sermon of the day would be complete. Looking earnestly down at them he would enquire: "And tell me, dearly beloved, if with me now, you were to depart . . . are you ready?" He would pause sadly then, accusingly, point his long finger. "Are *you* ready?" And a great groan would arise from the congregation. For they never were. Which would lead him straight to his electrifying conclusion as, raising up on his toes as if he verily meant to fly, raising his arms up, straining his gaunt face heavenwards in what must, surely, be his final, heroic convulsion, he would cry out in a tremendous voice: "Yet the time is now, even now, I see him coming with all his angels; He is upon us. He has us. He clutches my heart, and yours. He is here. Now. Now!"

At which, with a crash, he would fall back, before staggering down from the pulpit again and being supported to his seat by two helpers. Meredith's last sermon was the best thing he had ever done.

He was a little surprised therefore, just as he was beginning this sermon in St Lawrence Silversleeves, one January afternoon, to observe that two of his congregation, Martha and Gideon, were slipping out.

Jane and Dogget were lying on her bed together when the door suddenly opened and they found themselves face to face with Martha.

Martha had been thorough. It had not taken her long to get the truth from Gideon. Once directly challenged, he had not felt he could lie. "I do not know," he had said defensively, "but I think it is so."

"Even now?"

"Perhaps."

Now, as well as Gideon, she had another neighbour with her. "There must be proof," she had told Gideon. And the proof was there. The neighbour looked shocked, Gideon embarrassed. Martha's face was taut and white. Having seen, she left.

An hour later, having heard Jane's account, Meredith looked grim. "It's the very thing I always feared. I could see the way the wind was blowing even before they killed the king. Now the Puritans have changed all the laws . . ." He shook his grey old head sadly. "Curse these saints with their moralizing and their witch-hunts," he muttered. "And now you are taken in adultery."

"At my age," Jane shrugged, "it sounds absurd."

"But you forget," Meredith warned her urgently. "The penalty for adultery nowadays is death."

Young O Be Joyful sat on the edge of his seat. It was strange to see Mrs Wheeler and Uncle Dogget, as he called him, standing together like criminals. But then of course they were. Everyone knew it now. Even Dogget's children understood that their father was wicked. Martha had seen to that.

The trial of Jane and Dogget took place in the Guildhall. The courtroom was packed. There was, even amongst the good Puritans and the crowd, some wry amusement at the age of the accused. Yet there was no sense, it seemed, of the deeper irony of the event.

That here, before a stern judge and a jury of twelve solid

citizens, was a woman, entering old age, absent from her husband for over a decade, who was prosecuting another woman older than she, for doing something with her husband which, if truth were told, she did not even wish to do herself. Why? Because she had been made a fool of; because she was jealous of both for loving each other; because her God was a vengeful God.

The judge was grave. He knew what the verdict would be.

The evidence was irrefutable. The crime had been seen; the witnesses were reliable. The accused, upon the advice of a lawyer found by Meredith, pleaded not guilty. The witnesses, they said, had misunderstood what they had seen. No carnal act had taken place. But there was not a single soul in that courtroom who believed this manifest lie. The business did not take long. Everyone knew what the penalty for their crime must be. There was no needless mercy, no extenuation in the London of the saints. Their justice was a great, dark rock. The court became quiet as the judge instructed the jury. Nor did the twelve good men take long to consider their verdict. After only minutes they signalled that they were ready. Solemnly the jury foreman stood before the judge, to answer the awful question: "How do you find?" And clearly his voice rang out. "Not guilty, my lord."

"Not guilty?" Martha was standing, trembling with rage. "Not guilty? Of course they are guilty."

"Silence!" the judge thundered. "The jury has spoken." He nodded to Jane and to Dogget. "You are free to go."

"This is an outrage," Martha cried. But no one was listening.

The judge sighed. The verdict had been exactly as he expected. For if, in their zeal, the saints had passed stern, Old Testament laws, they had overlooked one thing: the trials resulting still had to go before an English jury. And the ordinary citizens had not entirely lost their humanity. The idea of hanging a man and a woman for adultery, however much they disapproved of the culprits' conduct, offended their sense of fairness. So they refused to find them guilty. Of the twenty-three known cases brought to court in the London area, only one secured a conviction. "So does this mean they are innocent?" O Be Joyful asked Martha. "No," she replied irritably, "it does not." Nor, she saw to it, did the weakness of the jury mean that the guilty couple escaped all punishment. There was still the community to deal with. As minister at the church, Meredith had to explain the situation to them. "You can't stay in the parish," he told them both. "They won't have you." And the truth of this was quickly seen.

Dogget's life was made simply unendurable. His two children hardly knew him, and out of sheer force of habit followed Martha's lead. No one would speak to him. As for Jane, it was worse. If she stepped out of her house into the street, she was greeted with cries of "Whore!" The man down the street stopped bringing her firewood. The water carrier did not stop for her. People in the nearby Cheapside stalls would ignore her if she tried to buy anything. One day she returned to find 'HARLOT' painted on her door. By the end of the month she said sadly to Meredith: "You're right, we must go."

The snow was falling on the late January day when, Dogget having previously conveyed all her possessions away by cart, he and Jane stepped into a wherry down by the Vintry and were rowed away upstream. Their destination was a little settlement beside Westminster. A century ago some French merchants had for a time formed an enclave there, convenient for doing business with the royal palaces of Westminster and Whitehall, and ever since these streets had been known as Little, or Petty France. Petty France was regarded as a place for misfits; though more recently some literary folk, including John Milton, had taken lodgings there. "At least," Meredith had advised, "Martha and her friends won't bother you in Petty France. You can live quietly there."

1660

During the decade of the 1650s no man in England was more loyal to the exiled House of Stuart than Sir Julius Ducket. But while Oliver Cromwell and the saints were masters of England, there was little that any Royalist could do. And so he read, and he pondered. He read the Bible, in its entirety, twice, and realized that it is the greatest book of history ever written. He read the classics; he studied English history and made notes upon the development of England's constitution. And he waited.

Superficially, Cromwell's rule was strong. His great, round

wart-marked face seemed to Julius to hang over the land like a grim mask from the pagan age. He had executed the king, and chased his son away to France. The Scots were cowed, the Irish massacred and bloodily crushed. All this he did in only a few short years so that even Julius grudgingly admitted: "His sword is mighty indeed."

Yet if the aim of the Commonwealth was to build a shining city on a hill, it was necessary to change men's hearts as well as the laws. And was it really working? For Julius, the turning point had been the trial and acquittal of Dogget and Jane. "The Puritans have gone too far," he told his family. In smaller ways, also, there were signs of unregenerate human nature at work. "Some of the watermen," Julius reported one day, "have started a competition to see who can get fined the most times for drunkenness within a year." It was as though, he reflected, the main streets had been swept clean for the Puritans, but the alleys were still full of sinners.

Nor was the case of religion any clearer. Anything it seemed, except bishops, was tolerated. In St Lawrence Silversleeves, Meredith had generally made use of the Presbyterian Directory but then, about the time of his celebrated Last Sermon, abandoned that for a form of Protestant prayers and hymns that Martha entirely approved of. Other churches were similar. So tolerant was Cromwell in these matters that one year he even forced Parliament to pass a law allowing Jews to enter England again. There had been none in the kingdom since Edward I had banned them back in 1290. Many Puritans, led by their hero William Prynne, who hated Jews, protested vigorously. But the thing was done; and soon afterwards Julius discovered a little community of Jews who had moved in near the Aldgate. "They even plan to build a synagogue there," he told his family. Indeed, Julius perceived only one real religious hardship: the Church of England's Book of Common Prayer, being deemed Royalist, was banned. Londoners were required to conduct christenings, marriages and funerals only before a magistrate now. Yet even so, in one or two churches, Anglican clergymen still secretly used the Prayer Book; and when Julius's son was to marry, his father reported with a smile: "I've found a loyal clergyman who will perform the ceremony in our house."

But greater than all these confusions was the fact that nobody, including Cromwell, could make up his mind how the Commonwealth should be governed.

Everything was tried. At first, Parliament was to rule; but Parliament agreed to nothing, quarrelled with the army and refused to dissolve itself. Cromwell kicked them out, as he did their successors in a series of constitutional experiments. Cromwell had already made himself Protector, and what was left of the Parliament was so weary of the army by now that they suggested he become king under the old constitution. "We didn't fight for that!" the army of saints cried. "But he very nearly took their offer," Julius noted. "So much for Puritan rule."

Patiently, therefore, he waited. If Martha and Gideon ruled the parish, he did nothing to provoke them. Meredith delivered his Last Sermon many more times and when he finally departed, he did so in style. Giving the sermon at St Paul's Cross itself, before an audience of hundreds, and having chosen from the Book of Revelation for his text, he had reached his crescendo, his gaunt face upturned just as the sun, breaking through cloud, smote upon it. "I saw a new heaven and a new earth," he cried. "He carries me away to a great and high mountain, and shows me that great city, the holy Jerusalem, descending out of heaven." Looking now at his audience for the last time he called to them: "Come with me, dearly beloved, come to that place." Then, staring up, straight at the sun, his arms outstretched towards it: "He calls to me, He that is Alpha and Omega, He calls to me now: 'Come hither. Come hither.'" At which he fell, with a crash, from the pulpit, never to rise.

Despite his differences with Meredith, Julius had come to tolerate him, and after his death he became quite friendly with Richard, the preacher's son. He was a clever young man, had studied at Oxford and, as he confessed to Julius, would have liked to enter the priesthood if he could have done so as an Anglican. Instead, he had studied medicine and was setting up as a physician. He had his father's secret scepticism and enquiring mind.

The only subject which continued to embarrass Julius was Jane Wheeler. He heard that Dogget had died three years after their departure; he was very glad indeed that she remained safely distant, down in Petty France.

But if he was sometimes haunted by guilt over Jane, his secret mission, and his loyalty to the late king's two sons, did much to salve his conscience. He was not alone, of course. Together with a dozen other loyal souls, he continued to send letters with every kind of intelligence to the exiled Stuart king-in-waiting in France. And he was overjoyed when, in 1658 Oliver Cromwell unexpectedly died.

The collapse of the Commonwealth took just over a year. Cromwell's son, who was pleasant but unambitious, gave up the succession almost at once. Parliament and the army continued to quarrel. Having watched for nine months, Julius dared to write in person:

> If your Majesty will compromise with Parliament, which your father never would, and if you pay off the army, which the present Parliament doesn't want to, then this kingdom may be yours.

One day, a discreet messenger arrived with tidings that gladdened Julius's heart.

"The king thanks you for your steadfast loyalty, which neither he nor his father ever forgot." Here the messenger grinned: "He is a much merrier fellow than his father, you know. Says he'd sooner compromise with a barrel-load of monkeys than stay an exile all his life. By the way," the man added as he was leaving, "he knows you lost Bocton through your loyalty. It will be returned to you, as soon as he is king."

Finally in the spring of 1660, Julius heard with almost inexpressible joy the cry: "The king is coming. King Charles II reigns. Long live the king!"

Chapter 13

London's Fire

1665

Ned was a good dog: medium size with a smooth, brown and white coat, bright eyes, and devoted to his cheerful master. He could catch any ball his master threw in the air; he could roll over and play dead. Sometimes, if his master was not looking, he would chase a cat for fun. But above all, he was a good ratter. There was not a single rat in his master's house. He had killed them all long ago.

It was a hot summer's day. His master had gone out early, so he was guarding the house in Watling Street. He hoped his master would return soon. There were a number of people about, as usual; but there was one stranger Ned did not like. He had been standing in front of the door of a house further down the street. When Ned had gone to investigate him, the stranger had tried to hit him with the long pike he carried. Ned had yelped, and kept away after that. A woman had come to the house about an hour ago. He caught a smell from her as she went past. He did not know what the smell was, but it was something bad. A little while ago, from the same house, he had heard the sound of weeping. There was no doubt, people were behaving oddly.

It was just then that he saw the monster.

The Ducket family was ready. Two coaches, as well as a cart, awaited them at the gate and Sir Julius surveyed them with satisfaction: his wife, his son and heir, his son's wife, two children. A manservant and two female servants were also to accompany them, together with the chest of clothes and other items in the cart. "But we've room for one more," he said. "And I am determined not to leave him behind." For the third time that morning, he went out into the street. Where the devil was the fellow?

Sir Julius Ducket was, in his sixty-third year, a very contented man. Now he was prosperous and honoured, friend of the king. And it was a delightful thing to be a friend of King Charles II. Tall, where his father had been short; informal where Charles I had been reserved; bursting with humour – his father was rather serious; and, most remembered of all, a huge and cheerfully open womanizer where his father, whatever his faults, had been very chaste. King Charles II knew everything there was to know about life's gutter. He would do whatever necessary to keep his throne because, as he assured everybody: "I have no wish to go on my travels again."

King Charles's court at Whitehall was the jolliest place. The Banqueting Hall, scene of his father's execution, was in regular use and his subjects could come to watch him dine there. Just west of Whitehall, he laid out the wooded open space into a new St James's Park where he could often be seen walking the pretty little spaniels he so delighted in, or, with his cavalier courtiers in the long tree-lined alleyway on the park's northern side, playing at pall mall – a curious game, halfway between croquet and a primitive form of golf – at which he was adept. All London enjoyed this lighter mood also. Sports were played; the maypole came out again. Theatres were opening, including a new one near the Aldwych, at Drury Lane, where the king's own company of players was performing and a buxom young actress called Nell Gwynne had just made her début. If His Majesty's somewhat puritan subjects were shocked by the genial immorality and extravagance of his court, no one wanted to return to the miseries of the Commonwealth.

Above all, this Charles had no illusions. He knew he was there, not by Divine Right, but because the English Parliament had decided he should be. "Parliament and I need each other," he remarked to Julius one day. Common and Lords were back, just as they had been half a century before; and Charles would get as much as he could from them. But he never pushed them too far. It was the same with religion. His young Portuguese wife was Catholic; so was his sister, married into the French royal house; but he knew perfectly well that many of his subjects were Puritans. "I would be happy to grant them all tolerance," he declared. Parliament wasn't. So the situation more or less like the settlement under good Queen Bess was reached. All must conform to England's Church with its ceremony and its bishops. Those who did not suffered minor restrictions and were debarred from public office. But that was all. The message from the king was clear.

"Be loyal. Then go play, or go pray, as you please." This was the royal court and settlement known as the Restoration.

The merry monarch had little desire for vengeance. One or two of his father's murderers had to be executed. The corpse of Oliver Cromwell was dug up and hanged at Tyburn. "Looks better now than when alive," Julius sourly remarked. But Charles made no attempt to pursue his enemies. His friends, however, he warmly remembered – including Sir Julius Ducket.

"Parliament won't allow me to buy Bocton for you," he apologized. "But I can give you a state pension – for life. So live long, dear friend." The pension was generous. With no more Roundheads to question his every move, Julius was also able to spend the remains of the treasure, and to start trading vigorously. A year ago he had been able to buy Bocton back, at a modest price, since the house was in a sorry state. Within months, he had put the whole place in order.

Indeed, all England seemed to be in a state of optimism and excitement. Her commerce was increasing: her colonies yielding rich results. Even the king's recent marriage to a Catholic was easily tolerated when it was discovered that she brought with her, as a dowry, no less a place than the rich Indian trading port of Bombay! England's mastery of the seas, too, was growing even greater. Last year her trading rivals the Dutch had been pushed out of several colonies including one quite promising settlement in America. New Amsterdam, they had called it, Julius heard. "So our naval squadron have called it New York." In the opinion of Sir Julius Ducket, the state of England had never been better.

At least, until about ten days ago. Just at this moment, however, he was not so sure. And it was with a trace of anxiety now, looking around, that he wondered: where the devil was young Meredith?

* * *

Ned's hackles rose. He got to his feet, growling; bared his teeth, took two paces forward. The monster was still advancing down the street. Ned's growl grew more savage. For he had never seen such a creature before in his life. The monster was at least as tall as a man. It was made of waxed leather. Its body was shaped like a huge cone and it reached all the way to the ground. The beast had two arms, and huge leather hands. It was holding a short stick. But most fearsome of all was the creature's head. For between two huge glass eyes, with rings round them, was a huge leather beak. On its head the monster wore a black, broad-brimmed leather hat.

Ned barked, growled, barked again, backed away. But the monster, having seen him, had turned and was coming straight towards him.

Doctor Richard Meredith had been the happiest man in London until an hour ago. The honour conferred on him the day before was great, especially considering his youth. He had set out in the morning with a spring in his step. Until, at the Guildhall, they had shown him the document.

If the Restoration had taken place a few years earlier, young Meredith might have been a clergyman. But he had no wish to be a Puritan minister and his old father had warned him: "Look at what I had to do to survive." So at Oxford, he had decided to become a physician. It was another way of serving his fellow man. It also suited his intellect, since he had a naturally enquiring and analytical mind.

Medicine was still a crude affair – a mixture of classical knowledge and medieval superstition. Doctors still believed in the four humours: they applied leeches and bled their patients because they supposed their blood needed thinning. They also used traditional herbal remedies – some effective – common sense and prayer. Indeed, in some cases the miraculous was considered a normal cure: no doctor discouraged the lines of people suffering from scrofula dutifully filing past the king whose touch, it was confidently believed, could cure that ailment. The natural sciences were in a similar state. Educated men still disputed whether unicorns' horns had magical properties. But in recent decades a new spirit of rational enquiry had been growing. The great investigative genius of William Harvey had shown that blood actually circulated in the body:

he had also begun to study how the human foetus develops. Robert Boyle, through careful experiment, had formulated laws for the behaviour of gases. And of all the places in which he might have lived none, surely, could be better than London. For London was the home of the Royal Society.

The Royal Society of London had begun as an informal discussion club twenty years before. Meredith's first introduction to it had been in the year of the Restoration, when he was allowed to attend a lecture given by a leading young astronomer – like himself a clergyman's son – named Christopher Wren. Membership of this club was restricted, though as a doctor of medicine, he was welcome to attend any lectures, which took place on Wednesday afternoons. King Charles too became a member and had granted the organization a royal charter after which it had become known simply as the Royal Society.

Some months ago, with great timidity, Richard Meredith had even delivered a short paper which had earned him kind words from Wren and several others. Yet even so, he had never expected the wonderful news of the day before.

"Doctor Meredith, you have been elected a full member of the society." No wonder that his cup of joy had been full. At least until an hour ago.

Doctor Meredith had not taken much notice of the trouble when a few cases appeared in May. Sporadic visits like this had been a feature of summer in London for centuries. Nor was he worried when more appeared in June. There were none in the parishes along Cheapside; Watling Street was untouched. No significant outbreak had occurred, he reminded himself, for nearly twenty years and nothing really major since the reign of King James I. So when people asked him if they had cause to worry, he had reassured them: "Avoid the area to the west by Drury Lane and Holborn. The city is hardly touched, though." The weather was exceedingly warm that month. "This dry heat," most medical men concluded, "will increase the element of fire in men's blood. This will produce yellow bile and make them choleric." Perhaps, he supposed, that was causing the sickness to increase. By July, he heard of growing numbers down in Southwark and on the road to the east, outside Aldgate. But this morning, when they had shown him the document, he had received a severe shock.

The Bill of Mortality was a document produced every week. In two long columns it noted the numbers who had died, of each of some fifty causes, in the city and surrounding parishes of London. Most of the numbers were small. "Apoplexy: 1. Dropsy: 40. Infants: 21." But near the top of the second column, the clerk had pointed to one, terrifying number: 1843. And beside it the single, awful word: Plague.

Plague, Contagion, the Black Death: all names for the same condition. "Do you mean to leave London?" the clerk had asked.

"No. I am a doctor."

"All the doctors I've seen so far this morning," the clerk smiled, "are leaving. They say they have to attend their rich patients, and as the rich will leave, they have to do so too. However," he said approvingly, "if you really mean to stay, we have something you had better wear."

Ned tried to hold his ground, but the monster was coming directly at him. Where could he attack the creature? It had no legs. Its arms were too thick to get a grip on. His snarls and barks grew furious, but did no good.

And then the monster did something extraordinary. It took off its head. Pulling off one huge leather glove, it held out a hand for him to sniff, and called his name. It was his master.

The huge leather outfit which the clerk at the Guildhall had given Meredith was terribly hot. The great beak was stuffed with aromatic herbs which he had just bought at an apothecary's. For many believed that the contagion was spread through foul air.

"Poor Ned!" He was laughing. "Did I give you a fright?" He patted the dog affectionately. "Let's go in." He had just opened the door when Sir Julius reached him.

"My dear Meredith." As Sir Julius looked at the remarkable uniform he realized how much he liked the young man. "What news of the plague?" he asked.

Meredith told him about the Bill of Mortality.

"As I feared," Sir Julius said. "Meredith, I beg you, come with us now. We are going to Bocton. Plague seldom comes into the country. Stay with us till it's over."

"I thank you," Meredith replied warmly. "But I feel my duty's here."

With a sigh Julius left him; and for half an hour he made his family wait before once more returning to have a last try at persuading the young man. But he discovered that Meredith had already gone out again, leaving only Ned guarding the door.

Sadly and thoughtfully he went back to his house, took his pistols, as he always did when they were travelling over the empty roads down to Kent, and having loaded them, ordered his family to get into the carriages. A few minutes later they were moving down Watling Street towards London Bridge. It was only then that he ordered his carriage to stop for a moment. For there was at least one small service he could perform for his young friend.

Ned wagged his tail as he saw Sir Julius approaching the house again. He knew he was a friend. He started to get up. He liked to greet friends even if his master was not there. Sir Julius was quite near now. He had paused for some reason. He was holding out his hand. No, he was pointing at him. Why was he doing that?

The great bang, the puff of smoke, and the huge blow that slammed him back against the doorstep were a single, flashing, unreal moment to Ned. There was a huge pain in his chest. Something warm in his mouth. That was the end of what Ned knew.

When Sir Julius had shot Ned, he tied the dog by a length of rope to the back of the cart and dragged him behind them. At the river, Ned was thrown in. Sir Julius had no doubt about the rightness of this action, sorry though he was to do it. After all, didn't most sensible people know that dogs and cats carried contagion? But knowing Meredith's affection for the dog, Julius knew he'd never have the heart to do what was necessary himself. At least Ned wouldn't infect his master now. "It was," he said, "the least I could do to save that brave young man."

"The dog was a good ratter," his son remarked. "Meredith hadn't a rat in his house."

"True," Julius replied. "But hardly relevant."

* * *

By mid-August the Mortality Bill was at four thousand a week; by the end of August, six thousand. Each day, Richard Meredith put on his great leather uniform and went out.

At times he almost thought he must be in some other city – like London, yet different. The streets were almost empty, the stalls in Cheapside all gone, and the houses shut up as though they meant to stop their mouths and noses against the contagion. The court had gone clean away to the West Country city of Salisbury. Since late July a stream of carriages and wagons had been rumbling out to the bridge or the gates: gentlemen, merchants, the richer artisans even, all bound for safety. With only a few exceptions, it was the poor who remained.

How eerie it was. As he wandered from parish to parish, Meredith could see that the mayor's regulations were being enforced. The moment the plague was confirmed by the city examiners, the house was closed, a watchman with a pike set on guard to stop anyone entering or leaving, and a terrible red cross painted on the door with, usually, the sad words: "Lord Have Mercy". Only a doctor dressed like himself could visit the patient then. When a household signalled it had a corpse, the searcher came to verify the cause of death, and soon after, most often at eventide, the bearers arrived with their cart, ringing a handbell and calling out the haunting, mournful cry:

"Bring out your dead. Bring out your dead."

Some parishes, almost a quarter in total, were free of the plague. On the last day of August, walking by St Paul's, he encountered a man named Pepys whom he had met several times at gatherings of the Royal Society. Pepys was an official at the Navy Board and, Meredith knew, had access to information of all kinds. "The real number of deaths is higher than the Mortality Bills show," Pepys told him. "The clerks are falsifying the accounts and some of the poor aren't being counted. The bills show seven and a half thousand last week."

"And the real figure?"

"Nearer ten," Pepys replied grimly. "But perhaps, Doctor Meredith," he added more cheerfully, "if God spares us both, I shall have the pleasure of hearing a lecture from you one day at the Royal Society, upon what is the true cause of the plague."

No subject, indeed, could have been nearer to Meredith's heart. As he had gone from house to house, seen people –

whole families – feverish, delirious, screaming in the agony of death, he had felt a terrible sense of helplessness. He was a physician; yet the truth was he could do nothing about plague and he knew it. And why, he considered? Because of his, and everyone else's complete ignorance. How could he suggest a remedy, or even alleviate the condition when he had no idea what caused it; how to protect his patients when he did not even know how it was transmitted?

He had formed certain suspicions. It was assumed that people gave the plague to each other: hence the attempts at quarantine. Certainly, as he went into some of the worst areas – Southwark, the parish of Whitechapel outside Aldgate, the road up to Shoreditch, Holborn – and saw whole streets where nearly every door bore the dreaded cross, this seemed a fair assumption. But why was the plague so concentrated in these places? Many people were smoking pipes because the smoke was supposed to cleanse the air. It was said that not a single tobacconist had caught the plague yet. But if it was carried in the air, then why did he find plague in one city parish, yet not in the parish a street away? Nor could he discover anything in common between the worst affected areas – one marshy, another dry and airy. It can't just be the air, he decided. Some other agent carries the plague. But what? Dogs and cats? He had heard from a neighbour that it was Sir Julius who had shot Ned and removed him. For a week he had been furious, but now he was no longer. God knows how many cats and dogs had been destroyed by now on the mayor's orders. Twenty or thirty thousand, he guessed. But even if it were dogs or cats, how did they pass it on?

A possible solution to the question of transmission came to him early in September, when he was attending a dying man down in the Vintry.

The plague came chiefly in two forms: in one, the bubonic, about one in three who caught it lived; in the other, pneumonic form, hardly any survived. The patient's lungs filled; he sneezed a lot, coughed up blood, had sudden, terrible fits of fever and chill, and then fell into a deep sleep, that grew deeper and deeper, until he was still. The poor fellow before Meredith had been a humble water carrier, with a bent back and six children. Shivering with the chills, he looked hopelessly at Meredith. "I'm going," he said simply. Meredith did not deny it. One of his little children came over to comfort him. And then the fellow sneezed. He could not help it. He sneezed into the child's face. The child winced. And Meredith, with a terrible instinct, rushed to the child, seized a rag, and wiped off its face. "Keep them away from him," he cried to the mother. "Burn this cloth." For it must be so, he thought. The phlegm and spittle of an infected person must carry contagion, since they derive from the most affected part. A week later, the child died.

Martha still hesitated, though her stepson Dogget was insistent.

"I'm safe where I am," she said. Though they had returned from Massachusetts together, she had not, for a long time, felt close to the younger Dogget boy. He lacked spiritual direction. Indeed, though she did not like to frame the thought, she was glad he was not her own. He had married and become a waterman instead of taking up a craft. But he came to see her every week and she reminded herself that there was good in almost everybody.

"I see what it is." A soft chuckle. "You think you're safe, old girl, don't you? 'Cause God's on your side." Dogget put his arm round her affectionately. "You think it's just us sinners that are going to die." And though she disapproved of his tone, Martha did not deny the charge. It was exactly what she thought. For Martha knew what caused the plague: wickedness.

Most people in a general way would have acknowledged this. Plagues and disasters, after all, were in the hands of God and had been sent to sinful mankind ever since Adam and Eve were cast out of the Garden of Eden. And if there were any doubt about this case, she would point out: "Where did the plague begin?" In Drury Lane. Why Drury Lane? Every Puritan knew the answer to that. The new theatre, patronized by the king with his women, and his lewd, extravagant court. Hadn't London been warned half a century ago when Shakespeare's Globe had burned down? Now, in the moral ruin of what should have been God's shining city, Martha could see the truth clearly. She could not think it likely, therefore, that the plague should visit her.

Yet it was certainly coming. From the Vintry, last week, it had steadily been making its way up Garlick Hill towards

Watling Street. It was not surprising that her family should be concerned about her.

If only Gideon were still there, but he had died three years ago. His place had been taken, as far as was possible, by young O Be Joyful; but though the woodcarver was nearly thirty now, and the delight of her old age, he had not the authority of his father. He was still a journeyman, rather than a master and could only just make out his letters. It was nonetheless O Be Joyful who now decided the issue.

"We are going too," he told her quietly, indicating his wife and two young children. "Please come with us, Aunt Martha, and be our spiritual guide." So, reluctantly, she agreed; and half an hour later, that warm September morning, she and the two little families walked solemnly down the hill to the riverside, where Dogget put them all in his wherry and began to row. Only as they got out into the stream did Martha stare ahead and ask in horror: "We are going to that?"

Their destination was certainly the strangest sight. It lay in midstream and, though large and growing before her very eyes, it was hard to say exactly what it was. "Waterman's Hall, I call it," Dogget said genially; for it was the river folk who had thought of it. Consisting of scores of rafts, wherries and other little craft lashed together, the whole structure formed a sort of huge, ramshackle, floating island. Even as they approached, men were hard at work enlarging it, adding decking and constructing little shelters upon it. Their reasoning was instinctive, but logical enough. If they could remain out in the river, isolated from the contagion, they might hope to survive. "There's water. There's fish. All we need is to build some shelters," Dogget continued. And when Martha enquired what he and his friends would do if anyone on this watery refuge developed plague, he grinned. "Throw them in the river," he said.

By mid-September it had become harder and harder to cope with the plague. The living were no longer obeying the mayor's orders. People were no longer observing the quarantine rules. Plague victims were being concealed; people were refusing to remain cooped up in infected houses, or trying to smuggle their children out to safety. And with the limited number of watchmen, it was impossible to control them. In an attempt to separate the sick from the healthy, the mayor had ordered that numerous poor victims should be kept apart in the city hospitals. But there were so few: there was old St Bartholomew's, another hospital dedicated to St Thomas, in Southwark and St Mary's up by Moorfield. They were full to bursting. The city had opened extra ones – called pesthouses – to the north and east of the city, and at Westminster. They were full too. Even more shocking, to Meredith, was the condition of the dead. The parish graveyards had not enough space. Great plague pits had been dug, mostly outside the walls, into which bodies were flung by the dozen. But still, Meredith observed, sextons were continuing to pile the bodies into the graveyards until the top ones were covered by only a few inches of earth. In one yard, he had actually seen feet and arms sticking out of the ground.

He frequently went over to the pest-houses at Westminster, and it was one day, starting back towards the city, that he was accosted by a watchman with a request that he would come to a house nearby where a patient had need of a doctor. Minutes later he found himself entering a small but pleasant house in Petty France.

Six days had passed since Jane Wheeler had begun to feel feverish. At first she had tried to ignore it. The twinges of pain in her arms and legs, similarly, she dismissed. After all, she reminded herself, I am over eighty years old. By that evening she felt weak, but could not sleep. The next day she began to feel giddy. At midday she decided to go out, but she had only gone ten yards when suddenly she began to stagger. Hardly knowing what was happening to her she had turned to go home. A neighbour came to help her. She remembered little of the next few hours. She thought her neighbour had come again in the evening, and the following morning. Then a strange woman came whom she had never seen before. A nurse of some kind. But by that time she could only think of one thing. It was in her neck, her armpits and between her legs. Great lumps: she could feel them. And the pain. The terrible pain.

Meredith sighed. If the pneumonic form of the plague killed swiftly, the other form, called the bubonic, was even more terrible to behold. The old woman before him had the bubonic plague and was suffering the final stages.

With bubonic plague, the lymphatic glands become horribly inflamed, swelling into lumps – buboes, as they called them. The body bleeds under the skin, causing dark spots and purple blotches. Patients are often delirious. At the very end – and this is what Meredith now saw – rosy-coloured spots often appear on the body. But, in this last crisis, the old woman was lucid. And it seemed she wanted something.

"Can you read and write?"

"Of course. I'm a physician."

"I want you to write my will. I'm too weak." She shivered. "There's pen and ink in the corner." He found them and, sitting down on a chair, he took off one of his gloves and prepared to write as she began: "I, Jane Wheeler, being of sound mind . . ."

So that's who this woman was. She had no idea of his identity; but though he had not seen her since he was a boy, he remembered the scandal about her. Poor woman, he thought, what a way to depart.

The will was short and to the point. She had no children. She left her little fortune, which it seemed had been diminished by time, equally to all the surviving children of John Dogget deceased, with the exception of the child by Martha. Hardly surprising, Meredith thought privately. "Is that all?" he asked.

"Nearly," she said. "But there's one thing more."

Richard Meredith was not aware, as he was writing, that under the floorboard of the room a black rat had just died. Nor could he have seen for it was very small indeed, the flea that had just come through the crack between the boards.

The flea was in poor condition. For several days it had been feeding upon the blood of the black rat, which had the plague. The bloodstream of the rat had contained hundreds of thousands of the plague bacilli, and some tens of thousands had been transferred to the flea. Inside the flea's stomach, the plague bacilli had multiplied, blocking the entrance. As a result, the flea was very hungry. Now the flea, finding its host lifeless, was looking for another body on which to feed. As soon as he punctured the skin of the next creature, he would try in vain to ingest blood through the blocked entrance to his stomach; meanwhile thousands of bacilli would seep into the new host where, they would quickly multiply, and multiply; and multiply again. The flea was death. It hopped on to Meredith's coat.

The last paragraph of Jane Wheeler's will was startling.

> Finally, with this my last testament, and with my dying breath, to Sir Julius Ducket, thief and liar, who has stolen my rightful fortune and caused my ruin, I bequeath my curse. May God, who is just, send him to hellfire for his sins, and may his family be cursed hereafter and his inheritance stolen as mine has been. Amen.

"Are you sure you want to say that?" Meredith asked.

"I am. Have you written it? Show me. Good," she breathed. "Give me the pen." She signed with difficulty. "You and the nurse witness." Meredith did so. The nurse made her mark.

The flea hopped on to Meredith's sleeve.

"I must go now," Meredith said, and pulled on his glove again. Jane hardly seemed to hear him. Suddenly she cried out in pain. The nurse and Meredith looked at each other. It would not be long now. He decided he would not tell poor Sir Julius that he had been cursed.

The flea could get nothing from the coat. He was just preparing to try Meredith's bare hand when it vanished inside the long leather glove. As Meredith went towards the door, the flea leaped on to the nurse.

By the month of October, the plague seemed to pass its peak. For the first two weeks the Bills of Mortality were in the four thousands; by the fourth week, fewer than fifteen hundred; then about a thousand for three weeks. Then a falling away. Although cases would continue to crop up into February, by November London was cautiously opening up again. By late January, the carriages of even the wealthiest citizens and their doctors were rolling back into town.

The total official death toll of the Great Plague is over sixty-five thousand. The true figure was certainly more, perhaps nearly a hundred thousand. One curious feature of the plague however, which is often overlooked, was the colony of folk living on floating islands in the Thames. There were a considerable number of these huge and curious structures. Altogether some ten thousand people lived on the river like this for several weeks. As far as is known, few if any of them caught the plague. It was a fact which Doctor Richard Meredith noted, but was still, to his chagrin, unable to explain.

So it was, at the end of November, that Dogget and his family finally ventured back to their lodgings, to find they had gained a small inheritance.

If Richard Meredith was saddened at his failure to understand the plague, nobody else did either. Not for almost two centuries would the true nature of the disease and its carriers be identified. Until that time it was remembered only for the fact that no herbs could cure it and for its symptoms – the rosy rash or the sneezing – recorded in the song which, a little time after, the children began to sing.

Ring a ring o' roses
A pocket full of posies
Atishoo, atishoo
We all fall down.

In later times, in North America, the "Atishoo" of the song, not understood, was changed to "Ashes". But there were no ashes – only, that year in London, the terrible sneezing before death.

1666

September the 1st was a quiet night. Sir Julius lay peacefully in the big house behind St Mary-le-Bow. It had been a long, pleasant summer and the family had only returned from Bocton the week before. It was Sunday tomorrow. About midnight he awoke briefly and went to the window. The air was pleasantly cool, with a hint of breeze coming from the east. He took a few deep breaths, then went back to bed.

At about one o'clock in the morning he arose again. Had he heard something? He looked out of the window. Was there, perhaps, a faint sound coming from the direction of London Bridge? Outside, the courtyard was like a dark well. A faint sheen of starlight touched the steep rooftops all around. He listened, but after a minute or two decided he had heard nothing so he returned to bed and fell asleep.

It was nearly four in the morning when his wife woke him. This time there was no doubt. Over the rooftops on his left, he could see a faint glow. Flames and hot ashes must be rising into the sky somewhere near the bridge. Probably not close. "But I'll go and see," he said.

He pulled on some clothes and left the house.

It was a fire, but not a very big one. It had begun some time after midnight in a baker's house down a narrow street off East Cheap, called Pudding Lane. A maidservant who had panicked and run up into the roof had been trapped and burned to death. The fire had spread to about a dozen of the huddled little houses now, but he had often seen worse blazes than this. The men were throwing buckets of water on it, without much conviction. As Julius turned to go home he met the mayor.

"They called me out," the mayor said irritably.

"It seems no great affair," Julius remarked.

"A woman could piss it out," the mayor grumbled, and stomped off.

This crude and famous verdict would not have gone down in history, and the fire in Pudding Lane would be entirely forgotten if it had not been for one extra factor which neither man noticed at the time.

The wind was getting up. By the time Julius was safely back in his bed, the breeze was sprightly. At the moment when, with his arm round his wife, he fell asleep again, the wind had carried the sparks and embers across to the next street, which led straight on to London Bridge. At dawn, the church of St Magnus the Martyr went. Soon afterwards, the fire reached the bridge. By mid-morning it was threatening the warehouses along the river.

By the time Julius went out again and made his way over to a vantage point near the top of Cornhill, he could see a huge conflagration spreading all round the head of the bridge. Two, perhaps three hundred of the tightly packed houses, he guessed, might be in flames. The crackle and roar reverberated all around the city now. So fascinated was he that he stood up there for more than two hours before making his way down the hill, skirting the fire as close as he dared, and then walking back up Watling Street. It was there that he encountered young Richard Meredith talking to a gentleman he introduced as Mr Pepys. This gentleman, who seemed to have seen more than most, was scathing.

"I saw both the king and his brother at Whitehall," he was saying. "They sent orders to pull down houses to make fire-breaks, but because the city authorities are afraid the owners may demand compensation, they're leaving the houses untouched!"

"Have you seen the mayor?" Julius asked.

"Five minutes past. First he almost weeps; then he says no one will obey him; then he says he's tired and going to dinner. Contemptible."

"So what will happen?"

"The fire," Pepys said, "will rage."

During the afternoon O Be Joyful told his family to be ready to move. The fire had been growing steadily. A stream of carts piled with people's possessions had been labouring up Watling Street from the London Bridge area for some time.

O Be Joyful had been increasingly conscious of his responsibility in the last few months. The time on the river and the general disruption of the plague had left Martha somewhat weakened. That spring he had persuaded her to live with them and her daily proximity could not fail to remind him that he was expected to take Gideon's place. With four children to think of now, as well, he knew it was his duty to give leadership. If only, he wished, these things came to him more naturally.

Nonetheless, he acted decisively now. A friend with lodgings at Shoreditch had agreed to take them in. If need be, they would be ready. And he was satisfied that his duty had been done when Martha had suddenly announced: "I want to go and see if my old friend Mrs Bundy is safe."

He knew this godly woman slightly and offered to go himself. "But you've never been to her lodgings," Martha had pointed out; so they set off together. As they descended Watling Street and crossed Walbrook the billowing smoke over the bridge area rose several hundred feet. As they passed the London Stone, Martha indicated a narrow street on the right and, with a resolute face, headed downhill, straight towards the fire.

If any explanation of the fire's unstoppable growth were needed, the scene before them certainly provided it. The narrow street, the wooden and plaster houses (the orders to build in brick or stone were always ignored, every century), the upper storeys that jutted out, each one further than the one before until they practically touched the house opposite: this huddled mass of tenements, courtyards and wooden structures that leaned this way and that, sagging and stooping like a row of drunken old gossips, was in reality nothing more or less than a huge tinderbox. Worse yet: people trying to put out fires in a hurry had already broken open the wooden water-pipes in the street to fill buckets, then left them gushing; consequently, the water cisterns, even from Myddelton's New Canal, had all run dry. As O Be Joyful looked down the street, he could see the fire steadily eating its way from house to house.

Yet strangest of all, he realized, was the behaviour of the people. For if the richer citizens were making off with their valuable goods, the poor, with nothing except the roof over their heads, were often remaining huddled in their houses in the hope that the fire might somehow stop before it reached them. He could see whole families coming out of tenements even after the roof of their house had started to burn.

The tenement Martha sought lay halfway down the street, some fifty yards from the edge of the fire. When they got there O Be Joyful offered to go in but she told him: "I know where she is. Keep watch outside." And he saw her enter the hallway and disappear up the stairs.

The progress of the fire was frightening, yet also fascinating. The brown and grey smoke rose above him now like a great wall, shutting off the whole sky. The heat was soon so great that he had to put his hand over his face. The air was full of glowing sparks and embers. Several fell close by him. He could see others lodging on roofs where little fires were breaking out. Above all, he was struck by the terrifying sounds of the fire, the crackle, the bursting bangs, the growing roar as it ate its way from house to house. Soon it was only thirty yards away. But where was Martha? Surely, even if Mrs Bundy was in there, she could not be much longer?

The bang, and the roaring tongue of flame that shot through

the house took him completely by surprise. The hot wave of air almost knocked him off his feet. As he scrambled up, he could see glowing flames at some of the windows. Smoke was starting to billow under the roof. How had that happened? And then he suddenly realized: he had forgotten about the rear of the houses. The fire had come roaring in from the back.

He ran to the hallway and the foot of the staircase, calling out Martha's name. But the roar of the fire all around must have prevented her hearing him. Somewhere above he could hear a crackle of flame. Smoke was oozing out from under the floorboards. He started up the stairs, still calling.

Then another great crack and a rushing sound, above him. God knew what was happening up there. He hesitated. He was not sure what part of the house she was in. He turned, ran back down the few stairs he had climbed and went out into the street.

"Martha," he cried. "Martha!" The fire had attacked houses right up the street. He glanced around to make sure he still had a line of retreat. "Martha!"

Then he saw her. She was at a small window, up on the top floor under the roof. Frantically he waved at her to come down. She made a sign he did not understand. Was she trapped? He signalled he was coming, and rushed inside. Moments later he was running up the stairs.

Crash. Something, a beam he thought, had fallen up above. Bang. Another. A pall of smoke hung over the stairs ahead of him. From his left, at the rear of the house, a loud crackle. Some plaster fell, only ten feet from him. Flames came through. He must hurry. He pressed on. The stairway creaked as he went up. A burst of flame shot out from the top floor. He gasped, stood still. And then his heart failed him. He went no further, but turned and fled. Moments later he was looking up at Martha again. He made a sign to her, as though to indicate that the stairs were impassable. Her pale round face continued to gaze down at him.

"Jump," he cried; but only to salve his conscience. Had she done so it would probably have killed her; anyway, the window was too small. "Martha!" Smoke was billowing out from under the eaves. Was she crying out? They just stood, looking at each other, for fully a minute until, with a roar, he saw the roof turn into a torch. Timbers started to fall; flames

were pouring out of her window. And then he saw she was no longer there.
The fire was coming so close that he could not stand the heat. He backed away, wondering if by some miracle she might come running out.

The mayor was relieved of his responsibility for fire control on Monday morning. The wind was strong; but the fire was so large now that it seemed to create winds of its own. Not only was it being blown right along the riverbank westward towards Blackfriars, but it was marching north, almost as fast, up the slope of the eastern hill. Early in the morning, soon after Julius had supervised the third cartload of possessions to leave the house and told his family to make themselves ready for a return to Bocton, he heard the good news that the king's brother James, the Duke of York, had arrived in the city with a body of troops. James was a solid fellow, a naval man. Perhaps he could restore order.
Sure enough, as soon as he went out, he saw the duke's handsome figure directing his men at the bottom of Watling Street. They were about to blow up half a dozen houses with gunpowder. He went to pay his respects.
"If we enlarge this street," James explained to him, "perhaps we can make a firebreak." They retreated a short way and took cover. There was a huge boom. "And now, Sir Julius," the duke asked smilingly, "are you helping us?"
A few moments later, to his great surprise, Julius found himself with a leather helmet on his head and a fire-axe in his hand, working alongside the duke and a dozen others similarly clad, pulling down walls and timbers to make the firebreak. It was hard work and he might have been glad to stop when, glancing at another man who had just started to work beside him, he realized that there was something familiar about the big, swarthy fellow; and a moment later, with a little rush of joy and excitement, he saw that it was the king.
"Should Your Majesty be doing this?" he asked.
"Preserving my kingdom, Sir Julius!" The monarch grinned. "You know how I try to hang on to it."
The firebreak did not work, even so. The fire's impetus was so strong that, an hour later, it leaped the gap.

* * *

It was on Tuesday morning that the most awesome event took place. O Be Joyful watched it from the bottom of Ludgate Hill.

His own house had gone on Monday afternoon. As arranged, he had taken his little family up to Shoreditch and then remained there. News had come all the time. In the evening he heard that the Royal Exchange was in flames; at dawn he knew that St Mary-le-Bow was no more. A little later he had decided to go and see for himself. Walking down to the city gates, however, he found his way blocked. The troops would not let anyone enter. "It's a furnace," they told him. The open ground at Moorfields had been turned into a huge encampment for dispossessed people. He had made his way round the old walls, past Smithfield where another little camp had formed by the gates of St Bartholomew's Hospital, and so had come to Ludgate. There was a crowd of people there. He saw good Doctor Meredith who had stayed behind in the plague amongst them. All had their eyes turned up the hill, awestruck.

For St Paul's was burning down. The huge, grey barn whose long line had hung over the city for almost six centuries; the dark old house of God which had stood sentinel on its western hill since the days of the Normans, enduring storm, lightning and the ravages of time; ancient St Paul's was slowly crumbling before their eyes. He watched it for over an hour.

He had turned and was walking out along Fleet Street. As he was approaching the Temple, he saw a group of youths. They had backed a young fellow against a wall. It looked as if they meant to harm him. He heard one of them cry: "String him up."

For a moment he hesitated. They were only youths, but there were a dozen of them and they looked sturdy. He crossed the street to avoid them and proceeded towards the Temple. He heard the young fellow cry out. And then stopped, ashamed.

He still had not told his family exactly what had happened to Martha. From the moment when he had backed up the burning street, he had told himself that there was nothing he could have done. So powerful was his need for this to be true that he had even managed to sleep a whole night believing it. He had still comforted himself with the belief on his way down to the city and all the way to Ludgate. But there he had seen Meredith.

Doctor Meredith, son of the preacher; Meredith who had, unlike most of his profession, stayed in London through the plague, risking his life, no doubt, scores of times. Meredith who, with no claims to any religious calling, had shown himself, in his quiet way, to be stout-hearted.

And what was he? Like an arrow penetrating armour, the question had struck through O Be Joyful's defences, causing him a spasm of pain. Faint-hearted. Even if Martha could not have been saved, had he really tried? Hadn't he lost courage when he ran down those stairs? And now it suddenly occurred to him: if you walk by on the other side, you prove your guilt. He turned back, and a moment later was confronting the youths.

"What has he done?" he asked. The young man himself began to respond, but the youths cut him off.

"He started the Fire of London, sir," they cried.

Even the day before, the rumours had begun. A fire like this could not be the work of chance. Some said it must be the Dutch. But most – perhaps half the good people of London – had a sounder suspicion by far. "It's the Catholics," they said. "Who else would do such a thing?"

"But," the poor boy cried in his broken English, "I am not Catholic! Am Protestant. Huguenot."

A Huguenot. Despite Englishmen's fear of the popish leanings of the Stuarts, to any Protestant living in Catholic France the kingdom of England had seemed a safe haven indeed. Massacred by the thousand by a pious French king in 1572, they had been protected from actual violence for a generation by the Edict of Nantes. But these devout French Calvinists were still subject to constant restrictions, and a modest but steady stream of them had come into England where they had been allowed to worship discreetly. Huguenots, they had come to be called.

The young fellow before him, O Be Joyful guessed, was not more than seventeen. He was a slim, intelligent-looking boy, with fine brown hair, but his most noticeable feature was the pair of spectacles he wore, through which he was peering short-sightedly at his assailants.

"You are Protestant?" Carpenter demanded.

"*Oui*. I swear," the boy replied.

"But he's a foreigner. Listen to him," one of the boys protested. "Let's give him something to think about."

O Be Joyful found his courage. Stepping in front of the boy he told them firmly: "I am O Be Joyful Carpenter. My father Gideon fought with Cromwell, and this boy is of our faith. Leave him alone or fight me first."

He would never be sure what would have happened next if a small patrol of the Duke of York's men had not ridden into sight from St Clement Danes. Reluctantly the youths went off, and he found himself left alone with the young Huguenot.

"Where do you live?" he asked.

"Down by the Savoy, sir," the young man replied. There was a little French Protestant community and church there, Carpenter knew. He offered to escort him back.

"You are new here?" he enquired, as they walked.

"I arrived yesterday. To live with my uncle. I am a watchmaker," the boy volunteered.

"I see. What's your name?"

"Eugene, sir. Eugene de la Penissière."

"De la what?" O Be Joyful shook his head. The French name was too much for him. "I'll never remember that," he confessed.

"How should I be called, in English, then?" Eugene asked.

"Well," O Be Joyful considered. The only English word that seemed anything like it was ordinary enough. "I think," he said, "you'd do better with Penny."

"Eugene Penny?" The young fellow considered doubtfully. Then his face brightened. "You saved my life, sir. You are a very brave man. If you say I should be called Penny. *Alors*," he shrugged and smiled. "Penny. And how may I find you, sir, to give you my proper thanks in future?"

"No need. My home's gone anyway. But my name is O Be Joyful Carpenter. I'm a woodcarver."

At the Savoy, the two men parted.

"We shall meet again," Eugene promised him. But just before turning away he said: "Those boys who wanted to kill me. They were not completely foolish. *Non*. For this fire – it was surely the work of Catholics."

* * *

And still the fire raged. St Paul's was gone, a huge, blackened ruin; the Guildhall, Blackfriars, Ludgate. By late Tuesday and Wednesday it even spread outside the walls, along Holborn and Fleet Street. St Bride's was gone. Only in the open greens around the Temple did the flames meet a firebreak they could not pass. In the east, a huge break created by the Duke of York saved the Tower of London. With this and a small number of other exceptions, the old medieval city within the walls was entirely lost.

But to two people the plague and the fire brought a more inward crisis. To Doctor Meredith the plague had brought a profound sense of failure. His only role, he freely admitted, had been to comfort the dying. His medicine was useless and he knew it. The quest for medical knowledge would go on but until the time when doctors actually knew something, "I might as well try to save their souls," he concluded. As he had watched St Paul's burn from Ludgate he had decided. "I shall take holy orders and become a clergyman, as I first intended." There was nothing to stop him continuing any medical studies at the same time. There would still, thank God, be the Royal Society.

Only for O Be Joyful Carpenter did the fire bring despair. For after parting from Eugene, he had not returned to his family, but walked about watching the fire; and as he did so, the boy's words had come back to mock him. "A brave man" indeed. It was no use, he told himself, to pretend that Martha's death had been inevitable. "I could have brought her down and saved her. Yet by my fear and cowardice I let her burn." Was he the son of Gideon, the spiritual heir of Martha? No. He was unworthy.

And what of their vision of the shining city? What had become of that now? As the fire made its way along Fleet Street, like some powerful chariot of destruction, its crackles seemed like the grinding of huge wheels upon the road, and their message was terrible yet plain: "All gone. All destroyed. All gone."

Medical opinion is still divided on why, after the Great Fire, the plague scarcely returned to London again. The causes of the fire similarly remained in dispute. Most Londoners believed it was the Catholics. The view of the Parliamentary

Committee called to report on the Great Fire soon afterwards was more measured. The blame, it concluded with great firmness, could not be placed upon any group of men, either foreigners or even Catholics. London's fire, it stated plainly, was an Act of God. It was God's Fire.

Chapter 14

St Paul's

1675

The sun was catching the southern face of the strange little building on the hill. Eugene Penny waited patiently for the two men to finish their conversation. The building cast a long shadow down the green and silent slope. Far below, the Queen's House gleamed white by the waterside at Greenwich. He wondered whether Meredith would be up there at night, gazing through the great tube at the stars. He felt a rush of embarrassment when he thought of what he had to tell the kindly clergyman, for he knew that Meredith would tell him he was mad.

Though Richard Meredith saw Eugene waiting for him, he could not easily break away, since he had a problem with Sir Julius Ducket. It was all the more irritating as he had been looking forward to the celebration of the opening of the building.

It had been especially appropriate, Meredith thought, that his friend and fellow member of the Royal Society, Sir Christopher Wren, the astronomer who had so brilliantly turned his mathematical talents to architecture, should have been the one to design the building. For the small brick, octagonal structure that now presided over the slope above Greenwich was the first of its kind in England: it was the Royal Observatory.

Strangely enough, its primary purpose was not to study the stars – though it contained a telescope of course. The main objective, as Meredith had explained to Sir Julius earlier that morning, was entirely practical.

"It's to help our mariners," he told him. "A sailor at present, by using a quadrant, can measure the angle of the sun at its zenith, or certain stars, and work out how far north or south he is. But what they do not know," he continued "is how far they are to east or west – their longitude. Until now, sailors have had to make a rough guess, usually by how many days they have sailed: hardly satisfactory. Yet there is a way of discovering one's longitude."

"For consider, Sir Julius. Each day, as the Earth makes its way round the sun – as, despite the old objections of the Roman Church we know it does – the Earth also spins. Because of this, as we know, the sun appears over the eastern horizon here in London, for instance, several minutes before it is seen in the west of England." Indeed, so well aware of this were men that local time was a highly variable affair. Each city normally set its own clocks according to the hours of daylight, so that the western port of Bristol kept a different time from London.

"We calculate that a difference of four minutes represents one degree of longitude; an hour is fifteen degrees. So you see, if a mariner could take his own time, which he can by the sun, he has only to compare it with our time here in London to discover how far east or west of us he is."

"If he had a clock that kept perfect London time he could do it."

"Yes. But we haven't discovered how to build a clock that will keep time like that at sea. However," Meredith continued, "we can make such accurate tables of the moon's position against the backdrop of the heavens that, by reading off his sightings in an almanac, a mariner will know what the time is, at a particular moment, in London. By comparing this standard astronomical clock, as it were, with his local time, he'll be able to know his longitude."

"Will it take long to complete these tables?"

"Decades, I should guess. It's a huge task. But that's what the Royal Observatory is for: to make a great map of all the heavenly bodies and their motions."

"So all sailors – from other countries too, I should think – will work out their bearings from a standard London time?"

"Precisely," Meredith smiled. "If they want to know where they are they'll follow the time of the Royal Observatory. We shall call it Greenwich time," he added.

But having taken Sir Julius to the Observatory and shown

him its telescope, clock and apparatus, Meredith had suddenly been sidetracked into this stupid conversation. Worse still, he had to admit, it was largely his own fault.

It was a month now since he had allowed the matter to slip out. In doing so – of course he saw that now – he had carelessly assumed that as he himself did not take the matter seriously, the baronet would feel the same. He had been entirely wrong; Sir Julius had been deeply concerned. In fact, he had been terrified; rich Sir Julius Ducket, friend of the king, had shaken with fear, all because poor Jane Wheeler, dying of plague, had laid a curse upon him.

"If she was a witch," Sir Julius was saying urgently, "aren't there prayers you could say? Or do you think," he continued, "we should dig her body up and burn her?"

Meredith sighed. Was this all, after seeing the Observatory that would chart the heavens, his friend could think of? It offended him, as a man of science, that people should still believe in all this superstition, yet he knew very well that even educated men still believed in witchcraft. There had been a crop of officially sanctioned witch-burnings in the countryside only recently. Nor was this just a hangover from the medieval religion of Rome: the stern Puritans of Scotland and even Massachusetts, he had heard, were positively eager to burn witches.

"She wasn't a witch," he said calmly. "And anyway, you can't dig her out of a plague pit."

"But the curse . . ."

"It died with her." He could see, however, that Ducket was by no means satisfied. Sir Julius was not his parishioner. After the Great Fire, the little church of St Lawrence Silversleeves, along with several others in the area, had not been rebuilt. Nor had Sir Julius continued to live in the city by St Mary-le-Bow, but moved westwards, while a new mansion, built on the site of his old house, had now become the official residence of the mayor. Soon after his ordination however, Meredith had been lucky enough to get the living at St Bride's in Fleet Street.

Although it went against his common sense, he comforted the older man. "I will pray for you," he reassured him gently. But he was not sorry, a few moments later, when Sir Julius left and he could turn his attention to the patiently waiting Eugene Penny.

Meredith liked the Huguenot, even if he was a member of an alien Church. O Be Joyful Carpenter had first introduced them and he had been able to help the young watchmaker to find a place with the great London clockmaker Tompion, who was installing the timepiece in the Royal Observatory. He listened carefully to what Penny had to say and then, as expected, he gave his judgement: "You must be mad."

The Huguenots of London formed a thriving community; the pastor of the French congregation was as busy as he could wish. They had also fitted in well. Some like the rich Des Bouveries family, had already risen to social prominence. Their French names – Olivier, LeFanu, Martineau, Bosanquet – had either acquired an English sound or they had been converted, as Penny had, to an English equivalent: Thierry into Terry, Mahieu into Mayhew, Crespin into Crippen, Descamps into Scamp. Their liking for such culinary delicacies as snails might seem strange, but other dishes they brought with them, such as oxtail soup, were soon popular with the English. Their skills in making furniture, perfumes, fans and the newly fashionable wigs were welcome; and though, like all newcomers, they were regarded with some suspicion, English Puritans respected their Calvinist religion. As for the king, he had reached a reasonable compromise. The first French churches – at the Savoy and at Threadneedle Street – might use a Calvinist form of service as long as they remained loyal and discreet. Any new churches must use a form of the Anglican service, in the French language; though if a few differences crept in to salve their Puritan consciences, they were unlikely to be troubled. Strangely enough, because they were devout and, unlike so many English Puritans, anxious not to offend, the Anglican bishops of London were usually rather protective towards them.

So why should Eugene Penny want to leave?

"Is it the riots?" Meredith asked. There had been several attacks on Huguenots in the eastern suburb of the city that year, and he supposed this might have worried Penny. Yet since he was convinced that the real cause of the trouble had little to do with the Huguenots as such, he continued immediately: "For if it is, let me reassure you."

It was true, of course, that there was always some friction between the "foreigners" – which still meant anybody from outside the city – and the Londoners who feared competition for their skills and jobs. But the real problem, Meredith realized, had come as a direct result of the Great Fire; and it concerned the city's ancient government.

In the first months when the old walled city was a charred and empty ruin, people had even wondered if it might be abandoned. Gradually it was rebuilt, but its medieval structure had gone. New fashionable developments were starting to spring up around the court area at Whitehall; the rich were more inclined to live there. Craftsmen meanwhile, who had been obliged to carry on in the northern and eastern suburbs of the city, found it cheaper to stay put. The mayor and the aldermen lacked the will to extend their authority over all these spreading areas, and the guilds felt much the same. If a man wanted the freedom of the city, and the benefits of guild membership, the old rules and the apprenticeship remained the same. But if traders and craftsmen chose to evade the rules and operate in the suburbs, there was not much the guilds could do about it. So when a group of Huguenot silk-weavers had moved into the little suburb of Spitalfields, just outside the city's eastern wall, and their hard work and imported skill had brought them instant success, some of the low-wage earners in the area had grown jealous.

"It's just a local affair," Meredith told him. "The Londoners aren't against the Huguenots, I promise you."

But Eugene was shaking his head. He had taken off his spectacles and was polishing them – a trick he often had when he was embarrassed. During his twenties, his face had become thinner, so that now it looked finely chiselled. His eyes, though short-sighted, were a deep, lustrous brown. He's a handsome fellow, thought Meredith; he might almost be Spanish. But the real problem for Eugene Penny was that he was French.

He had been sent to England by his father. Cautious, always planning ahead, quietly persistent, they both agreed what must be done. "The kings of France have sworn, by the Treaty of Nantes, to allow us to worship freely in perpetuity," he had told Eugene. "But the Church of Rome is strong; the king is devout. Go to England therefore. If we are sure we are safe here, you can return. If not, you must prepare a new home for your brothers and sisters there."

But after his last trip back to his family, Eugene had been overcome by a terrible homesickness; and with every month it had grown worse. Now, with an apologetic face, he confessed to Meredith: "I just want to go home to France. My family has come to no harm there. It cannot really be necessary for me to be here."

Meredith hardly knew what to say. He could not counsel Eugene about the situation in France, but it concerned him that the young watchmaker should leave such a good master. "At least write to your father first to seek his permission," he suggested but he doubted that Eugene would take his advice.

When Meredith had gone, Eugene Penny walked back slowly. He acknowledged the wisdom of what the older man said, but his heart was very torn. Making his way across the top of the slope to the broad expanse of Blackheath, he picked up the old Kent road and began the long descent towards Southwark. It was a good four-mile walk, but he did not mind. As he came down from the ridge he saw all London spread out before him – the charred city, still rebuilding, the distant palace of Whitehall, the more distant wooded slopes of Hampstead and Highgate. And wherever he looked, from London Bridge, extending downstream past the Tower and all the way along the Pool of London to beyond Wapping, he saw the ships; a forest of masts so thick that they seemed, like trees, almost to touch one another. There must, he thought, be over a hundred great vessels there, proof positive that the mighty port of London would never allow anything – plague, fire or even war – to stop its worldwide trade. How could he want to leave such a place?

On a warm afternoon a few days later, a group of men gathered in a circle at the centre of a huge, empty ruin on the city's western hill. Several of them were simple craftsmen and stonemasons wearing their aprons – which was appropriate since the pleasant, intelligent-looking man who had summoned them together was not only England's greatest builder but also a devout Freemason himself.

"Today", announced Sir Christopher Wren, "we begin a rebirth."

The rebirth of London was already a remarkable feat. The city that was rising out of the ashes might, certainly, have been grander. Wren and others had submitted plans for a splendid series of noble squares, circuses and avenues that would have been the wonder of the northern world. But the huge difficulty of compensating the thousands of people who had property rights along the existing street lines, the fact that the need to commence work was urgent, and the sheer expense of such grandeur had forced the king and his government to take a more modest course. The layout of the new city was a modified version of the old medieval plan.

But there all resemblance ended. For now, with seven centuries of huddled, overhanging wooden buildings burned to ashes, there was a chance to avoid the mistakes of the past, and the government took it. Regulations were drawn up; streets were to be wider; some of the gradients of the hills were smoothed; houses were to be built in handsome terraces, in a simple classical style, according to precise and uniform dimensions – two storeys plus a cellar and garret in side streets, three or four storeys for the main streets. And above all, strictly enforced this time, they were of brick or stone with slate or tile roofs. When one or two merchants tried to break the rules, their houses were promptly pulled down.

Now, all around London, were brickfields, where men dug up and baked the London clay and the rich brickearth that a tropical sea and, later, Ice Age winds had deposited so generously millions of years before.

A few medieval landmarks remained. The Tower still stood sentinel by the waterside. Inside the eastern wall, a Gothic church or two survived; out at Smithfield, St Bartholomew's kept its quiet peace from the days of the crusades. And on the river itself, one curiosity was retained: the tall old houses on London Bridge, which, though scorched, had mostly come through the fire, were left standing and were to remain, as a charming relic of London's medieval glory, of the days of Chaucer and the Black Prince, for another ninety years.

But the medieval city was gone: and in its place was arising something not unlike the Roman city that had been there once before. True, there was no amphitheatre looming over the western hill: the Guildhall occupied that site and men's love of bloodshed had to be contented with public executions and cock-fights instead of gladiatorial conquests. True, it would be another two centuries until central heating was rediscovered, seventeenth-century roads would have made any Roman laugh, and literacy was almost certainly less widespread than in the ancient world; but despite these drawbacks, it could still be said that the new city had nearly returned to the standards of civilization enjoyed by the inhabitants of Londinium fourteen hundred years before.

Of all the builders of the new city, none was greater than Sir Christopher Wren. The astronomer turned architect was everywhere. Already he had rebuilt St Mary-le-Bow with a magnificent tower and classical steeple. As a charming and witty addition, he had put a little balcony in the tower overlooking Cheapside as a reminder of the old grandstand where once kings and courtiers had watched the jousts. St Bride's in Fleet Street was going up, and numerous other projects were already in hand. But nothing compared with the vast undertaking before them now.

St Paul's. Huge, almost roofless, cavernous: its high, blackened walls had stood for some years after the fire. Since gunpowder was too dangerous, Wren had ordered them slowly pounded with a battering-ram and section by section, they crumbled and fell. Except for the west wall, they were only a few feet high now. And in place of the tall old Gothic church Wren had designed a magnificent new edifice that would be the glory of London.

And all the assembled craftsmen were smiling – except one.

O Be Joyful Carpenter had never got over the Fire of London. Indeed, in a sense, it had destroyed him. The fire of truth had sought him out and exposed him, naked, for what he was: a coward. But no, it was worse than that. He was a Judas. Hadn't his whole life afterwards proved it?

Until the death of Martha, the modest woodcarver had always supposed that he was one of the chosen. This was not out of any pride on his part: far from it. But hadn't he walked with God, in the company of Gideon and Martha, all his life? Didn't he carve for the Lord? Wasn't he simply one of a family, therefore, whom God had chosen to do His work? He had been, until he had killed Martha. You let her burn, he had told himself again and again, to save your skin. Where was your trust in God? When God confronted you, you turned away. Your faith is a sham. And for many months he had suffered great agony in his soul.

One day in the spring after the fire he had gone down from Shoreditch to the ruined city. Even after all these months the buildings of London were still quietly smouldering. He could walk through the wider streets, but many of the blackened stones were still too hot to touch. Acre after acre of charred desolation, smoke arising in tiny columns from innumerable ruins, a tart, choking smell wherever he walked: this, he thought, must be like the endless burning marl of the pit of hell itself. And then, with a dull, blank despair, he realized he was not one of the chosen at all; he was one of the damned, and his hell had already begun.

He seemed to lose energy after that. He had to rouse himself to work, but the joy had gone out of it. He prayed only with his family, for form's sake. He had little occasion to sin, but he made no great attempt to lead a godly life, since there was no longer any point.

He might have drifted still further into depression if there had not been so much to do. For in the years after the fire, houses had been going up by the thousand and as a journeyman carpenter, working for several masters, he had been kept busy. Doors, panelling, wood-carving of every kind – the demand for woodwork was huge.

It was a chance meeting with Meredith that had changed his life. Having known O Be Joyful all his life, Meredith had always kept on friendly terms. He had been delighted to help Carpenter's friend, the young Huguenot, and he had already secured O Be Joyful several small commissions in his new parish of St Bride's. Seeing the craftsman's gloomy face coming down Ludgate Hill one morning he had suddenly had a happy thought, that might cheer him up.

"My friend Wren has recently engaged a wonderful wood-carver who needs assistants. Why not let me take you to him?" he suggested. Thanks to his entreaties, that very afternoon Carpenter had met the remarkable Mr Grinling Gibbons.

Gibbons was a quiet craftsman like himself. Carpenter had heard of him by repute some months before when, emerging from seclusion, he had presented a magnificent carving to the king. Now, for the first time, he saw Gibbons's work; it was astounding. The human figure, animals, trees, fruit, flowers –

there seemed to be nothing he could not carve. More than that, these were not just the usual forms of such things. Even a simple apple in a lavish festoon of fruit to decorate some piece of wooden panelling had such an individuality, a lightness about it that you almost reached out to touch it believing it was real and ready to be eaten. "He is a sculptor, not just a carver," O Be Joyful whispered to Meredith as they looked round the master's workshop.

"There's no one in London who comes near him," Meredith agreed. "My friend Wren is commissioning him," he went on, "to work on his new churches. Would you like to join him?"

O Be Joyful gazed around in silence. What could he say? He might be condemned for all eternity himself, but there were things which out of a lifetime of habit he still could not bring himself to do. Martha and Gideon might now be looking down at him with pity or disgust; but to work in one of the king's churches, with their Prayer Book, their vestments, their bishops – sunk though he was in sin, he could not insult their memory by doing that.

Yet he had never seen anything like this carving. He knew with absolute certainty that he would never find a master in all his life like this. He could hear Martha's voice chiding him from above: "These are graven images – idolatry. A sin." He knew it was true. This was a love of worldly beauty utterly at odds with all he knew to be Puritan and holy.

He looked at Meredith. He looked at the workshop. "I should like to work for Grinling Gibbons," he said.

It was some months before his real woes began. The rebuilding of St Paul's had been long delayed because the costs were huge. The solution to the problem, however, was simple. The authorities announced a tax on coal. Every time the ships from Newcastle docked at London with the coal for its home fires, the unloaded sacks were taxed. And for every three shillings of tax, fourpence halfpenny went straight to St Paul's. Wren's great cathedral would be paid for, therefore, with coal.

By now this fund was beginning to mount up, and a new plan had been called for. Gibbons had shown O Be Joyful the rough wooden mock-up that had been made of Wren's initial design – a simple structure with galleries which had pleased Carpenter because it reminded him of a Protestant meeting house. But now, it seemed, the king wanted something grander. "They are making a model of the new church," Gibbons explained. "And I am sending you to help them."

The next morning, O Be Joyful had turned up at the workshop expecting to find one or two others at work on something the size of a small table. Instead, a team of craftsmen was already busy on a monumental model. At a scale of half an inch for every foot of the building itself, it was twenty feet long and almost eight feet high. More daunting yet, it was being made of oak, which was exceedingly hard to carve. And more impossible still, every detail, every cornice, was to be exactly reproduced inside and out. "Dear God," he murmured, "it'll be easier to build the real thing."

The drawings from which they were to work were coming in piecemeal, but the outline of the building was clear: a splendid classical structure in the form of a Greek cross, with large Roman windows, and porticoes with pediments at the ends. The drawings for the roof had not been supplied yet so he did not know how that would look, but there was no shortage of work meanwhile. The columns and pilasters of the great basilica were all of the Corinthian order and he was set to work on these. He was delighted by their chaste simplicity. "But they're the devil to carve," he admitted. For more than a month he laboured, every day, as the walls rose. Wren would come in frequently, say a few words, then dart out. Despite himself, O Be Joyful began to feel quite proud of his task.

One afternoon, just as work was ending for the day, Meredith came by and, beckoning to O Be Joyful, said, "There's something you should see." A few minutes later, the two men were at the site of the old St Paul's, where Meredith showed him a hole in the ground.

To ensure that his greatest work would last, perhaps to eternity, Wren had decreed that the foundations must be deep and firm. Boreholes had been sunk at the site to test the ground. Ten feet, twenty, thirty, down they had gone, past the existing foundations, past those of the church before that, past Saxon remains; but still the great architect had not been satisfied, and urged them: "Deeper still. Go deeper."

"See –" Meredith opened a box nearby and showed Carpenter some fragments of Roman tiles and pottery, "this is what they found, from the days when the city was Roman."

But they had gone further still, finding sand and then seashells. Meredith smiled. "It seems that once this place lay under the sea. Perhaps in the time of Noah. Who knows?" And O Be Joyful marvelled to think that the foundations of the new church should grow in this manner from the days of the Flood. "Then at last they came to hard gravel, and clay, over forty feet down," Meredith explained.

But the next morning when O Be Joyful arrived at work, a shock awaited him. They had brought in the drawings for the roof.

"He's putting that on a church?" he cried. He was not the only workman to gaze at the drawings in horror. For over the central crossing Wren had designed a huge drum, ringed with columns; and over that, rising magnificently into the sky, an august and mighty dome. "He cannot!" the carver protested.

No one there could possibly have missed its significance. No church in England had ever been disgraced with such a thing. From the shape of the dome, the Corinthian columns – every detail had suddenly fallen into place – this was clearly, if not a copy, then the very brother of that infamous dome that hung over what every Puritan knew was the great house of iniquity itself. "Dear Lord!" he cried. "It's just like St Peter's – at the Vatican. It's the church of Rome." And, in terror, he ran out of the workshop.

"The form of the building does not affect the religion," Meredith assured him an hour later, after the terrified carver had come to his house. "The Catholics themselves," he pointed out, "worship in churches of every possible shape. Wren himself," he added encouragingly, "is the son of an Anglican clergyman. He's no papist." But still, he could see, O Be Joyful was unconvinced.

"Wren may be all you say," he cried. "But what about the king?" And that, Meredith thought, was not so easy.

When Charles II had been restored to England, it had all seemed straightforward. The Church would be Anglican – the Church of his father and grandfather, the compromise of good Queen Bess. Puritans might not like it, but popery was at least banned. And that, for better or worse, was that.

Or was it? The Stuart court had always had Catholic overtones, but since being exiled during the Commonwealth, it had become still more so. The king's wife was Catholic, so was his sister in France, so were many of his friends. Charles II, it was true, had always played his Anglican role staunchly. Yet as the years went by, it seemed to many that he was on rather too friendly terms with his kinsman Louis XIV, the most Catholic king of France. When they had joined together recently to try to crush England's trading rivals, the Protestant Dutch under William of Orange, the English Parliament had grown restive.

"Weaken the Dutch: yes. They're our rivals. But don't destroy them. They are also fellow Protestants. And we don't want all the seaboard opposite us in the hands of the Catholics, do we?" As Charles's friendship with Louis continued, Parliament had begun to wonder. And to make sure of their ground they had suddenly sprung a new measure on the king. The Test Act of 1673 demanded that anyone holding public office must not only be Anglican, but must deny the miracle of the Roman Catholic Mass under oath. No conscientious Catholic could do that. They waited to see what would happen. And two months later, the Duke of York, the king's own brother, resigned as Lord High Admiral. He was a secret Catholic.

James was a decent, conscientious man. Few disliked him; most remembered his role in the Great Fire. All agreed that he had acted honourably now, but the shock was severe. Though Charles II had, as far as was known, some thirteen bastard children, none of his legitimate babies by the queen had so far lived. James might, therefore, be next in line. Charles, fortunately, seemed in rude good health. Perhaps he'd outlive his brother. And James's own two daughters were declared to be Protestant. It was not a crisis. Royalists like Sir Julius Ducket rallied round to assure everyone that the king was sound, the English Church secure. "But is it?" O Be Joyful now asked Meredith.

"It is. I promise you," the clergyman said.

Sadly, with doubt in his heart, O Be Joyful had returned to work. More than once he had asked Gibbons to give him other tasks, but his work was too good to be spared. Slowly he carved the columns and capitals round the great dome, sadly he put the finishing touches, from a ladder, to the top; miserably he watched as the junior workmen and apprentices polished the huge oaken model until it shone like bronze. "It's a work of art," Meredith told him, when he was shown it. But he was glad, soon afterwards, to return to other work, and he tried to put the model out of his mind.

He had been greatly surprised a few weeks ago when Meredith, chancing to see him in Cheapside, had smilingly approached. "Come," he said. "I have something that will please you." Leading the way past the site of St Paul's, the clergyman took him into a drawing office nearby where he pointed to a large sheet of designs on the wall. "The great model you worked on has been refused," he explained. "The Church authorities didn't like the popish dome either. So this is what has been approved."

O Be Joyful stared. The drawings on the wall were remarkable. One could see parts of the classical building remaining, but it was longer, thinner, more like an ordinary church. No dome now rested over the central crossing. Instead, supported on a similar framework, stood a tall spire – classical in form, but clearly echoing the spire of the previous building. It was, it had to be confessed, a somewhat ungainly-looking design, not at all what one would have expected from Wren, but it satisfied the main requirement.

"As you see," Meredith confirmed, "no dome. Work is to start at once," he added.

So here he was with Grinling Gibbons and Wren's other chief craftsmen to witness an impromptu ceremony – not a formal affair for the great men of the city but, typical of the great architect, a modest gathering, called at short notice, for the ordinary workmen. Nothing special had been prepared. Everyone except O Be Joyful was cheerful. He was so deep in gloom that at first he did not notice that the rest of the company had turned to look at him and that they were laughing.

Christopher Wren had just decided he needed a stone to mark the central spot of the new church and he had asked someone to bring him one from the churchyard outside. A stonemason was just setting off, when the great man's eye had fallen upon Carpenter and he remembered his unusual name.

"O Be Joyful," he announced, "what more perfect name for such a mission! Go with this fellow, O Be Joyful, and find me a stone." The company laughed, with simple good humour.

To O Be Joyful however, as he accompanied the mason outside, the laughter contained a note of mockery. They were laughing not at his name, but at his foolishness. Did they all know the secret then? It was unlikely. But Wren, his master Gibbons and doubtless many of the others were sure to be in the plot, and they were laughing because they supposed he had not guessed. He cursed them all in his heart as he did their bidding.

He and the mason looked about for several minutes in the churchyard and, feeling they should not take too long, they finally chose a flat piece that had obviously broken off a gravestone. On it was written a single word. The mason could not read. O Be Joyful slowly made out the letters, but they meant nothing to him. He shrugged. "It'll have to do," he said. They carried it back; and were both rather disconcerted when Wren, seeing their stone, most uncharacteristically clapped his hands in delight.

"O Be Joyful," he cried, "you are a wonder. Do you know what this says?" And he made them turn the stone so that all could see the single Latin word it bore: RESURGAM.

"I shall rise again – that is the meaning," Wren explained. "Here," he beamed, "was the hand of providence indeed."

They put the stone face up in the centre of the great church's floor.

But O Be Joyful did not even smile. He felt nothing but humiliation, for he knew very well what was to rise over this cursed stone. It had come to him the very day after Meredith had shown him the new drawings, and looking at Wren's laughing face now, he was utterly sure. It was inconceivable that the great architect truly planned to build that ugly, clumsy structure he had seen in the drawing office. It could only mean one thing therefore. The designs for St Paul's were a fake to keep everyone quiet while Wren played for time. He was planning to build a papist cathedral, with a papist dome. He looks like an Anglican, O Be Joyful thought. He says he's a Freemason, but really he's a Jesuit, full of lies.

And so, ashamed of himself though he was, and bound for damnation anyway, out of age and pride O Be Joyful made a secret vow. "If he builds a dome, I'll refuse to work in this church, even if Gibbons dismisses me." He might know the evil secret of St Paul's, but at least, for once, he would take a stand.

1679

The event which finally convinced Sir Julius Ducket that Jane Wheeler's curse upon his family had failed took placed on a July day in 1679.

As his carriage jingled down Pall Mall he felt, despite his seventy-six years, as excited as a young man. Who would have thought, at his age, that such a call would come? He was so pleased that besides having his tailor make him a new set of clothes he had made one other dramatic change to his appearance: Sir Julius Ducket was wearing a large grey wig.

The fashion, like most fashions, came from the court of the mighty King Louis XIV of France. King Charles had started it at Whitehall just after the fire; and though a man of Sir Julius's years would have been forgiven if he had come to court without one, he had decided that today he must be fully up to the mark. Nor was his wig a trivial affair. Imitating the long hair-style of the cavaliers, its tightly rolled curls not only covered the head but its heavy flaps fell to the shoulders. It was expensive; and oddly enough would remain in one shape or another the essential accoutrement of the upper classes for over a century, and of the English courtroom for long after that.

It was not only his new finery that made Sir Julius feel younger: the whole scene around him suggested a vigorous new life. In addition to the new city that was arising at London, the developments out by Whitehall were growing every year. To the north, classical Leicester Square was being laid out. To the west, along the northern edge of St James's Park, the former tree alley of Pall Mall had recently become a long street lined with fine mansions. Gentry, nobility, even Nell Gwynne the actress, currently the king's favourite mistress, lived there. Above Pall Mall, St James's Street, Jermyn Street, and stately St James's Square were all nearing completion. This was the West End, the new home of the aristocracy. Compared to its broad, straight thoroughfares and open piazzas, even the Romanized city seemed cramped. For Sir Julius, this burgeoning of London had also meant a burgeoning of his fortune. He had obtained a grant to build several streets of houses on the old hunting grounds – still known by the ancient huntsman's cry of "Soho" – above Leicester Square. The profit had been huge.

But, above all for Sir Julius, it was the sense of being needed that had raised his spirits. The monarchy was in trouble again; and his king had called for help.

The business in a way was absurd – though it concerned the succession. Charles II of England still had no legitimate child. He had any number of bastards of course, and one of them, a brilliant young Protestant called the Duke of Monmouth, was highly popular. "But you can't make a bastard king," Sir Julius would point out. "Apart from anything else, there are so many that if you start down that road you invite a civil war from all the rivals." Legitimacy was key; which meant that after Charles would come his Catholic brother James.

James only had two daughters, Mary and Anne, both of whom were indisputably Protestant. And though, after their mother's death, the Duke of York had, to everyone's displeasure, married a Catholic, the marriage had produced no children. Better yet, in an effort to reassure his Protestant subjects, the king had married his niece Mary to that most utterly Protestant Dutchman, William of Orange, mortal foe to King Louis of France and to all things Catholic. "So," Ducket would conclude, "even if, one day, the king should predecease his brother, we should have James for a few years and then, very likely, one of the most Protestant royals in Europe. There is simply nothing that any reasonable man need worry about."

But there was: his name was Titus Oates.

History has seen many hoaxes, but few more devastating than the great hoax of 1678. Titus Oates, bow-legged, lantern-jawed, a known – though unsuccessful – trickster, suddenly devised a way to make himself famous. Working with an accomplice, he uncovered a plot so terrible that it made all England tremble. The plotters, he claimed, were papists. Their plan was to kill the king, put his brother James, Duke of York, on the throne instead, and proclaim the kingdom subject to the Pope. It was the Armada, the Inquisition, everything that Puritan Englishmen dreaded. It was also, from start to finish, a fabrication. Some of the details were absurd. When told that the papist army was to be led by an elderly Catholic peer – whom Oates clearly did not realize had long since been bedridden – King Charles burst out laughing. But as usual in politics, the truth was not only different, it was irrelevant; all that mattered was what people believed. While the king's friends in Parliament protested, the more puritan-minded and those who wanted to see the power of the Crown reduced clamoured for justice. Oates's supporters paraded in the streets of London wearing green ribbons. Catholics were hounded and abused. Oates himself was given apartments near Whitehall and looked after like a prince. And above all, the cry arose: "Change the succession!" Some spoke of William of Orange, some of the bastard Duke of Monmouth; but loudest of all was the call: "Exclude Catholic James! No papist king!" The House of Commons already had a Bill, with majority support. Even the House of Lords was wavering.

The supporters of the king, who believed that the hereditary principle must remain inviolate, had even acquired a nickname. "Tories" they were called, which meant "Irish rebels". They in turn described the king's opponents with an equally rude epithet: "Whigs", which meant "Scottish thieves".

For Sir Julius Ducket there could be no doubt. Quite apart from his own calm assessment of the succession, and his disbelief in the preposterous Oates, he was bound by personal oath and by a lifetime of loyalty. Sir Julius was a Tory.

At the end of Pall Mall stood the Tudor gateway of the little palace of St James, a cheerful brick building which the king sometimes liked to use and which gave easy access to the park; and a few minutes later Sir Julius was walking across the grass to the long avenue of trees, known simply as the Mall, which ran down the centre of the park and where King Charles II was genially taking the air.

How strange it felt. Sir Julius was suddenly reminded of that other meeting, over forty years before, when he had gone with his brother Henry to see the first King Charles at Greenwich. Yet what a contrast. He thought of that small, quiet man, so obviously chaste, so politely formal, and compared him to the large, rather swarthy man who was approaching him now. There was nothing formal about Charles II. At the Newmarket race meetings he so loved, he would cheerfully mix with the crowd, and any man who pleased might talk to him. As to being chaste, the bevy of women who were walking with him in the Mall included his favourite, Nell Gwynne. Now, as the pretty little royal spaniel sniffed round the older man's feet, the king greeted him warmly.

"Well, good Sir Julius, have you chosen your new name?"

For Sir Julius Ducket was to be made a lord. Charles II liked to reward his loyal friends with titles – just as he had made most of his bastards into dukes. But in the case of Sir Julius the need was practical. Of a sound city family with no trace of popery anywhere, and a man whose opinion carried respect, Sir Julius was just the sort of man he needed in the House of Lords when the question of succession came up again that autumn.

"I should like to be Lord Bocton, Your Majesty." The ancient family seat; it had been an easy choice.

The king nodded thoughtfully. "We may count on you to support us over this Exclusion Bill? You will not desert my royal brother?"

"I gave my oath to your father, sir, to support his sons."

"Ah. Loyal friend. I think" – the king suddenly turned to his companions – "we can do better for Lord Bocton here. The barony of Bocton is yours, my dear lord," he said with a smile, "but how would you like to be an earl as well, eh?"

"Sir?" For a moment Sir Julius was too astonished to speak. A barony, the normal rank of an English peer, was a fine thing. Above that came the viscounts, but higher still came the three ranks of the upper aristocracy: the earls, marquesses and dukes. When a family reached that dizzying height, there was nothing above it save the monarch and, presumably, the portals of heaven itself. "An earldom?"

"What title would you like now?" King Charles laughed.

Another title? Sir Julius was so taken aback that he could hardly think.

As he dithered, Nell Gwynne cried out good-naturedly, "Come on, Lord Bocton! We can't stand around in St James's Park all day waiting for you to become an earl. Think of a name!"

"Could I be Earl of St James?" Julius asked in some confusion, seizing upon the words he had just heard.

"You can and you shall," Charles cried, in the greatest good humour. "Ladies," he admonished, "show respect for a loyal friend. We have not so many of them. You are Earl of St James, sir, and Baron Bocton, and I count on you." The earldom would secure him support through hellfire itself, and cost him nothing. He only wished he could find a hundred such fellows and make them all into earls.

An hour later, the newly created Earl of St James was bowling back along Pall Mall, his mind in a whirl. The implications of what had just happened were so wonderful that he just sat there, turning them over in his mind again and again. His eldest son would be called Lord Bocton now, while he was the earl. Over the Ducket coat of arms, there would be a crown bearing the decoration of strawberry leaves reserved for earls. His father had always told him that the family had been chosen, by which he had meant that they were God's elect. But, though he could not admit it, in his heart Julius knew that an earldom was more desirable even than the promise of heaven.

His carriage had just passed the top of Whitehall and was approaching the old Savoy when he noticed a party of men, carrying the green ribbons of the Whigs, clearly on their way to the palace to stage a little demonstration. Seeing them, he shrugged, and would not have given them a second thought if he had not realized that one, round-faced, rather gloomy figure at the back was vaguely familiar. The Temple was already in sight before he remembered who it was: O Be Joyful, of that cursed Carpenter family. And with the memory of the Carpenters came the memory of Jane and her curse on his family. He had not thought of her for weeks. Now, with a smile, he reflected that if anything was needed to prove how futile that curse had been it was today's events.

It was during the summer that O Be Joyful realized the full extent of the popish deviousness of Sir Christopher Wren.

The usual procedure when building a large church had always been to start at the eastern end and complete that first. In this way, services could at least be held while the rest of the church went up. But whenever O Be Joyful went past it seemed to him that the workmen were being employed in a different place, and soon it became clear that Wren meant to lay out at least the entire foundations before building up. Having seen the master architect do this already with several smaller churches, O Be Joyful did not pay too much attention, but his suspicions were further aroused one day late in 1677 when, curious to look at the drawing of the cathedral with its spire once again, he called in at the office which Wren and those directing the work now used. He had found the office empty except for a clerk who was friendly enough. He explained that he worked for Gibbons, and asked if he might see the plans.

"The plans aren't here," the clerk explained. "Sir Christopher took them all away."

"There must be something," O Be Joyful objected, but the clerk only shook his head.

"I know it's odd, but there isn't. We've a ground plan but no elevations, no models, nothing. All Wren does is provide drawings of the sections we're working on. I suppose it's all in his head."

The signs in the heavens began the next spring. No one had ever seen anything like them before, and not only was their message clear; it was insistent. There were two eclipses of the moon, and of the sun first one, then another, then a third. Amidst these terrible signs, Titus Oates confirmed all O Be Joyful's worst fears. There was a popish plot, and Sir Christopher Wren, O Be Joyful felt sure, was involved.

He would like to have denounced Wren; but if he did that, he would simply lose his job and nobody would believe him. He did join some Whig marches, but all that year and through the next, as the revelations of Titus Oates kept coming, and the popish court still held out, he could only reflect, with increasing bitterness: what would Martha have said?

O Be Joyful's greatest confusion had been caused by Meredith. Once or twice he had reminded the clergyman about his fears over Wren's papist cathedral, but even after Oates had revealed the conspiracy, Meredith refused to worry. Most puzzling of all, however, had been his reaction to the eclipses.

"The eclipses are welcome," he told Carpenter. "By these events we may measure the heavenly motions precisely."

"Are they not a sign from God?" asked O Be Joyful anxiously.

Meredith smiled. "They are a sign of how wonderfully He has made the universe." And as best he could he explained to the craftsman how the solar system worked and how eclipses took place. "All these eclipses may be precisely predicted," he told him. "Why, even the wandering stars, the fiery comets which used to frighten men, these too, we may suppose, travel in paths we shall be able to discover." This at least was the idea of a fellow member of the Royal Society, Edmond Halley, who had just returned to London from a voyage to the southern hemisphere where he had been mapping the stars of the southern sky. "Eclipses, comets, all the heavenly motions, these are determined by huge physical causes, not by the puny actions of men," he said reassuringly. But O Be Joyful was not reassured at all. The universe as Meredith described it sounded like a machine, strangely godless.

"You mean that God cannot send us a sign by an eclipse or a comet?" he demanded.

"Well, I suppose He can," said Meredith with a laugh, "since all things are possible to God. But He doesn't. So you needn't worry." But O Be Joyful worried even more. I wonder, he thought, if his science, his Royal Society and Observatory may not all be the work of the Devil too. After all, Wren was an astronomer. It pained him to think that Meredith, whom he knew to be a good man, might unwittingly be on the path to hell.

It was not until the summer of 1679 that O Be Joyful truly understood the cunning of Sir Christopher Wren. He was hard at work carving a pulpit for the old church of St Clement Danes which Wren was rebuilding, and often walked by the cathedral on his way home. He had paused to chat one evening with a mason working on the eastern end when, glancing down the length of the huge interior, he noticed that not only were the foundations arising all the way down the church, the walls were going up too. "Apart from the extreme west end, he's building the whole cathedral up in a single piece," the mason confirmed. "At least, that's how it seems to us. I don't know why."

Suddenly O Be Joyful knew exactly why. He only wondered why he hadn't guessed it before.

"He's building it like that," he said bitterly, "so that by the time people realize what he's really doing, it'll be too late to change anything. They'll either have to let him finish it his way or knock it all down and start again." He could not help admiring the architect's cleverness, wicked though he knew it was.

"So what's he up to?" the mason asked.

"Wait a few years," Carpenter replied. "You'll see."

Given all that he knew, it came as no surprise to O Be Joyful that autumn when Parliament reassembled, and the House of Commons voted to alter the succession to exclude Catholic James, that the House of Lords should have rejected the Bill and decided in favour of James. He was well aware that throughout the bitter debate the newly made Earl of St James had been prominent, arguing persuasively for the king and his brother.

The conspiracy was deep. The shining city on a hill was being prepared, before his very eyes, for the rule of the Evil One. It was only to be expected, he supposed, that the former Sir Julius Ducket should be of the Devil's party, leading them all to hell.

1685

The two children were clinging to him, terrified. One of the troopers, still mounted, was shaking nuts from the tree while two others had just trussed up a pig and slit its throat with a sabre. The officer in command of the dragoons looked at Eugene with a cool insolence.

"We shall need all three of your bedrooms."

"And where are we to sleep?" Eugene's wife asked.

"There is the barn, Madame," the officer shrugged. He eyed the two little girls. "Their ages?"

"Not yet seven, Monsieur le Capitaine," Eugene answered drily. "I assure you." If only, he thought, I had never returned.

Despite the protection of their cherished old Treaty of Nantes, the Protestant Huguenots had found his most Catholic Majesty less and less tolerant of their religion with every year that passed. Not only had their Calvinist synods been forbidden; their pastors had to pay special taxes and they were forbidden to marry good Catholics. To encourage them to mend their ways, they were offered tax concessions if they would abjure their heresy and return to the Catholic fold; but, more recently, King Louis had introduced a sterner measure. Any Huguenot child over the age of seven could be converted, without their parents' consent. Another year or two, Eugene knew, and his girls would be under pressure. Such things would not have happened if he had stayed in London.

His return to France had not been happy. His father had been furious. "You were to prepare the way for us," he had reminded Eugene coldly, and for a year refused to speak to him. Only when he had married a Huguenot girl whose father was a shipper at Bordeaux, did the rift begin to heal. They were on good terms when, five years ago, the older man had died and Eugene found himself head of the little family. Not that the family strife had ended. Within a year, his father's young widow had converted, left the house and married a Catholic with a small vineyard. As a result, Eugene had not only his own two little girls to look after, but his unmarried half-sister, who had refused to be a Catholic and accompany her mother.

Difficult though life had been for Huguenots, however, it was only in the last four years that King Louis XIV had made it intolerable. His method was simple: he quartered his troops on them. Time and again Eugene had heard how parties of dragoons had arrived, eaten all the family's stores, broken furniture, even terrorized the Huguenots' wives and daughters. Technically, the French king could still say they were free to worship, but in practice it was a policy of persecution. Many times recently Eugene had wondered whether he should emigrate to England again with his family; yet he was unwilling to leave the area he so loved unless he had to – and there was a large financial consideration.

"The king has forbidden any of his subjects to leave France without his permission. That means," he warned his wife, "that if we try to sell our house or furniture, we'll almost certainly be arrested on suspicion of leaving. If we go, we'll only have what we can carry." His business as a watchmaker brought a modest living; but the family's capital was in the house with its orchards that he had inherited. Like the other Huguenots in the area, therefore, they had prayed with their pastor, often in their own house, and read their bible, and hoped for better times. Until today.

"And how long," he now asked the officer, "will you and your dragoons occupy my house?"

"Who knows?" the officer replied. "A year? Two years?"

"And if I became a Catholic?"

"Why, Monsieur. We could be gone tomorrow."

But if the officer thought this short-sighted, bespectacled watchmaker with his little girls was going to be frightened into capitulation he was entirely wrong.

"Welcome to my house then, Monsieur le Capitaine," he said with quiet irony. "I hope your stay will be a pleasant one."

He made no complaint during the next two months while the family slept in the barn and the soldiers occupied the house. Once, it seemed to him, the officer meeting him one morning had even looked embarrassed. "We shall still be here when they have gone," he told his children. "Be patient." Things continued as they were until one afternoon when the officer, looking quite grave for once, clattered into the yard.

"I have news for you which will change the situation here entirely," he announced. "The Edict of Nantes has been revoked. Toleration is ended." After an appalled silence he continued. "All Huguenot pastors are banished; any caught will be executed. All Huguenots like yourselves will remain; none may leave. Your children will all become Catholic. That is the new law."

They retired to the barn in silence. That night, at nearly midnight, Eugene quietly woke his children. "Wrap up as warm as you can and put on your boots," he told them. "We're leaving."

As a man of God, Meredith knew he should not have done it, but as he came up the hill from London Bridge towards Eastcheap and caught sight of O Be Joyful's woeful face heading directly towards him, he looked for cover. Thanking God for His providence, he stood in the shadow of a doorway waiting for the danger to pass.

With horror, therefore, after a brief pause, he heard a shuffling of feet, then a sigh, and saw not six feet away the familiar back of the craftsman as he sat down on the step right in front of him. Damn it, thought Meredith, now I'm trapped. There was only one choice. He must go up the stairs behind him. And five minutes later he was gazing out from the top of the Monument of London.

There were few more striking sights in London than the Monument. Designed by Wren as a single, simple Doric column to commemorate the Great Fire, it had been erected close by the spot in Pudding Lane where the huge conflagration had started. Constructed in Portland stone, it stood two hundred and two feet high and over its summit, made of gilt bronze, was a flaming urn that glowed and flashed when it caught the sun. The endless spiral staircase gave on to a balcony just below the urn, from which the drop was so sheer that it made many people dizzy. Having enjoyed the view – one could see up and down the Thames for miles – Meredith peeped over the edge to see if it was safe to descend. It was not: O Be Joyful was still there.

It would not be surprising if the woodcarver had things on his mind; it had certainly been an eventful year. In February, quite unexpectedly, without any sign that he was even unwell, King Charles had suddenly died. His Catholic brother James had therefore become King James II and all England had waited to see what would happen. To general relief, he had scrupulously observed the Anglican rite at his coronation in the spring; but there were hints that he hoped for more toleration for his Catholic subjects and clear signs that he would not have them abused. That summer, Titus Oates, finally exposed as a complete fraud, had been tied to a cart tail and whipped through the streets from Aldgate to Newgate. Personally, since he had no doubt that Oates was a rogue and a fraud, Meredith hadn't the least objection to the sentence. More dangerous had been the Protestant rising that young Monmouth, foolishly thinking his popularity a much more powerful thing than it was, had tried to start down in the West Country. The regular troops, under the capable command of John Churchill, had easily crushed the rebels and poor Monmouth had been executed. But the sequel had been more disturbing. Judge Jeffreys, in summary trials that were immediately called the Bloody Assizes, had sentenced the rebels to hang by the dozen, and James had been so pleased that he had promoted Jeffreys to be his senior judge. Such thoughts, Meredith knew, were enough to cause O Be Joyful to plague him for hours.

As he grew older, Meredith found that he had less and less desire to concentrate upon such things. What, in the end, were these temporary affairs of men compared to the great mysteries of the universe? Especially when one of the greatest of all mysteries was being unravelled that very year in London?

It had been Halley's idea, supported by Pepys, the then president, that the Royal Society should publish the theories which Isaac Newton, a rather dyspeptic Cambridge professor, had been expounding. For months now, as he prepared his great theory for publication, Newton had been sending a stream of requests to the Greenwich Observatory for astronomical information. From all this Meredith already had a fair idea of Newton's system of gravity and it fascinated him. He knew that the attraction between two bodies depended upon the square of the distance between them; he also understood that two objects dropped from a height, regardless of their mass, should fall together at the same speed. And now, looking down, it suddenly occurred to him that the Monument itself would be an excellent place for such a demonstration. Indeed, he considered wryly, two objects dropped together just now should land on O Be Joyful's head at exactly the same time.

Carpenter, two hundred feet below, was oblivious to these dangerous ideas. It was not the first time he had come to the Monument. Some months before, when he was admiring the fine carving of the panels at the base, a kindly gentleman had translated one of the inscriptions in Latin which accompanied it. Having described the course of the Great Fire, an additional sentence had been added a few years later:

> But Popish frenzy, which caused
> these horrors, is not yet quenched.

"For you know," the gentleman had explained, "it was the papists who started the Great Fire."

The fact that it was in writing, and upon such a great structure as the Monument must, O Be Joyful supposed, prove it beyond a doubt. And for another half-hour, while Meredith became rather cold above, he sat there and gloomily wondered what terrible things the Catholics would do next.

When everything was ready, they prayed. Then they put the children in the barrels.

Eugene's father-in-law was a stout, sturdy man, not unlike a barrel himself. Eugene knew that the Bordeaux merchant was better placed to help them than most and he had also guessed that the sooner they left the better. "There will be so many other Huguenots trying to do the same thing that the escape routes will soon be jammed – or discovered by the authorities," he told his wife.

Louis XIV, the Sun King as they called him, was an autocrat whose power even Charles I of England, with his belief in Divine Right, could hardly have dreamed of. The king who built the vast palace of Versailles and nearly destroyed the Protestant Dutch, and who could tear up the Treaty of Nantes, would certainly be thorough. Only an hour after they had sneaked into the merchant's house, one of his children reported that the troops were on the quays, inspecting every ship.

Eugene's faith in his father-in-law had not been misplaced. "The ship I'm putting you on is English. The captain and I have done business for years. He can be trusted." He had sighed. "It's your best chance." It was sailing to the English port of Bristol.

Eugene thanked the merchant for putting himself at risk in this way and asked if he intended to follow them.

"No," the older man replied sadly. "I shall have to convert." He shrugged. "You're younger. You also have a craft – you can work anywhere. But I'm a wine shipper. All I have is here and I still have five children to look after. So, for the moment anyway, I'll have to be a Catholic. Perhaps in time the children will follow you." It obviously caused him grief.

The main problem had been how to smuggle Eugene and his little family aboard. The merchant had been confident, though. "Five barrels among a hundred. You'll be stacked towards the centre." Tiny air holes had been drilled in the top of each cask. "I hope the captain will be able to let you out once you're safely at sea," he had continued. "But just in case . . ." His wife had provided each occupant with a flagon of water and two loaves of bread. "Remember, you may have to stay in there a long time," he had carefully warned them all. "So you must eat and drink as little as possible."

By mid-morning, the carts carrying the casks of wine were rumbling along the quay to where the English vessel was waiting. There was nothing in the least unusual about the sight. The shipper's men and the English sailors began to load them, but in quite a leisurely fashion. The young officer in charge of the troops came over to watch carefully, placing himself near the merchant, whom he eyed from time to time, suspiciously. Suddenly he noticed that the men carrying one of the barrels seemed to be slightly off balance. He strolled over, drew his sword, and ordering the men to put their load down, drove it through the top of the barrel.

1688

How massively, how graciously it rose upon its western hill. Already the walls were up and the roofing had begun. The huge Roman temple of St Paul's stared down upon Ludgate as if it had been there first. And though over the cathedral's central crossing there was as yet nothing but a great, gaping cavity, open to the sky, it was entirely clear from the arrangement of the supporting pillars what was to come. King James had thrown his full weight behind the project. Extra taxes for the building had been raised, and even if nobody had seen any drawings yet, everyone knew that Wren's great cathedral would soon be surmounted by a mighty, popish dome. Though it was somewhat modified, O Be Joyful had no doubt that he was looking, essentially, at the great wooden model he had helped to make a dozen years ago. And with a Catholic king now on the throne, he knew that the conspiracy was complete.

Although, to his shame, he had continued to follow Grinling Gibbons's orders, O Be Joyful had always tried when he could to avoid projects that seemed too papist. His work some years before in the rebuilt Mercers' Hall in Cheapside had given him special pleasure, while two years ago he had managed to escape working on the frieze for a statue of the new Catholic king. At present he was working in the little palace of St James, and this too his conscience could allow him to enjoy.

But now on this bright morning of 9 June 1688, O Be Joyful Carpenter paused by St Paul's and wondered if he had been right in the advice he had given last night to his friend Penny, recently arrived from Bristol. Certainly the Huguenot had seemed astonished.

"You, O Be Joyful, now support a papist king?"

"Yes. Yes, I do." He supported King James. After what had happened recently, it had seemed to O Be Joyful that he must.

But as he thought of the Huguenot's urgent voice and his worried face he wondered: was this all a trap?

It was twelve o'clock that morning when Eugene Penny caught up with Meredith. He had gone first to St Bride's where the clergyman's housekeeper had told him he was out, but suggested one or two places where he might have gone. Since then he had tried Child's in St Paul's, the Grecian near the Temple, Will's by Covent Garden, Man's at Charing Cross, three others in Pall Mall and St James's, but at last it was in Lloyd's, that the Huguenot found the clergyman sitting comfortably at a corner table and smoking a pipe. Surprised but delighted to see him after all these years, Meredith motioned him to sit down.

"My dear Mr Penny! Will you take coffee?" Of all the many conveniences of the new city since the fire, none had pleased Meredith more than the institution of the coffee house. There seemed to be a new one every month. Open all day, serving hot chocolate and coffee – which was always drunk black, though usually with sugar – the coffee houses of the city and the West End were more gentlemanly places than the old taverns and were rapidly developing strong characters of their own. Wits went to one, military men to another, lawyers to a third. Meredith, who enjoyed good conversation, liked to visit a different one every day, though he tended to avoid Child's because it was full of clergymen. The clientele of the newly opened coffee house of Lloyd's tended to be merchants and insurance men. It was a good clientele to have. There had long been rudimentary schemes for insuring ships and their cargoes amongst merchants, though house insurance, before the Great Fire, had been unknown. But that huge disaster, together with the fact that the new brick and stone London houses were far less likely to burn down, had given a huge impetus to the whole insurance business. Many of the better houses, and almost all ships, were now comprehensively insured. The assessment of risk and the provision of cover was becoming an informal science. Meredith himself had investigated the mathematics of it and delighted to discuss such arcane subjects as the proper premium to be paid on a vessel bound for the East Indies, with the men who gathered at Lloyd's, where business was booming.

Having accepted a coffee and polished his spectacles, Eugene Penny diffidently enquired: "I was wondering – can you help me get my job back? I'd like to return to London."

Until recently, it had seemed to Penny, providence had been on his side. Certainly three years ago, when the captain of the English sailing ship had cracked open the top of his barrel, told him that they were now safely at sea, and cheerfully informed him that an officer had stuck his sword right through the barrel next to him – which fortunately had been full of wine – he had reasonably assumed that God meant him to survive. Their reception in Bristol had also been encouraging. There was already a Huguenot community in the western port, and in the months that followed it greatly swelled. Nor were the English unwelcoming. Even in London where, especially in Spitalfields, there was now a flood of immigrants, many of whom had suffered great danger and hardship in leaving France, there was remarkably little resentment against the hard-working foreigners. The tale of their persecution shocked the Protestant English. When they heard, as they soon did, of Huguenot pastors in France being broken on the wheel, they were outraged. Scores of thousands of Huguenots like the Penny family came into England in these years, bringing the total French population in England to some two hundred thousand – a number large enough to ensure that, in due course, three out of every four Englishmen would have a Huguenot somewhere in their ancestry. With so many of his countrymen in London, Penny had decided to remain in Bristol, had found work and modestly prospered.

But he missed working for Tompion. There were some fine clockmakers in Bristol, but nobody like him. And so, two days ago, he had journeyed up to the capital, found his old friend Carpenter, and set out to plead with his former employer for a position.

But the great clockmaker had been annoyed when Penny had suddenly left before and he was not minded to forgive him now.

Penny had not been surprised, but it had been a bitter blow, especially when he had seen in the workshop the wonderful watches the great craftsman was making. So this morning he had sought out Meredith to ask him if he would intercede on his behalf.

"I do know Tompion," Meredith agreed, but it seemed to the clergyman that there was still something more on Penny's mind. After an awkward pause, an offer of more coffee, and a gentle enquiry as to whether there was anything else he could do to help, Meredith saw the Huguenot take a deep breath.

Penny had been in Bristol nearly a year before any suggestion of trouble had reached him, and even then he was not sure what to make of it. The king, wanting more tolerance for his Catholic co-religionists, had started appointing a number of Catholic officers to the army and some Catholics to his Privy Council. The courts had agreed, albeit reluctantly, that he was within his rights; but many people were outraged. "What about the Test Act?" the Puritans cried. The Bishop of London refused to stop his clergy preaching publicly against it, and was suspended. Penny was not sure what all this meant, but in the months of peace that followed he had put it out of his mind until, the following spring, a new development left all England stunned.

"It's a Declaration of Indulgence," Penny told his astonished family one April day. "Everyone is free to worship as they please." Catholic King James, it seemed, irritated by opposition from the Church, had called in no less a Protestant than William Penn, the patron of the Quakers, and with his help had designed this remarkable edict. "It means that the Catholics are free to worship and to hold public positions," he explained. "But it also means that all the other faiths may do so too – Calvinists, Baptists, even Quakers." Such religious tolerance was not unknown in northern Europe. In Protestant Holland, for instance, Dutch Catholics and Jews worshipped freely and were never troubled by William of Orange. The Declaration would override the Test Act until Parliament repealed it.

In Bristol, Penny noticed, most of the nonconformist Protestants welcomed the news. The number of Catholics who would benefit was small, the number of Protestants far larger. "It benefits us," a Baptist remarked to him, "so we welcome it." They even sent the king a vote of thanks. But Penny himself was more cautious. He began to pay close attention to the news that came from London. He read broadsheets; asked questions. He learned that the papal nuncio had gone to Windsor in state; all over the country, he discovered, the king was replacing the lord-lieutenant and the justices of the peace who ran the counties with Catholics. News came from Oxford that King James was trying to turn one of the colleges into a Catholic seminary. At the end of the year there was even news that the queen was pregnant again – though since, in fifteen years of marriage, she had never done anything but miscarry, nobody was much concerned by that. But taken together these things disturbed Penny profoundly. The phlegmatic English might accept them, but the Huguenots he knew, who had experienced the French king's persecution, found them ominous. That spring, when King James announced that a Parliament would be called to turn this tolerance into law, and ordered his Declaration read in churches, Penny remained sceptical. "We were protected once, by the Treaty of Nantes," he remarked. "And look what happened to that."

Since there was little he could do about these fears, he had come to London to see Tompion anyway, and found his old friend Carpenter as well. But it was O Be Joyful who had provided the greatest surprise of all. Although the woodcarver hated popery, it seemed he was ready to support the king.

"So are the aldermen of London and the guilds," he explained and then added, almost apologetically: "Things have changed."

As he discovered what had passed in London, Penny saw how clever King James II had been. Since he wanted his Declaration passed into law, he needed a Parliament to vote for it. As the Tories, his natural supporters, were mostly Church of England men, they could not be relied on. But the opposition Whigs, inheriting some of the old Roundhead character from Cromwell, favoured toleration. King James II had therefore been securing Whig dominance in boroughs all over the country, so that they would send Whigs to Parliament. And nowhere had he been more thorough than in the city of London.

"By royal dispensation," O Be Joyful explained, "you no longer have to be Church of England to join the livery companies or become an alderman. The Dissenters have been flooding in. The Weavers, the Goldsmiths, even the grand old Mercers company have sent addresses thanking the king. The very things my father fought for are being granted. Most of the city officers are Puritans and Dissenters now. Why, even the mayor's a Baptist, I believe!"

But the woodcarver's greatest excitement had come the previous afternoon. No less than seven Church of England bishops had signed a petition protesting against the toleration. Yesterday they had been brought before the king's council charged with sedition.

"They've been sent to await trial in the Tower. Taken there by boat. I saw it myself," Carpenter said. Good Anglicans were shocked, but the craftsman could not conceal his glee. The king against the bishops – who would ever have thought it?

Penny, however, was unable to share this optimism. That same afternoon, curious to see how the West End had developed in the dozen years he had been away, he had strolled down towards Whitehall. With the royal family spending more time at St James's, the old Whitehall palace had become more of a series of royal offices than a residence. The old tiltyard where courtiers had once practised jousting was now a parade ground known as Horse Guards. As he walked down beside it he had to confess that the soldiers exercising in their red coats looked rather cheerful in the afternoon sun.

The colourful troops of soldiers had become a feature of the London scene during the last two decades. Originating from forces raised on both sides of the Civil War, they were all the king's loyal regiments now. The infantry troops on the parade ground Penny recognized as the smart Coldstream Guards. And a few moments later, a squadron of the Household Cavalry, the splendid Life Guards, came jingling into view. He was watching with some admiration when an elderly gentleman standing nearby addressed him.

"A fine sight, sir, are they not? Yet I wish," the older man continued, "there was not a huge camp of soldiers only ten miles outside London, under Catholic officers. The king has other camps like that all over the country. What does he mean by all these Catholic troops? That's what I'd like to know."

The squadron had reached them. How large the dragoons seemed on their magnificent mounts; how brightly their breastplates and helmets flashed; how proudly they rode. And how clearly, with a sudden, sickening resignation, it came to Eugene Penny that he did understand, very well, what the troops meant. He had seen dragoons like this before and he knew what they could do.

These English, he thought. They fought a civil war against an obstinate tyrant; but his son is more cunning. He will trick them into servitude. He may take his time, just as the French king did, but he will do it; and with terrible anguish he wondered whether he had fled the persecution in France, only to find the same thing in England, too. He had argued unsuccessfully with Carpenter the night before, and now addressed Meredith sternly: "It's a trap."

The Reverend Richard Meredith only sighed as he sipped his coffee. The publication of Newton's great work, he had to admit to himself, was far more important to him than twenty books of sermons. He had read the Declaration of Indulgence from his pulpit without a qualm and, though he felt duty bound to support his bishop and the others who had protested, he did so with no personal conviction. On the Catholic question he was cynical. For though King James himself undoubtedly believed that huge numbers of his subjects would flock to the Catholic Church if given the chance, Meredith was quite sure in his own mind that this was just another example of the Stuart's family's inability ever to understand their Protestant English subjects. As a former physician, he was also privy to two pieces of information unknown to Penny. James II of England was far from well; and he had also, more than a year ago, contracted venereal disease. The Catholic monarch would probably not live long, and the chances of his producing a healthy male heir were remote.

"England will stay Protestant," he assured Penny. "Even with dragoons, he can't impose Catholicism by force. You're safe. I promise."

Penny, however, seemed unconvinced.

O Be Joyful liked working in St James's Palace. The main carvings that Grinling Gibbons had undertaken were completed, but there were numerous small commissions which he had been given to do. The guards were used to seeing him go in and out and since he was always careful to choose a spot to work where he would not disturb anybody, he was allowed to move about pretty much as he pleased. He had chosen a panel over a doorway that afternoon where he carved some fruit and flowers, not as fine as Gibbons's work, but good, and he was proud of them. The carving was actually complete, but he wanted to apply some beeswax to the wood and polish it. In order to work more comfortably, he erected a little scaffolding over his side of the doorway and here he had contentedly ensconced himself. This corner of the palace seemed to be empty this afternoon; the door was just ajar, but half an hour passed before he heard anyone coming, and then it was a pair of murmuring voices he heard, and a faint rustle as two men approached the doorway. As they did so, their voices stopped. He saw the door open, a head quickly look round it to make sure the room was empty, and then, standing just the other side of the entrance, the two men continued their conversation. The head which had looked in, he had just been able to see, belonged to a Jesuit priest; and, somewhat embarrassed, he was about to make a noise to alert them to his presence when the other man spoke.

"My only fear is that the king is moving too fast."

O Be Joyful froze. Presumably these two men were papists. What would happen if they discovered him? Yet, suspicious as ever of any Catholics, he could not resist the desire to listen. A second later, as the first voice continued, he received a shock.

"The king is determined to bring all England back to Rome, but you must urge him to be cautious. It can't be done overnight. Not even by force."

O Be Joyful went cold.

"My dear Father John." The Jesuit spoke in English but the accent was French. "We all regret, of course, that this toleration must be granted to Protestant sects for the moment. But Holy Church has time on her side. That is well understood. And you need not accuse us of impatience, for we have already been working with this royal family for some time."

"With James, of course. But he has only been king a short time," the English priest countered. His words were followed by a short pause, and O Be Joyful wondered if the conversation was over. But then he heard the Frenchman again, in a lower voice this time.

"Not quite. There is perhaps something you do not know. His brother died in the true faith."

"King Charles? A Catholic?"

"Oh yes, my friend. He kept it from his people. But when he died . . ."

"The Archbishop of Canterbury attended him."

"True, but as the archbishop went down the front stairs, our good Father Huddlestone came secretly up the back. He heard Charles's confession, gave him extreme unction."

"I did not know."

"You must not say it. But I will tell you something more. Long before that King Charles II entered into a secret treaty with King Louis of France. In it, he promised to declare his true faith and return England to Rome; and King Louis promised him whatever forces he needed to do it. Nobody but a handful at the French court know this. Charles even deceived his own closest ministers. But the conversion of England has already been in preparation for fifteen years. I only tell you so that you shall better understand the work you are asked to do."

King Charles a secret Catholic all along? O Be Joyful was trembling. Although he had always believed in a Catholic plot, to hear it confirmed so blandly by another person was terrifying. And the real conspiracy was even deeper than the one Titus Oates had invented. The French king ready to use force? The toleration edict only temporary? Penny was right then. It was all a trap. He was so frightened he could hardly breathe and he thanked the Lord when, a few moments later, he heard the two men walk away.

His first impulse was simple. He must tell people. But who would believe him? They would say he was another Titus Oates, a scandal-monger; and there was no way that he could prove he wasn't a fraud. The alternative was to say nothing, to keep his terrible secret to himself, live his life in peace and quiet. No one would ever know. And if England was delivered up to Rome? It was fate. He was bound for eternal damnation anyway. Even the vision of Martha, rising up to admonish him for his cowardice, was not enough to dispel his apathy. He was helpless, he was damned, and, in all probability, all England with him. For fully five minutes he lay there meditating his course of action, and feeling more ashamed than ever.

Suddenly, he sat up. To his own surprise O Be Joyful was overcome by a huge indignation, a rage unlike anything he had known before. It was as if all his disgust with himself over the years and all the resentment he felt at the way these royal papists had so contemptuously duped him, had focused in a single point of fury. It was, though he did not realize it, the same sullen anger that his father Gideon had felt. No, he decided. This time, whatever the cost, he would stand up to them.

He came down from his place of concealment and made his way out of the palace. He would go to the Protestant Lord Mayor of London himself. And all the guilds too, if he must. His terror and even his rage were replaced now by a kind of wild excitement.

He was still in this state of furious elation when, about a hundred yards down Pall Mall, a carriage drew up a little in front of him, and an old man stepped out and moved slowly towards the entrance of one of the fashionable mansions. Just before reaching the steps to the door, he turned to glance at O Be Joyful, and the two men recognized each other.

It was nine years since old Julius had been made Earl of St James, and he had not expected to live so long. Yet, at the age of eighty-five, he had remarkably little to complain of. He was stooped; his eye was a little rheumy; an arthritic leg meant that he had to walk, rather painfully, with a stick but in his eighties he had acquired the same stiff dignity that had been the hallmark of his father, Alderman Ducket, back in the days when Shakespeare was still living. As he glanced at Carpenter now, in the manner of the very old who know they are soon to depart, he gave a smile of vague, uninterested curiosity.

But that was not what O Be Joyful saw. He saw the persecutor of his family, the hated Royalist, the thief who had taken an earldom to vote for a Catholic king. He was sure to be part of this papist plot. Worst of all, protected by wealth, titles, even his age, the evil old devil was grinning at him now because he thought he had got away with it.

Scarcely considering what he was doing, the craftsman rushed forward and in a voice of rage and blistering contempt he yelled: "You old devil! You think you've hoodwinked us all. Well, you haven't." Emboldened further by Julius's look of surprise he continued shouting. "I *know*, do you understand? I've heard your priests in the palace. I know all about your Royalist papist plot. And in an hour the mayor and all London will know too. Then, my lord, we'll string you and the king and all the priests up together." And with a cry, he ran off.

It took Lord St James several seconds to recover from this verbal assault; but as soon as he had he clambered back into his carriage and barked out a sharp order: "Drive like the wind!"

Twenty minutes later O Be Joyful, hurrying along Fleet Street near St Bride's, saw Meredith coming towards him. As the clergyman hailed him in his usual friendly manner, he halted.

"Why, what's the matter, Master Carpenter? You look as if you've seen the Devil himself."

O Be Joyful was glad to see the clergyman. Despite his rage and determination, the prospect of facing the Lord Mayor was rather daunting. By saying what he had to Lord St James, he had burned his boats; but he still had no idea of how to get the mayor to believe him. Seeing Meredith now, however, he suddenly realized that if he would accompany him to the mayor, it would be a different matter entirely. Meredith, at least, he could trust.

"There is something terrible . . ." he began.

"Come into the church," Meredith suggested. "It's quieter there."

So inside the handsome new church of St Bride's O Be Joyful told an astounded Meredith what he had heard.

When he had finished, Meredith, with a thoughtful nod, beckoned him. "Follow me," he said. "There is something I must show you." He led him down a passageway to where a heavy door guarded the stairs that led down into the crypt. Lighting a lamp, he gave it to Carpenter and asked him to lead the way. Only when the craftsman was more than halfway down, did Meredith close the heavy door and turn the key in the lock, as Lord St James had told him to do.

Then he went back through the church, leaving O Be Joyful a prisoner.

"Do you believe him?" Lord St James asked Meredith. They were sitting in the parlour of the clergyman's house.

"I'm sure he believes that what he says is true."

The earl said nothing for a moment, then asked: "Can you keep him there?"

"The poor fellow could shout his head off down in the

crypt and no one would hear him. But do you really think it's necessary?"

"Just for today. I need to think." The old man rose to leave.

As the hours passed, Julius discovered it was not easy to work out what to do. Like most old people, it was not the recent past that was vivid in his memory, but the days of his youth. And despite all that had passed between them in the Civil War, he still felt, as keenly as if it were yesterday, the guilt over Gideon himself, Carpenter and the Spanish Ambassador. Unlike O Be Joyful he was sure that if the craftsman took his story of a new popish plot around London he would be believed. Quite apart from the trouble that might stir up, he was in little doubt about what King James would do. With Judge Jeffreys in charge the fellow would be lucky if he escaped with his life. I sent the father Gideon to a whipping, he thought. I can't stand by and watch the son go to something worse. It was this that had prompted his dash that afternoon to St Bride's in the hope that Meredith could help him prevent the woodcarver doing something foolish. But how could they stop Carpenter placing himself in peril?

This dilemma, however, was better than the other he faced. The popish plot: had Carpenter misunderstood what he had heard? Could this French Jesuit, for whatever reason, have been lying? James's Catholicism was one thing, but had Charles really deceived his faithful supporters all those years? Had he really promised to deliver England to Rome, and bring in French troops to do it? The idea was unthinkable, a treachery not to be borne.

Lord St James supped alone. He took a little brandy. Unable to sleep, he found himself keeping a vigil through the night, just as he had once before, long ago, on the eve of the execution of the martyred king. Except that this time it was not the sad, chaste face of the first Charles who came before his mind's eye, but the swarthy, lecherous, cynical face of the second.

Could his king, to whom he was bound by his sacred oath, really have done such a thing? Could his own faith be shaken by some foolish tale from one of the cursed Carpenters? How could it be, he wondered, as midnight silently passed, that in his heart he now believed O Be Joyful rather than his king? The answer, though it came to him like a tiny voice, also came from a lifetime of experience. The loyalties of the Stuarts had usually lain outside England. And the Stuart men – yes, even the martyred king if truth be told – were nearly always liars.

The crypt of St Bride's was a musty place. It was dark. No sound could escape and the door was utterly solid.

It was the betrayal that hurt O Be Joyful most. Even Meredith, it seemed, was in the popish plot. Was there anyone in London he could trust now, apart from Eugene Penny? As the hours passed, he wondered what lay in store for him. If they were coming to arrest him, why were they taking so long?

At last he went to sleep, awoke, dozed again, then lost track of all time. His family must be wondering where he was. Penny, very probably, would be out looking for him. But there was not the slightest reason why anyone should look for him in the crypt of St Bride's. Some time around what he supposed to be dawn, it occurred to him that perhaps Meredith meant to leave him there to die.

On Sunday morning Lord St James ate a light breakfast. He still did not know what to do about Carpenter.

At mid-morning he went to church and heard the service. He had hoped it would give him inspiration, but it did not. When he returned to his house he found a polite note from Meredith reminding him that they could not keep O Be Joyful locked up in a dungeon for ever. "At least," it ended, "I ought to give the poor fellow some water – and some explanation."

Finally, somewhat past the middle of the day, they finally brought Lord St James news that quite unexpectedly changed everything.

"You are sure?" Meredith asked when Julius told him.

"That is the official news. The question is," the earl continued, "is it possible? As a physician, what would you say?"

"It's more than a month early. You say it's healthy?"

"'Bonnie' was the word that was used to me."

"It sounds," Meredith weighed his words carefully, "unlikely." He paused. The two men looked at each other. "She has always miscarried before," he said slowly, "and the king is now . . . unhealthy. That he should have a 'bonnie' son just now seems to me" – he made a face – "convenient."

* * *

O Be Joyful had no idea at all what time of day it was when the door above him opened. As he clambered weakly up into the light he saw not soldiers, but Meredith and Lord St James standing there, smiling.

"I'm sorry we had to keep you here," the clergyman said. "It was for your own safety. We believe every word you've said. And now I want you to go with Lord St James here. We can't force you, but I think it would be best. You'll be back in a week."

"Go with him? A week?" He blinked at them in the light, confused. "Go where?"

"To Holland," the older man replied. "I'm going to see William of Orange."

The events of the summer of 1688 marked a watershed in English history, but to refer to them as the Glorious Revolution is rather misleading. There was no revolution; nor was there anything glorious about the business at all.

When, on Sunday 10 June, King James II of England announced to an astonished world that his wife had at last given birth to a son and heir, loyal Englishmen were put into a quandary. If the child lived – and all reports said it was healthy – this baby would inherit the throne. He would also, undoubtedly, be Catholic.

"But we only put up with James," good Protestants pointed out, "because we knew we were getting William and Mary next." Indeed, long before this, some of the more concerned Protestants had discreetly approached William of Orange to suggest that he should at least urge his father-in-law to moderate his papist ways – though the cautious Dutchman had preferred not to interfere. This baby boy, however, changed everything.

For Lord St James, already appalled by the revelation from O Be Joyful, and wrestling with his conscience about what to do, the news had been a blow. To others, less loyal than he, it was a call to arms. The Whigs were disgusted; the Tories – who had just seen seven of their Anglican bishops put in the Tower – were thoroughly alarmed. Others too, besides St James, set out for Holland. By the end of the month, an invitation had been sent to William from some of the greatest men in the land: "If you want your kingdom of England," they told him, "you'd better come and get it now."

How could Julius, whatever the circumstances, desert the path of loyalty which was his birthright, and break his oath to the king who had even made him an earl? Wasn't it against all he stood for? Rooted equally deep in his character however was that other, binding injunction received eighty years ago from his father. The rule which, in the end, proved stronger than all the others: "No popery."

For what really astonished the people of England, what caused Lord St James and Meredith to look at each other so sceptically, was the fact that this baby – Catholic and royal – had been born at all. A healthy boy after nothing but miscarriages? More than a month premature?

"I'll tell you exactly what I think," Lord St James told the still dazed O Be Joyful, as their vessel made its way down the long Thames Estuary. "I think the queen had a miscarriage and that they substituted another baby. Meredith thinks so too." So did most of England. Medical history has since conceded that the baby was probably legitimate, but as Protestant England turned to William of Orange in 1688, it was widely claimed that the Catholic baby had no right to inherit at all. He had been smuggled in, so the story would finally go, in a warming pan.

Cautious William took his time. On 5 November he landed in the West Country. James went to Salisbury. Parts of the north declared for William; James hesitated. Then James's best general, gallant John Churchill, went across to William, who marched slowly up to London, and James fled. By January, Parliament had gathered, decided that James, since he had gone, must have abdicated and, after some haggling over terms, offered the Crown to William and Mary jointly. This sequence of quite unheroic events was called the Glorious Revolution.

It was, nonetheless, a great watershed. For with the new settlement, the religious and political disputes which had troubled England for more than a century reached a lasting resolution. The great and final loser was the Catholic Church. William and Mary, if they had no children, were to be succeeded by Mary's Protestant sister Anne. The Catholic descendants of James were omitted entirely from the succession.

Most significant of all, no person in the future who was, or even married, a Catholic could ever sit upon England's throne. As for ordinary Catholics, they were liable to extra taxes and debarred from any public position whatsoever.

The Puritans too were debarred from most public offices, but were free to worship as they pleased. Mary still hoped they might be included in a somewhat broader Anglican Church.

More subtle, but deeply significant, was the political aspect of the settlement. Though Parliament claimed it was only restating old rights, this was not so. Parliament was to be called at regular intervals – this was made statutory. No army could be raised without its agreement. Free speech was guaranteed. And, as it soon made clear, Parliament would always henceforth ensure the king was short of money, and ultimately subject, therefore, to Parliament's will. The attempt of the Stuarts to edge England towards an absolute monarchy like the French had failed. Parliament, having won the Civil War, had finally won the peace.

One small political change that a few at Westminster noticed was that from this time the old Earl of St James, who God knows had always been a Tory, started voting with the Whigs. He said to their surprise that he now thought kings should be subject to Parliament. But he never said why.

It was best in Julius's judgement that the secret of Charles II's treachery should be quietly buried. "It can do no good to stir that up," he told Meredith. Nor was O Be Joyful so eager to pursue the matter now that James and his Catholic heirs were gone. The extraordinary and treacherous agreement which had, indeed, been made between the Stuart King of England and his kinsman the King of France, was to remain secret for another hundred years.

One thing was very clear: there was no longer the faintest chance of the English monarch forming any threatening alliances with Europe's Catholic powers. The English and the Dutch now shared a Calvinist Protestant king whose greatest enemy was Louis XIV of France. The Huguenots like Penny could be certain that the island kingdom was a safe refuge. As for the English, they might still be trading rivals, but the Dutch were now their allies. The two countries had much in common. Their languages were similar and God knew how many Englishmen were descended from the Hollanders' Flemish neighbours. Catholic Spain, all through the Reformation, had been their common enemy. Englishmen admired Dutch craftsmen and artists, taking from them words like "easel", "landscape" and "still life". English sailors served in Dutch ships and cheerfully employed the Dutch terms "skipper", "yacht" and "smuggler". If King William told his English subjects that their Dutch cousins were in danger from the papist French, they were ready to help them defend the Protestant cause.

The Earl of St James lived to a very great age. In 1693 he passed his ninetieth year, and though he walked with difficulty, his mind remained keen. Nor was he ever lonely; for apart from his children and grandchildren, a stream of visitors came to talk to the man who had been born on the last day good Queen Bess was still the queen of England. From the Gunpowder Plot to the Glorious Revolution: "He's seen it all," they said. And in 1694, the last year of his life, he was allowed to see one thing more.

In that year, after much discussion, the city of London gained a new institution. Financed by a number of prominent London merchants, it was a joint stock bank. Its function was to finance long-term government debt by issuing bonds on which interest was payable. They called it the Bank of London.

"I told the first King Charles it could be done," the earl explained to his visitors, with perfect truth. "But he wouldn't listen. Perhaps," he would nowadays concede with a smile, "it was just as well." It also pleased him greatly that for its first premises the new bank should have taken offices in the rebuilt Mercers' Hall in Cheapside. "Our family's livery company," he remarked proudly. And indeed he might have added that by choosing this location, the new institution, which before long was being called not just the Bank of London but the Bank of England, was beginning its life on the very site where once had stood the family house of Thomas Becket, London's martyred saint.

Two months after the Bank of England's founding, Julius died, one peaceful dawn. He therefore missed by a year a small event that would have given him pleasure. Richard Meredith, like his own father, had married late; but he had married well, and in 1695 he was blessed with a son.

A month afterwards, one rainy morning, Meredith received a visit from Eugene Penny.

The Huguenot had come with a present contained in a little box, which he opened with evident pride. Inside, Meredith saw, was a handsome silver watch. But as Penny drew this out, the clergyman also noticed that there was something unusual about it.

Taking his spectacles off to give them a careful wipe, Penny smiled. "Look," he said, and opening the back of the watch he pointed with his little finger to explain its workings.

It was twenty years since Tompion of London had started making watches with a hair spring, but now the great clock-maker had devised a new refinement that was to carry London watchmaking to a position of prominence in all Europe. The tiny mechanism to which Penny pointed, and which was termed a cylinder escapement, made possible one great improvement in the portable watch. It allowed all the cog wheels within to be arranged horizontally, making the watch flat, so that it could be slipped into a pocket.

"It's the neatest thing I ever saw in my life," Meredith exclaimed.

It was to celebrate the birth of his son, and to say thank you for the kindly clergyman's help in getting the Huguenot his job back with Tompion the master clockmaker.

Soon after the new century dawned, there was one other addition to Meredith's life. In the year 1701 his friend Wren designed a splendid steeple for his church of St Bride's. It was a remarkable affair. Set over a fine square tower, like that of St Mary-le-Bow, it consisted of a series of eight-sided hollow drums, with open arches and pillars, arranged in tiers, each smaller than the one below, like an inverted telescope, and completed by an obelisk on top. Taller even than the Monument, the new steeple of St Bride's could be seen the whole length of Fleet Street, and made the church one of the landmarks of the city.

1708

They were still in good time. He had not told them where he was taking them, but he had obtained special permission and he wanted it to be a surprise. Though O Be Joyful had passed his three score years and ten, he felt fit enough for the task he had set himself as hurrying cheerfully along he led his two favourite grandchildren up Ludgate Hill. It was a sparkling late October day and the people thronging the streets were in festive mood. It was the day of the Lord Mayor's procession.

Except for the Commonwealth period when such festivities were banned, the ancient annual ceremony had been growing more elaborate with every decade. Earlier on, in his official residence behind St Mary-le-Bow – Sir Julius Ducket's place, as O Be Joyful still thought of it – the mayor had put on his robes before emerging and riding down to the river. Then, in his magnificent barge, escorted by the barges of all the livery companies, he had been rowed to Westminster where like a feudal baron of olden times he performed his oath of fealty to the monarch. After this, the barges would turn, disembark their passengers by Blackfriars, and then the mayor, aldermen and all the liveries of the city would ride, in a magnificent and brightly coloured pageant, up to Cheapside and thence to the Guildhall. And what better place for the two children to see the whole affair, Carpenter had thought, than from the great outside gallery of the dome of St Paul's?

There it was, looming in the sky ahead of them, the monarch of the city's western hill, the mighty dome. Even now, the last finishing touches were still being made to the great stone lantern tower that rose over fifty feet above the apex of the dome to conclude in a golden cross, a dizzying three hundred and sixty-three feet above the cathedral's floor. The dome: just as it had been in the great wooden model he had made almost thirty-five years ago, just as he had always known it would be. Yet with this one difference: Wren's final dome was taller, even more august, than the original model.

Carpenter had watched it go up with fascination. Wren himself was often there, an old man now, but still gamely letting the workmen pull him up into the dome in a basket so that he could inspect the work. Carpenter had been especially intrigued to see that the great structure was not in fact one dome at all, but three. Between the domed ceiling seen from the interior, and the metalled exterior roof which actually rose fifty feet higher, there was, not exactly a dome, but a massive brick cone, almost like a kiln.

"And that," Wren told him one day, "is what will support the lantern on top, and hold everything else in place as well." A week later, taking the terrified woodcarver up in the basket with him, he conducted him into the scaffolding of the roof and showed him some of its secrets.

"Around the base of the dome," the architect explained, "lies a great double chain. This is an extra protection to stop the weight above pushing the walls outwards. Then, all the way up the inner cone, I have placed bands of stone and iron chains which hold everything tight, like the metal hoops round a barrel. And everything needs to be very firm," he added a little sadly. "For the outer roof was to have been made of copper. But they made me use lead. It saved them a thousand pounds, but it added six hundred tons to the load the building has to bear."

Around the inside and the outside of the lower parts of the dome there were galleries; and, now that the huge building was completed, stairs even took the bravest up to the very pinnacle of the lantern tower itself. The view from the gallery was splendid, and thanks to Grinling Gibbons and Wren, O Be Joyful had been granted permission to go up there today. Feeling rather proud of himself, he reached the top of Ludgate Hill and led the way towards the great western portico with its huge pillars.

It amused him to notice that as the two children came to the door they hesitated for a moment before going in, but it did not surprise him. Indeed, in a way, he was rather pleased.

Gideon and Martha: his two favourites of the seven grandchildren. How proud, he used to think, their namesakes would have been if they could have seen them with their quiet but determined characters, their serious faces and rather solemn eyes. They had been strictly brought up in the Puritan manner too. For since the toleration granted after 1688, the Dissenters, as all Protestants outside the Church of England were now called, had flourished. Over two thousand meeting-houses were now operating in England, with London of course the most vital centre. True Puritans seldom dressed in black or wore high hats, these days, but you could see hundreds of good folk, in plain brown or grey, flocking to hear the pastors preach on any Sunday. The harsh moral laws of the Commonwealth might have gone, but every child of one of these congregations knew that ornament in dress was sinful, that worldly pleasures were corrupting, and that, if they committed fornication, or got drunk, or gambled, the quiet, disapproving eyes of the whole community would be on them. The Puritans might be out of power, but their conscience was still a mighty force in England, and those Dissenters who felt they had a part to play in public life would take communion in an Anglican church, for form's sake, perhaps as Church of England men. "I give the sacrament to five good Dissenters," Meredith once told Carpenter. "I know what they're doing and they know I know. Nor does it worry me. We are just getting round some legislation that shouldn't be there."

There was no such compromise in the Carpenter family. Now that they were not compelled to attend the Anglican Church with its bishops, the heirs of old Gideon and Martha did not do so. Neither little Gideon, aged nine, nor Martha, aged eleven, had ever entered an Anglican church at all. As for this popish-looking cathedral in front of them . . . they looked at their grandfather uncertainly.

It had rather surprised O Be Joyful, during the last decade, to find himself a revered figure in the family. Though he knew only too well that he did not deserve it, he felt for the sake of the next generations that he should at least try to fill the role. So when his grandchildren begged: "Tell us how Gideon fought with Cromwell against the king," or asked him, "Did old Martha really sail in the *Mayflower*?" he did his best to satisfy them. He had even, God help him, been forced to keep up the old lie that he had tried his best to save Martha in the Great Fire.

Since his grown-up children had all expected him to help them instruct his grandchildren, he had also been forced slowly and painfully to teach himself to read again. It had not been easy. He had even had to ask Penny to take him to a good spectacle-maker for his tired old eyes. But he had done it, and by the time little Martha was five, he was reading the Bible to her every day.

Even more than the Bible however, there was one book that

the family always wanted him to read. Written by a great Puritan preacher in the last part of King Charles II's reign, it told in allegorical form the story of a Christian man who, suddenly overcome by the sense of his own sin and the death that soon awaits him, sets out on a quest. It was a very Puritan pilgrimage: no saints, no Church authority, nothing but faith and the Bible guided poor Christian. The land through which he travelled was a vast moral landscape of the kind so familiar to stern Puritan congregations. The Valley of the Shadow of Death, the village of Morality, Doubting Castle, Vanity Fair, the Slough of Despond – these were the sort of places he encountered on the way to the Celestial City. The people he met, likewise, had such names as Hopeful, Faithful, Worldly-Wiseman, Mr No-Good, or the Giant Despair. The book's tone was that of the Bible – the Book of Revelation, really – but it was still so neatly couched in plain man's language that it could be enjoyed by any simple, unlettered fellow. Nor was its message harsh: on the contrary, poor Christian falls into all kinds of error from which he constantly needs to be rescued. Puritan it was, certainly, but *The Pilgrim's Progress* of John Bunyan which O Be Joyful had learned to read and to love was kindly and very human.

As they looked at the Anglican cathedral, O Be Joyful reassured the two children: "It's only a building. It isn't the Slough of Despond." Taking their hands he led them in.

The truth was, he had come to love the great cathedral. His vow never to work under that popish dome seemed unnecessary now. For whatever he had once thought, there was certainly nothing to fear from Rome any more. William and Mary had been succeeded, some years ago, by Mary's Protestant sister Anne. After Anne, it was to pass to her equally Protestant cousins, the German House of Hanover. Not only was the throne safe. In recent years the English army and their Dutch allies, commanded by the great John Churchill, made Duke of Marlborough now, had smashed the forces of mighty King Louis XIV of France and made all northern Europe safe for the Protestant cause.

As for the building itself, even the great dome no longer seemed so sinister. Thanks to the huge, plain glass windows, the cathedral's interior spaces were so light and airy that a visitor from Holland might well suppose himself in some big

Dutch Protestant church. St Paul's, it now seemed to Carpenter, was not so much a threat as a great English compromise – a Protestant spirit in a Roman form – just like the Church of England itself, in fact.

Apart from the verger who greeted them, it appeared for a moment that they had the whole place to themselves. Advancing slowly up the mighty nave, O Be Joyful could see that the two children were awestruck. Suddenly however, halfway up the aisle, the silence was broken by two sharp bangs that reverberated round the great central crossing ahead, and which were met with an impatient snort from the verger. What could it be, Carpenter enquired?

It turned out to be Meredith.

"Up there all morning," the verger explained in a voice that suggested he doubted Meredith's sanity. And sure enough, as they emerged into the space under the dome, they were just in time to see the clergyman scientist up in the gallery above. He gave Carpenter a friendly wave, then disappeared, and a few minutes later reappeared on the cathedral floor.

"I was just trying it out," he explained, as Carpenter and the children helped him pick up the various objects he had dropped from above. "This dome, you see, is the most perfect place to test Newton's theory of gravity. Precisely measured spaces; controlled conditions; the air is perfectly still. Much better than the Monument. The Royal Society, you know," he continued, "plans to conduct a series of experiments here very soon." And with another cheerful wave, and escorted by the disgusted verger, he made his way out towards the western door, leaving O Be Joyful alone with the children once more.

There was much to show them. He pointed out the 'RESURGAM' stone and explained what it meant. "I put that there," he told them, enjoying their surprise. Then he led them up into the choir.

Of the projects he had worked upon during the last twenty years, several had given him special pleasure. He had been proud of the ceiling he had carved for the new dining hall of Myddelton's New River Company; he had loved working on the fine new wing out at Hampton Court and Wren's splendid building at Chelsea Hospital. But nothing could compare with the magnificent carving of the choir stalls in St Paul's.

They were huge. There were not only the long, dark rows of

gleaming seats for the clergy and choristers; there was also the massive casing for the organ. The project had been a joint effort: Wren had designed the outline and had models made; but when it came to the job of planning the decoration of all this, the great designer had turned to his friend Mr Gibbons.

The result was breathtaking. Within the framework of simple classical forms – rectangular panels, pilasters, friezes and niches – a sea of carving appeared: rich, voluptuous, yet always controlled. Spreading leaves and sinuous vines, flowers, trumpets, cherubic heads, festoons of fruit burst from cornice and capital, panel and pediment, baluster and bracket. There was nothing quite like it in all England. The quantity of oak, scores of tons, was prodigious; the workmanship, thousands of feet of carving, vast; the cost stupendous. Indeed, the cost was so great that even the coal tax could not meet the current expenditure so that investors, including the great masters like Gibbons himself, had to lend money to the project to be repaid in future years, plus interest. "I financed the choir stalls," Gibbons had remarked to Carpenter, "at 6 per cent."

For three years O Be Joyful had worked in St Paul's, and they had been the best of his life. Every skilful joiner and woodworker in the city seemed to have gathered there for the great task. The atmosphere was quiet and pleasant. Once, at the start, he had complained to Gibbons about some of the profane language of the labourers; within a day Wren had issued an order forbidding all bad language. So great was the atmosphere of dedication that he could almost believe, despite the fact that it was still an Anglican church, that he was doing God's work by carving there.

Though the two children knew, of course, that their grandfather was a skilful carver who had worked in many places, they had never seen any large examples of his craftsmanship. It was with some pride therefore that he now led them along the gleaming stalls, explaining their features. "See this panel?" he asked. "This is of English oak. But that one," he pointed to another, more richly carved, "that came from Danzig in Germany. The German oak is less knotty, easier to carve." Then pointing up: "See that cherub?" It was normal for Grinling Gibbons to make a master model for a feature like this, which

O Be Joyful and the other assistants would copy. "I did that one," he told them. "And that."

"Now this panel," he explained, as they came to one of the most elaborate pieces of carving, "is not oak at all. It's lime-wood, which is softer. This is the wood Mr Gibbons likes to work with best."

He showed them the stall where the Lord Mayor sat, and the organ casing, but finally they came to the place which made him proudest of all. For at a corner of the stalls, surmounted by a splendid canopy carved with great festoons, stood the grandest seat of all, the masterpiece of the entire stalls: the bishop's throne.

"Mr Gibbons and I carved this seat together," he announced. Triumphantly he indicated the fantastic workmanship of the area above. "See the mitre; and below, a pelican in her piety as they call it. An old Christian emblem, that. And see the fine palm leaves? You can't even tell," he proclaimed, with perfect truth, "where his work ends and mine begins." It was the best work of his life.

The two children stared in silence. Then, glancing all around the magnificence of St Paul's, they looked at each other. Finally, young Martha spoke. "It is very fine, grandfather," she said quietly. "It is," she searched for a word, "very ornate." He could hear the doubt and disappointment in her voice. But now Gideon was tugging at her sleeve and pointing up to the mitre.

"Who sits here, grandfather?" he asked.

"The bishop," Carpenter answered, and saw the boy lower his solemn eyes in embarrassment.

"You made a throne for a bishop?" he asked. And then: "You could not refuse?"

Of course, he had failed them. What a fool he had been, in his pride over his workmanship, to neglect the essential. God knows, in a way the boy was right. Old Gideon would certainly have refused such a commission. "When you work for a master like Mr Gibbons," he answered lamely, "you must work as he directs, and still do the best work you can." But he could see that they were both confused and unconvinced.

Nobody said anything as they left the choir and entered the cathedral's central crossing again. Martha looked pale, the little boy thoughtful. But then, as they walked under the great dome, it seemed that little Gideon had an inspiration. Embarrassed by his grandfather's unexpected fall from grace, he was evidently anxious to give him the chance to redeem himself. Turning his face up to him eagerly, therefore, he suddenly asked: "Tell us, grandfather, how you tried to save old Martha in the Fire."

Carpenter fell silent. He understood exactly why the boy had said it. He saw, too, that the children needed him to be their respected grandfather again; to be valiant, like old Gideon and his saints. But it would also be a lie: another act of cowardice to add to the original one. His grandchildren wanted to have faith in him, but what was the value of basing their faith on a fraud?

"The truth is, Gideon," he heard himself confess, "I did not really try to save her. I saw her up there, but I lost heart."

"You mean," the boy was open-eyed, "you let her burn?"

"I'd tried to go up there once but . . . yes. I let her burn." He sighed. "I was afraid, Gideon. It's a secret I've kept for forty years. But it's the truth."

Then after a glance at the boy's stricken face, he bade them follow him to the staircase that led up into the dome.

It was a long climb up the broad spiral staircase into the dome, for the inner gallery of St Paul's is a good hundred feet above the cathedral's floor. O Be Joyful had time to reflect, as he led the way and the two children followed silently behind. Had he lost their respect, even their love? Their thoughts seemed to rest upon his shoulders like a weight, making the climb even harder. The years he had spent finding a modest happiness in his work suddenly vanished, leaving him once more with the remembrance, as keen and cold as it had been forty years before, that he was a coward. And now his grandchildren knew it. By the time he finally reached the base of the dome and entered the gallery that runs round its interior, he felt deeply tired, and indicating to the children that they should wander round, he sat down and rested.

The inner gallery of St Paul's can be a little frightening. Peeping over the parapet, newcomers suddenly realize that they are suspended in space, hanging with nothing, apparently, below them, over the awesome central void. Glancing up at the huge dome rising another hundred feet above them, they feel as if they have somehow become miraculously attached to that surface and may be expected to fly over the yawning chasm at any moment.

From where he sat with his back against the wall, dully watching the two children across the space, Carpenter could see them taking turns to go to the edge, and then see their heads vanish again as they retreated to the safety of the wall. It was totally quiet. Whatever was passing outside, the three domes kept out every sound. The children, at the far side, had temporarily disappeared. Perhaps they were resting too. He closed his eyes.

And then he heard them. He heard their voices, one coming in at his right ear, the other at his left, as clearly as if they were beside him. He had forgotten to tell them that other great wonder of St Paul's: that up in the gallery under the dome, the wall is so perfectly circular that even the softest sounds, reverberating on the curved surface, will travel unhindered all the way round. For this reason it was called the Whispering Gallery. With his eyes closed he now heard, as though etched upon the silent emptiness below, the whispers of the children in the dome.

"Did he really let Martha die?" Gideon's voice.

"He said so."

"Yes. But grandfather . . ."

"He lacked courage. He lacked faith, Gideon."

"It was brave of him to tell us, don't you think?"

"We must not lie."

There was a pause. Then the boy.

"He was just afraid. That's all." Another pause. "Martha. Do you think he'll still go to heaven?"

The girl was obviously considering. "Those who are chosen, go," she said at last.

"But won't he?"

"We don't know who is chosen, Gideon."

The boy seemed to think for a while.

"Martha." The whisper came loud and clear. "If he's sent to hell, I shall go down and rescue him."

"You can't."

"I shall try." A pause. "We can still love him, can't we?"

"I think so."

"Let's go back to him now," the boy said.

* * *

The outer gallery of St Paul's is higher than the Whispering Gallery, so it was necessary for Carpenter to lead the children upstairs again before they came out on to the balcony that circles the base of the almighty leaden dome.

They emerged into brilliant daylight. The sky was crystalline, the lightest breeze teasing the surface of the Thames below the city so that it sparkled. And all around them, as they circled the gallery, the panorama of London. Even in his desolation, it was hard for Carpenter, feeling the sharp autumn air on his face and seeing this wonderful sight, not to experience a bracing of the spirit.

They looked northwards over the newly rebuilt Guildhall, over new London's Roman streets, past old Shoreditch and the woods of Islington to the green hills of Hampstead and Highgate; eastwards they gazed, over the city's other hill, over the pinnacles of the Tower, the suburbs of Spitalfields where the Huguenot weavers lived, past the forest of ships' masts in the Pool of London and out towards the long, eastern estuary and the open sea beyond. Southwards they stared at the river, and the huge, curious old form of London Bridge with its tall, medieval gabled houses hanging over the river, and to the untidiness of Southwark on the opposite bank. But from the west came the most glorious vision.

The barges were returning. First, the great, majestic gold barge of the mayor; then the splendid vessels of the companies – pinnacles flying, awnings fluttering, reds and blues, greens, silvers, cheerful stripe and rich embroidery, their banks of oars pulled in perfect unison by the liveried watermen – and following them, score upon score of lesser vessels, all brightly adorned: the great, gilded procession filled the whole river. When the Lord Mayor of London came up the river in full state, there was nothing like it in all Europe except the sumptuous pageants of Venice. O Be Joyful watched, as the two children gazed in wonder.

And despite his sadness, he smiled. The children were right, of course. As he looked out from the dome over London, under that still greater dome of the clear blue sky, he knew it very well. He was not destined for eternal life.

Yet, as he looked at his little grandchildren, it seemed to him now that it no longer mattered very much. His own life, even the fate of his immortal soul, no longer seemed so important. Old Gideon and Martha had departed, but in a sense they had returned. Little Gideon, purer, more godly than he, the valiant little boy who was ready to brave hellfire to rescue his faltering grandfather, would succeed where he himself had so miserably failed. Perhaps these children might even, one day, build that shining city on a hill.

Far below, the barges were approaching Blackfriars. A few moments more, and the mayor would disembark.

Just then, the bells began to ring to welcome the mayor to his city. There were many fine peals of bells all over the city and the suburbs now, for more than ever had been installed in the churches that had risen again since the Great Fire. From one after another of Wren's fine towers and steeples that rose over the rooftops all around, from churches everywhere they began to chime. From Cheapside and Aldgate, Eastcheap and Tower Hill, from Holborn, from Fleet Street and the Strand. Many had their own particular tunes and, standing side by side with the children, he began to identify them, giving each peal the little rhyme by which it was known.

Oranges and lemons
Say the bells of St Clements

You owe me five farthings,
Say the bells of St Martin's

When will you pay me
Say the bells of Old Bailey

When I grow rich
Say the bells of Shoreditch

When will that be
Say the bells of Stepney

I do not know
Says the great bell of Bow

"That's St Mary-le-Bow," he explained. "Old Bow Bells, the very soul of London."

But more and more bells were joining in – single bells, peals of bells, tolling and clanging with that manly clamour that only the bells of England make. For the glory of English bell-ringing is not as in other countries its tunefulness, but, on the contrary, the stern order of the permutations, as the bells are led through their changes, as strict as the mathematics of the heavens. Louder and louder now their mighty ringing grew, clanging and crashing down the major scale, drowning out every puny tune, until even the dome of St Paul's itself seemed to be resonating in the din. And as he listened to this tremendous sound echoing all around him, so strident and so strong, it suddenly seemed to Carpenter that he could hear therein a thousand other voices: the Puritan voice of Bunyan and his pilgrim, the voice of his father Gideon and his saints, of Martha; why – even of the Protestant Almighty himself. And, lost in their massive chorus, for a moment forgetting everything, even his own poor soul, he hugged his grandchildren and cried out, in exultation:

"Hear! Oh, hear the voice of the Lord!"

Then all the bells of London rang, and then O Be Joyful was joyful indeed.

Chapter 15

Gin Lane

1750

Number seventeen, Hanover Square. It is past noon on a late April day. Spring is in the air. And inside the handsome, four-storey house with its big sash windows, five across, Lady St James is about to take her bath.

Two footmen have appeared – crimson livery, white silk stockings – carrying the metal hip-bath and have set it down in the middle of my lady's chamber. They return three times, bearing huge, steaming ewers of hot water; they fill the bath, then retire. Her ladyship's maid tests the water with a small, plump finger; indicates that all is well.

And now, my lady comes from the great bed with its richly embroidered coat of arms. She walks across the floor, her nightgown a wonder of blue ribbons and white lace. She hovers by the bath. A dainty white foot appears, an elegant ankle peeps from under the hem of the nightdress. Her foot touches the surface of the water and there is a tiny ripple. Now a little of the lace parts and a slim, bare calf is revealed. Her ladyship's maid stands close, reaches up to take the nightgown. There is a faint rustle, the whisper of satin flesh upon silk; the maid's arms draw back.

And – at last – she has emerged: slim, flawless, delicately scented. Her leg has slipped beneath the still water which now surrounds her high, round breasts, and laps those alabaster shoulders.

Her maid is attentive. Soap first. Then oils, to keep the skin soft. My lady lingers in the bath a while, but not too long, lest that dry out the skin. When she is ready to rise, a huge towel is held out. She will not be rubbed however, but gently pressed and patted dry. Then puffs of powder, unguents for her pretty feet, sprinklings of scent around her neck.

My lady hates imperfection. It is the only thing she fears.

She rests in a chair, robed in a long silk gown, sipping a cup of hot chocolate thoughtfully. When she is done, the maid brings her a little silver basin of water and a brush; sprinkles a powder on the brush. Carefully but thoroughly, her ladyship brushes her pearl-like teeth. Then she is handed a small, curved, silver scraper. Elegantly, making a pout, she sticks out her pink tongue and, while the maid holds a looking glass, she scrapes it to ensure that not a trace of dark chocolate nor of whitish fur disgrace its surface.

Could it be that the Countess of St James is preparing for a sexual encounter? It could: this very evening. In this very house.

Seventeen, Hanover Square. It was halfway up one side of the great, paved and cobbled rectangle named after the present royal house and what name could be more appropriate to convey its aristocratic ease?

The German Hanoverians might have only a tenuous dynastic claim to the English Crown, but Parliament had chosen them. They might speak English poorly, but they are Protestant. They might be stupid, but their rule had brought peace and prosperity. The dynasty is secure. Five years before, in a romantic but hare-brained escapade, the last of the Stuart line, young Bonnie Prince Charlie, had landed in Scotland to lead a great rising. But the English redcoats had marched; the rising had soon broken up, and been easily crushed at Culloden. The Jacobite cause, espoused by Prince Charlie's supporters, was dead.

True, there was always trouble brewing abroad, as the various powers of Europe ceaselessly watched for advantage but since the triumphs of Marlborough a generation before, England had suffered no cause for alarm. As for the spreading British colonies, their rich trade, from America and the Caribbean, to India and the fabulous Orient, brought an ever-increasing flow of wealth, while at home, improved agricultural methods were increasing the income of many landowners.

Only one event had taken place which might have shaken the confidence of the English themselves. In 1720, in the first massive stock market madness of the new, all-capitalist order, the entire London Stock Exchange first inflated and then collapsed in the disaster known as the South Sea Bubble. Great men and small, who had speculated in largely bogus companies, convinced that prices could only rise, lost all they had. So many were hit that the government had to intervene. Yet so vigorous was the nation's growth that a decade later it was almost as if the Bubble had never happened. Business was booming again.

Small surprise, then, if London was growing to match. The expansion begun by the Stuarts outside the city walls had continued. In a broad and splendid sweep towards the west, aristocrats, gentlemen, speculators, were all busy building. And if the motley, house-by-house ownership of old London had stymied any grandiose town planning within the city walls, the big landholdings of this new West End were a very different case. Nobles with estates could lay out whole areas of splendid squares and streets with vistas, which bore their family names: Grosvenor Square, Cavendish Square, Berkeley Square, Bond Street. Nor was it only individuals: livery companies, Oxford colleges, the Church and the Crown all owned land in the West End. Westward into open country therefore – parkland, field and pasture recommencing wherever the building ended – the broad and handsome streets and squares spread out. The houses, for the first time in history, were numbered. Their terraced façades were simple, inspired by classical antiquity, and because the Hanoverian kings of that time were all called George, their style became known as Georgian.

It was a classical age. Aristocrats made the Grand Tour and returned with Italian paintings and Roman statues for their houses; ladies and gentlemen went to the old Roman spa of Bath to take the waters; and great writers like Swift, Pope and Doctor Johnson modelled their poems and satires on those of Augustan Rome. It was an age of reason, when men aimed, at least, to possess the same restrained dignity and sense of proportion as the Georgian squares where they lived. It was, above all, an age of elegance. And elegance was everything, at number seventeen, Hanover Square.

At one o'clock, Lady St James was reviewing her plans.

Balthazar the hairdresser had arrived. His work would take

an hour, so she had let the lady's maid go downstairs to join the other female servants for their dinner. Balthazar inserted a pad. The design he had concocted for today would raise her golden hair a foot above her head, to be surmounted by a tightly drawn bun and a little circlet of pearls, to match the pearl choker she would wear around her neck.

Nearby, on a French gilt chaise, her dress was laid out. It was made of stiff silk brocade, its gorgeous design like a rich, dark forest of flowers, from the Huguenot silk weavers of Spitalfields. God knew what it had cost per yard, nor how many hours her dressmaker had spent, double-stitching every seam – my lady would spot it at once if she hadn't.

Before her rendezvous, Lady St James had to attend a dinner party, then an assembly. The fashionable world was a ceaseless round and those, like Lady St James, who were invited everywhere, had a duty to be seen.

"It is," she would say with a bright smile, "why God placed us where we are." The splendid squares and houses had to be populated; the elegant show must go on.

After that however, later tonight . . . She gazed at the window.

She thought she could trust the servants. She prided herself on her cleverness there. It was normally the master, not the mistress of the house who engaged the staff, but early in their marriage she had persuaded Lord St James that he was too busy, and as a result, both the butler and the housekeeper owed their allegiance to her. The two footmen obeyed the butler, but she took care to keep them sweet, and the maids received gifts of money and clothes. The cook, the pastry chef – whose fantastic creations regularly brought applause at dinner parties when dessert was announced – and the coachman were admittedly her husband's; but both the grooms were in love with her because, when they held her stirrup, she would sometimes give their necks a little touch.

So if this evening, a certain person were discreetly to enter the house while his lordship was out, and if that person were to go into her ladyship's chamber, into which, without her express permission, his lordship was forbidden to enter – "It is the only thing," she once melodramatically told him, "the only courtesy I ask" – she could be sure there would be no tittle-tattle, no peeping at keyholes or listening in passages. Nothing would disturb the silence of the house unless, within the sanctity of her chamber, it was the little rustle of silk, the soft creak of the bed, a tiny moan.

Several minutes passed as Balthazar worked on her hair and she contemplated this prospect. Finally, having reassured herself that her plans were in good order, she allowed her gaze to wander to another figure close by her side. For, as well as Balthazar, one other person had also been allowed into the room and he was now sitting silently on a little stool, just within her reach if it amused her to take notice of him, which she now did by stroking his head. He was a round-faced boy, eleven years old, dressed in a little crimson coat like the footmen, and he looked at her with large, adoring eyes. His name was Pedro. He was black.

"Aren't you lucky, Pedro, that it was I who bought you?" her ladyship asked; and the boy nodded eagerly. For no fashionable household was complete without a pretty, dark-skinned plaything like this. Pedro was a slave.

If a black man had been an object of curiosity in London a century before, he certainly was not now. The busy British colonies had seen to that. Nearly fifty thousand slaves a year were being shipped from Africa to work the sugar plantations of the West Indies and the tobacco plantations of Virginia. Even Puritan Massachusetts was engaged in the trade. Often such shipments came through England; and though Bristol and Liverpool were the greatest ports for slave-ships, nearly a quarter came from London where Negro boys were often bought as toys and domestic servants.

"Tell me, Pedro," she teased, "do you love me?"

Technically the boy was a slave, but he lived with the servants; and the servants in aristocratic houses lived exceedingly well. Beautifully clothed, well-enough housed, well fed and reasonably paid, they formed an élite. Footmen especially did well because they were often lent out to others. The serried ranks of footmen at an assembly, even in the greatest ducal households, would mostly have been borrowed from other noble friends. Tips could be generous. A London footman who knew how to make himself agreeable could probably save enough in due course to set himself up in business. Similarly, Pedro the slave knew that, if she chose, Lady St James could set him free one day and put him on the path to prosperity.

Black butlers and shopkeepers were not unknown. Yet if he had gone to a Virginia plantation . . .

"Oh yes, my lady." And he covered her hands – it was a liberty which amused her – with boyish kisses.

"I bought him and he loves me," she laughed. "Don't worry, my little man," she glanced down and chuckled, "you are becoming a little man, aren't you? You shall never be sold. If you're good."

It always seemed to Lady St James that everything, and everyone, in London was for sale. Slaves were for sale, fine houses were for sale, fashion was for sale, social position too – for old money, in Georgian London, certainly mixed with new. Even her husband's title, like so many others, had once been bought. The votes of numerous members of the House of Commons, her husband assured her, were daily for sale. There was only one trouble. And it was this, now, that made her grow quietly thoughtful again. A certain person, it seemed, was not for sale.

Captain Jack Meredith. She pursed her lips. It was difficult to buy him; she wished she could. She wished it very much. To have him, for her very own . . .

Her thoughts were interrupted by a knock upon the door. When Pedro opened it, it was her husband who entered.

The third Earl of St James was not in a very good humour. With one hand he dismissed Pedro and Balthazar. In the other hand was a sheaf of bills.

He was neither good-looking nor bad-looking. Taking after his fair, conventionally pretty mother, you could only say that his looks were bland. Not that he was stupid: his investments, though cautious, had been shrewd; the Bocton estate was well run; he was an active member of the House of Lords in the Whig interest. (Hanover Square was much favoured by Whig politicians.) He had put on his powdered wig and was wearing a richly embroidered blue coat, in whose broad opening he exhibited the first beginnings of a respectable paunch. In his early forties now, Lord St James, in another decade, would probably look rather impressive. His hands, always beautifully manicured, were universally agreed to be fine. The wad of bills in his left hand, however, was large. He made only a brief bow to his wife before he began.

"I think you will agree, madam, that I satisfy most of your desires."

Lady St James made no reply, but eyed him cautiously. She had to be careful what she said. She had wanted him, for instance, to tear down the old Jacobean manor house at Bocton. "Quite inadequate for an earl," she would tell her friends. A Georgian mansion with a pillared portico, even half the size she recommended, would look imposing on the hill above the deer park. His cautious lordship was still thinking about it and, for all she knew, might decide to do it. He had steadfastly refused to allow her to make over the whole town house in the French rococo manner. "Though you see it is the highest fashion," she had constantly reminded him. So far she had only been allowed a Chinese papered drawing room as consolation. Indeed, so much was she subject, nowadays, to his will, that she could only remember one complete success – and this was one which she would never publicly acknowledge. She had managed to change his family name.

To be Earl of St James was a fine thing. As plain Miss Barham, the prospect of becoming his countess had certainly been enticing. But Ducket: that was another matter. Why, half the memorial tablets in London proclaimed some Ducket or other to have been an alderman, guild member or merchant. Earls they might recently have become, but the family was rooted in trade. And here was the remarkable thing: fashionable young Miss Barham found this humiliating.

History is the servant of fashion. To the end of the Stuart age, the younger sons of the gentry were still becoming mercers and drapers, as they always had. Nowadays however, if they possibly could, they avoided it. Instead, they favoured the army – which had scarcely existed before – or the Church, which their grandfathers would certainly have looked down upon. They might also, at a pinch, become lawyers. History, obligingly, supplied the example of the feudal knight or Roman senator as model to back the fashion up; and so, from the middle part of the eighteenth century, the upper classes of England came genuinely to believe the adage: "Gentlemen do not engage in trade." It was a piece of historical nonsense that continued to govern men's lives for more than two centuries to come.

Their merchant forefathers were forgotten or suppressed.

Gentility and trade could not be mixed. The fashion was redeemed by only one concession to common sense. A gentleman could marry trade. Even in the most snobbish and august decades of that century of Georgian elegance, gentlemen and noblemen, including even the ducal families, cheerfully and publicly married the daughters of merchants. Their French or German counterparts would have been appalled. They didn't give a damn. In England, it was only the male line that counted.

But the male line of the house of St James still carried the tradesman's name of Ducket and it was hard for Miss Barham to bear. To oblige her therefore the young earl, who at that time was quite dazzled by her – she was the belle of every ball – changed the spelling to the French-seeming, if improbable, de Quette. It was, she told her friends, the older form of the name which only time had corrupted; and it was soon generally accepted that the earl's family name must have come over with the Norman conquest. Some ancestors are born, others made: the de Quettes were not the only family to perform some carpentry on their name.

"Though it is pronounced," she would say, with a show of English firmness, "Ducket."

But that, she thought sadly, was the last time he had really tried to please her. She had her name now, her house; but as for the rest . . .

"These bills, madam. Have you seen them?"

Lady St James made a faint sound that might have meant anything. She never looked at bills.

"They are large, Lady St James," he said.

"Are we in difficulties?" she asked innocently, "must I sell Pedro?" She sighed. "Pray do not tell me, my lord, that we are ruined."

"Not quite," he remarked drily. He knew that she suspected he was richer than he cared to admit; and indeed, as with many of his class, the burgeoning colonial trade and improved farming methods were yearly increasing his already substantial income. Even the expense of the London house was mitigated by the fact that most of the meat and produce consumed there was brought in by cart, once a week, from the estate in Kent. That very morning, though he had no intention of telling her, he had received plans for a new mansion at Bocton. "If we are not ruined, it is because I live within my income," he stated. "Madam, I have here bills from tradesmen that total three hundred pounds."

Lady St James threw up her eyes, and might have thrown up her head too, except that it would have disturbed Balthazar's work on her hair.

"Perhaps we need not pay them all," she suggested. Lady St James's generosity, so pleasantly shown to her servants, did not extend to tradesmen.

Lord St James began to read them out. A hatmaker, milliner, Twining the tea-seller, her shoemaker, dressmaker, two perfume-sellers, Fleming the baker, even a bookseller. To most of these she replied with a little groan, or a murmur. "Robbery", or "Impossible". Finally he came to an end.

"The dressmaker must be paid," she said firmly. She would never find another as good. She thought for a moment. She suspected all the bills were justified, but the baker's annoyed her. She had held a huge party and decided, as she put it herself, to decorate the room with cakes. The party had not been a success. "Give me the baker's bill," she cried. "I'll make the fellow eat it." Actually, she meant to throw it in the fire. Fleming the baker could wait. He was not important.

She hoped, now, that her husband would go. He did not. Instead he cleared his throat.

"There is another matter, madam, that I wish to discuss." She waited, offering nothing. "The family of de Quette, madam. I am the third earl. I still have no heir." There was another pause. "Something must be done." He gazed at her steadily. "I do not doubt that I am able."

"Yes. Yes, of course." Faintly.

"When, madam?"

"Soon. We are so busy at present. The season . . ." She collected herself. "Shall we not be at Bocton this summer? In the country?" She contrived a smile. "At Bocton, William." It was his name.

But even though she smiled, it was difficult for Lady St James to convey even the modicum of encouragement necessary for her own self-preservation. A wife might avoid, but could not absolutely refuse her husband. If only, in his presence, she did not feel so discouraged.

Why was it so? she used to ask herself. What had he done?

He was quite a good-looking figure of a man. If only, she sometimes told herself, he was not so cautious. If only he would take some wild risk – though not one, she admitted to herself, that could jeopardize their comfort. What did she want, then? A year ago she could scarcely have said. But now?

Now she wanted Jack Meredith. And as long as he was in London, her husband was insupportable to her.

"You gave me," he reminded her gently, "an heir once before."

She closed her eyes.

"I know." Dear God, she thought, why must he mention that?

"I'm sorry. Poor little George."

It was an area of darkness, the thing they did not mention. The death of the baby boy eight years before. Even now, Lord St James remained mystified by the business, and for her ladyship, who had been quite devastated at the time, it was the subject that must never be discussed. Lord St James had just broken the rule. But today, it seemed, he was not prepared to act the penitent entirely.

"Summer is a long way off," he said briefly, and retired, leaving Lady St James staring into silence.

Lady St James sat quite alone.

That night. The horror of that night, eight years ago, when the child had been born.

Her labour had been long; afterwards she had lain exhausted for a time and dozed a little, glad that it was over. She had not enjoyed the business of being pregnant. To be so big, so clumsy: it was terrible. But now, at least, she had felt a sense of achievement. The baby was born a boy, to be called George, after his grandfather. But what really mattered to her was that he was the heir to an earl, with a courtesy title of his own from the moment of birth: little Lord Bocton. Hearing the baby cry, she had told the nurse to bring him to her. Smiling, she had held the baby up, to inspect him by the candlelight. And then her face had fallen.

She had expected the child to be pretty. Fair at least, like its parents. But the little creature already had hair that was dark. Stranger yet, there seemed to be a curious white streak in the middle. Even this, however, was nothing to what she found next. For as she had taken the baby's tiny fist and opened the hand with her finger and thumb, she had discovered something else.

She let out a little scream. The baby's fingers were webbed.

"It's not mine," she shrieked. "You've brought me another child. Where's mine?"

"No, your ladyship," the nurse promised. "It's yours."

"Witch! Thief! It can't be." But just then the doctor entered and assured her that this was, indeed, just how the child had been born.

Dear God, she thought, how could she show such a thing to her friends? A sense of horror filled her: horror at the baby; horror at herself – but no, this could not be her fault; horror at her husband therefore, who had caused her to have such a thing.

"Take it away," she cried, and fell back on the pillow.

It had been fortunate that, soon afterwards, Lord St James had been obliged to make a journey to the north of England, leaving her alone in London. For by this time she had formed her plan.

The interview with the wet-nurse had given her the idea. It was, of course, unthinkable for a lady of the countess's station to suckle her own child. A buxom young woman had been found, who was due to give birth the month before. And it was during the interview that the girl had casually remarked:

"I've always plenty of milk, my lady; enough for yours to share. Unless my baby dies. Then yours will have it all."

"Do so many babies die?" the countess had asked. She knew vaguely that they did, but had never troubled her mind about the matter before.

"Why indeed, my lady," the girl had replied. "Scores every day, in London." Even the rich were at risk: any fever could carry off an infant. As for the poor in their crowded, insanitary tenements, hardly one newborn baby in three lived to the age of six. Abandoned babies, dead or dying, were a sadly common sight. This information, together with certain other enquiries she had made, gave Lady St James the basis for her plan.

All she had needed, next, was an accomplice. That had not been difficult to find. The shabby, green-eyed woman she had finally selected in a dark corner of Covent Garden had no idea who the strange lady wrapped in a cloak might be, but the payment of five pounds, together with the promise of another ten when the business was completed, had been more than enough to secure her cooperation, with no questions asked.

The servants at Hanover Square had been astonished when suddenly, two days after his lordship had gone, her ladyship had suddenly become anxious.

The child was sick, she announced. The wet-nurse was at fault. The girl was dismissed. Goat's milk must be found. "None may come near the child," my ladyship insisted, "but myself." Nobody had ever seen her like this. They offered to call the nurse, the doctor. She seemed to consider it, but decided: "I trust no one." Then, one terrible dawn, there was a scream. Her ladyship, distracted, rushed downstairs, carrying the baby, wrapped in a shawl. She gave orders: the fast post-chaise must be ready within the hour. She was going to Bocton. To Bocton, if you please, which she never liked, and at this hour of the morning! She would take no one with her but the coachman and a groom.

"Country air," she cried. "The baby needs air. Give him country air," she insisted, "and he will be well." Then she rushed out into the square with the baby – who would dare stop her? – and disappeared for nearly an hour.

What a mad drive that was. Clattering over London Bridge, through Southwark, out on the old Kent road that leads up to high bare Blackheath and the long drag of Shooter's Hill; the groom riding postilion, half-terrified of highwaymen; hour after hour they went, only stopping to change horses at Dartford and later at Rochester. How her ladyship drove them on, would not even leave the carriage when the horses were changed but told them to bring her a chamber pot. It was dusk already, that March day, when they came at last to the ridge and the wooded park of Bocton, where the astonished housekeeper had to hurry to make up the chamber to which her ladyship, holding the child close to her, immediately retired.

And it was a most astonished doctor from Rochester, summoned the next morning, who announced:

"This child has been dead a whole day at least."

But Lady St James, it seemed, was far gone by then, insisting distractedly that, now it had country air, the baby would be well, and the doctor had wisely taken the little corpse away with him.

Ten days later, when Lord St James returned from the north, it was to find that his heir was safely buried in the little churchyard by the deer park at Bocton and that his wife was practically out of her mind with grief – so much so that for a time he had feared she might go mad.

This was the dark memory that assailed her ladyship as she sat alone in her chamber at Hanover Square, nearly eight years later, with her hair so perfectly coiffed.

For her real child, whom she had exchanged for the dead one during her early morning disappearance, she felt nothing. When the woman from Covent Garden had asked her what to do with it, she had hissed: "Do what you like. So long as I never see it again." Nor had she. I did not kill the child, she told herself. She just hoped that it was dead.

But that was long ago. And hush, her ladiesmaid has entered the room, to help her ladyship into that gorgeous dress, so that she can go out.

Isaac Fleming could afford to be happy. His account to Lady St James was for no less than thirty pounds; since the huge order of cakes he had sent her had been, he knew, of the finest quality, he hoped that it would lead to a profitable business. Like many who have not had the good fortune to serve a truly fashionable clientele, Isaac Fleming was under the impression that the aristocracy always paid their bills.

"Perhaps," he told his family, "she will recommend us to her friends."

Isaac Fleming's present ambitions were not large, but they were precise. He wanted a bow-fronted shop.

In his grandfather's day, when the family was still in haberdashery, such things did not exist. After the fire, terraced, brick-built shops had begun to replace the wooden stalls of old London, but they were mostly quite simple affairs – a plain counter, the goods on racks, a sanded wood floor. More recently things had begun to change.

As a boy, Isaac would often walk out of Ludgate along Fleet Street to where, just after the ancient church of St Clement Danes, it widened into the broader carriageway that passed the old Savoy and was known as the Strand. He liked the Strand: it was a fashionable sort of place containing such delights as the Grecian Coffee House, the New Church Chop House and other haunts where lawyers and gentlemen gathered. What really took his fancy though, was a single, narrow shop into which he ventured every time he passed: Twining's Tea Shop. It sold only tea, but how beautifully, how elegantly it did so. Great painted jars were set in the window; inside, the barrels were all ornately labelled; on the counter, as well as weights and measures were several beautifully inlaid tea-caddies. It wasn't just a shop, it was a work of art.

"I want a shop like that, when I grow up," he would tell his father.

Since, a few years later, he had begged to be apprenticed to a humble baker, it had seemed to Isaac's father that he was unlikely to have need for such an elegant shop, but he had reckoned without the boy's initiative. Within a year of setting up his own little establishment beside the Old Cheshire Cheese tavern in Fleet Street, young Isaac had taken to making cakes. He did it very well. Within a few years the takings from the cakes were more than half those from the daily bread. "Your only mistake," his father warned him, "is that you put so much into the cakes that they're hardly profitable."

"I need to make a name first," Isaac replied. "Then I can raise my prices." One day, he hoped, he'd be able to move along the street that crucial quarter-mile that would take him next to Twining's in the Strand. "That's where I'll get customers," he would say, "like Lady St James."

Secretly he had an even greater hope. It was a dream really – though before my son takes over from me, he promised himself, I will do it. He would dispense with the bread altogether and make nothing but cakes. And he would move to Piccadilly.

Piccadilly was fashion itself. The name, originally, had been a joke, because the merchant who had bought up the land had made his fortune supplying 'picadils' – ruff collars – to the Elizabethan and Stuart court. But it was no joke now. Lying between the court of St James and Pall Mall to the south, and the fine new developments like Grosvenor and Hanover Square to the north, Piccadilly could not fail to be a place for the best society. And it was there, just by the little market at St James church, that there stood a shop so splendid, so utterly magnificent, so entirely surpassing anything else in London, that before it Isaac Fleming could only bow the head. If Twining's Tea Shop was his model, this was his inspiration; if Twining's was a church, then this was the Holy City itself, beyond mere human aspiration.

Fortnum and Mason. The two friends had set up the shop in 1707 when Fortnum, a footman in the royal household, had retired from service. It was astonishing what you could buy there: all manner of groceries, strange delicacies – Harts Horn, curious pieces, exotic candies – imported through the East India Company. But most amazing of all were the store fittings: magnificently dressed windows, brilliant lights, tables arranged as if one had entered a fashionable drawing-room in an aristocratic town house. It must, Isaac knew, have cost a fortune. The scale of the thing was quite beyond his reach. But one day he would dwell within sight of it and his own more modest window of cakes would be seen by the same illustrious folk who visited Fortnum's. It was a dream; but it might, just, be attainable.

The first step towards this distant goal was the improvement of his present shop; and the way to do that, without a doubt, was to alter the façade. First, he had to change his sign. For although most ordinary shops still had the old, hanging sign outside their doors, just as in medieval times, the smart new purveyors of goods were writing their names on neat boards over the windows, sometimes even in gold. And secondly, he needed a bow window.

The bow window was a very intelligent idea for a retailer. Not only did it look elegant; not only, by coming discreetly forward into the street did it seem to offer itself to the passer-by, in a friendly sort of way, inviting him to pause and come in; but in the simplest and most practical terms, its extra footage allowed the shopkeeper to increase the size of the window display substantially. "You see it well before you reach it, too," Isaac would point out. "So you also see it longer." That very day, therefore, he had finally taken the decision. The modest bakery shop in Fleet Street was to have a fine new bow-front put in. No expense spared.

"Can we afford it?" his wife asked a little nervously.

"Oh I think so," he answered cheerfully, his narrow, concave face positively glowing at the prospect. "Remember. I've thirty pounds due, from the Countess of St James."

Piccadilly was not only home to London's finest shop. At five o'clock that afternoon, a litter carried by two runners, and containing the elegant person of Lady St James, joined a hundred others and numerous emblazoned carriages as it passed through the gateway and into the colonnaded courtyard of a huge, stone Palladian mansion which stood back, in proud, Roman seclusion, from the northern side of the street across from Fortnum's. This was Burlington House.

The fashionable squares of the West End contained some very large houses, but there were still some aristocrats, mostly dukes, who were so massively rich that they could afford small palaces of their own. One of these was Lord Burlington. And though the Burlingtons, for many years, had preferred their other, exquisite Italian villa out at the western village of Chiswick, the huge Piccadilly house was still used from time to time for social gatherings.

Everyone, of course, was there. Nobles, politicians and, this being Burlington House, home of aristocratic patronage, a sprinkling of men from the world of arts and letters: Fielding, whose novel *Tom Jones* had given such amusement last year, was there with his blind half-brother John, both good company; Joshua Reynolds the painter; even Garrick, the actor. It was the rule with great assemblies to pack as many people of note into one place as possible – and Burlington House could probably have accommodated five thousand and still had room for a spare hundred or two by the staircase. Lady St James moved elegantly from group to group, saying a few words here and there, making sure that she was seen. But all the time, her eyes were secretly looking only for him. He had said he would be there.

He was.

When Lady St James came close to Captain Jack Meredith, before their affair had started, she used to find that she blushed like a child. It had been disconcerting. Or finding herself in a group of people, of whom he was one, all her elegance – which she had worn for so long now that it belonged to her as much as her arms and legs – would suddenly drop from her like an unfastened dress; and she would stand there, as awkward as some gawky girl, wondering if anyone had noticed.

Nowadays, as she approached him, it was different.

It was, first, a fluttering of the heart; then a tiny trembling which even the perfect arrangement of her dress and her tightly drawn coiffure could not quite disguise. Then a tingling warmth. It began in her breasts whose tops were so deliciously exposed, it gathered together somewhere in the centre of her body and then, in a great, hot river, rushed downwards bringing so great a burst of life to her whole being that it was almost terrible.

His embroidered coat was the colour of burgundy; she knew at once, before he looked at her, that it would suit his brown eyes. He was, momentarily, standing alone, his tall, lean form turned towards one of the great windows in the huge room. Aware of her presence as she drew close, he was careful not to face her at once, and as he half turned his head and smiled, as he might at any other woman, she noticed the handsome, manly line that creased his cheek. A fleck of powder from his wig had fallen on his cuff.

They stood, a little apart, aware only of each other's presence; they spoke quietly, so as not to attract attention.

"You will come?"

"At eight. You are sure he will not be there?"

"Certain. He is at the House of Lords now. Then he goes out to supper and cards." She sighed. "He never changes."

"Plays for damnably low stakes as well," Meredith remarked. "I've never got more than five pounds off him at the club."

"At eight then?"

"Of course."

She made him a little nod of her head and moved on as though she had hardly deigned to notice him. But her heart was secretly dancing.

It was oysters for supper over at Seven Dials. Harry Dogget surveyed the gaggle of children before him. They all looked like street urchins, which they were. The two seven-year-old boys, Sam and Sep, were both barefoot and smoking long pipes; but it was common enough for children to smoke in Georgian London.

"Oysters? Again?"

The children nodded and somewhat nervously indicated the stairs. Dogget cast up his eyes. They all knew what this meant. As if in answer, there was a muffled bang from the room above; and then the floorboards announced, with several irregular but apparently heartfelt creaks, the imminent arrival of Mrs Dogget or, as Harry appropriately called her, "my Trouble and Strife".

Harry Dogget sighed. But still, he thought, things might have been a lot worse. At least the children were shaping up well, even if, truth be told, he couldn't be sure exactly how many of them there were. One thing though, he reassured himself, as a thud announced that Mrs Dogget was about to attempt the stairs:

"Every one of them's a cockney. That's for sure."

Harry Dogget was a cockney and proud of it. People might disagree about where the term came from. Some said it meant a bad egg; others that it meant an idiot; others yet claimed something else. Nor could anyone quite say how or when it came to be applied to the Londoners – though Harry had heard it was not much used before his grandfather's day. But one thing everyone agreed on: to qualify as a true member of this notable company, you have to be born within the sound of the great bell of St Mary-le-Bow.

Admittedly, that sound might have been carried some distance on the wind. Most of the inhabitants of Southwark, across the river, would claim to be cockneys and people living out in places like Spitalfields, east of the Tower, would usually reckon they were cockneys too – unless, as was often the case, they preferred to be thought of as Huguenots. And westward, out along Fleet Street and the Strand to Charing Cross, Covent Garden and Seven Dials nearby, men like Harry Dogget, hearing the peal of the old bell on a still Sunday evening, would nod and say: "I'm a cockney all right, and no mistake."

Nor was it surprising that the London cockneys should be famous for their wit. Hadn't men – old English, Viking, Norman French, Italian, Flemish, Welsh, God knows what else besides – been living by their wits in the port of London for centuries? Sharp-eyed market-traders, loud-mouthed watermen, tavern-keepers, theatre-goers, steeped in the salty, subtle and vulgar tongue of Chaucer and Shakespeare, the street people of London were swimming naturally, from their birth, in the richest river of language that the world has ever known. No wonder then that the quick-witted cockneys loved to play games with words; and, as people have from the earliest times, they liked to make rhymes.

Harry would tell his children, as soon as they could talk: "Holy Friar: that means a liar. Loaf of bread: that's your head. Rabbit and pork: a lot of talk. So stop rabbiting on and use your loaf. Field of wheat," the lesson would continue, "that's the street." Then with a grin: "What's cobblers's awls?"

"Balls!" his children would cry.

"No," he would respond, serious as a preacher. "They are the little spikes what is used by the makers of shoes for the piercing of holes in the leather. Right?"

"Cobblers!" the children would happily shout.

And so as Mrs Dogget staggered down the stairs, Harry muttered: "Here's 'Trouble and Strife'." He meant his wife.

She was flushed bright red already, as she reached her waiting family; but it was not through any exertion. The trouble with Mrs Dogget was Aristotle – in other words, the bottle. And the contents of the bottle was Needle and Pin.

And that meant gin.

Mother's ruin, they also called it, but it was more like family ruin. For God knows how many a family in London had suffered because of it. The trouble was that the clear spirit was so cheap to produce, and when Dutch King William had introduced this drink, so popular in his native Holland, the poorer classes in the towns had soon become so addicted that, by now, it was the greatest curse of the times. "Drunk for a penny, dead drunk for twopence," the saying was; and Mrs Dogget, alas, spent more than tuppence on many a day. "A little bit of comfort," she would call it, whenever she began, and there was nothing, it seemed, you could do to stop her.

She was a small, round woman. The drink had made her eyes puffy, but through the two slits remaining, it was clear that she could see well enough. Harry Dogget accosted her firmly, but not unkindly.

"Oysters again?" The catch in the Thames Estuary had become so huge that oysters were one of the cheapest items on the market stalls.

"Needle and pin," one of the elder children remarked.

"But I gave you a shilling this morning," Dogget pointed out. "You can't have drunk all that, old girl."

And now, fighting red though she was, Mrs Dogget looked genuinely puzzled.

"I didn't spend but tuppence," she muttered, frowning.

"So who had it then?" he demanded, while all the children shook their heads.

Though, had he looked more closely, he might have detected a faint smile of complicity pass between the two seven-year-olds. For Sam and Sep knew very well. And they had no intention of telling anyone.

Seven Dials was a funny sort of place. Seven streets, none important, had apparently decided to meet there. At the centre of the intersection, a Doric pillar of stone with a railing round it, on top of which pillar was a clock, rather remarkable for having seven identical faces, one pointing at each little street. Lying as it did, just east of Covent Garden, where there was now a daily flower market, and only a five-minute walk from Piccadilly, it ought by rights to have been a respectable location. But the seven streets lacked the moral character of their neighbours and preferred instead to lapse, all together, into a common sink of genial depravity.

If you wanted to find the cheapest gin, you came to Seven Dials. Gin Lane, some called the area. If you wanted female company, not too bad-looking and quite likely not diseased, go down to the clock and you'd encounter a dozen women on the way, not so much regular prostitutes as the wives of working men, ready to earn a little on the side. And if, by chance, you wanted your pockets picked, why you could walk down any one of the seven streets and someone would be sure to oblige you.

But to Sam and Sep, Seven Dials was a friendly place. They had been born there after all, in a courtyard tenement not a minute from the Dials. Everybody knew them. And even those whose tempers might be uncertain, or habits dangerous, were unlikely ever to trouble Sam and Sep. After all, their father was Harry Dogget: a man of some importance.

There had always been street-sellers in London – the men and women with basket or barrow who hawked their goods from door to door; but nowadays there were more than ever.

The reasons were simple enough: an ever-growing population; and the increasing conversion of the old street stalls into regular shops.

Poor people did not frequent the new shops. Things cost more in there and besides, few shopkeepers encouraged these ragged folk to defile their premises and put off their better customers. The humble street vendors would go on their perpetual rounds, therefore, their cries and shouts filling the air so that often it seemed as if some great and noisy market had decided to up sticks and form a procession. "Hot pies!" "Buy my fat chickens!" "Oranges and lemons!" "Cherry ripe!" Or some, like the muffin man, would simply ring a bell. The hubbub was amazing.

But of all the street-sellers, the very princes of these cockney traders were the costermongers. And Harry Dogget was a costermonger.

The name originally came from "costard", a type of large apple, and "monger", a seller. A costermonger like Harry Dogget owned his own, splendidly painted barrow, and his own donkey to pull it. He sold fish, fruit and vegetables, depending on the day and season. The greatest costermongers were the unofficial rulers of each area, keeping order amongst the other traders and passing their position down from generation to generation in cockney monarchies. And though just below this ultimate élite, Dogget the costermonger was not a person to be trifled with. Fair in his dealings, the first to crack or to see a joke, generally liked – and by the women too, it was well known – with the same red kerchief always tied loosely round his neck, Harry Dogget was only medium-sized but very square.

"He hit me one time," the two boys had once heard a sturdy butcher confess. "Mind, I asked for it."

"What was it like?" someone had asked.

"I'd rather," the butcher said thoughtfully, "be kicked by a dray-horse."

Indeed, Harry would have been a fortunate man – if it wasn't for Mrs Dogget.

"It's not that she costs so much," he would explain, "but she don't bring nothing in neither." A man in his position, even a costermonger, expected his wife to add in some way to the family income.

Everything had been tried to wean her off the gin. Ordinary tasks, like taking in laundry, remained unfinished. One spring he had tried taking her out to Chelsea and Fulham for a week. People from the West Country and even from as far afield as Ireland would work in the huge market gardens owned by Mr Gunter out there. But she had still managed to find gin, become drunk and smashed into a greenhouse. That summer, Harry thought he had found a solution when a friend who worked at the Bull brewery in Southwark had suggested Mrs Dogget and the children go out for the weeks of hop-picking in the big Bocton hop-fields in Kent. "I don't think she could get any gin out there," he had suggested. But Mrs Dogget had refused to go. "Stuck better than a mussel on a rock, she is," Harry sighed. And that was that.

Sometimes he would wonder if it could be his fault. Had he driven her to drink? Was it his other women? But he didn't think so. Whatever her faults, Mrs Dogget had always been easy-going. As for his occasional lapses, he fancied she might not be guiltless in that respect herself. "Some get driven to drink," he concluded. "She just took to it." But whatever the cause, it meant that Harry, even with his barrow, could never really get ahead; and it caused him to warn his children, all too often:

"You must look sharp now, and learn to look after yourselves."

Which was exactly what Sep and Sam were doing.

Sometimes Sep worried about Sam's stealing. "The Bow Street Runners will get you," he would caution.

It was just the previous year that Henry Fielding, who as well as writing such novels as *Tom Jones*, was also a magistrate, had set up the first attempt at a proper London police force, which operated out of Bow Street near Covent Garden.

Sam only laughed at his brother. "You don't have to look out for me," he would say.

The two boys were not identical twins, but very alike, with the same shock of white hair and the webbed fingers which, though they had skipped Harry Dogget, had been passed down from the costermonger's father. Sam was the jollier of the two, always ready to joke; Sep was inclined to be more serious. Like all the other children, they were always busy. While the eldest boy helped his father with the barrow, however, and their sisters either kept the house or went into domestic service, the twins worked together, picking up odd jobs, running errands – anything to get a little cash which they carefully hid from their mother. But Sam, being bolder, had branched out into outright crime. His method was cunning.

For the last eighteen years, the most splendid theatre in London had been the new one at Covent Garden. When the audience came out after dark, besides the ranks of sedan chairs for hire, there would also be a crowd of fellows with lamps on sticks – the link-men – offering to guide those who preferred to walk home through the unlit streets. Many a gentleman, deciding to patronize the cheerful little boy standing among them and finding himself five minutes later deprived of his money by some ruffian near Seven Dials, would have been surprised indeed to discover that despite his apparent terror and tears during the assault, a calm and cynical Sam would collect his reward from the robber the following morning.

"The Runners won't trouble with me," he'd reassure Sep. "Anyway, they couldn't prove nothing."

When it came to his other line of theft, however, Sep joined him gladly. They stole from Mrs Dogget. It wasn't, they agreed, really even stealing. After all, it was only their rightful share of the family's money. If they didn't take it, they knew where it would go.

"Better us," Sam said, "than Needle and Pin."

If asked what he needed the money for, Sam at least could answer precisely. He wanted to be a costermonger like his father; and since his elder brother was going to inherit the barrow, he needed money to set himself up and buy his own. Street-sellers were not licensed; there was no guild, so you could start when you wanted as long as the senior costermongers let you. "I'll do more trade than him by the time I'm fifteen," he had sworn with a grin. And until he was five Sep had supposed that he wanted the same thing. Until, that was, he had made an exciting discovery.

There were a number of great events that marked the year in Georgian London. Most, of course, had been going on for centuries: Christmas, Easter, May Day, and the great water procession for the new Lord Mayor. But during Harry the costermonger's childhood a new, though more modest attraction had also been added. It was a boat race, run at the very start of August: six boats competed, each rowed by a single waterman, from London Bridge upstream to Chelsea for a prize of a rich coat and a solid silver badge. It had been set up by the will of a comedian and theatre manager. But the thing that seemed truly wonderful to young Sep was the name of this benefactor of the watermen. For it was Thomas Dogget. His own family name. And Dogget's Coat and Badge Race was watched by all London.

"Is it something to do with us?" little five-year-old Sep had eagerly asked his father when he had first been taken to watch.

"'Course it is. That was my old Uncle Tom," the costermonger had cheerfully lied. Whether Thomas Dogget, who had originally come from outside London, was even remotely connected to his own humble family, Harry had not the faintest idea, but it amused him to see the little boy flush with pride.

From that moment, however, in Sep's mind, the river and its watermen had acquired a completely new significance. A costermonger, of course, was a fine thing to be; but how could it compare with the glory of the river – the river where Doggets, he felt, truly belonged? Hardly a day went by when he did not dream of joining the colourful fellows on the water. And rather to his surprise, when he had confided this to his father one day, the costermonger had encouraged him. Not only was the waterman's life a pretty fair one, Harry informed him, but there was another side to it he had not realized.

"You could be a fireman as well," he explained.

It was the insurance companies who had started the fire brigades. Realizing that the simplest way to limit claims was to put the fires out wherever possible, each company had its own cart with water barrels, buckets and even primitive pumps and hoses. The policy holder was issued with a metal badge bearing the company's name and insignia, which was fixed on the front of the house so that the firemen could identify it as theirs; if you did not display the badge, they would leave your house to burn. As firefighters, the insurance companies hired the Thames watermen, who were always fit and ready for anything. Dressed in bright company livery, with stout leather helmets, Sep often saw the firemen with their engines racing through the streets. The crews from the Sun Insurance Company seemed to him the most glamorous.

"And they make good money too," Harry said.

By the age of seven, then, young Sep was in a position not granted to all boys his age. He knew where he belonged, in the bosom of the famous Dogget family; he knew his destiny, to be a fireman; he knew, already, almost all there was to know about the life of the London streets and his place in them.

Indeed, there was really only one thing about himself that he did not know. Though whether it mattered, who could say?

It had been quite early in the morning, seven years before, when Harry Dogget had taken his barrow out into the muddy street by Seven Dials. He had been in a contented mood. His new son, Sam, had been born the week before and this was a double blessing: not only had he hoped for a boy, but the new baby would occupy Mrs Dogget who had started drinking even more. He was whistling cheerfully, therefore, as he approached the pillar with its seven clock faces and noticed the little bundle.

It had been placed just inside the railings that ran round the pillar, and it was crying.

Henry had sighed. There was nothing surprising about a little bundle like this, but he always hated to see them. He didn't even blame the mothers who abandoned them. Unwanted children were an occupational hazard in a place like Seven Dials, and what was an unmarried girl to do? A certain Captain Coram, he had heard, had recently started a hospital for orphans; but to get her child in, the mother had to turn up and explain herself. And even then, there were so many that the orphanage had had to choose the children by lottery. No chance for this child, anyway. It was going to die and there was nothing to be done. Yet even so, he could not quite bring himself to pass by. He had stepped over to examine it.

The baby was not a newborn, but less than a month old, he guessed. A baby boy. It seemed healthy enough. But then he frowned. It was odd – the baby's hair seemed to have a tiny white streak in it, like Sam's. He shrugged, stuck out his finger for the baby to take – and a second later started back in surprise. Another child with webbed hands? What kind of coincidence could that be?

Harry Dogget stood silently and considered his misdeeds.

There had been the shoemaker's wife. When had that been? But he had seen her often since. She hadn't been pregnant. There was the girl at the bakery. About the same time. When had he last seen her? A month ago. Not that one therefore. But then . . . . Ah yes. There was the young woman he had met in the fruit and flower market in Covent Garden. She was working on a stall when he had met her. Two or three times they had sneaked off together. That had been about ten months ago – the right time. And then she'd vanished. Could be her, then. Had she, or somebody left the child here by chance, or because they thought the father lived by Seven Dials? No knowing. People do strange things. He inspected the baby again closely. There was no question about the hair and the fingers. Surely this couldn't be a coincidence. It seemed to him now that the child even had the same face and eyes as Sam.

"Ain't you the lucky one, then?" he smiled. "Found your father straight away, didn't you?" And he picked the baby up.

He was honest with his wife. Told her everything, very straight. She sighed, inspected the infant and agreed:

"He looks just like Sam."

"I couldn't leave him to die."

"'Course not." She shook her head, then grinned. "I must've had twins, Harry. Just never noticed." And from that moment, with never another reference to the subject, Sam had a twin brother. The other children, if a bit puzzled, soon forgot. A few neighbours laughed about it, but then passed on to other gossip. Nobody could afford to enquire too closely about children in Seven Dials. When, a few days later, Harry took the baby to the vicar to be baptized, the clergyman, who knew his flock only too well, far from scolding the father thanked God in his providence that the child had a home. Upon learning that Harry had no particular name in mind, he suggested with a laugh:

"Why not call him Septimus? It's Latin for 'Seventh' – and you found him by Seven Dials!"

Within a day, in the Dogget household, the name had contracted to Sep. And Sam and Sep grew up together. As for Harry and Mrs Dogget, the incident only sealed for ever the affection he had for her. So that now, even though she was red-faced, unkempt and minus the shilling he had entrusted to her, the costermonger looked down at her lovingly and said cheerfully:

"You're a good old girl. That's what you are."

At a little before eight o'clock that evening, Captain Jack Meredith came out of the door of White's Club in St James Street and started up towards Piccadilly.

It was only in the last few years that some of the smarter coffee-houses had turned into gentlemen's clubs with restricted membership, but already White's had established itself as the one with the most dashing style. Too dashing for some. For gambling was the thing at most of these clubs, and at White's they played high. Very high.

Captain Meredith was certainly dashing. As for gambling – he needed to win. He needed to win a great deal. His grandfather, a clergyman like old Edmund, had done very well and put by a tidy fortune. His father, having served under Marlborough, had married a well-endowed widow and left Jack a rich young man. Rich enough to lose five thousand pounds in a single evening at cards. Twice. But not three times, as he had finally done. Dashing Captain Jack Meredith kept a house in Jermyn Street, where the servants had not been paid for six weeks and he owed tradesmen a total of over a thousand pounds. And his regimental captaincy – for military commissions were bought and sold in the British army – had already been mortgaged to a moneylender who lived in an alley near Lombard Street.

Only one friend, a cynical fellow-member of the club, knew about the true state of Captain Jack's affairs and his advice had been blunt.

"You play well enough if you drink nothing and keep your head. We need to find you a victim to fleece. Some young fellow just up from his country estate who wants to cut a dash with us men of fashion. Come to the club each day and I'll keep my eyes open." Had they found their sacrificial lamb that day, Meredith would even have been ready to miss his appointment with Lady St James.

"I wouldn't take his estate off him," Jack had sworn. "Half would do."

As he walked calmly up St James Street however, on his way to the rendezvous with his mistress, no one would ever have guessed the state of his affairs. In the first place, Captain Meredith had a remarkable talent for putting aside distractions and concentrating his whole mind on the matter in hand. It made him a wonderful lover, and also one of the finest swordsmen in London. In the second place, he had simply too much style.

You could not say that Jack Meredith was vain. He was too manly for that. He was a good officer as well as being a fine sportsman. He looked after his men and could enjoy a broad joke with the best of them and out-box almost any man in the regiment. Splendid with men, tender with women, he was a successful and considerate lover, all the more devastating because, at all times, he knew exactly what he was doing. His relationship with Lady St James, however, went beyond the others. It had a special quality all its own. At times, in the last months, she had been an obsession. Her nakedness absorbed him. He would sit in White's, thinking of her body and how he might possess her, in a dozen, perhaps even a hundred ways. But he had been through that with so many women before and always become satiated in the end. With Lady St James there was something more. With her it was as though, each time, he were finding a new woman all over again; and the key to this lay not in her flesh but in her person. Her resilience, her artifice – frankly her fashionableness – were enough to intrigue him for years, perhaps even for a lifetime.

Yet if he was not vain, it might be said that Captain Meredith belonged in St James Street. The knowledge that his ancestors came to England with the first Tudor court, his club, his clothes, his connections, the very fact, even though it was a secret, that his mistress was a countess – these things were his life. Take them away and, like some fine Georgian house gutted by fire, he could not be what he was.

To ensure his survival in this condition, therefore, he was prepared to do whatever it took. If necessary he would kill. He could even justify it. For were not these the ancient rules of the aristocratic, knightly class? The rules of the game. There were many men in the clubs of St James who would have agreed; and to this extent, it might have been said that his heart, though warm enough, contained a place that was cold.

He had just come to the corner of Piccadilly when the three men stepped out of the shadows and seized him. Two took his arms from behind; the other stood in front of him.

"Captain Meredith? You are arrested, sir. For debt."

The door opened slowly. Lady St James felt a little tremble pass through her body. At last. He had come.

It was already half-past eight and once or twice in the last half-hour she had even feared that he might have changed his mind.

She had dressed with care. Her loose silk gown, exposing her shoulders, hinted that, at a touch, it would slip deliciously away. Her hair was now held by a single tortoiseshell comb. That too could fall, at the right touch. Her breasts felt taut against the silk. The door opened fully.

Lord St James entered the room.

Her face fell. She could not help it. "You?"

"This is my house." His bland face contracted; the beginning of a frown. "You were expecting someone else?"

"No." She strove to recover herself. "You always knock."

"My apologies." He said it a little drily.

What did he know? Where was Meredith? Was her lover about to arrive as well? She must warn him, or somehow get rid of St James. At all costs she must keep calm.

"I understood you were returning late this evening."

"I changed my mind. Does that displease you?"

"No, no. Of course not."

A knock at the door caused Lady St James to go pale; but a second later it was the ladiesmaid who discreetly entered. Did her ladyship require anything? She looked her mistress carefully in the eye.

Clever girl. She should have a present for this.

"I think not." Lady St James glanced at her husband. "You are not going out again?" He shook his head. She looked at her maid and smiled. "I shall not require anything further." The maid nodded. If Captain Meredith appeared near the house, he would be warned off. Lady St James silently breathed a sigh of relief. The maid left.

"You were preparing to retire?"

"Yes." She turned away. "I am very tired."

It was true. Quite apart from the great wave of disappointment that broke over her as she realized that she had lost Jack for the evening, the very fact of her husband's presence in her bedroom always had the same effect upon her. Everything in her body seemed to sink; a sense of tiredness, listlessness invaded her spirits. She would draw quickly away to create a distance between them.

Her husband was eyeing her thoughtfully.

"I am sorry you are tired," he remarked. She said nothing; prayed he would go. But he stood his ground. "We spoke this morning," he continued, "of my need for an heir."

"We said this summer . . ." Her voice was weary.

"But I do not wish," he said quietly, "to wait so long."

He moved across the room to the chaise. Deliberately, he took off his embroidered coat and hung it over the chaise, then turned back to face her. Standing there in his white silk stockings and breeches, and his long waistcoat, he was quite a good-looking man. Could she have found that body attractive if it had belonged to another man? She hardly knew any more. His eyes were resting on her exposed shoulder; they moved to her breasts.

She had become adept at avoiding contact. Not only was her bedroom forbidden to him without permission; if they returned from an evening assembly or ball together, she either complained of feeling unwell or feigned sleep. But even so, there were inevitably times when it was impossible to escape her marriage bed without risking an open admission of her feelings. On these occasions, she had a dozen small ploys which would usually serve to dampen his ardour, keep his activity to a minimum, or even cause him to abandon the business altogether. A complaint that he was tickling her, followed quickly by an apology, a stifled yawn, a sudden turning away of the head as if his breath offended her, or even a little cry of discomfort. Had Lord St James been less polite or less sensitive, these tricks might have been useless, but as it was, she had usually been able to make him a stranger without exactly refusing him.

Sometimes however, in order to make him believe that he still had a marriage, and a wife to be pleased, she would suddenly reverse these tactics and appear before him in the most seductive manner imaginable. Once or twice in the last year, when she had judged this necessary, she had closed her eyes and tried to pretend that it was Jack Meredith who pressed into her; but she had not always been able to bring this off to her own satisfaction.

Tonight however, the case was different. He had caught her prepared to receive Jack. Her claim that she was tired had been ignored. Did he suspect? If so, her only safe course was to welcome him with open arms. Playing for time, she smiled, half closed her eyes and watched carefully.

Her doubts were set at rest a moment later.

"The fact is, Lady St James," he blandly informed her, "that I have decided your conduct towards me is going to change." She opened her eyes fully, wondering what was coming. "You will no longer require me to ask if I may enter this room. I shall enter when I like."

"And when did you decide this, my lord?"

"This morning," he replied. "You told me to wait for my heir. Why should I wait? I've already waited far too long." His face creased into what was almost a little smirk. "Your marriage vows include the word 'obey'. I think it's time you did."

Lady St James had her answer. But not the answer he thought he had given her. It was the smirk that told her. A man who suspects his wife, a man who is fighting to win back his woman, does not smirk like that, she thought. It was a little smile of self-satisfaction, nothing more. He was preening himself, damn him. She felt a flash of irritation, so intense that it actually made her shiver. She saw him looked pleased, read his mind at once.

Dear God, she thought, he thinks if he is masterful that I shall like him better. And she thought of Jack, who did not need to be masterful and, fairly or not, despised the man before her.

Lord St James was unbuttoning his long waistcoat.

"No!" She could not help herself. "Not now, my lord. I beg you, not now." Why, after years of artifice, didn't she either find a way out, or give in gracefully? It was all she had to do. Lady St James hardly knew herself. Perhaps it was the combination of events – the shock over Meredith's failure to appear, together with her husband's self-satisfied smirk – but for once she was not in control of the situation. She simply could not face it.

He took no notice.

"My lord," her voice, though it had an edge of fright, was also icy. "I do not desire you now. Please leave."

He took off his waistcoat and coolly laid it on top of his coat.

She flushed as she lied: "My monthly curse is come."

"Really? We shall see."

"You are not a gentleman," she cried.

"I am an earl." He turned and took her by the wrist. "And you belong to me."

She tried to snatch her hand away, but he held her easily. She pulled again, violently, with all her force. His grip only increased. His free hand now caught her other wrist and, holding each he calmly drew them wide apart until her breasts were forced to brush against his chest. She found to her surprise that she could do absolutely nothing. She had never realized before how much physically stronger he was than she. Suddenly humiliated, she forgot even her own elegance, and jerked her knee sharply up to catch him in the groin.

It was a mistake. He swivelled just in time; her knee only hit his thigh; but she felt a spasm, then a great welling of rage suffuse his body, and knew, as though a red light had suddenly ignited in the back of her brain reminding her of ancient, more primitive human times, that he had the power to kill her with a single mighty blow.

He did not kill her. Letting go of one wrist, he slapped her hard in the face so that her head jerked back. Then, seizing her and lifting her bodily, he strode across and flung her on to the bed. A moment later, he was over her, holding her pinned.

"Now I will show you," he breathed, "who is master."

In the minutes that followed, despite the pain, it was his face that she chiefly remembered. Emerging through the bland mask he always wore, she saw features she had never seen before. Broad, hard, unyielding, it was the face of the ancient Bulls – yet, where theirs had been terrible when roused, in this face there was something petulant, spoilt, and therefore hateful.

Lord St James did not rape the countess – for the simple reason that law and custom both declared that such a word could not be applied when the victim was his wife. With a savage suddenness, he ripped her gown open and tore it off. Then, pausing only enough to loosen the flap of his breeches, he rammed himself into her viciously so that she cried out; and thrust with all his force, again and again, and again.

She was being hurt, badly. Her face was throbbing, too, from the blow he had given her. She could taste blood in her mouth. As much as the pain, the sense of being violated, humiliated, was terrible. She nearly screamed to the servants for help. Surely one of the footmen would hear. But what could they do? Challenge her husband and be dismissed? In any case, she was too proud to let them see this. Instead, summoning up all her remaining strength, she fought.

She had never had to fight before, but she did so now, like a wild cat. She tried to scratch, to kick, to bite, but found it was no use. The large, heavy man on top of her had her completely in his power. He was out to prove he was master. He was the earl, she was his wife. Her title, her house, her spending money and now, he was proving to her, her body, all belonged to him. And because God had made him a man, and her a woman, he had, in the end, the physical strength to dominate her and brutalize her as well.

"You will be mine, from now on, when I say, and as I please," he said coldly, at last, when he had finished. Then he left the room.

Captain Jack Meredith sat on the little wooden bench and shivered. It was cold. The cell was small. Almost every crevice in the old stone walls could be seen by the light of the gnarled remains of a candle that guttered on the wooden table. For the last two hours he had pondered his situation, and always come back to the same conclusion. There was no way out.

He was in the Clink.

There were several prisons for debtors in Georgian London. The largest were the Fleet, outside Ludgate, and the Marshalsea in Southwark. But, as often happened, both were full that day and so he'd been sent to the nearest lock-up with a vacancy, which happened to be the Clink. The little medieval prison of the bishops of Winchester had never been much of a place. Even in feudal days, when bishops ruled over the Liberty of the Clink and the brothels of Bankside, there had only been a few cells. Since the days of the Tudors and Stuarts, a few religious dissenters and suspected traitors had found their way there, but mostly it was used for debtors.

It was no joke to be a debtor in Georgian London. If your creditors obtained a judgment against you – as several of Meredith's had done – you could be seized without further warning and put in gaol. There, until your debt was discharged, you remained. It could be for ever. And what sort of life could you expect in gaol? It was just this question that was occupying the mind of Jack Meredith when he heard the sound of a large key turning in the lock, and, a moment later, became aware that the door of his cell was starting, slowly, to open. Whoever was coming, it seemed, possessed a lantern. He also, clearly, believed in taking his time.

First came the tip of his nose.

The nose, whoever it belonged to, was clearly no ordinary affair. The dimensions even of the tip suggested that this was a nose of consequence, and not to be taken lightly. By the time it was halfway through the door, the daunting scale of the thing was becoming apparent. But when, at last, the whole, huge protuberance came into view, one could only gaze and surmise that there was none other like it, under the sun.

Behind it, as though in procession, followed two mournful eyes. Then a wig so dingy that it looked as if it had been used to clean the floor. And finally the whole, stooping person stood before the captain and addressed him thus:

"Ebenezer Silversleeves, sir, at your service. I am the keeper of the Clink."

It was, like many such positions, an inherited post. Before Ebenezer, his father, and his father before him, had exercised their shabby authority over the little prison. You might almost say it was in their blood, since even before then, when the family were still in Rochester, they had been petty clerks or gaolers, ever since the days when Geoffrey Chaucer had encountered Silversleeves at the assizes four centuries before. Yet, prison-keeper though he was, when Ebenezer Silversleeves said he was at Meredith's service, he meant it, every word. Captain Meredith was just the kind of prisoner he liked.

The rules of the Clink, like those of most prisons, were very simple. If you wanted bread and water, it was yours for the asking. If you wanted anything else, you paid Ebenezer.

"Oh dear, sir," his opening gambit always began. "A gentleman like you shouldn't be in here." He would indicate the dark little cell with disgust. He had a quite commodious chamber next door, he would then explain, in the remains of the old bishop's palace, that was much more suitable and could be had for – depending on his guess at the gentleman's means – a shilling or two a day. Naturally the gentleman would be wanting a decent dinner, a bottle of wine. Why in a day or two he could probably be almost as comfortable as if he were at home. For a price, of course.

And how was a gentleman in debt to pay for such things? It was amazing what Silversleeves could arrange. No matter how disastrous their finances, fine gentlemen nearly always had items of value upon them. A gold watch, a ring – he'd sell it for you and bring you most of the money in no time. Better yet, he could send a fellow discreetly to your house to remove small items of value from under your creditors' noses. Gentlemen had friends, too. They might not pay the debt, but would often keep the gentleman in modest comfort during his incarceration. When you had got through all this, Silversleeves could still be of service. Your fine coat could be sold and another, serviceable enough, would replace it while you lived a few weeks more on the proceeds. He'd even get a price for your wig. And when even the clothes on your back had been sold and all your friends had quietly departed – why there was always the dark cell, snug enough for a beggar in your condition, and a nourishing diet of bread and water to sustain you for as long as you were able to live.

"Give me a gentleman whom his creditors have fleeced," he would tell his children, "and I'll show you how to skin him."

So when Captain Meredith informed him that he had no money at present, serviceable Ebenezer was not put off at all; Meredith had no sooner turned out his pockets than the helpful keeper spied a metal disc. A theatre token, allowing the bearer access to the Covent Garden theatre for the rest of the season. "Why I could get a few pounds for that, sir," he declared, "and you'll hardly be needing it now." And he took it in a trice.

Would the gentleman, he asked, be wishing to communicate with his friends?

Jack Meredith sighed. He had been wrestling with that problem for the last hour. As soon as he did so, all London would know. His humiliation would be public. His chance of a game of cards would vanish over the horizon. Soon, he supposed, people would know anyway; but he'd like another day to collect his thoughts.

One letter however, in common courtesy, was due. He must at least explain his failure to appear to the Countess of St James. The question was, how much should he tell her? Could he trust her? He was not sure.

"Can you arrange," he demanded at last, "for a letter to be delivered with discretion?"

Eleven o'clock had just struck when the man, who had been waiting for Lord St James to go out, approached the door of number seventeen, Hanover Square and, shortly afterwards, was admitted to the chamber of her ladyship to whom he now handed the letter. Respectfully he waited to know if there was a reply. He noticed that her ladyship looked pale.

Lady St James was sitting on the chaise. She had propped herself up with a pillow behind her. Spread over her legs was a shawl. There were great, dark rings under her eyes. She had not slept.

When her husband had left her the previous night, and she had risen, shakily from her bed, she had not called her maid. All alone, she had filled a basin of water from the pitcher on the night stand and, as best she could, straddled over the basin, and tried to wash all trace of her husband away. Then she had sat down on the chaise, covered herself, and remained there for the rest of the night.

Once, very quietly, she had wept. Several times she had suffered little fits of shaking. She was aching. She felt bruised in body and in mind. For hours she just sat, staring ahead of her. But gradually, before dawn broke, she began to recover herself.

If her husband thought she would submit, she would not. She had managed to have her own way so far and she would do so again. Tonight, he had merely made himself repulsive, untouchable, for ever. But what could she do? Run away and leave him? She'd have almost no money. Find a rich protector, a lover presumably? Easier said than done even for a society beauty. I should probably have to go abroad, she thought. Would Captain Meredith flee with her? She supposed he could afford to, but was not sure he would. Whatever the solution, she knew one thing: she refused to be helpless. Her shivers subsided and ceased. Her shock and hurt were slowly converted to a silent, burning rage. If Lord St James thought she was weak, and that she could be humiliated, he would learn better. A serpent, too, may be stamped upon, she thought. But take care when the serpent slips away and then rises. By the light of the morning, her anger was controlled, hard, and deadly.

"I will strike him," she vowed, "like a snake." And she wondered, hour after hour, how she would do it.

Now the letter from Captain Jack Meredith gave her an idea.

"Tell him," she told the messenger from the Clink, "to be patient a few hours. I may be able to help him in his troubles."

Sam Dogget also had an idea.

The start of May was a jolly time. On the May Day holiday, the maypoles were erected. Apprentices dressed in their best clothes, milkmaids wore garlands, and pipes, drums and hurdy-gurdies were heard in the streets. Since time out of mind, a big fair had been held in the area north of St James so that even now, when the elegant streets and squares above Piccadilly were filling up the area, it still kept the old name of Mayfair.

And – a more modern but charming touch – the chimney-sweeps, of whom, thanks to all the fine new houses, there was now a veritable tribe, had their own procession through the streets.

Sam and Sep were standing in Grosvenor Square watching the sweeps go by, when Sam thought of it.

The sweeps were a cheerful enough crowd: grimy and soot-covered on working days, they were scrubbed clean and dressed in sparkling white shirts and breeches for May Day. But what really caught Sam's attention were their assistants. Each sweep had one or two of these – small boys, some as young as five or six. These were the little sweeps who were sent up the chimney itself when the long-handled brush could not negotiate a corner. Their job was filthy: half-choked with soot, they might have to climb thirty feet up the blackened tunnel. And their lot was often very hard. If the sweep was their father, they were probably all right; but if they were orphans, or sent out to work by their poor family, their treatment might be harsh. It was quite common, however, for a householder, or even one of the servants, to take pity on these little fellows and slip them some money or a present of food. If you were clever, Sam had heard, you could make some money. Something else had occurred to him, too.

These sweeps got into the grand Mayfair houses. They visited every room. His face broke into a grin.

"Sep, I think I know how we can make some money."

The Clink's best room was certainly a great improvement. It had a decent bed, a writing table, a rug on the floor and a narrow medieval window with a view of an overgrown little garden. Jack Meredith felt more himself as soon as he was installed. The message from Lady St James, if unclear, had been encouraging and he had decided to take no further action until he heard from her again.

At noon, Silversleeves brought him a meal: a chicken, a pastry and a bottle of claret. Also a journal to read.

"Most of my gentlemen take the *Spectator*," he observed.

After his meal, Meredith contented himself with that periodical for an hour before there was a knock at the door and a visitor was announced. Though he was half expecting Lady St James, the visitor's face was so entirely hidden under a hat and a silken scarf that for a moment he was not quite sure if it was she. Only when the door was closed did she remove the wrap; and Meredith received a shock.

Lady St James had taken great care over her appearance. The cheek which her husband had struck had been carefully slapped by her maid with a wet towel for an hour before she left, so that the entire side of her face was now horribly swollen and puffy. Further, her ladyship had even knelt down and bumped the other side of her face against the bedpost so that she had a black eye too. She did not lack courage.

The captain, who had risen to his feet, gazed at her in horror.

"Who has done this to you?"

"Who do you think?"

"St James? My God! How? Why?"

She shrugged, indicated that she needed to sit down. Then

slowly, letting him coax it from her, she told him about her husband's assault.

Lady St James did not exactly lie. There was no need. After all, she had been assaulted and considerably hurt. But by the time she had related all to Jack, the scale of the violence had mounted to match and even surpass the injuries she now displayed. Cynical man of the world though he was, Meredith was appalled.

"He must be stopped," he cried. "The blackguard!"

She made a sad little face. "How?"

"By God, I'll stop him," he declared.

"You are in prison," she reminded him. "You can do nothing." She paused. Then gently: "Would you really be my protector, Jack?"

He looked at her, remembered her message and in the back of his worldly mind guessed that there was some artifice here; but even so he could not fail to experience a great rush of protective feeling towards her. She, watching his thoughts, now quietly interposed:

"Jack, if you don't save me, I'm condemned to a lifetime of this, and I don't know what I shall do."

"That mustn't be." His voice was low, manly.

"Well, Jack, there may be a way to save us both. But there's a price." She smiled a little wanly. "And as I don't know if you really love me, I don't know if you'd be prepared to pay it."

"What is it?"

She gazed at him. Then, suddenly it seemed as if she might dissolve into tears. "You can't guess?"

He did not speak.

She sighed. "I'm at the end of the road, Jack. I can't face all this alone. I don't want to." She looked down, so as not to meet his eye. "If I'm to live, I only want it to be with you."

Jack Meredith paused, thought, and made his decision. He understood that she had come to bargain. But she was a beautiful woman in distress and, God knows, he had nowhere else to go.

"I am yours," he said, "for ever."

Then she told him her plan.

Fleming stared at the surface of Fleet Street and shook his head. He had forgotten about the paving.

The quality of the London streets was remarkably uneven. There was no public roadbuilding in the city – the residents and tradesmen were responsible for paving their own streets, each paying for his own frontage. In poor quarters therefore, the lanes and alleys were like middens; but in big thoroughfares the residents often insisted on the finest paving. Now, in Fleet Street, they had decided upon resurfacing with the finest cobbles. And poor Fleming had just been informed how much he must pay.

"Fifty pounds!" He glanced miserably at where his new bow window was to have been. "That'll have to be delayed," he sighed. "This isn't much of a May Day, I must say. And the trouble is," he added, "I haven't got the money."

"You'll have to go to Lady St James," his wife said. "She owes you thirty."

"I suppose," he agreed, "I shall." He did not like to bother a great lady like that, and was afraid it might offend her.

"You've no choice," his wife said gently.

It was four o'clock when he came to Hanover Square. He was wearing his best brown coat, which was too hot for the day, and he was sweating under his hat. With trepidation he approached the big door fronting the square, noticed briefly that the house was protected by the Sun Insurance Company and rang the bell. A footman answered. But before he could even ask if his lordship or her ladyship were at home, that liveried personage, seeing at once that he was a tradesman, told him to go to the back entrance of the house and slammed the door in his face.

Fleming might have been less discouraged had he understood that in aristocratic houses even a gentleman personally acquainted with the owner, especially if that were so august a person as an earl, would be highly unlikely to secure an interview with anyone beyond the butler, or his lordship's secretary, unless he was expected. To the mews behind he went therefore, getting his best coat muddy along the way, and approached the entrance near the kitchens.

But there, more amiably, they told him that both Lord and Lady St James were out; his suggestion that either, when he or she returned, might grant him an interview was treated with a scornful laugh.

"Leave your account," they advised, "and go your way."

But this was not what he had come to do. So instead, he returned to the square and, taking up his position near a post where some sedan chairs were waiting, he kept watch on number seventeen. Half an hour later, it seemed that his patience was rewarded when a smart carriage, bearing the arms of the de Quettes, drew up before the door. He started forward.

The groom was already at the carriage door. He had placed a step before it and was holding out his arm to help the occupant down. Fleming could not see the face of the lady because she held a silk scarf against it, but he was certain it was Lady St James. Placing himself a little before her he made his best bow.

"Lady St James? It's Fleming, my lady, the baker." He smiled hopefully. The lady with the covered face gave no sign of recognition. It seemed to him that she made to move past; but without realizing it, he was blocking her way. "My lady was kind enough," he began, before the groom turned on him, with a peremptory wave of his arm.

"Move away, there."

Out of the corner of his eye, Fleming was aware of the coachman getting down.

"It's Fleming, my lady," he tried to begin again, then, getting confused, he held out his bill.

He had copied it out again that morning in his best copperplate; now, however, he suddenly saw that, while he was standing, holding it in his hand, his sweating palms had made the ink run and so it was a poor, soggy thing that he now proffered in his inky fingers. Lady St James instantly recoiled.

"Please, my lady," he blurted out, and took a step towards her.

The coachman's whip cracked just beside his ear. It did not actually touch him. The coachman could have flicked a fly off his nose without leaving a mark if he'd wanted to. But it sounded like a pistol, and it gave him such a fright that he lurched forward, slipped on the cobbles, and began to fall. Reaching up, without thinking what he was doing, his inky hand closed on something soft which came away in his fingers as he went down.

It was the end of Lady St James's silk scarf. A second later he found himself looking up into her uncovered face, and gasped.

Lady St James, finding herself exposed, did not try to cover her bruised and swollen face. She scorned even to run past the baker. Instead she decided to give him a piece of her mind.

"How dare you accost me, you vulgar little tradesman? Are you trying to dun me in the street? You rogue. Your bill is infamous anyway. No one of my party would touch your cakes. You may be sure you will never sell them to anyone in society again. As for your conduct here, if I even hear from you once more I'll have you arrested for assault. I have witnesses." She indicated the footman, who nodded vigorously. "I think," she called back to the coachman, as she sailed forward into the house, "that he may have blacked my eye." At which the coachman grinned, and gave Fleming a cut across the legs with his whip that made the poor baker howl.

Sadly he stumbled down to Piccadilly. He had been whipped and humiliated. His custom was destroyed, his hopes of a bow window dashed. And he was down thirty pounds. As he dragged himself past the great houses and elegant shops of Piccadilly, the whole fashionable world seemed to be mocking him. By Fortnum and Mason he sat down and wept.

And how the devil was he going to pay for those cobblestones?

A starlit night on the water. It might have been Venice. Like a gondola, the boat passed softly up the darkened Thames. The only sounds were the faint splash of the boatman's oars dipping in the water, and the tiny rattle of glass in the lamp that swung over the prow.

But who was the tall figure who lay back so elegantly in the passenger seat? He wore a three-cornered hat, a domino – the black hooded cloak in the Italian fashion – and a white mask over his face which, in the darkness, gave him a phantom-like appearance, blank and mysterious. A gentleman going to a Venetian ball? A lover on his way to some secret assignation? An assassin? A figure of death? Perhaps all these.

It was much in fashion, and had been for a generation, this Venetian masquerade. Half the parties in London seemed to demand a disguise, from the great balls where fantastic costumes were *de rigueur*, to the ordinary nights at the theatre where, scanning the boxes, one might see a score of ladies and gentlemen wearing masks. For what was life, to the fashionable world, without theatre and artifice and, best of all, a *frisson* of mystery?

Leaving the houses of Bankside behind, the boat passed slowly round the great curve of the river. On the right, the familiar old buildings of Whitehall Palace loomed along the bank. As Westminster itself came in sight, however, a less familiar shape appeared.

During the last sixteen hundred years, London had always had to make do with a single, crowded old bridge as its only road across the river. Recently, however, spanning the Thames in a few graceful arches, another had appeared. It had only been completed this year – to the fury of the Westminster watermen and the owner of the old horseferry – and the costs had so far overrun the estimates that the city had held a lottery to raise the extra money. But now, here it was, crossing sedately from Westminster to the Lambeth bank not far from the Archbishop of Canterbury's gardens. As the boat slipped under it, the passenger slowly sat up, scanning the river in front, and began to prepare himself for what lay ahead.

As he thought about what he must do that night, Jack Meredith kept a cool head. So far everything had been straightforward. Officially, he was still in the Clink; but for a fee, Silversleeves was always happy to allow his gentlemen a brief exeat, as long as they promised to return, and Lady St James had given him five guineas. As for the morality of the business, Meredith had few scruples. He despised St James. Besides, he was going to play by the rules, cruel though they were.

Soon, beyond Lambeth Palace on the southern bank he saw, like a string of pearls glimmering along the waterfront, the lights of his destination. Five minutes later he was stepping out at the pleasure gardens of Vauxhall.

Since the old, medieval days when it was Vaux's Hall, the little estate had undergone several transformations; but nothing to compare with the most recent. An entrepreneur named Tyers, with help from his friend, the painter Hogarth, had laid out a spectacular garden for entertainments and social rendezvous. Like their rivals at Ranelagh across the river, the Spring Gardens at Vauxhall, as they were called, were a huge success. The Prince of Wales was a regular patron, and entrance, except when the place was taken for a private party, was a shilling or two. Perhaps the place's greatest triumph, so far, had been the previous spring, when the first public rehearsal of Handel's *Music for the Royal Fireworks* drew a crowd of twelve thousand.

Meredith went in. The entrance to the gardens was through the doorway of a large Georgian building; but immediately afterwards he was gazing down a long, tree-lined walk, illuminated by hundreds of lamps. To the right of this avenue he could see the outlines of the bandstand; to his left was a splendid, sixteen-sided rotunda building in whose lavish interior dances and assemblies were held. Nearby were the boxes where patrons could listen to concerts. Decorated with charming painted panels by Hogarth, young Gainsborough and others, these boxes were Meredith's favourite spot. He did not pause by them this evening, however, but went in search of his quarry.

It was an evening of masquerade. Some wore only a black half-mask that covered the upper half of the face. One or two women had chosen to dress in veils. Usually, of course, people in society recognized each other, but not always: Meredith had enjoyed some delicious surprises. He glanced in at the rotunda, but did not see him there. He went down the long avenue where numerous couples were strolling. Off to the side were darker, tree-lined alleys where meetings of a more clandestine kind sometimes took place. When finally he saw him, it was in a group of gentlemen talking and laughing in a semi-circular arbour, enclosed by a little arcade of classical columns.

It was simple enough to attach himself to the group. Lord St James had been easy to spot, but Meredith pretended not to recognize him behind his mask. Two or three of the gentlemen there he really did not know. The talk was of politics, and he took no part. But after a time they moved on to gossip; and then, at a moment that seemed natural, he added his own voice.

"They say that the latest scandal concerns Lord St James."

There was a hush. He saw one of the gentlemen glance towards the earl enquiringly, before quietly asking: "And pray, sir, what is that?"

"Why," he continued to sound like a foolish fop, "they say, gentlemen, that the earl has taken to beating his wife." He paused for effect. "The joke is that he does not know why. For in truth, he has more to complain of than he understands." Here he let out an insolent, braying laugh. "As those, like myself, who have enjoyed her favours should know!"

It was done; and nicely done, he thought. The earl, if he was to retain any kind of honour, was left with no possible alternative. With a pale hand that quivered only a little, St James removed his mask.

"May I know the name of the blackguard I am addressing?"

Meredith removed his mask in turn.

"Captain Meredith, my lord. At your service," he answered stiffly.

"My friends will wait upon you, sir."

"I shall be at my house in Jermyn Street within the hour," Jack answered; then made his bow and turned upon his heel.

It was the privilege of the party challenged to choose the weapons to be used. When the two gentlemen from the earl called upon him that night, therefore, Meredith told them.

"I choose rapiers."

He had already got his own two seconds from the club. It was agreed that the matter should be settled straight away, at dawn.

Lord St James had half expected his wife to be asleep when he got back, so he was surprised to find not only that the door of her chamber was open, but that she was waiting for him.

All the way back from Vauxhall he had been wondering: should he confront her, or should he go to the duel without a word? There was also another matter on his mind. If by any chance he died, the whole St James estate, as things stood, would devolve upon his wife; for until he had a son, there were no surviving heirs. Yet did he really want to leave all his fortune to a faithless wife? If not, should he summon a lawyer, even though it was the middle of the night? Yet how would he change his will? He was not sure. It was with all these doubts in his mind that he found himself face to face with Lady St James who now beckoned him into her chamber and closed the door.

She looked better than she had earlier. Her face was no

longer swollen. Careful application of paint and powder had nearly hidden the black eye. And still more to his surprise, it seemed she wished to try for a reconciliation.

"My lord," she began gently, "you used me very ill last night. All day I have waited for some word from you – an apology, some message of tenderness. None has come." She shrugged, then sighed. "But I know I gave you cause. I loved society instead of my husband. I put my pleasure before my duty to give you children, and I am sorry for it. Can we not be reconciled? Let us go to Bocton at once."

He stared at her.

"And give me an heir?"

"Naturally." She smiled a little grimly. "It is possible that you already have one after last night."

St James looked at her thoughtfully. Was this a subterfuge of some kind?

"There is something, my lady," he said slowly, "that I must tell you. A certain person has informed me that he has been your lover. Naturally, I have defended my honour, and yours. What have you to say?"

If it is possible to register shock and disbelief and innocence with a single facial expression, Lady St James did so, without a hint of overacting.

"Who? Who could say such a thing?" she gasped.

"Captain Meredith," he answered coolly.

"Jack Meredith? My lover?" She stared in astonishment. "And you mean you are to duel?"

"How could it be otherwise?"

"Dear God!" She shook her head. Then, almost to herself. "That poor well-meaning fool." She sighed. "Oh, William. This is all my fault."

"You mean he was your lover?"

"Dear Heaven, no. Never in my life. I have had no lovers." She paused. "You see," she went on softly, "Jack Meredith pretends to be a rake, but the truth is different. In secret, he is a kind man who long ago confided his unhappiness in love to me. He became a friend. And when yesterday you had used me so cruelly, and I did not know what to do, I went to seek his advice. He was very angry, William. But I did not know he would go to attack you as he did."

"Why tell me he was your lover then?"

She looked genuinely perplexed. "I suppose to make you fight him. He must think I need defending. Surely you do not believe him?"

Lord St James shrugged.

"After all," she continued, "consider it, William. Whatever Meredith is, he is certainly a gentleman. If such a thing were true, can you imagine him crying such a thing out to a group of strangers in Vauxhall?"

This, St James had to admit, was true. Even in his angry state on the way home, the thing had struck him as odd.

"He is a gallant fool," she added. "And the fault is mine for making him think you a brute."

St James still said nothing.

"William," she cried, "this foolish duel must be stopped."

"The insult was offered, and in public. I'd be the laughing stock of London if I did nothing."

She considered. "Honour," she suggested, "may be satisfied with a prick, may it not? A drop of blood will do?"

"I suppose so." Many duels resulted in only a small wound, often in the arm, at which both pairs of seconds would hastily end it. Deaths happened, but were rare.

"Then I beg you," she cried, "do not kill him, for he has certainly not deserved it. I shall write to him now to scold him and to tell him we are reconciled and that he has no cause to defend me in this foolish way any more."

"You do not think you need defending from me?" he asked.

"That is forgotten. We are reconciled, are we not?" She kissed him. "I have never betrayed you, my dear lord, and I never shall." She smiled. "Go and rest now, while I write my letter."

Soon afterwards, the swift footman was carrying her sealed missive to Jermyn Street. As for Lord St James, he did not sleep; but in due course came and lay by his wife who held his hand for several hours. She had dozed off when he kissed her and, a little after dawn, he went out with a lighter heart.

It only took him five minutes to reach Hyde Park.

For centuries the old deer park, which lay immediately west of Mayfair, had belonged to the monks of Westminster, until King Harry took it from them when he dissolved the monasteries. The Stuarts had opened the place to the public, and the long carriage drive round it, the *route du roi* (or Rotten Row, as the common people soon pronounced it), was nowadays a fashionable place for a lady to be seen in her carriage. A still more charming addition had been made when the little Westbourne stream was dammed, to make a large, curved pond called the Serpentine. But in the early hours of the dawn, its ancient oaks and quiet glades were convenient for another purpose: the fighting of duels.

The issuing of challenges between gentlemen had an ancient history, from the days of medieval combat and long before. But it was only in the elegant eighteenth century that arranging private duels became fashionable. Why this was so is hard to know. Perhaps the West End of London, where huge numbers of people with leisure, and all claiming gentility, lived close together, provided a breeding ground for social disputes. Perhaps it was the influence of the increasing number of regiments, with their chivalric military ethos. Or perhaps the upper classes, led by the aristocrats who had made the European Grand Tour, were aping the customs of the French and Italians. Whatever the reason, they duelled upon points of honour and courtesy. And though, to later and more timid ages, the practice seemed barbarous, it certainly provided an incentive to be polite.

The law was mild concerning duels. The courts, after all, were run by gentlemen who understood these matters. There was no question of murder, since, by definition, both parties were consenting to the business. If you killed your opponent in a duel, you risked a fine, or perhaps a nominal three months in jail. That was all.

There were seven men present: the duellists, each with two seconds, making six, and a doctor being the seventh. The carriages remained a little way off. The place the seconds had chosen lay in a dell, screened from view, additionally, by the spreading oaks all around. Though there was not a soul in the park, St James was keenly aware of the company of the birds, whose morning chorus filled the air. The seconds had inspected the swords. He took off his cloak and handed it to his second, then took the rapier. He was wearing a linen shirt with loose sleeves: a sensible choice, just heavy enough to keep out the slight chill that was still in the morning air. He noted a little dew on the grass. He must take care not to slip.

As the two men, facing each other, each made a courteous bow, lowering their swords, the sun was just touching the tops of the oak trees, causing them to glisten. Now the two sword points rose, and hovered, very still, close to each other, like two silvery snakes involved in some silent dance whose true meaning is known only to them, before darting towards each other, with a rasp of steel.

St James was a fair swordsman, but Meredith was far better. It surprised Jack, nonetheless, that his opponent did not seem to be pressing him very hard and he concluded that this was probably a ruse. He waited cautiously, therefore, almost a minute before he saw his chance, and then, with a single swift and deadly lunge, he shot his rapier straight into Lord St James's heart.

The seconds cried out. The doctor ran over. But within seconds, the earl was dead.

"My God, sir, was that necessary?" the doctor exclaimed.

But Meredith only shrugged. That had been the bargain he made with Lady St James. And even if he might, faced with his man, have changed his mind, the note he had received from her in the middle of the night had made sure he would not.

"For God's sake take care, Jack," it read. "He means to kill you."

It was late that night, after he had blown out the candle, that Jack Meredith became aware of the door to his room in the Clink quietly opening and a figure softly stealing in.

Though he could only just make out her pale form in the darkness, he could tell who it was immediately by the scent she wore. She came over, touched him gently on the lips with her finger, then kissed him on the forehead.

"We cannot be seen together for a little while," she whispered, "but I have been active on your behalf. Since it was St James who called you out, and I told them he meant to kill you, they will take a lenient view in your case."

She went over to the window, where there was a chair. He could hear her starting to take off her clothes. He offered to strike a flint to light the candle, but she did not want him to.

When she came to his narrow bed, she had on only a short nightdress, as far as he could see. It seemed to be of a coarse material of some kind, which rather surprised him; but soon he thought no more about it.

Then Lady St James, dressed in the linen shirt, still spotted with blood, in which her husband had been killed, made love to his killer and so completed her revenge.

As the pleasant month of May progressed, the only thing Sam and Sep could not agree about was the stealing.

The chimney-sweeping venture was going very well. As their partner, they had found a young man, a little simple in the head, but whom they taught to perform well enough for their needs. Calling at a house with one of them, he would send the boy up the chimney with a few rough words, then leave him up there while he went round to the next house with the other brother and did the same thing. Returning to the first house, he would wait until there was someone by, then curse Sam or Sep, whichever it was, for taking so long and promise them a whipping; and they, in turn, would cower, and look so pitiful that there was scarcely a house where they did not get an extra tip of some kind. Covering two houses at a time in this way, they were splitting the payment, but not their tips, with their simple-minded partner and making a handsome living.

But, as Sam pointed out, they could do better.

"It's the little things you want," he'd explain. "Don't take anything too valuable or they'll see it's gone. Just something small they won't even miss. If you see a golden guinea and some small change on the table, leave the guinea but take a piece of silver. They'll think they lost it if they ever notice." But a silver coin here and there, an ivory comb, a gold button – these things mounted up. And Sep's reluctance to avail himself of this obvious opportunity was trying Sam's patience.

How could Sep explain? He did not understand it himself. Some deep instinct inside him seemed to say that property must be respected, even though he himself had none. Perhaps it was the ancient voice of the Bull ancestors of whose existence he was so profoundly ignorant. Perhaps it was something else. But he did not want to do it. Only after two weeks of listening to Sam's complaints did he finally agree.

"All right. If I get the chance."

"Good," replied his brother. "Because tomorrow we're going to those big houses, in Hanover Square."

Isaac Fleming the baker was never more astonished in his life than the morning in mid-May when the door of his shop opened, and Lady St James walked in. He was astonished not only to see her at all, but by the fact that her face was as serene as if their hideous encounter had never happened.

There was not a mark on her face. The death of her husband, which had been in all the London papers, had seemingly left her untouched. She even smiled as her eyes rested upon him with the same calm indifference as if he were part of the landscape on a sunny day.

"I need," she remarked casually, "a wedding cake." And, since no other explanation of either her presence or the need for the cake was offered, Fleming bowed low, and wondered what to do.

For Lady St James, things were going nicely to plan. The magistrates, as she had supposed, had taken a lenient view; and since Meredith had no money to pay a fine, and was in prison anyway, they had decided to bring no charges and let the matter drop. There remained only one thing to do then: she must make sure of her man.

The bargain she had made with Jack Meredith had been in two parts. First, he must provoke the duel with St James and kill him; second, he must marry her. In return, she would discharge his debts with the fortune now at her disposal. "And then," as she had put it, "we can live happily ever after." So far he had certainly fulfilled his part of the bargain, but Lady St James was cautious. Before doing anything else, she took care of herself. Taking all the family jewels and a substantial quantity of money, she secreted them. Once married, her fortune would pass into the control of her new husband, and whatever else befell her, she did not intend to be dependent upon any man again. As for securing Meredith, she would leave nothing to chance there either. Before setting him free from prison by settling his debts, she would marry him. She decided to do it straight away. Then they would leave England for a year, travel in Europe, and return to life as normal.

True, there would be those who might find this speedy marriage to a man who killed her husband a little shocking; but she had already begun to take care of them. Rumours of St James's cruel treatment of her had begun to circulate, thanks to her friends. She had let it be known that she had suffered in silence for years. One woman, who scarcely knew her, but hoped to, had described her as "a martyr, an angel". She could marry safely.

But how do you marry a man in a debtors' prison? And do it in a hurry? In 1750, in London, nothing was easier.

If the Clink and the Marshalsea were ancient houses for debtors, there was one greater still: the Fleet. The old prison house outside Ludgate had contained debtors of all kinds since the days of the Plantagenets. Small tradesmen, lawyers, knights and even peers might be found in there but its particular speciality was members of the clergy. They were often there by the dozen. And how should a clergyman in debt pay for his keep, or even attempt to satisfy his creditors? Why, by performing the function for which, despite his debts and his lack of a church, he was still licensed: he married people.

Anyone could get married in the Fleet. No banns were read, no questions asked. You might already have a wife, you might give a false name: but if you paid your fee, a regular priest would marry you and register you in the Fleet, and the thing was as valid as if you had been married in St Paul's Cathedral. Some of these clergymen did so well that, paying a fee to the gaoler, they set up little shops outside the prison where they touted for custom to passers-by in the streets. This strange little side-show to the Church of England, carried out not half a mile from the Bishop of London's great cathedral, had been going on quite unhindered by the Church authorities for several generations. It was known as a Fleet Marriage.

Lady St James had already made arrangements with one of the more venerable of these ecclesiastical gentlemen who would come, as soon as she summoned him, to the Clink and perform the ceremony there. Only when it was done, she had decided, should Jack come out, relieved of his debts, to play.

Only one thing irked her, as the days went by. The lack of social occasion. She was determined that Jack should remain safely shut up until she had her marriage. They also knew that discretion dictated they should instantly depart London for a while. And yet – she was a creature of society. That was what she was there for. Surely there must be some way that this all-important event could be marked by a social gathering. Without a party, it seemed to her, the business was not hallowed, was scarcely real. And it was while she was seeking for some excuse in her mind that she remembered Fleming.

He had seen her when her face was so swollen and bruised. His presence had infuriated her at the time, but now it suddenly occurred to her that he could be rather useful: a witness, the only one, to her ill-treatment. As she thought of it, she saw exactly what to do. A small gathering, a few friends, a wedding cake – something special, of course, worthy of remark – from Fleming. And a word to a friend or two:

"I always use Fleming. Quite the best. And a good little fellow. He saw me once, you know, after St James had . . ." She could hear her own voice trailing off. "But I feel I can trust him to keep his mouth shut, just as I trust you." Her friends would be round at Fleming's shop in a trice.

Secure now in the knowledge that a social gathering was truly needed, she had begun to plan a little gathering for a day or two after the marriage in the Clink. Just a few of her closest friends. Very select.

"I want a cake," she told Fleming, "that will be remembered. Something quite out of the ordinary. If I am satisfied, I will perhaps even relent and recommend you." She gave him a nod which, in so far as the vast social gulf between them made possible, was almost friendly.

All the time Fleming, a little wiser now in his dealings with the upper class, was wondering if he'd get paid.

"If I am pleased," she remarked casually, "I shall even pay your present account as well. Shall we say, a total of forty pounds?"

Forty pounds. If she paid, he'd be almost in the clear. For the price of making one wedding cake, even the finest, he couldn't afford not to take the chance. Which she knows very well, he thought to himself. But his concave face creased into a smile that seemed to indicate genuine delight and gratitude.

"That's very generous, your ladyship," he said. "We'll see what we can do – to really surprise them," he permitted himself to suggest. Lady St James departed in very good humour.

"And what sort of cake will it be?" his wife asked him afterwards.

"I haven't an idea," he confessed glumly. "And I bet she won't pay me either."

The marriage of Captain Jack Meredith and Lady St James took place quietly the following day. There were no bridesmaids. The elderly clergyman from the Fleet officiated. Ebenezer Silversleeves, who had changed into a magnificent coat which had belonged to a former inmate, since deceased, was best man.

"And now, Jack," the bride announced, as soon as it was done. "I'm off to pay your debts."

"So when do I get out of here?" he asked.

"Tomorrow," she said with a bright smile. "I expect."

There were few more fashionable places to be seen in London than the Foundling Hospital in Coram Fields above Holborn. That such a surprising venue should be so blessed was thanks mostly to the composer Handel who, during his long residence in London, had become an active worker for several good causes. In recent years, having taken an interest in the new venture for orphan children, he had not only donated an organ to the place but trained an excellent children's choir there. He had already, that year, given several performances of his *Messiah*, to which all London came, and which raised the notable sum of seven thousand pounds – making the great composer one of the few to be remembered almost as much for his philanthropy as for his genius. And it was to one of these performances that Captain and Mrs Jack Meredith, as they now were, decided to go that very afternoon, from the house in Hanover Square.

Mrs Meredith, that day, was a happier woman than she had ever been before, and Jack had only been home from prison a few hours.

Only now could she feel sure that if life and love were a treacherous battle, she had won. She had got everything she wanted; she had caught her man and brought him safely in. Around her home she could see only peace and security. It was a new feeling; she supposed it would take some getting used to. Even the little party she had so carefully planned for the next day suddenly seemed unimportant; the year-long tour of Europe might be curtailed. Perhaps six months would do, she thought. Then I could have him all to myself at Bocton. This thought had been filling her imagination for several delicious minutes as she prepared to go out when the quiet of the house was suddenly disturbed by a shout, followed by a piteous cry.

"What the devil can that be?" Jack remarked as he went to the door and vanished down the passage.

He appeared, a minute later, grinning broadly at her, and holding firmly, by one ear, a boot-blackened urchin.

"Dear heavens, Jack," she cried half in horror, half amusement, "don't bring the filthy thing in here. Why are you holding it?"

"Why, because," he informed her with a wink, "this is a dangerous criminal. Your footman's just caught him stealing a shilling off the kitchen table. He was supposed to be sweeping the chimney." He turned to the boy. "We'll call the Bow Street Runners, you little monster. What do you think of that?"

"I never stole nothing," the boy cried.

"You did."

"Never before, sir. I promise. Please don't be hard on me." It was said with such conviction one would almost have believed him.

"Take the creature away, Jack," the lady of the house pleaded, "whatever you do."

But Jack Meredith, who hadn't the least intention of doing anything more than boxing the boy's ears and kicking him out, was rather enjoying the spectacle of all this soot threatening his wife's spotless chamber. The urchin, who had now started to cry, most obligingly shook his head, scattering soot and causing my lady to scream in vexation. The tear streaks left white marks down his blackened cheeks. It had to be admitted that he looked a rather pitiful sight. Like a small animal caught fatally in the claws of some much larger predator, he seemed suddenly to give up, hanging limply at the captain's side, and quivering with fear. Even the fastidious lady of the house began to feel a little sorry for him.

"What's your name, boy?" she brought herself to ask more kindly.

No answer.

"Do you always steal?"

The head shook vigorously.

"Don't you know it's wrong?"

The head nodded with real conviction.

"Does someone tell you to do it?" Meredith asked.

An unhappy nod.

"Who?"

No reply.

Just then, as the two adults looked at each other and shrugged, the little boy made a sudden, desperate bid to escape. With a wrench that must have caused his ear agonizing pain, he jerked his head away, whipped round, and scuttled down the passage.

With three rapid strides and a long arm, Jack caught him this time by the hand, whirled him back to where he came from, and then exclaimed in surprise.

"Here's a strange thing. Look at this."

He held up the boy's hand. Then he took the other hand, remarking that it was the same. He noticed also, at that moment, that the boy's hair, out of which most of the soot had now fallen, had a curious white patch in it. "What an odd little fellow," he remarked. "He's got spirit, though." And glanced back at his wife.

She stood transfixed, white as though she had seen a ghost, staring at the child speechlessly.

"What is it?" he cried in alarm.

But Lady St James, as she had become again in her own mind at that moment, could say nothing, except, "Oh, my God. It cannot . . . surely . . . oh, dear God."

And Meredith was so flabbergasted that he scarcely realized that he had let go of the child who, seconds later, had vanished into the street, not to be seen again.

She would not speak. She would tell him nothing. Neither cajoling nor even, at last, a show of anger would get it from her.

"It was something about the boy, wasn't it?" he demanded. "Shall I go and find him?"

"No! On no account," she cried.

Whatever it was that had so shocked her, she would not speak of it. They drove to the recital in silence. Afterwards, she spoke of other things – the party the next day, their departure for the Continent – yet with a pale absence. Whatever the secret was that she had determined to keep locked inside her, he could see it was torturing her. Yet she still would not share it, even with him.

Until the dark and silent watches of the night.

Was it the suddenness of the shock? Was it the secret toll of the last three weeks' events when she had so coolly diced with life and death? Was it, perhaps, that having at last secured love herself, her heart had begun to open, and soften? For it was not only horror and it was not only guilt that racked her body and tortured her mind in her sleep. It was the pain, the longing, the great, overpowering emotion of the mother that caused her, without knowing it, to cry out to her new husband, again and again in the early hours:

"The child. Oh, my God. My lost child."

When she awoke, she found Meredith sitting quietly in a chair beside the bed. Gently but firmly he took her hand and asked her:

"What did you do with the child? Don't deny it. You spoke in your sleep."

"I gave it away," she confessed. "But, oh, Jack, it was long ago. It is all over. There is nothing to be done now. Let us go away, today, and forget it."

"Whose was it?"

She hesitated. "It doesn't matter."

"I think it does. Was it St James's?"

She paused. Then at last nodded.

"The heir to the estate, then?"

"Our son. We shall have a son. He'll have the estate. The other was . . . you saw for yourself." She shuddered at the old memory. He was . . . his hands . . ."

But then Captain Jack Meredith knew what he must do to save his soul, and hers.

"I've killed the father. But I'm damned if I'll disinherit the child," he said quietly. "If you don't take the child back, I will leave you."

And she knew that he would.

"You may not find him, anyway," she said at last.

It did not take him long. Though the Dogget boys had decided to avoid Hanover Square after the disaster of the day before, it was just after turning into Grosvenor Square that he caught sight of a blackened urchin with a sweep's broom who, after one look at him, dropped the brush and began to run. The little fellow made off down Audley Street and dodged about, but Meredith was fit, and by Hay's Mews he laid hold of him.

"Take me to your father," he ordered, "or it'll be the worse for you."

So together they set off in the direction of Seven Dials.

They encountered the costermonger in Covent Garden, where the flower market was still in progress. He was standing by his barrow, with a cap on his head. As he often did when pushing the barrow, he wore a pair of leather gloves. His eyes just then had been resting on a rather pretty young girl selling at one of the stalls, but seeing Meredith and the boy advancing he turned without ceremony and enquired: "What's up?"

"Your boy was stealing in a house yesterday," the captain answered.

"Never," the costermonger replied. "'E'd never do such a thing."

"I think he would," Meredith cheerfully countered. "But that isn't why I'm here."

"No, sir?" Dogget grinned. "You ain't come for a fight I s'pose, 'ave you?"

"Not today. What I'd like to know is, how did you come to possess this boy? Was he born yours?"

"I dare say." Dogget looked wary.

"Is that yes or no?"

"An' 'oo for that matter, sir, might you be, an' why are you askin'?"

"I'm Captain Meredith," Jack replied pleasantly, "and I've reason to think this boy may have been given away by" – he lied smoothly – "a servant who was discharged from a certain house. That's all I can say at present. But if the boy's yours, we'll say no more."

And now Harry Dogget became very thoughtful indeed.

"I've been this boy's father since 'e was a tiny baby," he said at last. "Given 'im a good home. I can't let 'im be taken off just anywhere."

"Take a look at me, then," the captain said.

"You look a reg'lar gentleman, I'll allow," Dogget agreed. Then he told Meredith exactly how he had found the baby, at Seven Dials.

"Then I must tell you," Meredith explained, when he had heard it all, "that this is undoubtedly the missing child."

"But Dad," cried the little boy, in real distress. He had conceived no affection for the tall stranger and was now hopelessly confused.

"Shut your north and south," the costermonger said kindly, "you little thief. You don't know wotcha talkin' about 'cos you wasn't 'ardly born."

The boy reluctantly kept quiet.

"But how d'you know it's 'im?" Dogget enquired of the captain.

"Oh, the hands. And the hair," Meredith explained. "Remarkable."

Yes, the costermonger agreed, they were.

So, leaving his barrow with one of the stallholders he knew, Harry Dogget accompanied them back to Hanover Square, whistled when he saw the house, asked – "You mean he'll live 'ere, not a servant, like, but one o' the family?" – and being told yes, he shook his head in wonderment. He declined Meredith's offer to go in but asked: "Can I come back tomorrow to see 'im? Just to make sure 'e's all right." Indeed, he was told, he could, and should.

Thus George, the former Lord Bocton and now the new Earl of St James, was restored to his home.

For Isaac Fleming, however, dawn had brought no such joy, but only a sense of hopeless failure.

If only it had not been for that forty pounds. The money weighed upon him crushingly. It was not just that he needed the money so much – that was bad enough. But whether he got it or not all depended upon this one cake. The result was that every time he thought of a design that might please her ladyship, the money hovered over him as if to say: "Is that all? For forty pounds?" He thought of a castle, a ship, even a lion except that he couldn't make it. Yet each, within the hour, seemed trite, obvious, unremarkable. It's no good, he thought. I'm not up to it. I lack the genius. It even came into his mind that perhaps Lady St James had been right when she told him that his earlier cakes had been failures.

"I should give this up," he told his wife miserably. But he needed forty pounds.

By the time he woke up that day, he was in despair. The bill for the cobblestones was still there, unpaid. Even the modest shop on Fleet Street, he concluded, was too much for him. He'd have to move, he supposed, to some cheaper part of town. "I'm finished," he murmured. He would like to have said it out loud, to wake his wife, but he did not do so. Instead he went sadly downstairs, to prepare the oven for baking the morning's bread.

Just after he had put the first batch of bread in he stepped outside. Fleet Street was still quiet. There was not yet a cart moving. Eastwards, somewhere over Ludgate, the sun was sending a bright glow across the heavens. The high, wavy clouds in the pale blue sky were like the tresses of a woman's hair. Towards Ludgate, high over the rooftops, he could see the splendid spire of Sir Christopher Wren's St Bride's with its tiers of octagons piled one above the other up heavenward.

St Bride's, he thought. Just the right name for a church, if you were having a wedding.

And then he had a most wonderful idea.

The guests were all assembled: just two dozen of her very dearest and most particular fashionable friends.

They all knew, of course, how badly she had been treated by St James and were full of sympathy. They knew about Fleming the baker too, whose special cake, though it had not yet been brought in, was promised to be remarkable. One lady, more zealous for information than all the rest, had already slipped out to send a footman over to the baker's shop to get the first description of what exactly Fleming had seen that day.

"Be sure to find out which eye was blacked: the left or the right," she had ordered him. "I won't be made to look a fool by getting it wrong."

But even this drama, and the sudden wedding, food for such delicious speculation for weeks to come – even this was quite put in the shade by the latest revelation to emerge from number seventeen, Hanover Square – the discovery of the heir.

It was astonishing. An evil servant switching the child, it seemed, when the young wife had been practically out of her mind with worry and the discovery that the lost child was a sweep. It had to be true, it was agreed, because there was no conceivable reason why either the lady or her new husband should invent such a thing. They clamoured to see the boy, but were denied.

"Too much for him," his mother told them. "I must protect him."

Indeed, she had insisted, and Jack had agreed, that the urchin – who could scarcely speak in any language fit to hear, let alone read and write – must spend at least a year in seclusion with a tutor before he was fit to be seen.

"But to do all this at once, and then leave town," one of the ladies complained. "Why, she has upstaged us all! I'm mad with jealousy."

As for the new Mrs Meredith, who had nearly, though by no means completely got over the shock of the day before, her social triumph – which was to make her immortal for an entire season – was crowned by the arrival, carried by two footmen, of the wedding cake.

The idea that had come to Isaac Fleming the morning before was so simple, yet so striking, that it was – the people in the room knew it as soon as they saw it – an instant classic. It was not one cake but four, each a little smaller than the last, encased in hard white icing and arranged, one on top of another, in tiers supported by little wooden classical pillars, also coated with icing. It was, as near as a cake could be, an exact replica of the spire of Wren's St Bride's. No such cake had ever been seen before. No wedding would ever be complete again without one. The guests broke into applause.

And their hostess was so pleased that she very nearly remembered to pay the baker, the next day, before she left the country.

She might, however, have been a little less pleased by an interview which took place at the corner of the street, at the moment when the applause was breaking out. It was between Harry Dogget, and the new Earl of St James.

"Everything all right, then?" the elder genially enquired.

"It's amazin'. But you have to be awfully clean and they make me wear shoes. In summer! That's 'orrible."

"Never mind."

"They're going to make me read an' write."

"Won't do you no 'arm."

The boy was thoughtful. "Just one thing, Dad."

"What?"

"Well, 'bout a year ago, when me mum was drunk, she said something about me an' Sep."

"Oh, yes?"

"She told me you found Sep by Seven Dials."

"Maybe I did."

"Well, if it was him you found and not me, then what'm I doing here?"

"Fate," said Harry Dogget cheerfully. He considered a moment. "See, it was you that went into the house and tried to steal a shilling, right?" Sam nodded. "So it was you they found."

"But I'm your son, aren't I?"

"'Course you are."

"And Sep's not."

"Ah. Now that," said Harry, with impeccable logic, "is something we don't know. When I found him, I reckoned he was mine. They lost one like him, so they say. Come to think of it," he added helpfully, "maybe he don't really belong to neither of us. But it don't signify now. What I do know is," said Harry Dogget emphatically, "that you, my son, have just got a bit of a leg up in the world."

"I'm a lord," the boy confessed.

At this revelation his father laughed so hard that he had to hold on to a nearby railing.

"It don't feel right," the boy complained.

"Look," his father said firmly. "Use your loaf. You want to live all your life in the bread and butter? Look at this 'ouse. 'Er ladyship says you're 'er Bath bun. You'd better keep quiet and be glad of it. Don't you want to be a lord?" he demanded.

"It ain't so bad," Sam admitted. "You should see the food. Not a bleeding oyster in sight."

"Well, then," his father declared. "Have a good life. If you get in trouble you know where to find me, but if you give this lot up I'll take a strap to your backside till you'll wish you was a lord again."

"All right." He paused. "Dad."

"What?"

"Tell Sep he can have all my savings."

His father nodded.

"Goodbye, Sam." And the costermonger went off, whistling a merry tune.

It was the subject of fashionable mourning which lasted fully a day, when Mrs Meredith, formerly Lady St James, died in childbirth the following year. Her husband, though he married again, continued to act as guardian to the young Earl of St James, which obligation he carried out fully and faithfully, taking only a perfectly proper fee from the estate for his trouble. The young earl was very fond of him. Those who remembered the old earl, however, would remark that the son was a much more amusing fellow than his father.

Sep Dogget, who had indeed been born Lord Bocton, was happy as a fireman, and, as he never realized he was owed a legacy, never missed it.

But the greatest legacy, perhaps, was that of Isaac Fleming, whose invention brought him fame and wealth, and a fine, bow-fronted shop – though still in Fleet Street – and whose wedding cakes will continue as long as there are weddings.

Chapter 16

Lavender Hill

1819

Soon, he thought, he would be in paradise.

As the Dover to London stagecoach came over the long, straight drag of Shooters Hill, the young man sitting up on the box had to wipe the dust from his spectacles twice. He was anxious not to miss anything. On his head was a large cloth cap with a peak; a woollen scarf flapped loosely round his neck. Eager, excited, eighteen-year-old Eugene Penny was making his first entry into London.

Just as they reached the end of Shooters Hill and saw the metropolis laid out below them, his expression changed first to one of surprise, and then, as they descended the slope and the afternoon suddenly grew darker, to one of horror.

"This is London?" he cried. And the coachman laughed.

If those who seek patterns in history were to look for a time when civilization moved beyond the glories of ancient Rome, then in the English-speaking world, they would surely have to choose the reign of King George III. His was a long reign which lasted, nominally – since the poor king, who suffered from porphyria, was declared mentally incapable for extensive periods – from 1760 to 1820; and it spanned two epic events.

Nothing could have been more Roman than the character of the thirteen American colonies who had proclaimed their independence from the British monarchy in 1776. Even those states which had begun as religious refuges had, by then, developed into societies not unlike those of the city states of independent farmers and merchants which formed the nucleus of the early power of Rome. Stoic General Washington with his patrician views, his country villa at Mount Vernon and his million acres of land behaved not unlike a Roman noble. The framers of the Constitution, with its elected Congress and its élite Senate, too were mostly men steeped in the classics. Most of the new American states even repeated the practice of the Roman republic with their massive use of slaves.

As for the great cataclysm of the French Revolution a dozen years later, it openly proclaimed itself to be Roman. Inspired by the Enlightenment – the triumph of classical reason over what was seen as the medieval tyranny and superstition of a Catholic monarchy – the revolutionaries quickly adopted every attribute of the ancient Roman age. The king's subjects were called 'citizens' like Roman freemen. Liberty, equality and the brotherhood of man soon found their new champion in Napoleon who made his armies march under Roman eagles, who gave France and much of Europe a system of Roman law, and whose favoured artists, furniture makers and artisans developed the 'Empire' style, inspired in every detail by models of imperial Rome.

On the island of Britain, however, the re-emergence of the Roman world was more appropriately measured in pragmatic ways. Before the reign of George III, to be sure, the splendid classical squares of London and the Palladian country houses of the aristocracy had probably surpassed those of Roman Britain. During it, although admittedly such amenities as public baths and central heating still had to be introduced, the Roman feature that had done most to bring order to the barbarian world began at last to reappear: the system of roads.

In Roman times roads had crossed the island like an iron framework. Then, neglected and overgrown, they had mostly been forgotten. Through the long centuries of the dark ages to the modern Stuarts and early Hanoverians, the roads of England were little more than prehistoric tracks and rutted Saxon lanes. In the case of the old Kent road from Dover and Canterbury along which young Eugene Penny had just travelled, the Roman road had remained in use, but its metalled surface lay buried so deep that even it appeared as nothing more than a cart track.

All that had now changed. The turnpike roads of the late eighteenth century were owned by private trusts and joint stock companies and run for profit, but with such success that within a generation they had covered much of the country. Sometimes they followed a straight Roman route, more often a curving Saxon path. Their surfaces were nothing like as sophisticated as those of the ancient world, but smooth and hard enough to permit a carriage to maintain a brisk and constant pace. Journeys that once took a day or two were now accomplished in hours. Entrepreneurs with fleets of express coaches rushed both mail and people out from London coaching inns to the furthest parts of the country. Suddenly the swelling capital was accessible to every town in the kingdom. It was, truly, both the return of Rome and the beginning of the modern age.

Yet the prospect that now greeted young Eugene's eyes was not at all what he had expected.

The metropolis of London had continued to grow during George III's reign, but it had done so mainly north of the River Thames. On the south bank, Southwark had grown, but only in a modest fashion. West of Southwark, though lines of houses were growing along the roads that led to Westminster Bridge, the great parish of Lambeth was still mainly orchard, market garden and field, with a scattering of timber yards along the waterfront; while further upriver, the old villages of Battersea and Clapham had only suffered the addition of some handsome villas and gardens belonging to prosperous merchants and gentlemen. Below Southwark, the riverside areas of Bermondsey and Rotherhithe were turning dingy with acres of crumpled brick housing; yet even this soon gave way to open marshland. Further downstream, the village of Greenwich with its huge white palaces was hardly altered at all.

But across the Thames, northwards, westwards, eastwards, the mighty city was spreading like a leviathan. Or so Eugene had heard. For he now encountered a problem which neither Stuart nor Tudor, nor even Roman had ever known. The city was invisible.

"That, sir," the coachman said, "is a London fog."

It lay over the city like a dark grey pall. Judging by its hazy edges, it seemed to Eugene that the great cloud of dirt was spreading outwards; and indeed as they came down the old Kent road it came out to meet them. By the time they entered Southwark borough, the sky was dark and the houses were becoming indistinct in an oily, greenish, mist through which their lights could only signal with an orange glow. By the time they reached the High Street, the coach had slowed and

Eugene could not even see the heads of the leading horses. When they turned into the courtyard of the George Inn for all he knew he could have been entering the gateway to hell itself.

The boat made a soft, grating sound as it emerged from the fog and came to rest on the mud below the stairs on the river's northern bank. One of the men climbed out and turned round to take his leave of the other who remained in the boat, his strange tall hat slouched on his head, his gnarled hands resting on the oars.

"Goodbye Silas," the standing figure said softly.

The other, for a moment, made no response; when he did, his voice was deep as the river, thick as the fog that shrouded it. "What'll you call her?"

"The baby? Lucy." His wife had chosen the name. He liked it.

"So you don't want to join me, Will?"

"I don't like what you do."

"You ain't getting rich yourself, are you?"

"I know."

Silas spat between his feet, and began to shove off. "You'll never go nowhere," he grunted, and a moment later he and his dirty old boat were swallowed up in the mist.

But I still wouldn't care to go where you're surely going, William Dogget thought, as he started to make his way home.

Penny's instructions from his father had been specific: as soon as he arrived in London, he was to go at once to the house of his godfather, Jeremy Fleming. But, judging that the fog made this impossible at present, Eugene decided to spend the night at the inn. He was cheerful enough. This inconvenience, he told himself, would only delay the start of his new life by a few hours.

What Eugene did not yet realize was that the fog which covered London was an integral part of the new life he was seeking. For no sooner had England resumed the standards of its Roman past than it had forged ahead into the great expansion called the Industrial Revolution.

It is often supposed that Britain's Industrial Revolution was a matter of huge factories manned by armies of the oppressed; and it is true that in the north and Midlands big iron foundries, steam-powered cotton mills, and coal mines which sent children underground did exist. But in reality, the Industrial Revolution was led by England's traditional woollen cloth trade and followed by cheap manufactured cottons. Though mechanical spinning and weaving made vast expansion possible, this manufacturing was mostly carried out by small masters with modest works and sweat-shops. But they all used coal: and the volume of smoke and soot from the city's now myriad fires became so great that in the right atmospheric conditions its dark vapours settled like a blanket, trapping even more fumes below; and then, as a mist arose, thickened into this choking, impenetrable horror in which men muffled their faces and a thief could walk beside you a hundred paces unseen. So was born the 'pea-souper', or London fog.

In the warm glow of the George's main parlour, Eugene could forget about the evil presence of the fog outside. The innkeeper brought him a steak and kidney pie and a bottle of porter, as dark beer was often called, and chatted to him from time to time. Eugene looked eagerly at the faces around him. Being a coaching inn, there were all kinds of travellers there – coachmen in their heavy coats, merchants, a brace of lawyers, a clergyman, a gentleman returning to the country, together with numerous locals, mostly shopkeepers.

It was about nine o'clock that the curious figure entered. He came in alone and ordered a tankard of porter, carrying it silently to a corner of the room where he sat by himself. There was a momentary hush as he entered. The smooth surface of conversation seemed to open, and people edged away from him; then it closed as quickly as possible in his wake. He was somewhat shorter than most men, but very heavy-set and he moved with a surly slowness. His big, heavy coat was of an indeterminate colour; and on his head he wore a high, black and shapeless woollen hat folded into a rim which touched his thick, black eyebrows. His eyes were big and angry; under them, the skin gathered into dark rings. The overall effect was one of deepset menace. And whether it was the pallor of his skin, or the strange, webbed hand which held the tankard, it seemed to Eugene as if this apparition had emerged from the depths of the dark and foggy river itself.

"Who is that?" he enquired of the innkeeper.

"That?" the man replied, with a look of disgust. "He is called Silas Dogget."

"What does he do?" Penny asked.

"You don't want to know," the other answered, and would say no more.

Not long afterwards, Eugene retired to bed, glad to think that with any luck he would never see Silas Dogget again.

It looked as if a riot might begin.

The wind had got up at dawn and blown the London fog away; only a tiny residue of grime over the city was left to mark its passing. The day was bright with a tingling breeze, and the fair weather no doubt encouraged the crowd of four hundred people who were gathered in front of the handsome house in Fitzroy Square to hear the figure standing in the open upstairs window proclaim his shocking message.

"Do we believe," he cried out, "in the Brotherhood of Man?" The crowd signified, with a roar, that it did. "Do you *acknowledge* –" this last word, said with particular emphasis, was Zachary Carpenter's trademark as an orator – "I say, do you *acknowledge* that every man born has rights? Isn't that common sense? Aren't these the Rights of Man?" As a murmur of recognition greeted this, he positively exploded: "And do those *inalienable* rights not include," he hammered the next words out like a drumbeat: "No taxation without re-pre-sent-a-tion?" And his small stout body and large round head fairly bounced.

It might seem strange that these doctrines which came straight from the writings of Tom Paine, the great propagandist of the American Revolution, should be proclaimed in a London street. Yet medieval Englishmen had said much the same thing in the days of Wat Tyler's revolt and plenty of men nowadays possessed grandfathers who could remember old Levellers from the days of England's Civil War. The free House of Commons, the Puritans, the Roundheads, the now independent Americans and the radical English were all different streams that had branched out from the same old river of freedom. King George III might have been furious with the Americans for breaking away, but many of his ordinary subjects had read Paine and sympathized with the plucky colonists.

"Did I make a mistake," Zachary now asked the crowd, "or did Parliament abolish slavery?"

The crowd assured him that this was correct. Slavery had been outlawed within England since 1772, and, thanks to the efforts of reformers like the great William Wilberforce, the slave trade had more recently been forbidden even in Britain's far-flung possessions overseas.

"Are you or are you not free-born Englishmen?"

The crowd let him know, with another roar, that they were as English as roast beef.

"Then why is it," he cried, "that here, in this parish of St Pancras, we are treated no better than slaves? Why are free men trampled by a tyranny? Do you *acknowledge* that this is so?"

They did. They did with a bellow that shook Fitzroy Square.

Carpenter's accusation was absolutely true. Even now, the old controversy over who should control the parish vestry, which had so infuriated Gideon Carpenter back in the days of King Charles, had still not been settled. Although the ancient area of the twenty-five city wards was still ruled by the mayor, aldermen and the now largely ornamental guilds, the vast and spreading metropolis outside had no central authority. Peace was preserved, streets paved, the sick and the poor were provided for by the parish. The parish built and organized. And of course to pay for it, the parish also taxed.

The parish of St Pancras was huge. Its base extended westwards from Holborn for over a mile; but from this base it swept up through city streets, then suburbs, then open field and sprawling village all the way to the hills of Hampstead and Highgate four miles to the north. Within this great domain now lived some sixty thousand souls, who were ruled by the parish vestry.

There were two kinds of parish nowadays. In one kind, the vestry was elected by at least some proportion of the householders. These vestries were termed "open". In the other – a minority, but a significant one – the vestry, whose composition was laid down by Parliament, nominated itself without any reference to the people of the parish. Such vestries were said to be 'close' or 'select'. And in this year of Our Lord 1819, thanks to a powerful aristocratic clique within it, the mighty parish of St Pancras which had been open had just been closed by Act of Parliament.

"This," Carpenter thundered, "is an iniquity."

Zachary Carpenter was a well-known figure. By trade he was a furniture maker, and a good one. Having served his apprenticeship with the firm of Chippendale he had briefly worked as a journeyman for Sheraton, but then set up on his own, specializing in the miniature domestic writing desks known as davenports. Like many cabinet-makers, he operated in the great parish of St Pancras, where he had a workshop with three journeymen and two apprentices; and, like many craftsmen and small employers, he was a fervid radical.

"It's in the blood," he would say. For though the details were vague, the family tradition of Gideon Carpenter's career as a Roundhead still remained. Zachary's own father had been a religious reformer. Zachary had vivid memories of being dragged out of bed when a boy and taken to the great hall up in Moorfields where old John Wesley himself was still preaching his message of pure and simple Christianity. But the subject of religion had never interested him much: Zachary sought purity, but he wanted to find it in the institutions of men.

He was eighteen when the French Revolution, with its promise of Liberty, Equality and Fraternity, had broken out, and twenty-one when Tom Paine's mighty tract *The Rights of Man*, with its demand for 'One Man One Vote' was published. Within a week of reading it, he had joined the London Corresponding Society, whose tracts and meetings were soon providing a network for radicals all over England. By the age of twenty-five, he was gaining note as a speaker. He had been speaking ever since.

"And isn't this parish just an example," he cried out, "of the great injustice done in every constituency in Britain, where free men may not vote and members of Parliament are chosen, not by the people but by a clutch of aristocrats and their creatures? It is time for this infamy to end. It is time for the people to rule." After this incitement to revolution, he turned and went inside, to wild applause.

Something was certainly peculiar about the scene. Fitzroy Square, designed by the Adams brothers, lay in the parish's most fashionable, south-western corner. Odder still was the presence, clearly visible at Carpenter's shoulder, of the owner of the house, who had been nodding in warm agreement all the time. Oddest of all was the fact that this person was that epitome of aristocracy, the noble Earl of St James himself.

It was seventy years now since Sam had become an earl. Indeed, as the years of his childhood passed he had gradually forgotten his early years in Seven Dials. Vague whispers, little flashes of memory would come to him sometimes, but he had been told so firmly and so often by his stepfather Meredith that he had been rescued and returned to the state that was properly his, that he came to believe it. By the time he was a young man he had actually forgotten about Sep, and if now and then he had been discreetly observed by a costermonger, he had not even been aware of it. As for his life since he came of age – the Earl of St James had been too busy enjoying himself to think of anything else. He was enjoying himself now, supporting his radical friend Carpenter.

As the two men, the rich aristocrat and the homespun tradesman, entered the room arm in arm, Lord St James's expression turned to irritation as he saw two men waiting for them.

"What the devil are you doing here, Bocton?" he exclaimed sharply, addressing the suaver of the two men.

Though the paternity of Lord Bocton was not in the slightest doubt, one would never have thought it to see him and his father together. The old earl adopted the dress of the more flamboyant young bloods of the next generation, who were known as the Regency bucks. Instead of breeches and stockings he wore tight trousers secured under the instep. He favoured a cutaway tailcoat, brightly coloured ruffled shirts, a floppy bow-tie or a cravat. He liked to wear a tall hat and carry a cane, and his collection of waistcoats was dazzling. He was as rakish as the Regency bucks too, for it was said that he had never missed a prize fight or a race meeting and was known to bet upon anything.

Lord Bocton did not bet. Though he had a white flash in his dark hair, like his father, he was tall and thin like his mother's family. He still wore the silk stockings and silver buckled shoes fashionable twenty years before, a black, buttoned-up waistcoat, a stiff white collar and a coat that was always dark green, so that his father used to remark, with perfect truth: "You look like a bottle."

"Who's this?" he enquired, nodding towards his son's companion.

"A friend, father," Lord Bocton began.

"Didn't know you had any," the earl snorted. "How did you like the speech?" He knew very well that Lord Bocton had not liked it at all. "Bocton here," he continued to Carpenter, "is a Tory, you see."

There were three political allegiances a man could hold in the reign of George III. The Tories, the party of squires and clergy, were for King and Country. Protectionist, since their income usually came from modest landholdings, they supported the Corn Laws whose tariffs on imports kept the price of their grain artificially high, and were naturally suspicious of any kind of reform. Stubborn old King George, mad or sane, suited them pretty well. The Whigs, as they always had, believed in keeping the king under Parliament's thumb. A merchant party still led by great aristocrats whose wealth often included mining and trading interests, they were sympathetic to free trade and modest reform. It was absurd, they agreed, that while a handful of voters could send a member to Parliament from one place, some growing commercial cities had no representation at all, leaving the government of England, as Carpenter truly pointed out, not unlike the vestry of St Pancras. They were also sympathetic to the religious Dissenters, the Jews and, some at least, even to the Catholics who under the old Test Acts were still unable to hold any public offices. Their cause of reform might have prospered even under King George, but for one problem.

The French Revolution might have promoted freedom in much of Europe, but in England it did just the opposite. Even in the early years, the ferocity of the revolutionaries – the Jacobins as they were called – and the awful bloodshed of the Terror and its guillotine, alarmed many peaceful Englishmen. But then Napoleon had risen to power in France and tried to invade the island kingdom. When gallant Admiral Horatio Nelson put a stop to that by smashing the French fleet at Trafalgar, the French emperor tried to destroy England's trade in Europe. No wonder then if most men in England, including the Whigs, rallied around the Tory prime minister Pitt, the incorruptible patriot, to defend England from this menace. Not only that, to most men of property the revolution became associated with the war, and the people's rights it proclaimed seemed to promise only fearful bloodshed and disorder.

"We want no Jacobins here," the English Parliament declared, and battened down its hatches against these treacherous revolutionary seas. Combination Acts were passed, forbidding unions and unlawful assemblies. To advocate reform of any kind during these years made a man suspect; and even after Wellington had terminated Napoleon's career at the Battle of Waterloo in 1815 this fear of revolution persisted.

There was, however, a third political group – a small band of radical Whigs known as Jacobins who continued to speak out for reform, for tolerance and freedom of speech. Their leader, during the darkest years of the struggle with Napoleon, had been Charles James Fox – dissolute, debt-ridden, lovable but, even his opponents conceded, the greatest orator England had ever known.

While he had declaimed in the Commons, Fox knew that in the House of Lords he could always count on the vote of the sporting Earl of St James. In Lord Bocton however, Fox possessed a younger, but implacable enemy.

"Since you ask, father," he replied, "I thought the speech unwise." He looked severely at Zachary Carpenter. "We should not agitate the people."

"You fear a revolution, my lord?" Zachary enquired.

"Of course."

"And you fear the people?" the radical pursued.

"We all should, Mr Carpenter," Bocton calmly replied.

This exchange not only signalled the two men's dislike for each other; a more profound, philosophical chasm was apparent in their precise – though different – use of language. It was a difference that marked a divide not only between English political parties but also between the two halves of the English-speaking culture – the Old World, and the New.

When an American spoke of the Revolution, he meant the act of free, mostly property-owning men breaking away from a corrupt aristocracy and a despotic monarch. When he spoke of "the people", he meant responsible individuals like himself. Carpenter the radical, by and large, meant the same things. But when Lord Bocton spoke of revolution, he carried in his mind a historical memory that dated all the way back to Wat Tyler's revolt. Indeed, the last really huge London disturbances – the so-called Gordon Riots of forty years before, which had started as an anti-Catholic protest and then turned into a vast horror of looting and slaughter – were still a vivid memory to many. Similarly, though he had no fear of his footman, or the individual estate workers he had known since childhood in Kent, when he spoke of "the people" he had visions of a terrifying, lawless mob. Nor was this just because he was a lord. Many respectable shopkeepers and craftsmen, though they might want reform, had the same fear of general disorder.

"My immediate fear, Mr Carpenter," Lord Bocton coldly observed, "is that you and my father are about to provoke a riot."

There was good cause for this fear. The ending of the war with Napoleon four years before might have brought peace to Europe, but it had certainly not brought tranquillity at home. Large numbers of returning soldiers were still unemployed; the textile industry was adjusting to the loss of its large orders for military uniforms; grain prices were high. Naturally the government was blamed and many believed the radicals who told them that all their troubles came from a corrupt, aristocratic clique who ruled the land. There had been some scattered riots; the government had been alarmed. But then, just weeks ago, troops had charged a crowd in the northern town of Manchester and more than a dozen people had been killed. It had become known as the Peterloo Massacre, and every public meeting since then had been tense.

"I cannot understand your letting this happen in your house, father," Lord Bocton complained.

The Earl of St James was unabashed. "What my son really means," he cheerfully explained to Carpenter, "is that if *he* had this house, there'd be no radicals here. What he can't understand is why I'm still here at all. He thinks I've lived too long already – eh, Bocton?"

"That is outrageous, father!"

"Then he'll have the money, you see."

"I am not thinking of money, father."

"Just as well." The earl looked at his son with glee. "Money, money, money," he said happily. "It's there to be enjoyed. Perhaps I'll spend it all." In fact the earl was far richer than his son realized and this amused him hugely. "Did you know, Bocton," he suddenly remarked, "I'm going to build a new house next year? In Regent's Park."

During those times when poor King George was incapacitated, his heir ruled, as the Prince Regent; the last period had lasted so long that it had become known as the Regency. And whatever one thought of the Prince Regent – he was certainly vain and lazy – no one could deny that he had style. It was his architect, Nash, who had built the sweeping, colonnaded thoroughfare of Regent Street; and already he had begun an even more splendid development of stucco terraces and magnificent villas around the great horseshoe of parkland to be known as Regent's Park. The earl watched as Lord Bocton, who had known nothing of this, was unable to prevent his face from twitching at the thought of the expense.

"You have a grandson to consider as well as a son, sir," he said with reproach. At the mention of his grandson the earl's eyes softened a little. Young George was a very different matter. But he was not going to spoil his fun. "Are you not in any case, father, a little old to trouble yourself with such a move?" Lord Bocton went on.

"Not at all," his father genially declared. "I shall live to be a hundred. You'll be over seventy then." He glanced out of the window. "No riot," he observed. "All's quiet, Bocton. You can go home now." And putting his arm through Carpenter's, the sporting old rogue led him off.

When they were well away from the house Lord Bocton turned to his lugubrious companion.

"What do you think, Mr Silversleeves?"

Silversleeves shook his head. "An interesting case, my lord," he agreed, before pausing regretfully. "Though I cannot . . ." he almost said "in conscience" but thought better of it, "I cannot yet do what you propose."

"But there is hope?"

"Oh yes, my lord." Silversleeves considered professionally. "His sense of responsibility: diminishing, without a doubt. Believes he'll live to be a hundred: delusion. Spending all his money: incapacity. His radical notions – that, sir, I take to be the kernel of it – that is what will ripen into madness." He sighed. "I've seen it time and again, my lord: a man gets an idea, it grows, finally it gets him. From enthusiasm to obsession; from obsession to lunacy. It's just a question of being patient."

"So you'll be able to lock him up?" Bocton asked bluntly.

"Oh, I'm sure of it, my lord. Sooner or later."

"Sooner, I hope," Lord Bocton remarked. "I count on you."

For Mr Cornelius Silversleeves was the deputy superintendent of the great Bethlehem Hospital, recently moved to a vast new premises in Southwark. Or, in the common vernacular, Bedlam.

Penny was lucky in his godfather. Jeremy Fleming lived in a pleasant, narrow old house off Fleet Street only a short walk from where his grandfather's cake shop had been. A widower whose children had married and left home, his concave face creased into a smile of delight at the thought of having company and he assured Eugene he might live in his house for as long as he pleased. He was also sanguine about Eugene's prospects of working in the financial world; for in his lifetime as a highly respectable clerk in the Bank of England he had acquired an encyclopaedic knowledge of the City.

The first day, Fleming showed Eugene the Tower and St Paul's. The second day they visited Westminster and the West End. On the third day he informed Eugene: "Today we begin your education." And at nine o'clock sharp they set off in a hired pony and trap, clattered over London Bridge and made their way out to Greenwich.

"If you want to understand the City," Fleming explained, as they looked out from the slope above Greenwich, "you need to come here first."

The scene before Eugene was certainly very different to the one that had greeted him three days before. There was a bracing easterly wind, an open blue sky; the distant city was so clear it might have been a painting and the great curve of the river lay gleaming below. But it was to a series of other patches of water, like huge ponds near the river that Fleming now directed his attention.

"London dock over there at Wapping; there's Surrey dock over on the left; West India directly opposite; East India further off." His face broke into a happy smile. "The docks, Eugene: aren't they grand?"

In the last twenty years the river, which had scarcely changed since Tudor times, had been transformed. The Pool of London below the Tower had become so crowded that something had had to be done. First one, then another huge dock and canal system was cut in the marshlands along the river; quays and roadways were built; and the gigantic system of London's docklands had begun. It was necessary. Eugene's head was soon swimming as Fleming related the volumes of trade flowing in from Britain's ever-growing commercial empire – the mighty sugar trade of the Caribbean, the tea trade of India where, thanks to some brilliant military campaigns, Britain now effectively ruled a large part of the subcontinent – and the vast commerce with Europe, Russia and the Americas north and south. During the last hundred years London had transformed itself from a major port to the hub of the greatest trading metropolis in the world.

"But you must never forget," Fleming went on, "that this is only possible because of one thing." He indicated two frigates moored just upstream at Deptford. "The navy."

After two centuries of struggle against the Spanish, Dutch and French, the vessels fitted and supplied at Tudor King Harry's naval base at Deptford had confirmed their supremacy of the seas. If Queen Elizabeth's buccaneers had begun England's trading empire, Nelson and his successors had now guaranteed it. "No navy, Eugene," his godfather remarked, "no city."

Eugene asked many questions. Had, for instance, the War of Independence with America affected commerce?

Fleming shrugged. "Not much. You see trade's like a river, really. You can try to stop it but it usually seeps through. Tobacco used to be the thing, but it's cotton now. They grow it, we manufacture. Independence or not, bad feeling or not, trade carries on."

"Not always, though," Eugene pointed out. In the long conflict with Napoleon when the mighty French emperor had barred English trade from most of Europe, only the smugglers had managed to get through.

"That's true," Fleming agreed, "and it was thanks to our sea power that we could take up the slack in other places. For Asia and South America, you know, are the emerging markets now.

But there was something else too, Eugene, that even Napoleon couldn't control."

"Which was?"

"Money, Eugene. Money." He grinned. "You see, while Napoleon was turning Europe upside down, every foreigner with money to spare sent it to London for safe keeping – including the French! Old Boney made us the money centre of the world." And he chuckled at the thought of the striking phenomenon of capital flight.

The following afternoon, announcing that, as he had business to attend to, this would be their last expedition together for a while, Fleming led Eugene along Cheapside to the Poultry, and there, with scarcely suppressed excitement, he paused. Ahead of them at the foot of Cornhill was the imposing outer façade of the Royal Exchange. To their right stood a splendid classical house. "The Mansion House," Fleming explained. "The Lord Mayor's official residence. Built in my father's day." His tone changed entirely as he pointed to another long, blank Roman façade, to the left of the Exchange and separated from it by a narrow lane known as Threadneedle Street.

"That, Eugene," he said with hushed reverence, "is the Bank of England."

Since it began its life in the Mercers Hall as a joint stock company, the Bank of England had outlasted all its rivals. "The South Sea Company burst with the South Sea Bubble of 1720," Fleming reminded him. Even the mighty East India Company had been so mismanaged that the Bank had helped the government take it over. Time and again, as England was forced into wars, the Bank had found the funds and seen the country through. His godfather proudly described the way it had helped the government through every crisis, how its clerks now administered most of the government's accounts, paid the army and navy overseas, and even administered the state lotteries. Though the Bank was, strictly speaking, a private company, it had become practically part of the constitution.

"So mighty are its reserves, and so carefully managed, that all the money houses and merchants in London look to it for funds when they need them," Fleming explained. "The Bank's authority is complete. It's only the Bank, in London, that has a charter to issue banknotes for the general public. And that's because money must be sound, you see. For a note from the Bank of England, Eugene, is as sound as . . . why, as sound as . . ." Here, at last, words failed him.

"And this soundness was achieved through caution, Eugene," the clerk cried, with a kind of ecstasy. "The Bank is cautious." He beamed. "Caution, Eugene, is the key to life."

Eugene was just about to thank him politely for this information when Fleming, with a look of immense satisfaction, continued: "I have some news for you now, Eugene. Thanks to an old friend of mine, I have been able to secure you a position." He paused for what was, to him, a delicious moment. "A position, Eugene, in the Bank of England."

"The Bank?"

"Yes." He smiled happily. "The Bank itself." He even laughed with delight at what he had been able to do for his godson. "Security for life, Eugene!"

Eugene had to think quickly what he should say. He was not a brilliant young man, but he was quite ambitious and, like his Huguenot forebears, very persistent. He had sensed quickly that his godfather's idea of a good position and his own were not the same. "If I joined the Bank of England," he asked cautiously, "how well could I do?"

"Oh, quite well. As a senior man you could live . . ." Fleming spread his hands to indicate that his own circumstances were not to be sneezed at.

"The trouble is, sir," Eugene gently began, "I had something else in mind. "I have come to make my fortune."

"Your fortune, Penny? You are sure of this?"

"Yes. I am."

"Ah." Jeremy Fleming fell silent for a time.

As they walked home, Eugene was afraid that Fleming had been offended, but that evening, over a supper of pickled herrings, the older man calmly enquired: "Was it stockbroking, or one of the private banks you had in mind?"

What followed surprised Eugene even more. In his quiet way, Fleming seemed almost pleased by his godson's initiative, and a new look, quite a sharp one, came into his eyes as he discussed the merits and drawbacks of the various firms.

"Amongst the stockbrokers, on the whole, I think the Quaker houses are the soundest, but I don't suppose you'd care to become a Quaker. As for the private banks, there's

Baring's of course – very grand, but as you've no great connections that mightn't do. Rothschild's all family. What I really think you need is a go-ahead little house, active in all the new markets." He tapped his fingers on the table thoughtfully. "Give me a day or two to ask around. In the meantime, young man," he remarked with a briskness that was entirely new, "no offence, but you don't know much."

Fleming taught Eugene all the following day; and the next, and the one after. He explained the operation of the markets, the politics of the City and its conventions. Spicing his conversation with all the liveliest gossip of the last forty years, he outlined the financial virtues to be cultivated and described in detail all the meanest of the dealers' tricks with a quiet relish. At the end of the third day, Eugene ventured to say: "I'm surprised, godfather, that you never went into business for yourself."

Fleming gave a little smile. "I dreamed of it once, Eugene."

"But you did not do so?"

"No." And here Fleming sighed. "Want of courage, Eugene," he confessed regretfully. Then he brightened. "By the way, you have an interview tomorrow."

Meredith's Bank was a tall brick house set in a narrow courtyard, reached by a little lane off Cornhill. It was typical of many small city firms of its day in that while the building itself was severely Georgian, the arrangements within it were still essentially medieval. On the ground floor was the counting-house, a large room, fitted with a counter and several desks and high stools for the clerks. Above this level lived not only Mr Meredith and his family, but the junior clerks, just like apprentices. In a comfortable parlour off the first landing Eugene found himself sitting opposite a handsome gentleman in his thirties, who introduced himself as Mr Meredith, and a much older gentleman in a wing chair, who seemed to be watching the proceedings as if it were some kind of sporting event.

Meredith was careful to put Eugene at his ease, talking pleasantly about his business before he asked about his family and name. When Penny explained its Huguenot origins, Meredith seemed well satisfied. "There are many Huguenots in finance you know," he observed. "They do well. I expect you work hard." Eugene assured him that he did. "And you want to rise?"

Eugene did not want to seem to be pushing himself too aggressively, but he confessed that, if he could prove his ability, he hoped to rise.

"Quite right," said Meredith obligingly. "It'll all depend upon how useful you can make yourself, you know. All of us here" – he grinned at the old man in the wing chair – "are free to rise – or fall."

He went on to ask a number of questions to determine what Eugene knew about the rules of finance, which thanks to his godfather's coaching, Eugene was able to answer. They had just come to the end of their interview when the old man suddenly spoke.

"What does he think about free trade?" he demanded.

The question was so abrupt that Eugene was almost startled. But Meredith only smiled. "Lord St James would like to know your view on free trade," he said.

Thank God, thought Eugene, thank God indeed for Fleming. Because of him he knew who the old man was and also what he must say. "I agree with the Whigs, my lord, that free trade in principle must be for the betterment of mankind, but until it is reciprocated by our trading rivals, English merchants may need some protection here and there." This was, of course, exactly the view of the Whigs' merchant and city supporters: they were all for free trade – as long as it suited them.

"That was all right, St James," Meredith laughed. But it seemed the earl meant to have a little more sport. Fixing Eugene with his sharp old eye, just as if he had been a horse he was thinking of betting on, he rapped out: "So what about the gold standard, young man, eh? What do you think of that?"

Once again, Eugene silently blessed his godfather. If there was one subject in the year 1819 that could be calculated to raise tempers in the city and in Parliament, it was the great question of gold.

Traditionally, when banknotes were issued, they represented gold bullion for which they could always be exchanged. This limited the number of notes in circulation and kept the currency sound. But early in the conflict with revolutionary France, the English government, through the Bank, had to borrow so much money – and therefore issue so many promissory notes – that the amount of money circulating in the London market swelled enormously. Indeed, by the end of the Napoleonic Wars, about 90 per cent of government income went in paying interest. In these circumstances there was simply not enough bullion to back all the banknotes needed; and so the Bank of England had been allowed to print money that was no longer, strictly, backed by gold.

These banknotes were still sound. They had the Bank's massive credibility, and the government's ability to raise money through taxes, behind them. But to many solid Tories in the country, the whole thing seemed like a trick.

"If it's not gold it's not real," they complained. "And besides," the sharper of them pointed out, "if there's no gold behind the currency, how can we trust these fellows not to print money whenever it suits them?" If this insulted the integrity of the Chancellor of the Exchequer and the governors of the Bank of England, they couldn't care less. In the summer of 1819 they had got their way. Parliament had declared that over the next few years it would return to gold. But there was one difficulty.

"Gold is sound, my lord," Eugene now said carefully. "But I think the sudden return to it is dangerous. The Bank will have to reduce the amount of currency in circulation to match it to the limited bullion. That means that with less money about prices will fall. All businesses will be hurt. Worse, with all this money being sucked out of the market, our merchants, already in trouble, will find it impossible to get credit to tide them over. The whole system could collapse."

This was precisely the view of the City. It had been urged repeatedly upon Parliament by Rothschild and other great bankers. The collapse they feared would be known to a later age only too well as a classic depression, caused by contracting the money supply.

Eugene's response drew from the Earl of St James a single word. "Remarkable."

Eugene had talked himself into a job.

1822

Lucy was four when her brother was born, one cold December dawn. At first they thought he would die.

"We'll call him Horatio," her father said. "After Nelson." Perhaps, they all hoped, the great hero's name would give the baby strength to live, and it seemed to have worked. Lucy would always remember the day, a month later, when her mother, judging that the child would live, told her: "This baby is yours too. You'll always look after him, won't you?" He had been hers ever since.

Death and hardship were no strangers to the Doggets. The children's father William had been only three when his father, old Sep Dogget the fireman had been killed when a blazing house collapsed. Will's mother had been Sep's second wife and she had done her best to bring him up alone. Will's elder half-brother had helped, but not much, since he had his own children, including Silas, to care for. By the time he was a young man, Will had drifted into the huge parish of St Pancras where he occupied three rooms with his wife and Lucy and sickly Horatio, the only two of his five children to survive. Infant mortality was an urban curse. Fewer than half of London's children reached the age of six.

He shouldn't worry, Penny told himself. After all, it was only a shot in the dark. Meredith undoubtedly knew what he was doing. Eugene had asked his godfather what he thought, but Fleming had advised him not to concern himself.

Meanwhile, his life at Meredith's was delightful. The first two years, he lived in Meredith's house, visiting Fleming or sometimes his parents in Rochester on Saturdays and Sundays. He was like an elder brother to Meredith's four boisterous children; secretly he was in love with pretty Mrs Meredith – of course, she and her husband were well aware of this – and if one day he could live as they did, he thought, he would be a lucky man indeed.

Though it held balances for a number of country gentlemen, the business of Meredith's, like most private banking houses, was in making commercial loans mostly to merchants in the import and export trade. None were made to manufacturers: "For then I should have to understand what they do," Meredith said. The manufacturers of the early Industrial Revolution raised their capital from friends or sometimes from aristocratic backers, hardly ever from banks. Short-term loans for cargoes, letters of credit, the discounting of bills – this was the bread and butter of small banks like Meredith's.

Business was not easy; the City's fears about the gold standard had been partly justified. There was less money about, credit was tight, stock prices were down, and everyone was jittery. "We need new clients. Look for specialist merchants; they often survive," Meredith told his clerks. Eugene had found several, including a trader who specialized in Indian dyes, and in tortoiseshell and mother-of-pearl. But the huge growth, in which he dreamed of involving Meredith's, came from the great foreign loans.

These were massive: loans to governments like France, Prussia and, most lately, the South American countries. Far too big for any one bank, this lucrative business was syndicated, numerous banks each taking a share, including Meredith's.

"But it's the agent banks, the ones who put the deal together, who really make a fortune," Meredith explained, "because they get fees as well." Baring's and Rothschild's were the leaders here because with their international connections they could arrange for banks all over Europe to participate. "Baring's are slipping, though," Meredith would say. By 1820, it was common knowledge that the younger generation of Baring's with their grand country estates were not paying enough attention to the details of their business.

Some people, Eugene knew, felt that sending money out of the country like this was somewhat unpatriotic. But the banker explained: "Money knows no boundaries, Eugene. After all," he pointed out, "in times past the Lombards and other foreigners lent money to England. Now it's our turn to be the bankers. And long may it last!" he added.

The counting-house was a merry environment. The six clerks, all under thirty, went out drinking together most evenings. The City was also a great place for practical jokes. One favourite was to go round to the Royal Exchange and offer obviously bogus stocks. Any unwary taker was then hooted with derision by all the onlookers. One offer – Chinese Turnpikes – was so successful it was tried on newcomers regularly. A more serious case that year had been an enterprising rogue's offer of bonds in a South American country he had invented, called Proesia. Having taken a considerable amount of money, he then vanished. Two unlucky investors had actually been ruined, but Meredith's traders were young and brutal: they howled with mirth.

But though he was enjoying himself day to day, Eugene never lost sight of his objective. What was he worth? This was the expression one heard every day in the City. How else, in a financial community, could a man be measured? So far, apart from the modest amount he would one day inherit from his parents, the answer was: not much. True, it was early days yet, but there were plenty of stories of ambitious young men working their way into partnership and riches in less than ten years. "Look sharp about you, Eugene," the other clerks told him. "That's the name of the game."

One way to make a little on the side was to dabble in stocks, but with very limited funds he was not sure how to get started. A young stockbroker friend enlightened him. "Futures, Eugene," he assured him. "I'll show you how they work."

The futures market was a lively business. Instead of buying a stock or bond and holding it, a man could agree to buy it at a future date, in effect taking a bet on what its price would be then. But then, if he could find another buyer, he could sell this option to purchase at a higher price, and pocket any profit having put practically no money down at all. This trading of options, which a later age would call derivatives, had first begun back in 1720 at the time of the South Sea Bubble. Although it had since then been made technically illegal, it was carried on every day.

Eugene soon found it was a good way to train himself in the intricacies of taking risks. He kept a little book detailing all his trades, and after a year he was starting not only to show a modest profit but to develop strategies for offsetting one risk against another. "You're getting the idea," his friend told him. "It's just like hedging your bets at the races!" Yet it was this kind of training that gave rise to Eugene's first feeling of disquiet.

Without particularly meaning to, Eugene realized that he was forming a picture of the Meredith Bank's activities, too. He began to make a catalogue of the principal people they dealt with and started to assess their businesses. And slowly he found himself coming to a rather uncomfortable conclusion. "I can't be sure," he had told Fleming, "but if some of these firms were to fail, I think Meredith could go under, too."

"But you must assume," Fleming comforted him, "that the Earl of St James is behind him." As everyone at the bank knew, it was Meredith's grandfather who had brought up the old earl and as a debt of gratitude St James had staked Meredith when he started his bank. The old man still liked to drop by from time to time: the business seemed to amuse him. "So I dare say," concluded Fleming, "he'll see you through."

Besides the Bank and the Royal Exchange, there was one other growing place of business in the City. Housed only recently in premises close by the Bank in a narrow enclave called Capel Court, this extended trading room was known as the Stock Exchange and was mainly used by the men dealing in the innumerable issues of government debt. Its inmates had decided they were going to live like perpetual schoolboys. They even had a big stall that sold them cream buns, doughnuts and candies. But perhaps its most surprising feature was number 2 Capel Court, which the great prize-fighter Mendoza ran as a boxing saloon where young brokers and other young bloods could come and take a turn either with each other or with a professional bruiser.

Chancing to pass Mendoza's with Meredith one day, Eugene saw a curious sight. The young fellow was on the short side but very compact. Stripped to the waist he had a boxing stance like a professional. He had a white flash in his hair and, for some reason, kept a red kerchief round his neck. He had just knocked down a broker and cheerfully asked if anyone else wanted a fight when Meredith hailed him.

"Hello, George! What brings you here?"

"Hello, Meredith!" He grinned. "Fight?"

"No thanks. George, this is Eugene Penny." He introduced them. "Penny, this is Mr George de Quette." And Eugene realized that he was looking at the Earl of St James's grandson.

Everybody had heard of George de Quette. Taking after his sporting grandfather rather than the sour Lord Bocton, he was renowned as the wildest, and jolliest young buck in England. He could ride like a jockey, fight like a turkey-cock and took no account of social rank. As for women, his exploits were legendary. He had been away for two years, sent by his father on a tour of the Continent, from which he had returned quite unchanged. Pulling on a shirt now he stepped out of the ring and chatted with them very pleasantly for several minutes.

It was typical of him that, seeing Penny in the street the following week, George remembered him at once and invited him into a coffee house. They had a delightful conversation, discussing the latest sporting events, but Penny discovered that the young aristocrat's interests were wider than he had supposed. He had a considerable knowledge of France and Italy and had read quite widely. He even liked poetry.

"Everyone reads Lord Byron, of course. It's the fashion," he declared. "But I like Keats as well. People laugh at him because he's not a gentleman, but did you read his 'Ode to a Nightingale' last year? It's beautiful."

He seemed interested in the bank too, and asked Eugene all about his life there. Eugene even told him about his own trading in futures.

"I suppose banking's like racing, really," the young aristocrat remarked. "Study the form. Hedge your bets. I learned all I know from my grandfather. He's a shrewd old devil, you know." He smiled. "'You've got to be ruthless.' That's what he'd tell me. 'If something doesn't work, get out, cut your losses, move on.' That's the art of all dealing, isn't it?"

He was right, of course, Eugene thought. But if Meredith's Bank got into trouble, he asked himself, would his lordship cut his losses? Just how ruthless, he wondered, would the sporting old Earl of St James turn out to be?

"I think," said Lord Bocton to Silversleeves, towards the end of that year, "that my father shows promising signs."

"Of seeing reason, my lord?"

"No, of madness. Indeed," Lord Bocton continued, "he could go to prison."

"You would wish that?"

"Certainly not. But we could save him from prison if you declared he was mad."

"Might not prison serve your purpose, though?"

"Bedlam's better," Lord Bocton snapped.

"What exactly," Silversleeves enquired, "has he done?"

It had disappointed Lord Bocton that his father had given

him no great cause for complaint in the last two years. The development of villas in Regent's Park had been slow and so Lord St James, who could not bear to be still, had instead purchased one of the stately, but far less ruinous terraced houses now lining the park's eastern side. As for the earl's dangerous politics, the situation had been calmer recently and with two forward-looking Tories, Canning and Robert Peel, joining the government, there was even a whisper that some modest reform might be desirable. If the earl was going mad, one had to admit that the present circumstances did not let it show to best advantage.

Help had come from St Pancras. In 1822 the select and aristocratic vestry of St Pancras had decided to build a new church that would be truly worthy of them in a suitably fashionable quarter. It was in the Grecian style and the vestry were delighted with it – as well they should be since it was for themselves. "God will not be troubled," Carpenter pointed out, "by any prayers from poor people in there." Its cost ran into tens of thousands, so the vestry had to increase the parish taxes. "The ordinary people of St Pancras will pay three times the former rate," Carpenter protested. And then the Earl of St James, declaring that the whole business was monstrous, had refused to pay.

At first the vestry was embarrassed. They really didn't want a scandal. But one or two members, who happened to be acquaintances of Lord Bocton, assured their brethren that they could not let this pass. "If he does it, hundreds will follow," they warned. And three applications having been made to the earl, a warrant was now being considered for his arrest.

"We'll let them arrest him first," Bocton said with satisfaction. "Then we'll save him."

On a cold December morning Eugene looked up from his desk in some surprise to see a worried-looking George de Quette enter the counting-house and ask for Meredith. A few minutes later, he was summoned into Meredith's parlour himself.

"Lord St James has been arrested," Meredith explained quickly. "He's refused to pay the parish rates."

"I'd pay them myself," young George explained, "but my allowance won't run to it."

"Couldn't Lord Bocton help?" Eugene ventured.

The other two looked at each other. "I'm paying," Meredith said swiftly. "God knows, George, I owe him everything."

"It has to be carefully done," George explained. "If he ever found out we'd interfered. . . ."

"We need someone not known. Someone discreet," said Meredith.

It turned out to be relatively easy. As soon as he made his offer it was clear to Eugene that the senior clerk in the vestry office was extremely relieved.

"You say this money comes from . . . ?"

"Well-wishers in the parish, sir."

"I did not catch your name."

"I act for unnamed parties, sir. As you will see, this entirely clears Lord St James's obligation."

"Yes. It certainly does."

"In which event, surely, his arrest. . . ."

"No longer necessary. Quite."

"But if he refuses to pay?" objected a junior clerk.

"He can refuse to pay till Doomsday," the senior clerk retorted with asperity, "but if he *has* paid, or someone has, we've no claim against him, have we? He can't go to gaol," he added with satisfaction, "even if he wants to." He turned to Eugene again. "I'm much obliged to you, sir – to those you represent. Saved us a deal of embarrassment. All charges dropped. He'll be out within the hour; I'll see to it myself."

Eugene strolled towards Holborn, happy with the way his business had gone. But after he had walked a quarter of a mile, he was stopped by a cry of "Hey! Stop, sir!" followed by the sound of hurrying footsteps behind him, and he turned to see the tall, bottle-green person of Lord Bocton, advancing towards him, accompanied by a lugubrious man with a long nose.

As it happened, Lord Bocton and Silversleeves had just called in at the vestry office to make sure their quarry had been safely trapped before they set about the rest of their plan. Now they caught up.

"Were you in the vestry office back there?" demanded Lord Bocton.

"I may have been," Eugene replied. "But then again," he added sweetly, "I may not. Might I ask what business it is of yours?"

"Never mind that, sir! Are you trying to pervert the course of justice?"

"No." He wasn't.

"Do you want to be arrested?"

"I don't believe so."

"What is your name, sir?"

Eugene allowed a look of delicious puzzlement to steal over his face. "My name?" he frowned. "Why, sir, that's strange. I can't remember." And while they gazed in stupefaction he abruptly turned a corner and vanished into a side street.

For several moments Lord Bocton and Silversleeves stood staring at each other. Finally Silversleeves spoke. "He could not remember his own name, my lord. Now that is a sure sign of insanity."

"Oh damn your insanity!" cried Bocton, and furiously strode away.

1824

They had gone further than usual that day, since a kindly neighbour had offered them a ride in his cart.

Lucy and Horatio were a well-known pair in their humble little street. The thin, pale five-year-old girl would take the toddler out with her every afternoon if he was well enough, because they told her it would make him stronger. And tiny Horatio, with his shock of white hair, would hold her hand and struggle along gamely beside her.

Their neighbour, having business near the Strand, dropped the two children at Charing Cross and promised to return to pick them up in half an hour. It was a good place for the children to wander. The space before them, which would in due course be enlarged and laid out as Trafalgar Square, was gently sloping. On its southern side were the entrances to the stately streets of Whitehall and Pall Mall. Just visible to the right was the handsome classical façade of St Martin-in-the-Fields, and immediately before them stretched the buildings of the Royal Mews where the king's horses and carriages were kept.

The summer afternoon was hot and dusty, sweet with the smell of horse dung. Great brown clouds of flies rose with a huge buzz each time a passing cart disturbed them. In the middle of the open space some stall holders had set up a little market; and from the classical pediment of St Martin's, pigeons and doves would swoop down to pick up scraps from around the stalls. Several street vendors moved about, crying their wares. As the two children wandered contentedly about their attention was caught by one young woman with a basket and the gentle cry – "Lavender! Buy my lavender!" – which somehow sounded to Lucy more haunting than the rest. The woman came over and offered them a sprig, and when Lucy explained that she hadn't any money, she laughed and told her to take it all the same. The smell of it was wonderful and Lucy asked the girl where it came from.

"Lavender Hill, of course," the girl replied. "It's out by Battersea Village," she explained. "Between that and Clapham Common." The market gardens on these slopes, which were less than three miles away, grew acres of lavender, she told her. It sounded a delightful place.

"This your brother?" the girl asked. "Sickly, is he?"

"He's getting stronger."

"Does he know the Lavender song?"

Lucy shook her head and the girl obligingly sang it to him.

"Lavender blue, dilly dilly,
Lavender green -
When I am king, dilly dilly,
You shall be queen."

"Only", she remarked, "as it's me singing it, I suppose it ought to be 'when *you* are king,' the other way round really. You should sing it to him," she told Lucy cheerfully, and moved off.

Lucy and Horatio were just about to start walking back to Charing Cross, when they saw their neighbour's wife hurrying towards them from the Royal Mews. Her face was sweating; her red cotton dress was sticking to her body. Walking rapidly, she scattered a crowd of pigeons in her path in her anxiety to reach the children.

"You better come along with me," she said, taking Lucy's hand.

* * *

They had laid Will Dogget on the bed and he was still breathing, but as she held her little brother's hand, Lucy knew it was death.

That dusty summer afternoon Will had been passing by a scaffolding, where they were working on a line of elegant houses beside Regent's Park. For no reason he had looked up – just in time to see the great hod of bricks come crashing down.

Will was groaning a little. His breathing sounded strange, rasping. He did not seem to know that the clergyman was there, nor did he see Lucy or little Horatio. By six that evening he was dead.

Lucy's mother's face was grey. It was a terrible thing to lose a husband. Because of death in childbirth, women's mortality rate was high. But a man could marry again and the new wife would look after her children, whereas if a working man died, how was his widow to live?

Will Dogget was buried the next day, in a common grave. There were only three mourners. Lucy had heard her father say that there were some other Doggets, aunts or uncles perhaps, but it seemed they lived far away and her mother did not know who they were. Only one other person turned up, a strange, stocky figure wearing a shapeless old black hat. He watched silently as the work was done, then came over and said a few gruff words before departing. He smelled of the river and he seemed to Lucy a sinister presence.

"Who's that?" she asked her mother.

"That?" Her mother made a face. "That's Silas. I don't know how he discovered about your dad. I never asked him to come here."

"He said he will come again."

"I hope not."

"What does he do?" the girl asked curiously.

"You don't want to know," her mother replied.

So what was he worth? As Penny walked across from Meredith's Bank that October afternoon, it had suddenly started to matter. It mattered because of a pair of wonderful brown eyes and a kindly voice with a soft Scottish brogue, belonging to the person of Miss Mary Forsyth. It mattered rather urgently because he was about to encounter her father for the first time.

In the last eighteen months, Eugene had done rather well. He had managed to put a little money by and started to make some promising investments. A new level of confidence had been growing in the City during the previous two years, led by the swelling market for foreign loans. Meredith's had already done very well out of Buenos Aires and Brazil and had just joined a huge syndicate for Mexico, though the bank had prudently declined opportunities to lend to Colombia and Peru. Encouraged by these vast and profitable shiploads of money passing through the City, the stockjobbers had been busy selling lesser bond issues and even joined stock companies like a flotilla in the great loans' wake. A great bull market, in short, was gathering itself together and surging ahead. All investors, since all prices were rising, looked wise. And Eugene Penny, playing steadily as was his nature, had already made himself more than a thousand pounds. But would it, he wondered, as he entered the Royal Exchange, be enough to satisfy the redoubtable Hamish Forsyth?

The Royal Exchange had always been a busy place, but nowadays it was full to bursting. Every few yards of the world trade emporium seemed to be dedicated to some special trade. There was the Jamaica Walk, the Spanish Walk, the Norway Walk, where gaggles of jobbers sold stocks to buyers from every land. Eugene passed through a group of Dutchmen, then some Armenians, before he passed from the noisy and colourful scene to the quieter regions of the mezzanine floor above. There, in a large and impressive hall, Mr Forsyth's place of business was to be found.

Lloyd's of London was not to be taken lightly. The old business of Lloyd's coffee shop had long since evolved into a carefully regulated partnership of the highest repute. Some of the smaller insurance brokers in town, Eugene knew, were little more than dressed-up barrow boys and card-sharps, but the men of Lloyd's were of a very different stamp. In this solemn hall, which they leased from the Exchange, was kept the Lloyd's Register of Shipping. Here, through syndicates rather like those used by banks for the greatest loans, the largest ships, no matter how valuable their cargo, were safely insured by the underwriters sitting at their desks. And of all the hundred or so underwriters, none was more solid or more awesomely principled than the dour figure who now, though he did not rise, granted Eugene a nod.

It was said of Mr Hamish Forsyth that he looked like a Scottish judge who had just passed sentence. His Presbyterian ancestors had been bleak as granite. But, though as stern as they, Hamish had preferred to transfer those feelings from the Kirk of God to the London insurance market. His brow, crowned with a few strands of grey hair, was noble; his nose, beak-like. From time to time he took large pinches of snuff, so that his conversation was punctuated by a series of huge sniffs – which gave to his utterances an air of finality which suggested that no ship *he* had insured would ever dare to sink.

"We'll go across the street," he said. Leading Penny out, he made his way to a coffee shop in Threadneedle Street where, with the air of one who confers a favour, he bought him a cup of coffee.

"You've met my daughter," he remarked. Penny agreed that he had. "You'd better answer for yourself, then," Forsyth declared, taking a pinch of snuff.

Penny felt rather as though he were a vessel being inspected to discover if it is seaworthy. Forsyth asked the questions. He answered. His family? He explained them. His religion? His ancestors were Huguenot. This drew a sniff, it seemed of approval. He himself, he admitted, was Church of England, but even this seemed to pass. "It's respectable," said Forsyth. His position? He explained he was a clerk at Meredith's. Forsyth looked thoughtful, then, like the Presbyterian minister he might have been, announced: "A man who invests in Mexico may be saved. In Peru . . ." Sniff. "Never."

Required to declare his own fortune, Penny told all, truthfully and, asked to do so, related his dealings in detail. This elicited a sigh. "This market is over-heating, young man. Get out or you'll be burned."

Eugene would have liked to argue, but was too wise. "When should I get out, sir?"

Forsyth gazed at him as he might at a man hanging by his fingers over a cliff, before he decided whether to tread on the fingers or help him up. "By Easter," he said definitively. And then, quite suddenly, as if he considered he had been much too kind: "You wear spectacles, Mr Penny. The truth, man. How bad are your eyes?"

Eugene explained that his father and grandfather had been short-sighted too. "But it doesn't seem to get any worse," he added.

Whether this satisfied Forsyth, Eugene could not tell, but he soon found himself asked a series of questions about banking and finance which warned him that the Scotsman's mind was very sharp indeed. Most he knew how to answer, but the final question made him pause.

"What, Mr Penny, do you think of the return to gold?"

Eugene remembered how he had answered the Earl when he had asked the same question, and he knew how most people in the City still felt, but he also reckoned, if he had judged his man correctly, that another answer was now required.

"I am in favour of the gold standard, sir," he said.

"Ye are?" For once he had surprised the Scot. "And why, may I ask, would that be?"

"Because, sir," Penny boldly replied, "I do not trust the Bank of England."

"Well." Even Forsyth, for a moment, was speechless. Penny kept a straight face. He had been right. "It is not often," Forsyth finally confessed, "that a young man can be found in the City with such views." Eugene had hit. Even the Bank of England, to Forsyth, was a weak and broken vessel. For a moment or two the older man sat thoughtfully, before recovering himself sufficiently to take another pinch of snuff. "So," he returned to the attack, "you care for Mary? You must admit though, she's no beauty."

Mary Forsyth had a slim figure, and a head which some might have thought a little large. Her brown hair was parted in the middle, and she had a somewhat studious look. There was nothing fashionable or coquettish about her. Her beauty lay in her kindly nature and her high intelligence. Eugene sincerely loved her.

"I beg to differ, sir."

Sniff. A pause. "So then," Forsyth blandly remarked, "it's her money you're after, I dare say." He watched Penny, almost amiably.

Eugene considered. Though not known as a rich man like some of the bankers, there was no doubt that Forsyth had a very solid fortune, and Mary was his only child. To pretend he had no interest in this fact would be absurd and disingenuous. He took stock of his man. "I should never seek to marry a woman," he began carefully, "whom I did not love and respect, sir. As to her fortune," he continued, "it's not so much money I look for. But I desire to marry into a family," he paused for just an instant, "that is *sound.*"

"*Sound,* do you say?"

"Yes, sir."

"Sound? I am sound, sir. You may be sure of that. I am very sound indeed!"

Penny inclined his head and said nothing. Forsyth also paused and took a pinch of snuff.

"You are young, Mr Penny. You must get established. And, of course, Mary may get a better offer. But if not, in a few years, we'll look at you again." He nodded, apparently with general approval. "In the meantime, you may call to see Mary. . ." Here, a huge and definitive sniff ". . . from time to time."

Lucy passed the place nearly every day, but she always looked away in case the sight of it brought her bad luck. It was the one place the family had to avoid.

The workhouse was the dread of every poor family, and the parish workhouse of St Pancras was as bad as they came. Lying in the angle between two dingy thoroughfares, it had long ago been a gentleman's residence. But there was nothing gentlemanly about it now. Nearby stood a broken-down old stocks and a cage once used for prisoners. Its filthy yard was strewn with refuse. They had been obliged to enlarge the old house some years back, for into it were crammed God knows how many poor souls, filling every hole and cranny, making it a sort of rabbit warren of the destitute.

In theory, the parish workhouses were to help the poor. Those unable to fend for themselves were to be housed, the children apprenticed to trades, the adults given work to do. In practice it was different. People had been complaining for centuries about the parish poor: to pay taxes for a fine new church was bad enough, but at least you had something to show for it; whereas when you spent money on the needy, they only seemed to ask for more. In practice, therefore, parishes spent as little as they could. Supervision was perfunctory. Most of these places filled with the sick – and poor folk who came there healthy seldom stayed so for long.

Soon after her father died, Lucy had nervously whispered to her mother: "Could we have to go to the workhouse?"

"Of course not," her mother had lied. "But we must both work."

Her mother had found work in a little factory nearby that made cotton dresses. But the hours there were very long, and the owner would not allow little Horatio in there. So each morning accompanied by her brother, Lucy would walk past the workhouse on the way to her new job in Tottenham Court Road.

Whatever he might think about the general state of the world, the furniture business had been good to Zachary Carpenter. "I can sell as many davenports and chairs as I can make," he would confess. He had taken extra space and employed ten journeymen now and an extra apprentice. His total workforce was twice this number, but the others were neither journeymen nor apprentices: they were little children.

"Their small hands, when properly trained, can make for very neat finishing work," Carpenter would explain. He did not know of anyone in his line who did not use them. As for whether it was right, that social reformer would say: "They ought to be in schools. But until there are schools, I at least keep them from starving." Or from the workhouse.

Carpenter, like most masters, did not employ children under seven, but he had made an exception for Horatio. Since the tiny boy was eager to help, he gave him a little broom and let him sweep up the wood-shavings for which, from time to time, he would reward him with a farthing.

It took both Lucy and her mother to replace even the majority of Will Dogget's wages. He had usually brought home between twenty and thirty shillings a week. His widow earned ten shillings, Lucy five. The picture was the same all over England: woman was paid about half a man's wage; a child, something over a sixth. These were the economics of avoiding the workhouse.

In the Easter of 1825, Eugene Penny took the advice of Mr Hamish Forsyth and reduced all his investments to cash and safe government stocks. If he's right and I don't follow his advice, he'll never forgive me, he reasoned; whereas if I do, and he's wrong, it puts me in a slightly stronger position with him.

Whether the dour Scot was correct it was hard as yet to say. The foreign loan boom continued. "We've never made such profits!" Meredith declared. But as Penny looked at some of the wilder excesses of the stock market he had to confess it was over-valued. In the commodity market, too, people were borrowing money to buy anything. "Copper, timber, coffee – they can't all go up for ever." But spring and summer passed and still the boom went on.

Penny had attained some seniority in the firm now. Since the affair with the old Earl of St James, Meredith had entrusted him with a number of tasks needing discretion and he was used to confiding in him about the bank's business.

"We've followed Baring's and Rothschild's," Meredith said. The two leaders in the foreign loans market had utterly shunned the stock speculation. "Our own positions are pretty sound. But what I do fear," he admitted, "is a general decline. It's very hard for a small bank like ours to protect against that." He shrugged. "It all depends on who goes down."

The danger to Meredith's Bank which Eugene had originally surmised was endemic to all such small operations. If some of those who owed Meredith money went under, he could be in peril. "But the real danger," he went on, "is not so specific. It isn't a bad investment or a shaky loan – it's nothing you can even predict. It's loss of confidence. That's what can kill us."

"I've never really seen that happen," Eugene confessed.

"Pray," said Meredith, "that you never do."

Eugene saw Mary every week. There was no doubt, they felt, that they would marry; but how soon was another matter. Eugene's salary had increased considerably; his position looked secure, but he had not yet reached a standing that would satisfy Mr Hamish Forsyth.

The trouble began in the autumn. "Batten down the hatches, Penny," Meredith announced. "I think we're in for a storm. The word is," he explained, "that the Bank of England is tightening up."

By October there were murmurs. By November there were cries. The markets began to falter, then to fall. "This can't go on!" Meredith declared. "The Bank must loosen up or everyone's going to panic."

Early in December, the Bank of England did conclude that it had gone too far and, started granting credit. It was too late.

On Wednesday 7 December it was confirmed that Pole's, a private bank closely linked with no less than thirty-eight provincial county banks, had been bailed out over the weekend by the Bank. On Thursday the 8th, a big Yorkshire bank called Wentworth's suddenly went under. Over the next few days, gentlemen all over England were rushing to their local banks to take out their money. News came back to London with the stage-coaches from every county town. "Gold. They all want gold!"

That weekend, Pole's stopped all payments. By Monday 16 December, in consequence, three dozen country banks had collapsed.

Fog had spread over the city before dawn that Monday. It made everything so quiet. At times, it almost seemed to Penny that the world might have come to an end as they waited in that yellow-lighted counting-house for someone to come and tell them it was all over.

The morning passed uneventfully. There was no trading to be done. From time to time one of the clerks would be sent out for news, vanishing into the oblivion and returning with reports: "The Exchange is full of people demanding money!" "Williams's in Mincing Lane is besieged. Don't know if they can hold out . . ."

Meredith's own preparations had been thorough. During the last week he had seen almost all the bank's major clients. "I think I've squared them all," he told Eugene. "But if the panic really takes hold . . ." He shrugged. The fog, he suspected, was actually a help. "People will have to seek us out. They won't just think of us as they pass in the street." He had also laid in as much gold coin as he could. "Twenty thousand in sovereigns," he announced. Though Penny noticed that when he remarked, "That should do it", Meredith had muttered: "It'll have to."

Only a few people came to withdraw money in the morning. At noon, miraculously, a merchant came in and deposited a thousand pounds. "Took it out of Williams's," he explained. "Safer with you." While news came of more banks in difficulty in the afternoon, the panic had still not spread to Meredith's.

Just before closing time, a stout, elderly country gentleman, wrapped in a brown greatcoat, appeared in the misty doorway and asked, in some doubt, "Is this Meredith's?" Being assured that it was, he advanced to the counter. "The name's Grimsdyke," he said. "From Cumberland. I'd like to make a withdrawal."

"By God," Meredith murmured, "that old gentleman was one of my first depositors! I'd almost forgotten what he looks like. He must have travelled all night."

"Certainly, sir," said the clerk obligingly. "How much?"

"Twenty thousand pounds."

There was really no need to take out so much, Meredith had calmly assured him, the bank was perfectly sound. But the old gentleman had not come all the way from the north of England to change his mind now. He took it all, and made the clerks carry it to his carriage. When the door was closed Meredith called Eugene over. "Strike a balance, Mr Penny," he said quietly, "and bring it to me in the parlour."

"We can't get through another day," Meredith concluded as he and Eugene looked over the books. "These three" – he pointed to the names that had troubled Penny several years before – "all owe us too much, and any of them could go under. I truly don't know if we're solvent or not. As for withdrawals: I can get hold of another five thousand in cash, but some time tomorrow that will probably be gone and we'll have to close our doors."

"Would the Bank of England tide us over?"

"They've yet to show willing. We're too small for them to bother about, anyway." They were both silent.

"There's the Earl of St James," Eugene said at last.

"I can't." Meredith winced. "He's done so much for me already. Besides, he already told me he'll never bail me out." He sighed. "I can't go to him, Penny."

"Let me go then," said Eugene.

"Trust the old devil to be out of London," Eugene muttered, as the coach bowled along that evening. The earl had gone down to Brighton. Accordingly Penny had hired a post-chaise and set out on the turnpike for the seaside resort, fifty miles away to the south. "At least," he chuckled grimly, "it gets me out of the fog." With luck, he estimated, he might get there before the earl had retired to bed. The only thing that embarrassed him a little was that he had had no time to change his clothes, and the person with whom the earl was staying in Brighton happened to be the king.

It was after ten o'clock when Eugene, after much explanation to doormen, lackeys and persons of importance, found himself alone in a gorgeously decorated ante-room with the Earl of St James. Although the old man had clearly drunk a number of glasses of champagne, it was remarkable how suddenly his eyes had become hard as Eugene explained his reason for being there.

"I said I wouldn't bail him out. He knows that."

"He does, my lord. I begged him to let me come."

"You?" St James stared at him. "You're one of his clerks, and you come to see *me*? Here?"

"Mr Meredith entrusts me with business."

"You've certainly got a nerve," St James said, without rancour.

"A steady nerve is all the bank needs," Penny said quickly. "If you'd just tide us over."

The old man paused. Then, suddenly, he turned his eyes fully on Penny, and they were as sharp as those of any bookmaker at the races. "Is the bank solvent?"

"Yes, my lord." He looked him straight in the eye. He said it with total conviction although he knew it was a lie. But he was doing it for Meredith.

"I'll lend him ten thousand at 10 per cent," St James said abruptly. "I'll come to London tomorrow. Will that do?"

Eugene Penny took the mail coach before dawn and was in the City by mid-morning. The fog had cleared. The streets were busy. When he told Meredith the news, the banker was so overcome he could only shake his hand. But, as soon as he found his voice, he had to explain. "I'm afraid though, it's probably too late . . . We've two thousand left. Money's been leaving at a thousand an hour. By noon, it'll be over. I've tried everywhere but I can't get another penny. I can't just close the doors until late afternoon when St James's money comes, because if I do that, there'll be a real run that not even his ten thousand could stop. We need four hours at least, Penny. What the devil can I do?"

And it was then that Eugene had his most brilliant idea. "You've two thousand left? Take it round to the Bank at once! In a handcart," he cried. "This is what to do!"

Half an hour later, the little crowd waiting to be paid in the counting-house was addressed by a now cool-as-cucumber Meredith. "Gentlemen, our apologies. We asked the Bank for sovereigns and they have sent us only change. But we have plenty of it. You shall all be paid. A little patience, please."

The two clerks at the counter started slowly paying out in shillings, in sixpences, but mostly in pennies. By the time the small coins were carefully counted out, the money was flowing out at only three hundred pounds an hour – but it never ceased. The earl himself arrived just before closing with ten thousand in gold, to find all but the most panic-stricken depositors starting to drift away out of sheer boredom. From that day, for many years after, the City would say of Meredith's: "They pay; but you only get pennies there."

The great banking crisis of 1825 did not end on that Tuesday. On Wednesday, for many – though happily not for Meredith's – it was worse. By Thursday the Bank of England, dropping all its severity, and backed in the cabinet by the iron Duke of Wellington himself, was bailing out every financial house in sight.

On Friday, the Bank of England ran out of bullion, too. In the evening it was saved by an infusion of gold gathered by the only man in England, or indeed the world, who could have done it: Nathan Rothschild. Rothschild was king of the City.

The winter Lucy was eight had been hard for the family. Her mother had been troubled by a hacking cough, though she had managed to get to work each day, but little Horatio had been more worrying. They had noticed that the boy's legs were getting weaker. By the turn of the year, he sometimes had to stay at home while Lucy went to work for Carpenter. By the spring, he did seem to be better but sometimes, as she led him by the hand, Lucy would see that he was crying silently.

One warm summer evening, when all the family was feeling better, Lucy was surprised to see the burly form of Silas Dogget tramping up the street to their door. Uninvited, he entered the house, sat himself at the kitchen table and gruffly announced: "I need help. Got a proposition."

"Never!" Lucy's mother cried, as soon as she heard what it was.

"I'd pay you twenty-five shillings a week," he continued. "Keep you out of the workhouse."

"We aren't in the workhouse."

Silas said nothing for a moment. "You're a fool like your husband," he observed.

"Leave us alone! Take yourself off!" her mother shouted now, in a real rage.

Silas shrugged and slowly got up. As he paused in the doorway his eyes rested upon Lucy. "Your boy's a weakling, but the girl looks strong. Maybe in a year or two she won't be as proud as you." He rested his heavy hand on Lucy's shoulder. "Just you remember your Uncle Silas, girl," he said in his deep voice. "I'll be waiting."

Lucy and Horatio had come back from their work at Carpenter's one September afternoon, not expecting that their mother would have returned, when they heard a strange sound coming from the room where they all slept. Opening the door, they saw their mother lying on the bed. Her face was very pale and she was making a hoarse sound. As they approached her, though she turned to look at them, she seemed to be gasping for breath. Hustling her brother out of the room, Lucy ran to fetch a neighbour and waited anxiously while the woman helped her mother until the fit was past.

"What is it?" she asked the woman desperately. "Is my mother dying?"

"No," the woman replied. "There are many people in this parish like that, Lucy. It is asthma."

Lucy had heard of the complaint but had never seen it. "Is it dangerous?"

"I've known people choke and die," the woman answered truthfully. "But though it makes them weak, most live with it."

"How can I make it better?" Lucy cried.

"More rest. Less worry." The woman shrugged. She gave the girl a kindly pat.

A month went by and, apart from a few small attacks, her mother carried on well enough. But then, one morning, she was struck again and could not go to work; and then Lucy raised the subject.

"Let me work for Uncle Silas, mother. He is kind," she pointed out, "to offer so much."

"Kind? Silas?" Her mother shook her head in disgust. "To think of you doing what he does . . ."

"I think I should not mind."

"Never, Lucy, while I have breath," her mother cried. "Do not even think of it again."

Eugene Penny decided to bring matters to a conclusion in September of 1827. Meredith's Bank had come out of the crisis rather well. Lord St James had been repaid his money and remembered the young clerk with some admiration. Meredith was in his debt. Word even filtered back to Hamish Forsyth that the twenty-five-year-old Penny was considered a fellow with a future. He had now nearly two thousand pounds of his own – a substantial amount when an ordinary Bank of England clerk made around a hundred a year. The time was approaching when other City firms might start approaching him with offers of a position, perhaps a lucrative one. But he also knew that the way to impress Hamish Forsyth was to show consistency.

One Monday morning he faced Meredith in the parlour. "I have good news," he told him. "I am glad to tell you that I am to marry the only daughter of Mr Hamish Forsyth of Lloyd's. She comes into his entire fortune, you know."

"My dear Penny!" Meredith, genuinely delighted, was about to call his family in, but Eugene stopped him.

"There is something else, Meredith. I think you may agree that I have earned a junior partnership here. My position as Forsyth's son-in-law also makes it appropriate. Indeed, if you don't, I'm sure Forsyth will feel I should look elsewhere."

"My dear Eugene!" It did not take Meredith long to calculate Forsyth's probable fortune, nor to admit that Penny had indeed made himself valuable to the firm, "I was thinking just the very same thing," the banker replied.

Penny had no sooner drunk the glass of sherry that Meredith pressed upon him than he walked straight across to Lloyd's.

"Mr Forsyth," he said boldly, "I have been made a partner in Meredith's. I have come to ask for Mary's hand."

"A partner?" the Scot enquired. "That is definite?" Eugene nodded. "Well, then, I suppose ye're right. It is time." He paused thoughtfully, and took a pinch of snuff.

"Have you a ring?"

"I mean to buy one today."

"Aye, well. A ring's a necessity. But if you will take my advice, do not get anything too expensive. I can take you to a man who will let you have something perfectly" – sniff – "reasonable."

The Pennys' first child was a healthy boy; and a second was already on the way when Mary said she would like to live outside the metropolis. So she was delighted when Eugene told her he had found a house in Clapham.

His choice of a village on the Thames's southern bank was sensible. Even Hamish Forsyth agreed about that. "The southern bank's the place to be," he nodded. Three new bridges – Waterloo, Southwark and Vauxhall – had made it far more accessible and the open fields by Lambeth were being laid out in handsome streets so that the carriage drive out to the villas of the well-to-do in Battersea and Clapham seemed likely to pass through quite a fashionable suburb. At Clapham itself, around the ancient common, there were a number of handsome houses. The church in the centre was a gracious classical edifice. And though Forsyth felt that the six-bedroom house Penny found was larger than strictly necessary, he seemed mollified when Eugene pointed out that their family would be growing.

"It'll save you the cost of moving later," Forsyth conceded. And to celebrate the event he even bought the couple a fine set of Wedgwood china. "Wedgwood keeps the same patterns," he pointed out. "If you should break a piece, it can be replaced without losing the value of the set."

Eugene found that his office was just over half an hour from home. But the feature which pleased his wife best was the fact that, not a hundred yards from their own pleasant garden, began the great fields on the slope down to Battersea where they grew lavender. Whenever people asked where she now lived she would tell them: "Oh, out at Clapham, just beside Lavender Hill."

1829

The boat nosed slowly through the brown water out into midstream. The little craft was dipping so low that from a distance, in the April evening's dulled light, it looked almost waterlogged. Once it had reached the middle, halfway between Blackfriars and Bankside, it paused and then, as though held by an unseen line, remained still.

"Hold her steady," Silas's voice, deep from the stern. The oars obediently stroked the water. "Steady. Good."

Although it was a year since Lucy, now ten, had started to work for Silas, she had still not grown used to it. So great now was the quantity of effluent, of sewage, of coal dust that washed down from the metropolis into the Thames that not even the sea-tides could carry it away. At high tide the water was murky; at low tide, a sickly smell hung over it. For the first time in history the fish in the river were dying: their mottled and blistered carcasses would be found amongst the rubbish on the mud flats. When a pea-souper descended, it seemed that the fog and the river were one and the same, the gaseous and liquid forms of a dark, putrid element. As Lucy plied the oars, she would often feel a piece of sewage gently nudging the blades.

Suddenly Silas reached over the side and plunged his hands into the water. A moment later there was a bump as something heavy struck the boat. Reaching back with one hand, he took a length of rope from between his feet, tied it round the object in the water and secured the other end to a ring on the stern. After this he occupied himself feeling about in the water again. Giving a grunt of satisfaction he sat up and, opening his big webbed hands, showed Lucy half a dozen gold sovereigns and a fob watch. Depositing these at his feet, he leaned over once more, staring intently at the face of the corpse that floated just below the surface. "That's him all right. Ten pounds for him," he observed.

This reward had been offered for the recovery of the body

of a certain Mr Tobias Jones who had disappeared a week before, but such corpses often carried valuables upon them, increasing their yield. A corpse was a fine thing indeed for Silas and Lucy to find.

For Silas was a river scavenger – a dredger as they were called. Dredgers took in anything. Crates or barrels that had fallen off a boat, wooden spars, baskets, bottles – and, of course, corpses. There was something about these water-borne vultures that made most men shun them. Yet the best, like Silas, could make a good living; for the dirty old river yielded up something every day.

Even now, Lucy was not sure why he had chosen her as his helper. "You're my kith and kin," he would say. Certainly the money he gave her had kept the little family out of the workhouse. Yet if Silas was so devoted to the family, there was one thing that puzzled her.

Though she called him uncle, she knew that in fact Silas was her cousin. "Your father and his father were brothers," her mother had told her. "There were sisters, and Silas had a brother too." When she had asked Silas about these other Doggets, he had only shrugged. "Don't you worry about them," he had said. "They've gone." Though whether this meant they were dead, or had left London, she could never discover. It occurred to her that perhaps the other Doggets did not care for Silas; but whatever the reason for their absence, Silas would often remind her: "I'm all you've got, young Lucy." She depended upon him entirely.

It had taken nearly a year, but her mother's asthma had taken its toll and she had been unable to work. Eventually, when the family was down to five shillings and Lucy had pleaded, she had weakly agreed: "Go to Silas, then."

If Lucy was out at work, it was little Horatio who helped keep the household going. At seven years old, he was still a pale, spindly little boy. His legs were thin as sticks, but in his quiet way he would not give up. Each day when she returned, she would find him waiting for her with the kettle filled and a meal laid out; and when she asked: "How is mother?" he would answer cheerfully: "Mother can breathe today." Or, more quietly: "Mother is tired," which meant that she could not.

Sometimes, when the weather was warm, and if their

mother was well, Horatio would go with Lucy to the river. She would not allow him to come in the boat in case she and Silas encountered a body, but he would sit in the sun by one of the riverside boathouses, or, if the water was low, wander on the mud flats, where there were always other children mudlarking. Though he could never keep up with them when they rushed to inspect a new find, he would often meet Lucy with a happy smile and show her some small treasure he had discovered in the grey old mud.

Every night, as she held him in her arms, he would promise: "One day I'll be strong. Then you shall rest at home and I'll go out to work for us all."

She would rock him gently and sing to him, always ending with his favourite, the song that the lavender-seller had taught her, singing it over and over, very softly, until he was asleep.

It was a pity that Silas did not like him. His heavy, angry eye would rest upon the boy and he would say: "He's sickly, like your mother."

"He grows stronger!" she would protest. Silas would shrug. "He'll never pull an oar."

Now, Lucy changed places with Silas, and he took the big oars, rowing with slow, heavy strokes towards the Tower of London while she sat in the stern, aware only of the corpse being drawn along below the surface just behind her.

"Your brother will die," Silas remarked suddenly. "You know that, don't you?"

"He will live!" she cried defiantly. "And pull a better oar than you."

For a time, Silas said nothing, but as they drew level with the little steeple of All Hallows church above the grim old Tower he gruffly declared: "Don't love him too much. He will die."

When Zachary Carpenter rose to speak nobody in the hushed hall in St Pancras would ever have guessed that he was convinced he was wasting his time. After all, he had spent half a lifetime agitating for reform and got nowhere. Nonetheless he addressed the crowd with his usual eloquence. His theme was a good one; he had perfected it in the last few years.

"Do you not *acknowledge*," he cried, "that this nation is being fed upon by bloodsuckers? What are the king, his Parliament and their many friends? They are eaters of taxes. They feed upon your flesh. I can give you proof positive of the rottenness of this kingdom. Do you want proof?"

The crowd in the hall said that they did.

"Go down to the Mall, then!" Carpenter cried. "Go to the Mall, look down to the end of it, and tell me what you see. I will tell you what you see: not just brick and mortar, not just stone, and tower, turret and pinnacle. You see a scandal, my friends, rising up to mock you. There is your proof." He was speaking, of course, of the building of Buckingham Palace.

Of all the many embarrassments which the Prince Regent, now king, had inflicted upon England, none – not his debts, not his roaming wife, not even his strange coronation – could begin to rival the ongoing scandal of Buckingham Palace. Originally an aristocrat's house bought by the royal family, George IV had decided to convert it to a new palace. His friend Nash, the architect, had been called in and Parliament, very unwillingly, had voted two hundred thousand pounds which had soon been spent. The radicals protested, Parliament protested, even the loyal Duke of Wellington exploded with rage. The king went blithely on. By now the expense was a staggering seven hundred thousand pounds.

To Carpenter Buckingham Palace was a safe bet. He only had to point out to his audience that such outrages would continue until there was reform, and his case was made. Yet was there any point? Nothing ever changed. Last year that staunchest of Tories the Duke of Wellington had become prime minister. True, the Iron Duke had somewhat modified the Corn Laws to help the poor, but not enough to do any damage to the landowners. True, also, the duke had repealed the Test Act so that Wesleyans and Dissenters like Carpenter were no longer debarred from public office. But Carpenter was not deceived by that. "Wellington's a general," he judged. "It's a tactical move to strengthen his position with the middle classes."

The present ministry showed every sign of wanting to impose the firm stamp of authority. The Home Secretary, Robert Peel, not satisfied with the old Bow Street Runners of the previous century, was even proposing to enforce law and order on the country with a uniformed police force under central authority – a frightening idea indeed. While the City of

London had already declared it would have no police force that was not subject to the Lord Mayor, decent people elsewhere were muttering: "The duke and Peel want to return us to the stern old days of Cromwell and the generals." As far as Carpenter could see, the cause of reform was further off than ever.

So as the crowd was leaving the hall Carpenter was greatly astonished to see, of all people, the bottle-green figure of Lord Bocton approaching him, not with a frown but a smile. Holding out his hand, that die-hard Tory remarked: "Mr Carpenter, I agree with every word you say!"

Carpenter looked at him with suspicion. Penny-pinching Lord Bocton might well agree about the absurd cost of Buckingham Palace, but surely not about anything else.

Seeing his surprise, Bocton coolly continued: "You and I, Mr Carpenter, may be closer than you think. Indeed" – and now he moved closer – "I have come here to ask for your help."

"My help?" What the devil was he up to?

"Yes. You see, Mr Carpenter, I am standing for Parliament." He smiled again. "I am standing for Reform."

As Lord Bocton watched Zachary Carpenter, he was pleased to see that he had judged human nature correctly. The proposals he put to the radical had been very carefully calculated. Bocton meant to get what he wanted.

The system of representation about which Carpenter complained was certainly hard to defend. Great commercial cities had no member of Parliament; many rural seats were under the effective patronage of great landowners; and last and most scandalous of all were the pocket boroughs – the rotten boroughs as they were often called – where a handful of electors had the right to return a member. Most of these were not independent men, but placemen who could be bought.

Some radicals even favoured a secret ballot.

"To me," Bocton confessed, "that seems a cowardly underhand sort of method which no honest man should support. But perhaps, Mr Carpenter, you can convince me otherwise."

But the real test came over the question of who was to vote. "Is it really your belief, Mr Carpenter," he asked, "that every man – the journeyman you have to dismiss for drunkenness, the apprentice, the beggar in the workhouse even – should have the same right to elect the country's governors as you?"

And just as he suspected, Carpenter hesitated. It was a question that had been haunting the reform movement for years. The purists believed that all men, no matter what their condition, should vote. Ten years ago, Carpenter would have agreed; but as he grew older, he had started having doubts. Were the twenty people he employed really ready for so much responsibility?

"Men who pay taxes should vote." Solid citizens. Men like him.

"Precisely," said Lord Bocton.

That women also might vote had never occurred to either of them.

"My title," Bocton reminded Carpenter, "as the heir to the Earl of St James, is only a courtesy title. My father sits in the House of Lords but I may sit in the Commons." It was a route that politically minded aristocrats often liked to follow. "At the next election I intend to stand for the St Pancras seat," he continued. "Though I am of course a Tory, I give you my word that I will vote for reform. I want you to support me."

"But why?" the bemused radical demanded. "Why should you want reform?"

The reason why Bocton, and a number of Tories like him, had suddenly swung round in favour of reform had nothing whatever to do with the merits of the case. It had to do with the Catholics in Ireland.

The previous year, in an unexpected by-election, a prominent Irish Catholic had been elected to the British Parliament. Under the existing rules, he could not take his seat. "But if we force the issue the Irish may revolt," Wellington regretfully concluded. "The king's government must be carried on." To his pragmatic soldier's mind it was a question of duty. And after considerable arm-twisting the Tory ministry had actually combined with the Whigs to pass a law giving Catholics the same rights as Dissenters. But it was a politically dangerous course.

By the spring of 1829, solid Tories in the shires found themselves agreeing with Wesleyan shopkeepers. "England's Protestant," they declared. "Why else did we throw out the Stuarts? The government and their placemen are selling us down the river. If they'll give way over Catholics, what will they give way over next?"

"Indeed," Bocton told Carpenter with disarming frankness, "some of us are even wondering if we'd be better off with men elected by sound fellows from the middle classes, than these placemen with no principles. I don't much like reform, but perhaps sensible reform is better than chaos."

The two men looked at each other. They had a mutual interest. They did a deal.

One thing puzzled Carpenter a little. Having come to an understanding with his former enemy, he ventured to ask: "So does this mean, my lord, that your father is pleased with you now?"

For a moment Bocton did not answer. Then he permitted himself to look pained. "I do not know," he replied; and after another brief pause: "Tell me, Mr Carpenter, do you suppose my father would agree with you about Buckingham Palace?"

"I suppose so."

"Yet he does not. He says the king should spend as much as he likes." It was perfectly true. Because the monarch was his friend, the pleasure-loving earl didn't give a damn how much he spent on the palace.

Carpenter hesitated. He was a little shocked, if not entirely surprised about Buckingham Palace. "He may not always be consistent," he allowed.

"I hope that is all," Lord Bocton said with filial sincerity. "The truth is, Mr Carpenter," he admitted, "that his family are worried about him. They have long been concerned that he may not be, nowadays, quite —" he hesitated a last time " – quite sound of mind." He gazed at Carpenter earnestly. "You observe him often. What do you think?"

"I think that he is well enough," Carpenter replied with a frown. For a lord, he would like to have added.

"Good. Good. I am so glad to hear you say so. If ever you should have any doubts Mr Carpenter, it would be a kindness, in confidence of course, to let me know."

Lucy would always remember the day they went to Lavender Hill.

It was pleasantly warm as they made their way down Tottenham Court Road. Lucy had a flask of water, and some food wrapped in a napkin and tied to a stick she carried over her shoulder. Every mile or so, they stopped for Horatio to rest and in this manner they slowly reached the Strand and crossed over Waterloo Bridge.

Years earlier, it would have been a more pleasant walk along the bank of the Thames, with timber yards along the riverside on their right and open market gardens on the left. But many of the timber yards were turning into little factories now, and the gardens disappearing under rows of houses for workmen and artisans. By the time they reached the old wall round the grounds of Lambeth Palace, the day was growing hot. From there they had another long stretch down to Vauxhall, where the old pleasure gardens were still open. A distillery and a vinegar factory on the riverbank in front of them, however, had destroyed the fashionable aspect of the palace.

As they came to Vauxhall, on the hot and dusty road, Lucy noticed that Horatio was beginning to limp.

The noonday bells had finished pealing only minutes before as Mary Penny came past Vauxhall. The pony trap had just begun to bowl up the long drag from there to Clapham when she noticed the two children, hand in hand, at the side of the road.

"Oh, do stop!" she cried to the coachman. "Let's help those children. They look so tired."

To her great relief, a moment later, Lucy found herself and Horatio perched beside the kind lady. When she heard where they were going she cried out: "Why, that's just where I live! It's an enchanting place."

"And you mean to walk all the way back to St Pancras?" she enquired, after Lucy had answered her question about their expedition. "That seems a very long way," she remarked, eyeing Horatio's legs. "Mind you have a good rest at Lavender Hill first."

Lavender Hill after noon. The August sun shone down with its great, broad heat. All around, thousands, perhaps tens of thousands of lavender bushes had turned the slopes into a vast, bluish haze, over which there hovered the continuous, droning buzz of the numberless bees. The scent was overpowering.

Lucy had been half afraid, as she unwrapped their food, that the bees might bother them. But it seemed they were far too busy attending to the lavender. To keep the sun off, she put the napkin over Horatio's head.

And there the two children stayed, for an hour, then another, too contented to move, drinking in the warm, sweet, hazy air as if it were a magical elixir that would give them new life. No wonder the lady had said the place was enchanted. As Lucy sat in the lavender, under the blue afternoon sky, it was as if she had entered a dream.

"Sing me the lavender song," Horatio murmured sleepily. Then, after she did, "You'll never leave me, will you Lucy?"

"Of course not. Never!"

He dozed for some time after that. "I think I'm getting stronger, Lucy," he said when he awoke.

"I know you are."

"Let us go home to mother, now," he said happily, "and take her some lavender."

When they reached the edge of the field, they were quite astonished to find the pony trap waiting for them in the lane.

"The lady gave orders that I'm to take you home," the coachman explained. "Up you get now."

On the way back, the two children sang to each other all the songs they could think of. And especially the lavender song, again and again.

It was the good fortune of reformers like Zachary Carpenter that 1830 turned out to be a cataclysmic year. In Europe, the political order which had been re-established after the mighty upheaval of the French Revolution and the career of Napoleon was by no means stable. The churning forces of democracy unleashed by the French were still active just beneath the surface; and now, in one country after another, eruptions began to occur.

In England, the boom market of recent years had suddenly halted; the harvest of the previous summer had been a disaster; and Wellington's revision of the Corn Laws had not been nearly enough to meet the case – the price of bread had soared. Then in June the king died, his extravagant London palace still unfinished, and was succeeded by his brother, a bluff sailor who became William IV. And in July, came the news from France. After over a decade under the putrid rule of the restored royal regime, the French had had enough. They revolted.

Within days, it was all over and a new liberal monarchy had been set up. As always, Europe looked to France. Signs quickly appeared of more revolts in Italy, Poland and Germany. It was at this point that, as if on cue, the riots in England began.

In fact the Swing Riots, which so terrified England that August, did not touch the cities. Named after one Captain Swing (the gentleman, it later turned out, never existed) they broke out in the south and east where the high prices of basic food that year had hit especially hard. The rioters were blaming everything: the government; agricultural machinery; the landowners. Week after week the trouble broke out, first in one place, then another, with great gangs roaming from village to village.

For Carpenter, however, the year brought growing excitement. In the early months he had been intrigued by a development in the north of England, where several attempts were now being made to bring together organizations of small masters and working men into unions who could, in effect, lobby for their interests with the political class. The purposes of these newly born unions was not clear yet. "But the fact that men are combining at all, in an orderly fashion, can only mean change in the long run," he judged.

But the real boost to his morale came with the election he fought with his new ally Bocton, that summer. It was a matter of convention that when a monarch died and a new king succeeded, an election should be held. So Wellington called one. It was not even a very significant affair since most of the seats were unopposed. But for Carpenter and Bocton the case was different. The St Pancras seat was contested. A well-spoken lawyer, supported by the gentlemen of the vestry, was standing and had assumed he would carry the day. The surprise candidacy of that gloomy Tory Bocton, standing on a Whig platform of reform, seemed an incongruous intrusion.

The tactic Bocton and Carpenter worked out was extremely simple. Whenever the candidate spoke at a public meeting, Bocton would do so too. First, he would agree with every word the Tory candidate had said. Then declare: "But unfortunately, it won't work." And then – he did this so well because it was what he truly believed – he would paint them a harrowing picture. Revolution in France, unions forming in the north, huge gangs of starving labourers sweeping over London Bridge at any moment; and finally he would cry: "Is that what we want? I have represented the aristocratic interest all my life, but I tell you it can't go on. Revolution or reform. The choice is yours."

Carpenter's speeches to the reformers and radicals who were his own constituency boiled down to an even simpler formula. "Bocton's a Tory but he's seen the light. He's our best bet. Vote for him."

Carpenter had seen less of the sporting earl in the last few years, but when they had met he had noticed, regretfully, that St James, now in his mid-eighties, did not quite look his old self. His clothes seemed loose. His hands looked reddish-blue and were swollen. In his eyes, there was a certain irritability.

It was in the middle of one of Bocton's speeches that Carpenter saw the earl. He was standing with his grandson George, a little removed from the crowd, watching intently. Bocton's voice carried clearly to where they were standing. He was speaking rather well. With a cheerful smile, therefore, Carpenter went over to greet the old man and casually remarked: "So my lord, have you come to support your son?"

For a moment, he thought the earl had not heard him, and was about to repeat the question when St James suddenly burst out: "Support Bocton? That traitor? I'm damned if I will!"

Young George, Carpenter noticed, said nothing.

"Damn you all," said the earl, presumably to Carpenter, and stumped off with George following.

When the St Pancras election was held Lord Bocton was returned with a large majority. In almost every one of the contested seats reformers had been easily returned. "I do believe," Zachary declared, "the tide is turning." Many of the Tories were wavering now.

The state of the country, however, remained volatile. The Swing Riots continued, breaking out in one locality after another, without warning, so that the government was unable to control them. The Whig opposition derided the government daily and told them the middle classes wouldn't stand for this much more. And as for the waverers: "They are starting," Bocton reported from Westminster, "to get jumpy."

The Duke of Wellington, however, held the line. The sole concession his government made to the people that year was to allow formerly unlicensed small producers to make cheap beer. This would compensate, he reasoned, for the higher cost of bread. But to the less battle-hardened waverers in the Commons, the riots in the countryside still seemed terrifying. Bocton was amused when, one day, a flustered member came up to him and, unaware he was the author, assured him: "It's reform, now, Bocton, or revolution."

At the start of November, apparently supposing that it was time to form a square, the gallant Duke of Wellington coolly informed the country that, as far as he was concerned, there would be no reform at any time in the foreseeable future. Even some of the Tories thought this was going a bit far. Two weeks later, in the House of Commons, the government was defeated on a vote; and Bocton, as a matter of courtesy, rode over to Carpenter's workshop to tell him: "The king is sending for the Whigs, Mr Carpenter. You have your reform."

For Lucy, the year brought pain. Even the warm weather that spring did not seem to improve Horatio's condition. Tired though he often was however, whenever he felt up to it during the hot days of summer, he would struggle down to the Thames and wander about on the mud while she and Silas worked. Once, as a treat, she took him from London Bridge, where they had been working, up to the Bank. From there, the previous summer, an enterprising man had started a new mode of transport: a huge carriage seating twenty passengers and pulled by three strong horses, it made the journey from the Bank to the western village of Paddington. An omnibus, the fellow called it, and the two children took it all the way back to the bottom of St Pancras. It cost them sixpence.

But still, she could tell, Horatio was getting weaker. In her heart she knew that in their dreary lodgings, and down by the damp, dirty old river, and in the terrible London fogs he would never be well. And though she could scarcely bear the thought of parting from him, she told Silas: "He must get away from here. He must."

Silas said nothing.

Several times, trying to think who could help them, she

begged the boatman: "Can't you think of any family, any friends who might help him? Have we no relations anywhere?" To which the answer always came, in his deep gruff voice: "No."

Once, on a bright October day, as Horatio was wandering on the mud flats by Blackfriars, she and Silas heard him give a cry, and then saw him waving to them. Silas, with a quiet curse, finally agreed to row back and Lucy, fearing something was amiss, ran over the damp mud to him so that her legs were speckled black by the time she reached him. He was not hurt though, but in his hand, which he now proudly held out, were no less than five golden sovereigns.

"Five sovereigns!" He smiled. "Are we rich, now?"

"Oh, yes!" cried Lucy.

"Does this mean you could stop working? At least for a little while?"

"We shall have a fine feast," she promised him instead.

For another hour Lucy and Silas plied the river that afternoon, and whenever Lucy looked back she could see the little boy standing there, smiling at her, a strange, unhealthy glow upon his pallid face and she thought, with a tremor of fear, how ethereal he looked, like a person from another world.

The most famous House of Commons vote in the history of modern England took place on 23 March 1831. The great Reform Bill, introduced by the new Whig ministry, had gone through amid stormy sessions. A hundred seats, after all, were to disappear. The entire political establishment was to be drastically rearranged. "I think, even now," Bocton had warned Carpenter, "that the vote will be close." He was right. The historic measure which ushered in modern democracy to England, passed by exactly one vote.

"Mine," Bocton claimed, with a wry smile.

Not that the thing was done yet. Within days, a wrecking amendment had got through and the Reform Bill lay in ruins. This last stand by the die-hards did not distress Carpenter much. "The Whigs will go to the country now," he judged. "And they will win." Sure enough, the Whig prime minister, Lord Grey promptly called an election. The Whigs were returned with a large majority. Reform was now inevitable.

One small event did puzzle both men. Carpenter had just gone for a meeting with Bocton at the start of the new election. Finding him in a large, crowded lobby beside Westminster Hall, the craftsman remarked with total innocence: "I see your son George is standing now, as well. For a pocket borough."

Bocton gazed at him in astonishment. "Is he?"

A moment later, walking stiffly by in the company of several other elderly peers, they caught sight of the old Earl of St James, whom Bocton now approached.

"Did you know, father, that George was standing for a rotten borough?"

"That's right, Bocton. I bought it for him."

"You did not tell me."

"Didn't I? Must have slipped my mind."

"I shall look forward to walking through the Aye lobby with him. Father and son," Bocton remarked drily.

The fact that a man was standing for a rotten borough, of course, was no indication that he supported the system. There were plenty of Whigs who had got into Parliament via rotten boroughs who were committed, as a matter of principle, to voting their own seats out of existence.

"Really?" The old earl shrugged. "I've no idea which way he'll vote."

For a moment Carpenter thought he had misheard. "He'll vote for reform like you and me, my lord," he coaxed the cross old man. "That's why you put him there."

"Oh." Did the old earl look a little vague, now? Had he lost the thread of what they were saying, or was this just another little game to annoy his son? He stared at Carpenter. "What sort of odds can one get on this election?" he suddenly demanded. "Who's making a book? Any idea?"

"No, my lord."

"I suppose I'd better go and find out." The earl paused. "I don't think," he remarked with a frown, "that I've been to the races for some time."

September fog, thick and brown, smothered the river. Had the boat been going round in circles? Were they opposite Blackfriars, or down by the Tower, or out in the reaches by Wapping? Used as she was by now to the river, she had no idea; and when, after an hour, she asked Silas, he only grunted.

How he expected to find anything in this brown miasma, she could not imagine; yet still, from time to time, he would give her an instruction: "Pull to port. Hold her steady." So that she could only wonder what he knew in the opaque, undivided firmament of water and fog, that other men did not.

As the boat drifted, Lucy's thoughts drifted also. For a time, after he had found the gold, Horatio had seemed to be better. At Christmas, he and Lucy had prepared a splendid feast for their mother, and he had even sung his family a carol he had learned. But in January he began to cough up phlegm, and in the first week of February he was so racked by a raging fever that at times Lucy wondered if his frail body could stand it. The infection that had taken over his lungs was as thick and evil as the London fog. For two months he had sat at home, his chest wrapped up in shawls. Sometimes his mother would try hot compresses to draw the infection, and he would thank her with tears of pain in his eyes. But only in May had the evil presence seemed to withdraw, for the time being at least, leaving him weak all through the warm months of summer; and now, with the chill and fog of September beginning again, she trembled to think of the sickness's awful return.

"Keep away from him, or you'll catch it," Silas would say.

"He must get away from this place," she repeated, though Silas gave her no encouragement.

She could see Silas well enough as he sat a few feet from her, and as he rested his chest thoughtfully on the oars it seemed to her that even he might be thinking of calling it a day. They seldom exchanged more than a few words but, sitting alone in the fog, Silas for some reason decided to be more companionable.

"You've got pluck. I'll give you that. Out here in this fog and you never complain."

"It's nothing," she said. And then, encouraged by this unusual turn of conversation she ventured: "How can you tell how to find things, Silas? Even in this?"

"I don't know, really," he confessed. "Always could."

"Were you on the river as a child?"

He nodded.

"And your father?"

"Waterman. Whole family on the river. Except my sister," he added thoughtfully. "She hated it."

Lucy's heart missed a beat. He had a sister. He did not seem to have noticed her surprise. He was gazing into the fog, his mind apparently elsewhere.

"She didn't stay then?" Lucy asked softly.

"Sarah? No. Married a coachman in Clapham," he mused. "They set up a shop there." And then, suddenly realizing that he had given away a piece of information he had never before divulged, he hastily added: "Dead now of course. Long since. Both of them. No children neither."

And she knew, she positively knew, that he was lying. "Oh," she said. "I'm sorry." But her mind was beginning to race.

By October 1831 Zachary Carpenter could truly feel for the first time in his life that all was right with the world. The September fogs had lifted; the weather was fine. Two weeks ago, as expected, the Whig Reform Bill had passed easily through the House of Commons. Lord Bocton and his son George had passed through the lobby together. So the measure has even brought unity to that family, he thought. Today the bill was going through the House of Lords. After that the king would sign it and the thing would be law.

Yet, for all the huge importance of the Reform Bill, another much smaller measure recently passed through Parliament had given him even greater delight. For in 1831, Parliament had calmly made the closed vestry of the parish of St Pancras illegal.

It therefore came as a great shock to Carpenter, late that evening, to receive a message from Bocton, which caused him to pull on his coat, permit himself two or three full-blooded oaths, and storm off towards the house by Regent's Park where the old Earl of St James now lived.

Never in all his life had Zachary Carpenter been more angry than he was now, as he faced the earl. St James was wearing, over his shirt and stockings, a gorgeous silken dressing gown which, Carpenter calculated irritably, could not possibly have cost less than fifty pounds. It was as if for the first time he had seen behind the sporting, reformist mask to the rich, capricious, selfish old soul who, all the time, had been lurking there behind it. He did not trouble to mince his words.

"What the devil were you doing, you old humbug?" he cried.

The House of Lords, by a narrow majority, had just thrown out the Reform Bill. And the Earl of St James had been one of the peers who voted against it.

Carpenter did not know what response he expected to this outburst, and he did not care. Knowing St James, he imagined it would be something sharp. He was surprised, therefore, when the old man seemed to hesitate. He frowned, looking a little confused. Then fumbling with the cuff of his silk dressing gown, as if he thought he had discovered a fly there, he mumbled. "They were going to take away George's seat."

"Of course they were! It's a rotten borough," Carpenter cried impatiently; but St James only frowned again, as if he had forgotten something.

"I couldn't let them take away George's seat," he said.

Carpenter was so blinded by the earl's behaviour that he failed to observe what should have been plain enough. The Earl of St James was not in full possession of his faculties. He was eighty-eight years old; and he was confused.

"You old fool!" shouted Carpenter. "You evil old aristocrat! You're the same as all the rest of them. Ordinary men are just a game to you. They're just something to bet on. Nothing ever touches you, does it? Tell me this, my so-called noble lord, who do you think you are? Who –" he was bellowing right into the old man's face now "– do you really think you are?" He turned on his heel and stormed out, slamming the door behind him. So that he never saw the Earl of St James staring after him in genuine puzzlement.

"Who am I?" he asked the empty room.

It was just after dawn at Southwark. Lucy knew she had no time to lose. The day after the fog, Horatio had started coughing. By the end of September the fever had returned and he seemed to be burning up before her eyes. She had fetched a doctor, using one of Horatio's sovereigns; but after a careful look at him the doctor had only shaken his head sadly and advised them to wrap damp towels round him to try at least to bring his fever down.

Would he be better off out of the city, in a more dry and airy place, Lucy had asked? Perhaps, the doctor had told her with a shrug. Then he had given her the sovereign back.

On 6 October, Horatio had coughed up blood. She could see the little boy was getting weaker. He'll never get through the winter like this, she thought.

Lavender Hill. In the chilly days of early October, the vision of that glorious blue haze haunted her. If she could only get him up there. And now she knew she had a cousin there, at Clapham. A cousin with a shop, up on the high ground to the south-west. Only the very worst of the pea-soupers made it out there. Within days she had formed a picture of her cousin: a warm, kindly, motherly sort. A person who would welcome the little boy in, and care for him and, perhaps, save his life. There could not, she supposed, be that many shops in the village of Clapham. A few enquiries and her cousin would surely be found. She had hoped to go out and search for the shop herself, but there had been no time and suddenly now, seeing the little boy coughing blood, she was overcome by a blind desire to get him out at once.

She had told no one. She knew Silas would not help her. She was not sure about her mother, but dared not take the chance. The day before, she had found a carter who agreed for a shilling to take them down to London Bridge at dawn. Leaving Horatio, wrapped up in a coat and scarf, by some river steps she went across to Southwark to get the boat.

"What will we do when we get to Lavender Hill?" he asked weakly. "I do not think I can walk about while you look for our cousin."

"But we can go to the house of the kind lady who took us in the pony trap," she reassured him. "We know where she lives."

"I should like that," he agreed.

The light was just lifting along the river when Lucy brought the boat to the steps and carried Horatio down into it. His teeth were chattering, but he did not complain. Minutes later, the boat was moving slowly upstream.

Another figure was also moving through the early light that morning. He was wearing a greatcoat and he had crammed an old three-cornered hat on his head so that, at first glance, it seemed as if he were some old watchman or lamplighter left over from the previous century. But under the greatcoat there was a brightly coloured silk dressing gown, and on his feet, instead of rough boots, a pair of highly polished court shoes. He was followed, nervously and at a distance, by a footman.

About the same time as Lucy and Horatio were passing under Westminster Bridge, the Earl of St James reached Seven Dials.

There were people about. Nearby, in Covent Garden market, business was already starting. From somewhere there came the smell of baking bread. Overhead, the sky was overcast with high, grey cloud, but the day felt as if it might get tolerably warm. When he got to the little monument of Seven Dials the earl paused for a moment, as though looking for someone. Then he made a little tour of the place, coming back to the railings round the monument. And there, still watched by the footman, he remained for a while until, by chance, he noticed a costermonger approaching with a barrow. The costermonger, who was a friendly fellow, and who soon figured that the old gentleman might not be quite right in the head, talked to him gently enough. Only one thing puzzled him. The old gentleman was talking in broad cockney.

"'Ave you seen me dad?"

"Who might that be, sir?"

"Harry Dogget, the costermonger. I'm lookin' for me dad."

"I should think, old fella, that your dad's been gone this many a year."

The Earl of St James frowned. "You never heard of Harry Dogget?"

The costermonger considered. The name, now he thought of it, was vaguely familiar. He thought he had heard of the Dogget family once, when he was a boy. But that was forty years ago.

A woman with a basket of oysters joined them now, sensing that there was some amusement to be had. "Who's he?" she asked.

"Looking for 'is dad," the costermonger said.

"Oh." She laughed. "What about your mum then, dear?"

"Nah." St James shook his head. "She won't do me no good."

"Why's that?"

"Needle and pin, that's why," he said sadly. Then, "I gotta find Sep," he went on.

"Sep? Who's that now? And why's that?"

"Should've been 'im up the chimney, not me," his lordship said.

"He's really gone in the 'ead, he has," the woman said.

"Where's Sep?" St James cried out with sudden urgency. "I gotta find Sep!"

Just then a carriage drew up a few yards away, out of which stepped Lord Bocton, accompanied by Mr Cornelius Silversleeves.

The journey had been very slow. The boat was heavy and Lucy was rowing against the current. By the time they passed under Vauxhall Bridge Horatio, having shivered continuously, had fallen strangely still. As they approached Chelsea, his head sank forward on to his chest and she could see beads of sweat on his pale brow. He had begun to make a rasping sound as he breathed.

The place for which she was heading lay just past the long reach beside Chelsea. At the end, a curious, rather ramshackle old wooden bridge crossed the river which, immediately afterwards, curved sharply left. A little way along this next, southward stretch, a stream came down to the river by the ancient village of Battersea, and from here it was only a short walk up to the slopes of Lavender Hill and the pleasant plateau of Clapham Common.

It was mid-morning when she pulled into the bank. The spot she selected was a little jetty just by the village church. It was an old church, people said, from the days when the Conqueror came.

Horatio was so limp when she tried to get him out of the boat that she had to carry him. "Look Horatio, we have arrived," she told him, but he hardly seemed to hear. With some difficulty she got him out on to the bank and wondered what she should do. Looking about, she noticed that in the little churchyard there was an old family tomb with a broad ledge round it, so picking him up, she carried him there and, sitting with her back to the tomb, rested his head against her chest and rocked him gently.

The churchyard was quiet. It seemed that few people came by the place at that hour of the morning. Some sparrows were chirping in the trees; river birds scudded along the bank now and then with shrill cries. For a few minutes the sun even broke through the film of grey cloud and she turned his face towards it, hoping its rays might revive him. Eventually his eyes opened and he gazed up at her, blankly.

"We're here," she said. "Look!" And she pointed to the slopes not far away. "You can see Lavender Hill."

It took him a little time, but he managed to smile.

"We'll just go up there," she promised, "and you'll feel better."

He nodded slowly. "I think," he said softly after a pause, " we should stay here a little longer."

"All right," she said.

He was silent for a time, though she could see he was staring up at Lavender Hill. Then his eyes took in the churchyard. "God lives in churches, doesn't He?"

"Of course He does."

Then he said, "Lavender Hill", and closed his eyes for a time before coughing. It was a deep, thick cough that she had never heard before as though his lungs were full of liquid. She held him gently and stroked his brow.

Very quietly, he said: "Lucy?"

"Yes?"

"Am I dying?"

"Of course not."

He tried to shake his head, but the effort was too great. "I think I am."

She felt his body shudder a little, before he gave a shallow sigh.

"If I could live," he said faintly, "I should like to live with you, at Lavender Hill." He was silent for a moment. "I am glad you brought me here," he murmured.

"Don't leave me," she begged. "You must fight!"

He did not answer. Then coughed again. "Lucy," he whispered finally.

"Yes, my love?"

"Sing me the lavender song."

So she did, very softly, cradling him in her arms as she sang.

"Lavender Blue, dilly dilly
Lavender Green,
When you are king, dilly dilly
I shall be queen."

He sighed, and smiled. "Again."

So again she sang the little song as though, by some magic, it could make him well. And yet again, keeping her voice as steady as she could, although she thought her heart would break. Whether it was the fifth or sixth time she could not afterwards remember, but it was just as she reached the words "When you are king, dilly dilly", that she felt his frail little body quiver, and then go limp, so that, though she went on singing to the end of the verse, she knew that he was gone.

"It is a most remarkable case," said Silversleeves. "A complete transference of personality. Notice the change of voice. He even seems to suppose he has another family."

"So is he mad?" Bocton asked.

"Oh, entirely."

"You can lock him up?"

"Certainly."

"When?"

"Now, if you like."

"That," Bocton replied, "would suit me admirably. It will even help the political process."

So great was the general public fury at the action of the Lords the night before that by mid-morning Sir Robert Peel's new police, and the mayor's police in the City, were preparing for riots. Within an hour of the vote in Westminster, members were saying that the king would be obliged to create more Whig peers to get reform through.

"The absence of my father," Bocton remarked drily, "will reduce that necessity by one."

At eleven-thirty in the morning a closed carriage entered the gates of the great hospital of Bedlam in Lambeth and from it the Earl of St James, looking frail and confused, was led into its splendid entrance hall.

* * *

He was not destined, however, to remain there very long.

It was the practice of the Bedlam, as long as you were a respectable person and purchased a ticket, to allow members of the general public to visit. Thanks to this liberal-minded policy, the curious could enter and observe all the persons whom either the criminal courts or Silversleeves and his friends had declared to be mad. Some, harmless enough, could be talked to. Several gentlemen believed they were Napoleon and would strike splendid, brooding attitudes. Others would laugh or gibber. Yet others were chained to beds and would sit there sullenly staring or perhaps might take their clothes off and perform acts of strange lewdness. It was really, most people agreed, quite amusing. One old man, half an hour after admission, said he was the Earl of St James.

It was not long after noon that Meredith arrived. Young George, as soon as he discovered what had happened to his grandfather, had gone to him for advice.

The Meredith Bank had prospered considerably in the years since the near-crash of 1825, and Meredith was tolerably rich now. The greying of his temples had lent his tall figure a look of patrician distinction. His advice to George had been quite bleak. "I think your father will almost certainly succeed, with Silversleeves's help, in getting your grandfather declared incapable. What we must do is get him out of Bedlam. You probably can't because Bocton will have warned them to expect you. But I might."

"And then?"

"I'll have to find somewhere to keep him in tolerable conditions. I dare say something can be done." He smiled. "I still owe him my bank, remember."

"But they'll come and demand him back."

"They'll have to find him first."

"But that's kidnap, Meredith!"

"That's right."

"You'll have to hide him somewhere straight away though," George pointed out.

"I can think of a place," Meredith said.

His approach to Bedlam was cunning. Sending a boy ahead to ask for Silversleeves, the boy ascertained that he had departed with Bocton for an hour or two. No sooner had this information been brought back than Meredith's carriage swept into the courtyard, and stalking into the building, he told the doormen to fetch Silversleeves and bring him to him immediately. Ignoring their assurances that he was not there, he strode down the hall demanding to see St James. The moment he found him, he took him firmly by the arm and led him back to the entrance.

"Where the devil is Silversleeves?" he repeated irritably. "I have orders to escort this patient to another place at once."

"But Mr Silversleeves and Lord Bocton said –" the head doorman began, only to be cut off instantly.

"You do not understand. I am the personal physician of His Majesty the King." Meredith gave the name of the distinguished doctor in question. "My instructions are from the king himself. You know, I suppose, that the earl is his personal friend?" He was not the grandson of dashing Captain Jack Meredith for nothing. The combination of his tall, commanding presence and this awesome list of names overcame them entirely.

"Tell Silversleeves," he called, as he led the old earl out, "to report to my house immediately."

Moments later, his carriage had rattled off, apparently towards Westminster. Once out of sight, it made a little detour and headed away in another direction entirely. And so it was that it was not little Horatio Dogget but the rich old Earl of St James who found himself, that day, in the sanctuary of kindly Mrs Penny's house on Clapham Common, by Lavender Hill.

"Damn!" said Lord Bocton, when he heard his father had escaped. "We should have chained him up."

The Great Reform Bill finally passed into law in the summer of 1832. Apart from giving members of Parliament to the new towns and abolishing the rotten boroughs, it gave the vote to a fair spread of the middle class. Women, regardless of their status, of course, still could not vote.

With her brother gone, and only her mother and herself to think about, Lucy had wondered for some months now whether she could afford to stop working for Silas. She had considered many prospects, including working in the little factory her mother had left. She had even wondered if she could get some assistance from the cousin she had learned about at Clapham. But after making three separate expeditions there in the spring, she had been unable to find any trace of her or her family.

The issue was resolved for her quite unexpectedly one summer day when, arriving as usual for work one morning, she was greatly surprised to find Silas standing by the mooring without his boat.

"Where's the boat?" she asked.

"Sold it," he replied. "In fact, I don't think I'll be needing you any more, young Lucy. I'm doing something else now." He led her back to an alley where a dirty old cart was standing. It contained nothing. "I'll be going round with that, collecting," he explained.

"But collecting what?"

"Rubbish," he said with satisfaction. "Dirt. People will pay you to take it away. Then you make a huge heap of dust in a yard somewhere – see? I got a yard near here. Then you sift through it and see what you can find."

"So it's like what you did on the river?"

"Yes. But there's more money in dust than in water. I've looked into it." He nodded. "You can come and help sift if you want, but I'll only pay you pence."

"I don't think so," she said.

"You and your mother'll be hard up."

"We'll manage."

"Maybe I'll help you," he said, then turned away.

For Eugene Penny the year brought one expense; but it was an expense which, fortunately, he could afford.

The stay of the old Earl of St James with the family had been, by far, the most trying three weeks of Penny's life. On some days the old man was lucid and demanded to go home. Eugene himself had been forced, physically, to restrain him, which he found embarrassing. At other times the earl was docile, but once or twice, in a confused state, he threatened Mary Penny with violence. It was a relief when Meredith finally came and removed him to a quiet place in the West Country.

From then on, Eugene had been so busy at the bank that he had hardly had time to think of anything else, until, one day, walking down Fleet Street, he had seen a stooped and sad-looking figure in scuffed shoes shuffling along towards St Bride's, and suddenly recognized with a pang of horror and of guilt that it was his godfather, Jeremy Fleming.

It was two years he realized since he had been to see him. Why had he not done so, when he had received such kindness at his hands? He had been busy. That was no excuse. And what in the world had happened to him?

Fleming's story was soon told. "It was Wellington's Beer Act, you see, in 1830," he explained. "You remember, when everyone was complaining about prices, he made a law that anyone could make and sell beer? Well, I had nothing to do with my life, Penny, so I set up a little brewery myself, up there," and he nodded northwards in the general direction of St Pancras. "And for a year, Penny, I made beer."

"I thought you were too cautious a man for such an undertaking," Eugene said.

"Very true. But I so admired the way that you had led your life, Penny, I said to myself: 'There, see what you might have done, Jeremy Fleming, but for your want of courage.' And I thought to myself: 'Everyone wants beer.' But they did not want mine. And then I lost caution and pressed on." He shook his head and smiled sadly. "Lost all I had, you see."

"I did not know! You never told me." And, Penny thought, I never asked. "How do you live?" he went on.

"My children are kind. They are good children. Better than I deserve, Penny. They give me what they can. I do not starve."

"Your house?"

"I live in a smaller place now. Nearby."

"You shall come to supper with us this very day," Penny cried. "You shall come to stay."

And from that time Mr Jeremy Fleming's rent was paid, and a new suit made for him at least once a year, and he came often to the house at Clapham where, at Mary's special request, he became an extra godfather to her children.

"You are good to him," she said sometimes with approval to her husband.

Eugene would only polish his spectacles, shake his head and say: "But very late, Mary. To my shame."

Yet all the same, as he took his walks with her on warm summer evenings, it seemed to him that most things had worked out for the best, up there by Lavender Hill.

Chapter 17

The Crystal Palace

1851

Everything had been carefully planned. By three o'clock precisely the whole family would gather at the big house up on Blackheath – for, as any of his four daughters or their husbands could tell you, it didn't do to be late for the Guv'nor. Besides, it was the dear old man's birthday. Unthinkable to be late for that.

But the August day was still young. Her husband had calculated that they could afford two hours and forty minutes of pleasure; so it was with some excitement that Harriet Penny and he approached the huge structure that flashed and glittered before them like some magical palace from a fairy tale.

Nothing like it had ever been seen before. Almost seventy feet high (even a great elm tree had been left growing inside) and four times the length of St Paul's, the monumental edifice stretched over six hundred yards along the southern edge of Hyde Park. And, most astonishing of all, it was almost entirely made of iron and of glass.

The gigantic hall of the Great Exhibition of 1851 – the Crystal Palace, as it was immediately called – was a triumph of British engineering. Designed exactly like a vast prefabricated greenhouse, its nine hundred square feet of glass, mass-produced in standard units, and thousands of cast-iron girders and pillars created nearly a million square feet of floor-space, yet had been built in only a few months. Light and airy, its hollow iron supports neatly doubling as drainpipes, the Crystal Palace represented everything that was modern and progressive. The only old-fashioned feature in the whole thing had been the importation – at the suggestion of the old Duke of Wellington – of a pair of sparrow-hawks to deal with the birds that had infested the galleries. The idea for this international exhibition and its great hall had come from the young Queen Victoria's clever German husband, Albert, who had both masterminded and seen the whole project through to completion. The royal couple were hugely proud of it.

And already it was declared to be a triumph. People from all over England had flocked to see it. French, Germans, Italians, travellers from America and even the Far East had come, not just in their thousands but their millions to see its wonders. Nor were these only people of the better sort. On most days, ordinary folk could come in for only a shilling.

Harriet had not been to the Great Exhibition before, although it had been open since May. Her three sisters had seen it, but she had waited until she could go with her husband. She took his arm contentedly. She had been lucky in Penny. Her older sisters, Charlotte and Esther, had been over thirty when they were married, both to ambitious, younger men. They seemed happy enough. And then there was her younger sister, Mary Anne. But Mary Anne, of course, was different.

Harriet had been twenty-three when she met Penny and though he was two years younger she had been attracted at once by the bespectacled young man with his cautious, quiet, determined manner. His father, the banker, had made handsome provision for all his children in several trusts, but young Penny had ambitions of his own, in insurance. If her elder sisters had been married for their fortunes, Penny had not needed Harriet's. It was just that it would never have occurred to him to marry a woman without a fortune, and she liked this about him too.

If the Crystal Palace itself was impressive, its contents, they soon discovered, were breathtaking. Every country of note in the entire world had a section. There was a stuffed elephant bearing a magnificent jewelled howdah from India; the fabulous Koh-i-noor diamond was on display, illumined by gaslight, too. From the United States came agricultural machinery including a cotton gin, Colonel Colt's revolvers and a missionary floating church that went up and down the River Delaware. From Russia's Tsar, magnificent sable furs; there was a Turkish pavilion, porcelain from China, all manner of useful goods from Canada and Australia, mineral specimens from South Africa. From France came a remarkable envelope-folding machine used by de la Rue and a fountain flowing delightfully with eau-de-Cologne. Berlin sent scientific instruments, lace-making machines. . . . But these were only a tiny handful of the wonders, artistic and manufactured, that continued acre after acre in the huge palace of glass.

Largest of all however, nearly half the space, was the exhibit of Britain herself. Carriages, engines, textile manufactures, the new electroplate system, clocks, furniture of the newly ornate style that would be known as Victorian, Wedgwood pottery; even, for the historically curious, a recreation by Mr Pugin, the brilliant architect and designer, of an entire medieval court – though when this was discovered to contain a popish crucifix amongst the decoration, it was felt to be un-English and rather disapproved of. Despite this one unfortunate lapse, the message of the exhibition could not be missed: Britain was prosperous, led all the world in manufacture, and was head of the greatest empire under the sun.

Apart from the loss of its American colonies seventy years before, the British Empire had never stopped expanding. Canada, the West Indies, great tracts of Africa, India, Australia, New Zealand were all under her sway, so that it was literally true that over the empire the sun never set. But this was no Oriental despotism. True, the British navy dominated the seas. True, also, some local resistance to the spread of her trade and enlightenment had been sharply put down. Yet Britain's military might on land was actually tiny. The more sophisticated dominions, for all practical purposes, were growing towards a form of self-governing affiliation; the rest of the empire remained what it had always been – a patchwork of colonies run by traders, settlers, some scattered garrisons and a few, usually well-intentioned administrators who believed in a Protestant God and in trade. For commerce was the key. It was not tribute, but raw materials – especially the all-important cotton – that flowed back to Britain where they were manufactured and re-exported world-wide. It was commerce, encouraged by invention, that was raising its people to affluence and bringing civilization to the most distant quarters of the globe.

For two and a half hours Harriet and her husband toured the exhibits arm in arm, and only when they finally emerged back into the sunny open spaces of Hyde Park did they glance up at the sky and then look at each other, with a mixture of amusement and trepidation.

"I wonder what's happened to Mary Anne?" said Penny.

Esther Silversleeves and her husband were early as they walked across London Bridge. Mr Arnold Silversleeves was a very respectable man. He was tall, taller even than his father who had presided over the Bedlam. His nose was large and long and he had never been known – though he was quite without malice – to see a joke. But he was already a partner in the firm of Grinder and Watson Engineers, where, apart from his undoubted competence, it was recognized that he had mathematical abilities that were close to genius. His affection for his wife and children was simple and straightforward; though if his life contained a real passion, then it was for cast iron. He had taken his wife to the Great Exhibition once, to show her the machines, but three times, before that, to watch the Crystal Palace being built and to explain to her the principles of its engineering.

He had a most curious way of walking. He would take ten or twenty paces at one speed, then stop for no obvious reason, then proceed, usually at a much brisker pace before quite suddenly changing to a slower speed or simply stopping again. Only his wife, through the long practice of obedience, could ever keep pace with him. It was in this manner, therefore, that they reached the southern end of the bridge and a few moments later entered the large shed-like building where their transport awaited them.

Arnold Silversleeves smiled. It was painted green, except for its brasswork, which was gleaming. Behind it were half a dozen chocolate-brown carriages. It hissed and it steamed contentedly and, occasionally let out a cheerful sort of snort. On the platform beside it, two uniformed guards in peaked caps looked as proud as if they were on guard at Buckingham Palace. The London and Greenwich Railway (the first London line, Terminus London Bridge, opened just as Queen Victoria's reign was about to begin) was so pleased with itself that the engines seemed positively to puff with pride.

As well they might: for if the age of Queen Victoria was one of huge progress, that was because it was the age of steam.

Though the first steam engine had been invented back in the days of George III, the introduction of steam power had been surprisingly gradual. The steam-powered engines of the textile works up in the north, primitive steamships, a locomotive for hauling coal in collieries, even a steam press for printing *The Times* of London had all been used since the days of the Regent; but then, with Queen Victoria, came the first passenger railway.

The expansion was amazing. Within a dozen years, there were railway companies competing with each other all round London. Euston Station had opened up the Midlands and the north. Three years ago, Silversleeves and his company had been busily engaged in building a great terminal across the river from Westminster, called Waterloo, from which trains ran to the south and west. If the stagecoaches could carry ten passengers along the turnpikes at, perhaps, eight miles an hour, the carriages rattling along the iron tracks behind a steam locomotive could take a hundred people at forty miles an hour. It was the steam trains that had brought people from far and wide to the Great Exhibition in the Crystal Palace. Without the new trains, most of those from the provinces could not possibly have come.

It had also had one other unforeseen effect. Railway trains required a railway timetable; but, despite the gradual adoption of Greenwich Mean Time on the world's oceans, the provincial cities of England were still keeping their own local time just as they had in the days of the Stuarts. Trying to publish train schedules in such conditions was confusing; and so recently the provinces had begun for the first time to adopt a standard London time. The steam locomotive was bringing order to the kingdom.

Silversleeves loved order; order meant happiness, and progress. "And it's all a question of engineering," he assured his wife. Even the poorest folk could benefit. The new railway lines from Euston had destroyed whole areas of rookeries and slum tenements. "These people will all be rehoused," he would explain. He even predicted that one day many of the ordinary folk, those who did not have to live directly beside their work, would be housed in clean new settlements outside the city and be shipped in each day by rail. Still more remarkable were his ideas for the centre of London. With the ever increasing population, the horse-drawn omnibuses – hundreds of them nowadays – and the thousands of cabs and carriages, the whole area from Westminster to the centre of the old city was jammed solid for several hours every weekday. It could take an hour to get from Whitehall to the Bank of England. "But we can solve that by running trains underground," he assured her. "From one end of London to the other in minutes. It's just a question of air vents and disposing of smoke so that people don't suffocate."

He had a solution for the smelly old Thames, too. "A new sewer system!" he told his family enthusiastically. Only last year, on his own initiative, he had made a personal study of the problem, diving down, notebook in hand, into the endless labyrinth of drains, sewers, subterranean water channels and cesspits under old London every spare day he could find. He had memorized the entire system, hundreds of miles of it, and flushed with this remarkable if malodorous achievement, had designed an entirely new system which he had pressed upon the city authorities, so far without success.

The railway from London Bridge ran on high brick arches that cut, like a giant aqueduct across the roofline of the huddled dwellings of Southwark towards the green spaces of Greenwich and Blackheath, affording an excellent view across the area as one went along. Esther had just listened to her husband's plans for the sewers once again, and thought what a visionary he was when, glancing out of the window, she chanced to catch sight of a spectacle which made her interrupt:

"Oh, Arnold! Do look! I think it's Mary Anne!"

For several seconds after the Earl of St James had unrolled the designs on Captain Jonas Barnikel's dining-room table, the worthy mariner did not speak. Young Meredith, who was representing his father, watched with interest. Then, Barnikel stroked his great red beard and delivered his opinion: "It's the most beautiful thing I ever saw in my life," he said gruffly.

"You can beat the Americans in this," St James declared. "I'm betting on it."

The designs were for a sailing ship. Though steamships were steadily claiming a share of the traffic of the seas, the overwhelming majority of the world's trade, in the year of the Great Exhibition, was still carried by sail. And of all the sailing ships, the swiftest, the more elegant and romantic was that greyhound of the seas, the clipper. The lovely lines of the designs before them suggested that this vessel might be the fastest clipper ever built.

It was the Americans who had changed everything when, only two years ago, their famously swift cotton clippers had been allowed to enter the English tea trade. Leaving London with a variety of cargoes, the ships would catch the north-east trade winds down the Atlantic, round the southern tip of Africa, and let the great roaring forties blow them to the Far East to unload their cargo. Then, in high summer, they would arrive at the Chinese ports of Shanghai or Foochow, anchor amongst the junks and sampans, and await the first batches of tea-leaves of the year's new crop. As soon as they had it, then what a commotion there would be as the ships were towed out, all flags flying, the other ships firing salutes, for the great race home. Back they would come on the south-east trade winds; lookouts would spot the first ships from the Kent coast; crowds would race down past the Tower to the London docks. And in the last two years the American clippers had come in so far ahead of the English vessels that it was humiliating.

Competition was the spur. London's mariners were not going to accept defeat. Already they were busy commissioning new vessels designed to be swifter than anything seen before. Two to three hundred feet long, sleek and sturdy as the old Norse ships that were their ancestors, but carrying a forest of sails on their three tall masts – some, with thirty-four sails, would carry thirty thousand square feet of canvas and more – the new class of clippers would be able to sail a thousand miles, fully laden, in three days and complete the entire voyage from China in a hundred or less. They were being built, mostly, in Scotland. And this new ship before Barnikel now was to replace his present one in as little as a year.

"So, what shall we call her?" the earl asked him. "You choose."

"We'll call her the *Charlotte*," Barnikel replied.

For God knows, he thought, he owed all this to her. True, he was a first-rate sailor, and as good a skipper as he knew, but it was marrying the Guv'nor's eldest daughter that had allowed him to buy a share in a vessel and make himself a captain in the first place. The pleasant Georgian house and garden they occupied in Camberwell Grove, on the genteel wooded slopes that gazed down on the crowded docklands of Deptford, had been purchased with Charlotte's money. I'd still be living down there, like as not, if it wasn't for her, he would acknowledge to himself; and though he was making a fortune of his own now, it gave him pleasure to think that when, in a short while, he took his plain wife and their children across the high ground to Blackheath, he'd be able to tell his old father-in-law: "The earl and I have just named the clipper after Charlotte."

Jonas Barnikel would own a fifth of the *Charlotte*; Meredith the banker, who had sent his son today, another fifth; and the sporting Earl of St James who, like his grandfather, would bet on anything, three fifths. The earl's statement that he would bet on the new clipper was not made lightly either. Huge wagers were placed every year on which of the tea vessels would be first home. The earl therefore intended to have his money three ways: he would own most of the vessel, also the cargo and bet on the race as well. It was five years since he and Jonas Barnikel had made each other's acquaintance and they trusted each other entirely.

Young Meredith however was an unknown quantity. Only recently out of school at Eton, he had asked his father to let him have a year of travel before he joined a regiment; and since Barnikel was shortly to make a voyage to India, the banker had asked the sea captain if he would take the boy along. Today was their first meeting and already Barnikel had allowed himself a few shrewd glances to size the young man up. He was a handsome fellow, a good height, auburn hair, and with an athletic figure. A fine young gentleman certainly: but what was he really made of?

"We are going over to dine with my father-in-law shortly," he remarked. "Perhaps Mr Meredith would like to come with us?" It was an impromptu suggestion.

"Well," the young man hesitated and glanced enquiringly at the earl, who nodded. "I shall be delighted. If you're sure your father-in-law wouldn't mind."

"Oh, the Guv'nor won't mind," Barnikel predicted confidently. "He always likes to see new faces."

Half an hour later, the Barnikel family, together with Meredith, were sitting comfortably in their carriage as it rolled up the old Kent road towards Blackheath when the young man drew their attention to an object in the sky. Charlotte Barnikel put her hand to her mouth and exclaimed: "Oh, Jonas! It must be Mary Anne!"

There was only the lightest breeze, just enough to make the journey. Mary Anne's fingers tightened on the side of the basket which lurched and creaked terrifyingly as the grounds of Vauxhall Gardens started to shrink in the most alarming way below them.

"Are you frightened?" her husband called in her ear.

"Of course not!" she lied. The operator gave them both an encouraging grin while, with a silent rush, the huge blue and gold balloon above them rose, imperious and unstoppable, into the clear sky towards the sun. For several moments more, Mary Anne experienced the awful terror of those who for the first time realize that they are soaring into the air with nothing underneath them. For horrible seconds she wondered if the bottom would fall out of the basket. Her hands were gripping the edge so hard now that they were probably permanently clamped, and she could only smile wildly as Bull shouted gamely: "Well, this is what you wanted!"

The scene below at Vauxhall Gardens was unattractive. It was not just the mean streets which had spread all round the gardens with the evident intention of choking them; but the iron tracks of the railway line raised on a brick viaduct had now arrived, its rattle, clank and smoke shattering the former quiet of the place. Vauxhall Gardens was in its last, dingy decline. But it was still the place from which balloons took off, and they frequently did. People used them to sketch panoramas of the city, to make daring journeys, with many bets being laid, to places as far off as Germany. Recently one man had insisted on going up not in the usual basket but sitting on his horse. Quite a crowd had turned out to see that. And today, watched by only a few curious locals, Mary Anne and Bull were making a short ascent which would terminate, if all went well and the wind did not change, somewhere on Blackheath.

The idea had been a whim. When, months ago, her husband had asked her what she would like for her birthday, which fell just after the Guv'nor's, and she had said, "a balloon ride", it had been a joke. In fact, she had quite forgotten about it. So she had been completely taken aback three days ago when he had casually announced: "I've arranged your balloon ride, Mary Anne. Wind and weather permitting, we'll go up on Saturday morning." He had grinned. "If you still want to, that is." She could hardly draw back after that.

Her sisters had been horrified. "How can you be so foolhardy? What will people say?" they cried. And finally: "Why do you always have to be different, Mary Anne?" She had made them promise not to tell their husbands. Nobody had told the Guv'nor.

It was also very expensive. But then, as they all knew, that was not a problem, for Edward Bull was going to inherit the brewery. Mary Anne was the only one of the Guv'nor's daughters who had married young. But Mary Anne was pretty. Slim, vivacious, with wonderful hazel eyes and a flash of white in her curly brown hair that made her look rather distinguished, she had an elegance and style that her sisters lacked. Edward Bull, just a year older than she, had no need of her money, though the Bulls certainly liked their wives to be women of fortune.

In seconds the balloon was at three hundred, then four, five hundred feet and climbing. But then the balloonist checked the pace, the balloon seemed to hover, and to her surprise Mary Anne felt her panic begin to leave her. She managed to stare outwards, across London, and was greeted with a magnificent view. The pace of building in the last twenty years had not slackened. On the south side of the river, the houses swept in an almost unbroken swathe from Southwark up to Clapham; to the north, the villages of Chelsea and Kensington were completely swallowed up in an endless succession of mock-Georgian terraces, and further off, above the City, the woods of Islington were going under even now. Yet these growths, seen from above, only seemed like so many stubby fingers from London's grimy palm, stretching into the green country all around. Lavender Hill was still a scented field; most of Fulham was still orchard and market garden; above Regent's Park, it was open country up to Hampstead.

Only as she glanced down again did she notice something a little alarming. Their journey was based on their belief that the breeze was coming from the west, and so should take them clean across south London towards Blackheath on whose huge open spaces they could easily land. But now she realized something else. "Edward! We're drifting north!"

Indeed they were: their path, directly over the Thames at this point, had already carried them to Lambeth Palace. If nothing changed, they would finish up looking for a place to land in the fields past Islington. "And then we'll be really late for the Guv'nor," Bull groaned.

But Mary Anne, as she overcame her fright, suddenly felt a surge of wild exhilaration. "I don't care!" she cried. "This is wonderful!"

Her husband laughed. Their route, he saw, was going to provide them with another unexpected benefit. "Look," he remarked. "We're going directly over Parliament."

The Houses of Parliament, in 1851, were an interesting sight. Seventeen years before, some functionary had decided that the records of the ancient English Exchequer should be tidied. Finding in the musty cellars, neatly bundled, the tens of thousands of little wooden tally sticks – stock, foil and counterfoil – some of which had lain there since the days of Thomas Becket, he decided they should be burnt. His minions obeyed his order with such thoroughness that they set the whole Palace of Westminster on fire and by the next morning it was all, except for sturdy old Westminster Hall, burned to the ground.

In its place, built round the old Norman hall, a palace now arose that was really much finer than the one that had burned down. Designed in honey-brown stone by the Londoner Barry, its gorgeous medieval-style interior by Pugin, the Gothic-inspired building was a fitting companion for the Abbey beside it. Already the House of Commons was completed; work was proceeding on the House of Lords; and at the eastern end, nearest Westminster Bridge, Mary Anne could look down upon the empty socket of the great clock tower which would soar above the rest.

From Westminster, they floated north over Whitehall up to Charing Cross. A few years ago, the area where the Royal Mews had stood had been completely cleared to form a huge piazza called Trafalgar Square, with a tall column supporting a statue of Nelson in the middle; and they were just about to sail over the great naval hero when the wind obligingly shifted and began to carry them back to the river again.

"We may be in time for the Guv'nor after all," Bull grinned. Sure enough, a few minutes later, they were floating lazily across Bankside and over Southwark in the general direction of Blackheath. "Look," he nudged her, "there's the brewery."

In fact, it would have been hard to miss it. For if the essential process of brewing had remained the same since the days when Dame Barnikel had stirred her huge brews beside the George Inn, the scale of the operations had altered out of all recognition. The Bull Brewery was huge. The high, square chimney stack of its boilerhouse towered over the roofs of Southwark. The main building, where the malt was mashed, the beer brewed, cooled and fermented, was seven storeys high, its big square windows staring out with a solid self-satisfaction from the high redbrick walls. Then there were sheds containing the brewery's massive old vats, large yards where the casks awaiting shipment were stacked in pyramids, and enormous stables for the mighty horses that pulled the drays. And over it all presided the family of Bull – cheerful, prosperous, rock solid.

They sailed over Camberwell and continued eastwards until the balloonist was able to set them down, with only a modest bump, on the wide expanse of Blackheath, not half a mile from the Guv'nor's mansion.

It was a happy and excited Mrs Bull who stood again on firm ground, kissed her husband and remarked triumphantly: "I do believe we'll be the first there!"

It was mid-afternoon when one other person set out. Leaving the district of Whitechapel in London's East End, this solitary traveller passed down on the eastern side of St Katharine's Dock, where the tea clippers came, and continued along the waterfront down to Wapping. From there, this lone East Ender meant to cross the river and proceed towards Blackheath. For the Guv'nor was to receive an unexpected visitor that day.

If the West End had been expanding for two centuries, the development of the East End was more recent. Immediately east of the Tower, the docklands began with St Katharine's and extended downstream through Wapping and Limehouse to where the great loop of the river formed the promontory of the Isle of Dogs, in which the huge basins of the West India Docks had been created. Above this line of docklands, starting out from Aldgate in the city wall, there had always been a succession of modest settlements: first Spitalfields, where the Huguenot silk-weavers had congregated, then Whitechapel, Stepney, Bow and Poplar above the Isle of Dogs. But nowadays all these were joined into an untidy, sprawling suburb of docks, little factories, sweatshops and mean streets, each with their own particular community. It was to the East End that poor immigrants usually came. And few were poorer than the latest influx of folk who had crowded into the streets of Whitechapel.

There had always been an Irish population in London. Since the previous century, a thriving community, mostly of labourers, had existed in the rookeries of St Giles's parish just west of Holborn. But this was nothing compared to the great wave of immigration that had taken place in the last seven years.

It was caused, as much of the western world now knew, by the failure of a single crop. For years a large and relatively dense population, living on some of the best agricultural land in Europe – much of it in the hands of absentee English landlords – had subsisted on that highly nutritious American native vegetable, the potato. When, for several years running, that crop had failed, the people of Ireland had faced a sudden and terrible crisis. And when the efforts at relief had proved utterly inadequate, the option had been stark: emigrate or die. So had begun that huge and terrible exodus from which Ireland would not recover for over a century and a half. To America, to Australia and to the English ports they had fled. To London also, of course. The largest group in London had settled in Whitechapel where there was work in the nearby docks. It was from a street of mostly Irish folk that the Guv'nor's unexpected visitor had started out.

The Guv'nor liked to have all his family round him. With his white beard and his rosy old face he looked like a benevolent monarch. He favoured, even in summer, a heavy frock coat, a white silk cravat fastened with a pearl pin, and his shoes were so polished that they twinkled. His Georgian mansion at Blackheath was beautifully run by a butler with a staff of eight. It was said that he had an income of ten thousand pounds a year. Quiet, kindly to all his sons-in-law, the Guv'nor asked nothing except that people should be punctual. If they were not, he could grow cold. But only a fool would fail to show proper affection and respect to a father-in-law with ten thousand a year.

It was five o'clock, after the grandchildren had all been taken away by their nannies, when the butler announced dinner. The Guv'nor, being old-fashioned, liked to dine at an early hour. Apart from this, however, everything was done in the modern manner. The gentlemen led the ladies into the big dining room. The Guv'nor said grace and then they all sat down, a lady between each pair of gentlemen. The huge table, covered with a white damask cloth, was a noble sight. In the centre stood a huge, ornate silver épergne – an object like a massive, five-branched candlestick except that it supported not candles but bowls of fruit. At each place, in the new and fashionable manner, there was an array of different wine glasses and of knives and forks – silver for the fish and fruit – all heavy and elaborate. The first course was a simple choice of soups: *julienne* of vegetable and vermicelli. This was followed by fish: boiled salmon, turbot, sole *à la Normande*, trout, mullet, and lobster rissoles. The salmon had been brought by train from Scotland.

Because he was a widower, the Guv'nor would usually ask one of his daughters to take the other end of the table and act as hostess, and today his choice had fallen upon Mary Anne. Accordingly, she found herself with an elderly gentleman neighbour on her right, and on her left, the boy whom Barnikel had brought along. During the soup she had made polite conversation with the old gentleman. Only when the fish arrived did she turn her attention to young Meredith.

Mary Anne was in a cheerful mood: in fact, she did not think she could remember a happier day in her life. She was still flushed from the triumph of her balloon ride. There had been no question of keeping it from the Guv'nor once it was done, and indeed she and Edward had met the old man, walking across the heath with his ebony stick to inspect the balloon as soon as it came down. He had been much surprised to see them, and had given Edward a rather old-fashioned look, but by the time the rest of the family arrived, he seemed to find the whole affair amusing. "I'm glad to see you all," he announced, "and very glad that Edward and Mary Anne could 'drop in'." As Harriet had remarked to her with a sigh: "He always did let you get away with anything, Mary Anne."

She and Edward had been too busy with her sisters and their children to take much notice of the young man before the meal, though she had vaguely thought that he seemed a nice-looking boy. She realized that she must be only two or three years older than he, but there was a world separating a young wife and a youth, however handsome, who was only just out of school. She noticed that he had accepted a second glass of white wine with the fish and she wondered how, without offending him, she could suggest that he should not drink too much.

She found him very agreeable: his manner was quiet and polite, but not at all shy. His eyes, she noticed, had a delightful way of lighting up as he spoke of the things that interested him. There was, she realized quickly, a fineness about him lacking in the others at the table. She asked him about his time at school and what things he liked to do. He admitted to being a good athlete and extolled the joys of hunting. But under a little closer questioning he confessed modestly but without embarrassment that he liked poetry and was fascinated by history.

"Should you not consider going to university then, Mr Meredith?" she asked.

"My father is against it," he replied. "And to tell the truth, I have such a desire to go out and see the world. . . ." he smiled.

"Mr Meredith!" She laughed. "I think you must be much more adventurous than the rest of us."

"Oh no, Mrs Bull." He came back at once. "I don't think so at all. For you see, *I* have never been up in a balloon!"

Her laugh of delight caused several heads to turn in her direction. She blushed a little, because she had not meant to laugh so loudly. But then she saw that it had attracted someone else's attention. From under his bushy old eyebrows, the Guv'nor was staring towards her too.

When the Guv'nor gave a dinner party, he liked to be entertained. He thought it was his due. New guests would often suppose that the rich old man had scarcely noticed them, yet in fact he might have scrutinized them quietly for an hour or more before suddenly asking them to give an account of themselves. His deep voice came gruffly down the length of the table. "I hear Mr Meredith is to travel for a year. Perhaps he would like to tell us something of his plans?" The entire table fell silent and everyone looked at Meredith.

"Oh, father!" Mary Anne protested. "Poor Mr Meredith, to be quizzed like this. He'll wish he hadn't come here."

But the young man was taking it in very good part. "Not at all," he replied. "An unexpected guest, Mrs Bull, enjoying such lavish hospitality, should expect to sing for his supper. The truth is, sir," he addressed the Guv'nor, "my plans are somewhat imperfect. My first desire, however, is to travel round India for several months." He paused, uncertain whether more was expected. The Guv'nor seemed to digest the information.

"Capital, Mr Meredith!" Silversleeves evidently thought he should say something to encourage the young man. "You will surely see opportunities in India for the development of a vast railway system. Perhaps greater than any on earth. The trade of India, large though it is, could be incomparably greater with better transport and engineering – wouldn't you say, Jonas?" he turned to Barnikel.

"Indian tea, hemp, cheap cottons," said the captain.

"I shall certainly hope to see all that," said Meredith.

"So you're going to look for railways?" the Guv'nor demanded.

"No, sir," Meredith smiled. "I'm not sure I'm going to look for anything so specific." And again he paused. But if the Guv'nor's sons-in-law had felt that he deserved a little help before, that help evidently had come to an end. From halfway down the table, there now came a gentle cough.

Despite the fact that their two families were linked through the bank, the younger generation of Pennys had never been warm towards their contemporaries in the Meredith clan. There was something just a little too aristocratic, too carefree about the Merediths that offended the cautious Calvinist and Scots nature of the Penny children. They did not mix. And listening to this young scion of the Meredith line now, the insurance man felt a twinge of irritation.

"One does not just gad about for months, halfway round the globe, without some definite object, surely," he suggested, with more than a trace of disapproval in his voice. "Or are you travelling for pleasure?" he acidly enquired.

Mary Anne glanced at Meredith, saw him flush at the implied insult, and glared at her brother-in-law. She glanced over at Edward, but got no response.

"I have a project in mind," Meredith replied evenly. "There is much to learn about India. Its civilization is so old and so varied. I thought I might spend a few months studying the Hindu religion and its gods." And he nodded to Penny politely.

There were circles in England where this statement might have been well received. Some of the administrators of the East India Company were deeply knowledgeable. A recent renaissance of the study of Indian culture in the subcontinent itself had actually been led by English scholars rather than Indian. But the Guv'nor's family at Blackheath was not such a circle. Even the Guv'nor seemed to be at a loss for words.

"How would you do this?" Mary Anne gently asked, hardly certain what she thought.

"I suppose that I should go to their temples and seek instruction from the priests," he replied seriously. "Perhaps," he added, "I should live amongst them for a while. It would be interesting to come to know them really well, I should think."

The company looked at him in appalled silence.

"But Mr Meredith," Esther Silversleeves said at last, "these people are heathens!" Esther was the most religious of the family. "Surely you cannot wish . . ." her voice trailed off.

"The heathen temples in India contain carvings that no God-fearing man would care to see," Captain Barnikel said quietly.

"Savages," said the Guv'nor. "Bad idea."

Edward Bull laughed. He did not laugh with any particular malice, he just laughed because Meredith's plan struck him as so obviously absurd. "Well I can tell you one thing," he informed them all with a chuckle. "There are no Hindus in the brewery. I can promise you that." He turned to Meredith. "I'm sure your father must know people out in India who could guide you, Mr Meredith. Pity to waste your time. And your father's money."

It was not exactly said with rudeness, but the tone was

clearly patronizing and dismissive. Mary Anne found herself suddenly flushing with annoyance. Heathen gods or not, why should her family treat this nice young man like this? "I think Mr Meredith's desire to know more about the peoples of our empire is most commendable," she cried. "It sounds fascinating." And though she had hardly been thinking about what she was saying, it suddenly occurred to her now that she knew nothing about the Hindu temples of India and the gods who dwelt therein. It really did sound interesting, and rather exciting. She looked at Meredith with appreciation.

Her husband was having none of it. "Don't be silly, my dear. It's all nonsense!"

She gave him a look. Edward might have given her a balloon ride, but he'd better not think he could start dismissing her, too. She glanced at young Meredith, to see how he was taking this treatment. He had bowed his head slightly, but she could see that he had done so out of politeness: he did not want to argue with them; he was a guest in their house. Not only that, she suddenly realized: a guest who was much better bred and far more intelligent than they were. He couldn't care less what Edward thinks, or any of the rest of us, she thought. And he's absolutely right. We're all – she hated to use the word, but it was inescapable – we're all so vulgar. Even her good and kindly husband, with his hard blue eyes, his broad, fair face and manly ways: even Edward, though no fool, was made of coarse cloth compared to this young man. She had married the Bull Brewery, with all its virtues, strengths, and limitations. And that was that.

"Ah!" cried Charlotte gratefully. "Here comes the meat."

There were two ways to cross the River Thames at Wapping. The first was to take a wherry. With the numerous bridges now spanning the river upstream, the traditional occupation of the watermen in the City and the West End was rapidly disappearing; but down in the docks, apart from the many commercial activities which occupied them, watermen could still be hired to ferry a passenger across. So long, of course, as the passenger could pay. For those who could not, however, at Wapping there was another way to cross.

The Guv'nor's uninvited guest descended slowly. At the

ground level, the circular building with its big Georgian windows looked like a handsome though rather dingy classical mausoleum. As one descended from the light and airy entrance, the great circular pit grew sombre, then dark. Gas lights appeared in the walls, but their little flames only served to make the surrounding shadows deeper. Down at the bottom in the dismal, gaslit gloom, a pair of arched entrances appeared side by side, behind which two dank, forlorn roadways receded.

This was the Thames Tunnel. It had been designed, and its construction supervised by Brunel and his son – two of the greatest engineers England had ever known, although the father had actually come from France. Technically it was a masterpiece, boring through the deep, prehistoric Thames mud for a quarter of a mile, linking Wapping to Rotherhithe on the southern bank. Commercially though, it had been a failure. The carriageways leading down to the tunnel had never been built. Only the staircases for pedestrians were in use and it was a brave, or poor, person who ventured through it now, at risk of being robbed or assaulted by the vagabonds and footpads who lurked down there. But then the Guv'nor's visitor had no money at all.

It was only by chance that she was approaching him – chance and a newspaper article. Few people in the Whitechapel street where she lived could read; but one man could, and it was he, one day, who had pointed out the Guv'nor's name to her. "Lord Shaftsbury's *Society for Improving the Condition of the Labouring Classes*," he read out, "has received a most handsome donation from a gentleman residing at Blackheath." There followed the Guv'nor's name and address. "He must be a kindly old gentleman," he remarked.

She was not quite sure who the Guv'nor was and she wondered if she should write to him. "I would write it out for you," her friend offered. "I'll pay for it too." With the newly organized penny Post, even a poor person in Whitechapel could afford to send a letter. But after thinking about it for a week she had finally decided to go to see this kindly gentleman in person. The walk from Whitechapel to Blackheath, via the tunnel, was only about six miles. "Perhaps if he sees me he'll help me," she told her friend. "Worst he can do is say no."

Lucy Dogget was pregnant.

* * *

Is there any smell in the world better than a joint of roast beef as it is being carved, piping hot, on the sideboard? Crispy brown outside, then a layer of rich fat, then the meat, rosy, a little bloody at the centre; the carving knife slips through it as though it were soft as butter, as the juice runs off. Not unless, perhaps, it is the spring chickens, the mutton cutlets *à la jardinière*, the veal in rice, the duck *à la Rouennaise*, or the ham and peas.

The Guv'nor's dinner party had resumed its jovial progress. Claret – an excellent one – was served with the meat. With the arrival of this course, Mary Anne had politely turned to renew her conversation with the old gentleman on her right. Glancing down the table towards the Guv'nor she could see that everyone had chosen to forget the embarrassing foolishness of young Meredith. The Guv'nor himself was describing the rhododendrons he was importing from India to improve his garden. Silversleeves was explaining to an old lady how smoke might be extracted from an underground railway. Captain Barnikel was describing the beautiful lines of his new tea clipper. Penny was wondering aloud what use the Crystal Palace might be put to after the Great Exhibition was over and his wife was explaining that the queen herself had made one of her many visits to the exhibition only the very day before she had been there herself. Without quite meaning to, Mary Anne also stole a glance at Meredith.

In less than a year, she thought, whatever he does in India, he will have joined a regiment: he'll be in uniform. It was not difficult to imagine him in a scarlet tunic. He would look very handsome. She wondered if he would grow a moustache. He was clean-shaven now, but as she mentally added the moustache to his face she unconsciously gave a tiny gasp. It would be auburn chestnut, like his hair, quite long, rather silky. The women will be all of a flutter and no mistake, she thought; and hardly realizing what she was doing she gazed into the middle distance until a gentle cough from the old gentleman on her right made her aware, with a little start, that she had completely forgotten him.

For the final course, even the Guv'nor relaxed his somewhat puritan rule a little, and more than six dishes were allowed. But then the final course, at a Victorian dinner, consisted of two distinct kinds of dish. For those who were either still hungry, or did not have a sweet tooth, there were savoury dishes: quails, a mayonnaise of chicken, turkey, heavily larded, or green peas *à la française*. These could be 'removed' – in other words, the palate cleansed – with a soufflé or an ice. But for those who liked a sweeter ending, there was a magnificent choice: a *compote* of cherries, Charlotte Russe, Neapolitan cakes, Madeira wine jelly, strawberries, pastries. More claret or a sweet wine was offered here.

People round the table seemed to be talking in little groups now. After some minutes of making dutiful conversation with the old gentleman, Mary Anne was glad to be able to turn to young Meredith again. Feeling rather conspiratorial she ventured to ask him: "Tell me about the Hindu gods. Are they really so dreadful?"

"The religious books of the Hindus are as old as the Bible, perhaps even older," he assured her. "They're written in Sanskrit, you know – which has a common root with our own language." His enthusiasm was infectious, and he talked so well of Vishnu and Krishna that she begged him to tell her more and he described the fabulous palaces of the maharajas, their elephants, their tiger hunts; he conjured up visions of steaming jungles and of floating mountains. It occurred to her that this aristocratic young adventurer, her junior by only a few years, would soon be far more worldly, far wiser, far more experienced and more interesting than she would ever have the chance to be. "I wish," she said softly, hardly thinking of the implication of her words, "that I could come with you."

Then she noticed that Edward was watching her, intently. He understood certain things very clearly. One of these was the brewery. He understood that his beer must be sound and that his word as to its quality must be sacred. He understood how to be a hale and hearty fellow and a good sportsman, because this was good for his business in this sporting age. He understood efficiency and simple accounting, and the fact that his assets, being ancient, were worth many times their value as shown on his balance sheet. In short, he was that most solid thing in all the world – a good brewer.

He understood, too, that the population of London was rapidly growing, that thanks to the empire, all classes, except the very lowest, were becoming more affluent, that the Bull

Brewery was producing more beer every year and that if this went on the dear old brewery with its cheerful brick buildings and its thick, malty smell was going to make him a very rich man indeed.

He also understood that his wife and young Meredith were paying too much attention to each other. It did not really matter: he knew perfectly well that Mary Anne would not be seeing Meredith again. He would make sure she didn't. But it annoyed him all the same. He felt like putting this tiresome boy in his place.

His opportunity soon came. The Pennys, still talking enthusiastically about the Great Exhibition, had just remarked on the splendid French and German sections, when Silversleeves joined in.

"The French, being more southern and Celtic," he pointed out, "are wonderfully artistic; but the machinery in the German section – that was the really impressive thing. But then of course," he added, "the Germans are like us, aren't they? Good, practical people. The Romans of the modern age." He glanced down the table. "It's practical people who build empires, Mr Meredith. You'd do better to study the Germans than the Hindu gods."

It was a view that had become rather popular in England recently. After all, people said, the Anglo-Saxons were a Germanic race; Protestantism had started in Germany, too. The royal family was German; the queen's husband who had inspired the Great Exhibition was very German. Industrious, self-reliant, northern Germanic folk, not too artistic but highly practical: this was how the Victorians had decided to see themselves. The fact that racially they were just as much Celtic, Danish, Flemish, French and much more besides had somehow been forgotten.

Edward saw his chance. "Yet there is a difference between our empire and that of the Romans," he genially pointed out. "And Mr Meredith might like to consider this also. Our empire is not one of conquest. There's hardly any compulsion at all. The Romans needed armies. We don't. What we offer all these backward countries is simply the benefit of free trade. Free trade brings them prosperity and civilization. One day, I dare say, when free trade has made the whole world peaceful and civilized, there won't be any need for armies at all." He smiled blandly at Meredith.

"But Edward," Mary Anne objected, "we have a huge army in India."

"No we don't," he replied.

"Actually, Mrs Bull," Meredith politely intervened, "your husband is quite right. The vast majority of troops are Indian regiments, raised locally and paid for by the Indians. Almost a police force, you might say," he added with a wry smile.

"I am glad you agree," Bull took him up. "And please notice, Mary Anne, another phrase Mr Meredith has just used: 'Paid for by Indians.' The British army, on the other hand, is paid for by the British taxpayer, out of his hard-earned income. If Mr Meredith becomes a serving officer, his purpose in life will be to protect our trade. And since" – he was going to put the younger man firmly in his place now – "I shall have to pay for Mr Meredith and his men, I think the cost of them should be as low as possible. Unless," he added drily, "Mr Meredith feels I don't pay enough in taxes."

It was, of course, insulting. Mary Anne blushed with embarrassment. Yet, as Bull knew very well, he was on firm ground. Few people would have disagreed. True, there were a few with a broader vision of England's role. At a City dinner recently Edward had found himself next to Disraeli, a tiresome politician, he thought, with his head full of foolish dreams of imperial grandeur. But Disraeli was an exception. Most men in Parliament were far more inclined to go along with solid Whigs like Mr Gladstone, who espoused free trade, sound money, minimum government expenditure and low taxes. Even a rich fellow like Bull was only paying income tax at the rate of 3 per cent. And that, he felt, was quite enough.

"I do not seek to raise taxes," Meredith said quietly.

"Surely," Esther reminded her brother-in-law, "the religion of the peoples of the empire is important? We sent out missionaries . . ." she trailed off, hopefully.

"Certainly Esther," he replied firmly. "But in practice, I promise you, religion follows trade."

It was too much. First Edward insulted Meredith, now he was being smug. Mary Anne was beginning to feel furious with all of them. They were so ignorant, yet so sure of themselves. "But what, Edward," she asked with mock innocence, "if the Hindus and the other people of the empire do not want our religion? They may prefer to keep their own gods, Esther, don't you think?" It was outrageous, of course. She meant it to be. Esther looked shocked. Penny was shaking his head sorrowfully. She heard Harriet murmur: "Mary Anne, you are incorrigible." But if she wanted to annoy Edward, she seemed to have failed.

"It is a question of time." He corrected her like a schoolchild. "As the less civilized peoples of the world come into increasing contact with us, they will see that our ways are better. They will accept our religion, very simply, because it is right. From the Ten Commandments to the Gospels. The moral and religious law." Here he gave Meredith a steely blue stare. "I hope Mr Meredith will agree with me, Mary Anne, even if you do not." He turned to the Guv'nor. "Am I right, Guv'nor?" he asked.

"Absolutely," the Guv'nor replied. "Morals, Mr Meredith. That's the key."

Now the butler appeared with decanters of Madeira and port, which he placed in front of the Guv'nor. This was a signal for the ladies to retire to the drawing room at once, while the men, in true eighteenth-century fashion, sat alone over port. Accordingly, Mary Anne rose as a signal to the other women, and some of the gentlemen politely escorted them to the door. It was there, pausing and smiling for a second, that Mary Anne gave Meredith her hand, as though to say goodbye – a gesture of no special significance, except for one tiny thing which made him blush. She was entering the drawing room, however, before her sister Charlotte caught her arm and whispered to her.

"You squeezed his hand!"

"What do you mean?"

"I saw. Oh, Mary Anne! How could you?"

"You could not possibly see."

"I could tell."

"Really, Charlotte? You must be an expert, then. Whose hand have *you* been squeezing?"

Charlotte knew better than to argue with Mary Anne. You never won. So she contented herself with murmuring, rather fiercely: "Well, you'll never see him again, make no mistake."

* * *

The Guv'nor's house was very large. Set well back with a handsome circular driveway, its more than a dozen windows stared out towards Blackheath with a dull reserve that told you clearly that the square, brown brick mansion to which they belonged could only be the property of a very rich man.

Uncertainly Lucy made her way to the door, her feet crunching on the gravel. Nervously she pulled the handle of the doorbell chain, and heard a bell sound somewhere within – wondering, just as she did so whether she should have gone round instead to the tradesmen's entrance. There was a long pause and then at last the door opened to reveal, to her terror, a butler. Stumbling with her words, she asked if this was the Guv'nor's house, learned that it was and then gave her name and asked if he would see her. After giving her a somewhat baffled and then a quizzical look, the butler himself seemed a little uncertain what to do. Was she expected, he enquired. Oh no, she told him. Did the Guv'nor know her? She believed so, was all that she could say. Deciding finally that he could not, on this basis, let her in, the butler, not unkindly, asked her to wait outside while he went to make enquiries.

To Lucy's surprise, he returned some minutes later and conducted her into the hall, past closed doors, behind which she could hear conversation, and down the stairs into a bare little parlour in the basement. There he politely left her alone, closing the door and, rather less politely, locking it after him. It was about twenty minutes she supposed before at last she heard the key turn in the door, saw the door open, and a moment later found herself face to face with the Guv'nor, who was staring at her, cautiously. She realised that he probably did not recognize her, but there was no mistaking him.

"Hello, Silas," she said.

It was hard to believe that this rosy-cheeked old man, with his neatly trimmed beard, his beautifully tailored frock coat, and twinkling shoes – even the nails on his strong old hands, she noticed, were manicured – was really Silas. The transformation was astounding.

"I thought maybe you'd died," he said slowly.

"I'm alive."

He continued to gaze at her, thoughtfully. "I looked for you once. Couldn't find you."

She stared at him. It might be true. "I looked for you," she said. "Couldn't find you either." But then, that had been a long time ago.

She had seen Silas only once more, after that day when he had given up the boat. It had been a year later when, one grey morning, he had come trudging into their lodgings and told her gruffly: "You come with me today, Lucy. Got something for you." She had not wanted to go, but her mother had begged her, and so, reluctantly, she had accompanied him to the smelly little cart he drove, and they had gone off. Their route had taken them down into Southwark and across into Bermondsey until at last they had turned into a large yard, enclosed by a high, ramshackle old wooden fence, and she had found herself gazing at a most remarkable sight.

Silas Dogget's dust heap was already almost thirty feet high, and it was evidently still growing. Fresh cartloads of material were constantly arriving – if fresh was the appropriate word. For there was nothing fresh about the contents of those carts. Dirt, rubbish, muck of every kind, the scrapings, leavings and refuse of the metropolis piled up in a single, putrid, stinking mountain. But most remarkable of all was the activity taking place on it. A swarm of ragged people was climbing it, burrowing into it, getting lost inside it for all Lucy could tell. Some dug with trowels, others used sieves, others scraped with their bare hands – all under the gimlet eye of a foreman who inspected every one of these human ants before they were allowed out through the gate at the end of the day, to make sure they took nothing with them. And what did they find? It was astonishing, she soon learned, as Silas took her round: bits of iron, knives, forks, copper kettles, pans, quantities of wood, old clothes, coins galore, even jewellery. Each of these items, and many others, was carefully placed in bins or subsidiary heaps where Dogget himself would assess their value and how to dispose of them. "This pile," he said with satisfaction, "will make my fortune."

And she – this was the generous offer he now made – could help pick it over with the others. Not only that: the pickers, being casual labour, were paid only pence a day, but Silas would pay her a weekly wage of thirty shillings. "Your being family," he had explained. "Maybe one day I might find you something even better," he suggested. "I told you," he reminded her, "that I'd help you."

But as she had gazed at the filthy heap, and at the grim slovenly form of the former dredger, Lucy's heart had sunk. She had pulled bodies from the river with him; poor little Horatio had dug in the Thames mud for coins, just as these poor, ragged folk were climbing up his precious mountain of dirt and slime. She had done all this before: the memories were too painful. She had refused him.

He had not said much. He had driven her home. When they got there he turned to her. "You'll never get a better offer. This is your last chance."

"I'm sorry."

"Obstinate like your father."

"Maybe."

"You can go to hell then," he had said, and without so much as giving her a shilling, he had flicked the reins and driven his cart away.

That had been the last she saw of him. Five years later, when her mother died, she had half expected him, in his uncanny way, to appear. But he had not. A month later, wondering what had become of him and his heap, she had gone down to Southwark and found the yard. But the heap had vanished and so had Silas. Nor did anyone there seem to know where he was.

She had moved soon after that. She had found employment with a button-maker in Soho and took lodgings with a family in St Giles's parish to be nearer her work. There she had stayed for the next ten years. It turned out that she had a talent for matching colours. Show her any piece of material and she could mix the dyes to reproduce that colour exactly. She could make buttons to go with anything. But the big vats of dye, which were in an upstairs room with little air, made a pungent smell; and at last their sharp fumes seemed to be affecting her breathing. Afraid that she would get asthma like her mother, she had given it up.

It was at about this time that she met her friend. He was a cousin of some Irish people she knew in St Giles, but he lived in Whitechapel. It was he who had found her work in a shop run by friends of his, in his own neighbourhood; it was because of him that she had moved, it was he who, in those years, gave her friendship and even affection. There was no one else, really, to do that now. He could read and write, quite well, too, which had allowed him to get a job as a clerk in a big shipping yard nearby.

And gradually, that kindness and friendship had turned into something more, until at last, some months ago, finding themselves alone, the inevitable had happened. And then again, several times more.

"I'm sorry for coming when you're busy," Lucy now remarked. "Sounds as if you've got company."

"Company?" He was still watching her cautiously. For just a second she thought he looked awkward, but then it passed. "Nothing much," he shrugged. "Just a few friends."

"Oh," she said. "That's nice." Lucy did not know he had a family. Even twenty years ago, when he already had four daughters, Silas had never seen fit to mention the fact. If he had felt any interest in Lucy's father or in her, that interest did not extend to allowing them even to imagine they had any claim on his own children. He had taken care never to let Lucy discover any of her other relations who might have given away his secret.

"And this house," Lucy gestured around. "This is all yours?"

"Maybe."

"You must be rich."

"Some people think I am. I get by."

It was, of course, a lie. By the time Lucy's mother had died, Silas had already finished with the Bermondsey heap. But he had built three more in west London. Soon after that, he found he could do even better by building heaps and then selling them to others to exploit. The hugest heaps he had sold for tens of thousands of pounds. Waste, then as subsequently, was big business. By the time he retired, Silas had sold ten heaps, and was a very rich man indeed.

"So why are you here?" he said.

She explained very straightforwardly that she was going to have a baby. Why had she let it happen? There had been two men before now who had wanted to marry her. But though she had liked at least one of them, she had resisted. For they were both as poor as she: simple labourers like her father. A single accident and they could be crippled, or gone. And what then? Destitution: the same sort of life, for her children, that she and Horatio had known. She did not want that, and no better alternative had offered. So why had she allowed it to happen with her friend? Perhaps because she loved him. Perhaps because he was a clerk with a little education, the sort of man she might have hoped for. Perhaps because time was passing – she was over thirty now. And perhaps, too, because he had shown her affection.

"Your husband. What's he do?"

She explained she had no husband.

"You mean you've a man who won't marry you?"

"He's married, Silas," she said.

Then Silas, forgetting for a moment that he was the respectable old Guv'nor now, made a grimace of disgust and spat. "You were always a fool. So what do you want?"

"Help," she said simply, and waited.

Silas Dogget considered. It was ten years since he moved to Blackheath, though he'd had quite a decent house down in Lambeth before that. To most people he was a rich and respectable old man. Some knew he had made his money in dust heaps, but not many. Once he had started building and selling them, he had managed to make his participation almost invisible. As for his dark years as a dredger – not a soul in Blackheath knew, nor did he intend that they should.

Of his daughters, only Charlotte could really remember the dingy lodgings in Southwark when he came home stinking from the boat. Sometimes, alone, she would shudder at the memory before pushing it from her mind. The middle girls, by the age of ten, were attending a little private school for young ladies; Mary Anne had been taught by a governess. They had still been in Lambeth when Charlotte reached a marriageable age and Silas had not really done much to bring her out into the local society because he wasn't quite sure how to do it. But none of the girls could be said to have suffered from their lowly background. Few men trouble themselves unduly about the origins of a rich young woman's fortune. Even with their plain looks, the eldest three Dogget girls had all found good husbands; and pretty Mary Anne had had her pick. During a twenty-year period, therefore, not only had Silas moved from rags to riches, but his entire family had evolved from the squalor of the backstreets to a middle-class respectability and a protected affluence that, in the case of the Pennys and the Bulls, might even lead to the higher reaches of society. Such transformations had always been known; but nowadays, in the vast, ever-expanding commercial world of the British Empire, they were becoming quite commonplace.

Having risen so far, the Guv'nor had no intention of being dragged down by the embarrassment of Lucy. He wished he had never troubled himself with her. At the time, she had seemed useful and he had been helping his kith and kin. But now he could see it had been a mistake. What should he do with her, though? He supposed if he gave her a small amount each month, on condition she stayed away from his family and kept her mouth shut, she would probably go quietly enough. But one thing he could not tolerate.

"Let's hope the child dies," he said. "But if not, you must give it up. We'll find an orphanage or something." To have a poor and unwanted relation was one thing; but to have a fallen woman polluting what was now the respectable Dogget family name was another. He would not have it, not even if she threatened to expose him.

"But I wanted help to bring the baby up," she told him.

"It must go. Have you no shame?"

"No, Silas," she said sadly. "I haven't much now." And then – she had not meant to but she could not help herself: "Oh, Silas, won't you take pity on me? Let me have the child. Can't you see? It's all I'll ever have." She had lost Horatio when she was a child and never had anyone since. "It is hard for a woman to live all her life and have no one to love," she cried softly.

Silas watched her impassively. She was an even bigger fool than he had thought. Walking over to a table in one corner where there was pen and ink, he wrote down a name and address on a piece of paper. "This is my lawyer," he said, giving it to her. "Go to see him when you're ready to get rid of the child. He'll be told what to do. That's the help you'll get from me."

Then he turned round, went out and locked the door behind him. Several minutes passed before the butler reappeared, took her out by the tradesmen's entrance, gave her two shillings to get herself home, and sent her on her way.

The butler did not forget his orders that on no account was she ever to be admitted to the house again.

Chapter 18

The Cutty Sark

1889

On the stage below, the colourful chorus of gondoliers was working its way, faster and faster, towards a brilliant crescendo. The audience – men in evening coats and white ties, women with frizzed hair and silk taffeta bustle dresses – were enjoying every moment. Nancy and her mother had taken a private box. While her mother sat behind, Nancy was leaning forward excitedly, her hand holding a fan, rested upon the parapet.

His hand was only an inch away from hers. She pretended not to notice. But she wondered: was it coming closer? Would they touch?

There were three levels of entertainment in late Victorian London. At the apex was the opera at Covent Garden. For the poor, there was the music hall, that wonderful mixture of song, dance and burlesque – the precursor to vaudeville – that was now spreading into theatres in even the meanest suburbs. But between these two in the last decade a new spectacle had appeared. The operettas of Gilbert and Sullivan were full of easy tunes, and charming comedy; yet Sullivan's music was often worthy of opera and Gilbert's lyrics, for verbal brilliance and satire, had no equal. *The Pirates of Penzance, The Mikado* – every year a new production had taken London, and soon would take New York, by storm. This was the year of *The Gondoliers*. Queen Victoria had loved it.

It could not be said that there was anything very remarkable about Miss Nancy Dogget of Boston, Mass. Her complexion, certainly, was good. Her golden hair was parted in the middle and modestly drawn back in a way that was perhaps a little childish for her twenty-one years. But her china-blue eyes were truly remarkable. As for the man who was sharing the evening so attentively at her side, he seemed everything that a man could be. Warm, charming, educated; he had a fine house and a lovely old estate in Kent. At thirty he was old enough to be a man of the world, but young enough for the girls back home to envy her. And then of course, as her mother had announced when she had first discovered him: "My dear, he's an earl!"

Not that family grandeur could be anything new to a girl from Boston. In the words of the rhyme:

> This is good old Boston
> Home of the bean and the cod:
> Where Lowells talk only to Cabots
> And Cabots talk only to God.

The old Boston families – Cabots, Hubbards, Gorhams, Lorings – not only knew exactly whom their ancestors had married but also, with a grim satisfaction, what the family had thought of them at the time. The Doggets were as old as most. They had come over with Harvard. It was rumoured they had even embarked on the *Mayflower*, "then jumped ship", a few unkind friends would remember. Their trust funds went down into the bedrock. And if from time to time, one of the family was born with webbed fingers, it caused no great concern: not even their greatest admirers claimed that the old East Coast families were renowned for their beauty.

Mr Gorham Dogget was a true Bostonian. He had been to Harvard; he spoke out of the side of his mouth; he had married a girl from a rich old New York family. But he was also adventurous. Investing in the railroads that had opened up the great Midwestern plains, he had trebled his already solid fortune. In recent years he had also been spending time in London. Though the United States was expanding mightily, the City of London with its vast imperial trade was still the financial capital of the world. American bankers like Morgan and Peabody spent most of their careers there and raised the money for huge projects like the American railroads. His visits to London in this connection had given Gorham Dogget several ideas for further projects.

Like other Americans made richer than ever before by the new industrial age, Gorham Dogget had also discovered the pleasures of Europe. Like English aristocrats in the previous century, they made the Grand Tour: and what better place to base oneself than London? The Doggets had already spent a month in France and another in Italy, where Nancy had made many sketches and acquired a smattering of those languages. Some fine paintings had also been bought. This was now the third time that mother and daughter had stayed, enjoying London's social life, while Mr Dogget returned briefly to Boston. But it was not only paintings and culture that could be acquired in Europe.

"Do you think St James would be a good husband?" Nancy had asked her mother. She had learned already that even their wives often referred to aristocrats by their titles in this way. "That would make me a countess."

"You should think of the man, not his title," her mother reminded her.

"But you do not object that he is a lord," Nancy gently remarked, and saw her mother blush.

"I think he is a good man," Mrs Dogget replied, "and I'm sure your father will like him."

"He hasn't made any declaration yet," Nancy said a little sadly. "He may not be interested anyway."

But as the finale of *The Gondoliers* had just reached its climax, the Earl of St James allowed his hand to brush against hers very lightly.

She would have been surprised to see him an hour later.

The first-floor parlour in the house by Regent's Park was used by the present earl as a library and office. Unlike his forebears, he had an intellectual and artistic turn of mind. His books were well chosen; he even had a small picture collection. Sitting at a French bureau, he was gazing rather sadly at the figure opposite him.

"Well, old girl," he sighed. "I suppose I shall have to marry Miss Dogget." He looked up and his eye caught a delicate little picture of the Thames he had bought recently. "The only person who can save me is Barnikel." He smiled ruefully. "Don't you think that's funny?" But it was always difficult to guess what Muriel thought.

The previous earl had married twice. From the first marriage, only Lady Muriel survived; from the second, the present earl who was fifteen years younger. Yet looking at the slim, handsome peer and his half-sister, it was hard to believe they were even related. Lady Muriel de Quette was so fat she could scarcely squeeze into the big leather armchair in the library. She seldom spoke. She did not ride or walk or read. But she ate continuously. At present she was consuming a large box of chocolates.

"Mind you, she's a nice little thing." The earl shook his head and sighed again. "We'd still have been all right, you know, if it hadn't been for grandfather."

Lady Muriel pushed another chocolate into her mouth.

When cautious, conservative Lord Bocton finally got his hands on his father's money soon after the Great Reform Act, he had put most of the family fortune into agricultural land, but even the vast extravagance of his son George, the present earl's father, would not have destroyed the family's wealth if it had not been for the railway. When Mr Gorham Dogget invested in the railroads that opened up the American midwest, he sealed the doom of many English gentlemen. The huge quantities of cheap grain that came from the American plains caused grain prices to tumble and with them the value of much agricultural land. When the present earl inherited, he had been forced to sell twenty thousand acres, at poor prices, to pay off his father's debts. The big London house, and the old Bocton manor remained, but there was little income. Soon one, perhaps both of these would have to go. If Lord St James was going to find an heiress, therefore, he knew he had better do it soon. Not that he was setting out to deceive anyone about his financial condition. He was not a fraud. But a lord who was still clinging on to a fine London house and an ancestral estate looked a lot more eligible, and dignified, than a lord – even an earl – who had neither.

Getting up and reaching into his waistcoat pocket for his keys, Lord St James moved over to a closet door, which he unlocked. Inside the closet was a small safe which he carefully opened, drawing out several leather boxes. While his sister watched impassively, he brought these over to the bureau and laid them out, lovingly lifting the lids to reveal the sparkling contents. "We've still got these, old girl," he said.

The St James family jewels were extremely fine. The ruby necklace in particular was noteworthy and it was widely known that whoever became the Countess of St James would get to wear it. For the earl, however, they were also a lifeline. Though he liked women and had enjoyed two long affairs, he liked his freedom and only felt compelled to marry from a sense of family duty. Without an heir, the earldom of St James would become extinct. Yet if he failed in his quest, the sale of Bocton and the jewellery would still, he calculated, provide him with enough income to live as the private cultivated gentleman which, in truth, he would rather have been. "I'd always look after you, old girl, of course," he would promise Lady Muriel on these occasions. There was no chance, he knew, of her getting married.

Having completed his inspection, he locked the jewels up in the safe and turned to his sister again. "It's curious, isn't it?" he remarked. "If Nancy Dogget were English, she probably wouldn't be an heiress at all." Though Gorham Dogget had a son as well as a daughter, he had always made it clear they would share his fortune equally; but among the old families of England such an arrangement remained almost unknown. Great estates went to the eldest son; married daughters often got nothing, unmarried daughters were usually supported during their lifetime by family trusts or expected to live at home. Lady Muriel herself had only what her half-brother chose to give her. "So," the earl came back to his theme, "I'll have to keep her warm until the new year, and then – it'll depend on Barnikel."

The reason the earl was not hurrying his courtship of Nancy lay some ten thousand miles away on the high seas: and her name was the *Charlotte Rose*.

The tea run of the sailing ships from China was over. It was the opening of the Suez Canal twenty years ago, and the consequent short cut to the Far East through the Mediterranean, that had finished it. The steamships with their huge cargoes, plodding along regardless of wind, could beat the sailing vessels on that route now. But the glorious days of the clippers were not yet past, for they now carried wool from Australia. The finest fleece, loaded at Sydney in Australia's spring – which was autumn in the northern hemisphere – was raced back to London for the January wool sales. Blown by the roaring forties the sailing clippers drove eastwards across the dangerous Antarctic waters of the southern Pacific, rounded South America's Cape Horn, and picked up the trade winds to fly up the Atlantic. On this run no steamship could catch them. A year before he died, the last earl had invested in a quarter share of a new clipper, even swifter than the *Charlotte*, which Barnikel had christened the *Charlotte Rose*. And on this the old sea captain, who should have retired years ago, was making brilliant runs each year: his average time from Australia in the last three years had been eighty days. In addition to the commercial profits of the voyage, there was the betting. Each of the finest clippers had its particular characteristics, each captain his own strengths and weaknesses. People could study the form. Huge wagers were made. And few larger or more daring than the wager placed some months ago by the financially embarrassed Earl of St James.

It was perfectly logical. The odds he had got were excellent: seven-to-one. The amount he had bet was one year's income. If he lost, it would not make a great difference: unless he married, he'd be forced to sell up anyway. If he won, on the other hand, he'd have another five years of living in style before facing a crisis again – and who knew what might turn up during that time? In six weeks from now, if the *Charlotte Rose* got back from Australia first, Lord St James would have no further need to marry Nancy Dogget. His intention therefore – since he had no wish to hurt her – was to keep her interested without committing himself too far, so that he could either advance quickly or retire with grace when the time came.

"The *Charlotte Rose* has had a refit. There's only one vessel afloat that could beat her, and if he spreads all his canvas, Barnikel's sure he can outrun her too," he assured his sister. "So there it is, old girl." He grinned. "We've just got to beat the *Cutty Sark*!"

There had been times lately when Mary Anne had wondered whether she and her daughter Violet could remain in the same house. Neither her three sons, nor Violet's two sisters had given her such trouble. But it was the effect Violet was having on her father's temper that was worst of all.

"You're like your father," she complained to the girl. "There's never any compromise with you. Everything's always either black or white!" According to Bull, however, the trouble was that Violet was too like her mother. A rebel. "But I was never unreasonable," Mary Anne would retort.

Violet had always been irritating. Mary Anne remembered the time when she had found her as a little girl trying on her clothes. The child had been soundly smacked for that, of course. A few years ago when Violet was sixteen, Mary Anne had noticed that she was getting really too close to her father. She would fuss over him, bring him his pipe, try to go about with him. Bull seemed rather to enjoy this, but Mary Anne had taken her daughter to one side and told her firmly: "I am his wife; you are his daughter and just a child. Please behave accordingly."

But the real trouble lay with her education. Like most girls of her class, she had a governess – a scholarly woman who told them Violet was gifted and who had taken her far beyond the standard required. "You should have seen what she was up to and put a stop to it," Bull had complained bitterly to Mary Anne when he dismissed the poor governess that autumn. It was certainly the governess's fault that the girl had got the foolish idea that she should go to university.

The idea, of course, was preposterous. Until forty years ago the possibility did not even exist. Though there were small women's colleges attached to Oxford and Cambridge, only a handful of women attended them and they were still not accepted as full members of the university. Thinking the girl could not really be serious her mother had remarked: "Your father would never allow you to live away like that, unchaperoned." But Violet had immediately objected: "I could stay at home and go to university in London."

As her mother soon discovered, she was right. The University of London was a curious affair. Started just before Queen Victoria came to the throne, as a place where religious dissenters, still denied access to Oxford and Cambridge, could study, it was a progressive institution. Its buildings were scattered; there was no requirement that students live in university colleges; and for several decades now, it had allowed women to take degrees. But what sort of woman would do such a thing? Mary Anne had no idea. Her eldest son Richard had been to Oxford. He had gone up as a gentleman of course and had told her proudly that he had never read a book while he was there.

When she asked him about the women undergraduates he had only said: "Bluestockings, mother. We avoided them." And he had pulled a face. Others she asked were just as discouraging. Besides, what would Violet do with all this knowledge? Become a teacher, or a governess? This was not at all the thing the Bulls had in mind.

Edward Bull had done even better than he had hoped. His greatest stroke of luck had come in the fifties when Britain fought its brief and unsatisfactory war with Russia in the Crimea during which he had been awarded the government contract to supply the army with drink. If everyone else remembered the Crimean War for the nursing activities of Florence Nightingale and the heroic charge of the Light Brigade, Edward Bull remembered the war because it had made him a very rich man. It was Edward who lived in the big house on Blackheath now; like other rich brewers at this time, he was almost ready to make himself a gentleman. And the daughter of a gentleman had only one destiny: to be a lady of leisure. "She may employ an educated woman as a governess I suppose," Edward remarked, "but she certainly can't become one." So Mary Anne, herself the daughter of Silas the dredger, discouraged her own daughter from getting any higher education because it might make the rising family look too middle class.

"You're not plain," she assured the girl. "You'll find a husband. But men don't like women to be too intelligent, you know; and if you are, you must learn to conceal it."

Yet Violet had still been obstinate. Unlike the other Bull children, who all had fair hair and blue eyes, Violet's wide-spaced eyes were hazel and her brown hair had a white flash in it. "I've no wish to marry a man who's afraid of intelligent women!" she retorted. For the last two months, she had been impossible. There was not the smallest possibility of Edward Bull giving way, nor the least chance that Violet would back down. The atmosphere in the house had been like a perpetual thunderstorm. Most irritating of all had been Violet's attitude to her. "I know you wouldn't understand," she would tell Mary Anne with a note of contempt in her voice. "You're perfectly happy doing whatever papa says. You've never wanted anything else in your life."

And how, her mother thought to herself, would you know?

Her thirty years of marriage to Edward had not been so bad. He could be obstinate and overbearing of course; but most men were. If sometimes she might have wished for something more – that his friends' senses of humour were a little lighter, that at least one of them had read a book – she kept it to herself. If perhaps there had been moments when she felt like screaming with boredom and frustration, those moments had passed. Marriage was about not screaming; and the rewards of marriage – the comfort, the children – had been blessings indeed. So if I could get through it, Mary Anne thought grimly, then so can she. "Life isn't the way you think it should be," she told the girl bluntly. "And the sooner you realize it the better."

Thank God there was at least one piece of neutral territory where, by unspoken agreement, these hostilities ceased. Every Wednesday afternoon without fail Mary Anne and Violet got on the train into London and, taking a hansom cab, rattled over to Piccadilly. That broad street had kept its fashionable eighteenth-century character. New mansions, fronting the street, were taking the place of the grand old palaces of the former age, though Burlington House – it was the Royal Academy now – remained in splendour behind its walled courtyard. Fortnum and Mason was still there. And a few doors further down, the sanctuary where even Violet would forget their differences.

On a cold December afternoon three weeks before Christmas, Mary Anne and Violet made their usual expedition. They had not let the weather deter them, and just as they were crossing Westminster Bridge, with the Houses of Parliament and the high tower of Big Ben looming above them, it started to snow. Passing up Whitehall and skirting the edge of Trafalgar Square, it was not long before they reached Piccadilly and the best bookshop in Victorian London, Hatchards of Piccadilly. Indeed, it was more than a bookshop: it was almost a club. There were benches outside where servants could rest while their employers browsed inside. There was a snug little parlour at the back, where regular customers could chat and read the paper in front of the fire. Royalty came to Hatchards; the grand old Duke of Wellington had loved it; the political rivals, Gladstone and Disraeli, both went there; Mary

Anne had once even found Oscar Wilde, who sent his plays to Hatchards for their opinion, standing just beside her, and had received a charming smile.

For both Mary Anne and her daughter Hatchards was a place of escape. Edward had no particular objection to Mary Anne reading; her most prized possessions were the sets of Dickens and of Thackeray she had purchased there. A friendly assistant had encouraged her to try Tennyson's poems too, and she was quite in love with the splendour of his verses now. As for Violet, she used to buy works of a philosophical nature, from Plato to such modern British thinkers as Ruskin; which Mary Anne, with some misgivings, used to conceal among her own books in case Edward should see them.

Today, however, they were searching for Christmas presents; and Mary Anne had just found a book on shooting which she thought might amuse her eldest son, when she became aware that a tall figure across the table was quietly observing her. As she glanced up to see who it was, he turned towards an assistant who was approaching him.

"I have the book you wanted, Colonel Meredith," the assistant said.

It was unfair. How could a man of her own age look so devastatingly handsome? His hair, clipped rather short, was still auburn; the greying temples only improved him. The lines around his eyes were those of a man who, she imagined, had seen much of the world in all kinds of weather. His body looked lean and hard. There was a hint that when the circumstances demanded it he could be dangerous. With his long silky moustache he was every inch a distinguished colonel; yet there was something else, a gentleness and an intelligence that suggested he was more than a military man.

"Mrs Bull? Is it Mrs Bull?" he enquired, as he came over to her. Mary Anne tried to nod but to her horror succeeded only in blushing. "I don't suppose you could possibly remember me."

"But, yes!" She found her voice, realized that Violet was coming over. "You were going to India. To shoot tigers." What sort of nonsense was she babbling?

"You are quite unchanged." He really seemed to mean it.

"I? Oh! Hardly. My daughter Violet. Colonel Meredith. Did you shoot any?"

"Tigers?" He smiled, then looked at them both. "Many."

It seemed Colonel Meredith had only been back in England a few months. Thirty years of travel had taken him to many lands. The staff at Hatchards knew him because very shortly a book of his own was to come out: *Love Poems, translated from the Persian.* He had a house in west London, large enough to keep his collections. He had never married. But perhaps, next Wednesday, she would like to come to tea?

"Oh, yes!" she said to her own and her daughter's astonishment. "Yes!"

As the dinner hour grew ever later, the Victorian English had taken up the Oriental custom of afternoon tea. It was simple, ensured a brief visit, and could be offered with propriety by ladies and by bachelor gentlemen.

The next Wednesday, a little after four o'clock, Mary Anne Bull, accompanied by Violet, arrived at Colonel Meredith's house in Holland Park. Mary Anne had wondered whether she ought to go, but told herself it would have been rude to change her mind; so she had taken Violet, somewhat under protest, to act, as she put it, "as my chaperone".

There were in London two particular suburbs where gentlemen of ample means and artistic tastes were apt to live. One, lying just above Regent's Park, on land that had once belonged to the old crusading order of the Knights of St John, was St John's Wood. The other was Holland Park. Passing along the southern edge of Hyde Park, past the little palace of Kensington where Queen Victoria had been brought up, one soon came to it. The focus was the fine old mansion and park owned by the Lords Holland. Around this, in pleasant tree-lined streets, were handsome houses where a gentleman might live quietly yet be only a ten-minute carriage drive from Mayfair.

Even for Holland Park, however, Colonel Meredith's house was striking. It stood in Melbury Road and, set in a garden with clipped trees, it looked not so much like a house as a miniature castle. In one corner was a circular tower with a turret. The windows were large, with leaded panes, and the entrance porch was massively heavy. There was something rather magical about it. But what really astonished the visitors was that, instead of the usual butler, the door was opened by a tall and magnificently turbaned Sikh who silently ushered them into the colonel's library.

On the walls were conventional pictures of his ancestors; in front of the fire, a leather-padded fender on which one could sit, and two wing chairs. But there English tradition ended. Over the fire hung a pair of ivory tusks; on the tables were ivory caskets, Chinese lacquer boxes, a wooden Buddha. By a desk, an elephant's foot made a waste-paper basket. In one corner was a rack of Indian daggers and a silver ankus, the gift of a friendly maharajah; in another hung some lovely Persian miniatures. Near the fire were a pair of Oriental moccasins with curling toes, which Meredith wore in private. And in the middle of the floor on top of the turkey carpet lay a magnificent tiger skin.

Tea was served at once, a choice of Indian or China, which the colonel insisted on serving himself. He seemed in high good humour and it was not long before, in answer to Mary Anne's questions, he began to reveal something of his fascinating life.

If Britain's empire had flourished as a purely commercial affair, the last few decades had seen a subtle shift of emphasis. Recognizing the need to control India, which had seen a mutiny in the 1850s, and to protect the passage of Egypt's Suez Canal, in which Prime Minister Disraeli had bought a majority share, the merchant island of Britain had been forced to adopt a more imperial, administrative role. They had done it rather well. The Indian Civil Service was of the finest quality. Its highly educated élite had a profound knowledge of the subcontinent. In the army, officers were often proficient in local languages and scholar soldiers like Colonel Meredith were not unknown.

When he remarked that he had never found time to marry, he was partly speaking the truth. He had spent time in India, China and Arabia and his exploits, though he did no more than hint at them, were legendary to his inner circle. The Sikh who served him so faithfully did so because Meredith had saved his life. As for his amorous conquests, he said nothing, but many in India could have told Mary Anne that they too were legendary. Only the wives of his brother officers were sacrosanct. Just. At least a hundred beautiful women, none of whom should, closed their eyes with a secret sigh quite often, and thought of Meredith's embraces.

For Mary Anne the effect was simple, unexpected, and searing. If she had supposed that the visit might rekindle the sympathetic attraction she had felt all those years ago, by the first cucumber sandwich she was experiencing that same giddying sensation that she had once felt when the balloon rushed her up into the sky. She had to hold on to her china cup firmly to make sure she did not swoon. By the time he served them walnut cake, and sat there quietly watching her, she knew only that she wanted to leave her house, her difficult daughter and her husband and to come to rest, for as long as he would have her, in Meredith's arms.

To force herself back into the context of her family she remarked: "Violet wants to go to university. What do you think?"

The girl had been rather sulky when they first arrived, but during the course of conversation she had noticed the curious volumes round the walls and asked Meredith about them. Besides the usual English classics, and a sporting section with titles like *Big Game Hunting in Bengal*, they were a fascinating assortment. There were books in Persian, in Arabic, even some strange, thin, concertina-like scrolls of parchment, pressed between wooden boards and tied with string which, Meredith explained, were written in Sanskrit.

"Can you read all those?" Violet had asked. He had admitted that he could. "How many languages do you know?" she had persisted. "Seven, and a few dialects," he had told her.

Now, in answer to Mary Anne's question, he looked at Violet and considered for several moments before replying. "I suppose," he said quietly, "it depends what you want to go to university for."

"Because I'm bored," she replied bluntly. "My parents' world is ludicrous."

Meredith seemed to take her rudeness in his stride. "Not ludicrous," he said. "I wouldn't agree with you there at all. But if you mean that you want wider horizons" – and he glanced round the room and at the bookcases – "university as such won't do it for you, though I dare say it can help. I never went myself." He smiled. "It's really a matter of the spirit. Destiny, I expect."

This seemed to keep Violet quiet, and Mary Anne was grateful to Meredith for handling it so well. But it seemed that, if she couldn't succeed in getting the colonel's support, the girl was still determined to make trouble. Just as they were due to leave, glancing at the moccasins by the fire and noticing a long Indian wooden pipe on a table, she suddenly interrupted:

"Do you wear those moccasins and smoke that pipe every evening, Colonel Meredith?"

"As a matter of fact I do," he confessed.

"Won't you show us before we go? I'm sure," Violet boldly continued, "that my mother would like to see you in your natural state."

"Really, Violet!" Mary Anne felt herself blushing helplessly.

Meredith, however, seemed to find it rather amusing. "Just wait a moment," he said, and left the room.

When he returned a couple of minutes later he was wearing a magnificent red dressing-gown of Oriental silk brocade and on his head he wore a red fez. His feet, encased in white silk socks, slipped easily into the moccasins, and he sat down very comfortably in the chair by the fire, expertly filled the pipe, kneading the tobacco into the bowl, lit it, and began to draw.

"Will that do?" he enquired, looking at them both.

But if the sight of Meredith, as her daughter had put it, in his natural state, was disturbing to Mary Anne, it was nothing to the sensation she had when, as they finally left, he took her hand, pressed it discreetly, and said softly:

"I hope we may meet again."

"It's a quandary, old girl. There's no doubt about it." The Earl of St James shook his head. "The trouble is, you see, the *Cutty Sark*'s never been beaten."

That was, in fact, only half the trouble. The first and most urgent problem was that two days before, Mr Gorham Dogget had arrived from Boston and declared that, immediately after Christmas, he was taking his wife and daughter away from the damp winter for a three-month cruise on the Nile and the Mediterranean. Whether Nancy and her mother were to return to London afterwards was not decided.

The problem with the *Cutty Sark* was her sturdiness. Her

redoubtable captain could put on more canvas than any other master would dare and still the clipper would plough safely on in the roughest seas.

"Barnikel may say he can beat her, and he may be right, but it's too great a risk," the earl continued. "We're out of time."

Lady Muriel had a box of dried fruit. She was munching thoughtfully.

"There's nothing for it," St James concluded. "I'm going round tomorrow to propose."

There were some people who laughed at Esther Silversleeves behind her back, though this was a little unfair. She certainly meant no harm.

Perhaps she would have been more confident, if only her sisters' husbands had not been so successful. Jonas and Charlotte Barnikel, though the sea captain had made a small fortune from his many voyages, had remained very comfortably the solid, seafaring tradespeople that they were. The Pennys, on the other hand, being a well-established City family, moved in a far more elevated circle, attended the City livery company dinners and even went to the opera at Covent Garden now and then. As for the Bulls, they had become so rich now that their children were mixing with young ladies and gentlemen on almost equal terms. With Arnold Silversleeves and his wife however, it was rather different. Their house was pleasantly situated, some four miles out from central London on the northern hill of Hampstead, not far from the big open spaces of Hampstead Heath. Many of the houses there were fine, or charming. Theirs – though neither of them realized it – was not. Its tall, awkward gables reminded one of the angular Mr Silversleeves himself. It was spacious however and, thanks to her money, they were never in the slightest want.

Arnold Silversleeves had remained a partner of Grinder and Watson until his recent retirement. His engineering was respected. Yet somehow the projects in which he involved the firm never seemed to be very profitable. Either he chose them for their technical challenge, or his own perfectionism eroded the profit margins. Well before his retirement there was a faint trace of impatience perceptible in the other partners when they addressed him. As for rising in the social scale, it would simply never have occurred to him. The family was respectable and provided for: what more could one want?

He had, however, as all his partners would admit, one of the finest engineering brains in London. And it was undoubtedly for this reason that he had recently been put on retainer by the rich American gentleman whose presence a week before Christmas in her house had caused Esther Silversleeves to go all of a flutter.

If Arnold Silversleeves had dreamed of projects for the betterment of mankind, or at least the Londoners, it gave him some satisfaction that many of them had come to pass. When, in the late fifties, Parliament finally decided on a complete remaking of the London sewers, it did not award the work to his own firm, but to the great engineer Bazalgette. Characteristically, he had at once offered his own drawings of the existing system to the great man, who used them as a check upon his own. "Your plans," he generously told Silversleeves, "I found to be perfect in every particular." The resulting Thames Embankment, which now swept along on reclaimed riverside over the new main drains from Westminster to Blackfriars gave the worthy engineer almost as much pleasure as if he had profited from it himself. More directly, he had actually been called in as a consultant on another colossal engineering feat now arising in the Thames. The two huge towers of Tower Bridge were clad in stone and modelled in high Victorian Gothic style to blend with the Tower of London and echo the Houses of Parliament downstream. "But the stone casing is just a disguise," he told his wife gleefully. "Inside is a great framework and a huge machine all of steel." It was the great bascules – the massive pair of steel drawbridges that opened to let the tall ships through – for which he had acted as consultant to the engineer Barry; and Brunel, Barry's partner, had called him in again to check all the complex mathematics of the system that would support and pivot the two mighty hundred-foot spans. His greatest enthusiasm, however, was reserved for the new project for which the American had retained him.

"This will be the way of the future," he told Esther excitedly. The dream he had always had of a London underground had partly been realized. A system of deep cuts and of tunnels with air vents had already been constructed for steam trains;

but it was hot and sooty and without clearing or undermining much housing, it could not be expanded into the more elaborate system London now needed. "But if we went deep down, maybe forty feet, we could safely build a whole network," he would explain. "The clay down there is easy to cut through. Then we build a tube. The train would run in a tube." But it would be utterly impossible to run a steam train through a deep tube. "So," he concluded happily, "the trains will be electric."

Electricity. To forward-looking Arnold Silversleeves, it was the herald of the modern age. It had been 1860 when Swan invented his electric lamp, but not until ten years ago had the first system of electric lights been installed in London, on the splendid new Thames Embankment. But since then, progress had been rapid. In 1884, the first electrically powered trams began to replace a horse-drawn version in the streets. Five years ago Parsons perfected a steam-turbine to drive a dynamo, opening the way for public power stations. And this very year, work was already under way on a deep tube which would contain an electric train. Silversleeves, who had already built his own dynamo and installed – to Esther's terror – several electric lights in their house, was all enthusiasm. "The electric train will be clean," he assured her. "And I calculate that, correctly engineered, it could be amazingly cheap to run. The working man will be able to afford the fares."

The only problem was finding men bold enough to build and operate them. Governments did not invest in such things, nor had they the money to do so. The tube, like almost everything in Victorian Britain, would be a commercial enterprise, and British investors, so far, were cautious about the new technology. But the Americans were not. And when Mr Gorham Dogget had last visited London he had approached Arnold Silversleeves.

"Electric rails have worked in Chicago," he told him. "London is the most populous city in the world, with a crying need for more transport. I want you to do me a feasibility study. I'll find the investors. This thing can be done!" And he had paid him, cash down, the first part of a fee that had made the engineer blink.

Mr Gorham Dogget's presence in her house had sent Esther

Silversleeves into a tizzy. She had asked the Pennys to give her support. The Barnikels, though they were fond of her, were apt to get impatient with her social efforts; the Bulls, though always friendly, had moved apart. But the respectable Pennys could be relied on. They had also brought their son, a bright young man in the City, very smartly dressed she was pleased to see. The gentleman from Boston seemed to find them acceptable company. The food – Arnold only liked plain food, but she had secretly had the cook prepare some puddings that were really rather daring – seemed to be finding favour. The maid's uniform had been starched twice. The only thing she had been unable to make up her mind about, wondering how and whether to handle it, did not finally come out until the duck was served.

"My maiden name was Dogget, the same as yours," she ventured.

"Really? Your father a Dogget? What did he do?"

She saw Harriet Penny glance at her nervously; but she had prepared for this.

"He was an investor," she said with only the faintest blush.

"Sounds a good man! We came over with the *Mayflower*," said Mr Gorham Dogget, and turned his attention back to young Penny who, it seemed to him, had some interesting ideas.

If Esther had found the Bostonian a little abrupt over some of her conversational gambits, this was made up for by the pleasure he seemed to take in the younger generation. Her own eldest son Matthew and his wife had evidently found favour. Matthew was a lawyer with a good firm of solicitors and the Bostonian had already indicated that he might have some work for him. As for young Penny, he was eager to push the family insurance business into an exciting new area. "For the first time in history there is sufficient prosperity not only in the middle class but in the small shopkeepers and even the skilled artisans for them to afford life insurance," he informed Dogget. "The size of each policy, naturally, will be small; but the volume of numbers is potentially huge. The Prudential Insurance Company is already active here, but there's plenty of room for us, too." The Penny Insurance Company had recently taken on the younger Silversleeves son as an actuary.

"Get the numbers right and offer cheap rates and there's nothing we can't achieve," young Penny assured them all.

"A sound, forward-looking young man, your son," the Bostonian murmured to Harriet Penny.

But it was when her desserts were being served that Esther Silversleeves really got her chance to shine. For it was then, glancing around the table, that Mr Gorham Dogget casually enquired: "Does anyone here know anything about a fellow called Lord St James?"

Oh, but indeed she did. Flushing with pleasure at the connection she could claim, Esther began: "I hope you won't think we are getting above our station . . ." This little phrase, used whenever she became socially self-conscious, made the Pennys secretly wince and had caused the Bulls to become rather distant. "But I can tell you all about the earl. He and my brother-in-law are partners together in shipping."

"A vessel, you mean?"

"Yes indeed. She's called the *Charlotte Rose*: a clipper. They think she can beat the *Cutty Sark* herself!" She became rather confidential. "In fact, the earl has bet on it so heavily that I believe his fortune may rest entirely on my brother-in-law's shoulders. He's the captain, you see." And she beamed at them all, thinking how well she had done, while Mr Gorham Dogget looked thoughtful.

Time was running out for Lucy Dogget. If she wanted to try to save the girl, she knew she must make the effort soon.

Lucy Dogget was seventy that year, but she looked more. Compared to Silas's daughters, she would have seemed not a decade but a generation older. Sometimes now, as she sat hour after hour at her worktable, she would wonder what had happened to her life.

It had been hard for a single woman with a child in Whitechapel. Some had it worse: families with six or seven children and a father out of work. Thieving and prostitution were the only way for them, and disease and death usually followed soon. For Lucy, it had been keeping her little boy out of that condition that was the great struggle. His father had tried to help surreptitiously in the five more years he had lived, but after that she had been alone.

She had worked at a variety of menial occupations to feed

herself and the child. She had managed to persuade the boy to attend a parish school, for which she had to pay a few pence. But he had grown bored, preferring to run about and find odd jobs. By the age of twelve, though he could read a little and write his name, young William was working most of the day at a boat-building yard where out of kindness the master had agreed to let the boy apprentice to the trade. But he would not stick at it and by sixteen he was seeking casual work at the docks. By nineteen, he had married the daughter of another docker. By twenty he had a son of his own who died at six months; then another; then a daughter followed by two more, both sickly, who died. Eight years ago he had lost his wife in childbirth. Such things happened; men married again. But William did not. He took to drinking instead. And so, at the age of sixty, Lucy had found herself, in effect, a mother again.

Whitechapel itself had changed significantly by this time. In the early 1880s in Eastern Europe a series of terrible pogroms forced a large section of the Jewish population to emigrate. Many were able to flee to the United States, but a large number, some tens of thousands, made their way to tolerant Britain; and many of these new refugees, like others before them, found their first home in the East End by the Port of London.

The transformation was astonishing. Some English and Irish stayed, others moved into neighbouring districts to make way, as street after street of Whitechapel became Jewish. The new arrivals were usually, like most refugees, very poor. They wore strange clothes and spoke Yiddish. "They keep themselves to themselves and they don't give any trouble," Lucy noted approvingly. But she moved into nearby Stepney with her neighbours all the same. And there, while her son sometimes worked, and sometimes remembered not to drink his meagre wages, she found work at a factory that made waterproof clothing and did her best to help two grandchildren to survive.

In one respect she did a little better. Since 1870 it had become compulsory for children to attend school, and even in the East End schools of some kind were now to be found in every parish. Not that it was possible as yet to enforce the law in practice. Few children attended more than sporadically and with the boy, Tom, she was forced to give up when he was ten. "You'll end up like your father," she warned him. "I 'spect I shall," he would reply casually, and she recognized that there was nothing she could do for him. But his sister Jenny was quite another story. By the age of ten she was earning a few pence helping the master teach the other children how to read. Something good, Lucy prayed, might finally come out of the sacrifice she had made all those years ago, to keep her disappointing son. Jenny could yet be saved.

Five years ago, because her legs were weak, Lucy had been obliged to give up going out to work. But for a woman sitting at home in the East End of London, there were still ways of making a few pence, and the surest, though the most tedious, was making matchboxes. She only needed the materials, a table, and a paste brush to assemble a matchbox. She was given the raw materials except for the paste which she had to buy herself. The work was not difficult. Bryant and May paid her tuppence ha'penny for every gross she delivered. Lucy could make seven gross in a day if she worked fourteen hours; so in a ninety-eight hour week she earned four pounds ten shillings. With young Jenny helping her a few days a week they could pay the rent and buy a little food. But what would become of Jenny when Lucy was gone?

As she looked around her, the signs were not encouraging. Her son was a drunk. Young Tom had taken up with some of the rowdier youths of the Jewish community; and though these Jewish boys did not drink so much, they were always gambling. "Which is just as quick a way of losing your wages," she pointed out to Jenny. Then, the previous year, there had been the terrible murders of Jack the Ripper in Whitechapel. So far the victims had been prostitutes, but with madmen like that about, what girl was safe?

There was something else that worried Lucy, too. The first sign of trouble in the East End had been last year at the Bryant and May match factory, when the girls there, led by a vigorous outsider called Annie Besant, had walked out in protest at their starvation wages. This year, more ominously, another woman called Eleanor Marx, whose father Karl Marx, they said, was a revolutionary writer who lived in the West End, had come to help the gasworkers organize a union; and soon after that, there had been a huge strike down at the docks.

"I'm not saying they're wrong," Lucy told Jenny. She knew all about the pay of the matchworkers; and her son had often described the terrible scenes at the docks where casual labourers were allowed to fight each other for the shift-work. "But where will it lead?" Whatever the future held for the East End, she wanted to find Jenny a safe haven, before she herself was no longer there to protect her. But how? Every year the East End had grown larger as the population swelled and immigrants came in. Villages like Poplar had completely disappeared in the endless, dreary wasteland of docks, factories and long rows of mean houses. Lucy could think of only one possible hope. And so, on a cold December day, she set out on a journey she had not attempted for over thirty years.

In the universe of lawyers there is no place more august and dignified than the big square near Chancery Lane known as Lincoln's Inn Fields. A noble old hall adorns one side, lawyers' chambers and other ancient offices stand quietly round the rest. And in one corner, up handsome, shadowy stairs which, somehow, suggested an appropriate air of dignified obfuscation, were the offices of Odstock and Alderbury, Solicitors.

Lucy had never gone to see Silas's lawyers, since she had not given up her child. Nor, given the circumstances, had she ever mentioned Silas to her son. But she could not help hoping that at his death at least he would do something for her. What other kin had he, after all? She had tried to discover what had happened to him and at last, a dozen years before, she had learned from an old newspaper of his death. She wrote to the lawyer and, receiving no response, wrote again to ask whether her kinsman had remembered her. This time she received a brief and curt reply: he had not.

She could think of no one else who could give her what she wanted: a nice place for Jenny in a decent house as far from the East End as possible, where she would be treated kindly. And besides, might not some tiny drop of Silas's great fortune come the girl's way?

At ten o'clock in the morning, therefore, she presented herself at the office in Lincoln's Inn, gave her name and asked if she might speak to Mr Odstock.

He kept her waiting two hours, a bent, severe, grey-haired

old man who was certainly surprised to see her, but who also, clearly, knew well enough who she was. He interviewed her in a small, book-lined office, nodded carefully, and after some thought replied: "I am afraid I cannot help you. I know of no such situations, though no doubt they exist."

"My kinsman left no word about me at all?"

"Apart from his original instructions, nothing."

"But what became of all his fortune?" she suddenly burst out.

"Why," he looked a little surprised. "His daughters . . ." Then, seeing her look of mystification, he shut up like a clam. "I'm afraid there's nothing I can do," he told her, opened the door and before she quite knew what was happening, ushered her out.

For fully ten minutes, Lucy sat in the cold of Lincoln's Inn Fields and pondered. There was no doubt about what the old lawyer had said: Silas had daughters. Might one of them, perhaps, take pity on her and the girl? But who were they? And where?

It was then that Lucy remembered something she had been told. At the start of her reign Queen Victoria had ordered that all births, marriages and deaths, usually only registered in each parish, should in future also be recorded in a single, combined register in London. The register could even be consulted by the public. If I could find any of his daughters' marriages, Lucy thought, then I could at least discover their names. Nervously approaching a lawyer walking past, she was informed that the office she sought was not far away. And by early afternoon she found herself, along with several others, in front of the huge registers. They were arranged by each quarter of each year, beautifully inscribed in copperplate on thick parchment paper, and contained every marriage in England.

Lucy had no idea there were so many Doggets in the world. At first she wondered how she would ever find anything; but gradually, working her way forward, she began to make sense of it. She missed Charlotte, because the family had not yet moved to Blackheath when she married, but a little later, just before the office closed, she came to another entry, in what looked like the right place. It read: Dogget, Esther, to Silversleeves, Arnold.

Could this be a daughter? Where was she now? How in the world could one discover an address? For several minutes after she left the registry she wondered how to proceed, and then remembered something else she had seen, a directory of sorts, while she was waiting in the lawyers' offices.

Just after he returned from a very good lunch old Mr Odstock happened to encounter young Mr Silversleeves, the promising grandson of Silas Dogget whom he had been glad to welcome as a junior in his office.

"Do you know," he began cheerily, "I saw, this very morning, a most curious kinswoman . . ." he was about to say, "of yours", but suddenly remembering Silas's clear instructions, he thought better of it.

"Kinswoman?" young Silversleeves enquired.

"Nothing," the old man corrected. "Cousin of mine. Wouldn't mean anything to you."

Since he had plenty of time and was in a cheerful mood, the Earl of St James had decided to walk.

His proposal to Nancy had been a great success. He had had the happy idea of taking her for a carriage drive. The weather had been kind. Under a cold, clear blue sky, the frosty ground was sparkling as the carriage left Piccadilly, passed the noble residence of Apsley House which the old Duke of Wellington had built, and entered Hyde Park. The scene had been like something from a fairy tale. The icy trees seemed to be made of glass as the carriageway took them by the site where the great Crystal Palace once stood. A tall, ornate monument to Prince Albert marked the place now while opposite, just outside the park, rose the huge oval shape of the new Albert Hall. They had sat gazing out in the magical silence until, just as they reached the place where the western section of Hyde Park turned into Kensington Gardens, he had asked her to marry him.

She had asked for time to consider – that was the form, of course – but only for a few days, and he had little doubt from her manner that the answer would be yes.

"Though of course you will have to ask my father," she had reminded him. He was still not quite sure, as he made his way along now, whether he would be seeing the father or the daughter first.

Either way, he had felt so cheerful, had so positively told

himself he really liked the girl a lot, that he had paused to buy himself a present.

There were many picture dealers in London, but his favourite was a Frenchman, Monsieur Durand-Ruel whose gallery lay in New Bond Street. The earl had been collecting pictures of the Thames recently; he had no idea why he should have felt so drawn to the river, but he was. He had bought one by the American, Whistler, who lived in London, but Whistler's prices, at over a hundred guineas, were too stiff. For less, at Durand-Ruel's he could purchase the work of an unfashionable but wonderful French artist, Claude Monet, who often came to stay in London to paint the river. And he had just agreed to buy a new Monet, for a very modest price, before he set out for his rendezvous.

His route from New Bond Street took him westwards along Oxford Street. The old Roman approach road from Marble Arch to Holborn was turning into a shopping street nowadays. He paused once or twice to glance at drapers' windows, crossed Regent Street, continued on to the bottom of Tottenham Court Road and then came down through Seven Dials and Covent Garden until he reached his destination on the Strand.

Both his wife and his daughter had noticed that Gorham Dogget seemed preoccupied since yesterday. He had been out on business twice and now, as he waited in the lobby, it appeared that the dry Bostonian was uncharacteristically nervous. It was certainly strange, for he was in his favourite place in all London.

There was nothing perhaps in all Europe quite like the Savoy Hotel on the Strand. The brainchild of D'Oyly Carte, the manager of the Gilbert and Sullivan operettas, the recently opened hotel, built on the site of the old Savoy Palace where John of Gaunt had lived and Chaucer been a frequent guest, had imported an up-to-date level of American comfort, mixed it with European grandeur, and created a masterpiece. Instead of the usual walk to a bathroom, which was routine in even the best hotels, the lavish suites of the Savoy each had their own. The chef was none other than the great Escoffier; the manager, probably the finest who ever lived, César Ritz.

Ritz – entrepreneur, discreet confidant, the ultimate arranger of everything.

Dogget seemed pleased, even relieved to see the earl, and invited him to a quiet corner where they could talk. Smiling pleasantly, he explained that his wife and daughter would be down in a little while and asked whether, in the meantime, there was anything St James wished to discuss. The signal being clear, the earl politely asked for his daughter's hand.

"I can't answer for her," the Bostonian replied, "but you seem, Lord St James, to be a fine man to me. As her father though, I have to ask a few questions. I assume you can support her?"

The earl had thought carefully about how to answer this. "Our wealth has been much reduced, Mr Dogget. The income from the land is small, though I have other interests. But the house and the Bocton estate are all in good order, and there are things like the family jewels. . . ." He was too well-bred to add the other obvious item – the title.

"You've enough to live on, though?"

"Oh, yes." It was true, for the time being.

"And you sincerely love my daughter, for herself? I have to tell you I believe in that, Lord St James. I believe in it strongly. For richer for poorer, as they say."

"Absolutely." A downright lie, the earl reminded himself, was not a lie when it meant being gallant towards a lady.

"That's good. Of course, I dare say one day Nancy will have something of her own," the Bostonian cautiously allowed, and was only prevented from expanding further by the unusual sight of Mr César Ritz, that most discreet of managers, hovering when he was not wanted.

"Excuse me, sir," he quietly interrupted, and handed Dogget a slip of paper, at which the American glanced irritably.

"Not now, Mr Ritz!"

"I'm sorry, sir." The manager did not move.

"I said later," Dogget growled.

"You said the matter would be dealt with this morning, sir," Ritz reminded him. "We had understood that as soon as you arrived. . . ." Dogget was glowering at him now but it seemed to make no difference. "Your wife and daughter have been here for weeks, sir. This cannot go on."

"You know perfectly well there's no problem."

"We have received a reply to an enquiry we made to your bankers in Boston, sir."

At this Dogget went pale. It seemed to St James that the American aged visibly before him. He crumpled. Then he replied gruffly: "I still have a house in Boston, Mr Ritz. The Savoy will be paid; you may just have to wait a little while. I'm due to leave in a day or two anyway." He glanced at St James in some embarrassment. "Some bad investments I'm afraid, Lord St James. Seems my fortune's gone. But, as I was saying, I still hope to do something for Nancy in due course. I'm not too old. I made a fortune once so I dare say I can do it again. Maybe you'll come along for the ride," he suggested, with a hint of family warmth.

But the Earl of St James, whether out of embarrassment or some other pressing reason, was excusing himself and beating a hasty retreat.

Mr Dogget was silent, shaking his head sadly for some moments after St James had left. Then he glanced up at César Ritz.

"Thank you, Mr Ritz."

"Was that all right, sir?"

"Oh yes. I think we smoked him out."

The letter was written in a beautiful hand – neat and scholarly but also very manly. Violet was in the room when Mary Anne opened it.

"It's from Colonel Meredith!" she said, before she had time to think.

"Oh mama!" The girl gave her a knowing look that Mary Anne considered most unsuitable. "What does he say?"

"That he is to give a reading from his Persian poems in two weeks' time, at Hatchards. Anyone may attend but he thought to let us know in case it would amuse us, as he puts it, to come." And how cleverly done, she thought. An invitation to a rendezvous, yet perfectly innocent if it should happen to be seen by anyone else. It was not even necessary to respond. No commitment. She could go with Violet, or she could go alone. Or, of course, as she knew very well that she should, she could stay away and not go at all. Whatever she decided to do, she wished that she had not blurted it out to the girl.

"Will you go, mama?"

"I don't think so," said Mary Anne.

So many things had been happening lately, Esther Silversleeves could hardly remember when there had been more to think about.

Mr Gorham Dogget's visit had certainly put things in such a whirl. Three days after Christmas, her son was summoned to the Savoy and given a great pile of legal documents to work on. As for Arnold, she had never seen him so busy. She hoped it was all right at his age, but he seemed very happy.

"These Americans have such bold dreams," he told her. "I wish I could have worked for men like this one all my life."

But the truly astounding thing was that the very next day, the Bostonian had asked her brother-in-law Penny if his son would like to accompany him and his family on their cruise.

"Just up sticks at the drop of a hat, take the boat from Southampton and be off for three months – down the Nile!" Harriet Penny had told her excitedly. "I do believe he means our son to keep his daughter company," she added. "And he's going!"

"Oh, my dear!" said Esther in awe. "We shall be getting quite above our station."

Sadder, even a little worrying, was that just after the New Year the *Cutty Sark* had returned, beating all opposition easily while so far no word had come of the *Charlotte Rose*. "He'll be all right," her sister Charlotte had said of her husband when Esther had gone out to Camberwell to see her. "He always comes home." But Esther could see that Charlotte was worried.

Least important, though strangest, had been the tiny incident that had taken place three days before. Though it fascinated him less than sewers and electric trains, Arnold Silversleeves had been delighted by the coming of the telephone in the last decade. In the capital, amongst the richer sort, the new invention had spread rapidly and Arnold had been eager to get one as soon as there was an exchange serving Hampstead. Many provincial cities could not be reached yet but, as he assured her, "it's the thing of the future".

But who, she wondered, could the strange female voice be who had called three days before:

"Mrs Silversleeves?"

"Yes?"

"Would you be the daughter of the late Mr Silas Dogget, of Blackheath?"

As soon as Esther answered yes, the caller had hung up. She was just wondering about it for the hundredth time when the doorbell rang, and a moment later, the maid announced: "There's a Miss Lucy Dogget to see you, ma'am."

Lucy had insisted that she could not state her business until they were alone. Esther had wondered if she should refuse to see her, but her curiosity got the better of her, and the quietly dressed old woman seemed harmless enough. Lucy had spent two days searching and borrowing enough clothes from the families she knew to make a respectable appearance. She had even borrowed a pair of boots from the vicar's housekeeper – a size too small, so that she could almost weep with the pinching pain after walking a mile from the bus. But in her grey coat, black hat, simple black dress and clean brown stockings, she could have passed for a respectable housekeeper or lady's maid in quiet retirement.

"I wanted to see you alone," she explained, "because I didn't want to embarrass you."

She told her story simply and when she had finished Esther Silversleeves gazed at her in horrified silence. She did not doubt Lucy's tale, but it opened up before her such a terrible abyss that she had to grip the arms of the chair.

"The rich relation, you mean, was. . . ."

"Up at Blackheath. Very fine gentleman he was, I must say. You must have been very proud of him."

"Yes. But. . . ." Esther gazed at her with dread. "You said your little brother died on the river. . . ."

Just for a second Lucy looked into her eyes with perfect understanding before dropping her gaze to the floor. "That was ever such a long time ago," she said softly. "Not sure I even remember it."

The dark chasm was there: the faint splash of an oar in the fog, the dull thump of a body, things Esther had scarcely known, but always dreaded. A cold, damp nightmare, invading the respectable house by Hampstead Heath. Esther thought of Arnold, of her sons, of young Penny cruising the Nile, of the Bulls, of Lord St James. And of Silas the dredger. For a moment she lost her voice. At last, hoarsely, she asked: "Do you need money?"

Lucy shook her head. "No. I didn't come to ask for money. I wouldn't do that. No, it's a decent place the girl needs. In service, you see. In a decent house, where she'll be safe and looked after. I hoped perhaps you might know somewhere. That's all. I didn't come to ask for anything more than that."

"How long is it since you came to see my father?" Esther asked at last.

"Thirty-eight years."

"You must have known great hardship."

"Yes, truly I have," said Lucy. And then, taking herself completely by surprise, she suddenly broke down, and for a moment could do nothing except lean forward in her chair, her hands gripping her knees through her old black dress, and her body quietly shaking as she murmured: "I'm sorry. I'm so sorry."

"She shall be safe. She shall come here," said Esther Silversleeves, greatly to her own astonishment.

For a man who always looked immaculate, it had to be said that the Earl of St James did not look quite himself that day. He had pulled on a greatcoat with shoulder capes over his open shirt, crammed a bowler hat on his head and seized a red silk scarf which he absent-mindedly wound round his neck as he ran out of the door and hailed a hansom cab. He was in such a state he even forgot his keys. Barnikel and the *Charlotte Rose* had just arrived, three weeks late.

The last month had been grim for St James. There had been the embarrassing business of Nancy. A gentleman was not supposed to go back on his word, but the marriage, of course, could not have gone forward. He had written her a letter suggesting that something in his own past made it necessary – indeed, though he did not say what, he implied it was only decent – to withdraw. He could have said he was penniless, too, but he was so furious about the whole thing that he was damned if he would. He comforted himself with the reflection that, having lost his fortune, the Bostonian was unlikely to appear to embarrass him in London again. The only mystery had been a rumour, shortly afterwards, that Mr Dogget had gone to the Nile after all.

As the days passed he waited anxiously for news of the clippers. First had come the crushing blow that the *Cutty Sark* had been sighted coming up the coast of Kent; then her arrival in the Port of London, and the knowledge that he had lost his bet. Then, day after day, the wait without news when he wondered if he had lost the vessel and his friend Barnikel too.

At the wharf it did not take Barnikel long to explain. Sadly the old mariner told him how, trying to outstrip the *Cutty Sark*, he had got caught in a storm, lost a mast and had to put in to a South American port for a refit. "We were ahead of her once," he said defensively. And glancing across to where the sleek, three-masted *Cutty Sark* lay quietly at her moorings he sighed. "I know it now if I didn't before: no vessel afloat will ever catch that one."

"She's ruined me," the earl said bleakly, and left.

There was really nothing left for him to do now, he reflected as the cab took him slowly home. The Regent's Park house would have to go of course. It was far too expensive. The thought of sharing a smaller house with Lady Muriel was not a happy one, however. Perhaps, he reflected, he should go to live in France. The English pound went a long way on the Continent and many an English gentleman was able to keep up appearances in France or Italy when they might have been severely embarrassed back at home.

In a grim but thoughtful mood he arrived back at the house, to be greeted with the news, unusual but not unwelcome, that his half-sister had gone out. "She didn't say when she was returning, my lord," the butler added.

Glad of some time to be alone with his thoughts, St James went upstairs to his library, and sat down in the big armchair.

It was some minutes before he noticed something odd. The door to the closet where the safe was had been left ajar. He got up slowly and went to close it. But as he did so, with a frown of surprise, he noticed that the safe was open. It was also empty.

"The jewels!" he cried. How had a thief got in? He was rushing to summon the butler when he saw his keys on the library table. Beside them was a single sheet of white paper on which, scrawled in his sister's large and childish hand, were just three words: I HAVE GONE.

With a howl of bitter rage, the poor Earl of St James cursed them all. He damned Muriel, and Nancy, and Gorham Dogget, and Barnikel.

"And damn you, too!" he cried. "You cursed *Cutty Sark*!"

It was just as well that the earl did not witness the scene which took place when Barnikel returned to his wife Charlotte at Camberwell that evening. After she had fed him, and made him his favourite grog, and sat him very comfortably down by the fireside, and affectionately stroked his hoary old beard, she remarked: "I'm sorry it didn't go better, but there's one compensation."

"What's that?"

"We made a tidy bit of money."

"How do you mean?"

"I put a bet on the race. Well, I had our son do it for me."

"You bet on me? Like St James?"

"No, dear. I bet on the *Cutty Sark*."

"You bet against your own husband, woman?"

"Well, somebody had to. I knew you couldn't win. The *Cutty Sark* had too much sail." She smiled. "We made a thousand pounds!"

After a long pause, Captain Barnikel started to laugh into his grog. "You're as bad as your old Guv'nor sometimes!" he chuckled.

"I hope," she said, "I am."

The arrangement agreed between Esther Silversleeves and Lucy was very simple. As soon as they had both recovered their composure, Esther found that she could think with a clarity she had not known she possessed.

"You are sure the girl knows nothing?" she asked Lucy.

"Nothing at all," Lucy promised.

"Then tell her that you found me through an agency," Esther ordered. "But you must tell her that since my own maiden name happened to be the same as yours, I do not think it appropriate that she should be a Dogget. She will have to change it." She considered. "Let her be Ducket. That will do."

Lucy was perfectly agreeable to this. But if she had any

misunderstanding about the arrangement, it was entirely dispelled when Esther declared with a vehemence that was quite frightening: "If ever, however, there is any word, any *hint* about any relationship to my father or about . . . the past, then she will be out on the street within the hour, and without a reference. Those are my conditions." Only after Lucy had promised her faithfully they should be met, did Esther's manner relent again. "By the way, what is her name?" she asked.

"Jenny."

So early in February 1890 Jenny Ducket, as she was now called, came to train as a housemaid for Mrs Silversleeves.

The spring of 1890 should have been a time of unparalleled joy in the household of Edward and Mary Anne Bull. In late March, Edward announced a breathtaking piece of news.

"The Earl of St James is selling his Bocton estate in Kent," he told the assembled family at dinner. "And I am buying it, lock, stock and barrel! We could move in tomorrow." He smiled at them all. "There's a deer park and a fine view. I think you'll like it." And then with a grin at his son. "As you've become such a gentleman, I should think it will suit you rather well."

"Us too!" cried two of his daughters. Eligible young men liked girls whose fathers had a place in the country. Only Violet did not trouble to give more than a vague smile of approval.

In recent weeks, Violet had taken to going to lectures. At first her mother had insisted upon accompanying her, but after three or four long and tedious afternoons at the Royal Academy or some place associated with the university, she had given up and allowed the girl to go to these dull but respectable affairs on her own. The only thing she wondered was where this was intended to lead. "I suspect," she confided to Edward, "she's up to something."

In the first week of April Violet came into her room one evening and closed the door behind her.

"Mother," she said calmly, "I think there's something you should know."

"If this is to do with university . . ." Mary Anne began wearily.

"It isn't." She paused. "I'm going to marry Colonel Meredith." And then she had the impudence to smile.

For perhaps a minute Mary Anne was not able to speak. "But . . . you can't!" she stuttered at last.

"Yes, I can."

"You aren't of age. Your father would forbid it."

"I'm nearly of age. Anyway, I could always elope if you force me to. There's nothing, actually, that anyone could do about it."

"But you hardly know him! How. . . ."

"I went to the poetry reading at Hatchards, mother. The one you didn't go to. I've been seeing him at least two days a week ever since."

"The lectures. . . ."

"Exactly. Though we do go to lectures, or galleries. Concerts too."

"But you should be marrying a young man! Why, even university would be better than this."

"He is the most educated and the most interesting man I shall ever meet in my life."

"He's done this behind our back. He has never dared come to see your father."

"He will. Tomorrow."

"Your father will turn him out of the house."

"I doubt it. Colonel Meredith is rich and a gentleman. Papa will be quite glad to have me off his hands. If not," Violet added coolly, "I'll make a scandal. He'd hate that."

"But, child," Mary Anne wailed. "Think of his age. It's unnatural. A man of that age. . . ."

"I love him! We are passionately in love."

At the word "passionately", Mary Anne gave a little involuntary start, then, suddenly feeling very ill she looked at the girl, full in the face. "Surely," her voice was husky, "you don't mean. . . ."

"I shouldn't tell you if it were so," the girl said blandly. "But after all, mother, one thing is certain anyway. *You* can't have him."

Chapter 19

The Suffragette

1908

Young Henry Meredith was weeping. He had just been soundly beaten. The fact that Mr Silversleeves, house-master and teacher of mathematics, was a relation had not made any difference. Nor was his punishment unusual. The cane, the birch and the strap were liberally used in England, America and many other countries. The reason for his punishment hardly mattered. While Eton and one or two other schools might promote a more individualist ethos, Charterhouse was one of the broad swathe of public schools whose principal mission was to knock the nonsense out of their charges. They often failed, but they did their best, and Silversleeves was only doing his duty, as both he and young Meredith knew.

There was also another possible reason for the boy's misery. He was ravenously hungry.

The Charterhouse school had started in 1614, some seventy years after the last monks had been ejected from the site by Henry VIII. More recently, the school had moved to a new location, thirty miles south-west of London. It was a fine old school and parents paid good money to send their sons there. Yet strangely, they either did not know or did not think it mattered that, once there, the children they undoubtedly loved were given almost nothing to eat. Thick slices of bread thinly buttered, stew or gruel in tiny amounts, cabbage boiled until it was bleached, wads of almost inedible suet pudding – this was the fare of privileged schoolboys. "Mustn't spoil them. Boys should be brought up hard." The survivors would rule the empire. Had it not been for hampers sent by his mother, Meredith could almost have starved.

But as he returned to his hard bench in the classroom and

the desk scored deep with the names of earlier sufferers, it was neither the electric pain nor the hunger pangs that caused Henry Meredith to choke back the tears. It was the article that an older boy had showed him in a newspaper that morning.

As the trap passed through the park gates at Bocton that autumn day, Violet still found it strange to think that her mother would not be there. Mary Anne had died the previous year and, of the four Dogget sisters, only Esther Silversleeves was left now.

The drive was long, and Violet nervously clutched her six-year-old daughter's hand the whole way down. There was no going back now. I'll hold my head high, she promised herself and gripped the child's hand tighter as she saw her father waiting for them in front of the house.

What made it worse was that old Edward Bull had been so good to them. Because Meredith had remained so strong and slim, she had supposed he would live to a great age. He had fathered their two sons and, when just over seventy, their little daughter Helen. So when he had suddenly died three years ago she had been taken by surprise. A massive heart attack, half a day when he could not speak, a tender look, a squeeze of her hand, and he was gone, leaving less money than she had thought. They were not exactly poor, but to keep up an appropriate household and educate the children she had found that her income was a little stretched. She had been grateful when her father had stepped in to pay for the children's schools.

For two whole hours while he walked them round the deer park and played with his granddaughter in the old walled garden Edward Bull said nothing. Only when Helen had been removed by the housekeeper and they were alone in the library did he take a folded newspaper, drop it down on the sofa beside her and remark:

"I see you've been talking to the Prime Minister."

Violet waited to see whether this was the prelude to an explosion.

The subject on which she had accosted the great man was not new. Since the Great Reform Act of 1832, democracy had been marching slowly forward. Two more Acts had enfranchised first the middle, then the better-off working class. Some two thirds of all adult men in Britain could now vote – but no women.

A respectable group of ladies known as Suffragists had been quietly protesting against this injustice for forty years, but got nowhere. Five years ago a new group led by the fiery Mrs Pankhurst had appeared on the scene. "Suffragettes" these new crusaders were soon dubbed. Their motto was Deeds Not Words and they lived up to it. They began to sport their own colours – purple, white and green – on sashes, banners and posters. They held public meetings and interrupted parliamentary elections. And, with unpardonable bad manners, Edward Bull thought, they had taken to accosting politicians in the street.

A week before, two respectable-looking Edwardian ladies, wearing the large, wide-brimmed hats decorated with feathers that were fashionable and looking as if they had just come from shopping in Piccadilly, waited quietly outside the Prime Minister's residence at 10, Downing Street. As Mr Asquith emerged, to the delight of *The Times* journalist and the photographer who had been tipped off, the two women fell into step on each side of him and stayed with him all the way down Whitehall, politely enquiring what he was doing about votes for women, until he was able to escape into the sanctuary of the Houses of Parliament. One of them was identified in the newspaper the next day as Violet.

"You're lucky you weren't arrested," Bull said gently.

Edward Bull had mellowed since he came to Bocton. His sons ran the brewery now and he enjoyed the life of a country squire. He had even discovered in the manorial records that the estate had once belonged to a family called Bull. "Nothing to do with us, of course," he had cheerfully remarked. He did not even get angry when Violet had announced her sympathy for the suffragettes, though his own attitudes had remained entirely unchanged. "Medical science has discovered that women's brains are smaller," he triumphantly informed her. Women should grace the home, he felt – and not only most men, but many women agreed. A women's organisation against the franchise had been formed. Mrs Ward, a prominent novelist, wrote in a similar vein. Women would be polluted by politics. Chivalry would die. It was a curious feature of late Victorian and Edwardian life that, partly because of a revival of Arthurian knightly literature, and partly because increasing affluence was bringing leisure to larger numbers of women, even middle-class women were imagining themselves to be as delicate and pampered as eighteenth-century ladies of fashion – an idea that would have greatly puzzled their ancestors.

"This is all because I wouldn't let you go to university," her father concluded.

"No, papa." Why could he never take her seriously? "Is it right that a woman can be a mayor, a nurse, a doctor, a teacher – or a good mother for that matter – yet be denied a vote? Why, things were better in the Middle Ages! Did you know that women could join the London guilds then?"

"Don't be silly, Violet." Edward knew the City: the idea of any of the livery companies admitting women was absurd. He would have been astonished to know that his own brewery had come to him from Dame Barnikel. He sighed. "In any case, it's all a waste of time. Not a single political party supports you."

Unfortunately this was true. There were those for and against in every party, but none of the leaders could decide whether it would be to their own political advantage to add a female vote. Even the most radical were far more interested in enfranchising more working-class men than worrying about women.

"Then we shall go on until they do," she replied.

"What infuriates me about your campaign is that it sets such a bad example," he confessed. "Can't you see that if people like us start publicly agitating, it only encourages the other classes to do the same? And, God knows," he added, "things are dangerous enough as it is."

Violet could sympathise with this last assertion. As the old century had departed, and old Queen Victoria with it, the new King Edward VII faced an increasingly uncertain world. A war against the Dutch-speaking Boers in South Africa had been won only with difficulty, and some doubt about its moral purpose. Murmurings against British rule had begun in India. The German Empire, although the Kaiser was King Edward's nephew, was expanding its colonial and military might in a rather threatening way. Britain's trade, too, was meeting stiff competition now, so that even staunch free-traders like Bull were beginning to wonder if the huge bloc of the British Empire should protect itself with tariffs after all. The issue of whether to give Ireland Home Rule had split the Liberal Party, too, making old political certainties harder for men like Bull. But the most disturbing aspect of the new Edwardian era lay even closer to home.

The huge inequalities and problems of the new industrial age had not been solved. While King Edward VII amused his subjects – the less puritan of them anyway – with his racy court and his splendid style, the uncertainty of these unresolved tensions increasingly troubled them too. Although the great socialist revolution predicted by Marx had not yet come, the Trades Unions which had grown up in the 1880s had two million members by the turn of the century, and four million expected soon. In recent elections they had fielded their own political party which was already emerging as a growing third force. At present the Labour Members of Parliament, only some of them true socialists, were ready to go along with the Liberal government whose radical wing, led by the brilliant Welshman Lloyd George, was pledged to introduce welfare provisions for the poor. "But they won't be able to do much, and the Conservative House of Lords will vote down even that," Bull predicted. "And what will happen then?" It was precisely this vague but growing fear of social unrest that made him deplore the demonstrations of the Suffragettes. "Trouble breeds more. You're stirring it up," he complained. "Have you considered your children?" he went on. "Do you think this is very kind to them? Is it a good example?"

Violet was furious. How could he use her children against her like this? "The children are proud of me!" she stormed. "They know what I'm doing is for a good and moral cause. I'm showing them how to stand up for what is right. And I'm sure they know it."

"Are you sure?" he answered.

His brother Herbert could be rather foolish sometimes with his clowning, thought Percy Fleming. But that was Herbert. A little crowd had paused to look at him as he stood in the middle of Tower Bridge.

"Decide, Percy!" he called out. "I shall stand here even if the bridge opens up until you do!"

One of the crowd was a young woman – well, perhaps a

year or two older than he was, Percy supposed – very respectable-looking. He wondered what she thought of it.

"Well?" cried Herbert, striking an attitude in the fashion of a melodrama at a music hall. "Oh, Percy, you will kill me!"

"I shall if you go on like that," said Percy – quite wittily, he thought. He glanced at the respectable girl to see if she thought so too.

Percy Fleming was a lucky man. In the fourth generation, the descendants of Jeremy Fleming, the Bank of England clerk, totalled thirty in number. Like any other family, some had prospered and some had not. Many had left London. Percy and Herbert's father had kept a tobacconist's shop in Soho, just east of Regent Street, which was a jolly area nowadays. When Percy was a child, the Metropolitan Board of Works had built two great roads in Soho – Charing Cross Road going northwards from Trafalgar Square, and Shaftesbury Avenue which descended to Piccadilly Circus: and before long Shaftesbury Avenue had become lined with theatres. But while Herbert had always loved raffish, theatrical Soho, Percy had always been drawn to the quieter side of Regent Street which merged, as one walked westwards, into sedate Mayfair. There were still some stately old firms of Huguenot clockmakers and craftsmen to be found there, but the chief occupation of the place, spreading out from the street behind old Burlington House called Savile Row, was that of the London tailor.

Though a tobacconist by trade Percy's father had many acquaintances in the business. "The golden mile they call it," he used to tell Percy. "I can always tell, the minute I see a customer step in the door, if he's wearing a West End suit." As for the new ready-made suits which had begun to appear in some clothing stores, his concave face would assume an expression of quiet contempt as he explained: "God did not make men in standard sizes. Each has his own shape and stance. A well-cut suit so perfectly fits that a man can't even feel he's got it on. But a stock item, even if you alter it, will never have any style." Percy had even seen his father hide his better cigars from a customer wearing a ready-made suit.

To Percy, the golden mile was a wonderful place. As a child, he watched the apprentices and the trotters who took samples round and ran errands. Through his father he made friends with some of the cutters, the all-important men at each establishment who cut the patterns for each customer's individual shape, always on to strong brown paper which would be kept, usually hung on a string, for re-use with the customer's next order. It was no surprise then that while his brother Herbert, after a brief flirtation with the theatre, soon settled down as a clerk, Percy was eager to serve the five or six year indenture to qualify as a tailor. And when, all on his own, he persuaded a master tailor to take him on and came back to report the fact to his father, Fleming senior had been truly impressed.

"Tom Brown!" he cried in delight. "Now that, Percy, is what I call a *real* gentleman's tailor."

At Tom Brown's, Percy had spent six very happy years learning the art of tailoring and learned it so well that at the end of that time Mr Brown had made him a good offer of employment. But Percy had other ideas. It was not unusual for a skilled tailor like himself to work independently. He was sure Tom Brown would continue to use him, and working for himself he could take in orders from other tailors too. If you were good, and you were happy to put in long hours, you could make more than you would as an employee, and you had your independence too. But the real impetus had come from Herbert.

"I don't see enough of you, Percy," he'd said, "and you're all that's left of the family now." Both their parents had gone by the old century's end. "Why don't you come up and live near Maisie and me? The air's much better up at Crystal Palace, you know. It'd be better for your cough."

When the vast Crystal Palace had been dismantled after the Great Exhibition, an enterprising group had bought it and reassembled it upon a splendid site on the long ridge, some six miles south of the river, that formed the southern lip of the London geological basin. Until recently, it had been mostly woodland and open field. Gipsy Hill, close by, had been what its name suggested. On the southern slopes of the ridge, even now, the houses soon gave way to open country that stretched away to the wooded ridges of Sussex and Kent as far as the eye could see. But on top of the ridge now, with magnificent views clear over the London basin to the distant hills of Hampstead and Highgate, were streets of houses – mansions in large gardens along the crest, modest houses and suburban villas on the slopes below. The air was excellent, safely away from the London smog in the basin beneath. Crystal Palace, as the area was now called, was a desirable place, and Herbert and his wife Maisie had lived there ever since they married.

"The station's close. I take the train into the City every morning," Herbert had pointed out. "But there's another you could take that goes to Victoria Station. Perfect for the West End. You could get from your door to Savile Row in under an hour."

Herbert was right about his cough. He had been feeling the effects of the London fogs recently. And if he were to leave Tom Brown and work from home, he would not need to go into London every day. But still it was a big move: he had hesitated to make it.

Percy and Herbert would sometimes meet on a Saturday, when Herbert's clerical work in the City ended early at two in the afternoon. Today, after a meal in a pub, and since the autumn day was quite fine, the brothers had gone for a walk. Herbert had not mentioned the subject of Percy's future however, until approaching the old London Stone in Cannon Street, he had pointed to a large structure opposite and remarked: "Now then, Percy, you know what that is!" Cannon Street railway station was a large affair. It covered most of the site where, when the road had still been called Candlewick Street, the Hanseatic merchants had lived – and indeed, where a Roman Governor's Palace had stood a thousand years before that. The busy station had its own iron bridge across the river. "That's where I get my train, Percy, to Crystal Palace."

He had been relentless after that. They had walked down past Billingsgate to the Tower of London, and all the way Herbert pressed him. "You're looking very pale, Percy. You must get out. Maisie's promised to find you a wife. She says she can think of several nice girls. But they'll want to live up there. Come on, Percy. You'll make more money, too!" and finally, as they walked over Tower Bridge, he had decided to play the fool.

"Oh, all right then!" Percy said. "I will."

"He's decided!" Herbert let out a cry. "Ladies and gentlemen," he addressed the bystanders, "you are all witnesses. Mr Percy Fleming here has just promised to set up on his own and move to the salubrious environs -" he went into full music-hall style – "the *rarefied* regions, I say the clean, the clear, the home of the *cr*ème de la *cr*ème, the very *cr*est of *cre*-ation, I am speaking, of course of the Crystal Palace . . ."

There was no doubt about it, Herbert was certainly a card.

Percy glanced round and was relieved to see that the onlookers were smiling. But Herbert was not done yet.

"Madam." He had gone up to the girl Percy had already noticed. "Will you be a witness, that my brother here – he's very respectable you know, and" – a stage whisper now – *in need of a wife* – has agreed to live at Crystal Palace, and that there can be *no turning back*?"

She smiled. "I suppose so," she said, and Herbert gave a little shout of triumph.

"Shake my brother's hand," he insisted, and as soon as she had hesitantly offered a gloved hand: "There, Percy. That's it!"

While Herbert turned to talk to another bystander – it was amazing the way he could do that, and people never seemed to mind – Percy found himself left with the girl. "I'm sorry about my brother," he said. "I hope he didn't annoy you."

"It's all right," she said. "He's just having a lark."

"Yes," he said. "He does that sometimes." He wondered what else he could say. She had very nice brown eyes, he thought. Nothing cocky about her though, like some girls: very quiet, kept herself to herself, he would think. She looked as if she might have suffered a bit. "I'm quieter than he is," he explained.

"Yes," she said. "I can see that."

"You don't live around here, then?" he said.

"No," she hesitated a fraction. "Up at Hampstead."

"Oh."

"That's a long way from Crystal Palace," she pointed out.

"Yes." He looked down. "I often come here on a Saturday like this, walk about, go into the Tower sometimes," he lied. "Just by myself usually."

"Oh," she said. "That's nice."

Herbert was ready to move on now, so Percy had to go. He nearly said, "Perhaps I shall see you again," as they said goodbye, but that would have been a bit forward.

* * *

Edward Bull knew the form. A short walk with his grandson around the grounds of Charterhouse, and it all came out. The teasing had been constant: "How's the Prime Minister, Meredith?" Or more unkindly: "Have they arrested your mother yet? Could she plead insanity?" Once, over his bed, he had found a huge placard saying: "Votes for Women".

"Pretty bad, eh?" Bull asked.

"I had to fight one fellow," Henry admitted miserably; and though he did not say so, it was obvious that he did not think the cause was worth fighting for.

Still, when Bull suggested he treat four boys to tea, there was no shortage of takers. Not a boy in Charterhouse would refuse the chance of food. At a tea shop, he did them proud.

Twenty years as squire of Bocton had added a massive and deep-seated authority to Edward's already powerful presence. To the boys, the solid Kentish landowner was an awesome figure. As for Bull, he had not run a brewery for nothing and he soon got the measure of the boys. There was one in particular they all followed. With his huge acquaintance in the city and elsewhere, there were not many people Edward could not place somewhere, and turning to the boy he casually asked: "Millward you say your name is. Now I know a broker called George Millward. Is he one of your people?"

"My uncle, sir."

"Hmm. Give him my best wishes when you see him." It was very clear that it was Bull who was conferring the favour.

He talked a little about how Charterhouse had been when he had been there, discovered another boy's father had hunted with the West Kent, of which his own son was now joint master; but kept his best move of all until, at the very end of the huge tea, he leaned back, smiled meditatively and remarked to Henry: "I miss your dear father, you know, Henry." And then by way of explanation to the boys: "Colonel Meredith, you know, was a most remarkable sportsman." And with a nod of admiration: "He had probably shot more tigers than any other man in the British Empire."

This, to the boys, was a hero indeed. Before he left, Bull tipped them each half a crown and gave Henry a whole one. His grandson, he rightly guessed, would have no more trouble at school that term.

* * *

As she went down into the bowels of the earth, Jenny Ducket wondered what she was doing. And on a cold day too. Not that it was cold down in the tube.

Arnold Silversleeves had just missed seeing his dream of an electric tube system come true. Gorham Dogget's conclusion after a year of trying to raise finance – "We're a decade too soon" – had been about right; and early in the new century it had been another American entrepreneur, a Mr Yerkes from Chicago, who developed and organized most of the London tube. Just as Arnold Silversleeves had envisaged, the electric trains ran deep underground; and at high points like Hampstead, the shaft down from the surface had to be so long that it seemed almost like descending a mine.

From Hampstead, Jenny's route would take her down to Euston Station where she would take another tube to the Bank of England. She could walk from there. Though I'm going to look a right idiot walking up and down on Tower Bridge freezing my bottom off, she told herself again.

Mrs Silversleeves didn't go out much nowadays, but when she did there were two places she liked to visit. One was Highgate Cemetery where, as he had wished, Arnold Silversleeves had been buried under a cast iron tombstone of his own design. The other was Tower Bridge; for that massive iron machine, whose bascules he had helped design, had been a source of such pride to Arnold Silversleeves in his final years that when Esther took her carriage down to the bank of the Thames she would gaze at it and declare: "Now that is my husband's true memorial."

The previous week however, she had not felt up to going out and had said to Jenny: "You go down there for me. You can take the carriage, have a walk and tell me how it looks." And this was what Jenny had been doing when she met the Fleming brothers.

Dear old Mrs Silversleeves. How vividly Jenny remembered her first arrival in the big, gabled house. She had been so nervous, with her new name of Ducket and all her grandmother Lucy's warnings and instructions ringing in her ears. "But they will give you a home, Jenny," her grandmother had told her, and in their way they had.

Life as a servant was hard work. Often Jenny would leave her tiny room up in the attic at five in the morning. As the youngest she had had the worst jobs, carrying the coal scuttles upstairs, cleaning out the grates, polishing the brass and scrubbing floors. At nights she would sink into bed exhausted. But compared to the life she had known in the East End, it was heaven. Clean clothes, clean sheets, enough to eat. She was expected to go to church every Sunday with the family, but she didn't mind that. And if at first she had found it difficult to remember to bob a little curtsey to Mr Silversleeves or to be properly respectful to the housekeeper, she knew it was only the proper order of things. "For we none of us, Jenny," Mrs Silversleeves would gently tell her, "need to get above our station."

Gradually, little changes had taken place. There was always a present at Christmas. Old Mr Silversleeves had shown her how to look after her tiny savings and augmented them from time to time with a guinea. As for Mrs Silversleeves, as Jenny progressed over the years to housemaid and finally to her lady's maid, she realized that the old lady was very fond of her. She would often say, "Here's a silk scarf you might like for your days off, Jenny." Or a pair of gloves. Or even a coat. Often they were hardly worn and once or twice she suspected that items of clothing had been bought with her in mind all along. Quite often, since being widowed, Mrs Silversleeves would have her remain in the sitting room with her, ask her to read the small print in the newspaper to her and talk to her. Only one subject seemed to be forbidden. When Jenny went, twice a year, to see her father and her brother in the East End, she never mentioned it to her employer. If she did, the old lady became distant and remarked: "We don't want to hear about that, Jenny."

There had been no men in her life. When she was a girl, some of the delivery boys had tried to flirt with her, but she had soon sent them packing. Over the years, through the other women working in the house, she had made a few friends and had met men occasionally, going out with them. There had been a young coachman, a greengrocer and a tramdriver who had all shown an interest in her. "I don't know why, I'm sure," she had confided to the cook, "because I'm nothing much to look at, all pale and thin." But as soon as these advances began, she had quietly discouraged them. She had her reasons. And in recent years, she sensed that old Mrs Silversleeves had so grown to rely on her that she would have felt guilty about leaving her anyway.

So why was she going to Tower Bridge? There was something about Percy, with his concave face, a little sad perhaps but determined, which made him look reliable. And when his brother had said that he needed a wife, she had suddenly felt that yes, she could do that. On Friday she had decided she'd just go for a walk on Hampstead Heath on her day off. She only gave her overcoat a good brush because it was time it had one anyway. And if now, on Saturday, she was making her way to Tower Bridge after all, she told herself it didn't signify. "Because he won't be there anyway."

She was really quite surprised to see him then, an hour later, standing in the middle of the bridge, trying to look casual and pretending he wasn't half frozen after waiting.

"Hello," Jenny said. "Fancy seeing you here!"

There were several regular places where Violet took her children, because it was good for them. Some they liked better than others. The Botanical Gardens at Kew was popular in summer, because they took a boat upriver to get there. Madame Tussaud's waxworks was a favourite too. The pictures in the National Gallery were a duty, though they enjoyed feeding the pigeons that swarmed in Trafalgar Square outside. More often requested was a visit to South Kensington.

So great had the profits of Prince Albert's Great Exhibition of 1851 been that the government had been able to use them to purchase a whole area running down from Hyde Park to South Kensington and here, on each side of a broad avenue called Exhibition Road, several magnificent museums were clustered. As well as the Albert Hall by the park, the new Victoria and Albert Museum was almost completed, and opposite, in a vast, cathedral-like structure, was the Natural History Museum, where fossils, rocks and wonderful drawings of plants all gave evidence of the scientific discoveries and the Darwinian ideas which had been changing the intellectual world in the last two generations. The children loved in particular the huge reconstruction of skeletons of the long-extinct dinosaurs.

For Violet herself there was one excursion that far surpassed all the rest, perhaps because the huge site it occupied lay in the heart of Bloomsbury, the quiet brown-brick Georgian area just east of Tottenham Court Road. It was here that many of the buildings of the University of London, which she would have liked to attend, were to be found. Its collection of antiquities was unrivalled anywhere in the world, and at least once every holidays her three children were taken to the magnificent splendours of the British Museum.

This grey December day, as they were looking at the Egyptian mummies and their cases – always a favourite section with the children – Henry asked casually: "Mother, you aren't going to go on being a Suffragette, are you?"

Violet stared at him blankly. Like many Edwardian parents, she assumed that children remained in a childlike, unquestioning state until they suddenly became adults. She had never discussed her activities even with Henry, except to tell him that women were suffering a great injustice and that she and other brave women were trying to correct it.

Two of her three children believed her implicitly. Little Helen, naturally, wanted to copy her mother in every way, but she had noticed once or twice during the autumn, when her nanny took her to school, that the other nannies had given them strange looks. As for Frederick, too young for Charterhouse, but already boarding away at a preparatory school, the news of his mother's escapade had hardly reached him. To the eight-year-old boy she was the angel, the kindly vision he dreamed of when he was lonely. But, just as naturally, he hero-worshipped his older brother Henry. If Henry and his mother were in dispute therefore, he closed his mind to the whole subject.

"It depends on what the government does," Violet answered.

"Well, I wish you'd drop it," said Henry.

Violet paused. It was so difficult, without her husband, to know how to react to what, she couldn't help thinking, was a great impertinence. "Your father was very much in favour of votes for women," she said carefully.

"I dare say!" Henry replied. "But would he have let you run about in the street and harass the Prime Minister?"

This was going too far, especially in front of the other children. "You arc not to speak to me like that, Henry!"

"You should hear how they speak to me about you at school," he said gloomily.

"Then the worse for them," she said stoutly. "I hope you know that the cause is right."

"No one else seems to think so," he remarked bitterly. "Couldn't you just help them without getting in the newspapers?"

"I am very sorry that you cannot see it is my moral duty to go on," she replied with dignity. "Perhaps in time you will."

"I shall never, mother," he said with equal gravity. It seemed to Violet, as he turned his face away, that some bond between them had suddenly and unexpectedly snapped for ever. Oh, she thought to herself with anguish, if only his father were here to share this burden with me now.

1910

Few of those who buy a West End suit realize that the top half and the bottom have almost certainly been made by different people. When customers came to Tom Brown, their jacket was made by a coat-maker, their vest (English customers called it a waistcoat, though tailors and customers from America still retained the older term of vest) was made by a waistcoat-maker, and their trousers (Americans still said pants, from the pantaloon breeches of the previous era) by a trouser-maker.

Percy Fleming was a trouser-maker and by now he had become very skilled indeed. "I don't know how you do it," Mr Brown had remarked to him recently, "but in the last year we haven't needed to alter a single pair of your trousers, even at the last fitting." Several other fine establishments could have said the same, and as a result, Percy was making a very good living indeed. Which was a good thing really, because he was planning to get married.

He and Jenny had taken their time. They were both cautious, and as they were able to meet at most once a week, he had never been sure during the first months whether he had even established a friendship. But he had persevered, and by the autumn of the previous year she seemed to have relaxed enough even to suggest a rendezvous herself. "I've never been to the zoo," she had said. "Would you like to go there next week?" Yet it had not prevented her, the following month, claiming that she was too busy to see him for three weeks.

"She's playing hard to get," Herbert told him when Percy consulted him. But Percy was not so sure. It had seemed to him that behind her studiously casual friendship, there lay a fear.

Percy's lodgings were on the top floor of a house on the slopes near Crystal Palace, overlooking Gipsy Hill railway station and the parkland around the suburban village of Dulwich beyond. The bedroom was tiny, but there was a large, light attic and this he had arranged as his workroom. As he cut, and stitched, and pressed, he could look up, glance out of the window and see right across London, to the hills of Highgate and Hampstead on the other side. It was a long way, there was no doubt about it. Worlds apart, most people would say. With the material progress of the Victorian age, London had strangely become more divided. The separation of the rich West End from the poorer East went back to the days of the Stuarts, but it was only in recent decades that another division had taken place: the split between north and south of the river.

It was the bridges and the railways that had done it. Always before, the river had been London's thoroughfare. There might have been only one bridge, but there were watermen, literally thousands, to ferry folk across to the theatres, pleasure gardens and other entertainments along the southern bank. As the bridges of the nineteenth century appeared, however, the watermen disappeared and the river slowly lost its colourful life. Then the railways had come, carrying the ever swelling population further and further out to suburbs north and south until now they were even spilling over the distant rims of Highgate in the north and Crystal Palace in the south. The stations – Waterloo, Victoria, Cannon Street, London Bridge – that lay along the river's banks had covered the old areas like Bankside and Vauxhall with railway lines. And so, as the vast, sprawling metropolis spread even further outwards, the two worlds had slowly separated. Middle-class and clerical folk came in from southern suburbs to work in the City or the West End, but were swiftly carried back to their homes, miles away in suburbs. Labouring men, though there were cheap fares to help them travel, usually lived close by their work, in one or other of the two worlds. And the River Thames was the great divider.

When the afternoon light faded and the distant hills of

Hampstead turned a purplish brown, Percy would be overcome by a sense of sadness. He would wish that he could go to Jenny, there and then, see her pale face, feel her eyes on him, just be in her presence. Yet still a week, perhaps two or three would go by before she would see him.

They always met somewhere in central London. Once, when he had suggested they could go for a walk on Hampstead Heath, she shook her head firmly and told him: "No. That's ever such a long way to come, just for a walk." And he had understood: it was too much of an invasion of her territory, implied too much commitment. They had always met in the safe and neutral zone after that.

It was hard to say exactly when he had detected a change. Perhaps it was the moment in Hyde Park when, for the first time, she had linked her arm in his. Their meetings had always been by day: a walk, a visit to the Tower, a visit to a tea shop, but as summer began he had determined to attempt something more daring: he would take her out one evening. He hardly knew what to do until Herbert had come to his aid.

"The Palladium, Percy," he declared. "It's all the rage."

What a night that had been! The huge new theatre, which had only just opened in Piccadilly Circus, was offering the biggest and most splendid music-hall entertainment in London. He had never seen Jenny so animated. She had even joined in when the audience sang along with some of the musical numbers. Flushed and happy, she had let him escort her back to Hampstead in a cab afterwards.

At the gates of the tall gabled house, she had let him kiss her on the cheek. Then he had walked all the way back through the warm night to Victoria Station where, having missed the last train, he lay contentedly on a bench and took the first train at dawn.

All this week the weather had been wonderfully fine. Each morning he had been up at dawn, and as he looked across London, where a hundred thousand roofs glistened with the dew, the faraway ridges of Hampstead were now so green and sparklingly clear that it seemed as if he could reach out and touch them. With the aid of a map, he had worked out exactly at what point on the skyline the Silversleeves house must be. He would imagine Jenny, getting up, going about her business; and from time to time as he stared across the place he would murmur: "I'm waiting for you, girl."

One other milestone of huge significance had been passed that wonderful evening. Before he left her at Hampstead, Percy had extracted a promise that, the following Sunday, she would come to Crystal Palace.

'We'll go and have Sunday lunch with Herbert and Maisie," he'd said. "I can meet you at the station."

Jenny had only paused a moment before she said: "All right, then."

He was sure it would all go off well.

East End. No end. Grey streets, grimy streets, streets without number, streets without meaning, streets that spread on and on under the dull, dreary eastern sky until, somewhere out past the miles and miles of docks they dissolved like an estuary, into a sea of nothingness. East End. Dead end. The East End was not a place, it was a state of mind.

The street where Jenny's family now lived was a short, dingy terrace that had apparently been cut off just as it meant to get started by a high warehouse wall. Their three rooms, on the ground floor of one of the mean little houses, had to contain her brother and his wife, three children, and her father who, though only fifty-six, had discovered that he could no longer work.

It was always the same. Jenny would visit, give him a few shillings, and her brother rather more. And her father would say, with the heavy sentimentality of a drunk: "You see, she never forgets her family." Her brother would say nothing, but his thought was as clear as if he had spoken it aloud. "It's all right for some."

Her brother worked in the docks: some days he found work and some days he did not. But he was better off than some, for the friendships he had formed with the wilder Jewish boys of which old Lucy had so disapproved had turned out to be fortunate.

The trade in second-hand clothes was a lively business. If the better-off classes had their clothes made for them, most poor people in London dressed in second-hand garments and there were plenty of East Enders, usually Jewish, in this trade. And since one of his betting friends had settled into this trade, Jenny's brother was often able to get some extra work driving the cart or minding the store. The sturdy old coat her father wore had once belonged to a sea captain; her brother's three children at least had boots of approximately the right size. And if her brother may have supplemented his income in other less legitimate ways from time to time, while his wife did what jobs she could, Jenny knew very well that they did what they thought they had to.

When her brother's wife, in her solid blouse and frayed skirt, came up to her and saw the clothes Mrs Silversleeves had given her, so neatly laundered and starched, when she could smell how clean Jenny was – "She smells of lavender water," she sadly remarked – and looked at her own roughened hands and chipped nails, when she tried to imagine what kind of house Jenny must live in and glanced at her own tiny rooms with their threadbare pieces of carpet, it was impossible for her not to feel envy. And it was impossible for her brother to keep a trace of malice out of his voice when he greeted her:

"Here's my sister Jenny, then. Ever so respectable."

Jenny did not blame them, but she felt awkward. She knew she could not quite disguise her own repugnance. The musty smell of long-boiled cabbage that pervaded the place; the stinking privy outside that three families shared; the general meanness of everything and, worst of all, the acceptance of these things. It was not that she had forgotten what it was to live like this. She could remember her poor grandmother Lucy with the miserable piles of matchboxes; she could remember hunger, a life far worse than this. But above all, she remembered the last words, spoken with a terrible urgency, that old Lucy had ever said to her. "Don't come back, Jenny. Don't you ever, ever go back to where you've been."

Respectable? For someone like Jenny, respectability meant clean sheets and clothes; a man with a steady job, food on the table. Respectability was morality, and morality was order. Respectability was survival. No wonder then that it was so highly valued by so many of the working class.

The meeting that Saturday had been the same as all the others. They had sat, talked a little. She had brought little presents for her six-year-old nephew and his little sister. She had played with the youngest, a baby girl of only two. She had wondered if perhaps she should mention Percy, but although she was going to see his family at Crystal Palace the next day, there was nothing really, as yet, to say. And the visit would have ended inconsequentially enough, like all the others, if it had not been for the pale and scrawny woman who appeared at the door, just before she was due to leave.

She had red hair, which might have been striking enough, though it was stringy and unkempt; but what made an even greater impression upon Jenny were her eyes, sunken with fatigue and staring. Holding her hand was a filthy child who was bawling because he had cut himself. A quick inspection showed Jenny that the cut wasn't serious, but the poor woman claimed she had nothing to bandage it with. They found something, quietened the child, and also two more of the woman's children who came wandering in. They all looked undernourished. After they had gone her brother had explained.

"Her husband died two years ago. Four children. We all give her a bit of help but . . . ." He shrugged.

"What does she do?" she had asked. "Matchboxes?"

"No. You can get more stuffing mattresses at home. But it's heavy work, you see. Wears you out." He shook his head. "Lost her man, see?"

Soon after that she had left, kissed her father and the children goodbye, and her brother, unusually, had walked with her a little way. At first he remained silent, but after they had gone about a quarter mile he said quietly:

"You done well for yourself, Jenny. I don't begrudge you that, you know. But it's more than that."

"How do you mean?"

"You did right not to marry." He shook his head. "That one you saw. Her husband had a good job, you know. Plasterer he was. And now he's gone . . . ."

She was silent.

"If anything ever happened to me, Jenny, you'd keep an eye on my little ones, wouldn't you? I mean, not let them starve or anything? You not being married, that is. You could do that, couldn't you?"

"I suppose," she said slowly, "I'd do my best."

It was a very jolly party the next day. Percy was looking so pleased and happy as he met her at Crystal Palace Station. She was wearing a pretty little straw hat she had bought herself, a very nice green and white dress, quite simple but very good material, that she had got from Mrs Silversleeves. She had even, though she had never done such a thing before, taken a little parasol. She could see Percy felt proud of her.

The villa where Herbert lived was a nice little house, two storeys over a half-basement, the front door being up a few stone steps. There was a little patch of lawn at the front with a privet hedge around it. There was an evergreen tree in the garden next door which perhaps made the place a little bit dark, but inside it was very nice. Indeed, Jenny's practised eye took in at once, every square inch of the place was polished and gleaming. As soon as she met Maisie, she could see why.

For the greatest social change wrought by the Industrial Revolution in London concerned the suburbs. The vast scale of trading operations, the growing banks, insurance companies and imperial administration in Victorian and Edwardian London required an army of clerks. And because there were now trains, and the spreading suburbs were both cheaper and more salubrious, this hugely expanded class commuted into work in their thousands and their tens of thousands. Men like Herbert Fleming, whose parents or grandparents had been shopkeepers or craftsmen, put on their suits and took the train to the office. Their wives, who would formerly have lived by their workshop or helped in their shop, were left alone at home and considering themselves a cut above women who worked, took on, in whatever small ways they could afford, the mannerisms of ladies of leisure.

Maisie was rather short. The first thing Jenny noticed was that she had a small birthmark on her neck; the second that she had a red mouth and tiny, sharp-looking little teeth. She had a single housemaid, whom she worked to death, and another girl who came in to help. Her sitting room had antimacassars on every chair, a large potted plant in the window and, in pride of place on the wall, a painting of a mountain which, she explained, her father had bought in Brighton. Had Jenny ever been to Brighton? she politely asked as they sat before the meal. Jenny said she had not.

The dining room was rather small. There was a round table in the middle and Jenny found she could only just squeeze into her place.

"I always like a round table. This is the one we had when I

was a child, though it went in a bigger room," said Maisie. "Do you like a round table?" Jenny answered that she liked them well enough.

They had roast chicken, with all the trimmings, carved with a number of theatrical flourishes by Herbert.

Despite these high domestic standards, it was soon clear that Herbert and Maisie also prided themselves on being very jolly. Once a month, without fail, they went to a music hall. "And then I get the whole performance back from Herbert the next evening!" Maisie laughed.

"She's no better with her drama society," Herbert rejoined.

"Maisie has a lovely singing voice," Percy added.

But their favourite activity in summer, Jenny learned, was to go for a bicycle ride on Sunday afternoons.

"Have you tried it?" Maisie asked her. "Herbert and I go for miles sometimes. I do recommend it."

It had not escaped Jenny's notice that Maisie's eyes, which were sharp, had been looking thoughtfully at her clothes ever since she had arrived. When the chicken was done and a fruit pie had been served, she evidently thought it was time to make a few enquiries.

"So," she said brightly, "Percy tells us you live at Hampstead."

"That's right," said Jenny.

"It's very nice up there."

"Yes," said Jenny. "I suppose it is."

"Before we bought this house," said Maisie, with just the tiniest extra clarity on the word "bought", so that Jenny should understand their financial position, "we did think of living up there." Just before she had married, Maisie had inherited the sum of five hundred pounds. It was not a fortune, but enough to buy the house and leave some over. She and Herbert were quite well set up, therefore. "Your family's always lived up there?" she enquired.

Suddenly Jenny realized they didn't know anything about her. Percy hadn't told them. She looked at him for guidance, but all he did was smile. "No," she said truthfully. "They don't."

Percy had never brought anyone to meet Herbert and Maisie before. He had supposed vaguely that they would all like each other. He realized of course that Jenny might not seem a great catch in Maisie's eyes; but it had not occurred to him that she would feel it affected her. Maisie's social aspirations were quite modest and with her house and her popular husband they were nearly satisfied. But if her husband's brother, living nearby, went and married beneath them, what did that do to the name of Fleming in the locality? She had planned – it had been her little project – to find him a nice girl who would do credit to them all. She had to make sure this mysterious girl from Hampstead was safe.

"So what keeps you in Hampstead?" Maisie persisted, quietly.

"That's what I keep asking her," Percy cut in, rather cleverly he thought. "She's so far away up there I never get to see her." And he started to describe in detail the time he had had the week before when he had missed the last train home from Victoria. He and Herbert had a good laugh about that. Maisie was silent.

As for Jenny, she felt only a kind of sullen misery. Was Percy trying to conceal what she was from his family? What was the point?

The meal was over, and the two brothers had just gone outside together when Maisie quietly turned to her.

"I know what you do," she said softly. "You're in service, aren't you?"

"That's right," said Jenny.

"I thought so. Those clothes." Maisie nodded. "We've never had anyone in service in our family, of course. Or Herbert's."

"No. I don't suppose you ever will, either," said Jenny.

"Oh." Maisie looked her straight in the eye. "That's all right then."

When, an hour later, in the handsome park around Crystal Palace, Percy asked her to marry him, Jenny said: "I don't know, Percy. I really don't know. I need some time."

"Of course. How long would you like?"

"I don't know. I'm sorry, Percy, but I want to go home."

Esther Silversleeves waited two weeks before she spoke to Jenny. By then she was worried.

"Jenny, you've been here most of your life. Now please tell me what's the matter." She waited patiently for her to speak.

Though Jenny had a few friends, there was no one she really felt she could confide in; so for the previous two weeks she had thought about it alone. And the more she thought, the more it seemed that everything was impossible. For a start, there was Percy to consider. Maisie and Herbert have probably talked him out of it by now, she thought. I expect he's wishing he'd never proposed. What's Percy want with an old thing like me with no money? she said to herself. Maisie could find him a young girl who'd do him much better. There was her brother and his children, also. I may be poor, she considered, but working as I do, if anything happened to him I could keep those children from starving. And dear old Mrs Silversleeves really needs me, Jenny thought. I'd be walking out on her, too.

"It's nothing, really," she said.

"Tell me about him," the old lady said quietly, and when Jenny looked surprised: "Out late and all dressed up on a Saturday night; then off with a straw hat and a parasol the next Sunday? Surely," she continued, as Jenny looked up ruefully, "you can't think me such a fool that I hadn't noticed."

So, haltingly, Jenny told her some of it. She said nothing about her brother and his family because that subject was forbidden, but she told her a little about Percy and his family, and her doubts.

"I couldn't leave you, Mrs Silversleeves. I owe you so much," she concluded.

"You owe me?" Esther stared at her, then shook her head. "Child," she said gently, "you owe me nothing. I cannot possibly live many more years, you know. I shall be looked after. Now as to this Percy," she continued firmly. "You only suppose he's having second thoughts. If he loves you, nothing this Maisie says is going to affect him in the least."

"But it's his family."

"Oh, damn his family!" said Mrs Silversleeves, surprising them both so much that they laughed. "Now," she said, "is that all?"

It wasn't. Every day the memory of the woman she had seen at her brother's, the desolation of her own childhood, those last words of poor Lucy – "Don't ever go back" – came to visit her. The stark reality was still, as far as Jenny could see, very plain. Marriage to Percy, some children perhaps: all right enough. But if Percy died, what then? A life like the poor folk in the East End? Probably not quite that bad, but hard. Very hard. Her brother had a point. She'd done well not to marry. She had the security of the Silversleeves house; a good character; some savings. After Mrs Silversleeves had gone, she knew she'd find a good position. A housekeeper even, or lady's maid.

Young girls got married without a thought; women like Jenny didn't, despite the fact that she longed to be loved and to live with Percy so much that it hurt.

The pains in her stomach had started a week ago. Sometimes they seemed like a knot. Twice she had been sick and she knew she was very pale. She was not surprised when Mrs Silversleeves said gently:

"Jenny, you don't look very well. I'm going to call the doctor."

If Mayfair had always remained a fashionable residential quarter, the area above Oxford Street had taken on a more professional air. Baker Street, on its western side, had been immortalized by Conan Doyle as the abode of his fictional detective Sherlock Holmes, but Harley Street near its eastern edge had achieved world fame all on its own.

Harley Street: it was, so to speak, the Savile Row of the medical profession. The men who practised in Harley Street were no ordinary doctors, but the most eminent specialists and were usually granted the title of "Mr", rather than "Dr". They also had the reputation for being rude – for the simple reason that they could get away with it. After all, if a man is only treating you for the common cold, you need not put up with much nonsense; but if he is going to cut a piece out of your liver, you normally prefer to humour him.

With some apprehension, the following week, Jenny made her way down Harley Street until she reached the door which a brass plate announced was the sanctum of Mr Algernon Tyrrell-Ford.

The Silversleeves's family doctor had not been able to find anything seriously wrong with her; but he had confessed to Mrs Silversleeves that, had Jenny been able to afford it, he would have sent her to a specialist just to make sure. Esther had been adamant. "Of course she must go!" she said. "Refer all the bills to me." And despite Jenny's protests she had sent her there in the carriage.

Mr Tyrrell-Ford turned out to be a large, portly and brusque gentleman. He ordered her sharply to undress and then examined her. It left Jenny feeling awkward and humiliated.

"Nothing wrong with you," he stated bluntly. "I'll write to your referring doctor, of course."

"Oh," she said weakly. "That's nice." She tried to mumble more thanks; but he did not seem interested. Then, just as she was nearly dressed he casually remarked: "You know you can't have children, I suppose."

She stared at him in horror for a moment. "But why not?" she managed at last.

Seeing no point in wasting words which such an insignificant woman could not possibly understand he merely shrugged. "It's the way you're made," he said.

Percy had suggested by letter that they should meet at Tower Bridge and she had agreed. She understood it was his way of saying that he hoped the place would bring him luck.

Now that she knew what to do it was almost a relief. When she had told Mrs Silversleeves, the old lady was not sure. "He might not mind, Jenny," she had suggested. But Jenny had known better. "He told me he wants a family," she explained. "I know Percy. If I tell him the truth now, he'll say it doesn't matter. But it does." The old lady had sighed.

Though it was summer, it was a dull day. As she had expected, he was waiting for her in the middle of the bridge, just as he had before. She gave him a smile, linked her arm in his in a friendly way, and then began to walk, leading him instinctively to the southern side, as if she were returning him to his own territory. They walked a little way down Tower Bridge Road then turned right towards London Bridge Station where there was a little tea shop where they could sit down.

"What's it to be, then?" he asked.

"Just a cup of tea," she said quickly, so he ordered tea and for a minute or two they talked about nothing at all, until the tea was poured.

"So," he said again, looking at her meaningfully this time. "What's it to be, Jenny?"

"I'm sorry, Percy," she said slowly. "I'm so flattered, I

mean, really honoured, Percy. You're such a kind friend. But I just can't."

He looked shaken. "Is it something Maisie . . ."

"No," she cut in. "It isn't that. I don't care about her. It's my fault. I like going out with you very much, Percy. I've really enjoyed it. But I'm happy where I am. I don't want to get married. Not to anyone." She had thought of telling him there was someone else, to make it more final, but she knew that was absurd.

"Maybe," he said, "I can persuade you to change your mind."

"No." She shook her head. "I don't think we ought to meet for a while."

"Well," he began, "we can still . . ."

"Percy," she cut him short quite sharply with a little show of cruel impatience that she had been practising in her mind for days. "I don't want to marry you, Percy. I never did and I never shall. I'm sorry." And before he knew what was happening, she walked out.

She walked quickly back towards Tower Bridge. She was just about halfway across when she noticed that a ship was approaching from upstream and that the bridge was about to open. She was already hurrying down the northern side when she thought she heard a cry, far behind her.

Percy had been running. For a moment or two he had been so stunned in the shop that he had forgotten to pay for the tea and had been called back. Then he had run as fast as he could back towards Tower Bridge. He saw her from the approach road, cried out, "Jenny!" and was just running out on to the great bascules when a burly policeman stopped him.

"Sorry, you can't go now, lad," he said. "Bridge is up." And as he spoke, Percy saw the road ahead begin to tilt before his eyes as Arnold Silversleeves's mighty mechanism went smoothly into operation.

The raising of Tower Bridge was an awesome sight. It happened about twenty times a day. To Percy it seemed as if the road before him rising up like a huge, hundred-foot wall blocking out the light, severed him with majestic finality from the one he loved.

"I've got to cross now!" he shouted foolishly.

"Only one way to do it, son," the policeman said, and

pointed up to the walkway which ran along the top. With a cry of anguish Percy ran towards the nearby southern tower.

He ran, panting and puffing, up the two hundred steps and more. Gasping he raced across the iron walkway that seemed to stretch before him like an endless, iron tunnel. Then he charged down the iron staircase in the northern tower to the other roadway.

There was no sign of Jenny. She had simply vanished. There was only the grim, old Tower of London behind the trees on the left, and on the right, the silent grey waters of the Thames.

Percy wrote to Jenny three times after that. None of the letters was answered. Maisie introduced him to another girl, but nothing came of that. As he looked out from his window to the faraway ridges across London, he still felt mournful.

1911

Helen Meredith had never felt so excited in all her life. Of course, she was used to being smartly dressed. Like most girls of her class, she was expected to put on a coat and white gloves even for a walk in Hyde Park. She was a child, to be dressed and treated accordingly. But not today. As she gazed at herself in the glass in her long white dress, with her sash of purple, white and green, she felt so proud: she was dressed exactly the same as Mummy. And they were going to march together, side by side in the Women's Coronation Procession.

The Edwardian era, though unforgettable, had only lasted a decade. Already well into an over-indulged middle age when his mother, old Queen Victoria died, King Edward VII had been showing signs of being unwell for some time, and his death the previous year had not been entirely unexpected. Now, after a suitable period of mourning, his son George V – correct, monogamous and dutiful – was to enjoy his coronation with his devoted wife Mary.

On Saturday 17 June, the weekend before the royal event, the Suffragette movement had decided to hold a coronation procession of their own. It was going to be huge.

There was no question that in the last three years, the Suffragette movement had made astonishing advances. Some of the tactics of its members had seemed outrageous, some rather cunning. Their ploy of chaining themselves to railings in public places, for instance, not only brought publicity, but allowed them to make lengthy and well-prepared speeches while the police had to saw through the chains. Discovering that if they walked on the pavements they could be arrested for obstruction, they took to walking with their placards in the gutters at the edge of the roadway where the police were powerless to stop them. When some of their more enthusiastic members had broken windows because the government refused to see their deputations, they were arrested. When they went on hunger strike in prison, many people thought it unjustified. But when there were well-documented reports of policemen assaulting and even beating demonstrating women, and of brutal force-feeding in jails, there was public disquiet. It was not just publicity that the movement had achieved. A detailed plan for moderate legislation had been prepared and a truce on all illegal acts had been called while the government considered it.

But above all, the years had brought supporters. With their headquarters in the Strand and their own publishing house, the Women's Press in Charing Cross Road, the movement was now large and professional. All over the country, affiliated organizations had sprung up. And today, symbolically marking the start of the new reign, the movement was going to demonstrate to all the world that it had come of age.

"Come on," her mother said with a smile. "We march together." Helen felt great pride as they set off together for Sloane Square underground station.

Lying immediately west of the walled grounds of Buckingham Palace and just below Knightsbridge at the eastern end of Hyde Park, Belgravia which belonged to the rich Grosvenor family, had been developed by Cubitt into a series of streets and squares of white stucco houses. Architecturally undistinguished, they were large, grand and expensive. The grandest of all was Belgrave Square. Then, running westward, the long rectangle of Eaton Square with the more modest Eaton Terrace, to which Violet had moved after Colonel Meredith's death, at its western end. Sloane Square, which marked the border between Belgravia and the start of Chelsea, lay only a short walk away, and contained an underground station.

As the two Suffragettes walked through this fashionable quarter some of the other inhabitants looked at them with disapproval. Helen had never experienced such a thing herself.

"People are glaring at us," she whispered to her mother. She never forgot her mother's reply.

"Really?" Violet smiled airily. "Well I don't mind. Do you?"

To Helen this seemed so free, so wonderful and so funny that she burst out laughing.

"I think that they all look terribly silly," said Violet gaily as they entered the underground.

The procession, when they emerged on the far side of Westminster, was like nothing Helen had ever seen in her life. The Suffragettes had learned that the way to disarm criticism that they were unwomanly was to dress with great care. The women, in their tens of thousands, were all wearing long dresses, mostly white, and could have been taken for matrons, or their daughters, from the strictest days of republican Rome. The only exception was the figure riding a horse near the front and dressed as Joan of Arc, whom the movement had adopted as their own saint. There were deputations and floats not only from all over England but from Scotland, Wales, and even India and other parts of the empire. The whole procession was four miles long. It would wind its way from the City, past Big Ben and the Houses of Parliament, and on to Hyde Park and the great rally – tickets all sold out long ago – in the Royal Albert Hall.

"And remember," her mother told her, before the huge procession moved off, "our cause is just. You must be prepared to fight for a noble cause, Helen, my child. We are marching for our country, and for a better future."

Although she never forgot these words, nor the amazing sight of thousands of women with their white dresses and sashes and banners, it was the extraordinary sense of marching that the girl remembered. Marching in unison, marching for a cause, marching side by side with her mother, into the new world.

* * *

There were other signs in these years that a new age was dawning. When, for instance, in the year that King Edward VII died, Halley's comet was seen it was treated as a simple, scientific event. More significant, perhaps, was the development of the motor car.

The English had been rather slow to make use of the internal combustion engine. There were some motor-buses now and a few motorized cabs; but so far the small numbers of motor cars in use were only for the very rich. Rolls-Royce had only been going for half a dozen years, but Penny owned one and early on Saturday, 17 June 1911, he came to pick up old Edward Bull.

The Penny family had always remained close to their Bull cousins; and thanks to his marriage to Gorham Dogget's daughter Nancy and to the huge success of the Penny Insurance Company, he was quite as rich as old Edward. The plan was that they would drive over to pick up Bull's two grandsons, the Meredith boys, who were both at Charterhouse now, and take them back to Bocton. The following day at tea-time, Penny would take them back. Even old Edward Bull, who had scarcely been in a motor car, was secretly rather excited by this expedition. "Though I don't know whether I should let you drive me in this contraption with your short sight," he had cheerfully remarked.

The day was fine, the country road beautiful. They averaged nearly twenty miles an hour and arrived at Charterhouse comfortably before lunch. Far from being tired, old Edward felt in excellent spirits and was considerably put out when Penny, having been given a telephone message by the boys' housemaster, announced that he had to go back to London.

The boys' faces fell too. It seemed the drive in the car and the weekend were to be lost, but Henry leaned forward.

"I wonder, grandfather," he said politely, "if I could make a suggestion."

There was no doubt about it, Bull thought, as the Rolls-Royce bowled into London two hours later: his grandson Henry Meredith was a fine young man. He knew what he'd been through at school, and not just on his own account either. Several times he'd been in scraps defending his younger brother from merciless bullying after their mother's name and photograph had appeared in newspapers. Finally Henry had declared that he personally supported the Suffragette cause – which he didn't in the least – and that anyone in the house who didn't like it would have to fight him first. As he was now tall and very strong, few cared to dispute with him.

"I do respect Mother because she believes in her cause," Henry had told his grandfather. "It may even be that women should have the vote, I suppose. I hate the Suffragettes' methods, but when she tells me that the polite, old-fashioned way gave women nothing, I can't deny it. I wish she could drop them, or at least support them quietly, but she feels she cannot. So in the end, grandfather, I support her because she's my mother."

"If you're going to return to London anyway," he had suggested, "couldn't we go too? We could spend the night at home instead and go back on the train to school tomorrow." And then, giving his grandfather a sidelong glance, "We've seen the newspapers, grandfather, so we know Mother's going to be out marching today. Why don't we all of us go round and give Helen a surprise? We could take her out for tea."

It was early evening and Helen's feet were quite sore when she and her mother reached the house. Even so, she felt a sense of triumph: they had marched on a famous day. She was surprised when the maid who opened the door looked rather frightened, and said something to her mother that she did not hear. Then, from the doorway to the drawing room she heard a familiar voice. Her mother whispered, "Go up to your room, Helen," but she didn't, and a moment later, unnoticed, peeped round the door.

Her grandfather was in there; so was Henry. If Frederick had come with them, he must have been sent to another part of the house. Her grandfather looked frightening and even Henry looked grave, and somehow older. Her grandfather spoke first.

"Am I to understand that you have dressed up Helen, an innocent child, as a Suffragette?"

"Yes." Her mother's voice was defiant.

"And taken her to a demonstration that could have turned into a riot?"

"It was perfectly peaceful."

"They have turned into riots before. In any case, a child's

place is in the nursery. You have no business dragging her into such affairs. These things are not for children. She shouldn't even hear about them."

"She is only eight, mother," Henry added quietly.

"Are you telling me I shouldn't even mention the subject of votes for women to my own daughter?"

"I see no need," Bull said evenly.

"That's just because you don't agree with it."

"No. She can decide for herself one day. But she is a child. Children should be protected from ideas."

"It would be wrong to take her to church then. She might hear ideas."

"That is blasphemous," Bull said quietly. "You are speaking of our religion. I must tell you, Violet," he went on steadily, "that if you ever use this child in this disgraceful way again, I shall remove her from you. She can live with me at Bocton."

"You can't!"

"I think I can."

"I'd take you to court, father."

"And a judge might well agree with me that you are an unfit guardian for a child."

"This is absurd! Henry, say something."

"Mother, if such a thing ever happened I should testify against you. I'm sorry. You're unfit." And he burst into tears.

Helen shook with terror until a pair of hands seized her from behind and carried her upstairs to the safety of the nursery.

There had not been a morning like it at Tom Brown since anyone could remember. The worst of it was that Lord St James himself was in one of the fitting rooms when it happened. What if he wanted to come out?

A lady had entered the premises.

She was very old. Very respectable, certainly. All in black, walking with an ebony stick. She had asked for Mr Fleming who, as it happened, was due to deliver some trousers that very morning. "Do you suppose we could hide her in another fitting room?" the salesman whispered.

"You will do no such thing," said Mr Brown calmly. "You will offer her a chair and make sure his lordship is fully dressed before he leaves the fitting room."

It had not been easy for Esther Silversleeves to decide what to do. She had respected Jenny for her decision to send Percy away, and as the months had passed and the letters from Percy finally ceased, she had sighed to herself and decided that this was fate. She had sent the girl on a week's holiday to Brighton that summer to cheer her up, which it had seemed to do – until a week ago, when another letter had come and Jenny had been visibly upset.

"It's Percy," Jenny said. "Says he's waited a year before writing, but that he'd like to see me again. Just as a friend. Says he's been sick, but didn't say what so I don't know if it's serious or not."

"You could see him, couldn't you?"

"Oh, madam, I don't know. I just don't think I could bear it." And the tears had welled up.

Esther Silversleeves had been meaning to go down to the West End for some time. Two years before, an American gentleman named Selfridge had opened a huge new department store in Oxford Street. When she was younger, Esther had always liked to go once a year before Christmas to the huge emporium of Harrods in Knightsbridge. Selfridges, she had heard, not only planned to rival it but had so much, including a restaurant, that you could spend the entire day in there. So she had instructed her old coachman to leave her there at ten and return at three; and no sooner had he gone than she had walked rather stiffly along to Regent Street and down to the premises of Tom Brown.

Neither she nor Lord St James knew who the other was when that nobleman emerged from the fitting room, shot her a glance of amusement, and made his way back to the quiet bachelor quarters of Albany, where he now lived, in nearby Piccadilly.

When Percy arrived at half past eleven, he was greatly surprised to encounter Mrs Silversleeves, whom he had never seen before. At her request he escorted her back to Selfridges and took her to the restaurant where she ordered a little cake and a cup of tea. She asked him a few questions about his health, nodding slowly, then asked him if he still cared for Jenny. Having satisfied herself with his answer, she explained her mission.

"Jenny herself, Mr Fleming, has no idea that I have come to

see you, and I do not wish her to know. But I am going to tell you something. What you do with the information, of course, is entirely up to you."

It had taken a little gentle persuasion from Mrs Silversleeves before Jenny had agreed to go. The second letter, saying that he was going away for the whole winter on account of his health had done it. "I think, if you can bear to, that it would be a kindness to see him," Esther said when Jenny consulted her. And so, two weeks later, in a nice little café called the Ivy, just off the Charing Cross Road, she found herself sitting opposite Percy again, having tea.

He looked cheerful enough, though a little pale. They made the usual enquiries. Her life was the same as ever. She had been to Brighton. Mrs Silversleeves was well. Maisie and Herbert were involved in a Christmas pantomime with Maisie's drama club. His lodgings at Crystal Palace were as nice as ever. Not until after the first ritual cup of tea did Jenny approach the big subject.

"So, you're going away."

"That's right." He shook his head thoughtfully. "It's silly really, I suppose, but the doctor said I should." He smiled a little wanly. "It was that cough of mine. They were afraid it was tuberculosis, actually." It was the curse of the time. "It wasn't, but the doctor says to me: 'If you really want to get well, you should go somewhere warm for the winter.'"

"That's just like the rich people, Percy. They go to the south of France."

"I know." He smiled. "Funnily enough, that's just what I'm doing. It turns out if you go to a little guest house or something, it's much cheaper in France than in England. And I've actually got quite a bit saved up now. Not being married," he smiled a little sadly. "I've nothing to spend it on. So," he continued cheerfully, "it's off next week for a five-month holiday in the south of France! They think when I get back in the spring I shall be fit as a fiddle."

"Oh, Percy! *Parlez-vous?*"

"No. Not a word. I'll have to learn I suppose."

"You'll be meeting all those French girls, Percy." She managed to laugh quite easily and was pleased with herself. "You'll bring back a French wife."

Percy frowned and seemed to hesitate. Looking at her a little oddly, he remarked: "I'm not sure about that, Jenny." He was silent again for a moment or two. "Actually, it turns out you did better than you knew when you turned me down. When they were doing all these tests on me trying to find out what was wrong with me, they told me something else. I can get married – and all that – if you see what I mean. But it seems there won't ever be any children. No little Percys. Pity really, but there it is." He nodded thoughtfully.

"Oh," she said.

It was dark when old Edward Bull came out of the lodge and walked from the Wallbrook up towards St Paul's. He intended to spend the night at his club.

There had always been a great many Freemasons in the City of London. Some found their secret ceremonies, their initiations and hidden membership sinister. Personally, Edward Bull had never found it to be any such thing. He had become a Mason as a young man, knew a great many City men through it, and regarded the whole business as a sort of club, with admittedly some rather quaint and medieval rules, but which was mainly concerned with doing charitable works, rather like a medieval City guild. It was the pleasure of these associations that had brought him into London that spring day in 1912, for a meeting of his lodge.

He had just started up Watling Street when he picked up a newspaper from a stand and saw the headline.

He found Violet in a cell. The police had been very kind to him, taken him to see her at once, even asked him if he'd like a cup of tea. They seemed to think it was a pity for such a respectable old gentleman to have such a daughter.

She was astonished to see him. "I've been trying to get a message to the lawyers," she explained, "but by the time I was brought here they'd gone for the day. You've got to bail me out, father. I need to get home to Helen."

"I understand that you have been smashing windows," he replied steadily.

The Suffragette campaign of smashing windows had begun, together with attacks on the grass of golfing greens, and even some arson – though carefully chosen so that no one would be hurt – the previous November after the Liberal government, backed by the worthy but conservative-minded King George, had ignored all their suggested reforms and then added insult to injury by giving more votes to working men, and none to women at all. "It's an outrage, so women are replying with outrages in return," she had explained at the time.

Violet herself had not been involved until now, nor, as it happened, had she intended to be that day. But when, walking back from a meeting, she had seen some women who had just rather carefully broken a window being roughly handled by a policeman, she had taken her umbrella and banged it against the broken window herself in a fit of rage. It had been enough, in the heated moments that followed, to secure her arrest.

"I'm sure you could persuade them to let me go for the night," she suggested.

"Yes," Bull agreed gravely. "I dare say I could." Then he shook his head. "But I'm afraid, Violet, that I am not going to."

"But, father! Helen . . . ."

"I shall go to pick up Helen now, Violet. I'm sorry, but we can't have this sort of thing. She shall come with me to Bocton."

"I shall come straight away and take her back!" she cried.

"I doubt it. I think it is far more likely, Violet, that you are going to prison."

He proved to be right. She got three months.

The marriage of Percy Fleming and Jenny Ducket – though the marriage certificate, to Percy's surprise, gave her name as Dogget – took place that summer. It was attended by Herbert, and by Maisie, who was not at all pleased, and by old Mrs Silversleeves. Because of the old lady – at least, that was the reason she gave herself – Jenny had not invited her father or brother. Mr Silversleeves, the lawyer, at his mother's particular request, came and gave her away.

The surprise came just after the old lady had left, when Mr Silversleeves took the couple to one side. "My mother has entrusted me with your wedding present," he explained, "and I am to hand it over to you in person. It is a cheque."

It was for six hundred pounds.

"But . . . I can't!" Jenny cried. "I mean, just for doing my job and looking after her . . . ."

"She is most insistent that you accept it," he said. "Those are my instructions." And he gave her a particular smile which she could only have understood had she known what, when he, too, had protested at the amount, the old lady had told him.

So Jenny and Percy were married and bought a little house up in Crystal Palace. It pleased Jenny that she could look right across London to the place where the old lady had been so good to her.

A still greater surprise to them both, however, occurred the following spring. At first Jenny said nothing. After another month, a little alarmed that something was wrong with her, she went to see a doctor. When she told him it was impossible, he assured her that it was not. And when, that night, she consulted Percy, he first stared, then burst out laughing.

For his own part, he knew that he had lied to her about his ability to have children, but the other part he had not foreseen and their son was born that summer.

The eminent Mr Tyrrell-Ford of Harley Street had been talking through his hat.

Chapter 20

The Blitz

1940

MORNING

"I was born lucky, I suppose." By rights Charlie Dogget should have been dead some hours ago.

The sun was already up. Overhead there was a pale blue sky. Charlie looked up as they drove across Tower Bridge and saw dozens of seagulls wheeling about over the river and filling the air with their cries. He and the other firemen had taken their helmets off, glad after their long, hot vigil to feel the cool morning air on their faces. Behind them smoke was still rising from the fires all over the East End and the City. They had just endured another night of Hitler's Blitz – and, in Charlie's case, they had seen a miracle.

But then when you thought about it, things had always turned out all right for the cheerful cockney with the white flash in his hair. Even in the hard days in the East End, he had always seen the bright side. Take his father and his Auntie Jenny. "Your rich Auntie Jenny doesn't want to know us any more. Never even invited us to her wedding," his father would always say. It was a refrain he had heard a thousand times. But she used to send them Christmas presents and to Charlie her very existence was a sort of inspiration. If one of the family could get out of the East End and get on in the world, then so, he felt, could he.

He could understand why his father and most of the men he knew were bitter. There wasn't enough regular employment in the docks and even when you got a job, you weren't safe. One day his father had been sacked for just looking at a foreman. "What are you looking at me for?" the foreman had shouted. "You're off!" And his father had never been able to work in that yard again. It was the same all over the docks and people heard that conditions in other industries, like the mines, were even harsher.

Of course, if you had a skill, life could be much better. His best friend when he was a boy had become a plasterer. He had an uncle in that trade who'd got him into a company where he'd served his apprenticeship. He'd done well and was living outside the East End now. But Charlie never quite had the patience for something like that. "I'll take my chances in the docks," he'd said. "You'll never get out," his friend had told him. But he was wrong there. "I got kicked out, and into a better life," Charlie would declare cheerfully.

His marriage to Ruth – what a row there had been! It was one thing for his father to have Jewish friends in Whitechapel, but when he fell for Ruth, that was quite another matter. Some of his own friends warned him: "They're still foreign, Charlie. They're not like us." But the real trouble came from Ruth's father. He was a small, bald man with pale blue eyes, who had his own little business. He had always been friendly enough before, but now he would start shouting whenever he caught sight of Charlie. "'A thief' he called me," Charlie reported. "Said I was stealing Ruth from her faith."

"He's right, actually," his father had pointed out. "You'd better leave it alone, son. You're meddling where you shouldn't."

"Doesn't seem to worry Ruth," Charlie replied.

When they had married, Ruth's family had cut her off entirely. Even her childhood friends deserted her, and she had told him: "Charlie, I want to get out." It was Charlie's friend the plasterer who had come up with an acquaintance with lodgings in Battersea: three upstairs rooms in a house just below what had still, until a generation ago, been the open fields of Lavender Hill. Both of them had been nervous about the move. Charlie wasn't sure what it would be like moving into an area where he wasn't known and as for Ruth, she had never lived in a place which had no Jewish community, though as fair-haired, blue-eyed Mrs Charlie Dogget, she fitted in easily.

Once again, Charlie felt he'd fallen on his feet. While Ruth got a job at a piano factory nearby, he found work on the buses. And best of all, after a year or two, he managed to get them a nice little house to rent in the safest part of the area.

The Shaftesbury Estate was a well-run community of workmen's houses, set up by the philanthropic Lord Shaftesbury for respectable workers and artisans. By the time their first child was born, things were looking up for Charlie.

In general, however, things were not all that much better for the working man. The Trades Unions had slowly improved things for working folk, and their representatives, the Labour Party, had become so numerous in Parliament that they could now be in a position to form a government. But in the difficult years after the Great War jobs were still scarce, money short. Some people hoped for a complete change to a socialist state and Charlie had heard a wonderful speech once by a man called Carpenter, a member of the socialist Fabian Society, who had promised a bright new world. But like most Londoners of the working classes, Charlie was a bit sceptical. "I don't know about a revolution," he would say, "but I'd like to see some better pay and conditions for the working man."

Only once had he come out on a big strike and that was the General Strike of 1926. The whole Trades Union movement had done so in sympathy for the coal miners who they felt, with justification, were being shabbily treated. "We'll come out, of course," he told Ruth. "I mean you have to." But he had a feeling it wouldn't do any good. He had been a bus conductor on the 137 route then, that went south from central London all the way out to Crystal Palace. The day before the strike he had taken a pair of brothers down from there. Respectable working men, he remembered, one a tailor and one a clerk.

"If you stop working, we shall walk to work," they had told him. "You won't stop us." If the tailors and clerks and the rest of them were against the strikers, he didn't think they'd get far. The bright young things of the upper classes also did their bit to break the strike. He had been walking with another busman up on Clapham Common when they had seen a 137 bus careering around it, driven by a young man and with a fair-haired girl conductor hanging gaily out of the back. "There's no passengers," his friend had remarked. "People are expressing solidarity with the working class." But Charlie was not so sure. Would anyone get on, with that young idiot driving, he wondered?

The General Strike collapsed in less than ten days. Slowly,

however, there were some signs of improvement. Modern factories like the Hoover factory, or the huge Ford Motor works east of London had been bringing jobs and steady wages to the capital. Houses had electricity, country roads were properly surfaced, people were driving cars – though as the smell in any London street would tell you, there were still plenty of horses and carts about. Progress was being made, inch by inch. There was still a Union Jack, and an empire, and a king, a good and modest fellow on the throne. "It's not all bad, is it?" Charlie would say.

On this September morning they turned west at the southern end of Tower Bridge and drove along the line of the Thames. They passed Westminster and looked across at the comforting sight of the great tower of Big Ben. As they came to Lambeth they could see the four huge chimneys of Battersea Power Station a mile ahead of them across the railway lines and goods yards of Vauxhall.

And the vehicle that these gallant firemen were driving was, like the majority of fire vehicles in the Blitz, a London taxi.

In shape and dimensions it was actually a motorized version of the old horse-drawn hackney cab: roomy inside and highly manoeuvrable. Fitted up with ladders on the roof and pulling a trailer pump behind, it dodged about the burning streets rather effectively. Anyway, it was all that the Auxiliary Fire Service had. AFS volunteers like Charlie had been given a rigorous training by the London firemen so that, when the war began, a number were taken on at once as full-time members at three pounds a week. There had been teething problems: Charlie and his fellow recruits had been stationed for a while in an old building near Vauxhall where they had all caught fleas and scabies. More hurtful to morale had been the suggestion, in the early months of the war, that the auxiliary firemen had volunteered to dodge the army, and many had actually left. But the last few days were giving the despised firemen the chance to show their mettle. For in September 1940, a year after the war was officially declared, Hitler began his famous offensive to bring England to its knees: the Blitzkrieg upon London.

Charlie could remember the Kaiser's war very well. There had been some Zeppelin raids on London then which had seemed shocking at the time. They'd all known of course that this time it would be a very different story, but even so, nothing could have prepared anyone for what was now taking place. The Blitz was not just a raid: it was an inferno. Night after night the bombs rained down on the docks. Sugar refineries, tar distilleries, more than a million tons of timber blazed, exploded and sent up walls of fire that the men in the converted taxis could scarcely hope to quench. But the most terrible fires of all that grim September had been the huge cylindrical tanks of oil that poured black smoke up into the atmosphere for days on end, and that could be seen almost a hundred miles away in the West Country.

Up on the roof of one oil tank last night, Charlie had not heard the warning cries of the men below. The first he saw of the Messerschmitt was when it was about five hundred yards away and coming straight for him. More from instinct than anything else, he did the only thing he could and pointed the hose at the pilot as he came. No one was sure how it was that Charlie was still there three seconds later as the fighter wheeled up into the air again.

"That's funny! I thought being a fireman was supposed to be safer than going in the bleeding army," he remarked cheerfully as he came down. But as they made their way back to Battersea that morning the thought did occur to his friends that a man can only have just so much luck, and Charlie seemed to have used up rather a lot of his last night.

AFTERNOON

"Something wrong?"

Normally Helen slept another hour into the afternoon, so when she appeared in the drawing room at Eaton Terrace at only two o'clock, her mother looked up sharply. "Rest some more," she continued.

"I can't sleep." There were rings under her eyes.

"Ah." Violet said nothing for a moment, then gently enquired: "Same trouble as the other day?"

Driving an ambulance in the midst of so much horror and death, it was not surprising that Helen should occasionally be haunted by premonitions of death. Most of the time, she told her mother, she was too busy to think about it, but sometimes such thoughts visited her and she would give her mother's arm an extra little squeeze of affection as she went off.

"You've had these feelings before," Violet said softly. "And here you still are."

"I know. I think I might go for a walk. Would you mind?"

"Of course not. Off you go." A moment later, hearing the door bang, Violet was left alone with the silence. Only after a long pause, during which she heard nothing but the quiet ticking of the clock, did she allow herself to sigh.

She had lost one child already. Must she lose another?

Henry. Henry who had never forgiven her for the campaigning which had made him suffer at school, Henry who had supported old Edward against her when, in the eighteen months that she had been in and out of prison, the old man had Helen with him at Bocton. "He's given the family a home," he had said to her bitterly. "You haven't." Yet despite that, it had been Henry who had come to visit her in prison. No one else from the family had.

Over a quarter-century had passed since that time, yet to Violet now, at the age of seventy, it seemed only too painfully close. She had been imprisoned three times. A sort of fever gripped many in the movement at that time. Enraged by the cynical contempt shown by even the Liberals, some of the movement had turned increasingly to acts of carefully calculated outrage. Several houses, including Lloyd George's, had been burned down. Emily Wilding Davison had even thrown herself in front of the king's horse during a race and been killed. With her father implacable at Bocton and her sons against her, she remembered telling a colleague: "I may as well be hanged for a sheep as a lamb." A week later at a demonstration she had been arrested again. Three months in prison that time, but in company with a dozen other women she knew. What a camaraderie they had felt! Soon after they were released, they had all been put in gaol again - six pale, determined women, shamefully treated in their fight against a cruel injustice.

Henry had come to see her then. A week later – dear God, she would remember *that* to her dying day – they had gone on hunger strike. She had never known what real hunger could feel like. And then the awful force-feeding: the powerful hands dragging open her clenched jaw; the threats to break her teeth. That cruel tube rammed down her throat, the awful searing agony, her throttled screams, the raw, burning pain that remained in her throat, hour after hour, until they came to do it again. The third time she fainted.

It had come as a shock, when she finally emerged, physically broken, to realize that the country was drifting towards war. After all, Germany might be an imperial rival to Britain now, but the two countries had always seemed to be natural friends. The king and the German Kaiser were cousins. Germany might be jealous and aggressive, the politics of Central Europe might be a tinder box, but somehow things would be patched up. Who could have foreseen that in a welter of botched diplomacy and misunderstanding the powers of Europe would get themselves into a position where they were forced to declare a war that none of them wanted? And who could have realized that after a skirmish or two the whole silly business would not have been over in a few months?

It had been the end of July 1914, just a week before war was declared. Henry had been due to go up to Oxford that autumn and even then none of them could believe that a war would prevent it. Within the family there had been a truce since Violet's release. Her father was really very old now, shocked by her treatment in prison and desiring only to see his family living in peace. They had all been reunited at Bocton and for some months she had made only a few trips to London. On one of these she had decided to take all three children to the British Museum. As usual she had led them up to its grand portals – only to be refused admission.

"I'm sorry, madam," the doorman explained, "but no ladies are being allowed in. It's those terrible suffragettes," he confided. "We're afraid they'll set fire to the place or start smashing the glass cases."

"I will take responsibility for this lady," Henry had offered, and so, after some hesitation, the doorman had let them in.

"By the way, mother," he had whispered, as soon as they were inside, "which glass case do you want to smash first?"

Dear Henry: a month later he had volunteered and was in uniform.

She had discovered what mustard gas could do when he had finally been invalided home after Ypres in 1915. "I suppose I should be glad to be alive," he told her wryly. Indeed, had he been older, he probably would have died. "These very young men have hearts that will take almost anything," the doctor told her. But he was a shadow, grey and almost lifeless all the same. And so he had stayed all through the long years of the Great War, while others were dying in the huge futility of trench warfare. By the end, Violet scarcely knew a single family who had not lost someone.

The war brought one other great change. So severe was the shortage of men at home that women stepped in to do their jobs – and were welcomed. They worked in the munitions factories and on the railways, they served behind counters, worked the telephones, toiled and dug. The Suffragettes had given up their campaign for the duration of the war; their service, it soon appeared, made their case for them. As people saw what women were doing, even the most stalwart conservatives found their own opposition to women's votes melting away. Violet knew her cause had finally triumphed when old Edward who had been taken ill and had to spend a few days in hospital told her: "The whole place was run by women, Violet! Porters, ambulance drivers, everything except the doctors. Very well run too."

In 1917, with hardly a murmur against it, Asquith, the Prime Minister, gave women the vote, declaring: "They have earned it."

The following year the Great War ended – and with it, Violet had supposed, the terrible loss of life.

Whether the great pandemic of Spanish 'flu at the end of 1918 was more dangerous than other influenzas, or whether it was just that, weakened after the long trauma of the war, people were more vulnerable, it was hard to know, but it spread right round the world with astonishing speed. The global death-toll in a six-month period was greater than that of the Great War itself. In England, more than two hundred thousand were estimated to have died. One of them was Henry.

Since then the memory of that winter had dissolved into a grey blur out of which his poor, pale, ravaged face arose to haunt her. And again and again over the years she had asked herself: should she have let the others do the marching? Why had she given such pain to the child who was gone?

As she sat alone in the house while Helen went for her walk

it was hard to come to terms with the grim thought that she had not confessed to her daughter. Helen had not had her premonition alone. Violet had had it too.

Helen walked through Sloane Square then turned up Sloane Street towards Knightsbridge and Hyde Park. It still felt odd to look at the familiar streets which she remembered as a débutante and see all the windows taped against bomb blast and the piles of sandbags by every doorway. The place seemed strangely quiet, like a Sunday.

As she passed Pont Street, a few drops of rain began to fall. By the time she was nearing Knightsbridge it had turned into a shower. To escape it she dived left into the Basil Street Hotel where she waited, gazing out of the window as the raindrops streamed down it, feeling sad.

She had no wish to die. She did not think she particularly deserved it. Hadn't she at least tried to serve some purpose all her life? She had always known that her mother was right to serve a cause, despite what the others had said. When she had been taken away to live at Bocton as a child her grandfather had tried to pretend that her mother was mysteriously called away, too, though she had known perfectly well from her brothers that she was in gaol. This had not detracted from the respect she had felt for the old man: she could see from the obvious respect that everybody had for him that apart from his disagreement with her mother his opinions were probably sound. Sometimes, having nobody else to talk to, he had discussed the issues of the day with the little girl as they sat in the old walled garden or went to look at the deer. And even now she could hear him, as clearly as if he were beside her, explaining gently:

"It's the socialists who are the real danger to us all, Helen, far more than the Germans. Mark my words, that will be the battle you face in your lifetime. Not only in Britain either, but in the whole world."

Had he lived just a little longer, to the end of the war, how right he would have seen his words to be. The Bolsheviks. The Russian Revolution. She had still been at school when these horrors occurred. The Tsar and all his children murdered. A wave of sympathy and disgust had passed across all Europe. As the horror of the war and the misery of the great flu epidemic receded, the Bolshevik menace was spoken of whenever people turned to serious conversation. Could such a thing, as the Bolsheviks themselves confidently predicted, come to Britain too, destroying everything she knew and loved?

In a way – her mother said so, everybody said so – a revolution in English society had already begun. The death duties introduced by Lloyd George had been cutting a swathe through the upper classes. There had been large sums to pay when old Edward had died at Bocton. Numerous gentry and aristocrats were being obliged to sell up. The coalition government during the war had been continued afterwards, on and off, but with the great difference that when the recently enfranchised troops returned demanding a better post-war world there had been a huge increase in the Labour Party supported by the Trades Unions. To many people's astonishment, in 1924 the Labour leader Ramsay MacDonald had even briefly been called upon to form a government. "If it's not a bloody revolution, we shall just be dispossessed," Violet had predicted.

The answer for some, she knew, was to ignore the whole thing. For many of her friends, there had been a sense of adventure in the air. The war was over. Those who had survived were relieved to be alive; those, like her brother Frederick, who had been just too young to fight, were anxious to prove themselves by doing something daring. And parents, if they could, wanted to reassure themselves that the world was returning to something like normality. Helen had been a débutante. It was rather quaint really, but she understood that her mother's sorrow about the death of Henry had made her determined to give her other children a good time if she could. She had wondered if her past as a militant might have put the other mothers against her, but it seemed all that was forgotten. Besides, handsome young Frederick Meredith was considered an asset at any party, especially with the shortage of men after the losses of the war. His little sister Helen therefore, as the saying was, "came out".

What a time she had had! There had been the traditional balls of course, but the new generation of 1920s débutantes were less demure than their mothers had been. Young men were allowed to take liberties which would have been almost unthinkable before. Helen knew scarcely any girls who would go "all the way", but that did not mean they wouldn't go a very long way indeed. She was pretty – she had her father's good looks, together with the bright blue eyes and golden hair of her Bull ancestors. She was vivacious and intelligent. By the end of her season she had received three offers of marriage, and two of them would have been very good matches indeed. The only trouble was that the young men didn't interest her. "They're insipid," she complained.

"You could still do worse," her mother had said weakly. "I just want you to be happy."

"You chose an interesting man," Helen had pointed out.

But where to find one? There had been the Frenchman. She had met him thanks to Frederick who had taken up flying. He had flown her across the Channel to an aerodrome in France, and it was there, one astonishing summer day, that she had met him. He had a plane. And a château. She had spent a wonderful summer. Then it had been over. There had been other interesting men, since then. "But the interesting men don't seem to marry," she had confessed to her mother sadly. What was she to do with her life?

"You're still a flapper, Helen," her brother Frederick would tease her affectionately. "Always looking for excitement." A flapper – that was what they had called the bright young girls of the 1920s.

"Why shouldn't I?" she demanded. "You obviously do." Frederick, having gone into the army, looked every inch the dashing hussar, but she suspected that his occasional disappearance to Europe might have something to do with a more secret life. But it was not only a question of excitement: she wanted a cause to which she could devote herself.

The General Strike of 1926 had seemed to offer such a chance. "This is the revolution that those Bolsheviks have been waiting for," Violet had announced. "We've got to beat them." Helen did not know anyone who thought otherwise. How they had all worked during those heady days! She had acted as a conductor on a bus driven by a young man from Oxford she knew. They had operated the 137 route from Sloane Square to Crystal Palace. Other people ran the underground and the other public services. Thank God, she had reflected, that this was Britain, where people behaved decently.

There had been little violence. The strike had been broken. And the whole country, unions and all, had drawn back from the awful communist threat.

After that, she seemed to drift. She had found a job as a secretary to a Member of Parliament. It was hard work, but she enjoyed it and felt she was doing something useful. When it came to the larger issues however, she experienced a growing sense of disappointment. There were great tasks to be accomplished. She was inspired by the aim of the League of Nations to rid the world of war – but saw it crumble. She watched in admiration as America responded to the Depression with the New Deal. Yet no great initiatives for a new world were coming out of the Mother of Parliaments. Under the canny but uninspiring Prime Minister Baldwin, there seemed only one strategy: to muddle through and keep the British Empire – only held together by goodwill – out of trouble. Helen's passionate nature secretly rebelled. "You had a cause to serve," she would tell her mother. "I haven't got one."

It was Frederick who provided it.

When Hitler had come to power in Germany, like many people in the western world Helen had supposed that it was probably a good thing. "His supporters are unpleasant," they agreed, "but he does seem to be a bulwark against communist Russia." As he strengthened his rule and ugly rumours about the character of his regime spread, she had chosen to discount them. As for his military intentions, when the rogue politician Churchill, still disappointed to be out of office, started his campaign for rearmament, she had believed her own MP. "Churchill's insane," he said. "Germany can't fight a war for twenty years."

During one of his fleeting visits to London, Frederick disabused her. He had been sent as a military attaché to the British embassy in Poland the year before and his assessment was blunt. "Firstly, Churchill is right. Hitler is rearming and means to go to war. Secondly, my dear Helen, this is news only to the English at home. Every embassy in Europe knows it perfectly well. Every military attaché, including myself, has been filing detailed reports which London is studiously ignoring. Our attaché in Berlin, a brilliant man, has just been sacked for reporting the German troop movements that he saw. Those politicians who know this either think the public won't stand for the truth, or have persuaded themselves they've done a deal with Hitler. The whole thing's a scandal!"

"The MP I work for says Germany won't be ready to fight for twenty years," objected Helen.

"That's the received wisdom. It's based on a first-rate report done by the War Office. There's only one problem – the report was written in 1919."

She had started to gather information after that. Friends in the army, a diplomat she knew, even one or two sympathetic people in Westminster had given her facts which corroborated her brother's charges. She and Violet built up a detailed dossier. Some of their friends thought them a little mad; others, remembering Violet's militant past, smiled and shrugged. Among the other secretaries in Westminster, most of whom came from families like her own, her cause became known as "Helen's crusade", and she soon discovered that several of them had relatives in the diplomatic corps who felt the same way. "You should talk to your boss about it like I do," she would say. "After all, he is in Parliament and you see him every day." Once she even tried to speak to the Prime Minister herself. When the abdication crisis of 1936 had come up, and everyone else was talking about the new king and Mrs Simpson, Helen shrugged. "I'm sorry for him, of course," she declared. "But it hardly matters if Hitler is going to invade."

It was not surprising that there were complaints. "You're upsetting people," her boss explained to her, "and agitating the other girls. I must ask you to stop."

"I can't," she said.

She was out of a job. She looked for another in Westminster but found nothing. She decided to travel and spent some months touring on the Continent, in particular in Germany. She intended to write a little book about it, but within a month of her return, the great crisis of Europe had begun and, just as she had feared, the country drifted towards war.

When it came, she had volunteered to drive an ambulance. It was frightening, of course, and dangerous, but she did not mind. "I'm single, mother," she had remarked the previous week. "So if someone has to get killed, it really may as well be me."

London had never seen anything like Hitler's terrible Blitzkrieg before. Many had predicted that a war with modern weapons would bring the world to an end and, she supposed, if it went on long enough the whole capital would be in ruins. But she did not think about that as she went about her work. She couldn't.

As the rain slackened off she left the hotel and turned towards Hyde Park. Usually she liked to walk right across past the waters of the Serpentine, but today she decided to turn left and continue westward past the Albert Hall and into Kensington Gardens.

In many ways the park with its quiet avenues of trees and its wide open lawns retained its Stuart and eighteenth-century air. As she caught sight of the small brick palace of Kensington sitting so discreetly under the pale sun, with the lawns in front of it shining softly from the rain, Helen could almost imagine that at any moment a horse-drawn carriage might emerge from it and roll away into the trees. Yet looking around, the rude sights of twentieth-century war were all too evident. There were trenches everywhere. She passed an anti-aircraft gun. As she came on to the open ground by the Round Pond in the middle of the gardens, she could see barrage balloons by the dozen, tethered in the blue sky. Most incongruous of all, an entire section of the open lawn had been converted into an enormous cabbage patch. "Dig for Victory!" Londoners had been told. Food supplies would be ensured during the war, even if every inch of park had to be turned into a vegetable allotment.

It was time to turn back. Helen allowed her eye to run round the quiet scene, drinking it in for perhaps the last time. She sighed. She was sorry that she might not see it again.

EVENING

Though the huge glass palace itself had burned down four years before, the area was still called Crystal Palace. From Percy and Jenny's little garden, you could see right over London. Now they stood with Herbert and Maisie, gazing across to the distant line of Hampstead.

The sky in the west was red, a presage of things to come. In the east, the dark shadow of night was spreading in from the estuary. As for the huge sprawl of the metropolis which filled the whole basin, the black-out was being rigidly enforced. The usual glimmering of a million tiny lights was absent. London was a vast blackness waiting to become invisible.

There were just the four of them. Herbert and Maisie had never had any children. Percy and Jenny's son was in the army; their daughter married and living down in Kent. Although Maisie and Jenny had never been close, they had learned to get on together and that afternoon, to take their minds off the Blitz, the two women had gone to see *Gone With the Wind*. The previous night they had stood together in the garden, watching as the waves of planes droned over London again and again, and the red fires lit up, flickering here, bursting out there into great clouds of burning cinders that soared up into the blackness of the night sky. The East End had got it again last night. Where would the bombs land tonight?

"Will you be staying here?" Jenny asked.

"No, not tonight," Maisie replied.

"Time to be off," said Percy.

He and Herbert, now in their sixties, worked at nights down at the little Fire Brigade substation nearby, helping out. "I couldn't just wait around and do nothing," Percy had explained. Maisie felt that Herbert should have stayed with her. "But it's good for them to be together," Jenny had told her.

"Right then," said Herbert. "Let's be going."

At six o'clock sharp, Charlie was off again. Before he went, though, there was an argument. The subject had always been the same ever since the three older children had been evacuated, and Ruth had refused to leave Charlie. Every night he worried about her and the baby.

"Where are you going to spend the night, then?"

There were three places where Ruth could go. The first was the shelter. In central London this would probably have meant the tube or some other place underground. But out at Battersea it simply meant a converted building, well sandbagged, where people could go and share the danger. A near miss and you were protected; a direct hit and you all died together. "All according to preference," as Ruth said drily. The second choice was an Anderson shelter. The Anderson shelters were quite effective. Essentially a semicircular tube of corrugated iron, just high enough to walk into stooped, it could be half buried in the garden, sandbagged, and covered with soil. So long as a bomb did not fall directly on top of it, the chances of survival in an air raid were rather good.

The narrow back garden of the house the Doggets rented below Lavender Hill had already been put on a wartime footing. First, beside the little concrete path, the grass had been dug up and a vegetable patch substituted. Next to that was a pen with three chickens which provided eggs. Beyond that was the Anderson shelter.

Ruth hated it. "I just can't bear being cooped up in that little thing," she complained, "It's damp anyway, so it's bad for the baby," she insisted, though Charlie found it perfectly dry. But he knew Ruth: obstinate as could be. So that left the third choice, which was to stay in the house, under the stairs. Charlie had sandbagged the back door and window. It was as safe as he could make it. "If the bomb's got our names on it, there's nothing you can do anyway," she had told him – and six out of seven Londoners felt the same way. But even so, he still tried to persuade her into the Anderson shelter each night before he left.

"I can't stay and argue any more," he said finally.

"I know," she said. "We'll be all right."

So with his uniform on, and carrying his helmet and his boots, Charlie Dogget set off for his dangerous night's work.

At a quarter past six Helen Meredith kissed her mother goodbye. She looked so well in her uniform, with her fair hair pinned up under her cap. "I swear you don't look a day over twenty-five," Violet said with a smile.

Helen smiled and nodded. "Thank you."

"Helen," her mother gently took her arm as she was turning to go. "Don't worry. It'll be all right."

Neville Silversleeves was a man who naturally collected responsibilities. It was not his fault: people asked him to do things and he did them very well. At an early age he had succeeded his father as head of the respected old firm of Odstock, Alderbury and Silversleeves, Solicitors. If he joined any society, within a few years he was inevitably asked to be its secretary. He was tall, with thinning black hair, and a very long nose. "That nose," a cruel barrister had once remarked, "collects petty authority like a flypaper."

As a good churchman, whose firm had done work for the diocese, Neville was a verger of St Paul's and, given his position, had become one of the select group of ARP wardens in the City and Holborn. In recent months the wardens all over London had been unpopular for their ruthless enforcement of the blackout – a policy they had only followed because they had been informed, quite incorrectly, that even a lighted cigarette could be seen from a German bomber five thousand feet above. In the City itself, the residential population was small, but with so many banks, offices and churches to protect, the wardens had important responsibilities. They were also at considerable risk from bombs and fires themselves. But to Neville Silversleeves, this was just another of the burdens which he believed it was his destiny to bear.

He was on duty that night.

The Fleming brothers' substation lay in section 84, at the outer edge of the London region's authority. It was an evacuated schoolhouse. The equipment consisted of four taxis with ladders, three trailer pumps, a van and two motorcycles.

The crews had all arrived by soon after six, but there might be hours to wait before they were summoned to back up the hard-pressed crews in the centre. There were two women on the telephones. There was the substation officer, who had been a regular fireman, and the crews, all Auxiliary Fire Service men. Percy and Herbert did the back-up tasks and Percy usually looked after the kitchen.

The men had set up a darts board in the main schoolroom; and Herbert had made himself a popular figure by playing all the favourite music-hall songs on the old upright piano there. The only problem, as Percy saw it, was the food.

It was unfortunate that the AFS administration had not done so well in the matter of provisions. Percy only had some rice, cabbage and a tray of corned beef which, it seemed to him, had a rather greenish look. "It's not much of a meal," he had remarked to Herbert.

There was nothing to do but boil the rice and wait for the first drone of the German planes as they passed – sometimes directly overhead – on their way to central London. Darkness had long since fallen and Herbert was busily playing a music-hall number when Percy, who had walked to the door to look out, heard the sound of a single approaching engine coming straight towards him, saw two lights and then, after a brief pause, something huge and fiery red that made him tremble.

"Oh, my God," he said.

Admiral Sir William Barnikel stood six foot three; his chest was reminiscent of the prow of a battleship and his beard was huge and red. He looked exactly like the descendant of Vikings that he was. "My grandfather Jonas was an ordinary sea captain," he would admit modestly enough, "and before that we discovered the family were common fishmongers." Having little knowledge of the City, the admiral had no understanding of the importance of the members of the ancient Fishmongers Guild. But whatever his antecedents, once Barnikel was on the quarterdeck he was a stupendous leader of men.

The authorities had taken a calculated risk in putting the admiral in charge of a large part of the London Auxiliary Fire Service. "He is not always diplomatic," certain bureaucrats gently suggested. His bellow could astound a frigate. "It is not a diplomat we need," Churchill himself had remarked, "but a man to raise morale." And so Admiral Barnikel's mighty heart and mighty temper had been let loose upon the AFS.

It was his great red beard that Percy now saw bearing down upon him as the Admiral arrived unannounced, as was his habit, to inspect this little outpost of his vast domain.

"Oh, my God," he murmured again.

The firemen all followed the admiral round. "More sandbags by that door," he jovially commanded. Then, seeing the piano, he roared: "Give us a song!" As Herbert bashed out *Nellie Dean*, he boomingly joined in. "Well done." He clapped Herbert on the back. "Best I've heard in any station. But is that piano in tune?"

"Not quite," Herbert confessed.

"Tune it, man!" he bellowed.

He inspected their uniforms and boots, pounded his fist on a cracked helmet until it disintegrated, produced a fresh one from his car and told them all that they were heroes. Then he entered the kitchen.

"Who's in charge here?" he demanded

Percy nervously said he supposed he was.

"But you just prepare what they give you?"

"Yes, sir," Percy replied truthfully. "And thank God," he said shortly afterwards, "that I did."

Having given the rice and cabbage a disgusted glance, Barnikel began to inspect the corned beef. If there was one thing Admiral Sir William Barnikel understood, it was rations. A well-fed ship, he knew, was a contented ship. He also knew that many of the fire-fighters still suspected that nobody really cared about them. He lifted up a slice of the greenish corned beef with a fork, eyed it and sniffed it. He took a bite, chewed it, screwed up his face and spat it out.

"It's gone off!" he bellowed. "This is the food they supplied for your men? Good God, you'll all be poisoned!"

And then Barnikel became very angry indeed. He twisted the fork so violently that he almost knotted it. His great fist pounded the kitchen table so hard that one of its legs fell off. He seized the tin tray of corned beef, marched outside with it, and hurled it away over the station roof into the sky – as far as anyone knew it might have landed in Berlin, for it was never found again. Then he went in to the telephone, called headquarters and ordered them to put a proper dinner in a staff car and bring it round to Crystal Palace immediately. "If necessary, you can send my own supper too." He turned to Percy.

"Your name?"

"Fleming, sir."

With his blue eyes blazing, the red-bearded admiral tapped his huge finger on Percy's chest. "Fleming, if you are ever given food like this again, you are to pick up the telephone, ring HQ and ask for me personally. If they argue, you tell them I told you to. I'm trusting you to do that. Do you understand?"

"Oh yes, sir," said Percy. "I do!"

"Good. Next time I come, we'll have a song on that piano." He looked at Herbert. "I shall eat supper with you."

And after a brief private word with the station chief, the Admiral was off to galvanize and put heart into some other unsuspecting outpost.

* * *

Charlie listened: the drone had begun. Soon it became a roar as they came over, wave after wave of Heinkels and Dorniers, escorted by buzzing clouds of Messerschmitts. The barrage was beginning now, a huge chorus of bangs, thuds and rattles, and of bursts of light in the night sky; the searchlights waved back and forth like strange, silver wands in the darkness above. The first few nights the barrage had been an exercise in noise, just to make the Londoners feel that they were being defended; but the operation was improving now and some enemy planes were actually being hit.

Soon he could hear the thud and boom of the high-explosive bombs crashing down. They sounded closer than they had last night, and sure enough a few minutes later, the telephone rang with the first request.

"It's the City. A serious fire near Ludgate. Off you go, lads."

There were two categories of big fire. The largest of all would be an entire block: this was termed a conflagration. A serious fire was the other category, but would still require over thirty pumps, which meant that AFS taxi-trailers from all over London would be converging to help the handful of proper fire-engines of the regular service.

Charlie's team crossed the river at Vauxhall Bridge, made their way along past the Houses of Parliament, up Whitehall and into the Strand. St Clement Danes flashed by. Then they found themselves joining a line of similar vehicles crawling down past the newspaper offices that lined Fleet Street, towards the church of St Bride's.

It was quite a sight. A single high-explosive bomb, Charlie guessed, must have struck, ripping out the guts of two houses. But a cluster of magnesium fire bombs had also fallen and it was these that were really doing the damage. Though in themselves the fire bombs were not very fearsome – they burned like a large roman candle firework and you could actually kick them away or put them out – they often lodged somewhere practically inaccessible and before the firemen could get to them, the fire had frequently taken hold. In this case, half a dozen houses were already blazing furiously. The last house in the row had not yet caught, but there was an incendiary on the roof.

"Lines!" the officer in charge was calling. "More lines!"

They were close enough to the river to run hose lines

straight down to its waters and pump from there. Already a dozen hoses were in operation.

"Come on," said Charlie, "let's go up there." While the others started undoing the ladder, he and the senior man on the team ran up the narrow staircase. They could hear a crackling sound coming from the next house, but the walls were quite thick and they knew that if the fire came through underneath them they could move along the roof, or have a ladder run up to them.

Once on the roof, they saw the incendiary easily enough. It was lodged up beside the chimney. "Here," said Charlie. "I could get that with a grappling hook." He started climbing up towards it. His foot went through once, but he managed to grab a hold on the chimney to steady himself. "Lovely view!" he shouted, and, at a signal from his companion that the coast was clear, he took aim, swung, and knocked the fire bomb clean off the roof into the street below.

They had just neared the bottom of the stairs when they noticed the smell. For a second they looked at each other in surprise, then Charlie's companion grabbed the stair rail. "I feel dizzy!" he cried, and Charlie had to catch hold of him. Charlie grinned. "Here," he hissed, "get a grip on yourself and come with me." They descended the stairs until they came to the cellars which, like many in this part of London, ran along under several houses. As they entered, they could see that the ground floor of the neighbouring house was burning. Falling embers would start a conflagration in the cellar at any moment. The dizzying smell was almost overpowering, but its cause was now obvious. "Alcohol," said Charlie.

The ground floor of the next door house was a liquor store; the fumes were from the broken bottles. They could be heard popping and exploding above and soon the same thing would start down in the cellar where the crates were stored.

"No way we can save this lot," his companion whispered.

"No," said Charlie, "but look at that." On the floor, not twenty feet away, was an open crate full of miniature bottles. Neither man spoke as they moved towards it.

A fireman's boot stretched well up his leg and had a large top. It was amazing how many miniatures would fit in there. A bit of floor fell in near them, but they took no notice until they had finished.

"Charlie," the other whispered, "you have all the luck!"

* * *

Helen drove through Moorgate. It seemed astonishing that even when there was an inferno in one street, the next could be pitch dark. Twice they had to stop to negotiate around a bomb crater. On the second occasion, they had only just seen it in time. There were just two of them in the ambulance – a sturdy old van with faint markings on its sides. It might have seemed a little primitive, but it carried a stretcher and a full complement of first aid materials, which was a great improvement on the situation some months before when she had been asked to drive her own little Morris and to find scissors and bandages for herself.

There was a lull in the bombing. Though a few searchlights stalked the sky, the drone of the bombers had died away. The quiet would certainly not last. Although the Spitfires were out there searching for prey, most of the bombers were not only getting through but were returning to base, reloading and coming back for a second run.

The tenement block came into sight. A single fire appliance was hosing down the corner where a bomb had neatly taken down a section of wall, leaving the interior exposed like a child's dolls' house. The firemen had brought an old lady out and laid her on a blanket to await the ambulance. It only took Helen a moment to ascertain that one of her legs was badly broken. The pain must have been considerable. But the old woman's response to it all was not unusual.

"I'm sorry, dear, to give you all this trouble." She tried to smile. "Should have gone to the shelter, shouldn't I?"

Helen strapped the old woman's leg to a splint and was just moving her on to the stretcher when she saw a fireman look up and heard the drone of the next wave of bombers approaching.

"Better hurry, Miss," he said.

She bent down to pick up one end of the stretcher and then realized that the old woman was trying urgently to say something to her. Patiently she leaned over her.

"Please, dear, if I'm going to hospital," the old woman pleaded, "I just realized. Could you help me? I forgot. . . ."

Helen did not need to let her finish.

"Your teeth."

It was always the same. They always wanted their false teeth. They had nearly always been left on the mantelpiece.

The blast had always blown them somewhere else. And, if she possibly could, she always went in to look for them. Keeping their teeth was the one little bit of dignity they still had. "Besides, with the war on, you never know when you'll get some more," an old man had once pointed out to her.

"What floor?" she sighed.

"Raid's beginning," the fireman called.

"A bomb never hits the same place twice," she said calmly, though she knew there was no reason why it shouldn't.

As the drone turned into a roar, and the barrage erupted above her, Helen walked through the door into the tenement building.

The premonition that had been troubling Violet was not of a definite kind. She had not seen a vision of Helen lying dead, or injured, it was more general: a sense that something important – she could not exactly say what – was coming to an end. When Helen had gone out for her walk and she had been sitting in her chair, she had closed her eyes and suddenly heard a sound, quite sharp, as though someone had abruptly closed a book. She told herself it was nothing, but she suspected that as people came close to some great watershed in their lives they might become a little psychic. After Helen had left that evening, the feeling had grown stronger.

Only after the first raid of the night had passed did it occur to her that it might be her own life rather than Helen's which was about to be snapped shut. There had only been a few bombs on Belgravia, presumably aimed at Buckingham Palace, but of course it was possible. She wondered whether she should try to do anything about it. She sighed to herself. She was over seventy. Did she really have the energy?

It couldn't have been the corned beef since that had never been touched, but, whatever it was, by midnight Auxiliary Fireman Clark was in no state to go out. Crew number three, therefore, was a man short.

When the news came through that the Bull Brewery had been hit, the station officer looked round for an extra man. He had always hesitated to use the older men like the Flemings. As both were in their sixties, they really belonged in the Home Guard and, in fact, though neither of them knew it, they were only there because he felt Herbert's performances at the piano were good for morale. Just now, however, he was a man short and faced with a conflagration. Thoughtfully, he looked at Percy.

"I suppose," he said, "you wouldn't like to go along?"

"Come on, Percy!" the others cried. "It's a chance to get in the brewery. We'll have a party!"

"All right, then," he said. "I'll go."

Now it was really coming down on every side. Incendiaries were falling, both magnesium and oil ones. Again and again, Charlie heard the scream and the awful thump of a high-explosive bomb. One fell in Blackfriars, another somewhere near the Guildhall. Above, the sky was full of starbursts as though they were witnessing a huge firework display put on by madmen. The roars, cracks and bangs were deafening.

They had been sent up to St Bartholomew's after Ludgate. On their way there, they had passed the high dome of the Old Bailey criminal court whose elegant figure of Justice holding the scales had presided over this quarter of the City for the last thirty years. Thinking of the illicit bottles in their boots, Charlie and his mate grinned at each other as they passed her.

The St Bartholomew's fire proved to be small and quickly dealt with. But they were not left idle: within minutes a dispatch rider told them to go over behind St Paul's. An office building between Watling Street and St Mary-le-Bow had caught fire. A dozen other appliances were hastening towards it.

Just as they were leaving, Charlie, who was driving, caught sight of something gleaming as white as an angel, drifting slowly towards them over the dome of the Old Bailey.

"Hello," he murmured. "We're in luck again."

Of all the agents of destruction dropped from the skies during the Blitz, perhaps the most devastating were the landmines. Drifting quietly down attached to a parachute, the landmine would strike the ground without burrowing into it and then detonate. One of them could easily wipe out half a street of small houses. The casualties they caused were terrible. Yet as these angels of death drifted down people were frequently seen running not away, but towards them.

The reason was the parachute. It was made of silk. If you could keep far enough away from the mine to avoid the blast, but then rush in quickly before anyone else, you could cut yourself a good piece of the silk parachute. They made up very nicely into shirts and dresses.

Luck was indeed on Charlie's side that night. While they took cover, the landmine obligingly landed in the open space of Smithfield where it made a large hole in the ground, but did no other serious damage. Within three minutes the parachute had disappeared into the back of the converted taxi, and Charlie and his men went off to risk their lives again.

•

Maisie could never sleep until the All Clear was sounded at dawn. And though she did not like to admit it, she wished now that she had stayed the night at Jenny's.

Just after one in the morning she slipped out of her house and began to walk up to the crest of the ridge. Even if Jenny were asleep, she knew that the front door would not be locked. As she reached the top, where the road led down towards Gipsy Hill, she paused.

Below her London was pulsating with molten red light, as if some vast geological change had taken place and the whole shallow bowl had transformed itself into the mouth of a volcano.

Just then, a wave of enemy planes started to drone over high above her. She was not worried, however: they were undoubtedly bound for the centre. An anti-aircraft gun spluttered into life too late and she was just about to turn down towards Jenny's when she became aware of a buzzing, whining sound.

Fighters. At first, she could hardly see the profile of the half-dozen planes as they swooped in the black night sky, but she could see the tiny flashes from their guns. The Messerschmitts swarmed up like angry hornets from the enemy convoy. Over Dulwich, on towards Clapham and the river, the planes looped, wheeled and spat death at each other in the darkness. It was, in its way, rather thrilling.

She watched them fly over towards Vauxhall; then it seemed to her that two planes—or perhaps here were more—had detached themselves from the rest, and were heading back over Crystal Palace. They wheeled directly over her only a few hundred feet up, fragmentary shapes against the reddened sky, soaring high into the night, rushing down again, flattening off just above her and then wheeling eastwards.

Where were they now? She gazed up fascinated, her small red mouth forming into a little circle as she stared into the sky where men were battling for their lives. Without even realizing what she was doing, she waved her arms and cried out: "Come on! Get him! You can do it."

But now another wave of bombers was coming over the high ridge. The anti-aircraft guns erupted into a frenzy. She craned her neck and spun round to look for the fighter. Would they return? The whole sky was flashing. She never saw or felt the sudden hail of shrapnel that crashed into the back of her head and caused it to explode like a little cherry.

When it got as hot as this, Charlie knew you had to keep your face down in front of the fire. The heat all around was so great that he had reluctantly taken the bottles of spirits out of his boots and dumped them in a pot-hole for fear they might burst and catch fire.

The main danger, apart from falling masonry, was the cinders. The burning dust could get into your eyes all too easily and cause painful burns. He'd already been treated for this twice. Charlie Dogget might not be averse to a bit of harmless looting, but once he was on the job there wasn't a braver firefighter in London. Only after he had been going non-stop, high up a ladder, right at the face of the fire for half an hour did the fire officer in charge order him to take a break.

There were hoses running down the lane from St Mary-le-Bow. Charlie followed them and then turned left, towards the corner of Cheapside, opposite the end of St Paul's. He was grateful to feel a little cool breeze on his face. Though he was not supposed to, he took his helmet off to cool his head. At the corner, a large crater was all that was left of two buildings that had been destroyed the night before. It was nearly twenty feet deep. Settling himself on some rubble that remained by the rim, he took a few deep breaths and sat quietly, gazing westward at St Paul's.

It was an awesome sight. Somehow, Wren's mighty, leaden dome remained intact. All around, the burning roofs created a surrounding lake of red, from which the massive temple of London arose dark, immovable, silent, with a rock-like indifference. It was as if, Charlie thought, the old cathedral was declaring that even Hitler's Blitz could never touch the City's ancient heart and soul.

After a few minutes, Charlie glanced down into the crater beside him. It seemed like any other, bigger and deeper than most, perhaps, but nothing very special about it. It was clear that the bomb had gone clean through the foundations of the houses that had been standing there. He could discern lines of earlier foundations of stone, too. In the flickering light from the surrounding fires, he thought he could make out a piece of tiled floor of some kind. From a nearby building, a little explosion caused a flash of reddish light to illuminate the pit further for a moment, and as it did so Charlie noticed a faint glint from something down at the bottom. Curious, he glanced about to check that no one was looking, and clambered over the edge. A second or two later he was feeling about in the dark. The faint glint seemed to have come from under a lid of some kind, covered over with rubble. He must have been looking from the top of the crater at just the right angle. He felt inside, frowned, whistled softly, and then drew his hand out carefully. The coins were heavy. He guessed they might be gold, but he hadn't enough light to see.

Then, all of a sudden, a powerful torch cut down from the rim of the crater and in an instant he saw that he indeed had a fistful of solid gold coins. The metal lid belonged to some sort of box and in the beam of light he saw that it contained a quantity of similar coins, and saw, too, that there were other containers like it nearby. Charlie Dogget, though he could not possibly have known it, had found the stolen bullion left by Roman soldiers one sunny afternoon nearly seventeen hundred years before.

"What are you doing?"

The owner of the torch was a tall man wearing an ARP warden's tin hat. By the light from the fires, Charlie could see that he had a large nose.

"You're looting! It's against the law," said Neville Silversleeves.

"No, I'm not. This is buried treasure, this is," Charlie riposted. "I'm entitled."

"The building, as it happens," Silversleeves said officiously, "is Church property. You are entitled to nothing. Now get out of there at once!"

"If you ask me," said Charlie firmly, "another bleeding raid's starting and it's you who'd better move!"

For the air suddenly erupted with the sound of anti-aircraft fire from every side, while overhead a fresh, droning roar of approaching bombers was heard.

Charlie had no intention of being shifted from his gold, and it seemed that Silversleeves was equally determined to stay at his post to make sure that the fireman didn't sneak off with any of it. The crash and thud of approaching bombs was heard, but neither man moved. The bangs grew louder.

"I shall report you," called Silversleeves.

"Suit yourself," muttered Charlie.

Then the bomb fell. It must have fallen, Charlie supposed, a hundred yards or so behind Silversleeves. The flash and roar were so great that for about twenty seconds he could not even make out what had happened. Then he realized that the unconscious body of Silversleeves was lying half-way down the opposite side of the crater from where he had been standing.

"And I hope you broke your bleeding neck," he murmured. Reaching in again to the coins, Charlie quickly began to stuff them into his boots. Ten, twenty, thirty. He had just got to his fourth handful when he realised that he was going to die.

The sound made by a high-explosive bomb just before it lands is a whistling scream. Charlie had heard plenty of those in the last two weeks. He had become quite an expert at sensing where they were about to fall. As he heard the pitch of the bomb's scream above him he knew at once that it was subtly different from any he had heard before. It was coming directly for him.

He dived frantically for the side of the crater. Hampered by his boots weighted down with gold, he started manically scrambling upwards, the rubble crumbling under his hands. As the bomb crashed on to the exact spot where he had been standing just two seconds before, he was still, ludicrously, scrambling. He continued to scramble until he reached the top. The bomb had not yet exploded.

Charlie Dogget sat shaking on the edge of the crater looking in. The bomb, all eight hundred pounds of it, was half-buried in the centre where the gold had been. Silversleeves was still lying unconscious where he had landed in the blast. Charlie stared at the bomb, half expecting it to explode. But nothing happened. Unexploded bombs – UXBs – were not uncommon, but they could go off at any time. Charlie got up slowly and wondered what to do. He supposed he ought to summon help and get Silversleeves out, but there was, of course, the matter of the gold. Was it all buried under the bomb now, or was it possible he could still get some more out? "If I'm lucky enough not to be killed by the Messerschmitt last night or this bomb now," he thought, "I should think my luck will hold good." Slithering down into the crater again, he started towards the bomb.

There was more light now. Some other building must have been set ablaze nearby because a wall of flame suddenly leaped into the sky behind him. By its light he saw one gold coin lying near the bomb, but nothing else. "I know what it is. It's God up there, sparing my life but keeping me from temptation," he thought. "Just when I think I've struck it rich, He goes and buries all the money under eight hundred pounds of high explosive." He reached down slowly for the gold coin only to be interrupted, from behind, by a roar that made him jump half out of his skin. He whirled round, looked up, and beheld a most awesome sight.

Standing on the edge of the crater, his huge form seeming even larger against the wall of flame filling the sky behind him, his great red beard appearing almost to be on fire itself, the mighty person of Admiral Sir William Barnikel was staring down into the pit. His arm, like that of some avenging Viking god, was raised and pointing at him.

"My God," thought poor Charlie. "He's caught me at it."

But Admiral Barnikel knew nothing of Charlie and his Roman gold. As his car came by St Paul's, all he had seen was the figure of Silversleeves being tossed by the blast into the crater, and now this gallant little fireman with his shock of white hair going down beside an unexploded bomb to get the warden out.

"Well done that man!" he thundered. "By God, you deserve a medal! Hold fast there. I'm coming!" Striding down into the crater himself, Admiral Barnikel cried: "You'll never haul him out alone, man! Here we go." Charlie took Silversleeves's long legs and Barnikel his arms, and they hauled the unconscious warden up to the roadway where the admiral flagged down a passing ambulance and told the two women in charge to take the ARP warden straight to St Bartholomew's. A moment later Helen was on her way with Silversleeves, still out cold, in the back of her van.

"Now then," cried the admiral cheerfully, "I want you to come with me. I need your name and station." He took Charlie over to his car. "I think," he said in a low voice, "we might also get out of here. You never know when one of these unexploded buggers is going to go off." Thirty seconds later, it did.

When an exhausted Percy got home from the big brewery fire at nine o'clock the following morning, Jenny did not tell him about Maisie.

"He's been out all night and he'll feel he's got to do something. Let him sleep," Herbert had insisted. So the brothers did not share their grief until the evening.

When Helen Meredith arrived home, however, she received a severe shock. The house in Eaton Terrace had been completely destroyed by a high-explosive bomb. One glance at it told her that no one could possibly have survived in there. She was still standing in the ruins unable to take in what had happened when her mother Violet walked round the corner.

"It's the strangest thing, my dear," Violet explained. "I had this extraordinary feeling I was in danger, so I went round to the shelter in Sloane Square Underground. I must say," she added confidentially, "it's what you might call rather *close* down there. But," she beamed at the charred remains of her house, "wasn't I lucky?"

Until recently, though acts of conspicuous gallantry in the military could be rewarded by the famous Victoria Cross, there had been no equivalent honour for civilian gallantry. This had now been remedied by the institution of the George Cross and the George Medal.

If there had ever been any doubt about the gallantry of the members of the Auxiliary Fire Service during the Blitz, that doubt was utterly vanquished when a number of fire-fighters won the George Cross. One of them, on the personal recommendation of Admiral Barnikel himself, was Charlie Dogget.

For Charlie it was rather an embarrassment. Though, as any of his colleagues could have attested, he'd earned a medal many times, he knew he hadn't deserved this one. But what could he say? Even Silversleeves, who remembered nothing at all of the moments before the explosion, had insisted upon visiting him and thanking him personally. He also had a letter from his Auntie Jenny when she saw it in the papers.

He had visited the place once, out of curiosity, but there was no sign of any gold. He kept the Roman coins he had, though, in a little box, and later gave them to his son.

Chapter 21

The River

1997

Sir Eugene Penny, chairman of the mighty Penny Insurance Company, member of a dozen boards and alderman of London, was feeling rather virtuous. Few possessions had been more treasured in his family than the collection of river landscapes, a number by Monet, that his father had bought just after the Second World War from the estate of the last Lord St James. And today he had just given the whole lot away.

The trouble with going on to the boards of charities and good causes, he thought wryly, was that sooner or later you always started putting your own money into them. As a trustee of the Tate Gallery it was impossible not to be excited by its plans, both for the original museum of modern art in its lovely classical building by the river and for the vast new gallery they planned to open in the old Bankside Power Station on the south side of the river, just near the reconstructed Globe Theatre. When a fellow trustee had hinted that really, those Monets of his ought to be seen by a wider audience he had felt bound to agree. After signing them over that morning, he had paid a visit to the nearby Chelsea Flower Show, followed by lunch at his club and a visit to Tom Brown, his tailor. He was in an excellent mood, therefore, when he turned up for his visit to the site by the river this afternoon.

In recent years he had become interested in the Museum of London. His interest had first been sparked by an exhibition the museum had mounted on the Huguenots. As a Huguenot himself, Penny had always known a fair amount about the French community, which still had its own association and charities. He had even known that three out of four Britons had some Huguenot ancestry. But the exhibition had been a revelation. Silk-weavers and generals, artists, clockmakers, famous jew-ellers like the Agnews, firms like his own – the exhibits, as well as showing off some wonderful arts and crafts, had revealed the Huguenot origins of any number of concerns that one thought of as quintessentially British. The thing had been so well done that he had begun to take more notice of the museum, and a little later, secretly hoping to find more evidence of Huguenot genius, he had gone to another show they had put on.

"The Peopling of London" had been very well done; but it had also been a surprise.

"I thought I knew something about my British heritage," he remarked to his wife. "It turns out I didn't at all." In his schooldays the history of England at least – if not of the whole of Britain – had been about the Anglo-Saxon race. "We knew about the Celts, of course. And then there were the Danes and a few Norman knights." But the exhibits on the peopling of London told a completely different story. Angles, Saxons, Danes, Celtic folk: they had all been found in London. But even back in the days when the Tower of London was built, Penny learned, there had been Norman and Italian merchants, then Flemish and Germans. "The Flemish people kept coming all the time, and they settled all over the island too, right out into Scotland and Wales." In more recent times, the big Jewish community, the Irish, and still later, the people from the former empire – the Indian sub-continent, the Caribbean, Asia. "But what is really so striking," he concluded, "is that even from the Middle Ages there is no question – London was always a city of large numbers of aliens who quickly assimilated. In historical terms, London has been just as much a melting pot as, say, New York." He had grinned. "I knew I was of immigrant stock, but it turns out that everyone else is too!"

"So the much vaunted Anglo-Saxon race . . .?"

"Is a myth. The northern half of Britain is more Danish and Celtic; and even in the south," he shrugged, "I doubt very much whether our Anglo-Saxon ancestry would make up one part in four. We are, quite simply, a nation of European immigrants with new graftings being added all the time. A genetic river, if you like, fed by any number of streams." The museum had produced a book on the subject. He kept it in the drawing room for guests to see.

"So how would you define a Londoner, then?" Lady Penny asked curiously.

"Someone who lives here. It's like the old definition of a cockney: someone who's born within hearing distance of Bow bells. And a foreigner," he added with a grin, "is anyone, Anglo-Saxon or not, who lives outside."

Now that he thought of it he had seen the process in the huge offices of the Penny Insurance Company. In the decades after the Second World War, there had been massive immigration from the Caribbean and from the Indian subcontinent into London. In a few places – Notting Hill Gate above Kensington, and Brixton, south of the river – there had been friction and even riots. Yet recently as he toured the office and found himself talking to the young generation in their twenties, he had realized that they all – black, white, Asian – not only talked with the local accents of London, but had taken on the same sports, the same attitudes, even the same irreverent cockney humour as the London folk he had known as a child. "They're all Londoners," he concluded.

It was quiet in the trench. Sarah Bull glanced at her co-workers and smiled to herself. She had been on many digs before, but she had particularly wanted to join this one because it was being conducted by Dr John Dogget.

Dr John Dogget was a Londoner through and through. "My grandfather was a fireman in the Blitz," he had confessed to her once. He was also a curator of the Museum of London where she had recently come to work.

Sarah loved the museum. Perched up on a big pedestrian area a few minutes' walk from St Paul's, its windows looked out on a large, handsome fragment of the old Roman wall of London. It was a growing tourist attraction and the parties of schoolchildren who were brought there seemed to love the place. The whole museum was arranged as a walk through history, from prehistoric times to the present day. The curators had created whole scenes, accompanied by the appropriate sights and sounds, into which the visitor walked: a prehistoric camp, a seventeenth-century room, a whole eighteenth-century street, Victorian shops – even a model of old London which lit up as you heard extracts from Pepys' diary of the

Great Fire. Accompanying each exhibit were articles from the time, from flint arrowheads to a real, fully stocked costermonger's barrow.

Behind it all, Sarah knew, lay hard scholarship, As an archaeology graduate, this was what had attracted her to the place. There were new finds, often huge discoveries, being made all the time: the little Temple of Mithras and then, only a few years ago, the discovery that the old Guildhall was actually standing on the site of a huge Roman amphitheatre. Roman roads and medieval buildings were regularly being uncovered. A charming recent find just by the old wall had been the remains of some coins and moulds used by a Roman forger and, by the look of it, jettisoned in rather a hurry. The curator in question had been able to demonstrate exactly how the forging of the coins was done.

And then, of course, there had also been young Dr Dogget. With his cheerful temper and the white flash in his hair, he was as popular as he was easily recognized. Rather curiously, he had webbed fingers. "Good for swimming and digging," he had wryly informed her. He was always so busy, and she, as a new recruit, was of course so junior, but she was hoping that at this dig he might notice her for the first time. The question was, as well as Roman artefacts, did he also like blue-eyed blondes?

The trench was on a small site overlooking the Thames. It was not often that archaeologists got the chance to dig in the City of London, but when a building was demolished and another built in its place, arrangements could be made for an excavation. There had been so much building since the City and East End was devastated in the Blitz that its quality was uneven. Some of the work, like the huge developments of the docklands now that containers and huge vessels had taken the dock activity far down the estuary, Sarah thought was good. The building where they were excavating had, in her opinion, been inferior, so she was doubly glad to see it qreplaced. The owners of the new building had even agreed that, if the archaeologists uncovered anything really exciting, they would construct an atrium and build round it, so that the remains could be viewed by the public. They had already gone down ten feet below the old basement, which this meant that, standing in the bottom of the trench, at her eye level she was looking at a layer of gravel that would have been the surface in the time of Julius Caesar.

It was mid-afternoon, and only a few puffy white clouds had appeared in the bright spring sky when the deputation headed by Sir Eugene Penny arrived. He inspected the place carefully, came into the trench, listened carefully while Dr Dogget explained to him exactly what they were doing, asked a few questions – Sarah had made sure that they were intelligent – and having thanked everybody, left. When he was introduced to Sarah he shook hands politely, then paid no further attention to her whatsoever.

No one at the museum had any idea that her family owned a large brewery, and certainly not that Sir Eugene Penny, alderman, was her cousin. She preferred it that way. But the museum, like all such institutions, was always short of funds for its ambitious projects and if anyone was likely to find a way of getting them, she thought it was probably her cousin.

After he had gone, for a few minutes Sarah allowed herself to walk by the quiet river. It was cleaner now than it had been for centuries. You could even catch fish in it again. It was also carefully managed. The gradual tilting of the island that had been raising the water level for so many centuries had been counteracted by an elegant flood barrier across the stream. London might have some things in common with Venice, but it certainly wasn't going to sink under the water. Allowing herself a last look down to Tower Bridge and up to St Paul's, Sarah returned to the trench.

It was amazing how quiet London could be. Not only in the big parks, but in great walled enclosures like the Temple, or in the old churches like St Bartholomew's, there was a silence that seemed to take one back for centuries. Even here in the City the office buildings rising high over the narrow streets provided a screen so that the sounds of London's busy traffic could scarcely be heard. She glanced up at the sky. Still blue.

Dr Dogget had gone. One other archaeologist was in the trench at the moment, scraping away patiently at the surface. Sarah went down to join her. As she did so, she remembered a talk she had heard John Dogget give to a party of older schoolchildren. He had outlined the work of the museum, and of the archaeologists too. And then, to put this work into focus, he said something she had liked very much.

"Imagine", he had said, "a summer. At the end of it the leaves fall. They lie on the ground. They almost dissolve, you might say, but not quite. The next year the same thing happens again. And again. Thinned out, compressed, those leaves and all the other vegetation build up in layers, year after year. It's the natural process. It's organic.

"Something similar happens with man, and especially in a city. Each year, each age, leaves something. It gets compressed, of course, it disappears under the surface, but just a little of all that human life remains. A Roman tile, a coin, a clay pipe from Shakespeare's time. All left in place. When we dig down, we find it and we may put it on show. But don't think of it just as an object. Because that coin, that pipe belonged to someone: a person who lived, and loved, and looked out at the river and the sky each day just like you and me.

"So when we dig down into the earth under our feet, and find all that is left of that man or woman, I try to remember that what I am seeing and handling is a huge and endless compression of lives. And sometimes in our work here, I feel as if we've somehow entered into that layer of compressed time, prised open that life, a single day even, with its morning, and evening, and its blue sky and its horizon. We've opened just one of the millions and millions of windows, hidden in the ground."

Sarah smiled to herself. She had liked that. And standing there in the trench, looking at the place where perhaps Julius Caesar had stood, she reached out her hand, and touched the past.

Acknowledgments

I am deeply indebted to the following, all experts in their respective fields, who gave advice, provided information and in many cases read and helped me correct text that I had written. Any errors that remain are mine alone. Ms Susan Banks, Museum of London Archaeology Service; Mr David Bentley, Museum of London Archaeology Service; Mr John Clark, Curator, Museum of London; The Reverend Father K. Cunningham, St Etheldreda's, Ely Place; Mr A. P. Gittins, Tom Brown, Tailor; Mrs Jenny Hall, Curator, Museum of London; Mr Frederick Hilton; Mr Bernard Kearnes J.P.; Dr Nick Merriman, Curator, Museum of London; Mrs Lily Moody; Mr Geoffrey Parnell, Curator, Tower of London; Mr H. Pearce; Mr Richard Shaw, Lavender Hill Reference Library; Mr Ken Thomas, Archivist, Courage Breweries; Mrs Rosemary Weinstein, Curator, Museum of London; Mr Alex Werner, Curator, Museum of London; Mr R. J. M. Willoughby.

I am grateful to the Directors and librarians of the Guildhall Library, the Museum of London Library, and, as always, the London Library for endless courtesy and assistance.

No thanks can be enough to Ms Eimear Hannafin and Mrs Gillian Redmond of Magpie Audio Visual for their unfailing help and good humour in the typing and constant altering of the manuscript.

Special thanks are also due to David Bentley and Susan Banks in the preparation of maps, and to Andrew Thompson, Siena Artworks, London, for map design and execution.

As always, I should be lost without my agent, Gill Coleridge, and my two editors, Kate Parkin of Century and

Betty A. Prashker of Crown Publishers. I thank them all for their unfailing support and encouragement.

To my wife Susan, my children Edward and Elizabeth and my mother, I owe a huge debt for their respective patience, support and hospitality.

Finally and most importantly, I must record that without the curators, especially John Clark and Rosemary Weinstein, and the staff of the Museum of London, this book could not have been written. The Museum of London has been for me, throughout this book's long gestation, a source of constant inspiration.